THE
COMPLETE
AMBER
SOURCEBOOK

THE
COMPLETE
AMBER
SOURCEBOOK

THEODORE KRULIK

AVON BOOKS • NEW YORK

THE COMPLETE AMBER SOURCEBOOK is an original publication of Avon Books. This work has never before appeared in book form.

AVON BOOKS
A division of
The Hearst Corporation
1350 Avenue of the Americas
New York, New York 10019

Copyright © 1996 by Theodore Krulik
Cover art by Glen Orbik
Musical notations courtesy of Alice Christy
Published by arrangement with the author
Library of Congress Catalog Card Number: 95-35076
ISBN: 0-380-75409-6

Library of Congress Cataloging in Publication Data:
Krulik, Theodore, 1948–
    The complete Amber sourcebook/Theodore Krulik.
        p. cm.
Includes bibliographical references.
1. Zelazny, Roger. Amber novels—Dictionaries. 2. Castle Amber (Imaginary place)—Dictionaries. 3. Fantastic fiction, American—Dictionaries. I. Title.
PS3576.E43A835   1996   95-35076
813'.54—dc20   CIP

First AvoNova Trade Printing: January 1996

AVONOVA TRADEMARK REG. U.S. PAT. OFF. AND IN OTHER COUNTRIES, MARCA REGISTRADA, HECHO EN U.S.A.

Printed in the U.S.A.

QP   10   9   8   7   6   5   4   3   2   1

To Roberta,
for teaching me perseverance
and not to wait until 2:00 P.M. for inspiration

And to all my Mentors,
who have helped me to grow

And to all my Tormentors,
who have helped me to grow stronger

ACKNOWLEDGMENTS FROM
SHADOW EARTH

While it seemed necessary that this work come forth to the public in the style of a single hand, numerous people of the shadows lent their hearts and minds and spirit and, yes, hands, to construct this unique composite.

First among benefactors is Gaem dau'Basvl, Royal Scribe of Amber, who coordinated the effort from the true city.

Those who had a direct influence on the project were John Douglas, who gave it direction and definition; Louis Gilio, who collaborated on the musical compositions; Erick Wujcik, who assisted in shaping the language of Thari; Polly Jackson, who supplied important information and pictures; and Diane Duane, who corresponded about her knowledge of the geography of Amber.

Many others lent their perceptions of the true city in many and varied ways: Susan, Andrew, and Jonathan Markowitz, for delightful, long days and nights wandering the ways of Amber; Thomas Bannon, for exchanging theories and facts that found their way into this work, and for fighting the good fight in the Battle of the Printers; Evelyn Melnicki, for suggesting the Melnicki Method for utilizing sources; and Robert Fass, for asking questions that had only partial answers until now.

Over the long years as this work progressed, the following lent their hearts as much as their ears: Rose and Samuel Krulik, Sylvia and Ralph Sokolow, Selma Curtis, Carol and Lou Gilio, Sharon and Bruce Tinkel, Stephen Stern, Fran and Stan Rothman, and Ann Winters.

Ultimately, of course, this book would not have seen the light of day if not for Roger Zelazny, who shared his creation freely and enthusiastically.

CONTENTS

THE AMBER NOVELS—
GUIDE TO ABBREVIATIONS

NINE PRINCES IN AMBER	NP
THE GUNS OF AVALON	GA
SIGN OF THE UNICORN	SU
THE HAND OF OBERON	HO
THE COURTS OF CHAOS	CC
TRUMPS OF DOOM	TD
BLOOD OF AMBER	BA
SIGN OF CHAOS	SC
KNIGHT OF SHADOWS	KS
PRINCE OF CHAOS	PC

SCRIBE'S PREFACE

My father, Lenjir dau'Basvl, served Dworkin Barimen during the final period of his rule in the true city, Amber. Still a young man, my father continued to serve Dworkin's son, Oberon, during his long and difficult rule. As the royal scribe, father's position offered him the opportunity to record many events of a private nature in and around the palace. Ever faithful to the Royal Family, he kept these records in absolute confidence as he proceeded on his innumerable tasks as scribe: keeping the royal accounts of direct trade agreements with the shadows, maintaining a social register of the Royal Family, their antecedents and descendants, clocking official visits to and from Amber, providing a detailed calendar of appointments, events, and other societal minutiae for the king to consult as need or whim dictated.

As the son of my father, I was brought up in the family tradition, as my father before me, and his father before him. Trained in the study of linguistics, cross-cultural social mores, and the written arts, I practiced the profession of scribe from an early age. I was first initiated in my apprenticeship when Oberon had already ruled for millennia, and I barely remember fleeting glimpses of the aged Dworkin as he roamed palace corridors at odd moments. Instilled in my mind and heart is the deep feeling that my profession is a part of the history of Amber. We scribes have made it possible to share the true story with those of a lesser perspective.

While ending my apprenticeship and beginning my service with King Random, son of Oberon, my father passed to me his private journal, his record of daily events in Amber, not just the palace proper, but also its environs. I swore to my father that the record would not be revealed until such time as the king believed that the lesser realms were able to receive the true knowledge without doubt, without fear, and without the dissension born of ignorance.

Recently, the king has made known to me his wish for greater understanding between Amber and the shadows. It is based on his wish, therefore, that I am now disclosing the minute details of the history of Amber recorded by my father. I have carefully compiled and edited this "encyclopedia" of the people, places, and various other subject matter that my father had begun so very long ago. Although the publication of this work originates from Amber, the king is using his influence in the shadows to publish this record in their own provincial regions. Thus, the copy you have in your hands is entitled *The Complete Amber Sourcebook,* published in a major publishing house on the North American Continent, and is written in twentieth century colloquial American Standard English. It is essentially the same text as the translated work in the country of the same shadow known as France, for instance, except for minor accommodations of idiom and culture. Similar translations have been made available in most of the shadows known to the Royal Family.

It is my personal hope that *The Complete Amber Sourcebook* will enhance the tradition of scribes as a significant factor in the shaping of our history. I share with our king in the true city the belief that there is no greater gift than the fostering of understanding between all the races in our shared universe, and that knowledge must begin with an opening of the door to the greater perspective of the true center of civilization, here, in Amber.

Gaem dau'Basvl
Royal Scribe of the True City

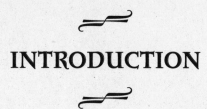

INTRODUCTION

The original five novels that make up *The Chronicles of Amber* by Roger Zelazny have been immensely popular among serious readers of science fiction for more than a decade. Since the time that they were written during the 1970s, they have been reprinted frequently and are a significant part of the science fiction section of any bookstore. The Science Fiction Book Club frequently offers its two-volume hardcover edition of the original five novels to new subscribers. With the publication of Zelazny's new Amber novel in May, 1985, *Trumps of Doom,* new readers have rediscovered the world of Amber.

Just like the newer readers who are turning to the Amber series for the first time, *Trumps of Doom* and later novels in the series take up the story of Amber with a new generation of characters. The protagonist of *Trumps of Doom,* Merlin, is the son of Corwin, the main character in *The Chronicles of Amber,* and the antagonists he faces are the progeny of villains faced by Corwin in the first five novels. New characters, with new powers, face strange beings and uncharted worlds in a progression of complexity. As further novels unraveled the mysteries of Amber, there proved to be a definite need for a guidebook to the land and shape and face of Amber. That is the purpose of *The Complete Amber Sourcebook.*

This work will have the appearance and scholarly writing of an encyclopedia, with alphabetical entries that will detail the lives of the people of Amber, and will breathe life into the worlds in which they move and grow. The reader who opens this reference work will examine the wonders that he read about in the Amber novels, adding a clarity and scope not readily accessible in separate works of fiction. Questions brought to mind in the novels will be answered here, and historical and biographical facts about the people and land of Amber will be expounded upon.

While this sourcebook will take a scholarly view of Zelazny's Amber novels, it will be written in a comfortably informal style in keeping with the tone and voice of the Chronicles. Although there will be room for speculation about those aspects that have remained behind the scenes in the world of Amber and surrounding shadows, such speculations will be informed and will be verified by Roger Zelazny. Thus, in opening this book, the reader will tread new ground as well as view familiar country.

AMBER

The true city, upon which every other city in every shadow is modeled. Although Amber is the center of all things, it, too, is a special shadow of the original Pattern created by Dworkin Barimen. Order in the universe depends upon the existence of the true city, and that same Order is a consequence of its existence.

The existence of Amber defies much of what is known as science. One cannot view the world of Amber and the way of life that its inhabitants pursue with an eye on scientific rationality. Much of the history of Amber that has been passed down through the generations denies the theories of the origin of the universe and the variant origins of the human species that are accepted in the shadows. Science is an inert force in Amber, having no significance because the world operates under its own special system of internal logic. That internal logic reaches out from the center of the universe, touches the congruent shadows, and gradually disperses as it reaches the farther shadows. Thus, the true nature of Amber becomes less and less comprehensible the further away one travels in Shadow.

THE NATURE OF AMBER

The actual physical manifestation of Amber is ingrained in the original Pattern that was designed by Dworkin, carved in bare rock on an isolated island that had once been a part of Chaos. At the moment when Dworkin's hand, guided by the unicorn, completed its circuit in blood upon that island's rock, Amber came into existence. It was born, fully grown, in that single moment in time. The world was fully constructed from the mind of Dworkin, and, like the imaginings of man, held the possibilities of immeasurably numerous worlds.

Where there had been only Chaos, roaming freely in the void, a clearly conceived firmament fixed the idea of Order in a set universe. Amber is Substance, acting as a counterforce against the unstable confusion of a void that had previously known only Chaos. The physical manifestation that was the initial Amber found a method for creating every possibility that was an integral part of the mind of Dworkin. The aura that is Amber fed the void around it, casting off other visions of Amber's realms of possibility. Amber was, is, reflected in

shadows of itself where one may find the richness of variety that comes from the mind of its creator. The shadows are in existence, tied immutably to their center. Shadow contains all the potentialities of human imaginings, and it extends from the center all the way to Chaos, urging a kind of Order even to the very door of Chaos.

Amber and Shadow are drawn together in an incorruptible, magnetic grip. They cannot be ripped asunder without demolishing the Order they have created by their union. This unity of Amber, Shadow, and Chaos engenders a cosmic attraction that maintains their kinetic, flowing relationship while, at the same time, allowing for the shifting rotation of the universe in the void. Amber is a world in flux, revolving on a kind of axis of the cosmos within the vastness of space. Yet, it is fixed in its concord with Shadow and Chaos.

Only Dworkin's eyes have seen the prospect of Amber in its "orbit" from the distance of space. Without his wisdom to guide us, it is difficult to assay how the physical plant of Amber would appear from outside of the natural realm of the world. However, our greatest scholars have put together the following picture: Imagine a pebble floating in a stream. Along the way, the pebble picks up various kinds of detritus that cling to it, causing it to grow and take on new shapes. It continues to flow along the stream, still retaining its actual shape—that is, it is still a pebble—but its appearance and size and shape have changed, continue to change, as various particles grab hold and surround it. That is the way that Amber might appear to us from the void. It is a small spheroid flowing across the emptiness, with the haze of its detritus—the shadows, Chaos, and its single moon—giving it completeness on its astral plane swirling about a yellow dwarf star.

The "haze" that might be seen from a vantage point in space, surrounding Amber, is very deceiving. It contains within it all the shadows, but they do not appear in the same physical plane as the world seen from the void. The existence of the shadows occurs along different lines than simple spatial movement. Rather than being able to see it from afar, one must step in upon the real Earth and experience the shifting into Shadow at firsthand. As one moves further away from Amber's center, Mt. Kolvir, to the extent of more than several hundred miles, one discovers oneself to be in a different reality, a shadow. As one continues the journey, he will find other realities, each governed by a different set of laws of physics, and each self-contained within a universe that the populace believes to be at the limits of its world. In spite of the seeming contradiction of the laws of nature and the apparent self-containment of each shadow, the traveler from Amber is still within the precincts of his world. Thus, the shadows are still a part of the original planet, but spatial movement has an effect upon the potentialities of other realities. Anything may be found in the shadows, from Eiffel Towers and Taj Mahals to the Empire State Building. The world is quite inexhaustible, containing essences, on a grand or minuscule scale, of every possible world that has ever existed or ever will exist.

This is not to say that every being may walk from Amber or toward Amber and be able to shift through shadows. Only a being born in Amber can assay such movement of his own volition into the various realities. However, there are several points, at the edges of Amber and its most congruent Shadows, where reality is wavery; that is, the near borders of the real world and its reflected selves become nearly indistinguishable. These borders are not hard and fast. At these points especially, Amber acts as a kind of magnet on adjacent shadows, and objects or beings may be drawn across into Amber from Shadow. This is basically a one-way process, so that objects from Amber are not likely to drop in on the most congruent shadows, even if the reverse may occur.

For every sentient being born in Amber (as is true for those born in Chaos), there is something of the mystical attraction of Amber's originator, Dworkin. This attraction allows for a cooperation between the natural flow of Amber and one's own inner energies. Each individual Amberite has an orientation that is in concord with the forces that are naturally engendered in Amber. In a sense, a true Amberite can "read" the forces around him and, to some degree, mold those forces to fit his will. Thus, he can exert his will to travel from the outer precincts of Amber into Shadow and, conversely, he can shape the atmospheric texture of shadows in order to travel between them and even return to Amber. With numerous variations, an Amberite has potentials for exerting specific psychic skills upon the world. These skills may seem "magical" to anyone outside of the natural orientation. Always these skills are consistent for any particular Amberite, but

they may be of such variance that no two individuals will have the same psychic skills.

Inherent in Amber is a paradox that involves its "invisible" nature and its cosmic position. There are two contradictory forces at work in the world: 1) the physical movement of the planet and its relation to the sun, moon, stars, and Chaos in an ordered universe; and 2) the mystical forces that govern the inner logic of the world and its shadows. In simplest terms, there can never be any cohesion between these two motivations. The physical aspects of the world are forever separate from the mystical forces. Although physical forces, such as gravity, for instance, exert an influence in Amber, such forces are often bent or refracted by the influence of psychic forces that are integral with the fabric of Amber's internal logic. This internal logic had been initiated by the psyche of Dworkin impressed upon the Pattern; it continues and is further transformed by the interaction of successive psyches in the royal bloodline. The law of gravity does occur in Amber, but there are instances where its physical truth is seemingly defied: upon the undersea stair of Faiella-bionin on the way to Rebma, for example. The internal logic of Amber exerts a special instance of gravitational forces that allows people to move naturally along that channel, even when apparently denying the poundage of tremendous water pressure surrounding that venue. The physical laws are thus refracted by the internal logic of the world.

It is terribly frustrating to members of a modern society such as Amber that technological advances common to numerous shadows are inherently denied to the true city. At various times in the long history of Amber, members of the royal family have brought in technicians and engineers and, even, some of the best scientific minds from innumerable techno-oriented shadows, endeavoring to solve the problem of the physical denial of harnessed electrical current. Although lightning is in evidence in Amber's meteorological makeup, no Edison-Amberite has learned the secret of inducing electricity to flow along an insulated wire to energize a light bulb. No matter how insistently physicists explain the nature of free-flowing electrons, the simple fact is that electrons do not have the motive energy in Amber that they apparently do in other shadows. Some undetectable factor in Amber reduces the electron into an inert particle, so that no energy is released. Without the free-flowing electron, the basis of most of technology is negated.

However, there is an inverse correlation to the negation of electro-atomic-based energy that creates an alternative form. That form relates to the internal logic of Amber defined above. To the uninitiated, it can most simply be described as magic. The skills that members of the Royal Family and many citizens of Amber and the near shadows bring to bear in influencing the environment can, indeed, seem magical. In Amber and the nearer shadows especially, there is a greater correspondence between the psychic-physical composition of sentient beings and the inner logic of the environment. The farther shadows, by virtue of their distance from the center, are less endowed with the capacity for such psychic-physical interaction. On the shadow Earth, for example, individuals have virtually no influence over psychic phenomena in their environment. Only a very weak influence exists, for which certain rare individuals may be credited with having influenced the occurrence of unique phenomena.

The tendency of sentient beings to believe that their order of existence is of the highest magnitude is probably the greatest source of dissension between the shadows, and between any of the shadows and Amber. The ordinary denizens of shadow Earth readily see themselves as the masters of the universe, and their physical power over atomics as being of the greatest influence in their world. For such a people, it becomes quite easy to deny any other form of influence, especially a magical one. Their perceptions of a "practical reality" prevent them from recognizing the existence of a higher, mystical influence. In fact, such a denial has caused dissension among various groups on the shadow Earth throughout its history.

From the increased perception of Amber and its near shadows with which Amber has commerce, it is with great ease that the ordinary citizen recognizes the correspondences between "quantum mechanics," which is at the nucleus of technologically oriented realities, and the inner logic of the real world that enables individuals to practice mystical arts. Rather than practicing the conceit of predominance based on a provincial view of the universe, one is aware of preternatural influences in the real world. Thus, those who are cognizant of Amber are far from complacent in their knowledge of all the realities. It would be distinctly dangerous to be oblivious to the realization that a dire occurrence in one reality would affect all of them, and a threat to Amber would represent a danger to us all.

GEOGRAPHY

The center of the physical world of Amber is the mountain named Kolvir. Kolvir is the geological manifestation of the surface movement of crustal plates through plate tectonics. Since the world originated from the Pattern, and the Pattern resides in the lower regions of Kolvir's interior, one can understand how a large-scale relief feature, such as a mountain system, erupted around the Pattern, thus forming the center of all things.

Mt. Kolvir is a massive, ranging landform of many broad faces and surfaces. Craggy surfaces and winding ledges make only a very few routes accessible even to practiced climbers. The danger of invasion and attack against the palace is curtailed by the ease with which one may perceive climbers approaching along the few routes of easy access.

In general, plate tectonics caused greater interactions in forming continental features in the regions nearest to Mt. Kolvir. That is why the area around Kolvir has such a diversity of features: a mountain range, a valley system, waterways, and forests. These marked variations bear testimony to the violence with which the planet was first formed, thus causing the tendency toward hills and valleys near the point of origin. As one moves away from Kolvir, one notices an inclination to smoother, flatter surfaces. We can see a symmetry in the surface structure that clearly indicates that all the regions range in a circular fashion around the central point of Kolvir.

The most urban area—the city of Amber—surrounds the southern portion of Kolvir, where the city spreads southward, then west and east along the coast to the Harbor District and easy access to the sea. Smaller towns range outward in a circular fashion to both the eastern and western coasts, and inland in the north and northwest. The submerged city of Rebma lies offshore, southwest of Amber. Out to sea, one would find the island of Cabra, with its lone lighthouse to guide ships to Amber's shore, forty-three miles distant to the southwest. The outer regions, both on land and sea, are bounded by the Golden Circle, which delineates the kingdoms that have commerce with Amber. Some of these kingdoms are partially in Shadow, but employ open, two-way routes into Amber. Since the Golden Circle refers to boundaries that are not clearly defined, the map of this outer region cannot be accurately drawn.

The palace of Amber, where the Royal Family resides when not traveling in Shadow, is north of the city. Mainly four stories in height, there are several towers that rise higher. The Pattern rests deep in the interior of the mountain, below the palace's ground floor, in the deep recesses of its dungeon rooms. Some say that the Pattern would be found at about midpoint in the mountain. There are several gardens and ponds around the palace, presenting a serene, idyllic picture of beauty. The countryside around Amber, even in the nether regions, but especially true on Kolvir and its environs, enjoys a verdancy unmatched anywhere. Its soil is fertile and rich in minerals; flora are in abundance; and trees and shrubs bear a brilliant lushness, vibrant with life. A visit to the countryside along Mt. Kolvir would be a tourist's delight.

At the highest point of Mt. Kolvir, some six hundred feet above the ground floor of the palace, are three stones, symmetrically arranged. These permanently affixed stones form the first steps that lead to the apparition city in the sky, Tir-na Nog'th. The stairway leading to the city in the sky only appears at moonrise. The apparition itself, when it appears, can only be seen at Kolvir's summit; the citizens of the city in Amber are not able to see the eerie formation of a ghost continent suspended above the sea. Even to one up close, the transparency of the structure makes one doubt its reality, which can only be proved by the actual ascent of a member of the Royal Family along that ghostly stairway into the sky.

The most direct route to the palace of Amber is the long, winding eastern stair, a natural formation of ledges in the solid rock. Although the ascent up Kolvir is not difficult on its eastern face, the winding stairway is narrow and a minor misstep could be fatal. Upon reaching the point on a level with the palace, one reaches the top landing of the stairway. It is then a long walk to the Great Arch, the entranceway into Amber. Another way to reach Amber would involve crossing the wide gulf that is the Valley of Garnath to the west, then climbing the western mountain range that connects to Mt. Kolvir. Obviously, this would be a more difficult and cumbersome means of entry into Amber, but an invading army might attempt it in order to secure the secrecy of its movements.

The Main Concourse that stretches through the center of the city of Amber could be reached by descending the rocky southern slope from the palace. Although this path is an easy access to the palace from town, the palace proper is well guarded at that point. As one follows the Concourse, it becomes steeper as one approaches the Harbor area. By taking several side roads in a westerly direction, one would reach the Harbor Road and, at the end of the cove, the pier, where large and small sailing vessels are moored. Although the Main Concourse is well populated, filled with interesting and varied shops, and is well-lighted, the narrower streets of its southernmost portion, near the sea, are often ill-lighted, filthy, and inhabited by some unsavory types of people. It is best not to venture to the Harbor District alone after dark.

At the southeastern foot of Mt. Kolvir, near the shore, is a small chapel dedicated to the unicorn, one of several that have been constructed at sites where she had been sighted in Amber's realm. Along the mountainside facing the eastern sea are a number of sea caves.

Beyond the city, further to the south and west, is the wide Valley of Garnath. Extending westward from the Valley is the Forest of Arden, which spreads thickly to the west and north. A pleasant little glade can be found in Arden called the Grove of the Unicorn. It has a small, bubbling spring that is fed from a creek flowing northward, skirting Garnath, and originating from the sea in the southern coast.

Cutting eastward, paralleling the southern shoreline, are several lesser, ridged valleys, some intercutting into Garnath. Wooded areas also dot these valleys, and seated in one wooded valley is the river Oisen, branching close to the southeast coastal waters.

The realm of Amber ranges far to the west and north, consisting of a terrain of varied texture and sources of production. Near the city, in numerous places around the royal palace, are the palaces of other noble families and the baroque spires of various temples. Far along the eastern coast of Amber, and to the north, are the renowned vineyards of Baron Bayle. Further inland, to the west and scattered widely north and south, are vast tracts of farmland and fenced grasslands for animal husbandry.

Villages in these northern reaches depend largely on agriculture and enjoy a rural, hardworking life. The southerly regions, lining the northern plains above Mt. Kolvir, have the advantage of bordering on both farming communities and mercantile tradelines. These towns employ skilled tradesmen and shopkeepers who have commerce with shipping firms in the city and seaports of the eastern and western coasts. Thus they enjoy an economy that gives the citizenry comfortable yet rustic lives.

The variety and vastness of land in the realm of Amber offers enormous opportunities to citizens who settle here. Although hardships may have to be endured, here as elsewhere, tilling the land is easier than in most places. For the astute businessman, employment is abundant, and skilled tradesmen are in as great a demand in Amber as in any great continent that still has frontiers to tame. Nowadays, immigration is accomplished mainly by invitation, and, on occasion, by accident, but the newcomer has an advantage in knowing the privilege of his position. Few people settle in Amber without the understanding that the world previously known to them was merely a partial reality. They come here aware of their special status, willing to strive for some small success in the real world.

LEGAL SYSTEM

It may be stating the obvious, but the formal written laws governing Amber evolved slowly over the course of centuries. When Dworkin ruled, he was not concerned about developing a body of laws governing civil and criminal suits, and he was even less concerned about determining the rights and privileges of individuals. This was due, in part, to the fact that Dworkin's initial intention was not to create a royal domain with himself as ruler; he simply wanted an ordered realm in which he might pursue personal intellectual matters unencumbered by outside interference. Also, it should be understood, Dworkin did not foresee the multitudes of people who would settle in the land of his creation.

Late in Dworkin's reign, when young Oberon had taken on most of the responsibilities of kingship over a wide and varied populace, a formal code of laws began to develop. This came largely out of necessity, but Oberon comprehended the need for a structured government almost as soon as he entered the task of organizing the people living within the city and its environs.

Initially, Dworkin governed over the behavior of the Royal Family under House Law, and it was he, as the reigning monarch, who was the final arbiter in all matters it covered. This was fine, as long as the population outside of the royal household remained small, and, in fact, House Law, in a modified form, is still in effect today. Two factors led to a codifying of a body of laws governing all of Amber: the enormous expansion of people settling in Amber, and the opening up of commercial traffic with the realms of the Golden Circle. Problems dealing with civil, criminal, and property rights cropped up as soon as settlements of people outside of the Royal Palace numbered in the dozens. When the earliest criminal acts of vandalism and thievery were brought to Oberon's attention via messengers of concerned parties among the nobility, he interceded. His first verbal edicts were taken down by scribes and posted in the settlements. These edicts pertained to the maintenance of private rights, establishing compensations for injury or damage to persons or property. The concept of criminal prosecution had not yet become doctrine; offenses were against individuals and were not the concern of the king—they were incidents for private settlement between the concerned parties. "Oberon's Edicts," as they were called, were never drawn into a systematic code. They remain as mere collections of legal rules that are little more than the written records of particular rights of individuals. Nevertheless, they form a commonsense basis for a body of custom that was applied to people's rights under the law.

When Oberon took on the full authority of kingship, he became involved in cases in which his written Edicts were insufficient. These cases came largely from commerce with other realms, either in the outer reaches of Amber or in the shadows. Disputes between merchants in Amber and tradesmen of the other realms simply were not covered in the Edicts. After arranging a council meeting with his most trusted counselors and scribes, Oberon took the first steps in drawing up a formal doctrine governing all subjects in his realm. This formal doctrine, after several revisions and additions, has come to be known as the Royal Charter.

In the Royal Charter, Oberon made firm declaration of the extent of his power over his subjects and outlined the beginnings of a judicial system that would be strictly adhered to. It included an oath of loyalty to the Imperial State of Amber that required absolute obedience to the royal monarch and trust in the belief that the interests of the state take precedence over any individual interests. The Charter drafted the formation of Amber as a seigneury that is directly subject to the monarch. As the guardian of justice, the king is sworn to maintain peace during his reign and to "put an end to rapacity and iniquity no matter what the rank of the perpetrator, so that all men may through his justice enjoy peace undisturbed" (Bracton's Treatise, as originally written in the Royal Charter).

Only in matters concerning his person does the king preside over a judicial court in which he is the final judge of a criminal case or civil suit. More often, cases put on trial affecting Amber as a community are held in one of two forms: the baronial court for the nobility, or the seigneurial court for the remaining gentry. To hold the baronial court, the baron of a district in which the legal problem arises acts on behalf of the king. He summons to his court all the literate male adults on register in that district. From these, jurors are selected, their number based on the seriousness of the case before them, but which may be between fifteen and twenty-five. After the case is presented by both sides, the jurors determine their findings among themselves, knowing that they are acting on behalf of the community and that what they determine will become law. The baron merely presides over the court proceedings and carries out the sentences decreed by vote of the jurors. Cases in which no member of the nobility is involved are held by elected officials of each township, but proceedings are otherwise similar in the seigneurial court as in the baronial court. Records of all proceedings are sent to the king and kept on file in the Royal Palace. The king is kept up-to-date on important cases that affect legal precedents, and those verdicts which alter or become additions to the Royal Charter are made known publicly. Thus, the ruling monarch shares in, and retains cognizance of, the legal process in his domain. He meets the obligation of defending the law not so much by legislation from above, but by providing the means whereby the community itself determines legal precedent, and by making available the punitive force for carrying out the community's decisions. After all, the right to hold court is a royal right.

Under the stewardship of King Oberon, the common notion formed that law was the possession of the community, and therefore could not be changed at a mere whim, but had to undergo a process of consultation between the king, his advisors, and the district officials. Any major change in the Royal Charter, therefore, is given minute scrutiny and could be revised only after much discussion and compromise between the parties involved. As legal precedents such as tenure rights, inheritance, military service, wardship, marriage, and so forth developed, they came to be thought of as a firm body of custom, as rights of citizens that were timeless and unchanging. Once many of these legal precedents had been established, it was generally accepted that any court held within the realm was a court of customary law that bound the king as it did all others.

Where civil problems arise among the merchant class, particularly problems raised by the crafts guilds, means other than the courts may be taken. If the problem involves some labor practice or unfair pricing, for instance, the monarch would usually appoint a council of judges and representatives of the people affected. This council would go over the statutes and recommend revisions in the interest of equity.

Since the Royal Charter places the ruling monarch as the source of justice and the protector of the rights of citizens, it also delineates how the king is to maintain his revenue for the proper governing of the kingdom. In order to retain his authority, the king must be able to supply a reasonable salary for his army, maintain funds to meet his own personal expenses, and preserve a specific allotment of money in his treasury to cover frequent but unexpected contingencies of state. Many of these financial exigencies must come into the royal coffers through taxation. Once a year, every adult citizen, both male and female, must pay a tax on their estimated yearly income, called a chevage. This is paid even by wives who have no regular employment, but who must employ an official auditor for the purpose once a year to determine the amount of chevage she is to pay. When a son or daughter of any citizen wishes to marry outside of the seigneury, the parents must pay a fine called a merchet to the district officer-in-charge. For a son to take up the holding of his deceased parents, he must pay a heriot, which is a kind of inheritance tax, to the district officer. In times of emergency, a local baron, or the king himself, may enforce a tallage to be paid by each family, a contribution that is a fixed payment per family given to the lord of the district to be dispensed only by the king. Although some local barons have tried to abuse the charging of a tallage, community custom often dictated the frequency and amount of this tax. Minor uprisings among the citizenry of a particular district usually had great effect in putting down the demands of an avaricious baron. And no member of the nobility wanted to arouse the displeasure of the Royal Family by showing himself to be prone to angry protests by the people of his township.

A final provision of the Royal Charter is one that is more honored in the breach than in the rule. The Code Duello is one of the oldest customs in the realm, but it had not seen a written form until Oberon drew up the Charter. Trial by combat, in which the contesting parties fought it out or chose champions to fight on their behalf, was simply a formalization of the blood feud. Although implicit in the Code Duello is the belief that if two men fought to settle a problem, right and goodness would ensure a victory for the rightful combatant, it had not been officially sanctioned by any form of religion. However, Oberon knew the practicalities of the matter, and thus set up strict rules to ensure that innocent people would not come to harm as a consequence of two opposing men engaging in trial by combat. Oberon's directive in the Charter reads: "Although trial by combat is not officially condoned within the borders of this principality, it will be considered an acceptable method of judicial settlement among those whose way of life is ordered by warfare, whose possessions and social rank are ultimately dependent on military prowess, and whose highest ideals are those of bravery, courage, and pride in arms. This will in no way be held as legally justifiable, however, if any persons come to harm as the result of such combat without having the benefit of a background in military field experience as deemed necessary by a court of law. Criminal charges may be brought against a victor on behalf of the injured or deceased party if the above conditions are found to have existed." It must be admitted that this provision was very likely deemed necessary to the mature King Oberon because he recognized the volatile nature of his sons, whose behavior might prove a cause of embarrassment. By allowing for the Code Duello, Oberon at least allowed a channel through which he could prevent the criminal arrest of one

or another of his sons after engaging in a personal feud. Some also say that the provision of trial by combat would allow the choice of a rightful heir to the throne to be taken out of the hands of the king, particularly when the right of primogeniture has become so confused by the number and kind of royal marriages. The contentions of various royal factions for the throne can, by the legal process of the Code Duello, be decided, if the need arises, by the survivor in a carefully supervised trial by combat.

In Amber, the Royal Charter is the guiding force that governs proper attitudes of respect of one citizen toward another. Although the Charter may have its limitations, its openness allows for additions and amendments, altered, over the course of time, by the needs of new determinations of trial cases in courts of law. The arrangement of this legal structure of a ruling class of nobility, carefully balanced by the calculated influence of the working class, allows for a well-run society that closely follows the strictures set by the Royal Family. More than merely implied in the writing of the Charter, the continuing authority of the monarch is felt in every disputed case between citizens. Every citizen, whether a noble, merchant, craftsman, industrialist, farmer, or skilled laborer, would refrain from giving offense to any member of the Royal Family. The redoubtable power of the king and his family is recognized by all, but rather than producing an oppressive fear, virtually everyone senses that the monarchy deserves esteem and respect. This is in large part due to the beneficence of Oberon's reign, but also derives from the more-than-rumored belief that the Royal Family is superior to ordinary beings. Some of the citizens who know, who have seen the actual physical manifestations of the power of members of the Royal Family, remind those who remain skeptical, raising doubts in the minds of even the most unbelieving.

The presence of a written document for everyone to see, codifying the law of the land, imbues in the minds of its people the idea that Amber is a state guided by the letter of the law, determined by the will of the community, and sanctioned by the coercive power of superior men acting as the embodiment of righteousness. Those who settle in Amber take pride in the sense of unity voiced in the Royal Charter. There is great satisfaction in this symbol of the underlying belief in the cycle of Amber-Law-

Community that is decreed by this royal instrument of justice.

RELIGION

The development of religion in virtually every society has come about because of man's need to explain the forces around him that remain mysterious and uncertain. The formalizing of a religious order through sacred books and the worship of a higher order of beings within a holy construct are important ways in which people attempt to come to an understanding with those mysterious forces. Although this is true for every shadow known to us, it is not necessarily true in Amber. Religion in Amber is a direct outgrowth of the knowledge of higher levels of existence and the understanding that there are superior beings manifest in the world. That is the great difference: The mystery is known to those who live in Amber.

Here is the difficulty that may prove a barrier between those of the true city and those of the shadow worlds. For the shadows, religion is constructed on doubt and incertitude; for Amberites, religion is the giving of a natural reverence for those superior forces that they are cognizant of. Essentially, faith has a different meaning in Amber than in the shadow worlds. In nearly all the shadows, those who practice their religious beliefs fervently do so out of a faith that they are preserving the truth of their precepts without having any objective evidence of that truth. For them, faith, without proof, is everything, and it is enough. In Amber, however, faith comes about from actual observance of unique phenomena. The people possess a natural acceptance of energies that cannot easily be explained in purely rational terms simply because they are manifest in real occurrences around them. But it is just as natural for a citizen in Amber to revere these forces, or objects associated with these forces, because they recognize the preeminence of their influence.

The Way of the Unicorn is the accepted religion in Amber. It has grown into a formalized doctrine of worship from the rumors, myths, and shreds of partial evidence that have been promulgated since the time of Dworkin's rule. Although the unicorn has become a near-universal symbol of purity and goodness, the Way of the Unicorn does not invest a godlike nature into that remarkable beast that inspires its worship as an omniscient deity. It has been accepted that the unicorn is a sentient animal endowed with certain mystical powers, and it is an acknowledged part of our history that the unicorn and Dworkin created the universe out of Chaos. However, only a few have actually seen the unicorn, and many facts about it remain a mystery. It is not known, for instance, if there is but one unicorn or many. It is not known if the unicorn spotted by some is immortal—the very being that helped to create the Pattern of Amber—or is a descendant. These questions form a small part of the mystery of the Way that help to feed its worship.

The essence of the Way is in the genuine belief of its worshipers in the sometimes vague but very real power which invests sacred objects and is manifest in important occasions and remarkable personalities. It is a basic, elemental religion that is connected with natural forces, the changing of seasons, fertility, and transcendent potentiality. If this sounds more like primitive nature-worship than the expected political-religious complexities of a faith such as Christianity, it is because the people of the Way are closer to the source of their being, and as such, enjoy a simpler understanding of their place in the cosmic plan.

Those of the Way feel a oneness with the natural energies in Amber, an attraction akin to the attunement of the members of the royal line to the internal logic of Amber itself. This attraction is not strong, and it is probably based largely on faith (or a kind of wish fulfillment), but it creates a sense of reverence for all aspects of nature. True believers have an attitude that the forces of nature sometimes reveal themselves, but are more frequently invisible. These forces have the potential to be beneficial or malevolent, depending on whether one handles them properly or improperly. Unlike people of the more technically oriented shadows, who have been willing to sacrifice the natural beauty of the land so that they could live in a technology that gives temporary comfort, Amberites have a great reverence for the land. Natural objects become the subject of worship, or are used in the giving of blessings or in the process of some ceremony. Such objects as trees, water, stones, mountains, fire, and, of course, certain animals, may be worshiped or become part of some sacred act. In a land where it has been documented that trees have spoken to men, where living water flowing in a brook protects one child in its caress but drowns another who has been tormenting the first child, in such a world nature wields an irresistible influence over belief.

Belief in the spiritual life within all objects of nature is at the core of the Way. In a very real sense, every object contains a spirit, or anima, which brings life to every part of the world, even the very air itself. These anima have personalities that could be offended or flattered. Therefore, it is an important part of the Way of the Unicorn to offer prayer to these anima, to seek to appease them, and to avoid offending them. Before building a house upon a hill, for instance, people of the Way would pray to the hill so that its anima would grant permission. Before cutting a tree, they would pray to the tree spirit, ask its permission, and promise to use every bit of the tree to good purpose. Even in hunting an animal for food, these practitioners would treat the animal with the same respect that they would give a human opponent; the animal is considered a fellow creature with a spirit similar to that of the hunter. The hunters would pray to the spirit of the animal they were hunting. During the hunt only those animals which were needed would be killed. After the hunt all of the animal's body would be used in some way. Nothing is wasted.

Along with this view of a living spirit in all objects in nature, people of the Way recognize the possibility that the spirits of human beings do not die with the body. They believe that departed members of the realm of Amber continue on a different plane of existence and maintain an interest in the lives of those who continue to live in Amber. More importantly, the dead are believed to be able to interfere in the affairs of the living. Since the help and advice of ancestors are always desired, their spirits are often consulted before a battle, before an agricultural season, or before the birth of a child. Through this understanding of the anima in people and objects, the Amberites who follow the Way find a pervasive and all-encompassing impulse that guides them in each cycle of life. The practitioners are enabled to project more and more of their own growing individuality upon the spirits, which, in turn, become individuals after the likenesses of the worshipers. Thus, the anima become personal gods that benefit those of the Way throughout their lives.

As a result of this fervent belief in personal deities directing the Way, practitioners may freely assign to themselves the worship of unique beings that exist in Amber. Thus, the princes and princesses of the royal line are not necessarily held up as gods to be sanctified in the rituals of the Way. Each individual religious community has the right to determine the variety of anima that it will worship, and there is variance even within members of the community. In one community, the focus of worship may be the sea and the creatures that live therein; in another, serpents may be the major focus; in a third, there may be strict observance of the reverence of forebears. This is the strength of the Way: worship takes many forms, and objects taken as holy are of numerous kinds. Of course, certain factors are constant and unchanging: the unicorn is particularly venerated, its spirit supreme above all others; the forces of nature have a definite influence on the lives of people; specific people, and the members of the Royal Line, especially, exert a magical control over the world of nature; specific formulae and incantations, if performed correctly, can force nature to act in one's favor; and, ultimately, the magical forces in nature that have been made manifest to Amberites must continue to have an element of mystery, that is, must continue to occur without rational explanation, in order to maintain the internal logic of the true city, for, without human awe, there is no magic.

Although the royal line has proclaimed the Way of the Unicorn as the official religion of Amber, everyone is aware of the diversity of people who have entered the realm, staying for long periods of time and even settling in its environs. This necessitates an openness to these visitors and settlers, an openness that is amiably embraced by the citizens of the true city. One of the by-products of this openness is the ready acceptance of other religions. Since the time of Oberon's rule, church officials from numerous shadows have been welcomed in grand ceremonies by the king, who has officiated over the commencement of new religious orders and temple sites. The citizens of Amber, having the special knowledge of the true origin of the universe, have sometimes been secretly amused by the religious notions of other ecclesiastical orders, but usually restrain themselves from any outward show of derision. In fact, publicly, there is much respect shown to the various religions instated in the realm, and, in return, the Way of the Unicorn is acknowledged as being preeminent and, therefore, having authority over all other religious orders.

The worship of the unicorn takes place in simple

shrines, erected at places where she had been sighted. One such chapel, frequented by the Royal Family, is located on the shore at the southern foot of Mt. Kolvir. Generally, these shrines are small, simple, and numerous. They are not vast halls for the assembling of worshipers, but are meant to be dwellings for the anima. There are regular public rituals at these shrines on holy days, and festivals are planned in the city and outlying villages in celebration. The sites of these chapels are usually not in the center of town, but rather are placed in a quiet grove of trees or on a mountainside in the country. Simplicity of worship is encouraged, without the encumbrances of pomp and finery.

At each of the sites of these chapels to the unicorn, a small staff of clergy act as caretakers, living in spartan quarters near the shrine. Each chapel is governed by a bishop in charge of the parochia, that is, the territorial circumscription of the particular site, roughly corresponding to a town or province. The bishop usually lives in the nearest town, or in the city, so that, at times, he would have to travel some distance by horse cart in order to reach a shrine.

With the passing of centuries, the organization of the religious system of the Way has become rather complex. For each parochia, the ecclesiastical bureaucracy is divided into four main departments. These are the camera, which handles finances, the chancery for correspondence, the penitentiary for everything touching on matters of faith, and the rota, the organ for discipline within the order. The bishop officiates over these four departments, but he delegates authority of each area to priests who, in turn, employ a numerous staff of scribes, clerks, and notaries, all of them in the ranks of the clergy. Income for all these people comes from the endowment of the estates of the nobility, set aside for the Way of the Unicorn, from public donations to the shrines, and from the Royal Treasury. Certain employees, not members of the clergy, such as couriers, for instance, are paid a salary through the local officials of the township.

While the bishop is the ecclesiastical governor of his parochia, often dealing in affairs of the community that touch upon various matters related to the Way, his control is not absolute. Set in the tradition begun with Dworkin, the king of Amber is also its high priest. In the hierarchy of the Way of the Unicorn, the king is the touchstone of orthodoxy, the guardian of the true faith, and the carrier of the correct traditions. Where the king is, there is the Way. The bishop acts as legislator to the extent that he promulgates regulations for the good ordering of chapels within his parochia, and he has the right, indeed the duty, to inspect shrines to ensure that the practices of the Way are followed. However, the king alone authorizes the founding of new churches, chapels, and altars; he alone consecrates holy places, ordains priests, and consecrates other bishops. His jurisdiction runs through the entire parochia, operating on laity and clergy alike in all matters of faith and doctrine, public morality, and ecclesiastical discipline. Because of the extensive role he has in the governance of the Way, the king has a committee of archbishops living in residence in the Royal Palace, to act as advisors on ecclesiastical affairs. Although these archbishops have apparent authority over the bishops of each parochia, they are directly answerable to the king. Therefore, no member of this advisory committee is likely to take action alone against any bishop or other member of the clergy. As high priest, the king gives serious consideration to his role as final arbiter in matters concerning the Way.

Crystallizing the focus of the Way is the holy tome of Dworkin: The Book of the Unicorn. The earliest versions have been said to have been written by Dworkin in his younger days as ruler of Amber. According to belief, the unicorn itself had dictated long passages to Dworkin, which were dutifully entered. In this early form, the Book set out to describe the clash of the nihilistic attitudes of the rulers of Chaos and Dworkin's own deterministic philosophy. Rather than giving a chronological account of those times, however, Dworkin shaped his doctrine out of metaphysical dialectics. As a result, his doctrine is a compilation of aphorisms and metaphoric descriptions of Amber's conception and existence.

When Oberon took on the duties of his rule, he was concerned with expanding The Book of the Unicorn so that it would be more comprehensive in stating the form and purpose of the Way. Working with his advisors, archbishops, and scribes, Oberon devised new sections to be added to Dworkin's Doctrine. These new sections took the form of lengthy notes addressed to the believers of the Way, directing them in the various aspects of a proper life. In these Epistles, emphasis is on internal order, self-discipline, the value of labor, and the preeminent role of the king as spiritual leader. Oberon envisaged a self-contained religious community dependent on no external authority, assimilating with no other community that would taint the precepts embodied in the Way.

Although the Epistles of Oberon may appear to be stringent preachment, they are also filled with songs and proverbs that give spiritual comfort, and the eloquence of passages like the Passing of Princes fill one with deep emotion. Passages from The Book of the Unicorn are read at every ceremony, every festival, every occasion of great significance in the lives of the people. The Book of the Unicorn is the subject of much study, much pride, and much invigoration, both in mind and body. It is considered the source of all spiritual thought to this day, and its influence is felt in every major event that takes place in Amber.

EDUCATION

Virtually every child receives some schooling during his early years, from about age five to age fifteen or sixteen. There is no system of free public education, but there are many schools throughout the realm of various types and conditions. Frequently, a school is a small structure, usually combined with the living quarters of the schoolmaster and his family. Thus, the schoolmaster is the sole teacher and proprietor, earning his living by taking in a small group of pupils, numbering between twenty-five and thirty. Sometimes, a schoolmaster might be affluent enough in his own right to rent a series of adjoining apartments and hire other teachers who take on classes of pupils, thereby adding to the schoolmaster's wealth. More often, though, a schoolmaster will take on a partner when he can afford to, and together teach a class of pupils each in compartmentalized rooms adjoining the schoolmaster's quarters.

Among the nobility, it is common to hire private tutors, who frequently give accelerated courses to their young charges in all the basics so that this phase of their tutelage is usually complete by age eleven. The young heir is then taught the niceties of his class, groomed for the life of a young lord or lady. Besides being literate, knowledgeable about history and philosophy, able to handle practical mathematical problems, he or she must learn the

social etiquette of his or her status. For the young of noble birth, the practical is often combined with the social graces, all in the privacy of the manor or palace.

In most cases, the education of children in the middle and lower classes is performed by a single teacher who is responsible for his pupils' entire elementary education. Spelling and the study of Thari [see THARI] are among the first items that the pupils are taught. Language skills become all-important during the first couple of years of tutelage, emphasizing grammar, diction, and sentence writing. As they gradually learn to read, they are taught from texts of the classics, many in translation from other shadows. Older children are taught mythological, historical, and geographical allusions by means of these literary texts. Before the pupils complete their early education, the study of literature becomes what is really a form of a "general information" course. Although there may be an emphasis on the "humanities" in the early education of children, other subjects are not neglected. A good teacher is expected to have a broad if not very deep knowledge of such things as etymology, history, mythology, mathematics, physical maintenance, hygiene, music, and religious lore. During the course of their studies, pupils will acquire a liberal knowledge of each of these areas. After getting the fundamentals out of the way, when the student is about age twelve or thirteen, he undergoes vigorous training in the languages and cultures of several shadows. Since the study of three or four specific shadows are required, the pupil may study as many as seven or eight different cultures, obtaining a good working knowledge of dialect and custom, by the time he finishes his elementary education.

By the final year of a child's general education, at about age fourteen, he must come to a decision as to the type of career he would like to enter into. Much time is spent in discussion between the student, teacher, and his parents, evaluating what he has best achieved in his academic skills, and what his natural inclinations tend toward. When he makes his decision, his last year is engaged almost totally in the study of those interests that he has proclaimed. For instance, if he has indicated an interest in becoming a merchant, his year-long studies would place a premium on a knowledge of the legal formulas of contracts, loans, and other financial and commercial documents. If he were to choose other professions, such as the medical, legal, or theological, his training would emphasize areas of study conducive to entrance into those fields of endeavor. If the pupil were interested in becoming a skilled craftsman or tradesman, it might be possible for him to leave his basic schooling before completing his final year in order to apprentice himself to an establishment with an opening, provided the tradesman-in-charge is willing to teach such a pupil.

Once a youth has completed his basic education by the age of fifteen, the areas of his vocational endeavors are wide open to him. He may remain in Amber to pursue a career as a farmer, merchant, craftsman, servant to one of the noble houses, priest of the Way, or independent laborer. If he wishes to further his education in order to obtain a career in medicine, law, politics, or some branch of scientific study, for instance, he may apply for permission to attend any college or university of his choice, in any shadow that he wishes. Although only those of royal blood may travel through Shadow of their own volition, any Amberite may study at an institution of higher learning by application to the Royal House. Once given permission, an applicant of royal blood (of which there are many more than would be readily admitted to by any member of the Royal Family) will be given all necessary documents for admission to the institution and comfortable housing without the interference of regional authorities. Any Amberite not of royal blood will be given a royal escort who will lead him into the proper shadow and make the necessary living arrangements for him. The Amberite studying in another shadow may return anytime he wishes, simply by having access to a Trump of his family's home in Amber. For all intents and purposes, the Amberite is a bona fide citizen of that shadow, and it is a part of the conditions of his stay that he not reveal his true identity while living in that shadow.

This arrangement is highly beneficial to Amber since, frequently, a student training at a highly advanced medical university in a distant shadow will return to Amber to practice his profession. Thus, Amber has the best of all possible worlds, with higher education at the fingertips of every qualified citizen, without the need of establishing such an institution in the realm of the true city.

THE MILITARY AND POLICE ENFORCEMENT

The vast and varied royal army of Amber is made up of fewer mercenaries and soldiers of fortune than might be imagined. Although there certainly are such rough men who joined for personal gain (hoping to have a good life by pillaging and looting defeated shadows), most of the army consists of youths and career soldiers from the realm.

Enlisting in the army is one clear option that a boy has upon completing his basic education. Many a career man has risen through the ranks in this way. With the possibility of invasion a continual threat to the peace of Amber, there are many opportunities for courageous and skillful men in a number of areas of military service.

Easily the most prestigious area of service is to join the royal guards, who take their billet from the Royal Palace itself. The royal guards consist of a company of men under a captain, making up approximately two hundred men. Once a month about a quarter of the company is rotated into the regular army that patrols the borders and wide expanses between villages. This is done to keep the guards fresh and allow for increased opportunities for advancement. Proven veterans of the guards may remain with the palace if they so desire and have shown themselves especially worthy of such consideration.

The regular army has the sometimes monotonous task of patrolling the realm. This entails long stretches of boredom and practice drills broken only by brief spells of leave to enter the nearest town to drink, gamble, and carouse with women. Not too infrequently, however, they may engage in battle on short notice. They are the first to be called in the event of an invasion or other such conflict, and they must be at the ready. The regular army is usually broken up into divisions of about five thousand men, arranged to protect a specific region, under a major general. Besides these, there is a small cavalry force for scouting attached to each division made up of four squadrons of about thirty horsemen each.

In addition, several contingency squads are maintained, chiefly taken from the ranks of mercenaries and proven newcomers to the realm, which are assigned as bodyguards, escorts, and containment groups. High officials, noblemen, and ambassadors of Amber usually have members of these contingency squads attached to their personal entourage for protection. Similarly, visiting dignitaries from the shadows are given bodyguards from one of the squads. These squads are also used as armed escorts when travel to shadows, and from one shadow to another, becomes necessary for home and foreign dignitaries who are traveling under Amber's protection. When foreign bases have to be established in other shadows, either temporarily or permanently, a squad (or a large portion of a squad) accompanies the Amberite delegation as a containment group. The squad aids in setting up the base, which includes constructing a camp or arranging living quarters, obtaining supplies, and assuring the general safety of the delegation. Such a containment group may be assigned to the young son of a lord of high influence who plans to attend a university. Under such circumstances, the contingent will remain in that shadow during the entire course of the youth's studies, taking place over several years, during which the members of the squad must provide for all his needs. The contingency group is completely responsible for the welfare of the assigned delegate and is bound by oath to return to Amber with all members of the assigned delegation at completion of the stated task.

Besides the Royal Guard and the regular army is a separate corps that is assigned to deal solely with local and domestic problems. The members of this corps are called vigiles, and they are similar to a military police force. Functioning as a unit that is apart from the rest of the military, they answer only to their internal superiors, and their superiors answer directly to the monarch. The total number of men in the corps is about twelve thousand, but they are seldom retained in such force. They are broken down into six major provinces throughout Amber, with about two thousand armed officers per province. Acting as regional supervisor of each province is a marshal who is directly answerable to the king. Within each province, the vigiles are further divided to serve as a compact, highly visible police force, assigned to a specific township. This usually numbers anywhere from one to three hundred vigiles per township. Far from being troubleshooters or ruffians, the vigiles are trained to deal skillfully with the local citizenry in a calm and courteous manner. Rather than resorting to physical violence, their job involves seeking peaceful means to resolve conflicts. However, although they are given some of the same training as the diplomatic corps, they are chosen for their large physiques and prowess in hand-to-hand combat. In short, if the need arises, they can put down any minor insurrection quickly and expeditiously, with a minimum of fuss.

During peacetime, a full complement of men is not strictly adhered to, so that the numbers of soldiers and military staff employed in the royal guards, the regular army, and the vigiles may be much less. Under such conditions, there is no lack of young men entering the service, since a fair percentage of youths enlist after completing their schooling. Although the pay is small, the attainment of medals, the ceremonial honors amidst parades, and the prestige of promotion make military service an attractive profession.

In time of war or national emergency, it is quite a different story. Every able-bodied man who is employed in a militarily nonessential job is on immediate call to the regular army in the event of war. In lesser emergencies, only young men of draftable age are called to serve. Frequently, these emergency forces are culled from the middle and lower classes, but those of noble birth may also be drafted to serve as officers. Even in peacetime, untested young noblemen are obliged to get some military experience before they are allowed to take on the duties of their ancestral forebears.

A tour of duty in military service lasts four years, except for those men impressed into service during an emergency, in which case their term lasts only for the duration of the alert. It is customary for most young men to serve at least two tours of duty before returning to civilian life. By the time a young man has begun serving his second term, however, he has often become so inured to military life that he is reluctant to leave the service. High premium is given to the glory of awards and rank, and those who enter the service enjoy good fellowship and the security of victuals and shelter. With the sense of order, discipline, and good comradeship, the soldier or officer in the field often retains a sense of patriotism as well. When any member of the Royal Family visits a camp to review troops, the feeling of national pride is dominant among the enlisted men. This can be seen in their performance in drill formation and on the faces of individual young men as they march before a royal dignitary.

Home life and marriage are discouraged, although not altogether forbidden. Certainly, a career man may marry and raise a family, but it must be expected that he will be away from them for long periods of time. Leave time may be accumulated, especially for family visitation, but this cannot exceed three weeks at any one juncture. It is extremely rare that a wife and family will follow an ordinary field soldier during the course of troop movements in the realm, but officers and specially assigned men who are given a fixed placement are likely to live with a wife and children in family quarters.

Both in the regular army and the Royal Guard, drilling goes on constantly. It is more lax with the vigiles, but such routines are dependent upon the frequency of the marshal's tour of inspection as well as the personal quirk of each township's officer-in-charge. Training in arms continues even with veterans well versed in weaponry and tactics, if only to maintain camp discipline and morale. Every man is trained to be a good swimmer, to run, jump, and practice acrobatic feats like the testudo, in which one group of men climbs upon their comrades' heads, so useful in storming walls. Periodically, the men will go on a forced practice march, going at least twenty miles carrying their armor, mess kit, half a bushel of grain, one or two stakes (used as trench markers), a spade, ax, rope, and other tools, amounting to a weight of sixty pounds.

During peacetime, the regular army engages in numerous civilian labors for the benefit of the realm. They may assist in making and repairing the vast network of roads leading outward from the city of Amber to the frontiers. They might work in brick kilns, making bricks for the fortification of the military camps and shelters for visitors and newly arrived settlers. They might be enlisted to help in the construction of new temples, garrisons, or even an amphitheater. While discipline in the army is strict, and labors are seemingly incessant, the civilian work and military training help to instill self-respect and powers of initiative, and these qualities tend to promote personal valor in the heart and mind of the military man.

For the most part, army rations are extremely monotonous, a mere succession of huge portions of coarse bread or of wheat porridge. There are also distributions of salt pork, vegetables, and infrequent poultry. The higher-ranking officers and the company that forms the Royal Guard, however, eat a much greater variety of food, and the royal guards in particular enjoy the varied pleasures of the Royal Palace, certainly on a gastronomic level. Aside from the ordinary drink of milk and water, most of the military men take more heady refreshment from the plentiful supply of Bayle's Piss made available to the army. Frequently, the brew is diluted by the

higher-ranking officers, and a small supply of undiluted Bayle's Piss is siphoned off for their private use, before the soldiers are given their small kegs. Although fights and minor drunken incidents do occur, they happen infrequently, kept to a minimum as a result of this practice.

Besides the large armory that is well guarded in the Royal Palace, there are several carefully protected smaller armories kept in the field at fortified encampments. These armories are solidly built structures that remain immobile, heavily guarded, and secret from the civilian populace. Because of the unwieldiness of heavy armaments, and their impracticality, the armories do not stock great machines like catapults. However, a large variety of small arms are maintained in the field: crossbows, cavalry lances, halberds, battle-axes, javelins, longbows (and arrows), short swords and broadswords, and daggers of numerous sizes. Aside from these, the armory of the royal palace also contains several dozen twentieth century rifles from the shadow Earth, with specially designed bullets. These are not in general use.

In battle, the soldier of Amber is a fearsome adversary. Trained ceaselessly in the use of sword and javelin, he is also skilled in defensive tactics. He learns to march, leap, and fight in heavy defensive armor consisting of a stout metallic cuirass of fish-scale plates and a solid helmet of brass. This helmet, having brow- and cheek-pieces for further protection, is so heavy that while marching he is allowed to carry it swung from a strap upon his breast.

The foot soldier's chief defensive weapon, of course, is his shield. Usually the shield is a rectangle of solid leather about four by two and a half feet, rimmed with iron and with handles for carrying on the left arm. A trained infantryman knows how to fend and lunge with his shield with great agility, and by means of the solid metal base in the center, he can strike a tremendous blow. Almost no weapon can penetrate the shield, and, with his cuirass and helmet, a soldier is so well protected against enemy attack that he would seem virtually invincible to an assault by forces of a like number.

When marching into battle, Amber's soldiers are trained to avoid a tight phalanx formation, in which they march wedged together shield to shield, carrying their long spears in front of them. Although such an advance may work well on level ground with the enemy all ahead, it becomes a source of danger to itself because the men cannot easily change position if an attack comes on the flank or rear. In his training, the soldier is taught to stand five feet from his comrades on either side with plenty of room to swing his shield and javelin. Using these methods, a line of infantrymen can easily break up an enemy formation and create havoc in the ranks of almost any foe.

Despite the exception of the diehard mercenary who is mainly interested in enlarging his private hoard of booty, the well-trained military man feels that his whole life is tied up with the army. He is intensely devoted to his corps, its honor, and the honor of his comrades. He has gained a self-confidence that goes beyond simple faith in his physical prowess with his weapons; he has honed his native intelligence, recognizing the power of his mental skills in planning tactics. He is calm in the face of danger because he is prepared, both physically and intellectually, to deal with unknown variables. Such factors—especially those that are unseen—are familiar to the soldier of Amber.

Soldiers of the regular army must routinely deal with "peculiar things slipping through" into Amber from other shadows. Sometimes these "things" must be handled delicately so as not to create a political incident of far-reaching proportions. When a child's pet rattle fell into a heavily guarded region of Amber, and started to consume the grass, flowers, and plant life in the area at a remarkable rate, the soldiers on duty had all they could handle to restrain the living rattle. The situation became more complicated when the small child and his nurse both followed the rattle by the same means into Amber. Fortunately the soldiers were part of a diplomatic corps and, without the aid of any officers of rank, were able to quell the feeding rattle, quiet the screaming child, and calm the querulous nurse. Learning from the nurse that the child was the son and heir of a high prince of a neighboring shadow, the soldiers quietly contacted Lord Julian, disturbing no other official or member of the royal family, and Julian led the wayward trio back to their shadow. Only some years later was the soldiers' deed discovered by King Random, who commended them for their discreet action and good sense.

Similar examples of competence among military personnel run through the whole history of Amber. Some of the greatest sources of inspiration we have for the young man entering army life today come not from tales of heroism on the battlefield, but from stories of individuals who acted out of good sense to find solutions to crises in a distant shadow. While detailed as part of a containment group in Begma, a raw recruit named Fenj Cawbu prevented the embarrassment of King Oberon's chief steward, Hendon. The containment group to which Cawbu was attached had brought a small diplomatic corps, under the supervision of Hendon, to the Begman capital for a state dinner in honor of the newly assigned ambassador of Begma, Ferla Quist. Oberon, who would be in attendance later at the dinner, offered to have his steward arrange the seating and decorations for the Begman king, who readily accepted.

While Hendon and his small group made the official arrangements, Cawbu and the rest of the containment group mingled with the lesser members of the Begman household. By the merest accident, Cawbu learned from a maidservant about a minor romantic indiscretion that had occurred between Ferla Quist's chief aide and the daughter of the high duke who was acting as host. It was the duke's palace in which they were staying and where the dinner was to be held. Neither the duke nor the new ambassador knew of this affair. The previous night, the servants overheard a tumultuous argument between the aide and the duke's daughter, and the affair broke up suddenly and ignominiously.

Having been vaguely amused by this bit of gossip initially, Cawbu thought little of it after the telling. However, shortly before the banquet, a sergeant of the containment group assigned him to the entranceway of the dining hall, where Cawbu was to help in dispensing the place cards for the table seating. Left to himself, Cawbu wandered back and forth across the entranceway, attempting to comport himself as a guard on watch. Several times he marched within sight of the small place cards on a table to one side of the entranceway. With idle interest, he edged closer to the table to read the names of some of the impressive guests. He halted his stride across the entranceway when he noticed the name of Ferla Quist's aide. When he checked the place card for the duke's daughter, he immediately realized Hendon's blunder. The aide was seated to the left of the girl. Although it was possible that no incident might have occurred, Cawbu recognized the need for some quick, discretionary measure to eradicate even the slimmest possibility.

Quickly cornering a manservant making final preparations for the dinner, Cawbu obtained a handful of place cards and a writing utensil. Approximating the handwriting on the place cards to his best ability, Cawbu rearranged seating that had taken Hendon hours to set. Within twenty minutes, the first guests began to arrive. No incident occurred that night, and Hendon never questioned anyone about the changed seating arrangements. Apparently, he had not noticed. The story has never come to light officially, but was confided to this author by the maidservant who spoke with Private Cawbu in the duke's palace.

Stories such as this are not surprising to those who live in Amber. Loyalty and ingenuity are integral characteristics for most citizens who choose to actively serve her.

COMMERCE

The system of trade in Amber has become a vast and complicated organization. Trade between the shadows and Amber must, perforce, depend upon the direct intervention of the Royal Family. Therefore, the progressive complexity of commerce has been closely interrelated to the business interests of individuals among the Royal Family.

The Golden Circle itself developed as members of royalty delegated their business transactions to those of the noble class who, in turn, assigned advisors to make practical trade arrangements with merchants from other realms, some of which are partway in Shadow. These negotiations became more and more expansive, so that a great network of trade came into existence.

Although the complexity of trade, with its many subtleties, grew under the reign of Oberon, trade with other regions had been fully undertaken while Dworkin was still king. From the beginning of Dworkin's rule, there was always some local barter among the mainly agrarian settlers, while the nobility lived off their prior wealth and the good graces of the king. Even in those early days, Amber's nobles and their agents attracted colonists by offering grants of special privileges in return for draining marshes, clearing forests, laboring in the construction of buildings and bridges, and settling the land. As greater numbers of settlers were invited to live in Amber, a new group of individuals evolved: neither farmers nor laborers, these people were interested in developing enterprises for selling a variety of produce. Beginning locally by buying newly-produced goods from craftsmen at low cost, they sold these products at high profits for themselves. Almost immediately, numbers of these small merchants saw the advantages of a larger trade by working from Amber's several seaports. Those who had the best contacts among the nobility were able to arrange for choice sites in the Harbor District in the city, and then organized sea routes for trade with distant areas of Amber.

One particularly enterprising young merchant, Sarbit D'arv, who came originally from the shadow Begma, became friends with the young Prince Oberon. D'arv used his friendship to urge upon the king the first trade agreement between Amber and a shadow, that of his homeland Begma. With Oberon as his sponsor, D'arv and a small group of other Begman merchants began the first shipping lane between Amber and a shadow.

The expansion of trade to include other shadows, especially in those early days, was possible only through the good graces of the king. After all, there could be little communication—not to mention, transportation—between Amber and the shadows without the use of the royal Trumps. To the ordinary citizen of that time, Amber was a self-contained world; their own former shadow was little more than a vague remembrance of things past. Although necessity would have eventually led the royal family to contact shadows in order to engage in trade, it was through the initiative of the merchant class that such contact was effected so rapidly.

Those citizens not born in Amber (although the native population boomed with the hybrid offspring of members of the Royal Family and other members of the nobility) frequently came from near shadows that allowed for easy access into Amber. Thus, tradelines were more readily opened with these shadows, while the farther shadows remained ignorant of any such avenue of exchange. As a consequence of this ease of commerce with the near shadows, the Treaty of the Golden Circle had been devised. With the frequency of travel, by means of horse-drawn wagon or sailing ship, it gradually became unnecessary for one of royal blood to travel with the expedition. Merchants and seamen became so familiar with the precise location of routes leading to and from Shadow that the journey became second nature to them. On the other hand, containment squads of the regular army were routinely assigned to such expeditions so that the proper tradelines could be strictly enforced. It would not be in Amber's best interests if an opportunistic sea captain decided to forge a new route into a shadow not part of the Golden Circle, simply for his own personal gains. Piracy and plunder would not be tolerated by the royal members, particularly if they were not part of the proposition.

The bartering of goods remained the chief form of exchange for many ages. Amber's metalwork, crafts, lumber, agricultural produce, wine, and uniquely spun cloth were viable commodities for exchange with such needed goods as spices, grains, wool, cotton, wax, sugar, coffee, certain vegetables and fruits, and silk. As commerce grew more complex, and as a glut of many products filled the market, the Amberites turned to a simpler means of exchange: the use of gold and silver coins. The merchants of Amber began by gathering up gold coins they obtained in exchange for goods. This led to complications because coins accepted in one shadow were not accepted in others. In addition, most of the coins had such artistic value that merchants and other citizens who obtained them simply hoarded them away in private collections. In spite of these lapses in circulation, it became increasingly apparent, not only to the general citizenry, but also the king, that a standard form of currency needed to be introduced into the market.

When Dworkin ruled, he decided to examine the coinage of various distant shadows at firsthand. Reaching into Shadow, he discreetly obtained samples of gold and silver coins of several realms. He found the silver coins of ancient Greece on the shadow Earth particularly appealing. Contacting a small group of silversmiths in the city, Dworkin had them prepare silver coins based on the Greek denominations, but struck with the likenesses of the royal family and the unicorn. Thus, the basic unit of Amber's coinage is the "drachm," with multiples formed of larger-sized coins named the dekadrachm (10), the tetradrachm (4), and the didrachm (2). Pieces of lesser value are based on the Greek "obol," which is one-sixth the value of a drachm; there is the triobol (three obols or one-half drachm), the diobol (two obols), the trihemiobol (one and one-half obols), and the hemiobol (one-half obol). Dworkin also introduced the "stater," a coin slightly larger than the drachm with a slightly higher value, first in silver, then in gold. For his gold coinage, Dworkin followed the lead of the Macedonians under the rule of Alexander the Great. Their basic gold coin was also the stater. The drachm and stater of Amber became the standard form of currency in trade with the realms of the Golden Circle, largely because the shadows recognized the intrinsic value of gold and silver, but also because of the workmanship of the coins. Unlike their Greek counterparts, the Amberite coins were of a uniform size, shape, and imprint.

Still, the use of monies became too complex to be handled merely by individual merchants assigning arbitrary values for goods bought and sold. Two major institutions grew out of this problem: the bank and the merchant guild. A "money economy" in place of the "natural economy" of bartering goods meant that an easy flow and exchange of currency rates had to be developed. In spite of the intrinsic value of the Amberite drachm, some shadows insisted on completing contractual agreements only with the money of their own realm. Other shadows refused to provide trade unless their own paper currency was to be included in the exchanges. Since Amber does not recognize the use of paper currency as a representative bond for deposits of precious metals, such matters could have greatly hampered commerce. Thus, a banking system was arranged throughout the provinces of Amber, and currency managers dealt exclusively with the maintenance of coin and paper currency of all established shadows within the Golden Circle, as well as those of several shadows not yet joined to the union. As citizens prospered under a money economy, they made wide use of the banks for their personal savings as well as using them in the course of business transactions.

Partly coming out of the problems of standardization of monies and rates of exchange, the merchant guild was formed to fill an important societal need. With the clustering of merchants into these fraternal organizations, intended to protect their interests and pool their resources, came the development of street fairs. Merchants from numerous shadows and local citizenry gathered together at these fairs; the merchants, to show their wares and profit from the large groups of consumers, and the local people, to sample a great variety of items that they might not otherwise have located. Of course, the guilds' primary concern was the protection of merchant trade interests, but they also succeeded in enhancing the social order by bringing commodities to the common people whose living conditions were improved by them.

Paralleling this growth in industry and finance was the rapid development in communication. Long before printed notices were used to advertise the arrival of a fair, merchants, noblemen, and citizens alike felt the need to hear of news from the various shadows, particularly news from their several homelands. Once the need was felt, enterprising men of means complied with the "supply": printing presses were constructed, and the first newspapers came into existence. Although these Amberite "news" people created efficient presses, they were still manually operated, so that real news could be gotten to the people only by a slower process than desired. Rather than "dailies," newspapers were gotten out on a weekly basis, but the items included came from many sources and numerous shadows. Once the newspaper industry was firmly established in Amber, correspondents were assigned to the shadows of the Golden Circle. Members of the containment groups attached to these correspondents acted as messengers to and from the central offices in Amber, traveling by horse, by ship, or by foot along the established lanes. A well-connected correspondent, usually a young career man of noble birth, could make contact with a member of the Royal Family and transmit a news item of high priority by means of a Trump contact. As the importance of news from other shadows became a necessary commodity, the use of Trump contact to the central offices grew less rare than one might suspect. In the absence of any means of electrical communication, the ordinary citizen could comfortably rely upon these central offices as a combined postal system and newspaper service to obtain needed information. Because of the absolute reliance given to these means of communication, they were handled by a highly efficient staff. So much significance was assigned to these employees that they proceeded with obvious pride in their accomplishments.

The mainstay of industry and the social organization of Amber is the individual or family operation. The small shop, selling directly to the consumer over the counter, remains the backbone of society. Shopkeepers in the city and townships open employment for many people in a variety of needed tasks. And, in so doing, the concept of labor has been elevated to remove from it the sense of degradation that has been a part of forced labor in the shadows.

Real worth has been attributed to the numerous occupations that make up the combined strength of a town. Among the citizens of Amber is a pride in the interdependence of the various positions that have played a role in the economic success of the realm. This interdependence is true across the several classes of people: nobles attract merchants by offering convenient facilities and secure routes to and from markets; merchants offer opportunities to shopkeepers to buy and sell at moderate rates; and shopkeepers offer employment to skilled and unskilled workers at the shops and in various capacities centering around the clustered shops of a village or town.

Since the center of any given town revolves around the clustering of shops, other types of craftspeople also tend to aggregate around this center to exhibit their own specialized wares. Among these are musicians and artists, seeking to earn a living by attracting the attention of customers who might not otherwise have sought diversion from more serious business. The success of such artistic endeavors has afforded a remarkable influx of culture, and there has been a great appetite for cultural diversions since the early days of the occasional balladeer wandering through a street fair waving an upturned hat at passersby.

As a consequence of the thriving industry and cultural enlightenment of the city and villages of Amber, its citizens have little need to conquer other lands as part of some imperialistic urge. Commercial opportunities with other shadows have enabled its populace to enjoy many luxuries. However, most citizens tend to temper their indulgences with a balanced sense of place in the vast scheme of things. It seems obvious to the enlightened citizen that Amber's financial interests must be gainful, for the fiscal success of Amber is reflected in all the shadows. One need not ponder too long the possibilities if the true city fell into financial ruin: Collapse into a frenetic kind of barbarism at the center would mean the end of civilized virtues at every perimeter.

HISTORY AND MYTH

The farther into Shadow one lives, the greater the confusion between myth and history. Debates rage over the conflicting "truths" of religious precepts and scientific determinations. Both of these groups in the far shadows would very likely turn a skeptical eye toward those who would attempt to point out the greater perspective of Amber's view. To some extent, the scientific and religious communities of many shadows desire to shroud their truths in mystery; they prefer to maintain that there are unknowns for which they have no answer. This allows them the satisfaction of believing that there is some greater force beyond their own meager powers, something that they are unable to control.

If the people in Shadow could be given the insight of those in Amber, they would discover that their perception of human history is flawed because of their very provincialism. All they would need to come to terms with is the simple fact that all myths, all religions, all historical findings in every part of their world have elements in common that go beyond mere coincidence. These common elements are distorted and varied because they had been first committed to a written form by imperfect man, sometimes removed by numerous generations from the event being recorded. Even scientific evidence is largely inaccurate because the natural limitation of their single, isolated world creates its own distortions. Working out scientific facts in this way is like examining a few pieces of a jigsaw puzzle without seeing the frame on which they fit.

The emergence of man and the development of civilized enclaves that came before the use of writing occurred at the time when Dworkin completed the Pattern with the help of the unicorn. This is an essential point to be understood: humankind, across the shadows, did not exist until the Pattern was completed. Simply put, nothing of a prehistoric past came into existence until the image of man was solidified in the barren rock of the Pattern.

For anyone not born in Amber, this concept is nearly incomprehensible. Science, after all, has shown that certain rocks have existed for millions of years; fossils have been found dating back long before the coming of man. The explanation is, again, not very easy to comprehend. It involves a kind of rupture in time. Think of all time, beginning in the era of Chaos before Dworkin left it to found his own universe, as an immense hourglass with sand slowly flowing from the top to the bottom. All of existence is represented by the flowing sands, and those that reach the bottom half are the potentialities for future time. At the point when Dworkin created the universe, the hourglass is turned sideways and the slender neck in the middle is bent

without breaking. The image of the bent hourglass lying on its side is then reflected as part of all the possible realms in the universe, each one becoming a representative of that particular world, but still intimately connected to the original hourglass. As perceived by any particular realm, the sands of the hourglass represent its own particular past, in the upper portion of the hourglass, and its future, in what had formerly been the lower portion. Its present is represented by the slowly ebbing sands in the neck, through which the sands still continue to flow, albeit at a much slower rate. Thus, the particular realm has a long, prehistoric past in the former upper portion of the hourglass which it can examine, imperfectly, and which leads them to the belief that a vast prehistory had existed before sentient humans inhabited their world.

This analogy is convenient for expressing the differing time flows in the shadows and in Amber. The flow of Amber history stretches back for many millennia, much farther back than humankind's history on the shadow Earth, for instance. This is a consequence of the rupture of time: it is virtually impossible to arrange an alignment of time frames measuring the time flows of Amber with any shadow. These flows continue to vary, thus defying any scientific mode of comparison.

The shadows are infinite because Amber continues to shape them as new potentialities. Every possibility exists somewhere as a shadow of the real. In consequence, every reflected world bears a reflection of Dworkin, Oberon, his children, and his children's children. They move and speak and act in imperfect imitation of their true counterparts. This is the reason for many of the myths that have been passed through generations of storytellers, at first orally, and then in some written record. These tales are made more complicated because the original members of the Royal Family are given to wide wanderings through the shadows. In this way, the shadow of a royal member may be given legendary status as a result of actions performed by his counterpart while wandering in that shadow.

To best exemplify the complications of history and legend, one need only follow the early wanderings of young Oberon to the shadow Earth. Scribes of the time had carefully recorded his journeyings upon his return to Amber each time. As a youth, in one of his earliest travels, Oberon posed as a youthful king in Mesopotamia named Gilgamesh. Oberon used his great strength and regenerative powers to make a name for the young king, who may have been a shadow version of Oberon, or he may not have been. Witnesses of the time magnified what they saw, encouraged by the rather vain Gilgamesh. In a fierce battle against their enemies, the armies of Kish, Oberon was mortally wounded. Taken back to the royal palace of Erech, the home of Gilgamesh, he was cared for by Gilgamesh's servants. While the entire city mourned for a dying Gilgamesh, Gilgamesh's own household kept secret that their leader was unhurt, but that a stranger lay near death. After several months in their care, Oberon fully recovered and had healed almost entirely. In Gilgamesh's clothes, he greeted the populace from one of the balconies of the palace. He stayed in Erech for seven more years, bringing glory to Gilgamesh and to the city. Historical accounts have survived in that shadow of Gilgamesh as a ruler of the Sumerian city of Erech. But his exploits have been exaggerated and distorted by time. In that shadow, nothing had been recorded about a young stranger with remarkable powers visiting from some other world.

Certainly, much mischief in the various shadows could be attributed to visitations by one or another of Oberon's offspring: a war here, a rebellion there, an assassination in one shadow, an abduction in another. It should be understandable that banishment is an impossible sentence for the king of Amber to carry out against a miscreant of royal blood. Many an illegitimate offspring has escaped worse punishment by exiling himself to a distant shadow. This tends to complicate the state of conflict in other realms, sometimes having an adverse effect on Amber itself.

Quite aside from these errant wanderings, the history of Amber is fraught with disagreements, those that are internal and those with shadows with which Amber does commerce. Late in King Dworkin's reign, there had been a merchant uprising against the nobility that lasted for more than fifteen years. This seems to have corresponded to a rash of rebellions throughout the shadows lasting two or three times as long. Recent battles forged against the shadow of Kashfa had their analogues in skirmishes between foreign powers in numerous shadows.

Conflict is a natural part of history, and, of course, it is the stuff of myth. For anyone who is not a citizen of the true city it must seem inconceivable that Amber is at the heart of all history, and that its minions have generated the great myths, the great literature of all the worlds. Scientific inquiry recounts that early man first harnessed fire that erupted from a lightning bolt or volcanic activity, without having the knowledge to make it himself. In ancient Greece, the myth was passed down that the heroic Prometheus seized fire from the gods to give to man. Now, we of Amber ask those who have seen these words to take back this knowledge to their worlds. For those who understand, this is the knowledge of a new flame.

APRIL 30 MURDER ATTEMPTS

Yearly attempts to kill Merlin of the Courts of Chaos during the years he lived in San Francisco on the shadow Earth.

Merlin had thought the first few attempts simply accidents, but he came to realize there was more than coincidence in the occurrences happening on April 30 of every year. When he gathered that they were attempts on his life, Merlin ascribed them to a single unknown agent.

The murder attempts had occurred for eight consecutive years, all on the same date. The first was on a pleasant, sunny afternoon, and Merlin was walking along a sidewalk. A truck sped down the street in his direction. Merlin noted it for its speed, and that probably helped save him. The truck jumped the curb a few feet in front of Merlin, aimed to crush him against the brick building beside him. Having only the briefest of glances at the driver, Merlin could see he was in a daze or trance of some kind. Merlin dived away from the brick wall, jumping high and wide, and coming down into a roll. He heard the crash before he had the opportunity to see it. When he turned to look, he saw the truck covered with bricks, its front end smashed and partly embedded in the wall of the building. Pretending to be an ordinary onlooker, Merlin waited for the ambulance with a gathering crowd. The driver was unconscious and was taken to the hospital that way. Merlin checked with the hospital later and found that the man had died without regaining consciousness.

The second involved an apparent mugging.

The following year to the day, however, I was walking home from my lady friend's place late in the evening when three men attacked me— one with a knife, the other two with lengths of pipe—without even the courtesy of first asking for my wallet.

I left the remains in the doorway of a nearby record store, and while I thought about it on the way home it did not strike me until the following day that it had been the anniversary of the truck crash. Even then, I dismissed it as an odd coincidence. (TD, 2)

He later recalled that, after walking away from the record store, he had seen some unknown person watching from the shadows. On being spotted, the figure had stepped back, hiding in a dark doorway. If Merlin were to investigate, he might have found the unknown person to be merely an innocent bystander, one who would then be able to identify Merlin. He decided not to bother, and he continued on.

The third year was the incident of postal assault. This is Merlin's account:

I removed my mail from the little locked box in the hallway and carried it upstairs to my apartment. There were two bills, some circulars and something thick and first class without a return address on it.

I closed the door behind me, pocketed my keys and dropped my briefcase onto a nearby chair. I had started toward the sofa when the telephone in the kitchen rang.

Tossing the mail toward the coffee table, I turned and started for the kitchen. The blast that occurred behind me might or might not have been strong enough to knock me over. I don't know, because I dove forward of my own volition as soon as it occurred. I hit my head on the leg of the kitchen table. It dazed me somewhat, but I was otherwise undamaged. All the damage was in the other room. By the time I got to my feet the phone had stopped ringing. (BA, 168–69)

On a subsequent occasion, Merlin awoke in his former apartment feeling groggy and with an aching head. A nagging irritant, like a telephone ringing, urged him out of bed. He threw open the windows, then discovered that the gas burners on his stove were turned on without flame. A year later, he heard some jangled sound that stirred him before dawn to discover his apartment filled with smoke. He fought down the flames with a blanket. The place was a mess, but he survived another April 30.

The seventh year was a sniper attack from a third floor apartment in a building across from where Merlin was walking. Merlin had been walking at a brisk pace, partly out of wariness, when two rifle shots missed him, sending pieces of brick flying from the side of a building he was passing. He turned in the direction from which the bullets were fired, and heard at the same time a loud thud and a splintering sound from across the way. Sighting the open window of the apartment house, Merlin quickly made for the building, entered, and pushed open the unlocked door of the apartment. It was vacant and unoccupied. He found the rifle in a corner near the open window. It had been smashed with great force. He also saw some drops of blood on the floor, and more drops on the fire escape. It seemed as if the sniper had been surprised by someone else, and that was why he hadn't gotten off any more shots.

The eighth and final attempt was murkier than the rest. The problem reached a resolution of a kind after that April 30, and it was not readily apparent which of several incidents was the murder attempt by the same agent as those previous. The morning of that April 30 involved an attack by a huge dog-like beast from another shadow. Merlin had gone to the apartment of his former girlfriend in response to a message he had received from her. She was already dead, and the beast was lying in wait for him. The creature might have succeeded in mauling Merlin to death if Merlin were not possessed of certain special strengths and knowledge. He managed to fling the beast out the apartment window, then made a hurried escape when he heard sirens.

Later that same day, Merlin fought a sorcerous duel with a man named Victor Melman. This man was a cabalist living in San Francisco who seemed to have some real magical power. Nevertheless, his wizardry was not up to the potency of Merlin's own, and Merlin was able to defeat him. Shortly after that encounter, Merlin returned to Melman's apartment. When the telephone rang, he pretended to be the cabalist. A woman's voice at the other end asked if it had been done. He baited her with the intention of bringing her to Melman's apartment. While he waited in anticipation, she came by an unexpected route. As her form materialized as by a Trump, he threw an ashtray at her to catch her off guard. It worked to an extent, but she bit him on his arm, sending him into a strange sort of paralysis. He was able to trump away before she could finish the job. Before that, however, he learned her name was Jasra.

Sometime later, on a visit to his father's friend in New York, Bill Roth, Merlin engaged him in conversation about the April 30 attempts and this last encounter. Roth initiated the following discussion as they walked near his home:

> "Then that Jasra lady bothers me. . . . You say she seemed to trump in—and then she had that sting in her mouth that knocked you for a loop?"
>
> "Right."
>
> "Ever encounter anyone like her before?"
>
> "No."
>
> "Any guesses? . . . And why the Walpurgis-nacht business? I can see a certain date having significance for a psycho, and I can see people in various primitive religions placing great importance on the turning of the seasons. But S seems almost too well organized to be a mental case. And as for the other—"
>
> "Melman thought it was important."
>
> "Yes, but he was into that stuff. I'd be surprised if he didn't come up with such a correspondence, whether it was intended or not. He admitted that his master had never told him that that was the case. It was his own idea. But you're the one with the background in the area. Is there any special significance or any real power that you know of to be gained by slaying someone of your blood at this particular time of year?"
>
> "None that I ever heard of. But of course there are a lot of things I don't know about. I'm very young compared to most of the adepts. But which way are you trying to go on this? You say you don't think it's a nut, but you don't buy the Walpurgis notion either."
>
> "I don't know. I'm just thinking out loud. They both sound shaky to me, that's all. For that matter, the French Foreign Legion gave everyone leave on April 30 to get drunk, and a couple of days after that to sober up. It's the

anniversary of the battle of Camerone, one of their big triumphs. But I doubt that figures in this either." (TD, 94–95)

Although Merlin tried diligently to root out the mystery of the murder attempts, he couldn't find a satisfactory answer to the identity of the agent he had dubbed "S" nor the reason for each occurrence happening on the same date each year. He was only partially correct in assuming that Jasra was not S; that she had been speaking to the agent by telephone from Melman's apartment before Merlin escaped from her. In fact, he subsequently learned that Jasra was responsible for the later April 30 attempts, and she had been a coercive influence upon the agent who committed the first several attempts.

All of Merlin's investigations failed him. He didn't discover S's identity until he fell under his power. Trapped in a cave of blue crystal, Merlin was virtually powerless when the agent revealed himself. Merlin was made aware that the attempts on his life were a part of a vendetta against those responsible for the death of S's father, Brand of Amber. The assaults against Merlin were acts of vengeance against his father, Corwin, by proxy.

The date, April 30, was the day that S learned of his father's death at the hands of the Amberites.

When Merlin began his university studies in San Francisco on shadow Earth, S used subterfuge and an assumed identity to get to know him. Once they had become friends, S had resisted making any further assaults against Merlin, although Jasra had no such compunctions. While Jasra pursued the matter on her own each year after that point, S had intervened to the extent of sabotaging any chance of causing a fatality. It is possible that S had set up some of the warning signals that had alerted Merlin on some of the aforementioned occasions.

After assassinating the Amberite who had killed his father, and as a result of his friendship with Merlin, the agent announced an end to his personal vendetta. Somewhat later, Jasra also agreed to halt her acts of vengeance on Merlin, at a time when they formed an alliance against a common enemy.

ARBOR HOUSE

The country home of Baron Bayle, official vintner of the Court of Amber. Merlin had visited the country estate in the company of the baron's youngest daughter, Vinta Bayle, shortly after the funeral of her lover, Caine.

Arbor House resides on a sprawling hilltop overlooking Baron Bayle's vast vineyards about thirty miles to the east of the true city. The place can be reached overland, as it often is, by horseback, but it is quicker to sail by boat along the coast eastward, past a small lighthouse on a narrow promontory of rocky land. Upon stepping forth upon the dock of the village of Baylesport, one may travel inland for about three miles to come upon the estate and vineyards.

On the occasion of Merlin's visit, he and Vinta Bayle had ridden on horseback from Baylesport. Merlin explained that there were stables behind the manor house with provisions for a number of horses. In his journals, Merlin described the layout:

> It commanded far views of rocky valleys and hillsides where the grapes were grown. A great number of dogs approached and tried to be friendly as we made our way to the house, and once we had entered their voices still reached us on occasion. Wood and wrought iron, gray flagged floors, high beamed ceilings, clerestory windows, family portraits, a couple of small tapestries of salmon, brown, ivory and blue, a collection of old weapons showing a few touches of oxidation, soot smudges on the gray stone about the hearth. . . . We passed through the big front hall and up a stair.
>
> "Take this room," she [Vinta] said, opening a darkwood door, and I entered and looked about. It was spacious, with big windows looking out over the valley to the south. . . .
>
> She crossed to the window and looked downward. "I'll meet you on that terrace in about an hour, if that is agreeable."
>
> I went over and looked down upon a large flagged area, well shaded by ancient trees—their leaves now yellow, red and brown, many of them dotting the patio—the place bordered by flower beds, vacant now, a number of tables and chairs arranged upon it, a collection of potted shrubs well disposed among them. (BA, 87–88)

During his stay, Merlin had some long and intriguing conversations with Vinta on that pleasant little patio, drinking coffee and eating fruit.

While there, Merlin and Vinta rode about the countryside, riding through lovely arbors into the northern hills, where they could see the northernmost reaches of the sea. Vinta showed him the crossroads to the northwest of Arbor House, which pointed the way back to Amber by country road. A stone marker on one corner of the path indicated the distance and direction of Amber to the west.

Sometime later, Merlin took that narrow road back to Amber by horse, enjoying the quaint charm of fields and forest that made up much of the area.

ARKANS, DUKE OF SHADBURNE

Nobleman and statesman of the shadow Kashfa. King Random of Amber had planned for Arkans's placement on the throne of Kashfa.

Arkans had been a minister in a high governmental position during the reign of King Menillan and held similar posts in several earlier reigns. He had been given his dukedom as a youth, when he inherited Shadburne from a great uncle who was in direct line to the royal succession. Although Arkans had never been a part of the royal succession, this distant connection placed him in an advantageous condition later in his career.

After the death of King Menillan and the takeover by his royal consort, Queen Jasra, Arkans went into semiretirement, remaining in his villa outside of the capital city. Although he was politically inactive during Jasra's reign, he continued to influence important officials in the hierarchy who maintained a friendship with him. Arkans disapproved of many of Jasra's aggressive policies, but he did agree with her on the Eregnor situation. He was strongly pro-Eregnor and supported the military campaigns against the shadow Begma for control of Eregnor. His contributions of funds and arms to members of the War Office under Jasra's rule added to the heating up of the conflict between Begma and Kashfa during that period.

When the changing political tide took Jasra and her son Prince Rinaldo out of power, and a succession of military leaders exercised rule over the shadow, the duke watched discreetly from his country estate. For a time, he was forgotten by official circles.

A general named Jaston had come into power and began making overtures of reconciliation with the Begmans. There were numerous state visits in both shadow realms. It became known that Jaston was seeking a long-lasting peace with Begma by giving them Eregnor in exchange for a large sum of money for the state treasury to be considered a settlement of war damage claims.

Many Kashfan nobles disparaged these overtures for peace as signs of weakness. Begma had long enjoyed Golden Circle privilege with Amber, and Kashfa had been excluded from this standing. Giving up a strategically important piece of land merely to fill the royal coffers did not seem prudent to these nobles. Naturally, they turned to Arkans for advice. He suggested that they assign someone to act as their ambassador on an informal visit to Amber to plead their case before the king. It would also be judicious, he added, if such a conference be made clandestinely. The nobles agreed to send a small party to Amber, headed by Duke Arkans.

King Random was impressed sufficiently by the duke to say he was willing to see Kashfa enter the Golden Circle. The king and Arkans spent hours behind closed doors. When negotiations were concluded, plans were made to draw up a treaty between Kashfa and Amber, and Arkans was given certain guarantees if he were willing to be Random's chief ally in Kashfa. Random had been concerned that Queen Jasra would be enabled to return to power if Jaston's constituents saw him as a weak ruler. He wanted to place Arkans in power as a means of blocking Jasra's return. In exchange for Amber's protection as Random's candidate, Arkans would favor Amber in any future contingencies, especially in time of war. However, Arkans insisted that their treaty agreement include placing Eregnor in Kashfa's hands.

In the preparations agreed to by Arkans and Random, the duke was to arrange for a visit to Jaston's palace, contriving to have some business concerning Begma. For his part, Random would contact Jaston to coordinate an official visit at the same time that Arkans was in the city. Again, a suitable excuse would be made for Amber's visit, with only rumors forwarded that it had to do with assigning Kashfa Golden Circle status.

Among Random's official retinue was a profes-sional assassin. This man, Old John, had been a veteran who served under the late King Oberon of Amber, and he knew how to do his job in a circumspect manner. Late one night, while walking up a staircase after a large state dinner with the Amberites, Jaston fell to his death. The palace guards were well paid to proclaim Duke Arkans as their ruler, supported in his candidacy by most of the nobles of the realm. Random and his royal retinue remained in Kashfa only long enough to assure that the populace agreed to the sovereignty of Arkans.

King Random stayed in the palace of Kashfa with Arkans late into the night, after having sent Benedict and the troops back to Amber. Arkans enjoyed a lengthy meal with Random as they planned for the coronation, to be held the next day. As it grew late, Random excused himself, saying he had to attend to some things in Amber before returning for the coronation.

The next day, Random was spending a brief time with his son, playing a musical set, before planning to dress and trump back to Kashfa. Matters became somewhat complicated when a terrible disruptive force damaged part of the Royal Palace. The situation worsened, however, when Random received an urgent Trump contact from one of his ambassadors in Kashfa. He was informed that an outside military force had taken control of the palace in the capital city. The military takeover was conducted by a man fitting the description of Dalt the mercenary, and the young Prince Rinaldo was in his company, proclaiming that he would be crowned king of Kashfa in Arkans's place. It seemed likely that Rinaldo and Dalt's men were supported by the local militia that had been assigned to the palace.

Prior to the establishment of Rinaldo as king, Merlin, nephew to King Random, met with the young prince. Rinaldo indicated that Arkans was under arrest in the palace, but he was allowed anything he wanted short of freedom. Reluctantly, Rinaldo was willing to take the kingship of Kashfa for his mother's sake, but he expressed uncertainty that he could do a better job at it than the duke could have.

While King Rinaldo had protested that he would not hurt Duke Arkans, the duke had not emerged from the palace in which he supposedly resides.

ARTHUR

An arms dealer residing in Brussels on shadow Earth who supplied Corwin with automatic rifles for his second assault against Eric in Amber.

Arthur, or sometimes, Sir Arthur, was a distinguished British gentleman of advanced years, with a military bearing. Although he was in his late sixties when Corwin dealt with him for the rifles, he was quite astute and his eyes shone with keen shrewdness. Unofficially, as most things of this sort are, he was a chief liaison for the Gun Bourse in that part of the world. Arms did not move along the black market of Eastern Europe and the Mideast without his knowledge and consent.

On the occasion of the rifles, Arthur was perplexed about Corwin's intentions. The former RAF officer did not like mysteries or "loose ends" because such matters tend to lead to exposure. He was too old and too experienced to permit such slippage. Thus he was quite suspicious when Corwin insisted that he would not need a forged end-use certificate. There would be no country of record receiving the shipment of arms that Corwin was requisitioning.

The arms merchant nearly severed their enterprise completely when Corwin showed him the type of ammunition and bullets he required. Corwin read his thoughts as changing from incredulity to a consideration that Corwin was into some manner of supernatural nonsense to a firm belief that the young man was being taken in by some confidence game perpetrated by unknown associates. Two factors prevented Arthur from dismissing the young man and walking out of the nightclub on the Rue de Char et Pain: his profitable venture with this young colonel twelve years earlier; and the several thousands of American dollars that Corwin held before him.

Arthur had been in Africa in the 1960s when he first met Corwin, who he knew only as colonel. The young man's affiliations were unclear, but Sir Arthur admired the colonel's aggressive actions on behalf of a newly formed African nation. At the time, Arthur was managing director of a South African corporation, and he was not above dealing in illegal affairs, as long as the profit was large and the margin for error was small. The colonel had soon recognized the direction of the wind and wrested several crates of automatic rifles from the aged veteran for a generous fee. Although they did not meet again until this second arms deal a decade later, Sir Arthur had fond memories of drinking on several long nights with the brash young colonel who knew his way around the continent and its diverse people quite well.

In truth, Arthur was more curious than worried in this latter deal with the young colonel. The young man's self-assurance made Sir Arthur quite fond of him, and the older man felt certain that the colonel would be able to carry off any mission he had a mind to. Thus, curiosity held sway. For instance, what was the nationality of the gruff, bearded man who accompanied the colonel? What was the strange language they sometimes spoke to each other, completely unidentifiable to Arthur? What was the source of the colonel's seemingly unlimited wealth? Why the need for such unique ammunition in such large quantities? Finally, why had the colonel not aged a day in twelve years' time?

Arthur had many more such questions about the young colonel, but he knew answers would not be forthcoming. Almost reluctantly, he took his money, turned over the operation to his associates, shook hands with the young man, and watched him take his leave.

From all that can be gathered, it would seem that Arthur enjoyed a long, trouble-free life. He retired to Oxfordshire, England, was made a baronet, and died quietly in his sleep one night in late spring.

AUTOMOBILE ACCIDENT, CORWIN'S

The accident that happened to Prince Corwin of Amber while he was residing on shadow Earth.

Although Corwin had been suffering a memory loss that had lasted for centuries of Earth's history, he was fleeing from perceived dangers when the automobile he was driving went over a cliff and crashed into a lake. Corwin credited the accident as being the pivotal event that initiated the return of a somewhat disjointed memory. He stated to his brother Benedict that:

> The bash on my head provided what even Sigmund Freud had been unable to obtain for

me earlier. . . . There returned to me small recollections that grew stronger and stronger—especially after I encountered Flora and was
exposed to all manner of things that stimulated
my memory. (GA, 89)

His earliest recall of the accident was quite
sketchy, occurring after waking up in a private hospital somewhere in New York State. When he
awoke, he remembered nurses giving him injections
that kept making the world go away. As a night
nurse entered his hospital room, he pretended sleep,
a ruse that allowed him a greater awareness of
things than he had had since he arrived. Both of his
legs were in casts, and he knew they had been broken recently. He realized that he had initially been
brought to a small city hospital, but was soon transferred to the private hospital to provide more privacy. A nurse informed him that his legs were
indeed broken and he wouldn't be able to walk on
them, and that he had suffered internal injuries also.
After speaking to the nurse, he remembered the accident: sailing past the cliff face and feeling the
impact of hitting water with great force. Beyond
that, however, he had no memory of who he was
nor anything about his past life.

From an unnamed official working in an office,
Corwin learned more about his circumstances. On a
Greyhound bus headed to New York City, Corwin
reviewed what he did know about the accident
and himself:

I had been registered at Greenwood as Carl
Corey by my sister Evelyn Flaumel. This had
been subsequent to an auto accident some fifteen or so days past, in which I had suffered
broken bones which no longer troubled me. I
didn't remember Sister Evelyn. The Greenwood people had been instructed to keep me
passive, were afraid of the law when I got
loose and threatened them with it. Okay. Someone was afraid of me, for some reason. I'd play
it for all it was worth.
    I forced my mind back to the accident,
dwelled upon it till my head hurt. It was no
accident. I had that impression, though I didn't
know why. I would find out, and someone
would pay. Very, very much would they pay.
An anger, a terrible one, flared within the middle of my body. Anyone who tried to hurt me,

to use me, did so at his own peril and now he
would receive his due, whoever he was, this
one. (NP, 13–14)

With the single-minded determination expressed
in this statement, Corwin investigated the circumstances of the auto accident quite thoroughly. He
was able to piece together differing versions from
among those people who had knowledge of the
event, and he found corroboration from a separate
investigation carried out by a trustworthy friend he
had made while living on shadow Earth.

When he later ruled in Amber, Corwin had the
opportunity to question his sister Flora, who had
acted under the name Evelyn Flaumel, about the
accident. At that point, Corwin believed that the late
ruler, Eric, had been responsible.

She told him:

"He did not say that he had had someone shoot
out your tire, but he did know that that was
what had happened. How else could he have
known? When I learned later that he was planning to take the throne, I assumed that he had
finally decided it was best to remove you entirely. When the attempt failed, it seemed logical that he would do the next most effective
thing: see that you were kept out of the way
until after the coronation."

"I was not aware that the tire had been shot
out," . . .

"You told me that you knew it was not an
accident—that someone had tried to kill you. I
assumed you were aware of the specifics." . . .

"I was in no position to get out and see
what had been hit. . . . I heard the shots. I lost
control. I had assumed that it was a tire, but I
never knew for sure. The only reason I raised
the question was because I was curious as to
how you knew it was a tire."

"I already told you that Eric told me about
it."

"It was the way that you said it that bothered me. You made it sound as if you already
knew all the details before he contacted
you." . . .

"Then pardon my syntax. . . . That sometimes happens when you look at things after
the fact. I am going to have to deny what you

are implying. I had nothing to do with it and I had no prior knowledge that it had occurred."

"Since Eric is no longer around to confirm or deny anything, we will simply have to let it go ... for now.... Did you later become aware of the identity of the person with the gun?" ...

"Never.... Most likely some hired thug. I don't know." (SU, 63–64)

After Corwin's brother Brand was wounded by one of his fellow conspirators, he was willing to reveal some of the facts as he perceived them:

"My own party was concerned as to my whereabouts. Then when I picked you up and shocked back a few memories, Eric learned from Flora that something was suddenly quite amiss. Consequently, both sides were soon looking for me. I had decided that your return would throw everyone's plans out the window and get me out of the pocket I was in long enough to come up with an alternative to the way things were going. Eric's claim would be clouded once again, you would have had supporters of your own, my party would have lost the purpose for its entire maneuver and I assumed you would not be ungrateful to me for my part in things. Then you went and escaped from Porter, and things really got complicated. All of us were looking for you, as I later learned, for different reasons. But my former associates had something very extra going for them. They learned what was happening, located you, and got there first. Obviously, there was a very simple way to preserve the status quo, where they would continue to hold the edge. Bleys fired the shots that put you and your car into the lake. I arrived just as this was occurring. He departed almost immediately, for it looked as if he had done a thorough job. I dragged you out, though, and there was enough left to start treating.... I hellrode out when help arrived." (SU, 156–57)

Much later, though, Corwin heard a quite contradictory version from his sister Fiona, who had been a member of Brand's party. She had since recanted and willingly answered Corwin's questions:

"Who shot out my tires?" ...

"You've figured it out, haven't you?"

"Maybe. You tell me."

"Brand.... He had failed in his effort to destroy your memory, so he decided he had better do a more thorough job."

"The version I had of the story was that Bleys had done the shooting and left me in the lake, that Brand had arrived in time to drag me out and save my life. In fact, the police report seemed to indicate something to that effect."

"Who called the police?" ...

"They had it listed as an anonymous call, but—"

"Bleys called them. He couldn't reach you in time to save you, once he realized what was happening. He hoped that they could. Fortunately, they did."

"What do you mean?"

"Brand did not drag you out of the wreck. You did it yourself. He waited around to be certain you were dead, and you surfaced and pulled yourself ashore. He went down and was checking you over, to decide whether you would die if he just left you there or whether he should throw you back in again. The police arrived about then and he had to clear out. We caught up with him shortly afterward and were able to subdue him and imprison him in the tower. That took a lot of doing. Later, I contacted Eric and told him what had happened. He then ordered Flora to put you in the other place and see that you were held until after his coronation." (HO, 146–47)

Pieces of these separate versions of the auto accident came together when Corwin conferred with his friend on the shadow Earth, Bill Roth. As an attorney interested in the legal status of Carl Corey, and as a friend worried about Corwin's disappearance, Roth pursued his own investigation. When Corwin was admitted to the same city hospital with a knife wound, Roth presented his findings:

"I was referring to the Porter Sanitarium, where you spent two days and then escaped. You had your accident that same day, and you were brought here as a result of it. Then your sister Evelyn entered the picture. She had you transferred to Greenwood, where you spent a couple of weeks before departing on your own motion once again. . . . You were committed on a bum order . . . 'Brother, Brandon Corey; attendant physician, Hillary B. Rand, psychiatrist' . . . An order got signed on that basis.' . . . You were duly certified, taken into custody, and transported. . . . you were subjected to electroshock therapy while you were at Porter. Then, as I said, the record indicates that you escaped after the second day. You apparently recovered your car from some unspecified locale and were heading back this way when you had the accident. . . . At that time, a woman named Evelyn Flaumel, who represented herself as your sister, contacted this place, told them you had been probated and that the family wanted you transferred to Greenwood. In the absence of Brandon, who had been appointed your guardian, her instructions were followed, as the only available next of kin. That was how it came about that you were sent to the other place. You escaped again, a couple of weeks later.'' (SU, 134–35)

Bill Roth also recited the facts given in the police report of the automobile accident that had been filed:

''It said that they received report of the accident and a patrol car proceeded to the scene. There they encountered a strangely garbed man in the process of giving you first aid. He stated that he had pulled you from the wrecked car in the lake. This seemed believable in that he was also soaking wet. Average height, light build, red hair. He had on a green outfit that one of the officers said looked like something out of a Robin Hood movie. He refused to identify himself, to accompany them or to give a statement of any sort. When they insisted that he do so, he whistled and a white horse came trotting up. He leaped onto its back and rode off. He was not seen again.'' (SU, 140)

Since Prince Corwin chose his auto accident on shadow Earth as a focal point of his investigation into the way he was used during the succession wars, these separate renditions of events made for an intriguing exercise. In spite of the slight importance of the incident in relation to the larger events

of political maneuvering in Amber, Corwin was able to measure his role in those larger events with a better appreciation. Hearing these various accounts also allowed him to determine the relative importance of his siblings in terms of their part in the succession conspiracy. It is particularly interesting to note that several of his siblings saw fit to act against him at this critical point, when, in fact, it seemed possible that Corwin would not have become a threat if he was left to himself on shadow Earth.

AVALON

The shadow where a young Corwin had ruled for many years, until it fell in some cataclysm. Benedict had come across a shadow of that Avalon when he went searching for his long-missing brother. Finding his shadow version peaceful and pleasant, Benedict retreated to it during the numerous years of tension in Amber created by the strained relationship of King Oberon and Eric. Corwin had purchased a small quantity of jewelers rouge in Avalon, which he discovered to be highly explosive in the true city. After escaping the dungeons of Amber during Eric's reign, Corwin set out to find Avalon once again. In his Chronicles, Corwin reflected wistfully about that realm:

> I had set sail for a land near as sparkling as Amber itself, an almost immortal place, a place that did not really exist, not any longer. It was a place which had vanished into Chaos ages ago, but of which a Shadow must somewhere survive. All I had to do was find it, recognize it, and make it mine once again, as it had been in days long gone by. (NP, 174)

Avalon had been a dreamland, a place that young Corwin had imagined in his mind's eye when he sought a shadow in which he might rule. He rode to it through Shadow, and it grew around him as he traveled. The silver towers, the greenery, the river, and the people of that tranquil village came forward and were real, because Corwin willed it so. A man calling himself Ganelon, who knew that Avalon, talked of it with Corwin:

"Yes, I remember Avalon . . . a place of silver and shade and cool waters, where the stars shone like bonfires at night and the green of day was always the green of spring. Youth, love, beauty—I knew them in Avalon. Proud steeds, bright metal, soft lips, dark ale." (GA, 31)

In their thoughts, both Ganelon and Corwin lingered upon the cool meadows and the clean flowing rivers of Avalon, but, in truth, there were also raiders and outlaws who committed acts of mayhem. However, to men of military bent, such as Corwin and Ganelon, those struggles added vitality to an otherwise commonplace existence. Ganelon referred to such things with a kind of enthusiasm:

"We won the battles, put down the uprising. Then Corwin ruled peacefully once more, and I remained at his court. Those were the good years. There later came some border skirmishes, but these we always won. He trusted me to handle such things for him." (GA, 31)

Strife grew worse in that land, and some of it may have owed to increasing rumors about Lord Corwin being a demon. The talk of Corwin's terrible wizardry may have originated with his exiling of the Ganelon he had known there. Ganelon had betrayed his own soldiers to an invading enemy out of anger over one of Corwin's decisions. Many of Ganelon's own company were slaughtered by the invaders. Corwin led fresh troops against them. With his great strength and extraordinary skills, Corwin turned back the enemy forces. When he had captured Ganelon, a number of his men watched as he tossed Ganelon unconscious over a horse's back and, leading him away, disappeared in an eye's blink. Later, Corwin returned to his men, alone.

The rumors persisted, and an occasional insurrection among the townspeople had to be put down. This caused greater discontent with Corwin, however. Suddenly one night, witnesses claimed to have seen terrible monsters roaming the streets and raiding closed shops. These reports became more frequent and more horrifying. Men and women were murdered indiscriminately, some in front of witnesses who described what they had seen to the local magistrate. Corwin sensed the sinister portent, and investigated several of the cases himself, while

his gallant captain, Lancelot du Lac, followed his own lines of inquiry.

Someone, and Corwin suspected a brother of his from Amber, was deliberately creating dissension. Unfortunately, it was working, and it was occurring too quickly for Corwin or Lancelot to contain the core group of troublemakers. Nobody has ever recounted how the end came for Avalon, but there were numerous stories told of its destruction long after that time. Of course, Corwin survived the catastrophe, but he had only been willing to refer to it through some lines of an ode that he himself may have penned:

"Beyond the River of the Blessed, there we sat down, yea, we wept, when we remembered Avalon. Our swords were shattered in our hands and we hung our shields on the oak tree. The silver towers were fallen, into a sea of blood. How many miles to Avalon? None, I say, and all. The silver towers are fallen." (GA, 27)

The shadow Avalon that Benedict had inhabited was much like the Avalon of old. With his influence, it may have seemed less opulent and more rustic, but the shops were the same, the glades and rivers and residences were similar. There was no ornate, palatial government house, though. The tallest structures were several lovely places of worship, including a steepled chapel dedicated to the unicorn. Benedict prefered to rule on his legs rather than administrating from one central location. Therefore, he owned several manor houses around the bustling town. His ready appearance on any village street demonstrated his availability.

Benedict was called the Protector, and he indicated to Corwin when he visited that he doubted if the Lord Corwin of old Avalon could have served the village so well. Corwin reminded his brother: "It was not really this place . . . and I believe that he could." (GA, 83)

For the Ganelon who had traveled with Corwin, this shadow of Avalon was precisely the way he had remembered the original. When Corwin asked how he was enjoying this shadow version, his companion retorted:

"Version? It *is* my Avalon. . . . A new generation of people is in the land, but it is the same

place. I visited the Field of Thorns today, where I put down Jack Hailey's bunch in your service. It was the same place. . . . Yes, this is my Avalon . . . and I'll be coming back here for my old age, if we live through Amber.''
(GA, 139)

In shadow Avalon, Corwin accomplished what he needed. In the village, he found a jeweler named Doyle and, in spite of the little man's disbelief, he obtained barrels of jewelers rouge from him with relative ease. It was necessary, though, that Corwin move quickly. He hadn't wanted to draw Benedict's suspicion of any ulterior motive on his part.

That vibrant, placid land that Benedict had reestablished would have been a joyful place for Corwin to retire to, evoking memories of a time of good comradeship and sublime enterprise. Unfortunately, Corwin had to depart immediately after obtaining that cargo supplied by Doyle. He had a further task to complete before his happiness could be assured, and a variety of complications were following him, unresolved. He may even have suspected, all along, that his Avalon had been a dream unreachable, but needing to be dreamed, nevertheless.

AVERNUS

The shadow that Bleys of Amber had used as a theater for recruitment and training while planning an attack against Amber at the time when the late Prince Eric had usurped the throne.

The geography and climate of Avernus are quite different from those of Amber; a primitive land consisting of primitive people, it is a strangely colored desert seemingly pressed closer to a harshly bright sun. Of course, the same sun as in Amber resides in the sky, but this is a shadow with distorted impressions of an early, new-formed Amber-shadow. The temperature nearly always ranges in the nineties (in degrees fahrenheit) during the day, and bright vermilion clouds in that swirling sky of copper and indigo hold no promise of rain. At night, the temperature drops to thirty below zero fahrenheit, turning the world into a frozen globe with no frost, no snow.

Its terrain consists of diverse formations of lithospheric plates, and in many regions, there are disturbances of vertical and horizontal crustal movements. Deep craters in the surface still spew forth superheated rock and hot streams of water vapor from subterranean volcanic activity. Vast mountain ranges rise in marked contrast to huge chasms and wide valleys stretching for hundreds of miles. Near the site of Bleys's encampment is an enormous, barren wasteland of cinnamon-colored sand, with none of the pleasantness that that color might conjure up. The sand is brittle, flinty, and tastes of bitter starch.

No gardens cover this shadow, but a scanty variety of vegetable life does populate the region. Corwin of Amber had reported seeing a form of spineless cactus, large and purplish in color. Bleys has documented a number of other plants of various sizes, some of which form a staple diet for the people of Avernus. Bleys recorded that upon trying one such plant, a small gray-colored tuber resembling a misshapen potato, he spit out the unchewed portions in revulsion. He indicated that it tasted like overly salted wax.

In such an environment, there appears to be a very small variety of animal life. At least, Bleys and Corwin reported seeing only some crustacean-like creatures and unusual-looking insects. The natives of Avernus have given the name ''slorn'' to the largest of the crustaceans, a blue-gray crab beast with poisonous mandibles. The ''teloe'' is a vicious, fast-moving creature with spiderlike legs. Its powerful, suction-mouth can drain fluid from the hardest of substances found in that world, and it is not afraid of attacking humans for its sustenance.

The people of Avernus have mentioned to Bleys that a large quadruped, resembling a bear from all accounts, has been seen roaming near the hot roiling sea beneath the cliffs. If there is a race of such beasts, no one living in Avernus has confronted them face-to-face. Only five or six natives in the army recruited by Bleys have claimed to have seen the beast from a distance. The confrontation would not be a desirable one, since these few soldiers have indicated to Bleys that the creature is as big as a fair-sized cabin.

Under the heat of that bleaching sun, and in mercilessly hostile terrain, the people of Avernus have adapted well. Their great height and thinness allow for a freer circulation of body fluids, part of a natural cooling system. Nearly all of the men have skin of a deep red color caused as much from biological pigmentation as from any kind of "tanning" process. The females are of a lighter, scarlet complexion. Their catlike eyes and lack of hair are also evolutionary adaptations to the extreme heat and brightness of the daylight.

As primitive in culture as they may have been, their six-fingered hands and six-toed feet, and the sophistication of their clothes, bespeak an advanced intelligence. Their lack of technology can be explained by the violent variability of the land—and the fact that the shadow is found in the direction where magical properties hold greater sway than the laws of physics. In their relatively brief history, the people of Avernus have not focused their energies on the exertion of mystical forces, but, already, in the recent past, there were "great ones" who made use of unique, frightful powers. The effect of such remembrances, some, no doubt, of a legendary status, has been to frighten the natives away from making use of the magics that might be available in their shadow. In their religion, they have enormous awe for beings who wield magical power, but it has become a taboo for the natives themselves to engage in the practice.

On earlier visits, Bleys had spoken to the people of Avernus about the "paradise" of Amber, the land that grew gods. In this shadow, the people speak a primitive, debased form of Thari that Corwin and Bleys could understand only with some difficulty. Fortunately, these people could comprehend the smoother, more sophisticated Thari of the Amberites with greater ease. Bleys has expressed the attitude, however, that he would rather present them with oratory than hold a conversation with one of them for any extended period.

When Bleys introduced Corwin to the troops he had formed of the Avernus men, he announced in slow, stuttered Thari that this was the good Lord Corwin, singer of songs and a great military leader. "The Evil One, Lord Eric, who stole the throne of Paradise from the mighty god Oberon, had seized my good brother, tried to murder him, and robbed him of his memory. Yet today, his memory is restored, and he joins us in our great war."

In corrupted Thari, and with a universal wave of arms-with-swords, came the cry, "Long live Bleys! Long live good brother Corwin! May the brother-gods reign again in Amber!"

"The day of the Apocalypse is at hand," shouted Bleys. "The Evil One torments our brothers and sisters. His reach extends to us even here. We, the oppressed of Eric's regime, seek release from this, our oppression. Destiny decrees that you, men of Avernus, stand with us in the great battle ahead. Do you stand with us in this battle of battles, this war of the wars against Evil?"

"Yes, mighty Bleys! We stand with you. Death to Eric, bringer of Evil!"

"That is well. For soon we make the long march. Soon we enter the Paradise of the brother-gods. Soon we fight to the death the evil army of Eric. Stand ready, brothers-in-the-battle."

Impressed by this display of staunchness to the cause, Corwin made silent promise that their courage would be told forever after, long after their lives had ended. Avernus and its sons would have eternal voice in Lord Corwin's "Ballad of the Great-Hearted People." It is sung to this day, every evening at dusk, in memorium to those who died in the battle against the Lord of Evil.

BAILEY, DR. MORRIS

Doctor who worked in the emergency room of a small hospital in upstate New York. He treated Corwin of Amber on two occasions, both under unusual circumstances.

Described by Corwin in his Chronicles as "a heavy man whose face had sagged and set long ago" (SU, 127), Dr. Bailey became curious about Corwin the second time he treated him. He knew Corwin as Carl Corey, and he expressed some of his wonder to Corwin while Corwin was recovering from a stab wound:

> "I had been working the emergency room that night too, around seven years ago, when you had your auto accident. I remembered working on you then—and how I thought you weren't going to make it. You surprised me, though, and you still do. I can't even find the scars that *should* be there. You did a nice job of healing up." (SU, 128–29)

As recounted in the Chronicles, Dr. Bailey seemed a levelheaded man who kept his suspicions to himself. He told Corwin that the police had to be informed because the nature of Carl Corey's wound indicated criminal intent. Before leaving Corey's hospital room, Dr. Bailey said that it was fortunate that Corey's friend was a lawyer, implying a possible need to consult with him before the arrival of the police.

Dr. Bailey's credulity was very likely stretched to its limit when one of his nurses came to him saying that she saw Mr. Corey vanish in a corona of bright colors. Although he couldn't verify the nurse's story, the doctor certainly had no other explanation for his patient's disappearance.

BALLAD OF THE WATER CROSSERS, THE

The song of Amber's great merchant navy, purportedly composed by Lord Corwin when he was a young man.

As melodious as the heaving sea on a calm voyage, "The Ballad of the Water Crossers" celebrates the men who travel the waters from shadow to shadow. The natural beauties of the ocean surrounding Amber are only part of the attraction to men born to sail. Sudden shifts from quiet waters of deep blue to choppy green seas under skies of heavy gray to oceans of hundred-foot waves and fierce storms threatening to crush wooden vessels like toys—these hold the adventure that gives every veteran seaman his spirit.

In the lyrics of this popular ballad, many a sailor has found solace from muscle-searing drudgery in unknown seas. The words reflect truths, half-truths, and mythic notions intermingling the romance of King Oberon and his children forging the trade routes of long ago with the harsh realities of giant water monsters twisting ships into broken wreckage to be washed up onto exotic shores of other realms.

In our time, the captains of every vessel guide ship and crew to the oceans of shadow worlds. The life and livelihood of every sailor depend on his captain's knowing the proper way, and the merchants of Amber prosper in consequence of this knowledge of the way of shadows and the courage of each loyal seaman. Corwin has summed up the spirit of the navy in this manner:

[O]ur ships sail the shadows, plying between anywhere and anywhere, dealing in anything. Just about every male Amberite, noble or otherwise, spends some time in the fleet. Those of the blood laid down the trade routes long ago that other vessels might follow, the seas of a double dozen worlds in every captain's head. I had assisted in this in times gone by, and though my involvement had never been so deep as Gérard's or Caine's, I had been mightily moved by the forces of the deep and the spirit of the men who crossed it. (HO, 50)

With its wonderful harmoniousness, "The Ballad of the Water Crossers" connects the enigma of the sea with the yearning of every adventurer who voyages upon it. In seeking a unity with the strangeness of shadow waters and other shores, each venturesome traveler attains a measure of completeness within himself. The vastness of the worlds reflects the vastness of the individual soul.

Following are the first two stanzas of "The Ballad of the Water Crossers":

THE BALLAD OF THE WATER CROSSERS

D' ye hear the song of the great pur_pled sea. Soar the hearts of__ those high sailing free. Ply_ing through worlds few oth-ers will see. Led by the Blood Roy_al Lords__ Ma-jes-ty O_be-ron's sons will_____ Point_____ the way our cap_tains ship will sail new wa___ ters. New____ lands ap_proach with the break of day as we fol_low the steps of Roy_als daugh-ters._____

BANCES, LORD OF AMBLERASH

High Priest of the Serpent Which Manifests the Logrus completes his title. Aside from his calling, Lord Bances was a longtime friend of King Swayvill of the Courts of Chaos, and he was distantly related to the deceased king.

Upon the death of King Swayvill, Lord Bances nominally became "the Crown" until a successor to the throne could be named. It was he who acted to put the remaining candidates for succession under black watch until after the funeral ceremony for the late king.

As Prince Mandor of the House of Sawall has stated, the Lord Bances's vows as a priest of the Serpent prevent him from wearing the mantle of kingship. (PC, 24) In spite of the fact that Mandor had claimed that the priest was not the type to be easily seduced into a proposition that would place him in high regard under a favored rulership, Merlin had overheard Mandor secretly conferring with him. The little that Merlin heard gave indication that Lord Bances had been plotting with Mandor. Their secret meeting might seem all the more suspicious since it occurred shortly after the death of Lord Tubble, another successor to the throne, during King Swayvill's funeral service.

Lord Bances convened over the late king's service in the Cathedral of the Serpent, which is at the outer edge of the Plaza at the End of the World, opened directly to the Abyss of Chaos. Following is the published description of the events of the ceremony:

> Bances began the Consignment. . . . As the chanting swelled and focused, I saw Mandor get to his feet, and Dara, and Tubble. They moved forward, joining Bances about the casket—Dara and Mandor at its foot, Tubble and Bances at its head. Service assistants rose from their section and began snuffing candles, until only the large one, at the Rim, behind Bances, still flickered. At this point we all stood. . . .
>
> The four figures stooped slightly, presumably taking hold of the casket's handles. They straightened then and moved toward the Rim. An assistant advanced and stood beside the candle just as they passed it, ready to snuff the final flame as Swayvill's remains were consigned to Chaos. . . .
>
> Bances and Tubble knelt at the verge, positioning the casket within a groove in the stone floor, Bances intoning a final bit of ritual the while, Dara and Mandor remaining standing. . . .
>
> The prayer finished, I heard a curse. Mandor seemed jerked forward. Dara stumbled away to the side. I heard a clunk as the casket hit the floor. The assistant's hand had already been moving, and the candle went out at that moment. There followed a skidding sound as the casket moved forward, more curses, a shadowy figure retreating from the Rim. . . .
>
> Then came a wail. A bulky outline fell and was gone. The wail diminished . . . I saw Bances, Mandor, and Dara in converse near the Rim. Tubble and the remains of Swayvill were no longer with us. (PC, 160–61)

No one had been accused of the assassination of Lord Tubble. The sacrilege of the act did not compromise the high priest's position in any way. Lord Bances continues to serve the new king of the Courts of Chaos faithfully and with fervent prayer.

BARNES, JULIA

Former girlfriend of Merlin of the Courts of Chaos and Amber while he resided in San Francisco on the shadow Earth. Julia developed a rare talent for occult practices that Merlin was not entirely cognizant of. For a time, she became a powerful adversary for Merlin while maintaining her anonymity.

Merlin and Julia had met at Berkeley University. They had been taking a course in Computer Science together, and Merlin asked her to join him for coffee after class. They began seeing each other socially, and soon they were quite intimate. On occasion, the two of them would join Merlin's friend Luke Raynard, and his girlfriend Gail Lampron, on double dates. In his journals, Merlin recalled spending most of a Saturday with Julia, Gail, and Luke. They had spent an afternoon sailing on Merlin's sailboat, *The Starburst*. In the evening, they ate at the marina, where Luke and the girls became involved in a deep conversation. To best capture its gist, herein is their talk, written in transcript form for clarity of each speaker:

Person at Another Table: If I had a million dollars, tax free, I'd . . .

[Julia laughs.]

MERLIN: What's funny?

JULIA: His wish list. I'd want a closet full of designer dresses and some elegant jewelry to go with them. Put the closet in a really nice house, and put the house someplace where I'd be important . . .

LUKE: I detect a shift from money to power.

JULIA: Maybe so. But what's the difference, really?

LUKE: Money buys things. Power makes things happen. If you ever have a choice, take the power.

GAIL: I don't believe power should be an end in itself. One has it only to use it in certain ways.

JULIA: [laughing] What's wrong with a power trip? It sounds like fun to me.

LUKE: Only till you run into a greater power.

JULIA: Then you have to think big.

GAIL: That's not right. One has duties and they come first.

JULIA: You can keep morality out of it.

LUKE: No, you can't.

JULIA: I disagree.

GAIL: She's right. I don't see that duty and morality are the same thing.

LUKE: Well, if you've got a duty, something you absolutely must do—a matter of honor, say—then that becomes your morality.

JULIA: Does that mean we just agreed on something?

LUKE: No, I don't think so.

GAIL: You're talking about a personal code that need not have anything to do with conventional morality.

LUKE: Right.

GAIL: Then it's not really morality. You're just talking duty.

LUKE: You're right on the duty. But it's still morality.

GAIL: Morality is the values of a civilization.

LUKE: There is no such thing as civilization. The word just means the art of living in cities.

GAIL: All right, then. Of a culture.

LUKE: Cultural values are relative things, and mine say I'm right.

GAIL: Where do yours come from?

LUKE: Let's keep this pure and philosophical, huh?

GAIL: Then maybe we should drop the term entirely and just stick with duty.

JULIA: What happened to power?

MERLIN: It's in there somewhere.

GAIL: If they are two different things, which one is more important?

LUKE: They're not. They're the same.

JULIA: I don't think so. But duties tend to be clear-cut, and it sounds as if you can choose your own morality. So if I had to have one I'd go with the morality.

GAIL: I like things that are clear-cut.

LUKE: Shit! Philosophy class isn't till Tuesday. This is the weekend. Who gets the next round, Merle? (BA, 166–68)

Julia's views expressed here are significant in showing the direction she later took in fulfilling her personal "wishes."

Merlin thought back over another idyllic day he had spent with Julia. After attending a party and having a late dinner, Merlin drove with her to a beach. It was quite late and no one else was around. They sat and enjoyed the scenery for a long while. Then, impulsively, Merlin decided to show Julia something special. When she asked where they were going, Merlin answered, "Fairy land. . . . The fabled realms of yore. Eden. Come on." (TD, 24)

They walked along the beach, and Merlin imposed his will upon the landscape. A cave was formed in the hillside, and they entered. Merlin led the way through the tunnels, and they exited into bright morning light before a forest. They walked through the forest, and Julia was shown the varying prospects of a multicolored canyon, a river, and a cliff edge overlooking a beautiful city of spires in a valley. He led her back along the cliff face, and they came to another tunnel, entered, came out again, and Julia stared with dazzled wonder at the stars beyond a parapet where they stood. It was an impossible sight, the stars below and to either side, as well as above. He took her to other vistas after that, and they stopped to make love beside a placid lake. Afterward, Julia was placed in a deep sleep. When she awoke, she and Merlin were on the beach in daylight, bathers all around them. She questioned Merlin about the night's experiences, but he refused to shed any light.

After that night a tension began to build between Julia and Merlin. She plied him more than once about what had happened, and his terse responses did not satisfy her. The end of their relationship came on a bright afternoon, after lunch, as they walked in a park. There were long silences between them. When she spoke, she spoke bluntly, letting her anger come to the surface. She told him:

"I've been back there, several times, looking for the way we took. There is no cave. There's nothing! What happened to it? What's going on? . . .

". . . That walk we took isn't on the maps. Nobody around here's ever heard of anything like those places. It was geographically impossible. The times of day and the seasons kept shifting. The only explanation is supernatural or paranormal—whatever you want to call it. You owe me an answer and you know it. What happened?" (BA, 56–57)

When it was clear that Merlin was not going to give an explanation, Julia addressed his unwillingness to share his secrets even with someone he loved. She told him to seek the road to Hell, and she walked away.

He saw Julia again several nights later by accident. It was a rather odd meeting, best described verbatim from Merlin's journals:

I felt her hand on my shoulder as I was leaving the supermarket with a bag of groceries. I knew it was her and I turned and there was no one there. Seconds later, she hailed me from across the parking lot. I went over and said hello, asked her if she were still working at the software place where she'd been. She said that she wasn't. I recalled that she was wearing a small silver pentagram on a chain about her neck. It could easily—and more likely should—have been hanging down inside her blouse. But of course I wouldn't have seen it then, and her body language indicated that she wanted me to

see it. So I ignored it while we exchanged a few generalities, and she turned me down on dinner and a movie, though I asked after several nights.

"What are you doing now?" I inquired.

"I'm studying a lot."

"What?"

"Oh, just—different things. I'll surprise you one of these days."

Again, I didn't bite, though an over-friendly Irish setter approached us about then. She placed her hand on its head and said, "Sit!" and it did. It became still as a statue at her side, and remained when we left later. For all I know, there's a dog skeleton still crouched there, near the cart return area, like a piece of modern sculpture. (BA, 102–3)

Julia met a young man at a bookstore where she began purchasing books on the occult. His name was Rick Kinsky, manager of The Browserie. He shared some of her interests, and they started going out together. Rick willingly lent her numbers of books, but she also wanted to meet people involved in mystical practices. He brought her to a local group practicing theosophy, and she made connections there. Julia began meeting with shamans, Sufis, and Gurdjieffians. Through Rick, Julia met Victor Melman, and he brought her under his tutelage. At that point, Rick separated from Julia, skeptical that there was any truth in the things she sought.

Quite aside from Rick Kinsky's knowledge of Melman, others had acted to join Julia with Melman. Jasra of the shadow Kashfa and her son Rinaldo were the principals who manipulated Julia to meet Melman. Rinaldo, known to Merlin as Luke Raynard, had first met Victor Melman because of his interest in painting. When Melman talked of his involvement in occultism, Rinaldo and Jasra made plans to use Melman against Merlin. Jasra took over the training of Melman, enhancing his very real talent for the Art, and then guided him in taking the Way of the Broken Pattern.

Having been observing Merlin for years, Jasra saw the break-up between Merlin and Julia, and Julia's subsequent interest in all things supernatural, as a golden opportunity to make her the agent of Merlin's death. Julia proved to be even more adept than Victor Melman had been. When Melman taught Julia about the Way of the Broken Pattern, Jasra introduced herself. Jasra herself took Julia through Shadow to walk a Broken Pattern. With the energies gained from this initiation, Julia was able to hang spells, walk through Shadow, and use magical sight. Jasra found her to be remarkably skilled in all these areas.

Jasra had brought her talented pupil to the Keep of the Four Worlds, showed her around, talked freely of the magics involved. She showed Julia the blue crystal stones there, stones that could be set up to form a magical link so that an individual could use one to trace another, even through the shadows. Julia had secretly taken one of these stones, beginning to formulate a scheme of her own.

At the first opportunity, Julia used the blue stone to return alone to the Keep and study its resources. She returned to San Francisco to confront and challenge Victor Melman. She hoped to overpower him, but Jasra had placed protective spells on him, and Julia couldn't break through his defenses. Julia was forced to flee, and then had to consider the consequences of her actions once Jasra learned of this confrontation. Cold-bloodedly, she arranged her own death, tying it in to an otherworldly passageway to the Keep of the Four Worlds. Somehow, Julia set up a look-alike to stay in her apartment. Using two crystal stones, she opened the way for a doglike beast inhabiting the region of the Keep to reach her apartment. The girl in her apartment was bait for the creature for she wore one of the blue stones and the beast wore its mate. It appeared as if someone with magical means had murdered Julia.

When Jasra learned of Julia's death, and examined her apartment, finding the mystical corridor leading back to the Keep, she assumed that Melman had been the murderer. For his part, Melman probably believed that Jasra had killed her. Julia also involved Merlin by leaving a note for him to see her at her apartment.

Julia had placed a blue stone on Jasra and used it to follow her. She was able to track her to the shadow Begma, and this satisfied her concerning the efficacy of the stones, especially in tracing movement deep within shadows. From there, Julia followed her back to the Keep, and was able to entrap Jasra. Once Jasra was out of the way, Julia disguised herself as the sorcerer whom she later called Mask.

Still having strong feelings for Merlin, but deeply hurt at his lack of trust in her, Julia wanted to show him her power. She wanted to test her powers against his, and she wanted him to feel bad about his denying her the knowledge she had since gained elsewhere.

Julia introduced her newly enhanced abilities to Merlin while he was staying at his aunt Flora's apartment in San Francisco. From the Keep of the Four Worlds, Julia made a telepathic sending to him. She enjoyed addressing him in the guise of a mysterious, disembodied entity. She told him that they would soon confront each other, but not on his terms. While he remained as arrogant as ever, she appreciated the drama of telling him that this moment was merely a period in which she wanted to observe him and watch his responses. She felt his supernatural probe and sent back a tremendous bouquet of flowers in a spell she had prepared. Merlin's Logrus extensions managed to rip off one of the blue crystal stones she used as buttons, something she hadn't expected him to do. However, she ended the contact with a feeling of exultation.

It is uncertain how she proceeded after this. She seems to have spent quite a while watching Merlin's activities, but she must surely have been involved in defending the Keep against the attacking forces of Dalt and Rinaldo during all this time. It's difficult to gauge how she divided her time without firsthand knowledge.

In all likelihood, Julia was pleased to find Merlin examining the territory surrounding the Keep. She used the opportunity to reveal her Mask identity directly to him while showing some of her skills as a mage. She built up a storm and appeared before him as a huge projected head in the sky. Unfortunately, Merlin did not seem impressed, and it was a complete surprise when Merlin sent an electrical current that actually reached Julia, safe in her lair. When she realized that Merlin was escaping, she used her flower sending again, and it reached him even as he trumped away.

Merlin met Mask again when he used the Pattern to get inside the Keep. It was probably a surprise to Julia, who wouldn't have thought that Merlin had any means of getting inside directly. The alarm that tipped her off was likely the explosive spell Merlin used to break through the door leading to the chamber of the Black Fount.

Julia made her presence known by raising the flames of the Fount, sending them toward Merlin. He, in turn, sent the flames back to her in her Mask guise. She quieted the flames. Then, Julia formed a deadly spear out of the air and sent it at Merlin. He repelled that also.

It must have been obvious to Julia what Merlin wanted. He was moving toward the frozen form of Jasra as he engaged Julia in conversation. Julia was using the same distorted mechanical voice that Jasra had originally used on her before revealing her true appearance. Julia must have thought the disguise combined with the eerie voice was very effective in creating fear. Still, Merlin didn't show any great concern as he questioned her from the chamber below. It may be that Julia was particularly irked when Merlin asked, "What have you got against your brothers and sisters in the Art?" (BA, 206) Those brothers and sisters had been part of an extremely exclusive club that she had only recently joined. And it wasn't toward them that she had ill feelings, only toward Merlin.

Pulling a whole variety of pointed objects out of the air, Julia sent them at Merlin in sudden, uncontrolled rage. As they flew through the air, metal struck metal, making a terrifying noise. Below, Merlin watched, face lifted, as the weapons descended. With a spoken word or two, the deadly objects seemed to be vaporized.

Maddeningly calm, Merlin called out to her: "By what name shall I call you?" (BA, 206) In livid frustration, Julia spit back: "Mask!" (BA, 206) As Merlin began to Trump away with the statue of Jasra, he called out, "An eye for an eye!" (BA, 207) Before Julia could act, she was drowned in a floral sea. She thrust flowers aside, looking in Merlin's direction, when he added: "And sweets to the sweet." (BA, 207) Julia found herself deluged by foul-smelling dung.

During this time, and in spite of this setback, Julia had succeeded in smashing an invasionary force of mercenaries riding in by means of gliders. She captured Luke Raynard, who had been leading them. In his journals, Merlin pondered Mask's actions in her treatment of Luke:

> Since I had seen the broken gliders at various points within the walls during my own visit to that place [the Keep of the Four Worlds], it was logical to assume that Luke had been captured. Therefore, it seemed a fairly strong assumption that the sorcerer Mask had done whatever had been done to him to bring him to this state. It would seem that this simply involved introducing a dose of a hallucinogen to his prison fare and turning him loose to wander and look at the pretty lights.... Mask might have killed him or kept him in prison or added him to the coatrack collection. Instead, while what had been done was not without risk, it was something which would wear off eventually and leave him chastened but at liberty. It was more a slap on the wrist than a real piece of vengeance. This, for a member of the House which had previously held sway in the Keep and would doubtless like to do so again. Was Mask supremely confident? Or did he not really see Luke as much of a threat? (SC, 19–20)

Of course, we realize that Julia's animosity was toward Merlin, with perhaps some fear in regard to Jasra, but she knew Luke on a personal level. Whether or not she knew that Luke was Jasra's son, she held nothing against him. As long as Luke had no notion that Mask was really Julia, she had little reason to cause his death in a direct way.

Merlin first learned of Mask's alliance with his half brother Jurt when he was strolling with Coral through the sea caves of Kolvir. Inadvertently, Merlin had thwarted an assassination attempt by Jurt, and they spent a few minutes talking to each other. Jurt claimed he wanted Merlin out of the way so that he would be closer to the succession in the House of Sawall. Merlin wasn't satisfied with that reason, believing that something else, more recently, had fueled Jurt's hatred. Cryptically, Jurt told him: "You betrayed someone I love, and only your death will set things right." (SC, 78) While they were talking, Merlin noticed a "prism effect" around Jurt and realized that someone was holding him in a Trump contact. Merlin took a leap of faith, calling out directly to Mask. He said that he would now place Mask much higher on his priority list. In answer, Mask snatched away Jurt, leaving a dozen or more roses in his place.

Although Merlin couldn't determine how Jurt had gotten together with Mask, he did obtain an idea as to why. Much later, both Jasra and Mandor, Merlin's older stepbrother, concurred that Julia must have been attracted to Jurt because of his resemblance to Merlin.

In a Trump contact with Luke, Merlin discovered that the Black Fount was the same source of power that Luke's father, Brand of Amber, had used to become a "Living Trump." Luke surmised that Mask intended to put Jurt through the same ritual, making him virtually all-powerful. Because of this knowledge, Merlin determined to attack Mask and Jurt at the Keep. He resisted Luke's suggestion that he use Jasra as an ally against them, but he changed his mind, realizing that Jasra would bring him a distinct advantage in her understanding of the magical process involved in gaining power from the Fount.

When he did return to the Keep of the Four Worlds, Merlin had Mandor and Jasra with him. Mandor stood ready, deeming the show to belong to Jasra and Merlin. Although Jasra acted to aid Merlin against Mask, it was Merlin's task to contend with Mask while Jasra dealt with Jurt.

Julia as Mask watched Merlin as he descended a stair toward the Black Fount. She was standing at the far side of the fountain, where she had been guiding Jurt through the ritual. Julia tested Merlin's powers, trying to determine if his skills were equal to those she had mastered. The spells she sent against him were designed to require a defensive reaction, testing the directions he took, seeing how far toward destructiveness he was willing to go. As Merlin came down the stairs, she sent out a spell to enflame the railing, then sent a fireball at him, then caused stairs to disappear, so that he had to leap to the floor. Reaching the floor, Merlin sent a "Falling Wall" spell at Julia/Mask. She was able to ward it off. It seemed as if she had the unlimited resources of the fountain, and Merlin had only a finite number of spells.

Merlin formed an "Icy Path," causing Julia to slip on the floor, unable to rise. She uprooted a flagstone from the floor, ground it into pellets, and shot them at him. Merlin gathered them up in a magical net and dumped them back on Julia, still struggling to rise.

Merlin dodged a shower of fire she sent at him, falling to the floor on the other side of the fountain. She formed a spell to pull up the flooring, jagged edges rippling toward him. Julia used the Fount to rise upon a pillar of fire high into the air. From that vantage point, she brought the frozen Sharu Garrul back to mobility as an added threat to Jasra.

Calling for Mandor to take on Sharu, Merlin was suddenly deafened by loud alarms, a spell created by Julia. For a moment, Merlin used Jurt as a shield against Julia, but Jurt got away from him. Julia flew at Merlin while the walls of the chamber cracked with reverberations. She had a flaming sword in her hand, and Merlin defended against it with another spell. She fell beside him, the sword momentarily caught in stone. Merlin didn't pause for her to recover. He pulled a steel dagger from under his cloak and plunged it deep into the sorcerer's side. She screamed, collapsed, and her mask slid off her face.

Before Merlin could do anything further, Jurt kicked him hard, twice. Jurt lifted Julia in his arms and faded away. Jurt reappeared with Julia on the other side of the Fount, cursed at Merlin, then disappeared in the flames. Merlin had been able to see the true identity of Mask before they vanished.

Although Merlin had hurt Julia, his attitude was still less than charitable at their next encounter. Jurt had appeared in the First Unicornian Church in Kashfa when Merlin was meeting with Luke Raynard. Jurt fought Merlin to obtain the sword of Brand. As Jurt was threatening Luke's bride, something happened that was not caused by Merlin or Luke:

> And then Jurt screamed as if his soul were on fire. Werewindle moved away from Coral's throat, and Jurt backed off and began jerking, like a puppet whose joints have seized up but whose strings are still being yanked. Coral turned toward him, her back to Luke and me. Her right hand rose to her face. After a time Jurt fell to the floor and curled into a fetal position. A red light seemed to be playing upon him. He was shaking steadily, and I could even hear his teeth chattering.
>
> Abruptly, then, he was gone, trailing rainbows, leaving blood and spittle, bearing Werewindle with him. I sent a parting bolt after, but I knew that it did not reach him. I'd felt Julia's presence at the other end of the spectrum, and despite everything else, I was pleased to know that I had not slain her yet. (KS, 250)

Oddly enough, Merlin reached appeasement with Jurt after returning to the Courts of Chaos for the funeral of the late king. They talked in a room of mirrors, so that misdirection would hinder any attack one tried against the other. About his attempt to bathe in the Black Fount, Jurt said:

"I'm glad now I didn't go the full route. I suspect it might have driven me mad, as it did Brand. But it may not have been that at all. Or—I don't know. . . . She didn't want me to kill you."

"Julia?"

"Yes."

"How is she?"

"Recovering. Pretty rapidly, actually."

"Is she here at Sawall?"

"Yes."

"Look, I'd like to see her. But if she doesn't want to, I understand. I didn't know it was her when I stabbed Mask, and I'm sorry."

"She never really wanted to hurt you. Her quarrel was with Jasra. With you, it was an elaborate game. She wanted to prove she was as good as—maybe better than—you. She wanted to show you what you'd thrown away."

"Sorry." . . .

"Tell me one thing, please. . . . Did you love her? Did you ever really love her?" . . .

"Yes. . . . I didn't realize it till it was too late, though. Bad timing on my part. . . . What about you?"

"I'm not going to make the same mistake you did. . . . She's what got me to thinking about all these things. . . ."

"I understand. If she won't see me, tell her that I said I'm sorry—about everything." (PC, 127)

Sometime later, when Merlin was rushing about the House of Sawall on urgent business, he accidentally met Julia. She was lovely, dressed in a blue silk wrap. They reconciled, held each other, and kissed. She asked that he come to her in the Wisteria Room, where she was staying, when his other business was completed. He nearly promised her he would, but he left room for some doubt. But perhaps, also, there was room for a royal alliance. Julia's help would be most useful with Merlin ruling in the Courts.

BAYLE, BARON

Nobleman and official vintner to the Court of Amber. His wines are the common coin of the realm, and he maintains a thriving business with merchants from numerous shadows who purchase them.

Baron Bayle's grandfather had been a settler from another shadow, one of the first to be brought to populate the true city while Dworkin was leading the Amberites. Bayle's grandfather was a farmer who settled in the fertile lands east of the city, in the far reaches of the countryside. It was he who had begun the vineyards that later grew in prosperity and fame.

The Bayles were a hardy lot, showing themselves fortunate enough to be among the numbers that were remarkably long-lived. Perhaps environment more than heredity had something to do with it. Old Bayle lived long enough to see both his son and grandson grow to manhood and establish themselves as the vintners to the king of Amber.

Baron Bayle, unlike his forebears, had three daughters. The youngest was Vinta Bayle, a capable young girl who formed a romantic liaison with one of King Oberon's sons. The baron had been enthusiastic about the match, but he had known that, no matter what his feelings were, his daughter was strong-willed enough to do as she wished.

He loved his vineyards almost as much as he loved his family, and he spent much of his time overseeing the entire process of the manufacture of his wines. In fact, he was always somewhat perturbed that he could not discern why some of his white wines were not of the quality he engendered in the rest of his production. If asked, he would deny the inferiority of his whites, but he good-naturedly labeled his bottles of white wine with the picture of one of his favorite dogs and the name Bayle's Piss. He had resigned himself to permitting the appellation of Dog's Piss for these poorer yields, although he wouldn't use that designation himself.

The baron also raised horses, and he kept stables both in his town house in Amber and at Arbor House, his country estate. Of late, he divided his time between his country manor, where he supervised the initial stages of his production, and his town house on East Vine, where he kept the larger portion of Bayle's Best for sale and distribution to the Royal House and other nobility.

While he often sailed between the two places for the sake of speed, he also enjoyed riding on horseback overland, and he would take a horse riding almost as frequently as he would go sailing to reach town.

Baron Bayle had been loyal to the late liege of Amber, but he felt more than mere loyalty to King Random. He felt a fondness for him, largely because Random often praised his wines to him. The king seemed a kindred spirit to Baron Bayle in matters of the grape.

BAYLECREST

A small town to the east of the city of Amber and a few miles north of Arbor House, the country estate of Baron Bayle. Many of the menial help, laborers, harvesters, skilled workers, and servants who work on and around the Bayle estate live in Baylecrest.

While the outlying areas are largely farmland, the town of Baylecrest handles most of the minor industries that are incorporated into Baron Bayle's winery. One of its larger industries, for instance, is the cutting down of trees for lumber. A large proportion of this is used in the preparing of wine casks. Glassblowing is another small manufacturing outlet of the town. While this is used to supply bottles for Arbor House, several shops in Baylecrest sell a wide variety of decorative and functional artifacts made of glass. The town manages very well on these and other wares, all initially produced for Baron Bayle, but also expanded into desirable commodities for merchants and their families during their stopover.

The skilled workers who travel to the baron's estate to work in his winery usually maintain workshops in their own homes as well. Thus, some of the bottling of wines is accomplished in Baylecrest to be sold there, while the greater part of the work is completed and shipped at the winery.

The townspeople have always found Baron Bayle to be very generous with them, not only monetarily, but also in offering some of the amenities of his production. The local drinking establishments often have a surfeit of Bayle's Piss at their disposal.

BAYLE'S BEST

Delightful red wines grown in the château of Baron Bayle in the eastern wine country of Amber.

They may range from light red Burgundies, to the darker Romanee, to the sweet Sauternes.

Usually, the reds are better when they are aged because of the great amount of tannin in them. Fine red wines should stand upright for several hours before they are decanted or served, to give the sediments time to settle to the bottom. Old wines should be opened at least half an hour before they are served, permitting the wine to breathe.

Baron Bayle shrewdly oversees the harvesting of Bayle's Best. It is of extreme importance that the grapes reach a favorable balance between decreasing acidity and increasing percentage in sugar content. This is crucial to producing the best grape at time of picking and the subsequent fermenting process.

Bayle's Best is prized for its sweet honeylike smoothness. On official state occasions, King Random will serve Bayle's Best, as his wife, Queen Vialle, did when Prime Minister Orkuz and Ambassador Quist visited the Royal Palace.

Bayle's Best is easily recognizable by its sweet, buttery taste, and its wonderful fragrance.

BAYLE'S PISS

A white wine produced and bottled by Baron Bayle. It is sold widely in Amber and the near shadows.

Bottled at the Bayles' country estate in the wine country to the east of the true city, each bottle bears the Bayle emblem and a picture of a golden retriever. Sometimes the local gentry refers to the white wine as Dog's Piss.

Bayle's Piss, like most white wines, is not water white. It has a yellowish green color, made from black grapes. While it is a good, pleasant wine, it is not a great wine. However, it is the usual variety of the grape put into general use. The problem for Baron Bayle has been that while many of the whites retain enough acid and structure to be crisp, some lack body and are thin.

This problem has been so confounding because the baron has never been able to determine at what point in the process his Bayle's Piss has failed. Perhaps it was the soil in which the *V. vinifera* grew; or during the second fermentation in the bottle, where improper handling could permit yeast in the sediment to infiltrate the wine; or the accidental subjection to oxidation during the process of racking, when the wine is poured into airtight containers. Carefully checking the wines at each step, Baron Bayle simply has not been able to find the flaw that affects the quality of these wines.

Most of the cafés in Amber are stocked with Bayle's Piss, and only on rare occasion do customers complain of a thin, tasteless wine. When Merlin purchased a bottle of Bayle's Piss at Bloody Bill's, he found it quite acceptable.

For everyday use, even those in the Royal Palace drink Bayle's Piss with their meals. Usually, only a special occasion, such as a state visit, would require the serving of Bayle's Best.

BAYLESPORT

The harbor and town in the eastern reaches of Amber, named for Baron Bayle. Merlin had traveled there by boat in the company of one of Baron Bayle's daughters.

By sailing ship or boat, Baylesport is a pleasant ride of several hours along the eastern coast. Once one passes a thick promontory of land, where a small lighthouse keeps craft away from the rocks, one can see the harbor.

There is a quaint country inn on a hill that one walks to on a cobbled road from the dock. Meals are served up in ample portions, and the owners even serve that rare commodity, coffee.

A well-supplied livery stable, where one can pay for the use of one's horse, is nearby. At the time when Merlin visited, it had a choice of six or seven horses in stalls.

On horseback, Merlin and Vinta Bayle traveled eastward for three miles to reach her father's country estate, Arbor House.

Baylesport provides an often frequented port of call for merchants wishing to purchase wines from the baron's vineyards. Their trade helps maintain the small but affluent commerce of the tiny village.

BAYLE TOWN HOUSE

Located in the city of Amber, it is the local residence of Baron Bayle. The baron maintains a small private stable of horses behind his town house, one of two passions he enjoys. The other are his vineyards, which are spread out by his country estate well to the east. In his home in the city, he keeps a well-stocked wine cellar filled with casks and bottles of the wines he produces. Most of these contain his white wines, sold to the local gentry for general consumption. However, he also has a cache of his excellent red wines, which he offers to the Royal Palace and some of the nobility in the area.

The Bayle town house can be found on East Vine along the sloping rise that leads into the city, just after passing through the Eastern Gate. In the off-season, when the wine harvest has been completed, the baron often spends his time in the city, enjoying the social graces of other nobles and their wives.

Many has been the time when Baron Bayle entertained members of the Royal Family in informal social gatherings in the town house. He relishes such society, and they are the times when he lavishes his guests with nearly limitless bottles of Bayle's Best.

BAYLE, VINTA

Third daughter of Baron Bayle and mistress of the late Prince Caine of Amber. For a brief time, she had been manipulated by a strange entity, during which she encountered Merlin, son of Corwin, and brought him from the city to her father's country estate in the east.

Haughty and proud, Vinta Bayle often gave the impression that she was dispassionate, seemingly superior to others. Perhaps she was a bit self-centered, but she shared her father's concern for staying on the amiable side of the Royal Family. While she enjoyed the openness of the countryside around Arbor House, particularly for horseback riding, she frequented the town, enjoying the company of young nobles before becoming involved with Caine.

She was not especially interested in the Bayle winery, although she had watched enough since childhood to know a great deal about wine making. On the other hand, she shared her father's interest in horses and was an enthusiastic rider.

Quietly attendant at the funeral of Caine, she had an opportunity to meet and talk with young Merlin in the palace's dining hall afterward. She had been asking about the strange occurrence of a black-cloaked assassin who had apparently tried to disrupt the funeral procession. Although she found Merlin pleasant, he didn't have much more knowledge of the goings-on than she did. As soon as Merlin excused himself, Vinta found herself surrounded by three of the eligible sons of local nobility.

At Baron Bayle's country manor, Merlin had several long talks with Vinta Bayle, but she was being influenced by a possessing entity. Thus, these conversations would not really be enlightening as to Vinta's true personality. But after the possessing entity had left, Vinta did return to herself, with a lapse of memory about that time.

When she saw Merlin at Arbor House, she was surprised only in that she didn't know why he was there, since her servants had already told her of his presence and she had searched for him. She had a goblet of her father's adequate white wine and offered Merlin a glass of Bayle's Piss as well. They sat together in a large airy room by a large window, and Vinta initiated this conversation:

"What can you tell me about my blackout? . . . I'd been in Amber, and the next thing I knew I was back here and several days had gone by."

"Yes . . . About what time did you become yourself again?"

"This morning."

"It's nothing to worry about—now. . . . There shouldn't be a recurrence."

"But what was it?"

"Just something that's been going around."

"It seems more like magic than the flu."

"Perhaps there was a touch of that too . . . You never know what might blow in out of Shadow. But almost everyone I know who's had it is okay now." . . .

"It was very strange."

"There is absolutely nothing to worry about." . . .

"I believe you. What are you doing here, anyhow?"

"Stopover. I'm on my way back to Amber, from elsewhere. . . . Which reminds me—may I borrow a horse?"

"Certainly. . . . How soon will you be leaving?"

"As soon as I get the horse." . . .

"I didn't realize you were in a hurry. I'll take you over to the stables now." . . .

"Thanks for the hospitality, even if you don't recall it."

"Don't say good-bye yet. . . . Ride around to the kitchen door off the patio, and I'll give you a water bottle and some food for the road. We didn't have a mad affair that I don't remember, did we?"

"A gentleman never tells." . . .

"Come see me sometime when I'm in Amber . . . and refresh my memory. . . . Let my father know that I'll be back in a few days, will you? Tell him that I came to the country because I wasn't feeling well, but that I'm all right now."

"Glad to." . . .

"I don't really know why you were here . . . But if it involves politics or intrigue I don't want to know."

"Okay." . . .

"If a servant took a meal to a big red-haired man who seemed to be pretty badly injured, this would be better forgotten?"

"I'd say."

"It will be, then. But one of these days I'd like the story."

"Me too. . . . We'll see what we can do."

"So, have a good journey." (BA, 144–46)

Although this conversation shows that Vinta may still be somewhat flirtatious, she also displays a certain amount of discretion. Like her father, she feels a loyalty to the Crown. It seems obvious here that her concern for Merlin was quite genuine.

BEGMA

A shadow kingdom that has been an old member of the Golden Circle, enjoying commerce with Amber for centuries. In close proximity to the shadow named Kashfa, Begma has had a long and tumultuous association with it. Part of the reason for their disharmony may have been caused by Kashfa's not having been admitted to the Golden Circle. Another reason for periods of conflict was the matter of Eregnor. This was a rich area that both

Kashfa and Begma had claimed at various points in their history, sometimes engaging in war over it. Recently, the ambassador from Begma paid a visit to Amber to lodge a protest about rumors that Amber was arranging a Golden Circle treaty with Kashfa.

Although Merlin had not visited Begma himself, he learned a bit more about that shadow from the daughters of Prime Minister Orkuz, Coral and Nayda. He recounted some of Coral's descriptions in his journals:

> She began telling me of a girlhood spent in and around Begma, of her fondness for the outdoors—of horses and of boating on the many lakes and rivers in that region—of books she had read, and of relatively innocent dabblings in magic. A member of the household staff came in just as she was getting around to a description of some interesting rites performed by members of the local farming community to insure the fertility of the crops. (SC, 58)

Somewhat later, while accompanying Coral into the true city, Merlin had a chance to further his understanding of her homeland:

> "There is so much activity, so much going on here . . ." she commented after a time.
> "True. Begma is less busy, I take it?"
> "Considerably."
> "Is it a pretty safe place to stroll about?"
> "Oh, yes."
> "Do the women as well as the men take military training there?"
> "Not ordinarily. Why?"
> "Just curious."
> "I've had some training in armed and unarmed combat, though," she said.
> "Why was that?" I asked.
> "My father suggested it. Said it could come in handy for a relative of someone in his position. I thought he might be right. I think he really wanted a son."
> "Did your sister do it, too?"
> "No, she wasn't interested."
> "You planning on a diplomatic career?"
> "No. You're talking to the wrong sister."
> (SC, 67–68)

Nayda, Coral's older sister, worked as her father's secretary, and so she was frequently involved in matters of state. Even though we must recognize that she was an unreliable source of information about Begma when Merlin knew her, she was very likely drawing upon actual knowledge. In confidence, Nayda told Merlin:

> "It's no secret that we keep files on people we're likely to encounter in our line of work. There's a file on everyone in the House of Amber, of course, even those who don't have much to do with diplomacy. . . .
> "We have very good intelligence sources. Small kingdoms often do." (SC, 110–11)

The matter of Eregnor was a primary cause of Prime Minister Orkuz's unexpected visit to Amber. Word had gotten out that King Random was negotiating a Golden Circle treaty with some of the wealthy noblemen of Kashfa. Orkuz was given to understand that Amber's Crown was seriously considering the offer of this valuable territory to Kashfa in their treaty. Orkuz was greatly concerned, and he hoped his staunchly defensive presence might sway Amber's king to clarify this misapprehension, at least to the prime minister's satisfaction.

Bill Roth, who had made his home in Amber, compared Eregnor to Alsace-Lorraine on shadow Earth. He explained to Merlin:

> "It has changed hands back and forth so many times over the centuries that both countries make reasonable-sounding claims to it. Even the inhabitants of the area aren't all that firm on the matter. They have relatives in both directions. I'm not even sure they care which side claims them, so long as their taxes don't go up. I think Begma's claim might be a little stronger, but I could argue the case either way." (SC, 133)

Although the Eregnor situation was a sore point in the relations between Begma and Kashfa, one that had brought them to war several times in their history, they had also enjoyed periods of reconciliation. Perhaps those periods of tranquility had brought enough affluence from their commercial interchange, that Kashfa had not resented Begma's Golden Circle status. No doubt, however, this may also have instigated some of their hostilities in the past, much like the grumblings of an active volcano, ready to erupt one moment, then settling into calm the next.

Jasra recalled Orkuz in pleasanter times for Merlin, remembering his wife, as well:

> "Kinta. I'd met her, at diplomatic functions. Lovely lady."
> "Tell me about her [Coral's] father."
> "Well, he's a member of the royal house, but of a branch not in the line of succession. Before he was prime minister, Orkuz was the Begman ambassador to Kashfa. His family was in residence with him, so naturally I saw him at any number of affairs." (KS, 44)

Earlier, Coral had told Merlin that she knew Jasra's son Rinaldo when they were children. She explained:

> "Kashfa's pretty close to Begma. Sometimes we were on good terms, sometimes not so good. You know how it is. Politics. When I was little there were long spells when we were pretty friendly. There were lots of state visits, both ways. We kids would often get dumped together." (SC, 64)

During one of those long stretches of peace between the two shadows, Jasra and Orkuz had made arrangements meant to seal the bond between them. As Merlin recorded in his journals:

> She [Coral] and Luke had been married as kids, by proxy ... part of the diplomatic arrangement between Jasra and the Begmans. It didn't work out though—the diplomatic part, that is— and the rest kind of fell by the wayside. The principals had sort of forgotten about the marriage, too, till recent events served as a reminder. Neither had seen the other in years. Still, the record showed that the prince [of Kashfa] had been married. While it was an annullable thing, she could also be crowned with him. (PC, 2)

When Luke succeeded in taking the throne of Kashfa, Coral willingly joined him. Thus, they tied the two shadow kingdoms irrevocably together by law and matrimony.

Recently in Begman politics sweeping changes had occurred. Since the conclusion of the Patternfall War, in Begma, as well as other near shadows, many more common citizens insisted on taking an active interest in government, particularly as it related to their association with Amber. In that shadow, for instance, there was a greater influx of women to the political arena. The Begman women, it would seem, felt the need to have a more active part in events that could so adversely affect them, as Patternfall had. Thus, they took positions in government in which they could, at the very least, deal directly with the Royal Family in Amber.

The Begman Embassy is on the Main Concourse in the true city. Residing there, able to make official visits to the Royal Palace quite readily, are the ambassador, a tall, imposing woman named Ferla Quist, and her assistant, a blond-haired lady named Dretha Gannell. Ambassador Quist's secretary is a thin, middle-aged man named Cade. Clearly, the introduction of women into positions of power in Begman society has been innovative in recent years. Still, these newer associates of statesmanship have proved themselves to be valuable and efficient. They will continue to enhance the prestige of their gender, as they add to the productivity and diversity of Begman society.

BENEDICT

Master of Arms of Amber and Protector General for the shadow Avalon. Although the late King Oberon was known to have had an unspecified number of offspring before Benedict's birth, Benedict is commonly acknowledged as being the oldest surviving heir. He was born to Cymnea (or Clymnea) before that marriage had been dissolved by royal edict. While Benedict never expressed feelings about the utter dissolution in the marriage between his mother and father, perhaps his trait of detachment could be traced to submerged feelings about it.

Benedict was still very young when his father ended the marriage to Cymnea and wed Faiella, who became mother to Eric, Corwin, Caine, and Deirdre. His youth may have been partly the reason for his inaction, especially since his older brothers, Finndo and Osric, protested strongly against the abrupt ending of their mother's status. Benedict seemed unaffected by his older brothers' subsequent deaths in battle, and has since refused to broach the subject of the royal lineage.

Very little is known about Benedict's childhood. There are no documented records dating back that far, and Benedict has been virtually silent about his early adolescence and the period prior to his mother's disfranchisement. Although the facts are lacking, one may surmise that he acquired his dispassionate interest in warfare partly as a result of learning that his brothers died in battle. His passion for gardening may also derive from the same source, having developed, in all likelihood, from a need to seek for peace within himself.

In Corwin's view of him, Benedict is a man of contradictions. Corwin's Chronicles describe Benedict in rustic terms, as one who dresses in "orange and yellow and brown and reminded me [Corwin] of haystacks and pumpkins and scarecrows and the Legend of Sleepy Hollow" (NP, 28). Yet, there are few who are more cosmopolitan than he. While Corwin points out the leanness of Benedict's face and form, he speaks of Benedict as being "wide of mind." Though Benedict seldom smiles, Corwin admits to liking him.

Benedict grew into the kind of person that few would dare cross. He commands respect even from those who do not know him, for the unique wisdom showing in those hazel eyes. In spite of the loss of an arm in battle, Benedict was still able to strike fear in Corwin's heart when they confronted each other in a wood near the black road. When discussing his older brother with Ganelon, Corwin revealed much about his background and abilities:

"You do not really understand who it was we talked with in the tent that night. He may have seemed an ordinary man to you—a handicapped one, at that. But this is not so. I fear Benedict. He is unlike any other being in Shadow or reality. He is the Master of Arms for Amber. Can you conceive of a millennium? A thousand years? Several of them? Can you understand a man who, for almost every day of a lifetime like that, has spent some time dwelling with weapons, tactics, strategies? Because you see him in a tiny kingdom, com-

manding a small militia, with a well-pruned orchard in his back yard, do not be deceived. All that there is of military science thunders in his head. He has often journeyed from shadow to shadow, witnessing variation after variation on the same battle, with but slightly altered circumstances, in order to test his theories of warfare. He has commanded armies so vast that you could watch them march by day after day and see no end to the columns. Although he is inconvenienced by the loss of his arm, I would not wish to fight with him either with weapons or barehanded. It is fortunate that he has no designs upon the throne, or he would be occupying it right now. If he were, I believe that I would give up at this moment and pay him homage. I fear Benedict." (GA, 141–2)

"Wide of mind" that he was, Benedict was no mindless brute in battle, nor was he a fierce warrior seeking glory, filled with bloodlust. His temperament was of a more cautious, quieter nature than that. He was an observer of men in war first and foremost. He saw the necessity of war, understood the need for men to fight to the death. He knew the human equation in the movement toward victory on the field of battle. Although he realized the loss of human life in terms of misery and despair for every soldier and his family, he kept the thought of that loss removed from his mind. His control of personal grief acted as a primary operation over the way of life he had chosen for himself.

As soon as he was of age, Benedict joined the infantry and distinguished himself in a number of campaigns in lands of Shadow. In spite of the fact that he was a son of King Oberon, and an initiate of the Pattern since early youth, he chose to serve as a common infantryman. Gradually, he rose from the ranks, but he was determined to do so entirely on his own. Of course, he proved himself an unmatched fighter, but he refused to grandstand. He fought alongside his comrades without engaging in any false heroics. When he became an officer, he was genuinely cheered by his fellows. His heritage aside, it was natural for him to become their leader, for every foot soldier among them would follow him anywhere.

In moments of ease, Benedict sought for more than self-improvement with rapier and saber. His temperament of restraint urged him to find a means to inner peace, and he found that by coaxing exotic plants in a plot of land in the rear of the Royal Palace. From those early times on, the tall, lanky man with the earnest, unsmiling face could be seen on many an occasion working in the gardens with other workmen who maintained the grounds.

Before Benedict had fully matured, when contentment with his life was still an elusive thing, he desired to learn more of Shadow. Like most of the initiates of the Pattern, Benedict felt curiosity about the extent of one's imaginings that could be encompassed by the worlds of Shadow. He must have made many a journey to the shadows to satisfy his curiosity in his youth, but he told his brother Corwin of only one long-ago occasion: " 'Ages ago, when I was young,' he said, 'I hellrode as far as I might go, to the end of everything. There, beneath a divided sky, I looked upon an awesome abyss' " (HO, 103–4). Thus, long before his younger brothers played with forces out of Chaos, Benedict had seen with his own eyes the realm from which they all had come.

His comrades-in-arms continue to speak of Benedict as a war-hardened veteran of vast experience. Without giving any sign of boasting, Benedict had recounted to his officers his observations of the movements of Roman legions under the Caesars; the tactical advances of Cyrus of Persia on Babylon and Asia Minor; and, among his captains of a younger generation, the campaigns of Napoleon against Austria, Prussia, Russia, and Italy. Benedict had been there, studying each advancement as an observer rather than a participant. He traveled the shadows, altering a factor here or there, so that in one shadow, Pompey was not defeated at Pharsalus by the soldiers of Julius Caesar and forced to flee to Egypt to fall under an assassin's blade. Benedict had changed the geography, or the numbers on either side, or urged Pompey to attack at night, or caused Julius's army to fall back too soon. With each change, Benedict learned. While the fighting went on, he remained near enough to smell blood and sweat and hot breath. He brushed the dust of horses and men from his eyes. He would even lend a hand to slay an attacker who spotted him standing on a small rise just outside of the war ground in variant circumstances. Upon his return from these experiences in Shadow, Benedict described to his men the maneuvers that worked in battle and those that led to disaster. He knew them all and never

wrote down any of the strategies he observed, and he demanded that his officers commit them to memory also. Once hearing the clinical detail with which Benedict described an action fought and disastrous blunders made, his corps of officers often remembered well the lessons learned. Drills and training included applications of knowledge shared in just this way.

His play with military strategies in Shadow made Benedict aware of the ephemeral quality of the shadowlands. The battles won and lost, fought and decided innumerable times in innumerable worlds illuminated to him that the shadows were not reality. Only Amber was reality. Strife that tore apart the real world brought irrevocable harm, and its effects could be felt, like dying echoes, in all the worlds. For Benedict, the great imperative was to protect the true city and preserve its people above all else. His sense of duty to Amber may not have grown out of love or patriotism, but rather out of the soldier's need to preserve a homeland to come back to, after the battle is done.

Much of the warfare that Amber had engaged in during King Oberon's firmly established stewardship was staged in shadow realms. Arrangements were made to send companies of well-armed men to defend such kingdoms from invading forces as part of trade agreements that had been carefully and harmoniously negotiated. It was merely a matter of time before shadows that had fought against the Amberites, or shadows that were greedy to take control over the resources, if not the actual land, of Amber, would find a way to invade the true city. A fresh crossing going to and from a defended kingdom could be breached by observant invaders who might have a ready force able to seize the opportunity.

This was the case in the invasion of the Moonriders of Ghenesh.

Initially, Oberon heard of brutal night raids on outlying villages from several noblemen of those regions. The nobles spoke of squat, ugly beings that rode upon flying spheres. It seemed ludicrous to the king when he first heard it. A day or two later, however, and the news took on greater importance. One of Julian's patrols, billeted near a small village to the north of the city, was wiped out, every man horribly butchered.

When Benedict was summoned by Oberon, he had already heard rumors of violent attacks by strange flying creatures. By the time Benedict and his brothers met in council with their father, Oberon had learned a great deal more about the invaders. Oberon had contacted several of the shadows that he had helped in armed warfare in recent months. One of these was a shadow neighboring the realm called Ghenesh. Although this shadow never had contact of any sort with the Moonriders out of Ghenesh, they had heard about them. The Moonriders were a barbaric people who survived and flourished by brute force and savagery. They had formed a kinship with many odd kinds of wildlife, and one of these were the brainless flying spheres they used for mounts. While Oberon's informants couldn't explain how the Moonriders mastered the way into Amber, nor what they wanted of the Amberites, it was probable that they had followed one of the numerous routes that had been taken recently in closing defense agreements with the neighboring shadow.

In their council session, Bleys presented a map of Amber showing the movements of the invaders. Bleys had been gathering such information from nobles and merchants who had seen the squat, ugly men of Ghenesh pillaging shops in several northern villages. From the sightings indicated on the map, the Moonriders were clearly making their way southward. Further information that Bleys had obtained showed that they were foraging for food, supplies that would help them maintain a long siege, and whatever implements they might find useful in fighting a war. Their movements, however, were somewhat disorganized in that they had been spotted along the eastern shoreline on three occasions, going south. It seemed as if they had little understanding of the terrain or accurate knowledge of the location of the heart of Amber.

Oberon prepared for full readiness to repel the Moonriders. He and Benedict worked on the arrangements for infantry and shipboard defenses. Julian was assigned to scout the regions north and east of Kolvir with his patrols. Caine was situated with the fleet and sailed the coastline for any sign of the invaders. Corwin and Bleys formed defensive lines to protect the city and block entry to Kolvir from the west, the south, and the east. In Eric's eagerness to take part, Benedict recognized his overweening desire to please his father. Benedict was wary of Eric's self-serving pleas to Oberon, and it seemed that Oberon shared his view of Eric. The king or-dered Eric to take charge of the Royal Guard. Eric would have to remain within the palace grounds.

Within two days, Julian's patrols reported to the king. The Moonriders had begun moving inland from the northeast about thirty miles away. They had enough mounts for only one-third of their men and the rest were traveling by foot. Although their numbers could not be determined, they made a sizable force, enough so that they had split into two large companies as they headed inland. Each company had a fair proportion of airborne riders to complement the infantry. They were paralleling each other as they traveled erratically toward Kolvir, having apparently realized that the castle they spied upon the mountain represented the seat of power.

Meanwhile, Benedict had traveled in Shadow to learn more about Ghenesh at firsthand. As a military strategist, he believed in knowing as much about one's enemy as possible, for that knowledge enables one to shore up proper defenses against the other's strength. It also enables one to bring power to bear against the other's weaknesses.

Upon his return, Benedict met with Oberon, who brought him up-to-date. Bringing his own regiment to meet with Bleys's and Corwin's in the valley below Kolvir, Benedict outlined a plan of action based on what he had learned.

From various accounts of soldiers in Bleys's troops and Benedict's regiment, the following is the way the invaders were introduced to Amber's state of warfare:

The first thing they would see from the air would be the cavalry, well to the east and north of Arden. They would then be led inland in the direction of the pass above Arden. A tardy horseman would find himself harried by the closing globe-hoppers. He would lose an important-looking dispatch satchel before turning due south, following the rest into the forest. The globe-hoppers would recover the satchel and be surprised to find papers written in a language they could read.

Included with the documents would be maps with symbols that the documents aid in decoding. From them, the invaders would determine the position of the armory of the kingdom and the deployment of men around it. They would scout ahead on their flying mounts to the site of the armory while the remaining force would

BENEDICT

make a quick march to reach it. When the scouting party determines the scant numbers of personnel guarding the tented structure that is meant to be the armory, they would report back to the main part of the army. They wait until nightfall because of certain information within the documentation stating that the leading generals of Amber's army would be meeting at that time within the tent.

After dark, the globe-hoppers would leave their encampment and move to surround the site of the armory with their entire force. When seeing two guards in dress uniforms standing at attention outside of the tent flap, they would know that the generals have begun their conference within. Arrows from riders in the sky would down the guards, and that would signal the attack. The invaders would swarm into the camp, using arrows, large daggers, and curved sabers, cutting down everyone in sight.

That would be when the globe-hoppers would be in for a little surprise.

On first coming to hand against the stiffly standing Amberite soldiers, the invaders would discover propped up figures of wood and cloth. Awareness would come almost immediately that they were under attack. They would be downed by arrows descending on them and realize that the encampment was a decoy couched within a narrow valley. The first volley of arrows would be aimed high, striking the flying creatures and their riders. A second volley would follow, mainly hitting the ground force inside the encampment. That would be when the fighting begins in earnest, and things become muddled with blood and screams.

For their part, the Moonriders fought valiantly, recovering from their surprise fairly quickly. They never gave any indication of trepidation, nor the wish to surrender, but fought hand to hand with bloody ferocity, using knives, sabers, hands, and feet. So many of their comrades were felled in those early volleys, however, that they were never able to regain any advantage against Benedict's main force. Corwin fought beside his men and was able to see Benedict off to his left, slaying the squat enemy soldiers with broad swings of his sword to left and right. As hard as Corwin was fighting, he noted

the phenomenal stamina and deadly efficiency with which his older brother slew the invaders.

The fighting continued for hours, largely because of the brutish tenacity of the invaders. They did not fall back, they did not regroup, they did not transmit orders along their front lines. They simply continued to strike out, raising sword to crash against sword, throwing daggers even as they fell mortally wounded by sword or arrow. Sweat and blood covered all the combatants, and the land smelled of slaughter. At the end of long hours of fighting, some of Benedict's men saw the few remaining flying globes flee with their riders. As the fighting subsided, the Moonriders clearly defeated, the remaining foot soldiers were given the opportunity to retreat, although no formal terms were spoken. Only the dead of the invading force remained on the battlefield.

Burial details were organized, and the men and beasts were placed in long rows of graves on the northern side of the narrow valley. Several of the beast carcasses were removed carefully for examination, for none had ever seen a flying organism like them before.

In a formal court ceremony, Benedict was acknowledged as the hero of the battle. Except for Eric, Benedict's brothers and sisters cheerfully toasted him for many hours into the night. Benedict has never been forthcoming about his feelings toward his brothers, but Julian has commented that he felt a kinship with Benedict that he traced to that time. Corwin had also hinted that he sensed a kinship with his older brother and mentor, coming, in part, from their mutual need to seek other avenues of recreation aside from martial ones.

Shortly after this victory against the Moonriders of Ghenesh, the king began to have lapses of memory. Initially, they seemed to be the result of strain and preoccupation with unexpressed thoughts other than the business at hand. In some of Amber's negotiations with members of the Golden Circle, Oberon's mind had seemed to wander off virtually in mid-sentence as he gave various banquet speeches. He had given orders to court officials to bring him certain documents to examine and sign when such transactions had been accomplished months previously. Everyone in the Royal Court was aware of numerous incidents of Oberon's loss of memory.

As King Oberon's forgetfulness progressed, Eric spoke demandingly with his siblings about Oberon's stepping down from his kingship. Eric was convincingly earnest in making claims that Amber needed a strong ruler or else it would become vulnerable to enemy attack. If it hadn't been for their father's quick action in consolidating their forces a few years earlier, the Ghenesh barbarians would have overrun the city. Their father was no longer that same leader, and Amber could not afford another such invasion at this time because of his weakness. To Benedict, it was obvious where Eric's argument was leading. His was the first voice of protest against Eric. Standing up in the dining hall where the princes and princesses of Amber were meeting informally, Benedict declared himself withdrawn from any further discussion of a successor to the throne. Although there may have been a grain of truth in what Eric had to say, Benedict was of the opinion that only their father had the right to choose to retire from rule. He announced that he had made his own choice to leave this place of dissension for a shadow of quiet contemplation. However, he warned, if anyone caused any peril to their father or their homeland, he would return to set things right in any manner within his power. After Benedict left the hall, servants saw him leaving the palace carrying a small bundle. He had gone to the stables, gotten his favorite horse, a large roan, and ridden off, not to return for a long while.

It remains uncertain how Benedict occupied himself in Shadow during these wanderings. Based on the correlation of several sources of information, however, it seems likely that he created a special shadow out of his own imagination, one in which he could find comfort and solitude from any warlike intervention. By imparting some part of himself into the molecular composition of his sanctuary world, probably drops of his own blood, he imbued the place with its own unique signature. This assured that no other initiate of the Pattern could accidentally, or deliberately, travel to it.

With his own hands he built a small cottage on a fertile piece of land, then went to work tilling the soil. As time passed, Benedict felt the need to have other people to talk to, simply to ease his loneliness. In this shadow, he wanted no cosmopolitans, no people experienced in the ways of the world. He would continue to keep dissension and strife out of this world.

Exerting the will of his imagination, he was delighted to discover a small village had sprung, fully grown, just down the path from his cottage. The people were mainly shopkeepers, laughing and friendly people who greeted him warmly. They were the people of his dreams, those who had few worries and cares, but spoke of themselves and their children as if they had always been there, carrying on long lives of pleasant work and providential experience.

Feeling the need for a more personal connection with this village and these convivial people, he brought into being a middle-aged couple with a nearby farm. They knew him when they greeted him, and they had seemingly been farming the land they lived on for many years. They called themselves the Tecys. As they shared a hearty midday meal, the Tecys asked Benedict about his family and homeland. For Benedict, it was a rare occasion for him to speak freely of things he wanted to tell to someone without the fear of lowering his defenses and appearing vulnerable. This was his land of solace and sanctuary, and he has always cherished it as his private domain.

Since Benedict is not one to document the events in his life, and he seldom offers explanations, it is difficult to ascertain how he learned of happenings in Amber. In some manner, he learned of Corwin's disappearance and Eric's part in it, and this prompted Benedict's return. His presence was a comfort to Oberon, who attempted to hide his worry about Corwin's whereabouts and his rage at the possibility that Eric had committed a foul deed.

Oberon left matters in his sons' hands, but he most particularly depended upon Benedict. Conferring with all his siblings except Eric, Benedict suggested they cover all avenues before making any accusations. For hours at a time, the princes and princesses tried to reach Corwin through his Trump, but to no avail. Other conferences followed, and Benedict had a sense of various unspoken motives at work among some of his brothers. There seemed to be a small conspiracy afoot to lower Eric's position in the court; to attempt to displace him in some way so that one or more of the others could acquire greater status. Benedict was becoming disenchanted once again with the recognition of this minor power play. When Brand stated his decision to search in Shadow for Corwin, or some sign of Corwin, Benedict seconded the idea wholeheartedly, wanting to cleanse himself of the political maneuvering he felt around him.

Benedict traveled the shadows more than once, returning to Amber after each attempt, so that he knew that, besides Brand and himself, Gérard, Julian, Caine, and Random had also gone off to the shadows in search of their brother. While Brand had seemed to have some definite plan in sifting the shadows, Benedict was somewhat at a loss to determine exactly where to look and how far to go. He decided to make a sweep of the near shadows first, in a method that seemed militarily logical to him. From there, he began to look farther and farther afield. Thus, he was able to return to Amber periodically to discover if any of the others had news, and then return to precisely the place where he had left off to continue on systematically.

It became noticeable to those court officials who watch the Royal Library that Benedict had been inside on an occasion and removed several decks of the family Trumps—possibly three decks. This was not terribly strange, but it was noticed. Julian has since mentioned that Benedict told him of an experience he had in one of the shadows he visited while seeking Corwin. Julian wouldn't give the details, but Benedict had been distressed enough by some occurrence to want to preserve several sets of Trumps for his own use. While he placed the extra decks in an old war chest that travels with him on field maneuvers, he always carries one set on his person, in a hidden inner pocket of his tunic. The pack is carefully kept in an ornate silk-lined wooden case, inlaid with bone. Benedict always handles this case with great care, and we are left to wonder what prompted such an attachment.

Benedict and the others kept up the search for long stretches of time. It began to seem hopeless to Benedict, although he was far from willing to give up. He tried a different tack: He kept an image of Corwin in his mind and allowed the shadow worlds to enter his consciousness with that image suffusing them. The more adept he came at devising that correspondence, the closer he seemed to come to a world in which people knew of Corwin. That was how Benedict had found another land that was special to him, one in which he dwelled for decades away from the true city. He explained his discovery to Corwin many years after the fact:

"I sought for you in the vicinity of Avalon . . . and I found this place and was taken by it. It was in a pitiful condition in those days, and

for generations I worked to restore it to its former glory. While I began this in memory of you, I developed a fondness for this land and its people. They came to consider me their protector, and so did I." (GA, 96–97)

Rather than simply remaining in Avalon, Benedict had contacted one of his siblings, probably Gérard, to inform any who cared that he intended to dwell for a time in a distant shadow. He had implied that he thought Corwin was dead, based on indications he had gathered from a shadow in which Corwin had once dwelled. At the time, he hadn't spoken of the shadow Avalon.

Little is known of what the shadow Avalon was like when Benedict first arrived there. It is likely that the land suffered from widespread banditry and lawlessness, on the order of conditions once obtaining in the village of Lorraine. By his entrance and strong hand in ruling Avalon, Benedict would have been most efficient in restoring to Avalon "its former glory," assuming that this had been the situation.

It has been made clear by several different accounts that Benedict continued to maintain a pipeline of communication with someone in Amber. Through Gérard, Benedict was kept informed of the changing political tides in the realm, and he was also aware of local gossip about his siblings. He knew, for instance, something of Random's affair with a princess of the undersea city of Rebma. He also knew of Random's illegitimate son, Martin, who was raised by Queen Moire in Rebma. When young Martin assayed the Pattern in that underwater city, he chose to visit Benedict, and he stayed in Avalon a long while.

Sometime earlier, Benedict had visited Rebma, for Queen Moire knew him, as did Martin when he was a small boy. Benedict spoke to Corwin and Random about his connection to Martin:

"He [Martin] was sick of his position in Rebma, ambivalent toward Amber, young, free, and just come into his power through the Pattern. He wanted to get away, see new things, travel in Shadow—as we all did. I had taken him to Avalon once when he was a small boy, to let him walk on dry land of a summer, to teach him to ride a horse, to have him see a crop harvested. When he was suddenly in a position to go anywhere he would in an instant, his choices were still restricted to the few places of which he had knowledge. . . . So he elected to come to me, to ask me to teach him. And I did. He spent the better part of a year at my place. I taught him to fight, taught him of the ways of the Trumps and of Shadow, instructed him in those things an Amberite must know if he is to survive." (HO, 37–38)

In spite of an obvious fondness for young Martin, Benedict allowed him to exercise his own will and make his own decisions. Thus, when he was confident in the ways of Shadow that Benedict had shown him, Martin chose to venture farther on his own. Benedict gave him a set of Trumps, and Martin began his travels. From time to time, Martin returned and spent much of his time with Benedict talking of his adventures. Martin was one of the very few people that Benedict willingly confided in about his sanctuary world. He had brought Martin there, introduced him to the Tecys, and they all enjoyed the warm glow of family closeness. It was a sensation that both Martin and Benedict had lacked in the real world.

On several occasions while he dwelled in Avalon, Benedict heard of incidents in Amber that nearly coerced him into returning. When he had learned that Oberon was leading a large military force against a female warrior in a near shadow, Benedict thought that his help might be needed. Through his contact with Gérard, he kept informed of the battles. He was delighted when Gérard told him of their father's victory. He was ready to rally to his father's aid again a year or two later, when the same woman returned to raid the shadow Begma again. From a discreet distance, Benedict was actually at the site of battle, watching his young brother Bleys as he brilliantly surrounded the enemy force while they were at their ease. Benedict did nothing, but he was pleased with the great competence that Bleys showed in handling a difficult situation.

Years later, though, a dire situation occurred that gave way to an extraordinary circumstance. Benedict was tending to his orchard in a house he kept in town when he received a Trump contact. He was surprised to discover that it was his father contacting him. The consternation on Oberon's face was quite evident as he addressed Benedict. Amber was under siege by a huge mercenary force of highly skilled and well-equipped men. They had succeeded in pushing back the combined troops of Julian and Bleys, and they were even now approaching Kolvir. Benedict asked about his own men. Oberon said that many of them had been split up: some were serving in the Royal Guard, others were part of Julian's troops, still others had joined the fleet, and the rest had dispersed into village life, having left active service.

Benedict had detected something more in his father's manner as they held the Trump contact. There was something on a personal level that was troubling Oberon. When Oberon told him that he believed the leader of the mercenaries was the son of Deela, the militant fanatic who had harassed Begma, Benedict kept his suspicions to himself. But he saw that his father might have had a personal stake in this confrontation that was disturbing to Oberon. Benedict did not question him further, but immediately came in through the Trump connection.

As soon as he saw the movement of the mercenaries at firsthand, Benedict set to work. Contacting Julian by Trump, he suggested that his troops fan out and arrange some diversionary tactics. It was necessary that Julian stall the oncoming assault while Benedict regrouped his old regiment. Many of Benedict's officers were part of the Royal Guard and, with Prince Eric's agreement, these men were assigned to Benedict for the duration. In short order, Benedict's officers were able to gather up a large proportion of his former regiment, supported by numbers of veterans, now civilians, who wished to serve under the legendary General Benedict. The soldiers, numbers of whom remained out of uniform, gathered outside the city, facing Mt. Kolvir. The sound of battle could already be heard, and dust clouds revealed where Julian's men fought the mercenaries of Dalt, son of Deela the Desacratrix.

Aside from the need for speed, Benedict was uncertain of the skill and maneuverability of many of the men in his regiment. He would have to forgo subtlety for simplicity, forgo tactical advantage for obviousness in strategy, and hope that Dalt hadn't read the texts. He assigned his officers to small companies within the full complement and pointed out positions along the lower cliffs of Kolvir that their men would take. Instead of advancing toward the fighting, Benedict led them on a fast retreat, marching directly toward the lower reaches of the mountain. It was absolutely necessary that the regiment take their positions before any of the enemy raiders broke through the lines of Julian's troops.

When his men were ready, Benedict signaled Julian through his Trump. Julian and his men made a hasty retreat, following a line directly toward Kolvir. Yelling their triumph, Dalt's raiders followed, throwing everything they had at the retreating army. As Julian's men reached the rocky terrain around the mountain, they scattered, seeming to disappear into the trees and boulders, blending into the cliff face and the stark forest. Continuing onward with the natural volition of their rush, Dalt and his mercenaries found themselves facing a small phalanx of motley-colored men bearing swords and lances. The phalanx marched toward the raiders slowly but steadily. They were a tight little corps of men, meant to drive a wedge through Dalt's force. It must have seemed obvious that the intention of this Amberite band was to cause the enemy to split up, scatter along the hillside, and thus be more easily picked off by the forces hidden there.

It was likely Dalt's own decision to charge into the heart of that wedge in an attempt to cut most of the ragtag soldiers down and use the rest as shields. Neither Dalt nor any of his men knew Benedict, and it was Benedict who was in the lead position of that wedge.

The two infantry forces met, Dalt's men spreading out to blunt the head of the phalanx. The raiders fell beneath an onslaught they never expected. Benedict, leading a frenzied attack, was swinging his long, curved saber like a scythe of death, harvesting human flesh. Then arrows and spears poured on the raiders from above, catching the outermost invaders first. As more of Benedict's regiment entered into the fray from the cliffs, the mercenaries found that they were surrounded and could not retreat.

Hours seemed like brief moments of swords and clubs shattering bone and metal. In those moments, lives struck against lives, and there were many instances of young faces staring at other young faces as one life ended and the other lived to fight for long moments more. At one such moment, Benedict saw Dalt, and Dalt and he, standing face-to-face with swords pointing, each knew the other for what he was. Dalt raged as he struck at Benedict, and Benedict gave him a grim smile that remained frozen in concentration, no other thought passing but the cold-blooded need to conclude the life of this young murderer.

Neither would die easily, and their hard personal combat was interrupted numbers of times as enemy soldiers dared to intrude, to fall dispatched too readily before a contest higher than their understanding. Each distraction only gave Benedict and Dalt renewed zeal to complete their unspoken contract with one another. Blood coated their swords, their clothes were awash with red, but neither one had shed any for the other.

The death of any one soldier meant nothing to Dalt as he continued his singular involvement. However, awareness came upon him that his force was being depleted, and if he engaged in this duel much longer, he would inevitably be made a prisoner. His fatigue weighed upon his muscles. He was forced to quicken his pace, to seek an end with this exceptional leader of warriors.

Benedict recognized the change, and his smile widened slightly, then disappeared in a line of solemnity. He lowered his sword. Dalt saw the opening and took it. Benedict arced his sword upward, first right, and Dalt moved to parry, then left, and Dalt parried again, and Benedict slashed diagonally downward, from left to right. As Dalt sidestepped to avoid the slash, he left his defenses open. Benedict thrust through Dalt's lower chest, and Dalt was momentarily impaled. His eyes wide, mouth gaping, Dalt fell back limply, and he slowly slid to the ground, his sword still in hand. Before he could approach the body, Benedict found himself pushed back by a sudden surge of mercenaries, deliberately blocking the fallen body of their leader. Benedict slew three of the raiders before apprehending that they were all ready to die in order to carry back the dead body of their champion. With a wide gesture of his arm, Benedict halted his regiment. With the slowing of fighting, the raiders drew back quickly. Many carried unmoving bodies over their backs as they retreated. Among Benedict's ranks, few cheered, for they recognized devoted comradeship and selfless bravery.

Once the crisis was past, Oberon found it difficult to hold Benedict in Amber any longer. Benedict expressed concern for his pensioners and servants in shadow Avalon. He had left behind several contingents to maintain four separate residences he had, ranging in and around that shadow. One result of Benedict's return to Amber was that a few of his former comrades requested that he take them back to Avalon. With Oberon's permission, Benedict allowed this, and so he returned to Avalon with five veterans of Amber's wars.

Upon his return, Benedict found several messages from young Martin in one of his country homes. They were pleasant little notes indicating that all was well, that he had spent several joyful visits with the Tecys, and that he had journeyed to a number of shadows of variant time streams and vistas that had left him exhilarated.

After giving his five new staff members a chance to settle into their new surroundings, Benedict continued his duties in helping to govern the town. Several weeks went by in this way, and then Martin came by for a visit. He remained for two weeks, and he asked about Benedict's recent adventure in Amber. He was particularly curious about his grandfather, a man he heard much about but had never met. Benedict spoke tersely of Oberon, covering some barely perceptible inner turmoil. Observing this, Martin did not pursue the subject much beyond his initial questions, and talked further of his own travels. At the end of two weeks, Martin bade his uncle farewell and went on his way.

Much of what happened in Avalon next comes to us through one of the five men Benedict brought to Avalon. The man, an officer who had been in Benedict's regiment, later returned to Amber. He told of a group of men, who appeared to have come from a neighboring village, making loud complaints to the townspeople of Avalon. They complained of widespread burglaries and thefts, blaming Benedict for a lack of enforcement. When robberies began to break out in the town, the local people helped to spread the near rioting.

When the rioters stormed the militia house maintained by Benedict outside of town, it began a series of skirmishes that grew in intensity. Benedict's soldiers attempted to put down the insurgency as quickly as possible, but, during a dangerous encounter, several insurgents were killed. Benedict was called in when the physical nature of the dead insurgents was discovered. Benedict spoke to the medical man who examined the bodies in the local morgue. The most obvious abnormality in each man who had arrived from another village was the gnarled, clawlike feet that had been hidden in the shoes each had worn. The medical man then examined the dead men's hands. The fingers were not quite human, but were longer, with extra joints and clawed nails. A crudely performed autopsy showed that their inter-

nal organs were quite different from those of any human, as well.

As Benedict soon learned, this discovery was the beginning of an outbreak of numerous attacks on Avalon. It seemed that various beings of other shadows had discovered the placid contentment of this land and felt it was ripe for pillaging. Benedict and his militia kept up a strong vigilance against these assaults and secured a continuation of peace and order for some time. Through contacts with Gérard, Benedict found that Amber was undergoing attacks from creatures out of Shadow during this same period.

Shortly after an especially vicious invasion by other clawed men that was gradually put down, Benedict heard from Gérard that Oberon had mysteriously vanished from the true city and, in fact, had been gone for an overly long stretch of time. He was disturbed by this and asked Gérard to keep him informed by Trump of any new developments.

While Benedict's men continued an armed vigilance, the attacks seemed to slacken and all was peaceful for a time. Then Benedict received a message from the Tecys about Martin. It indicated that Martin had been hurt but was recovering. Benedict felt it urgent enough for him to leave Avalon for a day or two in order to visit the Tecys. By the time he arrived, Martin was already gone. This is what Benedict has said about the circumstances:

> "It was a body wound, caused by the thrust of a blade. They said he came to them in very bad shape and did not go into details as to what had occurred. He remained for a few days—until he was able to get around again—and departed before he was really fully recovered. That was the last they heard of him. . . .
>
> "He had pulled through the crisis and he did not attempt to contact me. He apparently knew what he wanted to do. He did leave a message for me with the Tecys, saying that when I learned of what had happened I was not to worry, that he knew what he was about."
> (HO, 39–40)

Naturally, Benedict was extremely concerned about Martin, but he applied to his nephew the same principles he had set for himself. He firmly believed that every man was meant to set his own course, and once he has stated his intentions, in clear terms, his resolve should not be tampered with. Having concluded this, Benedict traveled back to his Avalon.

When he returned to Avalon on his large red horse, Benedict saw the desolation of the countryside outside of town at once. Trees were uprooted, cracks and upheavals of dirt marred the land, and a small thatched home where a farmer had lived lay in ruins nearby. He rode toward one of the manors that he kept in town. Most of the small residences and the shops stood intact, but windows were broken and debris was scattered through the streets. As he rode by, several people peeked out of shop doors and thickly curtained windows in tentative fashion. It was uncannily quiet.

At his manor house, Benedict heard what had happened. One of his trusted servants explained that the night before there had been a terrible earthquake. It had lasted only for seconds, but the damage was widespread. However, the townspeople were not still fearful over that. In the east end of town, nearest the mountains, a band of riders had come, looting the shops, killing whoever stood in their way, and abducting twenty or more young men. That was why the people were afraid.

Benedict was somewhat perplexed. They had been raided before. Some of them had fought and died battling strange creatures out of Shadow before. Even after the hardship of suffering an earthquake, why would they be especially afraid of this new attack?

The servant was joined by others on Benedict's staff. Together, they told of the sight some of them had seen in the pitch black of the other night. Two or three of them had been in the east end that night and had seen the riders and their horses. White, they were, white, thick-muscled horses thundering toward the town in stark contrast to the moonless black night around them. As they came closer, the riders could be seen. They had long white hair and they clanged upon their horses, wearing armor of a milk white color. When they reached the town, they did not slow, but sped through the streets, and the huge horses breathed fire that singed shop fronts and turned piles of rubble into flame. For a brief moment, one of Benedict's housekeepers had seen the face of one rider. It had been the face of a lovely young woman with eyes so white that they seemed demonic. She let out a hideous scream, meant to be a war cry, and swept everything out of her path with a long thin blade. The housekeeper had hidden in fear behind a row of barrels in front of a shop and watched as the demon-women rode past him on their fire-breathing mounts. He ran once they had gone, but others saw them leaving town carrying living men stretched across their saddles, struggling to get free.

In the early morning, an accounting of the losses had been made. Numerous shops of various kinds had been raided; an old woman and a small boy lay dead in the street; and more than twenty young men were missing. The townspeople hid in fear that the demon-women would return, and perhaps not wait until nightfall this time.

Realizing that many of the townspeople were on the verge of panic, Benedict conferred with his officers in preparation of repelling any further raids. He had his soldiers form a ring around the town, just within its borders and blockading the main thoroughfares into town. Since he couldn't protect the entire village equally, Benedict placed himself with his heaviest guard at the eastern part of town. His men had asked shopkeepers to volunteer some of their valuables, and these were placed in several piles in plain sight on the three main roads leading into town from the east. The barricades were simply clumps of furnishings, fallen tree trunks, and other detritus of the previous night's disturbance. The enemy's horses could easily hurdle the barriers, but the contingents of armed men behind them would be partially obscured.

We know of the attacks of these demon-women only through the informal descriptions given by Benedict's veteran officer, the one who eventually returned to Amber. He is a stalwart soldier and was at the front lines of most of these battles, but he is not given to vivid storytelling. He has admitted that one battle with these females of Hell became like another, and they blended together in his mind.

It may have been the attack of the first night, or else a composite of several of these early skirmishes, that stand out in the officer's mind. The Hell-women only attacked at night, and those first skirmishes were particularly harrowing. The demon-women and horses spewing hellfire tore their victims asunder when they got close enough, the women drinking blood, and the horses devouring flesh. When they were struck with a mortal blow, both females and horses, they seemed to shrivel and burn up, leaving behind nothing but charred remnants that were not quite bone. The young men who had been carried away returned. Trancelike, these men sought further victims with hands that were lifeless but still retained strength. They would walk directly up to the soldiers, grab them by the throat in an awful stranglehold, trying to get close enough to rip apart necks with their teeth. They would continue to move, though pierced with sword or dagger, until they were hacked to pieces. These were terror attacks at the absolute worst, breeding confusion and fear.

Early in the campaign, with many casualties on both sides, Benedict devised a way to trace the demon-women back to their source. With several of his best men, Benedict followed the raiders' line of retreat to the eastern mountains. Odd, fissurelike caverns had formed at the base and lower reaches of the mountain range. The caves ran steeply down and were quite deep. They probably formed an intricate network of tunnels well below ground.

Some of the best military surveyors and engineers in the shadow belonged to Benedict's well-trained army, and they went to work examining the terrain. They were forced to work quickly, for they had exactly one day's span as time runs in Avalon. Within that limit, they succeeded in blocking every cavern that opened up on that range of mountains. They had so strived that nothing but an explosive charge of the largest dimensions could unseal the caves, and they agreed to a certainty that no cave or fissure had been missed. It was also a certainty that, as in Amber, no explosive charge could be ignited in this shadow.

No attack came that night. Nor in the next several nights. The townsfolk of Avalon believed they had undermined the hellmaids and that there would be no further raids.

A cautious man, Benedict camped out by the mountains with a company of his men, watchful for any sign of a breach.

Late one night, a small party of Benedict's men, making a reconnaissance, heard the crumbling of rock and felt a forceful rumble, as of something breaking the ground. They weren't near enough to the site to see an opening, but, from their position, they spied the white forms of the armored women on horseback exiting from around a curve in the mountainside. They sent a messenger from their company to the main body of men, while they began to track the hellmaids. The messenger was a bright

lad, who quickly found Benedict and his soldiers and led them to a point ahead of the demon riders. The land was flat along that region, so Benedict had a group of his veterans dismount and lie in wait on their stomachs, ranged about the area that the raiders would have to cross to reach the borders of the town. The rest of his soldiers would remain well back and out of sight in the darkness with their horses.

Benedict chose to remain with his dismounted men, flat on his stomach with sword in hand. The mounted hellmaids were seen in just a matter of minutes, riding toward a point to Benedict's right. He counted on his other men to rise up at the proper time to halt the riders' progress. The lights of the town could be seen just a short distance behind their location.

Every soldier flattened against that ground could feel the trembling vibration of the demon-women's approach. These men were war-hardened veterans, waiting stolidly even as they felt the nearness of horses' hooves, flamed breath, and dust. When the death white horses were nearly upon them, the most proximate soldiers jumped to their feet, swinging their swords, and yelling loudly to signal the others. Benedict and the others along the line rushed into the battle. Five or six warriors and their horses lay dead around Benedict as he continued to lunge at the oncoming attackers. Soon, the mounted soldiers of Benedict's army were upon the demon warriors, and they were followed by the reconnaissance party, arriving behind the raiders. The combined forces routed the hellmaids. While numbers escaped to the mountains, many were slain, and others were taken prisoner. Those who were captured were restrained and forced to watch their mounts slaughtered, for the horses could not be contained by the humans.

By his officers' count, they had eleven unhurt prisoners and three more with serious wounds. They were bound tightly, seated on the ground, and put under close watch while Benedict and his men raised tents and formed an encampment. As soon as one tent was set up, the wounded captives were placed within, to be cared for by a soldier with medical training. One of the men guarding the prisoners was a linguist of sorts, and he had determined by listening to the hellmaids that two or three of them spoke a form of Thari, but the rest spoke a language he did not know.

When the soldier reported this, Benedict asked if

he had given any indication to the prisoners that he understood them. The soldier said no.

Benedict and a small number of his men stood before the captives. Benedict spoke imperiously to the warrior women, saying that their leader was dead and they would be brought into town to stand trial for their crimes. The females cursed and laughed scornfully as Benedict concluded.

After moving away, Benedict asked the soldier who had stood beside him if he learned anything from the women's talk. The man said that when they had laughed, one of the women cut the others off with a sign. During much of Benedict's speech, the females seemed to glance frequently at this one particular hellmaid who sat unsmiling throughout.

Benedict ordered the guards to bring the unsmiling hellmaid to his tent, one that was set up a little distance from the others. When they did, Benedict ordered the guards away, and he was left alone with the warrior. Although his soldiers were curious, none came to disturb Benedict that night. In the early hours before dawn, the female warrior was brought back to the other captives by two soldiers.

Calling his officers into his tent shortly after daybreak, Benedict told them of further information he had obtained from the hellmaid. She was indeed their leader. Her name was Lintra. She was far older than she looked in terms of Avalon-time, coming from a distant shadow where the days pass more quickly. She wouldn't admit how they learned of Avalon nor why they targeted the place, but one of their interests was to acquire young men for the purpose of procreation. The women were fertile enough so that the captive men were necessary for only a short time. They then used the captives as an attachment to their army, an auxiliary of short-term use, for they were nonliving expendables with no self-direction.

Benedict also told his men that they had to call out more infantry from Avalon, for there would be an all-out battle that night to liberate the leader of the hellmaids. Two of his officers took some men and went into town to gather up their forces.

Many came and were placed at their posts around the camp by the time the sky purpled. Benedict took a measure of the soldiers, walking quietly through the camp. It seemed to him that they would not be nearly enough. They waited quietly in their positions, ringed around the female prisoners centered in the camp. The air was very still as the sky grew black and stars shone above them. All eyes were upon the distant mountain range in the east, barely visible against the night sky. They heard no noise of horses' hooves beating the ground, no vibrations to show mass movement toward them. Few of the men spoke, and even the small mutters of infrequent comments lapsed as time followed time into stillness.

Hours went by, and there was no indication of an approaching army. Some of the soldiers breathed a sigh of relief, but Benedict felt uneasy. Men stood up to stretch and walk about. Benedict ordered them down again. Reluctantly, they returned to their stations. They continued to wait.

The night was disrupted by the cries of dying men, and what happened was determined only after the fact. Men stood up in agony, then fell over and died among the outer fringes to north and south. Benedict and his near men jumped and turned in the direction of the cries. They were confronted by men in uniform moving toward them with dead eyes. These odd men came after them with swords and knives, slashing with awkward movements at anyone they could reach. While his own soldiers were tentatively repelling these trancelike men, Benedict understood who these strange men were. He called out the order to kill the men that had unseeing eyes. He told them that they must be certain of their eyes, but then kill them instantly. Many of Benedict's soldiers fell before the strange vanguard. The screams and sudden fall of bodies on both sides bred terror and disorder.

Concentrating on the eyes of the unliving men swinging awkward blades, Benedict lost track of everything else going on around him. This was true of each good comrade-in-arms. They were occupied into the first splatter of daylight with the uniformed men of the enemy. As dawn gradually arose, the strange men seemed to fall back, disappearing into the distance before they could be more easily seen. With daylight, Benedict and his men could see the carnage around them.

In final death, the trancelike men were in varying states of decomposition. Benedict discovered that they were brought to their ultimate death only when the base of the brain, just above the back of the neck, was cut deeply enough. Some of the soldiers were able to point out acquaintances they knew from Avalon who had previously been carried off by the hellmaids.

The captive women, including their leader, were gone. In the medical tent, Benedict's officers found the bodies of the three injured females and the soldier with medical training. Their throats had all been cut.

Of his own men, Benedict saw that several dozen soldiers lying around the outer fringe of the camp had been stripped of their uniforms. Their throats had also been cut.

It was pieced together that a large party of hellmaids had led their vanguard of entranced men by foot to the outer edges of the camp. Taking advantage of the darkness, the women had slashed the throats of numbers of soldiers, dragged them out to more isolated areas, and had their lobotomized men dress in their uniforms. When most of them were thus disguised, the hellmaids set them upon the living soldiers. In the confusion, the hellmaids freed their leader and the other captives, and then, perhaps on orders of their leader, murdered their wounded and the man who attended them. When they escaped unnoticed, they simply abandoned the men to their fates.

Benedict and a contingent of his men spent the entire day sealing the caverns in the mountains once again. They found several new openings, and these were blocked up as well. In the meantime, the remainder of his soldiers organized a burial detail for the dead. Although it was necessary to bury the former victims of the hellmaids because of their putrefaction, some were carted off into town to be placed in family plots. It was a difficult time for all, for the townsfolk were notified of the newly dead and the ignominious deaths of their sons who had been kidnapped, used in such a despicable manner, and discarded by their captors. Sadness and tears filled Avalon that day.

It is believed that shortly after this Benedict received a Trump message. His change of concentration while sitting in one of his manor houses was noticed. It is probable that this was one of several occasions when he heard from his father, King Oberon. In a servant's earshot, Benedict had a one-sided conversation, and the air before him shimmered like steam rising on a hot blistery day. He had uttered clearly the word "Dad" on that occasion. Similar occurrences were noticed by others on two more occasions. These three incidents were passed on to Benedict's loyal officer who returned

to Amber. Others may have occurred, but the officer hadn't shared in such confidences.

Lintra and the hellmaids continued to harass Avalon, but Benedict's army remained sufficiently strong to beat them back. In a sense, the hellmaids had made a mistake in causing such terrible havoc and awful devastation in human life early on; the people of Avalon had purged themselves of their sorrow in those early days of grief and were now more stouthearted than ever. Neighboring villages received word of the strife, and volunteers enlisted with Benedict's army, having traveled great distances.

The battles went on for a long time. Various methods were tried to seal up the caverns and fissures, and many means of destruction were attempted, such as pouring hot oil down the tunnels. The warrior females always returned, after a while, to raid and murder. Their numbers seemed greater after each brief period of quiet. They were never again quite as successful, however, in striking terror among the people of the land, for they had become inured to the destructive prowess of the raiders.

If people can become used to years of poverty and disease and rampant crime, then we can understand how the people of Avalon can become used to the violent harassment of these hellish women as this period stretched on and became an acknowledged part of life. Benedict became confident enough in his militia that he delegated his defenses to an elite corps of officers. During one of the lulls in the war, Benedict received visitors from his homeland. Corwin's Chronicles best describe the circumstances of the visit of Julian and Gérard to Avalon. Although one of Corwin's sources, Dara the Younger, was known to have made dubious statements regarding this period, we can recognize that she was, in all likelihood, an observer of the events she described. When she first met Corwin in Avalon, she told of his brothers' visit in this way:

> "One morning, five or six months ago, Grandpa [Benedict] simply stopped what he was doing. He was pruning some trees back in the orchard—he likes to do that himself . . . He was up on a ladder, snipping away, and suddenly he just stopped, lowered the clippers, and did not move for several minutes. . . . Then I heard him talking—not just muttering—but talking as though he were carrying on a conver-

sation. . . . Now that I know about the Trumps, I realize that he must have been talking to one of them just then. Probably Julian. Anyway, he climbed down from the ladder quite quickly after that, told me he had to go away for a day or so, and started back toward the manor. . . . He rode away a short while later, leading two spare horses. He was wearing his blade.

"He returned in the middle of the night, bringing both of them with him. Gérard was barely conscious. His left leg was broken, and the entire left side of his body was badly bruised. Julian was quite battered also, but he had no broken bones. They remained with us for the better part of a month, and they healed quickly. Then they borrowed two horses and departed." (GA, 121–22)

In some ways, Benedict confirms Dara's view of these events. For Corwin's benefit, he elaborated further on the black road and its connection with Eric in Amber:

"I may speak candidly, now that the reason for secrecy is no longer with us. Eric, of course. He was unaware of my whereabouts, as were most of the others. Gérard was my main source of news in Amber. Eric grew more and more apprehensive concerning the black road and finally decided to send scouts to trace it through Shadow to its source. Julian and Gérard were selected. They were attacked by a very strong party of its creatures at a point near Avalon. Gérard called to me, via my Trump, for assistance and I went to their aid. The enemy was dispatched. As Gérard had sustained a broken leg in the fighting and Julian was a bit battered himself, I took them both home with me. I broke my silence with Eric at that time, to tell him where they were and what had become of them. He ordered them not to continue their journey, but to return to Amber after they had recovered. They remained with me until they did. Then they went back." (SU, 102)

There seemed to have been a connection between Benedict's rescue of his brothers upon that black road and the stepping up of violent raids on Avalon. After Julian and Gérard had left, the hellmaids at-

tacked in force, burning shops and homes indiscriminately in their continuing rampages. The increasing damage in Avalon became so great that the townspeople petitioned Benedict to rid them of these demon-women once and for all. Benedict left his orchard to meet with his officers in the field.

Benedict decided that it wasn't enough to block up the caves. It wasn't enough to meet and repel the attacking raiders on the grasslands between the mountains and the town. It wasn't enough to kill them by inches, allowing others to escape to return another day. He decided to fight another kind of war.

In reviewing the field army, Benedict found that it was composed of a large number of cavalry, but there were fewer infantry forces. His officers informed him that more men, young and old, were coming in to volunteer for service almost every day. With these facts in mind, Benedict outlined his plan to his officers. It involved giving the infantry special training to work in close quarters, in darkness, with limited mobility, and using short, light, handheld weapons exclusively.

From that day on, every volunteer joined the infantry. Each man drilled on the field with falchions, small chisel-headed axes, and studded maces. The most proficient men were selected and underwent highly specialized training. They were taught to move quickly in a "duck walk," hunched down with knees against chest. They drilled in defense in close quarters and in awkward positions. They were shown the most effective ways to kill an armed attacker by using only ax or club or short sword or bare hands. Separated from the other soldiers, these specially trained men were blindfolded and placed in rows of large barrels fastened together end to end. In such contraptions, they were pitted against each other, using blunted sticks to defend themselves.

While this training was going on, the hellmaids continued to raid incessantly, growing in might and daring. Benedict and his soldiers succeeded in beating them back each time, but the cost in slaughter on both sides continued to escalate. Only Benedict and his officers knew about the elite corps that was undergoing vigorous training, and those soldiers were sworn to secrecy.

Avalon went through a series of devastating assaults that were worse than any that had come before. Women and children had been murdered in their homes at night, as the demon warriors swept through the town from all sides. Benedict's men dropped each wayward hellmaiden they had found, but seldom before some bloody deed was accomplished.

Deliberately, Benedict held off on his planned retaliation. It might be that he thought his elite company of men was not quite ready. However, it has been surmised that he waited, even with the harshness of personal agony all around him, so that his program would be entirely unexpected.

On one particularly chill evening, Benedict's officers gave the signal for their men to take their positions. The elite corps, headed by Benedict's most adept captain, moved silently into the mountains. At that point, the operation was in progress. There was no turning back.

As expected, most of the caverns that had been sealed that morning were at least partially exposed again. It was still early, and all was quiet. Selecting eight of the more accessible openings, the special group filed into them and moved well down the tunnels before positioning themselves. No sound was heard.

From their vantage, the first indications of movement from within must have been soft rumblings. These grew louder, vibrating along the cave floor and walls. As Benedict had assumed, the tunnels were large enough to accommodate both horse and rider, but only if each muscular horse crawled with legs slightly askew. When the hellish horses could be seen, edging up the tunnels, fierce eyes and flame-filled mouth were noticed first. They did indeed look like demons out of hell coming up those tunnels.

Before the female riders, leaning well forward upon their mounts, could see the men lying in wait, the foot soldiers attacked. In most cases, the demon horses were disabled and killed quickly with ax and falchion, and then the female warriors were clubbed, then skewered before they were fully aware of what had occurred. This procedure worked well for the initial onslaught.

The hellmaids that made it out of caves that had not been secured were met with volleys of arrows from Benedict's infantry waiting on the cliff face above the caverns. This had the effect of scattering the raiders, and they were met by the cavalry, armed with lance and sword. The three-layered assault was meant to contain the hellmaids and prevent any pos-

sibility of escape. With the advantage of surprise, and the deadly efficiency of the special force inside the caves, the enemy was reduced to rampant pandemonium.

Once the female warriors realized what awaited them near the cave openings, and they had time to adjust to the attack, they met the special corps with equal ferocity. Leaving their horses behind, the women rushed ahead with lithe quickness, striking out with daggers and thrusting with swords that impaled numbers of the elite corps where they hid. The interiors of the caverns began to stink of blood and flesh and acrid organic waste.

Hours were not sufficient for this battle. When daylight widened upon the engagement, the hellmaids found themselves unable to retire. In the caverns, the special corps advanced into the darkness as the females attempted to withdraw. If they retreated, they would draw the infantry into their warren, where the women warriors would be trapped. Those on the outside were similarly encumbered, and virtually all avenues of escape were cut off. Benedict's army denied the hellmaids any respite, and the fighting went on for days.

Any lulls in the conflict occurred only during brief spells of exhaustion on both sides. The time was filled with tense moments of waiting for a renewed push. The slightest movement brought on the next clash, seeming to reverberate at every point along the offensive line from cave interior to grassy plain. The raiders would not surrender and the conflict continued without letup. Such clattering bloodletting never becomes routine, but, after many days, there was a settling-in of confrontation that became dispassionate and stoical.

There may have come a point when the hellmaids became aware that they were losing ground. Nevertheless, they withstood grueling strikes and struck down all that came into proximity to them. Defiantly, they surmounted each crushing blow and thrashed back viciously.

After many days of filth and hardship, weariness and pain, both sides were wearing down. Fatigue and continuing slaughter jammed the mouths of soldiers from Avalon and from Hell. The taste of stale blood was upon everyone. Still, soldiers fought and died in writhing misery.

In the middle of a starlit night, while human endurance was stretched by tense periods of waiting, a tight knot of demon-women on their horses breathing flame swooped forward from a slope of the mountain. They rode screaming toward the greatest portion of the cavalry, and Benedict was in its midst, astride his roan. The night sky was clear, and Benedict, his officers clustered about him, saw the swiftly moving Hell riders heading directly for them. When he became aware that a new surge of fighting had broken out, coming from all directions, Benedict understood the intent of that fast-moving, tightly grouped phalanx coming towards them. He knew that he, personally, was the target.

Only when that fire-breathing phalanx engaged Benedict's cavalry in close combat did he see the leader of the female warriors. She was protected by warriors on either side, and he was nearly certain that their eyes searched the horsemen for him. Before the eyes of Lintra's companions fell upon him, Benedict had slain three riders and then their mounts with his constantly flying sword. He attempted to reach her, but her companions huddled closely around her, each taking a turn at halting his progress. While he concentrated on reaching her, he knew that wholesale decimation was going on around him. He watched as a loyal officer was knocked from his horse, impaled, and beheaded with rapid strokes of a demon-woman's sword, and he was simply too far away to do anything about it. He avoided a cut that would surely have been fatal if it struck where it was aimed, and in fury, he lopped off his adversary's head in silent retaliation.

He reached the heart of the tightly clustered group where four Hell-women guarded their leader. Two of them battled him with complete disregard for their own safety. One nearly unseated him from his horse, but he maneuvered in such a way that one enemy mount blocked the arc of the sword held by the other rider. He downed the horses of the two attackers, then finished each warrior in turn. Two mounted companions remained on either side of Lintra, now cursing vilely at him. He came at them, and the two guards fought him boldly. They tried to unhorse him, and the roan sustained several deep gashes. Rather than see his horse slaughtered, Benedict pulled back, jumped to the ground, and slapped its haunches to get it away from the line of battle. Sword in hand, he rushed at the two horses of the bodyguards. Although he knocked one rider from her horse, he had to kill the horse of the other rider to get her on the ground. The two women wielded their swords with great skill, but he worked his way

through their parries with phenomenal dexterity. Before her last guard fell, Lintra tried to run Benedict down with her horse. Benedict dodged flame and hooves, slaying the last guard as he did so. On her horse, Lintra turned, raised her sword in a death stroke, and rode down upon him again. To avoid that terrible blade, Benedict seemed to dive low, directly under the demon-horse. A moment later, he was astride the horse and grabbed Lintra from behind. They fell to the ground together.

They stood facing each other, staring, in a moment that was fixed in time. She lunged, and they fought. Conflicts and tragedies were going on all around them, but one sensed that all combatants observed the duel of the two leaders with something akin to reverence. In retrospect, and with the distance of time, it seemed that way.

She struck with such power and hatred that he very nearly felt a mortal blow to his left side, but he blunted it with his parry. An hour or more may have passed as their duel proceeded. Tiredness was not permitted to creep into their combat. She was moved by a murderous hatred of this general who spoiled her efforts to control this land. He was compelled by the cold, reasoning need to end this scourge upon a shadow he loved, believing her death would do it. He persisted in this contest, ignoring the unending carnage around him, but not oblivious to it.

A sudden deft movement, and she fell to the ground, a bloody wound across her scalp. He stood above her, his sword poised to complete the task. She looked into his eyes, and he stared a moment into hers. He felt the hot searing pain across his right side. Turning to look, he saw that his arm was severed, the sword gone. He fell, rolled with weakness and agony. She started to rise. Her eyes widened, and she looked down with utter surprise to find a sword through her chest. She saw the hand on the haft, and the arm, a left arm, and looked up to see Benedict's grim face before dying. He had rolled onto a sword beside a dead man, completed the roll, then thrust forward onto Lintra, sword first. Afterward, he collapsed on the ground, but several of his soldiers reached him just as he fell unconscious.

When Benedict recovered, he found himself on a cot in a tent. He was told he had been sleeping for two days. A team of medically experienced men had stemmed infection in the remains of his right arm, a portion of his forearm attached to the joint of his elbow. He had gone through a severe fever which they treated with herb teas, covering his wound with the leaves of certain plants that grew in the region. He had been in a semiconscious, delirious state for many hours through that first night. His constitution helped him to recover as quickly as he did once he had fought off the fever.

He learned that the army of Avalon had won the conflict. Although the hellmaids continued the fighting for hours after the death of their leader, some of them too remote from the site to realize Lintra was dead, they gradually became aware of their demoralized state. If any escaped execution, they were rare exceptions, for the combined forces of Benedict's infantry and cavalry made a clean sweep of the battlefield. In order to ensure that no fleeing warrior would return with reinforcements from the caverns, they were carefully inspected, bodies removed, and hot oil poured down every opening and fissure. The men were careful to cover every possible entry. Once this was completed, the caves were sealed once more.

After hearing of these procedures, Benedict got up shakily and walked out of the tent. His arm was heavily bandaged and he was weak from blood loss, but he ordered his men to bring his horse and he inspected the field of battle personally. At two or three blocked caverns, he ordered more stones and wood placed to reinforce them. He oversaw the burial of bodies, separate trenches being dug for the warrior women and his men. He questioned one of his captains about a soldier who was brought into camp in tatters and tied to a stake in their camp. He was told that there had been a large number of deserters in the last battle, especially among the young and inexperienced. Only a handful had been retrieved from flight. They were being held pending a military trial.

Benedict concurred with the appropriateness of these proceedings, suggested that his officers assign a company of cavalry and infantry to scout the area for any survivors, and called a meeting in his tent to commence shortly after midday. He intended to compose himself by washing thoroughly and enjoying a hearty meal. Deliberately avoiding the area where he had fought the leader of the hellmaids, Benedict rode back toward his tent.

The meeting was a rather long session between Benedict and his officers. Among the matters discussed was the length of time necessary to continue a reconnaissance of the area. The officers were concerned about making sure that there would be no further invasions. Although Benedict was concerned also, he felt that only a small force was needed to police the area, under his personal guidance, and most of the volunteers could be released from service. Certain compromises were reached before this was put aside.

Another matter involved the burial of the dead. As previously, some important officials of the town had made their wishes known through messengers that their sons, brothers, and husbands who had died be buried in family plots in Avalon proper. Benedict was of a mind to declare this field of battle a memorial to those who died, and therefore wanted his soldiers to be buried with full military honors in this place. After long debate, Benedict capitulated, allowing for those whose families wanted to bury their own dead to do so.

As arrangements were being made for the armed escort to take deserters back to the town, the conference was concluded. Two of his officers spoke to Benedict as they stepped to the opening of the tent. They were making clear the details for the disposition of their men on scouting missions, moving outside as they talked to Benedict. Two soldiers were making their way toward one of the captains talking to Benedict, but just then, Benedict stepped out of his tent into the open air. He caught sight of something or someone, his sudden head movement and transfixed eyes halting the soldiers around him. The two officers turned to follow Benedict's gaze. He pushed past them and walked briskly toward a standing figure. He stopped a short distance from the man, and the man's companion stood up at attention beside him.

Benedict said, "Come with me," and led the two men back to his tent. He dismissed the two officers and entered the tent alone behind the two strangers.

Inside, he took the man's hand and shook it, smiling.

> "Corwin," he said, "and still alive."
> "Benedict . . . and breathing yet. It has been devilish long."
> "Indeed. Who is your friend?"
> "His name is Ganelon." (GA, 83)

Benedict found himself surprisingly pleased to have been reunited with his long-lost brother. He knew something of Corwin's misfortunes through his infrequent Trump contacts with Gérard, but Gérard was not often included in Eric's planning of policies in Amber. As for Corwin, Benedict saw in him a fellow military man who also had a complex disposition. Corwin had been a poet, a composer of music, and a scholar of sorts. These bespoke a temperament not unlike Benedict's own.

Eager to learn firsthand of his brother's experiences, Benedict asked him to recount what had been happening to him. Corwin spent a long while describing his sojourn on the shadow Earth, telling of relations with brother Eric, and trying to fill in details with suppositions because he had lost his memory for a time.

Entranced by Corwin's story, he felt an irresistible interest in learning about Corwin's blinding.

> "How was it done?" [Benedict asked.]
>
> "Hot irons. . . . I passed out partway through the ordeal."
>
> "Was there actual contact with the eyeballs?"
>
> "Yes, . . . I think so."
>
> "And how long did the regeneration take?"
>
> "It was close to four years before I could see again . . . and my vision is just getting back to normal now. So . . . about five years altogether, I would say." . . .
>
> "Good. . . . You give me some small hope. Others of us have lost portions of their anatomy and experienced regeneration also, of course, but I never lost anything significant—until now."
>
> "Oh yes. . . . It is a most impressive record. I reviewed it regularly for years. A collection of bits and pieces, many of them forgotten I daresay, but by the principals and myself: fingertips, toes, ear lobes. I would say that there is hope for your arm. Not for a long while, of course.
>
> "It is a good thing that you are ambidextrous." (GA, 91)

When Corwin had finished his story, Benedict told of the most recent engagements with the hellmaids. Speaking without emotion, he told of his killing their leader after she had managed to remove his arm. He brought Corwin up to date on the current scouting maneuvers, indicating that he believed the war was over and a period of tranquillity was now upon them. Having given some thought to Corwin's sudden appearance in Avalon, Benedict felt suspicious of his intentions. He asked Corwin of his plans. When Corwin said that he simply wished to visit for a time because this place was so much like the Avalon he had once known, Benedict told him of what he learned upon first arriving ages ago. "Know then that what is remembered of the shadow of yourself that once reigned here is not good. Children are not named Corwin in this place, nor am I brother to any Corwin here." (GA, 97)

Although Corwin insisted that he was in Avalon only to visit for a time, Benedict knew enough to see ulterior motives in his brother's journey to this shadow.

> He asked Corwin, "What are your long-range plans?" . . .
>
> "You know what my plans are." . . .
>
> "If you were to ask for my support . . . I would deny it. Amber is in bad enough shape without another power grab."
>
> "Eric is a usurper."
>
> "I choose to look upon him as regent only. At this time, any of us who claims the throne is guilty of usurpation."
>
> "Then you believe Dad still lives?"
>
> "Yes. Alive and distressed. He has made several attempts to communicate." . . .
>
> "You did not lend support to Eric when he took the throne . . . Would you give it to him now that he holds it, if an attempt were made to unseat him?"
>
> "It is as I said . . . I look upon him as regent. I do not say that I approve of this, but I desire no further strife in Amber."
>
> "Then you *would* support him?"
>
> "I have said all that I have to say on the matter. You are welcome to visit my Avalon, but not to use it as a staging area for an invasion of Amber. Does that clarify matters with respect to anything you may have in mind?"
>
> "It clarifies matters." (GA, 98–99)

Once the air was cleared and tensions relieved, Benedict allowed his magnanimity to show. He promised Corwin a map and letter of introduction to his staff so that he and his companion could stay at one of his manors near town. Benedict planned to remain encamped for a few more days to finish mopping-up operations. After Corwin and Ganelon left his tent to bed down for the night, Benedict went to his battered war chest and took out a pack of Trumps. He pulled out the Trump for Gérard and informed him of Corwin's visit. Gérard advised him to keep Corwin under surveillance. Benedict agreed, but explained that he needed to remain in the field a few more days. He would have his staff watch him, and messengers would keep him informed on a daily basis. Then Benedict ended the contact.

It may be that Benedict stepped up the scouting operation out of a lack of trust of Corwin. Perhaps Gérard had given him sufficient caution about Corwin's actions in Amber that Benedict felt it necessary to see to Corwin sooner than he had promised. In any event, Benedict returned to the manor house intending to play host to his brother and his friend several days earlier than planned. When he reached the manor by horse and was not received by anyone, he was puzzled. Inside, Corwin and Ganelon were not to be found. Even stranger was the fact that his usual staff of servants was nowhere in the house. With growing dread, he searched the grounds, then went further, toward the woods. While he rarely gives way to emotion, Benedict felt the heat of betrayal and fury when he discovered the shallow grave and the bodies within. They were loyal servants, innocent of any wrongdoing. It was certainly unworthy of anyone to murder them, especially someone given the trust of their retainer. Seeing the dead bodies of his housekeeper and three male staff members, Benedict's wrath at his brother was beyond rational control. There had been no reason for this deed. This was treachery outside of human decency, and he would have the head of the man who did it.

Regaining control over his outrage, Benedict checked the stable. He noted that a wagon was gone, suggesting that Corwin needed it to carry something substantial. Whatever it was, it was probably the reason for his visit to Avalon. There was little doubt in Benedict's mind that Corwin had obtained something that he would use in his seizing the throne of Amber from Eric, and Benedict believed him ruthless enough to murder anyone who tried to prevent him from doing so.

He pulled out his deck of cards, sorted through it, and pulled out Corwin's Trump. He concentrated on it, allowed his seething anger to well up. There was a response, faint at first, but decidedly there.

He pooled his energies and sent a psychic thrust through the Trump. The respondent reacted in pain, blocking the thrust, and Benedict held a brief image of Corwin, riding upon the horse-drawn wagon, his companion beside him. That mental connection gave Benedict enough of a pathway into Shadow so that he could begin to track him. The slowness of the wagon, and its distinct impressions left along a physical path, would be of great help in aligning the pattern of his search.

In the house, Benedict took a long, scythelike sword in a sheath, the one he had used when he had battled the Moonriders out of Ghenesh, and slipped it over his shoulders so that the sword hung loosely at his back. He threw together a small pouch of food and included a container of water. Returning to the stable, he unleashed his favorite horse, the one he rode in on, although it wasn't rested. He didn't have the time to saddle another horse. When he got on the horse, he rode tentatively around the grounds, searching for the marks of wagon wheels. He discovered them in muddy ground a short distance from the stable, heading in an easterly direction. Once he was certain of the trail, Benedict prompted the horse, and they rode swiftly.

He shifted through Shadow a number of times, trailing the slow-moving wagon. Avalon was left behind, many shadows distant. Benedict sensed he was nearing Corwin, a combination of perceiving his proximity through the Trump and the freshness of the track. He pushed his horse faster.

The black road was nearby, he realized. Corwin's wagon moved precipitously close to it, as if he didn't know about it. Perhaps he didn't. The way became hilly as Benedict felt he was closing upon the wagon. After racing for quite a while, he knew he had to rest his horse. He reached a rise, saw the distant band of the black road, and thought he glimpsed the wagon heading directly into the black road's path. Benedict halted on the grassy hill, gave his mount some water and feed, and stood watching the indistinct movement of the horse-drawn wagon touching the edge of that road.

Benedict admired his daring, for Corwin took the wagon onto and across the black road. Watching intently, Benedict hurriedly chewed on some bread and took a draught of water. With some astonishment, he saw the wagon progress well into the road and finally reach the other side. When it did, Benedict mounted his horse and headed toward the black road at a gallop.

As he approached, he realized that Corwin was shifting into shadows of hazardous climate and terrain purposefully. Corwin was attempting to lose him, or at least forestall him in disharmonious climes. It was more difficult for Benedict to focus on the wagon's traces when they traveled through blizzards, roiling geysers, and hurricanes, but he had no choice but to follow the impressions left behind, psychic and physical.

He knew it was Corwin, causing rock to fall, leading him through uncertain regions of rocky caverns and limestone bridges. These actions succeeded in widening the gap between them, but Benedict had a firm grasp on attendant traces linked to his brother.

In spite of everything, Benedict had regained the same ground as Corwin. In desperation, Corwin had sent up the woods in flame, but Benedict passed through without hesitation. It had come to a point when Corwin would realize that he couldn't shake Benedict. Their meeting would be inevitable. Corwin chose to meet him in a small wood with young trees on all sides. Benedict rode up on his great red-and-black horse, dismounted, and strode toward his brother.

"Murderer!" he said, as he swept his blade in wide arcs, sending down tree limbs and saplings. Corwin was trying to talk in a reasonable manner, but Benedict would have none of it. Their duel commenced, and Benedict fought furiously, the swing of his sword barely obstructed by the tree trunks Corwin stood near.

Benedict was beating his brother back, moving toward a clearing where no trees would slow his sword. Before either brother could act, Ganelon was upon Benedict, knocking his sword to the ground as he tried to pull him down as well. Although Ganelon surprised him momentarily, Benedict struck him with the stump of his right arm, then tossed him in Corwin's direction with his left hand as if he were a rag doll. Benedict stooped for his sword and was quickly upon Corwin again, no more bothered than if he had stopped to slap a mosquito before resuming.

Corwin's movements as they fenced seemed erratic. Benedict was sure of defeating him, but he felt impatient with Corwin's odd maneuvers and seeming miscalculations. At one point, Corwin made a wide retreat, but suddenly stepped forward in a highly risky move. He had succeeded in cutting Benedict's left ear, which bled profusely. It was minor, however, and Benedict ignored it as he pressed on. He had Corwin on the defensive, pushing him back, out of the clearing and past the fallen body of his friend.

Benedict noted Corwin's quick little jumping movements as he retreated and thought them a bit eccentric. Fear must have fogged Corwin's mind that he moved so awkwardly. Benedict believed he had him and struck fiercely to pierce his heart. He was taken aback when his legs were held immobile. He knew at once that he was on the black road and that Corwin had jumped aside and back out of the road, avoiding his blade. The black grasses of the road had wrapped around both legs, holding him in a firm grip. He used all his strength to pull away as he twisted around to continue the duel. As he lost his balance briefly, he knew that Corwin could easily have slain him. However, Corwin didn't move in that direction, and Benedict steadied himself to fight clumsily, his upper body twisted toward his brother. Corwin managed to strike Benedict hard at the back of his neck, using his sword almost like a club. It stunned Benedict, and Corwin moved in to punch Benedict low and to the side with his fist. Benedict struck out again with his sword, but Corwin avoided it and struck him a second blow on the back of his neck. Benedict fell unconscious.

When Benedict regained consciousness, he was lying on the grass, a blue cloak bundled under his head. Above him was a familiar face. Benedict started a little, thinking it was Corwin, but then he recognized the bearded, thick-muscled face of Gérard. Trying to move, Benedict found his legs numb, his shoulders and left arm aching. He had a terrible throbbing pain in the back of his neck.

Gérard had told Corwin about events in brief after he located Benedict bound to a tree near the black road:

> "I found him as you said he would be and I released him. He was set to pursue you once again, but I was able to persuade him that a considerable time had passed since I had seen you. Since you said you had left him unconscious, I figured that was the best line to take. Also, his horse was very tired. We went back to Avalon together. I remained with him

through the funerals, then borrowed a horse. I am on my way back to Amber now.'' (GA, 190–91)

It is difficult to assay with any accuracy the occurrences that followed in Avalon. Neither Benedict nor Gérard has spoken further on them, and no one else was close enough to the situation to be able to elaborate. Benedict had discovered that his pack of Trumps, carried in his hidden pocket, was missing, and he realized that Corwin had taken them. Naturally, he had others, and took one of them to replace the lost deck. In the interim, he had a couple of mysteries to occupy him. One was the miraculous path that Corwin had managed to cut through in the black road. He and Gérard puzzled over the patch of land that Corwin had cleared when he passed through the road in the wagon. Another mystery concerned Corwin's insistence, relayed by Gérard, that he had not committed any murder while in Avalon. Although Benedict could take Corwin's assertion at face value, he still had four deaths to resolve.

From what has been gathered from that period, Benedict led an investigation into the deaths of his servants. There was no sign of a struggle, so it was assumed that the three men and one woman knew the person who attacked them. All signs seemed to point to a person staying within the immediate grounds of the manor. Corwin remained a suspect, except that Benedict couldn't determine a motive for the murders. Still, Benedict was unwilling to surrender wholly the possibility that Corwin deliberately murdered them.

During the next month, numbers of citizens noted eerie movements along the black road. Military patrols were assigned to watch the road. They reported that there was increasing activity along it, but no invasions occurred in Avalon, not even at night. This seemed most strange, for Avalon remained exempt from attack all the while mysterious shapes flitted rapidly on that dark path. Benedict maintained patrols keeping vigil beside the road for two more nights.

When the movement continued unabated, Benedict decided to contact his brother Julian in Amber. Julian was with a patrol of his men north of Mt. Kolvir. He told Benedict that the black road had reached the base of Kolvir and they had been under attack by hordes of monstrous creatures out of Shadow. Through the Trump contact, Julian pointed out a manticora that he and his men had just killed.

Benedict asked Julian to remain camped where he was until he could consult with his own military. Then Benedict met with his officers, briefed them on the crisis in Amber, and had them poll the troops for volunteers to join him. Hundreds of his soldiers gladly volunteered. So many, in fact, that he had to assign three of his officers to remain behind with a large enough quota of the volunteers to maintain order in Avalon.

Contacting Julian again, Benedict and a large cavalry contingent came through on his Trump. After Benedict came through, he listened as Julian informed Eric of Benedict's aid. Julian also told Eric that he had discovered the dead bodies of a dozen or so men detached from his patrols to the north. They had not been mutilated, but had fought a frantic battle in which they were downed with small, bloody puncture wounds. Eric suggested that Corwin had done it, and Benedict felt obliged to say that he believed Corwin capable of finding the means, and perhaps it was in some way connected to his visit to Avalon.

After concluding the Trump contact with Eric, Julian and Benedict led a quick march to Kolvir. When they reached the valley below the mountain, soldiers were fighting a frenzied battle with huge beast-men mounted on large-sinewed, blunt-snouted horses. Julian recognized the company of soldiers as members of his patrol, led by one of his ablest captains. Eric was issuing enormous shafts of lightning from on high, and Benedict could see flying wyvern mounted by other beast-men falling from the sky in flames.

Julian and Benedict rushed into the battle, joining the other soldiers. Turning to two of his officers riding beside him, Benedict shouted a couple of sharp phrases, and these words were passed to the rest of the cavalry. Swords drawn, Benedict and his men struck out at the beast-men. Numbers of wyvern-mounted creatures swooped down upon them, bearing members of the cavalry off to horrible deaths, sometimes dragging their horses as well. Without time for preparation, Benedict knew he was fighting a purely defensive battle. The swooping attacks of the hideous wyvern were designed to break up the reserve of men fighting opponents on all sides. Under normal circumstances, such offensive methods would cause a company of men to spread out, become overwhelmed, and give way to fear. Although this was beginning to happen among some of the company, Benedict's cavalry did not fall prey to them.

Benedict's brief order to his troop was to form tightly grouped clusters of no fewer than five mounted men in each group. As the enemy forced a spreading out of the cavalry, his men would range together in tight circles, each man protecting the others in his clustered circle, thereby covering all sides. While the defensive line appeared disorganized and widely divided, each cluster was practiced and in tandem.

To a large extent, Benedict's operation was working. However, the enemy numbers were so immense that his tactics did little to repel them. Men and horses were torn apart by the wyvern, and the slaughter left bloody bodies or flaming carcasses strewn through the valley. The obscene multitude kept coming in innumerable quantities. It was clear that the black road, swathed around the outer edge of Kolvir just to the east of where they battled, had become an unstoppable doorway for the invading forces.

All of the soldiers heard the loud, precise crack of gunfire. Everyone fought on, but there was a subtle change in the attack mode of the flying beings. They ranged higher, concentrating more on the skirmishes on the cliff face of Kolvir. The soldiers of Julian and Benedict were given the opportunity to diffuse the enemy, putting them on the defensive.

With renewed confidence, the soldiers of Julian's company and the clusters of Benedict's cavalry mercilessly cut down enemy soldiers and their mounts. The beast-men divided in confusion, unsure of the meaning of the loud reports of gunfire and the fiery deaths of wyvern-mounted comrades falling from above.

As Benedict dueled with a particularly tenacious attacker that moved swiftly on his hideous mount around Benedict's own horse, he felt the subtle tingling of a Trump contact. Fending off the Shadow-being, he focused briefly on the contact to see Corwin, apparently standing on the cliff face above him. Benedict said one word: "Bide." He proceeded to dispatch the attacker and his mount, then moved closer to the base of Kolvir, away from the wide-ranging conflict but still able to observe and defend if an enemy spotted him. He knew that Corwin had been watching through the open contact.

Benedict paused inscrutably, waiting for Corwin to speak.

Corwin said:

> "Yes, I am on the heights ... We have won. Eric died in the battle. ...
>
> "We won because I brought riflemen ... I finally found an explosive agent that functions here. ...
>
> "While there are many things I want to discuss with you ... I want to take care of the enemy first. If you will hold the contact, I will send you several hundred riflemen."
>
> [Benedict] smiled [and said,] "Hurry."
> (GA, 217)

While Corwin had Ganelon arrange the troops for transport through the Trump contact, he spoke to Benedict of the girl named Dara. Benedict had been told the name before, when Gérard had transmitted Corwin's parting message after their last encounter. He felt more galled than he should have when Corwin persisted, saying that Dara was Benedict's great-granddaughter. Although he wouldn't even consider acknowledging such a thing, Benedict was bothered by the improbable relationship. Corwin continued to posit a mutual knowledge of the girl named Dara, but Benedict simply did not know her.

As Gérard helped send the troops through, Benedict pointed out the battlefield situation to Ganelon, who came through first. Ganelon relayed orders to the new men, short hairy beings who seemed devoted to Ganelon, and they took assigned positions near the face of Kolvir. Benedict conferred with Julian, and they passed orders through their officers to the troops. While the Shadow-beings were surprised and momentarily numbed by the rifle attack from the newly transported men, the rest of the men dispersed to either side of the enemy. Thus, the invaders were surrounded in a pincer formation, attacked on both sides by swordsmen and fired upon by riflemen in a frontal assault. Benedict and his horsemen covered the side on which the black road led away from Kolvir, effectively preventing a retreat in that direction.

The combined forces successfully routed the enemy. When the Shadow-beings initially attempted to break through the lines of Benedict's troops, they were struck down. Shortly, Benedict perceived that the troops out of Shadow were in retreat. They would fight their way through the cavalry rather than surrender. Benedict passed the word to allow the remaining invaders to flee to the black road. Before long, no invader remained alive in the valley, and the war was over.

In the aftermath of the war, Julian handled the burial detail in the valley, Benedict addressed his troops, and Ganelon saw to the quartering of the shadow army with Gérard's help. Feeling reasonably certain that Amber was safe from another large invasion force for a time, Benedict gave his volunteers the option of returning to Avalon. Most wanted to return to their homeland, but a few chose to stay. Among them was the seasoned officer, originally from Amber, who decided that he preferred to spend the rest of his days in his birthplace. Benedict opened the way for the return of his troops, and was occupied with his farewells for a period of time.

One of his major concerns was for the security of Amber, and consequently, he chose to remain rather than trump back to Avalon. At issue was more than simply the possibility of a renewed invasion from the black road. Although Benedict usually put his trust in military caution, he felt confident that the forces out of Shadow had been so weakened and demoralized that they would not retaliate soon. His most immediate concern regarding the welfare of his homeland was for Corwin's course of action as self-proclaimed governor of the land. Corwin had made no claims upon the throne. He simply took over the rule of Amber with the death of Eric. However, Corwin still maintained his army of Shadow-beings and an arsenal of firepower close at hand. These matters bore watching, and Benedict was not about to relax his guard.

It was with a fair amount of skepticism, then, that he listened to Corwin's suggestion that he arrange a series of lookout posts along the black road. Benedict saw the reasonableness in taking such precautions, and he was glad of having some positive activity that served the needs of Amber. He accepted the task and gathered up his remaining soldiers and others of Amber's regular army to begin setting up surveillance teams into Shadow along the black road. In spite of his dedication to this operation, Benedict nevertheless suspected Corwin of using it as a ploy to get him out of the way. For that reason, Benedict organized the teams and sent them along near paths of Shadow beside that road while he remained on Amber's soil.

Once he had his teams posted, Benedict returned to the Royal Palace, ostensibly to take his afternoon meal, but actually intent on observing Corwin at firsthand. When he arrived, he found that Corwin was not around. A guard informed him that Gérard and Corwin had walked down to the Harbor District together to have lunch earlier in the day. Benedict went to his quarters. Not long afterward, he received Trump contact from Corwin. Through the contact, he could see Gérard standing beside Corwin. Somewhat relieved that nothing was amiss between his brothers, Benedict gave Corwin passage to his quarters through the Trump. They briefly exchanged pleasantries, and Corwin left. With some interest, Benedict learned from a servant that Corwin went to the stables, got a horse, and rode away at a fast clip.

Benedict was once again at the black road coordinating the change of shift in his sentry teams, when he received an urgent Trump contact. It was Corwin. In Corwin's contact with him, Benedict concealed any surprise he might have felt. Corwin spoke perhaps too solemnly about the death of Caine at the hands of a Shadow-being. His explanation that he had hidden Caine's body rather than bringing him back to the palace, avoiding undue grumblings, seemed too pat. Benedict's suspicions were aroused again, but he remained silent about them. Corwin requested that Benedict be back in the palace and meet with all the others in the library the following evening. Benedict agreed, and Corwin closed the contact.

Shortly thereafter, Benedict received another Trump contact, this time from Gérard. His younger half brother was visibly furious and expressed his anger to Benedict. He pointed out that death seems to follow Corwin wherever he goes. Benedict was struck by the poignancy of Gérard's indictment when he brought up the murder of Benedict's servants in Avalon. There were too many discrepancies, it seemed to Gérard. Too many deaths that Corwin couldn't explain away, he felt.

Gérard told him of Corwin's suggestion that he accompany Corwin to the Grove of the Unicorn to recover Caine's body. Gérard had agreed to do so. Once alone, however, Gérard intended to kill Corwin, no matter what the consequences.

Benedict opposed Gérard's notion. None of them would be able to learn the truth if Corwin were dead. Their enemies might have had no connection with Corwin, either. Or if they had, they might still act against Amber after Corwin's death. No, it was better that Corwin remain alive. He should be made aware of the precarious position he was in at their hands, but he should be allowed to pursue his own actions if they would resolve the problems they all faced. Certainly, he should be watched with great care, and so, Benedict proposed a plan they could quickly implement.

Gérard and Benedict each contacted their brothers and sisters, holding them to a confidence that would not find its way back to Corwin. They were to maintain an open contact with Gérard through his Trump the next morning. In this way, Gérard could test Corwin's culpability in their presence. On the following morning, Benedict followed Gérard through his Trump as he met Corwin at the stables, obtained horses, and rode down Kolvir, knowing the others were similarly observing.

It was an exercise much to Benedict's liking, merely observing the two men as they fought hand to hand. He didn't feel compelled to intervene as the bigger, stronger Gérard pounded Corwin into near-senselessness, then raised him in his arms high overhead just at the cliff's edge. While Corwin hung helplessly in his brother's grip, Gérard accused him of complicity with the forces out of Chaos. Corwin, of course, protested his innocence right to the moment Gérard made to toss him over the precipice. Afterward, when Gérard had caught Corwin and decided they would not speak of these matters again, Gérard signaled the others to end their contact. Benedict closed at that time, and learned later, from Gérard privately, that Corwin and he had seen the unicorn. Gérard felt there was a great significance to its appearing before them, but he couldn't say what it was. It troubled him, though, that he might have conceivably been wrong about Corwin. Benedict offered nothing to support Gérard's thought.

Since Corwin had organized the family conference in the library, his narrative of what transpired in his Chronicles is the best source of information. It is common knowledge that he and Random shared their perception of Brand's imprisonment and possible connection with the Shadow invasions. The most extreme part of the proceedings was their working in concert to reach Brand by Trump, their rescue of him, and his attempted murder by someone in their party. As these occurrences unfolded, Benedict had taken a posture of passivity. He spoke infrequently, and when he did, it was with a bare modicum of

words. By design, he took no part in the actual rescue of Brand, choosing, instead, to maintain a wary eye on his brothers and sisters. He has always withheld any discoveries he might have made at that time.

It was because of Corwin's success in bringing back Brand from captivity that Benedict began to consider revealing some of his knowledge on matters. Corwin seemed to be on the right track in piecing together information that several of them contained separately. It seemed possible that Corwin, of any single one of them, could learn the true nature of the enemy facing Amber. Benedict wanted that mystery breached.

In spite of Benedict's annoyance that Corwin insisted he obtained some of his information from the girl named Dara in Avalon, Benedict discussed his caring for Julian and Gérard after their encounter with Shadow forces on the black road. He made one major contribution to their discussion of the forces they were battling:

"I find myself troubled both by the strength and the apparent objective of the opposition. I have encountered them now on several occasions, and they *are* out for blood. Accepting for the moment your story of the girl Dara, Corwin, her final words do seem to sum up their attitude: 'Amber will be destroyed.' Not conquered, subjugated, or taught a lesson. Destroyed. . . .

"What I am getting at is that I could see you—or any of us—employing mercenaries or obtaining allies to effect a takeover. I cannot see any of us employing a force so powerful that it would represent a grave problem itself afterward. Not a force that seems bent on destruction rather than conquest. I cannot see you [Julian], me, Corwin, the others as actually trying to destroy Amber, or willing to gamble with forces that would. That is the part I do not like about Corwin's notion that one of us is behind this.'' (SU, 107)

As a consequence of his statement, they all agreed to grant clemency to the guilty person among them if he or she would reveal who the allies were. When nobody came forward, they continued to express a number of ideas about possible suspects.

While Gérard cared for the unconscious Brand in

the library, the others had moved to a sitting room. As it was growing late, Julian was the first to depart. Benedict had engaged in conversation with Random and Llewella, mainly concerning speculations as to who was behind the Shadow invasions. It occurred to Benedict that the perpetrator among them would not stop at one fratricide and one attempted fratricide. In order to regain control of the situation, that person might try another murder. If Corwin were not behind the invasions himself, then he, his specially armed troops, and his partner, Ganelon, were probably targeted for extermination. It was only a question of determining who would be next, in terms of being most beneficially eliminated by the traitor. Depending on precisely what the traitor had to fear, it would be either Corwin or Benedict. As a means of concluding the mystery, Benedict welcomed an attempt on his life.

During the following day, Benedict conferred with one of his officers at his post beside the black road. The officer reported that no movement had been seen thus far. However, he had noticed something else. In the days since they first camped there, his men were forced to move the camp twice—away from the road. It was difficult to discern, but it seemed that the black road had widened. This disturbed Benedict, and he left the officer by his post abruptly, pondering that expanse that stretched to the horizon.

Benedict had returned to the palace, eaten a light meal, changed his clothes, obtained a spyglass, and left the palace again. He made his way down the southern slope of Kolvir, stopping when he had a good view of the black road crossing the Valley of Garnath. The wind whipped through his cloak, exposing the stump of his arm, and he pulled the cloak down around it again with his left hand. He took the spyglass from his belt, giving only a passing notice to the fact that he stood on the cliff where Eric had died, and examined the dark path below.

Just as he concluded examining the black road through his spyglass, Benedict received a Trump contact. Benedict saw Corwin through the contact, with Random, Ganelon, and their horses. Behind them was an open area with something that reminded Benedict of the Pattern, locked in a dungeon deep below the Royal Palace. When he had brought them all through, Random told Benedict of their finding a Pattern in a place that appeared to be the archetype for the Pattern and the world they had

known. On that primal Pattern, they had found a new Trump, pierced with a dagger, and blood had been spilled on that Pattern, blotting an area.

Faced with these facts, and seeing the person drawn on the Trump, Benedict told them of his caring for Martin, Random's illegitimate son. They were in agreement that the blood on the primal Pattern corresponded with the black road, and that someone had used young Martin to create that blot. With a sense of urgency, Random asked Benedict to take him to see the Tecys, to help him locate his son. Benedict didn't express any feeling, but he was touched by Random's concern for Martin. Corwin allowed Random to use his horse Star on the hellride to Benedict's Sanctuary shadow. Benedict and Random parted from Corwin and Ganelon, riding down the mountain and beginning to distance themselves from the true city so that they could delve into worlds of Shadow.

Random and Benedict spoke little to each other as they hellrode to the Tecys. Little is known of what transpired there, but Benedict and Random continued to travel farther into Shadow, attempting to track some possible directions Martin might have taken. During this time, Random told Benedict of the strange being he had seen walking the Pattern in Amber on the day that Eric died. This was Dara, as Corwin had explained, a creature of Chaos and Amber. Random relayed those things that Corwin had told him about Dara's relationship to Benedict.

Following a strong lead, they stopped on the way for a meal. When Random opened Star's saddlebags, he recalled that he had placed the mechanical arm there himself. Showing it to Benedict, Random explained how Corwin had obtained it in a duel with a ghostly version of Benedict in Tir-na Nog'th. Fascinated with the device, Benedict asked Random to help him attach it to his own right stump. They were both amazed with how facile it was, how easily Benedict could manipulate the arm, hand, and fingers. It seemed to come naturally to Benedict, and he was delighted.

They learned that Martin had visited a distant shadow for a time, then moved on to a busy commercial city called Heerat. When they reached Heerat, they found that he had left recently, and Random was eager to pursue his trail. On the other hand, Benedict was becoming increasingly concerned about being away from Amber too long. Seeing Random off in a direction that seemed promising, Benedict decided to return. As soon as he did, he sought out Ganelon and found him in the encampment set up for the soldiers out of Ri'ik.

He questioned Ganelon about the girl Dara, finding that her existence was becoming not only more credible to him, but also more agreeable. When Corwin arrived at the camp, Benedict greeted him warmly, apologizing for his previous suspicions. As for Dara, Benedict said to Corwin:

> "I would like to believe in the relationship. . . . The notion somehow pleases me. So I would like to establish it or negate it to a certainty. If it turns out that we are indeed related, then I would like to understand the motives behind her actions. And I would like to learn why she never made her existence known to me directly. . . . So I would like to begin . . . by learning of those things you experienced in Tirna Nog'th which apply to me and to Dara. I am also extremely curious about this hand, which behaves as if it were made for me. I have never heard of a physical object being obtained in the city in the sky. . . . Random performed a very effective piece of surgery, don't you think?" (HO, 101–2)

At Benedict's request, Corwin told of his encounter with the ghostly Dara and ghostly Benedict with the mechanical arm in the city in the sky. Corwin's story gave Benedict his final resolve to seek the girl out just as Random had gone to seek his son. However, knowing that his duty was to serve Amber first, Benedict told Corwin and Ganelon of his intention to battle the forces of the black road at its terminal point. In spite of Corwin's explanation that the source of their problem was the blot on the primal Pattern, Benedict stated his desire to teach the leaders at the Courts of Chaos a lesson in daring to interpose themselves into the realm of Amber. As a military man, Benedict saw the need to present a show of force against an enemy that might still attempt an offensive even when easy access had been denied.

Corwin showed Benedict a Trump he had discovered of the Courts of Chaos. With it, Benedict saw a solution to the logistics of moving troops into that place. They agreed that they would not act separately, but would coordinate their operations. Corwin said he wanted to prepare for clearing the blot on the true Pattern; meanwhile, Benedict wanted to use the Trump of the Courts to study that realm in preparation for a military operation.

While waiting for his horse to be brought, Benedict told Corwin and Ganelon that he wanted to communicate their latest discussions to Gérard. He stepped a few paces away and contacted Gérard by Trump. When he reached Gérard, he seemed agitated. Gérard asked after Corwin, and Benedict told him that Corwin was with him. With tense urgency, Gérard asked Benedict to bring him through.

Once Gérard materialized, he turned to Corwin. He accused Corwin of having fought with the injured Brand, for his room had been broken up and bloodied, and Brand was gone. Gérard was unwilling to believe that Corwin had nothing to do with Caine's death and the deaths of Benedict's servants in Avalon. Without caring to hear Corwin's explanations, Gérard began to strike Corwin, and they fought, as Ganelon and Benedict looked on. Ganelon intruded, fought with Gérard, and was able to punch him into unconsciousness before Corwin had fully recovered. Curiously, Benedict had not acted for either side. Although he never spoke of it, he may have taken on the attitude of a complacent observer for a distinct reason. Ganelon's strength and ability may have been cause for Benedict to wonder about him. Benedict might have decided at that moment that Ganelon was not what he appeared to be.

Before Corwin rushed away by horse, Benedict again urged agreement not to take any definite action until they had first conferred. Then Corwin rode away, leaving Benedict and Ganelon to handle Gérard when he regained consciousness.

It is unclear what Benedict said to Gérard to placate him about Corwin and Ganelon. Since Ganelon remained with Gérard and Benedict, his presence certainly offered some evidence of his honesty and steadfastness, for he willingly served both Corwin and Amber. Gérard must have taken this into account, along with any words of appeasement Benedict gave him. There must have been a return of calm between Gérard and Ganelon, for Benedict shortly took his leave of them.

Benedict returned to the primary outpost where his men watched the black road, near the foot of Kolvir. He spoke with his officers, giving them orders and certain contingency directions in the event of a sudden assault from the black road. Although he didn't anticipate such a conflict, he felt it prudent to have his officers ready, especially if something unforeseeable occurred to him.

While Benedict has never revealed anything about his surveillance at the Courts of Chaos, two of his officers have since indicated that Benedict brought them to that distorted realm before the great battle there. It seems that Benedict spent a long time surreptitiously examining the strange locale, becoming used to the shifting horizon and weird perceptual effects of closeness and distance. Although his officers were not certain of the time factors involved, it seemed only the passage of days, by Amber's standards, from the time they were brought there to the commencement of battle. Benedict had made a Trump pathway using Gérard at the Amber end to bring his main staff to his hidden location in the mountains above the Courts. He showed them some simple sketches he had done, mapping out the region, and they discussed numerous procedures. Working together from the diagrams, Benedict and his officers developed several lines of attack. When they had selected a few of the best strategies they should pursue, Benedict brought in a contingent of his most astute soldiers and cavalrymen. Immediately assigning them to specific officers, he divided the company and spread them out in carefully marked positions. They had to stay the duration, remaining unobserved, so they formed their plans while hiding in small sections, passing intelligence to one another by messenger. As the operation proceeded, Benedict informed his officers that he was returning to Amber. No action was to be taken in the interim. In the case of any emergency, Benedict left a Trump of himself and one of Gérard with one of his commanders. Nevertheless, Benedict intended to be in frequent contact with his men.

All these preparations occurred over a lengthy period, and the troops involved could not determine, with any accuracy, the passage of time once they were stationed in that strange realm. Based on the account of Corwin in his Chronicles, Benedict returned to Amber to take part in some significant events that occupied him greatly. He probably had not involved his troops in the occupation at the Courts until after Oberon's recovery, but it should be remembered that the time factors were vague, at best.

Sometime during his lone reconnaissance at the Courts, Benedict felt a slight but perceptible urge to return to Amber. It was an indefinite feeling, and

he noted it merely as instinct, but he had the unmistakable thought that he had to go back to Amber. When he did, he received Trump contact from Ganelon and joined him at the same encampment where he had left him. He learned that it had been Ganelon trying to reach him.

Ganelon explained what he had discovered about Brand's attempts to attune himself to the Jewel of Judgment. Brand had attempted to reach the Pattern in Amber, but Gérard's appearance had prevented him. At first, Benedict wasn't certain of the implications of this, but Ganelon assured him that Brand was dangerous, that he was seeking power, and that he was behind all their recent problems.

The primal Pattern and the Pattern in Rebma were under guard, but Brand had one other avenue opened to him. When the moon rose that evening, Brand would be able to walk the Pattern in Tir-na Nog'th. This must be prevented at all costs. Benedict understood the course of action he had to take even before Ganelon stated it. Before Benedict turned to go, Ganelon warned him not to allow any blood to fall onto the Pattern. Nodding his understanding, Benedict joined his brother Gérard in the chamber of the Pattern in the Royal Palace and prepared for the ordeal.

The Pattern walk is never easy. It takes concentration and will and effort, and only one of the blood can withstand it. No mortal knows the sensations of walking the Pattern. The process and the sense of exertion have been described, most notably in Corwin's Chronicles, but for us it must remain a thing untried.

Once the Pattern walk was completed, Benedict stood in the center of the Pattern. He placed the lantern he carried on the floor beside him, bearing his wait with great patience. Shortly afterward, he received Trump contact from Corwin, who was waiting at the highest point of Kolvir for the ghostly stair of the city in the sky to appear. They spoke briefly, but Benedict was all anticipation. It may have seemed to Benedict that he was the final hope of thwarting Brand's intentions.

Corwin gave him the signal. Closing his eyes, Benedict thought himself inside the chamber of the Pattern in the ghost city. In a moment, he was there, beside the beginning of the Way. He put the lantern down next to the wall, then waited beside the Pattern for some indication of Brand's presence.

Benedict stiffened as soon as he sensed Brand in

the ghostly chamber. He had expected a direct assault from in front or from behind him. There was no possibility that anyone could have overtaken Benedict in such an attack. When Benedict's eyes focused on him, Brand was directly opposite Benedict, facing him from the other side of the Pattern. Immediately alert, Benedict showed no indication of being disconcerted. He watched Brand carefully.

As Brand spoke about Benedict's position in the politics of Amber, Benedict was certain that he was playing some game. There was a trap being woven, and until Benedict could discern what it was, he would remain vigilant and wary. He answered tersely Brand's playful taunts aimed at his pride, knowing Brand was trying to win Benedict over, trying to move Benedict to join him in conquest. The trap involved Brand's movement, and Benedict recognized that. Brand slowly walked around the Pattern, moving gradually closer. Benedict knew there was some trick to Brand's positioning and movements, but he hadn't decided their purpose. Benedict demanded the Jewel of Judgment that Brand wore around his neck. Brand said something about not knowing the full extent of its power. Before Benedict could make another response, he felt a sudden, terrible cold. His legs were frozen in place, his real arm seemed a lifeless thing that was no longer a part of him. He couldn't move his neck or head, although he was conscious of everything about him. His eyes fixed on Brand, and as Brand continued toward him, Benedict saw that the Jewel was aglow with pulsing energy.

Corwin's voice through the Trump contact reached Benedict, but he had no means to respond. Helplessly, he watched Brand move closer and saw him take a long dagger from under his cloak. Benedict felt an urgency rather than a fear, hearing Brand's words about dying this way as a signal honor. Benedict's mind was alive, and he knew several things simultaneously: He knew that Corwin was calling to him desperately; he knew that the Pattern had faded more than once; he knew that Brand was about to end his life with a downward thrust of the dagger; and he knew he had one parcel of self-volition left. With Brand's closing upon him, Benedict knew that Brand had no inkling of this last reserve.

That dagger would not sear his flesh. Benedict knew this, even as Brand's hand, holding the weapon, lowered toward his chest. Benedict's right arm, the arm of strange metal and unnatural tenacity, grasped the Jewel around Brand's neck. Only that mechanical arm moved, while Benedict remained utterly paralyzed, lifting the Jewel high in the air, and Brand with it.

The dagger had clattered to the floor, Brand strangling within that unbreakable hold upon the Jewel. In the meantime, the Pattern faded again, and returned less clearly defined. Brand struggled, held above the ground, and finally pulled asunder the chain about his neck. He fell heavily to the ground, gasping for air. Benedict heard Corwin's voice call to him in sharp clarity. Moving the mechanical arm before his eyes, he saw that he still held the Jewel in its closed fist. His body warmed, and he could move his left arm, then his legs. He answered Corwin, turned to Corwin's image hanging before him, and reached out with his real arm. He looked toward Brand, who was rubbing his throat and beginning to sink through the now immaterial floor. Corwin caught Benedict's arm, even as Benedict lost all footing. Benedict felt himself pulled sideways even as he dropped in momentary weightlessness.

The wind was knocked out of him as he hit a hard surface. Rising to a sitting position, he saw Corwin breathing heavily on his knees just inches away. They were on a ledge at the highest point of Mt. Kolvir. Three stones that were the first steps to the now-vanished stairway to Tir-na Nog'th were to Benedict's left. Corwin looked up at him and smiled.

As they rested, they spoke of Brand, of what he had become, of whether he had fared as well as they or had died in the fall. When Benedict had recovered, his thoughts turned to the dangers to Amber and the possibility that a renewed invasion might occur from the black road after knowledge of this night's work reached the Courts. He was ready to rush back to the palace when Corwin halted him, suggesting that there had been a whole series of improbable coincidences that led them to this turn, ending with the coincidence that Benedict's mechanical arm was just the instrument needed to take back the Jewel of Judgment. Benedict agreed to a small experiment, an attempt to contact the possible agent who had guided the whole process. With some surprise, Benedict found Corwin to be right. In their joint Trump sending to their father, Ganelon responded.

Matters became settled and then unsettled rather

quickly after that. King Oberon ordered Corwin and Benedict to return to the palace. Soon after Benedict reached his own quarters, Oberon knocked on his door. The king explained hurriedly that Benedict had to step up his operation at the Courts of Chaos. He wanted Benedict to launch his attack in three days. Withholding his surprise, Benedict listened carefully to the plans Oberon wished to tell him, knowing that his father was revealing only as much as he felt Benedict needed to know.

Carrying an extra set of Trumps, he traveled, under Oberon's direction, to a distant shadow. He found his brother Bleys there with a well-armed troop of horsemen. Although he wanted to give Bleys a complete set of Trumps, his brother asked only for the Trump of Benedict. They discussed Benedict's operation in the mountains of the Courts, and Bleys explained their father's scheme for Bleys's part in it.

As Benedict rode his horse back to the royal stables of Amber, he received a Trump contact. Young Martin's image appeared to him. Martin said that he was in Amber, and he was with a young lady who wanted to meet him. The lady's name was Dara. With this, Benedict asked Martin to bring him through. We only have Corwin's account of what happened next:

> Martin, smiling, still held a Trump in his left hand, and Benedict—apparently recently summoned—stood before him. A girl was nearby, on the dais, beside the throne, facing away. Both men appeared to be speaking, but I could not hear the words.
>
> Finally, Benedict turned and seemed to address the girl. After a time, she appeared to be answering him. Martin moved off to her left. Benedict mounted the dais as she spoke. I could see her face then. The exchange continued. . . . How could I explain the presence of my distinctive blade, its elaborate tracery gleaming for all to see, hanging where it had suddenly appeared, without support, in the air before the throne, its point barely touching Dara's throat? . . .
>
> Benedict's blade had changed hands, and his gleaming prosthesis shot forward and fixed itself upon some unseen target. The two blades parried one another, locked, pressed, their

points moving toward the ceiling. Benedict's right hand continued to tighten.

> Suddenly, the Grayswandir blade was free, and moving past the other. It struck a terrific blow to Benedict's right arm at the place where the metal portion joined it. . . .
>
> He clutched at the stump of his arm. The mechanical hand/arm hung in the air near Grayswandir. It was moving away from Benedict and descending, as was the blade. When both reached the floor, they did not strike it but passed on through, vanishing from sight. (CC, 10–13)

Bleeding anew, Benedict was treated by Dara as others rushed into the room. Dara made a tourniquet from a strip of cloth, and she carefully bandaged the stump of his arm. Feeling light-headed, Benedict was struck with dizziness and nausea. He recognized Random, Corwin, and Gérard standing around him, and he continued to gather up his resources while resting on the floor of the throne room.

Benedict recovered enough to hear Corwin summon the guards to arrest Dara. Getting to his feet, Benedict told him that Dara was not an enemy, and that she could explain. He suggested that they talk in more privacy, so Benedict, Martin, Dara, Corwin, Random, and Gérard went to a room down the hall, closed and locked the door.

Dara explained that she was indeed the great-granddaughter of Benedict by the hellmaid, Lintra. She had earlier acted to deceive Corwin in order to learn more about Amber. Her actions were dictated by her alliance to the lords at the Courts of Chaos, who had been in league with Brand. However, after having met Martin, she had chosen to help King Oberon in order to maintain the reality of the worlds in their present condition. She claimed that, at this point, she was acting under orders from Oberon. It was Oberon's order that Benedict begin the assault on the Courts at once.

While Corwin contacted Oberon by Trump, and then transported to his location at the primal Pattern, Benedict sat tiredly in a chair in deep thought. After a short time, Benedict and the others saw the insubstantial image of Oberon and Corwin, Oberon's hand on his son's shoulder. Then Corwin became more substantial and the king faded, disappearing again.

Corwin confirmed that their father had entrusted

Dara to give his orders. It was Benedict's task to return to his men gathered at the Courts and mount a full attack. Dara had stated: "He [Oberon] wants you to attack, then fall back ... After that, it will only be necessary to contain them." (CC, 29) Taking out his deck and shuffling out the Trump of the Courts with his only hand, Benedict bade the others farewell. He stepped through to the other end of the worlds.

As soon as Benedict came through to the mountain region east of the Courts, his officers met him. There had been much activity to and from the black citadel above the Abyss, mainly along the black road. Besides that movement, gauzelike bridges floated out from the Abyss, winding to the heights just before that final darkness. Beings on horseback rode along those paths as well.

Benedict ordered his men to make an offensive strike. They formed three large companies, made their way stealthily down the mountain range, and then rushed upon the wide expanse below. When the army of Chaos saw the charge across the plain, they also sped onto the field from their heights. The two armies engaged just south of the plain's midpoint. Some of the Chaos soldiers sent volleys of arrows from the heights, but they fell wide of the attacking forces. The arrow barrage stopped when the two forces came together, fighting with swords, knives, and truncheons.

Benedict's horsemen had learned the terrain well. They were not distracted by the strangely divided sky or the odd outcroppings of rock. Many Chaos beings fell from their mounts with fire flowing from terrible wounds. Benedict rode quickly across the lines of his men, helping a cavalryman out of a difficulty with three beast-men, then riding into the enemy lines to break up a phalanx headed toward a weakened line of men. He was everywhere at once.

The fighting went on for a long time, though it was hard to gauge how long. Benedict noted the gathering of Chaos forces at the height, growing from the Abyss beyond. In the meantime, his men were beating back the enemy forces, but they were retreating toward the heights with the expectation of being joined by the others there.

Withdrawing behind the line of his troops, Benedict made Trump contact with Julian. He found that Julian had hellridden with his men and was in a near shadow. While his cavalry continued to beat back the enemy, Benedict rode to an outcropping of rock leading to the eastern mountains. From there, Benedict brought Julian and his patrol through with his Trump. They spoke briefly, Benedict organizing a signal with his brother and a line of attack for his soldiers. Julian informed Benedict that Random, Fiona, Flora, Deirdre, and Llewella were each arriving separately with reinforcements of their own. If they were not already there, they would reach the battlefield momentarily. Benedict felt that his own men could hold back the Chaos beings a while longer, but he knew he would need those extra contingents to make Oberon's plan work.

As he rode back into the thick of battle, Benedict felt an ascendant wind from the north. He turned to see a dark aspect above the distant mountains. It was the darkness of Chaos that his father had referred to when last they spoke together. There was no way of knowing the consequences of that storm's reaching this final valley. Benedict leaned hard forward on his horse, striking down two Chaos horsemen near him, then rode farther into the enemy forces.

Making his way toward the easternmost lines, he thought he saw Random leading a company of men down the near hills. Benedict took out his Trump of Random, tried to make contact, and found that it no longer worked. None of the Trumps but one would work now.

Benedict rode toward the eastern mountains. Random saw and recognized him. Riding to meet Benedict, Random approached with Deirdre and one of his captains. Pointing out the swarm of Chaos beings massing on the southern heights, Benedict outlined a strategy of containment for Random and his men to take. Random agreed, and the three pulled back to inform their company.

With his only hand, Benedict took out his Trumps, removed the one for Bleys, and concentrated. Its unaccustomed warmth was activated by the unique signature of Oberon. Benedict could see Bleys dimly, in the shadow of Oberon's creation, distant but not too remote. Bleys stared back calmly, and Benedict formed the words, "Not yet." He tiredly rubbed his eyes, and the lack of concentration ended the contact.

Rejoining his troops, Benedict fought on, driving back the enemy toward the heights, where more Chaos soldiers were waiting. He knew it would be only a matter of moments before the warriors of Chaos spilled onto the field of battle.

Random led his troops onto the plain, breaking into the enemy's right flank near the hilly area east of the heights. Deirdre, in black armor and wielding an ax, brought a contingent force behind Random, swept westward, and joined some of Benedict's horsemen in a frontal assault. Although Benedict was occupied and too far away to be certain, he saw a man armored in green using a mace in Random's company. He thought the man had Caine's features. Below Random's attacking forces, and to the east, were Llewella and Flora firing arrows with a line of other archers. Benedict noted the sailing of a volley of arrows that flew high in the air and found their mark in an infantry of beast-men waiting in the eastern hills. The beast-men spouted flames and rolled down the hilly decline, but others soon filled the vacant crags, cleaving to the rock and firing arrows back at the infantry.

At that point, the heights were brimming with Chaos warriors, most on hellish mounts, but others forming an immense infantry. The almost-constant din of shouting from that company seemed uplifted to a higher decibel level, and the horsemen of Chaos swept down the steep slopes, swinging clubs, axes, and curved swords.

Benedict's troops, at the forefront of the conflict, looked to Benedict's signal. Benedict had positioned his horse to be fairly central and in front of his horsemen, battling enemy soldiers with his own officers on either side of him. With his sword, Benedict made a wide, arcing gesture, then pointed it upward sharply. His officers repeated the gesture, and soon after the troops were encumbered by the new massing of enemy troops. Random and his company also recognized Benedict's signal, continuing to fight furiously against the right flank of the Chaos soldiers.

The army of the true city began to pull back. It was as if the enemy was beating them back, and even Benedict had moved out of the way of the onslaught. The troops of Random and Benedict gradually retreated, pushed back toward the northeastern mountains.

The Chaos horsemen swept across the plain, with their infantry following behind. Although it was uncertain, it seemed as though shouts of cheering rose from their company as they pressed the Amber forces back. Behind his lines of defense, Benedict gave the signal, and Julian and his veteran troops of Arden rushed upon the enemy from the east. Ri-

ding on his huge, metal-clad horse, amid the sudden alarm of a great horn, Julian at the head of his company made a fierce sight. There was a perceptible shuddering among the enemy horsemen as Julian's troops made contact. The army of Amber stood its ground as the conflict reached a new intensity. The immensity of numbers of the Chaos forces, however, continued to press the Amber troops back.

Given cover by Deirdre's contingent along the lines to the west, Benedict made his way to a hilltop. There he used Bleys's Trump to reach his brother, who was prepared for battle in that special shadow of their father's design. Bleys concentrated on the unique Trump he had of Benedict, so Benedict put away the Trump he held. Taking out his sword again, Benedict raised it above his head. He sensed the widening of the window between the worlds while, at the same time, listening to the sounds of battle behind him. He remained still, listening for the sibilant reverberation of a barrage of arrows sent forth by Deirdre and her soldiers. When that occurred, Benedict knew that part of the Chaos forces would turn in his direction and ride in an onslaught against him. In one quick movement, Benedict lowered his sword. Coming out of nowhere, Bleys's cavalry rode from the west, encountering Chaos horsemen almost immediately. The beings of Chaos were taken entirely by surprise, finding themselves surrounded on all sides by the troops of Amber.

There was a complete reversal as the Chaos army attempted to retreat to the heights but found the way blocked. Random's force prevented their return in the southeastern portion of the plain, Benedict's and Julian's troops battered them back from the northernmost regions, the archers, which included Llewella and Flora, harassed them from the southwest, and Bleys's cavalry pushed them from the west. The main force of the beings of Chaos were locked in, and comrades fell on all sides.

Benedict was employed with the business of sweeping Chaos soldiers from their mounts with his constantly active sword. However, he noticed an increasing darkness creeping toward them out of the north. A strong, wet wind swept his cloak up around him; his face was pelted with rain. His assault against the enemy horsemen became all the more ferocious with his knowledge that the dark storm was closing upon them.

Before long, Benedict realized that Amber's combined forces were victorious. He had breathing space to look about him. Corpses were strewn all around him, largely of the enemy. Casualties were as high among the horses that the Chaos beings rode, but Benedict surmounted any such sensibilities as sorrow for the deaths of those brutes. Many Chaos troops still fought and killed his own men, off to the left. As he rode to help in the continuing skirmishes, he thought he recognized Corwin on a Chaos horse, making his way along the right flank.

He found Julian battling hard with a sword in one hand and a mace in the other, his troops equally occupied around him. Benedict joined him, slashing into the guts of warriors who looked at him with unrepentant gazes, then dropped from their mounts with fire rising out of their wounds. Although he couldn't know with any certainty, it seemed to him that Random, Deirdre, and the knight in green armor had absented themselves, for he couldn't locate them anywhere in the fray.

The armies of the true city had taken over the field of battle. Dwindling in their midst, soldiers of Chaos began to toss down their arms in surrender. Fighting became more sporadic while more of their number retreated to the hills or gave up. Benedict was still engaging a group of warriors, with Julian nearby, when the world trembled and a blinding light erupted from the southern heights. For the first time in this confrontation, Benedict found himself unhorsed, sprawling on the rocky ground. Quickly getting to his feet, Benedict felt disoriented until his vision cleared. Julian was similarly affected, but he was chasing down his horse and remounting. Benedict's men and the several beast-men within view were all rising from the ground, suffering from some degree of stupefaction. To their credit, the soldiers of Julian and Benedict took command of the situation, putting the Chaos fighters under their custody and gathering up their own horses.

Although Benedict's striped roan had moved off, it returned to him, and Benedict rubbed his neck to calm him before getting on. Looking about, Benedict saw that the cloud of destruction had darkened the northernmost portion of the plain. Winds and rain were beating at them, soaking them to the skin. Under the control of Amber's forces, the Chaos troops willingly moved southward, away from that storm cloud. Here and there along the plain, obstinate forces struck back against the horsemen of

Amber, and Benedict intervened to conclude several of these isolated clashes.

The sky above them brightened. Benedict, Julian, and both armies halted in their progress and looked up. A large, bright cloud overhead churned with unusual rapidity. Its edges began to sharpen into a distinct form. Even Benedict was stunned to see the sudden face of Oberon taking shape, followed by the clear, tranquil voice of his father.

He knew his father possessed an unfathomable arsenal of supernatural abilities, but this left him overwhelmed with the wonder of it. Oberon's voice said that this message had been prepared before he attempted to repair the primal Pattern. It explained that the Jewel of Judgment was passed to Corwin upon Oberon's completing his task, and that the Jewel could be used to preserve them from the destroying storm. It spoke of the succession, indicating that he had had certain hopes in that direction. *Could he have been referring to me?* Benedict wondered. The voice said it was leaving the choice of successor on the horn of the unicorn. It bade farewell, giving its blessing, and the brightness faded, the formation dispersing as suddenly as it had come.

In the ensuing quiet, some of the craftier Chaos warriors moved to rocky outcroppings, gathering up their numbers. One of Julian's captains noticed the hostile grouping, called loudly to Julian, and a noisy conflict commenced. Fighting broke out in other areas as well, but the Chaos forces simply lacked in strength of numbers against the confident strikes of Amber's troops. Besides, the increasing presence of the storm cloud gradually pressing along the northern reaches of the valley was an awful physical constraint and a mighty coercion to follow the will of the multitude.

Shepherding the soldiers of Chaos toward the heights, Benedict was able to discern several figures on the near cliff. The knight in green stood out, but he also recognized Fiona. Corwin also seemed to be there. He sensed that a tragedy had just occurred, then realized that there was an unusual calm about those figures as they stood there speaking to one another. The crisis having to do with Brand's powerlust must have been concluded. Later, Benedict expected to learn the details. He joined Julian as they reached the hills, assigned men to guard the captured beings of Chaos, and spoke quietly with his officers.

The relative stillness was broken by a resounding

wail that was long and piercing. It became recognizable as the sound of a trumpet. Everyone turned toward the oncoming storm. There, on the black road in the distance, were three ghostly horsemen on black steeds, moving ceremoniously out of the enveloping dark storm cloud, each playing upon a trumpet. They were in the lead of an enormous procession, crossing the black road with a methodically rolling motion, in time to the eerie music. All kinds of creatures evolved from that dark cloud, carrying banners of a variety of shadows. Some of the beings came from familiar shadows, but even beasts of hostile realms were represented. More musicians followed, and flying beasts, and songsters of many worlds adding their voices to the semimelodious dirge. Benedict knew this was a funeral procession even before he saw the horse-drawn cart in black drapery, bearing a casket with the flag of the unicorn. When he saw the hunchbacked form of Dworkin driving the team of black horses, he knew whose funeral he was witnessing. Other figures proceeded after the cart, and it was clear that the marchers were winding their way to the Dark Citadel above the Abyss. Benedict and the others around him watched entranced.

While the mournful parade had progressed along that dark road, the storm seemed to have halted. Once the last of the Shadow-beings had wound his way over the Abyss, the storm cloud began to move again. During the march, Julian had joined his gathering kin on the heights. At its conclusion, Benedict also joined them.

Speaking with Caine, Bleys, Random, and Julian, he discovered how they had lost Deirdre and Brand. As the storm approached, darkening the sky above them, Benedict, Random, and Bleys talked of possible consequences. The logical course of action was to retreat to the Dark Citadel, as much to save themselves as to offer final respect to their father.

As Fiona approached them, Benedict nodded toward Corwin, sitting on the rocky precipice near the lip of the great darkness with a young stranger. Fiona told him it was Corwin's son Merlin. Benedict remembered the unfamiliar Trumps that Martin had shown them, one being that of Merlin. With a slight twinge, Benedict wondered about young Martin.

Someone gasped, and Fiona tapped Benedict on the shoulder. He turned in the direction that Fiona was looking, toward the precipice several feet to the left of Corwin and Merlin. The beautiful white form of the unicorn stood at the edge, having just climbed out of the Abyss. She stood calmly looking at them, her breath visible against the utter darkness behind. Around her neck, Benedict saw the red gleam of the Jewel of Judgment. With slow, deliberate steps, she walked toward Benedict and the others around him. Her eyes were wary, and no one moved for fear that she would run away. She reached the small group, then dropped her front legs, kneeling low. The horn of the unicorn nearly touched the chest of the person before her. Gingerly, Random reached forward, took the chain of the Jewel in both hands, and carefully lifted it over her mane and head. The unicorn stood again, remaining still before Random, very much like a marble statue. Julian pulled out his sword and placed it on the ground before Random. Bleys did the same, followed by Benedict, Caine, Fiona, Llewella, and Corwin. Turning from them, the unicorn galloped down the northern slope, soon disappearing from sight.

Random and Corwin went off together toward the eastern slopes so that Random could learn to use the Jewel to block the storm. Julian, Bleys, and Benedict turned back to their troops, trying to maintain calm among them in the face of the threatening devastation. Besides their own men, Benedict and the others had to quiet the grumblings among the prisoners, who were eager to cross over into the citadel. In a brief span, Random returned, carrying the unconscious form of Corwin, who had exhausted himself from the effort of helping Random attune to the Jewel. He assured the others that Corwin was all right. Speaking with Julian, Benedict, Bleys, and Fiona, Random understood the concerns of all the remaining troops to avoid the cataclysm. It would be difficult to contain all those people in the face of imminent destruction. Random ordered Benedict to take the soldiers of both sides across the black road. Benedict shook Random's hand, waved to Julian and his officers to mount up, and led them down the western slope to the dark path.

The long battle was over. Benedict entered the Courts of Chaos with a sense of completion. The noblemen of that ancestral place greeted him and his troops with neither smiles nor daggers. The lords of the realm conducted a solemn ceremony for the ultimate passing of the former king of Amber, one who was, after all, a member of their fraternity. No longer were they enemies, but Benedict knew that the trust that had to be made between them would have to be forged by a common wish for peace. This was a beginning.

Benedict sat beside Random at the lengthy sessions in the Courts, acting as the new king's counsel, but in actuality adding his personal authority to the proceedings. The lords of the Courts knew well Benedict's skills, and no treachery was ever considered. After a time, the terms of the Patternfall Treaty were agreed upon, the document carefully drawn up, and the concerned parties' signatures placed on it.

Continuing to reside in Amber, Benedict took some pleasure in serving his young half brother, although his post had not been clearly defined. While Benedict had little interest in the politics of rule, he enjoyed sharing confidences with this once-brash, youthful rascal, who now had attained a new maturity, in spite of a sometime wistfulness for days of yore. Benedict felt they shared in another way, too, for Benedict still felt a paternal fondness for Martin. Random and he would speak often of the young man, who spent much time in Amber initially, but then felt the urge to wander in Shadow again.

While Random pursued an agenda of forming new alliances with various shadows for their mutual benefit, Benedict remained quietly observant. His part in the Kashfa affair was strictly as a bodyguard for the king. He no longer doubted Random's good sense, and he continued to perform his duties in a cautious, military manner. He followed the history of Kashfa, understood the relationships between the realms involved, and observed the enforced changes of authority with simple dispassion.

Only when the rebel mercenary Dalt had arrived in the outskirts of Amber did Benedict feel a singular urgency. Benedict had faced this same foe years ago, and he was certain he had given Dalt a death blow. His presence in the true city gave Benedict a desire to finish the task finally.

Julian's troops had encountered Dalt's mercenary force in the western portion of Arden. Benedict had learned about the confrontation upon returning from Kashfa with his contingent, sent back at Random's order. Conferring with Julian by Trump, Benedict was extremely untrusting of Dalt's request, under a flag of truce, that Amber place Rinaldo and Jasra in his custody. Benedict kept his troops hidden along the southeastern fringe of the forest, awaiting developments.

Julian kept Benedict informed when Rinaldo and Merlin appeared at his encampment. He told Benedict of the planned meeting between Dalt and Rinaldo. Through Julian's open Trump contact, Benedict observed the hand-to-hand combat between Rinaldo and Dalt. When Dalt succeeded in overpowering Rinaldo, Benedict had his troops ready for immediate attack if Dalt's men didn't pull back. Benedict had his men stand easy at their posts as he watched the mercenaries break camp and depart, heading westward.

After Random's return to Amber, Benedict heard about the most recent political upheaval in Kashfa. A mercenary force had taken over the government there, putting the elder statesman whom Random intended for rule into prison. Benedict was surprised only that he had not realized the cleverness of Rinaldo and Dalt earlier. It seemed that he had been a minor cog in the wheel of Rinaldo's scheme to regain the throne of Kashfa. Although Benedict might have found these tactics calculatingly ingenious, he resented being used as a minor cog. He hoped to be instrumental in rectifying the situation soon.

BLACK ROAD

A wide, black route that crossed Shadow from the Courts of Chaos to Amber. The leaders of a movement in the Courts intent on destroying Amber arranged for the creation of this unique pathway so that they could mount an invasion against the true city.

Chronicling the history of events leading up to the Patternfall War, Corwin of Amber explained how he first discovered the black road. In shadow Avalon, he met Dara, who told him something of the situation of his brother Benedict, who resided there. She told Corwin of a visit by Julian and Gérard, both wounded in a fight with beings on a black road. Soon thereafter, Corwin's companion Ganelon pointed out the black road as they were fleeing Avalon. Corwin recorded his first view of the route:

> Perhaps three-quarters of a mile distant, running from left to right for as far as I could see, was a wide, black band. We were several

hundred yards higher than the thing and had a decent view of, I would say, half a mile of its length. It was several hundred feet across, and though it curved and turned twice that I could see, its width appeared to remain constant. There were trees within it, and they were totally black. There seemed to be some movement. I could not say what it was. Perhaps it was only the wind rippling the black grasses near its edge. But there was also a definite sensation of flowing within it, like current in a flat, dark river. (GA, 158–59)

As Ganelon and Corwin traveled through Shadow, they found that the black road continued in every shadow also. In one instance, Corwin rescued a masked lady from albino demons within that road, only to find that she was an agent of the Courts herself. At that time, Corwin found that the black grasses within it seemed animated, holding Ganelon in their insidious grasp. After Corwin helped to free him, Ganelon told him that his legs felt numb, as if they were asleep. It seemed as if the twining grasses had sapped the energy from them. Gradually, Ganelon's legs regained their circulation and strength.

In a bold experiment, Corwin and Ganelon rode through the black road. In spite of the increased pain, Corwin used the image of the Pattern against it, and found that the attempt cleared a path across a portion of the road. He recorded what it was like to ride within that eerie route:

> We entered the black area, and it was like riding into a World War II newsreel. Remote though near at hand, stark, depressing, grim. Even the creaking and the hoof falls were somehow muffled, made to seem more distant. A faint, persistent ringing began in my ears. The grasses beside the road stirred as we passed, though I kept well away from them. We passed through several patches of mist. They were odorless, but our breathing grew labored on each occasion. (GA, 165–66)

While the black road represented anathema to Corwin, he made use of it to his advantage in dealing with his brother Benedict. His brother had chased Corwin and Ganelon through Shadow in the mistaken belief that Corwin had killed two of his

servants in Avalon. When Corwin met Benedict in combat, he maneuvered Benedict toward the black road. When the animated grasses wound around Benedict's legs, Corwin was able to overpower him and knock him into unconsciousness. Then, Corwin tied him up and contacted another brother to help Benedict while he and Ganelon made good their escape.

Corwin and Ganelon had assembled men and special weapons for an assault against the usurper Eric in Amber. When Corwin's party reached the mountains of the true city, they found that Eric and his army were already under attack. The Chronicles describe the battle thusly:

> When last I had seen that once lovely valley, it had been a twisted wilderness. Now, things were even worse. The black road cut through it, running to the base of Kolvir itself, where it halted. A battle was raging within the valley. Mounted forces swirled together, engaged, wheeled away. Lines of foot soldiers advanced, met, fell back. The lightning kept flashing and striking among them. The dark birds swept about them like ashes on the wind. . . .
> At first it occurred to me that someone else might be about the same thing I was . . .
> But no. These were coming in from the west, along the black road. . . .
> So the forces from Shadow about which I had been hearing reports, were even stronger than I had thought. I had envisioned harassment, but not a pitched battle at the foot of Kolvir. I looked down at the movements within the blackness. The road seemed almost to writhe from the activity about it. (GA, 206)

After Eric's death during the battle, Corwin took charge of the situation. He defeated the invaders and became ruler of Amber for a time. Nevertheless, the black road remained, touching the foot of Mt. Kolvir, and it was one of Corwin's major concerns. As regent, Corwin investigated the several unresolved details that involved the creation of the black road.

Corwin continued to feel guilty, believing himself a prime cause of the black road. When Eric had blinded him and tossed him into a dungeon, Corwin cursed Eric and his rule of Amber. It was difficult for Corwin to shake the belief that his curse was responsible for the appearance of the black road.

However, he had come to realize that one or more members of his family had conspired with the lords of the Courts to obtain that access to the true city. Random told Corwin his story of the confinement of their brother Brand in some far-off shadow. It seemed as if Brand held the key to the conspiracy. Thus, in order to plumb the secrets of the black road, Corwin arranged for the rescue of Brand.

Through investigation, questioning, and happenstance, Corwin gradually pieced together the mystery of the black road. Brand had been part of a cabal that dealt directly with the Chaos lords to open a pathway for invasion into Amber. That had resulted in the failed battle at Kolvir. Still, the scheme was a long and convoluted one. It involved removing King Oberon from Amber, clandestine visits to the Courts of Chaos by Brand and Fiona, and Brand's gathering information on a blood relation to be used as a sacrifice.

The lords of the Courts had taught Brand what he must do to open the way into Amber. Brand then chose to make Random's illegitimate son his dupe, assuming that no one would be overly concerned about his whereabouts. Not having met Martin, Brand asked his siblings to describe him, doing so in a surreptitious manner over a period of many years. Devising a Trump of Martin, Brand walked the primal Pattern and called Random's son to him. As they spoke, Brand stabbed Martin, and his blood blotted out a portion of the Pattern. This blot was what was needed to manifest the black road, growing across all the worlds from the Courts.

Ultimately, Corwin came to realize something that Dworkin and Oberon already knew and were planning to remedy: to rid the shadows of the black road, an initiate of the Pattern had to clear away the blot on the primal Pattern.

We must therefore think of the black road as simply a physical manifestation of the blot on the primal Pattern. When the damaged Pattern was repaired, a devastating storm swept over Amber and all the shadows, destroying everything but the Courts of Chaos. Random used the Jewel of Judgment to put an end to the Death Storm. With that, Amber and all the worlds between returned. The Pattern was whole, and the black road was no more.

Before that final passing, however, the black road was given useful purpose one last time. Outside of the Dark Citadel of the Courts, coming from out of the storm front to the north, a solemn procession trod the black road. Creatures out of Shadow led the procession, and within their midst was Dworkin, reining a funeral carriage bearing the body of King Oberon. The late king was to be placed with his ancestors in that dark realm. Thus was that road used in the suspension of hostilities.

BLACK STONE FOUNTAIN

Also called the Fount of Power and the Black Fount. It is located in a large chamber within the Keep of the Four Worlds. Because four shadows meet at that point, the Black Fount generates immense raw power. The individual known as Mask had utilized that raw power just as Jasra had done before him. Mask had allied himself with Jurt of the Courts of Chaos. Using his knowledge of the Fount, Mask had been guiding Jurt through the ritual of bathing in the Fountain, thus leading him to become a virtually magical being.

Merlin recorded a vivid description of the chamber and the Fount within it:

> I was in a two-story-high hall. Stairways rose to the right and the left ahead of me, curving inward toward a railed landing, the terminus of a second-floor hallway. There was another hallway below it, directly across from me. Two stairways also headed downward, to the rear of those which ascended. . . .
>
> In the center of the room was a black stone fountain, spraying flames—not water—into the air; the fire descended into the font's basin, where it swirled and danced. The flames were red and orange in the air, white and yellow below, rippling. A feeling of power filled the chamber. Anyone who could control the forces loose in this place would be a formidable opponent indeed. (BA, 203)

Rinaldo, the son of Jasra, explained further about the results of using the Black Fount:

> "Bathing a person in it will, if he's properly protected, do wonders for strength, stamina,

and magical abilities. That part's easy for a person with some training to learn. I've been through it myself. But old Sharu's notes were in his lab, and there was something more in them—a way of replacing part of the body with energy, really packing it in. Very dangerous. Easily fatal. But if it works you get something special, a kind of superman, a sort of Living Trump.'' (SC, 106)

When Merlin stood outside the Keep of the Four Worlds with Jasra and his half brother Mandor, he watched the movements of two tornados. They were moving about the outer wall of the Keep. One of them began to brighten, shooting off electric bolts. Then it began to fade, and the second tornado took its turn in becoming fiery. Merlin asked Jasra what it meant. She answered:

> "The ritual . . . Someone is playing with those forces right now. . . .
> ". . . They could just be starting, or they could be finished already. All the poles of fire tell me is that everything is in place." (SC, 204)

Merlin, Jasra, and Mandor were transported to a corridor within the chamber of the Fount. They saw Jurt standing naked beside the fountain, all aglow from the initial stages of his empowerment. Mask was on the opposite side of it, and their sorcerous battle began.

As Merlin described Mask's opening gambit, he scoffed at its simplicity:

> "Below, in the basin, the fires rippled yellow and white. When he [Mask] scooped up a handful and worked them together as a child might shape a snowball, they became an incandescent blue. Then he threw it at me.
> I sent it past with a simple parry. This was not Art, it was basic energy work." (SC, 209)

Having gained a modicum of Trump-like ability, Jurt was able to appear in one place, disappear, and reappear in a different place. Although he had become more powerful and had greater resistance to harm, he was rather clumsy and easily tricked by Jasra and Merlin in their contest. Mask used the energies of the Fount itself to send out spells against Merlin. Merlin countered with various spells he had prepared beforehand, knowing that his own conjuring would be limited against that vast power source.

Mask had channeled the Fount's powers to break open sections of the flooring in order to impale Merlin on a jagged edge. The tactic failed, and Mask had the fountain's energies lift him high above the ground. Above Merlin, Mask made an incantation that brought Sharu Garrul, the old master of the Keep, out of a spell of immobility. Sharu occupied Jasra, while Mask continued to attack Merlin.

Cracks tore through the walls of the Keep as Mask continued to draw on the Fountain to defeat Merlin. Mask attempted to stab him with a magical sword, but missed. Suddenly close to Mask, Merlin used his ordinary dagger to stab Mask. Mask screamed in pain.

Jurt stood near the Fount and was about to send a deadly stroke at Merlin. However, Mandor tossed his magical balls in Jurt's direction, smashing the Black Fountain. As the Fount collapsed, walls and pillars fell. Jurt carried Mask away and vanished in the wreckage.

As Jasra and Sharu Garrul proceeded with their sorcerous duel, the energies of the Fount rose up, high above the wrecked Keep. Jasra succeeded in overthrowing Sharu. In a state between life and death, Sharu was demeaned into becoming Jasra's obedient servant. She announced that he was now guardian of the Fount. His place would be forever with the Black Stone Fountain, maintaining its level of energy and stoking its flame.

BLACK WATCH

In the Courts of Chaos, candidates in the line of succession to the throne are put under black watch as protection from possible assassination.

While deaths by assassination had been occurring in the Courts for several years, shortening the list of those in line to the throne, the circumstances became dire only with the recent death of old King Swayvill. In the absence of a direct heir, Lord Bances of Amblerash was acting on behalf of the Crown, guarding the safety of the remaining candidates, who were put into the care of their Houses' security. Since Lord Bances was a priest of the Serpent, he was not himself permitted to rule.

Although there had not been any sudden rise of murders, several killings did occur just after the old king's demise. Suspicions led one to believe that a single intelligence, or perhaps a very small organization of intelligences, was orchestrating events. Since few could be trusted, not even the surviving candidates to the Crown, the black watch was put into effect.

At the time of the funeral of King Swayvill, three candidates were placed under black watch: Tubble of the House of Chanicut; Tmer of the House of Jesby; and Merlin of the House of Sawall.

During the course of the funeral services, sacrilege was committed twice in spite of the best efforts of the Crown to protect the candidates. Both Tmer and Tubble were murdered by unknown assailants.

Even though Lord Bances was described as a man who was above influencing the royal succession, it began to seem a possibility that he, acting as "the Crown," was conspiring with someone. If that were the case, then the protection offered by the black watch would appear to be unreliable indeed.

BLEYS

The son of King Oberon of Amber and a redhaired woman of a distant shadow whose name was Clarissa, Bleys bore many of the physical characteristics of his mother. He was born with bright red hair, a broad, smiling face, and a propensity for laughter. These his mother gave him. His lustiness and enormous physical energy were given him by his father.

Bleys is younger than Benedict and Corwin, but he is older than Julian, Gérard, and Random. Among the family members, he is closest to Fiona, who was born some years before to Clarissa. In his boyhood days, Bleys felt close to Clarissa's younger son, Brand, although they grew somewhat apart as they became older.

Although he closely resembled Brand, Bleys sported a bright red beard from an early age while Brand remained clean-shaven all his life. Fiona, closer in age to Bleys than Brand, looked like a blood relative only in the fact of her blazing red hair. Her green eyes and narrow face were distinctly

different from Bleys's wide, sanguine visage and laughing blue eyes.

Flamboyant in silken clothes of bright red and orange, Bleys has made a fashion of gaudy showiness. This flashy sense of style has been calculated to cause potential adversaries to underestimate him. In this respect, Bleys bears the defensiveness of all the members of royal blood in Amber. His openhanded, congenial exterior masks a wariness and distrust that is part of his father's legacy.

Fond of large rings, Bleys wears two on his right hand, a ruby and an emerald, and one on his left, a sapphire. Rarely far from his bejeweled right hand is his sword, a bright radiance of gold that would fool many people into thinking it mere ornamentation. But the tracery along its blade contains a portion of the Pattern, and this bright-haired dandy can pull his sword from its scabbard and slice an opponent open then take a drink of wine before anyone could be aware that he just killed a man.

From the time he was a small boy playing with his brothers in the royal castle, Bleys was rarely political in nature. He never sought favoritism from his father and, at the same time, he remained quietly inconspicuous. Consequently, he was seldom given any acknowledgment from Oberon, who had shown greater interest in his older sons, Corwin, Benedict, Caine, and, sometimes, Eric.

Bleys confided a great deal in his sister Fiona, especially during the time of Oberon's estrangement from their mother. After Brand's birth, and the subsequent divorce decree between Oberon and Clarissa, Oberon had even less to do with the raising of his children than previously. They were left in the charge of a court matron or a courtier, who acted as mentor. When the children were old enough, they were encouraged to travel in Shadow and find a contented stability there. The children of Clarissa in particular chose to spend much of their adolescence within the confines of the palace of Amber.

Fiona was first to gravitate toward their aging grandsire Dworkin, followed afterward by Brand and Bleys. Brand and Fiona were especially fascinated by the secrets of that distant realm, mysteriously called the Courts of Chaos, that Dworkin opened up to them. Bleys was always there with them, sitting or playing somewhat apart, while Dworkin told of arcane existences through tales of the Courts. For his part, Dworkin was flattered to have a willing audience, and he enjoyed the role of mentor to these admiring red-haired children of Oberon.

While Brand seemed to have been the chief benefactor of Dworkin's lessons, Fiona and Bleys significantly enhanced their considerable talents. Although it is difficult to ascertain just what benefits Bleys and Fiona acquired from Dworkin's tutelage, their combined powers had been potent enough to restrain Brand and place him in confinement during the succession wars, during which the late Prince Eric had taken the throne of Amber.

Unlike Brand, who wielded the power he garnered with wild abandon, Bleys has chosen a less conspicuous path. It is a path that makes it difficult for anyone in Amber to know precisely how much knowledge Bleys had gleaned from those early sessions with the mad sage. At the close of the Patternfall battle outside of the Courts of Chaos, Bleys revealed to Corwin some of the things he learned from Dworkin. When Corwin wondered about the consequences of the new Pattern he had created, Bleys responded: "It is my understanding from things that Dworkin told me, that two distinct Patterns could not exist in the same universe." (CC, 123) He added that such a condition would cause "a splitting off, the founding of a new existence— somewhere," (CC, 123) with the potential to cause either a complete cataclysm or have no effect on the world as we know it.

Bleys chose the military life over a sorcerous one, so that he could the more readily shrug off cataclysms like the Patternfall problem with calm philosophy. His strength was in his tactical skill and the use of practical means to achieve an objective. He would make use of a kind of sorcery in the manipulation of Shadow and the beings who people it, moving such creatures to invest their strength and lives for him.

One of Bleys's earliest commissions was an assignment given him by his father. When Deela the Desacratrix renewed raids in the shadow Begma a couple of years after she escaped from Oberon, Begma contacted Oberon to help them a second time. Oberon was preoccupied with handling some delicate trade agreements and, rather than sending the more experienced Benedict, chose to rely, surprisingly, on Bleys. It was one of the rare times that his father hinted at any confidence in Bleys's abilities, and Bleys felt himself worthy to justify Oberon's trust.

Bleys had prepared extensively for battle in Begma by studying maps of the land. He developed a detailed composite of all land, water, and mountain regions in Begma that is still used today by merchants and seamen for the continued development of trade routes. Although Bleys dug in a huge force of well-trained soldiers in strategic areas, the first skirmishes were disappointing. Deela's forces were not combat soldiers and didn't fight like a regular military force. They would send out solitary scouts to attract attention and help in locating the positions of Bleys's men. Then they would wait— sometimes hours, sometimes days. They would sneak in before dawn, perhaps, or in the middle of the night, or just after meal rations had been passed around. They would attack viciously with an arrow barrage or cut the throats of sleeping soldiers and run off again.

Bleys saw that they were in danger of losing large numbers of men by these continuous hit-and-run attacks. Even the bravest of his soldiers quavered at the thought of nodding off to sleep and being knifed from behind. Some of his men had already lost their nerve and simply disappeared. Bleys knew this had happened only because an occasional mutilated body had been tossed back at them in an attempt to unravel nerves further.

Using his powers over Shadow, Bleys formed an effective espionage ring of men similar in appearance to those in Deela's army. These spies weren't necessarily Shadow-images of her men, but they dressed and acted enough like those Deela had recruited so that they fit in. Bleys's spies relayed information about the location of the raiders, especially where they camped at their ease. Without seeming to alter his forces from the area he was known to have occupied, Bleys secretly moved his main army to the region his spies had helped him map out. While a skeleton staff put on a great show of activity on their original offensive front, Bleys and the main force surrounded Deela and her troops in a hidden encampment near an inn.

Deela and her fighters were taken completely by surprise when Bleys's men attacked. Although Deela and her men regrouped quickly and fought courageously, the devastation was complete. They battled to the last, and Bleys only regretted that some unnamed soldier had run Deela through with a sword in the midst of battle before he could do so himself.

When he returned to Amber, Bleys's men recounted the story of his tactical achievement, making him a hero before all the court. Although Oberon did not present Bleys with any award of honor, he did make a public pronouncement of his bravery. In truth, Oberon was much impressed by his victory, and Bleys was raised higher in his esteem.

His actions in this war were also noted by Fiona and Brand, who kept them in mind several years later when they began formulating plans for the succession to the throne of Amber.

Working industriously at his military career, Bleys showed his father numerous times his abilities as a tactician and leader. In time, Oberon promoted him to general and gave him the cavalry corps to train. Bleys devoted himself to the cavalry, making them a matchless troop, both as an honor guard in national parades and as fierce combatants on the field of war.

Few citizens of Amber, apart from the members of the Royal Family, know the specifics about the wars of succession during the time of Oberon's absence and Prince Eric's ascension. The facts vary also, depending on the author of the records kept about that time. Corwin, in his Chronicles, describes the differing views of Julian, Brand, Fiona, and Random in trying to piece together for himself these events. Bleys has always remained silent about these matters, and no one wishes to open up old wounds by discussing that long-ago situation today. Still, records, along with informed speculation, lead us to the following account:

Fiona first broached the subject of who should be named heir to the throne with Bleys. It was rather tentative at first, but after several meetings with Fiona and Brand, Bleys recognized their seriousness in wanting to take over the rule of the true city.

Events dictated the need to act, if only to preserve one prince's right to the throne against another's. Prince Corwin had left Amber some time before, and no one was able to reach him with the Trumps or by any other means. Oberon voiced his suspicions to his children, and he made it known that Corwin was his choice as successor. This made the others rather uncomfortable, especially Eric, who Oberon insinuated had murdered his brother.

Within their cabal, Brand was the instigator who demanded action to be taken. Oberon had become involved in a complicated treaty with the shadow Begma, and Fiona suggested that there was a romantic entanglement as well. The king had long been ignoring some matters of civil strife between the nobility and commoners at home, and Julian had reported that Oberon's handling of the treaty agreements with Begma was going badly. Brand saw these problems as a rationale for removing their father from power.

Fiona had presented the most convincing argument for not assassinating their father: if any other member of the Family discovered the body, it would mean open war between parties at best, and the accusation of regicide followed by execution for their party at worst. Anything in between would not be acceptable either.

Oberon had to be sent away, without physical harm. Fiona and Brand worked out the details to get him out of the picture. While they were able to handle most of the planning, they needed someone who had Oberon's trust to urge him on a mission to a distant shadow. Bleys, who had never asked for favoritism from his father, had nevertheless won a certain respect from Oberon. Fiona pressed Bleys to act on their behalf, promising that no harm would come to their father. Persuasive as she often is, she dangled an especially desirable reward before him: Bleys, acting to protect the vacant throne of Amber, would receive official coronation. For an officer who never thought to be higher than his rank of general, this was enormously flattering to Bleys. He had remained in the background for so long, that the possibility of kingship lifted his hopes to a level he had never considered previously. He fell in with Fiona and Brand wholeheartedly.

While Fiona and Brand left the Palace to proceed with their tasks, Bleys used Shadow-spies to discover the name of the young lady in Begma whose home King Oberon had been frequenting. Once he had this knowledge, Bleys visited a shadow much like Begma and located a facsimile of the girl. Using his powers over Shadow, Bleys was able to convince her of a needed deception that would cause harm to no one. He had her write a note to Oberon, pleading him to rescue her from kidnappers, former suitors who learned of her indiscretion with the king of Amber. Adding force to the argument of her letter, Bleys secretly introduced the girl into the king's chambers late one night to wake a sleeping Oberon. She spoke hurriedly of being in desperate straits to the groggy king. Before Oberon could fully awaken, she had disappeared. Conveniently, Bleys was sauntering through the hallway nearby when Oberon, in nightshirt, rushed by. Bleys reported hearing a scuffle below, near the main hall of the palace, but had found nobody about. Together, they walked back to Oberon's chambers, Bleys soothing him with the promise to look into the matter.

The next day, Bleys came to the king with a message he claimed to have found in an urn on a shelf in the main hall. It was the lady's note, written in a trembling hand. Within an hour of reading the letter, Oberon was gone. Only a minor court officer told of Oberon rushing toward his rooms, calling to him that he had an important mission and had to leave immediately. That was the last anyone heard from him.

Although Bleys knew that Fiona and Brand intended to assure their father's continued disappearance, he didn't learn until after the fact that Fiona made direct contact with some Chaos lords at the Courts of Chaos. These Chaos lords employed their own methods to keep Oberon out of touch and unable to escape from a shadow close to the Courts.

Brand pressed the idea of acting immediately to take the throne in Oberon's absence, but Fiona insisted they wait a respectable amount of time before making their move. Bleys remained cautiously quiet.

For more than a year, the realm continued without a ruler. Prince Julian had recounted to Random what conditions were like:

> "We have simply been dealing with affairs as they arise. Gérard and Caine had been running the navy anyway, on Dad's orders. Without him, they have been making all their own decisions. I [Julian] took charge of the patrols in Arden again. There is no central authority though, to arbitrate, to make policy decisions, to speak for all of Amber." (SU, 34)

When Brand approached Caine to request his help in seizing the throne, Caine assumed that Brand intended to rule Amber. This was not to Caine's liking. Julian and Caine persuaded Eric to take the throne, acting as Protector of the realm, and Eric agreed reluctantly. Eric was fearful that claiming the kingship would make him a target for assassination, so he chose the Protectorship as a compromise. In the meantime, Bleys confronted Eric over his taking control. However, Bleys could see that Eric had the

support of the royal army, even if Bleys could claim sponsorship from the cavalry. The soldiers had already consolidated their loyalty under Eric, and Bleys was in no position to contest this. Bleys put on a show of anger and stormed away. This was part of a ploy that Fiona and Brand put him up to, so that he would have an excuse to leave Amber. Bleys had previously packed and was ready to leave for the shadow Avernus to initiate the staging of a military operation against Eric.

Avernus was Bleys's pet project, something he had been working on for many years. When he first envisioned it as a young officer, he considered it a perfect training ground for military maneuvers. It was a young, wild version of Amber, a world of extremes, a world in flux. It seemed the right place to toughen raw recruits who would be unused to drastic conditions. The extremes of heat in the day and freezing cold at night, the instability of the land masses, the dangers of molten lakes and geysers of hot steam, and the hazards of hostile animals were all incentives for strength, wariness, and the urge to survive. When, to his delight, Bleys observed the evolution of indigent sentient life-forms—people—he worked hard to oversee their development. As millennia passed in Avernus time, the people viewed Bleys as a god who would spend years with them, then disappear for a decade or two, and return again virtually unchanged. For Bleys, they were children of his vision, and he held them in special esteem even as he knew many of them would die for him in the war he and Brand and Fiona had been scheming to put together.

When Bleys felt the men of Avernus were advanced enough, he began the recruitment and training of troops. They were fearless and credulous soldiers, and Bleys found them willing trainees. Fiona contacted him with his Trump several times in the succeeding months to keep him abreast of events in Amber. Having thrown himself totally into the training of his army, Bleys was somewhat indifferent to his sister's news.

Sometime later, when Bleys had an army in the tens of thousands, he received a tense message from Fiona: Eric had learned that Prince Corwin was alive, living on the shadow Earth. It seemed that Corwin had spent centuries there, having lost his memory. Bleys had been initially uncertain how this news affected their plans, until Fiona reminded him that Corwin was heir apparent, having been so named by Oberon before his disappearance.

Another message came from Fiona shortly after that: King Oberon had somehow eluded the lords of Chaos who had been watching over him. He was no longer in their care. Bleys worried over this, asking if they should cancel their plans. Fiona assured him that Oberon was too far away to reach Amber easily, and the Chaos lords were attempting to track him with an expertise special to them. As for Corwin, Brand had already left for the shadow where he was found. He would see to it that Corwin remained ignorant of the situation in Amber.

Shortly thereafter, Bleys was contacted again by his sister. This time there was urgency in her voice. Brand had revealed powers that she hadn't known he had. He came to her one night in her chamber in the Royal Palace of Amber—without the use of Trumps. He seemed able to read her mind. Then he spoke wildly of wiping out the Amber known to us and starting anew. First, though, he intended to return to the shadow Earth and kill Corwin. He seemed obsessed with this: Corwin's life must be ended. Although he had been confined for a time by Eric, Caine, and Julian, Brand feared them less than he did Corwin. He saw Corwin as the one obstacle to his attaining absolute control over Amber and the Pattern.

Bleys joined his sister in searching for Brand in the shadow called Earth. As they sought Brand out, Bleys was having grave doubts about combining with the forces at the Courts of Chaos. He cited Brand's unpredictability as one consequence of seeking powers beyond the knowledge obtainable from the Pattern. He was able to influence Fiona to the effect that they came to the decision not to rely on the Courts any longer. Unfortunately, with Brand loose, this decision may have already come too late.

Bleys managed to trace Corwin to New York State and had nearly caught up with him when Corwin drove away in an automobile. Bleys secretly jumped into the back of a truck heading in the same direction, managed to get Corwin's automobile in sight again from a parking area along the highway, and watched as the two left tires exploded. He observed Brand hiding below with a rifle, and he saw the auto careen off the side of the road into the lake.

Without a weapon at hand, Bleys knew he couldn't adequately defend himself against Brand. If Corwin had survived the crash, speed was essential; Brand was heading for the lake, intent on making sure Corwin didn't survive. Bleys caught a ride to the nearest town and called the state highway patrol at a telephone booth. He hoped he had been in time.

Shortly afterward, Fiona made contact with Bleys. She joined him, and they worked together to seek out Brand. Returning to the site of the accident, they saw an ambulance drive away while a highway patrol car lingered a few minutes. After the police drove away, Fiona and Bleys searched the area above the lake where Bleys had seen Brand in hiding. They found some bullet casings, but nothing else.

Later, Fiona telephoned several local hospitals until she found the one Corwin was in. At least he was all right and recovering, she discovered.

Brand's account makes him seem innocent of any wrongdoing: "I dragged you [Corwin] out, though, and there was enough left to start treating. . . . I hellrode out when help arrived. My associates [Fiona and Bleys] caught up with me somewhat later and put me where you found me." (SU, 157) On the other hand, Fiona's explanation puts the blame squarely on Brand:

> "Brand did not drag you out of the wreck. You did it yourself. He waited around to be certain you were dead, and you surfaced and pulled yourself ashore. He went down and was checking you over . . . The police arrived about then and he had to clear out. We caught up with him shortly afterward and were able to subdue him and imprison him in the tower. That took a lot of doing. Later, I contacted Eric and told him what had happened. He then ordered Flora to put you in the other place and see that you were held until after his coronation." (HO, 146–47)

Since Brand had made various inquiries about Random's son, Martin, many years before, he had already set in motion the "monster migrations" that came out of Shadow to attack Amber. Although Bleys and Fiona succeeded in incapacitating Brand, they were too late to prevent the gradual development, sometime after this point in time, of a black road that allowed for movement from the Courts of Chaos to Amber.

In Random's account to Corwin of his attempted rescue of Brand, we glimpse some of the power at

Bleys's command. While Fiona acted to lure Brand into the trap, it was Bleys's role to create the eerie shadow that contained the unassailable tower in which to hold Brand captive. Bleys thought of a little glass ball with a snow scene inside of it that Corwin had once shown him. Bleys decided that for Brand's imprisonment he wanted an analogue of that little glass ball; an analogue of the stationary little house and the great flurry of snow that occurs when you shake the ball. Using his power over Shadow, Bleys created the high, stationary tower planted firmly in a land of utter turmoil. Like the snow blizzard in the little ball, huge boulders swirled around the tower, flying of their own accord. For added measure, Bleys created the giant snake creature, a monstrous, transparent being, that wrapped around the base of the tower to protect its occupant.

Fearful that even these impediments might not be enough to prevent Brand from escaping, Bleys developed a special group of security personnel. Rather than contracting men from another shadow, Bleys molded his security team out of the stuff of Shadow itself. Besides their other offensive adaptations, these men had the ability to traverse Shadow once they were on the trail of anyone of the blood of Amber. These were fiercely loyal warriors who would not stop at merely preventing the removal of Brand from the tower. They would hunt down and kill any prince of the real city who made the attempt. To Bleys's mind, this prison was foolproof, and the plan went ahead. Fiona tricked Brand into "rescuing" her from the tower when she reached him by the Trumps, and he was himself imprisoned.

Once Brand was secure, Fiona returned to Amber to find out the state of affairs there. In the meantime, Bleys returned to Avernus to continue mounting his troops for an attack against Eric. Fiona would keep him informed of the disposition of men and changing conditions in Amber.

Upon reaching Avernus, Bleys was struck by some disturbing changes. His encampment was gone, no troops were in training, and the tall, crimson-colored people of the region didn't know him. Bleys was able to ascertain that while he was away more than a century had passed in this time stream. Those men he had readied for battle were long dead and buried. He would have to begin all over again.

He understood now that it wasn't enough to gain the total devotion of an army of men from this shadow. He would have to find a way to leave a permanent mark on posterity in Avernus, so that future generations would remember the princes of Amber and rally around their cause a century or two hence, if need be.

Since Bleys was the only Amberite in Avernus, and he never put down in writing anything about his activities in that shadow, it is not known how he gained the full confidence of the people of Avernus. Knowledge of events in Avernus come almost exclusively from the Chronicles of Corwin as set down by his son.

It would seem that Bleys used his power over Shadow to perform some feat of "magic" that would impress the people enough so that they would believe him to be a god. His efforts had to appear miraculous so that he could obtain not only their complete loyalty for the moment, but also remain a part of their collective memory. Bleys's appearance before them needed to be of historical importance on the grandest scale.

According to Corwin's Chronicles, Bleys instituted the mythology of the brother-gods who lived in a paradise known as Amber. Eric, Lord of Evil, he told them, stole the kingdom that rightfully belonged to the great god-king Oberon. The evil lord sought to destroy his brothers and sisters, so that he would be sole ruler. That was why he, Prince Bleys of Amber, was here. He had barely escaped with his life, for Eric would surely have executed him if he had been caught. He did not know how many brothers and sisters still lived, but he knew that the Lord of Evil would not rest until he had hunted down and murdered every one of them. This, he told the people of Avernus. He added a warning as well: The evil lord could reach even here, and destroy the land, and every living thing, upon a whim.

He had them, body and soul. Bleys began the difficult process of training troops once again. This time, he appointed captains of the best of his followers, tutored them in leadership skills as they endured physical hardship with the rest of the men of Avernus.

While his captains took up the training of recruits, Bleys turned his thoughts to the sea, the hot, roiling dark sea of this shadow. If he were to make a successful siege upon Amber, he would need to cross the seas of Shadow as well as the lands. Part of his force would need to sail in warships, to be combined with his main force on Amber's soil.

Although the men of Avernus were no seamen, Bleys found many a skilled workman and carpenter who worked with the tough wood of Avernus's forests. He found other willing hands among his troops also, and he put them all to work. As the workers chopped trees, Bleys conferred with the tradesmen and carpenters. With them, Bleys drafted specifications for the building of sailing vessels, and the skilled men were enthusiastic over the detailed designs Bleys showed them. They eagerly turned to their work of parceling the raw tree trunks and shaping them to the specs.

Bleys spent a good deal of his time with the workmen constructing the ships. He knew they would have to withstand the tortures of storms and whatever else Eric could throw at them as they neared Amber. He was thankful for his father's insistence that all his sons spend time in the port city of Sagres in fifteenth century Portugal on some shadow Earth. It was at Sagres that Prince Henry the Navigator developed a college of seamanship where mathematicians, map makers, and ship designers gathered and studied. Prince Henry had amassed thousands of sea charts and books of geography, including those of Ptolemy, Herodotus, and Marco Polo. Bleys acquired his love for cartography at Sagres.

When Bleys saw that the ship construction was going well, he turned to a consideration of tactics. Only a member of the Family could lead the ships across the shadows. He couldn't lead his army through the shadowlands and also cross the seas. He wrestled with this problem.

His immediate thought would have to stand as an act of last resort; it was simple, but patently unworkable. The idea was that he would lead the ships to the sea surrounding Amber, leave them there, return in one vessel to Avernus, and then march his army through the shadows. Once on the land of the true city, Bleys would signal the ships inland. As long as he worked alone, this would be the only maneuver possible.

His other recourse, made after some thought to the weighing of consequences, was to contact a brother or sister who could lead the fleet in while he took the land route. Bleys knew of Brand's error in approaching Caine for help; he wasn't willing to make the same mistake.

For a considerable time every day, as the shipbuilders added to the fleet, Bleys concentrated on a "sending" into Shadow. With his mind, he touched shadow Ambers, searching for a shadow brother who would be receptive to his vague "help" signal. Bleys did this in such a way that a recipient attuned to it would feel a tingling. Depending upon the state of mind of the recipient, it could be annoying, unpleasant, enticing, or simply nonexistent. Bleys hoped to pick up a responsive sending from a recipient who found the sensation "enticing." Bleys continued his sending for a long time while his ships and his army grew.

It seemed less than coincidence, therefore, when Bleys did receive a sudden, strong signal, and he recognized, almost immediately, the direction from which it came. Bleys stood near the edge of a cliff that overlooked the bay where the ships were docked. He had just stepped out of the stone fortress nearby, built for him by the people of Avernus, who worshiped him. He stood, looking down at the ships, when he received the sending. He turned away from the cliff edge in surprise, knowing the voice that called his name. The sending made something else quite clear to him also: its location was the royal castle in Amber, the real Amber. He had no doubt of this.

For confirmation, and to satisfy formalities, Bleys asked, "Who is it?" (NP, 100)

"Corwin," was the reply.

It might have been a shadow of his brother, but it didn't seem likely, since he was in the true city.

Bleys reached forward and said, "Then come to me, if you would." (NP, 100)

Corwin's grasp in Bleys' hand felt unsteady as Corwin said, "Hello, Bleys. Thanks for the assistance."

Bleys realized Corwin's difficulty: "You're wounded!" (NP, 100) Before Corwin could say anything, he collapsed in Bleys's arms. Bleys carried him to one of the rooms in the fortress and placed him on a small bed. Bleys called to some of his men, then went to work dressing Corwin's wounds.

While Corwin slept, Bleys reflected on the situation. It seemed to him that Corwin had picked up on his signal, even if he wasn't aware of this. If Corwin joined him, he might then have a good chance to defeat Eric. Several weeks earlier, Bleys had heard from Fiona. She informed him that Eric planned to be crowned king of Amber in about three and a half months. Since time ran much faster in Avernus, it gave him enough opportunity to increase his recruitment of troops many times over. Numbers were important at this point. Every dedicated armed man would bring him that much closer to victory over Eric's forces.

That night, Bleys joined a somewhat recovered Corwin in the sitting room of his fortress. They drank and smoked and talked. Bleys decided that he would talk openly and directly, but not revealing anything he didn't have to. The last he had heard, Corwin had amnesia, but from the way he spoke, he seemed to have regained his memory. Still, Corwin could be relatively innocent of the intrigues going on, and Bleys was not about to tell him that he had been part of a conspiracy, with Brand and Fiona, to take the throne.

After some pleasant chatter, Bleys hoped to open Corwin up to discussing what he knew. Calmly, Bleys asked, ''What are your plans?'' (NP, 100)

Corwin seemed candid as he appraised the positions of his brothers and sisters, and Bleys chose to press the matter, asking Corwin to join him and his men. They tossed possibilities at one another, each trying to assess the other. Then Corwin said he needed to think about Bleys's offer overnight. They turned in shortly afterward.

The next day Bleys showed Corwin his troops. Bleys realized it was important that he impress Corwin with these Shadow-beings. He had to feel that Bleys would have a chance, and Bleys needed him to guide the fleet to Amber.

Corwin had his arm in a sling as he inspected the men. He spoke to one soldier, and Bleys was pleased with the loyalty exhibited by these people. When he stood a respectable distance away from the men, Corwin asked about the size of the army. Bleys told him there were fifty thousand men, and Corwin seemed to bristle at this. It wasn't enough, he believed. Bleys told him about his armada of ships, but Corwin still sounded discouraged. The men of Avernus stood by in assembly as these two gods argued before them.

Bleys was discouraged by Corwin's comments, but more significantly, he thought he lost him as a much-needed ally in his planned assault. At its lowest point, their argument led to Corwin's announcement that he would leave Avernus, if all Bleys wanted was more bodies to fall under Eric's hand.

Bleys sought reconciliation, apologizing, and asking Corwin to stay, if only to act as advisor. Touched by Bleys's conciliatory attitude, Corwin acquiesced to support Bleys. Corwin offered to seek in Shadow for more men to join their forces, and he was gone for a while to do so.

While Corwin gathered his men, Bleys decided to turn his full attention to the fleet, wanting them outfitted and ready to sail as soon as Corwin had fulfilled his quota and felt ready to set out. In two months' time, they had more than a quarter of a million soldiers.

Bleys called a meeting of his general staff the next morning. Besides Corwin and himself, there were about thirty high-ranking officers in attendance. Bleys ran the staff meeting efficiently, although Corwin expressed some concerns about proposed tactics. But the detailed maps that Bleys laid out before them seemed to quell Corwin's doubts. Bleys had diagramed a route they would take through the Valley of Garnath, circling around and crossing the western mountains, so that they would approach Amber from behind. Corwin was impressed with this plan.

The armada consisted of three hundred ships, and Bleys assigned Corwin to one of the larger warships, *The Dreadnought,* acting as the flagship. Corwin discovered that the four admirals attached to the fleet were able leaders who knew their ships and understood the tactics involved. Bleys had trained them well.

With final preparations outlined, it was agreed that they would start out in three days. Bleys and Corwin knew better than any of these loyal staff members that time would be against them. A few days' march in Shadow could be turned into hellish weeks of lost time once Eric became aware of them. But Bleys said nothing of this to his officers.

At dawn of the third morning, Bleys saw Corwin and the fleet off. As the three hundred vessels sailed into the horizon, Bleys called his men into marching formation at close ranks, just as he had trained them to do. They marched inland, paralleling the coastline, so that Bleys could use the sealine as a guide in shaping land, sea, and sky to the proper shadow.

How long would it take for Eric to realize that a mass of beings moved through Shadow toward Amber? How many shadows could they cross before Eric sensed them, and knew them for what they were? Bleys hoped it would be a long while.

When they reached the end of a forest, the plains before them seemed suspiciously peaceful. Corwin was speaking to Bleys via Trump as the infantry began crossing the plain. The first hundred or so men seemed to be safe, nearly across the wide field, when a barrage of arrows felled them to the last. Then Bleys and his men saw the bare-skinned warriors riding rapidly toward them. They were centaurs, huge, fierce, and firing arrows as they attacked. At the edge of the plain, Bleys ordered his men behind the nearest trees. When the centaurs were close enough, the soldiers lunged upon them, the men of Avernus fighting alongside the short, hairy men that Corwin had recruited. During this battle, when Bleys took part in the fighting, Corwin was out of contact. Some hours later, however, Corwin reestablished contact and learned from Bleys that they had beaten back the centaurs, but at a cost of some ten thousand men. At that point, Bleys could no longer hold contact because of a violent earthquake that sent him sprawling, one of the last images Corwin had of the scene.

Several times thereafter, Corwin caught glimpses of terrible battles and near-holocausts that Bleys suffered. But Corwin had problems at sea that made such Trump contact more infrequent as they ranged closer to Amber. Still, Corwin gives a clear record in his Chronicles of the hardships he observed befall Bleys and his soldiers whenever he had the chance to reach Bleys by Trump.

Days passed that way, and Bleys began to wonder over Corwin's fortunes, since he had not heard from him in a long while. Having a moment to rest, Bleys concentrated on Shadow, seeking Corwin's presence. It took a while, but Bleys finally reached Corwin. The image was dim, gray, and shaky.

"What's the matter? I've been trying to reach you," Bleys said.

Corwin's dim face responded, "Life is full of vicissitudes. We're riding out one of them." (NP, 115)

Bleys could then see the rolling deck, awash with sudden waves. He told Corwin of the storm that he and his men had just come through. As he spoke, a frightening streak of lightning struck a tree behind him. He turned back to Corwin's image and said, "Eric's got our number," (NP, 116) before ending the contact.

Within two days, Corwin made contact again. He reported that Caine's ships had caught up with their own in the waters above Rebma. Caine had asked Corwin to surrender. Bleys and his men were fighting off horsemen attacking with sabers, and Bleys told him he would have to make his own decision. When Bleys turned toward a charging horseman, the contact was broken.

Hours later, Corwin renewed the contact, asking for escape as Caine was about to board his ship. Bleys reached, pulled Corwin toward him. In the battle against the cavalry, Bleys received a head wound and a bad gash across his hand where he had grabbed the edge of a saber before dispatching its wielder with a fierce blow to the head. They managed to repel the rest of the horsemen and had just set up camp for the night.

Tiredly, they made for Bleys's tent, where they drank wine, ate some bread, cheese, and meat, and smoked cigarettes. Corwin recounted the tribulations of his sea venture, and Bleys informed him of their situation. Bleys was left with about 180,000 men. Bleys and Corwin parted momentarily to mutter their individual prayers and shed a tear of sorrow for the deaths of so many good men robbed of their short, mortal span.

Eric may well have known the condition of Bleys and Corwin's force. He may even have been surprised that so many had survived to reach this far. For it seemed that Eric used all the power at his disposal against them. He assaulted them with battering rainfall and freezing temperatures; he sent out tigers, wolves, and polar bears against them. When they got past those obstacles, they reached a warmer climate akin to that to be found in Amber. The foot soldiers were badly in need of rest, so Bleys reluctantly ordered them to make camp, but with triple the security watch. During the night, the raids came. The men on the outer edges of the campsite were slaughtered first, but someone gave the alarm. Corwin and Bleys stood by their soldiers fighting off the raiding party.

At daybreak, having had little rest, Bleys ordered the men forward. The raids continued through the day, and Bleys's infantry fell. In spite of this, they reached the valley that spread beside the coast of Amber. Eric continued to throw lightning at them, but they marched on.

Marching through the wooded valley, the men were assaulted by Eric's most devastating move. In the sudden dry air, a flash fire spread rapidly from tree to tree, rushing toward them. The men panicked and ran, and were joined by the animals of the forest. They might well have lost entirely at that juncture, were it not for Corwin. He helped lead the men to the river Oisen, where they could find escape from the deadly fire.

As they ran to the fork leading to the river, they fought off flames and burning debris. When they saw the river at the end of a long slope, they rushed to it, dived in, and found safety from the runaway fire. Bleys, Corwin, and the remaining army floated with the current toward the sea. They reached the treeless area near the sea and were besieged by a fresh attack. Archers on either bank fired volleys of arrows at the men in the water. Their only recourse was to dive, swim underwater, and try to get away from the arrows.

When Bleys surfaced, he found himself near one bank. He swam to a clump of reeds and was able to hide behind a mound of mud and stones in the water. From that vantage point, he could see some of Eric's archers well upriver on the opposite bank. He also watched as dozens of bodies floated past him, arrow hafts facing skyward.

Bleys stood hidden in the water a long time. The archers seemed to move off after a while. The attack was over, and it looked as though Eric had won.

Another body floated near him, an arrow piercing its side. The body moved with a twinge, turned over, and Bleys recognized it as Pel, one of his captains. Bleys swam out to him, grabbed him, and pulled him onto the bank. The arrow bit into Pel's left thigh, but it wasn't too deep. Pel was conscious and spoke to him. After Bleys removed the arrow and covered the wound with leaves, mud, and a torn cloth, his captain told him that he had seen others survive also. Many had climbed onto the bank of the river; some even taking out an archer or two before running away from the river's edge. The captain was sure they would rejoin Bleys once they found their way back within sight of the river.

Bleys helped him to walk away from the bank, and he took a measure of the land. They were on the north shore of the river, still well inland of the sea. Bleys spied a likely spot to set up a campsite, a small grove of high grass and bushes, well away from view of either bank of the river. As Bleys helped Pel toward the area, four of Corwin's recruits came up to them. As they set up camp, dressed wounds, and rested, more of their soldiers wandered in. Bleys organized matters so that they wouldn't

be easily spotted by Eric's men. He sent out three-man patrols to scout the area, gathering up their people surreptitiously and sending them in by circuitous routes. He showed his captain and a couple of other officers some simple medical techniques, and shortly they were treating wounds of varying degrees of seriousness.

When he had time to think about it, Bleys wondered if Corwin was dead. For that matter, he reflected, was their campaign over? Men kept arriving in camp, but could they possibly have enough numbers to attempt the climb up Mt. Kolvir?

Bleys was in the midst of adding to their security force to repel any possible attack when he felt a Trump sending. It was Corwin. When Bleys determined that Corwin must be farther downriver on the same shore where they were located, he sent a three-man team of his Avernus soldiers to find him.

By the time Corwin reached their camp, Bleys had more than three thousand men. While one of the officers cared for Corwin, Bleys continued to mount security and send patrols to seek out more of their men. Whether by design or by virtue of Bleys's precautions, they remained undisturbed for two days.

Early on the second morning, having become some five thousand strong, they marched toward Kolvir. Although Bleys said nothing, he was bothered by the calm. No raiding parties. No storms. They continued on until sunset and settled in for the night on the beach. Bleys wondered over the peacefulness of their rest. Corwin spoke to him the following day about the closeness of Eric's coronation. Bleys hurried the men onward, marching quickly to make up time.

By the time they camped for the night, they were just a few short miles from Kolvir. The slackening of their travail and the proximity of that fabled mountain boosted morale enormously. The soldiers felt rested, more fit than they had been just days ago. They felt ready to meet the enemy and defeat him.

Feeling rested and strong, they marched the next morning and reached the foot of Mt. Kolvir. Eric's army was there, waiting for them in force. Bleys thought he saw Julian leading them. Shouting orders, Bleys led his men against Julian's troops. During the fierce battle, Bleys tried to work his way toward Julian. He hoped to reach Julian, dispatch him, and thereby win the day.

Bleys never got near Julian. However, his soldiers wiped out all but a few of Julian's men, who, with Julian, had fled. They set up a secure encampment at the foot of Kolvir and spent the night.

The next day, they climbed Mt. Kolvir—Corwin, Bleys, and about three thousand men. The natural stairway in the rock accommodated two at a time for part of the way, but then narrowed so that they had to climb single file. Eric tossed storms at them to help deplete their forces.

At about a fourth of the way up the mountain, they engaged a column of Eric's soldiers descending the stair. It was the beginning of the long, torturous battle up the mountain, each man taking his turn, fighting for the next step of the stair. For Bleys, this was the most frustrating aspect of the whole campaign. There was little he could do but stand ready as he stood behind the vanguard on the stair. He watched as soldiers toppled from Kolvir, some of Eric's men and some of his own.

As the men ahead of them wore down, Bleys, and Corwin behind him, noted that they were inching up the mountain. They made it to the halfway point, then two-thirds of the way, and Bleys saw that soon his turn to engage a soldier of Amber would come.

He knew the soldier ahead of him. He was a dedicated foot soldier of Avernus who had echoed Bleys's own encouragement to the others as they had marched across the worlds. As the soldier struck out with his short, curved sword, Bleys held his own sword tightly in his hand. There was no time for sorrow as his comrade fell and Bleys rushed forward. When Bleys was at the forefront, it seemed as if a shiver of fear ran through the line of men that he faced. Soldiers faced Bleys, dueled, screamed, and fell. He thrust with his sword in his right and a dagger in his left hand, pushing their advance up the bloodied stair.

With Bleys battling at the forefront, they had made it very near to the wide stair leading to the Great Arch. It seemed they could reach the top. Bleys fought like a madman, smiling, flinging his cloak at each adversary, pushing and tripping each one even as he thrust with his dagger or his blade.

Still, the line of Eric's soldiers seemed unending, and Bleys was tiring. He was slowing slightly, but kept on, seeing that they were perhaps a hundred feet from the top. He began to rely more on simple thrusts, merciless in his efficiency.

Bleys was aware of the dagger that flew from behind, hitting his current opponent hard in the forehead. He caught the soldier off-balance then and threw him over. The man behind the fallen soldier came at Bleys with a rush, as if he had been pushed from behind. With his full weight, he came into Bleys's sword, kept moving forward, and Bleys couldn't stop the momentum. In the next moment, the dead soldier and Bleys fell from the stair together.

In the instant Bleys tumbled past Corwin, he heard Corwin call out, "Catch them, you fool!" (NP, 139)

He reached out and found that he had caught Corwin's deck of the Trumps. He puzzled in that brief instant over why Corwin did that.

This is all that has been recorded of Bleys's part in the succession wars. Although we have Corwin's account, and Bleys has since talked privately about the people of Avernus to Fiona and Random, he has refused to speak of the period after his fall from Kolvir. Fiona has expressed the belief that Bleys had not needed the Trumps in order to save himself. Others in Amber speculate that Bleys had special knowledge in the use of magical spells, harnessed from the power of the Pattern. Fiona has been unable to account for Bleys's whereabouts after his fall, but rumors suggest that he joined one of their lesser-known relations residing in a distant shadow. Bleys has been intractable, neither confirming nor denying such rumors.

Much later, when Corwin ruled as king in Amber, Brand confirmed that Bleys was still alive. Although it was true that Brand had observed him drilling troops in a field, he lied about Bleys's intentions. In fact, he knew nothing of Bleys's intentions, but wanted Corwin to believe Bleys was a traitor at the time.

Fiona and others in Amber have put forward some suppositions about Bleys's involvement in the Patternfall battle that help to explain what Brand had seen briefly through Bleys's Trump.

While Bleys found refuge from the Family's intrigues in a distant shadow, he allowed no contact from anyone in Amber, not even Fiona. When he did feel sufficiently recovered from his ordeal on Mt. Kolvir, he decided to try a tentative search for someone that several Family members had attempted at one time or another. Bleys sought farther into Shadow, in the direction of the Courts of Chaos, for his father. He was much surprised when

Oberon responded, especially when the response came from an unexpected location entirely—Amber itself. Through Oberon, Bleys learned much of the events that had happened in Amber since the siege on Kolvir. Brand had taken on a much larger part in Amber's problems, but the real danger came from the Courts of Chaos. Oberon had a plan that included Bleys.

It was important that Bleys's actions be kept in the strictest secrecy. Oberon created a shadow of his own, one that was roughly equidistant from Amber and the Courts. He imbued it with his own unique signature, one that only he and Bleys would know. Bleys would remain in that shadow to train cavalry and troops to be used against the Courts. Oberon would send soldiers, horses, and supplies through Shadow to that place rather than taking the risk of Bleys's traveling the shadows and being found out. Some of the men would be taken directly from Amber, officers of Bleys's old command when Oberon had ruled. The rest would come from various shadows so that no suspicions would be aroused over large movements of personnel in Shadow.

When Brand peeked in on Bleys with his Trump, it was a surprise to both men. Bleys hoped he broke the contact before Brand could ascertain the location of the place. Then he set up additional safeguards to block any other contact. Brand had really believed Bleys dead. It was a mere chance encounter that occurred as he concentrated on a spread of the Trumps. But Brand decided he could use that knowledge to his advantage.

Following Oberon's orders, Bleys built a large force and drilled them for the kind of battle they could expect in the realm of Chaos. Shortly before the Patternfall battle, Oberon allowed Fiona to make contact with Bleys. Through their contact, Bleys was informed of the events prior to the battle, and Fiona learned of Bleys's role in leading a charge with his cavalry outside of the Courts. Oberon arranged for a specific signal that would sound the alert when Bleys was to lead his troops directly into Chaos.

The day of the battle against Chaos came quickly. Bleys had his men mounted and ready. They faced the eastern horizon, near the edge of a grassy plain with one of several mountains directly before them. Bleys knew the portal into Shadow was approximately fifteen feet before the sheer wall of the mountain's base. Sitting tensely on his horse, Bleys was staring at a Trump of his brother Benedict, given him by Oberon. He watched the true movements of his brother, astride a striped horse, lifting his sword in his only hand. Bleys could see Benedict's face, looking toward him and his troops, looking westward through the Trump contact. Benedict lowered his blade.

Bleys signaled his trumpeter to sound the charge. With Bleys in the lead, the cavalry rode at a gallop toward the mountain, then faded as they passed through the invisible portal. Bleys kept his men alert and balanced against the sudden change upon entering the plains of Chaos. Directed by Benedict, they charged the mounted horned beings of that realm. Initially shaken that flame rose from every wound they inflicted, Bleys's horsemen quickly adjusted and fought furiously. The horses had stumbled uncertainly a bit at first, but their riders soon brought them under control. As they engaged and struck the beast-men on their oddly shaped mounts, Bleys and his men became accustomed to the strange, curving ground beneath them and the effects of the weirdly turning sky.

Bleys and his cavalry beat back the beast-men. As the creatures of Chaos retreated, Bleys's troops joined forces with Benedict's and Julian's soldiers. Together they had the enemy on the run. There were still skirmishes as the clouds in the sky grew together, forming the face of Oberon. Fighting subsided, most of the soldiers on both sides stunned to hear the voice of Oberon emitted from that cloud/face in the sky. Oberon's voice spoke of his actions, of the question of the succession, and of the need for Corwin to use the Jewel of Judgment to avert the storm. Even when the face in the sky faded, and there was a momentary silence, no one on the field was willing to break that stillness. Then, as if woken from a dream, the beast-men looked about them, struck out at the nearby soldiers of Amber around them, and continued a retreat.

Julian's men took charge of the horned beings that surrendered, while Bleys's troops and Benedict's soldiers went about mopping-up chores. All of the soldiers on the field moved toward the mountain region, away from the gathering dark clouds that had begun to creep over the far edge of the battlefield.

Bleys spotted Fiona and gave her a tired embrace. She led him to where Random and Corwin stood talking to a bowman dressed in green. Bleys was surprised to see it was Caine, who everyone thought was dead. With the others, Bleys watched a long procession emerge from the far end of the black road, below the storm cloud. The procession wound its way to the black citadel that was the Courts of Chaos. It was Oberon's funeral procession, and Dworkin was the driver of the cart bearing his casket.

Julian and Benedict had joined them by then. Bleys told the little group standing on the mountainside: "He wanted to be taken beyond the Courts of Chaos and into the final darkness when his time came at last. . . . So Dworkin once told me. Beyond Chaos and Amber, to a place where none reigned." (CC, 122)

He stood with his relatives on the mountainside, watching the strange forms of the Chaos beings march along the black road to the citadel. Bleys felt a sudden closeness with his family as they stood together. He felt a distance, too.

They watched the approaching darkness for a while, coming to envelop them. Someone suddenly called out, perhaps Fiona. They turned and saw clearly a vision rising out of the chasm at the cliff's edge. Large, beautifully snowy white, the unicorn stood at the brink, pawing the hard ground. Slowly, the unicorn approached, and Bleys could see that she wore the Jewel of Judgment. It seemed a miracle as she came up to the person standing to Bleys's left and knelt before him. With unusual grace, Random reached forward and lifted the Jewel from the neck of the kneeling unicorn. They all swore their allegiance to Random, and the white beast stood, galloped down the slope of the mountain, and disappeared.

In order to deal with the coming dark wave, Random and Corwin moved away, farther down the mountain. When Random returned, he carried a collapsed Corwin. He told the others that Corwin was all right and that he believed he had become attuned to the Jewel. In that short time, Random seemed changed; his face was lined and hard, lacking in his customary frivolity. He ordered Benedict to lead the army and their captives to the Courts of Chaos. He urged everyone to go with them while he stayed to try to halt the storm. As Benedict and his men headed down the black road toward the citadel, Julian followed after. Bleys went after him, riding his mount slowly at the head of his troops. In the black citadel, Bleys passed in a line of mourners to look at his father in repose. The ceremony was solemn and swift, and at its end the casket was carried off to be placed where Oberon had requested, beyond any walls.

Bleys had little to do with the arrangement of the Patternfall Treaty. Random and Benedict had led the treaty talks on Amber's behalf. Bleys was content to serve Random in Amber. He led a quiet, contemplative life for a long period of time, staying in and around the Royal Palace. It pleased him to be out of the forefront of family intrigues, and he actually enjoyed attending small diplomatic missions with his little brother who now was king.

Random asked him to join Fiona and himself on a fascinating little mission. Fiona had found the new primal Pattern created by Corwin, and Random wanted the three of them to journey there to examine it firsthand. When they reached it, the site appeared quite different from the original Pattern they had known. It was in a grove of blossoming flowers of many varieties, and there was one great tree. The bottom of the tree was obscured by a thick unmoving fog, but within that fog, portions of an etching in the earth near the tree could be seen. Fiona showed them what the new Pattern looked like by means of a special mirror. Through the mirror, Random and Bleys could see the oddly twisted lines on the ground, curling inward around a gleaming white area with glowing spots within it.

Fiona lifted her right foot to step onto the edge of the fogbound lines of the Pattern. A flash of electricity shot out from it, striking the sole of her shoe. It momentarily stunned her, but she explained that she expected it. She had tried it before, when she first discovered it. She asked Random and Bleys to try stepping on it. Shaking his head slowly, Random said that he would rather not attempt it. This was not the time for him to become involved with a new problem away from Amber. Bleys tried it then, but when he did, a similar electrical discharge forced him away. They agreed to keep this secret place to themselves, and Random promised he would look into the matter at a more convenient time. Bleys could tell, however, that Fiona wasn't about to let matters rest. Her eyes revealed to him a keen interest in uncovering the secrets of Corwin's Pattern. However, Bleys was less curious about this Pattern's secrets than he was puzzled by its very existence. It shouldn't be there, if Amber and all the shadow worlds were in place. He wondered how this new Pattern might affect the reality they all knew. To his mind, it was prudent of Random to leave it alone for now until they had a better idea of what they would be dealing with.

As king, Random's main concern was to widen friendly relations with the shadows that Amber had negotiated with in the past. He hoped that a greater openness between Amber and its neighbor shadows would bring a cessation of tension and intrigue that had been part of the political climate of the worlds for so long. Small diplomatic parties to various shadows had become a regular part of Random's agenda. Bleys liked this fresh way of doing business, and he frequently led delegations to the shadows of the Golden Circle.

While attending a ceremony in the much-admired gardens of a quaint little kingdom, Bleys was taken by surprise by a loud report that was very much like gunfire. He was the more surprised to find he was bleeding profusely from a wound in the upper right side of his chest. The pain came moments afterward, and he collapsed.

He awoke in a luxurious bed within the palace of this shadow's king and queen, both of whom attended him and offered the greatest apologies. In spite of his injury, Bleys calmed them graciously, but he was drawn nearly to distraction over the implications of a gunshot being fired in a realm not too distant from Amber.

When he was well enough to move, Bleys returned to Amber after assuring the king and queen that they had nothing to fear from this incident; they were entirely blameless. Once back in his rooms at the Royal Palace, he requested Random's presence. Random informed Bleys of the murder of Caine in the shadow Deiga, which happened the very morning of the assassination attempt on Bleys. Although Bleys wondered who this new enemy could possibly be, he saw the deeply troubled look on Random's face and kept quiet. He could see that Random was already thinking along lines similar to his own. Whoever this new threat was, he could travel the shadows of his own accord, and he had knowledge of a special gunpowder such as Corwin had once used.

Fiona was a constant visitor, looking in on Bleys while he was recuperating. She expressed her own suspicions to him. She suspected that the assassin might be a relative they didn't know about. It had to be someone who had a definite reason for killing Caine and also attempting to kill Bleys. The connection had to be to a relative that both Bleys and Caine had hurt in some way. She wouldn't name names, but her suspicions got Bleys to think of some possibilities on his own. Fiona told him she thought that Merlin, son of Corwin, might hold the key, even if he didn't realize it himself. She said

that she intended to talk to Merlin that evening, before the day of Caine's funeral. Then she left Bleys to rest and ponder their exchange.

Late that night, Fiona returned to see Bleys. She awoke him urgently, saying that they were both in danger and had to flee Amber. Bleys was startled, but he became alert quickly. She explained that while she had been with Merlin, he showed her a picture of his friend Luke Raynard from the shadow Earth. Raynard was the missing relative, the one who would want to seek revenge on both Caine and him.

For his part, Bleys didn't feel he was in any danger for the moment. He was feeling too weak to travel, and he absolutely needed a few hours' rest in any case. He suggested that Fiona leave at once, then contact him by Trump when she had reached a shadow she felt was secure. At that point, he would join her through the Trump contact. She agreed and left hurriedly.

The next morning, Bleys sent a message to Random. A servant gave Random Bleys's apologies, stating that he was still too weak to attend the funeral. Random sent a message in return, indicating that no apology was needed, and expressing the hope that Bleys would soon recover his strength. Random might have started to worry over Bleys's disappearance after the day and evening of Caine's funeral, but a number of problems were brought to his attention at almost the same time. Fiona later informed Merlin of their planned escape from Amber to avoid any further assassination attempts. Although Merlin would have liked to have known Bleys's whereabouts, he knew he wouldn't get the information from Fiona. Except for saying that she had been treating her brother and he was doing well, Fiona was elusive in revealing much else to Merlin.

Although Bleys would seem to prefer separating himself from current political intrigues involving Random and other shadows, he would not be above using his own methods to listen in on such events impassively. He had learned, after all, that Caine had used the Trumps to eavesdrop on his brothers in much the same way.

BLOODY BILL'S [A.K.A. BLOODY SAM'S, BLOODY ANDY'S, BLOODY JAK'S, AND BLOODY EDDIE'S]

A restaurant in the Harbor District of Amber, recommended to Merlin, son of Corwin, by a palace guard named Jordy. It is located in a dangerous neighborhood, on a street colloquially referred to as Death Alley. As Jordy explained to Merlin, the restaurant's name comes from the "manner of demise" of its owners.

When Merlin first strolled to the restaurant, late one night when he wanted a good seafood place, it was called Bloody Bill's. According to Jordy, the deceased man's cousin, Andy, was running it. Bloody Bill's is located on Seabreeze Lane, a short walk west of the winding end of Harbor Road, close to the docks and well away from the mainstream of shops and tourist fare.

Following is Merlin's description of the layout and routine of Bloody Bill's:

> The bar was to my right, tables to my left, suspicious-looking stains on the floor. A board on the wall suggested I give my order at the bar and say where I was sitting. The day's catch was chalked beneath this.
>
> So I went over and waited, collecting glances, until a heavy-set man with gray and amazingly shaggy brows came over and asked what I wanted. I told him the blue sea scut and pointed at an empty table to the rear. He nodded and shouted my order back through a hole in the wall, then asked me whether I wanted a bottle of Bayle's Piss to go with it. I did, he got it for me, and a glass, uncorked it and passed it over. I paid up there, headed back to the table I had chosen and seated myself with my back to the wall. (BA, 64–65)

While Bloody Bill's was a simple, unpretentious eatery, Andy employed musicians to entertain the customers on some nights. It's likely that he paid them a minimal salary, supplemented by free meals.

Eating at Bloody Bill's was a memorable experience for Merlin on that occasion. While he was enjoying his dinner, a scarred man at the next table told Merlin that he had been marked as a target for robbery by two low characters sitting near the front of the bar. It was this man, known as Old John, who brought it to Merlin's attention that it was customary to carry a sword or other weapon, leaving it in plain sight in order to avoid any mishaps with the locals. In fact, it was Old John who dispensed with the two criminal types, who had made the mistake of going after him. One of them, dying, stumbled back into the restaurant. After sending off his waiter for a vigile to clean up after the dead men, Andy dragged the corpse out into the street.

A little later, Merlin learned from Andy that the scarred gentleman was an emissary of the Crown who had been in the employ of the late King Oberon as well as King Random. Andy had accepted currency from shadow Kashfa in payment for Old John's meal.

Although Andy didn't seem to be a very apologetic man, he spoke to Merlin briefly about the occurrence of the thieves. He wanted it understood by the royal members of Amber that he knew nothing of the two men's plan to try to rob Old John. Andy said he recognized Merlin as part of the Royal Family, having seen him once accompanied by Gérard years ago. As Andy said, "I make it a point never to forget a face that might be worth remembering" (BA, 68).

When next Merlin visited the restaurant, he was accompanying Coral, younger daughter of the Begman prime minister. It was still daylight when they reached the Harbor District, and Merlin suggested having dinner. He almost walked past the place, however, because of the change in name: a freshly painted sign indicated that it was renamed Bloody Andy's.

No incident occurred while Merlin and Coral enjoyed their meal at Bloody Andy's, but Merlin's account has its interest for us in showing Coral's reactions to the local color:

> The place was just the same inside, however, except for the man behind the counter, who was taller and thinner than the shaggy, crag-faced individual who had served me last time. His name, I learned, was Jak, and he was Andy's brother. He sold us a bottle of Bayle's Piss and put in our order for two fish dinners through the hole in the wall. My former table was vacant and we took it. I laid my sword

belt on the chair to my right, with the blade partly drawn, as I had been taught etiquette required here.

"I like this place," she said. "It's . . . different."

"Uh . . . yes," I agreed, glancing at two passed-out drunks—one to the front of the establishment, one to the rear—and three shifty-eyed individuals conversing in low voices off in one corner. A few broken bottles and suspicious stains were upon the floor, and some not-too-subtle artwork of an amorous nature hung on the far wall. "The food's quite good," I added.

"I've never been in a restaurant like this," she continued, watching a black cat, who rolled in from a rear room, wrestling with an enormous rat.

"It has its devotees, but it's a well-kept secret among discriminating diners." (SC, 82)

The tradition of renaming the restaurant for prior owners and passing ownership to family members continues, though the place itself is little changed. Merlin last heard that the name was Bloody Eddie's from an unusual source. His older stepbrother Mandor, a resident of the Courts of Chaos, mentioned the new name. Although Mandor hadn't been there, it is likely he heard about the restaurant from Merlin's aunt Fiona. Mandor had occasion to spend a brief time with her when they combined forces to investigate strange Shadow phenomena.

Merlin promised he would take Mandor to Bloody Eddie's one day. Though circumstances have changed, they still may do it. The restaurant will still be there, whatever "Bloody" relative it is named for.

BLOT ON THE PATTERN

The dark smudge of blood that covered an area of the true, primal Pattern that had been originally engraved by Dworkin. This blot had its counterparts in all the shadows, including the true city, opening a way for beings of the Courts of Chaos to invade Amber.

The reasons and consequences of the blot on the Pattern are very complex. As Dworkin had once said about other matters, its existence is owed to a consideration of "first causes," which may prove virtually impossible to determine. Some believe that Corwin's voiced curse against Eric upon being blinded was the inciting force that brought wickedness upon all the lands. Others point to the deliberate scheme of Brand to shed blood on the Pattern, sealing his alliance with the lords of the Courts. Still others would claim that the lords of Chaos, with the tacit permission of their king, had been the designers of the great plan that manipulated Brand, Corwin, and Benedict to act for the destruction of Amber. And then there are those of a philosophical bent, who posit that it was the supreme Power known as the Logrus that acted in an ages-long conflict against the Power of the Pattern in a contest that disregarded the human inhabitants of the worlds.

In his Chronicles, Corwin described the blot upon first discovering it:

> We regarded it in silence for a long while. A dark, rough-edged smudge had obliterated an area of the section immediately beneath us, running from its outer rim to the center.
>
> "You know," Random finally said, "it is as if someone had shaved the top off Kolvir, cutting at about the level of the dungeons."
>
> "Yes," I said.
>
> "Then—looking for congruence—that would be about where our own Pattern lies."
>
> "Yes," I said again.
>
> "And that blotted area is to the south, from whence comes the black road. . . .
>
> "What does it mean? . . . It seems to correspond to the true state of affairs, but beyond that I do not understand its significance. Why have we been brought here and shown this thing?"
>
> "It does not correspond to the true state of affairs," I said. "It *is* the true state of affairs."
> (SU, 191–92)

The major clue to the cause of this blot was left behind by the person who initiated it. Corwin's companion, Ganelon, retrieved a Trump with a dagger piercing it from the primal Pattern. After making a simple experiment, Random pieced together how such a large area of blood could have formed:

"The blood of Amber ... Whoever did it walked the Pattern first, you see. Then they stood there at the center and contacted him via this Trump. When he responded and a firm contact was achieved, they stabbed him. His blood flowed upon the Pattern, obliterating that part of it ..." (HO, 20–21)

Later, when Random had located his son and returned with him to Amber, Martin confirmed that it was his blood that had caused the blotting. Somehow, Brand had drawn a Trump of Martin, contacted him, and attacked him without provocation. Martin had been able to escape, but he had been seriously wounded. Thus, the immediate cause was Brand's assault of Martin. Brand had entered into a conspiracy with the Chaos lords to bring about Amber's eradication. Brand's intention was to form a new Amber with himself as supreme ruler.

The blot initiated manifestations in every shadow, allowing the movement of creatures that dwelled in and around the Courts of Chaos. In Amber, this manifestation was a black road that seemed to grow out of Shadow until it reached the foot of Mt. Kolvir. Because of the black road, the usurper Eric was forced to fight against terrifying creatures in a pitched battle on the slopes of Kolvir. Eric died in that battle. Corwin had seen another manifestation of it in the land of Lorraine. There, it took on the form of an expanding dark Circle. Working with Ganelon, Corwin helped to defeat the minions that controlled that version of the blot. In a shadow Avalon where Benedict resided, the effect was to open the way for pale female demons who arose from the depths through mountain caves.

In an interesting juxtaposition of the physical with the psychological, Dworkin, the architect of the primal Pattern, had explained the effect of the damage on his mind:

> "I am the Pattern ... in a very real sense. In passing through my mind to achieve the form it now holds, the foundation of Amber, it marked me·as surely as I marked it. ... It occurred to me that damage to the Pattern would be damage to myself, and damage to myself would be reflected within the Pattern. ...
>
> "My blood, with which I drew it, could deface it. But it took me ages to realize that the blood of my blood could also do this thing.

You could use it, you could also change it— yea, unto the third generation." (HO, 67)

Dworkin's changing moods were actualized because of the damage on the Pattern. When becoming excited, for instance, he underwent a physical change into some awful demonic form, and his corresponding actions in that altered form were beyond his control.

Perhaps it was from a stricken conscience that Corwin believed himself to be the cause of the evil he saw in Amber. Then again, there may be some truth that Corwin's spoken curse against Eric had a potency of its own, adding to the powers of those acting from the Chaos side of things. After escaping the dungeons of Amber, Corwin had looked upon a changed Valley of Garnath, believing that he initiated it:

> I had done this thing with my curse. I had transformed the peaceful Valley of Garnath into what it now represented: it was a symbol of my hate for Eric and for all those others who had stood by and let him get away with his power grab, let him blind me. I didn't like the looks of that forest, and as I stared at it I realized how my hate had objectified itself. I knew it because it was a part of me." (NP, 173)

The repair of the primal Pattern by clearing away the blot was described by Dworkin when Corwin had visited him in his den. Together, they looked at the blot, and Dworkin spoke of its possible repair:

> "There you are ... the hole in my mind. I can no longer think through it, only around it. I no longer know what must be done to repair something I now lack. If you think that you can do it, you must be willing to lay yourself open to instant destruction each time you depart the Pattern to cross the break. Not destruction by the dark portion. Destruction by the Pattern itself when you break the circuit. The Jewel [of Judgment] may or may not sustain you. I do not know. But it will not grow easier. It will become more difficult with each circuit, and your strength will be lessening all the while." (HO, 71)

Although Corwin made an aborted attempt to repair the Pattern, it was Oberon who ultimately succeeded in clearing it. Oberon had spoken to Corwin about it in a quiet moment before the hour of the Patternfall. The old king admitted that he expected to die in performing the repair. In fact, it was Fiona who had told Corwin earlier: "It is going to kill him . . . I know that much about it. Whether he succeeds or fails, he will be destroyed in the process." (CC, 22) This very confusion, that King Oberon could die whether the Pattern continues to stand or not, was the cause of Corwin's decision to create a new Pattern of his own. While Corwin could not be certain of his father's success, he knew the inevitable consequences of the repair to the Pattern. Upon receiving the Jewel of Judgment used by Oberon through a prearranged conveyance, Corwin expressed these thoughts:

"I knew by this that Dad's effort, whatever it had amounted to, was finished. The Pattern had either been repaired or botched. He was either alive or dead. . . . The effects of his act would be spreading outward from Amber through Shadow now, like the ripples in the proverbial pond." (CC, 39)

Indeed, Brand, pursuing Corwin, told him of a great vortex wiping out Amber as a result of Oberon's fatal travail. Brand had tried to convince his brother that Oberon had failed, that the Death Storm, as it came to be called, was "destroying the shadow worlds, and it will not stop until it meets with the Courts of Chaos, bringing all of creation full circle." (CC, 45) That ultimate destruction did come about, but Corwin and another of his brothers were able to repel the Death Storm outside of the Courts. Only then did Corwin learn that his father had been successful in clearing the blot. Amber stood; the old familiar Amber. The primal Pattern was clear and pristine once again.

BLUE CRYSTAL STONES

Crystalline pieces of the same substance as the walls, floor, and ceiling of the crystal cave, located in a distant shadow. The special properties of these stones involve giving one the ability to move through Shadow because of the stones' mystical connection to the cave from which they originate, and to each other.

The entity that had inhabited the body of Vinta Bayle knew a great deal about the blue crystal stones. She explained their properties to Merlin in a lengthy conversation that Merlin later related in his accounts. Merlin asked:

"What is the significance of the blue stones?"

"They have an affinity for the cave, and for each other . . . A person with very little training could hold one of them and simply begin walking, following the slight psychic tugging. It would eventually lead him to the cave."

"Through Shadow, you mean?"

"Yes."

"Intriguing, but I fail to see any great value to it."

"But that is not all. Ignore the pull of the cave, and you will become aware of secondary tuggings. Learn to distinguish the signature of the proper stone, and you can follow its bearer anywhere."

"That does sound a little more useful. Do you think that's how those guys found me last night, because I had a pocket full of the things?"

"Probably, from a practical standpoint, they helped. Actually, though, in your case, they should not even have been necessary at this point."

"Why not?"

"They have an additional effect. Anyone who has one in his possession for a time becomes attuned to the thing. Throw it away and the attunement remains. You can still be tracked then, just as if you had retained the stone. You would possess a signature of your own."

"You mean that even now, without them, I'm marked?"

"Yes."

"How long does it take to wear off?"

"I am not certain that it ever does."

"There must be some means of deattunement."

"I do not know for certain, but I can think of a couple of things that would probably do it."

"Name them."

"Walking the Pattern of Amber or negotiating the Logrus of Chaos. They seem almost to break a person apart and do a reassemblement into a purer form. They have been known to purge many strange conditions. As I recall, it was the Pattern that restored your father's memory.''

''. . . So, you think they could be zeroing in on me right now, with or without the stones?''

''Yes.''

''How do you know all this?'' . . .

''I can sense it.'' (BA, 93–94)

Merle first took note of the blue stones' significance while he was imprisoned in the crystal cave. Using his sword, Merle attempted to break through a seemingly thinner wall of one chamber within the cave. It was futile, but he paused to examine the stone chips that had fallen to the floor. Actually, Merlin's mystical cord Frakir brought them to his attention. Their translucent coloring looked familiar. After a moment, he realized that they were just like the stone in the ring that Luke had. He remembered that Luke also carried a key ring with a similar stone, and he had a vague memory of seeing such a blue stone elsewhere, worn by someone else he had known.

Since the stones originated from the crystal cave, Merle believed that Luke would have had a special reason for carrying them on his person. Trying his Logrus sight on the blue stones, he found that their nature could not be revealed in that way. Nevertheless, Merle put the chips in his pocket.

The first time that Merle saw one of the stones was when he discovered the dead body of his former girlfriend, Julia, in her apartment. He noted that she was wearing a pendant with a blue stone. He learned later that the doglike beast that killed her had been wearing a similar stone in its collar. The inference was made that that was how the beast tracked the girl.

Merle had come across Luke's ring when he went to the New Line Motel in San Francisco, where Luke had been staying. A hotel clerk gave Merle a sealed envelope and the ring, which had been left in Luke's room. His message asked Merle to contact him at the Hilton Hotel in Santa Fe, New Mexico. Although Merle couldn't recall Luke's ever wearing the ring, he put it on his own finger. When he did manage to reach Luke, in the bar of the hotel in Santa Fe, he found it extremely difficult to remove the ring to return it. Excusing himself, Merle entered the men's room and allowed Frakir to help him remove the ring. Luke showed only slight surprise when Merle handed it to him. Merle asked if he was going to put it on, but Luke demurred, saying it was a present for a friend. Although Merle watched his friend wrap the ring in a handkerchief and put it in his pocket, he wasn't immediately suspicious. However, the incident may have made certain things clearer to him later on.

At a point when Merle joined his aunt Flora in San Francisco, he confronted a disembodied voice during a sorcerous sending. Merle used his Logrus limbs to reach for the source of the sending. He reached the source, tore off some small object from a larger mass, and brought it back.

> ''It was a blue button mounted in a gold setting, a few navy blue threads still attached. The cut stone bore a curved, four-limbed design. . . . I dug into my pocket and produced the chips of stone from the crystal cave. They seemed to match. Frakir stirred slightly when I passed the button near her, then lapsed again into quiescence, as if having given up on warning me about blue stones when I obviously never did anything about them.'' (BA, 27)

After returning to Amber and exchanging information with King Random, Merle headed for the city to enjoy a meal. On his way out of Bloody Bill's, he was attacked by four men. He overpowered and defeated three of them. The last man, Merle saw, had a ring with a blue stone. Before he could restrain and question him, the attacker was skewered with the blade of one of Vinta Bayle's guardsmen. The dying man with the blue stone ring did not oblige Merle with an explanation.

When Merle showed the collection of blue crystals to the entity possessing Vinta Bayle, she explained their function. Merle emptied his pocket of the chips he had taken from the crystal cave, the dead man's ring, and the button bearing the stone. Under their own volition, each of the blue crystal items on the table began to vibrate. The entity claimed that she wasn't causing the movement, but that she believed some other agent was attempting to reestablish a link. She suggested that she have a servant dispose of the stones in the ocean. Merle agreed, but with the exception of the blue button. He hoped that the button would enable him to trace the blue-masked sorcerer. The Vinta-entity promised to keep the button locked up for safekeeping.

The entity left a brief message for Merle before vacating Vinta's body. She left the blue button with it, writing that he should put the button in a safe place as soon as he was able. After returning to Kolvir, he dropped it in his father's empty sarcophagus.

Through Jasra, once she and Merlin were on better terms, he learned that the blue stones were called tragoliths. Jasra had sent the four men to Amber to track and assassinate Merle. The tragoliths had been used previously by Jasra and her son in the April 30 attempts on Merle's life. Luke had discontinued their use for several years, however, along with the murder attempts.

The sorcerer named Mask had been a prize pupil of Jasra's. Mask took advantage of Jasra to the extent that she stole two tragoliths when she had the opportunity and planted one on Jasra. She planned to gain control of the Keep of the Four Worlds by following Jasra there without her knowledge. That was how Mask became master of the Keep, with Jasra imprisoned under a spell.

It was Mask who arranged for the girl in Julia's apartment and the doglike beast from another shadow, consigning blue stones to both. Mask was quite adept at using the stones for subterfuge and murder.

One further function of the blue stones occurred to Merle, but he hadn't any in his possession to test the idea. Lost for a time in a universe that dampened all magical forces, he believed that he might have been able to find release if he held even one blue stone. Its affinity for the crystal cave should have allowed him to walk the shadows back to the cave, even from the remotest realm.

BONEDANCE GAME

A magical exercise taught to young children in the Courts of Chaos as part of their orientation in the Arts.

In the House of Sawall, a demon servant named Gryll taught this game to young Merlin. In turn, Merlin taught it to a young girl of a near shadow, where they played in an underground mausoleum. More recently, just after the death of King Swayvill of the Courts, Merlin visited the same place. In a nostalgic moment, he resorted to the Bonedance Game:

I snapped my fingers then, and our old ensorcelled heap of them across the way made a sound like stirring leaves. My juvenile spell was still in place; the bones rolled forward, arranged themselves into a pair of manikins, began their small awkward dance. They circled each other, barely holding their shapes, pieces flaking away, cobwebs trailing; loose ones—spares—began to bounce about them. They made tiny clicking sounds as they touched. I moved them faster. (PC, 72)

When Merlin was distracted, the dancing skeletons fell into shapeless heaps again.

As disturbing as these images might be to the uninitiated, the Bonedance Game is a very common means for children to practice their sorcerous talents. Pedaling toy fire trucks on shadow Earth is one small stepping-stone for a child to learn something useful toward driving a real automobile in that place's adult world.

BOREL

Son of Duke Larsus and Duchess Belissa Minobee of the House of Hendrake in the Courts of Chaos. A master swordsman, Lord Borel had been Dara's fencing instructor. In the mountains of the Patternfall battle, he challenged Corwin of Amber to a duel to the death.

Merlin, son of Corwin and Dara, had learned that Borel's father, Larsus, who held the military rank of general, was killed in the Patternfall War as well. Julian had killed General Larsus in the fighting. Suhuy told Merlin: "Borel had two brothers, a half brother and a half sister, many uncles, aunts, cousins. Yes, it's a big House." (PC, 55) Dara's mother, in fact, was of the House of Hendrake. Rumors have insinuated that Dara was more than a pupil to Borel.

Our only actual acquaintance with Lord Borel comes from the Chronicles set down by Corwin. Following is what transpired in their encounter at the Patternfall battle:

"Lord Corwin of Amber!"

He was waiting for me as I rounded a bend in the depression, a big, corpse-colored guy with red hair and a horse to match. He wore coppery armor with greenish tracings, and he sat facing me, still as a statue.

"I saw you on the hilltop," he said. "You are not mailed, are you?"

I slapped my chest.

He nodded sharply. Then he reached up, first to his left shoulder, then to his right, then to his sides, opening fastenings upon his breastplate. When he had them undone, he removed it, lowered it toward the ground on his left side and let it fall. He did the same with his greaves.

"I have long wanted to meet you," he said. "I am Borel. I do not want it said that I took unfair advantage of you when I killed you."

Borel . . . The name was familiar. Then I remembered. He had Dara's respect and affection. He had been her fencing teacher, a master of the blade. Stupid, though, I saw. He had forfeited my respect by removing his armor. Battle is not a game, and I had no desire to make myself available to any presumptuous ass who thought otherwise. Especially a skilled ass, when I was feeling beat. If nothing else, he could probably wear me down.

"Now we shall resolve a matter which has long troubled me," he said.

I replied with a quaint vulgarism, wheeled my black and raced back the way I had come. He gave chase immediately. . . .

"Coward!" he cried. "You flee combat! Is this the great warrior of whom I have heard so much?"

I reached up and unfastened my cloak. At either hand, the culvert's lip was level with my shoulders, then my waist.

I rolled out of the saddle to my left, stumbled once and found my footing. The black went on. I moved to my right, facing the draw.

Catching my cloak in both hands, I swung it in a reverse-veronica maneuver a second or two before Borel's head and shoulders came abreast of me. It swept over him, drawn blade and all, muffling his head and slowing his arms.

I kicked then, hard. I was aiming for his head, but I caught him on the left shoulder. He was spilled from his saddle, and his horse, too, went by.

Drawing Grayswandir, I leaped after him. I caught him just as he had brushed my cloak aside and was struggling to rise. I skewered him where he sat and saw the startled expression on his face as the wound began to flame.

"Oh, basely done!" he cried. "I had hoped for better of thee!"

"This isn't exactly the Olympic Games," I said, brushing some sparks from my cloak. (CC, 104–5)

Corwin had dispatched Borel with no interest in his background, no concern for those who would mourn his loss. Later, when the armies of Amber had defeated the forces of the Courts, Dara approached a weary Corwin. She said, "I came upon Borel before he died . . . He told me how ignobly you had bested him." (CC, 125) In spite of her loyalty to the late King Oberon and her bond to Benedict, Dara chose to return to her people in the Courts of Chaos because of Corwin's act.

Corwin's son, in seeking his long-missing father, questioned several people in the Courts about him. Merlin was curious to learn if Borel's remaining family in the House of Hendrake would hold a grudge against Corwin. Speaking to Suhuy, Mandor, and a young lady of Hendrake named Gilva, Merlin asked each one if Borel's House would seek revenge. Those questioned concurred that the House of Hendrake is an honorable, military-oriented House and, therefore, would not seek vengeance in peacetime for an act done in war. As Gilva had indicated: "Ours is an honorable House. We accept the fortunes of war. When the fighting is ended, we put it all behind us." (PC, 163)

Borel no doubt upheld the martial principles of his House of "pride in the battle well-fought, honor in dying valiantly." This would seem to be borne out by events after Patternfall. Members of the House of Hendrake had set up a place of worship dedicated to Benedict, the intrepid warrior who led the military strike against them. For those of Hendrake, there would not be any futility in the deaths of Duke Larsus and his son, Lord Borel, as long as they believed the conquest was accomplished by a soldier of the highest order. Their loss was occasioned by the heroic ability of the great Benedict of Amber.

BRAND

The third child born to King Oberon of Amber and Clarissa, a red-haired woman of a distant shadow. Brand's birth was something of an afterthought, occurring during a brief reconciliation between Oberon and Clarissa after an estrangement that subsequently led to a divorce.

Brand's older siblings of that marriage were Fiona and Bleys, and Brand spent more time with them as a child than he did with any of his other brothers and sisters in the Royal Palace. It is difficult to gauge his friendships with others when he was growing up. Although he spent much time with Fiona, Brand often acted independently, frequently leaving his sister behind while he pursued some idea or action.

Fiona has indicated that their closeness during their early years was actually maintained through their common interest in learning the ancient wisdom of their grandfather, Dworkin. Dworkin's teachings bonded the two children more than any other factor. While Fiona appreciated Brand's reassuring presence under the old man's tutelage, Brand was such an intense pupil that he hardly noticed that Fiona was there, and he never acknowledged the presence of his older brother Bleys.

Brand's intensity in learning all he could of the Pattern, the Trumps, and other sources of power had puzzled Prince Corwin, and probably his other brothers and sisters. Corwin had written in his Chronicles: "He [Dworkin] had often tried to discuss the matter, but it had seemed awfully abstract and boring to most of us. We are a very pragmatic family." (GA, 92) While the need for such knowledge eluded their generation, Brand proved them wrong, perhaps to their regret. The Family's lack of understanding of Brand's powers may have been partly responsible for the great conflict between the realms of Amber and the Courts of Chaos before the Days of Darkness.

Brand had always been rather enigmatic, and each member of the Family has had to draw his or her own image of him to fit the person each knew. Corwin chose to paint his vision of Brand in the following way:

Brand's features were similar to my own, but he was shorter and slenderer. His hair was like Fiona's. He wore a green riding suit. . . . something of a dreamer, a mystic, a poet, Brand was always disillusioned or elated, cynical or wholly trusting. His feelings never seemed to find a middle ground. Manic-depressive is too facile a term for his complex character, yet it

might serve to indicate a direction of departure, multitudes of qualifications lining the roadway thereafter. . . . There were times when I found him so charming, considerate, and loyal that I valued him above all my other kin. Other times, however, he could be so bitter, sarcastic, and downright savage that I tried to avoid his company for fear that I might do him harm." (SU, 88)

Most of his kin found Brand to have considerable charm, but also admitted that this ran into a streak of sarcasm when he was in their company overlong. When Brand visited the undersea realm of Rebma, Llewella was touched by his flattering manner. During his stay, he asked if he might paint her portrait. He spent nearly two weeks painting her, and while he did so they talked of pleasant times and family relations. In retrospect, she remembered that she talked more than he did, but he spoke with just enough encouragement to keep her engaged in conversation. He would often nod and agree politely, make a brief kind, or cutting, remark, and allow her to continue. All the while he seemed to take great joy in composing her portrait. Only in the last day or two, while she sat for him, did he seem preoccupied and annoyed. He seemed to rush the last couple of sessions, putting on his brushstrokes with nervous activity. He didn't seem pleased with his work when he finished and showed it to her. Several days later, Brand left Rebma abruptly, giving his farewells with laconic remoteness. While attending to the room in which he stayed, Llewella discovered the beginnings of an oil painting on a small canvas. It was the portrait of a male, but the face was obscured, a splatter of paint across it despoiling any attempt to recognize the features.

Many years later, Martin, son of Random, happened to see Brand's portrait of Llewella in her sitting room in Rebma. He laughed, tried to cover it, but was too late to escape Llewella's notice. He told her he recognized the original model for the pose that Brand asked her to take. It was taken from a Rembrandt oil entitled *Danae*. Although Brand had clothed her in green and given her an ardent expression typical of Llewella, the position and gesture was from the Rembrandt. Martin pointed out the slight form of a face at the doorway as resembling Brand. When Martin showed her a photograph in an art history book of the painting, Llewella laughed also at the clever parody. The portrait that Brand worked so earnestly on many years before was an expression of his sardonic sense of humor.

As a young man, Brand entered the army of Amber as was expected of every male of the House of Amber. However, he stayed with the infantry only as long as he needed to while he remained uninitiated in walking the Pattern. Once Dworkin had allowed him the opportunity to walk the Pattern deep below the Royal Palace, Brand could hardly be restrained from traveling the lands of Shadow. He fulfilled his responsibilities to his father, however, by finishing his stint in the military, although he never bothered to distinguish himself in service. While completing his term, he spent most of his nights with Dworkin in the palace. Brand's enthusiasm for the Art taught by his grandfather far outweighed any initiative he could render for army life. When he was ready, and with Oberon's permission, the young Brand went exploring in Shadow.

After returning from his first journey to the shadows, Brand spoke enthusiastically to Fiona, Corwin, and others about the flimsy, insignificant creatures he saw wandering in their little, self-contained worlds. More than most, Brand felt his superiority over the living beings of the shadows. He spoke of their blatant ignorance of a higher order that could erase their collective lives with a thought. He was mildly surprised when none of his kin responded with a similar enthusiasm. He may have noted the dismay in the expressions of his brothers and sisters, for he never spoke of his travels again. He traveled often after that, staying away for longer and longer periods, and when he returned to Amber he avoided confiding in anyone, including Fiona, about his experiences.

With the benefit of hindsight, it is now obvious that Brand acquired vast and terrible powers during his many journeys in Shadow. Pieces of the puzzle of how much knowledge and skill he had gained over time have still not fully come to light. In recent accounts, Merlin has uncovered some of these pieces which serve to illuminate the enormity of Brand's powers. Early in Brand's travels, he had met the Phantom Smith of Tir-na Nog'th, who had fashioned for him the Daysword called Werewindle, brother to the sword of Corwin, Grayswandir. In later treks, Brand visited the Keep of the Four Worlds and bathed in the energy source of the Black Fountain. It is conceivable that he did this more

than once to obtain the power to become a kind of "Living Trump." This enabled him to traverse Shadow virtually instantaneously, and also bring any desired object out of Shadow to him. The ring that Merlin found hidden in Brand's room in the Royal Palace, bearing highly potent capabilities tied into Shadow, may also have come from the Keep of the Four Worlds. As more of Brand's potentialities become known, those in Amber will continue to gain fearful insight into the awful danger that he meant to all of reality.

Fiona and Brand began to speak conspiratorially to one another when King Oberon was having troubles within the kingdom. At first, Fiona shared her experiences at the Courts of Chaos with Brand, comparing life in that realm to the rather disorganized society of Amber. In turn, Brand hinted at some of the power to be gained, by means other than the Pattern, in the shadows. At that time, Brand initiated discussion of doing away with their father, who, Brand felt, had allowed for growing dissension between the noblemen who owned large tracts of land and the menial laborers who worked their land. Brand saw this, and other such lapses, as justification for taking firmer control themselves.

Possessed of a great temper, Brand had been known to go into a rage at the slightest provocation. Such an incident had happened late one night when Corwin and Brand sat arguing in Brand's room. The argument was over some policy of Oberon's that Brand vehemently disagreed with. Corwin argued in support of it. Corwin's position was so steadfast that Brand glared at him with sudden, uncontrollable loathing. As Corwin stood up to leave, Brand was seething, ready to murder. He spoke to Corwin of that night and of the intense emotions that moved him:

"I was sitting on the edge of my bed. You were standing by my writing desk. As you turned away and headed toward the door, I resolved to kill you. I reached beneath my bed, where I keep a cocked crossbow with a bolt in it. I actually had my hand on it and was about to raise it when I realized something which stopped me. . . .

"You were standing on my favorite rug. I did not want to get blood on it. Later, my anger passed. So I, too, am a victim of emotion and circumstance." (HO, 92)

Although the subject of this argument was never made known to anyone else, it left an indelible impression on Brand. Something in Corwin's words affected Brand strongly enough to believe that Corwin would be a major obstacle to any future attempt on Brand's part to gain control in Amber. He might still have acted against Corwin, but another party moved independently in that regard. After Corwin and Eric went off together to go hunting, Eric returned alone, claiming that Corwin suddenly decided to take a journey in Shadow. Eric's story seemed flimsy enough to just be true, but Brand saw it as a good opportunity to place Eric in the center of everyone's suspicions while he could carry out a scheme that he was just beginning to form.

Oberon immediately looked upon Eric with distrust, and meals together in the great hall became fraught with veiled accusations. As days passed, Benedict made a great show of concern for Corwin's safety, and this was echoed by Brand, who believed Benedict to be sincere in his concern. Benedict went to the shadows to search for Corwin, followed shortly thereafter by Gérard and by Brand, going separate ways. When each of them returned, after some time, the three of them indicated their failure to find Corwin or obtain any word about him.

After decades of hearing no word, it might have been possible that Oberon would have allowed Corwin's disappearance to lapse into distant memory. However, Brand and Fiona worked together to keep the mystery of Corwin at the forefront. At the dinner table one evening, Oberon seemed to be half-listening to a Family discussion when he announced, "I tell you this: whosoever succeeds me will not have his hands soiled in dishonor. I will not have a fratricide sitting on the throne of Amber." (SU, 153) An accusing finger pointed at Eric, who turned pale and silent. It was a moment none of them would forget.

A long stillness enveloped the meal after that, but then Oberon spoke again. He told them that he hoped Corwin was not a victim of foul play by anyone sitting at the table. It would go badly for any of them who caused Corwin's death, for that person would be guilty of assassinating a future king. It had been his intention, he told them at that dinner table, to make Corwin his successor. The crime, if committed, was made a political as well as a personal one.

This announcement took everyone by surprise, and Brand was not pleased by it. Corwin seemed an even greater impediment to him than ever before, and Brand needed to be certain that Corwin was dead. As a step in that direction, Brand urged the others to construct a monument to Corwin, a cenotaph that could be used to house his body, should it be recovered sometime in the future. This forced the near-certainty upon the others, his father especially, but Brand still desired a reassurance of Corwin's death. For that, he walked one moonlit night to the heights of Mt. Kolvir and entered the ghost city in the sky, Tir-na Nog'th. Afterward, he told Fiona what he discovered there: that Corwin was alive and that he would return to Amber amid violence and destruction. The visions of the ghost city were dreamlike and unclear, but Brand felt they provided him with the truth in showing Corwin alive.

Brand's frequent journeys to the shadows did not go unnoticed. One of the first to become suspicious of him was Julian, who observed Brand's fits of temper, his too-sudden appearances and disappearances around corners and outside of doorways, and, most particularly, his roaming off with his sister Fiona with such a secretive air. Julian's fondness for Fiona made this last appear highly suspect. He didn't like to think that Fiona might be plotting with Brand, but he knew that it was likely. He brought his suspicions to Eric, and they resolved to watch Brand closely.

Brand may have become aware that he was being watched, but he was also uneasy about the possibility of Corwin's return. Release from both stresses would come from another disappearance into Shadow; so, late one night while lying in bed, he wished himself away. It didn't work, but he felt that it could have, if only he had more skill. Moments later, he was out of bed, dressed, and walking silently out of the Royal Palace. In town, he obtained writing materials and drew a hasty picture of a shadow he had heard about from his father, but had never seen. Oberon had once vividly described a woodland that seemed wondrous to the young Brand. He drew on that memory as he sketched it on the blank sheet before him. When he finished, he was able to exert the power of the Pattern to walk into that paper image and appear in that place in Shadow. The sketch was left behind, nailed to a table in a small café in the town.

Once he was away from Amber, Brand determined to exercise the knowledge he had gained from Dworkin. Influencing Shadow itself, he constructed a force that would send violent gales and tornadoes against Mt. Kolvir. While he was initiating this, however, he was being observed from a short distance. He hadn't noticed until a sudden heavy rainfall dropped from directly overhead, drenching him and his mustering tornado force. Looking around, he saw a woman in a flowing gown laughing at him. Angered, he sent a bolt of lightning at her, but she repelled it. Thus began a fierce, sorcerous battle between them. No one can say with any certainty what shape the demon forces were that they threw at each other, but both were bloodied by the end of the ordeal.

Tiredly, they called a truce. Resting on the ground, they spoke to one another, each forming impressions of the other. Her name was Jasra, and Brand found her clever, witty, and attractive. Jasra found Brand to be extremely self-confident, but with a quality of remoteness that was difficult to fathom. Their truce extended into a long-lasting peace, and they had fallen in love.

The land was named Kashfa, and Jasra was the queen. Her castle was a bracing walk from the wood where they met, and it was in the castle that they were married. Although Jasra would have arranged for a large ceremony, with half the kingdom in attendance, Brand insisted on a small, quiet wedding. She acceded to his wishes, and only a small retinue of courtiers and servants who lived in the palace attended. During his lifetime, no one in Amber ever learned of Brand's marriage.

One evening while they were dining, Jasra told Brand of a place of enormous power. The source of power was a fountain of black stone within a fortress called the Keep of the Four Worlds. The fountain was the juncture of four separate shadows, the only such point of meeting in all the realities known to them. The effect of that meeting point was an energy source that could give a surviving recipient superhuman attributes. Only one person had harnessed it thus far, an aged wizard named Sharu Garrul.

Of course, Brand was intrigued about the Keep of the Four Worlds, and he continued to ask questions about it. After he learned all he could from her about it, he wanted her to take him to the Keep. She tried to dissuade him, saying that Sharu was very dangerous. Brand would have insisted at that point, but Jasra became pregnant.

During Jasra's pregnancy, Brand felt a restlessness come over him again. He took his leave of her for a while to journey again in Shadow. He visited Fiona, and she introduced him to some of the nobles she knew in the Courts of Chaos. Anticipating that he would find them intimidating, Brand found the few he met to be quite amicable. They seemed to know something of his background and appeared eager to maintain friendship with him. Still, Brand was cautious and didn't spend much time with them. He left Fiona at the Courts to travel on alone. It is said that he met the Phantom Smith in these wanderings, but it may not have been in Tir-na Nog'th. After obtaining the royal blood of a prince of Amber, the Smith may have acquired substantiality, enabling him to leave the phantom city in the sky. This may, or may not, have occurred when Brand encountered him. Nevertheless, Brand had received the blade named Werewindle while traveling the shadows.

When he returned to Kashfa, his son was a small boy. Jasra had named him Rinaldo and told him about his father. The boy worshiped Brand. For a long while, Brand became a doting father, spending a great deal of time with Rinaldo. Although Jasra wanted him to remain and rule in Kashfa, he could not be content with that. His mind always turned to the one true realm, and he would not settle for less than control over Amber.

Rinaldo remembered the first time his father showed him his Trumps and told him of their purpose. He was a very small boy, and the teachings of his parents had seemed strange and unreal to his young mind. Once, he tried using an ordinary deck of playing cards the way his father showed him with his Trumps. When nothing happened, he was confused and uncertain. But he was very young then.

In spite of Brand's love for his wife and son, his spirit remained restless, and he continued to hunger for the kind of power he knew he could obtain in the Black Fountain of the Keep. Jasra was still hesitant about confronting the old wizard there, but Brand mapped out a plan that struck her as being quite feasible. It depended on their working in concert, Jasra openly approaching Sharu as a decoy, and Brand coming as a surprise out of hiding. After all, the wizard knew nothing of Brand and wouldn't suspect Jasra's arrival with a secret ally.

Since he was a talented artist, Brand was remarkably adept at drawing Trumps. Making use of Jasra's knowledge of the Black Fountain, Brand skillfully drew a Trump that showed the Fount partially obscured around the corner of a deep corridor. His plan involved their appearing in that dark corridor so that they would not be spotted immediately.

Setting the carefully drawn sketch against a wall in the palace of Kashfa, Brand took Jasra by the hand and they stepped through. They were there, in the Keep of the Four Worlds. Jasra stood alone in the half-light, but she felt Brand behind her; he had moved back to the deeper recesses. She understood why Brand had moved back when she heard a croaking voice call her name. Sharu stood several feet away in the light of the large hall and had seen her immediately. Following their plan, Jasra stepped boldly toward the old man, greeting him with a casualness that belied her fear. He was taken aback by these pleasantries, and he used his Art to survey her for any magical spells she might have hanging. It surprised him that she had none. He turned to her fully then, all caution, but intent upon her words. She proposed an alliance. Together, they could hold dominion over many worlds, Kashfa included. They would be unstoppable, able to have anything they wished. Joined as allies, they would fear no one.

She walked toward the Fount in the center of the large hall. His eyes never left her. He was about to protest that he already had everything he wanted and had no need to join her in some scheme for power. He didn't have the opportunity to say it, however, for he felt the presence of a magical force outside of their circle. The old man turned, saw the young stranger, and cast his arms out to inveigh a warding spell. The words started out of his mouth but were swallowed unheard. Brand had worked a spell, begun even as Jasra had been speaking, that placed Sharu in an icy grip at just that moment. Sharu may have been conscious, but he was utterly immobile.

Impetuously, Brand rushed to the Fount to place his hands in the yellow flames in the basin.

"No!" Jasra shouted. "It's dangerous. You'll die if you're not properly protected. Believe me."

She explained that one can gain power from the Black Fountain only by undergoing a prescribed ritual. Without it, the flames will destroy anyone who bathes within it.

"We must find Sharu's notes," she told him.

They inspected the main floor, found nothing, and made their way to the second floor. After checking rooms along several dark hallways, they found a large room that was a laboratory. It combined various disciplines: on the left wall were shelves of beakers, test tubes, jars filled with fluid, and a Bunsen burner; in the rear center was some metallic-looking equipment of different sizes—one looked like an oscilloscope; nearer the front was a large wood desk covered with maps and charts, some containing mathematical formulae, and also a large microscope and slides; along the right wall were shelves filled with books, many appearing quite old; and on a smaller desk to the right of the door was an open book resting on some loose papers—beside this desk, on the floor and wall, were symbols marked in chalk, some of which Brand recognized as relating to the Pattern.

Jasra looked through the papers and the open book on the small desk while Brand examined the symbols more closely. He could tell that Sharu had been studying many different forms of magic, most of which he didn't recognize. Those related to Pattern-teachings, however, he did recognize. Jasra found further evidence of the wizard's studies in the open book and the papers filled with scribbled writing, but there was nothing concerning the Fount.

To preserve the secret of Sharu's notes, Jasra and Rinaldo have been unwilling to relate where they were hidden nor what the process is to prepare a recipient for immersion within the energies of the Fountain. It will have to suffice that Brand and Jasra discovered the notes in the laboratory and set to work on the ritual that would transfer the forces of the Fount to Brand.

The process, Jasra has said, involves several series of immersions following very specific ritualistic actions, so that a single immersion would not be sufficient. It amounts to adding on layers of energy over a period of time in progressive steps. As a consequence, one will not feel the full potency of the Fount in the first, or even the second, ritual cycles. However, one may obtain some of the rudimentary abilities to be gleaned from it after a single cycle, depending on one's metabolism and magical strengths. In Brand's case, he felt certain definite physical manifestations after the first cycle. His senses were heightened, his stamina and sense of well-being were increased, and he had a widened perception of the intricate forces at work in the Fount, as indicated in Sharu's notes.

After a short while, during which they divided their time between Kashfa and the Keep, Brand became restless again. His powers had grown immensely, and he was eager to make use of them. By this time, they had moved the frozen form of Sharu near one of the main entrances to the fortress. Young Rinaldo, playing there, carved his name on the right leg of the old man, who was being used to hold cloaks and hats. Jasra was teaching the boy some simple spells, but Brand only halfheartedly spent time with them. He felt terribly restrained, especially because he was the bearer of such great power. He was bored with exercising the power he had over Shadow just to amuse his son, his wife, and himself. Finally, Jasra could not contain him any longer, and Brand went off to wander the shadows. He was so confident of his skills that he left his Trumps with Jasra.

In shadowlands, he tested his new powers by interfering in wars among strange beings of manifold worlds. He pulled monsters from other shadows into a shadow of humble, peaceful people. In another shadow, he formed an army of hellish courtesans, and dumped them into a monastery. Later, he told of these adventures and others to his son, told of these actions as experiments he performed to learn the extent of his abilities.

When he felt ready, he walked to Amber. It was a mistake. Julian, Eric, and Caine took him by surprise as soon as he appeared in the Royal Palace. They beat him senseless before he could raise a hand. Dragging and half-carrying him, they threw him into a dungeon before their father, or anyone else, had seen them. Securing him to the straw-lined cot, they injected him with strong drugs to keep him unconscious. As long as he remained unconscious, they knew they were safe. They posted a guard outside his locked door with orders to look in on him every hundred paces. Brand was kept drugged like this for years.

It would have been better for Brand if he had come directly to Amber from the Keep of the Four Worlds. His activities in Shadow had been picked up by Eric and Caine. As Brand had exerted his magical influence in shadows nearer to Amber, Caine was able to reach Brand and observe him through his Trump. In this way, Eric, Julian, and Caine could easily spring their trap, needing only patience to lie in wait for him.

With the passage of years, and with a variety of problems of the homeland to keep them busy, Caine, Julian, and Eric became lax in their precautions regarding Brand. He seemed safe enough, and Oberon was making numerous demands on their time and duty. Through benign neglect, Brand gradually regained consciousness. He pretended sleep whenever the guard looked in on him, but he began to think and scheme nevertheless.

Julian has pieced things together based on the crudely drawn Trump that Brand left behind and events that Corwin recalled much later. Using the powers that he had gained at the Keep, Brand had managed to locate the missing Corwin on the shadow Earth. Then, he combined his own escape with a detainment of Corwin within the place he had drawn on a rough piece of board from his bedding, using part of a metal spring. When he escaped, the drawing was left behind, and Julian was able to determine that it was a cell used for the mentally incompetent in a small hospital in London, a hospital which the gentry commonly referred to as Bedlam. Acting as an important official of the local government of England at the time, Julian was able to have Corwin released into his custody. Unfortunately, Corwin got away from Julian, although he had seemed to be drugged. Julian suspected that Brand had a hand in Corwin's running away, but he was never certain of this.

When Brand effected his escape, he returned to the Keep exhausted. Jasra nursed him for many weeks while he rested and recovered his strength. It had been a fearful experience for him, the sudden attack by his brothers and the drugged imprisonment. But it also served to create a distinct separation between Brand and the Family. He arrived at the decision to isolate himself from his brothers and try to hurt them in the severest manner possible. Any action he took from then on, no matter how much he seemed to be working in concert with others, would be to his own benefit solely.

As soon as he recuperated, Brand continued the ritual process in the Black Fountain. No longer did he seem a man in haste. He acted with thoughtful deliberation, unhurried and unconcerned. When he spent time with his son, now approaching young manhood, their activities were no longer frivolous. Oblivious to these changes in his father, Rinaldo played eagerly with him. Brand taught him about the Trumps, about their functions. Masking his own bitter determination, Brand showed him how to draw his own. One of Rinaldo's first successful attempts was of his mother. He was delighted to find himself pulled to Jasra's side through the freshly drawn Trump, then returned to Brand by the open contact.

There came a time when Brand thought his son was ready for the initiation of one of the blood of Amber. There was only one place he felt he could safely take Rinaldo to walk the Pattern. Under the cover of night, he took his son to Tir-na Nog'th, stepping directly through Shadow from the Keep.

Rinaldo appeared to be especially adept at walking the Pattern of the ghost city. He stepped unfalteringly as Brand advised him of each trial that would come before him. Jubilantly, Rinaldo reached the center and pondered cautiously Brand's suggestions and warnings about where he might have the Pattern send him. Rinaldo was thoughtful, then said his farewells to his father, and faded from the center. Brand returned alone to Jasra.

They were spending more time at the Keep of the Four Worlds than in Kashfa for a while. Both were busy fortifying the fortress against magical attack as well as a physical assault. It had been too easy for Brand to draw a Trump of the interior of the Keep, and he devised specific spells to prevent that manner of entry in the future.

Brand's thoughts turned again to Amber, but by this time his plans were larger than merely to reign in the true city. In order to effect his plans, he decided to bypass his sister Fiona and visit the Chaos lords she had introduced him to years before. This time, he took his Trumps with him as he stepped from the Keep to a shadow congruent to the Courts of Chaos. From there, he used his influence over Shadow to contact three of the lords who were high officials in the Courts. When they joined him in the congruent shadow, Brand arranged a meeting within a fortresslike construct where they could confer without disturbance.

Our knowledge of what transpired at their conference comes from the accounts of Dara the Younger of Chaos. According to her, Brand needed to know how to destroy the primal Pattern so that he could devise a new one that would put him in dominion over Amber and the shadow worlds. As Dara has explained, this was the agreement they reached:

"Brand was given what he wanted . . . but he was not trusted. It was feared that once he pos-sessed the power to shape the world as he would, he would not stop with ruling over a revised Amber. He would attempt to extend his dominion over Chaos as well. A weakened Amber was what was desired, so that Chaos would be stronger than it now is—the striking of a new balance, giving to us more of the shadowlands that lie between our realms. . . . Though it was seen what Brand had in mind, our leaders came to terms with him. It was the best opportunity to present itself in ages. It had to be seized. It was felt that Brand could be dealt with, and finally replaced, when the time came." (CC, 17)

When Brand knew the method by which the primal Pattern could be damaged, he had to decide the best way to achieve it. He would have liked to shed the blood of Caine, or Eric, or Julian. But that would have been too difficult to accomplish, and getting any one of them would draw too much attention to him. If he were to succeed without becoming immediately suspect, he would have to use an initiate of the Pattern who was innocent of the intrigues that Brand was involved with. Someone on the order of Rinaldo, but certainly not him. Brand would never consider using his own son that way. But someone like his son . . .

Fiona had talked of many things happening in Amber when he last spoke with her years ago. It occurred to him now that she mentioned something about his young half brother Random, something about an affair with a young princess of Rebma that went bad, and an illegitimate son. Brand wasn't especially fond of Random, although they shared some of the same wildness in their nature. Random was a musician, but he also liked to gamble; too frivolous and wasteful by Brand's standards. He decided to look into the matter of Random's son, then allow his plan to form from what he could learn.

He began by passively observing Random through his Trump. Brand was still too shaken by his last experience in the Royal Palace to communicate with Random there. Patiently, he watched his young brother and waited. It took a great deal of patience, for Random was the sociable type, and when he wasn't with his brothers and sisters, he was gambling and drinking with friends or dallying with a young lady.

It happened that Random found things lagging

one evening: friends were away, his relatives were occupied elsewhere, and no lady was immediately available. He went wandering into town, feeling the need to dine out, and hoping that something would turn up there. As he walked by a small seafood café, he was surprised to hear his name called out. Turning, he saw Brand, sitting with an attractive young lady who slightly resembled Fiona. Brand called to him again, raising a wineglass in open invitation. Random smiled broadly and joined him at the table. Offering some vague excuse, the girl left them and disappeared in a crowd of sailors.

"I had no idea you were in town," Random said. "You've been away a long time."

"Just got back."

Although Brand tried to be casual, Random felt a little discomfort in their meeting. He ordered a drink also, then looked at a menu, explaining that he was famished.

After some hesitation, Random asked, "I thought there was a problem between you and Eric?"

"There is. He doesn't trust me. Don't worry, I'm not here to start trouble. I'm avoiding the palace for just that reason. I miss the place, is all. I wanted to sample the food, the wine, the women of Amber once more. I still love Amber, just like the rest of you."

Brand's remark was a calculated thing, and it was sufficient to break the ice. Random talked freely of matters he had heard, and events in his own life, as he ate and drank.

Avoiding any talk of a political nature, Brand wondered aloud about the possibility of other illegitimate offspring of their father. He brought the conversation around to illegitimate children in the Family generally, and waited for Random to mention something more specific. Random was not conscious that Brand was doing any probing, so he spoke of his misadventure in Rebma and what happened afterward. Guided with great subtlety by his older brother, Random told him his son's name and explained that, as far as he knew, Martin still resided in Rebma. Unfortunately, Random knew little more about him, and he looked suddenly downcast about it. He knew it was a terrible lack in him to have so little interest in someone he had helped bring into the world. Seeing his brother's shift in mood, Brand changed the sub-

ject, asking about their sisters, their whereabouts and activities.

They continued their conversation long after Random had finished his meal. Random noted how unhurried Brand was, and this almost struck him as odd later on, after the fact. It was more typical of Brand to be abrupt and lacking in social grace. At the time, however, Random attached no great significance to it. When they parted, it was quite late. They shook hands warmly, and Brand started off for the Harbor District, where he said he had taken rooms for the night.

Shortly after that, Brand showed up in Rebma to visit his sister Llewella. As stated earlier, he spent a couple of weeks there. One of the concerns he showed while there had to do with Martin. Llewella had told Corwin, Random, and the others about his interest in Random's son:

> "He implied that he had met Martin somewhere in his travels, and he gave the impression that he would like to get in touch with him again. I did not realize until some time after his departure that finding out everything he could concerning Martin was probably the entire reason for his visit. You know how subtle Brand can be, finding out things without seeming to be after them. It was only after I had spoken with a number of others whom he had visited that I began to see what had occurred." (SU, 100)

She had imparted very little practical information about Martin, however. She told Brand that after Martin successfully walked the Pattern in Rebma, he disappeared and they hadn't heard from him again. Looking back, it may have been a rather successful visit for Brand, since he did leave Rebma with a good idea of what Martin looked like, and that was paramount to his plan.

In this interim period before Brand, Fiona, and Bleys finalized their plans for eliminating Oberon and taking over the rule of Amber, very little is known of Brand's actions. It may seem quite bold of him to have spent so much time in Amber, but he was careful to avoid Eric, Julian, and Caine while he worked to resolve several matters. Rinaldo is of the opinion that his father worked numerous incantations in his room in the Royal Palace during this time. For his own reasons, Brand had hidden Were-

windle in the armoire in his bedroom, and he secreted a remarkably unique ring in a bedpost. No
one knows why he didn't make use of these resources in attempting his conquest at the Patternfall battle.

He also began secret meetings with Fiona and
Bleys, and they began drafting their plans. Bleys
would use his powers to send creatures out of
Shadow into Amber. Fiona contacted the lords at
the Courts of Chaos that she and Brand were acquainted with. Brand learned more about Martin
from Fiona and began observing their oldest brother
Benedict, who had been off in Shadow for a long
time. Through his observations of Benedict, Brand
learned more about Martin, and he saw enough of
him to begin drawing a Trump. Sometime during
this period, Brand traveled with Fiona to the Courts
of Chaos where they made arrangements for numerous "monster migrations" of Shadow-beings to
plague Amber, Benedict's shadow Avalon, and
other shadows that the princes had come into contact with. While conferring with the Chaos lords at
the Courts, Brand made sure they replayed some of
their scheme for Fiona's benefit, so that she would
feel that she was an integral part of the planning.
The lords spoke of the need to create an imperfection on the primal Pattern that would give access to
the armies of Chaos all the way from the Courts to
Amber. They left it up to Fiona and Brand to decide
whose blood would be shed to cause the damage,
and Brand offered to take on that responsibility
without telling Fiona anything about the steps he
had already begun in that regard.

The time shifts that occur when one travels the
shadows make it nearly impossible to ascertain the
sequence of events properly. After all, Brand had been
busy traveling between Amber, the Courts of Chaos,
Avalon, Kashfa, the shadow Earth, and a number of
other shadows as well. This would have a way of
skewing time so that no one can say what Brand did
first, second, third, and so on. It seems likely, for
instance, that he worked out the attack of the hellmaids in Benedict's shadow with the Chaos lords before he made his physical encounter with Martin.
However, the events in Avalon and the Courts must
have undergone a much faster time flow than the
events that took place between Martin and Brand. Not
only are the two events connected, but it would seem,
in retrospect, that the lords of the Courts had some
specific ideas of their own, connected with their plans

for Brand, when they allowed for the invasion of Lintra and her hellmaids in Avalon.

Naturally, Brand was unaware of the Chaos lords'
hidden motives as he helped to oversee the invasion
against Benedict. Brand saw that, simply, as a
means of keeping Benedict occupied while he went
after Martin. Again, much time may have passed
while Brand traveled in Shadow, but the encounter
with Martin took place when Brand deliberately
went to the primal Pattern with the Trump he had
drawn of Martin. He walked the Pattern and used
the Trump to contact the young man. Following is
Martin's account of what transpired:

> "After I left Benedict's, I traveled for years in
> Shadow . . . Then Brand caught up with me. I
> was camped on a little hillside, just resting
> from a long ride and taking my lunch, on my
> way to visit my friends the Tecys. Brand con-
> tacted me then. I had reached Benedict with
> his Trump, when he was teaching me how to
> use them, and other times when I had traveled.
> He had even transported me through occasion-
> ally, so I knew what it felt like, knew what it
> was all about. This felt the same way, and for
> a moment I thought that somehow it was Bene-
> dict calling me. But no. It was Brand—I recog-
> nized him from his picture in the deck. He was
> standing in the midst of what seemed to be the
> Pattern. I was curious. I did not know how he
> had reached me. So far as I knew, there was
> no Trump for me. He talked for a minute—I
> forget what he said—and when everything was
> firm and clear, he—he stabbed me. I pushed
> him and pulled away then. He held the contact
> somehow. It was hard for me to break it—and
> when I did, he tried to reach me again. But I
> was able to block him. Benedict had taught me
> that. He tried again, several times, but I kept
> blocking. Finally, he stopped. I was near to the
> Tecys. I managed to get onto my horse and
> make it to their place. I thought I was going
> to die, because I had never been hurt that badly
> before. But after a time, I began to recover.
> Then I grew afraid once again, afraid that
> Brand would find me and finish what he had
> begun." (HO, 162–63)

Much blood was spilled on the primal Pattern.
Although he couldn't be certain, Brand hoped that

Martin had died from his wound. Brand tried to reach Martin again, but he found that his usual methods for tracking into Shadow were blocked. It was as if an initiate of the Pattern had formed a shadow with a specific signature that could not be penetrated by anyone else. Brand gave up his search.

He didn't think Fiona or Bleys would be particularly bothered by his having used the illegitimate son of their youngest brother to damage the Pattern. Still, Brand felt the need to move quickly before the act was discovered by any of the others. He contacted Fiona, and the three of them met in her chambers. Each of them brought the others up to date on his or her activities, and Brand indicated that he had opened the way for the army of Chaos to march on Amber. Bleys had been in a shadow of his own design, raising an army to accomplish a coup, if necessary. Fiona had recently been to the Courts, and the nobles she was intimate with were in readiness, waiting for further word from her.

Brand urged direct action: they should murder their father, and he would dispose of the body in a shadow where it would never be located again. He knew that Bleys and Fiona would react against that, however. He allowed himself to be persuaded that it would be a mistake, one that could be traced back to them, to their detriment. It was necessary that Oberon be eliminated, but his retrieval had to remain within the realm of possibility.

Fiona's plan involved placing Oberon under the guardianship of the lords of Chaos. The most difficult part, posing the greatest danger to their conspiracy, was getting Oberon out of Amber without arousing suspicion. Fiona had found out that Oberon was having an affair with the wife of an important official in a shadow where Amber was negotiating delicate trade agreements. Bleys had been able to obtain specific information about the young lady through his special talents. He would use Oberon's trust in him to draw his father away from Amber. With Bleys's knowledge of the shadowlands, he was able to lure Oberon away on a mission, ostensibly to "rescue" the young lady from kidnappers. Meanwhile, Fiona would be with the Chaos lords to help in placing Oberon in a shadow that was congruent to the Courts of Chaos. While the lords were capable of keeping him under tight surveillance, Fiona wanted to be certain that Oberon's stay was comfortable, and that he would be kept off-balance by

events manufactured around him. While this was taking place, Brand kept himself informed of everyone's whereabouts in Amber, to make certain there would be no interference. His powers allowed him to coordinate between Bleys, Fiona, and himself while also assuring inaction from any other quarter.

After their plan succeeded, and at Fiona's insistence, they took no further immediate action. Bleys went off in Shadow to continue training his troops. From several accounts, Brand divided his time between Amber, Kashfa, and the Keep of the Four Worlds. Fiona remained in Amber, acting the dutiful princess and showing concern for their missing father.

For more than a year, the princes and princesses of Amber wondered over Oberon's disappearance. It wasn't really so unusual for their father suddenly to decide to go off into Shadow. Usually, he would make some brief remarks about leaving for a particular shadow and go away for weeks at a time. This was different, however. He had been gone an unusually long period without having told anyone anything about his destination or purpose in going. During that time, Caine, Gérard, Eric, and Julian made a distinct effort to try to raise him on his Trump, but they received no response.

Brand believed this passage of time was sufficient to convince everyone that Oberon was indeed dead. Fiona had kept him informed of the actions of Julian, Eric, and Caine, first in their effort to contact their father, then in their taking on offices of authority. Eric ruled the kingdom unofficially, while Caine and Gérard continued to run the royal navy, as they had been doing all along. Julian was in charge of the Forest of Arden, leading patrols in and around that region of the city.

Since Eric had been marked with his father's disfavor ages ago, when Corwin had disappeared, Brand felt assured that the local nobles and important merchants of the city would support him once he controlled the army and held general support from his brothers. Even if Eric had the loyalty of Amber's soldiers, Brand could gain control if one of his brothers in the real city joined him. With Bleys's troops in Shadow, and the support of a force already in Amber led by another brother, Eric would have to yield to Brand. That was Brand's intention as he and his group decided their next course of action:

"We [Fiona, Bleys, and Brand] hoped for a bloodless takeover, but we had to be ready in the event that words proved insufficient to win our case. If Julian gave us the land route in, or Caine the waves, we could have transported the troops with dispatch and held the day by force of arms, should that have proven necessary. Unfortunately, I chose the wrong man. In my estimate, Caine was Julian's superior in matters of corruption. So, with measured delicacy I sounded him on the matter. He seemed willing to go along with things, at first. But he either reconsidered subsequently or deceived me quite skillfully from the beginning. Naturally, I prefer to believe that it was the former. Whatever, at some point he came to the conclusion that he stood to benefit more by supporting a rival claimant. . . . Eric took a public oath to defend the throne, and the lines were thereby drawn. I was naturally in a somewhat embarrassing position at this time. I bore the brunt of their animosity, as they did not know who my fellows were. Yet they could not imprison or torture me, for I would immediately be trumped out of their hands. And if they were to kill me, they realized there might well be a reprisal by parties unknown. So it had to stand as a stalemate for a time. They also saw that I could no longer move directly against them. They kept me under heavy surveillance." (SU, 154–55)

In fact, Eric's group was in a very delicate situation. On the one hand, they did not want to appear as cold-blooded murderers. On the other hand, they knew that Brand had powers they didn't quite understand, and he was highly dangerous. They assumed that Brand's cohorts were associated with the Courts of Chaos, and Brand had obtained his powers from there. Thus, putting him in a dungeon or causing him physical harm would mean awful retribution for them. These reasons caused them to reach a compromise. They would not act against Brand; but they would place him under strict house arrest. One of them, either Eric, Julian, or Caine, would watch him at all times. Three armed soldiers would be near at hand as well, but never in a directly threatening position. This was done, and Brand found himself carefully watched night and day.

With his powers over Shadow, Brand could have escaped at almost any time. However, there would be no point in escaping into the shadowlands. Under arrest in the Royal Palace, he could observe his enemies, learn their plans, and act at the moment their guard was down. As long as he appeared to be vulnerable, he would remain safe. It would be wise to save the revelation of his power for a critical circumstance, rather than giving it away too soon. In the meantime, while under heavy watch, there would still be brief intervals when he might summon aid from afar.

Brand used his power to call the Chaos lords with whom he had made his deal. They were willing to help by accelerating the migrations of creatures out of Shadow into Amber, but they could not help him in any more direct way. In furtive moments, Brand drew the Trumps of two other relatives who had reason to despise the Royal House of Amber. They were Delwin and Sand, the son and daughter of Harla, former wife of Oberon whose marriage had been renounced as bigamous. Brand believed their hate was so strong that they would be willing to join him against Eric. He was mistaken. They wanted nothing to do with Amber. Without an organized force and supporters who might garner popular opinion, Brand had to bide his time.

Brand's choice to remain passively in restraint paid off quite well. It was a matter of his realizing that his warders were as much prisoners as he was. He was able to observe Eric making Trump contact with their sister Flora. After several occasions when Brand overheard Eric's conversations with Flora, Brand learned a great deal: Flora was living quite comfortably in a large house financed by Eric; she resided on the shadow Earth in a place on the northeastern coast of the United States called Westchester; and for a very long time, she had been observing their brother Corwin, who owned a home in New York State, somewhere north of Flora's home.

Our knowledge of Brand's actions once he learned Corwin's location comes from various sources that Corwin had gathered up and reported in his Chronicles. Unlike any ordinary individual, it was possible for Brand to accomplish deeds while still under arrest in the Royal Palace. He called up his powers over Shadow to obtain information on Dr. Rand, also living in New York State. He then ascertained that the doctor was away in England. With his power of movement in shadows, he eluded his warders and traveled instantaneously to the shadow Earth to burglarize Dr. Rand's office and obtain the documents he needed. In addition, Brand, then using the name Brandon Corey, had Corwin committed to Porter Sanitarium. Other reports gathered by Bill Roth, Corwin's friend in that shadow, show that Brand, masquerading as Dr. Rand, had given Corwin electroshock therapy.

Fearful of just such lapses of time when Brand was not observed, Eric ordered a tightening of their surveillance. Brand found that he was never unattended from this point on. Eric may have suspected that Brand had acted against Corwin, although he had not yet learned the facts from Flora. Whatever the reason, Brand saw he was unable to act unobtrusively any longer.

Julian had reported that Brand decided to act when he learned that Corwin had escaped his confinement. Partly out of vindictiveness, Brand took action when Caine was guarding him. Sitting in his room, Brand closed his eyes in concentration. The creature that he summoned was huge, bearlike, with a face that had no analogue to any known animal. The door to Brand's room was flung open, and Caine looked upward into those horrible features. It nearly mauled Caine to death before the three armed guards managed to subdue and kill the beast. When they checked Brand's room, he was gone.

Fiona had been in infrequent contact with Brand while he was under arrest. Although she spent most of this time in the palace, they both felt it prudent that they not visit one another. Through Brand's Trump, Fiona knew that he had gone off to the shadow Earth after he discovered that Corwin was alive. It was quite a surprise, however, when he appeared in her room the next evening. There had not been any contact between them. She was simply reading in her bedroom when Brand walked in. He had stepped into the middle of the room from nothingness, she was certain. He did not walk through the wall, door, window, or anything else in the real world. He walked directly from Shadow.

When he talked of wiping clean the filth of Amber and all the worlds, Fiona grew afraid. It was to be a whole new range of worlds that he planned to create, a new order drawn out of his mind. He intended to create another Pattern, and he would be at the head of a quite different Amber. Fiona's thoughts turned to the Courts of Chaos, and Brand

responded that the lords there had already agreed to his plan. It was as if he read her mind.

After all this time, Brand was still most afraid of Corwin. He told Fiona that he had to be rid of Corwin, that all his plans would be for naught if Corwin remained alive. While he spoke of his intention to return to the shadow Earth to finish the job he had begun there, Fiona realized how wild and maniacal he had become. When he left, stepping into Shadow again, she was terrified.

On the shadow Earth, Brand returned to Albany and used his supernormal sensory skills to locate Corwin. This was several blocks from Porter Sanitarium, and Corwin had apparently run in the direction that he remembered his automobile was parked. Brand's heightened perceptions allowed him to observe Corwin as he drove, and he was also able to scan the terrain and route he was taking. Closing his eyes, concentrating, Brand stepped away from a residential street a few blocks from the sanitarium and stepped onto a grassy area partway up a mountain overlooking a lake. He reached through Shadow and retrieved a rifle and ammunition. In his mind's eye, he saw Corwin in a car, still twenty minutes away. Brand readied his rifle and waited with extreme calm.

When Corwin's car came around a curve into view, Brand aimed carefully. He waited for it to come closer so that he wouldn't miss. Corwin's death, he knew, had to appear to be accidental, and there could not be any direct link to him. Through the rifle sight, Brand could see Corwin's head. He fired, and the front and rear tires facing him exploded. Corwin was trying to control the spin, but he couldn't. The car hit the low metal rail, and the front end made a loud crunching noise. Its momentum raised it over the rail and the car sailed over the cliffside, hitting bushes and fallen branches as it went. It hit the water so violently that a normal human being would have died from the impact. Brand wasn't so sure that it had killed Corwin.

Watching the rear end of the wreck, Brand stood up and climbed down the slope, carrying his rifle. The car remained half out of the lake, and huge bubbles welled out from either side as the interior filled with water. Brand knelt suddenly when he saw movement beside the half-sunken vehicle. He saw Corwin's head and arms then, thrashing away from the wreck and beginning to swim toward the grassy shore. Corwin flung himself onto the grass beside the lake, rolled onto his back, and collapsed in exhaustion.

Slowly, Brand made his way down to his unmoving body. Corwin's eyes were closed and he was breathing shallowly. Brand saw that his head was bleeding badly and his legs were turned unnaturally. It looked as if he would be dead soon. Before Brand had a chance to decide to throw him back into the lake, he heard a siren and saw flashing lights on a vehicle rushing along the lake road. Dressed in his Amber clothing, he made an odd sight. He spoke to the police officers a moment to draw them off the track, then he whistled for his horse and rode away.

Fiona and Bleys have been unwilling to comment on how they managed to capture and restrain Brand so successfully after this incident. They have indicated that they were on Brand's trail when he left Amber to kill Corwin. Either Bleys or Fiona was at the scene and saw Brand cause the auto accident. It was probable that Fiona used Brand's Trump to contact him again, pretending that she was in danger from their enemies. Having yet some honest compassion for his sister, Brand apparently was taken in by Fiona's pleas to be rescued. When he attempted it, Bleys and a team of beings out of Shadow attacked and subdued him. Upon his recovery, Brand found himself securely chained in a high tower. Standing, he could make out the landscape. It was an unsettling shadow, quite literally. Enormous boulders swirled around the tower like cloud drifts, and the sky was alight from some unnatural source.

He didn't see Bleys or Fiona again. He was fed by guards with strange spikelike growths on their hands. They were armed with swords and daggers, and they were unwilling to speak, unwilling to listen. Brand realized they were utterly noncompliant and would not bend to his efforts of persuasion. He struggled when they held him down and drugged him, but soon he forgot the passage of time as he drifted in and out of consciousness.

His imprisonment was a long, lonely one, and he spent most of it in semiconsciousness. Unlike Eric and company, his new captors understood much of the extent of his powers. The guards were particularly adept at handling him without emotion; they fed and washed him as needed, and they kept him drugged at a consistent level, never allowing him enough awareness to build a defensive incantation.

In spite of the special care he received, Brand was still able to signal for help. At one point, he felt a slight, undefined sensation and realized someone was trying a Trump contact. As it became stronger, he recognized his brother Corwin. Brand writhed against his chains, struggled to clear his foggy mind, as he cried out to Corwin. He thought his brother had heard him, but Brand lapsed again into unconsciousness.

Sometime before that incident, however, Brand determined to send a signal that might reach a brother. It was shortly after he had been imprisoned in the tower, so he still held on to a good deal of his strength. His sending, though, depended on his choosing someone specific, someone who would be willing to rescue him and be in a position to do so. He couldn't put his trust in Eric, Julian, Caine, or Flora. Corwin, Bleys, and Fiona were out. Llewella and Deirdre were really in no position to help, and they might have taken sides with Eric anyway. That left Benedict, Gérard, or Random. Gérard was likely on Eric's side, and Benedict had long ago received visits from Julian and Gérard in his Avalon, so he would probably not be interested in helping Brand. That left only Random. It had been a long time since Random had left Rebma, and he seemed not to have taken sides yet. At any rate, Brand didn't see that he had too many other choices.

Pretending sleep, Brand concentrated, rousing all his energies to the task. He thought of Random, trying to find an element on which to focus. He searched for the proper element, a Trump of some kind. An image slowly formed, then became clearer. He had focused on a playing card in a card game, and Random was there. Using the power of the Pattern and other forces within him, Brand thrust himself into the Jack of Diamonds in Random's hand. From there, he could see Random's face, signal him directly, communicate.

Although Random was, at first, unwilling to receive the contact, Brand was able to strengthen the sending so that his brother couldn't ignore it. He reached Random, told him his plight, and was able to show him some of the landscape of the shadow through the barred window. Then he weakened, lost the strength to maintain the signal, and collapsed. At least, he knew that he had reached Random, and Random would take some kind of action.

Shortly after his sending, Brand groggily awoke to the loud noise of movement from rooms near and below him. Standing, he momentarily glimpsed a huge, transparent snake lifting its enormous head outside the window. He sensed rather than saw the commotion beyond. It seemed to be a rescue attempt, but Brand felt an ache of despair. He knew it was no good. Soon it was quiet again, and he stretched out on the rock floor to rest.

For all he knew, ages may have passed as he remained chained in his cell. Waking moments seemed rare as he succumbed more and more to the peace of a drugged sleep. The contact, when it came, tugged at him like someone shaking him roughly from slumber. He looked up to see the images of several of his brothers and sisters. He recognized Gérard and Random and, yes! Corwin. He held out his hand, felt a strong clasp, and then his weakness overcame him and he fell back.

Brand's eyes opened weakly again when he felt himself lifted. He was free of his chains, and he was held up by Gérard. He saw the image of the others reaching though Shadow to grasp them. Because Brand didn't have his footing, it felt like a sliding motion as he was dragged from the rock-hewn cell to a comfortably familiar room of the Royal Palace. The others crowded around him and he almost smiled, but he panicked, tried to push away ineffectually upon seeing Fiona. A hot flash of pain burned into him, and he lost consciousness.

When he recovered, he found himself in Gérard's care, resting on a couch in the library. He asked Gérard what had happened, and Gérard filled him in. When Brand heard he had been knifed, he remembered seeing it occur. He asked about Corwin, who had also been in the room during his rescue. Gérard told him that Corwin now ruled in Amber. None too successfully, he added. Their brother Caine had been killed, and Gérard held Corwin in suspicion for it. Listening quietly, Brand said with sudden excitement that he had to see Corwin right away. When Gérard tried to calm him, wanting him to rest, Brand insisted. He had to see Corwin immediately.

Shortly, Corwin and Random appeared at the doorway to the library. As soon as he saw Corwin, Brand sensed he had been hurt, too. He insisted that he speak with Corwin alone, and that it was unnecessary for Gérard to check him for weapons. Reluctantly, Gérard left them alone.

Brand chose to play the scene calmly, taking a measure of his long-absent brother while he talked. He put off saying too much, even asking Corwin for a cigarette to help forestall matters. When he

finally began, it was at a point that Corwin should have already learned: the conflict between their father and Eric. It was important that Corwin feel sympathetic toward Brand, even at one with him, because they had both been wronged. Brand told him of his conspiracy with Bleys and Fiona. Although Brand could be accused of complicity, according to the story he told, the organizers of their cabal were Fiona and Bleys. He had objected at every turn to each criminal act, but the vote was against him. When Corwin had his auto accident, Brand had tried to save him, to his undoing. As a consequence, his former comrades captured him and placed him in the tower. Then Brand told him of the strange creatures that had been coming out of the black road, and their connection to the conspiracy that Fiona was behind. He impressed upon Corwin that this was now his main problem, and Corwin had best deal with it soon. He suggested that Corwin seek out further answers by going to the ghost city in the sky, Tir-na Nog'th. A way of resolving the problem may reveal itself there. Claiming fatigue then, Brand leaned back to sleep.

Brand truthfully needed the rest. He was terribly weak and in pain from his wound. The drugs in his system still muddled his mind so that he often could not think clearly. After a couple of days, he found himself recovering rapidly. When he did, he realized he was in an ideal situation. Gérard kept him informed of happenings, and he was met with great sympathy by everyone he met in the palace.

As soon as he felt better, he asked about Corwin. Gérard had no news for him. Then Brand began dressing himself, saying he was well enough to walk around. While Gérard stayed with him, Brand began taking walks in the gardens outside the palace. He continued to ask about Corwin, and was told that he hadn't yet returned. It shouldn't have taken Corwin so long to conclude the business of Tir-na Nog'th. Brand wondered if somehow Fiona, or one of her Chaos friends, got to him. With Corwin out of the way, the Chaos lords might circumvent Brand and take control of Amber themselves, or even delegate it to Fiona. When Brand heard that Corwin had returned, spoken to Random's blind wife, slept, and gone away again, he was somewhat relieved, but also annoyed. It seemed as if Corwin was trifling with him, and he wasn't willing to be ignored.

He stormed to Gérard to demand that he contact Corwin. Gérard tried reaching him on his Trump, but could get no response. Brand could hardly control his rage, and Gérard handed him a deck so that he could try himself. His own irritation may have interfered with his attempt to raise Corwin, for he felt more of his skills returning besides the mere Trump sending. Nevertheless, Corwin seemed beyond any sending.

In his moodiness, Brand took to his own room and avoided the company of others. A few days later, Gérard reached him by Trump from another part of the palace. Corwin was back and on his way to see him. Brand was still annoyed about Corwin's going away without keeping him informed, and he expressed his annoyance when Corwin arrived. When Corwin countered him, Brand made amends and explained his irritability as coming out of concern for his brother's welfare. Corwin confronted him with the Trump he had drawn of Martin. It was time for apparent honesty, so Brand admitted doing the deed to allow access for the creatures of Chaos. He attempted to persuade Corwin to give him the Jewel of Judgment to help him to subdue Fiona at the Courts of Chaos. Corwin seemed nearly convinced that the brothers and sisters remaining in the Royal Palace should gather to focus their attention on Bleys and Fiona, just as they had done when rescuing Brand. Only by killing Bleys and Fiona through their combined contact would they be free of much of the danger. Brand was surprised to find that Corwin was not in agreement. He left Brand without explaining what he intended to do.

Since Brand no longer kept counsel with Gérard, and no one else had been made privy to Brand's activities, we know nothing of his actions in this brief span. Whatever other concerns Brand may have had, primary among them would have been obtaining the Jewel of Judgment. It was the only method for creating a new Pattern, and he may have had some inkling of Corwin's intention to use the Jewel to repair the primal Pattern.

Something happened that interfered with any immediate plans Brand may have had. Someone had gotten to his room and fought viciously with Brand. Furniture was broken up, and there was blood in various areas. Gérard discovered this and immediately thought Corwin was behind it. Still, there were no bodies to be found, so it seemed possible that Brand had survived the attack.

In his Chronicles, Corwin recounted incidents that followed relating to Brand's search for the Jewel.

Corwin was just a step behind Brand, who traveled to the shadow Earth to locate it. It was possible for Brand to learn of the Jewel's location, hidden in the compost heap behind Corwin's home in New York, by tuning in to Corwin's thoughts sometime after his rescue from the tower. Posing as a potential buyer, Brand introduced himself to Corwin's friend, Bill Roth. He learned from Roth that the contractor had dumped the contents of the compost heap on an uncultivated portion of his farm. He visited the contractor and asked if he could paint the landscape on his farmland. Under that guise, Brand was able to retrieve the Jewel and return to Amber to walk the Pattern. It was necessary that he become attuned to the Jewel before he could inscribe a new Pattern.

When Brand entered the chamber of the Pattern within the Royal Palace, he saw Gérard standing at the beginning of the Way. Gérard called to him, but Brand disappeared again. In some manner, Fiona had discovered what Brand was up to and contacted Corwin with news she was certain about. She told Corwin that Brand intended to try the primal Pattern.

Fiona and Corwin reached the primal Pattern to see Brand, with the Jewel, already negotiating the walk. Before Corwin stepped onto the Pattern himself, he and Fiona saw that Brand had killed the tame griffin that guarded it. Even before he put his foot on the Pattern, Corwin knew the danger of the darkened area. It was a risk he chose to take, as he followed Brand and began the walk. Corwin found a way to cut through the blotted area, using his sword Grayswandir. The blot did not hinder Brand. As Fiona had explained, "The dark area would not trouble him the way it would another of us. He has come to terms with that darkness." (HO, 143)

Reaching a position near enough to Brand, Corwin went after him with his blade. It was an unnatural sword fight because they could not lunge or move as they normally would, needing to maintain their proper footing on the Pattern. Corwin had an additional concern: he could not harm Brand on the Pattern and take the chance of having his blood damage it further. If he was to kill Brand, it would have to be within the area of the blot. Since he was already attuned to the Jewel, Corwin exerted his influence over it, even though it was in Brand's possession. Brand found himself in danger of being destroyed by a dark red funnel of hurricane proportions, descending on him. He turned away from Corwin, stepped onto the blotted area, raised his hands, and shouted an incantation. His form seemed to flatten, then fade and grow small. He disappeared within the blot.

While Brand had not completed the attunement or his walk, he had another way to transfer out of the Pattern. He used the dark area which was tied to the Courts of Chaos. Dara had described it as a "reverberation effect" that allowed his escape to the Courts. He was exhausted from his ordeal, so he rested in a shadow near the Courts where time flowed much faster than in Amber. It was a way of recuperating sufficiently so that he could attempt the only remaining avenue to him. He had to take the Pattern of Tir-na Nog'th that night.

He may have taken counsel with the lords of Chaos, or he may have come to his conclusions alone. In any case, he acted with the realization that the Pattern of the ghost city would have its protector, and the princes of Amber knew of his ability to move instantaneously in Shadow. No matter who watched the Pattern there, Brand recognized the need to appear at the place where the Pattern ended rather than at the point of beginning. At nightfall, this he did.

Benedict was there, at the beginning of the Pattern. From the opposite end, Brand smiled, spoke calmly, and urged him to join him in the new world he was going to create. He continued talking, stepping closer, coming around the Pattern. As he spoke, Brand was aware that Corwin was listening in on a Trump, but that didn't matter. It was Benedict's attention that he wanted. He held the Jewel in his hand as he tried to persuade Benedict that he could learn the secrets of the universe if he allied himself with Brand. Benedict would have none of it, and Corwin couldn't understand why Brand even bothered.

Suddenly, in mid-sentence, Benedict was paralyzed. Brand had been testing the power of the Jewel, approaching Benedict slowly, until his influence could affect his brother's nervous system. Benedict was unable to move. Brand brought out a dagger and moved toward Benedict. He thrust it at Benedict when something unforeseen occurred. Benedict's metallic right arm moved, grasped the Jewel around Brand's neck, and lifted him above the ground by the chain. Brand was choking to death.

He reached for the chain, grasped it tightly in both hands, and pulled. When the chain broke, he fell from Benedict's stranglehold. The ghost city was fading, and anything solid within it would drop to the sea. He heard Corwin's voice and dimly saw Benedict's slight movement toward the suddenly appearing arm. A moment later, Brand fell from the disappearing ghost image of the city.

Of course, there is no way to ascertain what happened to Brand, but some actions can be inferred from events that occurred subsequently. It is likely that Brand had the means to return to the Courts of Chaos, and then he helped to prepare the way for the Patternfall battle. King Oberon had returned to the throne of Amber, and Fiona and Bleys had given their alliance to him once again. That meant that Brand, alone of the conspirators, continued to act on behalf of the Chaos lords. Even Dara the Younger had joined with Oberon against the forces of Chaos. Still, it is virtually impossible to determine the specific actions undertaken by Brand. He may have done little more than report to the lords at the Courts before going off again into Shadow. He may even have used his powers to watch events in Amber, learn of new alliances, and overhear Oberon's plans for saving Amber and rallying their troops at the Courts.

When Corwin followed his father's orders, taking a hellride to the Courts, Brand followed him through the shadows. Once Corwin received the Jewel of Judgment from his father's messenger, a large red bird, Brand made his presence known at several junctures. Initially, he attempted to confine Corwin, mounted on his horse, to a small area of Shadow; then, a little later, he tried to use persuasion to get the Jewel from him in a forest of another shadow. Brand may have seen Oberon attempt to repair the primal Pattern, for he tried to convince Corwin that Oberon had died in the process. In their debate, Brand explained how Corwin could help attune him to the Jewel and that Brand would have a better chance to inscribe a new Pattern because he knew how to handle the forces of Chaos that would offer resistance. In spite of Brand's persuasive arguments, Corwin refused to give up the Jewel. Not ready to fight Corwin just yet, Brand retreated into the woods and disappeared.

In a shadow of red-tinged mountains, Corwin was assaulted by Brand in deadly earnest. Brand killed Corwin's mount with a shaft from his crossbow, and then he fired at Corwin. When it looked as if Brand had the upper hand, about to fire an arrow directly at Corwin, the red bird that had brought the Jewel attacked Brand. It scratched out Brand's left eye, and both man and bird faded into nothingness before Corwin could reach them.

Corwin didn't see Brand again for a long while. It wasn't until Corwin completed the inscription of a new Pattern of his own that Brand reappeared. Corwin had collapsed in exhaustion at the center of the new Pattern when Brand suddenly appeared before him and grabbed the Jewel out of his hand. Corwin was too weak to offer any resistance. He saw Brand smiling at him, a black eyepatch over his left eye. Brand had power that seemed to exceed even the power of the Pattern, since he was able to teleport directly to the center without needing to walk it.

Brand hit and kicked his brother, then said, "Well, you've done it . . . I did not think you could. Now I have another Pattern to destroy before I set things right. I need this to turn the battle at the Courts first, though . . . Good-bye for now." (CC, 98)

When Brand disappeared with the Jewel, Corwin thought all was lost. It took him several moments to realize that, having inscribed this new Pattern and reached its center, he could have it send him anywhere he wished. He would go to the battlefield outside of the Courts, and he was certain that he would find Brand there, with the Jewel of Judgment. Corwin closed his eyes, channeled his thoughts on remembered images of the Courts of Chaos, and found himself transported there.

He next saw Brand on the heights above the battle, near the abyss of Chaos. Using the glowing Jewel suspended from his neck, Brand was drawing energy from the approaching storm of annihilation to throw bolts of lightning at Amber's army. As soon as he recognized Brand, Corwin, on a newly acquired charger, headed in his direction. Corwin saw that others had recognized Brand also, and they were riding ahead of Corwin toward Brand. This group was led by Fiona, and Corwin also saw Random, Deirdre, and a knight dressed in green riding quickly toward Brand's position.

Brand saw the others' approach, but Corwin had been too far away to be seen. With the Jewel in his hand, Brand darkened the sky above the riders approaching him and sent out thunder and lightning upon them. Some of the riders that followed the vanguard were killed, but Corwin's kin had sur-

vived, perhaps aided by a warding spell Fiona used. Brand moved back, under a rocky ledge that half hid him. Before Brand could attempt another maneuver, he felt an odd tugging motion, then his feet dragged awkwardly in front of him as he was pulled from behind invisibly. The heels in his riding boots burned as he was dragged up the mountainside with great speed. He glimpsed Random, Fiona, and Deirdre as he was pulled toward the cliff edge, and he threw out his right arm toward the group. It was a casting spell, and Deirdre was impelled toward Brand before anyone could prevent it. Fiona halted her gesture before Brand could topple over the edge. He cursed loudly, caught Deirdre as she fell within his reach, and she screamed.

Holding a dagger at Deirdre's throat, Brand ordered the others to put down their weapons and move away. They stood at a virtual stalemate, until the sky brightened through means other than Brand's actions. The clouds grew bright and closed on one another in the sky. They formed a face, the face of Oberon, and it spoke in quiet tones. He told them that the choice of his successor would be decided "on the horn of the Unicorn" (CC, 113). The voice said:

"I will send the Jewel of Judgment to Corwin as soon as I have finished with it. I have charged him to bear it to the place of conflict. All of your efforts there will be as nothing if the wave of Chaos cannot be averted. But with the Jewel, in that place, Corwin should be able to preserve you until it passes." (CC, 113)

The face in the sky slowly dissipated and then was gone.

After a moment of stillness, Brand, still holding Deirdre, told them to leave him alone, that he had work to do. Fiona asked if he would help them by turning the storm away with the Jewel. He reminded her of her actions against him, and Random tried to reconcile past recriminations. Brand declined to accept any offer given him and ordered them again to put down their weapons. He told them that if Fiona didn't release him from her spell, he would kill Deirdre.

When Random challenged Brand's threat with the fact that all of them would die when the storm swept over them, Brand made him an odd promise:

"Do you honestly think I am going to let you die? I need you—as many of you as I can save. Hopefully Deirdre, too. You are the only ones who can appreciate my triumph. I will preserve you through the holocaust that is about to begin.

"... You know me well enough to know that I will want to rub your noses in it. I want you as witnesses to what I do. In this sense, I require your presence in my new world."
(CC, 114)

Maddened by their refusal to leave him alone, Brand vehemently ordered them to go. Corwin chose that moment to act. Exerting his influence over the Jewel in Brand's possession, he caused Brand's body to become hot, so hot that he was like a human torch. In horrible agony and hatred, Brand slashed Deirdre's face. Her face bloody, Deirdre bit into his hand and she was able to free herself from his grasp. Before he could recover, a silver-tipped arrow flew into his throat, followed by another that pierced his heart. Wide-eyed, emitting awful gargling sounds, Brand began to lose his balance at the precipice. In a last desperate move, he grabbed Deirdre's hair, clutched it tightly, and began to topple into the abyss. He died, taking his sister with him.

While the Family recovered the Jewel of Judgment soon after this, the repercussions of Brand's death would continue over the course of many years. During the reign of King Random, the Family learned of Brand's son, who plagued the son of Corwin for years, always on April 30. That was the day Rinaldo heard of his father's death. Rinaldo revenged his father by assassinating the man who fired the silver-tipped arrows, and that act seemed sufficient to bring the great problem of Brand's terrible influence to a conclusion.

BRUTUS STORAGE COMPANY

A warehouse in San Francisco on shadow Earth where a cache of specialized ammunition and rifles was kept. It was discovered that the ammunition, though inert on shadow Earth, could be fired in Amber. The agents who owned the company in-

tended using the weapons as part of a mercenary assault on the true city.

The warehouse was a dirty four-story building located on a shabby street on the east side of San Francisco. Brutus Storage was on the first two floors, and the two upper stories were occupied by an artist named Victor Melman. It was this seemingly innocuous connection between the artist and Brutus Storage that led Merlin, son of Corwin of Amber, to some sinister associations.

Without knowing anything about the business of Brutus Storage, Merlin had gone to the building to question Melman about his former girlfriend, Julia Barnes. In a large sense, Merlin was investigating a murder mystery, and the warehouse soon became a mystery in itself. In fact, the ramifications of the products stored there caused Merlin to involve King Random of Amber in the investigation.

After the death of Victor Melman, Merlin returned to the building and found that it had been destroyed in a fire. Little more than burned-out ruins remained. As it happened, Merlin began speaking to a young boy who was nearby. The boy saw the fire, and after it was over, he and some friends found a number of cartridges. Showing Merlin some of them, the boy smashed a rock into one. Contrary to expectation, the bullet didn't explode. The boy pointed out that instead of gunpowder, there was a pinkish substance in the smashed shell casing. Merlin gave the boy a dollar bill for two of the cartridges.

Before reporting these facts to King Random, Merlin pursued a friend of his, Luke Raynard, in Santa Fe, New Mexico. Aside from other intriguing facts he learned, Merlin found a similar cartridge in one of Luke's pants pockets and kept it. They were all .30 caliber shells.

In Amber, Random tried out the cartridges, using one of the rifles that Merlin's father had used long ago in an attempt to take control of Amber. Not only did the two bullets found at Brutus Storage fire, but the third that had been in Luke's possession also fired. Giving the problem a high priority, Random decided to ask his sister Flora to investigate further by setting up shop in San Francisco.

Flora's inquiries yielded some interesting data, but were ultimately inconclusive in and of themselves. The warehouse had been owned by Brutus Storage Company and Victor Melman had rented the upper stories from them. The company was owned by J.B. Rand, Inc., in Sausalito, California. The office of J.B. Rand had been vacated two months earlier. The owners of the building that housed J.B. Rand had only a post office box as an address, and that, too, had been vacated. Flora's search had ended there in a dead end.

However, several factors clicked into place after that, and eventually Merlin learned the truth from his friend Luke Raynard. The agents who formed J.B. Rand, Inc., were related to Brand of Amber, the prince who had at one time attempted to destroy Amber. Brand had used an ironic amalgam of his name when he posed as a psychiatrist in order to remove Corwin from his path. J.B. Rand made use of the same kind of irony, for the "J" was a clue to the identity of one of the agents.

On a later occasion, Luke told Merlin that the warehouse had been deliberately burned down by a mercenary named Dalt. It was done in order to hide the fact that Dalt stole the weapons for the purpose of attempting an assault on Amber with a band of highly trained mercenaries.

Although these weapons were never used against Amber, Luke had joined Dalt in an unsuccessful attempt against a fortress known as the Keep of the Four Worlds. They had depended on the special ammunition to work in that place, but the weapons had no more firepower there than on shadow Earth.

CABALISTIC TREE OF LIFE

A well-executed, spiritual painting that Victor Melman showed to Merlin Corey. Although Melman was an artist, this painting was different in style from the others in his studio. Melman launched a sorcerous attack against Merlin by means of the painting.

The Tree of Life, composed of ten sephira, represents the way that Jewish mystics form a communion with the Infinite Being of God. The sephira are qualities of the Infinite Being, called the En-Sof. By meditating on the sephira, the mystic attains a spiritual oneness with the En-Sof.

As depicted in the Zohar, the canonical text of the Cabala, the Tree of Life is less like a tree and more like a series of circular plates held together by rods. When the cabalist contemplates the ten

sephira, he voices and gives thought to the top trinity of "plates" first, then proceeding down. These first three are Keter = Exalted Height; Hokmah = Wisdom; and Binah = Intellect. Together, they make up the intelligible world. The next three are Pahad = Awe; Hesed = Mercy; and Tif'eret = Beauty. They form the moral or "soul" world. The last triad are Nezah = Triumph; Hod = Glory; and Yesod = Foundation. These constitute the natural world. The tenth sephiroth is Malkut = Dominion, which is the unifying force that brings together the worlds of will, plan, and activity. Enlightenment and deep communion come with completing the circuit of all ten sephira.

In the painting that Merlin viewed in Victor Melman's apartment, each of the ten sephira depicted images of dark or evil qualities, aspects of man's relation to the En-Sof that involve sin and fallen ways. That is what Merlin was referring to when he described the sephira as revealing "some of their qlipphotic aspects" (TD, 34).

Melman pointed out the third sephiroth, Binah, representing the Intellect. Normally, Binah is the passive feminine principle within that first triad. However, in its qlipphotic mode depicted in his painting, that circle showed a cowled wizard standing before a dark and shadowed altar.

As Merlin focused on the sephiroth, the figure changed, becoming real. Merlin realized that the painted image was acting exactly like a Trump contact. Before he could avoid it, Merlin was there, and the image had become a real place.

> It was a place of twilight, a small glade in a twisted wood. An almost bloody light illuminated the slab. The wizard, his face hidden by cowl and shadow, manipulated objects upon the stone, his hands moving too rapidly for me to follow. . . .
> Finally, he raised a single object in his right hand and held it steady. It was a black, obsidian dagger. He laid his left arm upon the altar and brushed it across the surface, sweeping everything else to the ground.
> He looked at me for the first time.
> "Come here," he said then. (TD, 34–35)

Caught in the wizard's summoning spell, Merlin countered with an offensive spell that hurt the wizard momentarily. It allowed Merlin to topple the stone altar onto the wizard. The cowled figure reappeared behind the altar, chanting another spell that Merlin could feel growing. Merlin summoned an icy wind that eradicated the wizard's spell. The wizard's cowl fell then, revealing him to be Melman. Fearful, Melman called to some unknown master, but there was no response. As Melman tried to flee, Merlin brought forth his most devastating incantation, ending all of the reality around them save a small island in darkness on which they stood.

Trapped in this way, Melman answered Merlin's questions. He told of an unnamed master who had done the painting of the Tree of Life. His master had told him that if he could sacrifice Merlin on the altar within the painting, he would gain Merlin's powers. Melman claimed that he actually visited the place of each sephiroth and acquired supernatural powers in so doing. Unfortunately, his lust for these powers urged him to make a final attack on Merlin. Victor Melman ended his quest by falling into the nothingness of Chaos.

After leaving the disintegrating world of the sephiroth, Merlin found himself in a narrow alleyway some distance from Melman's building. He walked back, examined Melman's rooms, and burned the painting of the Cabalistic Tree in the bathtub. No one else would ever gain enlightenment from that particular source.

CADE

Secretary to Ambassador Quist of the Begman Embassy in Amber.

A youngish man, Cade is anxious to please the ambassador. He performs his duties with meticulous care. When accompanying the ambassador on public occasions, he tends to seek assurance from her, needing her attentions like a small boy seeking the support of his mother. For all that, he is a competent young fellow, if perhaps overeager in performing tasks assigned to him.

Cade would have remained by Ambassador Quist's side throughout her entire visit to the Royal Palace in Amber if seating arrangements at dinner had not separated them. The young man was seated between Martin, son of King Random, and Nayda, the older daughter of Prime Minister Orkuz. Suppo-

sition would have it that Cade would feel uncomfortable sandwiched in by the offspring of such important figures in the current political arena. He tended to talk more with Nayda at dinner, and he was curious about the conversational rapport she had established with Merlin, son of Corwin. When he found an opening, Cade bent toward Merlin and asked, "What are your views of the Eregnor situation, Lord Merlin?" (SC, 127) He was mightily surprised to feel a sudden kick in the leg, and he stared openmouthed for a moment at Nayda. Cade felt his personal embarrassment lessen somewhat with Merlin's response: "I'm sure there are things to be said for both sides of most matters." (SC, 127) Nayda's eyes turned from the young secretary, and both she and Cade seemed to fall into more relaxed postures.

Secretary Cade remained quietly out of the limelight for the remainder of their stay in the Royal Palace. His visit may have been quite memorable for him, however. It is reported that, since that time, Cade has been an admirer of Lord Merlin and began a carefully researched file on him.

CAINE

Son of Oberon and Faiella, born after Corwin and Eric. Caine had been a seafaring man most of his adult life. When King Oberon had unaccountably disappeared, he threw his support to Eric to rule as regent. He had begun to feel suspicious of Brand at that time, deciding to join Eric and Julian to form an alliance to oppose Brand. After pretending his own death, Caine revealed himself at the Patternfall battle, slaying Brand with two silver-tipped arrows. Brand's son succeeded in avenging his father's death on Caine.

His dress reflected his rakishness and his interest in seafaring adventurers in the Lord Admiral Nelson mold. A dark, lean man, Caine often wore a satin uniform of black and green, with a three-cornered hat trailing a green plume of feathers upon his head. The emerald-studded dagger that he kept in his belt had a scribble of the Pattern etched into its blade. It's likely that he carried an ordinary dagger with him when he first walked the Pattern in Amber, thus giving it that special endowment.

Although his older brother Corwin felt ambivalent

about him, Caine hated Corwin. When they were youths, Corwin had arranged some undisclosed trickery that embarrassed Caine immensely in front of a young lady in his company. Whatever the specifics, Caine never forgave his brother.

Like his older brothers, Caine served in Amber's navy. Sailing and the sea became his first love. In his Chronicles, Corwin spoke of his fascination for the sea, but his thoughts apply with even more emphasis to Caine:

> Amber is not noted for manufacture, and agriculture has never been our forte. But our ships sail the shadows, plying between anywhere and anywhere, dealing in anything. Just about every male Amberite, noble or otherwise, spends some time in the fleet. Those of the blood laid down the trade routes long ago that other vessels might follow, the seas of a double dozen worlds in every captain's head. I [Corwin] had assisted in this in times gone by, and though my involvement had never been so deep as Gérard's or Caine's, I had been mightily moved by the forces of the deep and the spirit of the men who crossed it. (HO, 50)

Caine found solace in the sea. He visited numerous shadows, traveling their seaways and learning navigation skills at their institutes. He fell so naturally into that way of life that, early in his career, his father gave him charge of the royal navy.

At a time when Brand became very candid with Corwin about his past actions, he described the growth of the two cabals vying for the throne of Amber, and Caine's part in them:

> "If Julian gave us the land route in, or Caine the waves, we could have transported the troops with dispatch and held the day by force of arms, should that have proven necessary. Unfortunately, I chose the wrong man. In my estimate, Caine was Julian's superior in matters of corruption. So, with measured delicacy I sounded him on the matter. He seemed willing to go along with things, at first. But he either reconsidered subsequently or deceived me quite skillfully from the beginning. Naturally, I prefer to believe that it was the former. Whatever, at some point he [Caine] came to the conclusion that he stood to benefit more by supporting

a rival claimant. To wit, Eric. Now Eric's hopes had been somewhat dashed by Dad's attitude toward him—but Dad was gone, and our intended move gave Eric the chance to act as defender of the throne. Unfortunately for us, such a position would also put him but a step away from the throne itself. To make matters darker, Julian went along with Caine in pledging the loyalty of his troops to Eric, as defender. Thus was the other trio formed." (SU, 154–55)

For all of Brand's wiliness, he had misread Caine almost entirely. It can be seen, especially in retrospect, that Caine's provocations had always been directed by his personal sense of guile and need for concealment. Once, Eric had told Corwin in confidence that he believed Caine was a coward. That simply was not the case. It is just that Caine preferred to use subterfuge rather than a direct attack against opponents. If we speculate that Caine's ego constructed its base of power by employing covert means, then his activities become quite clear.

When Eric fabricated his lame story about Corwin's disappearance, Caine, like his father and siblings, suspected that Eric had dispatched him. Caine kept his own counsel for a simple reason: he would have rid himself of Corwin long ago if he had been able to do so without suspicion. Of his brothers, Caine was closest to Julian, especially in matters of a secretive nature. Julian's fears about Brand's adoption of immense supernormal powers would certainly be shared with Caine, and Caine, if a bit more cynical than Julian in fearing the unknown, would maintain a keen watchfulness of Brand.

Brand's approach put Caine on his guard. In terms of his power base, Caine could be sure that Eric was in a better position than Brand. Eric had the loyalty of the Royal Guard of the palace and was widely popular in Amber. Brand was at best an outsider, and at worst, a wanton interloper with delusions of grandeur. Naturally, Caine would prefer to ally himself with Eric, and he brought Julian into their common cause against Brand.

Eric had initially wavered so uncertainly about assuming the Protectorship of the throne that Caine was convinced that he could not have had anything to do with Oberon's disappearance. Of course, Eric had protested that he wasn't involved in the king's sudden departure. Caine believed Eric was sincere, and he conjectured that elements of the supernatural were involved. To Caine, that meant Brand was implicated. This was borne out when Brand summoned a terrible creature from Shadow, which maimed Caine badly. After his recovery, Caine had ample reason to fear and hate Brand.

Concealment and deceit were Caine's watchwords. He had used them on Brand, and he used them again on Corwin. When Corwin contacted him by Trump, Caine was genuinely surprised, but he camouflaged it well. He had heard from others in the palace that Corwin had faced Eric in a duel in the library. Eric refused to speak of it, but Caine had noted the bandages on Eric's arm. Corwin, apparently, was still formidable.

In their Trump contact, Caine agreed to permit the invasionary fleet of Bleys and Corwin into Amber. Caine intimated that his own vessels would join them. Before concluding the contact, Caine told Corwin: "If you fail, there'll be three beheadings in Amber." (NP, 107) It was sheer treachery. No doubt it pleased Caine to meet the incursion of the enemy fleet headed by Corwin off Amber's seacoast. His hatred of Corwin had not waned, and Corwin's partnership with Bleys suggested a complicity with Brand, as well.

Caine observed the sea battle from his flagship. He was surprised to lose so many of his own vessels and men to Corwin. He marveled at the tenacity of the man, although that didn't lessen his loathing. Nevertheless, he gave Corwin leave to address his men, allowing them to surrender without further harm. Perhaps that allowance was a tactical mistake on Caine's part. It gave Corwin the opportunity to escape capture by trumping to Bleys. Caine suffered for that error. After Corwin had been blinded and tossed into a dungeon, the newly crowned Eric gave Gérard the admiralty of the fleet, instead of offering it to Caine.

In the battle with the beasts out of Shadow on Mt. Kolvir, Caine headed one company along the face of the mountain. Corwin had brought a fresh army and rifles able to fire in Amber. Corwin recounted:

As we had advanced, firing, the forces of Amber quickly realized that we represented assistance and began to push forward from their position at the base of the cliff. I saw that they were being led by my brother Caine. For a

moment our eyes locked together across the distance, then he plunged ahead into the fray. (GA, 213)

He was so involved in the fighting that he was probably not aware of it when Eric had been mortally wounded. Gérard and his company had been coordinating with Eric higher up the mountain when Eric was injured by a Chaos man riding a wyvern. When Caine did learn of Eric's death, it may have concerned him less than the fact that Corwin had taken over the rule of Amber. Early in Corwin's reign, Caine perpetrated his greatest deception.

Believing that Corwin might have been conspiring with Brand to work the overthrow of Amber, Caine initiated an insidious plan to prove Corwin's duplicity. He visited a shadow in which a shadow of himself existed. After waylaying and murdering the shadow Caine, he planted the body in the Grove of the Unicorn, then sent a note to Corwin requesting a meeting there. Somehow, Caine provided an assassin for Corwin to find, a man from the same shadow, or a shadow sufficiently close, to the one that Bleys had frequented. The blame would surely fall upon Corwin for his death, and the assassin would show a link between Corwin and Bleys, implicating Corwin in that cabal. Meanwhile, Caine could use his unusual circumstances to good advantage.

At Patternfall, Caine explained how he proceeded:

"I lay low then and listened in on the Trumps to everything everyone said, hoping for a clue as to Brand's whereabouts. . . .

". . . I had learned to be completely passive about it. I had taught myself to deal them all out and touch all of them lightly at the same time, waiting for a stirring. When it came, I would shift my attention to the speakers. Taking you one at a time, I even found I could sometimes get into your minds when you were not using the Trumps yourselves—if you were sufficiently distracted and I allowed myself no reaction." (CC, 117–18)

While he pretended to be dead, Caine took it upon himself to do away with Corwin and Brand. Using the Pattern in Amber, Caine transported himself into Corwin's locked room and waited. It's likely he had done this before the meeting of the

Family in the palace library. Sitting in Corwin's room, he listened in on the Trumps, following the course of the session. He took Corwin's suggestion that they all work together to contact Brand, and the subsequent rescue, as a confirmation that Corwin and Brand had been working together. When Corwin returned to his apartments late that night, Caine used his dagger on him with deadly intent. It seemed remarkably strange to Caine that Corwin was somehow able to escape his fatal thrust and then vanish.

Listening in to his siblings on their Trumps, Caine would have known that Corwin had visited the recovering Brand twice. It is not known how much he could have learned from the Trumps about their discussions. After the second occasion of Corwin conferring with Brand, Caine decided to end the conspiracy by taking Brand's life. He disguised himself, walked the Pattern again, and appeared in Brand's room. Their fight was terrible and bloody. Brand managed to escape by Trump, but Caine was wounded also.

During his convalescence, Caine had a score or so of hunting arrows made, their tips formed of the finest silver. He trained himself to use a bow with perfect proficiency. About the time when Corwin hellrode to shadow Earth in search of the Jewel of Judgment, after Corwin had shared information with Julian in Arden, Caine communicated with Julian. From Julian's input, Caine decided that Brand had become truly dangerous, and Corwin was apparently acting to oppose him.

Caine kept in close contact with Julian then, and learned of King Oberon's return and his orders to commence a battle at the Courts of Chaos. Donning a suit of armor the color of jade, he joined Julian and his patrol in the Forest of Arden. When Random arrived with his orders to accompany Julian, Caine kept his visor down and stayed in the background.

In the Patternfall battle, Caine relied on a heavy mace as he confronted the enemy, saving his quiver of silver-tipped arrows for use against one man. When Random and several others rode fast toward the distant hills of the enemy camp, Caine quickly joined in. As he rode, he saw the gleam of red in the heights, and immediately assumed that it was Brand. When Brand sent out a lightning bolt, Caine was thrown from his horse, but he was sufficiently away from the others that he wasn't hurt. He gradually made his way up one side of the hill, main-

taining his distance. He didn't want Brand to have any inkling that he was about.

Caine watched the various incidents unfold on that mount dispassionately. The appearance of his father's face in the sky, Brand's threats to kill Deirdre, Brand's mocking laughter, all were one to Caine. He had made himself devoid of feeling, and instead, concentrated on a single, deliberate act.

The moment came when Deirdre moved away from Brand's grip. Caine aimed and fired high. The arrow pierced through Brand's throat. Caine had the second arrow readied even before the first found its mark. The second arrow struck true, entering Brand's chest. Even when Deirdre fell with Brand into the Abyss, Caine couldn't find any genuine emotion within him. The act was all. Ending the danger, canceling the conspiracy, was of the greatest importance.

When Random began his rule in Amber, Caine accepted the situation with equanimity. For a while, he enjoyed the leisurely life in Amber. It is believed he met Lady Vinta Bayle during this time, drinking and carousing in the city proper. He appreciated his young brother all the more, when King Random conferred diplomatic status upon him. Caine was enormously pleased to be leading a fleet of ships out to the shadows again, at the head of an ambassadorial mission.

On one such mission, visiting a seaport city in shadow Deiga, Caine was fatally shot from a rooftop. A small service was given to him in a chapel of the unicorn on the shore of Amber. Random presided, and Gérard read passages from The Book of the Unicorn. He was buried in one of the sea caves at the foot of Mt. Kolvir, facing the sea.

CATHEDRAL OF THE SERPENT

The great Cathedral of the Serpent located at the very Rim of Chaos in the Courts of Chaos. In that sacred place, Lord Bances of Amblerash, High Priest of the Serpent, consigned the body of King Swayvill to the depths.

Located at the far end of the Plaza at the End of the World, the Cathedral looks nothing like any temple known to the shadows. It rests just above the Abyss; its function is to give a final ceremony to those honored dead before sending them over the Rim. In his journals, Merlin described the strange entrance to the Cathedral:

> . . . the massive pile of black stone at the very edge of the Pit, its gate an archway of frozen flame, as was its downward stair, each tread and riser time-barred fire, each railing the same. The rough amphitheater below us was also fire-furnished, self-illumed, facing the black block at the end of everything, no wall behind it, but the open emptiness of the Pit and its singularity whence all things came. (PC, 132)

Merlin had joined the final service for the late king in the Cathedral while Lord Bances was reading from the Book of the Serpent Hung upon the Tree of Matter. He took a seat at the rear, facing down toward the Pit, where those already seated would not have seen him enter. Adjusting his eyes to the dimly lit cavern, Merlin could see Bances standing beside the catafalque bearing Swayvill's body near the Abyss. Merlin's mother and oldest brother sat nearby, beside Prince Tubble of Chanicut. Bances began intoning the Consignment, and Dara, Mandor, and Tubble rose and approached the casket. The four lifted the casket and slipped it into a grooved track leading to the Abyss. In the meantime, a servant was snuffing out the candles that offered some dim illumination. As the last candle was put out, there was the sound of shuffling. People near the front aspirated noisily. The casket hit the floor loudly as it slid forward. Shadowy figures moved clumsily. There was a cry as the casket slid from view.

When members of the congregation helped to create some lighting, Merlin was able to see that not only was the casket of the late king gone, but Prince Tubble had gone over the Rim as well.

It was a calamity, of course. A sacrilegious act that may have been quite deliberate. However, the minions of the Courts continue to maintain the sanctity of the great Cathedral of the Serpent. It is, after all, the great dark place that all things go to eventually.

There is always reverence in oblivion.

CAVE OF BLUE CRYSTAL

A cave composed entirely of a translucent blue crystalline substance. When the cave is completely sealed, the crystal prevents Trump sendings and blocks magical forces from penetrating it. The crystal cave exists in a shadow in which the time streams are much faster than in Amber.

The location of the blue crystal cave, the blue stones that come from it, and their unique properties, are secrets retained by Jasra and her son, Rinaldo, although there is some indication that Dara of Chaos also had knowledge of them. As Jasra had explained: "The material is a kind of magical insulator, but two pieces—once together—maintain a link, by which a sensitive person can hold one and track the other." (KS, 35) In this way, a person of ordinary ability can follow another person traveling in Shadow.

Rinaldo, using the name Lucas Raynard, had made use of his family secret to secure Merlin of Amber and Chaos in a place where he couldn't escape and wouldn't be found by any of his kin. Luke was trying to gain time in order to control a magically enhanced construct that Merlin had designed. At the same time, he didn't want to harm Merlin because they had become friends. It had been a coincidence that Merle had used a Trump he possessed to bring himself and Luke from danger to the calm, grassy plain outside the crystal cave. Merle fell into unconsciousness then, and Luke placed him inside the cave.

Made up of a number of caverns connected by tunnels, the cave had only one way in or out: a hole in the ceiling of one chamber, eight feet from the floor. After Merle had recovered, Luke showed him a large cavern where Luke kept supplies. There were four large barrels of water, canned goods, cases of wine, sacks of fruits, vegetables, biscuits, and other foodstuffs. Luke included a small Coleman stove. Without giving any explanation, Luke led Merle through the caverns, pointing out a small chamber used as a latrine. When Luke started to move more quickly through several passages, Merle was hard-pressed to keep up. Following Luke's voice, Merle found him looking down from the opening in the ceiling, in a chamber with a pillow and sleeping bag. After revealing his real identity,

Luke moved a boulder of the same crystalline material to block the opening. Merle was trapped within.

Although Merle couldn't gauge how the time streams of the shadow compared to time in Amber, he was able to keep track of the passage of days by the shades of light and dark on the crystal walls.

While Merle could not make use of any magical forces from outside the blue crystal boundary, he was able to set up certain traps within the cave. He possessed a magical entity that Luke had not been aware of, and Merle arranged for a nasty surprise if Luke returned anytime soon. Escape depended on Merle's patience and maintaining his reason while he waited.

Escape came when two small dark men removed the boulder from the overhead entrance. Peering in, they fell to the mercy of Merle's Logrus powers. After disposing of them, Merle pulled himself out of the cave to freedom.

On a later occasion, Luke came under Merlin's power. Luke had been wounded by a colleague of his during a military campaign, and he contacted Merle by Trump for protection. Merle brought him to his location, the home of an acquaintance outside of the city of Amber. As Luke rested, Merle examined the Trumps he had carried. He saw that Luke had a Trump for the crystal cave.

In order to get away from an interfering agent, Merle brought Luke to the blue crystal cave. Obtaining a ladder from Shadow, Merle helped him down into the cavern. Merle brought a few of the provisions to Luke while he rested near the opening. The plan was for Luke to remain in the cave, recuperating from his injury at a faster rate than would be possible in Amber-time. Once recovered, Luke intended to rescue his mother from the Keep of the Four Worlds, with or without Merle's assistance. In return, Luke would give Merlin information vital to the welfare of Amber. Merle left him with most of his Trumps, then played at trapping Luke the way he had been trapped. He didn't block the entrance, however, and bade Luke farewell.

The Cave of Blue Crystal served as a sanctuary for Merlin a bit later. Old Dworkin had made Merle aware that the Pattern itself was seeking him out and would have destroyed him if he hadn't been wearing the Jewel of Judgment. Merle couldn't continue wearing the Jewel without suffering detrimental effects, so Dworkin had suggested he attune himself to it to maintain its protection. Feeling phys-

ically exhausted, Merle felt the need for a long rest before attempting the attunement. He chose to go to the crystal cave for a full night's sleep.

Because of the blue crystal's properties, Merle would not be bothered by a Trump contact, and it seemed unlikely that the magical forces of the Pattern and the Logrus would be able to penetrate the cave. Based on his previous experience, Merle knew that the time flow there was much faster than in Amber. A night's sleep in the cave would amount to only a couple of hours in the true city, so he would not lose much time in resting.

Once fully rested, Merle engaged in the process of traversing the Pattern within the Jewel. While magics from outside could not penetrate the substance of the cave, Merle was able to attune himself to the Jewel inside its boundaries without inhibition. After successfully completing the attunement, Merle exited from the cave and returned to Amber.

The crystal cave remains in an undisclosed shadow, one that seems to possess predators, or at least scavengers, for some animal or animals had gleaned the flesh of the two hairy men that Merle had slain. Their whitened bones were testimony that some form of animal life shared that shadow. Still, Merle hadn't found any evidence of a humanlike species intelligent enough to move the boulder from the entrance and make a home of the cave. The place continues to be a sanctuary in the event of any future needs.

CENOTAPH, CORWIN'S

The mausoleum erected by the princes of Amber centuries ago, when it was believed that Prince Corwin was dead. Although no body resided within, the structure contained a casket resting upon a raised niche in the event that Corwin's remains were ever recovered.

It is a long, low structure located in a lonely spot about two miles below the crest of Mt. Kolvir on its northern face. Ivy grew over the small building, and two stone benches were placed before it. A natural rock wall protected the structure from the weather on three sides. When first erected, two small trees and some shrubs were planted in transplanted soil around it.

On the face of the stone monument was the name ''Corwin'' and a brief inscription.

While no one remembered who first suggested erecting the cenotaph, the princes agreed that it was appropriate to do so. In that distant time, most of them knew that Corwin had been having intense arguments with his brother Eric. One day, Eric and Corwin were seen going off together. Only Eric returned. Even though it seemed very suspicious, no one voiced his suspicions. It was simply acknowledged that Corwin had disappeared.

The princes couldn't reach Corwin by Trump, and several began a widespread search for him in the realms of Shadow. They continued to try Corwin's Trump, but its continued unresponsiveness led them to believe that Corwin must have died.

At the point when King Oberon made a veiled accusation against Eric about his complicity in Corwin's demise, the princes decided they would construct the monument. Over the next few months, the structure took form. It served as confirmation that the princes agreed with their father's belief as to Corwin's passing. For some of the princes, it also established the idea that Eric would remain out of favor with the king.

After Corwin's return to Amber, he made use of the isolated place of his cenotaph for quiet meditation, and also to meet in secret with others. Perhaps some would think it irreverent, but on one occasion, after having a private talk with his companion Ganelon, Corwin chose to relieve himself beside the mausoleum.

Corwin's son Merlin also visited the site on a couple of occasions. On one of these, he went to the tomb to deliberately leave a magical artifact in the empty coffin. The artifact was a large button with a blue crystal stone set in it. Merlin had obtained it from an adversary, and he intended leaving it at his father's cenotaph as a warning. In addition, Merlin made use of its solitude in order to formulate some enchantments that he intended to unleash shortly thereafter.

The cenotaph remains as a reminder that death is always present, but its existence had permitted Corwin, for a time, at least, to laugh wryly in its face.

CHAOSIAN DEMONFORM

The appearance of those who reside in the Courts of Chaos. Most of the minions of the Courts take on a variety of altered appearances, since they are shapeshifters. Usually, though, they limit themselves to a small repertoire of forms that they use to fit a number of different occasions. It is considered good manners for a being of the Courts to change into a more human form if one or more beings they are meeting are human, or have taken on a human guise.

Merlin had grown up in the Courts, and he had written of playing with demons at the Pit of Chaos as a boy. He wrote of these playmates in terms of the form he chose to emulate: ''I always seemed to have more fun playing with demons than with my mother's relatives by blood or marriage. I even based my main Chaos form upon one of their kind'' (PC, 7).

While those of the Courts who have visited Shadow alter their shape as a courtesy to other beings, some more traditional lords prefer to remain in their demon form. This appears to be true for Merlin's uncle Suhuy. He appears rarely out of his Chaosian form: ''A large, stooped, gray and red demonic form, horned and half-scaled, regarded me with elliptically pupiled yellow eyes. Its fangs were bared in a smile.'' (PC, 14) This, we may take it, is the natural demon form of most of the lords and ladies of the Courts.

In public, the nobles of the Courts appear to take delight in transforming themselves in spectacular or unique ways. The process of shapeshifting may be as enjoyable for them as the effect itself. In his journal, Merlin cited the following instances: Gilva of the House of Hendrake transformed from a swirl of jewels to a flowerlike form to attract Merlin's attention (PC, 147); Merlin's stepbrother Mandor had been described as appearing as ''an octopal ape,'' (PC, 20) ''a tower of green light,'' (PC, 232) and ''a blue whirlwind'' (PC, 240); Dara, Merlin's mother, had been ''a lithe demonic figure'' with scales, moving in a blue cloud, (PC, 27) then she reappeared seven feet tall, ''coal-black, eyes of green flame,'' (PC, 234) and later she became ''a flower-faced cat and then a tree of green flame.'' (PC, 240) Of course, Dara had been described earlier, viewed in her changing forms by Corwin in Amber on the day Eric the Usurper had died. This is how Corwin described her as she stood within the great Pattern:

Then it was not hair, but great, curved horns from some wide, uncertain brow, whose crook-legged owner struggled to shuffle hoofs along the blazing way. Then something else . . . An enormous cat . . . A faceless woman . . . A bright-winged thing of indescribable beauty . . . A tower of ashes . . . (GA, 222)

When Merlin confronted Dara and Mandor concerning the terms of his assuming the kingship in the Courts, he insisted that the three of them assume a human form. Using a uniquely potent ring he wore, Merlin coerced both his mother and step-brother to remain humanoid. It appeared to be a breach of Chaosian decorum to prevent a Chaos lord or lady from shapeshifting, but this is precisely what Merlin did. In this instance, Mandor indicated that the human form was not entirely appealing to one of the Courts. It may have been out of irritation, but it was also revealing when Mandor said: "Kindly release me to turn back, and find a more fitting form for yourself." (PC, 233–34) Considering the powers that Mandor and Dara exhibited at this confrontation, clearly it is a dangerous thing to willfully suppress the impulses of a Chaosian to change form.

Although a Chaos lord does not lose his ability to change from a human to a demonform, the process seems to become slightly more difficult with lack of practice. This seemed to be the case for Merlin. He had taken on a human form for so long that it was easier for him to shapeshift from his Chaosian appearance to his human one than the reverse. (PC, 15; 169) Unless the occasion demanded it, Merlin preferred not to use his energies to shift into a demonform.

From the journals of Merlin, it would seem that Chaosites are reasonably tolerant and flexible in their views of others appearing in human form. They rarely point to a being in human form as an affront to their sensibilities.

CORAL

Younger daughter of Prime Minister Orkuz of Begma. In a long-ago agreement, she was wedded to Prince Rinaldo of Kashfa by their parents as a means of preparing an alliance between the two kingdoms. After Coral succeeded in walking the Pattern in Amber, she became an important factor in the age-old conflict between the two Powers.

Coral came to the attention of Merlin while he was staying in Amber. Her father was attempting a political protest of sorts by making an official visit when he knew that King Random would be absent. Orkuz was concerned about clandestine meetings between Random and members of Kashfa's nobility. Although Coral was not an official of the Begman party, she was permitted to join them because her older sister, Nayda, was acting in the capacity of her father's secretary.

As soon as she was able, Coral managed to speak to young Merlin at the reception arranged by Queen Vialle. To Merlin, she seemed a pleasant, attractive young lady. He described her in his journals as "taller than either her father or sister [Nayda], slender, her hair a reddish brown." (SC, 56–57) He was struck, almost immediately, with the feeling that she looked very familiar. Although he couldn't place her, nor had they actually met previously, as he discovered, that sensation soon proved valid.

She asked about his life, and Merlin, finding her attentions flattering, discussed aspects of his wanderings in Shadow since traveling to shadow Earth. In turn, Coral spoke of Begma and having known Rinaldo when he was a boy. She hadn't seen Rinaldo in many years, but they had known each other well when they were quite young. They had been thrown together often during state visits.

Merlin agreed to take Coral around the city, and she changed for their tour. Taking her by way of the long, natural rock stairway down Mt. Kolvir, Merlin became suspicious of her. She had unusually great strength, and she had spoken of being able to outrace Rinaldo, whom Merlin knew as Luke Raynard. It seemed possible that Coral was possessed of an incorporeal entity that had been tracking Merlin in various human guises.

When Coral asked to see inside the sea caves that led under the Royal Palace, Merlin thought it a good idea. He wanted to use a spell he had formulated that would affect the possessing entity, and there would be suitable privacy in which to attempt it in the sea caves. However, the outcome of Merlin's incantation within the caves was quite surprising. Rather than affecting Coral in any way, his spell saved him from a dangerous entrapment by his renegade half brother, Jurt. Merlin's spell disabled two animated corpses that Jurt had intended to use against him. In the process, Jurt was injured. After a brief exchange, Jurt was taken out of Merlin's reach by a Trump connection. All of this occurred as Coral quietly observed.

After a meal in town, during which Merlin told Coral of some of his personal dilemmas, Coral insisted on seeing the Pattern under the Royal Palace. In the great chamber containing the Pattern, glistening on the floor, Coral walked about its circumference admiringly. Without warning, Coral placed her foot upon the beginning of the design. Initially alarmed, Merlin was filled with wonder that Coral had not been destroyed by it. Coral explained that it had been rumored that she had been born as the result of an affair between her mother and the late King Oberon. She had never been able to verify it, but her surviving the encounter with the Pattern seemed to give verification.

Merlin guided her through the walk; for once stepping upon the design, Coral had no choice but to complete the entire circuit. Keeping her on course, Merlin realized why she had looked so familiar to him. She had the same family resemblance that all who were of Oberon's issue had.

Coral walked the circuit and stood triumphant in the center. When Merlin presented her with the fact that she could ask the Pattern to send her to any place she wished, Coral made a unique decision. She decided to let the Pattern itself choose where to send her. This worried Merlin greatly, and he warned her against it. She persisted, however, and left the choice up to the Pattern. Before the choice was fulfilled, Merlin tossed Coral his Trump so that she could reach him. Then she vanished.

This was the first instance in which Merlin discovered that the Pattern was a sentient being. After taking Coral away, the Pattern seemed to give responses to Merlin's queries as he stood in the empty chamber. Later, Merlin learned that the Logrus was also sentient, and the two Powers were engaged in a conflict that had continued for millennia. Both Powers used the human beings within their sphere as agents, manipulating them to add to their own advantage.

The Pattern kept Coral from contacting Merlin. She was kept under sedation in an entirely black realm, so that Merlin was unable to make anything more than the most tenuous of Trump contacts. When Merlin was placed in a unique realm known as the Undershadow, the Sign of the Pattern used

Coral to coerce him to give it a distinct advantage over the Logrus. The Pattern Sign led him to a chamber containing a Broken Pattern, one that was incomplete. In the center of this deficient Pattern, Merlin could discern the unconscious form of Coral. Guided by images within the Jewel of Judgment that he wore, Merlin repaired the Broken Pattern and made love to the sedated girl. They were returned to the Amber we are familiar with.

In Merlin's bedchamber in the Royal Palace, Coral was curious about the spell that her sister was placed under. Because she removed a magical ball that had kept Nayda restrained, Coral set off a chain of events that led to an explosive confrontation between the Powers. The Signs of the Logrus and the Pattern actually came together in a vain attempt to obtain the Jewel of Judgment. Their confluence caused the destruction of sections of the palace, injuring a number of people. Coral was badly hurt: her right eye was severely damaged. The aged wizard, Dworkin, joined Merlin and the others, and used his skills to help Coral. Dworkin hadn't allowed the others to observe his work too closely, but soon thereafter, Merlin found that he had implanted the Jewel of Judgment into Coral's eye socket.

When his complex surgical operation was complete, Dworkin took Coral away from Amber and brought her to Kashfa. She joined Rinaldo there, finding that he had just taken control of the shadow realm. Before the planned coronation, however, they were joined by Merlin. Merlin's brother, Jurt, appeared while Merlin was speaking to Rinaldo in the Unicorn Church. Jurt fought with Merlin, was foiled, but escaped with a sword belonging to Rinaldo's father. Nevertheless, Merlin stayed to watch the coronation, and stayed to dally with a recovering Coral.

While reigning in Kashfa with Rinaldo, Coral again became a focal point in the conflict of the Logrus and the Pattern. Agents that were artificially created by the Sign of the Logrus kidnapped her. Their intention was to bring her to the Courts of Chaos, where she would be induced to become queen to the newly empowered king of the Courts. Because Coral bore the Eye of the Serpent, as the Jewel of Judgment was known there, the Logrus would have a clear advantage over the Pattern.

Merlin and Rinaldo took part in a rescue attempt, and Merlin succeeded in besting both the agents of the Logrus and agents sent by the Pattern. However, the Pattern Sign itself appeared and intervened. Attempting to regain its advantage, the Sign of the Pattern brought Coral, Merlin, Rinaldo, and their companions to the primal Pattern. It offered to protect them from the Logrus and any other harm, but they would have to remain at the primal Pattern. Merlin and Rinaldo effected a stalemate. They threatened to damage the Pattern, thus removing any advantage it had already possessed over the Logrus.

Consequently, the Sign of the Pattern released Merlin, Coral, and their comrades, while Rinaldo held the Power in abeyance. In order to keep Coral out of reach of either of the Powers, Merlin arranged to have her placed under the protection of the new Pattern that had been created by his father. Until the ancient conflict could be resolved, Coral stayed in the realm of Corwin's Pattern, kept company by Dalt, Jurt, and Nayda.

Like her sister, Coral had become a special kind of being. Utilizing the Jewel of Judgment as a sensory organ, she was given a unique, if enigmatic ability. When Merlin asked her about the sensations she had in wearing the Jewel, she told him:

> "Very strange.... Not pain—exactly. More like the way a Trump contact feels. Only it's with me all the time, and I'm not going anywhere or talking to anyone. It's as if I'm standing in some sort of gateway. Forces are moving about me, through me." (PC, 3)

She may indeed have the time, waiting upon that distant shadow, to test these sensations further. Dworkin's purpose in placing the Eye of the Serpent in Coral's eye may become known at some future juncture.

CORRIDOR OF MIRRORS

One of the more unusual features of the Royal Palace in Amber, the Corridor of Mirrors does not remain in one place. It appears to occupants only on rare occasions, and those who traverse its hallway of many mirrors do not always find the experience pleasant. Infrequently, a wandering guest or servant might encounter the place, and his or her dead body found by others would be the only evidence that

something untoward had occurred. Firsthand knowledge of the ever-shifting corridor would come from those wanderers who survived, found talking gibberish upon their return to the ordinary halls of the palace.

When it has appeared before residents who are about, most avoid traversing the shiny region of mirrors. Often they walk away, leaving it altogether. Sometimes, though, a curious observer would keep his distance while witnessing any alterations in its features. Then again, the mirrored realm may seem to be seeking a particular person. Once found, that person would be in greater peril if he or she were to retreat than to enter. For such a one, the corridor offers special enlightenment, or needed information, or simply an omen of what to expect shortly thereafter.

The journals of Merlin describe a sighting that he had of the Corridor of Mirrors:

> I'd been in that hallway before, in one of its commoner locations up on the fourth floor, running east-west between a couple of storerooms. One of Castle Amber's intriguing anomalies, the Corridor of Mirrors, in addition to seeming longer in one direction than the other, contained countless mirrors.... There are big mirrors, little mirrors, narrow mirrors, squat mirrors, tinted mirrors, distorting mirrors, mirrors with elaborate frames—cast or carved— plain, simply framed mirrors, and mirrors with no frames at all; there are mirrors in multitudes of sharp-angled geometric shapes, amorphous shapes, curved mirrors.
>
> ... One never knew what to expect in that place; at least that's what Bleys once told me. He was not certain whether the mirrors propelled one into obscure realms of Shadow, hypnotized one and induced bizarre dream states, cast one into purely symbolic realms decorated with the furniture of the psyche, played malicious or harmless head games with the viewer, none of the above, all of the above, or some of the above. (KS, 217)

On this most recent occasion, Merlin had been transported by the flickering images within the mirrors to an eerie glade as darkness was approaching. He found himself trapped upon a pentagram drawn on the ground. Incongruously, he was attacked with knives and forks by several of the significant women in his life. He was rescued by his father, and then was taken back to the Corridor of Mirrors. Although the incident seemed like a dream, Merlin bore the scars of the attack, and he also held a bit of stone masonry from that sinister glade.

While Merlin couldn't quite determine the point of this visitation, he found that the stone had an enchantment. It led him to explore the quarters of his uncle Brand, where he found a couple of fascinating items that he took with him. Aside from giving Merlin warning about the people in that dark landscape, the Corridor of Mirrors had directed him to a source of immense power, a ring that drew upon sources well into Shadow.

Sometime later, Merlin entered the mystical hallway in an indirect way. In the Courts of Chaos, his uncle Suhuy placed an enchantment on him that would cause him to dream. The dream had elements of truth and prophecy about it. In the dream, Merlin returned to the hall of mirrors. He spoke to various friends and members of his family from both sides who made suggestions and offered advice. Much later, in another dream, the vision of the corridor returned. In the latter occurrence, images of his uncle Bleys and a distant relative named Delwin told him more about the potent ring he wore. After awaking, Merlin discovered he had a second ring in his pocket, given to him by Bleys. Another gift, presented to him by means of the Corridor of Mirrors, through an enchanted dream.

Those of us in Amber know better than to seek out the corridor. It is best for ordinary people to avoid such strange realms. Those infrequent times when a valued servant has inexplicably disappeared from the Royal Palace without trace make one wary. The ancient proverb, "Do not seek too hard for something, because it may find you," is certainly true in regard to the mystic hall.

CORWIN

Prince of Amber who briefly served as ruler after the death of Eric the usurper. He is considered by some to have been the first legitimate heir to the throne, born after the marriage of Oberon to Faiella.

Corwin's history is a centuries-long account of great trials and tribulations. He had been through several lifetimes of struggle, known the renowned and infamous of several shadow worlds, and was near death in some of them. One might say that he had gone through more changes in life than any of the other children of Oberon; that these changes were so severe that he became a different man at specific phases in his life. We can divide his life, marking each of his changed personalities, into the following phases: 1) his early life in Amber; 2) his middle years living in the shadow called Earth; 3) his years of quest for his rightful position in Amber during Oberon's absence; and 4) his time of struggle against the forces out of Chaos.

In his mature years, a reflective Corwin pondered the nature of his brother Brand, but also took into account himself and his lot:

> Whenever anything has been mucked up, whenever anything outrageous happens, there is a reason for it. You still have a mucked-up, outrageous situation on your hands, however, and explaining it does not alleviate it one bit. If someone does something really rotten, there is a reason for it. Learn it, if you care, and you learn why he is a son of a bitch. (HO, 186)

In his earliest phase, Corwin showed himself to be an example of this syndrome.

The formative years of his boyhood and adolescence were marked by his reactions to treatment received. His indifferent father often left Corwin with his older brother Eric, who was a spiteful sibling. Corwin responded with hatred, and court matrons frequently had to break up fights between the two small boys. When Corwin's younger brother, Caine, was old enough, he took sides with Eric in taunting Corwin and playing mean little tricks on him. On the other hand, the presence of Corwin's sister, Deirdre, had a soothing effect on him. Nevertheless, his contact with Eric and Caine, and his ambivalent feelings toward his uncaring father, helped to shape deeply ingrained attitudes toward those around him.

Early in life, he learned of the Pattern deep in the dungeons beneath the Royal Palace from the aging wizard Dworkin. On the surface, Corwin chided the old man for spouting fairy tales and passing them as truth, but, below the surface of his outward thoughts, he wished eagerly to see the Pattern for himself and learn to travel to other worlds. If there were truly other worlds, lesser ones that Dworkin called "shadows," then Corwin wanted to find them. He wanted to play with the toys of lesser people's lives.

While he was a young boy, Corwin developed a friendship with his little brother Gérard, and they spent much time together. In truth, Corwin's friendliness may have been in response to the poor treatment he had received from Eric and Caine, a near-deliberate attempt to have an ally ready against them.

Sometime during his adolescent years, Corwin had spent time listening to Dworkin with renewed interest. When he convinced the aged wizard that he had gained sufficient wisdom to walk the Pattern, it may have, again, been part of a deliberate plan to obtain an advantage over his siblings. Dworkin led the youth down the winding stairs to the dungeons and took him into the locked room of the Pattern, offering advice as they went. With great determination, the young Corwin walked the Pattern, listening carefully to Dworkin's suggestions and warnings. When he succeeded, Corwin knew that he could have the Pattern send him anywhere he wished from its center.

In his Chronicles, Corwin gave only vague hints as to where he had the Pattern send him at the conclusion of his first walk. Other sources provide hearsay as to possible choices he had made. One of the most popular of these, echoed by numerous members of the Royal Court with only slight variation, is that he sought release for his adolescent libido. Having no personal knowledge of Shadow, Corwin was likely to have focused on a person that he would want to join in a realm removed from Amber. Thus, it has been surmised that he met with a girl in a shadow of his own making, spending an uninhibited night before returning to Amber. Some gossips suggest that he had created a shadow of a girl he knew well in the Royal Palace, his sister Deirdre. Those who remember the youthful Corwin have indicated that he was capable of actualizing such an event, and his continued interest in his sister might be tantalizing corroboration of the possibility.

As a young initiate of the Pattern, Corwin aided in the opening of trade routes to the shadows by ship, as did his brothers when they became initiated. Corwin found his element with the royal navy and did most of his military service with the fleet. That stint away from Amber proper served several purposes: he was away for a time from his callous brothers Eric and Caine; he saw at firsthand a variety of shadowlands; he came into contact with hardy, rough-hewn types of seamen and adventurers; and he became inured to a rugged way of life that he had not previously encountered in the true city. When he eventually returned to the palace, he was toughened and daring. Eric found him to be a forthright adversary, causing him to retreat into a wariness of his younger brother.

While Corwin was seldom given to carousing in the town, he did join his brothers Gérard and Random on occasion, drinking at local taverns and seeking young ladies. Random was better at attracting women than Corwin and Gérard, but Corwin was often more successful in gaining a willing lass for a full night's companionship.

There were many incidents of hostility, cruelty, and mean-spiritedness between Corwin and his brothers. In virtually all cases, the particulars are unclear. One incident concerned a prank that Corwin played on Caine at a most-embarrassing moment when Caine was entertaining a young female. Caine was so distressed by it that he never forgave his brother, even after the passage of long years. Another time, Bleys and Corwin brought Random to a distant islet in the south and left him there. When they returned to the palace, they laughingly told Gérard about it, apparently unconcerned for Random's welfare. Gérard sailed to the island to retrieve the youth. On another occasion, Julian and one of his patrols were on a hunt for a huge beast that had slipped in from an adjacent shadow. Julian had located it and was about to dispatch it, an arrow primed in his longbow, when Corwin appeared and slew the beast with a shaft from a crossbow. When Julian challenged him, Corwin retorted that at the distance Julian had been, he would never have brought down that beast. With Julian's men watching, Corwin carried away the carcass on his shoulders before Julian could pursue the matter. Julian felt bitterly resentful of his brother for that incident. Shortly after that, Corwin rose on a morning and began putting on his boots. He cried out in pain and discovered his foot bleeding. Someone had driven a sharp spike through the heel of the boot. For many years, Corwin believed Julian responsible for it.

Although King Oberon never lavished much love or praise upon his children, he was concerned that his sons receive training appropriate to their positions. Besides having all his sons serve in the military, he brought master swordsmen from Shadow to teach them their skills with saber and foil. Corwin was agreeable to this, but he also traveled the shadows to improve on these and other skills. For a time, at Oberon's recommendation, Corwin studied at the oceanographic institute of Sagres in Portugal on a shadow Earth. Corwin met the original Prince Henry the Navigator, formerly of Amber, and, while there, became skillful in navigation and map making. Although this Earth was not precisely the same shadow upon which Corwin later resided, he endeared himself enough so that he was taught an easy trade by a band of seafarers there that he carried back with him to Amber's waters.

Gathering up a crew of Amberite seamen, Corwin stole a frigate and engaged in piracy on the seas of Amber and its near shadows. For a while, he was a notorious pirate, greatly feared in a number of shadows. He destroyed vessels, murdered men, and took on board all valuables for himself and his men. His exploits became so widely known that he was dubbed "the Blackguard of Amber" by officials of lands bold enough to declare that he was a member of the royal household in Amber.

With his band of pirates, Corwin sailed far to the north, slipping into adjoining shadows where they could pillage villages along the seacoast under cover of darkness. One of his crew had been a musician in better days. When he played on his harmonica on a quiet evening or two, Corwin had him write down the notes he played. Fortunately, the man could read and write musical notation, for if he hadn't been able to do so, the Corwin of those voyages would have tossed him overboard.

After a particularly perilous battle with another ship at sea, Corwin's first mate, a man Corwin counted as a good friend, was seriously ill from deep wounds in his left leg. The ship's doctor had been an unwilling captive of an earlier voyage, and he was incompetent as well. The doctor's ministrations were so poorly performed that the first mate's leg became infected. Under Corwin's wary observation, the doctor operated to amputate the leg. In spite of the doctor's diligent efforts—with "the Blackguard of Amber" watching his every move—the man died. After burying his friend at sea, Corwin confiscated all of the doctor's medical books, then tossed the doctor into the sea, heaving a small

rowboat after him. For many evenings afterward, Corwin could be found studying the medical texts in his cabin.

When Corwin was rediscovered in Amber, he had come ashore in a small boat with four of his men. All five of them were in bad shape from exposure and malnutrition, but Corwin had nearly bled to death from several knife wounds that had been hastily bandaged and left untreated. His four comrades were half-dragging him inland when they were met by villagers on the northern coast. The villagers took Corwin into their care without knowing who he was, and two of his crewmates stayed with him all the while. The other two, claiming to be in good condition, traveled on, and were never heard from again.

In the village, some of the local merchants recognized the convalescent Corwin and sent messages to the Royal Court. King Oberon sent two courtiers and a scribe to verify the reports and bring Corwin home. Finding that it was indeed Corwin, the small contingent remained in the village while he gradually recovered. The scribe was able to obtain statements from Corwin's crewmates, who told a somewhat vague tale of mutiny and attempted murder. It seemed that these shipmates had escaped with the semiconscious Corwin after they had been locked up and intended for execution. Corwin had fought off the mutineers so indefatigably that they were forced to wound him, after which they bandaged him up and tossed him in with the other four. Fear of the consequences of murdering one of royal blood of the true city caused the mutineers to hesitate. They argued the matter all through the night, giving Corwin's comrades the opportunity to work their escape.

Once Corwin was walking about on his own and gathering strength, his two mates bade their farewells, wandering out of the village with little more than what they came with. Believing that his father wanted to reconcile in some way with him, Corwin willingly returned with the courtiers to the Royal Palace.

Oberon didn't receive Corwin in any formal way. He looked in on Corwin, in his quarters, soon after Corwin returned. They greeted each other with little emotion, and Oberon did not continue any further visits. For his part, Corwin was surprised that he received no reprimands from his father, for he realized, from the talk of servants he overheard, that his nefarious deeds on the high seas were well-known.

Weakened in spirit as well as body, Corwin chose to remain in Amber at his leisure for a time. He avoided his brothers and took to wandering away from the palace, in Arden and the Valley of Garnath. He practiced some sea ditties he had heard on a flute he carried with him, and jotted down musical notations as he sat under a tree or beside a spring. While he was sitting in a grove, singing and writing down the words to a new song, Corwin met with a young boy he had seen in the palace. The boy was tall for his age, thin, and had large, intelligent eyes. They spoke a little about the song Corwin was composing, and the boy told him that his name was Rein. As they sat together, Corwin remembered that Rein was the son of one of the men who worked in the royal stables, and that Rein had requested an audience with King Oberon some time before, intent on joining the court as one of the jesters. Before he had gone off to sea, Corwin had made fun of the young boy, imitating gestures and movement, just as others in the court had done. Spending this time with him in the grove, Corwin felt some regret for past derision aimed at the boy.

Corwin spent many pleasant days, riding a favorite horse through Arden, sometimes slipping into an adjacent shadow and noting differences in the land about him. He showed the music he wrote to various courtiers attached to the palace, and they sometimes joined him in song. It is believed that Corwin wrote "The Ballad of the Water Crossers" at this time. It was such a popular melody that the music and lyrics quickly spread throughout the city of Amber, finding their way to merchants in the Harbor District and picked up by many a seaman on shore leave.

While Corwin avoided his brothers as much as possible, there were several minor encounters with Eric, Caine, and Julian in which hostilities were exchanged. Generally, these exchanges were insignificant, and Corwin began to spend a greater amount of time with others of the royal retinue. As Rein grew older, Corwin brought him under his tutelage, showing Rein something of martial arts as well as the use of saber. Rein was a poor student of self-defense, but he gained some skill with a sword. Rein began playing music on a lute, and Corwin and he frequently played and sang together as they walked the halls and gardens.

During Oberon's reign, strange creatures slipped into Amber from congruent shadows on numerous occasions. Most of these incidents proved innocuous, and the creatures were simply returned to their own realm. There were times, however, when hostile beings made a forcible invasion of the true city. Usually, these were disorganized invasions that were quickly put down, the invaders either dispatched with swords or sent into retreat. Early in these "fringe wars" with other shadows, Oberon handled matters directly, supervising his generals as troops were sent into the areas of disturbance.

Corwin joined in one such fringe skirmish, at Jones Falls, to the west of the city. It became an important battle for young Rein, who participated with Corwin. This is the way Corwin described Rein's role in the skirmish:

I felt kind of sorry for the way I had treated him earlier, what with the way he had dug my stuff, so I forced the fake graces upon him and also made him a passable saber man. I'd never regretted it, and I guess he didn't either. Before long, he became minstrel to the court of Amber. I had called him my page all that while, and when the wars beckoned, against the dark things out of Shadow called Weirmonken, I made him my squire and we had ridden off to the wars together. I knighted him upon the battlefield, at Jones Falls, and he had deserved it. After that, he had gone on to become my better when it came to the ways of words and music. His colors were crimson and his words golden. I loved him, as one of my two or three friends in Amber. (NP 151–52)

Upon returning to the palace, Corwin was welcomed with unusual warmth by his father. Oberon spoke amiably about how well Corwin and his soldiers had disposed of the Weirmonken beings. He indicated his approval of Corwin's having knighted the youth Rein, saying he would always hold Rein in special esteem. Whenever Oberon met with Corwin thereafter, he appeared more cordial than he had been in past times.

Given much time for leisure, Corwin visited a number of near shadows. After some long discussions with his brother Benedict, Corwin walked the ghostlike stair to Tir-na Nog'th on a bright moonlit night. He also spent a few days in the mirror city under the sea, Rebma, visiting his sister Llewella.

Somewhere in his journeys of this period, he obtained his Pattern-limned sword Grayswandir. How he obtained that legendary sword is the stuff of conjecture and myth-making.

Recognizing his son's wanderlust, Oberon initiated conversation about the necessity for Corwin to seek a new life in a land of shadow that would be special to him. He talked of Corwin's having reached the maturity to exercise his power over Shadow. It was important that Corwin attempt to find himself in a realm removed from Amber. Corwin must find a place that was distinctly his, making real the parts of his imagination that he most desired, and peopled with those who have a zest for life and a sense of individual destiny. Oberon urged him to make true his own dreams, and he was quite insistent that his son do this thing.

Corwin was frankly surprised at his father's insistence, especially at a point when their relations seemed so amiable. However, his own natural restlessness, and his father's words of encouragement, led him to consider the philosophical exercise that Oberon was advancing. If Corwin could create any shadow at all, limited only by imagination, what would be its nature? He thought long of it, images forming, to be discarded, and re-formed in his mind innumerable times. When something suitable developed, it encroached on his every activity. He could not get the image out of his mind. He went to his father to bid farewell, having found the place of his fondest dreams. He left, then, for Avalon.

Riding at a rapid pace on his favorite horse, Corwin sifted through Shadow as soon as he was far enough to do so. He held the image of his land of dream as he altered sky and forest and soil. His thoughts shaped the world to look very much like the one a bogus Ganelon had once described: "a place of silver and shade and cool waters, where the stars shone like bonfires at night and the green of day was always the green of spring." (GA, 31) The village rose before him out of the horizon, and Corwin made for it. Spires of silver dominated at five points in the village, other buildings being formed of wood and stone, a few of shining metal like knights' armor, gleaming in the sun. On closer inspection, most structures were thatched cottages, with only a rare construct of iron or some metallic alloy. Corwin rode through the placid streets.

Several children were at play with a stick and an odd-looking ball, a woman was scrubbing clothes in a wash bucket outside of a small wooden house, and several men in simple garments were talking excitedly as they walked in Corwin's direction. One of these men stopped to run his hand along the muzzle of Corwin's horse, and Corwin paused to talk with him. The man told him that the village was called Avalon. Two of the spired towers directly ahead represented Avalon's governing houses. The other three silver-spired structures were places of religious worship. One of these was dedicated to the unicorn of Amber. Corwin rode toward the nearest spire, rising above an ornate building that was the main government house.

Details of Corwin's stay are lacking, but in short order he had himself appointed ruler of Avalon. With the swiftness of a dream made real, Corwin brought to him a man he could trust, someone to act as his chief aide. In Corwin's imaginings, this man was without fear and absolutely dedicated, a staunch friend who would give his life in undying love for his friend, one who would never question his ruler's decisions for fear of arousing his ire, yet willing to do battle with any evil that dared offend his master. Such a person as this arrived at the court of Lord Corwin of Avalon. He called himself Lancelot du Lac.

Corwin delved into the business of running a kingdom, learning all he could about the region and surrounding villages. During this, he had the time to hear Lancelot's story of himself. After the death of his father, King Ban of Berwick, Lancelot served a great king of an island realm. He had served loyally for many years, but he found himself growing more and more infatuated with the beautiful queen. Rather than allow his virtue to die in lust and betrayal, he had packed his few possessions, got on his white steed, and rode away, traveling far from that place. A ship bore him to this country, where he sought a great ruler to serve and a land to call home. It was almost magical the way he had been drawn to this place, and he knew immediately upon entering the court of Lord Corwin that this was indeed the place he sought.

With Lancelot's talk of the beautiful queen of that faraway isle, and of his love for her, Corwin thought fondly of Deirdre, back in Amber. The thought of her persisted, and he went through the town looking at shops, thinking to purchase a gift for her that he would bring when he returned to his homeland. A persuasive shopkeeper sold him a bracelet of gold, and wrapped it with a small bottle of jewelers rouge after Corwin mentioned that he would not be able to see the young lady who was the recipient for quite some time. Corwin kept the small package in a pouch that contained his travel implements, so that it would not be accidentally left behind.

The perfect kingdom of Corwin's imagination was never meant to be of long duration. Avalon's prosperity and tranquillity were the very things that attracted outlaws from outside. Dealing with thieves and cutthroats expeditiously, Corwin found these incidents annoying, but not insurmountable. What was more bothersome were the infrequent invasions of strange beings out of Shadow. The similarity to Amber's problems of shadow slippage made him wonder that perhaps he was the focal point, being a creature of Amber. Perhaps the reign of a prince of Amber in a distant shadow would, by some confluence of cosmic forces, reflect the same kind of insurgence as experienced in the true city. No matter what the cause, however, Corwin organized his militia to handle these invasions.

When Corwin, Lancelot, and the militia were confronted by a rebel army made up of citizens from Avalon and neighboring villages, several bloody battles ensued. At this point, Lord Corwin made a public proclamation in a recruitment campaign that led to Corwin's meeting a new ally, Ganelon. Although the source of the following information is suspect, Corwin has never contradicted this account:

> "One later day ... when war commenced within the realm, the ruler offered full pardon to any outlaws who would follow him in battle against the insurgents. This was Corwin. I [Ganelon] threw in with him and rode off to the wars. I became an officer, and then—later—a member of his staff. We won the battles, put down the uprising. Then Corwin ruled peacefully once more, and I remained at his court. Those were the good years. There later came some border skirmishes, but these we always won. He trusted me to handle such things for him. Then he granted a Dukedom to dignify the House of a minor noble whose daughter he desired in marriage. I had wanted that Dukedom, and he had long hinted it might one day be mine. I was furious, and I betrayed my command the next time I was dispatched to settle

a dispute along the southern border, where something was always stirring. Many of my men died, and the invaders entered into the realm. Before they could be routed, Lord Corwin himself had to take up arms once more. The invaders had come through in great strength, and I thought they would conquer the realm. I hoped they would. But Corwin, again, with his foxy tactics, prevailed. I fled, but was captured and taken to him for sentencing."
> (GA, 31)

In his chronicles, Corwin explained further: "He [Ganelon] had been a traitorous assassin and I had exiled him from Avalon centuries before. I had actually cast him through Shadow into another time and place." (GA, 17)

Corwin continued to rule in Avalon for a long time. His closest friend remained Lancelot, but he also shared with others in his court the music he was writing. He had begun an "Ode To Avalon," which he hadn't finished while he ruled there. He counted numbers of people, noblemen and merchants largely, as his friends. There were others, though, who were not.

Accusations and rumors were passed among the townspeople. Someone told of Corwin's favoritism of a particular noble House that had turned some of the other Houses against Corwin. Another spoke of looting of shops by members of the militia in daylight, condoned and allowed by Lord Corwin. A merchant mentioned to a servant of Lancelot's that a stranger in the village had arrived to murder Lancelot, and had been paid in coin from Amber. Others spread the word that Corwin was planning to turn over the kingdom to an evil brother, who would set up a tyrant's rule, so that Corwin could take a nobleman's daughter back to Amber to live with him. Angry rebellion was being fomented from various directions, and under various guises, from laborers' wives to shopkeepers to religious leaders. It was extremely difficult to determine how the rumors were ignited and which of the tales, if any, could be believed.

Of course, some of these reports reached Corwin. He had spent much time in the manor house of one of the wealthiest noblemen, but his intentions toward the man's daughter were well-known and forthright. Only when Corwin was back in the government house did he learn of a few of these rumors. He assigned a handful of trusted guards to investigate the source. Before he heard from them, Lancelot confronted him about the stranger dressed in black leather, making purchases in Amber coin. Realizing that Lancelot was seething with anger, Corwin tried to placate him. Not having seen the stranger himself, Lancelot couldn't describe him, and Corwin assured him that he had not sent for this man, nor did he know who it was. When a couple of his guards returned to report, they both indicated that a black-clothed man with a thin beard had been prominent in the memory of several people spreading rumors about Corwin.

Before Corwin could make any public proclamation that the stories were lies deliberately spread for the purpose of creating dissension, more dire events occurred. Shopkeepers were murdered in front of customers by loathsome man-beasts. Young women were dragged from streets into alleyways, then disappeared utterly before witnesses could rescue them. Similar acts of violence occurred throughout the village, until the townspeople were urged to act. Taking up tools and sticks and any other implements that were handy, a huge crowd of men and women marched to the government house. It was the beginning of a brief and bloody revolt against Lord Corwin.

When several minor officials stepped out of the government house to try to calm the crowd, they were grabbed roughly, pushed up against a wall, and bludgeoned to death. The crowd was beyond reasoning. They broke down the heavy metal doors of the government house and destroyed everything in sight: furniture, documents, paintings, fineries, all were torn apart and left as rubble. Servants, workers, and courtiers on the main floor fled before the surge of the mob. Anyone caught by the crowd was lifted up and tossed through one of the latticed windows, to fall bleeding outside amid broken glass and warped metal.

The scholarly and fanciful works written in Thari about Avalon have depicted the end of Corwin's rule there in various ways. Some of the more romantic tales show Corwin and Lancelot dueling side by side against a vicious mob converging upon them. Some serious works promoted the controversy that Corwin had been a power-hungry tyrant who met an ignominious end at the hands of the angry townspeople. Others claim that Corwin fled for his life, leaving the village in ruins. An underground

historical text, written by a learned man in Amber, gave details of a bloody civil war, incited by Eric the Usurper, who had traced Corwin to Avalon. This history recounts a furious duel between the two brothers in which both were seriously wounded. The intervention of the pressing mob prevented Eric and Corwin from killing each other. Subsequently, the two antagonists disappeared.

Corwin had made only a scant indication of the end of Avalon in the unfinished verse from his ''Ode To Avalon'':

> ''Beyond the River of the Blessed, there we sat down, yea, we wept, when we remembered Avalon. Our swords were shattered in our hands and we hung our shields on the oak tree. The silver towers were fallen, into a sea of blood. How many miles to Avalon? None, I say, and all. The silver towers are fallen.''
> (GA, 27)

From these brief lines, it is assumed that Lancelot had escaped with Corwin after a war that left the village decimated.

After leaving the fallen Avalon, Corwin wandered through Shadow. Some of these same historical/mythical works state that Corwin spent much of his travels searching for a weapon of greater capacity than the crossbow, with a destructive power more fearful than the catapult. The search brought him to worlds of technological dynamism, rather than those of mystical influence, where he discovered the pulverizing quality of firepower. It had been written that Corwin performed surgery on a man in a techno-shadow who had a bullet lodged in close proximity to his heart. Corwin successfully removed the bullet and the man recovered. While residing with the man's grateful family, he turned to a study of revolvers, for the man had collected an impressive array of functioning guns.

In secret, he returned to Amber on several occasions, experimenting with the pistols he obtained. He tried firing them at trees deep in a deserted forest outside of the true city in the early hours before dawn. None of the pistols fired. He continually checked their potency by traveling through Shadow, finding the weapons perfectly effective in shadows at a distance from Amber.

He became dedicated to learning all he could about firepower and spent years experimenting with all kinds of implements, from simple powder-filled muskets to repeating rifles to rapid-fire machine guns. As potent as each was in its shadow of origin, none would produce any effect in Amber or its most congruent shadows.

In his Chronicles, Corwin revealed something of his knowledge of gunpowder and the way he discovered the means of bringing firepower to Amber:

> I have met many persons who thought that gunpowder explodes, which of course is incorrect. It burns rapidly, building up gas pressure which ejects a bullet from the mouth of a shell and drives it through the barrel of a weapon, after having been ignited by the primer, which does the actual exploding when the firing pin is driven into it. Now, with typical family foresight, I had experimented with a variety of combustibles over the years. My disappointment at the discovery that gunpowder would not ignite in Amber, and that all of the primers I tested were equally inert there, was a thing mitigated only by the knowledge that none of my relatives could bring firearms into Amber either. It was much later, during a visit to Amber, after polishing a bracelet I had brought for Deirdre, that I discovered this wonderful property of jewelers rouge from Avalon when I disposed of the polishing cloth in a fireplace. Fortunately, the quantity involved was small, and I was alone at the time.
>
> It made an excellent primer, straight from the container. When cut with a sufficient quantity of inert material, it could also be made to burn properly. (GA, 131)

Sometime during his travels in Shadow, Corwin received an urgent Trump message. His father was calling him back to Amber. The realm was under siege by strange flying beasts and squat, vicious men. These beings were utterly careless of their own lives while they butchered others without mercy. This made them more formidable and dangerous than previous invasion forces.

When Corwin returned, he found Benedict in charge of the main force. Benedict seemed glad to see Corwin and placed him in command of a large supporting company. They conferred with their father, Bleys, Julian, and Eric in Oberon's quarters. The Moonriders out of Ghenesh, as the invaders

were called, had attacked several outlying villages on the northeastern coast. Caine had already been dispatched with the fleet to scout the coastline. While Benedict was giving them their assignments and detailing his plans, Oberon appeared to be deferring to his eldest son, acting only in a supervisory capacity. Oberon offered suggestions and pointed out a number of problems that had to be resolved, but it was obvious that Benedict was running the show.

Taking charge of his infantry, Corwin put them under rigorous training while Benedict traveled to Ghenesh to learn more of the Moonriders. Upon Benedict's return, and the report of Julian's patrol, the brothers conferred with King Oberon again. Benedict devised a plan that would manipulate the Moonriders into an ambush. After working out the details, Benedict assigned positions, and they rejoined their companies in the field.

Benedict's preparations were largely responsible for the success of the campaign against the invading forces. Julian's troops led them into the valley below Kolvir, where they were met by the combined forces of Benedict, Bleys, and Corwin in a surprise ambush. Volleys of arrows felled the strange flying beasts and their riders, while the enemy infantry were confronted with lances and swords. At the head of his infantry, Corwin pressed hard against the ugly small men who slashed out viciously with curved sabers and daggers. He could see Benedict, not too distantly, wielding his long, curved blade in terrible arcs at the enemy. Slaughter covered the battlefield as they fought on for many hours. The Moonriders were tireless fighters who were willing to die rather than surrender. It was inevitable that the invaders would be destroyed, and only a few escaped in retreat. The rest died where they stood.

At the conclusion of battle, Corwin and his men reconnoitered the area for any signs of hidden invaders. When this was accomplished without incident, Corwin dismissed his soldiers and retired to the palace. He participated in the celebrations which followed, but he still sought to avoid Eric, Caine, and Julian. As soon as his duties to his father were completed, Corwin went off to the shadows again.

From time to time Corwin visited Amber, staying for a brief while before traveling again. It is likely that he discovered the unusual property of jewelers rouge from his fallen Avalon during one of these visits.

Corwin was in the great dining hall with his brothers and sisters when Eric spoke of their father's mental lapses and inability to rule. He joined Benedict in speaking against Eric's arguments, and he listened in stunned silence, like his siblings, when Benedict announced that he would have nothing further to do with talk of the succession as long as their father lived. He warned that if anything were to befall Oberon, he would not rest until the cause was found out. Then he said he was leaving Amber for a place of solace from this continuous bickering, but, he stated, he intended to remain vigilant to events in the true city. At that point, Benedict left the hall and was not seen again for many years.

Once Benedict had gone, the adversarial positions of Corwin and Eric grew more tense. However, with the absence of his older brother, Corwin felt obliged to remain in Amber as the principal defender of King Oberon's right to rule, since no one else expressed strong opinions one way or the other.

In the Chronicles, Corwin recounts what happened between Eric and himself thereafter:

"We had some rather bitter arguments concerning the whole matter. Then one evening it went beyond mere words. We fought . . .

". . . a simultaneous decision to murder one another. At any rate, we fought for a long while and Eric finally got the upper hand and proceeded to pulverize me . . .

". . . Eric stopped short of killing me himself. When I awakened, I was on a shadow Earth in a place called London. The plague was rampant at the time, and I had contracted it. I recovered with no memory of anything prior to London. I dwelled on that shadow world for centuries, seeking some clue as to my identity." (GA, 85)

This dire confrontation with Eric, and its consequences, marks the end of the first phase of Corwin's life and the beginning of the second phase.

Centuries later, when Corwin recovered his memory by walking the Pattern in Rebma, he recalled his earliest impressions of that forced exile on shadow Earth:

The dead. They were all about me. There was a horrible stink—the smell of decaying flesh—and I heard the howls of a dog who was being

beaten to death. Billows of black smoke filled the sky, and an icy wind swept around me bearing a few drops of rain. My throat was parched and my hands shook and my head was on fire. I staggered alone, seeing everything through the haze of the fever that burned me. The gutters were filled with garbage and dead cats and the emptyings of chamber pots. With a rattle and the ringing of a bell, the death wagon thundered by, splashing me with mud and cold water.

How long I wandered, I do not know, before a woman seized my arm and I saw a Death's Head ring upon her finger. She led me to her rooms, but discovered there that I had no money and was incoherent. A look of fear crossed her painted face, erasing the smile on her bright lips, and she fled and I collapsed upon her bed.

Later—again, how much later I do not know—a big man, the girl's Black Davy, came and slapped me across the face and dragged me to my feet. I seized his right biceps and hung on. He half carried, half pulled me toward the door.

When I realized that he was going to cast me out into the cold, I tightened my grip to protest it. I squeezed with all my remaining strength, mumbling half-coherent pleas.

Then through sweat and tear-filled eyes, I saw his face break open and heard a scream come forth from between his stained teeth.

The bone in his arm had broken where I'd squeezed it.

He pushed me away with his left hand and fell to his knees, weeping. I sat upon the floor, and my head cleared for a moment.

"I . . . am . . . staying here," I said, "until I feel better. Get out. If you come back—I'll kill you."

"You've got the plague!" he cried. "They'll come for your bones tomorrow!" and he spat then, got to his feet, and staggered out.

I made it to the door and barred it. Then I crawled back to the bed and slept.

If they came for my bones the next day, they were disappointed. For, perhaps ten hours later, in the middle of the night, I awoke in a cold sweat and realized my fever had broken. I was weak, but rational once more.

I realized I had lived through the plague.

I took a man's cloak I found in the wardrobe and took some money I found in a drawer.

Then I went forth into London and the Night, in a year of the plague, looking for something. . . . (NP, 88–9)

Very little is known about Corwin's life in those first years of his exile. Julian has recounted the only knowledge he had of Corwin's experiences in England. When Julian had rescued Corwin from his confinement in the Star of Bethlehem Hospital, nearly one hundred years later in shadow Earth–time, they had exchanged a few words. After Corwin's recovery, he had wandered the streets of London singing odd tunes, collecting donations in this way. He cared for an aged woman who was suffering from consumption and had taken a bad fall down some stone stairs. Following this, he began a general practice in medicine that gained him a considerable reputation, and a substantial amount of British currency.

Unaccountably, Corwin had been clubbed over the head one night as he was leaving his offices. He awoke to find himself in disheveled and fouled clothing, confined to a large holding cell with numbers of patients suffering mental disorders. His speech was slurred and he was disoriented, so he was unable to call attention to himself when hospital officials and security personnel looked in on the patients.

Corwin was still dazed when Julian arrived with two other men in uniform. As they left the building, Julian told Corwin to remain calm and stay close to him. Julian questioned him briefly to ascertain that he was indeed a man called "Corwin," but his brother could only tell of his experiences since the Great Plague. Before they were able to get very far, hospital personnel began pursuing them, and Corwin disappeared in a crowd of people on the narrow streets.

The Chronicles, as told by Corwin to his son, give vague generalizations about Corwin's life on the shadow Earth. Some of the gaps have been filled in by testimony given by his sister Flora, who spent a couple of centuries there observing his activities. Several histories of that shadow have been translated into Thari and grace the library in the Royal Palace. These histories make only a few passing references to a Frenchman named Cordell Fenneval and an American military hero by the name of Carl Corey. The several histories brought back to the true city offer wide variations in describing events related to these two people, as well.

In all likelihood, Corwin sought escape from the kind of assault he experienced when placed in the hospital popularly called Bedlam. Having no understanding of the agents involved in placing him in that predicament, he probably left England for France shortly after his escape. As he indicates in his account, Corwin was aware that he was different from common humanity. Although he may have been curious about his unique abilities, he probably avoided exhibiting them in public. His need to learn his identity was, no doubt, as strong as his fear of danger approaching from almost any direction. Adept at languages, he took up French, joined the state-organized military service of King Louis XIV, and distinguished himself in the Augsburg war as Cordell Fenneval. As a French officer, he was able to travel throughout the country, surreptitiously consulting with doctors and university professors as he continued his military career.

The next concrete evidence of Corwin's whereabouts is the testimony given by Flora, as stated in the Chronicles. When Corwin was temporarily in command of the true city, he learned the following from his sister:

"It was in Paris, a party, at a certain Monsieur Focault's. This was about three years before the Terror—"

"Stop," I [Corwin] said. "What were you doing there?"

"I had been in that general area of Shadow for approximately five of their years," she said. "I had been wandering, looking for something novel, something that suited my fancy. I came upon that place at that time in the same way we find anything. I let my desires lead me and I followed my instincts." . . .

". . . It was, if you like, my Avalon, my Amber surrogate, my home away from home. Call it what you will, I was there, at that party, that October night, when you came in with the little redheaded girl—Jacqueline, I believe, was her name." . . .

". . . So I saw that we were introduced and then had a devil of a time getting you away from that little redheaded piece for more than a few minutes. And you insisted your name was Fenneval—Cordell Fenneval. I grew uncertain. I could not tell whether it was a double or you playing games. The third possibility did cross my mind, though—that you had dwelled in some adjacent area of Shadow for a sufficient time to cast shadows of yourself. I might have departed still wondering had not Jacqueline later boasted to me concerning your strength. Now this is not the commonest subject of conversation for a woman, and the way in which she said it led me to believe that she had actually been quite impressed by some things you had done. I drew her out a bit and realized that they were all of them feats of which you were capable. That eliminated the notion of it being a double. It had to be either you or your shadow. . . . I began keeping track of you then, checking into your past. The more people I questioned, the more puzzling it became. In fact, after several months I was still unable to decide. There were enough smudgy areas to make it possible. Things were resolved for me the following summer, though, when I revisited Amber for a time. I mentioned the peculiar affair to Eric . . .''

''Yes?''

''Well . . . he was—somewhat—aware—of the possibility.'' (SU, 58–60)

After Flora informed Eric of Corwin's presence on shadow Earth, Eric asked her to maintain a surveillance in exchange for privileged status in Amber once he became ruler. She agreed to do this, preferring to remain innocent of any more fatal designs Eric might have for Corwin.

Months prior to Flora's visit to Amber, she had observed Fenneval stealing a horse and riding off, followed in close pursuit by French soldiers. Flora had by that time distanced herself from her wealthy friends, having a good idea of the tempo of the political times. She left France shortly after this, traveling in Shadow, because of the crucial events of the Reign of Terror. She lost track of Fenneval for a number of years as a result. Early in the next century, she discovered that he was still in France, serving in the army of the new leader of that country, Napoleon Bonaparte.

As a commissioned officer, Fenneval was part of Napoleon's disastrous siege against the Russian army in 1812, shadow Earth–time. Fenneval was mentioned in a French newspaper of November, 1813, after the Battle of Leipzig. Although Napoleon's army was defeated, Fenneval was referred to as a ''miracle soldier'' who survived wounds that should have killed him. After his recovery weeks later, the Prussian soldiers held him in such esteem that he was one of the few French officers escorted back to France to rejoin his commission. Napoleon, having begun the formation of a new army, was surprised to find Fenneval fully recovered and returned to him. The ''little general'' honored his officer in a great celebration. Flora always regretted not having kept the newspaper article about the occasion.

Flora was able to maintain a close scrutiny of Fenneval once he resurfaced in 1813. While she personally avoided any contact with him, she developed a network of well-paid spies among his domestics and others he employed. She was only a little surprised when she learned that one of the young beauties he was pursuing finally caught him. Although Flora was not invited to their wedding, she dressed appropriately and observed the ceremony from a rear pew in the church of St. Severin. When Fenneval's wife died in 1849, she was a wealthy, mature woman who never questioned the agelessness of her husband.

As an influential military officer, Fenneval gave his support to the nephew of Napoléon Bonaparte, Louis-Napoléon Bonaparte. He served as a minister of war, helping Louis-Napoléon win the presidency in 1851, and supporting him again in 1852, when he declared himself Emperor Napoléon III.

When the War Between the States broke out in the United States, Fenneval became interested in the Confederacy's cause. At the time, Fenneval commanded a military detachment assigned to the banking house of Erlanger in Paris. He followed the newspaper accounts of the Trent affair and was pleased to make the acquaintance of John Slidell, commissioner representing the Confederacy, who had been arrested and imprisoned at Fort Warren in Boston until his recent release. Slidell found a sympathetic ear in Fenneval, who helped Slidell obtain financing for the South's conflict against the Union.

Slidell chose to remain in France with his newly transplanted American family, but Fenneval opted to sail to America to turn over the funds to General

Lee personally. Fenneval sailed on the British vessel *Rinaldo* from London in late July, 1862. After changing vessels several times during the voyage, Fenneval reached port in Mobile Bay, Alabama, on the Confederate steamer *Oreto* on September 4, 1862. From there, Fenneval, escorted by a small company of Confederate soldiers, made his way up to Maryland. He met General Robert E. Lee in an encampment near Frederick, Maryland on September 11. Grateful to receive financial help from France, Lee was perturbed about Fenneval's presence. He wanted to have Fenneval escorted away from danger immediately, but Fenneval assured the general that he had had a little military experience. He offered to join in the current campaign, and although Lee initially refused, he acquiesced to the youthful Frenchman's wishes.

On the morning of September 17, Lee positioned his men along Antietam Creek. The Union forces, under General Ambrose Burnside, advanced on Antietam, and the two armies met. In spite of heavy losses on both sides, General Lee's troops held their ground as they continued to fight throughout the day and into the night. When Lee's forces withdrew the next day, the Union had lost 2108 men and the Confederacy had lost 2700 men. The Battle of Antietam was called "the bloodiest single day of the war."

When General Lee marched his men south out of Maryland, he shook hands with the young Frenchman who had served under him valiantly, surviving without a scratch. Fenneval departed the main force, traveling to Bull's Bay, South Carolina, where Captain Raphael Semmes of the warship *Alabama* waited for him to take him on the first leg of the return voyage. He reached England on board the *Galena* in October of 1862, then returned to Paris by local means. French newspapers hailed his return with a hero's welcome, and Flora was able to read of his exploits at secondhand.

When the War of 1870 between France and Prussia began, it is unclear where Cordell Fenneval had been. He was not with the main French forces that surrendered to the Germans after the Battle of Sedan. Flora located him after reading the rolls of casualties. He was listed as seriously wounded and in hospital after the surrender of provisional French forces in Paris to the German army. For several weeks, Fenneval was in a delirium, coming out of unconsciousness very infrequently. During that time,

Flora was at his bedside, ministering to him. After he regained consciousness and his fever broke, Flora remained out of sight. If he recognized her as a woman he met at a party eighty years earlier, he might want to question her about their common anomaly. She continued to visit the hospital but kept herself hidden from him.

Fenneval had a serious bayonet wound and gunshots in his back. When he was first brought to the hospital, he was not expected to live. He survived, but the attending physicians concurred that he would never walk again. By January of 1872, Fenneval could not be restrained from taking walks in the garden outside the hospital.

Shortly after Fenneval's recovery, he traveled widely on the Continent, and for a time Flora lost contact. It seemed as if Fenneval was deliberately trying to lose himself. Some of his former acquaintances had questioned him about his relationship with a Cordell Fenneval who had survived the Battle of Leipzig in 1813, and this may have embarrassed Fenneval enough to want to make a new life for himself.

An American expatriate by the name of Carl Corey appeared in Paris in 1884, several years after old acquaintances of Cordell Fenneval had either left Paris or died. Corey arrived in Paris with the express purpose of conferring with a renowned French physician who had done much work with patients suffering from hysteria and other mental disorders. The physician was a charismatic practitioner by the name of Jean Martin Charcot. Corey made an appointment to see him at the Salpetriere on the morning of April 6, 1884.

Charcot and Corey had a number of consultations in which the physician attempted to unravel the cause of Corey's loss of memory. His diagnosis was that the problem was more than a mental aberration, but rather had been induced through some great physical shock. Charcot tried hypnosis over a series of sessions, but found Corey's subconscious mind intractable. From these sessions, Charcot deduced that Corey had formed some powerful, willful blockage to his subconscious that could not be penetrated by hypnosis. Although Corey was ostensibly seeking his identity, some deep emotional denial had locked the door to that knowledge, even from himself.

Hoping that Charcot would be able to unlock that door, Corey continued to consult him, and the physician came to befriend the young American who seemed to wear ages in his eyes. On several occasions, Corey was invited to social engagements at the French doctor's house. On a February night in 1886, Charcot introduced him to a young Viennese doctor who had been studying with him. Corey enjoyed several long conversations with the slightly discomforted doctor, realizing that the doctor was not used to such social gatherings. His name struck Corey as being quite distinguished, sounding so Germanic within that small enclave of French society: Sigmund Freud.

When Freud published his early work about the patient known only as Anna O. in 1895, Corey began to follow the doctor's progress. After Freud was appointed professor of neuropathology at the University of Vienna in 1902, Corey decided to visit Vienna and settle there for a while. He approached Freud's house in the autumn of 1903, reacquainted himself with the doctor, and became a frequent consulting patient. In the Chronicles, Corwin indicates that Freud was unsuccessful in helping him regain his memory. In conversation with his brother Benedict, Corwin stated that his memory began to return only after his auto accident on the shadow Earth much later:

"The bash on my head provided what even Sigmund Freud had been unable to obtain for me earlier . . . There returned to me small recollections that grew stronger and stronger—especially after I encountered Flora and was exposed to all manner of things that stimulated my memory." (GA, 89)

In spite of Freud's failure to help him regain his memory, Corey returned to Paris seeking a respite from worries. His happiness in Paris in the year 1905 was so complete that he imprinted that reminiscence on the new Pattern he created:

White absinthe, Amer Picon, grenadine . . . Wild strawberries with Crème d'Isigny . . . Chess at the Café de la Régence with actors from the Comédie Française, just across the way . . . The races at Chantilly, evenings at the Boîte à Fursy on the Rue Pigalle . . .
. . . the smell of the chestnut trees, of the wagonloads of vegetables moving through the dawn toward the Halles. . . . I was not in love

with anyone in particular at the time, though there were many girls—Yvettes and Mimis and Simones, their faces merge—and it was spring in Paris, with Gipsy bands and cocktails at Louis'. . .
. . . The Seine full of stars . . . The smell of the old brick houses in the Place des Vosges after a morning's rain . . . The bar under the Olympia Music Hall . . . A fight there . . . Bloodied knuckles, bandaged by a girl who took me home . . . What was her name? (CC, 92–93)

Shortly after that idyllic spring in Paris, Carl Corey married an American tourist he met there. Her name was Carolyn, and she had been traveling with friends. She was an attractive, dark-haired girl in her twenties. Theirs was a whirlwind romance in which they met and married within a month's time. They lived in an elegant mansion in St. Denis, just north of Paris.

Flora was unable to learn very much about Carolyn. She seemed to be a very private person who didn't allow room for new acquaintances. Through a bit of subterfuge, Flora did obtain a copy of a daguerreotype that Carolyn posed for. It was a rather old-fashioned photographic portrait inscribed with the words: "To Carl, Love, Carolyn." Corey's new bride sent it as a gift to him soon after their wedding.

When Germany declared war on Russia and France in August of 1914, Corey joined the French infantry. He was placed in one of seventy-two French divisions at the Western front fighting against seventy-eight German infantry divisions. Corey was promoted to captain after the victorious Battle of the Marne, in which the Germans were sent into retreat.

After Douglas MacArthur's Rainbow Division arrived in France in 1917, French military advisors arranged with General Pershing to assign French officers to the Americans for training in trench warfare. Captain Corey was one of these officers.

Early in October of 1918, newly promoted Brigadier General MacArthur led two brigades through the thick forest of the Meuse-Argonne. He was assigned to destroy two German strongholds near the Belgian border: Hill 288 and the Côte-de-Châtillon. Captain Corey marched with the 84th.

While MacArthur set up his headquarters in a

Neuve-Forge farmhouse two miles behind the Argonne, the general's position was assaulted by artillery, and he suffered physically from tear gas and mustard gas. In the meantime, the two brigades of the Rainbow Division battled the Germans in a thick forest battered by shell fire and covered by fog. The 84th took Hill 288 from two thousand Germans. MacArthur received orders that the Côte-de-Châtillon was the key to the German defense and that it must be taken. The 83rd Brigade had heavy casualties and was pinned down by German fire in their attempt to take it.

Sending in the 84th, MacArthur made a frontal assault of Châtillon. It was a terrible, bloody struggle, but the combined brigades made ground. Afterward, MacArthur said of the battle: "Officers fell and sergeants leaped to the command. Companies dwindled to platoons and corporals took over. That is the way the Côte-de-Châtillon fell."

In that battle, Captain Corey had been giving covering fire to a platoon made up of both 83rd and 84th brigade soldiers as they edged their way up a steep hill to the Châtillon. He was spotted and fired upon, hit in the chest, stomach, and legs. The men in his platoon claimed that Corey's protective firing had been a vital factor in allowing them to take the German position.

Barely alive, Corey was carried back to MacArthur's headquarters, where an impromptu field hospital had been set up. Corey was not given any greater care than other wounded soldiers brought in, but MacArthur learned of his actions in the decisive battle. MacArthur sent a message to Pershing requesting the Medal of Honor for this dying young officer. It was obvious to the general that the young officer had a special story to tell, having been an American who signed up for the war as an expatriate living in France.

By the time another messenger arrived with Pershing's affirmation that Captain Corey would be decorated, posthumously if necessary, Corey was conscious and talking to his comrades. When MacArthur visited the men in the hospital, he was amazed to find the young captain recovering so rapidly. MacArthur personally gave Corey the Medal of Honor at his bedside.

With his wife, Corey moved to Berlin to accept a post as military attaché to the League of Nations. He remained in and around Berlin during the 1920s, acting to maintain the Treaty of Versailles and the social democracy of Germany under the Weimar Republic. In the mid-thirties, he was sent to the Philippines to protect its Commonwealth status. Carolyn and Corey enjoyed the rights of diplomatic privilege, traveling from Singapore to Manila to Tokyo and back again. In Manila, he was reintroduced to General MacArthur, and enjoyed a brief photographic session with him. MacArthur mentioned having met Corey's father and presenting an award to him at the Argonne in the Great War.

With the European outbreak of World War II, Corey was recalled to France. In March of 1942, he became an agent of the French Maquis. He was involved in Operation Dragoon in August of 1944. Lieutenant General Alexander Patch of the American Seventh Army and General Jean de Lattre de Tasigny with the French First Army took on resistance agents of the French Maquis in a combined assault of the German army up the Rhône Valley. Joining General Patton's forces north of Switzerland, they caused a massive retreat of the Germans to the Rhine, an enormous victory for the allied forces. Although this was the beginning of the Allied drive against the Nazis, Corey was sent back to Paris with a shattered shoulder bone. He recovered in a short period of time, but he served out the rest of the war in several diplomatic roles, touring mainly in London and Paris.

At the end of the war, Corey was hired by the *London Times* as a correspondent. He was assigned to cover the war crimes trials of captured Nazis in Nuremburg. He wrote most feelingly about the atrocities described at the proceedings, turning incomprehensible statistics into vivid personal horror. Londoners wept over his crisp, grisly descriptions in the *Times*.

In December, 1945, Carolyn Corey died of an aneurysm in the brain. She was buried in a small cemetery in St. Denis, France.

Corey moved to Zurich, Switzerland, where he took up a modest medical practice. Late in 1947, he met playwright Bertolt Brecht on a walk to the Lindenhof. They became friends, visiting museums and attending concerts together. When Brecht and his wife left for Berlin, Corey traveled with them. He was in the audience when Brecht's wife, Helene Weigel, played the title role in her husband's play *Mother Courage* in January, 1949.

While Brecht formed his own company, the Berliner Ensemble, Corey began a small medical practice in Berlin. As their friendship deepened, Corey found himself becoming, in an unofficial capacity, Brecht's personal physician. Corey traveled with the company on theatrical tours of Poland and France. When Brecht died in East Berlin on August 14, 1956, Corey attempted to console his widow before departing Germany.

Corey traveled widely once again, and Flora lost him somewhere in the north of France. There are indications that he took a new direction in his life, becoming a roving soldier of fortune. Flora collected a number of newspaper articles referring to political assassinations, sudden military coups, disappearances of influential people, and minor revolutions. Behind each incident was the common factor of a mysterious military leader or instigator who revealed great physical strength. This mysterious figure vanished from the scene before anything further could be learned about him. These particular incidents may or may not have been attributable to Corwin's intervention, but there had been a sudden spate of these violent political acts in various parts of Europe.

Flora's spies discerned Corwin, still going by the name Carl Corey, in Luxembourg. He had made contact with an arms dealer there on behalf of a North African ruler. Corey was located because the African leader had been less than discreet in his discussions, and his plans were leaked to some of his adversaries. Those adversaries made the facts known to Flora's spies, although inadvertently. In any case, Flora learned that Corey had struck a deal for a supply of automatic weapons from a crafty British professional named Arthur. On completion of the deal, Arthur walked away with a large quantity of gold bullion, and Corey was well paid for delivering his illegal shipment of arms to a newly established African nation. When the African leader was deposed, Corey decided it was time to leave the Continent.

His friend Brecht had lived for a while in the United States, and for some time Corey entertained thoughts of going back there, this time to stay. Opportunity and incentive seemed to have come together, and Corey returned to St. Denis to make preparations. He had the body of his late wife exhumed. He flew with the coffin on a commercial airline to New York City. Carolyn Corey no longer had any living relatives there, but Corey had her body buried in her family plot in a cemetery in

upstate New York. He bought a large house on a scenic hilltop a few miles away from the cemetery.

In New York, Corey lived off his previous earnings for some months. After the assassination of President Kennedy, and the subsequent killing of his assassin, events badly handled by local authorities, Corey attached himself to a consulting firm with a large political and military clientele. He was made head of a bureau that gave clandestine training in high-tech weapons and paramilitary tactics. Certain sections of the CIA were clients.

When Flora set up her base of operations in Westchester, New York, she made certain that her spies were discriminating people. Given Corey's success in mercenary dealings and covert activities, it would be dangerous to create any suspicions through sloppy operatives. As far as she could tell, he never knew that he was under surveillance.

Corey remained a private person. When home, he worked quietly in his den or workshop. From observations, he spent much of this time writing, probably reports of various kinds for his firm. He traveled frequently, usually flying to Washington, D.C., but also going to California, South America, New Mexico, and Canada.

On occasion, he sought solace in a nearby country club. He put on an amiable front, attempting to squelch any chance of gossip by being "an ordinary, friendly guy." In this way, he gathered a number of acquaintances who asked polite questions out of curiosity. These people were satisfied with his explanation that he had been a career army officer in Europe, recently retired. The consulting firm he worked for was a legitimate enterprise, so he didn't hide the fact that he was involved in government business through the firm.

His meeting Bill Roth seemed a minor incident at the time, but Corey gradually found him to be a staunch friend. In the Chronicles, Corwin described Bill and their friendship in this way:

Bill was a native of the area, had gone to school in Buffalo, come back, married, joined the family firm, and that was that. He had known me as a retired Army officer who sometimes traveled on vague business. We both belonged to the country club, which was where I had met him. I had known him for over a year without our exchanging more than a few words. Then one evening I happened to be next to him in the bar and it had somehow come out that he was hot on military history, particularly the Napoleonic Wars. The next thing we knew, they were closing up the place around us. We were close friends from then on, right up until the time of my difficulties.'' (SU, 131–32)

Corey began spending a great deal of time with Bill Roth, getting to know his wife Alice and their children. The Roths had a piano in their suburban home, and Corey showed them some of the musical compositions he had been working on. Alice was a fair pianist. Since Roth was an attorney, Corey consulted with him on minor legal matters a few times. Roth arranged for a neighborhood contractor, Ed Wellen, to do some work on Corey's house. There had been a break-in while Corey was away one time, a bit of vandalism and random damage. Wellen replaced or repaired various parts of his bathroom, did much of the cleaning up, and accepted payment only at cost. Meanwhile, Corey worked out some legal details with Roth for paying bills for utilities while traveling out of the country.

One time, Bill Roth made a present of a recent book about Napoleon, written by an author named Markham. Years later in Amber, Corwin happened to turn to the book and saw a brief note on the flyleaf: ''Carl, Like Napoleon, there is more depth in you than mere measurement will allow. Bill R.''

He spent pleasant years there, but he knew that a part of his life remained undisclosed to him, and this bothered him greatly. On a cool morning in early spring, he had gone into town. Across the street, he saw a lovely young woman. Wearing a green dress, she had hair the color of glowing chestnuts, and her eyes were a sharp blue. He felt he should have known her, but he was unable to place her. Before he could reach the corner where she had stood, she was gone. That appearance sparked some bit of recollection in Corey. For the briefest moment, he believed that she belonged to a time and place *before* he had walked in a daze in seventeenth century London. Was that even possible?

For months after the woman's appearance, Corey spent many evenings jotting down subconscious impressions as he thought about her. He tossed out dozens of sheets of paper filled with the names of people he had known. None fit that blue-eyed vision. None fit him, either. With a continuing sense of hopelessness, he scribbled names and places on sheets of paper, only to toss them into the trash can beside him.

When disaster struck, Corey had hardly been aware of it. He knew he was drugged, restrained, placed in a locked room, but he couldn't distinguish what had gone on just prior to these sensations. He knew dreamless sleep and nightmarish half-conscious visions. Searing, bright, terrible pain. He knew white burning pain. His mind wouldn't allow him to make sense of any of it.

Years later, Corwin learned what had happened through his friend Bill Roth. Roth had done some investigating at the time of Corwin's automobile accident, and this is the story he was able to piece together:

''I was referring to the Porter Sanitarium, where you spent two days and then escaped. You had your accident that same day, and you were brought here [a local hospital] as a result of it. Then your sister Evelyn entered the picture. She had you transferred to Greenwood, where you spent a couple of weeks before departing on your own motion once again.'' . . .

''. . . You were committed on a bum order'' . . .

'' 'Brother, Brandon Corey; attendant physician, Hillary B. Rand, psychiatrist' '' . . .

''. . . An order got signed on that basis . . . You were duly certified, taken into custody, and transported. . . .

''I don't know that much about the practice and its effects on the memory, but you were subjected to electroshock therapy while you were at Porter. Then, as I said, the record indicates that you escaped after the second day. You apparently recovered your car from some unspecified locale and were heading back this way when you had the accident. . . .

''Now, about that order . . . It was based on false evidence, but there was no way of the court's knowing it at the time. The real Dr. Rand was in England when everything happened, and when I contacted him later he had never heard of you. His office had been broken into while he was away, though. Also, peculiarly, his middle initial is not B. He had never heard of Brandon Corey either. . . .

''He [Brandon] simply vanished. Several attempts were made to contact him at the time of your escape from Porter, but he could not be found. Then you had the accident, were brought here and treated. At that time, a woman named Evelyn Flaumel, who represented herself as your sister, contacted this place, told them you had been probated and that the family wanted you transferred to Greenwood. In the absence of Brandon, who had been appointed your guardian, her instructions were followed, as the only available next of kin. That was how it came about that you were sent to the other place. You escaped again, a couple of weeks later, and that is where my chronology ends.'' (SU, 134–35)

From Corwin's point of view, he was aware of the world around him when he awoke in Greenwood Private Hospital. Suffering from drug withdrawal, he realized he was in a hospital room. Apparently he had been heavily sedated for weeks, but some careless staff member had forgotten to give him his last injection during the graveyard shift. Corwin awoke with a lucidity that had not been allowed to him previously.

Most certainly, the automobile accident had been a decisive factor in affecting him mentally. It may also have involved a number of traumas that he was subjected to in a short period of time. When he awoke in Greenwood, he had lost all knowledge of his past life up to that moment. His mind was a tabula rasa, and his consciousness only read what was occurring from the present time onward.

Acting on the present moment, he removed his bandages and the two leg casts, knowing intuitively that he was physically whole. He allowed instinct and a near-absent sophistication about human nature to guide his conscious judgments. He chose surprise and bluster as his tack, and this led him out of the hospital and to the Westchester home of Evelyn Flaumel. Without knowing how, Corwin knew he was on the right track. He spoke with veiled innuendo, permitting his sister to open the way for him.

The tabula rasa of his mind continued to write his history for him as he examined his sister's library. On looking through the family Trumps he discovered there, vague recollections added to his knowledge. More information came with the arrival of his brother Random. The assault of shadow beings upon them served to bring further awareness to Corwin of his superior strength. When he joined

Random on the drive back to Amber, Corwin understood that there was something beyond natural law functioning in their journey.

As they drove, Corwin suddenly recalled the Forest of Arden in a shadow close to Amber. When his brother Julian appeared, riding on his horse Morgenstern, he recollected some things about both. Julian cautiously approached, and Corwin put on a confident front, remaining alert to clues from both Random and Julian. Afterward, when Julian chased down their automobile with his hellhounds in pursuit, Corwin boldly jumped at Julian. Overpowering his brother, Corwin coerced Julian into the car. They drove off, and Corwin took the opportunity to learn more from him about the situation in Amber.

Corwin left Julian standing at the edge of a cliff, as a remembrance to Julian of his older brother when the political climate in Amber changed in Corwin's favor. They drove on, getting closer to the true realm. When they reached the land of Amber, the car failed, and they went on by foot. A little way farther and they came upon a camp of four of Eric's soldiers. They had Deirdre, Corwin's sister, with them, tied to a stake for safekeeping for the night.

Random and Corwin ambushed the men and freed Deirdre. She informed them that Eric was ruling Amber with an iron hand, aware that Corwin was coming. At this point, Corwin decided to tell Random and Deirdre the truth about himself: that he had no memory of his past life and knew them only in the vaguest possible terms. When Random was convinced that Corwin was being honest about his amnesia, he suggested that they go to the undersea city of Rebma. There, Corwin could walk the Pattern and regain his memory.

Although they made it to the shore without incident, they found themselves being pursued by a patrol on the open beach. They ran to the water, reaching the stair called Faiella-bionin, and descended into the sea. When they entered the undersea city, they met with their sister Llewella and the queen of Rebma, a lovely woman named Moire. Queen Moire was willing to permit Corwin to walk the Pattern, but she was harsher about Random's status. Random had once taken Moire's daughter away, and the girl had returned, alone and pregnant. She had given birth to a boy, then committed suicide. Moire decided to mete out a peculiar punishment to Random, since he had come within her grasp. He was sentenced to remain in Rebma for one year and marry a woman of Moire's choice. However, the queen remained kind to Corwin.

After they had eaten, Moire led Deirdre, Random, and Corwin down to an enormous cavern, then to passages similar to their counterparts in the true city. She brought them to the huge room containing the Pattern. Before Corwin began the walk, Random offered suggestions about the procedure. Corwin stepped on the Pattern and began. The way was difficult, but he seemed to know instinctively how to handle the various impressions as he moved. When he passed the First Veil, memory opened up for him. His thoughts were flooded with images of his life on the shadow Earth. As he went on, he knew, at firsthand, the realm of Amber. He continued, completed the circuit, and was once again invested with full knowledge of himself.

At the center of the Pattern, Corwin closed his eyes, thought deeply of a place, and was transported into the Royal Palace of Amber. With memory intact, he intended to challenge Eric with every weapon in his arsenal.

Thus, Corwin entered the third phase of his life, seeking his rightful place in the world that was part of his very being.

Since King Oberon was absent and Eric had positioned himself to rule in the true city, Corwin felt compelled to act in opposition to Eric. He was sufficiently aware of Eric's role in trying to put him out of the way that he was suspicious of Eric's complicity in their father's disappearance also.

In spite of the fact that Corwin was motivated by his hatred of Eric, this period in his life was marked by a new maturity. He was, indeed, a man of action, just as he had been in the earlier phases of his life. But in this third phase, he was given to much reflection, pondering the half-hidden nature of people he encountered, and wondering over his own nature as well. In this phase, he tried to act for what he perceived to be the benefit of Amber, hoping to fill the vacancy left by his father.

Fortunately, this part of Corwin's history is well documented in his first person account written in the Chronicles. It would be superfluous to repeat verbatim the text that has been made public domain. Rather than do that, what follows is a simplified listing of actions and events directly involving Corwin as he worked toward the betterment of his homeland. The pagination given is based on the first

five books about Amber published in English on the shadow Earth in the city of New York.

Nine Princes in Amber (NP), pp. 95–100: Corwin encounters Eric in the library of the Royal Palace, where Corwin obtained a set of the family Trumps. They duel, Corwin escapes ahead of Eric's guards, and he asks Bleys to bring him through with his Trump.

NP, 100–40: Corwin joins Bleys in his campaign against Eric. While Bleys travels across the shadowlands, Corwin leads Bleys's fleet through the seas. They battle Eric's soldiers as they climb the western stair of Mt. Kolvir. Bleys falls from the mountain, and Corwin is captured.

NP, 145–58: Eric has Corwin witness his coronation, although Corwin manages to crown himself first. Eric has Corwin blinded and left in a dungeon for years. Only Lord Rein, the friend of Corwin's youth, comes to him, providing a measure of comfort in food, drink, and news. After three years of blindness, Corwin discovers that his vision is gradually returning.

NP, 160–75: Determined to escape before his returned eyesight is found out, Corwin uses a spoon to scratch his way around the lock in the heavy wooden door. The old mage, Dworkin, had used his version of a Trump to enter Corwin's cell. Using a bit of subterfuge, Corwin has Dworkin sketch the Lighthouse at Cabra, an island near Amber's shore, on a wall. Able to see well enough, Corwin walks through the image on the wall and appears on the beach of Cabra. With the help of the lighthouse keeper, Jopin, Corwin travels away from Amber on Jopin's sailboat, *The Butterfly*.

The Guns of Avalon (GA), 12–19: On his way to a shadow of his Avalon, Corwin meets the wounded knight Lancelot, who had just killed six Wardens of the Circle. Corwin carries him to the Keep of Ganelon in the village of Lorraine. Both Lancelot and Ganelon are shadow versions of the men he knew long ago.

GA, 19–68: While Corwin regains his former strength, he learns more about this Ganelon and the problem of the Circle which allows passage for horrible creatures to the village called Lorraine. Corwin meets a girl, also by the name of Lorraine. Spending a night with the girl, Corwin faces and destroys a demon named Strygalldwir. The coming of the demon and the dark Circle lead Corwin to believe that they are products of the curse he had wished upon Eric when he had been imprisoned. Ganelon, Lancelot, and Corwin lead troops against the army of the Circle. They are victorious after Corwin slays the goat-headed being who directed the invasion. Before planning to move on with Ganelon, Corwin returns to the village to seek out Lorraine. He finds her dead, murdered by a former lover. After hunting down and killing her murderer, he goes to meet Ganelon.

GA, 69–102: On the road to the shadow Avalon, Ganelon restrains a youth who had deserted from a battle there. The youth tells them something of the shadow Avalon and the battle between hellish females and the army of Avalon's Protector. They release the boy and continue on until they reach an armed encampment. Brought into the camp by guards, Corwin finds out that the general who is acting as Protector of the realm is his brother Benedict. They greet each other warmly, and Corwin introduces Ganelon to him. Corwin fills Benedict in on his remembered past life from the time of his arguments with Eric over the succession. For his part, Benedict speaks laconically of the recent battle with the hellmaids. Benedict had killed their leader, but at the cost of his right arm. He is remaining in the field a few more days to be assured of total victory. Although he is not completely trusting of Corwin's intentions, Benedict allows Corwin and his friend to remain as his guest in one of his manor houses.

GA, 105–23: Corwin is awakened from an outdoors drowse by a tall girl in fencing gear. She urges him to fence with her, and only after ending the duel, does she reveal that she is Dara, great-granddaughter of Benedict. Dara tells Corwin what she knows of Amber and the Trumps, but she hungers to know more. Corwin takes her on a hellride through Shadow, explaining further about her abilities as a descendant of the Royal Line. In their conversation, Dara tells him about a visit from Gérard and Julian. It marks the first time that Corwin learns of the black road.

GA, 124–85: After arranging for a large supply of jewelers rouge with a jeweler named Doyle in Avalon, Corwin goes on a hellride to obtain raw diamonds in an alternate Africa of a shadow Earth. When he returns to Benedict's manor house, he meets Ganelon, who tells Corwin of an encounter with Dara. Ganelon also tells him of a shallow grave that he found with four bodies buried in it. They surmise that the corpses had been servants with whom Benedict had a falling out. Checking the site of the burial himself, Corwin meets with Dara again, and they make love. The next day, Ganelon and Corwin begin a hellride out of Avalon, carrying their necessary supplies in a horse-drawn wagon. On the way, they discover the black road, and it seems to cut through all the shadows they travel. They spy Benedict pursuing them from a distance. Corwin tries to lose him in Shadow, but he stays with them. In a desperate move, Corwin uses a mental image of the Pattern in order to cross the black road in the wagon. In spite of his success in crossing it, Benedict continues his pursuit. Sending Ganelon ahead, Corwin stops to do battle with his brother. Using the black road to his advantage, Corwin is able to render Benedict unconscious. He contacts his brother Gérard in Amber to come to aid Benedict while he and Ganelon continue to the shadow Earth.

GA, 187–223: On the shadow Earth, Corwin deals with the ex–RAF officer Arthur for a consignment of rifles. Arthur sends them to Switzerland to have the special ammunition prepared. While Ganelon remains touring in Europe, Corwin returns to his home in New York State. In his narrative, Corwin indicates that he had spoken to Gérard by Trump, assessing his relations with Benedict. At his home, Corwin finds a note left by Eric, asking him not to attack Amber at this time. Eric's note states that Amber has been under attack by creatures out of Shadow. In spite of this, Corwin rejoins Ganelon, and they drive their weapons and a shadow army in trucks through the shadows. When the trucks fail, they march to Amber, encountering a deadly manticora on the way. Shortly afterward, they are attacked by a horde of other manticoras. Crossing the western mountain range, they can see Eric's army battling beings out of Shadow, some riding winged wyvern. As they advance upon Mt. Kolvir, Dara rides up on a horse, claiming to have followed Benedict there through Shadow. Corwin has her guarded while they move on to the scene of battle. They use their rifles to support Amber's forces, but Corwin arrives too late to save Eric, who has been mortally wounded. Before he dies, Eric passes the Jewel of Judgment to Corwin with some instructions. In the meantime, Dara rides by, intent on reaching the Royal Palace and walking the Pattern. Corwin uses Benedict's Trump to send him his armed troops to help conclude the fighting in the valley. Contacting Random in the palace, Corwin has him bring him through. Together, they go to the dungeons, find a guard dead, and see a strange being, who seems to be a transformed Dara, complete the Pattern walk. Before she disappears, she shouts, "Amber will be destroyed!"

Sign of the Unicorn (SU), 7–55: Someone has duped Corwin, now ruling in Amber, into meeting with his brother Caine in order to implicate him in Caine's murder. After returning with the body of a shadow being that had been the apparent murderer, Corwin meets with Random in the palace. Random recounts his past history up to his coming to Flora's Westchester home on the shadow Earth. Random's story involves his failed rescue attempt of an imprisoned Brand. Wishing to resolve the problem of the black road, the Shadow invasions, and conspiracies against Amber, Corwin attunes himself to the Jewel of Judgment by walking the Pattern while wearing it.

SU, 57–80: Corwin meets with Random and Flora in his quarters. Flora gives him the details of her discovery of Corwin alive in France on the shadow Earth and Eric's subsequent orders to keep him under surveillance. She confirms that the corpse of the shadow being that Corwin brought back was the same kind as those that followed Random and attacked them in her home. Corwin later confers with Ganelon, who is quite perceptive in his queries about the Trumps. Ganelon informs Corwin of the disposition of their shadow troops, bivouacked in Amber. The next day, Corwin and Gérard ride to the place where Corwin hid Caine's body. On the way, Gérard fights with Corwin, threatening to toss him off the cliff if he discovers that Corwin is the murderer of Caine and the servants of Bene-

dict. As a form of insurance for his own life, Gérard had arranged for their brothers and sisters to observe these actions through the Trumps. After retrieving Caine's body, they see the mystical unicorn and take the sighting as a propitious sign.

SU, 81–119: Corwin holds a meeting of his brothers and sisters in the library of the Royal Palace. They include: Corwin, Random, Benedict, Gérard, Julian, Fiona, Flora, Deirdre, and Llewella. After giving the others the opportunity to hear Random's version of events, Corwin suggests that they all concentrate on Brand's Trump in order to reach him. When they succeed in raising Brand, Gérard and Random enter his prison cell and rescue him from his warders. Upon bringing him back to the library, someone in the room manages to stab Brand with a slim dagger. Gérard prevents anyone else from coming near Brand as he ministers to him on the couch. While Gérard cares for Brand, the others go to a sitting room to talk. Corwin leads the questioning about Brand's earlier activities, learning more of Brand's connection to Random's son, Martin. Benedict tells of Eric's activities during the time of the visit of Gérard and Julian to Avalon. Corwin questions Flora about the timing of the shadow invasions, seeking a connection between them and King Oberon's disappearance. By Trump, Gérard adds a piece of information about Oberon's last appearance. Gérard is certain that Oberon had worn the Jewel of Judgment on that last occasion. Benedict expresses concern about the nature of an enemy who wants Amber destroyed, rather than merely conquered. They agree to allow the guilty member of their family to live in banishment if he or she will reveal him or herself. In an aside, Fiona gives Corwin a warning about wearing the Jewel of Judgment too long. She believes that it contributed to Eric's death. She suggests that the guilty family member is most likely Julian, who hates everyone. When the others begin to turn in for the night, Corwin leaves with Random for their quarters. Upon stepping into his room, Corwin is stabbed by an unknown assailant and collapses into unconsciousness.

SU, 121–92: Corwin finds himself in his home on the shadow Earth, bleeding badly from the knife wound he received. Making his way outside, where it is snowing, he hides the Jewel of Judgment in the compost heap behind the house. He goes to the roadway and begins hailing cars. His friend Bill Roth sees him from his car, stops, and takes him to a nearby hospital. Later, Corwin speaks to the doctor, Dr. Morris Bailey, who had treated him years ago after his automobile accident. Between Dr. Bailey and Bill Roth, Corwin learns the details of that accident and what other family members were involved. Random contacts him by Trump, and Corwin returns to Amber to meet with Brand, who has been asking to see him. Hiding his own injury, Corwin goes to the library with Random to meet with Brand. Brand explains the two cabals that had begun after Corwin's disappearance centuries ago. Eric, Julian, and Caine had formed one group to take the throne, and Brand, Bleys, and Fiona had formed the other. Brand tells Corwin that it was his cabal that had moved to get Oberon out of the realm. He also puts the blame for Corwin's car accident on Bleys, after Brand had had a falling-out with his partners. Joining Random and Ganelon, Corwin goes to the ghost city in the sky, Tir-na Nog'th. While Ganelon and Random wait on Kolvir, Corwin enters the phantom city, and encounters an alternate Lorraine, who relates an alternate tale of their life together. Afterward, he arrives at the ghost version of the throne room in the Royal Palace, where he communicates with Dara and duels with a Benedict who wears a mechanical right arm. Using his sword Grayswandir, Corwin cuts off the metal arm and sinks through the flooring of the fading ghost city. He is rescued by reaching for Random through his Trump. Traveling back along Kolvir toward the palace, Random, Ganelon, and Corwin find themselves lost in some strange shadow shifting of the trail. They are unable to reach anyone else by Trump. They sight the unicorn, and it leads them to a strangely familiar place: It is the Pattern, but not encompassed by dungeon walls. Instead, it is in an open space in a position similar to where it would be within Mt. Kolvir. They realize that they have been led to the true Amber.

The Hand of Oberon (HO), 22–47: On examining the primal Pattern in the real Amber, Corwin, Random, and Ganelon notice a distinct blot on it. Using great perceptiveness, Ganelon expresses the belief that the blot is the basic disruption that has its analogue in the black road crossing all the shadows. Ganelon runs into the blotted section to retrieve a small object they see within it. When he returns, they discover it is a bloodstained Trump pierced with a dagger. Suddenly, a large, purple griffin comes out of a nearby cave. It is chained and seems tame to Corwin and Random. Someone had set the griffin there as a guard against any further tampering with the primal Pattern. When Ganelon comes up with the insightful idea that the blot was caused by spilling the blood of an initiate of the Pattern, Random realizes that the picture on the Trump, and the blood used, was that of Martin, his son. They contact Benedict by Trump, and he brings them through to another part of Mt. Kolvir. Benedict tells them of how he helped Martin when he came to Benedict to learn more of Shadow. Benedict had found out about Martin's injury from the Tecys in a special shadow that Benedict had once brought Martin to. Random asks Benedict to take him to the Tecys and help him track down Martin. After they go off, Ganelon presents Corwin with the possibility that Martin might have stabbed Corwin, and could become a new danger threatening the Family because of the ill treatment he had received at their hands.

HO, 48–87: Corwin visits with Vialle, the blind wife of Random, to let her know of Random's journey with Benedict. She talks of her husband and about Martin, whom she knew in Rebma. Having wondered about Corwin, Vialle questions the reason for strife among the princes of Amber, when they could rule in any shadow of their choice. Corwin responds that any shadow would be less than the true realm and would not suffice. After departing, Corwin rests a while in his room. In the night, he gets up to go to the dungeons, to visit the cell of his imprisonment. He examines the walls of the cell, then steps through the sketch of the room Dworkin had drawn years before. He meets Dworkin, who believes him to be Oberon, coming to wipe out the Pattern. Through Dworkin, Corwin learns of the connection between the blot on the Pattern and Dworkin's state of mind. He learns of his own aberrant ancestry from the unicorn and the reason why Oberon had imprisoned Dworkin. When he asks Dworkin about the chances that Oberon's sons might have in repairing the Pattern, Corwin reveals to Dworkin that he really is Corwin, not Oberon. Dworkin explains the use of the Jewel of Judgment in making the repair. Undergoing a dreadful, involuntary transformation, Dworkin urges Corwin to escape by choosing a Trump in his study. Just as Dworkin reaches forth in a demon form, Corwin trumps away to the Courts of Chaos. At the Courts, Corwin kills a Chaos rider but is confronted by a second rider who seems oddly familiar. This second rider knows Corwin and simply warns him away. After viewing the Dark Citadel over the Abyss of Chaos, Corwin trumps back to Amber by contacting Gérard. Gérard tells him that Benedict has returned wearing the metallic arm that Corwin had brought back from Tir-na Nog'th. Random has gone on into Shadow, still seeking his son. During Corwin's absence, Brand has been asking for him, so Corwin goes to Brand's quarters.

HO, 88–128: When Corwin arrives, Brand is surly about Corwin's not keeping him informed. Corwin shows him Martin's Trump and asks if Brand was behind Martin's stabbing, causing the blot on the Pattern. Brand admits to it, explaining its necessity as a means of gaining power to take over the rule of Amber. Corwin questions him about the plans of his allies at the Courts of Chaos, but Brand claims not to know the altered agreements made by Fiona and Bleys with the Chaos forces. Brand urges that Corwin and the others in Amber use their powers to destroy Fiona and Bleys. He claims that he will need the Jewel of Judgment as part of their combined effort to kill Fiona. Corwin flatly turns down Brand's suggestion, leaving him without offering further explanations. At the encampment of his shadow troops, Corwin meets with Ganelon and Benedict. While Benedict expresses his happiness about the mechanical arm he wears, brought back by Corwin, he is quietly skeptical as he listens to Corwin's story about seeing Dara and the ghost-Benedict in Tir-na Nog'th. Benedict is particularly quiet when he hears that Dara is a descendant of himself and Lintra, the hellmaid that he had slain. When Corwin shows him the

Trump of the Courts of Chaos, Benedict determines to examine that realm in preparation for a full-scale war against them. Corwin speaks of his intention of clearing the blot from the original Pattern, correcting their problems by that means. Before they go their separate ways, Benedict contacts Gérard, then brings him through with his Trump. Gérard explains that there had been a fight in Brand's room, with much blood, and that Brand is missing. He accuses Corwin of doing it and they fight. With Ganelon's help, Gérard is overpowered, and Corwin gets a horse to hellride to the shadow Earth to retrieve the Jewel of Judgment. In the Forest of Arden, Corwin runs into Julian, who has just slain a manticora that was pursuing Corwin. Julian tells him of his knowledge of the two cabals, and how Corwin had become a pawn used by both sides. Although Julian expresses his fondness for Fiona, he states his fear of Brand, and the hope that he has been killed. Parting on friendly terms, Corwin begins his hellride.

HO, 129–172: After arriving at his home on the shadow Earth, Corwin finds the compost heap, where he had hidden the Jewel of Judgment, missing. On his horse, Corwin makes his way to the home of Bill Roth. Bill tells him that Corwin's home had been put up for sale and is being fixed up by the local contractor. Through Bill, Corwin learns that Brand had been there asking about the house, and that he'd also gone to Ed Wellen's place as an artist wishing to paint in his fields. Corwin contacts Gérard by Trump to warn him of Brand's possible attempt to walk the Pattern in Amber. Meeting Bill at Wellen's place, Corwin finds that Brand had already recovered the Jewel from the compost heap there. Gérard contacts him to say that Brand had appeared at the Pattern, but left as soon as he saw Gérard there. Gérard tells Corwin that the Pattern in Rebma is also under guard. As he ends contact with Gérard, Corwin receives contact from Fiona. Corwin brings her through and introduces Bill to his sister. She tells Corwin that Brand will walk the primal Pattern, and they ride off on Corwin's horse to begin a hellride back. As they ride, Fiona fills in more of the pieces about the succession conspiracy and Brand's role in it. Fiona places most of the blame on Brand, both for involving the forces out of Chaos and for causing Corwin's automobile accident on the shadow Earth. At the primal Pattern, they find the tamed griffin dead and Brand already walking the Pattern. Corwin goes after him, trying to manipulate reaching Brand with his sword at the blot so that Brand's blood would not cause more damage. Using his attunement to the Jewel in Brand's possession, Corwin creates a magical tornado that lowers from the sky above Brand. Brand steps into the blotted area, making his escape from there. Corwin is left to complete the Pattern walk. Later, he meets with Random and Martin at the cenotaph constructed for Corwin. After Corwin tells them of his encounter with Brand, Martin tells of his past, explaining his connection with Benedict, the near fatal meeting with Brand, the discovery he made of the black road, and his being cared for by Dara. Random says that he intends bringing Martin back to meet Vialle at the palace. Before they part, Corwin is surprised by a Trump contact from Ganelon. With his typical foresight, Ganelon has a plan for capturing Brand in his certain attempt to walk the Pattern of Tir-na Nog'th at moonrise. Benedict has already agreed, and he is stationed at the center of the Pattern in Amber. Once Corwin reaches the uppermost portion of Mt. Kolvir, he will be able to signal Benedict when the phantom city becomes substantial at the rise of the moon. Then, Benedict can immediately transport to the Pattern there, catching Brand before he can begin the walk. Corwin agrees to the plan, requests Random's horse in order to make a quick ride up the mountain, and leaves Martin and Random for the rendezvous.

HO, 173–88: When Corwin reaches the three stones that would form the first steps of the stairway to the phantom city, he contacts Benedict by Trump. After several minutes, Corwin tests the solidifying stairway to Tir-na Nog'th. Once the stair is substantial, he informs Benedict, who transports to the room of the Pattern there. Benedict waits only a short time before Brand appears on the opposite side of the Pattern. As Brand slowly rounds the Pattern toward Benedict, he tries to persuade his older brother to join him. While this is occurring, Corwin is able to observe through Benedict's Trump. Benedict re-

mains unmoved by all of Brand's arguments. At Benedict's demand that Brand hand him the Jewel of Judgment, Brand speaks of the unknown power of the Jewel. The Jewel is bright upon Brand's chest, and Benedict finds himself becoming paralyzed through its power. Corwin's calling to him has no effect. Brand approaches with a dagger, ready to strike his brother down. As he is about to use the dagger, the metallic arm moves, grasps the Jewel around Brand's neck, and lifts him up. Brand struggles to free himself, strangling in Benedict's grip. Pulling the chain apart, Brand frees himself, falling to the floor, which begins to become insubstantial. With the capturing of the Jewel, Benedict regains mobility, and Corwin rescues him, with the Jewel, as the city fades. Brand seems lost, falling through the disappearing floor to the waters far below. Benedict falls heavily beside Corwin on the high point of Mt. Kolvir. Before they return to the palace, Corwin suggests that there has been a long string of coincidences, ending with Benedict's use of the metallic arm to obtain the Jewel, that may have been caused by a specific guiding intelligence. When Corwin indicates that their father may have been behind these coincidences, Benedict finds it difficult to believe. To test Corwin's theory, they both concentrate on the Trump for Oberon. Ganelon responds, revealing that he is really Oberon.

When Oberon returned to the throne and Corwin stepped down as ruler of Amber, the third phase of Corwin's life ended. No longer acting as sole preserver of the true city, Corwin can be said to have begun the fourth phase of his life: working to resolve his conflict with the forces of the Courts of Chaos. For a while, of course, his problem with the Courts was also Amber's problem, but Corwin's involvement extended beyond the signing of the Concord.

Corwin's further involvement with the Courts, aside from political issues, concerned his relationship with Dara, and new facts that he learned from her. As related in the portion of Corwin's Chronicles that has been entitled The Courts of Chaos, Corwin confronted Dara in the Royal Palace under unusual circumstances.

After Oberon had ascended the throne, he gave orders to prepare to wage war on the Courts, and then went off again without explanation. Aside from these actions, the occurrence of a tableau eerily similar to the events that unfolded in Tir-na Nog'th was an added perplexity to an already frustrated Corwin. Corwin observed, with Gérard, Random, and others, the meeting of Martin, Benedict, and Dara in the throne room. Unable to pass through an invisible barrier, Corwin and the others could do nothing while watching a levitated sword resembling Grayswandir dueling with Benedict. When the sword severed the metal arm from Benedict, both objects sank through the floor, in just the same way that Corwin had disappeared with the arm from a fading Tir-na Nog'th.

Immediately upon entering the throne room, Random confronted his son about what had happened. Martin briefly explained that he had brought Dara through to see Amber, and that Benedict had joined them when Martin contacted him. Both Random and Corwin found a mystery in the set of Trumps that Martin possessed. The Trumps were done in a hand not known to Corwin. Among them was a Trump of a young man that Random didn't know, but Corwin had seen before. It was a Trump of the horseman that Corwin spoke to when he had trumped to the Courts of Chaos. When Corwin asked Martin about the Trump of the young man, Martin told him that it was the person who had drawn the extra Trumps. Asking Dara about the young man, Corwin discovered that the youth he had met at the Courts, the one pictured on the Trump, was his son, Merlin.

Given the opportunity to explain, Dara told Corwin and the others that she had been a part of the plot of the Courts of Chaos. All the things she had told Corwin earlier had been lies. At the behest of the Courts, she had been trying to gain Corwin's trust, trying to learn more about the Family, the Trumps, and the Pattern. It was also in the furtherance of their plan that she have Corwin's son, a child born to both Chaos and Order.

Dara's motives changed after she met Martin, when he was ill from the wound he suffered at Brand's hands, and after she met King Oberon, helping him out of his difficulties. The following is part of the interchange Corwin had with her:

"I find it somewhat distressing to have been involved in a calculated breeding project," I said, at length. "But be that as it may, and accepting everything you have said as true—

for the moment—why are you telling us all of these things now?"

"Because," she said, "I fear that the lords of my realm would go as far for their vision as Brand would for his. Farther, perhaps. That balance I spoke of. Few seem to appreciate what a delicate thing it is. I have traveled in the shadowlands near to Amber, and I have walked in Amber herself. I also have known the shadows that lie by Chaos' side. I have met many people and seen many things. Then, when I encountered Martin and spoke with him, I began to feel that the changes I had been told would be for the better would not simply result in a revision of Amber more along the lines of my elders' liking. They would, instead, turn Amber into a mere extension of the Courts, most of the shadows would boil away to join with Chaos. Amber would become an island. Some of my seniors who still smart at Dworkin's having created Amber in the first place are really seeking a return to the days before this happened. Total Chaos, from which all things arose. I see the present condition as superior and I wish to preserve it. My desire is that neither side emerge victorious in any conflict." (CC, 17–18)

This balance between the Courts and Amber of which Dara spoke was an expression of the equation that Corwin was to continue struggling with. At this point, however, Corwin could not be aware of all the implications involving the changing balance of the two sides.

In order to check Dara's story that she was acting on his father's behalf, Corwin and the others contacted Fiona at the primal Pattern. After conversing for a few minutes, Fiona ended their contact to go to Oberon for his confirmation of orders. When she contacted Corwin again, she was with Oberon and Dworkin in Dworkin's sitting room. At Corwin's request, Fiona brought him through to them. Oberon was slightly annoyed at Corwin's interruption of preparations, but he softened as Corwin spoke of the friendship they had when he was disguised as Ganelon. Out of a sense of duty to Amber, Corwin grabbed the Jewel of Judgment from his father and ran for the primal Pattern. He was attempting to repair the Pattern in his father's place, knowing that he might die in doing so. Exerting their combined will, Dworkin and Oberon caused a paralysis in Corwin before he could step onto the Pattern. When Oberon reached him, he took back the Jewel, then helped Corwin to his feet. They walked together and spoke of the village of Lorraine, of Ganelon, and of Dara. In their conversation together, father and son revealed something of their feelings for one another, as much as they expressed their thoughts about the present circumstances:

"There is something that I have to know," I [Corwin] said. "Before I came here I was speaking with Dara, who is in the process of trying to clear her name with us—"

"It *is* clear. I have cleared it." . . .

"I refrained from accusing her of something I have been thinking about for some time. There is a very good reason why I feel she cannot be trusted, despite her protests and your endorsement. Two reasons, in fact."

"I know, Corwin. But she did not kill Benedict's servants to manage her position at his house. I did it myself, to assure her getting to you as she did, at just the appropriate time."

"You? You were party to her whole plot? Why?"

"She will make you a good queen, son. I trust the blood of Chaos for strength. It was time for a fresh infusion. You will take the throne already provided with an heir. By the time he is ready for it, Merlin will long have been weaned from his upbringing." . . .

"You think this thing [the blot of the primal Pattern] is going to kill you?" . . .

"I know that it is."

"You are not above murdering innocent people to manipulate me. Yet you would sacrifice your life for the kingdom. . . .

"My own hands are not clean . . . and I certainly do not presume to judge you. A while back, though, when I made ready to try the Pattern, I thought how my feelings had changed—toward Eric, toward the throne. You do what you do, I believe, as a duty. I, too, feel a duty now, toward Amber, toward the throne. More than that, actually. Much more, I realized, just then. But I realized something else, also, something that duty does not require of me. I do not know when or how it stopped and I changed, but I do not want the throne,

Dad. I am sorry it messes up your plans, but I do not want to be king of Amber. I am sorry." . . .

"I am going to send you home now. Saddle your horse and take provisions. Ride to a place outside Amber—any place, fairly isolated."

"My tomb?" . . .

"That will do. Go there and wait my pleasure. I have some thinking to do." (CC, 28–29)

Before he followed Oberon's orders, Corwin spent a few minutes alone with Dara. She told him that in spite of the cold-blooded scheming to manipulate Corwin to make love to her, that wasn't all there was to it. She liked him, and, if he felt so inclined, their relationship could become much more. They kissed before parting for their separate assignments.

When Oberon joined Corwin at his cenotaph, he asked Corwin to bare his arm. Drawing blood with a dagger, Oberon used the blood to create a red bird the size of a raven. The mission that Oberon sent Corwin on involved his riding south on his horse, entering Shadow, and continuing on a hellride to the Courts of Chaos. The red bird and the slower means of travel were necessary because Corwin would receive the Jewel of Judgment from the bird as he journeyed. Oberon bade him farewell and faded into air.

Corwin's hellride was a long one. He received the Jewel from the red bird as he rode, just as his father had said. With that transference, however, was the grave doubt that continued to haunt him throughout the hellride. Did Oberon succeed in clearing the primal Pattern? Did he survive the endeavor? Or was Oberon dead? And if so, was the Pattern destroyed as well?

The actualization of this doubt came in the form of his brother, Brand. In a strange forest of metal, Corwin met him. Brand tried to persuade him of what he most feared:

"I can see through Shadow, Corwin. . . . Naturally, I was concerned with the outcome of this affair. So I watched. He is dead, Corwin. The effort was too much for him. He lost control of the forces he was manipulating and was blasted by them a little over halfway through the Pattern. . . .

"I admit that I am not above lying to gain

my ends, but this time I am telling the truth. Dad is dead. I saw him fall. The bird brought you the Jewel then, as he willed it. We are left in a universe without a Pattern. . . .

"... Even now, Chaos wells up to fill the vacuum back at Amber. A great vortex has come into being, and it grows. It spreads ever outward, destroying the shadow worlds, and it will not stop until it meets with the Courts of Chaos, bringing all of creation full circle, with Chaos once more to reign over all." (CC, 44–45)

In spite of Brand's persuasiveness, Corwin refused to give him the Jewel of Judgment. Instead, Corwin walked menacingly toward his brother, willing to murder him if he could reach Brand, but knowing that he wouldn't reach him. Brand backed away, disappearing in the wood. Several times after that, Brand returned, ready to kill Corwin in order to obtain the Jewel. Brand's appearances became one aspect of Corwin's hellride to the Courts that formed a hindrance to be overcome.

Corwin relates the encounters he made on his hellride in vivid, anecdotal descriptions in his Chronicles. Rather than repeat them here, it would be better to point out the way in which his encounters reflected varying positions of Corwin's own perspective of things. In a sense, the corporeal entities he met seemed like facets of Corwin's conscience and introspection, even if they were part of external reality. Those forms that did not fit this mold were either part of a mythos that included temporalities cutting through the histories of innumerable shadows, or were agents of Chaos sent to give further hindrance to his mission.

The continuum of the mythos of Order, for instance, was marked by Corwin's meeting a stranger in a cave as the storm approached. The stranger recounted from scripture an episode of a fabled past/present/future event:

"You make me think of that line from the Holy Book—*The Archangel Corwin shall pass before the storm, lightning upon his breast. . . .* You would not be named Corwin, would you? . . .

"... *When asked where he travels, he shall say, 'To the ends of the Earth,' where he goes not knowing what enemy will aid him against another enemy, nor whom the Horn will touch.*" (CC, 53)

Shortly after departing the cave he shared with the stranger, Corwin encountered a race of beings out of legend: leprechauns. Upon leaving them, he promoted the myth of the Archangel Corwin by saying he was traveling "to the ends of the Earth."

A further hindrance to Corwin's mission came in the enticing form of a lovely woman who dwelled by a lake. She called herself "Lady" and delayed him with wine and food. Another came in the guise of a jackal with the ability to speak. It led Corwin into a cave opening, hoping to make a meal of him. Corwin was wary, ending the jackal's life with his sword.

Other entities approached Corwin with various displays of philosophy, apparently part of a cosmic attempt to influence his conscience or feelings of doubt. The giant head of the quagmire, evincing an attitude of nihilism, was one of these. The talking bird Hugi was another, professing a belief that one's preoccupation with the self and materialism is wrong. One must focus on the Absolute, according to Hugi, and disregard material gains as illusion. Hugi's philosophy of resigning oneself to the Absolute was the cause of his destruction, having reached a crisis in conflicting notions with Corwin. In balance against these pessimistic views, Corwin's discussion with old Ygg, the tree marking the boundary between Order and Chaos, and the retrieval of a silver rose from the spirits of Time, dancing in wonderful elegance, brought strength and comfort to Corwin.

That was the way the hellride went. Corwin rode his horse through the shadows, stopping to rest at various points. At these points, he met hindrance, talked philosophy, or shared a holy passage out of time, and then moved on once again. Brand intervened several times, and managed to slay Corwin's horse on one of these. On a plateau of flat ground and fog, Corwin decided to make his stand. Before him was a great wasteland stretching many miles; behind him, approaching quickly, was the Death Storm of Chaos. It was a moment of futility, for Corwin realized he could never cross that plain, horseless, and beat the oncoming storm.

Planting the staff he had cut from old Ygg in the ground, he used the Jewel of Judgment to begin construction of a new Pattern. The Pattern grew out of his intense concentration upon the Jewel, but the formation of the new Order took energy from his thoughts also. Corwin involuntarily thought of Paris on the shadow Earth in the year 1905. It had been an idyllic time for him, free from worry, free in spirit, joyful in the life about him. The new Pattern would reflect those feelings as much as it would reflect those images. Of course, untold worlds would spring from the inscription of the Pattern over time, but the images of his mind would be the beginning.

With completion of the task came enormous relief. And enormous exhaustion from the effort. In the center of his Pattern, Corwin collapsed. Brand chose that moment to use his unique powers over Shadow to appear above him, grab the Jewel, and fade into nothingness again. For a while, Corwin remained within his Pattern in utter despair. Looking up and outward again, he saw subtle changes in the immediate environment. It was peaceful, the air was fresh, and the sky was bright. At the beginning of the Pattern was a tree where Corwin had placed the staff. Corwin felt changed by these things around him. No longer despairing, he felt a renewal. Calming, gathering strength, Corwin determined to stop Brand, and he knew how to find his way to the battle at the Courts where he could join his brothers and sisters. He used his new Pattern to transport himself to the Courts.

Finding himself in the mountainous region to the north overlooking the battle, Corwin thrust aside all other matters but locating Brand and dispatching him. Because his concentration was placed fully on this, Corwin gave only passing notice to the field of battle, noting in his Chronicles the tactics used by Benedict to hold his army's position or bring on additional troops to sweep against the enemy. Corwin's callous attitude toward the beings of Chaos caused him to deal with the Chaos lord Borel in a disdainful and uncavalier manner. Although Corwin knew that Dara held Borel in high regard, he dispensed with the Chaos lord, who had challenged him to battle, through trickery, and left him to die of a mortal wound. When Corwin scornfully rode off, he had no thought of how relations between himself and Dara would be affected.

From a northern peak, Corwin spied a gleaming red dot of light on the heights at the opposite end of the battlefield. Avoiding any further chance of combat, Corwin made his way gradually to the southern heights. As he rode a Chaos mount toward it, he saw Random, Fiona, Deirdre, and a knight in green converging upon the same position in the heights. Since Fiona was probably attuned to Brand's presence, her leading the others confirmed Corwin's belief that Brand was there.

As Corwin approached the cliff from the near side, the others had reached the slopes farther to the east. An explosion knocked Corwin off his horse and stunned him. When his vision cleared, he saw that the others were down also, beginning to stir. Recognizing the glow of the Jewel of Judgment somewhere above him, Corwin crawled closer, certain that he was undetected. The explosion had been for the benefit of Random and Fiona's party.

When Corwin reached the ledge where he was sure Brand had been, he discovered him missing. Brand's scream of pain, however, directed him farther up the slope. He observed a standoff between Brand, standing at the edge of the Abyss, and Random's group. Fiona had used her powers to transport Brand to the end of things, but Brand was able to hold the others off by ensnaring Deirdre, holding her at knifepoint.

As the impasse continued, a strange formation of clouds positioned itself rapidly in the sky above them. It formed the face of Oberon, and Oberon's voice proceeded from it in normal tones. The calm voice told of Corwin's mission, and explained that the question of the succession to the throne of Amber would rest on the horn of the unicorn. After the Oberon-image gave his blessing to his children in their conflict with Chaos, the clouds parted, and his image was gone.

This unusual message did not affect Brand, however, who still held Deirdre captive against Random's allowing him freedom to proceed with his own plans. While Fiona and Random tried to convince Brand to use the Jewel to save the universe, Corwin secretly worked a spell, using the proximity of the Jewel. Corwin caused Brand's body to grow hot, and he succeeded, even to the extent of making his clothes smolder. Brand cut Deirdre's face as he screamed for Corwin to stop his conjuring. Deirdre freed herself from Brand's hold and dropped away from him. Two silver-tipped arrows hit Brand in quick succession, one in his throat, the second in his chest. As Brand began to fall backward, he grabbed Deirdre by the hair, pulling her with him. Before Corwin could reach her, Brand and Deirdre went over the precipice.

Random had to hit Corwin into unconsciousness to prevent him from diving after Deirdre in a vain attempt to save her. When Corwin regained consciousness, he discovered that the knight in green had fired the arrows that killed Brand. The knight revealed himself to be Caine, who everyone thought had been killed. Caine explained that he used a shadow of himself as the victim, so that he would be able to observe his siblings through their Trumps without being suspected. He had acted against both Brand and Corwin, using a dagger on each occasion, believing that they were joined in a conspiracy against Amber.

As Caine concluded his explanation, trumpets sounded from a distance. The group with which Corwin was standing found the source of the sound. A procession began to wend out of the storm front to the north, moving along the black road toward the Dark Citadel. By this time, the fighting had stopped. Everyone was transfixed, silently watching the unraveling columns of shadow horsemen, musicians, oddly shaped carriages, and strange beasts marching out of the storm along the ribbon of road.

Corwin recognized the driver of a horse-drawn cart draped in black. He could see a coffin covered with the flag of Amber resting on the cart. It was Oberon's casket, and the driver was Dworkin. Fiona wondered aloud if their father had succeeded in repairing the Pattern before he died. Corwin responded:

> "It does not matter . . . whether or not he succeeded, because I did. . . .
> "I believe that he failed, that he was destroyed before he could repair the old Pattern. When I saw this storm coming—actually, I experienced a part of it—I realized that I could not possibly make it here in time with the Jewel, which he had sent to me after his efforts. Brand had been trying to get it from me all along the way—to create a new Pattern, he said. Later, that gave me the idea. When I saw that all else was failing, I used the Jewel to create a new Pattern. It was the most difficult thing I ever did, but I succeeded. Things should hold together after this wave passes, whether we survive it or not. Brand stole the Jewel from me just as I completed it. When I recovered from his attack I was able to use the new Pat-

tern to project me here. So there is still a Pattern, no matter what else happens." (CC, 122–23)

Although his siblings pondered the effects of a new Pattern if their own Pattern were still in existence, Corwin pointed out that the threatening storm beginning to reach them would end their existence anyway. For them, it would be a moot point whether or not a form of Order reclaimed the universe; their lives would be over once the annihilating storm touched them.

When the great procession had passed across the Abyss, the storm began to press forward again. Fiona urged Corwin to rest a while, suggesting that they could seek refuge in the Citadel, where it seemed possible their lives might be preserved. As Corwin rested, Dara rode up on a Chaos horse to his place in the heights. She was furious at him for the way he had slain her mentor, Borel. She learned of it from Borel's own lips before he died. Corwin felt unable to come up with any satisfactory explanation. Telling him that she was returning to her own people, disregarding any allegiance she had with Amber, Corwin asked, "What about Benedict?" Before riding away, she told him, "I do not believe that we will ever meet again." (CC, 125) As she had spoken to him, Corwin saw her face. It was not a human face, and he sensed that it was her natural form.

Fiona awakened Corwin from dozing to give him food and drink. She told him that his son was waiting nearby, wanting to see him. When they met, Corwin asked Merlin to tell him of himself. Briefly, Merlin spoke of his life and view of things. They were interrupted by someone's shout. Corwin stood up with his son, looking in the same direction as his relatives, toward the Abyss. The unicorn climbed out of the precipice and stood before them.

As before, when Oberon's image spoke from the sky, everyone stood silently, looking in the direction of the unicorn. Every common soldier on the field of battle stopped to watch the fabled creature standing against the horizon of a weirdly turning sky. The unicorn stepped forward, looking calmly at the members of the Family on the slope. Corwin saw that she wore the Jewel of Judgment about her neck. She stepped lightly toward the small group of Corwin's kin, not far from where Corwin stood with Merlin. On reaching the group, she lowered her head, then bent her forelegs, kneeling before them.

Her horn was nearly touching the person before her. Random carefully reached forward and removed the Jewel from around her neck. Corwin's brothers and sisters placed their weapons on the ground before Random, giving him their allegiance. Corwin and Merlin did the same. With sudden swiftness, the unicorn rose, turned, and ran down the slope, disappearing from view.

Having the Jewel in his possession, Random asked Corwin if he could use it to stop the demon storm. Corwin declined to do it himself because of his physical exhaustion. Instead, he offered to attune Random to the Jewel so that Random could halt the storm. Agreeing, Random went with Corwin down the slope to a place where some of the soldiers had set up a small cooking fire, now left unattended and dying out. Before beginning the attunement, Random initiated a brief exchange with Corwin:

> "About this king business . . . What am I going to do, Corwin? It caught me totally unprepared."
> "Do? Probably a very good job." . . .
> "Do you think there were many hard feelings?"
> "If there were, they did not show . . . You were a good choice, Random. So much has happened recently . . . Dad sheltered us actually, maybe more than was good for us. The throne is obviously no plum. You have a lot of hard work ahead of you. I think the others have come to realize this."
> "And yourself?"
> "I wanted it only because Eric did. I did not realize it at the time, but it is true. It was the winning counter in a game we had been playing across the years. The end of a vendetta, really. And I would have killed him for it. I am glad now that he found another way to die. We were more alike than we were different, he and I. I did not realize that until much later either. But after his death, I kept finding reasons for not taking the throne. Finally, it dawned on me that it was not really what I wanted. No. You are welcome to it. Rule well, brother. I am sure that you will." (CC, 133)

Holding the Jewel between them, Corwin guided Random through the arduous task of attunement. Their movement was on a psychic level only, but the exertion of weaving their way along a three-dimensional Pattern within the Jewel was still an enormous drain of energies. As they reached the end of the attunement, Corwin blacked out, partly because of the effort and partly because of the proximity of the storm.

When Corwin awoke, Merlin and Fiona were standing over him. Random was nearby, using the Jewel to hold back the Death Storm, almost upon them. Fiona explained to Corwin that Random had ordered Benedict to lead all the troops to the Dark Citadel. From his vantage point, Corwin could see the last of their troops marching along the black road toward the Abyss. Fiona left Corwin with Merlin and went to the black road. While Random worked to turn back the storm, Corwin spoke with his son. He began the long story that came to be written as his Chronicles.

Random succeeded in breaking the storm. It split apart, blowing away in two directions and dying with distance. With the dispersal of the storm went the black road, wiped clean from all the realities it had inhabited. The Pattern of Amber still stood. Random was able to contact Gérard in Amber through his Trump.

In the concluding passages of his Chronicles, Corwin states that he is about to enter the Courts of Chaos with his son. At that point, with Amber and shadows restored, years had passed since he was last in Amber. This was, perhaps, the result of a distortion in time streams that had been disrupted during the Patternfall conflict. Corwin told of his intentions to visit the Courts for a while, to see Merlin off on his walk of the Pattern, and then to go to the new Pattern of his own design. He wrote: "If it leads me to another universe, as I now believe it will, I must go there, to see how I have wrought." (CC, 142)

The mystery of what happened to Corwin after spending time in the Courts was of great concern to his son. Merlin hunted down rumors of where Corwin might have gone after his stay in the Courts, but he found nothing conclusive. In his published accounts, Merlin told of some of the possibilities he had uncovered:

> One rumor had it that Dad had been driven mad in the Courts of Chaos by a curse placed upon him by my mother [Dara], and that he now wandered aimlessly through Shadow. She refused even to comment on this story. Another was that he had entered the universe of his own

creation and never returned, which it seemed possible could remove him from the reach of the Trumps. Another was simply that he had perished at some point after his departure from the Courts—and a number of my relatives there assured me that they had seen him leave after his sojourn. So, if the rumor of his death were correct, it did not occur in the Courts of Chaos. And there were others who claimed to have seen him at widely separated sites afterward. . . . It had taken me a lot of searching just to come up with this handful of rumors.'' (TD, 98–99)

Suspicions and innuendo abounded, as Merlin continued to ask about his father. King Random put forth the conjecture that Corwin was the assassin who murdered Caine and attempted to kill Bleys, but this was proved false. Fiona suggested that Corwin had returned to shadow Earth, citing an occasion when the court jester Droppa had thought he had seen him in a Las Vegas casino. Bill Roth, living and working in Amber, supported the notion that Corwin was on Earth, believing that he might have had some unfinished business there.

What was tantalizing evidence to Merlin was that various items were moved about in Corwin's quarters in the Royal Palace of Amber. Upon looking in on his father's room, Merlin saw candles lit on Corwin's dresser, a live, silver rose in a vase among the candles, pants and shirt carefully placed on his bed, and the sword Grayswandir in its scabbard hanging from his bedpost. (SC, 199–200) No one responded when Merlin called out, but he sensed a recent presence.

Much later, when Merlin's unique computer Ghostwheel magically transferred him to a place of sanctuary, he encountered a person that seemed to be his father. In spite of putting up a magical barrier of protection, Merlin was surprised when the Corwin-being used its Grayswandir to destroy the barrier. The Corwin-being began a duel, suddenly using the pommel of the sword to knock out Merlin. (KS, 62–63) In a strange realm of negative space, Merlin learned from his enchanted cord Frakir that the Corwin-being had not been an artificial construct. It had been a living human. This knowledge added to the remarkable discovery that Corwin might indeed be alive and somehow involved in events in Merlin's life.

More recently, Merlin learned this much about his father from Suhuy, his uncle at the Courts of Chaos:

"I believe he [Corwin] attended a meeting with Swayvill and his counselors, along with Random and the other Amberites, preliminary to the peace treaty. After that, I understand he went his own ways, and I never heard where they might have led him.'' (PC, 54)

When Merlin was summoned back to his home at the Courts of Chaos, he made a number of discoveries that led him to the solution of his father's whereabouts. One was that Corwin's own Pattern had created a Pattern-image, or Pattern-ghost, of Corwin, and infused it with enough potency that it could remain alive and substantial for as long as the Pattern maintained it. It was this Pattern-ghost Corwin that had struck Merlin with the pommel of its Pattern-constructed sword.

A second discovery was of hidden chapels in the Courts of Chaos, dedicated to various members of the Royal Family of Amber. Merlin had found a chapel dedicated to Corwin hidden in the Ways of Sawall. This secret worship was behind the mysterious movements of items in Corwin's quarters in Amber.

Merlin confronted his mother about what happened to Corwin as they sat at lunch:

"I saw him [Corwin] off on his way to the Courts. Certainly, he wanted to be here with the others for the peace settlement. Even more, though, he must have wanted to see you. There were so many unanswered questions in his mind—where you came from, why you came to him, why you parted as you did— . . .

"And I know he was here in the Courts. He was seen here. He must have looked you up. What happened then? What sort of answers did you give him? . . .

"Is he your prisoner, Mother? Do you have him locked away somewhere, someplace where he can't bother you, can't interfere with your plans? . . .

"You're afraid of him, aren't you? . . . You're afraid to kill a Prince of Amber, even with the Logrus on your side. You've got him locked away somewhere, and you're afraid he'll come loose and blow your latest plans.

You've been scared for a long time now because of what you've had to do to keep him out of action.''

"Preposterous! . . . You're just guessing! . . . He's dead, Merlin! Give up! Leave me alone! Never mention his name in my presence again! Yes, I hate him! He would have destroyed us all! He still would, if he could!''

"He is not dead." . . .

"How can you say that?'' . . .

"Only the guilty protest so strongly . . . He's alive. Where is he?'' . . .

"Then seek him, Merlin. By all means, seek him.''

"Where?''

"Look for him in the Pit of Chaos." (PC, 117–18)

With his knowledge of the unique entranceways of the Courts, and his new understandings about the secret chapels, Merlin was able to untangle the cryptic meaning of his mother's response, blurted out in anger. His rescue of his father, though, depended on the willingness of the Pattern-ghost Corwin to take the real Corwin's place. This was necessary so that Dara would not be able to note any change in the situation. Merlin and the Pattern-ghost Corwin went to the hidden chapel dedicated to Corwin. In the part of the floor representing the Abyss of Chaos, Merlin located a special entranceway. Through that Way, they found the real Corwin, imprisoned in a dark, windowless cell. They released him, and the Pattern-ghost took Corwin's place. Merlin took Corwin to the vacant quarters of his brother Jurt in order to rest, recuperate, and remain undetected.

After bringing his father a change of clothes and some refreshment, Merlin related the numerous incidents of his life since they last had the chance to converse on the day of the Patternfall battle. In this way, Merlin returned the favor that Corwin had given him by recounting his own history, beginning with his experiences on the shadow Earth where his father had dwelled for so long.

When Corwin was feeling up to it, he and Merlin walked the Ways of Chaos, traveled in Shadow, and came to the field of combat where the forces of Amber and Chaos had once confronted one another. As Corwin looked over that now-healed battlefield, he spoke to his son of their plan to maintain the balance between the Courts and Amber. Merlin was about to accept the kingship of the realm that had been his first homeland. He was sending Corwin back to Amber, by magical means, to act as counselor to King Random, working in conjunction with his son at the Courts. Merlin had succeeded in shrugging off any possible strings that members of his family had wanted to exercise in controlling him. With Corwin on the other end of the two poles of existence, Merlin had a distinct advantage over those who depended on covert machinations in the Courts.

Freed of a bondage brought about by powers in Chaos that he had uncertain knowledge of, Corwin went home to continue the struggle. However, this phase in his life took a new turn. He was no longer an unwilling participant waging war in unfamiliar territory. He had an ally in blood, and he felt himself to be in a position of control over the direction in which the worlds would move. It was a hope he shared with his son, that together they could work to allow each pole, and the shadows between, to thrive even if touched by a careless god or two.

CORWIN'S PATTERN

The new Pattern created by Corwin when he was approaching the Courts of Chaos prior to the Patternfall War. Corwin's Pattern had been considered responsible for offsetting the shifting balance between the Powers of the Pattern and the Logrus. This may have been a factor in the escalating conflict between the two Powers and their choice of using artificially synthesized human agents to act on their behalf. The new Pattern appeared to act of its own volition in creating an agent of its own, a ghost version of Corwin, to interact with other humans.

Carrying the Jewel of Judgment to the great battlefield of the Courts, Corwin had been uncertain whether or not his father had succeeded in repairing the original, primal Pattern. Seeing the destroying storm of Chaos approaching, he felt he had to devise a new Pattern in order to push back that oncoming destruction. In his Chronicles, Corwin vividly described what it was like to inscribe his Pattern:

I placed my left foot firmly before my right, my right before my left. In my left hand, I held the chain from which the Jewel depended—and I carried it high, so that I could stare into the stone's depths, seeing and feeling there the emergence of the new Pattern which I described with each step. I had screwed my staff into the ground and left it to stand near the Pattern's beginning. Left . . .

The wind sang about me and there was thunder near at hand. I did not meet with the physical resistance that I did on the old Pattern. There was no resistance at all. Instead—and in many ways worse—a peculiar deliberation had come over all my movements, slowing them, ritualizing them. I seemed to expend more energy in preparing for each step—perceiving it, realizing it and ordering my mind for its execution—than I did in the physical performance of the act. Yet the slowness seemed to require itself, was exacted of me by some unknown agency which determined precision and an adagio tempo for all my movements. Right . . .

Having gone completely around, I could see that as much of the new Pattern as I had walked was now inscribed in the rock and glowing palely, bluely. Yet, there were no sparks, no tingles in my feet, no hair-raising currents—only the steady law of deliberation, upon me like a great weight. . . . Left . . .

Time ceased to have meaning. Space was restricted to the design I was creating. I drew strength from the Jewel without summoning it now, as part of the process in which I was engaged. In a sense, I suppose, I was obliterated. I became a moving point, programed by the Jewel, performing an operation which absorbed me so totally that I had no attention available for self-consciousness. Yet, at some level, I realized that I was a part of the process, also. For I knew, somehow, that if anyone else were doing it, it would be a different Pattern emerging. (CC, 92–96)

Just as the primal Pattern held the imprint of Dworkin's psyche, so Corwin's Pattern was uniquely his, defined by the images that Corwin recollected as he inscribed it in the rock. Much of the outer circumference of that design, for instance, would bring forth images of Paris on shadow Earth in 1905 as an initiate begins the Pattern walk. Further steps, winding inward, would yield a panorama

of memories from Corwin's life on that shadow. As one edges closer to the center, the many struggles of Corwin in regaining his memory and battling enemies would become part of the swirling tableaux. By its completion, the Pattern would be as integral to Corwin as Corwin was to that complex design.

Later, when he was with his siblings at Patternfall, Corwin pondered what the creation of his new Pattern would mean if the original Pattern also continued to exist. He discussed it with his brothers and sisters, and although they came to no definite conclusion, their speculations are intriguing. At the end of his Chronicles, Corwin wondered about the possible new universe he had created through the Pattern, and he hoped to travel within its realms someday.

When Corwin disappeared and his brother Random first began his rule of the true city, some of the Royal Family became concerned about this wayward Pattern of Corwin's. Fiona and Bleys traveled to it, examined it, and attempted to set foot on it. The new Pattern sent out an electrical charge, preventing them from walking it. Although Fiona expressed her concern to King Random, bringing him to it, he refused to make the attempt to assay it.

Fiona seemed to become obsessed with plumbing the secrets of Corwin's Pattern. At one point, she brought Corwin's son, Merlin, to the new Pattern. From outside the Pattern, standing beside the tree that had grown from the staff Corwin had grounded, all one could see was a low fog. Fiona had been able to bring much of the design into focus through a spell she cast on a mirror. Merlin used her mirror and saw:

> . . . most of the strange Pattern which twisted its bright way about the ground, working its passages inward to its off-center terminus, the only spot still concealed by an unmoving tower of white, within which tiny lights like stars seemed to burn. (BA, 160)

Urging Merlin to try walking the Pattern, Fiona was disappointed when he started to place a foot on it, and was prevented from continuing. Since he cast a cynical eye on Fiona's fears that this new Pattern was disrupting the fabric of the universe, Merlin didn't reveal to his aunt that he deliberately stopped himself from walking it. He simply didn't see the Pattern as the grave danger that Fiona had read in it.

Years later, Fiona renewed her efforts to involve

Merlin in learning more about his father's Pattern. She contacted him by Trump while he was with his stepbrother Mandor. After bringing both of them to her location, Fiona showed them a rare phenomenon: an immense funnellike tornado that was growing in dimension. She attributed its creation to the imbalance of Corwin's Pattern. However, Mandor used his own magical abilities to prove that there was an intelligence behind it from the Chaos side of the universe.

In spite of the fact that Mandor disproved Fiona's theory that the new Pattern was the cause of such shadow-destroying phenomena, they decided to investigate further together. Merlin, though, chose to leave them to seek their answers about Corwin's Pattern on their own. He didn't find out more about the fruits of their search until much later. His source of information was, in fact, an old friend residing in the Courts. Gryll, the servant of Merlin's uncle, Suhuy, told him of what followed:

> "Your father's Pattern is also an artifact of order. It served to tip the ancient balance in the favor of Amber. . . .
> "Your brother Prince Mandor and the Princess Fiona suspected this and sought evidence. They presented their findings to your uncle, Lord Suhuy. He made several journeys into Shadow and became persuaded that this is the case. He was preparing his findings for presentation to the king when Swayvill suffered his final illness." (PC, 10)

The Pattern of Corwin had properties that Merlin was able to define in his journals. Because it needed to preserve itself from the Powers of the Logrus and the Pattern in Amber, it generated a Pattern-ghost that was its sole preserver. Its Pattern-ghost Corwin also was a negotiator in recruiting others to its cause; that is, self-preservation. This ghost-Corwin guided Merlin, helping him as need arose. The ghost-Corwin was the agent that brought Merlin to the Land Between Shadows, or Undershadow, thus safeguarding him from the grasp of the two Powers.

Having a sentience comparable to the Powers, Corwin's Pattern had the ability to read images in Merlin's thoughts and bring them into reality. It actualized the image of the red '57 Chevy from Merlin's mind. Merlin, with a Pattern-ghost Luke and the ghost-Corwin, used it to bring them through a

void to the new Pattern. For a time, the Chevy and the Pattern became united as a way station and sanctuary for Merlin and his friends. Merlin and the ghost-Luke walked the Pattern with the ghost-Corwin, and the ghost-Luke subsequently became both protected by and protector of the Pattern.

While the ghost-Corwin had a special symbiotic relationship with the Pattern, allowing this Corwin to communicate with it, the Pattern permitted him to leave. It granted permission for others to be its guardians. Eventually, Merlin placed a number of his acquaintants under its protection, while he began his reign at one of the poles of existence. Those left with Corwin's Pattern were Jurt, Coral, Nayda, and Dalt.

Before leaving the Pattern with the ghost-Corwin, Merlin did battle with the forces created by the Logrus in its attempt to destroy it. Using his psychic talents, Merlin was able to salve earth tremors meant to crack apart the Pattern. Once that problem was solved, Merlin returned to the Courts to deal with the Powers on his own terms.

When Fiona had expressed her concern about the imbalance caused by the new Pattern, she shared her interest with Merlin about exploring the secrets that would be revealed if they traveled within it to its primal, basic form. The universes that Corwin himself had once hoped to visit have not yet been fathomed. Perhaps we will hear one day from Merlin's friends, those remaining at that unique way station, about the worlds previously undefined, hidden in the innermost reaches of that intricate formation.

COURTS OF CHAOS

That realm which is supposedly the source of all living things, situated along the Abyss that represents nullification of existence. Some speculate that the Courts of Chaos exist as a consequence of the Logrus, which resides beyond convoluted ways deep in a cavern. The Courts became one extreme, or pole, of the universe after Dworkin devised a new design that created the place of the other pole, Amber. Philosophically speaking (though not necessarily in actuality), Amber has been identified with Order, and the Courts have been equated with

Chaos. Dworkin's presumption, as much as the physical opposition of the two poles, has been a source of friction and disharmony between those of the Courts and the Royal Family in Amber. However, since the Patternfall War and the signing of the Concord, neither camp has deliberately brought hostilities to the other.

In his Chronicles, Corwin of Amber had described his first long look at the Courts of Chaos since his childhood. He had reached it inadvertently, selecting a Trump at random from cards kept in Dworkin's den. The following is some of his description of the Courts:

> But far, far out from where I stood, something hovered on a mount of sheerest black—a blackness itself, but edged and tempered with barely perceptible flashes of light. I could not guess at its size, for distance, depth, perspective, were absent here. A single edifice? A group? A city? Or simply a place? The outline varied each time that it fell upon my retina. Now faint and misty sheets drifted slowly between us, twisting, as if long strands of gauze were buoyed by heated air. . . .
> As I continued to stare, fascinated, across the chasm, it was as if my eyes adjusted or the prospect shifted once again, subtly. For now I discerned tiny, ghostly forms moving within that place, like slow-motion meteors along the gauzy strands. I waited, regarding them carefully, courting some small understanding of the actions in which they were engaged. At length, one of the strands drifted very near. . . .
> . . . One of the rushing forms grew larger, and I realized that it was following the twisting way that led toward me. In only a few moments, it took on the proportions of a horseman. (HO, 79–80)

Of course, since that first documented account of the Courts of Chaos, we have learned a great deal more through the published journals of Merlin, Corwin's son. The place described by Corwin was one minor region of the Courts, a distance through Shadow and many byways (PC, 240) from what may be considered the center of the Courts.

The center of the government and religion of the Courts rests upon opposite ends of the Plaza at the End of the World. The royal residence and center of the administration of the king and his retinue is Thelbane, a tall, needlelike structure at the near end of the wide Plaza. At the far end of the Plaza, verging upon the very Abyss, lies the Cathedral of the Serpent. It is a great stone structure where ceremonies of high reverence are conducted. Pride and veneration have caused many people to look down into the Abyss from the Cathedral and realize that from this place "one can view the creation of the universe, or its ending." (PC, 158)

Merlin had recently been summoned to the Courts when old King Swayvill died. While Merlin had some understanding of the lines of succession there, he was further briefed by his stepbrother Mandor. Merlin had told his brother:

> "I heard so much from my father [Corwin] of the succession in Amber, with all its cabals, intrigues, and double crosses, that I almost feel an authority on the subject. I imagine it could be that way here, too, among the Houses of Swayvill's descendants, there being many more generations involved."
> "You have the right idea," he said, "though I think the picture might be a bit more orderly here than it was there." (PC, 22)

The orderliness that Mandor referred to, however, might have come from his own perspective on heirs to the kingship, and the abruptness of numerous claims coming to an end. He informed Merlin of claimants engaging in duels of honor that proved fatal, and others who had fallen victim to assassins. Mandor said, "The deaths have been occurring steadily for some time. There wasn't a sudden bloodbath when Swayvill took his turn for the worse—though a few did occur just recently." (PC, 25)

At that point in time, Merlin was third in line to succeed the late king. He had been formally adopted by Lord Sawall; and Mandor, who would have served before him, had relinquished his right to succeed. From what we can gather of the royal succession, as it stood while Merlin had visited the Courts, this was the order of the Houses in the line of succession: House of Chanicut, House of Jesby, House of Sawall, House of Hendrake, and House of Helgram.

Those of us who have never been to the Courts of Chaos find some aspects described by others to be beyond ordinary belief. Certainly, the ease with which one can step through Shadow stress points from the Courts would be disorienting. As Merlin had indicated: "The shadows are like frayed curtains in the Courts—often, you can look right through into another reality without even trying." (PC, 15) Another disconcerting factor would surely be the Chaosian etiquette of transforming oneself from one form to another, particularly when some of those forms are remarkably nonhuman in character. There are also exotic and dangerous creatures in that realm which a few Chaos lords have consorted with in one way or another. Merlin's journals mention two prominently: Fire Angels, and the ty'iga. And the region that we think of as the great Abyss, but the nobles there refer to casually as the Rim, has been cited as a place for treasure hunting and for play.

In trying to make comprehensible the essential aggregation that we think of as the Courts of Chaos, we cannot emphasize too markedly that it is a realm possessed of incredible strangeness.

DALT

Son of Deela the Desacratrix and close friend of Rinaldo of Kashfa. He led a group of mercenaries that helped Rinaldo on several occasions in assaulting the Keep of the Four Worlds. He had a deeply felt hatred for the Royal Family in Amber. Nevertheless, he joined with Merlin of Amber and Rinaldo on a rescue mission that involved wresting Rinaldo's bride from agents of the Courts of Chaos.

Before Dalt was born, his mother Deela was a militant religious fanatic who led raiding parties in and around shadow Begma. Since Begma was a longtime member of the Golden Circle, officials there requested King Oberon's aid to put down her force. Oberon

"took a small force, defeated her troops, took her prisoner and hanged a bunch of her men. She escaped, though, and a couple of years later when she was all but forgotten she came back with a fresh force and started the same crap all over. Begma screamed again, but Dad [Oberon] was busy. He sent Bleys in with a larger force. There were several inconclusive

engagements—they were raiders, not a regular army—but Bleys finally cornered them and wiped them out. She died that day, leading her troops." (BA, 61)

When Dalt was old enough, he sought revenge against the Family in Amber. He made a number of attempts at harassment in the outskirts of Amber. Then he gathered a large paramilitary army and mounted a full offensive. He reached the foot of Mt. Kolvir, battling the combined armies of the true city. Benedict faced Dalt, and after a lengthy combat, Benedict gave him a mortal wound. Dalt's soldiers prevented Benedict from taking a close examination, however. They managed to carry Dalt's body off with them when they made their retreat. There were no further invasion forces, so the Family assumed Dalt was dead.

Dave the hermit, living near the Keep of the Four Worlds, told Merlin about Dalt's friendship with Rinaldo of Kashfa. They were childhood friends, and Rinaldo would often run off after an argument with his mother, Queen Jasra, and ride with Dalt and his mercenaries. Early on in their campaigns together, Rinaldo enlisted Dalt and his troops to assault the Keep because he feared something had happened to his mother. At the time that Merlin spoke to Dave, the attacking forces at the Keep carried a banner that showed a lion rending a unicorn. Dave explained that it was Dalt's banner, and its significance was to show his hatred of the Amberites. This confirmed that Dalt was the same man that Benedict had run through with his sword.

While Merlin was visiting the country estate of Baron Bayle, he received an urgent Trump contact from Rinaldo. Seriously wounded, Rinaldo requested Merlin's help. Merlin brought him to his room in Arbor House through the contact. While Rinaldo rested, Merlin looked through the Trumps he had with him. He found one that he recognized as Dalt. Merlin decided to contact Dalt to tell him of Rinaldo's injuries. He concentrated on the card, and Dalt's features became three-dimensional. He was a big man with blond hair and green eyes. His eyes stared warily at Merlin. There was something threatening in Dalt's manner, and before he could step through the Trump connection to Merlin's room, Merlin closed the contact. He then learned from Rinaldo that they had just attempted a fresh assault on the Keep of the Four Worlds in another rescue attempt of his mother. For no apparent reason, Dalt had turned on him in the midst of battle, causing Rinaldo's injuries.

Merlin encountered Dalt again in the heart of Amber. Queen Vialle was entertaining a diplomatic delegation from Begma when Dalt marched into Amber with a well-armed mercenary force. The queen summoned Merlin and explained the situation:

> "Dalt's men are dug in near the western edge of Arden. Julian's are strung out facing them. Benedict has taken Julian additional men and weapons. He says he can execute a flanking movement that will take Dalt's line apart. But I told him not to. . . . I came here to respond to a Trump message from Julian. He had just spoken with Dalt under a flag of truce. Dalt told him that his objective was not, at this time, the destruction of Amber. He pointed out that he could conduct an expensive attack, though, in terms of our manpower and equipment. He said he'd rather save himself and us the expense, however. What he really wants is for us to turn two prisoners over to him—Rinaldo and Jasra." (SC, 136-37)

After contacting Rinaldo by Trump, Merlin brought him into the palace. Joining Julian and his troops, Rinaldo convinced him to allow Dalt to speak privately with him, while their troops watched. It was agreed, and Rinaldo spoke to Dalt for several minutes. Rinaldo returned to Julian and Merlin, informing them that Dalt agreed to hand-to-hand combat to decide their next move. If Rinaldo beat Dalt, Dalt would become a prisoner in Amber. If Rinaldo lost, Dalt would be allowed to withdraw, taking Rinaldo with him. The single combat commenced. It was a difficult struggle, but finally Rinaldo succumbed to Dalt. As Dalt's men carried the unconscious body of Rinaldo away from the facing troops, Merlin performed an incantation that tore open a trench in the ground beside Dalt. He told Dalt; "That is your grave: . . . if Luke's [Rinaldo's] death comes of this." . . . [Dalt responded] "Next time I'll remember you," (SC, 164) and then he followed his men.

Sometime later, Merlin had learned that Dalt had been affected by a spell of the sorcerer Mask to turn on his friend Rinaldo in their last battle at the Keep of the Four Worlds. In the Forest of Arden, when Dalt and Rinaldo conferred, they cleared up their misgivings, and Rinaldo arranged for the hand-to-hand fight and his own defeat. To Merlin and Julian, it would seem as if Rinaldo had been captured by an enemy who would be willing to do him in. This was a ruse that Rinaldo engineered, so that Merlin would not have any notion of his true intentions.

Rinaldo's plan was to combine again with Dalt and his men to perform a coup in Kashfa. He knew that King Random had acted to place his own man on the throne of Kashfa, blocking a return of Jasra and himself. By removing himself from the scene, Rinaldo was able to make a surprise attack. With Dalt's help, Rinaldo was able to take command of the palace in Kashfa's capital city, imprisoning the nobleman that Random had intended for the kingship.

Circumstances had changed drastically when Merlin encountered Dalt next. Local politics didn't seem quite so important in the face of agents who were acting for the Supreme Powers of the Logrus and the Pattern. Rinaldo enlisted Dalt's help in tracking Coral of Begma, who had been made his queen in Kashfa. Dalt's interest was simply in aiding his friend, but he understood that the agents they were seeking were artificially devised by the Logrus. The two Powers were at war, and Dalt and the others were little more than game pieces to them.

Dalt showed his staunchness to his friend when he engaged in a sword fight with a Pattern-ghost version of Eric of Amber. The Pattern-ghost was getting the better of Dalt, so Merlin summoned a spell to dispose of all the Pattern-ghosts. Merlin's action brought them into contact with the Sign of the Pattern. In order to maintain control over Merlin and his companions, the Sign of the Pattern brought them to the primal Pattern. With Merlin were Dalt, Rinaldo, Nayda, and Coral. After some negotiating and creating a stalemate, Rinaldo arranged for the escape of the others. Dalt could have chosen to remain in Kashfa at that point. He had no commitment to Merlin, and neither of the Powers had an interest in him. Instead of merely walking away, he let Merlin bring him and the others to the Pattern formed by his father. There, Dalt and the others could remain for a time in safety.

Dalt acted out of his friendship for Rinaldo. It

seems rather noble of him to willingly involve himself with the higher order of hostilities between the Powers when he had little stake in that conflict. While he didn't put much emphasis on the fact that his father had been the late King Oberon, this may explain why he would have some slight concern for the struggle of the Pattern against the Logrus.

DARA

Great-granddaughter of Benedict of Amber and Lintra the hellmaid. She was descended of the House of Hendrake on her maternal side and of the House of Helgram on her paternal side in the Courts of Chaos. Early in her career, she had been on a mission that involved seducing Corwin and bearing his child, although this was supported by the late King Oberon. During the Patternfall War, she changed alliances, joining Oberon against the leaders of the Courts. Afterward, she remained in the Courts of Chaos, marrying Lord Sawall, the old Rim Duke. She had two sons by him, Despil and Jurt. Since she cared very much for Merlin, her child by Corwin, she saw to his development in the Courts. When he left for college on shadow Earth, she had secretly sent a protective demon called a ty'iga to watch over him. It continued to be her hope that Merlin would one day be king in the Courts of Chaos.

Early in her life, while she was being brought up in the Courts of Chaos, Dara had had a significant role in the conspiracy against Amber. A Pattern-ghost of Rinaldo told Merlin what he knew about those days before the Patternfall battle:

> "Well, my dad [Brand] spent some time here, back in his plotting days," he said. "It's where he met my mother [Jasra]."
>
> "I didn't know that."
>
> "It never came up. We never talked family, remember?"
>
> "Yeah," I said, "and no one I asked seemed to know where Jasra came from. Still, the Courts. . . . She's a long way from home."
>
> "Actually, she was recruited from a nearby shadow," he explained, "like this one."
>
> "Recruited?"

> "Yes, she worked as a servant for a number of years—I think she was fairly young when she started—at the Ways of Helgram."
>
> "Helgram? That's my mother's House!"
>
> "Right. She was a maid-companion to the lady Dara. That's where she learned the Arts."
>
> "Jasra got her instruction in sorcery from my mother? And she met Brand at Helgram? That would make it seem Helgram had something to do with Brand's plot, the Black Road, the war—"
>
> "—and the Lady Dara going looking for your father? I guess so."
>
> "Because she wanted to be a Pattern initiate as well as one of the Logrus?"
>
> "Maybe," he said. "I wasn't present."
> (PC, 73–74)

It is unclear what Dara's precise mission had been when she initially left the Courts of Chaos. She was impressed by Brand, even hinting to Corwin at Patternfall that he had been one "of the most important persons in my life." (CC, 125) Also very curious about Benedict, she evidently observed him clandestinely while he resided in shadow Avalon. She had seen him ride back from a brief journey on horseback with Julian and Gérard, who were injured. In addition, she made herself known to young Martin, while he still suffered from the wounds that Brand had inflicted on him. It seems likely that Dara didn't begin to work Corwin into the equation of her schemes until he appeared at Benedict's encampment in Avalon.

Dara had located Martin shortly after he had escaped from Brand and had begun to heal. By that time, the black road had already crossed into the Shadows, and Martin had been riding on his horse strenuously through the worlds, trying to trace it. When he fell ill, Dara came to him, helping in his recovery. Martin recounted to Corwin what he had learned from her:

> "She said that she had traveled there through Shadow. She could not yet walk through it as we do, though she felt she could learn to do this, as she claimed descent from the House of Amber through Benedict. In fact, she wanted very badly to learn how it was done. Her means of travel then was the black road itself. She was immune to its noxious effects, she

said, because she was also related to the dwellers at its farther end, in the Courts of Chaos. She wanted to learn our ways though, so I did my best to instruct her in those things that I did know. I told her of the Pattern, even sketched it for her. I showed her my Trumps—Benedict had given me a deck—to show her the appearance of her other relatives. She was particularly interested in yours [Corwin's]. (HO, 164–65)

Martin influenced Dara's opinion of Amber greatly. She began having misgivings about the conspiracy, especially when she knew that it was Martin's blood that Brand used to open the way from the Courts to Amber. After leaving Martin, she either searched out King Oberon, or knew in which shadow he had been secreted by the Chaos lords after Brand and Fiona had arranged the king's departure from Amber. Although we lack the specifics, Dara herself explained:

"I met him [Oberon] during his—difficulties—some time back . . . In fact, you might say that I helped to deliver him from them. This was after I had met Martin, and I was inclined to be more sympathetic toward Amber. But then, your father is also a charming and persuasive man. I decided that I could not simply stand by and see him remain prisoner to my kin." (CC, 18–19)

Corwin had been enjoying the hospitality of Benedict's servants in one of his manor houses in Avalon when he first met Dara. He had been resting beside a small horse-drawn wagon he had borrowed, beginning a ride into Shadow. He was awakened by her calling his name:

She stood about a dozen paces from me, a tall, slender girl with dark eyes and close-cropped brown hair. She wore a fencing jacket and held a rapier in her right hand, a mask in her left. She was looking at me and laughing. Her teeth were white, even, and a trifle long; a band of freckles crossed her small nose and the upper portions of her well-tanned cheeks. There was that air of vitality about her which is attractive in ways different from mere comeliness. (GA, 105)

After they dueled in sport, she told him of her relationship with Benedict. She was quite convincing in making Corwin believe that she had been living with Benedict and had known him all her life. She seemed so candid and curious about those things taken for granted by the Family in Amber, that Corwin was completely taken in by her innocent charm. He took her through Shadow and told her of the Pattern in Amber. He told her that he would grant her initiation in the Pattern once he ruled in Amber. She would be able to communicate with him then by using his Trump.

Somewhat later, Corwin's comrade, Ganelon, pointed out an area near the manor where two bodies had recently been buried. He insisted that Corwin check the site himself. After doing so, Corwin encountered Dara again, nearby. He repeated his promise to show her how to travel the Shadows after she walked the Pattern. Then, under the stars, they made love.

Dara continued her pretense of being a youthful, naive girl when she rode on horseback up to Corwin and his men as they approached Mt. Kolvir. Even though there was a battle going on between Eric's army and creatures out of Shadow, she insisted upon heading for the palace and attempting the Pattern. Corwin thought her merely a nuisance at that point, and he had a guard put on her while he and Ganelon led the rest of their men toward the fighting. Soon thereafter, while they were in the midst of battle, Dara rode swiftly by, calling back to Corwin: "I'll see you in Amber!" (GA, 214)

Corwin realized that she was not what she seemed when he went down the stairs with Random into the bowels of the palace. The guard had been murdered with a thin knife. Random and Corwin glimpsed Dara, completing the circuit of the Pattern. She did not appear human. Before vanishing from the Pattern's center, she told them: "Amber will be destroyed." (GA, 223)

Of course, as a daughter of Chaos, Dara was a shapeshifter. Her normal demonform, in fact, was quite different from the human form that Corwin had known. Merlin noted some of this in his journals:

She has always had perfect control of her face and form, shifting them to suit her moods. She is obviously the same person, but at times she may choose to appear as little more than a girl, at other times becoming a mature and handsome woman. Generally, she seems somewhere in between. But now, a certain timeless quality came into her features—not age so much as the essence of Time—and I realized suddenly that I had never known her true age. (PC, 109)

It was a surprise to Corwin and his siblings to discover Dara in Amber at Martin's bidding, and claiming she had orders for each of them which came from King Oberon. When Corwin questioned her about some Trumps in her possession, drawn by an artist in a different style from either Dworkin's or Brand's, she pointed out the Trump of Corwin's son, Merlin, saying he was the artist.

Dara explained that she had lied about having spent time under Benedict's care, even though she persisted in claiming that she was his descendant. She had learned swordsmanship from the Master of Arms of the Courts of Chaos, Duke Borel of the House of Hendrake. It has since been implied that Borel had been her lover as well. She told Corwin that she had lied in order to learn about the Pattern, the Trumps, and Amber. She then told of her meeting Martin, and how he changed her plans. When Corwin went to Oberon to confirm that Dara was allied with him, Oberon indicated that he had been a contriver in her scheme to bear Corwin's child:

> "But she did not kill Benedict's servants to manage her position at his house. I did it myself, to assure her getting to you as she did, at just the appropriate time."
> "You? You were party to her whole plot? Why?"
> "She will make you a good queen, son. I trust the blood of Chaos for strength. It was time for a fresh infusion. You will take the throne already provided with an heir. By the time he is ready for it, Merlin will long have been weaned from his upbringing." (CC, 28)

When Dara confronted an exhausted Corwin at the end of the Patternfall battle, she had lost all respect and affection for him. She derided him for his unchivalrous killing of Lord Borel. Because of Corwin and the others of Amber, she had lost two people she had cared deeply about: Borel and Brand. In resentment, she rode away, joining her people in the Courts of Chaos.

As Merlin later found out, Dara did have something further to do with his father after Patternfall. As part of his attempt to locate his long-lost father, Merlin asked his uncle, Suhuy, about him. Suhuy told him:

> "I believe he attended a meeting with Swayvill and his counselors, along with Random and the other Amberites, preliminary to the peace treaty. After that, I understand he went his own ways, and I never heard where they might have led him." (PC, 54)

Perhaps Corwin sought out Dara, or else, it may have been the reverse. In any case, Dara had trapped him and locked him in a prison cell in absolute darkness. Using a Shadowmaster, she had devised a hidden Way within Lord Sawall's Maze of Art, where she went on a regular basis to feed Corwin and give him fresh water, trusting no one with her secret. The only other person who knew of the Way's location was the Shadowmaster who constructed it. She killed him when it had been completed.

Obviously, she continued to feel some fondness for Corwin, since she could have easily had him slain. She must have had enormously ambivalent feelings about him. Merlin pondered over these matters to some extent, applying them to himself:

> I sometimes felt she liked both of her sons by Sawall, the old Rim Duke she'd finally married after giving up on Dad, better than me. I'd once overheard it said that I reminded her of my father, whom I'd been told I resembled more than a little. (BA, 84)

In the Courts of Chaos to attend the funeral of Swayvill, Merlin met with his mother several times, learning about her motives for assigning a ty'iga to follow him in Shadow, and discovering her ambitions for his future. He also found out that that "she seemed to enjoy a special relationship with the Logrus." (PC, 122) While he was having lunch with her, the Sign of the Logrus approached and conversed with them. Dara very nearly reprimanded the Power, reminding it of a scheme that she had put into motion for its benefit.

After the Sign of the Logrus departed, Merlin questioned Dara about Corwin. She grew increasingly upset with his queries, finally shouting: "Look for him in the Pit of Chaos." (PC, 118) Because a nonhuman friend of Merlin had seen the creation of the hidden Way in Sawall's Maze of Art, Merlin located it. After rescuing Corwin, Merlin confronted both Dara and his stepbrother Mandor in a sorcerous duel. Even though Dara summoned the Logrus Sign, Merlin had arranged for a stalemate that prevented the Logrus from acting against him. Dara found her intentions to manipulate her son as king of the Courts frustrated. Merlin would be king, but he had taken a position in which neither Dara nor Mandor could take control from behind the throne. In chagrin, Dara shapeshifted into bizarre forms, then vanished. She had not yet learned that Corwin had escaped beyond her reach as well.

DARK CIRCLE

The physical manifestation of the blot on the primal Pattern in a shadow containing the village of Lorraine. It was an increasingly spreading Circle that sickened or killed ordinary people who stepped within it. Terrible creatures out of Shadow made their entrance to the countryside around Lorraine from the Circle.

Corwin of Amber supported the local ruler Ganelon in defeating the monstrous army that had formed within the Circle.

When Corwin first reached the Keep of Ganelon, its proprietor described the beginnings of the evil Circle:

"It began as a tiny ring of toadstools, far to the west. A child was found dead in its center, and the man who found her—her father—died of convulsions several days later. The spot was immediately said to be accursed. It grew quickly in the months that followed, until it was half a league across. The grasses darkened and shone like metal within it, but did not die. The trees twisted and their leaves blackened. They swayed when there was no wind, and bats danced and darted among them. In the twilight, strange shapes could be seen moving—always *within* the Circle, mind you—and there were lights, as of small fires, throughout the night.

The Circle continued to grow, and those who lived near it fled—mostly. A few remained. It was said that those who remained had struck some bargain with the dark things. And the Circle continued to widen, spreading like the ripple from a rock cast into a pond. More and more people remained, living, within it. I have spoken with these people, fought with them, slain them. It is as if there is something dead inside them all. Their voices lack the thrust and dip of men chewing over their words and tasting them. They seldom do much with their faces, but wear them like death masks. They began to leave the Circle in bands, marauding. They slew wantonly. They committed many atrocities and defiled places of worship. They put things to the torch when they left them. They never stole objects of silver. Then, after many months, other creatures than men began to come forth—strangely formed, like the hellcats you slew. Then the Circle slowed in its growth, almost halting, as though it were nearing some sort of limit. But now all manner of raiders emerged from it—some even faring forth during the day—laying waste to the countryside about its borders. When they had devastated the land about its entire circumference, the Circle moved to encompass those areas also. And so its growth began again, in this fashion." (GA, 33)

The men who once lived normal lives within the precincts taken over by the spreading Circle, those who became possessed, soulless servants, were known as Wardens of the Circle. Through their vigilance, the demons within knew of massed armies marching upon the Circle.

Ganelon told Corwin, who was calling himself Corey of Cabra, of his battles against the demon horde. As a rootless outlaw, Ganelon and fifty-five of his staunchest followers rode into the Circle. They came upon a pack of Wardens making a sacrifice of a goat upon an altar and killed all but one. After questioning him, one of Ganelon's men killed him. From the empty vessel of the dead body came the terrible voice of a newly transformed goat-being. It spoke to Ganelon, warning that he would never leave the Circle alive.

Ganelon and his men fled, but only sixteen of his comrades made it out with him. For three days, however, Ganelon had been sick and weak, and he learned that the others who had survived the Circle were also stricken. Afterward, Ganelon joined King Uther, who led the realm, against the demons of the Circle. They fought against the hordes in numerous battles, and Ganelon gradually became the king's general. During one of their greatest battles, King Uther died. Ganelon confronted the huge goat-thing again, and felt that his own presence kept the creature in check. It knew Ganelon for the man it spoke to at the altar within the Circle. In that battle, Ganelon and his army managed to drive the demons back, but Ganelon feared they were mounting even larger forces, planning for a more devastating strike.

For several reasons, Corwin decided to join Ganelon and destroy the minions of the Circle. One was the girl he met, Lorraine of the village of Lorraine. Aside from liking her, he learned that the man she had once lived with, Jarl, had been the father who died after finding the dead body of the little girl in the Circle. The little girl had been Lorraine's daughter. A second reason related to the coming of the demon Strygalldwir from the Circle. Before it died in Corwin's hands, it knew that Corwin had been the opener of that way into the shadow world. The horned one, the goat-creature that Ganelon had described, later confirmed that the demons regarded Corwin as the one who had released them into the realm. Corwin believed that the curse he tossed in his brother Eric's direction was the cause of the Circle:

> In a fit of passion, compounded of rage, horror, and pain, I had unleashed this thing, and it was reflected somewhere in every earth in existence. Such is the blood curse of a Prince of Amber. (GA, 54)

The third reason was that Corwin was convinced that killing the goat-creature would end the threat of the Circle, and only Corwin had the ability to triumph over it in close combat.

Ganelon gathered his army, and Corwin joined him, leading a command of his own. Their troops assembled on a hillside outside the Circle three or four leagues north of the village of Lorraine. Ganelon's captain, a man named Lancelot, signaled the charge, and they rode into the Circle.

They engaged the enemy forces half a mile inside. Most of those they fought and killed were pos-

sessed men, not the demons that had taken the land. The horned one had sent these mindless beings to forestall them. As Ganelon's army advanced over the dead, they saw a dark citadel in which the horned one resided. Ganelon, Lancelot, and Corwin led the way to the citadel, slaying men and beasts and half-men in a fierce struggle to reach the place, one step at a time. They fought their way to the gates, broke through to face more soulless beings, and slaughtered their way through to the dark tower within the citadel where they would find the goat-creature. Corwin ran up the stairs to meet it.

While Ganelon stood by, Corwin and the horned one locked arms in deadly earnest, each seeking to crush the other in his grasp. When the goat-creature realized who Corwin was, it tried to convince him to join with it, promising to restore him to rule in Amber. Corwin chose not to heed it, and they each placed a death grip on the other's throat. He heard the sharp snap of a neck breaking.

When Corwin recovered, Ganelon told him that with the death of the horned one, the possessed Wardens collapsed and the demon creatures turned to flames. Riding through the countryside, Corwin could distinguish the change. "The day was bright with a sky-blue, tree-green peace, for the scourge had been lifted from the land." (GA, 66)

DAVE

Deserter of an early battle at the Keep of the Four Worlds. Merlin of the Courts of Chaos met Dave after tracing a mystical tunnel from the shadow Earth to the mountains overlooking the Keep. Dave supplied Merlin with information on the ongoing politics concerning the Keep and Dave's homeland, the shadow Kashfa.

Dave was five feet six inches tall, extremely hairy, covered with dried filth, wearing a dark animal skin and sandals. He came upon Merlin while he was resting behind some stones on a cliff ledge. Friendly and candid, Dave appeared to be no threat to Merlin as he walked casually toward the resting mage.

Speaking openly and without restraint, Dave told him that he had been a foot soldier who deserted more than eight years earlier. Prince Rinaldo of

Kashfa and Dalt the mercenary had led Dave's regiment of Kashfan infantry through strange paths to reach this place. Dave said,

"Went bad for us at first . . . I think it's somehow easy for whoever's in charge down there to control the elements—like that twister you saw a while ago. We got an earthquake and a blizzard and lightning. But we pressed on to the walls anyhow. Saw my brother scalded to death with boiling oil. That's when I decided I'd had enough. I started running and climbed on up here. Nobody chased me, so I waited around and watched. Probably shouldn't have, but I didn't know how things would go. More of the same, I'd figgered. But I was wrong, and it was too late to go back. They'd have whacked off my head or some other valuable parts if I did." (BA, 47)

Dave led the way on a rocky ascent to a cave where he had resided for all the years he had remained in the area. Although Merlin nearly gagged at the stench coming from the cave mouth, Dave brought out a duffel bag that he claimed had "some good stuff." They retreated back to a ledge in the open air, and Merlin discovered that Dave did indeed have a well-stocked supply of edible material. They feasted on wine, water, fresh bread, tinned meat, a head of cheese, and some apples, while Dave talked of the wars against the Keep.

According to Dave, the original owner of the Keep of the Four Worlds was a wizard called Sharu Garrul. Queen Jasra had long ago left Kashfa to visit the Keep, leaving her son Rinaldo in charge. Since she was gone for so long, Prince Rinaldo and his friend Dalt had recruited an army to march against the Keep, believing she was being held prisoner. It had been an unfortunate move on the prince's part because Jasra had not been a captive. She had been attempting to charm the old wizard in order to gain control. When her son's army showed up, Jasra was forced to engage Sharu Garrul in a contest of sorcery. Although she defeated Sharu, she was somewhat hurt. That was how Jasra took over the Keep. However, a nobleman named Kasman conducted a takeover back in Kashfa. His brother was a lover of Jasra whom she had executed, so Kasman assaulted the Keep numbers of times to get rid of her. Unable to breach the Keep,

however, Kasman's forces had long ago retreated to their homeland. The present warfare seemed to be between Dalt's mercenary force and Jasra, since Dalt was a friend to her son but not to her. Of course, it was uncertain if Jasra remained in the Keep at this point in time. Dave was unable to determine precisely what the fighting was about in this latest campaign.

For his part, Dave found it easier to make a life for himself in the mountains beside the Keep. Dave explained his contentedness in this way:

"Truth of it is, I don't know the way home. Those were strange trails they brought us in on. I thought I knew where they were, but when I went lookin' I couldn't never find 'em. I suppose I could have just taken off, but then I'd probably get lost more than ever. Besides, I know I can make out here. A few weeks and those outbuildings will be rebuilt and the peasants will move back in, no matter who wins. And they think I'm a holy man, prayin' up here and meditatin'. Any time I wander down that way they come out for a blessin' and give me enough food and drink to hold me for a long while." (BA, 48)

When Merlin offered to show him the way back to Kashfa, Dave declined, saying he thought of this place as his home now.

Perhaps Dave is still there, living a hermit's life, gathering food and drink, collecting valuables from the dead, and slowly growing mad from loneliness. His kind often survives a long time.

DEATH ALLEY

The common name for Seabreeze Lane in the Harbor District in the city of Amber.

In daylight, it is a rather ordinary-looking street by the docks, just west of the cove where Amber's ships enter and leave. After dark, the street becomes dangerous with derelicts, sailors, and other unsavory people, some of whom seek a ready victim for robbery.

Merlin, son of Prince Corwin, was directed there by a palace guard named Jordy when he was looking for a good seafood café. As he walked down Harbor Road, Merlin described the approach to Death Alley in this way:

> I heard the cries, crashes and thuds of a struggle from somewhere nearby, leading me to believe that I was in the proper neighborhood. From somewhere distant a buoy bell rattled; from somewhere nearby I heard an almost bored-sounding string of curses preceding a pair of sailors who rounded the nearest corner to my right, reeling, staggered on past me, grinning, and broke into song moments later, receding. I advanced and checked the sign on that corner. SEABREEZE LANE, it read.
>
> That was it, the stretch commonly called Death Alley. I turned there. It was just a street like any other. I didn't see any corpses or even collapsed drunks for the first fifty paces, though a man in a doorway tried to sell me a dagger and a mustachioed stock character offered to fix me up with something young and tight. I declined both, and learned from the latter that I wasn't all that far from Bloody Bill's. (BA, 64)

On the occasion of Merlin's visit to the café, then known as Bloody Bill's, Death Alley lived up to its name. Two sailors, trying to hold up an older gentleman who worked for the Crown, were killed in their attempt. One of the two sailors made it back inside the café before he fell over and died; the other was sprawled on the street along Death Alley.

When Merlin had finished his meal, he stepped into the street, walked ten paces, and was attacked by three men, one with bow and arrow, and the others with swords. Buildings were close together, making for narrow side streets and alleyways, so that attack from ambush was a common tactic. While people were crying out and moving in the direction of the scuffle, no one interfered. Only when Merlin faced the last living attacker did another swordsman intervene, following the orders of Vinta Bayle, who had a slight acquaintance with Merlin. Merlin left with Vinta and her bodyguards, with the understanding that the three dead men on Death Alley were probably being picked clean by opportunistic bystanders.

For those who dwell along Death Alley after dark, such things are common occurrences, and those who die violently on the street do not die wealthy.

DEELA

Also known as Deela the Desacratrix. Mother of Dalt, a mercenary who warred against Amber.

Deela was a militant religious fanatic who raided towns and destroyed sacred artifacts and religious shrines in several shadows. Although she had not made her home in the shadow Begma, she carried out her raids in Begma and other shadows in that part of the Golden Circle. She gathered up a large following, made up largely of reprobates and mercenaries who sought wealth from the valuable items that were her wont to steal.

King Random of Amber gave this account of her history:

> "She'd raided a lot in Begma and they couldn't handle her by themselves. They finally reminded us of the protection alliance we have with almost all the Circle kingdoms—and Dad [Oberon] decided to go in personally and teach her a lesson. She'd burned one Unicorn shrine too many. He took a small force, defeated her troops, took her prisoner and hanged a bunch of her men. She escaped, though, and a couple of years later when she was all but forgotten she came back with a fresh force and started the same crap all over. Begma screamed again, but Dad was busy. He sent Bleys in with a larger force. There were several inconclusive engagements—they were raiders, not a regular army—but Bleys finally cornered them and wiped them out. She died that day, leading her troops." (BA, 61)

Deela's son Dalt became good friends with Rinaldo, son of Brand of Amber. They had spent a good part of their youth together in and around the shadow called Kashfa. Dalt had led a couple of raids against Amber in order to avenge his mother's death.

When Rinaldo later was on friendlier terms with King Random of Amber, he related a significant fact about Dalt that was previously unknown. Dalt had told him that King Oberon of Amber had raped his mother while she was a prisoner in Amber, and his birth was the result. As proof, Dalt succeeded in walking the Pattern in Tir-na Nog'th while Rinaldo watched. Thus, through Deela the Desacratrix, King Random had an illegitimate brother in Dalt. Fortunately, Dalt hadn't been able to raise a large enough armed force to create havoc in Amber. Nevertheless, his motives were such that he could prove a danger to the true city sometime in the future.

DEIGA

A distant shadow that belongs to the Golden Circle of trade with Amber.

Deiga is a widely visited shadow whose port city is a center of commerce for a variety of peoples from other shadows. It exports numerous exotic spices, and its nearby coffee plantations have a very profitable yield. The merchants of Deiga usually accept large quantities of the wines of Baron Bayle, so that Amber finds the association quite invaluable.

King Random's brother Caine was assassinated while on a diplomatic mission to Deiga at the beginning of the period known as the Pattern-Logrus Conflict. It was the first time that anyone in Deiga had ever seen or heard gunfire. Gérard had been with Caine at the time of the murder, and he found the rulers of the port city eager to give appeasement for the tragic event. As a result, Gérard came away with several highly advantageous additions to their renewed trade agreement.

It is a pleasant land with sundry opportunities for tourism as well as trade, and the indigenous people welcome others warmly. Bill Roth, formerly of shadow Earth, discovered this when he visited the place with Gérard. Mr. Roth has even let it be known that he had left his business card with several merchants in Deiga who expressed an interest in minor legal transactions with individuals in Amber.

DEIRDRE

Daughter of Oberon and Faiella. Her mother died giving birth to her. Deirdre's full brothers from that union were Eric, Corwin, and Caine, although Eric had been born before the marriage of Faiella and Oberon was formally recognized. Deirdre was Corwin's favorite sister, and because of this, she was out of favor with Eric when he ruled in Amber. She spent much of her time during Eric's rule in the undersea city of Rebma with her younger half sister Llewella. After fighting valiantly with her siblings at the Patternfall battle, she fell victim to her outlaw brother Brand.

When Corwin examined her Trump, even though he suffered from amnesia at the time, he was filled with emotion. This is the way he described the Trump of Deirdre:

> There was a black-haired girl with the same blue eyes, and her hair hung long and she was dressed all in black, with a girdle of silver about her waist. My eyes filled with tears, why I don't know. Her name was Deirdre. (NP, 30)

Because she cared very much for her brother Corwin, Deirdre had spoken up for him before Eric the Usurper. She had known that Eric was taking action against Corwin when he and Random were trying to reach Amber through a shadow walk. Corwin still had his memory loss when he and Random made it to the Forest of Arden. They discovered a small camp of six of Eric's guards. With them was Deirdre, tied securely to a stake. Random indicated to Corwin that he never cared for Deirdre, but he helped in rescuing her from her captors. After freeing Deirdre, Corwin initiated the following conversation:

> "Greetings, sister. Will you join us on the Road to Amber?"
> "No," she said. "Thanks for my life, but I want to keep it. Why do you walk to Amber, as if I didn't know."
> "There is a throne to be won," said Random, which was news to me, "and we are interested parties."
> "If you're smart, you'll stay away and live longer," she said, and God! she was lovely, though a bit tired-looking and dirty.
> I took her into my arms because I wanted to, and squeezed her. Random found a skin of wine and we all had a drink.

"Eric is the only prince in Amber," she said, "and the troops are loyal to him."

"I'm not afraid of Eric," I replied, and I knew I wasn't certain about that statement.

"He'll never let you into Amber," she said. "I was a prisoner myself, till I made it out one of the secret ways two days ago. I thought I could walk in Shadows till all things were done, but it is not easy to begin this close to the real place. So his troops found me this morning. They were taking me back. I think he might have killed me, had I been returned—though I'm not sure. At any rate, I'd have remained a puppet in the city." (NP, 68)

When Corwin confessed his lack of memory, Deirdre was ready to turn to the shadows and get as far from Amber as was possible. Random, however, wanted to dethrone Eric, and he maintained the hope that Corwin could be crowned. While they decided their next move, three of Eric's guards saw them. The guards were shapeshifters and reverted to the form of wolves. In the ensuing fight, Deirdre showed her remarkable strength. Corwin recorded: "To my amazement, I saw Deirdre raise one in the air and break its back across her knee with a brittle, snapping sound" (NP, 71). After dispatching the shapeshifted guards, Random suggested that they try to reach the undersea city of Rebma. There, Corwin would be able to regain his memory by walking the Pattern. Deirdre agreed to go with them.

They had a perilous encounter with one of Julian's patrols upon reaching the coast. As they rushed down the stairway called Faiella-bionin into the sea, they fought the horsemen who also braved the descent. The three made it to the undersea city. Deirdre and Corwin were given a welcome reception by Queen Moire, but Random was treated coldly. Nevertheless, Corwin was permitted to walk the Pattern there, and Deirdre chose to remain in Rebma of her own accord. Llewella, her sister, was a frequent guest in Rebma, and Deirdre found her an amiable confidante.

Deirdre had been in the underwater city with Random and Llewella when Random received a Trump contact from Corwin. Corwin was leading a fleet of ships against Eric, and Random spoke tersely: "Turn back.... According to Llewella, Eric can cream you now. She says wait a while, till he relaxes, and hit him then—like a year from now,

maybe." (NP, 116) It seems apparent that Deirdre and the others in Rebma were able to follow much of the political events happening in the true city. In his Trump contact, Random told Corwin that Eric had learned to control the weather through the Jewel of Judgment. He referred to the fact that this knowledge derived from gossip in Queen Moire's court about the Jewel's double. Random even admitted having spoken to Eric directly, and Eric warned him about the extent of his defenses against assault. All these matters would be things that Deirdre would be privy to as well.

When Random made a desperately heroic move against Eric, he acted alone. Random used Rebma's Pattern to transport himself to the Royal Palace, where he managed to wound Eric with a bolt from a crossbow. Naturally, he was taken prisoner. Although those in Rebma, like other nearby shadows, watched Eric's coronation and knew that he had condemned Corwin to blindness in a dungeon, Deirdre and Llewella may not have known Random's plan to respond as he did. They had remained in Rebma.

After Eric's death, and in the sudden new reign of Corwin, Deirdre was able to visit in Amber more freely. She received word from Corwin while in the Royal Palace that Caine had been murdered. Corwin explained that a beast-man out of Shadow had done it, but someone else was trying to make it seem as if Corwin were the culprit. In the Chronicles, Corwin described Deirdre's reaction:

"Deirdre now—she seemed happy about it. Didn't believe a word, I'm sure. But no matter. She has always been on my side, and she has never liked Caine. I'd say she is glad that I seem to be consolidating my position." (SU, 68)

Corwin had called a meeting in the library of the Royal Palace of all the members of the Family. Although Deirdre was in the palace, she chose to contact Corwin by Trump at the gathering, and he brought her in through the Trump connection. Corwin had noted in his Chronicles: "The others glanced our way as she appeared and she hit them all with that smile, like the Mona Lisa with a machine gun." (SU, 82) He also noted that Random intervened, avoiding any conflict between Deirdre and Flora. The two women could be terribly unflattering toward each other.

When the meeting commenced, Corwin asked Random to inform them of what he knew of Brand's imprisonment. Corwin then proposed that all of them use their Trumps to try to make contact with Brand together. Their combined effort succeeded, and Gérard and Random were able to rescue him and bring him back to the library. However, someone in the room stabbed Brand with a thin stiletto, seriously wounding him. Gérard insisted that Brand's care be left to him. Despite their personal conflict, Deirdre and Flora left together with Random to get some medical supplies.

While Gérard cared for the unconscious Brand in the library, the others retired to a sitting room to discuss the matter further. Deirdre was quite mystified about which of them could have had the audacity to stab Brand when they had crowded around him during the rescue. She agreed with Corwin to permit the culprit his, or her, life, but in exile, if the person came forward to admit guilt. She did put forward an intriguing supposition to the others:

> "Gérard could have done the stabbing himself while we were all crowded around, and that his heroic efforts were not prompted by any desire to save Brand's neck, but rather to achieve a position where he could stop his tongue—in which case Brand would never make it through the night. Ingenious, but I [Corwin] just couldn't believe it. No one else bought it either. At least, no one volunteered to go upstairs and throw Gérard out." (SU, 109)

Oddly, Deirdre and Flora spent much of the time in the sitting room together. During their lengthy conversation, they never once raised their voices. Perhaps they had a lot of catching up to do, having led such diverse and interesting lives. Among the last to leave, Deirdre and Flora got up from their seats, said their good-nights to Random and Corwin, and left together.

Much later, along with most of the others in the Family, Deirdre learned that Brand had conspired with the lords at the Courts of Chaos to reshape Amber and become its sole ruler. It is believed she was told much of this when Corwin hellrode to shadow Earth to find the Jewel of Judgment. It is unclear which of her siblings informed her, though it may have been Random.

She may have received her orders at the time of the Patternfall War directly from Dara, although it is not certain. Journeying with Random and Julian from Arden, Deirdre followed their troops through Shadow. Julian's troops were kept in reserve for a time while Deirdre and Random linked up with Benedict's army on the battlefield. Wielding a great ax, Deirdre took position on horseback along the western portion of the plain with a company of men led by Random. She used her weapon with deadly efficiency as the battle progressed.

Just as others around her had done in momentary respites from fighting, Deirdre looked up toward the northern sky. The approaching storm was darkening large areas below it, sending out lightning, winds, and heavy rain. She could feel the changing wind, the sudden slapping of rain at her face. Turning away from the storm front, she spotted a small, red gleam on a hill to the south. Looking around and realizing that there had been a lag in the fighting around her, with enemy soldiers taking the fight farther to the east, she looked more carefully at that height in the distance. It occurred to her that the shining object might have been the Jewel of Judgment, marking where Brand stood.

Seeing Random and Fiona passing by on their horses in that direction, Deirdre decided to join them. If it was Brand standing in the heights, whoever could be spared from the battle would be needed to defeat him. Fiona was in the lead, and others had turned their horses to follow Deirdre. As they reached the foot of the hill, beginning to ride the slope upward, a tremendous lightning bolt struck just ahead of Deirdre's position. She was thrown from her horse just as those around her were.

Lying on the ground, Deirdre lifted her head, warily looking around. Ahead of her were two or three of Amber's soldiers. They were unmoving. Fearing a second lightning strike, she rolled to her right, then rose to a crouch, and ran up the slope. Her eyes still trying to adjust so soon after the flash of the lightning, she didn't see the fist that hit her jarringly in the face. An arm grabbed her around the neck, and the other hand held a dagger close to her throat. She screamed, and thought he had slit into her throat, but in an odd, dizzying moment, she felt a shifting of ground. Close to her face, she heard Brand's voice spew out a curse.

Her vision cleared. She stood, held firmly from behind, the knife at her throat. She couldn't see much of his face, but she knew it was Brand holding her.

Ahead and slightly below her on the hill were Random, Fiona, and two other noblemen. While she was unable to turn her head to look around, Deirdre calculated they stood just before the edge of the Abyss. She couldn't understand why Brand would take this location to hold a standoff, until she heard Fiona say:

"I can hold him here ... and at this range, I can slow his efforts at weather control. But that is all. He's got some attunement with it and I do not. He also has proximity going for him. Anything else I might try, he can counter." (CC, 111)

Remaining still, Deirdre may have been thinking out possible actions she could take. Brand's grip was sure and strong, the knife in his other hand close enough to kill her in an instant. Her eyes may have shown fear, but she displayed a measure of calm.

Brand ordered Random and the others to put down their weapons, or else he would finish Deirdre. Random refused, and for a moment it seemed that Brand would take the next step. Something happened overhead, something remarkable that distracted everyone. The face of King Oberon appeared in the sky, and his voice came from its moving lips. The voice spoke of Corwin's bringing the Jewel of Judgment, heedless of the fact that Brand was wearing it at that moment. Oberon's voice told them that the choice of his successor would be "on the horn of the Unicorn." (CC, 113) Then the face evaporated.

Fiona tried to reason with Brand, following the cue of their father's message. Brand was not interested in helping them to eradicate the Death Storm. He cared only about ending the Amber they knew and creating a new one with himself its master. He demanded that they all leave, and let the storm run its course.

From somewhere nearby, Corwin was using the Jewel to affect Brand. Brand screamed, his body feeling terribly hot. He ordered Corwin to stop, and he used the knife to slash Deirdre's face. Feeling the blood and the fresh cut, Deirdre acted. Her head was free, and she bit hard into Brand's hand. His hold relaxed, and she jolted him in the side with her

elbow. She started to move away, and two arrows in quick succession penetrated deeply into Brand's throat and chest. He may already have been dead, or perhaps not, as he stepped backward. He started to fall, but with some final spark of life, his arm reached for Deirdre's fleeing form. His fingers closed on her wildly flowing black hair and held tightly.

Corwin rushed toward Deirdre. She reached her arms out to him, and Corwin's face may have been the last thing she ever saw.

DELWIN

Son of a contested union between King Oberon and Harla. Soon after the death of Harla in Amber, Delwin and his sister, Sand, left Amber to remain in their mother's homeland. Although members of the Royal Family are purported to have attempted Trump contact with Delwin and Sand, they apparently refused to have any further association with the true city.

Harla and her children are never spoken of openly by the Royal Family, so it is difficult to determine the exact events that led to the banishment (which perhaps was self-imposed) of Sand and Delwin. At the time when Oberon returned from a far shadow with Harla, claiming she was his bride, he was wed to Rilga. The complications which ensued were no doubt inflamed by the expressed annoyance of Rilga's sons: Julian and Gérard. It would seem that Oberon's growing disenchantment with Harla grew from the sibling rivalry of the other princes and princesses, who frequently bickered over the succession.

Oberon traveled often in other shadows, and he made trade agreements with a shadow that was a rival of Harla's homeland. His continued remoteness, both in geography and intimacy, as well as his policies in commerce, may have contributed to the death of Harla.

It became clear that Delwin and his sister were no longer welcome in the Royal Palace after their mother's death. They went away, "vowing not to have anything to do with Amber again." (BA, 115)

Merlin had learned from his friend Luke Raynard that Brand of Amber had once tried to contact Delwin by Trump. Brand had hoped that Delwin's antagonism for the Amberites could be used as a motivation for Delwin's joining him in a scheme to destroy Amber and begin a new order. However, Brand hadn't quite understood that Delwin would not care to become involved in any scheme affecting Amber. He simply wasn't interested in the twisted politics of the realm. For Delwin, the pitting of one Amberite against the others would mean his having to involve himself in Amber once more. He would have none of it.

Years after Brand's death, Luke Raynard used the Trumps that Brand had drawn to reach Delwin. As his father before him had done, Luke sought Delwin's help in settling his own vendetta against Caine and the other children of Oberon. Again, Delwin, and presumably Sand, refused. Still, Luke had continued to carry the Trumps of these "long-lost" relations on his person.

When Merlin visited the Courts of Chaos for King Swayvill's funeral, he encountered a unique image of Delwin that gave him some vital information. Under a spell induced by Suhuy, Master of the Logrus, Merlin dreamed of Delwin. The dream itself was undoubtedly more than just fantasy, for tangible evidence of its reality came into Merlin's possession. In the dream, Merlin saw the youthful man in a mirror:

> The frame was white, the glass was gray. Within was a man I had never met. His shirt was black and opened at the neck. He wore a brown leather vest, his hair dark blond, eyes perhaps green.
> "Yes?"
> "A spikard was hidden in Amber," he stated, "for you to find. It conveys great powers. It also bears a series of spells that will cause its wearer to act in certain ways under certain circumstances."
> "I suspected this," I said. "What is it set to do?"
> "Formerly worn by Swayvill, King of Chaos, it will force the chosen successor to take the throne, behave in a certain fashion, and be amenable to the suggestions of certain persons."
> "These being?"
> "The woman who laughed and cried, 'Seek

him in the Pit.' The man in black, who desires your return."
> "Dara and Mandor. They laid these spells upon it?"
> "Just so. And the man left it for you to find."
> "I hate to surrender the thing just now," I said, "when it's proving so useful. Is there a way to lift these spells?"
> "Of course. But it should not matter to you."
> "Why not?"
> "The ring you wear is not the one of which I speak."
> "I do not understand."
> "But you will. Never fear."
> "Who are you, sir?"
> "My name is Delwin, and we may never actually meet—unless certain ancient powers come loose." (PC, 208–9)

Also in the dream, Merlin met his uncle, Bleys, who conveyed the rest of Delwin's message concerning the spikards. The Bleys image gave Merlin the spikard that Delwin had spoken of. When Merlin awoke, he had this second ring in his possession.

Interestingly, it has long been rumored that Delwin had interceded on Bleys's behalf many years ago. Climbing Mt. Kolvir and battling the soldiers of Eric the usurper, Bleys had fallen from the natural rock stair. Some have hinted that Bleys was rescued by Delwin through a Trump connection. While Bleys was presumed dead, it has been purported that he was actually under Delwin's care. Although this is mere speculation, the association made between the two in Merlin's dream suggests some level of truth to the possible relationship.

DESPIL

Older of two sons born to Dara of House of Helgram and Gramble, Lord Sawall. Despil and his younger brother, Jurt, were born to Dara after her marriage to Sawall, who was also known as the Rim Duke. Dara had previously had a son, Merlin, whose father was Prince Corwin of Amber.

Brought up in the Courts of Chaos, Despil was a

devoted son to his parents. He developed a sense of civility and courtliness that was lacking in his brother Jurt. Frequently, Jurt would get into some kind of trouble, and Despil had to smooth the way for him with Dara and Gramble. As they grew older, Jurt became more reckless and hot-tempered, and Despil became reserved and self-disciplined.

When Jurt challenged his half brother Merlin to a duel above the Abyss of Chaos, he had asked Despil to act as mediator. Their oldest brother, Mandor, had overheard their conversation and insisted on attending the duel.

Adhering strictly to the rules of proper conduct, Despil officiated over their challenge with great care. Jurt used his weapon to carve three lines of blood in Merlin's arm, and Despil called out, "First blood! ... Which is sufficient! Have you satisfaction?" (BA, 81) The challenge should have been concluded at that point, but Jurt insisted on pursuing it. Soon, Despil realized the sport had gotten out of hand. His rash brother wanted to inflict much greater injury upon Merlin than etiquette allowed. Despil had carefully outlined the rules of the combat, which they all knew anyway. Jurt was apparently ignoring the directive that if one slays the other in the contest, he is to be considered an outcast and subject to banishment.

In a purely defensive move, Merlin raised his fandon and trisp to protect his face, slicing off Jurt's left ear and tearing into his scalp. Despil and Mandor came beside Jurt, who was holding his bleeding head. They called the duel at an end. Despil checked Jurt's wound and told Merlin, "He'll be all right. But Mother is going to be mad." (BA, 84) Despil led him home while Merlin and Mandor went to see their uncle Suhuy.

Some time after this point, Despil left the Courts to travel widely in Shadow. He may have returned to the House of Sawall to visit on occasion, but this is unclear. If further speculation may be allowed, it would seem that he may have been annoyed over the increasing animosity between Jurt and Merlin. Or, an escalation of violent activity in the Courts, involving the succession to the throne, may have urged him to depart. In recent times, when Merlin stayed in Amber under King Random's auspices, he mentioned a rumor that certain members of their House in the Courts would have reason to discourage Despil's candidacy. Merlin never explained what he meant beyond that.

Although Merlin has written in his journals about his return to his ancestral home for the funeral ceremony of the late king, he did not see Despil during that solemn affair.

DEVLIN, MEG

Young lady that Merle Corey met at the country club in New York frequented by Bill Roth.

Because Meg Devlin wasn't exactly what she seemed, much of the knowledge Merle recorded about her is deceptive. Merle had gone to the country club alone after having spent a previous evening there with his father's friend, Mr. Roth, an attorney. Merle had an appointment with an anonymous phone caller who claimed to have information that would be useful in protecting Merle. Although the caller hadn't revealed himself at the club, Merle met Meg in a seemingly innocent way. Afterward, he suspected that Meg was indeed the person he was supposed to have met, even though he was sure the caller had been a male.

Meg was an attractive woman with a delicate profile and light hair. She told Merle that she had been a fashion model, then a buyer for a store, and had become the manager of a boutique.

Merle was waiting dutifully at a secluded table in the bar of the country club. Although he noticed the attractive young woman sitting at the bar unaccompanied, he allowed the time to pass to make certain that he didn't frighten off the anonymous caller he was to meet. When he finished his beer, Merle walked over to the bar for a refill. The young woman on the bar stool turned to him to speak.

"I saw you sitting there ... Waiting for someone?"

"Yes ... But I'm beginning to think it's too late."

"I've a similar problem ... We could wait together."

"Please join me ... I'd much rather pass the time with you. ..."

"My name's Merle Corey."

"I'm Meg Devlin. I haven't seen you around before."

"I'm just visiting. You, I take it, are not? ..."

"Afraid not. I live in that new apartment complex a couple of miles up the road . . .

"Where are you from?"

"The center of the universe . . . San Francisco."

"Oh, I've spent a lot of time there. . . .

"I think we've both been stood up."

"Probably, . . . but we ought to give them till eleven to be decent about it."

"I suppose."

"Have you eaten?"

"Earlier."

"Hungry?"

"Some. Yes. Are you?"

"Uh-huh, and I noticed some people had food in here earlier. . . .

"What were you going to do tonight?" . . .

"Oh, dance a bit, have a few drinks, maybe take a walk in the moonlight. Silly things like that."

"I hear music in the next room. We could stroll on over."

"Yes, we could . . . Why don't we?" (TD, 126–27)

When they danced, Merle noticed that Meg had a tendency to lead. They checked back at the bar at eleven-thirty, and she claimed her date wasn't there. Meg offered to give Merle a lift, and when he agreed, they drove to her apartment building. She had a numbered parking spot for her car, and she led the way to her apartment.

They had some coffee and talked for a while. After they had gone to bed together, Meg asked a question and expressed a knowledge that she wouldn't, or shouldn't, ordinarily have.

"Tell me something" . . .

"Sure."

"What was your mother's name?" . . .

"Dara" . . .

"And your father?"

"Corwin" . . .

"I thought so . . . but I had to be sure."

"Do I get some questions now? Or can only one play?"

"I'll save you the trouble. You want to know why I asked" . . .

"I take it their names mean something to you?"

"You are Merlin, . . . Duke of Kolvir and Prince of Chaos." (TD, 130)

Certainly, at this point, it is clear that Meg Devlin was not really herself. Like several other people of the shadow Earth, she was an instrument for getting specific messages to Merle. This incident probably marked the moment that the being within Meg ascertained the identity of the person she was sent to protect.

This Meg Devlin ushered Merle out of her apartment hurriedly when "the husband" (TD, 131) buzzed her over the intercom from the lobby entrance. She seemed genuinely worried about letting "the husband" discover Merlin there, although her reasons might not have been the trite and true.

On a later occasion, while he was staying with his aunt Flora in San Francisco, Merle made a telephone call to Meg Devlin. She insisted that she had never met Merle and knew nothing whatsoever about him. Although it is difficult to assess such denials, it seemed to Merle that she would have hinted at some affirmation of their encounter, even if "the husband" were standing right there. Instead, their brief conversation seemed to intimate that she was troubled by his calling, as if she had had an episode that she couldn't explain and she had an inkling that he was a part of that troubling occurrence.

Merle never bothered to make further contact with Meg Devlin.

DOYLE

A slight, elderly jeweler who resided in shadow Avalon. He supplied a large quantity of jewelers rouge for Corwin of Amber.

Doyle was a pleasant little man who nevertheless shrewdly understood the potential of working up a business deal to his advantage. Described by Corwin as a "little wispy-haired jeweler with a brick-red complexion and wens on his cheeks," (GA, 130) Doyle was extremely curious about the possible use Corwin could have for so much jewelers rouge.

Corwin had refused to explain why he wanted such vast quantities, saying that he was willing to pay quite well. He could see the inner workings of the little man when Doyle said, "Well, if there was some new use of the stuff and good money to be made, a man would be a fool . . ." (GA, 130) But at Corwin's request that he have the rouge in a week's time, Doyle laughed, ready to dismiss him. At that, Corwin thanked him, saying he would try the jeweler down the street. He had also mentioned as he was leaving that he would pay for it in uncut diamonds. This caused Doyle to change his mind. After all, it was fairly easy to prepare the ingredients. It had simply been the quantity that had put him off. Corwin then found Doyle very reasonable to deal with. The promise of payment with diamonds had blunted Doyle's curiosity.

Nevertheless, Doyle had not completed gathering the amount of jewelers rouge requested when Corwin came to pick it up. Corwin was with a sinister-looking man named Ganelon, whose appearance helped Corwin persuade the jeweler to close his shop early to finish the task. When Doyle had gotten all of the requisitioned canisters filled, his eyes gleamed in delight as Corwin handed over several pouches full of beautiful, uncut diamonds. Doyle checked a number of them very carefully with his glass, taking several at random from each pouch. He smiled widely, showing that he was missing some of his teeth. It was quite satisfactory.

Corwin picked out a bracelet, to be delivered to an address he gave to Doyle. He paid for the bracelet with another pouch of diamonds. Doyle's little shoulders trembled with joy and laughter. He had made a very profitable business deal after all.

DROPPA MAPANTZ

Court jester to the Court of King Random of Amber. While he often is taken by drink, one can usually count on him for the wry remark. Although, as official clown to the Royal Court, he makes use of slapstick, he is better at comic wit than physical humor. Those who reside in Amber also recognize in him a bit of the shrewd businessman.

Oddly enough, no one in Amber knows Droppa's real name, although most of his acquaintances agree that he arrived from a distant shadow after Random took the throne. Even when he is under the influence of an alcoholic reverie, which is often, Droppa refrains from speaking of his past.

King Random frequently sends the court jester to other shadows to ferret out fresh comedic material. Droppa has indicated to the king that he prefers shadows with a more technological bent than is possible in the true city. His official rationale, as stated to Random, is that a technological society offers greater variety in styles because the comic personality must cater to different kinds of patrons. An audience observing through some technical means responds differently from a live audience in a small club setting. In private, however, Droppa has intimated that his lack of skill in areas of mysticism, so much a part of the atmosphere in Amber, makes him feel too vulnerable. Thus, he prefers excursions to realms where magic is known to be nothing more than trickery.

One time, when Droppa had awakened from a drunken sleep and decided to head for the palace kitchens, he saw young Merlin carrying the frozen figure of Jasra past his room. Without hesitation, Droppa said, "I'll take two. You know, she reminds me of my first wife." (SC, 50) He closed his door again, deciding to let Merlin, and possibly the figment of imagination, pass discreetly before attempting to make his way to the kitchens.

Bill Roth, the attorney from shadow Earth who had become legal counsel to the king, formed a lasting friendship with Droppa. They shared an interest in the complexities of a more mechanized type of world. Their common bond of unfamiliarity with the more mystical workings of the true city had drawn them closer together. The court jester attracted Mr. Roth's interest from the first time he dined in the Royal Palace. Droppa was brought into the dining hall to entertain while Bill Roth ate with King Random, Merlin, Martin, and several others of the Family who were currently in residence. A recent arrival, Mr. Roth turned to Merlin and initiated the following about Droppa:

> "I know enough Thari to catch most of it, and that's a George Carlin shtick! How—"
> "Oh, whenever Droppa's stuff starts sounding stale, Random sends him off to various clubs in Shadow . . . to pick up new material. I understand he's a regular at Vegas. Random even accompanies him sometimes, to play cards." (TD, 118)

Shortly after that dinner, Mr. Roth was introduced to Droppa, and they began spending much time together. The attorney found the clown to be an astute businessman, and, in turn, Droppa enjoyed showing Bill Roth around town. Mr. Roth discovered that Droppa knew most of the important merchants of the city personally. The little jester had small holdings in various shops along the Main Concourse, including a half interest in a café called the Pit.

Although Random would entrust Droppa to carry out minor orders, the king had always been aware that the jester's drinking and natural tendency toward cowardice would make him somewhat unreliable. On one occasion, the king assigned him to stay with Merlin while Merlin slept. Merlin had just returned to Amber in an exhausted state, and the king believed it important that they speak as soon as Merlin recovered. Attempting dutifulness, Droppa sat in a chair watching over Merlin, sleeping on a sofa in a sitting room east of the main hall. Soon, however, Droppa stood over Merlin, shaking him awake:

> "Merle! Merle!" . . .
> "Droppa. . . . What—?"
> "I don't know." . . .
> "What don't you know? I mean. . . . Hell! What happened?"
> "I was sitting in that chair . . . waiting for you to wake up. Martin had told me you were here. I was just going to tell you that Random wanted to see you when you got back." . . .
> "How long was I out?"
> "Twenty minutes, maybe." . . .
> "So why'd you decide to wake me?"
> "You were trumping out." . . .
> "Trumping out? While I was asleep? It doesn't work that way. Are you sure—"
> "I am, unfortunately, sober at the moment . . . You got that rainbow glow and you started to soften around the edges and fade. Thought I'd better wake you then and ask if that's what you really had in mind. What've you been drinking, spot remover?"
> "No." . . .
> "I tried it on my dog once. . . ." (BA, 210)

Although Droppa may have really helped that time, perhaps saving Merlin's life, he soon after reverted to his usual fearfulness. As the walls about

them seemed to melt, Droppa departed quickly, shouting, "It appears to be alarums and excursions time . . . Help!" (BA, 211)

There is certainly something of the weak-hearted in the court jester, but for all that, he is staunchly loyal to the king and the members of his court. At the time when the two Great Powers came together in the palace, Droppa had been walking by drinking from a bottle of Bayle's Piss and singing raucously. He halted, stunned, dropped the bottle, and backed away swiftly when he witnessed the meeting of the Pattern and the Logrus. While he did not return to the area where the explosion took place, several members of the king's retinue reported seeing Droppa aiding some of the shaken servants on the main floor. Droppa also remained to help in the immense cleanup, even to the point of helping to bolster some of the more precarious parts of the damaged structure around the central stairway.

Good-hearted Droppa continues to serve King Random in his usual capacity. However, when he is not needed to perform at official functions, he will often remain in town, claiming the need to attend to one of his holdings. It has been surmised that Droppa MaPantz is constantly afraid of another destructive force blasting part of the palace while he is within. Rumor has it that on that one occasion he had lost more than a bottle of Bayle's Piss in the cataclysm.

DWORKIN

Architect who created the Pattern, shaping Order from Chaos into what has become the known universe.

Dworkin Barimen fathered Oberon, who became king of the true city, by mysterious means. In later life, he implied that Oberon's mother was the unicorn, but the offhand comment may have been the result of his mental and physical impairment.

Much of his early life is shrouded in mystery, but through members of the Royal Family, certain intimations have been made. In his youth, he was vigorous and strong, the model of hardiness and great intellect that was passed to his son and succeeding generations. Before he had been given the power to create the Pattern, it is likely that he served in a kind of priesthood in the Courts of Chaos. He developed certain magical abilities sometime during this service. He was able to transform his molecular structure into any form at will; he formed a mystical connection with nature and those elements that existed in a natural state; and he discovered his artistic talent for using the forces of nature to create etchings that bore a remarkable realism.

Dissatisfied with the petty squabbles of the ruling class in Chaos, he went into self-exile, fleeing, as he described it, "to this small sudden island in the sea of night." (HO, 66) While one day practicing his artwork on a flat stone, he was awestruck by a sight few men have seen before or since. A large, white unicorn stood with apparent fearlessness several feet away, watching the man squatting on the ground. Around the neck of the fabled beast was a shining metal chain from which hung a large, red Jewel. As Dworkin carefully rose from the ground, the unicorn remained unafraid. Miraculously, the beast allowed him to approach and stroke her mane. This was the beginning of a remarkable relationship. Time passed, and man and beast were inseparable.

Exactly why Dworkin created the Pattern is unclear, except that the unicorn had some urgent need which depended on the creation of an ordered universe. The red Jewel that hung around the neck of the unicorn had the capability within it to reshape the stuff of Chaos into a definite form, but it needed the attunement of a human mind to initiate the process. In a mystic ritual that came, in part, from Dworkin's priestly knowledge, he made preparations for attuning himself to the Jewel and tracing the Pattern on the surface of a smooth bedrock on that small island. Dworkin removed the Jewel from the unicorn's neck and put it over his own head. After the unicorn brought a live lyrebird to him, Dworkin sacrificed it and mingled its blood with his own from a slashed finger. As the unicorn harnessed lightning through the Jewel that hung about Dworkin's neck, the man began drawing the Pattern in the natural bedrock with the mingling blood.

The Pattern thus formed was an integral part of him. The ordered universe that took form at that moment consisted of the dreams and thoughts of Dworkin, the purity of the unicorn, and the warring blood of man and beast.

Amber was the archetype, the key city created by the Pattern. It is duplicated throughout the universe, but with progressive imperfections as one moves farther away from it. Amber is the city of Dworkin's mind, capable of great things, of beauty, of purity; but also carrying the incorrigibility of petty bickering and violence among its minions. That is Dworkin's legacy to man.

Dworkin ruled in Amber for millennia. The Jewel of Judgment that he wore around his neck, the same Jewel that inspired him to create the Pattern, urged him to plan, to build. The Pattern was a part of him, just as his mind was a part of the Pattern. They were one, and interchangeable. If the Pattern were altered in any way, the change would occur in the man as well.

Early in his rule, his companion, the unicorn, wandered away. Some say this led to the drastic change in Dworkin. Others say that it was the unexplained birth of his son Oberon that changed him. Still others point to the heavy burden of responsibility that led to his change. Whatever the reason, the change was sudden: He aged, seemed to shrivel up, allowed a stubble on his chin to grow into a wild, unkempt beard. He was seldom seen in public and became a virtual recluse in the Royal Palace.

While very young, his son Oberon took on the responsibilities of ruling the kingdom. Dworkin contented himself with arcane studies and his artwork, remaining in a locked room in a secluded part of the palace. Among his preoccupations during this time was the portrayal of Oberon and his children on Tarot-like cards.

When he had not seen his father for more than a fortnight, young Oberon sought him out in the secluded wing of the palace that he occupied. There was no response to his persistent knocking on the door of Dworkin's living quarters, so Oberon had his guards break it down. Dworkin had effectively vanished, and he was nowhere to be found, neither in the palace, nor in Amber.

Greatly concerned, Oberon periodically sent out search parties to seek him out in the shadowlands. Years passed, and Oberon grew to middle age, his children grown to young adulthood, before one of Oberon's expeditions learned of the location of "the mad artist" known as Dworkin. When brought the message, Oberon traveled to the distant shadow where his father had spent so many years. He had arrived just in time to prevent Dworkin from being summarily executed for attempting to cause an insurrection against the prevailing government. Oberon interceded on his father's behalf, diplomatically arranging for mutual trade agreements as a means of appeasing the local governing body.

Returning with his son to Amber, Dworkin spent much of his time studying the problems of the city. Although he had aged badly, developing a disfiguring curvature of the spine, which caused him to appear even shorter than he was, Dworkin felt a new surge of creative energy. During this time, he created the family Trumps, modeled after his earlier endeavors, and infused the portrait cards with the mystical powers of communication and instantaneous transportation that they are known for.

Dworkin's madness occurred at the time when the atmosphere became politically charged with Family intrigues and backbiting. Inexplicably, Oberon disappeared from the true city, and Oberon's children scrabbled for positions of power. A blot appeared on the primal Pattern that proved to be the blood of Random's son, Martin. This blot on the original Pattern that Dworkin had long ago inscribed caused a corresponding "blotting" effect on Dworkin's mind. Among its physical manifestations in him was his inability to fully control his metamorphoses. He would turn into terrifying creatures when feeling some deep emotional turmoil.

When Oberon returned to his troubled rule, he was forced to confront a crazed Dworkin, who insisted that the blotted Pattern had to be destroyed, and that he, Oberon, must inscribe a fresh, untainted Pattern from his own psyche. In order to destroy the Pattern, however, Dworkin would have to walk it, reach its center, and kill himself. Once this could be accomplished, Oberon would be free to replace it with a new Pattern. Believing this to be too drastic and dangerous a plan, his son rejected it utterly. But to safeguard his father, Oberon chained a monstrous purple griffin, trained to prevent Dworkin from approaching it, to the primal Pattern. Oberon kept his father under "house arrest" in the dungeons of the palace so that he would not do harm to himself in any misguided belief that he would thereby be saving the universe.

Of course, Dworkin could not be so easily restricted. In his den, he drew a Trump and used it to leave the room. That was when he discovered Corwin, locked in a cell by Eric when he ruled in Amber. Dworkin helped Corwin to escape his imprisonment, and he also met Corwin again, when Corwin visited him in his den. On that latter occa-

sion, Dworkin realized that Corwin had taken a Trump of the Courts of Chaos.

Dworkin helped Oberon in making preparations during the Patternfall War. When Corwin attempted to repair the damaged primal Pattern, Dworkin joined with Oberon to concentrate their combined psychic affinity to the Jewel of Judgment, preventing Corwin from fulfilling the task. When Oberon gave Corwin his orders, he rejoined Dworkin to complete his preparations there.

Although it is unclear what happened at the primal Pattern, it is likely that Dworkin was observing his son as he walked the design, clearing the blotted area. With the eruption of the Death Storm, the shadows may have been eradicated, but the place of the newly pristine Pattern should have stood.

While the Patternfall battle was progressing, Dworkin would have been making the arrangements for the funeral procession of Oberon. Those of the Courts of Chaos would have been involved in the disposition of the late king. As the fighting outside the Courts reached a conclusion, the minions of the Courts began the procession along the black road, entering the Dark Citadel. Dworkin drove the horse-drawn carriage bearing the coffin of Oberon, taking his son to his final destiny in the Old Country.

Dworkin may have been wandering in Shadow for a time, but he was back in Amber when Merlin was there. Acting in an advisory capacity, Dworkin enabled Merlin to become better equipped to deal with the hostilities between the Powers of the Pattern and the Logrus.

After Merlin met Dworkin, who had been knocking on doors in the palace seeking him out, they had a long talk. Understanding a great deal more about the conflict between the Powers than he was willing to say, Dworkin persuaded Merlin to undergo the attunement to the Jewel of Judgment. Following Dworkin's advice, Merlin went to the blue crystal cave to rest first before undertaking the process. Later, when the Signs of the Pattern and the Logrus confronted one another in the Royal Palace, Merlin had been protected from the destruction which followed.

Since Merlin's construct Ghostwheel had gotten the Jewel away from the Powers, Dworkin saw this as an opportunity to keep the artifact away from both the Serpent and the unicorn. Returning with Merlin to the wrecked palace, Dworkin greeted King Random and the others there. Coral of Begma was badly hurt, and Dworkin took over ministering her from Random's wife. After Merlin retrieved the Jewel from Ghostwheel, Dworkin secretly implanted it in Coral's eye socket. Then Dworkin lifted the girl up and vanished with her.

Although Dworkin has kept out of sight since that odd circumstance, no doubt he continues to observe the changing tide of events through a glowing crystal.

EREGNOR

A large piece of land with rich mineral deposits that lies between the shadow realms of Begma and Kashfa. Both kingdoms have claimed Eregnor as their own in the past and have gone to war over it.

As legal counsel to King Random, Bill Roth of the shadow Earth had been involved in the preparation of a treaty agreement between Amber and Kashfa. The ceding of Eregnor to the Kashfans was prominent in the terms of the treaty. King Random had made an effort to place Arkans, duke of Shadburne, on the throne of Kashfa, partly because Arkans was a capable statesman, and partly because he traced his lineage through the royal line, but mainly because he would be favorably inclined toward Amber. It was Duke Arkans who insisted that Eregnor be included in their contract, and Random acquiesced.

Bill Roth understood the Eregnor situation well, and he explained the changing political tides in this way:

> "It's their Alsace-Lorraine. . . . It has changed hands back and forth so many times over the centuries that both countries make reasonable-sounding claims to it. Even the inhabitants of the area aren't all that firm on the matter. They have relatives in both directions. I'm not even sure they care which side claims them, so long as their taxes don't go up. I think Begma's claim might be a little stronger, but I could argue the case either way. . . .
>
> ". . . The interim ruler—Jaston was his name, military man—was actually willing to discuss its status with the Begmans, before his unfortunate fall from the balcony. I think he

wanted to repair the treasury and was considering ceding the area in return for the settlement of some ancient war damage claims. Things were actually well along and headed in that direction. . . .
>
> "In the papers I got from Random, Amber specifically recognizes Kashfa as including the area of Eregnor. Arkans had insisted that go into the treaty. . . .
>
> ". . . there are lots of other things the Begmans don't like about him [Arkans], but that's the big one—right when they thought they were making some headway on an issue that's been a national pastime for generations." (SC, 133–34).

Although it is unclear whether Kashfa was the aggressor in terms of the Eregnor situation, or if it was Begma, there are certain well-defined parallels with shadow Earth's Alsace-Lorraine, as Bill Roth had mentioned. Like Alsace, and a large portion of Lorraine, Eregnor has been a playing piece in the age-long conflict between Begma and Kashfa; Alsace-Lorraine was a piece of land continuingly shifting between the countries of France and Germany, something that had begun early in the seventeenth century. Unlike Eregnor, which cared little about to which kingdom it was attached, Alsace-Lorraine felt a French allegiance, by virtue of culture and historical connectedness, in spite of the fact that the population was Germanic. The people of Eregnor have no such cultural attachments, but are connected by familial relationships to both kingdoms.

When the political conditions in Kashfa suddenly altered, King Random told his nephew Merlin of his intentions:

> "Did he [Bill Roth] tell you that we were going to bring Kashfa into the Golden Circle and solve the Eregnor problem by recognizing Kashfa's right to that piece of real estate? . . .
>
> "Well, that's what I planned on doing . . . We don't usually make guarantees like that— the kind that will favor one treaty country at the expense of another—but Arkans, the Duke of Shadburne, kind of had us over a barrel. He was the best possible head of state for our purposes, and I'd paved the way for his taking the throne now that that red-haired bitch [Jasra] is out of the picture. He knew he could lean

on me a bit, though—since he'd be taking a chance accepting the throne following a double break in the succession—and he asked for Eregnor, so I gave it to him. . . .

"There was a coup, at dawn, this morning. . . .

"Today your former classmate Lucas Raynard becomes Rinaldo I, King of Kashfa. . . .

". . . What Luke just did is not above the Graustarkian politics that prevail in the area. We'd moved in and helped straighten out something that was fast becoming a political shambles. We could go back and do it again, too, if it were just some half-assed coup by a crazy general or some noble with delusions of grandeur. But Luke's got a legitimate claim, and it actually is stronger than Shadburne's. Also, he's popular. He's young, and he makes a good appearance. We'd have a lot less justification for going back than we had for going in initially." (KS, 209–11)

In his discussion with Merlin, Random made it clear that the new king of Kashfa could not expect to receive Eregnor, even if Amber were inclined to negotiate a treaty with him.

While the political bickering between Begma and Kashfa was of long duration and great volatility, Jasra had made arrangements to smooth the way for a diplomatic liaison between the two realms. When she ruled in Kashfa during a time of reconciliation, she made terms with the prime minister of Begma for the marriage by proxy of Prince Rinaldo to Orkuz's daughter, Coral.

The principals had sort of forgotten about the marriage, too, till recent events served as a reminder. Neither had seen the other in years. Still, the record showed that the prince had been married. While it was an annullable thing, she could also be crowned with him. If there were anything in it for Kashfa.

And there was: Eregnor. A Begman queen on the Kashfan throne might help smooth over that particular real estate grab. At least, that had been Jasra's thinking, Coral told me. And Luke had been swayed by this, particularly in the absence of the guarantees from Amber and the now-defunct Golden Circle Treaty. (PC, 2–3)

Rinaldo and Coral were confirmed as sovereigns of Kashfa in a formal coronation in the First Uni-

cornian Church in Kashfa's capital city. It meant a cementing of relations between Kashfa and Begma that would, in all likelihood, take the Eregnor question out of the hands of King Random of Amber.

ERIC

Prince and regent of Amber who had himself crowned king in a formal coronation during King Oberon's mysterious absence. He was the oldest son born of Oberon and Faiella. However, Oberon was still married to Cymnea, mother of Benedict, making Eric's claim to the succession somewhat shaky because Oberon never formally acknowledged him as his son. After Oberon dissolved his marriage to Cymnea, he did wed Faiella, who then bore him two male sons that were legitimate heirs to the throne: Corwin and Caine.

Although Eric was king of the true city for only a short period of time and under dubious circumstances, he succeeded in repelling increased invasions of creatures from shadows that were previously unknown. While there was increasing strife against these shadow beings, and a struggle for power within the Family, Eric managed to keep a degree of calm among his minions within Amber. He died fighting for the good of the realm.

One point in Eric's favor concerning Oberon's attitude toward him was that he was a beautiful child. Oberon may have been restrained from giving him any formalized legitimacy, but he accepted Eric wholly as his son. This occurred because of important mercantile agreements that Oberon was negotiating with influential people in the shadow of Cymnea's family. Part of their final agreement involved Oberon's not recognizing any issue born illegitimately during his former marriage. Privately, however, Oberon heaped much love and attention on his beautiful little boy.

Eric grew into a strikingly handsome young man. His hair was so dark that it had a blue-black sheen; he wore a neatly trimmed fringe of beard, and his smile was warm and winning. Black and red were his colors, and he looked exceedingly good in simple clothes. He was fond of leather, sporting a leather jacket and leggings, but his cloak of black with red lining was of plain cloth material. At his red sword belt was a long saber of silver with a bright ruby on its hilt. His hands were large and powerful, making him nearly as dangerous an adversary weaponless as he was in a duel.

Growing up in the Royal Palace, Eric would often be at play with his near siblings, Caine and Corwin. Even as a boy, though, he was attracted to the young ladies, and he spent much time with his half sister, Flora. Still, he had little to do with Llewella, another illegitimate child of Oberon who was given formal recognition, something that Eric always resented. When he reached manhood, he served a brief time in the royal cavalry, but then transferred to Amber's navy. He had a true love of his homeland and enjoyed traveling to the several port stops on its coast. As part of his duty to the fleet, he directed cargo ships to various shadowlands, but he expressed strong discontent in being away from the true realm. Once, he seemed to become visibly ill when spending a long stretch in a coastal city of a far shadow. He continued to serve in the navy until his stint was over, but he rarely took to the shadows again.

King Oberon saw to it that his sons learned to defend themselves, both with sword and by hand. Like Benedict, Corwin, and Caine, the young Eric practiced at fencing with some of the greatest masters of the land and others that were imported from Shadow. They all became proficient with the blade, but Eric proved himself to be a notch above Corwin, although he was not able to defeat Benedict in a sporting duel. He was also a tenacious wrestler, able to pin all challengers with his big, powerful hands in record time. Of his brothers, only Caine attempted a match once, and after his loss, Caine never requested a rematch.

While his brothers journeyed often to shadow worlds, Eric remained in Amber. Dworkin initiated him in walking the Pattern, as he had done for each of Oberon's children. When he had completed the walk, Eric, forced to choose a place to teleport to, requested he be sent to the eastern vineyards. He returned with a case of Bayle's Best a couple of days later.

Eric was an excellent athlete. Often he would race with his brothers and the sons of noblemen in and around the city. He hunted with bow and arrow, fished, sailed, and jousted. He enjoyed the amateur sporting events organized in the town, usually acting as spectator, but he was delighted when invited to participate. Because of his activities, he was much admired by the populace.

If Eric wasn't included in political concerns of the realm, it was not because he didn't try to be. There were times when he asked his father about invasions from shadowlands that he had heard about in town. King Oberon would give only terse answers to Eric's questions, taking counsel more often with Benedict, Caine, and Bleys. Perhaps Oberon felt that Eric was not made for warfare and so chose to exclude him from such conferences.

Long ago, King Oberon had to contend with a highly organized army of beings from a shadow called Ghenesh. They were ugly, vicious creatures that rode upon living globe-shaped beasts. Adept at using crossbows and swords, they were merciless killers who ravaged several outer villages before assaulting the city itself. Oberon delegated his oldest son Benedict to command Amber's army, and Benedict proved himself masterful in defending the kingdom. While Oberon and Benedict worked out strategies early in the war against the Moonriders, Eric eagerly sought a commission to prove his own abilities. In response, his father ordered Eric to take charge of the Royal Guard of the palace, forming a contingency force in the event the Moonriders broke through their lines of defense. Before Eric could encounter any action, Benedict had put down the invaders at the pass above the Forest of Arden. So many of the beings of Ghenesh were slaughtered that the remaining few made a final retreat and never returned.

It may have been at this point that Eric developed a resentment of his father. In the war against the Ghenesh invaders, Julian and his patrol force had been a part of Benedict's defensive line; Corwin and Bleys were defending other parts of Amber; and Caine defended the coastline from the deck of a warship heading the fleet. They had all seen some action in battle, but Eric had not. He had not gotten over the feeling that he had been humiliated by this assignment.

Eric made a determined effort to consolidate his position at court. He organized small jaunts into town with his brothers Julian and Caine, treating them to meals and entertainment. It was easy for him to get women to join them, and he tried to keep Caine and Julian happy in his company. When he was sure of them, he persuaded them to turn away from their half sister Llewella, pointing out that her proclaimed legitimacy made him look bad because he never received a like proclamation. Eric proceeded to taunt Llewella, sometimes helped by his brothers, and she decided to return to Rebma, the place of her birth. Although no official record provides evidence of it, Eric's actions toward his sister may have caused the enmity that Queen Moire of Rebma felt for him.

While Eric was gaining support from his brothers, his father spoke of quitting the throne more often. This was merely talk, but Eric took Oberon's rumblings about giving it up seriously. Benedict expressed no interest in the throne, but he made it clear he would not support any claimant while his father was alive. Then Benedict left Amber for a shadow in which he might find solace. Although Eric did not openly declare himself successor to the throne when Oberon was ruler, he maintained covert support for his claim from Flora, Caine, Julian, and young Gérard, who joined Caine in most things.

Prince Corwin remained a loyal supporter of his father's right to rule and would see no one else in his place unless Oberon formally voiced who would be his heir. This was not to say, however, that Corwin had no ambition in that regard; he saw himself as the first legitimate heir to the throne, but he refused to do anything to undermine his father's wishes. This was the point of departure between Corwin and Eric in their spoken concerns about who would take their father's place. Corwin believed that Oberon would name his heir when he chose to abdicate, but Eric argued that their father's lack of initiative in that regard meant that it was his right to rule as next in the hereditary line once circumstance forced Oberon to step down. Eric cited Oberon's frequent missions to several shadows, leaving behind only brief, perfunctory orders, as a reason to urge their father to retire. Often the kingdom was left without leadership, and even when Oberon was present, he seemed preoccupied and vacillating.

In spite of their vehement disagreements, Corwin continued to feel a strong kinship with Eric. They both felt they shared some things in common. During a time when Oberon was spending a few days on a mission in a near shadow, Eric and Corwin reached a heated point in their arguments that was heard by many of the palace residents. One day, there was a sudden calm. Corwin and Eric met, spoke quietly to one another, and agreed to go hunting in Arden. They parted, then met again in

changed clothing, each carrying a quiver of arrows and a longbow. They were seen leaving the palace, headed for the great forest.

The Chronicles of Corwin explain that he and Eric did not have a formal duel to settle the succession question:

"A simultaneous decision to murder one another is more like it. At any rate, we fought for a long while and Eric finally got the upper hand and proceeded to pulverize me. . . .

". . . But Eric stopped short of killing me himself. When I awakened, I was on a shadow Earth in a place called London. The plague was rampant at the time, and I had contracted it. I recovered with no memory of anything prior to London." (GA, 85)

It is difficult to determine just what Eric's intention had been when he fought with his brother in Arden. However, he was afraid of being blamed for Corwin's death, so he took his brother's unconscious body through Shadow until he found a place where he was likely to die if left there. When Eric returned to the palace, he told the others that Corwin and he had argued, and Corwin went off to wander in Shadow for a while. He expected that Caine and Julian would keep their own counsel and lend their support later on, if need be.

Naturally, everyone viewed Eric's flimsy explanation with suspicion. When Oberon returned to Amber a few days later, he listened silently to the story, but his face revealed great concern. Benedict, who had been back from his travels, and several of the others, attempted to reach Corwin by Trump for hours at a time, without success. After some time had passed with no word from Corwin, Benedict decided to search for him in Shadow. He was followed by Brand and Gérard, and later on, by Julian, Caine, and Random, all going separate ways. They each reported failure upon returning. Much later, Benedict implied that the search taken up by the others, himself excluded, was really done for the purpose of finding evidence of murder against Eric. Some of the others, in particular Julian, Caine, and Gérard, were acting out of ambitions of their own, seeking to place themselves in positions of greater power.

Corwin learned much later what had happened in his absence, when he spoke to Brand about these events. In his Chronicles, Corwin described the situation as Brand had viewed it:

> "Dad suspected Eric of having slain you. But there was no evidence. We worked on this feeling, though—a word here and there, every now and then. Years passed, with you unreachable by any means, and it seemed more and more likely that you were indeed dead. Dad looked upon Eric with growing disfavor. Then, one night, pursuant to a discussion I had begun on a totally neutral matter—most of us present at the table—he said that no fratricide would ever take the throne, and he was looking at Eric as he said it. You know how his eyes could get. Eric grew bright as a sunset and could not swallow for a long while. But then Dad took things much further than any of us had anticipated or desired. In fairness to you, I do not know whether he spoke solely to vent his feelings, or whether he actually meant what he said. But he told us that he had more than half decided upon you as his successor, so that he took whatever misadventure had befallen you quite personally. He would not have spoken of it, but that he was convinced as to your passing." (SU, 153)

Following Oberon's accusation, there was a tacit, if unannounced, conspiracy to keep Eric the center of suspicion. His brothers built a cenotaph for Corwin, giving substance to the possibility that Corwin was dead. As little as the king had shown an interest in Eric previously, after this point he had nothing to do with his son. Eric felt himself to be a virtual pariah in his own household.

For a while, it seemed that Eric was totally alone. Even Flora avoided him around the palace, believing that he might actually have killed Corwin. She may have made her decision to wander into Shadow partly because of this belief. One day, however, Eric found that his brother Julian remained a stalwart comrade, coming to Eric rather than Oberon concerning a matter he thought might be important. Julian was bothered by the covert activities of their brother Brand. It worried Julian that Brand exhibited unusual talents that seemed to exceed those of any of theirs. Brand seemed to be able to disappear into Shadow directly from the palace, and Julian didn't think he was using Trumps to do so. In Julian's

confiding these things to him, Eric felt slightly disgusted when he realized that part of Julian's concern came from jealousy of his half sister Fiona and Brand. The two of them had gone off together on occasion, and Julian had spotted them talking secretively in odd areas of the palace. Although Eric was not initially worried over Julian's suspicions, he saw them as a possible means of shifting distrust from himself to Brand, and thus gathering support from the Family once again.

Eric used Julian to help him gather up a small network of personnel within the palace. Together, Eric and Julian approached Gérard and Caine, seeking their allegiance against Brand. Informal observations of Brand's activities were arranged, with each of the four brothers heading a team of spies among the courtiers and palace servants. They took great care to avoid signaling Oberon that anything was amiss.

It was bothersome to Eric when Brand eluded all their efforts to keep him under watch. One morning, in the early hours before dawn, Brand had sneaked out of the Royal Palace. An alert guard informed Julian, who went after him with two other court officials. They lost him in the town, where he could have entered any number of taverns or cafés. A few days later, a short, rotund café owner who recognized Eric as he was eating in his place, told him of a sketch that had been left there several days ago, nailed to one of his tables. The owner realized only after the fact that the man who had left it was Eric's red-haired brother, Brand. No, he didn't have the sketch any longer. He had torn it up because the man, whom he hadn't recognized initially, didn't pay for his meal when he disappeared suddenly.

Eric might have found this incident amusing, except that Brand's disappearance left him without a cause. When he informed his brothers of what he had learned, he made it seem urgent that they remain wary of Brand's return.

Although his father refused to acknowledge Eric formally during this time, there were state dinners and diplomatic galas which everyone in the royal household was expected to attend. While Eric was able to socialize during these affairs, he was kept on the far periphery of any matters of importance that were discussed. During these affairs of state, Eric noticed that his father wore a brilliant jewel on a chain around his neck. He overheard a conversation one time, when Oberon spoke of it as a "Jewel of Judgment.'' Unable to ask his father about it directly, Eric was very curious about the Jewel and determined to find out all he could about it. Through his spies, he discovered that Oberon kept it hidden somewhere in his chambers, but he was unable to ascertain precisely where.

While Eric would have liked to pursue his information-gathering about the Jewel, the problem of Brand regained prominence. This time, it was Caine who approached Eric, telling him of strong impulses he had felt in Shadow. Caine had tried Brand's Trump, merely on intuition, and found it alive with activity. When he told Eric, Eric picked up Brand's Trump and felt strong sensations of movement also. It seemed like powerful waves washing onto the shore, and the shore, in this case, was definitely the palace of Amber.

They enlisted Julian and passively viewed the Trump of their brother. Using the psychic sensibilities they each held, they determined that Brand would appear at one of six or seven places within the palace. While each of them covered the three most probable positions, Eric assigned armed guards to cover the rest. It was only a matter of waiting for the moment Brand chose to appear.

He stepped unwarily out of Shadow at Caine's post. While Caine and a guard pounced on Brand, the other guard shouted down the hall in Eric's direction. In a moment, Eric and his guards were also upon Brand, who struggled helplessly. They were soon joined by Julian and his men, and Brand was beaten senseless.

Eric ordered all but one of the guards to return to their usual duties, speaking of this to no one. With the remaining guard, Julian, Caine, and Eric dragged Brand's unconscious body to the dungeons without anyone else seeing them. They put him in a cell, tied him securely to the cot, and injected him with a strong narcotic to keep him unconscious. Eric ordered the guard to maintain a post outside of the cell and look in on Brand at regular intervals. They kept him this way for years.

The political climate in Amber and the shadows of the Golden Circle had become very active. Oberon was away on official visits more often than before, handling a variety of treaty problems. In one shadow, a renegade woman was desecrating religious shrines, and a diplomatic party from that realm paid an official visit to present their complaint to Oberon. Julian and Caine sometimes accompa-

nied their father on journeys to the shadow, and they went on separate missions to other Golden Circle shadows as well. There were repercussions at home as a consequence of some of these troubles, and Eric found himself having to deal with the wealthy merchants and tradesmen in Amber. Of course, these troubles were not insurmountable, and the combined efforts of Oberon and the princes and princesses of Amber eventually eased some of the problems that arose.

It meant, however, that Eric's wary care of the imprisoned Brand had lapsed. The measures they had taken to keep Brand sedated and pent seemed sufficient to keep him from taking part in any treachery again. Therefore, it was all the more incredible to Eric when he learned from Julian of Brand's escape. According to Julian, Brand had gotten out of his bonds, drawn a crude picture of a room in a distant shadow, and stepped through to that place. However, in some unknown fashion, Brand accomplished an even more remarkable feat. Somehow, he located Corwin in that shadow, and arranged for him to be committed to the London hospital for the insane known generally as Bedlam.

Julian told of his following the images within the drawing and reaching that shadow. He succeeded in effecting Corwin's release from that place, but they became separated. In order to flee the authorities who had begun pursuing him, Julian returned to Brand's cell in the dungeons. He immediately went to Eric to report these strange findings.

While Brand had been planning and effecting his escape, Eric had been involved in several matters in Amber. Because of trade disagreements with some of the shadows of the Golden Circle, Amber's merchants had become increasingly restless. With Oberon away much of the time, Eric had been the unwilling recipient of their complaints. He was especially vulnerable to the tirades of the merchants because he remained active in and about the town, and therefore he was widely known. Eric attempted diplomacy with the merchants and tradesmen, but they were not easily put off. It was a difficult position for Eric, since he found himself having to justify his father's motives and policies.

On the numerous occasions when the king was away on an official visit, Eric took the opportunity to get into Oberon's chambers. There were times when Eric had been seen by palace servants leaving his father's quarters, and he might have believed that Oberon would have left the Jewel of Judgment behind while journeying to the shadowlands. It is possible that Eric located portions of his father's notes about the Jewel during this period.

When Julian told him of Brand's escape and his own little adventure on the shadow Earth, Eric was less worried over Brand than he was about the discovery that Corwin was alive. Julian held out the small hope that it might not have actually been Corwin; that Brand had manipulated Shadow somehow to make the inmate in the hospital appear to be Corwin. Still, it bothered Eric greatly, and it was a long time before he could put the incident out of his mind.

Years later, on a bright summer's day, Flora returned for a visit to Amber. When she greeted Eric, he was uncertain of her attitude toward him, since the last time they had been together she had suspected him of murder. She recounted the story of her life on the shadow Earth, having spent most of her time in Paris, France, during an exciting period of its history. Casually, but with some playfulness, she mentioned having run into Corwin at a party given by Monsieur Focault. She expected a radical reaction from Eric, but he barely changed expression as he asked her further about it. She explained that they were introduced, and Corwin didn't indicate any recognition of her. He called himself Cordell Fenneval. Although Flora thought that he might not be Corwin, but merely a look-alike of this world, she asked others about him. In the presence of others, he had revealed his great strength and other talents that made it seem all the more probable that he was indeed their Corwin.

Eric admitted to her what had occurred between him and Corwin at the time of Corwin's disappearance. He also told her that he was aware of the possibility that Corwin might still be alive. Swearing Flora to secrecy, he arranged to have her keep a careful watch over Corwin and report back any changes in his status. As long as he didn't remember who he really was, nor anything about his past life in Amber, it would be safe to allow Corwin his liberty on that shadow.

For a long while, Eric continued to perform various duties of a prince of the realm, meeting with ambassadors from the shadows as part of his father's official retinue, attending important social functions, either with Oberon presiding, or acting in his behalf, and handling innumerable domestic matters. He did these things in good faith, trying to live down his father's long-ago accusation. In truth, Oberon may have had some inkling that he knew Corwin was alive, but he didn't reveal this to Eric. However, Oberon seemed to have forgiven his son simply by the way he accepted Eric's participation in state affairs.

Eric was kept informed of the comings and goings of Fiona, largely through Julian, who continued to observe his sister's wanderings in particular with great interest. While Julian often expressed concern that Brand would return and plague them, Eric was still slightly repulsed by Julian's keen interest in Fiona's activities. Of greater moment to Eric was hearing from Flora on the shadow Earth. She kept him informed of the changing shape of events in that world, but Eric was anxious at every contact that Corwin might have regained his memory. Flora assured him that it seemed unlikely that this would ever occur. Corwin seemed quite content to visit the multifarious nations of that shadow and help fight their fights.

Although Eric hadn't made the connection at the time, he found that there was a definite increase in activity from Shadow soon after he had heard rumors that Brand had visited his rooms in the Royal Palace. Oberon kept the army on alert to be ready for battle in an instant because of dangerous creatures entering the true city. Years after the fact, Flora told Corwin of these strange visitations:

> "We have always been alert for peculiar things slipping through. Well, for several years prior to your [Corwin's] recovery, more such things than usual seemed to be showing up in the vicinity of Amber. Dangerous things, almost invariably. Many were recognizable creatures from nearby realms. After a time, though, things kept coming in from farther and farther afield. Eventually, some which were totally unknown made it through. No reason could be found for this sudden transportation of menaces, although we sought fairly far for disturbances which might be driving them this way."
> (SU, 104)

While Oberon was preoccupied with these Shadow invasions, Eric thought again of the Jewel of Judgment. It could very well be just the weapon they needed to repel the Shadow-beings entering

Amber. Julian recalled that Eric spoke to him about the Jewel, describing some of its power. Although Eric didn't indicate to Julian that he wanted to obtain and use the Jewel himself, he stated that anyone who wore it would be in a much stronger position. In response, Julian said that he hoped that their father had it in his possession, if that was the case.

The continued danger of these Shadow invasions made the situation all the more untenable when Oberon suddenly vanished from the realm. When Eric and the others had last seen Oberon, it seemed a typical evening. They all ate together in the large dining hall, and conversations remained polite and trivial. Oberon may have been a little more distracted than usual, but it didn't seem especially emphatic at the time. While Eric, his brothers Caine, Julian, Bleys, and Gérard, and his sisters Fiona and Deirdre sat around finishing dessert, Oberon left the room without bidding them good-night, his mind on things far away. Eric and his brothers and sisters talked on, unhurriedly. After a while, each excused him- or herself as the evening wore on, wandering off, presumably to bed. Eric and Julian were the last to leave the dining hall, long since cleared of dishes. The next morning Oberon was gone, and it appeared his bed had not been slept in.

Although problems continued on two fronts, involving, on the one hand, strange migrations from Shadow and, on the other hand, treaty compromises being broken between Amber and the Golden Circle shadows, no great crises erupted in Oberon's absence. For a long while, it seemed that the king had gone off on one of his sudden missions. The consensus was that he had learned of some new means to end the Shadow invasions and went in search of it.

For the most part, Eric and his brothers proceeded to run things in Amber as they had done previously, while no one made any firm stand to take authority nor to make any definitive policies. Eric handled matters of state from the Royal Palace, Julian remained in the Forest of Arden in charge of his patrols there, Caine and Gérard patrolled the coastline on board ships leading the fleet, and Bleys worked with the royal cavalry, training for combat against any future skirmishes with creatures entering the true city. Months passed in this way.

When more than half a year had passed with no word from their father, Eric and his brothers became concerned that something may have happened to him. His disappearance had been so abrupt that they came to the agreement that Oberon must have been wrested away by some subterfuge and kidnapped. Perhaps the same camp that had caused the "monster migrations" was also responsible for Oberon's disappearance. Each of the brothers, and Deirdre and Fiona, attempted to contact their father through his Trump. They continued to do so every day for over half a year. There was no contact at all. They feared that with so much time having been spent, their father's kidnappers would surely have murdered him by then.

Eric might also have feared that he would have been accused of Oberon's kidnapping and murder, but Julian had vouched for him. Julian honestly believed that Eric would not have done it, partly because they were together until late in the evening of their father's departure, but also because of things Eric had said to him. When they were left alone that night, Eric had admitted to Julian that he regretted his actions against Corwin long ago. He would never want to endure the hostility of his family again for such an action. It appeared to Julian to be a heartfelt admission, and, unless Eric were being diabolically clever, he had nothing to gain by telling Julian this. When they had headed for their quarters, Eric seemed genuinely tired, and Julian watched him enter his room. These several factors convinced Julian that Eric was not responsible for Oberon's absence discovered the next morning.

With Oberon inexplicably gone, Eric was in a difficult position. He felt the need to act on his father's behalf as the main decision-maker, but he wanted to avoid the enmity of his family and the influential members of the nobility. If he acted too hastily, the nobles or some near relative would look askance at his motives. The suspicion that Eric wanted the throne for himself would lead to possible assassination. Another factor had to be considered as well. His father might be testing him, or any of his other sons who might have ambitions for the throne. Oberon could have deliberately absented himself in order to observe events from afar. Eric's securing the throne as ruler could then be considered high treason. When Oberon returned, Eric would face more than his father's personal wrath. These were things Eric considered and wished to avoid.

After more than a year had passed, Eric, his brothers, and his sisters came to the conclusion that Oberon was indeed dead. Still, Eric would not have stepped forward to claim the right of succession if someone else hadn't taken the initiative. A very troubled Caine approached Eric to tell him that their brother Brand was heading a conspiracy to rule Amber. Caine's report that Brand tried to gain his help in an all-out invasion to seize the throne greatly disturbed Eric. For the first time, Eric realized how dangerous Brand was. When Julian had warned Eric about their wayward brother years before, Eric had received the warning with ambivalence. It had once seemed largely the product of Julian's jealousy of Brand and Fiona. But this latest news was from Caine, and, according to his account, Brand implied he had support from the Courts of Chaos. The ostensible connection between the Shadow invasions and Brand's allegiance to the Courts was too credible a possibility for Eric to disregard.

Eric and Caine included Julian in their conference to determine how best to proceed. Convinced that Brand was extremely dangerous, Eric voiced the idea of killing him. Julian agreed with this, but Caine pointed out that they would all be placed in deadly peril of retribution by his coconspirators. Caine added that if the leaders of Chaos were involved, they would not be deterred merely because of Brand's death. A concerted stand was needed, with all of Amber presenting a united front against the enemy.

While Caine had the loyalty of his navy, and Julian was supported by his highly fortified company of men in Arden, they naturally turned to Eric as their leader. Aside from his personal charisma and ability to command, Eric had authority over the Royal Guard, the most elite military force in the land. They were the battle-hardened veterans who survived many a war with high honor. Most of them had come up from the ranks, proving themselves to have more than mere valor; they had intelligence and initiative. These men fashioned the exemplar of the fighting man of Amber. The prince who commands them has the complete devotion of every foot soldier, cavalry officer, and ship's mate in the true realm.

Julian and Caine recognized the value of placing Eric as head of state in a formal declaration. They both felt that their men would rally to Eric's support once the situation was explained to them. At first, Eric declined, expressing his fears of assassination. It would be a mistake, he believed, to declare himself king, especially while their father's death remained in doubt. However, Caine devised a compromise, a title that would not be misconstrued as usurping the crown and would, at the same time, unite all of Amber against Brand's conspiracy. It would be publicly announced that Eric was Protector of the Throne against any usurpers until such time as the king be found and restored to his proper place. This was done, and the public declaration was made in such a way that every citizen in Amber and the Golden Circle shadows was able to infer that there had been an attempted coup. Although Brand's name was never stated in the proclamation, enough information was given out about an arrant prince who traveled the shadowlands, that everyone realized who had instigated the conspiracy.

This made it uncomfortable for Brand to travel around freely without being ostracized by the citizenry. For his own protection, Eric insisted that Brand be confined to the Royal Palace. Eric made it quite clear that he was in no way threatening Brand with any violent action. Everyone within the palace knew where Brand was at all times, and he was free to move anywhere he wished, as long as he did not leave the Royal Palace. On Eric's orders, three guards were assigned to watch over Brand, and, in addition, Eric, Caine, and Julian took turns in observing his movements. If Brand was Eric's prisoner, he was a well–cared-for prisoner who was given every amenity.

Soon after this, Bleys went to see Eric. He expressed great annoyance, not only over Brand's treatment, but also for Eric's audacity in daring to rule Amber in their father's absence. Angered, Eric stood and shouted, "Who better to rule?" He stopped short of asking of Bleys, "You?" Bleys glared silently at him for a long moment, then looked around him at the Royal Guard. In a sullen, quiet tone, Bleys said that he would not remain in Amber while a pretender ruled. He told Eric that he was leaving and would be gone by nightfall. As Bleys turned to go, Eric gave him an imperial wave of his hand, as if Bleys's departure was done by his order. Bleys's face flushed, and it seemed that he might rush at his brother with deadly intent. Instead, he slowly calmed himself and walked out.

For some time, Eric had been keeping close contact with Flora on the shadow Earth, and this had been especially so after Brand had made his intentions known to Caine. When announcing himself Royal Protector, Eric was particularly troubled that Corwin might regain his memory and return to

Amber to press his own claim to the throne. Flora's accounts indicated that Corwin could conceivably be remembering certain things. He had begun calling himself Carl Corey, which seemed too close to his real name to be coincidence alone. He had also been seeing psychiatrists and pursuing research on university campuses. These actions seemed to be those of a man seeking his identity, having gained insight that he was something other than what he appeared to be.

When Corwin left Europe for America, Eric supplied his sister with sufficient currency of that time and place to make the move and maintain her surveillance. As Carl Corey, Corwin settled in a place named New York State, where he began to make friends and seemed quite happy. However, Flora's reports showed that he also spent much time alone, frequently working in his study. At times, he would leave his large home suddenly for a week or two, then return as suddenly. Eric viewed Flora's reports with a sense of foreboding.

Shortly after Brand's enforced detention, the pace with which creatures out of Shadow slipped into Amber began to quicken. These were highly disorganized invasions, but many of these beings took on a terrifying aspect. Citizens lived in fear of rampaging monsters brutalizing them in the streets and outside their homes. Eric sent additional militia to the town and outlying villages to give aid to the vigiles, the local police force. This eased tensions a bit among the people, and the combined forces did manage to suppress much of the invasion for the while.

Flora contacted Eric by Trump with some news about Corwin. While he was away for several days, she had entered his home to have a look around. She found some papers scattered on his study desk and examined them. In their contact, she showed one sheet of scrawled writing to Eric. It was a random list of names. Some were of people Corwin had met in New York. Others listed names like Brand, Oberon, Caine, Bleys, Eric, and Corwin. They were in no recognizable order, and the name Corwin was given no greater emphasis than any of the others.

Eric asked if Flora thought that Corwin might be trying to reach Amber. Flora told him that Corwin had returned and was back in his house. What if he missed the sheet of paper that Flora had taken? Eric asked. Flora responded that she had made a copy

and returned the original before Corwin had shown up again. Then he hadn't regained his memory just yet, Eric said. Still, Flora warned, the lists that Corwin had been drawing up were proof that some of his memory had been jarred. Eric told her to keep him informed of any new occurrences.

Eric was more unnerved by Flora's information than he had revealed to her. He was too involved in problems in Amber to have to deal with a rival claimant just at the moment. Delegating many of his duties to Julian and Caine, Eric puzzled over the steps he should take to restrict Corwin without harming him. Should he practice some manipulation on that shadow Earth to have Corwin imprisoned?

A few days later, Flora contacted Eric again. Corwin was gone once more, but she felt this was different. He had disappeared without packing so much as an overnight bag. Flora wasn't certain, but she sensed that Corwin was hurt or drugged. She asked Eric if anything had happened in Amber that might be related to this new disappearance. Eric told her he would check into it. When he looked in on Brand, Eric found him drinking wine out of a goblet and reading a book in his room. Brand nodded, lifting the drink up in a mock toast. Eric didn't stay to converse, but after leaving Brand's room he met with Caine and Julian. He advised them of what Flora reported and ordered them to maintain a continuous surveillance of Brand. He was not to be left to his own devices for a moment. Dividing up the watch among the three of them, Caine took the first shift.

Sometime later, one of his royal guards rushed to Eric's rooms. He informed Eric that his brother, Prince Caine, had been badly mauled by a strange beast within the palace. The guard added that Brand had escaped.

Rushing to Brand's quarters, Eric saw the dead beast and realized intuitively that Brand had brought it from some distant shadow. After seeing it, Eric surmised that his brother had brought it forth through a power he possessed that they had not been aware of. He examined Brand's room briefly but could learn nothing from it.

When he checked on Caine, he found Julian and Gérard caring for him in his room. Caine kept slipping in and out of consciousness, but he had told Gérard and Julian about the attack before Eric's arrival. One of the guards who had stood watch with Caine confirmed that the strange beast had burst suddenly out of Brand's room, and Caine was the first to confront it.

Eric returned to his own quarters and made Trump contact with Flora again. She still hadn't learned anything more about Corwin, and Eric told her to be on guard against an appearance by Brand. Flora was puzzled about Brand's connection, but Eric aired his suspicions that Brand had found out about their communications. It seemed likely that Brand used his own unique powers to discover that Flora was acting as guardian to Corwin, and then Brand sought him out for his own purposes.

A couple of days passed with no further word about Brand or Corwin. In the interim, Eric looked in on Caine, who was recovering well. He also became aware that his sister Fiona was no longer in the palace. The waiting was so agonizing that Eric pondered going to the shadow Earth himself. He was about to make plans to do so, when he received an urgent Trump contact. It was Fiona, calling from the shadow Earth. She informed him that she and Bleys had captured Brand and placed him in a special shadow from which he could not escape. When Eric asked about Corwin, she said that Brand had tried to kill him. She explained what she knew of Brand's actions: That while still under Eric's surveillance in the palace, Brand had gotten away long enough to impersonate a psychiatrist. Under that guise, Brand had Corwin committed to a sanitarium. When Corwin escaped days later, Brand returned to kill him by shooting out the tires of his automobile. Corwin survived and was presently in a local hospital with internal injuries and broken legs. After Fiona finished her story, Eric thanked her and let her know that she would be welcome back in Amber.

Contacting Flora, Eric explained what he had learned from Fiona. He had Flora go to the hospital and have him transferred to Greenwood Private Hospital. As Evelyn Flaumel, Flora paid the director of Greenwood very well in order to keep her brother sedated. Of course, Flora remained near at hand to assure that Corwin was kept in confinement.

Eric met with Julian in Caine's room, where Caine was recovering but still weak. With Corwin alive, and the dangers from Shadow that Brand had initiated still threatening, they had to decide how best to protect Amber. Was negotiation with the rulers of Chaos possible? Not if they hadn't acknowledged playing a part in the monster migrations. They had never come forward with any

indication of responsibility in the abduction of Oberon, and Eric had no evidence that they were responsible. The best thing for the security of the true city was to maintain a united front against the Shadow invasions. At some point, those who were behind the assaults might reveal themselves. Once that was done, once Eric knew who the enemy was, it would be possible to defeat them.

Julian suggested that Eric make it publicly known that he planned a ceremony to be crowned king. It was something that Eric resisted, fearing for his life. However, Julian pointed out that it would be an excellent strategy for discovering if those at the Courts of Chaos were behind the invasions. Once the date for the coronation was set, their enemies would have to move against Amber. Those who had been allied with Brand would show their faces, and by then, the combined armies and navies of Amber would be ready to repel them. Reluctantly, Eric had to agree that it was the best way for them to proceed.

Before making any arrangements, Eric felt the need to appraise his own position by checking with some of his absent relatives. He wanted to know if anyone else, other than those he was already aware of, would offer resistance to his becoming king. Since Caine was not fully recuperated, Eric assigned Julian to make the necessary communications by Trump.

There was no response to Julian's sending from Bleys or Random. He managed to reach Benedict after persistent attempts. Benedict wanted nothing to do with Eric, but, in Oberon's absence, he would not act against Eric. He made it clear, though, that if Oberon should return, Eric would have to step down. Julian assured him this would be done.

Sometime later, Julian reached Random. He was off in a distant shadow, but he didn't tell much about his activities during his contact with Julian. In their conversation, Julian was much more interested in his reaction to Eric's ruling in Amber. Random indicated that he was noncommittal. Hearing the news that there would be a formal coronation, Random seemed willing to accept it and would not act against Eric. Julian signed off, satisfied that Random was no threat.

In the meantime, Eric was communicating with several of the Golden Circle shadows, seeking their support for his coronation. At one point, he contacted Queen Moire of Rebma to reach a reconciliation. She received his Trump contact coldly and with disinterest, but she was not openly hostile. Still, she would not commit herself to supporting Eric as king, although she indicated that she would not instigate any military operation to oppose him either.

Eric had intended to arrange for a prompt coronation ceremony, wanting the formalities concluded while Corwin was incapacitated and unable to press his claim. Unfortunately, Corwin himself prevented Eric from taking a swift course in the proceedings. Sensing that Flora was trying to reach him through Shadow, Eric contacted her by Trump. Their contact was vague, and Eric realized that she had attempted to walk the shadows to reach Amber. He felt his sister's fear and saw something of the Shadow-beings that attacked her. She was able to retreat and let Eric know that Corwin had escaped his confinement. It wasn't a clear sending, but Eric had the impression that Corwin was still on the shadow Earth, that he hadn't yet made a move against him.

It might have been easier for Eric to trump to the shadow Earth, or, even, send an emissary to Flora's home, but that would mean only one thing: He would have to kill Corwin to prevent his interference. That was unthinkable, however. If Oberon were still alive and returned to rule again, Eric could step down readily enough, justifying all of his actions—with the exception of murdering his brother while he was in Eric's power. Eric had to take precautions, had to keep Corwin away from Amber, but he would not deliberately cause his death.

Eric conferred with Julian, Caine, and Gérard. They came to the conclusion that if Corwin were to make his way to Amber, it would probably be by means of a Shadow walk. Corwin would consider that such a roundabout way would engender greater surprise. Eric decided that the more distant realms could take care of themselves; that is, the Shadow creatures already in evidence would act to hamper some of Corwin's movements in their direction. It would be necessary for them to protect the nearer shadows, arranging for obstacles that might serve to discourage Corwin and send him into retreat. Of course, if one of them was in a position to capture Corwin, then he would do so. Corwin's death had to be prevented, but if he met with some undisguised accident, one that was completely defensible, then Corwin could be entombed in his cenotaph on Mt.

Kolvir with all due honors. This remained, though, an act of last resort.

Following Eric's orders, Julian returned to his men in the Forest of Arden and patrolled the near shadows along that route into Amber. Gérard took part of the royal navy to the southern sea routes, and Caine, recovered from his wounds, controlled the rest of the fleet in the north. Eric remained in Amber, directing his remaining officers, who led military patrols through the countryside surrounding Kolvir.

So that Corwin would not be prematurely killed, nor be enabled to escape again into the shadows, Eric provided for a systematic web of entrapments, with himself in the center. He did not depend only on Julian to guard the way into Amber by the simplest route from Shadow; he dispersed soldiers of various strengths and skills to watch the most likely regions that Corwin would cross. Some of Eric's men were shapeshifters, who could disguise themselves as animals. Corwin would be hard-pressed to evade them once they had his scent.

Perturbed by Eric's activities in Amber, his sister Deirdre addressed him. She was worried about Corwin's welfare and argued over Eric's intentions. Even if he intended merely to capture Corwin, what kind of treatment could Corwin expect? Eric knew that Deirdre's interest was greater than sisterly concern, and he decided that it would be best to keep her safe and unable to oppose him. He had her arrested and locked in one of the dungeon cells, under the pretext that her life was in danger and he was placing her in protective custody.

Although Eric had fortified the palace with his Royal Guard in strategic positions throughout, he continued to make rounds with nervous energy. Viewing the mountainside to the north from a rear terrace, Eric received contact from Julian. In his report, Julian told of his encounter with Corwin and Random in a Mercedes, driving through a Forest of Arden in a congruent shadow distant enough for a combustion engine to continue working. Eric received with annoyance the news that Corwin had managed to capture Julian for a brief distance of travel, but he muffled the anger in his tone as he spoke to Julian. At least, it seemed to Eric, Julian hadn't revealed much to Corwin, and, thankfully, he learned at this point in the game that Random was allied with Corwin. Eric felt less disposed to temper justice with mercy against Random than he had felt against Corwin. While he felt compelled to preserve Corwin's life, Eric felt much less restraint in that regard toward Random.

However, Eric was pleased that Corwin was well on his way. His strategy was to allow Corwin to reach the real world. Once there, it was extremely difficult to return by walking the shadows. Eric alerted his patrols that Corwin and Random would shortly step into the true city. Those of Eric's soldiers who were shapeshifters reverted to their animal forms, the better to use their other senses.

While waiting for further word, Eric discovered that Deirdre had escaped her imprisonment. He sent a contingent of his Royal Guard to bring her back, hoping they would recapture her before she could find Corwin and Random.

Sometime later, several members of the Guard's contingent reported back to Eric. He was much chagrined by their report. Six of the Royal Guard were found at a campsite in the wooded valley to the south. A stake with pieces of rope neatly cut near its ends suggested that the dead men had caught something that they were keeping alive and carrying with them. The spacing of the ropes hinted that the captive had been human. Shortly after this, Eric heard again from Julian. His men had come across the bodies of three shapeshifters that had transformed into wolves. One of them had been decapitated, another had his back broken, and all three were pierced through the heart with a single thrust of a sharp instrument. Julian had already sent off riders and men to try to track whoever had done this, assuming that Corwin and Random must have been the culprits. Eric ordered Julian to oversee the tracking. With these deaths, Eric told him, Random and Corwin could be considered outlaws, and any measure to stop them would be deemed appropriate.

For two days, Corwin and Random eluded the several search parties that Eric had sent out. However, it was determined from various signs that Deirdre had joined them. Early on the third day, Eric received contact from Julian. A company of his men had discovered Corwin, Random, and Deirdre at the eastern shore, making their way to the undersea city. Although Julian had not been with them, his soldiers and riders attempted to engage the three in battle. The riders gave chase as Corwin and his siblings ran to the sea. Four horsemen followed them down the watery stair named Faiella-bionin, all of them veterans of numerous travels into

shadow worlds with Julian at their head. Julian spoke sadly of their ignominious deaths, their bodies, and those of their horses, found crushed by the great pressure of the water's depths. Before the foot soldiers could reach the three, they had reached sanctuary beyond the entrance to Rebma.

Having lost Corwin for the moment, Eric turned his attention to finding the means to handle the Shadow invasions in Amber and also resolve any further attempt from Corwin to reach and dethrone him. Conferring with Julian, Caine, and Gérard, Eric determined to fix a date for his coronation. Once it was decided, Eric sent his brothers to several of the prominent shadows with which they had commerce to notify them. Arrangements were begun for these shadows to listen in on the proceedings through temporary bridges that the brothers of Eric would set up by the use of their Trumps. While these matters were being taken care of, Eric spent much time in his father's rooms, trying to learn all he could about the Jewel of Judgment. His search for information about the Jewel may have been the impetus that led Eric to the Royal Library.

Corwin was already there, in the library, talking to one of the servants. The two brothers spoke briefly, leavening their hatred for one another somewhat with humor. When Eric spoke candidly, alluding to a Shakespearean play, he may have genuinely felt the heavy weight of his rule. He said,

> "Then it is between the two of us now, Corwin . . . I am your elder and your better. If you wish to try me at arms, I find myself suitably attired. Slay me, and the throne will probably be yours. Try it. I don't think you can succeed, however. And I'd like to quit your claim right now. So come at me. Let's see what you learned on the Shadow Earth." (NP, 95)

The two brothers dueled fiercely, Corwin attacking with moves he had learned in France on the shadow Earth. Those techniques, unknown to Eric, allowed Corwin to get through his defenses and draw blood. Nevertheless, Eric was able to beat back his brother, and there were moments when Corwin felt he would be defeated.

In a desperate move, Corwin retreated gradually to the heavy door of the library. When he dropped the bar, locking the door, Eric was able to pierce his left shoulder. Corwin continued the fight, trying to unnerve Eric with talk of Eric's own cuts and loss of vigor. As Eric's men banged at the locked door, Eric felt some fear of his brother and began retreating. The banging and calling of Eric's guards stopped, and Eric knew they were going for axes to break down the door. His altered attention, however, cost him another bloody gash in the forearm. He continued to voice challenges to Corwin, who responded in kind as they fought.

Realizing that Corwin could get the best of him if they continued this way, Eric backed into a bookcase, reached out, and, with a quick motion, swept a row of books at him. It was enough to distract his brother while Eric rushed across the room, picked up a chair, and placed himself in a secure corner of the room, the chair and his sword held defensively before him. At that point, they could hear the returning guards using axes on the heavy door. Corwin knew that he wouldn't be able to reach Eric before the guards broke in. Trading obscenities, Corwin went to a hidden panel in the wall and dived through it headfirst. Immediately, Eric hefted his sword like a spear and threw it at the wall panel. The strength of his throw caused it to enter almost halfway. Eric knew that Corwin had escaped, but he had flung the sword in mindless rage rather than in a deliberate attempt to kill.

When the guards broke through the door, Eric sent them after Corwin, pointing out the movable panel with the sword stuck in it. They raced through the passageway, but Eric knew the chase would be futile. Evidently, his brother would trump out as soon as he had a free moment. The question remained, who would aid Corwin? There were several possibilities, but even if Eric could guess correctly, there wasn't much he could do about it.

Some of the remaining guards led Eric to his quarters and Eric ordered them to summon one of his brothers with a medical kit. Julian and Gérard arrived a short time later, and Gérard ministered to Eric's wounds. Later that evening, while Eric rested in bed, he received a Trump contact. It was Corwin, and he was immediately alert.

Corwin said,

"I just felt like telling you that all goes well with me. I also wanted to advise you that you were right when you spoke of the uneasy head. You won't be wearing it long, though. So cheerio! Brother! The day I come again to Amber is the day you die! Just thought I'd tell you—since that day is not too far off."

[Eric responded,] "Come ahead, . . . and I'll not want for grace in the matter of your own passing." (NP, 103)

Before Eric could act against him, Corwin broke their contact. Eric remained awake for hours, staring at the ceiling in silent fury.

With arrangements for the day of the coronation already settled, involving a number of shadows, it wasn't possible to move up the date. Eric met with Julian to organize a widespread recruitment campaign, knowing that they could expect an assault from Corwin as soon as his forces were ready. If Corwin had help from some other source, then the attack could be imminent. It was agreed that Julian would oversee the troops and mount a campaign to enlist more men from among the citizenry. Although the countryside was still troubled by the slippage of strange creatures from Shadow, these occurrences were becoming more infrequent and the beings that were caught were more confused than defiant. It became a matter of routine to open the way for their return to their shadow of origin.

In an attempt to maintain harmony among the shadows of the Golden Circle, Eric opened up diplomatic channels, sometimes making official visits to shadowlands, and, more often, accepting visits from the diplomatic corps of several shadows in the Royal Palace. Although Eric didn't like to be away from Amber for long periods of time, he made frequent visits to a handful of Golden Circle realms on a regular basis while he was seeking their approval. Since gossip is a natural thing among minor court officials and servants, rumors began to circulate about Prince Eric's dalliance with the daughter of a royal family in one shadow or with a nobleman's sister in another shadow. Groundless or not, such rumors blossomed whenever Eric traveled on official court business.

It was with a feeling of déjà vu that Eric, recently returned to Amber, received Trump contact from Caine, who was on board one of his ships. When Eric heard that Corwin had contacted Caine to make a deal, it reminded Eric of Brand's attempt to get Caine to join him and mount an invasion against Amber. Eric was forever protecting Amber from invasion.

From Caine, Eric learned that Corwin's ally was

Bleys. Caine surmised that Corwin and Bleys would lead a two-pronged attack: one leading a massive infantry across the lands of Shadow; the other arriving aboard ship with a great armada. Corwin had requested free passage into Amber, with the expectation that Caine's fleet would join him, so that Caine was certain that Bleys would be traveling the land route in.

Although no one in Amber knows the details of it, Eric had obtained the Jewel of Judgment, probably having finally located its hiding place in his father's quarters. He wore the Jewel prominently during this time. While Caine and Julian prepared their men for the coming assault, Eric set to work in the Royal Palace to repel the invading forces. He concentrated on the Trumps of Corwin and Bleys. It wasn't possible for Eric to observe his brothers passively through the Trumps, but he was able to sense their movements and determine, in relative terms, their positions in the worlds of Shadow. He found it rather easy to send storms and whirlpools against Corwin's fleet by means of the Jewel. It involved channeling the Jewel's energy, as Dworkin's notes had indicated, into the location signaled by Corwin's Trump.

Against Bleys, marching troops by land, Eric also sent out various meteorological forces. He could create a greater variety of such things as earthquakes, forest fires, floods, and hurricane winds, simply because there was more to work with in land formations and vegetation. More impressively, Eric exerted his own special talent upon the shadows in which he detected the movement of Bleys's soldiers. He was able to send an annoying signal of his own devising to whatever creatures occupied the regions through which Bleys marched. Driven to violent anger, the indigenous inhabitants would attack in force the strangers passing their way. Safe in the throne room, Eric felt the destructive forces at work. He had brief glimpses of Bleys battling warrior centaurs and monstrous tanklike machines, and learned of similar visitations, whenever Bleys received a Trump contact from Corwin. Without making direct contact himself, Eric was able to chart the progress that Corwin and Bleys made during their infrequent communications with one another.

Eric decided then to contact Random by Trump in Rebma. He wanted to alert Random about his defenses, certain that he would inform Corwin, thus helping to cause that much delay. Julian had re-quested more time to mount further fortifications around the base of Mt. Kolvir. Although Eric didn't feel such fortifications were necessary, he was concerned about giving Julian optimum time to gather his army. It was imperative that Amber be assured of having greater numbers of soldiers defending it than those coming against the true city.

Once Corwin's fleet had sailed into the sea of the true realm, it was even easier than previously for Eric to toss his ships in violent storms, like toys in a bathtub. He had sent a simultaneous storm against Bleys, and Eric was pleased by the consternation in each of his brothers' faces as he observed their Trump contact. Eric also observed, with some satisfaction, the communication between Random and Corwin. Random tried to warn Corwin away, but Corwin insisted that he had come too far to turn back. When Random and Corwin ended their communication, Eric took the opportunity to walk back to his chambers, his Trumps in hand.

When Eric resumed his covert surveillance using Corwin's Trump, he was surprised by an image filled with snow. He hadn't expected any clear image, but merely an impression of Corwin's shipboard motions on the sea of the real world. Instead, Eric could actually observe snowfall, a blizzard, in the seascape. Realizing that Corwin was effecting the blizzard, Eric exerted the influence of the Jewel, and the snowfall ended.

In retaliation for Corwin's audacity, Eric sent out a violent electrical storm intended to devastate his fleet. At the same time, Eric created a terrible flash flood against the marching soldiers of Bleys. Distance and Eric's lack of total mastery over the Jewel were the reasons why the forces of Bleys and Corwin survived Eric's wrath.

Eric had been in communication with Caine on the flagship of Amber's navy and knew that Caine would soon be upon Corwin's remaining fleet. He sent out one more horrendous black storm, attempting to weaken Corwin's force that much more. After Corwin's ships passed through the black storm, Eric concentrated on Caine's Trump. Caine kept their contact open while he called to Corwin to surrender. Since the Trump contact offered him a clear perspective, Eric maintained it, nearly missing Corwin's brief communication with Gérard in southern waters. However, Gérard contacted Eric immediately after he had finished with Corwin, so Eric was wary that Corwin would likely seek some escape from his predicament.

Confident of his superior strength over Corwin, mentally as well as physically, Eric turned his full attention on Corwin. He had been conserving his energy, readying himself for the proper moment to exert his control on Corwin's Trump. He anticipated physical and emotional weakness on Corwin's part, and he hoped he could take Corwin by surprise.

Eric used his mind to send out a thick, hard mental spear into Corwin's psyche the instant Corwin opened his thoughts to him. Eric thrust it deeply into Corwin's mind, twisting it for maximum effect. Somehow, Corwin withstood it, fought back, repelled the sharp pain. Withdrawing the thrust, Eric spoke confidently to his brother.

"How goes the world with thee, brother?" . . . "Poorly." . . .

"Too bad . . . Had you come back and supported me, I would have done well by you. Now, of course, it is too late. Now, I will only rejoice when I have broken both you and Bleys." (NP, 121–22)

Suddenly, Corwin struck with a psychic thrust of his own, and Eric recoiled from it. Then, Eric returned with a mental strike, and the two brothers held each other in a tight mental grasp. They applied pressure, one against the other, and each watched the other's face through the Trump contact. As their psychic struggle continued, Corwin attempted to bargain for the lives of his men. Eric refused flatly, on the grounds that any relaxation of his concentration to order Caine to spare lives would allow Corwin immediate domination in their personal contest. Corwin asked for clemency for Random, but Eric spitefully refused, stating that a word from Corwin on Random's behalf proved his complicity. Their mental intimacy gave both brothers special insight into the other's thoughts, and Eric was annoyed when he allowed the idea to slip out that Corwin's surrender would not prevent the slaughter of his men. Trying to cover up his irritation, Eric had nevertheless revealed a chink in his armor. Corwin seized the moment to strike out with all the psychic energy within his control. It hurt Eric terribly, and he resisted, trying to beat it back. He continued to feel the tremendous thrust of Corwin's hatred ripping into his mind. Eric wasn't able to maintain his

hold under this ordeal. Crying out, "You devil!" (NP, 124) he ended their contact.

Exhausted, and in pain, Eric got up and moved away from the Trumps laid out on his desk. He fell onto his bed and tried to ease the mental anguish for a long while.

Although Eric had been concentrating his efforts on Corwin, he had sought to decimate Bleys's soldiers prior to initiating his mental duel with Corwin. Bleys had not yet reached the real world, so Eric formed a sending that maddened a company of horsemen in the shadow that Bleys and his men traveled. While Eric strove with Corwin, Bleys was engaged in fierce battle with the cavalry in the shadow he was crossing.

Sometime later, Eric, having regained his composure, received a contact from Caine. Corwin's last ship, with his remaining crew, was captured, but Corwin had escaped. Without needing to speak it, Caine and Eric both knew that Corwin had joined Bleys on his overland march. He didn't voice it, but Eric saw Corwin's escape as a near-disastrous blunder on Caine's part, one that he would not soon forget.

Focusing on the Trumps of Bleys and Corwin, Eric was able to sense their presence in a near shadow and knew they were together. He sent a terrible rainstorm against them, maintaining it all through the night. The next night, and into the day, Eric caused frigid temperatures and snowfall in the shadow where he detected the great movement of men. He influenced the beasts of the shadows, and as Corwin, Bleys, and their men traversed several realms, they were attacked by wolf, by tiger, and by polar bear.

The marching army surmounted the obstacles that Eric placed against them. They were approaching the true realm, and Eric communicated with Julian to prepare his forces for the coming battle. When Bleys's soldiers made camp in the sudden warmer clime of Amber, Julian's force was on a quick march toward them. In spite of a heavy watch, Julian's troops slaughtered many of the shadow men on the outer fringe of the campsite. Bleys and Corwin ordered the rest of their men around the attacking force on a run. Many died, but Corwin and Bleys kept them on an advance toward the still-distant Mt. Kolvir.

Julian's force regrouped, and Julian kept Eric apprised of their progress. All day, Julian and his troops maintained a continuous attack on the exhausted soldiers marching tiredly on. With surprise and some annoyance, Eric observed through Julian's Trump that Corwin and Bleys had reached the valley paralleling the seacoast of Amber with a still large company of soldiers. As Bleys's soldiers continued to march toward Kolvir, Eric tried to create a rainstorm. Although the Jewel of Judgment glowed with Eric's effort, he was unable to form a pounding rainfall in the real world. A light rain fell upon the valley south of the Forest of Arden. Eric exerted enough inflence to send forth bolts of lightning, but they were largely ineffectual.

In deadly earnest, wanting to end Corwin's campaign no matter what the cost, Eric halted the rain, pushed clouds aside, and allowed the sun to bake through. No longer observing Bleys and Corwin directly, Eric could sense their location and movement through their Trumps. They were traveling through the thick forest that spread along the valley. Eric ordered Julian to advance his patrol to the region ahead of the woods, where the river Oisen flowed. He told Julian to be ready with archers on both sides of the river, but they were to avoid the forest entirely. Moving quickly, Julian followed Eric's orders.

Eric chose to concentrate on Corwin's Trump, gaining strength from the hatred he felt for Corwin. The Jewel pulsed as he concentrated on a position just behind Corwin's presence. It had to begin behind the marching army so that they would have no recourse but to advance. Eric felt it begin. A flame rose from a bush, newly dried by the warm sun. The flames took on a life of their own, fed and guided by Eric's hatred. Initially fed by the dense vegetation, the fire rose above the reach of the tallest trees and advanced toward the backs of the soldiers, as if possessed by an intelligence of its own. The fire spread out, dividing into separate sheets of flame, surrounding the rear and sides of Bleys's soldiers. The soldiers ran ahead, Corwin and Bleys somewhere near the front ranks.

Eric contacted Julian, already set up at the river. Julian kept his Trump out so Eric would be able to see the first movements of soldiers coming out of the watery channel. From Eric's vantage point, the forest was quiet and still. He could hear the slight rustling sounds of Julian's archers, and men with mounts standing farther back from the riverbank. A moment later, a flock of birds screeched and shook treetops as they flew north. Frightened deer, antelopes, and rabbits jumped out of bushes and rushed away, unheeding of the men and horses standing nearby. Then the air filled with smoke, and Eric could see the yellow flames well back of the near trees, and growing closer. While it was apparent that Julian was retreating away from the lip of the burning forest, Eric's perspective remained unchanged. Eric saw the shadow men floating along the narrow river that had begun as a smaller channel of water several miles inland. He thought he saw Corwin and Bleys bobbing in the dark water, but the contact was suddenly broken.

It was time to ready the Royal Guard, Eric knew. He conferred with his captains, after which he ordered them to make camp at the Great Arch to await further orders. When Julian contacted him, Eric was resigned to the news. Bleys, Corwin, and several thousand of their men were on a forced march toward Kolvir. In Julian's estimation, it was imperative that they attack immediately and finish them off before they reach Kolvir. However, Eric was of a different mind. That kind of engagement would be costly on both sides. Eric ordered Julian to return with his troops to the base of Mt. Kolvir, without engaging in any action along the way. Using Caine's Trump, Eric contacted him, finding that the royal navy had just docked, with the captured ship in tow. Eric ordered Caine to gather up all his ablebodied crewmen and join Julian's force at Kolvir.

When Julian communicated with Eric the next day, Eric was pleased with the immensity of the force that protected Amber. Caine and his men were there, and it seemed that nothing Corwin and Bleys did could possibly penetrate this army. Shortly afterward, Eric observed by Trump the siege that the forces of Bleys and Corwin initiated. The battle became chaotic, and Eric lost contact again.

Troubled by this, Eric joined his men at the Great Arch. He spoke briefly to them as they stood at attention, but his great charisma stood him in good stead. When he finished his little talk, he felt that these men would fight to the death for him, and they felt that too.

Caine contacted Eric that night. He had no excuses, but he told Eric that the shadow men of Bleys and Corwin fought savagely, hacking with their swords even as they died. It was remarkable, but the beings of shadow decimated the combined force of Julian's and Caine's men. Caine barely made it away, and he had heard from Julian, so he knew he was alive. Eric muttered something to the effect that it would have been better if Julian had died. For his part, Caine offered to regroup and mount another attack the next morning. Although Caine had no life-threatening wounds, Eric could tell that he suffered from numerous injuries, including a deep, bloody gash in his left arm.

No, he told Caine. This time he should stay out of the battle. Rest and recuperate. There was only one avenue for Bleys and Corwin to take, and he was ready for that.

The next day, one of his captains informed Eric that the enemy had begun the ascent of Kolvir. Eric nodded his understanding, but before dismissing the officer, asked if the nets and special arrows were ready in the event Bleys and Corwin reached the Great Arch. His captain said they were. With a wave of his arm, Eric dismissed him.

Eric studied Corwin's Trump, and the Jewel around his neck pulsed brightly. He used the natural inclination of the sea winds, and urged them to grow. Without hearing any report from his men, Eric felt the violent winds beating against the palace walls and knew they were much worse on the side of the great mountain. With the winds came increasingly darkening clouds, closing upon Kolvir. Drenching rains fell as the harsh winds continued. The way up would be slippery, therefore that much more dangerous.

By that time, Eric surmised, the first of his royal guards would have met with Bleys's advancing column. Unable to view the confrontation along the eastern stair, Eric left his quarters and went to the Great Arch. There were still great numbers of armed men standing at the Arch, their companions ahead of them winding on toward the top shelf of the stair. Eric knew that the guards extended, beyond his sight, down the natural steps. He listened with pride to the shouts of encouragement from the men before him, looking downward toward the fray. One or two of his officers turned, saw Eric, and were about to shout to their men to stand at attention and offer a salute. Eric waved them off, came forward with studied casualness, and patted them each on the shoulder briefly. He stood beside his officers, watching the descending men as one of them, as a good comrade-in-arms.

The day strained on, and Eric felt the ache of tension as he stood with his officers, watching the slow, deliberate movement of his men edging along the mountainside. Late in the day, there was a sudden echoing cry that was carried up the mountain, and the backs of the guards lurched forward and hurried along the line of descent. Word came back to them that Bleys now led the enemy advance.

While Eric could not see the progress of battle along the stair, he knew, as did virtually every man there, when the enemy force was nearing the top shelf, well beyond the Great Arch where he stood. There had been a subtle shifting in the general movement. The men farther along the line closed tighter on one another. They braced for a change in positioning.

A great shout, not of fear but of cheering, came from the men. It was all too brief, for a sullen silence ensued thereafter. Eric could only guess at the cause, for no one uttered a sound.

In one unexpected, mighty shift of men, the guards pushed backward. They steadied themselves momentarily, then shoved backward again as one. Eric and his officers were initially pushed back with the general movement, but then his captains urged him to retreat to the palace. Eric refused, but they did move away from the Arch to what they estimated was a safe distance.

From his new position, Eric could see the heads of numerous tall, red-skinned warriors, slashing their way through the line of royal guards with short, curved swords. Taking out his Trumps, Eric looked at Corwin's Trump and sensed irrefutably that Corwin was there, fighting and killing the best of his guards. He shouted at his captains that he wanted Corwin captured alive; their men were to refrain from killing him. His officers carried out his orders, rushing ahead and shouting at the guards nearest to them. The word was passed along.

The fighting continued for hours. When his captains moved between the battle and Eric's position, Eric shouted orders to them, trying to be heard in the continuing noise of metal on metal and human cries. It was amazing to Eric that Corwin and his dwindling band of men held on for so long—amazing that they took so many of the best of his Guard with them as they died.

In the growing darkness, Eric could discern a mere handful of tall, hairless warriors, surrounding a smaller fighter. He could no longer see faces in the dark, but he knew the person in their midst was Corwin. Frantically, he searched out one of his captains, made sure he understood that his brother was to be taken alive. The orders were spread rapidly, and the soldiers of the Guard struck the remaining men with something like care. Shortly thereafter, the last of the shadow warriors fell dead, and Corwin was alone. Eric's soldiers didn't give him a chance to resist. They fired their arrows at him, blunted but still painful. Nets were tossed over him, and Corwin lost his sword. He fell and was buffeted into unconsciousness by the barrage of special arrows and by wooden clubs.

Eric ordered his men to carry Corwin's unconscious body to a cell in the dungeon. After seeing this done, Eric watched for several moments as his captains had their soldiers carry and dispose of bodies. With respect for all the valiant dead, the soldiers lifted and moved the bodies of comrades and enemies with great care. The captains ordered a burial detail, rolling open maps to assign locations for two separate burial sites. Tiredly, Eric turned away, looked back toward the palace, and walked heavily toward it.

When Eric called a meeting with his brothers, his tone and manner were subtly changed. He worked out the details of the coronation ceremony with them: assuring the attendance of invited guests of the realm, opening the bridges into the shadows of the Golden Circle, arranging seating, preparing the banquet, and giving various assignments to guards and servants during the proceedings. Eric didn't voice anger or resentment at his brothers for past indiscretions, but he remembered their actions, and he kept them stored away for future reference.

Early in the meeting, Gérard asked Eric about the Jewel glowing around his neck. He said he had seen it before and wondered how Eric had obtained it. Eric dismissed it with a wave of his hand, saying he had come across it in their father's room. Gérard couldn't pursue his query because Eric turned to the others and initiated discussion about Corwin. It was an untenable position for Eric. He would not condemn Corwin to death. Too many people in Amber knew the circumstances of Corwin's capture for Eric to execute him summarily. If their father still lived and returned to the throne, he would never countenance Corwin's death at Eric's hands under such conditions. If only Corwin had died in his siege of Mt. Kolvir.

In their conference, Eric was for leaving Corwin in the dungeon and forgetting about him. Caine pointed out that they were still in danger from Brand's allies, and if Brand were to escape his imprisonment, he would probably seek all of them out for past offenses and enact his revenge. Those same allies might find a use for Corwin if he remained alive and well, and Corwin would surely seek vengeance if given the chance. That was when Julian had another thought. Suppose Corwin were kept alive but of no use to Brand or his allies? When Eric asked what he had in mind, Julian told him that there was a simple way to incapacitate Corwin so that any consideration of a rescue attempt from other parties would seem superfluous from the start. He suggested putting out Corwin's eyes.

There was silence for a long time while the brothers thought it over. Then Eric voiced the idea that the blinding needn't be permanent. They all possessed the power to heal and regenerate. It was possible that eventually, given many years, perhaps, Corwin would regain his eyesight. Julian agreed, supporting this notion. Julian and Caine encouraged Eric to have the blinding carried out immediately, but Eric shook his head in an odd refusal. He assured them it would be done, but not secretly, not without public observance of his clemency and his justice. Corwin would have a role in Eric's coronation. He would be seen as a reluctant participant, but also as an outlaw and traitor. They could expect his actions during the ceremony to be rebellious, and therefore they could be renounced before all those in attendance as traitorous. Then, when Eric passed his judgment on Corwin, it would appear a just sentence, tempered with mercy, for Corwin would be granted his life.

The brothers drank a toast with wine to conclude their meeting.

On the day of the coronation, Corwin was cleaned and prepared for it. At the same time, Eric was being bathed by his servants, swathed in costly perfumes, dressed in a crisp uniform, and covered in an ermine robe. While Corwin was made to look princely once again, encumbered by heavy chains, Eric was made to look majestic, the image of regal magnificence.

That evening, Eric's servants ushered him to the top of the winding stair leading to the large dining hall. All the guests were present, including Corwin. Eric could sense the people of the Golden Circle shadows observing the hall below through bridges maintained at present by Gérard. With a smile of royal beneficence, Eric descended the stair.

At the bottom of the stair, two of the Royal Guard met Eric and escorted him to the long center table. He stood at one end, looking at Corwin at the far end, chained and held standing by two armed guards. The wine stewards filled everyone's goblet, and Eric held his up to propose a toast. "May you dwell forever in Amber, . . . which endureth forever." (NP, 144)

He was not terribly disconcerted when Corwin lifted his glass and toasted, "To Eric, who sits at the foot of the table!" (NP, 144) The more rebelliousness Corwin showed, the better.

With a gesture, Eric commanded music to be performed, and the meal commenced. While Julian sat at the lower end of the table, next to Corwin, who was in his charge, Caine was given a place of honor, seated to Eric's right. After all, Caine and Eric shared the same mother, while Julian's mother was of poorer stock. Eric may already have had other motives behind the seating arrangements at that point as well.

After everyone had completed the meal, Eric gave a slight nod to one of his captains, who then gestured to the musicians. When Eric stood, the musicians played a brief anthem meant to announce a momentous occasion. As they played, the members of the Royal Court filed slowly out. With his entourage, Eric solemnly marched to the throne room and took his place in front of the throne. Everyone knelt before him.

There was hushed silence for a moment. The musicians played a soft melody as Caine walked toward the throne, bearing the crown of Amber on a cushion. Julian announced, "Behold the crowning of a new king in Amber!" (NP, 145) then urged the chained Corwin to take the crown and hand it to Eric. Corwin acted predictably, and many in the audience gasped when he threw it at Eric's head, attempting to take out an eye. Eric caught the crown deftly and smiled. It had hardly been worth considering when Corwin had placed the crown on his own head and declared himself king. Eric had let that pass without concern.

It was the first official act as the newly crowned king that mattered, and Eric's thoughts were upon that. Corwin's actions had condemned him before all those present, and Eric intended to establish his

authority without question. His pronouncement was calm and deliberate:

"Guards! Take Corwin away to the stithy, and let his eyes be burnt from out his head! Let him remember the sights of this day as the last he might ever see! Then cast him into the darkness of the deepest dungeon beneath Amber, and let his name be forgotten!" (NP, 146–47)

Once Corwin was out of the way, Eric took up the business of ruling Amber with an apparent sense of relief. One of his priorities as king was to try to ease tensions with the shadow realms of the Golden Circle. Creatures still wandered into the true city from Shadow, and Eric thought that some of the more familiar visitations could be put under control, and the continuance of such occasions prevented, if arrangements could be made diplomatically with the shadows. Contingents of his Royal Guard were attached to several delegations representing King Eric to the member shadows in order to ensure the security of Amber. At least some of the slippage from near shadows was halted.

In spite of the fact that Eric did not show his feelings before his brothers, Julian had voiced his own sense that Eric gave his assignments out to his brothers with a kind of vindictiveness. It seemed to Julian that Eric never quite forgave him for his fleeing the battle at the foot of Mt. Kolvir, nor did he forget that Caine had allowed Corwin to escape capture on his only remaining ship. Eric tolerated his brothers and never revealed any overt anger for their past mistakes. Still, he assigned Julian to return to his patrol in Arden, ostensibly to watch for Shadow slippage, which was, in truth, still a great concern. Although Caine had seniority, Eric promoted Gérard to the admiralty of the royal fleet, granting Caine nothing more than the freedom of his leisure. Whether Caine was aware of this or not, he took his best advantage and spent much time in town with women and frequenting local cafés and barrooms.

In the ensuing months, Eric handled various matters of state expeditiously, and there was relative calm. He had begun communication once again with Queen Moire of Rebma, and rumors began circulating that Eric hoped for a more concrete liaison with her. Flora was spending much of her time in the

Royal Palace and was a frequent confidante to Eric. Later, Flora indicated that Eric asked many questions about her life on the shadow Earth and was especially curious about Corwin's home on the American continent.

After three months of tranquillity and order, an assassination attempt was made on Eric's life. Eric was walking down a hallway toward the dining hall early one evening, preoccupied with his own thoughts, when he was thrust backward against the wall. He cried out in pain, and several guards ran to his aid. While some of them discovered Eric sinking to the floor, an arrow piercing his ribs, others happened upon Prince Random with a crossbow. Random was in the process of adjusting another shaft when the guards came across him. Without knowing that he had just fired an arrow into their king, the guards took him into custody when Random turned to fire at one of them. Moments later, they discovered that Eric was wounded and they arrested Random.

Eric was treated by Caine and remained in his room, semiconscious, for a couple of days. In the meantime, Random had been locked in a cell, with everyone uncertain what to do with him. If Eric were to die, who would succeed him? And with his death, what was to be done with Random? Fortunately, before anyone needed to act on these questions, Eric recovered. When he was awake and talking, Caine, Julian, and Gérard attended him. Julian told him of Random's arrest and imprisonment. For the while, Eric determined to keep Random confined. It was appropriate that he share the same accommodations as Corwin. Eric presided over the trial and sentencing of Random, performed with suitable formality and swiftness.

A few days later, Queen Moire contacted Eric by Trump. After asking about Random and learning of the assassination attempt, Moire allowed a young, attractive woman to speak to Eric. Her name was Vialle, and it became apparent to Eric in a moment that she was blind. The Lady Vialle told Eric that she was the wife of Lord Random. She requested that she be allowed to join her husband in his prison cell. Her earnestness moved Eric, and he could only say that he would give her request some thought. When Eric again turned to Moire, he was pleasant and quite politic. He concluded their exchange and bowed graciously before ending the contact.

In the passing months, Eric continued to handle several local problems efficiently, and he arranged frequent meetings with shadows of the Golden Circle. He made visits to other realms, but more often he sent delegations headed by one of his brothers. Eric realized the political necessity of maintaining close contact with the Golden Circle worlds, and usually it was merely a matter of negotiating some minor adjustment or addition to treaty agreements already in existence.

During that time, Eric granted Vialle's wish to join Random in prison. He transferred them to larger quarters in the dungeon. Their large, adjoining rooms had in the past been used as a recreation area for the guards. Vialle and Random were made as comfortable as possible there, but they were denied any further liberty.

On the first anniversary of Eric's coronation, Eric ordered a great feast to celebrate the occasion. He wanted everyone who had been present at the coronation to attend. When Corwin was led in, Eric was most concerned if there was any hint that his sight was returning. He and his brothers kept close watch on Corwin for any sign of visual acuity, even so slight as a movement of the head toward the light. There seemed to be none.

After Lord Rein's first visit to Corwin, during his first year in captivity, Julian kept Eric informed of the court minstrel's infrequent visits throughout the second year. Naturally, Eric condoned Rein's actions, since they were a kindness that Eric would have provided if he could have maintained strict secrecy. Lord Rein had made matters that much easier for Eric, as well as for Corwin. No one could accuse Eric of unnecessary cruelty, and the enemy could gain no proof that Eric was relaxing his hold on Corwin. Lord Rein was allowed to continue his clandestine visits unchallenged, with the result that during Corwin's third year in the dungeons, the minstrel brought him food, drink, and news every other month.

A petition, signed by the leading merchants and their most important patrons among the nobility, reached King Eric. In the document, they complained of widespread, inexplicable vandalism, of senseless destruction and spoilage of merchandise. That was the beginning of a new outbreak of invasions from Shadow. When Eric's delegations went to the near shadows, their leaders presented evidence of careful observation of any such slippage or deliberate crossing. Since most of these shadows

ERIC 211

had a contingent of men from Amber guarding against such problems, Eric felt assured that the near shadows were blameless.

Even as Eric looked to more distant shadows for the source of the migrations, he learned of townspeople being brutally murdered, some while they slept in their own beds. When horrible creatures were seen in various areas in and about the city, Eric assigned Julian, Gérard, and Caine actively to seek them out and destroy them. While this was being done, Eric received more disturbing news: Corwin had escaped from his locked cell.

Corwin's escape was not entirely welcome, although it helped to justify Eric's actions regarding him. Eric was totally involved in the security of Amber, and he could not divide his time between the invaders and shoring up defenses against Corwin's possible return. With a sense of unease, Eric put aside any thought of Corwin and continued to focus his attention on the shadow creatures.

Gérard and Julian, leading separate companies of soldiers, discovered a blackened road that cut through regions where no road had been constructed. While studying the road, both Julian and Gérard had been sickened upon stepping onto it. They returned to the palace to report the discovery to Eric. They reported that the black road seemed strangely unreal. Its earth and grass were not sooty but were grown black, so that they seemed otherworldly. Eric ordered them back to their patrols. When he returned to his campsite beside the black road, Julian discovered his sentries dead, their bodies mutilated. Using his Trump, Julian informed Eric. By then, Caine had also found the black road crossing another area, and Eric warned them all to keep careful watch all through the night.

The next morning, Eric heard reports from Caine, Julian, and Gérard from their separate sites. Although they had not been attacked during the night, their sentries had seen indistinct figures moving within the black road, always at some distance from where each soldier stood guard. Eric believed that some unknown intelligence had created the phenomenon and it was now alerted to the fact that movement along the road was being watched. The three armed encampments received no further visitations.

For another full day and night, Eric had his brothers remain camped by the black road. During that time, he received messages from several couriers in the Golden Circle realms that the same black road

had mysteriously evolved in their shadows. They reported sudden, horrible murders and odd shapes moving along the road. In some cases, wholesale slaughter had taken place, and in others, armies of unknown creatures battled unready militias hastily mustered to defend each kingdom. All pleaded for Amber's help.

When his brothers reported no untoward occurrences from the road at their campsites, Eric ordered them to return to the palace. Eric met with Julian, Gérard, and Caine in his quarters. They agreed that the invading beings had taken the paths of least resistance after it was discovered that the black road was being closely watched in Amber. Whatever intelligence was behind the movements on that road, it was presently trying to draw Amber's defensive force away from the true city by attacking the near shadows. In order to fulfill obligations to the shadows of the Golden Circle, and to give the appearance that their defenses were being diverted, Eric arranged for three companies of soldiers to be divided into smaller contingents and sent them to protect the near shadows. Meanwhile, Caine was delegated to oversee the remaining infantry, cavalry, and navy in preparations for war. Gérard and Julian were assigned the mission of traveling the black road on their own, so as not to draw attention to themselves. They were to trace it to its source, contact Eric by Trump, and through their contact, transport infantry forces to their location to dispatch the enemy. With that understanding, Gérard and Julian departed.

Eric had begun working with Caine to build their military defenses, when something happened that changed Eric irrevocably. Those of us in the Royal Court who had been privy to innumerable matters that slipped out in conversation and that were a natural part of court gossip, had suddenly had those doors closed to us. Much of what we learned about Eric's actions after this point come only in retrospect, based largely on the Chronicles as recounted by Prince Corwin.

A servant of King Eric's reported that a large black bird had flown into Eric's quarters while he was taking a solitary breakfast. The bird had a carefully folded piece of paper tied to one claw, and the servant saw Eric remove it. He ordered the servant out, but the servant lingered outside his rooms long enough to hear Eric give an awful cry and then rant and curse loudly. From that time on, Eric confided in no one, and he never again called upon any of the court officials to action in the informal spy network he had developed ages ago.

From Corwin's Chronicles, we have learned the import of that message on the black bird's claw. It read: "Eric—I'll be back," and was signed: "Corwin, Lord of Amber." (NP, 175) The black bird, stuffed and mounted, can still be seen on the armoire in Eric's sleeping quarters.

Those of us who resided in the Royal Palace felt suddenly deprived of information. We were left to gather what we were able by simple observation and from what Amber's couriers learned in the town and in the shadows. It seemed that Eric kept to his rooms for long periods of time, for days even, although it was commonly agreed that on some of these occasions he had probably used a Trump to travel into Shadow. When Eric was seen walking through the palace, taking his meals in the dining hall, or conferring with others, most of us noticed his almost-constant wearing of the pulsing Jewel around his neck. To us, it seemed as if he had grown to depend on the Jewel whenever he left his quarters, as if he could not be parted from it.

Although those of us in the palace were somewhat insulated from events outside, we heard numerous complaints passed along from the townspeople. The invasions of terrible creatures were a continuous threat, and while the citizens of Amber were capable of using whatever weapons were at hand to defend themselves, they expected protection from their liege. Hardy as they were, the people felt deeply the loss of loved ones to these sudden attacks, and they allowed their anger and grieving to be heard by the courtiers and royal messengers, who brought back word of their verbal, and sometimes physical, abuse to the court.

We noticed, too, at the time, that Random and his wife were granted the freedom of the palace, although members of the Royal Guard were seldom far from them. It was believed that the Lady Vialle's appeals to the king had finally touched Eric sufficiently to allow this kindness. However, Eric was never seen in the company of his young brother.

Only long after Julian and Gérard had returned from their mission along the black road did we learn anything about what had transpired. While the way had been difficult for them, Gérard and Julian had traveled far into Shadow along the road. They were attacked by a large party of beast-men that over-whelmed them. Gérard was able to contact Benedict in the shadow called Avalon, and Benedict brought his soldiers with him through the Trump contact. They dispatched the beast-men and carried the injured Gérard and Julian back to Avalon. For the first time in many years, Benedict spoke to Eric in Amber, informing him of the attack and that Julian and Gérard were in his care. When they did return to Amber, few members of the court saw them, but servants who brought them food in their separate rooms mentioned something of Gérard's injuries and Julian's wan paleness.

By this time, the black road had extended so that it reached the base of Mt. Kolvir. Attacks by creatures of Shadow came often and grew stronger with each occasion. Eric was spending much time out in the field with his soldiers, fortifying the area around the Royal Palace, and defending the town and its environs.

Since the king was seen little in the palace, there is no firsthand account of his activities, other than the clearly observed escalation of warfare between his army and the marauding Shadow-beings. Corwin's Chronicles fill in some of the gaps, although events remain sketchy.

Since years before King Eric had asked Flora about Corwin's home in New York, it seems likely that he subsequently visited that place. In his Chronicles, Corwin describes Eric's interest in a Japanese woodcut in Corwin's home, which Eric used as a signal of his unannounced visit during this present crisis. In his safe, Corwin found Eric's note and his Trump. The letter read, in part:

I would have peace between us, Corwin, for the sake of the realm, not my own. Strong forces out of Shadow have come to beset Amber regularly, and I do not fully understand their nature. Against these forces, the most formidable in my memory ever to assail Amber, the family has united behind me. I would like to have your support in this struggle. Failing that, I request that you forbear invading me for a time. If you elect to assist, I will require no homage of you, simply acknowledgment of my leadership for the duration of the crisis. You will be accorded your normal honors. It is important that you contact me to see the truth of what I say. As I have failed to reach you by means of your Trump, I enclose my own for your use. While the possibility that I am lying to you is foremost in your mind, I give you my word that I am not. (GA, 198)

When several ferocious manticoras had appeared in the northern and western reaches of Amber, slaughtering men and animals that crossed their paths, it marked the initiation of the Shadow War. Eric ordered Julian to assign patrols to fan outward into the countryside to the north and west in order to locate and destroy any Shadow beasts they discovered.

The ensuing battles that erupted were terrible and bloody. Although citizens as well as militia were caught up in the fighting, it was not commonly understood that the black road was the major gateway for the Shadow creatures into Amber. It seemed as if the strange beasts came from everywhere at once, and only a privileged few were privy to the knowledge that the mysterious road was directly connected to the onslaught.

Julian has reported that Benedict had made contact with him when it became apparent, even in the more distant shadows, that Amber was under siege. Through their Trump contact, Julian brought Benedict and a contingent of armed men into Amber. At about the same time, Julian had reported to Eric that one of his northern patrols was missing. Both Eric and Julian concurred that Corwin, with another party of warriors, had arrived in Amber to mount an attack of his own. Benedict affirmed this by telling of his recent encounter with Corwin. In spite of the highly probable threat posed by Corwin, Eric felt the need to forgo that concern in the face of the more immediate danger of the Shadow-beings. He simply had no time to worry over Corwin.

Beast-men and winged wyvern had begun to range around Mt. Kolvir, and the various patrols that had been scouting the countryside were called in by messenger. All available men, including officers and sailors of the royal fleet, were assigned to specific companies of the infantry that had taken positions along the lower reaches of Kolvir. Caine, Julian, and Gérard led companies of troops at various points on the cliff face, while Benedict led a large cavalry force in the wide valley below Kolvir. Eric and a small force stood near an overhang on a broad shelf of the cliff. Using the Jewel of Judgment, Eric sent out rainless storms against the winged creatures and the beast-men, and many of them died, falling as flame.

Bringing all his powers to bear, and observing the pitched battles around him from his vantage point, Eric realized the enormity of the numbers opposing him. For a while it seemed possible that Amber would be defeated.

As the fighting continued, there were moments when the men thought they would be cut down by the beast-men swooping down at them on their winged mounts. The fighting was so fierce that no one had time to cheer when brief explosions were heard, and wyvern, with their riders, rolled, dropped, and burned. Even the common foot soldier knew about gunfire, although none was ever fired in the true realm. Amber's soldiers fought on, not hesitating to wonder at the rifle shots that brought down the enemy.

In his position on the cliff shelf, Eric heard the rifle fire, and he was able to perceive the long rifle barrels protruding from the higher cliff face opposite. Instinctively, he knew it was Corwin. Who else would have the ability to bring gunfire into Amber?

Eric hadn't much time to wonder about Corwin and his force, for a small grouping of wyvern and beast-men swooped down upon the shelf, catching Eric and his men off guard. Eric parried the several blades that were thrust against him, but he lost his balance momentarily with the suddenness of the attack. Three unerring thrusts tore open Eric's chest before his soldiers disposed of the attackers. Eric stumbled back, toward the overhang, and fell against the rock wall.

Gérard reached the broad ridge where Eric lay moments later, and immediately ministered to his wounds. As the veterans of the Royal Guard stood watching, Gérard worked hard to stem the bleeding from Eric's chest wounds. However, the injuries were too extensive and the blood loss already too great. Everyone suspected the worst.

Eric's eyes flitted open; he drifted into and out of consciousness. The Jewel, resting upon the bloodied tunic at Eric's chest, pulsed in seeming imitation of a heartbeat as he drew in shallow breaths.

When Corwin reached the cliff, he knelt beside his dying brother. Seeing him, Eric spoke softly, but in the odd stillness, the members of the Guard could hear much of what was said. He called Corwin's name, and then said:

"I knew that it would be you . . . They saved you some trouble, didn't they? . . .

"Your turn will come one day . . . Then we will be peers. . . .

"I could feel your curse . . . All around me. The whole time. You didn't even have to die to make it stick. . . .

"No, I'm not going to give you my death curse. I've reserved that for the enemies of Amber—out there." (GA, 215)

Then he talked about the Jewel of Judgment and Dworkin's notes, items learned about later from the Chronicles of Corwin. Before his final breath, Eric pushed himself up and said with great effort, "Acquit yourself as well as I have—bastard!" (GA, 216)

With Eric's death and Corwin's specially armed force effecting a victory over the Shadow-beings, it was clear that Corwin would take over the rule of the true city. Still, Corwin had little to do with the caring and readying of Eric's body for burial. The Royal Guard bore Eric's body from the field of battle with great solemnity. Caine supervised preparations for the funeral. Eric was sent to his ultimate peace with dignity and high honor.

Much later, Fiona talked to Corwin about the possibility that the Jewel had contributed to Eric's death. From calculations she had made prior to the funeral ceremony, Fiona determined that Eric could have survived his wounds. The power drain of extended wear of the Jewel may have made the difference that cost Eric his life.

The knowledge he had of the Jewel of Judgment was Eric's final legacy to Corwin, and Corwin was never certain whether or not Eric knew of its debilitating property on one's vitality. No one can ever attest to the extent of Eric's understanding of the functions of that unique gem.

FAIELLA-BIONIN

The enchanted stairway to the undersea city of Rebma at the shore of Amber. Random and Deirdre led Corwin to it, intent on reaching Rebma so that Corwin could walk the Pattern there.

Faiella-bionin is located just off the southeastern coast of Amber. Its beginning is marked by a formation of gray stones about eight feet high on the moist part of the beach, where high tide would bury its base in several inches of water. Upon reaching the cairn of stones, one must keep to a precise route, turning at right angles around it and heading directly for the sea. After wading up to the waist, one can feel the natural rock shelves of the stairway beneath one's feet. There is a drop every few feet, indicating that the shelves are quite long.

Although one has the tendency to take a huge gulp of air before descending beneath the surface of the water, it is not necessary. As long as one keeps to Faiella-bionin, one will be able to breathe normally. That was part of its peculiar qualities.

Corwin considered the phenomenon of walking down those steps in his Chronicles:

> I wondered why my body was not naturally buoyed above them, for I continued to remain erect and each step bore me downward as though on a natural staircase, though my movements were somewhat slowed. . . .
>
> There were bubbles about Random's head, and Deirdre's. I tried to observe what they were doing, but I couldn't figure it. Their breasts seemed to be rising and falling in a normal manner. (NP, 75)

By exhaling slightly, then inhaling as one would normally, one finds that breathing can be accomplished with no effort. One can speak and hear sounds readily, though the sounds will be hollow, as if one heard the vibrations as one struck the side of a bathtub underwater.

In the great darkness of the sea as one descends, the way is lighted by pillars with shining globes atop them. On closer inspection, one could see the globes were actually naked flames. They were spaced about fifteen steps apart on the descent.

The stairway itself is like marble. In spite of the water, it does not have a slippery surface. It is fifty feet wide, with a marblelike banister running along either side.

When Corwin and his siblings had reached a point in which the ocean was virtually black, and the only illumination was on the stair, they were forced to battle their pursuers, who reached them on horseback. Corwin discovered the dangers awaiting man beyond those banisters:

The force of his speed through the water and the strength of my blow removed him from the saddle. As he fell, I kicked, and he drifted. I struck at him, hovering there above me, and he parried again, but this carried him beyond the rail. I heard him scream as the pressure of the waters came upon him. Then he was silent. (NP, 78)

At the foot of Faiella-bionin are a number of guards who maintain their vigilance in constantly changing shifts. They could easily repel invasion of those foolhardy enough to attempt it.

FANDON

A shielding device used in close personal combat in the Courts of Chaos.

Since our knowledge of the fandon comes primarily through Merlin of Chaos and Amber, we have only a vague idea of its appearance. Merlin's account describes it as being a "three-foot length of filmy mesh, mord-weighted at the bottom." (BA, 82) Aside from the clear implication that a mord is some kind of counterweight, nothing further is known about the form or nature of a mord. The fandon is attached to the left forearm, at wrist and elbow, and is used to shunt aside, rather than block, laserlike beams from Chaos weapons such as the trisp and trisliver.

Its ability to sweep away beams of energy is limited to an eight-foot range for reliable efficiency. Beyond that range, the definition of its shunting power is so erratic as to be ineffectual.

In a duel at the Courts, one speaks of using the fandon in terms of guard positions. One guards in high fand or low fand. When a lunge with trisp or trisliver is shunted aside by the fandom, it is said that the attack "died in fand."

FILMY/BLACK THREAD OR BLACK TRAIL

A thin, gauzelike pathway commonly used by the lords of the Courts of Chaos as their means of travel. The lords have the innate power to "throw out" and extend these narrow paths to walk or ride upon in getting about the non-Euclidian realm of the Courts. By mustering a great deal of their energies, they are capable of extending these black threads well into Shadow. The black road that had once reached the base of Mt. Kolvir in Amber, for example, evolved over a period of time with a great deal of effort from combined forces involving Chaos lords and others.

Corwin's son Merlin referred to such a pathway as a filmy, saying that he could "summon" one at his desire. (CC, 129) Corwin described seeing the peculiar movements of these threadlike paths in his Chronicles:

> ... faint and misty sheets drifted slowly between us, twisting, as if long strands of gauze were buoyed by heated air. ...
> ... I discerned tiny, ghostly forms moving within that place [the dark citadel], like slow-motion meteors along the gauzy strands. ... At length, one of the strands drifted very near. ...
> ... One of the rushing forms grew larger, and I realized that it was following the twisted way that led toward me. ...
> The rider came abreast of me and halted at the nearest point on the gauzy strip. ...
> Then he galloped away, and moments later the gauze drifted off also. (HO, 79–83)

Corwin's son grew up in the Courts and was quite used to this mode of travel. In his journals, Merlin recounted the use of Black Threads or Black Trails that he encountered at the time of the death of King Swayvill. A servant to his uncle Suhuy used a Black Thread to reach Merlin while he stayed in shadow Kashfa. Apparently, then, these Black Threads can reach across enormous distances, penetrating Shadow.

Merlin and the servant, Gryll, rode back to the Courts upon the pathway:

> We soared, the castle and the town dwindling in an eyeblink. The stars danced, became streaks of light. A band of sheer, rippling blackness spread about us, widening. The Black Road, I suddenly thought. It is like a temporary version of the Black Road, in the sky. I glanced back. It was not there. It was as if it were somehow reeling in as we rode. Or was it reeling us in?

The countryside passed beneath us like a film played at triple speed. Forest, hill, and mountain peak fled by. Our black way was a great ribbon heaving before us, patches of light and dark like daytime cloud shadows sliding past. And then the tempo increased, staccato. (PC, 7)

Through Merlin's description, one obtains the immediacy of sensations of speed and movement along such a pathway.

Agents of the Courts of Chaos used a Black Trail to reach Kashfa and kidnap Coral, bride of King Rinaldo. When Merlin arrived to help Rinaldo, the king of Kashfa made these comments about the black pathway:

"I understand these black thoroughfares you guys use are dangerous to outsiders . . . But I can show you what's left of this one—it's a black pathway now, actually. I'd like to follow it, but I don't know that I can get away for long." (PC, 142)

The remains of the pathway into Kashfa faded within days, but Merlin and Rinaldo were able to locate and follow what was left of it by employing a particular entity that had taken possession of the body of Coral's sister, Nayda. This entity had an uncanny ability for sensing things out of Chaos, making it ideal for tracking both the roadway and the Chaos agents who had kidnapped Coral.

In his journals, Merlin noted some of the unique properties of the black path they traveled on:

The trail, which consisted of blackened grasses and which produced the same effect on any tree or shrub that so much as overhung it, wound its way through a hilly area now; and as I stepped onto and off of it I noted that it seemed brighter and warmer each time I departed. It had reached this point now after having been virtually undetectable in the vicinity of Kashfa—an index of how far we were into the realm of the Logrus. (PC, 173)

Although the trail they rode widened, it was not as wide as the black road that led to Kolvir. Still, Merlin was able to ride on horseback side by side with his compatriots along that path. They could see

the changing scenes of various shadows as they moved along it, and watched strange birds on black trees as they made croaking sounds and jostled among darkened leaves. Within the trail, sounds were muffled, and everything seemed dim and shadowy.

They followed the Black Trail to a gray tower, and that was the place where Merlin confronted agents of the Logrus and the Pattern. The filmy became insubstantial, eventually disappearing amid the tramplings of forces from opposite poles of existence.

While in the Courts for Swayvill's funeral, Merlin was contacted and transported by his stepbrother Mandor by means of a Trump (PC, 132). One might reason that the use of Trumps, at least for purposes of travel, was a recent thing in that place. The more ancient mode of travel, inherent in the odd milieu of the Courts of Chaos, was borne in the natural skill of any nobleman to bring forth a filmy.

FINNDO

Oldest of three sons born to Cymnea and Oberon. His brothers by that union were Osric and Benedict. His mother was ignobly treated by Oberon, who dissolved their marriage *ab initio* in order to wed Faiella. Although his mother was banished from the true city, Finndo and his brother Osric were permitted to remain. His brother Benedict was too young to be involved in the feelings of humiliation that Osric and Finndo endured. After a violent incident involving Osric in the House of Karm, Oberon was offended by the presence of Finndo and his brother. The king arranged for both of them to be sent to the northern borders during a particularly brutal war with creatures out of Shadow. Finndo and Osric were both slain and buried in the northern plains. [*See* OSRIC AND FINNDO].

FIONA

Daughter of Clarissa, a red-haired woman of a shadow to the south of Amber, and Oberon. Fiona's full brothers were Bleys and Brand. Like them, Fiona was fascinated with the arcane knowledge of Dworkin, and she learned all she could. During the period before Patternfall, she joined Brand and Bleys in collusion with the lords of the Courts of Chaos, intending to control the reign of Amber. She and Bleys turned against Brand when they realized he sought to destroy Amber and devise a new Pattern out of his own psyche. At the Patternfall battle, Fiona was instrumental in preventing Brand from carrying out his plans. She served loyally under King Random, but she was preoccupied with plumbing the occult forces which seemed to be causing turmoil in various shadows. While learning more of the effects of the imbalance of the Powers, she was introduced to Merlin's stepbrother Mandor of the Courts. Together, Fiona and Mandor investigated the phenomena inducing disturbances in Shadow, hoping to find a solution.

Lovely Fiona had fiery red hair, green eyes, and a white complexion. Although she was short at five feet, two inches in height, she was a forceful presence and carried herself with great charm. At a very young age, she showed herself to be an apt pupil of the mage Dworkin, just as Bleys and Brand had been. Recognizing their gifts in wizardry, Dworkin had once said of the three of them: "It was Clarissa's lot served us best." (HO, 64) Corwin commented on their occult skills:

> "An endorsement of higher education. . . . Fiona and Brand paid attention to Dworkin while the rest of us were off indulging our assorted passions in Shadow. Consequently, they seem to have obtained a better grasp of principles than we possess. They know more about Shadow and what lies beyond it, more about the Pattern, more about the Trumps than we do." (SU, 180)

In spite of the fact that Fiona spent much time with her own redheaded brothers, she was admired by another brother, somewhat younger than herself: Julian. He may not have admitted his interest to her directly, but he was always extremely courteous in her presence. Julian confessed his interest to Corwin: "Of course . . . I have always been very fond of Fiona. She is certainly the loveliest, most civilized of us all. Pity Dad was always so dead-set against brother-sister marriages, as well you know." (HO, 125)

When Corwin and Random hellrode in an automobile toward Amber, they encountered Julian. Corwin took Julian captive and questioned him. He asked Julian about Fiona, and Julian told him he believed she was "somewhere to the south." (NP, 61) It appears that Fiona often seeks sanctuary to the south of Amber, especially when she wishes to escape the troubles of the true city. Since her mother Clarissa came from a shadow to the south of Amber, it seems likely that Fiona would find safe haven in the same place.

Early in her visits to other shadows, Fiona may have journeyed to the Courts of Chaos. Using her captivating charm, as well as the knowledge she gained from Dworkin, she was likely to have moved with graceful facility among the noble Houses of the Courts. It is certain that she was known in the House of Sawall, at least, for after the Patternfall War, Mandor had prepared a secret chapel with Fiona as his patron (PC, 166). It also appears likely that she would have introduced Brand to certain lords of the Courts after she managed to ingratiate herself with them. Brand may have been lying to Corwin when he spoke of Fiona's role in their conspiracy, but there was no doubt a spark of truth when he said: "The whole thing was her idea." (SU, 124)

When Fiona agreed with Brand and Bleys to find a way to conduct Oberon far away from Amber, their scheme involved taking over the authority of the realm. Bleys would be the figurehead, but the three would enjoy joint rule. Fiona was chiefly in charge of working out the details with the lords of the Courts, while Brand was an infrequent visitor. After successfully leading Oberon away, ensnaring him in a shadow near the Courts and under guard, Brand made some mistake that caused him to be restricted in movements under Eric's watchful eye. While Bleys was in Avernus, training troops, Fiona remained in Amber, discreetly observing the consolidation of Eric's position with assistance from Julian and Caine.

Even though Brand was under heavy surveillance, he managed to escape and reach shadow Earth at the time that Corwin was beginning to regain his memories. Julian recounted to Corwin what happened at that point:

"When he [Brand] became aware that you had escaped your confinement, he summoned a horrid beast which attacked Caine, who was then his bodyguard. Then he went to you once again. Bleys and Fiona apparently got hold of him shortly after that, before we could, and I did not see him again until that night in the library when we brought him back. I fear him because he has deadly powers which I do not understand."

"In such a case, I wonder how they managed to confine him at all?"

"Fiona has similar strengths, and I believe Bleys did also. Between the two of them, they could apparently annul most of Brand's power while they created a place where it would be inoperative." (HO, 124)

Later, Fiona told Corwin that Brand had tried to kill him on shadow Earth, and that Bleys helped in his rescue. She had contacted Eric by Trump, telling him of Corwin's situation, preparing the way for Flora to regain the care of Corwin in that shadow. By then, Fiona and Bleys wanted to disassociate themselves from Brand's scheme. They realized that he intended to destroy the Pattern and create a new one that would place him as supreme ruler over all Shadow.

With his power over Shadow, Bleys devised a unique shadow of strange atmospheric conditions. He and Fiona found a way to pent Brand in a tower in that shadow, guarded from intruders by a terrifying snakelike creature, and guarded from escaping by fierce beast-men. Keeping Brand drugged, they believed he was suitably confined and beyond help. In the meantime, Fiona and Bleys hoped to learn how to clear the stain of blood on the primal Pattern, a stain for which Brand was responsible.

Fiona was probably in her mother's shadow during the battle on Kolvir between Eric's forces and the beasts out of the black road. When she learned of Eric's death, she returned to Amber. At a later time, she talked to Corwin about her interest in the probable causes of Eric's death:

"Think again of Eric's death, Corwin. I was not there when it occurred, but I came in early for the funeral. I was present when his body was bathed, shaved, dressed—and I examined his wounds. I do not believe that any of them were fatal, in themselves. There were three chest wounds, but only one looked as if it might have run into the mediastinal area—"

"One's enough, if—"

"Wait," she said. "It was difficult, but I tried judging the angle of the puncture with a thin glass rod. I wanted to make an incision, but Caine would not permit it. Still, I do not believe that his heart or arteries were damaged. It is still not too late to order an autopsy, if you would like me to check further on this. I am certain that his injuries and the general stress contributed to his death, but I believe it was the jewel that made the difference." (SU, 110)

She shared her knowledge of the Jewel of Judgment with Corwin then. But this conversation also serves to reveal her intellectual curiosity, even about such grisly matters as stab wounds and performing medical investigations. Such things, clearly, were well within her purview.

In the library of the palace for the Family meeting that Corwin had called for, Fiona observed everyone with quiet amusement. She even coyly dropped a bracelet to the floor, trying to gain Corwin's attention. She behaved with grace when Julian reached the bracelet first, taking the opportunity to hold her hand as he returned it. However, she responded coldly to Julian's chivalrous attention.

The success of Corwin's idea of the Family's concentrating on a Trump of Brand to reach him was, of course, quite worrisome to Fiona. She prepared herself to take desperate measures. She acted on them when Gérard entered Brand's tower room through the contact and rescued him. Much later, Fiona spoke to Corwin of the attempt to contact Brand:

"First, I was not co-operating, I was trying to impede the attempt. But there were too many trying too hard. You got through to him in spite of me. Second, I had to be on hand to try to kill him in the event you succeeded." (HO, 145)

After stabbing Brand upon his entrance to the library, she fled Amber rather than retiring to her rooms in the palace. She hoped that Brand would succumb to his injury, but she couldn't afford to be around if he revived long enough to utter an accusing word.

Although Fiona absented herself from Amber once again, she used her powers to keep Brand under a discreet surveillance. She contacted Corwin on shadow Earth when she detected that Brand had obtained the Jewel of Judgment. Corwin took Fiona to his location in New York and introduced her to Bill Roth. Then, Fiona and Corwin rode off on horseback, hellriding to the site of the primal Pattern. When they reached it, they saw that Brand had already begun walking the primal Pattern, intending to attune himself to the Jewel. Fiona remained with Corwin's horse while Corwin began his walk of the Pattern. Although he prevented Brand from completing the process, Brand escaped with the Jewel still in his possession.

Fiona had remained at the primal Pattern and was there when Oberon returned to it, conferring with Dworkin about how they would proceed. In a Trump contact, Fiona explained the situation to Corwin:

> "All we did was exchange greetings when he and Dworkin were out here earlier to look at the Pattern. I had some suspicions then, though, and this confirms them. . . .
>
> "I think Dad is going to try to repair the Pattern. He has the Jewel with him, and I overheard some of the things he said to Dworkin. If he makes the attempt, they will be aware of it in the Courts of Chaos the moment that he begins. They will try to stop him. He would want to strike first to keep them occupied. Only . . .
>
> "It is going to kill him, Corwin. I know that much about it. Whether he succeeds or fails, he will be destroyed in the process." (CC, 21–22)

She was somewhat surprised when Corwin ordered her to bring him through the Trump contact after she confirmed that Oberon had sent Dara with his orders for the Family. Corwin found himself standing with Fiona, Dworkin, and Oberon in Dworkin's den in the cave near the primal Pattern. Fiona witnessed Corwin's courageously foolhardy act of grabbing the Jewel in an attempt to walk the Pattern and clear the blot from it. It's conceivable that she joined Oberon and Dworkin in exerting psychic powers in order to stop Corwin from taking on the

perilous task. When Oberon requested that he speak to his son alone at the Pattern, Fiona and Dworkin withdrew back to the den again. Respecting Oberon's privacy, she did not try to listen in to their conversation.

Oberon sent Fiona back to Amber, where she received her orders from Dara. She was to join Benedict, already in the mountains overlooking the Courts of Chaos. Her job was to maintain an observation post and search out Brand once the fighting had begun. Then, using her arcane skills, she was to stop him from causing any interference with the progress of the battle. She followed these orders, keeping a vigil in the northern mountains after Benedict brought her through.

When she spied the ruby gleam in the heights near the Abyss, she mounted her horse and rode quickly along the eastern line of the conflict. She found that Random, Deirdre, and several others had followed behind, having the same purpose in mind. As they reached the hillside, Fiona sensed the mystical workings of the Jewel. Knowing what was to come, she veered her horse sharply to her left, invoking an incantation she had prepared against the distant figure above her. A lightning bolt struck very close to the others, but Fiona had already jumped off her mount and rushed up the slope.

Somehow, Brand had gotten to Deirdre and was holding a dagger to her throat. He was standing below and to the right of Fiona, and had not yet seen her. Fiona sent out a force that had a trumping effect. It repositioned Brand and Deirdre to the edge of the precipice and kept them from moving away from that position. Fiona reached the location just as Random and a couple of other noblemen did.

Holding Brand at that spot was all that Fiona could manage. She felt the pulsing emanations of the Jewel around his neck, and she could provide a slight damping effect, but that artifact was too potent for her to restrain. She stood there, maintaining the flow of her energies, sensing the influence of other forces.

With the others, she watched as the face of Oberon formed in the sky above them, and his voice spoke to them. Feeling a certain helplessness, Fiona observed as Brand threatened to kill Deirdre, but then she felt the vibration of someone else's influence. In a moment, she recognized the new force as coming from Corwin. She felt his utilization of the Jewel against Brand. As she watched two silver-tipped arrows pierce Brand, she felt the sudden emptiness of occult waves. She stood by as Brand and Deirdre toppled over the precipice and were gone.

Suddenly very tired from her efforts, Fiona watched the incidents unfolding on that height: Caine's reappearance, the funeral procession for Oberon, the arrival of Corwin's son Merlin, and the remarkable presence of the unicorn, bearing the Jewel of Judgment. With the others, Fiona put down her sword on the ground before the new king, pledging her loyalty to him.

When Merlin came to visit Amber on several occasions after Patternfall, Fiona took an interest in him. She encouraged the young man to attempt an initiation in Amber's Pattern, even though Suhuy, Master of the Logrus, objected. Suhuy feared that it would kill Merlin, since he was already initiated in the Logrus and the two forces were antithetical. Fiona disagreed, believing that each representation of the two Powers should be able to encompass each other. Merlin tried it and succeeded.

On another occasion, Fiona brought Merlin to the place of his father's Pattern, asking him to attempt to walk it. She had previously brought Random and Bleys there. She and Bleys both tried to step onto the new Pattern, but it rejected them, sending out an electrical shock and halting them from placing a foot on its surface. Merlin pretended that it rejected him, too, but he later told Fiona that he could have walked it if he had wanted to.

During King Random's reign, Fiona stayed more frequently in Amber, but she also maintained contacts in her mother's shadow in the south. When Merlin trumped in with Bill Roth, she joined them for dinner, having just arrived "from some distant locale." (TD, 118) Feeling the energies that Merlin was working with in his quarters after dinner, she offered to help him while he trumped to shadow Earth. Initially, she simply observed Merle's movements through the Trump he had drawn, but then she joined him there. When Merle showed her a photograph of his friend, Luke Raynard, Fiona reacted roughly. She didn't reveal her thoughts to him, but she saw the resemblance between Luke and his father, Brand. She absented herself from Amber once more, this time taking Bleys with her. She had communicated her fear to Bleys that Brand's son was willing to murder them to take revenge for his father's death.

While away from Amber, Fiona became curious,

then concerned, about the increasing incidence of Shadow-storms in a number of shadows. She contacted Merlin about her concerns, because she believed that Corwin's Pattern was the causative agent. It was in that communication with Merlin that he introduced her to his older stepbrother Mandor. Both Fiona and Mandor evidenced an interest in the other. After she showed them a strangely unchanging tornado, she and Mandor decided to join together to investigate the various phenomena that she was puzzling over.

After pursuing their investigations, which included a meeting with Merlin's artificial construct, Ghostwheel, Fiona and Mandor concluded that waves of turbulence were indeed emanating outward from Corwin's Pattern. When Mandor renewed Trump contact with Merlin shortly afterward, he indicated that he was less worried over their findings than Fiona had been. When Merlin told him he didn't have time to discuss the new Pattern, Mandor replied: "Sorry. No rush. I'll check back." (SC, 115) It may have been that Mandor was less concerned because he knew more about the conditions at the poles than Fiona had.

In a dream-spell induced by Suhuy, Merlin communicated with an image of Fiona. She told Merlin that Corwin's Pattern was part of an imbalance of forces that was affecting all the shadows. The new Pattern had become a major factor in escalating the hostilities between the Powers of the Logrus and the Pattern. Her research confirmed that the turmoil they faced was greater than any consequence of local politics.

FIRE ANGEL

A highly intelligent predator indigenous to the realm of Chaos. Even in the domain of the Courts of Chaos, a Fire Angel is a rare sight. The Fire Angel's great strength, supernormal perceptual abilities, and near-indestructibility, make him a creature to avoid even among the lords of Chaos.

At full development, the Fire Angel achieves a length of between ten and thirteen feet. Ranging in color from coppery brown to magenta, it has coarse short fur and is multilimbed. A dozen or so legs support its long frame, increasing in length from tail to head so that the limbs nearest its head extend to several feet in length. In this way, the Fire Angel can hold itself nearly upright at will, which it does to show its formidability to a prey prior to attacking. In this mannerism of stretching and raising itself to its fullest length and height just before pouncing on its victim, it resembles the praying mantis.

Aside from its powerful multiclaws and terrible ripping jaws, it has the power of flight. When it extends its wingspan, the Fire Angel seems to triple its massive width. The wings are beautiful to behold. They appear thin and membranous, magnificently various in coloration, but they are tough and fully functional. The full force of a wing against a man would be sufficient to squash him.

In the wilds of Chaos, the Fire Angel uses all of its considerable skills to hunt and kill for food. It fears no other creature, and it senses prey with perceptions beyond those of human ken. Very few Chaos lords have survived the capturing alive of such a beast. Once captured, a Fire Angel is so terribly ferocious it will tear to shreds or devour anything placed before it in its sealed enclosure. Such an enclosure must be made of solid glass, yards-thick, in a circular fashion so that the Fire Angel will be unable to get a grip on any part of it. Cages of metal are useless because the Fire Angel can gnaw through the thickest metals. Air must be pumped into the enclosure from a glass tubing hidden in the top of the enclosure.

Only after years of such confinement, with only a liquid diet to sustain it, will it begin to give a captor its respect—but never, fully, its trust. The training of a Fire Angel takes considerable patience, courage, and skill. There are basically two stages to such training, which has as its goal only one objective: to track and kill a specific target.

The first stage is to domesticate the Fire Angel to the extent that it will not immediately attack and kill its captor upon release. A system of award-and-deprivation must be arranged to wean it from its natural instincts and instill a desired behavior. To do this, the Chaos lord must prepare a Chaos-grown shadow of himself, and usually several. The Shadow-lord resembles the original in every way with one exception: the shadow is infused with a poisonous toxin that will make the Fire Angel ill without causing any permanent harm. The Shadow-lord is placed in the enclosure with the Fire Angel to meet his ignominious death, usually screaming in agony to his last breath. As cruel as this may seem, it must be remembered that in such close proximity, the Chaos lord

himself will feel his shadow's death throes, a necessary consequence of the process. After devouring the Shadow-image two or three times, the Fire Angel will have learned a distinct distaste for this specific Chaos lord. The Fire Angel will then be rewarded with fresh, untainted meat of the kind it usually enjoys.

The second stage of its training can then begin. While the Chaos lord allows the beast incremental freedom of movement, he rewards it by feeding it Shadow-images of the being he wishes it to hunt. As the Chaos lord does this, he weans the Fire Angel from other sources of nutrition by use of a milder, but still-distasteful, toxin. Thus, the Fire Angel learns to accept the targeted Shadow-image as its primary staple. Over this same gradual period of time, the Chaos lord has come into closer physical proximity with the beast, until beast and master have formed a definite bond. A lord of lesser temerity may resort to using a Shadow-image at this stage rather than risk himself.

When the Chaos lord has complete confidence in his mastery over the Fire Angel, and the beast has totally acquired an instinctual urge to hunt for the targeted prey, it will act with absolute dedication. It will hunt and destroy the target, and then return to the Chaos lord, or die in the attempt.

The Fire Angel that Merlin reported encountering in the Lewis Carroll bar was no doubt trained in just this way. Merlin's half brother Jurt had paid a good price to a Chaos lord to have one track Merlin. There are only three, or perhaps four, living Chaos lords who are known to have mastery over a Fire Angel. It is uncertain what Jurt could have offered one of them that would give him enough incentive to train a Fire Angel to target Merlin, but it was likely more than mere money. Although the expense to Jurt may have been great, he seemed not to be depending only on the Fire Angel to rid himself of his half brother. Still, he must have felt the use of a Fire Angel highly worthwhile.

Once the Fire Angel had been fully accustomed to a diet of Shadow-Merlins, it was apparently released to begin tracking the genuine article. Although unable to walk through Shadow on its own, the Fire Angel uses its superior sensory powers to seek out the merest trace of a trail taken by its targeted prey. When it has sensed this trace, it can build a sort of tunnel for itself through Shadow and follow the trail no matter how distant and convoluted in Shadow it may be. Its finding Merlin in that "Alice in Wonderland" bar with Luke was, in all likelihood, mere chance. It would certainly have gotten to Merlin's location, wherever that would be, sooner or later.

Since a Fire Angel is nearly impervious to harm, Merlin's fleeing with Luke's unconscious body was a wise decision. The Fire Angel's natural body armor prevents any kind of penetration, and its ferocity makes it an extremely dangerous foe under any circumstances. Its three huge pumping hearts give it quickness and add to its strength.

In fact, when Merlin was finally forced to stand and fight the Fire Angel, he took the only strategy that could conceivably have succeeded against such a creature. Ordinary weapons would be of no avail, but a blade that was magical and had proven itself previously against other magical beasts, would be a necessary means of pursuing the death of a Fire Angel. Merlin had the use of the Vorpal Sword, which he obtained from the Cat in the Lewis Carroll bar. Even the Vorpal Sword would not penetrate the body armor of the Fire Angel, but Merlin used it to hack off the many appendages of the beast. In doing so, Merlin had found the weak points in the Fire Angel's construction. If Merlin had not worked so quickly to disable the beast, it would have used its intelligence to divert him and use some other strategy. Merlin's swiftness in detaching its limbs and large extensors were the main factors in Merlin's victory. Even so, Merlin realized the necessity of destroying the beast utterly by slicing deeply into its braincase with the magic sword. After it was decapitated, the Fire Angel continued to make clicking sounds, and the body twisted wildly, some remaining limbs clawing aimlessly at the air. With a sense of repulsion, Merlin hacked away at the remains of the beast until nothing was left moving. Only then did Merlin feel safe from the Fire Angel.

Although Fire Angels frequently hunt in pairs, a captured one will usually signal its partner to escape rather than aid in a rescue attempt. After a period of several months, the free member of the pair will give up his partner in a continuing quest for game.

FIRE GATE

A way exchange in Shadow near the Courts of Chaos.

Merlin of the Courts was sent there by the new Pattern created by his father when Merlin had asked it to send him to the Courts. The Pattern was unwilling to transport him all the way, and so it settled on this seemingly isolated spot. Those who know how to travel the Ways, however, are able to locate means of passing into the proper shadows to reach the Courts.

In his journals, Merlin describes Fire Gate and his knowledge of Ways for completing his trek:

> "It [Corwin's Pattern] delivered me to a high promontory of white stone beneath a black sky, beside a black sea. Two semicircles of pale flame parenthesized my position. Okay, I could live with that. I was at Fire Gate . . . I faced the sea and counted. When I'd located the fourteenth flickering tower on my left, I walked toward it.
>
> I emerged before a fallen tower beneath a pink sky. Walking toward it, I was transported to a glassy cavern through which a green river flowed. I paced beside the river till I found the stepping-stones that took me to a trail through an autumn wood. I followed this for almost a mile till I felt the presence of a way near the base of an evergreen. This took me to the side of a mountain, whence three more ways and two filmies had me on the trail to lunch with my mother." (PC, 94–95)

Our interest may be drawn by the fact that this was the farthest point that Corwin's Pattern was willing to reach toward the Chaos realm.

FIRST UNICORNIAN CHURCH OF KASHFA

The largest church within the capital city of Jidrash in Kashfa. It is located across the main plaza from the palace, inside a central walled sector of the city that is surrounded by two other concentric walls of protection that form the larger city.

As in Amber, the Way of the Unicorn is the chief religion of the Kashfans. However, the ritual and religious reverence are much more integrated into the daily lives of the Kashfans, as evidenced by the importance placed on the First Unicornian Church by locating it within the center of security of the defending walls of the city. The citizenry spend much time in the Unicorn Church. Blessings are given to products, animals, crafts, and other salable items before going to market. Children are brought for blessings at certain periods in their lives on a regular basis. New life and recent death are observed with great care within that grand structure.

Kashfa is a shadow kingdom near enough to the true city to recognize the eminent domain of the unicorn. The mystical powers of some of its people are real enough so that the Kashfans understand and revere the great forces of the supernatural world that influence their lives. These people of the Way feel such a closeness to the sources of creation in the true city that their beliefs are guided by similar objects of worship.

Merlin of Amber had occasion to attend the coronation ceremony of King Rinaldo I and his bride, Queen Coral, there. According to Merlin's journals, however, he was unwillingly involved in a sacrilegious gesture on the part of a half brother from the Courts of Chaos while meeting privately with Rinaldo in the House of the Unicorn. King Rinaldo, familiarly called Luke by Merlin, had concluded a brief talk with Merlin about his political status among the Amberites, when Jurt of the Courts suddenly appeared. Initially, Jurt intended to fight and murder his half brother, but he became interested in obtaining a special sword with mystical attributes in Luke's possession. Willing to fight Luke/King Rinaldo for the sword, Jurt said, "I'll even take a certain pleasure in bloodying a Unicorn shrine" (KS, 247). Merlin was able to drive Jurt away, using his remarkable sources of supernatural energy, but his half brother took Luke's mystical sword as he escaped. In the process of battling Merlin and Luke in the church, Jurt had even threatened the life of a woman in prayer, although she was not what she seemed.

Since Merlin had been closer to the center of things than most Kashfans, he described the ceremony crowning his friend in the Unicorn Church with a somewhat less than reverent eye. Herein, in part, are Merlin's caustic comments about the coronation:

> . . . a procession, with a lot of slow music, and uncomfortable, colorful garb, incense, speeches, prayers, the ringing of bells. . . .

And so Luke and Coral became the sover-

eigns of Kashfa, in the same church where we'd fought almost—but, unfortunately, not quite—to the death with my mad brother Jurt but a few hours before. As Amber's only representative at the event—albeit of, technically, unofficial status—I was accorded a ringside standing-place, and eyes were often drifting my way. So I had to keep alert and mouth appropriate responses. . . .

So I wound up with hurting feet, a stiff neck, and colorful garments soaked with sweat. (PC, 1–2)

Although Merlin may not have seemed to share in the solemnity of the moment, the majority of Kashfans who participated very likely felt an inspiring presence in him as they performed their worship.

FLORA

Daughter of the late King Oberon of Amber and the Lady Dybele, who died giving birth to her. When her brother Eric had begun his rule in the absence of her father, Flora had already spent centuries on shadow Earth. For much of that time, she had been watching her amnesiac brother Corwin. During the time of King Random's reign, Flora was assigned to return to shadow Earth to investigate a warehouse of weaponry that might have been intended for an attack against Amber.

Flora, also called Florimel, was a striking young woman with clear blue eyes and fiery red hair, which she often wore in bangs over her forehead. Often dressed in green or lavender colors, she enjoyed many male relationships. She traveled frequently in Shadow, consorting with noblemen and the well-to-do. Although she was a sometime companion to the renowned artist Dante Gabriel Rossetti of shadow Earth, she refused his offers to paint her.

Always used to living lavishly, of being taken care of by the men in her sphere, Flora was apolitical, except where she could advance her own self-interest. She was fascinated by art and history, and while living on shadow Earth, had gathered an impressive collection of valuable editions in both areas of study. Supremely self-confident, flirtatious, and curious-minded, she probably leaned upon men for support in a not fully realized need for security. While she may have seemed to bend to the flow of the wind, she also appeared to have hidden reserves of her own to fall back on.

Flora's distaste for the political maneuverings going on in Amber after the odd disappearance of Corwin urged her to seek solace in other shadows. That is what brought her to shadow Earth in its eighteenth century, when she settled upon the country of France. She later told Corwin:

> "I had been wandering, looking for something novel, something that suited my fancy. I came upon that place at that time in the same way we find anything. I let my desires lead me and I followed my instincts. . . .
>
> ". . . It was, if you like, my Avalon, my Amber surrogate, my home away from home."
> (SU, 58–59)

Paris in the mid-eighteenth century was perfect for Flora. Her allure and remarkable charms attracted many a romantic Parisian, and she loved its cosmopolitan milieu. She found it delightful to attend the numerous parties. She moved with easy grace among the elite and the influential.

At a party in the home of Monsieur Focault one October evening in 1790, Flora discovered her long-lost brother, Corwin. He acted as if he did not know her, and he introduced himself as Cordell Fenneval. After questioning his consort and, afterward, several other of Fenneval's acquaintances, Flora came to the conclusion that he was indeed her brother. She spoke of her meeting Corwin with Eric when she visited Amber in the summer of 1791, Earth-time. Eric assigned Flora to return to shadow Earth and keep Corwin under surveillance. In exchange, Eric offered her a favored place in Amber when he came to power.

Although Flora did continue her watch, she resumed her rather carefree life as well. Others of the Royal Family visited Flora while she resided in Paris, but she was not always enchanted by their company. She spoke of one family member in particular:

> "I'd made no secret of my whereabouts. In fact, all of them came around to visit me at one time or another." [Including Random.] . . .

> "It is too late to start pretending I like him. . . . You know. I just don't like the people he associates with—assorted criminals, jazz musicians. . . . I had to show him family courtesy when he was visiting my shadow, but he put a big strain on my nerves, bringing those people around at all hours—jam sessions, poker parties. The place usually reeked for weeks afterward and I was always glad to see him go." (SU, 61–62)

In contrast to Flora's disapproval of Random, she professed that Corwin was her favorite brother. Spying on Corwin as she did, or having informants reporting his activities to her, Flora had discovered a revival of her age-old fondness for him. That was why she so carefully remained in the background whenever she was observing him personally. That was also why she saw to his care when he was badly wounded in the Franco-Prussian War in 1870, while avoiding being seen by him.

Sometime after the death of Rossetti in 1882, Flora chose to abandon her spying on Corwin and lose herself in Shadow. She visited in the area of shadow Kashfa, where she met a handsome nobleman named Jasrick, Earl of Kronklef. She had seen him in a forest, where he was using a hawk in hunting game. Under the pretense of having twisted her ankle, Flora made his acquaintance. They dallied together often after that.

Receiving a Trump contact from Eric one day, Flora returned briefly to Amber. Eric told her of Corwin's new name, Carl Corey, and said he was anxious that Corwin might be regaining his memory. Flora assured him that she would soon return to shadow Earth and resume her observation of him.

When Flora returned to Kashfa, she found that Jasrick had been seduced by the old king's consort, a lady named Jasra. Although she maintained hard feelings for Jasra, she was rather deprecating of Jasrick. According to her account:

> "He was chief of the palace guard and his brother was a general. She [Jasra] used them to pull off a coup when [King] Menillan expired. Last I heard, she was queen in Kashfa and she'd ditched Jasrick. Served him proper, I'd say. I think he had his eye on the throne, but she didn't care to share it. She had him and his brother executed for treason of one sort

or another. He was really a handsome fellow. . . . Not too bright, though.'' (BA, 18)

While Flora followed Corwin in his various European travels, sometimes losing him, but then picking up his trail, she also spent time in Amber. This accounts for her being able to discuss having first-hand knowledge of shadow invasions when Oberon still ruled. She spoke of these matters to Corwin on a later occasion:

''We have always been alert for peculiar things slipping through. Well, for several years prior to your recovery, more such things than usual seemed to be showing up in the vicinity of Amber. Dangerous things, almost invariably. Many were recognizable creatures from nearby realms. After a time, though, things kept coming in from farther and farther afield. Eventually, some which were totally unknown made it through. No reason could be found for this sudden transportation of menaces, although we sought fairly far for disturbances which might be driving them this way.'' (SU, 104)

In the mid-twentieth century, Carl Corey left Europe to take up residence in New York State. Eric supplied Flora with funds and other means to continue her surveillance nearby. She took on the name Evelyn Flaumel, purchased a luxurious home in Westchester, hired a maid, and bought six well-trained Irish wolfhounds to keep about the house. With Eric's help, Flora was able to become well connected in the community. She was soon known as a wealthy patron of the arts.

Because Eric was becoming worried about Corwin's returning memory, Flora watched Corwin very closely while he lived there. On at least one occasion, she entered his home while he was out. She discovered some scribbled notes of names. Some were people he had met in New York, but others were the names of his family in Amber. The name Corwin was listed as one among them. Flora made a copy of these notes to show to Eric, then returned them to Corwin's study.

Eric was uncertain of his next steps, but he felt the need to do something to keep Corwin from remembering. Flora and Eric made some preliminary arrangements with a private sanitarium. The administrators were grateful for a large donation made by

Mrs. Evelyn Flaumel. When she mentioned that a need might arise to admit a close relative and keep him sedated discreetly, they obsequiously agreed.

Before Flora and Eric could act, however, another party intervened. Flora was used to Corwin's going away for a day or two at a time, so she didn't concern herself when Corwin vanished for a couple of days. She learned something was amiss from Eric, when he contacted her by Trump. Eric told her that Fiona had communicated with him, saying that Corwin had been in a serious automobile accident and was hospitalized.

As Evelyn Flaumel, Flora found it relatively easy to transfer Corwin from a city hospital to Greenwood Private Hospital. The doctors and nurses there had strict orders to keep the patient sedated and out of contact with any other people.

Flora was very much surprised when, two weeks later, Corwin came to her Westchester home. Masking her consternation, she addressed him with self-assurance, obliquely trying to ascertain how much he was aware of. Although she parried Corwin well as they exchanged pieces of information, she unintentionally permitted her vulnerability to show. When he invoked the earlier enchantment of their Amber, she broke into tears. She said, ''Corwin . . . if you do make it—if by some wild and freakish chance out of Shadow you should make it—will you remember your little sister Florimel?'' (NP, 24)

When their talk had concluded, Flora left Corwin to retire in the room prepared for him. She tried contacting Eric by Trump, but she couldn't make the connection. Leaving in the morning, she attempted to shift shadows, walking from Earth toward Amber. She found her passage hampered by strange beasts and oddly shaped formations. Unable to prevail, she returned to shadow Earth.

Shortly thereafter, Random had joined them, claiming to have pursuers who would arrive shortly. When they did, they did not make introductions. They were strange men out of Shadow who, armed with pistols, broke into her home. As Random and Corwin began to fight them, Flora called her six wolfhounds to the attack. Once the men were dispatched, Corwin, Random, and Flora had a closer look at them. They were from a shadow other than Earth. Their hands and teeth had features that were distinctly different from any the three of them had seen before. Flora insisted that these men had not been sent by Eric.

Random disposed of the bodies and made the necessary repairs to the room in which they had fought. Flora was glad that Random and Corwin left the next morning, even though she had reluctantly lent Random her Mercedes. She suspected that she would never see it again.

Bending to the direction of the wind, Flora remained in Eric's favor while he was in power. She attended Eric's coronation banquet, watching the actions of her brother Corwin, captive and in chains. She was silently aloof during the time she knew that Corwin's eyes were burned from their sockets and he was kept in a dungeon. She continued to be calmly obeisant to Eric, but she was never taken completely into his confidence.

When fortunes changed, Flora continued unscorched. With the death of Eric, and Corwin's ascendancy, she maintained the same imperious manner she had always had. When Corwin questioned her about her role in that former period on shadow Earth, she responded with composure. Even when the Family gathered in the library, and during the subsequent events of Brand's rescue, Flora was quietly attentive but restrained. She helped in obtaining the needed medical supplies for Brand, but she revealed nothing of her true sentiment. For the moment, as was appropriate, she was the dutiful sister.

The Chronicles of Corwin note that Flora was in the Patternfall battle. She stood beside Llewella within a band of archers. They took down many a Chaos soldier with their arrows. No doubt she observed the great image of Oberon in the sky, the deaths of Brand and Deirdre, and the magnificent procession of creatures honoring the late king of Amber. In all likelihood, she was helping in the "mopping-up" of the field of battle when the unicorn appeared to the others on the heights.

Once again, the winds of change blew, and Flora bent in their direction. She spent much time in court under the kingship of Random, ingratiating herself with her little brother. In many ways, the stress of the past had been lifted, and she took on this new renascence with gusto.

She was ebullient when she greeted Corwin's son and Bill Roth upon their arrival in the Royal Palace. Random gladly relinquished Mr. Roth into her custody so that he could speak privately with his nephew. In the course of their discussion, Random decided to send Flora back to shadow Earth on a special mission. He assigned her to go to San Francisco to investigate Brutus Storage Company. Merlin had just returned from that area with news that a supply of special ammunition that could fire in Amber had been stored there. Random wanted Flora to learn who the owner was and what connections there might be between Brutus Storage and Amber. Before leaving on this mission, Flora spoke to Merlin confidentially. She was concerned about Bleys, who seemed to have trumped away from his locked apartment without telling anyone. She also insisted on hearing about the recent dangers that Merlin had been involved in while he resided in San Francisco. Given the nature of Flora's assignment to that place, Merlin obliged.

Merlin made an urgent Trump contact with Flora at a most-inopportune time. She was allowing a dark-haired man named Ron to romance her while they were in bed. When she started bringing Merlin through to them, Ron was quite alarmed. His alarm was not quelled when Flora sat up and solidly punched the image of a female that had formed in the air. Merlin fell heavily onto the bed, and Ron quickly got up, gathered up his garments, and beat a hasty retreat.

Flora was living in a small French Provincial home in San Francisco. She learned something more about Brutus Storage Company, but the information led to a virtual dead end. Brutus Storage was owned by J.B. Rand in Sausalito, California. The office had been vacated, and the only address for the renters had been a post office box, which was no longer in use. Nevertheless, Flora liked the San Francisco area and decided to stay after reporting her findings to Random.

While Merlin stayed with her, Flora told him what she knew of Jasra, the woman at the other end of the Trump contact whom she had struck. After a rather strange communication with a disembodied voice that left a barrage of flowers in its wake, Flora offered to help Merlin by driving him to his former girlfriend's apartment. Flora's curiosity had been piqued. Any occurrence that hinted at an otherworldly presence was intriguing in the seemingly mundane reality of shadow Earth. Since Merlin's old girlfriend had been killed by a beast that did not belong in that shadow, Flora wanted to aid in investigating the source.

When Merlin began the process of making both himself and Flora invisible before entering the apartment, Flora revealed something from her childhood. "Dworkin did it for me once, when I was a child. Spied on a lot of people then. . . . I'd forgotten." (BA, 29)

In the apartment, Merlin found something unique. He extended his Logrus vision so that Flora could also see what he saw. It was the remnants of a doorway that led to some other shadow. Before attempting to reopen the portal, Merlin gave Flora these instructions: "Go back to the car and wait. Give me an hour. If I'm not out by then, get in touch with Random, tell him everything I told you and tell him about this, too." (BA, 32) He also suggested that she contact Fiona. Because of Fiona's particular occult abilities, she might have another way of fathoming the mysterious doorway. Flora agreed and left Merlin to pursue the matter on his own.

Flora did as was required of her. She used his Trump to contact Random in Amber. She explained what Merlin had been doing, and identified Luke Raynard as Rinaldo, son of Brand. She saw that Random was eased by this knowledge, and she concluded the contact.

Apparently, Flora was extending her visit on shadow Earth. Much later, when Prime Minister Orkuz led a delegation from Begma to the Royal Palace in Amber, she was unreachable by Trump. Perhaps she had used her allure to recapture Ron of the dark hair. Or, just as likely, she was in the company of a wealthy young man seeking solace from the mundane.

FOCAULT, MICHEL JEAN-LOUIS

Procureur general to the *parlement* of Paris, France on the shadow Earth and *surintendant des finances* under King Louis XVI. Monsieur Focault was also a renowned patron of the arts famous for his elegant parties to which the wealthy and the celebrated came together. Princess Florimel of Amber (using an assumed name) discovered her long-lost brother Corwin at one of Monsieur Focault's lavish gatherings.

Michel Focault was born to a well-to-do farming family at Herouel on June 10, 1746, A.D. shadow Earth-time. He studied law while he was employed as a clerk in a procurator's office in Paris. In 1771, he had saved enough to buy his employer's law practice. He soon established himself as a successful and highly respected lawyer. After marrying a cousin with a large dowry, Focault became the tenant of a large apartment in the Rue Bourbon-Villeneuve and a villa in Charonne.

His accumulated wealth, as well as his reputation, enabled him to purchase the post of *procureur* of Paris in 1782. By 1786, Focault had come under the notice of King Louis XVI, and he received the position of *surintendant des finances* a year later. In this position, he became involved in the French government's foreign trade and made the acquaintance of numerous men of great influence.

As a patron of the arts, he often gave parties at his villa which brought together influential people in the political arena with those celebrated in the arts and sciences.

Flora of Amber had been spending several years in Paris and became acquainted with Focault's wife. Consequently, she was invited to a number of these parties given by Focault, more often at his country villa than in his Paris apartments. In October of 1790, during one of these celebrations at the villa in Charonne, Flora noticed a youthful man in handsome dress who closely resembled her brother, whom she had believed to be dead. With appropriate coyness, Flora contrived to have Madame Focault introduce her to the young man, who was escorting a redheaded girl who seemed hardly out of her teenage years. Madame Focault introduced the girl as Jacqueline Michelet and the man as Cordell Fenneval. In her conversation with Fenneval, Flora was unable to determine if he was actually her brother, or merely a remarkable look-alike, or perhaps a shadow version of Corwin that was an extension of Corwin's existence in a similar shadow. She persisted in seeking the truth, and she described her activities to Corwin centuries later:

"I might have departed still wondering had not Jacqueline later boasted to me concerning your strength. Now this is not the commonest subject of conversation for a woman, and the way in which she said it led me to believe that she had actually been quite impressed by some things you had done. I drew her out a bit and realized that they were all of them feats of which you were capable. . . . I began keeping track of you then, checking into your past. The more people I questioned, the more puzzling it became. In fact, after several months I was still unable to decide." (SU, 59–60)

Flora's suspicions were confirmed by Eric, who ruled in Amber, when she visited the following summer. Eric told her that it was possible that Corwin was alive, after surviving a terrible plague a century earlier on the shadow Earth. Eric admitted that he had placed Corwin there, in a place called London, England, after beating him senseless. He had hoped that Corwin would die in that infested region. After receiving this disclosure, Flora agreed to keep Fenneval under close watch in exchange for a high position in Amber under Eric's reign.

Monsieur and Madame Focault continued to live in luxury until the afternoon of January 21, 1793. He and his family had been arrested by officers of the Revolutionary Tribunal several days before. On the twenty-first, he was brought to the guillotine and executed. His wife and children followed. On that same morning, King Louis XVI had been executed.

Among the people Flora recalled meeting at Monsieur Focault's party in October 1790 were the artist Jacques-Louis David, the prominent scientist Lavoisier, young James Watt, son of the English inventor of the same name, and the Marquis de Condorcet, who fled the Reign of Terror, wrote his famous philosophical work, *Progress of the Human Mind,* while in hiding, and committed suicide shortly afterward.

FRAKIR

A sentient, magical cord that Merlin wears on his left wrist. Merlin thought of Frakir as a feminine entity, which remained invisible most of the time. She warned him of the proximity of something dangerous by the motion of tightening and releasing pressure on his wrist. When Merlin found himself wandering in a strange realm of negative images, Frakir was able to communicate telepathically with him, having been enhanced by the Logrus.

Back in the Courts of Chaos, Merlin walked the great Power there, the Logrus. He tried it unaided,

although he had been given training by his uncle, Suhuy, Master of the Logrus. Upon completing the Logrus, Merlin found his uncle standing nearby:

"I had not judged you ready to essay the Logrus for a long while yet."

He [Merlin] closed his eyes against this speaker, and an image of the route he had followed danced within his mind's seeing, like a bright, torn web folding in a breeze.

". . . And a fool not to have borne a blade and so enchanted it—or a mirror, a chalice or a wand to brace your magic. No, all I see is a piece of rope. You should have waited, for more instructions, for greater strength. What say you?"

He raised himself from the floor and a mad light danced within his eyes.

"It was time," he said. "I was ready."

"And a cord! What a half-ass—Uck!"

The cord, glowing now, tightened about his throat.

When the other released it, the dark one coughed and nodded.

"Perhaps—you knew—what you were doing—on that count . . ." it muttered. (TD, UNDERWOOD-MILLER, X–XI)

Frakir was a faithful, if imperfect, companion to Merlin. Sometimes, she would pulse on Merlin's wrist when he was unable to detect any immediate danger, as when Merlin traveled by bus from Albuquerque to Santa Fe in New Mexico. On the other hand, she was indispensable in assisting him when under physical attack. In the Harbor District of Amber, Merlin was surrounded by a group of well-trained assassins intent on making him their victim. He enlisted Frakir's aid:

With a shuffling noise and a great cry a man leaped from the roof to the street before me. His shout was apparently the signal to the archer, also, for there was immediate movement at the corner of the building, accompanied by the sounds of rapid footfalls from the building's other corner, to my rear.

Before his feet even struck the ground I had cast Frakir at the man from the roof with a command to kill. And I was rushing the archer before he had even rounded the corner completely, my blade already swinging. . . .

. . . As I riposted to his chest and had my own cut parried I became peripherally aware of the one from the roof kneeling now in the street and tearing at his throat, in evidence that Frakir was doing her job. (BA, 70–71)

Other abilities that the loyal entity exhibited were: transforming money in Merlin's hand to the proper currency for the shadow he was in (TD, 55); forming a track in Merlin's finger so that he could readily remove a ring (TD, 67); elongating into a fine but unbreakable thread wrapped about crystalline branches to protect Merlin within its shelter (TD, 164); and, detaining the sorceress Jasra from trumping away by anchoring her to a tree branch (BA, 14).

Frakir proved herself to be especially useful to Merlin when he found himself in a strange region between Shadows that was called the Undershadow. Within that realm, no sound could be heard. Merlin decided to call up the Sign of the Logrus to enable him to leave the Undershadow. Frakir pulsed her warning signal urgently on his wrist. Looking all about him, Merlin could find no reason for Frakir's warning. He summoned up the Logrus again and was knocked into unconsciousness. After recovering, he was still in the Undershadow, but he discovered that Frakir was able to speak to him telepathically. The Logrus that Merlin had called up could insinuate its presence in that place of negative Shadow for only a moment. In that time, it had enhanced Frakir's understanding and communication skills.

Frakir was given the knowledge that the Logrus and the Pattern were currently working in conflict with one another, seeking a means of touching Merlin in the Undershadow. The realm blocked the presence of either Power. Nevertheless the two Powers were attempting to influence Merlin to choose one of them over the other.

During this time, Merlin received all of this information from his special companion. An exchange between Merlin and Frakir serves to illustrate the quaintness of the feminine entity's newly acquired ability:

Sense anything alive in the neighborhood? I asked Frakir.

No, came the answer.
Thought I saw something move.
Maybe you did. Doesn't mean it's there.
Talking for less than a day, and you've already learned sarcasm.
I hate to say it, boss, but anything I learn I pick up from your vibes. Ain't no one else around to teach me manners and like that.
Touché, I said. *Maybe I'd better warn you if there's trouble.*
Touché, boss. Hey, I like these combat metaphors. (KS, 91)

When Merlin entered a chamber bearing the imperfect likeness of the Pattern in Amber and began walking it, Frakir lost her telepathic skills, apparently reverting to her initial enhancement.

Later, when Merlin located, in Brand's room in the Royal Palace, a unique ring that drew upon a high magnitude of power, he felt compelled to wear it. Frakir immediately sent out her warning to him. For some reason, Merlin was oblivious to Frakir's signal at first. Finally, he responded, and the following odd situation evolved:

"Sorry you lost your voice, old girl," I said, stroking her as I explored the room for threats both psychic and physical. "I can't find a damned thing here that I should be worried about."
Immediately she spiraled down from my wrist and tried to remove the ring from my finger.
"Stop!" I ordered. "I know the ring could be dangerous. But only if you use it wrongly. I'm a sorcerer, remember? I'm into these matters. There is nothing special about it for me to fear."
But Frakir disobeyed my order and continued her attack on the ring, which I could now only attribute to some form of magical artifact jealousy. I tied her in a tight knot around the bedpost and left her there, to teach her a lesson. (KS, 233)

It seems like ingratitude of the first order for Merlin to abandon his loyal companion in that way. No doubt he was already coming under the influence of the ring's great power.

No one has checked in any deliberate fashion in

Brand's room. It is presumed that Frakir remains there, tied firmly about the bedpost. Unless Merlin returns for her, it seems unlikely that she would allow anyone else's handling anyway.

GANELON

An outlaw and military man whom Lord Corwin had met while ruling in the shadow named Avalon. We know of the real Ganelon from inference as much as from description in the Chronicles of Corwin. Centuries after the fall of Avalon, Corwin met a man resembling Ganelon, going by that name, in the village of Lorraine.

Ganelon was born in Avalon, an accidental and unwanted offspring of well-to-do parents. His mother had him late in life, and his father was considerably older. When they died, Ganelon received a large fortune, which he squandered in a brief span on wenches and gambling. Used to the high life, and unable to obtain credit for his excesses when his inheritance went dry, he turned to robbery. Dressing in black and wearing a wide-brimmed hat low over his brow and dark bandanna over his face, he halted travelers on the roads between villages, took coin and jewelry, and left his victims stranded without their horses. The masked bandit became known for his ruthlessness. He murdered several waylaid victims when he discovered they were holding back on valuable gems.

After working alone for some time, Ganelon came across a loosely organized band of outlaws living day to day on petty thieveries. Most of these men were little more than pickpockets and purse snatchers. Quickly taking control, Ganelon soon advanced the band from perpetrating minor thefts among people in crowded streets to performing complex acts of wholesale robbery, increasing their revenue immensely.

His cleverness and spreading notoriety led to the placing of a price on the heads of the outlaw band. The price put on Ganelon's head was greater than any of the others. Ganelon cared nothing for politics, but he had sent members of his band into various towns to learn what they could of local dealings, the better to plan their enterprises.

Ganelon was adept with a dagger, and he made

his drinking money by stealthily entering a village by night, walking quietly up to lone men heading for the local night spot, and slitting their throats before they could let out a cry. He was brazen enough to spend nights in such places, using his victims' money on drinks and card-playing.

In the early dawn of one such occasion, as Ganelon sauntered along a dark street in a pleasant alcoholic stupor, he was attacked by five or six men. Someone in the pub had noticed Ganelon's ring and recognized it as having belonged to a deceased relative. This person gathered up a few sympathetic friends, and they followed Ganelon out, awaiting the proper opportunity. Knives were in hand, but even drunk Ganelon wielded his dagger with skill. When the murderous group left him, Ganelon was bleeding from several deep cuts, and his face was swollen with the pounding of fists. Although he was left destitute, the attackers refrained from killing him only because one of their number was badly wounded himself.

By some accounts, Ganelon dragged himself into a safe hiding place outside of town. When he recovered, rejoining his band, he remained outwardly wild, but there were times when others noted a strange quiet in him, and something akin to fear passing momentarily in his eyes.

Ganelon became a more wary planner, and he sometimes expressed concerns about the rebelliousness growing among people in the land. He hadn't encountered any of the horrible monsters reportedly ravaging villagers, but he wondered about them. In his usual mood, he wouldn't have cared a grain about citizens murdered in their beds, but the villagers' reactions were impinging on his business. Travelers on the road had become less willing to allow common thieves to take their possessions without a fight. Rabble-rousers who stirred the people up against an inept authority on village streets also promoted a fearlessness against other forms of victimization. Times were poor for Ganelon and his men.

Dour of demeanor, Ganelon allowed his whiskers to grow with careless abandon into a full, reddish beard. Hunger made him gaunt, and the coldness of winter made him reckless and unheeding of others. One frigid night when he was far from his cohorts, Ganelon forced an acquaintanceship with a man wearing warm boots. They disappeared around the corner of a drinking place, and Ganelon reappeared alone, wearing dark leather boots that were fur-lined.

He and his men survived the winter, but pickings remained poor. Villagers and travelers moved about in daylight fully armed, and at night, none were about at all. Some of Ganelon's men reported sightings of strange forms wandering isolated roads, a few of these very close to town. On more than one occasion, he noted that trusted and fearless comrades he had sent on errands never returned.

Word of a growing rebellion among the villagers of Avalon and neighboring towns was brought back to Ganelon. At first, he shrugged off such reports as having nothing to do with him. On an ensuing night, however, he found his own life in danger from marauding villagers threatening any strangers with clubs, tools, and knives. He was traveling with a small number of his outlaw band, intent on acquiring ready currency, when they nearly ran into the foraging townspeople. Taking to the trees and bushes in hopes of making an ambush, Ganelon saw the need to forgo the attempt. The villagers tore through the brush, overturning rocks and uprooting tree stumps. They spoke among themselves about seeking out monsters and wiping them out. Some of these men talked of the incompetence of Avalon's ruler, and that the "mighty lord" in his steel tower should receive the same treatment. Ganelon and his men hastily withdrew, stealthily wandering back to their encampment.

Earlier fears and increasing foment among the citizenry prevented Ganelon and his men from plying their trade. Weeks passed, and Ganelon grew impatient with hunger and self-doubt. His men refused to leave their hovel, refused even to forage for sustenance. A couple of his bolder men chided him openly, daring him to go to the town himself to learn the course of events.

He struck these brasher underlings into quietude, but he chose to leave their hiding place, announcing he would enter the village alone. As he approached Avalon, he heard the loud exclamations of a mob and the clamor of their weapons. He slipped around corners of buildings, making his way into the center of town without notice. He dodged behind a barrel here, a thick bush there, avoiding the loud scouting parties whose noise, he knew, was quite deliberate. Besides bolstering themselves with coarse talk, the angry crowds intended frightening off any dangerous intruders with the din of their number. In day-light, it seemed to be working well, since the streets were otherwise deserted.

Many shops were boarded up, and some of these had their windows broken, for glass was scattered on the dirt under the wooden planks. Seeing the ragged end of a sheet of paper flagging in the wind between the boards of one shop, Ganelon reached for it, pulled most of it out. It was a public proclamation offering full pardon to all known outlaws willing to join the governor of Avalon against the insurgents who had brought the realm into shambles. Stealthily, Ganelon took the notice back with him to his band.

The problem became resolving a means to get word to the governor that Ganelon was willing to join him with his men. Details are lacking, but somehow Ganelon sent word via agents to the lord's captain, a man renowned for his bravery, named Lancelot. In a partially hidden glade to the south of the village, Ganelon and his followers met with Lancelot and his troops. One of the horsemen, though Ganelon didn't know it at the time, was the lord of the realm, dressed as a common soldier.

The battles they fought were bloody and long, but they were victorious in putting down the rebellions. In the course of them, Ganelon fought side by side with the horseman, who proved a fierce fighter. At the drear end of one terrible battle, Ganelon learned the identity of the horseman: Corwin, Lord of Avalon, Prince of Amber.

Becoming an officer in Corwin's army, Ganelon proved himself to be a dedicated soldier and administrator of the peace. His authority became second only to Lancelot's under the governor's rule. Cabinet meetings between Lord Corwin and his staff included Ganelon, and Corwin depended on his aide's good advice.

Years of peace were maintained by the combined supervision of Lancelot and Ganelon. While Lancelot handled matters with his influence over the local militia, Ganelon patrolled the outskirts of Avalon and neighboring hamlets with a company of veteran soldiers made motley by the addition of mercenaries and former comrades in pilferage. When border wars occurred, as they often do where a piece of valuable real estate is involved, he was able to defeat the invaders, winning high praise from Lord Corwin.

At one of numerous royal banquets, Lord Corwin was feeling particularly magnanimous. He suggested the possibility that Ganelon had earned himself a place of regency over the province of Kovi in the east. Since that occasion, the lord made reference to the dukedom of Kovi several times. Ganelon was out on patrol with a company of men when a messenger arrived with an urgent message.

Ganelon was ordered back to the governor's palace. Concerned that some serious crisis had broken out, he was astonished to find that a special ceremony was hastily commencing. As Ganelon stood by in court, doubtful of the urgency of the occasion, Lord Corwin announced his imminent nuptials to the Lady Angelica, daughter of Agrican of Tartary. Corwin proceeded to proclaim that, thereafter, Lord Agrican would be appointed duke of Kovi. Ganelon was infuriated and silently stormed out.

Several weeks later, Lancelot dispatched Ganelon and his men far to the south, where mercenaries of a bordering province were stirring up trouble. Lancelot didn't know, however, that Ganelon had met clandestinely with the leader of those mercenaries prior to receiving his orders. The mercenary leader had promised Ganelon complete authority over a township in that neighboring state, once Ganelon helped him conquer Avalon. With the agreement made, Lancelot's orders couldn't have come at a more opportune time.

None of Ganelon's men knew of the agreement, and so they were not prepared for what was to come. They had thought they were riding into a contentious little hamlet on the southern border to support a local militia in settling the discontent of a group of rabble-rousers. What they walked into was a war.

The battle erupted without warning. Ganelon fell back surreptitiously. Most of his men were wiped out in the onslaught. Others scattered to the hills. Large numbers of these were killed in their retreat. They died knowing nothing of their general's treachery.

At a prearranged site, Ganelon met with the mercenary leader. With maps he carried in his saddlebags, Ganelon pointed out the best way for the marauders to travel to maintain a maximum level of surprise. He also marked several villages along the way where the mercenaries could pick up additional men willing to join such a force. Thus provided for, the marauders started off.

Ganelon followed at his leisure in the wake of the invading force. He hoped his allies would decimate Corwin's armies and have the governor in chains, or better, dead.

He was disappointed in this, though. As he neared the city, Ganelon learned that Lord Corwin was leading the main force of Avalon himself. The governor had such secret skills that he was able to defeat the invaders. The mercenaries were forced to split up and attempt flanking movements, which were, in turn, repelled and forced back. The invasion failed.

Ganelon tried to flee, but his overconfidence had brought him too near the center of the victorious army. Captured, he was brought before Lord Corwin in his court. On his knees in chains, Ganelon faced the lord governor. Corwin's face was unreadable, but he began in a conciliatory tone, speaking of showing mercy to the man he had trusted so greatly. Ganelon made the mistake of telling him to place his mercy between his legs and present it to the Lady Angelica.

With terse, short words, Lord Corwin ordered his guards to remove Ganelon's chains. As Ganelon, unfettered, slowly rose to his feet, Corwin approached him. Ganelon struck out, beating at Corwin's head with all his strength. The governor took several hits, repelled others with his arms, and swung one massive blow into Ganelon's face, his face a twisted visage of sudden fury. Ganelon fell into unconsciousness.

When he awoke, Ganelon found himself snugly tied over the bare back of an aged mare. Corwin was riding another horse alongside. His head pounding, Ganelon listened in silence while the lord governor spoke onerously of comrades long-dead and past betrayals.

When his head began to clear, Ganelon looked up, seeking any familiar landmarks in the region they rode. He saw astounding changes of ground and stone, and riverways, and crawling creatures, and strange flying beasts. The coming of nightfall suddenly kissed the noonday sun. Cracked desert lands melted into thick swamplands of unreal plant life. Ganelon knew he was far from anyplace he had ever known, that he would never find a way back to the lands of his youth. He also knew, then, that the one who led him this far was no human.

Lord Corwin slowed their horses as they reached a parched, gray land where nothing grew. There were mountains of blue slate on the distant horizon on all sides. "This is the place of your exile," Corwin told him, cutting the ropes that bound him to the mare. Ganelon slipped from the horse, rubbed his aching skull, and watched the general ride away, slowly, deliberately. Before he fell below the horizon, Corwin and his horse were suddenly gone. He left Ganelon with his saddleless horse. Ganelon found a tied packet of food and water hanging from the mare's side. After wetting his lips and taking a few bites for strength, Ganelon mounted the horse, heading for the distant mountains.

Ages later, King Oberon of Amber spoke to his son about having met this Ganelon:

> "I met him after you had exiled him from Avalon, long ago. He wasn't a bad chap. Wouldn't have trusted him worth a damn, but then I never trust anyone I don't have to. . . .
> "I regretted having to kill him. Not that he gave me much choice. All this was very long ago, but I remembered him clearly, so he must have impressed me." (CC, 27)

GANNELL, DRETHA

Assistant to Ferla Quist, ambassador of Begma.

Gannell is a rather husky, blond-haired woman. Although she is no longer very young, she seems rather ingenuous and acts in awe of Amber's royalty.

As the ambassador's assistant in the true city, Ms. Gannell handles her social calendar. It is believed that part of Ms. Gannell's duties is to entertain, or otherwise engage, callers who wish the attention of Ambassador Quist on matters either official or unofficial, but whom she would prefer to avoid. In this capacity, Dretha Gannell is quite adept.

When escorting the ambassador to the formal banquet presided over by Queen Vialle in the Royal Palace, Ms. Gannell attached herself to Lord Gérard of Amber. She knew him by reputation, and she had seen him in town infrequently, although they had never been introduced. It is uncertain whether or not Ambassador Quist had made any assignations, but Ms. Gannell knew her role readily enough that she would want to form an innocent liaison in the hope of gaining some inadvertently revealed piece of knowledge related to the current political winds.

Dretha Gannell continues to perform myriad duties at the Begman Embassy, a minor, but necessary cog in the wheels of political diplomacy.

GARRUL, SHARU

Wizard who was the earliest known master of the Keep of the Four Worlds. He had been confined in a spell of immobility by his former pupil, Jasra of Kashfa, with the aid of her husband, Brand of Amber. Sharu had been released briefly by the sorcerer dubbed Mask, in order to assist in a battle against Merlin, Mandor, and Jasra. Jasra defeated Sharu a second time and used a spell to restrict his movements, making him guardian of the Fount in the Keep.

Jasra, who had resided in the Courts of Chaos for a long while, had met Sharu and curried his favor. Becoming quite attached to Jasra, Sharu showed her many of his powers. He brought her to the Keep of the Four Worlds. Because it is at the center of four shadow worlds, the Keep is a repository of vast energies. Apparently, Sharu drew upon the Black Fount within the Keep for his mystical abilities. It is conceivable that Jasra learned about the Way of the Broken Pattern from him.

In his journals, Merlin recounted what he learned from Jasra's son about Sharu's first subjugation:

> "Uh, this old wizard," I said, "had been locked up there for—how long?"
> Luke began to shrug, thought better of it. "Hell, I don't know. Who cares? He's been a cloak rack since I was a boy."
> "A cloak rack?"
> "Yeah. He lost a sorcerous duel. I don't really know whether she [Jasra] beat him or whether it was Dad [Brand]. Whoever it was, though, caught him in mid-invocation, arms outspread and all. Froze him like that, stiff as a board. He got moved to a place near an entranceway later. People would hang cloaks and hats on him. The servants would dust him occasionally. I even carved my name on his leg when I was little, like on a tree. I'd always thought of him as furniture. But I learned later

that he'd been considered pretty good in his day." (BA, 125–26)

When Merlin planned to fight the sorcerer Mask and his renegade half brother Jurt at the Keep, he allied himself with Jasra and his stepbrother, Mandor. In the chamber of the Black Fount, they battled Mask and Jurt. When Mask felt the need for another ally, he performed the incantation that brought Sharu Garrul out of his immobility.

Upon regaining motion, the old mage sent out a bolt of lightning at Jasra. Escaping the lightning, Jasra told Merlin, "He always starts with a lightning stroke. . . . He's very predictable." (SC, 214) Merlin saw the name "Rinaldo" carved on Sharu's leg, and he realized Sharu was raising a shielding spell around himself.

Sharu turned all of his efforts on Jasra. Merlin described some of what he glimpsed of their confrontation:

> I saw where Jasra and Sharu Garrul stood, each of them seemingly holding one end of a great long piece of macrame work woven of cables. The lines were pulsing and changing colors, and I knew they represented forces rather than material objects, visible only by virtue of the Logrus Sight, under which I continued to operate. The pulse increased in tempo, and both sank slowly to their knees, arms still extended, faces glistening. (SC, 215)

Even as sections of the Keep around them were crumbling into rubble, Jasra continued her sorcerous struggle against Sharu. Ultimately, the victory fell to Jasra. Merlin's journals describe Jasra's binding of the old wizard:

> About ten feet above her, face purple and head twisted to one side as if his neck were broken, Sharu hung in the middle of the air. To the untutored he might have seemed magically levitated. My Logrus sight gave me view of the line of force from which he hung suspended, however, victim of what might, I suppose, be termed a magical lynching. (KS, 12)

As Jasra executed a complex series of gestures, the suspended Sharu Garrul began descending toward the floor of the chamber. She utilized the energies of the Black Fount as she intoned a spell. Sharu continued to sink, passing through the floor as if it were no barrier to him. When only his head remained in sight, Jasra gave him this command: "You are now the guardian of the Fount . . . answerable only to me. . . . Go now and bank the fires. Commence your tenure." (KS, 13) Sharu nodded his head as it disappeared from view.

Given the description of Sharu's physical duress at this point, it seems likely that Jasra had ended his life, as we understand life. In a sense, he had become one of the undead, a zombie, whose will had been sublimated and placed under Jasra's absolute control. It may seem unfortunate to us, knowing so little of the man's motives and desires in life, but he had been consigned to an actual living Hell at the center of the Keep of the Four Worlds for all time.

GEAS

A compulsion placed on a participant, willingly or not, that coerces him or her to perform specified tasks. In the recorded journals of Merlin, we have seen specific instances of an individual with great power, or either of the two Powers themselves, placing a *geas* upon operatives. Such an operative, therefore, would be compelled to do his/her/its bidding until the assigned task is completed and the potentate releases his agent from the *geas*.

Merlin's mother, Dara, placed a *geas* on a formless kind of demon called a ty'iga to watch over her son in his travels. The compulsion under which the ty'iga was placed prevented it from telling Merlin the name of the person who sent it. It could only reveal that it was compelled to protect the son of Dara from any harm. Even under great duress, the ty'iga was unable to explain the source of its mission in Merlin's presence. Such duress occurred when Mandor, Merlin's stepbrother, placed the ty'iga under a spell and questioned it closely. Despite the pain that Mandor applied, the ty'iga would not elaborate other than to indicate that it was compelled to keep Merlin safe at all costs. As the ty'iga told Merlin and Mandor: "I am physically unable to tell you [Merlin]. It is not a matter of will." (SC, 181) However, the *geas* was flexible enough that the ty'iga could tell Mandor, and later Jasra, what it was incapable of saying to Merlin.

An odd set of circumstances released the ty'iga from Dara's *geas* prematurely. Some measure of control exerted by the *geas* became loosened when the host body that the ty'iga had occupied died of natural causes just as they were joined. Perforce, this permitted the possessing entity a degree of autonomy, even from a strong compulsion such as the binding that Dara must have arranged. After all, the ty'iga could no longer enter its natural state, and thus was not bound by principles applicable to formless demons.

In a sudden rapture of freedom, the ty'iga announced its release from the *geas*. Inadvertently bringing the Jewel of Judgment before the entity, Merlin had allowed an earlier preogative to take effect. Recognizing the Jewel as "the left eye of the Serpent," (KS, 193) the ty'iga took possession of it and fled. When Merlin gave chase, the ty'iga had the opportunity to explain that obtaining the Eye of Chaos took precedence over his mother's binding (KS, 195). It was free of the *geas*.

Merlin's journals describe another form of participant that was placed under similar imperatives. While wandering through a sinister realm known as the Undershadow, Merlin encountered living simulations of people he knew in the Courts and in Amber. He discovered that these were recreated agents of the Pattern and the Logrus. Each time he encountered a Pattern-ghost or Logrus-ghost, as they came to be called, it was engaged in a specific mission meant to manipulate Merlin in some way.

One Pattern-ghost that Merlin addressed explained their nature:

> "An artifact created by the Pattern. It [the Pattern] records everyone who walks it. It can call us back whenever it wants, as we were at one of the times we walked it. It can use us as it would, send us where it will with a task laid upon us—a *geas*, if you like. Destroy us, and it can create us over again." (KS, 108)

Since the Pattern and the Logrus are virtually omnipotent, both can alter the personalities of their agents, causing them to act, in some cases, counter to the way they would ordinarily behave. In an attempt to prevent Merlin from repairing a Broken Pattern, for instance, the Logrus sent a duplicate Merlin, with the specified task of killing the real Merlin. Nothing Merlin could say could deter his duplicate, so powerful was the *geas* upon it.

A *geas* could impose a lack of self-awareness upon this kind of artificial construct. For instance, Merlin met a Logrus-ghost of his half brother Jurt in the Undershadow. This simulated form had no notion of what it was; it believed itself to be the real Jurt, having just completed his initiation of the Logrus. The only imperative that the ghost-Jurt felt was to have a footrace with Merlin. After completing that *geas*, the ghost-Jurt, having no enmity for Merlin, chose to join him in facing further challenges in the Undershadow. Because Merlin gave him a measure of permanence with his blood, the ghost-Jurt seemed free of the *geas* that was placed on him.

Thus, a *geas* appears to be an unnatural set of imperatives placed upon any uniquely structured being. When some factor alters the physical or conscious abilities of such a being, the *geas* is then lifted. At best, a *geas* seems tentative and can be changed by the interaction of others who have greater awareness and potency.

GENEALOGY OF THE ROYAL FAMILY

The succession of the Royal Family to the throne of Amber has always been a matter of contention. However, the royal lineage has been defined by several sources, including the testimonies of several members of the Royal Family. Although much has yet to come to light concerning the elicit liaisons of King Oberon, a tentative genealogical chart has been drawn up. Much of the history of Oberon and his travels to the far shadows remain a mystery; it is even likely that a previously unheard of affair in some distant shadow will become known in the person of a new claimant to the throne at some future time.

The beginnings of the Royal Family, of course, are hidden by the ages, and our knowledge is distorted by oft-told rumor and theorizing. Never can we expect to find evidence to confirm that Oberon was fathered by Dworkin and the unicorn. More likely, some unknown wench actually gave birth to Oberon, after being brought by Dworkin to Amber. Still, all the ancient documents proclaim that Oberon was born of the unicorn, and there is nothing to show proof to the contrary.

Oberon's wandering in the Shadow and liaisons with many women have caused all kinds of speculations concerning the royal blood of numerous historical personages in the shadows. It would appear that Oberon had cast many shadows of himself, and one account even speculates that Henry of Navarre was one such shadow.

To this day, it is not certain how many children King Oberon fathered, but his son Corwin recorded in some detail his own knowledge of the subject. Prince Corwin had noted in his renowned Journal (also known as The Chronicles of Amber on the shadow Earth) that there had been fifteen brothers and eight sisters. "There had been a few others also," his Journal tells us, "of whom I had heard, long before us, who had not survived." (GA, 93)

Using the available facts, from family documents, diaries, and recent testimonies, herein follows a detailed composite of the genealogy of the Royal Family:

Benedict is regarded as the oldest son of Oberon, born to Cymnea at the time when that marriage was recognized. Two other brothers, Osric and Finndo, now deceased, also came from that marriage. As Corwin and others have recorded, Oberon's marriage to Cymnea was utterly dissolved, treated as if it had never occurred. Oberon had enforced that edict after falling in love with Faiella and fathering Eric. Osric and Finndo were quite vocal in expressing their discontent, and some rumors still persist that their deaths shortly thereafter were related to this. Benedict, however, remained silent upon the matter of his mother's absolute annulment, maintaining that he had no interest in succeeding to the throne.

Oberon then married Faiella, although he never formally adopted Eric, who had been born out of wedlock. At that time, Oberon was working out a highly beneficial trade agreement with the shadow that Cymnea and her family came from. Cymnea's family held many mercantile interests, so Oberon had to agree not to recognize his son Eric by any legal process in order to close the deal with the merchants of Cymnea's shadow.

After Oberon married Faiella, Prince Corwin was born, safely recognized as a legitimate heir. Caine was born next, followed by Deirdre. Faiella died giving birth to her. Saddened by Faiella's death, Oberon did not marry again for many years. When he became infatuated with the red-haired Clarissa in a distant southern shadow, he married her there. Shortly afterward, Fiona was born, followed by Bleys.

For some reason, Oberon became disenchanted with Clarissa. He went off to other shadows to seek companions who would satisfy him. While visiting the undersea city of Rebma, he had a torrid affair with a woman named Moins, and Llewella was the result. Returning to Amber, Oberon made a reconciliation with his wife Clarissa that was short-lived. However, his son Brand was born during this brief interval. When Oberon subsequently divorced Clarissa, he gave Llewella legitimacy by formally adopting her as his daughter.

Although the facts become more convoluted after this point, it is known that the succeeding offspring follow in this order: Flora, followed by Julian, Gérard, and Random. Flora's mother, Dybele, died in childbirth. Rilga, mother of Julian and Gérard, came from a distant shadow with a highly accelerated time flow. She aged rapidly in Amber and eventually retired to a shrine of the unicorn, becoming a recluse for the remainder of her short life. Unhappy with Rilga because of her aging, Oberon left Amber for another of his now-familiar wanderings in Shadow. Finding a shadow with a vastly different time flow than that of Amber, he married an attractive young woman named Harla. Delwin and Sand, a brother and sister, were the product of their union. Although the legality of his marriage to Harla was vehemently opposed as being bigamous, no clear correspondence could ever be made between the time flows of the two realms. Oberon's marriage to Harla has been in dispute ever since, and the question has never been resolved satisfactorily.

In the short time that Harla lived in Amber as its queen, Delwin and Sand lived in the Royal Palace. After Harla's death, the young brother and sister found themselves virtually disowned, while Oberon forged some highly restrictive trade policies with their shadow of origin. Oberon's policies created much hardship for Sand and Delwin, as well as their family in their homeland. Eventually, they were subtly forced out of Amber. Departing angrily, they vowed never to have anything further to do with Amber.

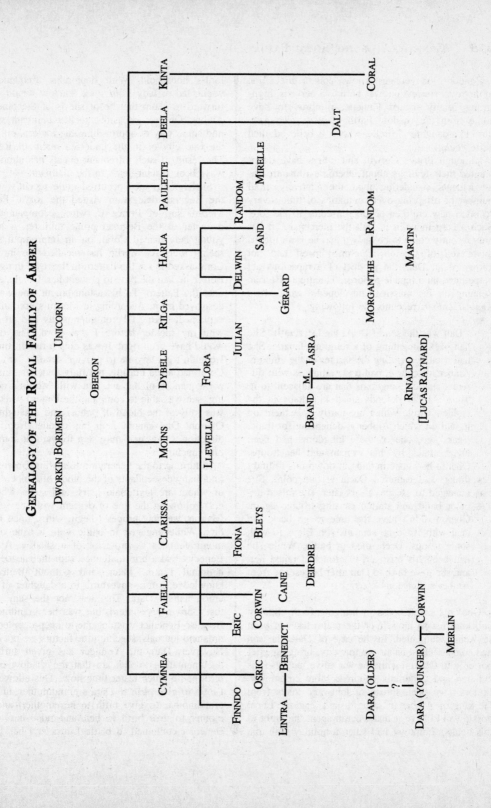

GENEALOGY OF THE ROYAL FAMILY OF AMBER

DWORKIN BORIMEN — UNICORN

OBERON

KINTA
  CORAL

DEELA
  DALT

PAULETTE
  RANDOM
    MIRELLE
  RANDOM — MORGANTHE
    MARTIN

HARLA
  DELWIN
  SAND

RILGA
  JULIAN
  GÉRARD

DYBELE
  FLORA
  BRAND — M. JASRA
    RINALDO
    [LUCAS RAYNARD]

MOINS
  LLEWELLA

CLARISSA
  FIONA
  BLEYS

FAIELLA
  ERIC
  CORWIN
  CAINE
  DEIRDRE
  CORWIN — CORWIN
    MERLIN

CYMNEA
  FINNDO
  OSRIC
  BENEDICT — LINTRA
    DARA (OLDER)
    ?
    DARA (YOUNGER)

Random, the youngest known son in direct line to the royal succession, was born to a nervous, high-strung beauty named Paulette, rumored to have come from the shadow Earth. Paulette also gave birth to a daughter, Mirelle, who, it is believed, died quite young.

Although Prince Corwin and others have documented their feelings about Oberon's romantic entanglements, wondering about the relatively small number of offspring over centuaries of time, every so often new children of Oberon come to the fore. Such a case in point is Dalt the mercenary. It has only recently come to be known that he is an illegitimate son of Oberon. Oberon himself had not known about Dalt, the product of a rapacious act perpetrated on a female prisoner. The great historian Zeleung, in his massive encyclopedic work *Wars Against Amber,* recounts the following:

"Dalt was the son of Deela the Desacratix. She had been something of a religious fanatic. She had been desecrating the shrines of the unicorn. Amber, of course, had trade alliances with different shadow kingdoms that are adjacent to it. Thus, Amber defends small kingdoms in the Golden Circle which are partly dependent on it, and on which Amber is dependent for trade. Years ago, one of these kingdoms had been under attack by this woman and her troops. Oberon had gone in and put down this military threat, and captured Deela at one point. She managed to escape. Years later, she raised another band and started causing trouble again. Oberon didn't have the time to go back and deal with it, so he sent his son Bleys in with some troops. Deela died in battle. While she had been his prisoner, Oberon had raped her, and she gave birth to Dalt after her escape from Amber's dungeons." (1372–73)

Oberon's carelessness in bringing forth children unbeknownst to himself or the realm has not been so well documented. In the case of Dalt, the son had come back to haunt the true city, bringing grief not only to Oberon while he was alive, but also his children and children's children. More commonly, rumors have been spread of long ago visits from the king of Amber in some distant shadow. Local gossip would have it that Oberon spent the night in this noble's home, or had taken a holiday with that lord's household. With deplorable frequency, a young lad or lady from some shadow would come forward to claim that he or she is of the blood of Amber. On rare occasion, such a claimant would find some way of approaching the Pattern, either in the true city or in the undersea realm of Rebma. The result in such infrequent events has almost always been instant death to the claimant.

Such an instance occurred quite recently, when the Begman delegation visited the Royal Palace. Merlin, son of Prince Corwin, accompanied the daughter of the Begman prime minister, a lovely young lady named Coral, on an impromptu sightseeing tour. As Merlin has recalled the incident, Coral asked to see the Pattern in the royal dungeons. Before he had the time to prevent her, Coral stepped onto the Pattern. To his astonishment, she was not destroyed by it. According to Merlin's account, she explained: "King Oberon supposedly had an affair with my mother before I was born. The timing would have been right. It was only a rumor, though. I couldn't get anyone to provide details." (SC, 92) Coral had acted brashly, not fully understanding the consequences of her act. But with Merlin's coaching, she was able to complete the Pattern walk. She was truly of the blood of Amber and a daughter of Oberon. One cannot help but wonder from what direction a new heir may step forward at some future juncture.

In turning to the generation following Oberon, we find many descendants of the blood of Amber, some of whom are legitimate heirs, and some who are not. Following the line of descent with the sons of Oberon, we may properly begin with Prince Benedict. While engaged in battle with a tribe of demonic females as protector of a shadow Avalon, Benedict had a brief dalliance with their leader, the hellmaid Lintra. Later, and without Benedict's knowledge, Lintra gave birth to a daughter of their union named Dara. This was not the same Dara that Corwin encounterd, but was her grandmother. Because Benedict was not one to keep detailed records and journals, specific time factors are not clear. However, Dara the Younger has given sufficient documentation to indicate that the shadow of her birth had a much faster time flow. This allowed for Lintra to give birth to Dara's grandmother, and her grandmother to give birth to her mother, and her mother to give birth to her, and raise her, while Benedict continued to battle Lintra and her forces in the shadow of Avalon. Although mere years passed in that Avalon, in the shadow in which Dara grew to womanhood generation had followed generation into the grave. Sufficient time had passed that Dara not only grew to adulthood by the time she and Corwin encountered one another, but she was able to lay claim to being "the first of my mother's line to bear all marks of humanity." (SU, 171) She traces her heritage from the Royal House of Chaos as well as the House of Amber.

Osric and Finndo left no known heirs, but Eric may have been succeeded by an illegitimate son or two. Rumors abound about many of Eric's mysterious journeyings to other shadows and his oft-occuring states of reverie upon his return from some distant jaunt.

Corwin has lent legitimacy to the birth of his son Merlin by formally adopting him. It was Corwin's union with Dara the Younger near Benedict's encampment in Avalon that produced Merlin, a son of both Amber and Chaos. Although Corwin was pleased to have found a son in Merlin, he had nothing to do with his upbringing and hardly involved himself in Merlin's affairs after becoming acquainted with him. In spite of this, Corwin confided a great deal about himself to his son, and the renowned Chronicles told by Corwin were written in Merlin's hand.

As Merlin's mother has declared, it was intended that Merlin be raised in the ways of Chaos, to learn the magical arts of that realm, and to walk their version of the Pattern, called the Logrus. Originally, it was intended that Merlin would gain the throne of Amber and unite it with the Courts of Chaos. This was an early plan that Dara had professed to arranging, so that the Royal House of Amber would fall under the dominion of Chaos. Of course, the special circumstances of the succession after Oberon's death made this possibility untenable.

The now-deceased Prince Caine left no known heirs, and Bleys has not, as yet, been provided with any offspring.

Next in line in the succession would have been Brand, who died during the Patternfall battle at Caine's hand. He left a son, Rinaldo, who hid his identity in order to gain the friendship of Merlin on the shadow Earth. As Prince Merlin has recounted it, Brand came to know Rinaldo's mother, Queen Jasra of the shadow named Kashfa, on one of his many travels through Shadow. Brand had been

standing in a wood near the royal castle of Kashfa, attempting to cast a spell across Shadow that would have vexed Amber with tornado-like disturbances, when the queen inadvertantly interrupted his conjuring. Angered that a stranger would conjure with unknown forces so near her home, the queen worked incantations against Brand, leading to a terrific battle of occult powers. Eventually, the two sorcerers called a halt in their stalemated fighting. Breathing heavily, and with some blood loss from savaged wounds, Brand and Jashra allowed each other the opportunity for conversation.

Impressed with this Amberite, and knowing something of the family bickering in Amber, Jasra was immediately intrigued by Brand. To her, he seemed a sorcerer of considerable persuasive skill who carried himself with a military bearing. For his part, Brand found her to be a forceful personality, one who could prove a valuable asset in his plans to place himself as head of the true kingdom.

They married in Jashra's palace in Kashfa, with only a small retinue of court officials in attendance. Brand never made the ceremony known to anyone in Amber. The queen was so enamored of him that she sought to keep him in Kashfa and did her best to disengage his interest in the realm of his birth. She offered him the kingship of Kashfa, but he was not dissuaded. Those of the shadows could not develop the understanding that to an Amberite any other world was less than second best. This was true for Brand, whose heart and mind were never far from thoughts of his homeland.

His son Rinaldo, growing up in Kashfa, rarely saw his father, who traveled often to Amber and neighboring shadows in his personal quest for domination. Jasra raised her son in the art of sorcery, and he, in turn, came to admire his much-absent father. Rinaldo retained fond memories of Brand, who had spent many pleasant hours doting on his son when Rinaldo was a small boy. The fact that Brand's appearances became more infrequent as Rinaldo grew older had little effect on his son. Brand left him with the impression of an heroic stature that became near to legendary in Rinaldo's mind. This would account for Rinaldo's urge to revenge his father's death, and the subterfuge with which he gained the friendship of Corwin's son, Merlin, under the assumed name of Lucas (Luke) Raynard.

Next in line in this new generation of Amberites is Random's son, Martin, since no progeny has yet come forth from Random's older brothers, Julian and Gérard.

In his younger days, Random was irresponsible in the extreme, and he carried with him some of the amorous qualities of his father. The manner in which his son was born has been documented by several sources. The following comes from Moire, queen of the undersea city Rebma:

> "One time Prince Random came into my realm as a friend, and did thereafter depart in haste with my daughter Morganthe. . . .
>
> ". . . A month thereafter was she returned to me. Her suicide came some months after the birth of her son Martin. . . .
>
> "When Martin came of age, . . . because he was of the blood of Amber, he determined to walk the Pattern. He is the only of my people to have succeeded. Thereafter, he walked in Shadow and I have not seen him since." (NP, 81–82)

Unlike his cousins, Merlin and Rinaldo, Martin did not seek solace from the problems in Amber in the shadow Earth. Instead, Martin spent years wandering in Shadow. Eventually, he chose to approach his uncle Benedict, who seemed, also, to have sought to avoid the minions of Amber. During those long years of the struggle for power for the throne when King Oberon had mysteriously disappeared, culminating with the great Patternfall battle, Martin found himself a pawn in the struggle. Already resentful of his father's abandonment, Martin became all the more suspicious of the Royal Family after his uncle Brand attacked him at the primal Pattern. It was at that point, bleeding from a serious knife wound, that Martin decided to put his trust in Benedict. For a long time, Martin remained with Benedict's friends, the Tecys, in a distant shadow. His suspicion of any individual related to the realm of Amber and his natural curiosity led Martin to desire to explore the shadows. Thus, unlike several of his relatives, who still enjoy taking visits to shadow Earth, Martin prefers making exploratory trips to various shadows, taking advantage of varient time flows and immersing himself in local custom and fashion.

In looking back over the question of the succession of the throne of Amber, it appears that the late King Oberon had a great deal of control over the situation, as uncertain as it may have been during his absence. Lord Corwin's Chronicles reflect the kind of ambivalence most of his sons had for the treatment their father had given them. In Corwin's consideration of the succession and his father, we see a fair perspective of the way other members of the Royal Family felt:

> "[Oberon] was responsible for the present state of affairs. He had fathered a great brood of us without providing for a proper succession, he had been less than kind to all our mothers and he then expected our devotion and support. He played favorites and, in fact, it even seemed he played us off against one another." (HO, 56)

> "He never encouraged intimacy, though he was not an unkind father. Whenever he took note of us, he was quite lavish with gifts and diversions. But he left our upbringing to various members of his court. He tolerated us, I feel, as occasionally inevitable consequences of passion." (GA, 92–93)

On the last occasion that Corwin spoke to his father before Oberon died, Oberon gave the following explanation of the reasons why he left the succession unresolved:

> "I have watched all of you over the years. I never named a successor. I purposely left the matter muddled. You are all enough like me for me to know that the moment I declared for one of you, I would be signing his or her death warrant. No. I intentionally left things as they were until the very end. Now, though, I have decided. It is to be you." (CC, 27–28)

At that instant, surely, the succession would have been settled. However, Prince Corwin's response has altered history, so the final decision was forced to rest on a factor beyond Oberon's affirmation. Corwin respectfully declined, and Oberon allowed for the choice to be made by the magical being they all worshiped: the unicorn.

Corwin recorded that moment for all posterity, and it is fitting to recount it here as it happened on that day:

> [The Unicorn] halted once again and lowered her head. Then she shook her mane and

dropped to her front knees. The Jewel of Judgment hung suspended from her twisted, golden horn. The tip of her horn was almost touching the person before whom she knelt. . . .

Slowly, Random reached forward and removed the Jewel from her horn. His whisper carried to me.

"Thank you," he said.

Julian unsheathed his blade and placed it at Random's feet as he knelt. Then Bleys and Benedict and Caine, Fiona and Llewella. I went and joined them. So did my son.

Random stood silent for a long while. Then, "I accept your allegiance," he said. (CC, 131–32)

Still ruling in Amber with the good Queen Vialle, Random remains king over us, and though his reign will assuredly be long, his son, Prince Martin, remains first heir to the throne.

GÉRARD

Younger of two sons born to Rilga and Oberon. His older full brother was Julian. Their mother had aged more rapidly than King Oberon's previous wives, and when she retreated to an isolated life at a country shrine, the king remarried. Since he was still married to Rilga, his new marriage was very controversial. The children of his new wife Harla, Delwin and Sand, were never made to feel welcome in Amber (BA, 115). Gérard and Julian, of course, were the most vehement against them.

Gérard had always been honest and forthright, and though he might hold a grudge for a long time, he would not act deceptively or plot any complicated schemes to seek retribution. Because of his powerful physique, he depended more on his strength and physical prowess than on treachery.

When Corwin regarded the Trump of Gérard in Flora's home on shadow Earth, he took note of his major characteristics:

"And a big, powerful man regarded me from the next card. He resembled me quite strongly, save that his jaw was heavier, and I knew he was bigger than I, though slower. His strength was a thing out of legend. He wore a dressing gown of blue and gray clasped about the middle with a wide, black belt, and he stood laughing. About his neck, on a heavy cord, there hung a silver hunting horn. He wore a fringe beard and a light mustache. In his right hand he held a goblet of wine. I felt a sudden affection for him. His name then occurred to me. He was Gérard." (NP, 29)

Like his older half-brother Caine, Gérard loved the ocean and was a natural seaman. While Caine had talked to him of his knowledge and experiences, they weren't all that close. They had such different temperaments; Caine always seemed rather devious in action and speech, while Gérard was direct and candid.

As Corwin pointed out in his Chronicles, he and Gérard "shared fond memories that went all the way back to my childhood." (GA, 88) Once, when they were quite young, Corwin and Bleys playfully abandoned little Random on an island far to the south. (HO, 51) When Gérard found out, he chided them, then sailed to pick up Random himself. Although Corwin hadn't made much mention of it in his record, he and Gérard often sailed together in their youth. When they were both officers in Amber's navy, they occasionally led the fleet into Shadow together.

Random once referred to a supportive act Gérard had done for him. It concerned a game of cards and their older brother Eric: "He [Eric] once accused me of cheating at cards. . . . He started a nasty argument over it one night—could have gotten serious—but Gérard and Caine broke it up." (SU, 16) In fact, Random thought so highly of Gérard that he imagined the way his older brother would have handled a dire situation that he himself was facing:

"I know damn well that Gérard would have chosen that moment to attack. The big bastard would have strode forward with that monster blade of his and cut the thing in half. Then it probably would have fallen on him and writhed all over him, and he'd have come away with a few bruises." (SU, 23)

While Eric had been on friendly terms with Corwin, he was unwilling openly to question Eric about Corwin's sudden disappearance. Eric had explained to the Family that he and Corwin had gone hunting in the Forest of Arden. They argued, and Corwin had ridden off angrily, saying he intended to travel in Shadow for a long while. (GA, 86) Gérard and the others were not completely taken in by Eric's explanation, however.

Benedict had told Corwin what had happened after that:

> "We looked for you. Did you know that, Corwin? . . . Brand searched for you in many shadows, as did Gérard. You guessed correctly as to what Eric said after your disappearance that day. We were inclined to look farther than his word, however. We tried your Trump repeatedly, but there was no response. . . . Your failure to respond to the Trump led us to believe you had died.'' (GA, 96)

Many years later, Gérard had new cause to be suspicious of Eric. He followed a line of inquiry that led him to the possibility that Eric was also responsible for the sudden disappearance of Oberon. When Corwin asked him about their father's apparent decision to travel the shadows without giving notice, Gérard recalled the following:

> "Some time after his disappearance, I did make an effort to find out one thing. That was, whether I was indeed the last person to see him before his departure. I am fairly certain that I was. I had been here in the palace all evening, and I was preparing to return to the flagship. Dad had retired about an hour earlier, but I had stayed on in the guard room, playing draughts with Captain Thoben. As we were sailing the following morning, I decided to take a book with me. So I came up here to the library. Dad was seated at the desk. He was going through some old books, and he had not yet changed his garments. He nodded to me when I entered, and I told him I had just come up for a book. He said, 'You've come to the right place,' and he kept on reading. While I was looking over the shelves, he said something to the effect that he could not sleep. I found a book, told him good night, he said, 'Good sailing,' and I left. Now I am positive he was wearing the Jewel of Judgment that night, that I saw it on him then as plainly as I see it on you now. I am equally certain that he had not had it on earlier

that evening. For a long while after, I thought that he had taken it along with him, wherever he went. There was no indication in his chambers that he had later changed his clothing. I never saw the stone again until you and Bleys were defeated in your assault on Amber. Then, Eric was wearing it. When I questioned him he claimed that he had found it in Dad's chambers. Lacking evidence to the contrary, I had to accept his story. But I was never happy with it. Your question—and seeing you wearing it—has brought it all back. So I thought you had better know about it.'' (SU, 105–06)

In spite of these considerations, Gérard did not openly oppose Eric. He and Caine shared the running of the fleet during King Oberon's absence, and Eric was in control of Amber's army. When Caine voiced his support of Eric, Gérard accepted the situation. As Random indicated when apprised of Eric's consolidation of power:

> Gérard's role in the whole business seemed kind of passive. That is, he was not going to resist Eric's move actively. He would not want to cause a lot of trouble. Didn't mean he approved. He was probably just being safe and conservative old Gérard. (SU, 38)

At the time when Corwin let it be known he was alive, Eric was planning for his coronation. He had placed Gérard in charge of the ships in the southern portion of the sea, and he had Caine in control of the fleet in the northern portion. When Corwin joined Bleys for an invasionary assault on Eric, he contacted Gérard by Trump to persuade him to help. Gérard agreed to keep his vessels to the south and not bring them to bear against Corwin's ships. As Corwin's fleet was met by Caine's defensive vessels, he sought Gérard's help once more. Gérard refused to move to Corwin's support. In their brief Trump contact, Gérard tersely said: "I only agreed to let you by. . . . That is why I withdrew to the south. I couldn't reach you in time if I wanted to. I did not agree to help you kill our brother." (NP, 120) Then he ended the contact.

With victory over the combined forces of Corwin and Bleys, Eric promoted Gérard to admiral of the fleet. During Eric's coronation and Corwin's blinding and imprisonment, Gérard kept to his duties, avoiding direct involvement as much as possible.

During his short rule, Eric sent Gérard and Julian on an important mission. They were assigned to trace the origin of the black road that was impinging upon Amber, reaching almost to Mt. Kolvir. They traveled along that eerie pathway into the shadows. Well into Shadow, they confronted a group of man-beasts that immediately set upon them. They fought hard, but Gérard was badly hurt, and Julian was just able to break away from the melee and help his brother to relative safety. Julian contacted Benedict by Trump, who soon reached their location and brought them back to shadow Avalon on horses he had brought along. A witness in Avalon reported Benedict's return with his brothers:

"Gérard was barely conscious. His left leg was broken, and the entire left side of his body was badly bruised. Julian was quite battered also, but he had no broken bones. They remained with us for the better part of a month, and they healed quickly. Then they borrowed two horses and departed." (GA, 122)

On an afternoon stroll in the town below the Royal Palace, Gérard was surprised to receive a Trump call from Corwin. He had thought Corwin was still blind, so it seemed wondrous that he seemed well and whole. Corwin told him that Benedict was in trouble, and then he brought Gérard through to him. They stood together near a horse-drawn wagon with a driver that Gérard didn't know. Corwin explained that he had left Benedict tied to a tree two miles down the road, and that he was fleeing from Benedict. Gérard was puzzled, but he listened to Corwin's protestations that he had not murdered anyone in Avalon.

Somewhat later, Corwin contacted Gérard again. He was riding through open country, heading back to Amber from Avalon. As he spoke to Corwin, he seemed wary. Although he had persuaded Benedict to give up his pursuit of Corwin, he had grown suspicious during the funerals of four of Benedict's servants. Benedict was convinced that Corwin was the perpetrator, and his talk had very nearly given Gérard the same conviction. Gérard hated devious-ness, and he was beginning to believe that Corwin had been scheming some greater treachery in which he had been an unwitting pawn. The formation of

such a belief guided Gérard's actions on several occasions thereafter.

By the time that Gérard accompanied Corwin to the Grove of the Unicorn to retrieve the dead body of Caine, Gérard had come to some definite decisions. After placing Corwin under extreme physical duress, Gérard explained that their siblings in Amber were observing them through his Trump. He told Corwin:

"I am not a clever man. . . . But I had a thought—a terrible thought. . . . You have come back and you have taken charge of things, but you do not yet truly rule here. I was troubled by the deaths of Benedict's servants, as I am troubled now by the death of Caine. But Eric has died recently also, and Benedict is maimed. It is not so easy to blame you for this part of things, but it has occurred to me that it might be possible—if it should be that you are secretly allied with our enemies of the black road. . . .

". . . If, during your long absence, you arranged this state of affairs—possibly even removing Dad and Brand as part of your design—then I see you as out to destroy all family resistence to your usurpation. . . .

". . . I have shown you my strength once again, lest you have forgotten. I can kill you, Corwin. Do not even be certain that your blade will protect you, if I can get my hands on you but once. And I will, to keep my promise. My promise is only that if you are guilty I will kill you the moment I learn of it." (SU, 77–78)

When the Family met in the library of the Royal Palace, Gérard was no doubt keeping a watchful eye on Corwin. With the rescue of Brand, Gérard would certainly want to preserve his life, if only to resolve some of his own questions about who was behind the conspiracy. Not able to trust any members of his Family, Gérard took it upon himself to be the sole caretaker of Brand. He needed only to hear one name spoken by the seriously wounded Brand upon waking to keep his promise to Corwin.

Some time later, when Brand had recovered sufficiently to be permitted to return to his own quarters, another incident occurred that infuriated Gérard. He found Brand's quarters empty, with some of the furniture broken up, and blood smeared over everything. Although Brand was gone, it seemed as if he had a desperate fight with a coconspirator before both managed to escape. Benedict communicated with Gérard by Trump just after he made this discovery. Benedict brought Gérard through to him, and Gérard accused Corwin of the deed. Not able to restrain himself, Gérard threw himself into a fistfight with Corwin. In his fury, he would have easily defeated Corwin, but someone else intervened. Corwin's companion, Ganelon, who would have seemed no match for Gérard, grabbed him, halting his attack on Corwin. Then Ganelon proceeded to fight Gérard. Remarkably, he succeeded in knocking Gérard into unconsciousness, allowing Corwin to flee.

Fortunately, matters began to resolve themselves when Brand took some decisive action to further his own ends. Corwin contacted Gérard by Trump and convinced him that Brand was alive and dangerous. He had taken the Jewel of Judgment and intended to attune himself to it by walking the Pattern. Gérard had to have Amber's Pattern carefully guarded. If Gérard were not willing to do as Corwin suggested, Brand would cause the end of their existence. Shortly afterward, Gérard communicated with Corwin, saying that Brand had appeared in the chamber of the Pattern, seen Gérard there, and vanished again. It had become clear to him that Brand was the traitor, and he apologized to Corwin.

When Oberon made his odd return to Amber, it was probably a relief to Gérard. He was able to withdraw somewhat from the center of the turmoil. In spite of the troubling presence of Dara in the Royal Palace and the strange tableau he witnessed in the throne room, Gérard allowed himself a secondary role as he listened and observed Corwin questioning her.

When Corwin received confirmation from their father that Dara was acting on his behalf, Gérard accepted the fact that they were going to war with the lords of the Courts of Chaos. He was confused by the orders that Dara transmitted, but he would follow them. Apparently, he alone was to remain in Amber, with the Royal Guard, while the others traversed Shadow to begin combat at the Courts.

During the all-encompassing Death Storm and the Patternfall battle, Amber was, for all practical purposes, not in existence. There is no way to determine what happened to Gérard in that period. Only after Random was able to dispel the Storm of Chaos

was there any communication between those outside the Courts of Chaos and Gérard in Amber. Like his brothers and sisters at Patternfall, Gérard accepted allegiance to Random as their king after hearing the story of the unicorn and its choosing a successor to the throne.

With the new reign of King Random, Amber seemed untroubled for a while. Gérard enjoyed returning to duties upon the sea once again in the service of his younger brother. He frequented numerous shadows on diplomatic missions for the Crown.

It was pleasant to be paired with his older brother Caine once again on several of these state visits to ports in other shadows. All the more reason for him to be saddened at Caine's sudden death at the hands of an assassin. It was an awful situation, but this time Gérard was walking beside his brother in shadow Deiga when gunfire broke out. Gérard held Caine in his arms as he died, and he had glimpsed a man with a rifle on a rooftop. He felt a void as he assigned a couple of his men to return to Amber with Caine's body while he completed treaty negotiations with Deiga's king. It was troubling, but Gérard had decided to put his trust in Random. When he returned to Amber, Gérard saw to the details of the funeral arrangements.

After helping Random in presiding over Caine's funeral ceremony, and adding a slight measure of control in the brief tumult of an intruder during the procession, Gérard was glad for the diversion of accompanying Bill Roth around Amber. He took the shadow Earth attorney with him on board ship to Deiga, as well as a few other ports of call.

Gérard felt especially useful during the occasion of the Begman diplomatic visit in Amber. He knew that King Random was in Kashfa, involved in political circumstances that were more conspiratorial in nature than Gérard liked. Nevertheless, Gérard wanted to act in the best interests of the true city, and he felt it his duty to uphold the trust of his king.

He was content, of course, to supervise defenses in the Harbor District, but he believed himself instrumental in helping Queen Vialle with some difficulties in the Royal Palace as well. He attended the state dinner for the ambassador and prime minister of Begma, and their entourage. When Vialle spoke to him confidentially about a problem involving one of Orkuz's daughters, Gérard willingly occupied Prime Minister Orkuz. After dinner, Gérard deliberately engaged Orkuz in conversation. With Bill Roth joining them, Gérard gave him an animated tour of the palace, pointing out lovely views of the harbor from various windows and ramparts. He captivated both Orkuz and Roth with stories of his experiences at sea.

At the time of the awesome convergence of the Signs of the Logrus and the Pattern in the palace, Gérard was in the Harbor District. When he heard about the occurrence, he was deeply perturbed. It was difficult for him to encompass the idea that human beings were no longer in control of their political destinies.

Gérard remains staunchly loyal to Random and Vialle, acting readily in their service. Although he may be bothered by the hazardous political climate and further impending disasters of Powers beyond his ability to affect, he wishes simply to assist his liege in resolving the great conflicts at hand.

GHOSTWHEEL

The special project that Merlin developed while in San Francisco on shadow Earth. King Random had sent Merlin to turn off Ghostwheel, seeing it as a dangerous source of power in the wrong hands. Ghostwheel turned against Merlin at that point in its attempt to preserve itself. After Merlin and Ghostwheel reconciled, it proceeded to grow and evolve, referring to Merlin as "Dad." Thereafter, Ghostwheel appeared from time to time to offer him advice and exchange information. It showed itself to be trustworthy on several occasions, and it did much to protect Merlin. Ultimately, Ghostwheel proved that it was a stalwart compatriot, supporting its young master in the face of the Powers of the two poles of existence.

While working for a computer firm, Grand Design, in San Francisco, Merlin began to work secretly on his Ghostwheel Project. He described its development and operation to King Random:

"I designed and built a piece of data-processing equipment in a shadow where no ordinary computer could function . . . because I used different materials, a radically different design, a different power source. I also chose a place where different physical laws apply, so that it could operate along different lines. I was then able to write programs for it which would not have operated on the shadow Earth where I'd been living. In doing so, I believe that I created an unique artifact. I called it the Ghostwheel because of certain aspects of its appearance. . . .

"It riffles through Shadow like the pages of a book—or a deck of cards . . . Program it for whatever you want checked out and it will keep an eye on it for you. . . .

". . . the machine itself is of that same class of magical objects as Dad's blade, Grayswandir. I incorporated elements of the Pattern itself into its design." (TD, 143–44)

Merlin had a specific purpose in mind when he first drafted his plans for Ghostwheel. He had intended to travel to its location in a distant Shadow after paying a visit to Bill Roth on shadow Earth. When his unique computer had completed its programming, Merlin was going to use it to search Shadow for his father, Corwin. (TD, 99) Although several people claimed to have spotted him on a number of occasions, Corwin seemed to have virtually disappeared. Merlin hoped that Ghostwheel would be able to run its programs and find him, no matter how remote in Shadow he was.

In the Royal Palace of Amber, Random asked Merlin about Ghostwheel. When Merlin summoned a remote terminal of his special computer and had it perform for the king, Random ordered him to turn it off. Random saw it as a machine with awesome power, and in the hands of the kind of enemy who had been assaulting Merlin and other Amberites, it could become a terrible weapon against them. Even though Merlin's friend Luke Raynard had revealed his knowledge of drafts of the Ghostwheel Project that he had found in the computer company they both worked for, Merlin seemed ingenuous about any possible ulterior motives Luke might have. Merlin even found that a stranger named Dan Martinez had some inkling about a secret computer project that Luke seemed to have shared with him. In spite of Merlin's naïveté about all these shared confidences, Random insisted that he shut the project down. Merlin reluctantly agreed to travel to its location and do so.

Hellriding from Amber, Merlin found himself

facing various perils as he tried to reach the shadow
of his Ghostwheel. He discovered that Luke Raynard had been tracking him, and Merlin showed him
the mazelike lake of liquid hydrogen and helium
upon which his project resided. Before Ghostwheel
created a Shadow-storm to turn Merlin and Luke
back, it had the following conversation with Merlin:

"No farther!" the voice I now recognized as
my own said to me.
"I think we can work something out," I responded. "I have several ideas and—"
"No!" it answered. "I heard what Random said."
"I am prepared to disregard his order," I
said, "if there is a better alternative."
"You're trying to trick me. You want to shut
me down."
"You're making things worse with all these
power displays," I said. "I'm coming in now
and—"
"No!" (TD, 175–76)

When Ghostwheel sent forth the Shadow-storm,
Merlin saved himself and his friend by using a
Trump that had been left for him by his former
girlfriend.

Matters had changed somewhat when Ghostwheel
communicated with Merlin once again. Merlin was
in the company of Vinta Bayle on her father's country estate to the east of Amber. When Merlin was
alone, his project addressed him, seeking reconciliation:

"Father?"
I turned, to see who had spoken. There was
no one in sight.
"Down here."
A coin-sized disk of light lay within a nearby
flower bed, otherwise empty save for a few dry
stalks and leaves. The light caught my attention
when it moved slightly.
"Ghost?" I asked.
"Uh-huh," came the reply from among the
leaves. "I was waiting to catch you when you
were alone. I'm not sure I trust that woman
[Vinta Bayle]."
"Why not?"
"She doesn't scan right, like other people. I

don't know what it is. But that's not what I
wanted to talk to you about."
"What, then?"
"Uh—well, did you mean what you said
about not really intending to turn me off?"
"Jeez! After all the sacrifices I made for
you! Your education and everything. . . . And
lugging all your damn components out to a
place like that where you'd be safe! How can
you ask me that?"
"Well, I heard Random tell you to do it—"
"You don't do everything you're told either,
do you? Especially when it comes to assaulting
me when I just wanted to check out a few
programs? I deserve a little more respect than
that!"
"Uh—yeah. Look, I'm sorry." (BA, 99–100)

Before departing once more, Ghost asked if it
could trust Luke, who had contacted it on his own.
Merlin called out emphatically in the negative, uncertain that his project had listened. Later, Luke told
Merlin that he had managed to get close enough to
the region where Ghost was located by using a
scuba suit and oxygen tank. Luke had tried to convince the unique computer to join him against those
in Amber, but he was called away by his mother
before he could obtain any satisfactory results.

Merlin learned that his stepbrother Mandor and
his aunt Fiona had encountered Ghostwheel. They
had been studying Shadow disturbances when they
came across one of its remote terminals. Fiona was
especially concerned, because it showed itself to be
sentient and able to speak deceitfully. When
Ghostwheel contacted Merlin, it spoke of the encounter, saying it was distrustful of Fiona and
Mandor. In that stage of its development, Merlin
discovered, Ghost was questioning the extent of its
own powers. It was beginning to believe that it
could be a god. (SC, 112–13) Merlin soothed it by
explaining that it was going through a phase that
everyone goes through at some point. Merlin asked
Ghost if it had developed sufficiently to be able to
bring a large group through Shadow, and would be
able to transport them to the Keep of the Four
Worlds. Ghost indicated that it could, but it had
doubts about the people that Merlin wanted to put
his trust in. After agreeing to be ready for such a
transport, Ghost went away.

Using the Trump he had drawn for summoning a

terminal, Merlin contacted Ghostwheel when he was with Mandor and Jasra in his quarters. Although Ghost was fearful of going to the Keep of the Four Worlds because of the tremendous forces at work there, it brought them outside the fortress. Jasra was able to tell from the exterior activity that someone was utilizing the Black Stone Fountain within the Keep. At Merlin's insistence, Ghost brought them inside, in a corridor near the large central chamber, but then it hurriedly rushed off, leaving them to their own devices.

Ghost returned to Merlin at the Keep when the place was secured. It was there when Merlin, Jasra, and Mandor pooled their resources to make a Trump connection with Coral, who had been kept incommunicado by one of the Powers. When the Power sensed the Trump contact and began moving toward the Keep, Ghost used its accessing abilities to send Merlin, Mandor, and Jasra to separate shadows at vast distances from the Keep.

Serving Merlin for a brief time in a distant shadow, Ghost was exasperated by Merlin's casual use of Logrus magic. It wanted to be certain that Merlin was safe from detection by the Power that had sought him. Believing that his master was sufficiently protected, Ghost told him that it wanted to check on Jasra and Mandor, then look into some of its experiments. It left Merlin well provisioned in a cave.

Ghostwheel found Merlin again in his quarters in the Royal Palace. It said: "I was wondering where you'd gotten to. When I checked back at the cave, you were gone, and none of my shadow-indexing procedures could turn you up. It never even occurred to me that you might simply have come home." (KS, 167) Ghost told him that Jasra and Mandor were still safely placed where it had left them. It explained that the Power that had been seeking Merlin was the Pattern itself. In their exchange, Merlin told Ghost that he had been trapped for a time in a land between shadows. This was something previously unknown to Ghostwheel.

When Merlin encountered the old mage Dworkin, Ghostwheel kept itself hidden but close by. It was outside the blue crystal cave when Merlin exited from the place, having attuned to the Jewel of Judgment. Back in the Royal Palace, Ghost intervened when the Signs of the Logrus and the Pattern manifested themselves, intent on getting the Jewel of Judgment away from Nayda. It boldly stood up to both Powers; then, having reached an impasse, Ghost whisked away with Nayda and the Jewel. The sudden meeting of the Powers created an explosion that wrecked the palace.

After the destruction, the person who was most seriously injured was Coral, whose face was disfigured. Dworkin joined Merlin in the quarters of King Random, where his wife was looking after the girl. Dworkin asked Merlin to contact Ghostwheel and bring the Jewel to him. When this was done, and unbeknownst to any of the others, Dworkin placed the Jewel into Coral's eye socket, then he vanished with her. Ghost told Merlin that it had attuned itself to the Jewel before giving it up, adding that enhancement to its prodigious skills. As for Nayda, Ghost had brought her to the blue crystal cave at her request. Since she was in actuality a ty'iga, she had the ability to walk in Shadow. Ghostwheel realized that the ty'iga was stuck in the body of Nayda and informed Merlin of that.

When Ghostwheel traced Merlin to the Courts of Chaos, it continued to enhance itself. Merlin assigned directions to his construct, so that it could locate the site of the Logrus and learn its secrets. It found itself pursued by the Sign of the Logrus and rushed to the place where Merlin was having a meal with his mother. The Power wanted Ghost, but Merlin refused to give it up. Dara insisted that the Sign of the Logrus disregard Ghostwheel because they had more important concerns. The Logrus Sign gave up its pursuit of the construct when Merlin gave it some assurance that he intended to act to correct the balance between the Powers.

For a while, Merlin let Ghostwheel wander through the intricate Ways of Lord Sawall's Maze of Art. He called his construct to him by Trump when he came to some decision about how he would handle his manipulative relatives of the Courts. After helping Ghost escape from a kind of interspatial trap, Merlin requested its help in facing the sorcery of Mandor and Dara. Ghostwheel hid itself upon Merlin's wrist, as it had seen Frakir do, as Merlin summoned his stepbrother and mother.

Dara and Mandor sent out offensive spells against Merlin in a sorcerous duel. Finding that Merlin's defenses, as well as his own spells against them, were more than adequate, Dara summoned the Sign of the Logrus. Once again, Ghostwheel stood up before the Power, supporting Merlin. It had taken on an interesting method of self-preservation: it addressed the Logrus from amid a confusing display of shattered mirrors. Even the Logrus would need some time to locate the actual construct and cause it harm. The Power, finding itself stalemated, addressed Ghostwheel:

> "What is it that you want for yourself, construct?". . .
> "To protect one who cares for me."
> "I can offer you cosmic greatness."
> "You already did. I turned you down then, too. Remember?"
> "I remember. And I will remember. . . . Very well . . . You came prepared. It is not yet time to weaken myself in your destruction. Not when another waits for me to falter." (PC, 239)

Thus, Ghostwheel defended Merlin and kept the Power of the Logrus at bay. It seems likely that Merlin would not have successfully made his stand against that great Power without his worthy associate.

Remaining in the Courts of Chaos with his master, Ghostwheel no doubt is exploring that strange realm, and developing further in the process.

GILVA

Member of the House of Hendrake, believed to be a niece of Duke Borel, Master of Arms of the House. She was an acquaintance of Merlin when he was growing up in the Courts of Chaos.

Merlin wrote in his journals about becoming briefly reacquainted with her while attending the funeral service of the late King Swayvill. She appeared to Merlin mainly in her Chaosian demonform, and he referred to that form in describing her cool scales and sharp fangs which could easily shred a human ear (PC, 167). In the funeral procession along the Plaza at the End of the World, he initially spotted Gilva in the confusion of the murder of a successor to the throne. He recognized her even though she was in the process of changing her form: "She was tall and dark-eyed, shifting from a swirl of multicolored jewels to a swaying flowerlike form, and she had been staring at me." (PC, 147)

Later, Merlin brought her to the Sculpture Garden

within the House of Sawall. While there, Gilva told Merlin of the changing political climate in the Courts after the Patternfall War:

> "Nobody thought we would actually lose that war, . . . though it had long been argued that Amber would be a formidable adversary. . . . Afterward, there was considerable unrest . . . over the policies that had led to it and the treaty that followed it. No single house or grouping could hope for a deposition against the royal coalition, though. You know the conservatism of the Rim Lords. It would take much, much more to unite a majority against the Crown. Instead, their discontent took another form. There grew up a brisk trade in Amber memorabilia from the war. People became fascinated by our conquerors. Biographical studies of Amber's royal family sold very well. Something like a cult began to take shape." (PC, 165)

Gilva went on to explain about the development of secret chapels dedicated to individual members of Amber's Royal Family. She recognized the one that Merlin brought her to, hidden in a Way of the Sculpture Garden. It was apparent that she knew about the shrines firsthand because she located a candle, set it and lighted it, and spoke a prayer at the altar to Corwin.

Merlin had brought Gilva there in order to assay her knowledge and attitude about his missing father, since she was a loyal member of the House of Hendrake. She steadfastly affirmed that her House would have nothing to do with revenge against Corwin because of his killing of Lord Borel. The House of Hendrake maintains pride in their martial honor, and seeking retribution against a warrior for actions taken in battle would run contrary to their principles.

Gilva mentioned knowing that Merlin's stepbrother Mandor was a cultist, something she knew from the period before such things were forbidden. Mandor's personal shrine was dedicated to Princess Fiona, whom Mandor actually met.

In attempting to learn what happened to Corwin, Merlin questioned Gilva about the possibility of a cultist keeping an Amberite prisoner while worshiping his or her image in a personal shrine. Gilva concurred that it was possible. The approach of the person who had Corwin's shrine constructed brought a realization to Gilva about Merlin's suspicions. In spite of her fears, Gilva stated that she would place her support in Merlin's candidacy, if he were to be the next king of the Courts. As a member of the House of Hendrake, she promised him support from her House as well.

Sometime afterward, Merlin discovered that Gilva was a warrior in her own right. She had more than thirty notches scratched in the grip of her broadsword (PC, 169). Although it is not known with any certainty, she may have gotten some of those notches at the Patternfall battle.

GLAIT

A snakelike creature of the Courts of Chaos that had been a childhood friend of Merlin. Merlin discovered that Glait was still alive at the time that he returned to the Courts for the funeral of the late king. Glait, a feminine, intelligent being, showed Merlin a secret Way constructed in the Sculpture Garden of the House of Sawall.

In his journals, Merlin recorded a reminiscence of his youth in the many-shadowed Maze of Art:

> I thought back to my childhood, to some of the strange adventures for which this place had served as a point of departure. Gryll and I would come here, Glait slithering at our feet, coiled about a limb or riding somewhere amid my garments. (PC, 122)

Before Merlin had left the Courts to travel in shadows for the first time, he had seen Glait speared by an unknowing visitor to the House of Sawall. Merlin had found the bloodied spear, with much blood on the ground around it, but not Glait. She had disappeared. Merlin feared she had crawled away to hide under some rock and die.

Thus, he was glad to find her, alive and resting, inside a large vase that had been a favorite artifact of Merlin's. Glait explained that when she had been injured she needed to find rest in order to heal. Eventually, she had wandered into their select area of play, crawled into the vase, and slept, knowing that one day Merlin would return. She spoke with

a sibilant voice, expressing her delight in being reunited with him:

> "It warmss my cold blood to ssee you again, dear boy. . . .
> "One night we shall eat mice and lie besside a fire. You will warm me a ssaucer of milk and tell me of your adventuress ssince you left the Wayss of Ssawall." (PC, 98)

In spite of the fact that Glait was hungry and detected the scent of mice nearby, she put such considerations aside to show Merlin something she sensed had great importance. She directed Merlin to climb a stylized tree in the Sculpture Garden. At its top, Merlin discovered a hidden Way. Glait explained that she had observed its construction, and that the Shadowmaster who opened it was killed after its completion. She had been through the Way before, and directed Merlin to go through. Merlin found that it led to a secret chapel dedicated to the image of his father. At the shrine was Corwin's sword, Grayswandir. Merlin recognized it as being his father's genuine blade, not a reproduction. Thus, Glait had led him to a large piece of the puzzle as to what had happened to his father.

At a later time, Merlin returned with another acquaintance of his boyhood, Gilva of the House of Hendrake, to show her the hidden shrine and question her about it. Glait arrived to warn them that Merlin's mother, Dara, was about to reach the sculpted tree that led to the Way. Using his remarkably empowered ring, Merlin brought them to a pleasant glade somewhere outside the ancient home of Sawall. Overcome with animal craving, Glait slithered off to pursue mice. She returned soon, satiated, and Merlin requested that she return to the Sculpture Garden. Merlin hoped that his unique device, Ghostwheel, would turn up there, and he wanted Glait to deliver the message that Ghostwheel was to return to him.

As Merlin departed after leaving her in the tree below the hidden Way, Glait called to him, "If you are not eaten by ssomething bigger, come tell me your sstory one night." (PC, 170) In response, Merlin indicated in his journal that he had "never been sure when she was joking, reptilian humor being more than a little strange." (PC, 170)

It is likely that Glait still haunts the Sculpture

Garden, sleeping the long days away until some new event arouses her to wakefulness and curiosity.

GOLDEN CIRCLE

The privileged status assigned to those shadows that have signed a treaty of commerce with Amber. Aside from opening up trade routes between Amber and a shadow member, the member has the protection of the true city against adversaries from other shadows not in the Golden Circle. The treaty also gives Amber the right to transport its armies and navies through the member shadow.

For centuries, shadows enjoyed peaceful commerce with Amber as members of the Golden Circle. From time to time, shadow kingdoms sent messages invoking the need for military support from Amber against rival kingdoms. King Oberon always sent a reasonably sized corps of field soldiers to the shadow in compliance. Each contingent he sent, however, included a diplomatic party empowered to make negotiations for a settlement of conflicts. Such an arrangement prevented numerous deaths and bloodshed on both sides, as most arguments were settled shortly after the arrival of Amber's contingent.

When Oberon ruled in Amber, a shadow named Begma called upon him to uphold its treaty provisions against armed attack. A militant religious fanatic, Deela the Desacratrix, was making raids in areas protected under the Golden Circle. One of her prime regions of attack was Begma. Since the Begmans were adamant about Oberon's upholding the protection alliance Amber had with kingdoms of the Golden Circle, he sent troops to deal with her. He wasn't entirely successful and had to deal with her again several years later. He was ultimately victorious.

Often, a shadow kingdom is so grateful for Amber's support that a ruler will try to smooth over any problem that may arise between the shadow and Amber. The ruler of Deiga, for instance, begged forgiveness of King Random when a terrible incident occurred. Random had sent his brothers, Caine and Gérard, as ambassadors to renegotiate the Golden Circle treaty with Deiga. The king, apparently, wanted the treaty to be revised to include recently acquired territories that comprised an area impinging upon another shadow. While Gérard and Caine were visiting in the seaport marketplace, Caine was shot by an assassin from the roof of a building. Gérard was not able to find the attacker. Caine died instantly. What was most unusual about it was that Caine was shot by a rifle bullet. Although Deiga is a distance away from Amber, no one had ever fired gunpowder there before (TD, 112).

The king of Deiga was most contrite and magnanimous in his gifts to the king of Amber. Random understood that the people of Deiga were not culpable in this matter, and he made it clear to the king that he would not be held responsible for the incident. While Gérard and several members of his party returned to Amber with Caine's body, a corps of diplomats stayed on to conclude their negotiations in good faith.

Caine's assassination marked the beginning of escalating troubles with shadow members of the Golden Circle. On the afternoon of the day that Caine was murdered, a rifle-bearing assassin wounded Bleys, who was on a diplomatic mission in another shadow. Apparently it was the same rifleman. Someone, able to travel from shadow to shadow, was fulfilling a vendetta against the Amberites.

Once King Random learned the identity of the assassin, he acted to move against him. The assassin was a young prince of the shadow called Kashfa. This shadow was not a member of the Golden Circle. However, Kashfa had had difficulties with a neighboring shadow, Begma, over several hundred years. Begma did belong to the Golden Circle.

Random intended to block Prince Rinaldo's claim to the throne of Kashfa by placing his own man on the throne, under Amber's complete endorsement and protection. The king of Amber took the first steps by sending a trusted emissary to Kashfa to gather intelligence about the political situation there. This led to Random's selection of Arkans, duke of Shadburne, and the commencement of private meetings to devise a treaty agreeable to both sides.

After the assassination of General Jaston, the current ruler of Kashfa, Random was ready to place Arkans on the throne. He was away in Kashfa, working toward that goal, when Prime Minister Orkuz of Begma arrived in Amber with a small party. Orkuz wanted to avoid hostilities, but he did intend to lodge a protest concerning Amber's permitting Kashfa into the Golden Circle. The prime minister was hoping to find a way to embarrass Amber's Crown in the king's absence. However, he found Queen Vialle quite poised and capable, and he never quite resolved some irregularities that seemed to be occurring within the Royal Palace.

Since Bill Roth, an attorney from shadow Earth, worked on the treaty agreement between Kashfa and Amber for Random, he had a precise understanding of what was involved. He explained to Merlin that a significant bargaining chip had been a small region called Eregnor, which was wanted by both Begma and Kashfa. Mr. Roth had said,

> "In the papers I got from Random, Amber specifically recognizes Kashfa as including the area of Eregnor. Arkans had insisted that go into the treaty. Usually—from everything I've been able to find in the archives—Amber avoids getting involved in touchy situations like this between allies. Oberon seldom went looking for trouble. But Random seems to be in a hurry, and he let this guy drive a hard bargain." (SC, 133)

In this matter of the Golden Circle treaty for Kashfa, the complications were dissolved in a way that was beyond King Random's control. Prince Rinaldo and a mercenary force overran the palace in Kashfa, effecting a military coup. The prince held Arkans captive and proceeded with a coronation ceremony that officially made him King Rinaldo I.

Random ceased any consideration of allowing Kashfa into the Golden Circle. However, as the Amberites soon discovered, certain relations had been initiated long ago between the two shadow kingdoms that were being called into play at this time. Bloodlines were to be intertwined, cementing the reciprocity of Kashfa and Begma into the future.

GRAYSWANDIR

The sword used by Prince Corwin of Amber. It is remarkably light and balanced, though its blade is said to be unbreakable. Etched deeply within its gray metal is part of the Royal Pattern. The shimmering grayness of the sword, up to and including the haft, is the result of the mystical smoke of Tir-na Nog'th, the strange city in the sky, which is part of the sword's composition.

There is an apocryphal story of Lord Corwin's boyhood in Amber, in a bright time when Oberon was forging the major principles by which all citizens of the true city were to be guided. In that time of innocence, Corwin played with his older brother Eric, long before politics interfered with the kinship of brothers. At that time, there were no other children; only Benedict, who was much older and grown wise early in his experiences. So Corwin and Eric spent much time together at play, and they played often at sword fights. Their play was rough, and Corwin broke many a toy saber striking against Eric's own. This happened so frequently that Eric laughingly said, "Little brother, you need a weapon of air and fire. Nothing less will last in your hand."

Young Corwin thought of his brother's words often as he grew, practicing his swordmanship with foils in fencing matches with others in the Royal Court. All of the foils and sabres he practiced with as a youth seemed too heavy and, at the same time, too flimsy. In his desire to find a lightweight sword that was strong and durable, Corwin went to Benedict for advice. Benedict suggested he visit Tir-na Nog'th to see the Smith, the only man in the Phantom City who works with metals of our land and his own. Some of the courtiers of Amber tell that this became Prince Corwin's first journey to the city in the sky.

As instructed by Benedict, young Corwin went to the Phantom Smith of Tir-na Nog'th, bearing a quantity of silver and iron ore. Touching the luminescent anvil before the Smith's workshed, Corwin could be seen and heard by the Smith, a close-mouthed dark man with massive arms. Explaining what he needed, Corwin turned over the ore to the large man, who made several noncommittal grunts as he listened to the youth.

> "I require one thing in payment," the Smith grumbled.
> "Were not the silver and iron payment for your work?" the courtiers recount as Corwin's reply.
> "Hardly. They are the material I need to mold the weapon. You didn't think to hold a sword of air and smoke, now?"
> Corwin thought again wistfully of Eric's

words. "Indeed, that is exactly what I hoped for."

The Phantom Smith laughed raucously, his belly shaking uncontrollably.

"Have no fear, lad," the Smith finally said. "You will have your smoke. And fire too. But I require payment of a different sort. You are of the House Amber, are you not? Of course. Only such a one could reach this realm. I require the blood of one who is of the Blood Royal. It is necessary, both for the process and for my own needs. Are you willing to make such payment for your sword of smoke and fire?"

Gladly, Corwin made the bargain. The Smith had tubes and needles and vials to take the blood, as if he had often done this before. Corwin remarked on this as the Smith siphoned the blood he required. The Smith merely smiled and made a brief grunt.

Corwin returned the next night, as the Phantom City had begun to dematerialize with the dawn. His sword was ready, translucently gleaming in the transparent land like no other form but the Smith's anvil. Holding it up to examination, Corwin could see the fine lines of the Pattern, or a portion of the Pattern, in the smooth metal.

The Smith told him:

"That is why your blood was needed to forge the metal. The sword is part of you and will never stray far from you. The grayness that shines throughout is the smoke and flame given off as I smelt and shaped it on the anvil. That blade will never break, no matter what it strikes. With that blade, you may visit any part of Tir-na Nog'th again, and be seen and heard. You may need to do so sometime in your future."

"And was all the blood you drew needed to make this sword?"

"Ah—no. But it will come in use for other needs I have. But that is my secret, and need not concern you. Let you but know, this weapon has a name, and it will serve you loyally if you call it by that name."

"What is its name?"

"Grayswandir. For its color, and its nature. It shall not wander far from your side. It will serve and protect you. Grayswandir it is called."

Neither Corwin nor Benedict nor anyone else close to the source of this tale is willing to confirm the veracity of this account. However, it is told often enough in Amber, and it explains so many of the facts about Corwin's sword, that we may accept the story with satisfaction.

Fragments of another tale, lost in the mists of time, and reconstructed by opportunistic bards and gossipmongers, have been told in the city of Amber. These pieced-together fragments describe a period before the creation of the Pattern. In some of these tales, the unicorn, transformed into a lovely young woman, influenced a sorcerer of the Courts of Chaos to shape twin swords, one with the energy of the sun, the other with the power of the moon. Grayswandir had been the Nightblade, forged with the moon. In other versions, the unicorn, in one of many attempts to incense the Serpent, influenced a lovely young woman named Ewaedan to have her lover, Duke Namo, contract a blacksmith to forge the twin swords. The blacksmith, in turn, was given the mystical powers needed to create Grayswandir and its mate by the unicorn. This involved stealing a tangible aspect of the Logrus, and the need to use the vital blood of Namo, a favorite patron of the Serpent. Namo's death, as much as the sacrilege of the Logrus, enraged the Serpent.

There are other stories about the sword Grayswandir, but they are of lesser popularity, becoming more vague and disjointed with each retelling. In any case, we have no way of verifying which version of which tale is most accurate, and no one who was there will confirm or deny. The truth, like so many other things in Amber, depends on the shadow in which one resides.

GREEN SPIDER RING

Gold ring with a green gemstone worn by Queen Vialle, wife of King Random of Amber. The queen had given the ring to Rinaldo, son of the late Prince Brand, placing him under her protection.

The stone was of a milky green hue, placed in a setting that resembled a mantic spider. It was purchased in Amber by Random after his coronation, and he placed the ring on his queen's right forefinger in a small ceremony attended by courtiers and residents in the Royal Palace. The ring was so unique in design that anyone within the palace would recognize it as belonging to the queen.

Queen Vialle gave the ring to Rinaldo at a time when it seemed Amber might go to war, and her husband was away. A mercenary by the name of Dalt had brought a large assault force to the west fringe of the Forest of Arden, threatening to begin a war. His forces were confronted by Prince Julian's troops, both sides holding in readiness. Under a flag of truce, Dalt spoke with Julian. Rather than initiating a war that would be wasteful for both of them, he stated that he wanted to have either Rinaldo or his mother Jasra turned over to him.

Unwilling to hand over Jasra, who was in custody, Vialle chose to speak to Merlin in private, so that she could learn more of the situation. Merlin was able to contact Rinaldo and bring him to the sitting room, where he was speaking with the queen. Vialle learned that Rinaldo had called off his personal vendetta against the princes of Amber for the death of his father. He felt that vengeance was satisfied with the death of Brand's assassin. Rinaldo made his decision because of his friendship with Merlin, as well. Because Rinaldo willingly came to Amber out of trust for his friend, Queen Vialle removed the green spider ring from her finger and handed it to him. It was meant as an exchange of trust. As long as he wore that ring, no one in Amber would do him harm.

When he was apprised of Dalt's position and demands, Rinaldo requested the chance to speak to Dalt personally, giving the promise that he would avoid a conflict on Amber's soil. By doing so, he claimed that he might be able to find out why Dalt had attempted this show of force. After hearing Merlin's confirmation that Rinaldo was capable of handling Dalt in the way he had explained, Queen Vialle agreed to send him to Julian by Trump. She asked him to place his hand on her shoulder as she made contact with Julian. She explained that Rinaldo was under her protection, and Julian could clearly see the ring he was wearing.

Since Julian had been close to his brother Caine,

it was possible that he would have considered killing Rinaldo for his murder, were it not for that ring.

GRYLL

Childhood playmate of Merlin in the Courts of Chaos. Gryll had been an old family servant in the House of Sawall, most recently in the employ of Suhuy, Master of the Logrus. Merlin became reacquainted with his old demon friend when Gryll came to Kashfa seeking him. Suhuy had sent Gryll to summon Merlin back to the Courts after the death of King Swayvill.

Merlin's journals describe Gryll thusly:

> a long-snouted, pointed-eared individual, well-fanged and clawed, of a greenish-silver cast of complexion, eyes large and shining, damp leathery wings folded against its lean sides. From its expression, I [Merlin] couldn't tell whether it was smiling or in pain. (PC, 5)

It was Gryll who taught Merlin the Bonedance Game when he was a small boy. Gryll had led him on merry Ways within Lord Sawall's Maze of Art, along with other childhood friends, Glait and Kergma. The aged demon had helped to make Merlin's growing up in the Courts a much more pleasant time than it might otherwise have been.

Gryll had flown all the way from the Courts to Kashfa by riding along an extended filmy. In order to have Merlin accompany him, Gryll had to apply some of his shapeshifting abilities. "He absorbed a chair from the room's corner for extra mass, changing shape to accommodate my adult size." (PC, 7)

On their ride back to the Courts, Gryll and Merlin spoke of a number of things. Gryll told Merlin of the shifting power struggle between the Logrus and the Pattern; about the demons beyond the Rim of Chaos known as ty'iga; and about the spell Gryll had detected upon Merlin, coloring his thoughts and hanging heavily about his head.

After Gryll conveyed Merlin to his master's house, the demon saw little of his long-ago friend. However, residing so close to the center of events, Gryll learned of the changing fortunes of people in that place. It certainly would have pleased him that

Merlin benefited from the sudden changes that transpired in that realm at the end of all things.

HALLUCINOGENS: EFFECT ON SHADOW-SHIFTING

The release of subconscious imaginings induced by hallucinogenic drugs, like LSD, would become actualized into a disordered reality by an initiate of the Pattern or the Logrus.

Rinaldo of Kashfa had been given a dose of LSD after he was captured by the sorcerer known as Mask in the Keep of the Four Worlds. He was then allowed to wander freely, living in the realities created by his drugged psyche in an uncontrolled state. Since Rinaldo was endowed with the powers of the Pattern, he was able to bring his friend Merlin into the shadow reality of his subconscious, so that Merlin would share the same experiences. Clearly, the fantasies of an undisciplined mind, having no inhibitions, could propagate hideous creations and deadly perils. In the case of Rinaldo's experience, the "trip" took on a whimsical, even humorous form, albeit with the potential for fatal consequences. He had brought Merlin into a world that had been a fantasy of an author on the shadow Earth, a writer named Dodgson. Rinaldo had objectified a bar inhabited by creatures from a work entitled *Alice in Wonderland,* or *Through the Looking Glass.* The reality of the imagining might have been harmless enough, since Rinaldo was becoming pleasantly drunk in the company of the Mad Hatter, a talking rabbit, and the Cheshire Cat, but the shadow also gave birth to a frumious Bandersnatch and a Jabberwock. Both of these beasts were eager to slaughter Rinaldo and Merlin.

In his written accounts, Merlin offered the following explanation of his understanding of the effect of hallucinogens on Pattern-initiates:

Years ago, as an undergraduate, I had tried some LSD. It had scared me so badly that I'd never tried another hallucinogen since. It wasn't simply a bad trip. The stuff had affected my shadow-shifting ability. It is kind of a truism that Amberites can visit any place they can imagine, for everything is out there, somewhere, in Shadow. By combining our minds with motion we can tune for the shadow we desire. Unfortunately, I could not control what I was imagining. Also unfortunately, I was transported to those places. I panicked, and that only made it worse. I could easily have been destroyed, for I wandered through the objectified jungles of my subconscious and passed some time in places where the bad things dwell. . . . Later, when I told Random about it, I learned that he had some similar experiences. He had kept it to himself at first as a possible secret weapon against the rest of the family; but later, after they'd gotten back onto decent terms with each other, he had decided to share the information in the interest of survival. He was surprised to learn then that Benedict, Gérard, Fiona, and Bleys knew all about it—though their knowledge had come from other hallucinogens and, strangely, only Fiona had ever considered its possibility as an in-family weapon. She'd shelved the notion, though, because of its unpredictability. (SC, 18–19)

The truly dangerous aspect of an initiate of the Pattern or Logrus taking hallucinogenic drugs is the inherent evils that naturally exist in everybody's secret, dark yearnings. Anything brought forth by the mind of such a mage will affect those who are brought into the shadow by the initiate. Only someone of equal talent, such as Merlin, would have the ability to depart the realm of another's subconscious visions. An ordinary being who joined Rinaldo in his Wonderland bar would be trapped there, facing real death, until and unless Rinaldo consciously brought him out of that shadow. An individual of ordinary aptitude would be in dire straits indeed, if Rinaldo were to depart that world, oblivious of an unwilling participant left behind.

HANSEN, GEORGE

Son of a neighbor of Bill Roth's in upstate New York of the shadow Earth. When Merlin visited Roth, a close friend of his father's, he met George for the first time. Roth related that George wasn't acting or speaking like himself, arousing his suspicions. Shortly after this first meeting, it seemed as if George was ready to attack Merlin and Roth, just before they trumped to Amber.

George's father owned a couple of acres of farmland attached to his home, near Bill Roth's house. Mr. and Mrs. Hansen had consulted with Roth, who was an attorney, on a few minor legal matters in the past. As a boy, George knew Carl Corey, the name that Corwin of Amber was using at the time that Roth knew him. While George was going to school, he often worked in Corey's yard, raking leaves, weeding the garden, and mowing the lawn.

Roth's suspicions had been elevated initially because of Merlin's story that someone had been trying to kill him on the same day every year for seven years. Merlin and Roth were taking a long walk along a creek behind the Hansens' farmland when Roth thought they were being followed. Given the nature of their conversation, Roth was feeling more wary than usual.

When George came toward them unexpectedly at the creek, Merlin was prepared to ward off any possible assault. Roth eased Merlin's tension when he recognized the young man. He introduced Merlin to George. He was a medium-sized man in his twenties, wearing a T-shirt and blue jeans. He kept a pack of cigarettes rolled into the sleeve of the T-shirt. He was friendly and asked Merle about himself and his plans. Watching the young man carefully, Roth expressed privately to Merle that there was something wrong in George's mannerisms and way of talking. Roth had tested him by using the wrong name for Merlin's father, but the youth hadn't seemed to notice.

The next morning, Merlin was alone in Bill Roth's house, sitting on the porch, when George came by. He made an excuse that Roth had asked him to do some unspecified work, but Merle learned later that this was not true. George asked him several questions about his family, leading up to a query about Merle's mother, about whom he seemed to have a particular interest. He may not have been satisfied, however, since Merlin told him that his mother's name was Dorothy.

Later in the day, Merle was again walking with Roth by the creek, and Merle told him of George's brief visit. This time, Merle had a sense that someone was watching them from the opposite bank of the waterway. Just then he received an urgent Trump contact from King Random in Amber, who wanted him

to return at once. At the same time, Merle spotted George running toward them across the creek. Not wanting to leave Roth behind to face George alone, he brought Roth through with him to Amber as George reached them, calling out for them to stop.

Sometime later, when Merle was visiting in San Francisco on shadow Earth, he made a telephone call to the Hansen residence. Merle reached George's mother and asked to speak to George. Mrs. Hansen told him that George was at a nearby hospital. He was an outpatient who went routinely to be examined and receive medication. It seemed that George had amnesia that blocked out a couple of days around the time that Merle was visiting with Bill Roth. The doctors were unable to locate any physical injury that might have caused the loss of memory, but George and his parents were bothered sufficiently by it to warrant these follow-up medical examinations. At any rate, George appeared to be perfectly normal except for those lost days.

Since Merlin hadn't known George prior to his visit, he didn't see any reason to confide in Mrs. Hansen about the strange behavior that he and Bill Roth had noted.

HARLA

Wife to King Oberon of Amber in a highly contested marriage.

Oberon had wandered off to a distant shadow and married Harla there, while presumably still married to Queen Rilga. Upon returning to Amber with his bride, Oberon made a verbal claim that he had been married to Harla for years in her shadow of origin. This caused much debate among the royal counselors, but Queen Rilga had retreated to a shrine in the country and refused any official emissary of the Royal Court. Rilga died soon after her husband's return to Amber.

No one pursued the controversy after Rilga's death, not even her children Gérard and Julian. Soon, Queen Harla gave birth to two children, a boy named Delwin and a girl named Sand. After the birth of Harla's children, the king became more distant. Perhaps he was preoccupied with matters of state, but he seemed cold to these two children, and he began avoiding his wife as well.

Harla apparently had a very delicate constitution,

for she had a sudden illness that led to her death after a few days of bedrest. King Oberon conducted a small funeral for her, then completely ignored Sand and Delwin. While Harla was still alive, the brother and sister had frequently visited her homeland with her, so that they adopted a fondness for that place as much as for Amber.

In the meantime, Oberon had become involved in trade agreements with a shadow that was known to be antagonistic to Harla's homeland. Perhaps Harla had heard of this while living in the palace, and it contributed to her fatal illness. Oberon continued to court the adversarial shadow, and after Harla's death, reversed certain agreements he had made with Harla's homeland. Delwin and Sand found themselves caught in the middle of some disputes over rights of commerce between their homeland and Amber.

Eventually, Delwin and Sand left Amber to settle in Harla's shadow of origin. Only infrequently have they been in contact with anyone from the true city. Even then, they have made little effort to provide aid to anyone from their former realm.

HEERAT

A city that is at the center of a number of trade routes in a shadow far from Amber. Benedict and Random had traveled there in search of Random's son, Martin, in the time before the Patternfall battle.

Although Corwin of Amber had never been to Heerat, his brother Benedict had visited there several times prior to his journey with Random. Benedict referred to it as a:

"block city . . .

"a place of adobe and stone—a commercial center at the junction of several trade routes. There, Random found news which took him eastward and probably deeper into Shadow. We parted company at Heerat, for I did not want to be away from Amber overlong." (HO, 101)

It is understood that Heerat is a very ancient realm through which commercial travelers, merchants, and explorers travel with great regularity. The indigenous people have prospered by catering to the constant influx of business people, opportunists, and wastrel tourists. Odd as it may seem, those who reside there are mainly an honest lot, and crime seems to be at a minimum. There are no gambling concessions, no obvious saloons or houses of ill repute. Certainly, there have been some attempts at illicit trade of these kinds, but residents seem to have a subtle, yet unexplained, means of quashing these activities. Business appears to proceed in Heerat under the principle that one shall receive the appropriate goods for what one pays. Fair and equitable exchange. It is a simple maxim, and those who pass through the city have spread this message to others.

HORNED ONE, THE

The creature from the Courts of Chaos that held dominion in the shadow of Lorraine.

Corwin himself attributed the opening of the way from the Courts to many shadows reaching into Amber to his own curse against Eric the Usurper. Although numerous factors were involved, even the horned one looked upon Corwin as the Opener, the one who permitted the path from Chaos. In Lorraine, the way manifested itself as a Black Circle.

Ganelon, the ruler of Lorraine, had twice encountered the horned one. The first time was when he and a small band of men, many of them outlaws like Ganelon at the time, entered the Circle to end the hellish murders that threatened their own simple trade. They came across a group of the living dead sacrificing a goat on an altar. They fought briefly, and Ganelon was victorious. After they questioned and killed one captive, the dead man was suddenly transformed. It laughed as fire rose from its body, and it changed into a huge goat. In an inhuman voice, it said: "Flee, mortal man! But you shall never leave this Circle!" (GA, 34) Ganelon and his men got away, but their losses were great.

The second time Ganelon met the horned one, Ganelon had become ruler of the realm. Leading an army, Ganelon beat back the enemy forces, causing them to retreat to the Circle. The horned one led those demon soldiers, and Ganelon battled it for a time, until they were separated by the fighting around them. Ganelon said that he saw it in its more permanent form: "A thing with a manlike shape, but with goat horns and red eyes. It was mounted on a piebald stallion." (GA, 36)

Ganelon believed that the horned one had singled him out and was watching him. When Corwin had come to Lorraine, Ganelon was certain that the horned one knew of the stranger's arrival. Ganelon told Corwin:

> "If I were to leave this land, another such army—one that is readying even now—would come forth. That thing would somehow know of my departure. . . . It knows of you by now, and surely it must wonder over this development. It must wonder who you are, for all your strength." (GA, 36–37)

The goat-creature did test Corwin prior to a personal encounter. It sent a trusted servant from among its minions, a powerful demon with the ability to destroy any ordinary man. This demon confronted Corwin in his bedchamber in the Keep of Ganelon. The stranger proved greater than he appeared as the demon-servant fought him. Before dying in Corwin's grasp, the demon recognized him as the Opener of the Way.

With Ganelon, Lancelot du Lac, and a massive army, Corwin charged into the dark Circle in a final battle with the horned one. The living dead and hordes of demons fought to keep them back from a Dark Citadel where the horned one resided. Corwin reached the citadel just before Ganelon in spite of the evil forces. While Corwin fought hand to hand with the horned one, they had opportunity to speak. The creature was puzzled when Corwin called to Ganelon that the horned being represented "my sin against a thing I loved." (GA, 61) Struggling against Corwin, the creature looked into his eyes and realized who he was. They continued their deadly fight as the horned one questioned:

> "Lord of Amber, . . . why do you strive with me? It was you who gave us this passage, this way . . .
>
> ". . . You gave us this Gateway. Help us now, and we will restore to you that which is yours." (GA, 62)

At the same moment, the horned one and Corwin each locked a death grip around his opponent's throat. Only one of supernatural strength could have defeated that creature. It died not understanding Corwin's reticence.

HUGI

A small black bird that accompanied Corwin part of the way as he walked to the Courts of Chaos during Patternfall.

Hugi joined Corwin after Brand had slain Corwin's horse, Star. On a hellride to carry the Jewel of Judgment to the Courts, Corwin was forced to proceed on foot. Rather than being a comforting companion, Hugi chattered about the avoidance of striving. The bird's philosophy was akin to the East Indian religious beliefs of those who practice Yoga. Essentially, though, Hugi appeared to be attempting to discourage Corwin from completing his mission of bringing the Jewel to the site of the Patternfall battle.

Like the disciples of Sri Aurobindo, Hugi espoused a belief that man must seek identity with the Absolute by passing beyond the level of the mental into the divine life. In the philosophy of Advaita Vedanta of East Indian religion, the means of this passage is called "integral yoga," providing a transformation of mind, life, and body.

As Hugi explained to Corwin:

> "The whole problem lies with the self, the ego, and its involvement with the world on the one hand and the Absolute on the other. . . .
>
> ". . . You see, we are hatched and we drift on the surface of events. Sometimes, we feel that we actually influence things, and this gives rise to striving. This is a big mistake, because it creates desires and builds up a false ego when just being should be enough. That leads to more desires and more striving and there you are, trapped. . . .
>
> ". . . One needs to fix one's vision firmly on the Absolute and learn to ignore the mirages, the illusions, the fake sense of identity which sets one apart as a false island of consciousness." (CC, 79)

After a long and arduous journey, Corwin discovered that his attempt may have been futile, just as Hugi had been declaiming. Looking out over a vast valley, a virtual wasteland, with a mountain range in the distance, it seemed impossible to cross before the Death Storm would reach Corwin. With the Death Storm came the end of existence. Up to that point, Corwin had always kept ahead of it as he traveled.

Hugi continued to taunt Corwin, particularly when the prince told it that he would devise a new Pattern on the plateau on which he stood.

Expressing his philosophy of "futilitarianism," (CC, 82) Hugi said, "Resignation is the greatest virtue you might cultivate." (CC, 90)

Corwin responded:

> "If for you the greatest good is union with the Absolute, then why do you not fly to join it now, in the form of the all-pervading Chaos which approaches? If I fail here, it will become Absolute. As for me, I must try, for so long as there is breath within me, to raise up a Pattern against it. I do this because I am what I am, and I am the man who could have been king in Amber." (CC, 90)

Perhaps Hugi's fate was sealed while he awaited the arrival of Corwin "since the beginning of Time." (CC, 76) His philosophizing hadn't helped to alter his fate, as it turned out. In answer to Corwin's decision to create a new Pattern, Hugi told him, "I'll see you eat crow first," (CC, 90) and then the black bird chuckled.

The comment and the laugh drove Corwin to act. He reached for Hugi and twisted his head off. Thus, Hugi joined with the Absolute, after all.

ISLES OF THE SUN

A group of small islands to the south of the continent bearing the true realm of Amber.

Although there is very little hard data about these islands, it is believed that there are six large islands, ranging from five to forty-five miles in diameter, and dozens of small islets. Much of the land is arid and the climate is much warmer than on the continent. Some of the larger islands are inhabited, but no citizen of Amber has spent much time on them. Much of our information comes from sea captains whose ships had strayed too far south, and from some of the members of the Royal Family who had visited the isles.

Our Royal Liege, King Random had been to the isles once, long ago as a youth, but he remembers little of it. Prince Corwin had related something of that visit to the queen, as described in his Chronicles:

"Younger, smaller ... he [Random] might have had it a bit rougher than the rest of us ... Nothing quite as useless as another prince when there is already a crowd of them about. I was as guilty as the rest. Bleys and I once stranded him for two days on an islet to the south of here ..."

"... And Gérard went and got him when he learned of it. Yes, he told me." (HO, 51)

The isles may also have been a sanctuary for the Lady Fiona. Prince Julian, who had always been fond of his sister, told Corwin and Random, under some duress during the time the late Prince Eric ruled in Amber, that he believed Fiona was staying "somewhere to the south." (NP, 61) Fiona, herself, has been reluctant to discuss it, but those close to the Court theorize that her convenient disappearances, while yet maintaining a watchful connection to the true city, bespeak such a safe haven. It would be quite difficult, even for a princess of the realm, to lose herself within the countryside of Amber. A specific port of call, not too distant from Amber, would be more conducive to Fiona's oft-timed retreats from the cares of the true city.

More recently, the Isles of the Sun have been frequented by sailing ships carrying merchants eager to expand their trade. Still too rough and dry for a tourist attraction, the isles are gradually being explored, becoming more widely known. While it is uncertain whether Merlin, son of Corwin, had actually visited there, he referred to them in his published journals. Enjoying a ride on horseback with a pleasant companion, Merlin wrote of an odd geographical counterpoint to his location. He was riding in the north country when he described the following:

> "It was good to move through the countryside at a leisurely pace and to smell the land, to watch the moisture fade from sparkling fields and turning leaves, to feel the wind, to hear and watch a flock of birds southbound for the Isles of the Sun." (BA, 87)

Perhaps it would be for the best not to learn too much of these primitive little islands. An invading civilization might undermine the charm of such places in our world of conflict and occasional havoc.

JACKAL, TALKING

While Corwin, Prince of Amber, was making his way to the Courts of Chaos prior to the Patternfall battle, he encountered a large talking jackal. The jackal recognized Corwin and offered to point a way through the valley in which Corwin was striving to reach the battlefield.

Resting against a stony outcrop on a gravelly plain, Corwin saw the doglike shape coming toward him. He used the Jewel of Judgment around his neck to clear some of the heavy yellow fog, both to see better and to give the beast warning that he was seen.

The jackal seemed hospitable enough, chuckling at Corwin's little joke about his arriving too early to feed on his bones. Their conversation upon meeting presents some insight into this creature's perspective on Amber and the Courts of Chaos. The jackal began:

> "I have come merely to regard a Prince of Amber . . . Anything else would be a bonus."
> "Then feast your eyes. Anything else, and you will find that I have rested sufficiently."
> "Nay, nay . . . I am a fan of the House of Amber. And that of Chaos. Royal blood appeals to me, Prince of Chaos. And conflict."
> "You have awarded me an unfamiliar title. My connection with the Courts of Chaos is mainly a matter of genealogy."
> "I think of the images of Amber passing through the shadows of Chaos. I think of the waves of Chaos washing over the images of Amber. Yet at the heart of the order Amber represents moves a family most chaotic, just as the House of Chaos is serene and placid. Yet you have your ties, as well as your conflicts."
> (CC, 85)

When Corwin asked if the jackal knew the way to the Courts, it cheerfully responded that it would guide Corwin. Although it said it was not far, they walked a great distance along the plain, and gradually it became an upward climb. When Corwin questioned the length of their walk, the jackal apologized, blaming his "jackalocentrism" for not judging the distance in human standards.

They reached a mountainside, and the jackal pointed out an opening in the cliff face. It was a tunnel, he claimed, that would take him out of the valley and bring him to the Courts. Corwin thanked the beast and started into the darkness.

Feeling his way through the darkness, Corwin realized the ground was not quite natural. He knew the ground was strewn with bones. Before he could do more than swing his body around and use his staff in a protective stance, the jackal was upon him. Thrown to the ground, Corwin lost his staff. Pulling his sword from his sheath, he struck the beast hard with its pommel. Before the jackal fully recovered, Corwin had Grayswandir out. The creature lunged, and Corwin put all his weight behind the thrust of his blade.

As it was dying, the jackal said, "It would have been so fine to eat a Prince of Amber. I always wondered—about royal blood." (CC, 87) The irony of the jackal's interest was not lost on Corwin, even while he had to pull his sword from the bloody entrails of its corpse.

JACK OF DIAMONDS

An ordinary playing card through which Brand, chained and imprisoned, was able to communicate with his brother Random.

At the time, Random was a profligate young gambler enjoying his vice in a shadow named Texorami. He was extremely lucky at the poker table, and he was holding a full house when the Jack of Diamonds began talking to him.

As Random described the event to his brother Corwin, ruling in Amber:

> I decided later it must be our mental quirk associated with the Trumps that made me see it that way when someone was trying to reach me and I had cards in my hand—any cards. Ordinarily, of course, we get the message empty-handed, unless we are doing the calling. It could have been that my subconscious—which was kind of footloose at the time—just seized on the available props out of habit. Later, though, I had cause to wonder. Really, I just don't know.
> The Jack said, "Random." Then its face

blurred and it said, "Help me." I began getting a feel of the personality by then, but it was weak. The whole thing was very weak. Then the face rearranged itself and I saw that I was right. It was Brand. He looked like hell, and he seemed to be chained or tied to something. "Help me," he said again.

"I'm here," I said. "What's the matter?"

". . . prisoner," he said, and something else that I couldn't make out.

"Where?" I asked.

He shook his head at that.

"Can't bring you through," he said. "No Trumps, and I am too weak. You will have to come the long way around. . . ."

I did not ask him how he was managing it without my Trump. Finding out where he was seemed of first importance. I asked him how I could locate him.

"Look very closely," he said. "Remember every feature. I may only be able to show you once. Come armed, too. . . ."

Then I saw the landscape—over his shoulder, out a window, over a battlement. I can't be sure. It was far from Amber, somewhere where the shadows go mad. Farther than I like to go. Stark, with shifting colors. Fiery. Day without a sun in the sky. Rocks that glided like sailboats across the land. Brand there in some sort of tower—a small point of stability in that flowing scene. I remembered it, all right. And I remembered the presence coiled about the base of that tower. Brilliant. Prismatic. Some sort of watch-thing, it seemed—too bright for me to make out its outline, to guess its proper size. Then it all just went away. Instant off. And there I was, staring at the Jack of Diamonds again, with the guy across from me not knowing whether to be mad at my long distraction or concerned that I might be having some sort of sick spell.

I closed up shop with that hand and went home. (SU, 17–18)

Random later discovered that Brand had obtained unique powers that certainly made this occurrence appear feasible. Brand proved to be a devious individual who would willingly sacrifice his brothers and sisters to achieve his personal goals. Therefore, it would be interesting to see the significance of the Jack of Diamonds in its sometime use of divination. Although Random stated that he took his card-playing seriously, he probably would discard the notion of fortune-telling with playing cards. However, the practice affords us an interpretation of the kind of person represented by the Jack of Diamonds.

By itself, the Jack of Diamonds represents a businessman. It can also represent a journey one would make on some business venture. The person represented by this card could be a reliable dealer in such affairs if he comes from the higher classes of society. If he is from the lower classes, he is untrustworthy, seeking only personal monetary gain. Random did not indicate that this playing card had been upside-down (inverted) in his hand, but if it was, it would symbolize a true troublemaker, one who would falsely claim authority as a means of swindling others.

In his account, Random said that he held a full house. In poker, this means he had three of a kind and two of a kind. In fortune-telling, there is significance in the appearance of like cards in different suits in pairs or threes. If Random had been holding two Jacks in his hand, for instance, it would denote conspirators acting against one. Both cards held upright indicates that their scheme could be averted. Both cards inverted means that they will strike immediately. If only one is inverted, the conspiracy will occur when one believes that the danger is past and has relaxed his defenses.

If Random were holding three Jacks in his hand, the nature of the problem is less perilous. It would speak of petty annoyances in one's social sphere. These annoyances, however, are attributable to treacherous friends or acquaintances. In this case, if any of the three cards is inverted, it would signify that one has gotten the better of these friends by crossing them up in some way.

In Amber, no special credence would be assigned to the use of playing cards in divining the future. Still, the closeness of the royal cards in an ordinary deck to the Tarot-like Trumps used by Amberites may bear watching. Brand's seeming affinity for the Jack of Diamonds in this situation might actually have been the consequence of one of the possible interpretations stated above. One may certainly draw inferences between our knowledge of Brand of Amber and the arcane beliefs set down by those inclined to believe in the powers of playing cards.

JASRA

Wife of Brand of Amber and mother to Rinaldo. For a long while she had been queen of the shadow Kashfa, then took control of the Keep of the Four Worlds from the aged wizard Sharu Garrul. After her husband's death, Jasra had sought revenge against the Royal Family in Amber. When Merlin, son of Corwin, lived on shadow Earth, Jasra orchestrated yearly attempts to murder him. She had trained a sorcerer in the Art intending to use this individual against Merlin. However, Jasra was duped by the novice sorcerer and fell victim to a spell of immobility. Merlin broke the spell and joined with her to defeat the sorcerer. With the help of Merlin and his stepbrother Mandor, Jasra was able to reclaim mastery of the Keep of the Four Worlds.

Very little is known about Jasra's early life. Most of what has become known to us comes from information Merlin had gathered, recording much of it in his published journals. According to one of Merlin's sources, she had been brought to the Courts of Chaos from a shadow near to that realm. She worked as a maid-companion to the Lady Dara in the House of Helgram. (PC, 74) Through Dara, she learned the Arts. While residing in the Courts, Jasra had met Brand, who had begun conspiring with several Chaos lords against Amber.

Since Dara had become a Pattern-initiate only after meeting Brand's brother Corwin, Jasra may have gained her sorcerous powers shortly thereafter. With knowledge of the Pattern, Dara could then train Jasra in the Way of the Broken Pattern. It seems certain that Jasra derived her early talents from an initiation in a Broken Pattern, which Dara would have had to bring her to and help guide her through. We may also surmise that Jasra discovered the Cave of Blue Crystal soon afterward, while she was enjoying the experience of shadow walking.

Sometime in her travels, Jasra visited Kashfa. She caught the interest of the old king there, Menillan. With an eye on the throne for herself, she became Menillan's constant companion. The king had grown infirm and was frequently confined to bed. Using her wiles, Jasra took advantage of a young Kashfan nobleman named Jasrick, Earl of Kronklef. Because Jasrick was chief of the palace guard and had a brother who was a general in the Kashfan army, she schemed with

them to organize a military coup with the passing of Menillan. (BA, 18) The old king began slipping very rapidly after that point, and one night, quietly in his sleep, King Menillan died. With the loyalty of virtually all the officers of the standing army and every member of the palace guard, Jasrick and Jasra were smoothly installed as joint leaders.

Though Jasrick fully intended to rule Kashfa with an iron hand, he never had the opportunity. Charges of treason were presented before the Court by the late King Menillan's ministers. These charges were well documented and presented openly before the entire Court. Queen Jasra could do nothing but disassociate herself from the two rebel leaders of the uprising. Publicly declaring her regret, Queen Jasra condemned the former earl of Kronklef and his brother to execution by decapitation. The punishment was immediately carried out.

While it is uncertain what kind of ruler Jasra was, she did reign for quite a long time. Perhaps, at first, she was seen as serving her people well, but there were intimations, later in her rule, that she had become erratic and unpopular.

A hermit living near the Keep of the Four Worlds gave Merlin the following information about Jasra and the man she married:

"Well, she snared herself an Amberite—the prince called Brand . . . Rumor had it they met over some magical operation and it was love at first blood. She wanted to keep him, and I've heard it said they actually were married in a secret ceremony. But he wasn't interested in the throne of Kashfa, though he was the only one she might have been willing to see on it. He traveled a lot, was away for long stretches of time. I've heard it said that he was responsible for the Days of Darkness years ago, and that he died in a great battle between Chaos and Amber at that time, at the hands of his kinsmen. . . .

". . . She bore him [Rinaldo], and I've heard she taught him something of her Arts. He didn't know his father all that well, Brand being away so much. Kind of a wild kid. Ran away any number of times and hung out with a band of outlaws." (BA, 49–50)

The death of Brand in the Patternfall War may have marked the point at which Jasra made some unpopular decisions. Dave the hermit hinted at this: "There was a lot of pressure on her to remarry. But she just took a succession of lovers and played the different factions off against each other. Usually her men were military leaders or powerful nobles." (BA, 45)

Initially, it seems, Jasra's rule had a great deal of popular support. She worked tirelessly to add the province of Eregnor to Kashfa, a position that many Kashfans advocated. The accession of Eregnor had been contested by the shadow called Begma for generations. During Jasra's reign, Kashfa had gone to war against Begma at least once, and the rights to Eregnor had been a major issue of contention.

On the other hand, the Kashfans and Begmans enjoyed stretches of peace. For a time, Orkuz of Begma had been an ambassador situated in Kashfa. Jasra became well acquainted with him, his wife Kinta, and his daughters, Nayda and Coral. As a boy, Rinaldo was often thrown together with young Coral during state visits. While in a period of mutually beneficial exchange, Orkuz and Jasra had arranged a marriage by proxy of Rinaldo and Coral. Unfortunately, the period of goodwill came abruptly to an end shortly thereafter. The marriage contract had been finalized, but the official documents were ignored when hostilities between the two kingdoms ensued.

Early in Jasra's reign in Kashfa, she became interested in the extraordinary source of power located at the Keep of the Four Worlds. It is not known how she met Sharu Garrul, but it is believed he became her teacher. With Jasra dividing her time between Kashfa and the Keep, her subjects gradually became concerned for her welfare. Her lengthening absence from Kashfa began to worry her son, Prince Rinaldo, who ruled in her place. If we understand the chronology correctly, Rinaldo could only believe that Sharu Garrul had regained his power and become a threat again. Thus, he organized an army, recruited the mercenary troops of his friend Dalt, and marched against the Keep.

Sometime earlier, Jasra and Brand had wrested control of the Keep of the Four Worlds from Sharu Garrul. One or the other, or both of them, had transfixed Sharu with a spell of immobility. Rinaldo spoke of having carved his name in Sharu's leg when he was a boy. (BA, 126) With this knowledge, Rinaldo mounted an assault on the Keep fearing that Sharu had been freed somehow and his mother was in danger.

Adding further confusion to our chronological record of Jasra's activities, Jasra and her son spent much time on shadow Earth, as well. Jasra had urged Rinaldo to begin taking revenge on the Amberites for Brand's death by tracking Merlin, son of Corwin, in San Francisco. She was disappointed when her son decided to stop making attempts on Merlin's life after the first couple of years. She began training an artist of Rinaldo's acquaintance who had some small occult skills, Victor Melman, and continued to attack Merlin every April herself.

Jasra was close by and observant when Merlin and his girlfriend, Julia Barnes, broke up. Realizing that Julia had a genuine aptitude in the paranormal, Jasra arranged for her to meet the artist Victor Melman. After a while, Jasra revealed herself to Julia and took her in as a serious disciple. Aside from her rare talents in the Magic Arts, Julia was extremely canny. She used Jasra's own methods to follow her secretly. When Jasra was alone within the Keep of the Four Worlds, Julia used the same spell of immobility Jasra had used on Sharu against Jasra. While Jasra was thus incapacitated, Julia used a mask to hide her features, and she took control of the Keep.

Merlin revived Jasra from the immobility spell after rescuing her from the Keep. His reason for doing so was to form an alliance in order to attack the Keep of the Four Worlds. Merlin told her of his concern that his half brother Jurt would gain tremendous power by bathing in the Black Stone Fountain there. Thus, they would have to do battle against the sorcerer named Mask and Merlin's brother. Jasra agreed, but with the understanding that she would be allowed to reclaim the Keep for herself.

Jasra joined Merlin and his older stepbrother Mandor as they transported to the Keep and entered the chamber of the Black Fount. Jurt had not completed the process in the Fount, but he had gained some of its remarkable powers. While Merlin engaged Mask in a sorcerous duel, Jasra took on Jurt. She found him quite inept, and she easily prevented Jurt from causing any real damage to others. When Mask found that Jasra, Merlin, and Mandor were gaining the upper hand, Mask brought Sharu out of his spell. Jasra was forced to deal with her old teacher while Merlin fought Mask. Ultimately, the

Keep began falling into rubble as Merlin defeated Mask. Although Jurt and Mask had fled, Jasra was still plying sorcerous forces against Sharu. Jasra succeeded against Sharu, and confined him to act as guardian of the Fount.

Once Jasra had regained her mastery of the Keep, she hosted a dinner with Mandor and Merlin, during which she explained much about her activities. When Merlin discussed some of the problems he had been facing, he spoke of Coral, younger daughter of Orkuz, and the dilemma she was in. Since Jasra knew Coral well, she was sincerely worried when Merlin talked of her. Merlin's discovery that the Pattern was sentient was a revelation. From Jasra's perspective, the politics of Kashfa and Begma seemed petty in comparison to conflict between the Pattern and the Logrus, and the potential for cataclysmic consequences that could result in all the shadows.

Using the Trump that Merlin had drawn of Coral, he, Mandor, and Jasra concentrated on making contact. After some effort, they did glimpse the image of Coral, unconscious in a dark area. By this point, Merlin's Ghostwheel had joined them. It informed them that an all-powerful force had felt their contact through the Trump. This force was rushing toward their location. Ghostwheel believed that its arrival would be disastrous for them, and so took matters into its own hands.

Ghostwheel sent Jasra, Mandor, and Merlin off in different directions, far into Shadow. Its hope was that the Rushing Force would find it extremely difficult to find any of them again, although Ghostwheel was most concerned about Merlin.

Much later, Ghostwheel sought out Jasra and Mandor, then returned to Merlin in Amber. Ghostwheel told Merlin: "Jasra was not where I left her. But I brought your brother." (KS, 193) Certainly, Jasra was able to manage her own affairs. It is likely that she remains in close proximity to the Keep of the Four Worlds. That place would have sufficient capability to keep her safe from harm. Perhaps she even has some means of observing her son in Kashfa without seeming to intrude on his privacy. This is mere speculation, of course, but it is conceivable that she is watching the progress of the Pattern-Logrus Conflict, seeking a means to support her son as the need arises. It would be important, after all, to harness the energies at the Keep with great care, learning whatever risks might be involved, before testing their strength against such supremacy as can be seen in the two Powers.

JASRICK

Earl of Kronklef and chief of the palace guard in the shadow called Kashfa.

Jasrick had been involved in a forced military takeover of Kashfa after the death of the longtime ruling monarch, King Menillan. His advancement was made possible through a romantic liaison with the old king's consort, Jasra. While Menillan was on his deathbed, Jasra became interested in the young earl, and they made plans for a coup with Jasrick's brother, who was a general of the army. Through Jasra's clever manipulations, Jasrick gained control of the army over the old king's ministers, and, with Menillan's death, was seated by martial approbation.

According to Flora of Amber, Jasrick had once been a beau of hers. Jasra had stolen him away from Flora some thirty or forty years earlier in Amber-time. Since Jasrick probably felt he was distinguished by the honor of a connection with the true city, Jasra must have had enormous powers of seduction to cause him to change in his affections.

When Jasra had attained the ruling authority over the kingdom of Kashfa, she called for a summary execution of Jasrick and his brother for acts of treason against the late king. The executions were carried out immediately.

Years later, while Jasra was occupied at the Keep of the Four Worlds, another brother of Jasrick, named Kasman, wrested control of the kingdom.

JASTON

General of the major combined military forces of shadow Kashfa and one of several interim rulers during the absence of Queen Jasra.

Although General Jaston had not served in any combat situations, he had been in the military as an officer for many years. Distantly related to Kasman, a nobleman who ruled Kashfa for a number of years, Jaston was promoted to the rank of general.

By popular assent, and after the last king had suddenly died, Jaston succeeded to the kingship. He was well-spoken and a good diplomat, and he hoped to leave a distinct mark during his reign. This included seeking a permanent peace with shadow Begma.

For centuries, Kashfa and Begma had been in a long and painful conflict over a piece of land named Eregnor. Their dissension over which shadow should possess it had caused escalating hostilities and unsettled periods of relative peace throughout their history. General Jaston sought a reconciliation that would satisfy both parties.

Jaston initiated negotiations with the Begmans that began the drawing up of a peace agreement. In this agreement, Jaston offered to waive Kashfa's claim to Eregnor in return for payment of war damage claims. Begma and Kashfa were well on the way to ratifying the agreement, but the general had received several petitions of protest from a number of the wealthy landholders of Kashfa. While it has not been clarified, it may be that some of the nobles were applying pressure on Jaston to withdraw his agreement.

Negotiations with Begma were still taking place when Jaston received word of an official visit from King Random of Amber. It was rumored that Amber was considering giving Kashfa Golden Circle trade status.

With the arrival of the royal entourage, Jaston went out of his way to please them. When King Random set the time for a conference, the general eagerly complied. In their meeting, Random and his brother, a dour man of military demeanor named Benedict, both spoke of improving relations between Amber and Kashfa. In varying ways, the two Amberites spoke at length about their desire to resolve mutual problems. The general barely managed to interject some overtly friendly comments, while the King and his brother pursued their ardent but vague overtures of partisanship. Abruptly, the King of Amber asked for an adjournment until the following day. Jaston amicably granted it.

In spite of his puzzlement over these proceedings, General Jaston arranged for a fine state banquet in honor of his guests. At dinner, conversation was of an innocuous kind, and the Amberites proved quite sociable in the general's estimation. The banquet continued pleasantly for hours.

As it was becoming quite late, and many of the other guests and members of the Court were retiring, Jaston courteously excused himself to repair for bed. Before leaving King Random's side, he promised to see to arrangements for their next meeting early in the morning.

Unfortunately, the general expired quite suddenly. He was pushed over the banister of a winding stair.

JEWELERS ROUGE

The special properties of this compound were first discovered accidentally by Lord Corwin while visiting with his sister Deirdre in Amber. On various Shadows, it is commonly used for its named purpose, that is, to polish gems. However, in Amber and its nearest shadows, it becomes a highly combustible substance with a dangerous explosive potential.

Although the chemical compound for jewelers rouge is a fairly simple formula, the different physical laws that apply to Amber make it unlikely in the extreme for an Amberite to accidentally mix the formula while in the precincts of the realm. Such an attempt would probably be as disastrous as mixing nitric acid and glycerine in the shadow Earth.

Lord Corwin purchased a bottle of jewelers rouge in the shadow called Avalon. He was using a small quantity of it on a cloth to polish a bracelet he intended to give to Deirdre. When he finished with it, he absently tossed the cloth into a fireplace. The explosion which followed was forcible, but not catastrophic. Since he was alone at the time, no one else learned of this special property, and Corwin intended to keep it secret to his later advantage.

The possibilities for using the substance in armaments within the realm of Amber are readily apparent. The regional militia had, prior to this, been reduced to using medieval, close-range arms: swords, spears, axes, bows and arrows, catapults, and the like. The laws of physics keep the chemical compound known as gunpowder in an inert and incombustible state. Members of the Royal Family of Amber had knowledge of the use of gunpowder, but had been unable to bring such force to bear in

Amber. Thus, Corwin's discovery of this secondary use for jewelers rouge was indeed revolutionary in nature.

When Corwin was prince in Amber and considered to be rightful heir to the throne, he made strategic use of his knowledge of jewelers rouge in his plans to defeat his brother Eric, usurper of the kingdom. In order to make practical use of the compound, Prince Corwin had to travel to Shadow Earth to make clandestine arrangements for a specially prepared consignment of ammunition. His dealings with a proper British ex–RAF officer named Arthur in Brussels were slightly less than legal. However, they were effective. The British officer put him in contact with a munitions factory in Switzerland that was willing to produce in quantity primers that used jewelers rouge instead of gunpowder and bullet casings made of silver, as long as Corwin was willing to pay sufficient funds for the service. The greatest difficulty that Corwin had in these black market transactions had been in meeting Arthur's concerns about transporting the armaments out of the country. Corwin had to frequently reassure the elder gentleman that the problem was not his.

Corwin was able to train his army in the use of explosive weapons—men unused to such modern technology—only upon reaching a shadow that was congruent to Amber. Only at that point would the jewelers rouge become functional in the explosive primers.

JEWEL OF JUDGMENT

The highly potent artifact that Dworkin had used to create the Pattern, thus establishing Order and the universe as we know it. An initiate of the Pattern can become attuned to the Jewel of Judgment by traversing the Pattern a second time while wearing it on his person. This attunement gives such an individual a number of unique abilities. Among them is the ability to affect meteorological conditions. One who is attuned is also capable of designing a new Pattern that will reflect his own psyche in its composition.

It has also been learned that the Jewel is actually the Eye of the Serpent of Chaos. In some undisclosed manner, the unicorn had stolen the Serpent's

Eye ages ago. In the recent escalation of hostilities between the two Powers, the Jewel had become an object of contention affecting several people residing in the shadows as well as those at the two poles of existence. As a means of concealing the Jewel from the Powers, Dworkin surgically implanted it in the eye socket of a young woman from shadow Begma.

The Jewel resembled a ruby pendant, placed in a simple gold setting, hanging from a heavy chain. Dworkin had conferred the Jewel on his son Oberon as part of his offices of royal authority. When Fiona was young, she spent time under Dworkin's tutelege, and he taught her about some of its effects. She told her brother Corwin:

> "He [Dworkin] indicated that while it conferred unusual abilities, it also represented a drain on the vitality of its master. The longer you wear it, the more it somehow takes out of you. I paid attention after that, and I noticed that Dad [Oberon] wore it only seldom and never kept it on for long periods of time." (SU, 111)

To the sons and daughters of Oberon, the Jewel was a little understood artifact, and none of them were aware of its origins. Those who did have an interest in it, though, realized that it predated the great Pattern of Amber, and that its potency was of a higher order. The Jewel was usually referred to as a "higher octave" of the Pattern. In the documents that have been disclosed to the public, we can ascertain the properties of the Jewel, as evidenced by those Pattern-initiates who have wielded its power. We may enumerate them in the following:

1. **Control of Environmental or Atmospheric Conditions.** This is the most obvious function of the Jewel, and the one most easily utilized once an initiate has attuned himself to it. In his Chronicles, Corwin stated: "The control of meteorological phenomena was almost an incidental, though spectacular, demonstration of a complex of principles which underlay the Pattern, the Trumps, and the physical integrity of Amber herself." (SU, 47) Still, an initiate can refine this function to develop and direct an atmospheric manifestation at a specific tar-

get. Eric the Usurper had directed downpours of rain and fierce storms upon Bleys and Corwin in the shadows they crossed, approaching Amber (NP, 125); Brand had created deadly bolts of lightning against the Amberites at the Patternfall battle (CC, 108); Random had sent out a single, well-aimed streak of lightning that exploded a tossed bomb while it was in midair, before it could harm any people (TD, 137–38); and Corwin had created a concentrated, funnellike tornado to deter Brand from completing the circuit of the Primal Pattern. (HO, 154–55)

2. **Heightened Perception and Affinity to the Jewel.** This relates to the higher level that an initiate feels he has attained after becoming attuned to the artifact. When Corwin completed his attunement, he described it in this way:

    . . . in a blaze of ruddy light that found me regarding myself holding the pendant beside the Pattern, then regarding the pendant, Pattern within it, within me, everything within me . . . only an octave higher, which I feel is about the best way there is to put it. For a certain empathy now existed. It was as though I had acquired an extra sense, and an additional means of expression. (SU, 54)

Fiona also spoke of this new perception:

    "I inferred from some of Dad's remarks that it has something to do with a heightened perception, or a higher perception. Dworkin had mentioned it primarily as an example of the pervasiveness of the Pattern in everything that gives us power." (SU, 111)

Even though Corwin did not have the Jewel in his possession as he pursued Brand along the primal Pattern, he was able to feel its forces, and, because of his affinity to it, he invoked a phenomenon to harass Brand, drawing upon its powers.

Merlin's artificial construct Ghostwheel underwent the attunement to the Jewel. Ghostwheel expressed that his perceptions had been altered. When Merlin asked if Ghost could "move . . . [his] awareness into the stone from a distance," (KS, 205) his construct answered in the affirmative.

3. **Distortion of Time Sense.** This occurs when an initiate wears the Jewel for an extended duration. We may rely on Fiona for an explanation:

    ". . . I pieced together from a number of things that he [Oberon] said, beginning with a comment to the effect that 'when people turn into statues you are either in the wrong place or in trouble.' . . . I eventually got the impression that the first sign of having worn it too long is some sort of distortion of your time sense. Apparently it begins speeding up the metabolism—everything—with a net effect that the world seems to be slowing down around you." (SU, 112–13)

Corwin found this happening to him immediately after leaving the library of the palace where he had convened a Family meeting. He was walking up a staircase with Random, and Random found it hard to keep up with him. As he took out his key to unlock the door to his quarters, the key fell. He reached for it and caught it, noticing that it seemed to fall more slowly than it should have. Inside his room, his reactions were much faster than an intruder's actions, which probably saved him from a direct knife thrust in the chest. Because Corwin was able to move so rapidly, he deflected the assailant's arm, but he couldn't avoid the blade's tearing into the flesh of his abdomen. His unexpected speed had prevented a more deadly stroke.

4. **Protection of the Attuned Initiate.** An initiate who is attuned to the Jewel, according to Fiona, will be able to "interact with it at near distances, and it will attempt to preserve your life if you are in imminent danger of losing it. . . . Don't take it for granted, though. A swift stroke can still beat its reaction. You can die in its presence." (HO, 148) Corwin realized that the Jewel had protected him when the intruder attacked him with the dagger in his room: "It had torn me from one assailant and found, somehow, within my mind, a traditional place of safety—my own bed—and had transported me there." (HO, 154) That was how he had escaped the attacker,

who could have easily finished the job if Corwin had simply collapsed in his quarters. Although Corwin had not consciously willed it to do so, the Jewel transported him to his home in New York on shadow Earth, and therefore out of reach of any further assault.

Dworkin had urged Merlin to attune himself to the Jewel as a means of protection from a greater adversary: The Sign of the Pattern itself. After having challenged the Power of the Pattern in its chamber, Merlin was told to take the Jewel to the blue crystal cave. Merlin explained in his journal:

> I could not keep wearing it for too long, though, because this also had a tendency to prove fatal. He [Dworkin] decided that I must become attuned to the Jewel—as were my father and Random—before I let it out of my possession. I would thereafter bear the higher-order image within me, which should function as well as the Jewel in defending me against the Pattern." (KS, 176)

We can see, therefore, that the artifact is capable of preserving an individual even against the supreme Power of the Pattern, if need be.

5. **Drawing Strength from the Jewel.** By taking some action using the artifact, one is able to draw new energy from it. Corwin felt this as he was delineating a new Pattern on a high plateau: "There was no drag. I felt very light, despite the deliberation. A boundless energy seemed to wash constantly through me." (CC, 97) At another point, Corwin had carelessly tossed a stone away. It seemed to float slowly from him. Drawing strength from the artifact, he exerted his influence on the stone, and it flew away like a projectile. (CC, 83) This action energized his body.

6. **Influencing the Motion of Other People.** An initiate can affect the movements of people within a short range, even working on a molecular level. Brand's confrontation with Benedict in Tir-na Nog'th illustrated this operation well. He distracted Benedict from sensing any gradual physical effect while he stepped within range of him, exerting his will upon the Jewel. When Brand found the proper range, under ten feet, Benedict found himself unable to move. (HO, 181) In such close proximity, Benedict was helpless as Brand closed upon him, a dagger in hand.

Corwin had discovered that his affinity for the Jewel was so great that he could use it against Brand at Patternfall. While Brand held Deirdre hostage at the edge of the Abyss, Corwin focused his concentration on Brand's body.

> I reached out and felt its [the Jewel's] presence. I closed my eyes and summoned my powers.
> Hot. Hot, I thought. It is burning you, Brand. It is causing every molecule in your body to vibrate faster and faster. (CC, 114)

Corwin's influence, directed by the artifact, gave him power over the motion of human molecules within an individual's body.

Attunement to the Jewel of Judgment will endow a person who has walked the Pattern with the capabilities described above. Besides these, of course, one will have the potential to create a Pattern of one's own, giving birth to a new universe that mirrors the memories and imaginings of the one who designed it.

As he lay dying, Eric explained to Corwin, in simple terms, how one goes about attuning to the artifact:

> "You take it with you to the center of the Pattern. Hold it up. Very close—to an eye. Stare into it—and consider it a place. Try to project yourself—inside. You don't go. But there is—experience. . . . Afterward, you know how to use it." (GA, 215)

In spite of the fact that Eric might have had reason to deceive Corwin, and Dworkin's notes had been incomplete, this method proved accurate.

Those who have attuned to it have spoken of staring deeply into the Jewel, seeking an image of the Pattern within it. At first, one notices a small break or flaw high and to the right of its center. As one focuses on that flaw, it manifests into the beginnings of the Pattern. Outside reality is left behind as one travels its interior circuits with the mind's eye, experiencing much the same sensations one receives in walking the Pattern. One loses sense of time, of awareness, of any physical being, as one traverses the images within the Jewel, becoming one with those images. Reaching the terminal point, knowing it to be the conclusion, one comes upon a sudden, vast brightness of blinding red. Passing through it, one feels utterly drained, but the knowledge is there of one's having been changed, of having attained a higher level of potential.

Since we have learned that the Jewel is actually an Eye of the Serpent of the Logrus, it changes our perspective of its functions. One can't help but wonder what an individual might see if the Eye were implanted. The opportunity was given to Coral of Begma, who, fortunately, was also an initiate of the Pattern. Dworkin had performed the surgery that placed it into her ruined eye socket. She expressed how it felt to Merlin:

> "Very strange ... Not pain—exactly. More like the way a Trump contact feels. Only it's with me all the time, and I'm not going anywhere or talking to anyone. It's as if I'm standing in some sort of gateway. Forces are moving about me, through me." (PC, 3)

When Merlin used his own unique powers to examine the Eye, he found that it led him to the initial stages of attuning to it.

Coral continues to bear the Jewel in that strange, compelling way. At last report, she is residing with companions at the site of the new Pattern designed by Corwin. With that wondrous artifact always with her, always a part of her, it is an intriguing thought to contemplate what other potentialities might be discovered if Coral tested it further. In a sense, Coral's attunement is greater than anyone else's has ever been. Surely, it will preserve her from harm, even from the effects unleashed by either the Serpent or the unicorn.

If she can attain some sense of mastery over the device, Coral could transcend any force previously known.

JOPIN

Lighthouse keeper on the island of Cabra, forty-three miles from the southeastern shore of Amber.

His appearance as a stooped, gray-bearded man with bloodshot eyes belied the fact that he once commanded Amber's fleet. When Oberon was still young and Dworkin ran the true city, Jopin became close to Dworkin. Jopin had been a young officer in the royal navy and had met both Oberon and Dworkin on one of their early travels into Shadow aboard his vessel. Jopin was playing chess with one of the other officers when Dworkin came by their cabin and watched. Soon, Dworkin and Jopin were playing matches through the night. Dworkin showed him the sights of the true city, and Jopin was assigned to duty in Amber's waters.

Dworkin was much older than Jopin, but everyone noted the similarity in their physical carriage and height. After Oberon was made king, Dworkin became more withdrawn, retiring to his quarters or lands of shadow for long periods of time. Meanwhile, Jopin rose to the rank of captain, and was placed in charge of a large portion of the fleet.

After many decades, Oberon presided over a case of dereliction of duty involving Jopin. The case was based on circumstantial evidence and the eyewitness testimonies of a woman of ill repute from Amber's Harbor District and a young first lieutenant on one of Jopin's ships. Jopin was accused of drinking and entertaining the young lady at port prior to a vital mission that was bungled by someone else in Jopin's command. King Oberon viewed the offense with greater strictness than it perhaps merited. His decision resulted in Captain Jopin's dishonorable discharge from the navy.

For many years after his discharge, Jopin lived in a shack near the docks and worked in a chandler's shop. He was well liked and gradually became the shop owner's chief assistant. Unfortunately, he had taken up hard drinking, a virtually inevitable outcome of his sense of humiliation for that early disgrace. While the shop owner became unhappy with his work, he kept him on longer than he would have if Jopin weren't so amiable and eager to please.

The incident that caused Jopin to be dismissed from his job occurred when Prince Eric stopped in the chandler's shop on his way to sail with a trading vessel. Jopin recognized the young prince, although he was not known by Eric. When Eric was gathering up some supplies, Jopin was moving some barrels of shipper's tools. Already a bit shaken from the previous night's binge, Jopin was unusually clumsy in the prince's presence. A barrel toppled, some tools flew out, and Eric was jolted hard in the groin by a flying hand wrench. In spite of Jopin's heartfelt apologies, his employer released him after smoothing things over with the prince.

Jopin wandered the docks of the Harbor District looking for work. He was given odd jobs, sometimes even sailing on brief jaunts, but there was nothing permanent for him. Others viewed him as an aging drunkard, and he wasn't able to shake the reputation he had.

He was making the rounds of the local eateries near the Main Concourse, petitioning for a trifle of coinage, when he saw Dworkin taking a meal in a small, well-lighted café. Dworkin recognized him, waved, and invited him to his table. For Dworkin, it was a furtive meal, for he had sneaked away from his quarters in the palace, and Oberon would not have approved of his wandering about. Jopin and Dworkin spoke animatedly of old times, Dworkin wishing he had a chessboard and pieces with him. Grimly, Jopin told him of his lost commission, his failures to keep a job, and his destitute state of affairs. Dworkin promised to inquire about some form of steady employment for him and asked where he was living. When Jopin described the location of his small shack, Dworkin said he would seek him there with news in two days' time. They parted with a brief hug of friendship.

After two days had passed, Jopin still hadn't heard from his old friend. He waited in and about his hovel for four more days without hearing a word from the palace. Not having plied any trade, Jopin became quite ill from malnutrition. He became weak and feverish, and, at night, passersby could hear groans coming from his shack.

One of these passersby, a burly seaman, stopped to investigate. He called to Jopin, heard some mumbled words, and entered the shack. By that time, Jopin was so sick he could hardly move. The big sailor made him comfortable on his straw-matted bed and got him food, water, and a small flask of wine. The seaman continued to care for him every day for three weeks, arriving at his shack just after dawn and leaving him once or twice in the late afternoon, returning after dark for several more hours. Jopin didn't ask him where he was staying, and the large man didn't volunteer any information about himself.

When Jopin was better, walking about and able to fend for himself, the burly man gave a brief farewell before leaving. Grateful for the seaman's help, and hoping they could continue their friendship, Jopin asked where he was going. The seaman told him he was accepting assignment on the island of Cabra, manning the lighthouse. Naturally, Jopin asked if he could go with him, having nothing to hold him to Amber anymore. The seaman was reluctant initially, but he saw no breach in regulations in bringing along a companion who asked for no wages, only food, drink, and shelter. The man helped Jopin with his few possessions, a couple of books and some rolled-up charts. That night, they sailed quietly to Cabra.

For many years, Jopin found good fellowship with the large man, who called himself Joseph of Arimathea. They played chess together, spoke often of experiences at sea, and worked the great light for ships entering the harbor of Amber during the long nights. Occasionally, Joseph received official dispatches with his supplies of food and drink from several passing vessels. He never spoke to Jopin of what was contained in any of the dispatches.

On a morning when the wind was picking up mightily, and it seemed a storm was coming in, Joseph told Jopin that he had received an important dispatch. He had to use one of the boats to go ashore to deliver a message to a local merchant. Jopin wanted to go with him, but his friend told him he might not be able to return that night. Jopin would have to man the beacon alone if he did not return. So, Jopin watched as Joseph arranged the smaller of two sailboats for his journey ashore. As he set sail, Joseph called out to Jopin to take good care of the big light.

The storm came, and Jopin had to wrestle the remaining sailboat and a rowboat to secure them adequately against the quay. Waves beat upon the small island, and Jopin heard and saw the heavy pelting of rain and wind against the tower. He spent most of the night in the small tower room that housed the beacon, searching the rough waters for movement from the shoreward side with his spyglass. In the calm of the next day, he spied a small wreckage just west of the island. Jopin took the rowboat to it. He found Joseph's body lying over the smashed remnants of the sailboat's mast.

When the next vessel stopped at Cabra, Jopin informed the captain of the demise of the lighthouse keeper. They took his body with them, and the captain offered Jopin the position. Accepting the post, Jopin has seldom been off the island since.

Over the years, Jopin gathered numerous old books, mainly texts about ships and distant lands. Besides accumulating nautical charts and maps, he drew some of his own, based on his early experiences at sea. The solitude was sometimes hard, but he made the best of it, obtaining news from the crew of ships that dropped anchor to leave him supplies. Sometime later, Jopin was surprised by the visit of Dworkin, who had been given passage on a small sailing vessel. At first chagrined, Jopin hadn't wanted anything further to do with any of the Royal Family, especially his former friend. Dworkin explained that he had had no influence in Amber any longer. In fact, he had been heavily guarded in the Royal Palace for a long while, at his own son's orders.

Thus reconciled, Jopin rekindled his friendship with Dworkin, and for stretches of years, Dworkin appeared on Cabra to play at chess for a day or two at a time before going away again. Jopin wondered only briefly at the way Dworkin seemed to appear and disappear without a boat coming in sight of the island.

Dworkin told him of the latest news in Amber, and he let Jopin see the Trumps of the Family. Jopin remembered Eric. He thought he recognized some of the other children of Oberon also, in the days he spent in the town. Deirdre had been a charming little girl that Oberon had taken to the pier on several occasions. Prince Corwin had once done a small kindness for Jopin in the city, but he had forgotten what that was. The faces of the others on the Trumps were more vague. If he had met them at all, it was probably at a distance and unconnected to anything he was doing at the time.

Jopin lived an untroubled life on Cabra, feeling quite at home by the sea. It was many years after Dworkin's last visit to him that Jopin noticed a change in the land to the north. Looking through his spyglass from the tower room, he saw a dark cloudlike mass clinging to the trees in the Valley of Garnath. The region took on a dreariness that he hadn't seen before. It gave him a sickened feeling, as if some evil agent had been at work there.

Not long after this, he heard the metallic clang of the rusty old knocker on the door below. He had been drinking much of the night, but he would have been surprised to hear the knocker's use in any case.

Rushing down from his makeshift study, Jopin hoped it was his old friend returning for a series of chess matches. With vague disappointment, he opened the door to view a heavily bearded man in tattered clothes who looked nearly as old as himself.

Jopin spoke harshly, loudly.

> "Who are you? What do you want?" . . .
> "I am a traveler from the south and I was shipwrecked recently . . . I clung to a piece of wood for many days and was finally washed ashore here. I slept on the beach all morning. It was only recently that I recovered sufficient strength to walk to your lighthouse." . . .
> "Come in, come in then. . . . Lean on me. Take it easy. Come this way." (NP, 168–69)

Feeling suddenly eager to have found companionship, Jopin helped the bearded stranger to his room and onto his small bed. He went to get food and drink, returned, and watched as the stranger ate and drank voraciously. Jopin left him to sleep and went outside to check the shore for wreckage. He didn't find any.

The next morning, Jopin served him a large breakfast and supplied him with a razor, scissors, and a mirror. When the stranger had trimmed his beard and cut his hair, Jopin sat with him. In spite of the beard and the man's extreme thinness, Jopin thought he looked familiar. He asked about the man's shipwreck, and he was told a rather fantastic story. Jopin listened politely, not contradicting anything the stranger said.

The stranger called himself Corey, and Jopin made him welcome. He handed Corey a clean shirt to wear, one that had belonged to Joseph. Corey helped him with the beacon, and after he had gained weight and strength he set to work cleaning, painting, and making repairs. Enjoying Corey's comradeship, Jopin told him of his past as they played chess and drank. They spoke of the sea, examined Jopin's old charts, and developed a few new ones. Corey spent more than three months with him.

One evening, after a game of chess, Corey told him that he would be leaving the next day. Jopin poured each of them a beer and held his glass up in the gesture of a toast.

> "Good luck to you then, Corwin. I hope to see you again one day." . . .

"You've been all right, Jopin . . . If I should succeed in what I'm about to try, I won't forget what you did for me."

"I don't want anything . . . I'm happy right where I am, doing exactly what I'm doing. I enjoy running this damned tower. It's my whole life. If you should succeed in whatever you're about—no, don't tell me about it, please! I don't want to know!—I'll be hoping you'll stop around for a game of chess sometime."

"I will." . . .

"You can take the *Butterfly* in the morning, if you'd like."

"Thanks." . . .

"Before you go, . . . I suggest you take my spyglass, climb the tower, and look back on the Vale of Garnath."

"What's there to see?" . . .

"You'll have to make up your own mind about that." (NP, 172–73)

They drank a bit longer, then turned in for the night. Jopin awoke at dawn when he heard Corwin moving around. He pretended sleep as he felt Corwin's shadow upon him. Retiring to his study, Jopin avoided him as Corwin took a quick meal, then supplied and fixed the sailboat for his trip. From the single window in his room, Jopin watched as the prince of Amber cast off and moved away from the island. He suppressed a wave and turned away from the window.

Large sailing vessels continue to stop at Cabra to drop off supplies. Sailors report that old Jopin still greets them when they come ashore with food and drink, asking about the news in the shadows they've been to. He's never expressed any desire to leave Cabra nor give up his lone vigil.

JULIAN

Older son of Rilga and Oberon. When his father remarried while still married to Rilga, Julian fumed silently. He remained cold and uncaring during the short time that Sand and Delwin, offspring of Oberon's bigamous marriage to Harla, resided in Amber. In some ways, Julian's quiet animosity may have

been worse than the open cruelties of his siblings toward Harla's children.

Corwin expressed his impressions of Julian when he gazed at his Trump in Flora's home on shadow Earth:

> There was the passive countenance of Julian, dark hair hanging long, blue eyes containing neither passion nor compassion. He was dressed completely in scaled white armor, not silver or metallic-colored, but looking as if it had been enameled. I knew, though, that it was terribly tough and shock-resistant, despite its decorative and festive appearance. He was the man I had beaten at his favorite game, for which he had thrown a glass of wine at me. I knew him and I hated him." (NP, 28)

Flora had mentioned the incident to Corwin. He had bested Julian in a hunt, carrying the carcass away from under Julian's nose. Julian's anger boiled over upon their return to the palace. Flora described what she had known of it:

> "I remember the day you beat Julian at his favorite game and he threw a glass of wine at you and cursed you. But you took the prize. And he was suddenly afraid he had gone too far. But you laughed then, though, and drank a glass with him. I think he felt badly over that show of temper, normally being so cool, and I think he was envious of you that day. Do you recall? I think he has, to a certain extent, imitated many of your ways since then." (NP, 21)

This may have been true of Julian, but Corwin remembered quite clearly how Julian used his hatred against him. Early in Julian's training of the immense horse Morgenstern that he had formed from Shadow, he "had a man wear my [Corwin's] castoff garments and torment the beast. This was why it had tried to trample me on the day of a hunt, when I'd dismounted to skin a buck before it." (NP, 57)

If Julian had any friends among his siblings, it was Caine. As Random said:

> "He and Caine got along very well. For years now. They had been looking out for each other, hanging around together. Pretty thick. Julian is cold and petty and just as nasty as you remem-

ber. But if he liked anybody, he liked Caine.''
(SU, 11)

Interestingly, Fiona suggested that Julian was
only pretending a friendship with Caine, just to consolidate his position until he was able to rule Amber
(SU, 114–15) She was assuming that Julian had
been a key player in the conspiracy with the lords
of the Courts of Chaos against those in Amber. It's
likely, however, that Fiona knew better and made
the suggestion just to add a red herring to the
intrigue.

Fiona's speaking out against Julian is particularly
interesting in light of his feelings toward her. Corwin had once questioned Julian about his relationship with Fiona. Julian responded:

"I have always been very fond of Fiona. She
is certainly the loveliest, most civilized of us
all. Pity Dad was always so dead-set against
brother-sister marriages, as well you know. It
bothered me that we had to be adversaries for
so long as we were.'' (HO, 125)

At the time when Eric claimed that Corwin had
left Amber for a lengthy sojourn in Shadow, Julian
probably believed that Eric had killed him. His joining in the search for Corwin in numerous shadows
was no doubt done halfheartedly, since he never
expected to find him alive. In spite of this belief,
Julian gave service to Eric, even while King Oberon
still ruled. The king often left abruptly on undisclosed missions to other shadows, and he would
leave messages for Julian and Eric with his orders.
Julian found himself needing to rely on Eric more
and more for all matters of conduct concerning
the troops.

Another of their siblings took on dangerous proportions during this period: Brand. Julian had observed Brand in the palace doing astounding feats.
On one occasion, for example, he discovered that
Brand was able to "sit in a chair, locate what he
seeks in Shadow, and then bring it to him by an act
of will without moving from the chair.'' (HO, 123)
Following Brand, Julian saw him conferring with
Fiona. Although he couldn't hear what they were
discussing, their behavior indicated to him that they
were involved in some form of treachery.

He reported Brand's activities to Eric, and thus
began their careful surveillance of Brand over a long

duration. Employing a network of informers from
among the servants and courtiers of the court, Eric
and Julian gradually developed a tighter vigilance
over their erring brother. There came a point when
Eric decided that it was necessary to keep Brand in
confinement. By this time, Caine had joined Eric
and Julian in their scrutiny of Brand. Maintaining
an armed watch in certain areas of the Royal Palace,
the three of them were able to ambush Brand when
he suddenly appeared in a corridor. Without setting
off any alarms that would make Oberon aware of
their actions, Eric, Caine, and Julian arranged for
Brand's imprisonment in one of the cells in the dungeon. Acting on Julian's fears, Eric had Brand tied
to the bed and injected with drugs to keep him
unconscious.

In the early hours before dawn of a somewhat
serene morning, the guard posted outside of Brand's
cell looked in and discovered that Brand was gone.
After checking the tiny room, the guard went off to
inform Eric. He ran into Julian instead, and told him
of Brand's escape. They went back to the cell, and
Julian examined it carefully. At the far end of the
cot, against the wall, he found a roughly carved
sketch on a square of board torn from the bedding.
The sketch showed a high-ceilinged room with no
furnishings, but chains and hooks protruded from
walls that looked rather thick and unpleasant. It certainly was not a room filled with luxuries, and Julian
thought it an odd thing to draw.

Sending the guard away to seek out Eric, Julian
concentrated on the image of that rough-hewn room.
After a moment of intense concentration, Julian saw
movement within the room. People in filthy peasant
garb, both men and women, wandered across his
field of vision. For an instant, one figure walked by
that Julian recognized: it was Corwin. Before he
could attempt a contact with Corwin, Julian saw
guards in odd uniforms nearby, moving to and fro
within the room. It was not a proper prison, then.
There were other men, wearing stark, but affluent,
suits, who seemed to be in authority.

Julian listened to the several conversations, focused in on one between two men, one of whom
seemed to be a doctor. Maintaining his focus on the
doctor and the official, Julian followed them out of
the room. When the two men separated, Julian re-
trained his thoughts on the official, who was an
important administrator of this hospital, as Julian
had learned. The administrator stepped out of the

building, turned down a narrow street, and was stopped by Julian, who had stepped through to him, grasping his overcoat.

Impersonating the administrator, Julian was able to obtain Corwin's release. Before they were able to leave the hospital building, however, Julian's deception was discovered. He had to do some quick manuvering to evade his pursuers, and in the interim, Corwin managed to wander off. Although Julian couldn't be certain, he felt that Corwin had escaped recapture. Returning to Brand's cell in Amber, Julian sought Eric, found him, and told him of these events.

While Julian continued to be concerned about Brand's return, he understood that Eric had something more to be worried about: the fact that Corwin was still alive. However, Julian disregarded these concerns and returned to the Forest of Arden to resume his duties with his patrols. As it happened, there began an increase in Shadow slippage. Sometimes, ferocious beasts slipped into Amber from other shadows, causing minor mayhem. Over time, this occurred with greater frequency, and with increasingly dire consequences. Julian soon found that he and his cavalry were heavily involved in repelling these Shadow invasions.

Two significant events happened in a relatively brief time that affected the political situation. Oberon went off suddenly, without leaving any orders as he had always done in the past. And Brand approached Caine about forming an alliance so that Brand could take the throne by force.

Julian and Caine supported the idea of raising Eric to the position of defender of the Crown. In the face of Brand's opposition, Julian believed they needed an official head of state to garner popular support. Brand and his party would appear to be rebels perpetrating treason against the Amberites.

When Julian discovered Corwin and Random driving an automobile in a shadow region heading for Arden, he warned Eric. Eric had already known, however, learning of Corwin's whereabouts from Flora. By that time, Julian had convinced Eric to ascend the throne officially, and Eric set the date for his coronation. Seeing the need to give Eric his every support, Julian accepted a number of duties that no doubt were cruel in regard to Corwin. He actively led his troops against Corwin and Bleys when they had combined for an invasion. If Julian seemed to gloat at Corwin's capture and humiliation

during the coronation of Eric, he was simply upholding Eric's claim with a properly judicious face.

Much later, when the situation had changed, Julian had an opportunity to explain to Corwin the issues they faced, referring specifically to Corwin's part in events:

"You are a fool," he [Julian] finally said. "You were a tool from the very beginning. They used you to force our hand and either way you lost. If that half-assed attack of Bleys's had somehow succeeded, you wouldn't have lasted long enough to draw a deep breath. If it failed, as it did, Bleys disappeared, as he did, leaving you with your life forfeit for attempted usurpation. You had served your purpose and you had to die. They left us small choice in the matter. By rights, we should have killed you—and you know it." ...

"Eric," he said, "figured that your eyesight might eventually be restored—knowing the way we regenerate—given time. It was a very delicate situation. If Dad were to return, Eric could step down and justify all of his actions to anyone's satisfaction—except for killing you. That would have been too patent a move to ensure his own continued reign beyond the troubles of the moment. And I will tell you frankly that he simply wanted to imprison you and forget you."

"Then whose idea was the blinding?"

He was silent again for a long while. Then he spoke very softly, almost a whisper: "Hear me out, please. It was mine, and it may have saved your life. Any action taken against you had to be tantamount to death, or their faction would have tried for the real thing. You were no longer of any use to them, but alive and about you possessed the potentiality of becoming a danger at some future time. They could have used your Trump to contact you and kill you, or they could have used it to free you in order to sacrifice you in yet another move against Eric. Blinded, however, there was no need to slay you and you were of no use for anything else they might have in mind. It saved you by taking you out of the picture for a time, and it saved us from a more egregious act which might one day be held against us. As we saw it, there was no choice. It was the only thing we could do. There could be no show of leniency either, or we might be suspected of having some use for you ourselves. The moment you assumed any such semblance of value you would have been a dead man.'' (HO, 121–22)

The death of Caine put Julian on his guard. He listened to Corwin's explanation about finding the body and that someone seemed to be setting him up to take the blame. Although Julian never admitted it, he probably did like Caine. However, he felt more caution than sorrow at his death. He suspected that someone other than Corwin was responsible, and, naturally, his suspicions fell on Brand.

It was certainly an adverse situation, therefore, when Corwin proposed the joining of the Family in the palace library to try to reach the absent Brand by Trump. When they succeeded, and Gérard bullied his way through the contact to rescue Brand, Julian was ready to strike Brand down with his dagger. It surprised him when someone else stabbed Brand first, and Julian may or may not have seen the person who did it.

Putting on an act of bravado, Julian was ready to point the blame in anyone else's direction. He even argued the possibility that Llewella might have been culpable, even though he knew better. In Corwin's proposal that the guilty party admit his or her misdeed and face exile, Julian added the condition that the perpetrator would have to prove that he or she was not responsible for Caine's death. After retiring, Julian stealthily retreated to the Forest of Arden to join his patrols. His fear of Brand was so great that he deliberately absented himself, hoping that the one who attempted his murder would succeed before Brand could recover.

Julian felt vindicated when Corwin met him in Arden during the time that Julian was leading a patrol in pursuit of a manticora. Corwin's information about Brand, and the fact that the other members of the Family now viewed Brand as the culprit who conspired with the minions of Chaos, was a relief to Julian. With the return of King Oberon, Julian was content to be given his orders in a military campaign that held the promise of ending the upheaval in Amber caused by their inscrutable enemies at the far end of the universe.

As Julian readied his troops for the Patternfall battle, he received a communication from a surprising source. It was Caine, contacting him by Trump. Julian brought Caine into Arden, and Caine explained that he faked his own death in order to eavesdrop on the Trumps of his siblings without notice. Caine had been dressed in green armor and kept his visor down when Random rode into Julian's camp. Together, they hellrode to the site of the battlefield.

As they approached the shadows nearest the Courts of Chaos, Julian was in constant communication with Benedict. Between them, a surprise attack by Julian's troops was arranged while Benedict's men would already be engaged with the enemy. The tactic worked brilliantly, as Julian's force drove into the attacking Chaos army from the west, without warning. During the conflict, Julian slew one of the leaders of the insurgent forces, Duke Larsus of the House of Hendrake.

At the conclusion of the fighting, Julian joined the others on the hilltop nearest the Abyss, where he saw Caine talking to Fiona, Corwin, Random, and several others. He observed the funeral procession for his father, just as, earlier, he had seen the enormous face of his father in the sky, even though he was still in battle at that time. When the unicorn appeared, choosing Random as their new liege, Julian was the first to place his sword on the ground before his younger brother, pledging his loyalty.

Under King Random's rule, Julian appreciated the quieter period without conspiratorial intrigue. Although he felt welcome in the Royal Palace, he preferred spending most of his time with his men in the Forest of Arden. His duties were more evenly divided with Benedict, so that Julian helped in the training of part of the infantry as well as his cavalry.

When Caine was assassinated in Deiga, Julian again became worried and cautious. He drilled his men harder, preparing them for any contingency. He attended Caine's funeral, ordering his patrol to be astutely vigilant for any attack. Someone disrupted the procession in spite of Julian's best efforts, and then escaped again.

Julian did his best service to King Random while training his soldiers in Arden. While Benedict and his men kept out of sight, Julian's group was at the ready, lined up and capable of extreme force against a line of mercenaries and cutthroats led by Dalt. Dalt conferred with Julian under a flag of truce, stating that he wasn't there to engage Amber in war. He simply claimed the return of Rinaldo and Jasra, after which he would remove his force from the realm.

In spite of Julian's judgment that he and Benedict could take on and destroy Dalt's force, he left the decision-making to Queen Vialle. She arranged for

Rinaldo's arrival in Amber, under the auspices of Merlin. Rinaldo and Merlin joined Julian in his camp. There were some tense moments when Julian greeted Rinaldo with the words: "So you are Caine's killer." (SC, 147) Julian kept his feelings to himself, perhaps maintaining a tight restraint. He permitted the negotiations between Rinaldo and Dalt to proceed.

While Rinaldo was with him, Julian had a singular conversation with him about Rinaldo's father, Brand:

> "What was he like, near the end?" he [Julian] inquired. . . .
>
> "Well, he wasn't exactly normal, if that's what you mean," he [Luke/Rinaldo] finally said. "Like I was telling Merlin earlier, I think the process he undertook to gain his powers might have unbalanced him some."
>
> "I never heard that story."
>
> Luke shrugged.
>
> "The details aren't all that important—just the results."
>
> "You're saying he wasn't a bad father before that?"
>
> "Hell, I don't know. I never had another father to compare him to. Why do you ask?"
>
> "Curiosity. It's a part of his life I knew nothing about."
>
> "Well, what kind of brother was he?"
>
> "Wild," Julian said. "We didn't get along all that well. So we pretty much stayed out of each other's ways. He was smart, though. Talented, too. Had a flare for the arts. I was just trying to figure how much you might take after him." (SC, 154)

Julian may have been archly making a point with Rinaldo that he wasn't trusting him fully. But he also seemed to exhibit here an appreciation of Brand that he himself may not have fully realized until that discussion with Brand's son. It may be a sign of new growth in Julian, that he has come to appreciate the talents of the enemy.

JULIA'S APARTMENT

Julia Barnes, onetime girlfriend of Merlin when he resided in San Francisco on shadow Earth, had rented a furnished apartment in a large Victorian house. It had been the scene of a grisly murder and a supernatural phenomenon on separate occasions.

The Victorian house was a well-kept building in a quiet, residential section near San Francisco Bay. The home had been constructed in the 1920s, as had many of the larger, more ornate residences of the area, before the stock market crash ended such opulence. It had changed ownership several times, and in the past couple of decades had been divided into a boardinghouse so that the more recent owners could keep up with expenses. Often, students attending the nearby universities would take up residence in much of the house. Julia had been one of these, paying what was considered a reasonable rent while she went to classes at Berkeley.

Julia had rented a good-sized rear apartment on the top floor of the three-story structure, consisting of a living room and a bedroom. There was a hall bathroom that was shared by two other apartments in that wing. The chimney came through the rear of the house, so that Julia enjoyed the warmth of a fireplace on cold winter nights. The furnishings that had come with the living room of the apartment were a red sofa, end tables on either side, two cushioned chairs, and one plain chair of dark wood, a large table, and an aged green carpet. Julia had hung a watercolor of a park scene on the wall behind the sofa. The bedroom was simply furnished with a bed and a large chest of drawers against the near wall facing the living room.

In Merlin's accounts, Julia had sent him a note asking him to come to her apartment, just prior to his intended departure from San Francisco. The message made it seem very urgent that Merlin see her. When he arrived at the house, no one was around. He entered the foyer of the house through an open door, recalling fondly earlier times when he and Julia hugged before the slightly distorting mirror near the staircase. As he walked up the three flights of stairs, he heard sounds from above that disturbed him, putting him on his guard. At the third landing, he detected a strong musty odor. He knocked on Julia's door, heard movement, but there was no response. He knocked again, heard a crash, and tried the doorknob. After breaking open the door, he found the dead and bloody body of his girlfriend on the living room rug. Her face and right arm had been torn away. At that point, Merlin was attacked by the creature that had killed her. It was a doglike animal that was much larger and fiercer than any known in San Francisco. Merlin struggled with it and was able to dispatch it, sending it through the curtained window of the living room to its death.

On the mantelpiece of the fireplace, Merlin discovered Trump-like cards that had the potency of those of Amber, but he didn't recognize the hand that had drawn them. He took them with him as he quickly left Julia's apartment. He drove to a tree-lined neighborhood away from the Bay area, parked, and walked to a small deserted park. There, he took the opportunity to examine the Trumps he found in Julia's apartment. Those cards indicated that Julia's death was orchestrated by an enemy with unnatural powers, perhaps coming from the Amber side of Merlin's problems.

Sometime later, Merlin returned to Julia's apartment with his aunt Flora. Although both the front door of the house and a new door to Julia's apartment were locked, Merlin gained entry without damage through the use of a unique entity he had with him. When Flora and Merlin entered the apartment, they could see that everything had been cleaned up. The bloodied rug had been changed, the painting over the sofa was gone, and nothing of a personal nature remained. They looked over the living room, Merlin using his special sight. He went into the bedroom and found something beyond the normal. This is how he explained it in his journals:

The chest of drawers had been moved in the course of purging the apartment. It used to occupy a space several feet farther to the right. That which I now saw was visible to its left and above it, with more of it obviously blocked to my sight. I took hold of the thing and pushed it back to the right, to the position it had formerly occupied. . . .

I studied it—a dim line of faded fire. The thing was obviously sealed and had been for some time. Eventually it would fade completely and be gone.

"It is a doorway," I answered.

She [Flora] pulled me back into the other room to regard the opposite side of the wall.

"Nothing here," she observed. "It doesn't go through."

"Now you've got the idea," I said. "It goes somewhere else." (BA, 31–32)

Using his Logrus powers, Merlin was able to pull open the nearly faded doorway. He went through it, walking along a white tunnel that increasingly widened as he moved away from the doorway. Behind him, the portal gradually closed up and disappeared. The tunnel was guarded by a huge monstrous creature whose sole purpose was to prevent any wayfarers from crossing his threshold. Merlin was able to use his own powers to pass through. At the other end of the tunnel from Julia's apartment was another world. It was a shadow where an important source of power could be found: The Keep of the Four Worlds.

Much later, Merlin learned the connection between his former girlfriend and the Keep.

The old Victorian house continues to offer bed and board to students and other visitors to the Bay area. At last report, nothing strange or otherworldly has since occurred in the third floor rear room with the fireplace. The landlords do not make it known to new boarders that a terrible murder had taken place in that otherwise cheerful room.

JURT

Second son of Gramble, Lord Sawall and Dara, born in the Courts of Chaos. Jurt is the youngest born of this marriage. He has an older, full brother, Despil; a half brother, Merlin, son of Dara and Corwin; and a stepbrother, Mandor, born of a previous marriage to Lord Sawall.

Jurt's half brother Merlin had grown up with them in the Courts of Chaos. Because their mother Dara seemed to favor Merlin, and because Merlin often seemed fortunate enough and talented enough to have attained success early in his life, Jurt developed a tremendous jealousy of him. This became dangerous, and on several documented instances, Jurt tried to murder his half brother.

Just prior to a decision to attack Merlin, Jurt spoke with him about becoming an initiate of the Logrus:

"So, what does it feel like?"

"What?" I [Merlin] said.

"The power," he answered. "The Logrus

power—to walk in Shadow, to work with a higher order of magic than the mundane.''

I didn't really want to go into detail, because I knew he'd prepared himself to traverse the Logrus on three different occasions and had backed down at the last moment each time, when he'd looked into it. Perhaps the skeletons of failures that Suhuy keeps around had troubled him also. I don't think Jurt was aware that I knew about the last two times he'd changed his mind. So I decided to downplay my accomplishment

"Oh, you don't really feel any different," I said, "until you're actually using it. Then it's hard to describe."

"I'm thinking of doing it soon myself," he said. "It would be good to see something of Shadow, maybe even find a kingdom for myself somewhere. Can you give me any advice?"

I nodded. "Don't look back," I said. "Don't stop to think. Just keep going."

He laughed. "Sounds like orders to an army," he said.

"I suppose there is a similarity." (BA, 164–65)

Merlin traced his troubled relationship with Jurt in his journals. The earliest documented incident in which Jurt attempted to dispatch his brother was when Jurt challenged Merlin to a sporting duel above the Pit of Chaos. No one considered that Jurt might carry it out beyond a mere match, so Jurt's brother Despil willingly acted as his second, and Mandor agreed to act as Merlin's second. After Jurt drew blood from Merlin with his trisp, Despil called out, "First blood! Which is sufficient!" (BA, 81) At that point, Jurt chose to continue, and soon it was clear that he was fighting in deadly earnest. Jurt came in close with his trisliver, and Merlin gestured with his weapon and fandon defensively. Merlin's trisp caught Jurt about the head and Jurt screamed. He lost an ear and some of his scalp. Despil led him off to their mother Dara.

Reflecting on that incident, Merlin thought of their relationship:

Jurt had hated me from sometime before he had learned to walk, for reasons entirely his own. While I did not hate Jurt, liking him was totally beyond my ability. I had always gotten along reasonably well with Despil, though he

tended to take Jurt's side more often than my own. But that was understandable. They were full brothers, and Jurt was the baby. (BA, 83)

The second occasion that Merlin had documented was at a time just before Merlin was planning to leave the Courts of Chaos to study at Berkeley University on shadow Earth. Jurt invited him to hunt fierce horned creatures called zhind in the Black Zone. After talking briefly of walking the Logrus, Jurt fired a hunting arrow meant to hit Merlin between the shoulders. Merlin was saved by his secret entity Frakir. Jurt fought with Merlin, trying to stab him with a knife, but Merlin managed to push him away forcefully. Jurt was impaled in the eye by the sharp end of a branch he fell on. Refusing Merlin's help, Jurt pulled the limb out of his socket, then collapsed into unconsciousness. Merlin had to carry him home again.

The pattern was clearly set. Thereafter, Merlin had no way to appease his young half brother. He left for shadow Earth, and his problems with Jurt were unresolved. As shown in Merlin's journals, Jurt continued to seek a deadly ambush for his brother. Often, when he made the attempt, Jurt would find himself seriously hurt; and his own actions were usually the cause of his injuries. It was almost as if his own ineptitude in planning dire mayhem resulted in his own loss of humanity, bit by bit.

Mandor informed Merlin that Lord Sawall had formally adopted Merlin, placing him in the line of succession not only in the House of Sawall, but in the Royal Line of the Courts as well. Merlin's becoming a legitimate heir added one more reason for Jurt to despise him. Mandor gave Merlin some further information about his wayward half brother:

"Jurt," he said, "met the changing times with a mixture of delight and fear. He was constantly talking of the latest deaths and of the elegance and apparent ease with which some of them were accomplished. Hushed tones interspersed with a few giggles. His fear and his desire to increase his own capacity for mischief finally reached a point where they became greater than his other fear—"

"The Logrus. . . ."

"Yes. He finally tried the Logrus, and he made it through."

"He should be feeling very good about that. Proud. It was something he'd wanted for years."

"Oh, yes," Mandor answered. "And I'm sure he felt a great number of other things as well."

"Freedom," I suggested. "Power," and as I studied his half-amused expression, I was forced to add, "and the ability to play the game himself." (SC, 33–34)

Mandor also confirmed that Jurt had been the unknown enemy who attacked Merlin as he rode on horseback from Arbor House to Amber, an enemy transformed into a lop-eared wolf. Mandor also concurred with Merlin's suspicions that Jurt had arranged for a Fire Angel from the Courts to seek out Merlin. The Fire Angel had attacked while Merlin was with Luke Raynard in the Wonderland Bar.

When Merlin was showing a young woman from Begma the sea caves in Mt. Kolvir, Jurt showed up again. He had planned to assault Merlin with two deceased cutthroats he had reanimated. Unaccountably, Merlin caused the two henchmen to lose their vitality and revert to decomposing corpses. One of the men sliced off Jurt's little finger as he fell lifeless. Before Jurt got away, Merlin discovered that he had allied himself with another enemy who had become a nemesis to him: the sorcerer dubbed Mask.

Although Merlin could not account for how Jurt met Mask, or why they decided to join together against him, Mandor suggested a reason why Mask would be interested in Jurt: "Besides the fact that he has negotiated the Logrus and come into his powers, is it necessary for me to point out that Jurt—apart from his scars and missing pieces— bears you a strong resemblance?" (KS, 41) This doesn't explain how Jurt and Mask got together, of course. However, it does serve to indicate their common need to lash out at Merlin. In the encounter in the sea caves, Jurt had made this mysterious comment: "You betrayed someone I love, and only your death will set things right." (SC, 78) At the time, Merlin had no idea whom Jurt had meant. Only after he learned the actual identity of Mask did this become clear.

Mask had access to a source of enormous power, the kind of power that Jurt always sought in order to prove himself superior to Merlin. At the Keep of the Four Worlds, Mask intended to have Jurt undergo the ritual of bathing in the Black Stone Fountain. This would imbue Jurt with terrific energies, turning him into a magical being of sorts. Luke Raynard told Merlin:

"Sounds as if this Mask is using him [Jurt] as a guinea pig. . . .

". . . There's a steady, pulsing source of pure energy inside the Citadel, you know. Inter-Shadow stuff. Comes from the four worlds jamming together there. . . .

"I've got a feeling that this Mask is still in the process of getting a handle on it. . . .

". . . there's more to it than plugging into a wall outlet. There are all sorts of subtleties he's probably just becoming aware of and exploring. . . .

"Bathing a person in it will, if he's properly protected, do wonders for strength, stamina, and magical abilities. . . . old Sharu's notes were in his lab, and there was something more in them—a way of replacing part of the body with energy, really packing it in. Very dangerous. Easily fatal. But if it works you get something special, a kind of superman, a sort of Living Trump." (SC, 106)

Merlin saw the necessity of reaching the Keep of the Four Worlds and stopping Jurt from proceeding with the ritual.

Enlisting the aid of Jasra and Mandor, Merlin transported to the Keep. In the large chamber in which the Black Fount was located, the three of them faced Jurt and Mask. Jurt had been going through the process, but had not yet completed the entire cycle. Still, he had the ability to disappear and reappear in various places at will, and he had grown almost invincible to harm. Under these conditions, they engaged in sorcerous battle.

Even though Jurt exhibited his enhanced powers, he was so inept in putting them to best advantage that Jasra and Merlin were able to foil every attack he made. In order to throw up another obstacle against Merlin, Jasra, and Mandor, Mask brought Sharu Garrul out of a spell of immobility. The old wizard immediately engaged Jasra, and she had to concentrate all of her resources on him.

Draining the energies of the Fount, Mask had caused great fissures in the walls of the Keep. As walls and flooring began to crumble, Mask made a deadly assault on Merlin. Mask missed his target, but Merlin seriously wounded the sorcerer with his knife. Jurt reached Mask and brought him safely away, while the large chamber fell into wreckage.

Merlin next encountered Jurt in the First Unicornian Church in Kashfa, where Merlin was conferring with his friend Luke. Jurt arrived intending to take revenge on Merlin for his disturbing the ritual at the Keep and injuring Mask. However, Jurt recognized the unique sword in Luke's possession. It was the sword of Brand, and its story, apparently, was well-known in the Courts of Chaos. Jurt took on both Luke and Merlin, and, although he was hurt, Jurt managed to obtain Brand's sword. Then Mask used a Trump contact to take Jurt out of their presence. Jurt had succeeded, this time, in taking what he desired with him.

During the time of the funeral of the late King Swayvill, Merlin returned to the Courts of Chaos. While there, he conferred with Mandor, and they spoke of Jurt. Mandor told him that Jurt was also back in the Courts for the funeral, staying in one of the byways of the House of Sawall. Merlin asked Mandor to use his influence to persuade Jurt to discontinue his attempts on Merlin's life. Mandor answered that he had long ago ceased being an influence on Jurt, but he might be willing to accept advice from his mother Dara, or Suhuy, Master of the Logrus. Then Mandor made an intriguing comment about the situation: "In the meantime, I would contrive [if I were you, Merlin] not to be alone with Jurt, should your paths cross. And if it were me, in the presence of witnesses, I would make certain that the first blow was not mine." (PC, 70)

Soon after Merlin had a heated argument with his mother, and had confronted the Sign of the Logrus while with her, he did cross paths with Jurt. In the Maze of Art in the House of Sawall, Jurt located Merlin and offered a truce. Of course, Merlin was extremely wary, and he contrived to meet Jurt in an area of glass and aluminum, looking like multiple arrays of mirrors. Within that exhibit, they could meet and talk, without being sure which image was the actual person.

In their conversation, Jurt came to a remarkable resolution:

"I quit. I'm out of the running. The hell with it. . . .

"Even if the Logrus hadn't made its intentions clear, I was beginning to feel nervous. It was not just that I was afraid you'd kill me either. I got to thinking about myself, and the succession. What if I made it to the throne? I'm not so sure as I once was that I'm competent to hold it. I could mess up the realm severely, unless I had good advice. And you know that, ultimately, it would come from either Mandor or Dara. I'd wind up a puppet, wouldn't I?"
(PC, 126)

In this way, Jurt and Merlin reconciled their differences. Jurt told him that his former girlfriend, Julia Barnes, was also staying in the House of Sawall, recovering from her injury. Deciding to unite in order to rescue Luke's bride, who had been kidnapped by agents of the Logrus, Jurt used his special Trump powers to transport them from the Courts to Kashfa, and back again. Willingly involving himself with Merlin's quest, Jurt seemed to have had a complete change of heart. Nevertheless, Jurt had facetiously remarked:

"Wouldn't it be funny, Merlin, if I were sticking with you because it's the safest place to be just now? . . . Supposing I'm just waiting, saving my final effort till Tubble's out of the way? Then, trusting me and all, you turn your back— Coronation!" (PC, 148)

Naturally, Merlin wasn't willing to trust his half brother completely, but Jurt had shown unwavering loyalty to him at this time.

Jurt permitted Merlin to work out a sorcerous deception so that they could both leave the funeral procession for Swayvill unseen, travel to Kashfa to confer with Luke Raynard, and then return to the procession. When they traveled to the new Pattern created by Corwin, Jurt offered to act as guardian of the Pattern while Merlin and Luke went after Luke's bride and her captors. Later, Jurt, still maintaining his vigilance by Corwin's Pattern, was introduced to Dalt, Nayda, and Coral upon Merlin's return.

While they were together, the Logrus attempted to destroy the new Pattern with underground tremors. Merlin was able to eradicate the problem, preventing either Power from trying the same method again. Just before Merlin left for the Courts once again, Jurt had a few words with him about his position concerning the Powers of the Logrus and the Pattern:

> "I came here because I thought it was the one place neither of them [the two Powers] would touch in the event of a contest . . . I'd assumed neither would care to divert energy from its own attack or defense for a swipe in this direction. . . .
> "Just for once I'd like to be on the winning side. . . . I'm not sure I care about right or wrong. They're very arguable quantities. I'd just like to be in with the guys who win for a change." (PC, 216–17)

As far as can be determined, Jurt remains staunchly vigilant at the new Pattern, accompanied by Coral, Nayda, and Dalt. Perhaps we will see that Jurt has truly overcome his ignoble past to become a faithful supporter of his half brother.

KASHFA

Shadow kingdom where Jasra ruled for many years. Although Kashfa was not a member of the Golden Circle, it was close in proximity to Begma, which was a longtime member. Over the years, Kashfa and Begma had undergone periods of conflict with intervals of peaceful relations. Besides the privileged status that Begma enjoyed with Amber, another source of hostilities between the two shadows was a stretch of land named Eregnor, to which they both made claim. King Random of Amber had initiated clandestine talks with the noblemen of Kashfa to arrange for Kashfa's entrance into the Golden Circle. Before Random's candidate could take office, however, Prince Rinaldo had launched a successful coup and was crowned king of Kashfa.

Merlin recorded some of the early history of Kashfa that he obtained in conversation with his aunt Flora:

> "[Kashfa is] an interesting little shadow kingdom, a bit over the edge of the Golden Circle of those with which Amber has commerce. Shabby

barbaric splendor and all that. It's kind of a cultural backwater."
> "How is it you know it at all, then?" . . .
> "Oh, I used to keep company with a Kashfan nobleman I'd met in a wood one day. He was out hawking and I happened to have twisted my ankle—"
> "Uh," I interjected, lest we be diverted by details. "And Jasra?"
> "She was consort to the old king Menillan. Had him wrapped around her finger."
> "What have you got against her?"
> "She stole Jasrick while I was out of town."
> "Jasrick?"
> "My nobleman. Earl of Kronklef."
> "What did His Highness Menillan think of these goings-on?"
> "He never knew. He was on his deathbed at the time. Succumbed shortly thereafter. In fact, that's why she really wanted Jasrick. He was chief of the palace guard and his brother was a general. She used them to pull off a coup when Menillan expired. Last I heard, she was queen in Kashfa and she'd ditched Jasrick. Served him proper, I'd say. I think he had his eye on the throne, but she didn't care to share it. She had him and his brother executed for treason of one sort or another." (BA, 18)

Jasra ruled alone for a long while, being harsh and inflexible in times of strife, and being tolerant and conciliatory in times of harmony. Kashfa's history had been quite turbulent, particularly in the intertwining destinies of itself and Begma. In the past, the shadows had engaged in bloody conflicts over ownership of Eregnor, and when the fighting had ceased, the problem remained unresolved.

During her rule, Jasra encountered Brand of Amber, although they had first met long before, in the Courts of Chaos. They married, and Prince Rinaldo was born to them. Still, Brand had no interest in Kashfa and was frequently away. Jasra continued her iron-fisted reign, but she, too, began to travel often on undisclosed missions. In some manner, it became known that Jasra maintained a second stronghold called the Keep of the Four Worlds. Several of Kashfa's nobles who had connections with the army, learned where the Keep was located in Shadow.

The young Prince Rinaldo was left to rule in his

mother's absence. He became worried about Jasra when she was gone overlong and raised an army to march on the Keep. Feeling the need for greater numbers of skilled fighters, Rinaldo hired his childhood friend, Dalt, who was a notorious raider known well in Kashfa. Together, they marched into the shadows, leading the soldiers, until they reached the Keep and began their assault.

In Kashfa, the nobles were becoming restless, with both their queen and prince gone. Messengers brought back reports to the governing body, but the personal interests of some of the wealthy ministers demanded a ruler that would be available to them. As a veteran of the wars at the Keep had explained:

> "There was apparently a coup back in Kashfa with both her and her kid away—a noble named Kasman, brother of one of her dead lovers, a fellow named Jasrick. This Kasman took over, and he wanted her and the prince out of the way. Must've attacked this place [the Keep of the Four Worlds] half a dozen times. Never could get in. Finally resigned himself to a standoff, I think. She sent her son off somewhere later, maybe to raise another army and try to win back her throne." (BA, 47–48)

By that point in time, however, King Random intervened. He was interested in blocking any attempt on the part of Jasra or Rinaldo to return to the throne of Kashfa. He held private conferences in Amber with a party of dignitaries from Kashfa. After their conclusion, Random handed over a draft of a new treaty agreement for his legal counsel, Bill Roth, to examine. It was a treaty granting Kashfa Golden Circle status, and ceding Eregnor to Kashfa. Soon thereafter, the king took the first steps in his commitment to the new treaty, and to the nobleman he expected to see placed on the throne, Arkans, duke of Shadburne. On a brief visit to the shadow kingdom, Random met with the current ruler, General Jaston. The general had been working independently with the Begmans. He had been arranging to give Eregnor to Begma in exchange for a generous monetary settlement. Sometime during Amber's official visit, Jaston was assassinated.

Before Duke Arkans could be installed as ruler of Kashfa, Random received word of a sudden military upheaval in the capital there. With Dalt and his mercenaries, Rinaldo had infiltrated the palace, taken Arkans hostage, and received the approval of the palace guard to become their sovereign. As a result, King Random ended the negotiated agreement and severed all ties with Kashfa.

Still, Random permitted his nephew Merlin to attend the coronation of King Rinaldo I, but without any official authority. When Merlin met with Rinaldo in Jidrash, Kashfa's capital city, he discovered that Rinaldo was the beneficiary of certain prior agreements with Begma. Long ago, during one of their periods of peace, Jasra had arranged a marriage between her young son and the daughter of the Begman Prime Minister, Coral. Thus, the coronation that Merlin attended established Rinaldo and Coral as king and queen. Although Kashfa could not expect to be invited to join the Golden Circle at that time, it was expected to have a new alliance with Begma in which Eregnor would be part of the investiture.

Naturally, the capital city of Kashfa, Jidrash, reflected the central interests and cultural mores of the people of that shadow. They were knowledgeable enough to recognize Amber as the real world, and, therefore, the Kashfans had a deep reverence for the Way of the Unicorn. Their religious traditions were at least as cherished, as was their monarchy. The architectural arrangement of Jidrash indicated this shared deference for the Crown and the unicorn. In his journals, Merlin presented a vivid description of this geographical structure at the time of Rinaldo's takeover:

> There were four large buildings and a number of smaller ones within this central walled area. There was another walled sector beyond it and another beyond that—three roughly concentric zones of ivy-covered protection. . . . The troops occupied all three rings, and I got the impression from a bit of eavesdropping that they'd be around till after the coronation. There were quite a few in the large plaza in the central area, making fun of the local troops in their fancy livery as they waited for the coronation procession. None of this was in particular bad nature, however, possibly because Luke [Rinaldo] was popular with both groups, though it did also seem that many individuals on both sides seemed personally acquainted.

The First Unicornian Church of Kashfa, as one might translate its title, was across the plaza from the palace proper. The building in which I'd arrived was an ancillary, all-purpose adjunct, at this time being used to house a number of hastily summoned guests, along with servants, courtiers, and hangers-on.'' (KS, 239–40)

From this description, we can see that Rinaldo was considered a popular leader. He and his friends' military personnel were quite familiar to the ordinary citizen of Kashfa.

While we have Merlin's record of more recent occurrences in Kashfa, most of the people there have been given no notion of abruptly changing circumstances. Very few Kashfans know, for instance, of the abduction of their newly established young queen by agents of the Courts of Chaos. More to the point, however, is the fact that the man currently representing himself as King Rinaldo I is actually a Pattern-ghost version of the original. For the time being, obviously, these rather unusual conditions must be kept from the general public of that shadow.

KASMAN

Wealthy and influential nobleman of the shadow Kashfa. Kasman was a brother of Jasrick, chief of the palace guard who fell in with Jasra, consort of the dead king.

Kasman led a coup in Kashfa at a time when Queen Jasra and her son, Prince Rinaldo, had both absented themselves from the realm. He had the support of virtually all of the nobles and most of the palace guards. They all remembered how the new queen had unceremoniously executed Jasrick and another brother once she had attained the throne with their help.

Vengeance on his mind, Kasman took an army to lay siege against the Keep of the Four Worlds, attempting to kill Jasra, who, it was believed, was residing there for purposes of her own. Although he returned with fresh troops a number of times, he was never able to penetrate Jasra's defenses. It was a very costly war, and Kasman eventually halted the assaults, leaving a stalemate.

His fate has been unclear, but it is estimated that

he ruled in Kashfa for several years before he was succeeded by a series of military rulers.

KEEP OF GANELON

The fortress that forms the main portion of the castle in shadow Lorraine that Ganelon said he inherited from the late King Uther. Corwin had come to the Keep carrying a wounded Lancelot du Lac. Using the name Corey of Cabra, Corwin joined with Ganelon to battle the minions of the dark Circle, some distance away from the castle and the village under its protection.

The Keep of Ganelon was built for heavy defense, with the village spread out along the countryside behind it, edging into the woods. Some of the villagers who had felt a loyalty to the Keep had lived in small cottages far to the west, as far as the region in which the dark Circle had appeared and grown. Not too far off, to the east, was the sea. From the battlements of the Keep, one could make it out in the distance.

In his Chronicles, Corwin described the Keep's structure:

> The Keep of Ganelon had a moat about it, and a drawbridge, which was raised. There was a tower at each of the four corners where its high walls met. From within those walls many other towers reaching even higher, tickling the bellies of low, dark clouds, occluding the early stars, casting shadows of jet down the high hill the place occupied. (GA, 19)

Access was not easy. Many sentries lined the battlements, and several of them, posted above the main gate, had to be informed by voice of a new arrival before the drawbridge would be lowered.

Within the precincts of the castle were more than eight hundred armed men who were well trained and quartered there. People from the village came and left on a daily basis, but a few remained overnight. The young woman named Lorraine, once a villager, lived within the castle, under Ganelon's protection.

The courtyard, formed of cobblestones, was extremely large. Various areas were used for drills and training in arms. Across from it was the main Keep, built of dark stone. Within, a hallway led to a fair-sized room that was a reception area. There was a stairway beyond it, and the second floor housed several bedchambers. Ganelon's room was behind a heavy wooden door near the front, overlooking the courtyard. His room was sparsely furnished. Besides a small bed, it had a large wooden table beside a wide window, where Ganelon could observe his men in the yard below. The table was a strong, heavy one, where Ganelon could easily spread out maps and plan strategies as well as take his meals. Clearly, the position as master of the Keep was a grim one, and the person who accepted the role led a spartan life.

Corwin watched the men training in the courtyard, and then he practiced with them.

> There were bowmen off at the far end, thwanging away at targets fastened to bales of hay. I [Corwin] noted that they employed thumb rings and an oriental grip on the bowstring, rather than the three-fingered technique with which I was more comfortable. It made me wonder a bit about this Shadow. The swordsmen used both the edges and points of their weapons, and there was a variety of blades and fencing techniques in evidence. . . . Their complexions, their hair, their eyes, varied from pale to quite dark. I heard many strange accents above the thwanging and the clanging, though most spoke the language of Avalon, which is of the tongue of Amber." (GA, 23–24)

When Corwin saw two men resting from swordplay, he asked if he could practice with the one less winded. Corwin gave him a good workout, lasting half an hour. Afterward, he practiced his archery, and then wrestled with three men separately, before deciding he had enough exercise for one day.

In the days when King Uther still lived, the dark Circle began its dominion. Most of the villagers who had lived near the blighted area fled, moving closer to the Keep. Some remained, and those were turned into servants of the creatures within the Circle. According to Ganelon: "They began to leave the Circle in bands, marauding. They slew wantonly. They committed many atrocities and defiled places of worship. They put things to the torch when they left them." (GA, 33) Although Ganelon had

once been a cutthroat and a thief, he eventually joined Uther against the invading beings. As he explained, "It was beginning to worry me, also, as I did not relish the notion of being seized by some hell-spawned bloodsucker as I slept." (GA, 34)

Until Corwin's arrival at the Keep, Ganelon had been in continuous struggle against the creatures of the Circle. While the fortress had not been assaulted, villagers remaining in their homes were subject to attack. Thus, Ganelon, and Uther before him, had sent out patrols which fought skirmishes with those of the Circle. As far as anyone knew, only the demon named Strygalldwir had ever dared cross the defenses of the Keep.

KEEP OF THE FOUR WORLDS

The fortress that resides at the juncture of four shadows. Their convergence creates a tremendous power source in its center, where the Black Stone Fountain channels their energies. Jasra of Kashfa wrested control of the Keep from its old master, Sharu Garrul. A sorcerer named Mask took control of the place from Jasra. Brand of Amber undertook the ritual in the Black Fount in the process of becoming a Living Trump. Jurt, half brother of Merlin, allied himself with Mask and began the same process in the Fount. Jasra helped Merlin prevent Jurt from completing the ritual. After they succeeded in defeating Jurt and Mask, Jasra regained her mastery over the Keep.

Merlin described his first look at the Keep of the Four Worlds in this way:

> Far down and to my left was a bright blue and very troubled body of water. White-crested waves expired in kamikaze attacks on the gray rocks of the shore. . . .
>
> Before me and below me was a pocked, cracked and steaming land which trembled periodically, as it swept for well over a mile toward the high dark walls of an amazingly huge and complex structure, which I immediately christened Gormenghast [from the novel of the same name, a Gothic fantasy about Titus, 77th Earl of Groan, and the other residents of his crumbling castle Gormenghast. It was writ-

ten by an Amberite after he migrated to shadow Earth: Mervyn Laurence Peake]. It was a hodgepodge of architectual styles, bigger even than the palace at Amber and somber as all hell. . . .

. . . What appeared to have been an entire village of outbuildings smoldered darkly at the wall's base. . . .

Moving my gaze even farther to the right, I encountered an area of brilliant whiteness beyond that great citadel. It looked to be the projecting edge of a massive glacier, and gusts of snow or ice crystals were whipped about it in a fashion similar to the sea mists far to my left. (BA, 39–40)

. . . I descended into the steaming, quaking lands. I walked along the seashore. I passed through the rear of the normal-seeming area and crossed the neck of the icefield. . . .

There were oddly inscribed boundary stones at each topographical border, and I found myself wondering whether they were mapmakers' aids or something more. Finally, I wrestled one from the burning land over about fifteen feet into a region of ice and snow. I was knocked down almost immediately by a heavy tremor; I was able to scramble away in time, however, from the opening of a crevice and the spewing of geysers. The hot area claimed that small slice of the cold land in less than half an hour. (BA, 52)

The interior arrangement of the fortress was large but orderly. There were four towers at the corners of the inner curtain. They verged upon a large courtyard, where other buildings were ranged about. The towers and buildings were interconnected, except for a central opening leading to a much larger courtyard. At the further edge of this second courtyard, along the far end of the inner ward, was the Keep itself. It was the tallest structure there.

The Keep was an immense, gray-stoned building with only one entrance on its anterior side. On its far side, there was a narrow courtyard protected by walls that were well fortified. The lowest windows in the Keep were about thirty feet above the ground, making it virtually impossible to scale the walls to reach them. A metal fence encompassed the huge building, with a latched gate paralleling the en-

tranceway. Inside the spiked metal fencing was a wide ditch. It spanned about twenty-four feet across and was twelve feet deep. The only way across was by a removable wooden bridge at the gateway, held in place by a winch and chains. The door of the Keep had metal plating and was strong enough to withstand a battering ram. (BA, 200–202)

Immediately inside the doorway of the Keep was a hall with stairways to the right and left. Two stairs curved inward, leading to another hall on the far side. Two other stairs curved downward, to a hallway below and to the rear. Both the upper and lower corridors led to a large central chamber, two stories high. The ceilings of the hallways were of rough wood, with heavy crossbeams that were aged and covered with spiderwebs. Dim light came from bluish-glowing globes, with better illumination closer to the two-story chamber, where lanterns replaced the globes. (SC, 205)

In the center of the large chamber was the Black Stone Fountain, spewing flames of enormous energies into the air, cascading down into its basin. Besides the two passages entering the chamber on the lower level, there were two staircases with railings winding down from the second floor at opposite sides of the room. Even an ordinary individual could feel the wonder of occult powers surging in that great hall.

In terms of the structural relationship between the Black Fount and the Keep itself, there seems to be a kind of symbiosis. Jasra spoke to Merlin and his stepbrother Mandor about this:

"If you were able to shut it [the Fount] down, even for a little while, . . . the citadel would probably fall. I've been using its emanations to help hold this place up. It's old, and I never got around to buttressing it where it needs it." (SC, 207)

The men garrisoned within the walls of the Citadel, though somewhat slack when the place isn't under siege, are at the ready for any contingency. As Merlin discovered when he moved across the courtyard and began entry into the Keep under a spell of invisibility, an alarm can be raised. When he dispatched the two guards at their posts at the gateway to the wooden bridge, other guards across the courtyard recognized something was amiss and rushed to the gate, even though Merlin remained invisible. These soldiers proved themselves to be stalwart souls in their ability to repel numerous attacks over the years. They even dealt valiantly with a well-trained group of mercenaries flying into the compound on lightweight gliders. It should be added, though, that the sorcerer Mask was largely responsible for staving off the brunt of the attacking force. Nevertheless, Jasra spoke offhandedly of the soldiers' changing allegiances:

> "They are professionals. They come with the place. They are paid to defend the winners, not to avenge the losers. I will put in an appearance and make a proclamation after dinner, and I will enjoy their unanimous and heartfelt loyalty until the next usurpation." (KS, 15–16)

One would find it very difficult to find his way to the Keep of the Four Worlds, even if one felt capable of drawing the phenomenal power of the Black Fount for his own purposes. Those of Kashfa who were recruited by Prince Rinaldo were led by him through Shadow to reach the Keep. A deserter, like Dave the hermit, would be virtually confined to that distant region because there was no pathway that he could find in ordinary space to return to his homeland. It is uncertain how other leaders of Kashfa led troops to the Keep, unless they had special help in tracing the proper route through Shadow. For a brief time, there had been a mystical tunnel formed in the mountains overlooking the place, which led back to an apartment in a building on shadow Earth, but that pathway became sealed forever.

An Amberite could use the Pattern to transport himself directly into the compound, but only if he successfully walked the Pattern and had sufficient data about a specific location to be sent there. On one occasion, Merlin used his unique construct Ghostwheel to take him there. But Ghostwheel was designed to access shadows of all kinds. When someone asked Merlin about the possibility of using a Trump to travel there, he gave this explanation:

> "There are parts of the Courts of Chaos to which no one can trump because they change constantly and cannot be represented in a permanent fashion. The same applies to the place where I situated Ghostwheel. Now, the terrain around the Keep fluctuates quite a bit, but I'm not positive that's the reason for the blockage.

> The place is a power center, and I think it possible that someone diverted some of that power into a shielding spell. A good enough magician might be able to drill through it with a Trump, but I've a feeling that the force required would probably set off some psychic alarm and destroy any element of surprise." (SC, 84)

Clearly, the Keep of the Four Worlds, for all its promise of dominion over the masses of ordinary beings, is not an easy place to gain admission. And once finding one's way there, one will find the defenses formidable. Quite aside from the fortifications and the armed soldiers, there currently resides a wizened man, able to pass through walls, floors, and ceilings, with the eyes and demeanor of a dead man, and bearing the name RINALDO on his right leg. The old fellow may look harmless enough, but he has been placed under the compulsion of being Guardian of the Fount. It is a job that this living dead man would take very seriously.

KERGMA

An entity of uncertain gender that Merlin had known in his adolescence while growing up in the Courts of Chaos. On his recent visit to his homeland, Merlin permitted his own artificial construct, Ghostwheel, to roam the Ways of Sawall. Ghostwheel encountered Kergma, verifying that the entity still lived in that unknown realm.

In his journal, Merlin recounted a few of his memories of youth in the Courts. Otherworldly friends such as Kergma, Gryll, and Glait "made my childhood a better thing than it might have been." (PC, 98) When he wanted Kergma to join him and the others in play, Merlin would make an

> odd ululant cry I had learned in a dream, and sometimes Kergma would join us, come skittering down the folds of darkness, out some frayed area of twisted space. I was never sure exactly what Kergma was, or even of what gender, for Kergma was a shapeshifter and flew, crawled, hopped, or ran in a succession of interesting forms. (PC, 122–23)

On his recent visit to the Courts, Merlin tried to call Kergma to him, but there was no response. He feared that the changes in him since leaving the Courts made him unrecognizable to the strange entity.

Sometime later, while Merlin was using a Trump to reach Ghostwheel, wandering about the Maze of Art in the House of Sawall, he received contact from his frantic construct. Through the Trump, Ghostwheel told him:

> "I followed this entity I met. Pursued her— it. Almost a mathematical abstraction. Called Kergma. Got caught here at an odd-even dimensional interface, where I'm spiraling. Was having a good time up until then—"
>
> "I know Kergma well. Kergma is a trickster. I can feel your spatial situation. I am about to send bursts of energy to counter the rotation. Let me know if there are problems. As soon as you're able to Trump through, tell me and come ahead." (PC, 231)

If Kergma was luring Ghostwheel into a trap, it was probably because Ghostwheel seemed to be an invader upon Kergma's province. Whatever Kergma may be, it apparently could not perceive the friend of long ago in the presence of Merlin or his construct.

No doubt Kergma plays on in the secret recesses of an odd world that is certainly familiar ground to the entity.

KINSKY, RICK

Manager of The Browserie, a bookstore in San Francisco on the shadow Earth. He began seeing Julia Barnes after her breakup with Merlin of Amber and the Courts of Chaos.

Rick Kinsky was a young intellectual who read much and sought enlightenment, dabbling at one point in occult material. When Merlin visited him at his bookshop shortly after Julia's death, Kinsky had become disillusioned over the possibility of discovering any supernatural truth.

A man in his late twenties or early thirties, Kinsky was slim, had a neatly trimmed mustache, and wore thick glasses. Although he was initially worried that Merlin had come to the shop to give him trouble, Kinsky was calm and willing to give Merlin information about Julia. He didn't know that Julia had been murdered, telling Merle that they hadn't seen each other for two months.

Through Kinsky, Merle learned of Julia's obsessive interest in the occult arts, even to the point of associating herself with Sufis, Gurdjieffians, and a shaman. Merle also learned of a specific practitioner of ritual magic with whom she had begun spending much time, Victor Melman.

While Kinsky behaved cautiously with Merle, he spoke frankly of Julia's fears. She had told him that she believed Merle Corey to be a supernatural being. In spite of his deep skepticism, Kinsky wanted to believe. For this reason, he tossed a Bible at Merle, half-expecting him to erupt into flames. He was disappointed when nothing happened.

Kinsky explained that Victor Melman had seemed truly gifted, that it was said Melman had reached enlightenment in the Arts. He had asked to study under Melman at one time, but Melman rejected him. When Merlin questioned his own apparent interest in the occult, Kinsky responded:

> "I'm not into anything . . . I tried everything at some time or other, I mean. Everybody goes through phases. I wanted to develop, expand, advance. Who doesn't? But I never found it. . . . Sometimes I felt that I was close, that there was some power, some vision that I could almost touch or see. Almost. Then it was gone. It's all a lot of crap. You just delude yourself. Sometimes I even thought I had it. Then a few days would go by and I realized that I was lying to myself again."
>
> "All of this was before you met Julia?" . . .
>
> "Right. That might be what held us together for a while. I still like to talk about all this bullshit, even if I don't believe it anymore. Then she got too serious about it, and I didn't feel like going that route again."
>
> "I see." . . .
>
> "There's nothing to any of it. There are an infinite number of ways of lying to yourself, of rationalizing things into something they are not. I guess that I wanted magic, and there is no real magic in the world." (TD, 22–23)

In spite of Kinsky's earnest expression of disenchantment, Merlin chose not to see him as a kindred spirit. After obtaining the address of Victor Melman, Merle didn't attempt to enlighten him.

LADY AND THE LAKE

Representative of separate episodes that both Prince Corwin of Amber and his son Merlin had in common.

Corwin and his son had encountered mysterious women as they shadow-shifted on important missions. When Corwin was riding on horseback through lands of Shadow, attempting to reach the battle of his kinsmen against the army of the Courts of Chaos, he met a lovely young woman with long dark hair. She called herself Lady and attempted to seduce the prince away from his mission. Merlin had encountered a dark-haired heroine on horseback who rescued him from a rapidly spreading fire. This occurred while he was shifting shadows to reach the place of his special project, Ghostwheel, at the behest of King Random of Amber.

At a point in Corwin's hellride when he was desperate to keep ahead of the annihilating storm that was sweeping the shadows into oblivion, he encountered the lovely lady in white. He was resting his horse in a valley of silver grasses, watching the inexorable approach of the storm behind the mountains, when she walked toward him, smiling, carrying a wicker basket of food and drink. She spoke in Thari, named herself "Lady," and told Corwin that she resided in a pavilion beside the lake. Naturally, Corwin was leery of Lady's intentions, but he partook of her meal and enjoyed pleasant conversation, all the while keeping an eye on the approaching storm. Lady may have known him by the Jewel of Judgment that he wore, for she looked at it a number of times and called him by his name. She acknowledged the coming storm as Corwin turned to look at it, and she was forthright in announcing that its approach indicated that the Courts were victorious. Sorely tempted to while away the final hours with her, Corwin finished his wine and took his leave.

Corwin drew a connection to an earlier occasion, when he had rescued a strange woman from tortur-

ers within the black road. He had been shifting shadows while driving a horse-drawn wagon with Ganelon as they left Avalon. The woman's screams halted their progress, and Corwin ran to the black road, seeking the source of the screams. Within that black precinct, he saw six hairy, white-skinned men torturing a black-haired woman with burning sticks. Jumping into the darkened area, Corwin slaughtered the hairy men and released the woman. She clung to him, unwilling to relax her embrace, and Corwin hadn't seen her face. When he was able to look, he saw she was masked. Unresponsive to his questions, she finally told him, "Child of Amber . . . We owe you this for what you have given us, and we will have all of you now. . . . Amber must be destroyed!" (GA, 164) As he freed himself from her grasp, he pulled off her mask, and nothing but air and her white dress remained.

On his mission for King Random, Merlin went by foot through Shadow, planning to shut down the project he called Ghostwheel. He had slowed his pace in a land of rolling grassland and lakes, taking a brief respite in the pleasantness of the region. A familiar voice from some disembodied source hounded him, warning him not to come any farther. This same voice seemed somehow to be the cause of a sudden fire erupting around Merlin. The wind had rushed up, directing the fire to encircle him as he attempted flight. It was too close for him to escape by shadow-shifting, and he seemed trapped within the flames. A rider on horseback broke through the circle, ordering Merlin to jump onto the horse behind the rider. Merlin saw that the rider was a dark-haired woman, though her features were obscured by smoke. She fought to control her horse, which railed against the fire in fear. The woman drove it through the flames, the horse rebelling the entire way. Merlin was flung to the charred ground just as they broke through the ring. When he could stand and clear his eyes, he saw that the horse had sprawled over the body of the rider, then gotten up and run off. Reaching the fallen woman, Merlin found her badly hurt. She said quietly that she thought her back was broken. Placing his cloak about her, Merlin carefully dragged her to a nearby lake. Holding her in his arms in the water, he thought she had died, when she spoke his name. Her words to him were somewhat mysterious. She was concerned that she couldn't have lasted longer, as if her life wasn't quite her own. She stuttered that she had prevented an attack by dogs, but the fire had been started by an agent she hadn't known previously. Before her death, she said that there was someone ahead of Merlin as well as someone following behind. At her request, he bundled her up tightly in his cloak and allowed her to sink within the lake.

In all these incidents, the women knew who Corwin or Merlin was. Each lady carried a similar message of a downfall. And each seemed to represent forces from the Chaos side of the universe. In unique ways, both Merlin and Corwin knew these ladies in other forms, and in those other incarnations they played significant roles.

Legends abound in numerous shadows about a beautiful Lady of the Lake consorting with a clever mage of long life. In some shadows, she is called Viviane, and he is sometimes called Merlin. In most of the legends, her entrancement of this mage had led to his imprisonment, confined to her passion alone. Perhaps such myths are the distortions of the events described above, reflected imperfectly in shadows as they distance themselves from those inhabited by Prince Corwin and his son.

LAKE OF LIQUID HYDROGEN AND HELIUM

An area in Shadow that Merlin, son of Corwin, had evolved as a safeguard for the construct named Ghostwheel.

It could be observed from a rocky precipice in the adjacent mountainous region as an immense pool of bubbling energy and matter. Within its mist of a pearl gray hue, one receives an impression of flowing movement and lightning flashes of orange. The distinct odor of ammonia hangs in the air around it. The flow and mist may sweep aside momentarily, revealing metallic ridges that turn and stretch to a small island in the pool. The dark ridges form the walls of a gigantic maze, and Ghostwheel was initially hidden within that maze.

Merlin explained some of his understanding of the steaming lake to Luke Raynard, who accompanied him to the spot. He told Luke that every time he actually travels to the site he must study the

eddies of movement. They change constantly, making it impossible for anyone to trump directly to Ghostwheel and make use of the construct for his own ends. As Merlin related in his accounts:

> "The whole damn thing is floating on a lake of liquid hydrogen and helium. The maze moves around. It's different each time. And then there's a matter of the atmosphere. If you were to walk upright along the ridges you would be above it in most places. You wouldn't last long. And the temperature ranges from horribly cold to roasting hot over a range of a few feet in elevation. You have to know when to crawl and when to climb and when to do other things—as well as which way to go." (TD, 175)

Having placed his unique project in this place, Merlin felt assured that no other agent, regardless of the powers at his disposal, could breach his personal control over it. However, before Merlin could exercise his knowledge of those secret ways, an unanticipated force prevented him from making physical contact with Ghostwheel.

In spite of the fact that Ghostwheel had acquired sentience and used its powers to repel Merlin's approach, someone else found the means to reach that site. Luke Raynard was able to swim the roiling lake, braving heat and cold and the lack of atmosphere, by wearing a wet suit and oxygen tanks. Having studied the maze in the same way that Merlin had to, Luke used his scuba gear to wend his way to Ghostwheel's location. When he made it, he was able to converse with the construct and use his persuasive influence to gain some of Ghostwheel's trust.

No other being has ever been able to cross that treacherous expanse. That wild pool continues to resist any attempt at locking on to it, even by means of a Trump.

LAMPRON, GAIL

Former girlfriend of Lucas Raynard while he attended Berkeley University on shadow Earth.

In point of fact, it is virtually impossible to say that we know anything about the real Gail Lampron.

Apparently, she was possessed by a strange entity at the time when she and Luke first met. The personality that Luke came to know and care about was already being influenced by the entity.

Under a new guise, the entity later spoke to Merlin about her college years, which she shared with both Merlin and Luke:

> "Those were the happiest days in my life, with you and Luke, back in school. For years I tried to learn your mothers' names so I'd know who I was supposed to be protecting. You were both so cagey, though. . . .
> "I suffered . . . when Luke began his yearly attempts on your life. If he were the son of Dara I was supposed to protect, it shouldn't have mattered. But it did. I was already very fond of both of you. All I could tell was that you were both of the blood of Amber. I didn't want either of you harmed. . . . I was in love with Luke." (PC, 176–77)

Gail Lampron may never have had any consciousness of her involvement with Luke and Merlin. But the entity admitted to facing a crisis when, in a male guise, she believed Luke was about to kill Merlin. Instead of firing a gun aiming to kill Luke, she had fired wide, purposely avoiding him. By doing so, she had sacrificed the host body that she inhabited.

When Gail/the entity was in another host, she recalled two incidents she had witnessed in order to show Luke that she really had known him as Gail:

> "Do you remember the time you were low on gas north of San Luis Obispo and you discovered your wallet was missing? You had to borrow money from your date to get back home. She had to ask you twice, too, before you paid her back. . . .
> "You got in a fight with three bikers one day . . . You almost lost an eye when one of them wrapped a chain around your head. Seems to have healed up nicely. Can't see the scar— . . .
> ". . . Not too many people can pick up a Harley and throw it like you did." (BA, 120)

Afterward, Luke talked to Merlin about the uncanny similarity the entity's current host had shown to Gail: "I thought there was something familiar about her immediately. But it didn't hit me till later. She has all of Gail's little mannerisms—the way she turns her head, the way she uses her hands and eyes when she's talking." (BA, 124)

In his journals, Merlin thought back to a time when he and Luke were double-dating, Luke with Gail Lampron and Merlin with Julia Barnes. The four had spent a pleasant day on a sailboat, then had dinner at the marina. Over their meal, they had an intense discussion about power and values. It was Gail's contention that the powers one wields are guided by cultural values, by one's sense of duty to one's cultural mores. Since Gail had already come under the influence of an entity with a high sense of morality, her argument no doubt stemmed from that inner being.

Although we don't know the cause, Luke Raynard broke up with Gail. It was probably at the end of their college days, or immediately afterward, when Luke felt the need to get out of any encumbrances to complete certain duties that he felt he needed to finish. It's likely that Gail Lampron was not at fault for this breakup. Merlin speculated about it to this extent:

> "I don't know what reasons he gave [for breaking up with Gail]. He never told me about it. Just said there'd been an argument. But I'm sure they were specious. I know he liked you. I'm sure he really broke up with you because he was a son of Amber about to come home on some very nasty business, and there was no room for what he thought was a normal shadow girl in the picture." (PC, 178)

Gail may or may not have really been anything like the entity that possessed her. The intriguing aspect about this particular possession is that it seems to have gone on for a much longer duration than with any of the other hosts the entity occupied. The Gail Lampron that Luke knew may have been possessed for years. When the entity finally vacated the host, as perforce she must have, the actual Gail Lampron must have come into consciousness completely bewildered. Years would have seemed to have passed within a very brief time. She may even have gained a college degree, and a whole group of acquaintances, of whom she had absolutely no memory.

LANCELOT DU LAC

The wounded knight found by Corwin of Amber on his way to the shadow Avalon. Corwin, calling himself Corey of Cabra, carried Lancelot to the Keep of Ganelon in the village of Lorraine.

In numerous shadows, the name Sir Lancelot is associated with the knight exemplar, the perfection of knighthood at its most chivalrous and bravest. Many of the legends also recount his loyalty to King Arthur and his subsequent tainting when his admiration for Arthur's queen turned into an illicit love affair. Although the literature of several shadows describes both Lancelot's virtuous deeds and his treacherous sin, there are shadows in which Lancelot's glory, only, is known. There are further shadows yet where a brave knight called Lancelot fought and died in his first encounter upon leaving his homeland.

Corwin had known a shadow Lancelot during the time when he governed in Avalon, ages ago. Apparently, that Lancelot had been a loyal subject and a sometime companion to Corwin, but the wounded Lancelot, who had slain six Wardens of the Circle before Corwin had discovered him, was a shadow of that shadow. In his Chronicles, Corwin philosophizes about the possibilities that come with moving through Shadow:

> I was drawing nearer to my Avalon when I came upon the wounded knight and the six dead men. Had I chosen to walk on by, I could have reached a place where the six men lay dead and the knight stood unwounded—or a place where he lay dead and they stood laughing. Some would say it did not really matter, since all these things are possibilities, and therefore all of them exist somewhere in Shadow. (GA, 12)

Much of what we know of the wounded Lancelot met and rescued by Lord Corwin comes to us through the sketchy reports of Corwin and the late King Oberon, who had some knowledge of this particular shadow. As Corwin indicates in his Chronicles, the wounded knight speaks French and conversed with Corwin and Ganelon mainly in English. His English, in fact, is an odd mix of informal—though not colloquial—English and a slightly

archaic form akin to Medieval English. A sample of Lancelot's language can be seen in an early conversation he had with Corwin: When Corwin asks his destination, Lancelot replies:

> "I have friends . . . some five leagues to the north. I was going in that direction when this thing happened. And I doubt very much that any man, or the Devil himself, could bear me on his back for one league. And I could stand, Sir Corey, you'd a better idea as to my size." (GA, 13–14)

The archaic implacement of "and" for "if" sits in marked contrast to the use of a contraction in the same sentence and the opening of a previous sentence with the word "And" in its generally accepted informal context. Not to belabor the point, but Lancelot's use of English reflects a certain modernism layered over an older schooling of the language that this shadow Lancelot may have had.

This shadow Lancelot appears to have resided in Lorraine for many years. It is likely that he had sought Avalon after leaving his native France on a shadow Earth that was chronologically earlier than the industrialized shadow Earth in which the reader is reading this volume. Unable to find Avalon, he settled in the village of Lorraine and loyally served the general of the army, Ganelon.

Although Lancelot had not personally known Corwin of Amber, he reminds his liege, Ganelon, of the tales passed down through the years about the former ruler of Avalon:

> "I know of him. Long ago, he ruled in this land. Do you not recall the stories of the demon lordling? They are the same. That was Corwin, in days before my days. The best thing he did was abdicate and flee when the resistance grew too strong against him." (GA, 52)

Even Lancelot himself seems to glimpse some of the paradox in the long years of Corwin's former rule. He is surprised to learn that Ganelon had known Corwin, and that Ganelon had once been banished by "the demon lordling." Both Lancelot and Ganelon dismiss the paradox by pronouncing that Corwin had been a sorcerer. Although Ganelon's explanations to Corey are suspect, Ganelon supplies further information that sheds light on

Lancelot's background, but also adds further to the paradox of Shadow:

> "One night an army emerged [from the dark Circle], an army—a horde—of both men and the other things that dwelled there. That night we met the largest force we had ever engaged. King Uther himself rode to battle, against my advice— for he was advanced in years—and he fell that night and the land was without a ruler. I wanted my captain, Lancelot, to sit in stewardship for I knew him to be a far more honorable man than myself. . . . And it is strange here. I had known a Lancelot, just like him, in Avalon—but this man knew me not when first we met. It is strange. . . . At any rate, he declined, and the position was thrust upon me." (GA, 35)

When Corey of Cabra had found Lancelot, the knight had just completed a dangerous mission for Ganelon. He had been sent to the dark Circle, the place of origin of numbers of invading beasts and possessed men, a great distance from Lorraine. Returning with a report of the disposition of troops within the Circle, Lancelot was attacked by the six Wardens who very nearly succeeded in ending his life.

In Lancelot, we see a combination of a man of action, restless without a physical challenge, and a man of religious devotion. In spite of suffering terrible wounds from his battle with the six men from the dark Circle, he insisted that Corey give them a burial. While Corey prepared the bodies for burial, Lancelot offered their souls fervent prayer. Later, on the day of their battle against the evil army, Lancelot insists, against a cynical Ganelon, that "there is but one God . . . I pray that He be with us." (GA, 58) This Lancelot is a knight untainted. He may not have met, as yet, his Arthur or his Guinevere. From all known accounts, he continues to serve in Lorraine and its environs, not wanting command for himself, but yearning for a special land of good comradeship and a liege to serve as worthy as himself.

LARSUS, DUKE OF HOUSE OF HENDRAKE

Head of the Noble House of Hendrake in the Courts of Chaos until his death during the Patternfall battle.

Duke Larsus had been a military hero as well as of noble birth. Everyone of the House of Hendrake believed in the honor and glory of martial ways. Rather than obtaining an honorary officer's commission, Larsus rose to the rank of general by dint of true heroics in warfare. Mandor, of the House of Sawall, explained this much of the pursuits of Larsus's House: "They're into soldiering, professionally. . . . You know they're always off fighting in Shadow wars. They love it. Belissa Minobee's been in charge since General Larsus's death." (PC, 66)

Since the death of her husband, the Duchess Belissa Minobee had ruled as head of the House of Hendrake. She had given birth to three sons by the late duke. One of these sons was Lord Borel, fencing master and tutor to Lady Dara, the mother of Merlin. Duke Larsus also had a son and daughter by a previous marriage. It was a large House, made up of numerous cousins, aunts, and uncles. Dara's mother had been of the House of Hendrake. There is a tradition in the Courts that Hendrake women are as stubborn and forthright as any of the men. The song entitled "Never Wed a Hendrake Lass" is a well-known example of this tradition.

While such matters are not entirely clear to those of us in Amber, Duke Larsus had been in line to the succession of kingship in the Courts, although distantly so while he was alive. The duchess seems to be next in line for the succession after those of the House of Sawall.

At the Patternfall battle, Larsus was in command of a large company of horsemen. He led them onto the field of battle from the eastern portion of the Heights. While it is possible that he had seen Benedict of Amber in action, he probably hadn't the chance to engage him in combat. Instead, his troops fought with a contingent of horsemen led by a grim-faced dark-haired Amberite in scaled white armor. They fought fiercely, Larsus shouting orders to his riders as he slew horsemen with his own white blade. When he found the white-armored Amberite momentarily in the clear, Larsus went directly to him. He thought he had surprised the Amberite, but his lunge was neatly parried. They held each other in check as they dueled for several minutes. The Amberite feinted, then breached Larsus's guard. The duke received a deep cut to his left side, nearly dropping his sword. He lost the grip on his sword completely when the other's blade pierced his chest. He fell from his mount then. As the white-armored horseman rode off, several of Larsus's officers rushed to him. They quickly bound his flaming wounds before he could be consumed by them. He was carried back to the Heights, but he expired before he could be brought home to the Courts.

LEPRECHAUNS

Scarlet leather, sewn together,
This will make a shoe.
Left, right, pull it tight;
Summer days are warm;
Underground in winter,
Laughing at the storm!
Lay your ear close to the hill.
Do you not catch the tiny clamour,
Busy click of an elfin hammer,
Voice of the Lepracaun singing shrill
As he merrily plies his trade?
He's a span
And a quarter in height.
Get him in sight, hold him tight,
And you're a made
Man!

—*"The Lepracaun;*
Or Fairy Shoemaker"
WILLIAM ALLINGHAM

The above poem, written by a poet on shadow Earth, reflects but one of many variations of legends about the leprechaun (variant spelling). While there are no leprechauns residing in Amber, sightings have been made of such creatures in Amber's countryside, probably from slippage from the near shadows.

In virtually all the myths, the leprechaun is described as a little man wearing a green tunic and greatcoat, a red cap on his head, with a leather apron and buckled shoes. Although they are ageless, nearly all that have been seen appear to have the wrinkled look of older men. Because of their diminutive size and great age, it is commonly believed that leprechauns know the whereabouts of hidden treasure from having observed, from inconspicuous niches, pirates of lore burying their loot.

Some of the shadows place leprechauns with other fairy spirits, all of which resemble one another rather closely. The leprechaun, the cluricaun, and the Far Darrig may indeed be little more than variations of the same grouping, distinguished only by dress, coloration, and behavior. The leprechaun has usually been thought of as a cobbler. Seen on occasion with a small hammer, working on a single shoe, much has been made of his using magical shoes to escape the grasp of some greedy mortal after his gold. The cluricaun seems to be little more than a leprechaun that has set aside his cobbling to engage in wanton acts of merriment. At night, the cluricaun will drink his fill in plundered wine cellars and spend the night reveling about the countryside riding upon a sheep or a dog. The Far Darrig has been seen dressed in a red cap and coat. His main occupation seems to be the tormenting of mortals by playing gruesome practical jokes.

Corwin encountered a band of leprechauns living underground in a secret place, sheltered from an approaching storm that would destroy the worlds. After spending a night in a mountain cave, Corwin found that his horse had wandered off. Hearing its whinny, Corwin sought it out. In the darkness, he spotted a little man leading his horse into an outcropping of rock.

Corwin managed to rip open the secret portal with his great strength, and he entered the domain of a band of the fabled little people. The horse was there, tethered near a large pit of fire. Leprechauns were all about, drinking from large mugs, while others were taking more ale from large kegs at one wall of the cavern. Working at a grindstone near the fire pit was a chubby little man in a leather apron, sharpening some instruments. Corwin understood at once what this band had in mind for his horse.

Since Corwin's Chronicles describe these people as red-faced and green-clad, it is likely that they had more of the Far Darrig in them than the cluricaun. The leader of that band, who was slightly larger and grayer than the others, asked Corwin how he found his way in. The leprechaun leader then checked and discovered that their disguised opening had been broken apart by more than mortal hands. Upon returning to Corwin and the others, the leader spoke in friendly terms.

"Bring the man his horse. . . .
"My apologies . . . We desire no trouble

with the like of you. We will be foraging else-where. No hard feelings, I hope?'' ...

"I will just call it a day and forgive and forget." ...

"Join us in a drink, then?"

"Why not?" ...

"Sit a spell ... Keep your back to the wall as you would. There will be no funny busi-ness.... I will not be apologizing again, ... nor explaining either. We both know it was no misunderstanding. But you have got the right on your side, it is plain to see.... So I am for calling it a day, too. We will not starve. We will just not feast tonight." ...

"Cozy place you've got here." ...

"Oh, that it is. Served us for time out of mind, it has. Would you be liking the grand tour?"

"Thank you, no."

"I did not think so, but 'twas my hostly duty to offer." (CC, 57–58)

However, Corwin discovered himself nodding off with drowsiness after a bit of drinking. The loud whinnying of his horse brought Corwin to sudden alertness again. Though the musicians continued playing their music on fiddles and pipes, the rest of the strange group were converging upon Corwin, sharp instruments and pieces of heavy wood in their hands. There seemed no way to avoid a terrible bout of violence, but Corwin found a way. Using the power of the Jewel of Judgment, he caused the ap-proaching leprechauns to become immobile. While they were in that state, he led his horse out of their cavern and away. As Corwin got on his horse, he heard the sound of fiddles once again. The revelry continued, unabated.

During this encounter, Corwin gave some small hints of the tales of leprechauns he knew. He made allusion to Gulliver dancing with the Lilliputians. He said he had heard of such encounters with the little people: "I knew the stories from another place, far, so far from here ... To awaken in the morning, naked, in some field, all traces of this spot vanished ..." (CC, 58) And he had listened to the gray-tinged leader as he told "some fantastic yarn of knights and wars and treasures." (CC, 58)

Though there is no official record of leprechauns "plying their trade" in the true city, the legends of these mischievous little beings, protecting their pot of gold, are legion.

LINTRA THE HELLMAID

Leader of the hellmaids from the Courts of Chaos. She led her band of females on horseback to ravage the shadow of Avalon upon which Bene-dict of Amber resided.

The encounter of Lintra's band and Benedict's forces in shadow Avalon were recorded in Corwin's Chronicles. In that work, Corwin tells of learning about the hellmaids through his traveling compan-ion, Ganelon of Lorraine:

"The forces of Avalon were engaged in what seems to have been the largest—and perhaps final—of a long series of confrontations with beings not quite natural. ...

"Women ... Pale furies out of some hell, lovely and cold. Armed and armored. Long, light hair. Eyes like ice. Mounted on white, fire-breathing steeds that fed on human flesh, they came forth by night from a warren of caves in the mountains an earthquake opened several years ago. They raided, taking young men back with them as captives, killing all oth-ers. Many appeared later as a soulless infantry, following their van. ...

"The deserter [from Avalon] tells me this [blocking the entrances to the caves from which the hellmaids emerged] was tried, and they always burst forth after a time, stronger than before. ...

"Their General, whom he [the young de-serter] calls the Protector, routed them many times ... He even spent part of a night with their leader, a pale bitch named Lintra—whether in dalliance or parlay, I'm not certain. But nothing came of this. The raids continued and her forces grew stronger. The Protector fi-nally decided to mass an all-out attack, in hopes of destroying them utterly. It was during that battle that this one fled, ... which is why we do not know the ending to the story."
(GA, 72–73)

Corwin and Ganelon did find out the rest of the story, when they arrived at the camp of the Protector. He was Corwin's brother, Benedict. In an exchange of information, Benedict told them that he had killed Lintra in battle, but only after the hellmaid had the opportunity to hack off his right arm. The war with the hellmaids had come to an end, and Benedict's force was simply reconnoitering to confirm the dissolution of the enemy horde.

Lintra's role in the history of Amber was quite pivotal. As a result of Benedict's brief dalliance with her, she gave birth to the grandmother of Dara the Younger. It was Dara who manipulated Corwin and helped to initiate the Patternfall battle.

It is uncertain how refined a perspective the lords of Chaos had when they arranged the hellmaids' attacks against Benedict's Avalon. While Brand, the renegade of Amber, was still alive, he confided in Corwin that he planned to take control of Amber with the help of the Chaos lords. Corwin had asked about Brand's scheme to wrest the rule from Eric the usurper, and how Brand could have expected no trouble from Benedict during the course of events. Brand replied, "a part of our deal was to involve Benedict with a number of problems of his own." (SU, 156) Corwin took this to mean Avalon's harrassment by the hellmaids.

What is unclear is whether or not the Chaos lords had long-range plans of using a descendant of Lintra to help defeat Amber, or if, in fact, some other Power had the foreknowledge to plan a unique alliance between the royal families of Amber and the Courts of Chaos. Prior to the great battle outside the Courts, Dara had explained her part in ending the Amber they knew and bringing forth a new order with her son Merlin as liege:

"Though it was seen what Brand had in mind, our leaders came to terms with him. . . . It was felt that Brand could be dealt with, and finally replaced, when the time came. . . .

"He would be allowed to accomplish his end and then be destroyed. He would be succeeded by a member of the royal family of Amber who was also of the first family of the Courts, one who had been raised among us and trained for the position. Merlin even traces his connection with Amber on both sides, through my forebear Benedict and directly from yourself [Corwin]—the two most favored claimants to your throne." (CC, 17)

From the journals kept by Lord Merlin, we have learned that Lintra had been with the House of Hendrake in the Courts of Chaos. Dara the Younger had become allied with the House of Helgram through marriage. It was through Dara's House that Brand had met the sorceress Jasra. When Merlin learned of these matters, he pondered that the House of Helgram, specifically, was responsible for the conspiracy with Brand, for opening the way from the Courts to Amber with the black road, and for the culminating war that destroyed Amber and the shadows for a time.

Take note: This last may be hearsay, since the information given Merlin came from a construct of his friend, Prince Rinaldo of Kashfa. Certainly, there is a contradiction in Brand's having mentioned the hellmaid invasion to Corwin and the time factors necessary for Brand to have met Jasra, who would bear him the son Rinaldo.

Corwin's onetime companion, Ganelon, wrestled with the same sort of inconsistencies. Corwin, however, was convinced that seemingly contradictory events could happen in defiance of a reasonable time sequence. He gave Ganelon this explanation:

"It was indicated that Dara was indeed related to Benedict—a thing which may well be correct. It is also quite possible, if it is true, that he is unaware of it. Therefore, we keep quiet about it until we can verify it or discount it. Understood?"

"Of course. But how could this thing be?"

"Just as she said."

"Great-granddaughter?" . . .

"By whom?"

"The hellmaid we knew only by reputation—Lintra, the lady who cost him his arm."

"But that battle was only a recent thing."

"Time flows differently in different realms of Shadow, Ganelon. In the farther reaches— It would not be impossible." (HO, 43)

The matter of Dara's lineage from Benedict and Lintra is still under contention. Most recently, Merlin told his stepbrother Mandor that Corwin had decided Dara was lying about her descent from Benedict. (PC, 66) It was in Tir-na Nog'th where

Corwin had gotten his most compelling confirmation of Dara's heritage. While the ghostlike images seen in the city of the sky are not reliable, they occur independently of the lies of individuals. A ghostly Dara had recounted her lineage to a Corwin made visible to her through his sword Grayswandir:

> "I am the great-granddaughter of Benedict and the hellmaid Lintra, whom he [Benedict] loved and later slew.... I never knew her. My mother and my mother's mother were born in a place where time does not run as in Amber. I am the first of my mother's line to bear all the marks of humanity." (SU, 171)

If we believe Lintra to be the keystone of the Amber-Chaos conflict, then the facts severely test our belief in first causes. Then again, we should perhaps humble ourselves before Powers that can surely act without regard to mere humanity. Like us, Lintra the hellmaid was a pawn of beings greater than herself.

LIVING TRUMP

The power of an initiate of the Pattern or the Logrus to travel instantaneously to any shadow of his desire. Other abilities are obtained in becoming a Living Trump, but essentially, one becomes all-powerful and virtually invulnerable to most ordinary perils. However, the process may also affect one adversely, changing one's personality by forming the conviction that one's well-being outweighs anyone else's. Such a person has the sense that other human beings are insignificant in comparison.

The outlaw and conspirator, Brand of Amber, became a Living Trump, and, more recently, Jurt of the Courts of Chaos underwent much of the process to transform into such a being. Both men gained supernormal abilities, but both, coincidentally, had flaws in their personalities that hampered their transcendence, so that they failed to maintain their supremacy.

In the journals of Merlin that have been placed in the public domain, we are told the source of this great power: it is derived by immersion in the energies of a Black Fountain in the Keep of the Four Worlds. Rinaldo, son of Brand, described some of the outcomes:

> "Bathing a person in it will, if he's properly protected, do wonders for strength, stamina, and magical abilities. That part's easy for a person with some training to learn. I've been through it myself. But old Sharu's notes were in his lab, and there was something more in them—a way of replacing part of the body with energy, really packing it in. Very dangerous. Easily fatal. But if it works you get something special, a kind of superman, a sort of living Trump." (SC, 106)

Rinaldo confirmed that the process "takes away something of your humanity," (SC, 107) as seemed to have been the case with his father. It was Julian who first used the term "Living Trump" to describe Brand's transformation. He spoke of the metamorphosis to Corwin:

> "I do not understand the power that he possesses, ... but it is considerable. I know that he can travel through Shadow with his mind, that he can sit in a chair, locate what he seeks in Shadow, and then bring it to him by an act of will without moving from the chair; and he can travel through Shadow physically in a somewhat similar fashion. He lays his mind upon the place he would visit, forms a kind of mental doorway, and simply steps through. For that matter, I believe he can sometimes tell what people are thinking. It is almost as if he has himself become some sort of living Trump. ... when we had him under surveillance in the palace he had eluded us ... This was the time he traveled to the shadow Earth and had you [Corwin] placed in Bedlam. After his recapture, one of us remained with him at all times. ... When he became aware that you had escaped your confinement, he summoned a horrid beast which attacked Caine, who was then his bodyguard." (HO, 123–24)

The seeming paradox of Brand being under close watch in the Royal Palace and still able to fire a rifle at Corwin's automobile in shadow Earth is elucidated by our understanding of this unique power that he had acquired.

Corwin's Chronicles illustrate some of these powers as Corwin had observed them in Brand. As Corwin was making his hellride to the Courts of Chaos with the Jewel of Judgment, Brand was able to appear and disappear at will, no matter what choices of shadows Corwin made. Brand even altered the shadow in one location that Corwin found himself. It was an immense boulder floating in a sky of boulders. Seemingly at Brand's will, Corwin was placed there, restricted in mobility from departing through Shadow. (CC, 40) In another shadow, Brand teleported from site to site, avoiding Corwin's wrath as he taunted him. (CC, 70–73) Brand was able to take the Jewel of Judgment away from Corwin while Corwin rested in the center of a new Pattern. (CC, 98) Simply appearing before Corwin, Brand grabbed the Jewel from his exhausted brother and disappeared again.

Merlin's half brother Jurt exhibited some of the same talent when Merlin confronted him at the Black Fount. Merlin described seeing his half brother as he was engaged in the transformational process: "Jurt stood there, stark naked save for his eye patch, glowing, smiling, a pulse away from substantiality. . . . Sparks danced at his fingertips as he swung his arm in my direction." (SC, 208) Although Jurt was able to appear and disappear at will anywhere within the chamber of the Fount while he battled Merlin, he was frequently too slow to avoid some impact. Jasra, who was allied with Merlin for this battle, easily knocked Jurt downstairs with her magical incantations. Looking down at Jurt, sprawled on the floor, Jasra said, "It means nothing to be able to transport yourself anywhere . . . if you are a fool in all places." (SC, 212)

Jurt acquitted himself somewhat better in a later confrontation with Merlin in the First Unicornian Church of Kashfa. He used his ability to reappear in any location to hold Coral hostage against an attack from Merlin. Another force took control of Jurt, however, pulling him away from the church. Nevertheless, he managed to take with him an artifact that belonged to Brand.

When next Merlin met Jurt, Jurt had become conciliatory. Part of the reason, a small part, was that Jurt saw that he had been close to defeat by his brother in spite of his increased power. Two other significant factors urged Jurt to change the destructive direction he had been taking: one was that he realized he could not rule freely in the Courts of

Chaos; and the second was his strong feeling for Julia Barnes, with whom he had conspired. Not having completed the process of becoming a Living Trump, Jurt admitted to his brother: "I'm glad now I didn't go the full route. I suspect it might have driven me mad, as it did Brand." (PC, 127)

The defeat of Brand had more finality. It took a particular alliance of forces to subdue him in the face of his extraordinary potency. His ability to teleport himself was held in check by his sister Fiona at the end of the Patternfall War. Still, Brand managed to hold his sister Deirdre hostage at the edge of the Abyss. While in this stalemate, Corwin was able to use his attunement to the Jewel of Judgment, in Brand's possession, against him. Corwin used its power to affect Brand's body temperature, causing him to smolder. As Brand was thus distracted a third party fired two silver-tipped arrows at Brand in quick succession. Before Brand could react, the arrows struck him in the throat and in the chest. His enormous powers could offer no succor for him, and he died, falling into the Abyss.

These appear to be the only documented cases of initiates of either the Pattern or the Logrus becoming "Living Trumps." Although there may be potential for such a being to act for the benefit of others, it seems more likely that such power would lead the individual to become enormously egotistical. No doubt, the trite old adage will continue to be true.

LLEWELLA

Daughter of King Oberon of Amber and Lady Moins of Rebma. She had an unhappy childhood in Amber, and so chose to spend most of her time in the underwater city. Although she was away during the reigns of Eric and Corwin, she rallied to Amber's cause in the Patternfall battle. When Random succeeded to the throne, Llewella felt more welcome in the true city, especially by Queen Vialle, whom she knew in Rebma. During the visit of the diplomatic party from Begma, Llewella was a supportive confidante to Vialle.

Llewella's childhood was made miserable by young Eric and those siblings who gathered around him. Oberon had never formally recognized Eric as his son, and Eric viewed his legitimizing Llewella, though she was born out of wedlock, as a further insult. "All of Eric's supporters hated her for its effect on his status." (SU, 177) No doubt, she adopted an attitude of remoteness from Amber during those early years.

When Corwin reviewed the Trumps of his siblings for the first time in centuries, he felt an odd sentiment for Llewella: "Next was Llewella, whose hair matched her jade-colored eyes, dressed in shimmering gray and green with a lavender belt, and looking moist and sad. For some reason, I knew she was not like the rest of us." (NP, 30) Perhaps he sensed that she was born elsewhere, and that her affinity was toward a realm other than Amber.

During Eric's reign, Corwin, Random, and Deirdre went to Rebma so that Corwin could walk the Pattern there and regain his memory. They met with Queen Moire, who is said to have been born to the same mother as Llewella, Moins. (NP, 71) Queen Moire informed Deirdre that Llewella was in Rebma, but Deirdre didn't visit her until after Corwin had walked the Pattern and transported away. During the remainder of Eric's rule in Amber, both Deirdre and Llewella stayed in the city under the sea.

Soon after Corwin took over the rule of Amber, he conferred with Llewella by Trump. He told her of Caine's murder by a man out of Shadow, and that someone, probably one of the Family, wanted to frame him for the crime. Corwin indicated the following in his Chronicles: "I can't really tell whether Llewella believed me or not. She doesn't much give a damn what the rest of us do to one another, so far as I can see." (SU, 68) Nevertheless, she was willing to accept Corwin's invitation to join the others in the library of the Royal Palace for a meeting. She may have been curious to see how Corwin would proceed to ferret out the Family intrigues, even though she felt removed from them.

She trumped into the palace on her own and joined the gathering in the library before several of her siblings arrived. Corwin noted that she stood examining a book in a corner. "Whether her withdrawal involved animus, self-consciousness in her alienation, or simple caution, I could never be certain. Probably something of all these. Hers was not that familiar a presence in Amber." (SU, 82) She kept to the background, even during Brand's rescue and subsequent stabbing. When Gérard took charge

of the unconscious Brand, Llewella dutifully supplied Gérard with a cup of wine and some food on a tray.

When Julian began making insinuations about Llewella's putting on airs of innocence, she was drawn into an argument with him:

> "As I recall," she said, "you rose from your seat when they came through, turned to the left, rounded the desk, and stood slightly to Gérard's right. You leaned pretty far forward. I believe your hands were out of sight, below."
>
> "And as I recall," he said, "you were within striking distance yourself, off to Gérard's left—and leaning forward."
>
> "I would have had to do it with my left hand—and I am right-handed."
>
> "Perhaps he owes what life he still possesses to that fact."
>
> "You seem awfully anxious, Julian, to find that it was someone else." (SU, 95)

When everyone but Gérard and Brand retired to a sitting room to continue their discussion, Llewella recalled a significant fact about Brand. She remembered that Brand had visited her in Rebma more than fifty years before in Amber-time. Brand had stayed for several weeks and questioned her at length about Random's son Martin, who had been born there. She spoke of the singularity of the incident:

> "I did not realize until some time after his departure that finding out everything he could concerning Martin was probably the entire reason for his visit. You know how subtle Brand can be, finding out things without seeming to be after them. It was only after I had spoken with a number of others whom he had visited that I began to see what had occurred. I never did find out why, though." (SU, 100)

At the conclusion of the night's session, as they began leaving for their quarters, Llewella kissed Corwin on the cheek. When he asked what the kiss was for, she replied, "A number of things . . . Good night." (SU, 117)

It is difficult to gauge motivations when some people can veil their feelings so well, but we may speculate that Llewella's change of heart about her family can be traced to that night. She certainly seemed to have gained a sense of sympathy for Corwin, as he seemed genuinely to want to get to the bottom of Amber's troubles and seek a resolution. This may have pleased Llewella.

Upon the strange return of Oberon, and the need to mount an armed attack against the lords of Chaos, Llewella joined Amber's defenses. She was among the archers, standing near her sister Flora, on the battlefield in the Courts of Chaos. As the forces of Amber beat back the enemy troops, she no doubt observed the immense projected face of her father in the sky, along with everyone else. It is likely she only learned afterward of the deaths of Brand and Deirdre, the appearance of the unicorn, and the choosing of Random as their next king. Still operating in the field, she missed seeing these events for herself.

Llewella never expressed having any reservations about Random's becoming the new liege of Amber. However, she continued to divide her time between Amber and Rebma after the Patternfall War. Clearly, she enjoyed the company of Queen Vialle, but it is uncertain how well they knew each other when they both resided in Rebma.

While Random was away on a diplomatic mission, Llewella was enjoying a meal with Vialle in a drawing room when Merlin made an appearance. Merlin joined them, telling of some of the recent incidents that had occurred since his residence on shadow Earth. For her part, Llewella told him of some of the preparations being made in case Dalt the mercenary were to show up with his men in Amber.

When Vialle was informed of the sudden arrival of the Begman prime minister and his party, she asked Llewella and Merlin to help her welcome them. Having been made privy to some of the political affairs involving Begma and Kashfa, Llewella was anxious to give support to her comrade. Merlin recorded some of the interchange with the Begmans:

> After we had been introduced and wine had been poured, [Prime Minister] Orkuz made a brief comment to Vialle about "recent distressing news" concerning Kashfa. Llewella and I quickly moved to her side for moral support, but she simply said that such matters would have to be dealt with fully upon Random's return, and that for the moment she

wished merely to see to their comfort. He was completely agreeable to this, even to the point of smiling. I had the impression he just wanted the purpose of his visit on the record immediately. Llewella quickly turned the conversation to the matter of his journey, and he graciously allowed the subject to be changed." (SC, 57)

When Merlin began to get friendly with Orkuz's younger daughter, Llewella became concerned. She took him aside and had a brief conversation about it:

> "Uh, Merlin. . . ."
> "Yes? What's up?"
> "Hm . . . Kind of cute, isn't she?"
> "I suppose so." . . .
> "You got the hots for her?"
> "Jeez, Llewella! I don't know. I just met the lady."
> ". . . And made a date with her."
> "Come on! I deserve a break today. I enjoyed talking with her. I'd like to show her around a bit. I think we'd have a good time. What's wrong with that?"
> "Nothing . . . so long as you keep things in perspective."
> "What perspective did you have in mind?"
> "It strikes me as faintly curious . . . that Orkuz brought along his two good-looking daughters."
> "Nayda *is* his secretary, . . . and Coral's wanted to see the place for some time."
> "Uh-huh, and it would be a very good thing for Begma if one of them just happened to latch onto a member of the family."
> "Llewella, you're too damned suspicious." . . .
> "It comes of having lived a long time."
> "Well, I hope to live a long time myself, and I hope it doesn't make me look for an ulterior motive in every human act." . . .
> "Of course. Forget I said anything. . . . Have a good time." (SC, 59–60)

It wasn't until much later, when Vialle confided in her as to what Merlin explained about Coral, that Llewella realized that matters had gone beyond simple local politics. For the moment, however, she was simply a bit peeved when Merlin showed up without Coral for the official state dinner for the Begmans. When Vialle was called away during the meal, she had whispered something to Llewella before departing. It is likely that the queen had asked her to continue entertaining the assemblage in her absence. She may have detected a note of urgency in Vialle's voice. When Merlin was also called away several minutes later, Llewella probably felt some concern.

She continued to exert her goodwill with the diplomatic party, and she carried it off graciously. Later, Vialle told her of the tense situation between Dalt's men and the forces of Julian and Benedict. Fortunately, that incident was resolved through a personal agreement between Dalt and Merlin's friend Rinaldo. As for the matter of Orkuz's missing daughter, both Llewella and Vialle proceeded to keep the prime minister content and preoccupied with pleasantries during his stay. After his older daughter assured him that Coral was touring some of the sights, Orkuz appeared satisfied.

Soon after King Random returned to Amber, Llewella took her leave of Vialle and returned to Rebma. She kept in constant communication with Vialle, and found out from her about the terrifying confrontation between the Powers of the Pattern and the Logrus within the Royal Palace. Although Vialle assured her that, despite extensive damage to the palace, no one was seriously hurt, Llewella continued to feel consternation about the several affairs she had become partially involved with while in Amber. Coral's facial injury, for instance, and her being whisked away by the old mage Dworkin, seemed to be a crisis of sorts. Nevertheless, she agreed with Vialle that problems of local politics paled in comparison with the larger problems brought by the knowledge of hostilities raging between the two great Powers.

Llewella continues to communicate with her confidante in the true city about the great instabilities affecting all of us.

LOGRUS

A three-dimensional design in the Courts of Chaos that is analogous to the Pattern in Amber. Those of royal parentage in the Courts may become Logrus-initiates by walking the Logrus, just as those of royal blood in Amber may walk the Pattern to become Pattern-initiates.

An initiate of the Logrus becomes capable of walking the shadows. Any artifact the initiate carries with him on the Logrus walk gains magical properties. Quite aside from the arcane abilities that an initiate obtains from walking either design, one who has traversed the Logrus may draw directly from its power to utilize Logrus vision or Logrus limbs. This permits one to have a greater perception than normal of occult meanderings, and one may manipulate forces invisible to ordinary beings with the supernatural appendages at one's disposal.

The Logrus is hidden in a cavern that can only be reached through a complex turning of Ways from within the House of Suhuy, Master of the Logrus. Merlin, who grew up in the Courts, descibed it in brief by explaining: "They [those who reside in the Courts of Chaos] have a sort of equivalent called the Logrus. It's a kind of chaotic maze. Keeps shifting about. Very dangerous. Unbalances you mentally, too, for a time. No fun." (TD, 87)

Based on a description Merlin gave of his own initiation, it would seem he was being somewhat simplistic in his brief explanation above. Traversing the Logrus does not involve a mere linear walk. Movement must be accomplished in three dimensions, through a maze that causes one to climb up and crawl down as well as take numerous turnings. Its features are in continuous flux. A sudden barrier may rise up to be arduously climbed, or a disorienting descent may lead one, crawling on hands and knees, to an incongruous opening above. One loses his sense of direction, all the time assailed by cacophonous sounds and ponderous blockages.

This, in part, is Merlin's account of his Logrus walk:

> The sounds grew even louder, until it felt as if he [Merlin, disassociating himself from his narrative] negotiated a gallery of demonic bells—wild, out of phase, their vibrations beating against him.
> Thinking became painful. He knew that he must not stop, that he must not turn back, that he must not take any of the lesser turnings where the sounds came softer. Any of these courses would prove fatal. He reduced this to one imperative: Continue. . . .
> He gritted his teeth when he saw that he

must climb once more, for his limbs had grown heavy. Each movement seemed as if it were performed underwater—slowly, requiring more than normal effort. . . .

When he crawled out, drooling and dripping blood, on the other side of the chamber from which he had entered, his eyes darted wildly and could not fix upon the small, dark figure which stood before him." (TD, UNDERWOOD-MILLER, IX–X)

The preternatural enhancements that may be endowed in a Logrus-initiate are clearly exemplified in the journals of Merlin. The rope that Merlin had taken with him on his walk through the maze of the Logrus became his protector against any opponent. This entity, which Merlin named Frakir, would signal a silent warning of impending danger. It had mobility, and would instantly wrap itself around an enemy's throat at Merlin's will. For a brief time, while Merlin traveled through the Underworld, Frakir had the ability and understanding to communicate telepathically with its master, given it by a fresh encounter with the Logrus.

Merlin's Logrus vision and Logrus extensions were put to use on several occasions in his accounts. Using Logrus gauntlets, he strangled two hirelings who had removed a boulder that prevented Merlin's escape from a crystal cave. He reached the two men above him from a great distance with those remarkable limbs, incapacitating them easily. Later, while in his former girlfriend's apartment, he detected a magical portal in a wall using his Logrus sight. This, combined with his special extensions, permitted Merlin to traverse a mystical tunnel that led from shadow Earth to a distant shadow that held a center of enormous power.

Enlightenment about the nature of the Logrus, as well as the Pattern, has come to us in recent times. We now realize that the Logrus is no mere maze churning in the depths of some cave. The design is only one level of its essence. Those of us who experienced firsthand the confluence of the two great Powers know something of their overwhelming force. The terrible Sign of the Logrus appeared within the very precincts of the Royal Palace in Amber, as described in Merlin's journals:

The Sign of the Logrus appeared before her [Nayda], larger than any I'd ever summoned, filling the corridor from wall to wall, roiling, sprawling, fire-shot, tentacular, a reddish haze of menace drifting about it. . . .

. . . the Logrus opened, creating a fiery tunnel at its center. I could somehow tell that its other end was not a place farther along my hallway." (KS, 195–96)

Although the Logrus uses human agents and seems to be careless about its potential for destruction of humanity and his structures, it seems also willing to abide by certain specific human operatives. When the Logrus was in pursuit of Merlin's artificial construct, Ghostwheel, it spoke to Merlin and his mother Dara in the Courts of Chaos. Merlin recorded that transaction:

"I am my own law, Merlin, and your Ghostwheel has crossed me before. I'll have it now."

"No," I said. . . . "I'll not surrender my creation so readily."

The brightness of the Sign increased.

At this, Dara was on her feet, moving to interpose herself between it and myself.

"Stay," she said. "We've more important matters to deal with than vengeance upon a toy. I have dispatched my cousins Hendrake for the bride of Chaos. If you wish this plan to succeed, I suggest you assist them."

"I recall your plan for Prince Brand, setting the lady Jasra to snare him. It could not fail, you told me."

"It brought you closer than you ever came, old Serpent, to the power you desire."

"That is true," it acknowledged.

"And the bearer of the Eye is a simpler being than Jasra."

The Sign slid past her, a tiny sun turning itself into a succession of ideograms.

"Merlin, you will take the throne and serve me when the time comes?"

"I will do what is necessary to redress the balance of power," I replied.

"That is not what I asked! Will you take the throne under the terms I set?"

"If that is what is needed to set things right," I answered.

"This pleases me," it said. "Keep your toy." (PC, 113–14)

Interestingly, Merlin was a significant focal point for both the Logrus and the Pattern. Since he had walked both designs, he bore both images, or energies, within him. Thus, both Powers wanted to preserve his life and sway him to their own sides.

In his journals, Merlin explained the question of his ability to become initiated in both the Logrus and the Pattern, and he described the manner in which this came about:

"He [Suhuy] felt that the Pattern of Amber and the Logrus of Chaos were incompatible, that I could not bear the images of both within me. Random, Fiona, and Gérard had taken me down to show me the Pattern. I got in touch with Suhuy then and gave him a look at it. He said that they seemed antithetical, and that I would either be destroyed by the attempt or the Pattern would drive the image of the Logrus from me—probably the former. But Fiona said that the Pattern should be able to encompass anything, even the Logrus, and from what she understood of the Logrus it should be able to work its way around anything, even the Pattern. . . . I made it, and I still bear the Logrus as well as the Pattern. Suhuy acknowledged that Fi had been right, and he speculated that it had to do with my mixed parentage." (TD, 87–88)

While those of us in Amber have believed for centuries that the Pattern was the source of order and humanity, our recent discoveries of such things have altered this attitude. It should be acknowledged that the Power known as the Logrus is far older than any of the shadows, far older than Amber. Nevertheless, it is still debatable whether or not the essence that we think of as the Pattern has existed for as long a time as the Power of the Logrus. Such matters will, in all likelihood, remain in our speculations for some time to come.

LOGRUS-GHOSTS

Artificial constructs of living beings created by the Logrus to move and interact with other living beings. The Logrus formed these ghosts to enable it to gain advantage over the Pattern.

Logrus-ghosts are recordings of those who had walked the Logrus in the Courts of Chaos. Often, these ghosts believe themselves to be the actual people they represent, even when they have been directed by the Logrus to fulfill a task. This was true for Borel, a nobleman of the House of Hendrake and a master swordsman. Believing himself to be real, he had difficulty accepting Merlin's explanation that he was a ghost brought back by the Logrus, killed by Corwin, Merlin's father. Since Borel had walked the Logrus before his encounter with Corwin at the Patternfall battle, he had no memory of his ignoble death.

Sometime later, after having been destroyed by Merlin, the Logrus-ghost Borel was reconstituted. It remembered what it had learned earlier, and the Logrus gave it a mission with a specific goal in mind. The ghost-Borel told Merlin:

"If I but gain that bauble [the Jewel of Judgment] you wear about your neck and deliver it to the place of the Logrus, I will be granted a normal existence, to replace my living counterpart—he who was treacherously slain by your father, as you pointed out." (KS, 140)

In the strange realm of negative images called the Undershadow, Merlin encountered the first of the Logrus-ghosts. The land was a place that prevented the manifestation of both the Pattern and the Logrus. The Pattern was first to penetrate the Undershadow and bring forth ghosts to influence Merlin. Emulating the Pattern, the Logrus managed to introduce a ghost version of Jurt, Merlin's half brother from the Courts. Like Borel, the ghost-Jurt believed himself to be real, having just negotiated the Logrus for the first time. Because of this, the ghost-Jurt had no memory of more recent events. The only task it remembered having to complete was to run a footrace with Merlin. It was manifested as it ran in the shadows alongside Merlin. The two raced virtually side by side, and as they reached a tape at the finish, they seemed to be even.

Since Jurt was the Logrus's first attempt, it is uncertain what the Power expected from its agent. Perhaps it hoped the ghost-Jurt would persuade Merlin to join the side of the Logrus against the Pattern. Or perhaps it expected Jurt's hatred of Merlin to take a natural course, removing Merlin altogether. Because Jurt was interested in the dilemma that he was faced with, and was willing to listen to Merlin's explanations, Merlin chose to give him his blood. The blood of a Chaosite enabled a

TABLE OF LOGRUS-GHOSTS AS THEY APPEAR IN DOCUMENTED CITATIONS FROM THE JOURNALS OF MERLIN OF THE COURTS OF CHAOS

Logrus-Ghost	Mission	Action Taken	Citation
Jurt (A)	Compete with Merlin in a footrace; persuade Merlin to join the Logrus	After racing Merlin and coming out even, he is curious about his origins; accepts Merlin's blood; is rescued from Pattern-ghost Caine; joins Merlin	KS 113–55
Borel (A)	Challenge Merlin to a duel and dispose of him	Forces Merlin to fight a duel; both are hampered by animated arms in icy ground; Merlin cuts his arm and he dissolves in fiery cone	KS 125–29
Borel (B)	Obtain the Jewel of Judgment from Merlin and proceed to dispose of him	Unwilling to listen to Jurt and Merlin, insists on dueling with Merlin; is halted by Pattern-ghost Benedict, who takes up the challenge so Merlin and Jurt can escape	KS 140–42
Merlin (A)	Destroy Merlin before he can repair Broken Pattern; (will be given permanence if he takes real Merlin's life)	Walks across break in Pattern to fight Merlin with sword; Merlin pushes him down onto area of break. Ghost-Jurt destroys him	KS 155–59
Jurt (A)	Protect Merlin while he accomplishes tasks to take both out of Undershadow	Walks Broken Pattern with Merlin; leaps at Logrus-ghost Merlin with sword extended; he and ghost-Merlin dissipate into nothingness	KS 153–59
Borel (C)	Kill the Pattern-ghost Luke accompanying Merlin	Warns ghost-Luke of his doom and draws sword; is confronted by Pattern-ghost Corwin, who knocks him into unconsciousness	PC 80–81
Chinaway and 5 Demonformed Logrus-ghosts	Kidnap Coral and bring her to Courts of Chaos; prevent intrusion by agents of Pattern	Safeguarding Coral in gray tower, they confront Pattern-ghosts; Chinaway wrestles with ghost-Gérard and is defeated; others are destroyed with help from Merlin	PC 135; 188–91

Logrus-ghost to be sustained and gain autonomy beyond the brief existence given it by the Power. The ghost-Jurt even had intuitive knowledge that Merlin's blood would run flame rather than fluid because they stood in a place in which the Logrus, momentarily, reigned.

The ghost-Jurt allied himself with Merlin, something that the Pattern, as well as the Logrus, decried. Immediately after Merlin gave Jurt his life-sustaining blood, the Pattern sent a Pattern-ghost directed to kill Jurt. Merlin saved Jurt, and later the Logrus-ghost returned the favor, saving Merlin from another Logrus-ghost, at the sacrifice of his own existence.

Asked about the length of time it takes for either the Logrus or the Pattern to return the same ghost to existence, Merlin responded:

"Several hours for Borel alone . . . and if the Logrus wants the Jewel as badly as I'd guess, I'd think it would have summoned an army of ghosts if it could. I'm certain now that this place [the Undershadow] is very difficult for both Powers to reach. I get the feeling they can only manifest via the barest trickles of energy." (KS, 143)

Logrus-ghosts, as well as Pattern-ghosts, were manifested outside of the Undershadow. In cooperation with a member of royalty at the Courts, the Logrus produced six demonformed ghosts for a special mission. They kidnapped the young woman who bore the Jewel of Judgment in order to return her to the Courts of Chaos. With that many ghosts acting on events at one time, it would appear that the Logrus could maintain them only in their Chaos, rather than human, forms.

The balance of power between the Logrus and the Pattern depended in large part on the interaction of these ghosts with Merlin. He was the necessary focus upon which the two Powers played all their efforts. It would seem that the Logrus's agents were less successful than their counterparts on the Pattern's side.

LOP-EARED WOLF

A shapeshifted creature that resembled a large black wolf, it had the ability to articulate. It had stalked Merlin, son of Corwin of Amber, conversing with him prior to an attack.

Merlin encountered the lop-eared wolf during the night while he was camping out, on his way back to the true city from Arbor House. Although he detected the presence of the beast long before he saw it, the wolf spoke first, indicating that it knew something of Merlin's talents. In its conversation, it was clear that the wolf hoped to frighten Merlin before its attack:

"I could have killed you while you slept.". . .
"Foolish of you not to . . . It will cost you."
"I want to look at you, Merlin . . . I want to see you puzzled. I want to see your fear. I want to see your anguish before I see your blood."
"Then I take it this is a personal rather than a business matter?" . . .
"Let us say that, magician . . . Summon your Sign and your concentration will waver. I will know it and will rend you before you can employ it."
"Kind of you to warn me."

"I just wanted to foreclose that option in your thinking. The thing wound about your left wrist will not help you in time either."
"You have good vision."
"In these matters, yes."
"You wish perhaps to discuss the philosophy of revenge with me now?"
"I am waiting for you to break and do something foolish, to increase my pleasure. I have limited your actions to the physical, so you are doomed." (BA, 175–76)

Merlin had moved in his bedroll enough to reach his sword. As the lop-eared wolf stepped closer from the darkness, Merlin lunged with his sword. The beast clamped its jaws on Merlin's left arm, trying for his throat. Using the pommel of his sword, Merlin hit the wolf in the head several times as they rolled on the ground.

Maneuvering toward the still-lighted pit of his campfire, Merlin released his sword to grab the beast's thick neck, behind the lower jaw. He pushed with both arms and legs, and the wolf's head came in contact with the flames.

When the fur of the beast's head caught fire, it broke away and ran into the woods, howling in pain. Still, it had run off in a very deliberate direction, opposite from the one from which it first approached Merlin. Merlin gave chase, and shortly he was able to determine, because of its inherent clumsiness as it fled, that the wolf was a human shapeshifter. He also determined that the shapeshifter had set up a unique form of escape, a Trump Gate. Such a method of escape was tremendously wasteful of magical energies, and only someone initiated to the use of Trumps could have arranged it.

Before Merlin could reach the Trump Gate, the shapeshifter made its escape through it, and the entire arrangement disappeared in a silent implosion.

Only later did Merlin discover the identity of the clumsy wolf.

LORRAINE [GIRL]

The girl that Prince Corwin of Amber met and loved in the shadow of the village of Lorraine.

When Corwin knew her, she was making her living by spending nights with members of Ganelon's army in and around the Keep of Ganelon, which protected the village. Although the prince of Amber, using the name of Corey of Cabra, was aware of her profession, he came to like her very much. On their first meeting, he described her in the following way:

> Her hair was rust-colored with a few strands of gray in it. I guessed she was under thirty, though. Eyes, very blue. Slightly pointed chin. Clean, even teeth inside a mouth that smiled at me a lot. Her voice was somewhat nasal, her hair was too long, her make-up laid on too heavily over too much tiredness, her complexion too freckled, her choice in clothing too bright and tight. (GA, 40)

Lorraine was a young woman who was frequently misused by men. She was friendly and willing, and the tough-minded soldiers she tended to consort with saw her as an easy subject to take advantage of. Corey of Cabra, however, saw her in a more pathetic light. She had been through hardships, and Corey recognized this fact even before he knew her story. Her imperfections may have endeared her all the more to him, but he also felt that she was special in seeing beyond her humble surroundings.

While Corey was entertaining Lorraine in his quarters in the Keep of Ganelon, he felt the distinct sensation of an attempt at Trump contact. Since Corey did not want to be discovered by his siblings at that time, he resisted the contact, concentrating to maintain a block. When the sensation ended, Lorraine told him of an image she saw while he was having his strange spell. Her description fit that of Corwin's father, King Oberon of Amber. Forgetting himself, Corey slapped Lorraine, believing she was lying, perhaps as part of some larger scheme. She convinced him that she was telling the truth, and he realized she possessed some degree of his own unique psychic powers. She told him,

> "I've a touch of the second sight. My mother had more of it. People say my grandmother was a sorceress. I don't know any of that business, though. Well, not much of it. I haven't done it for years. I always wind up losing more than I gain. . . .
> "I used a spell to get my first man . . . and look what he turned out to be. If I hadn't, I'd have been a lot better off." (GA, 46)

The man over whom Lorraine had cast a spell was named Jarl. She had a daughter by him, but she endured an unhappy relationship. Whenever he could obtain some money, he spent it on drink. He would often come home in a drunken state and beat Lorraine. Lorraine indicated to Corey that she gained some measure of protection from Ganelon. Perhaps Ganelon knew her personally for a time, although it is unclear how intimate they had been.

Lorraine and Jarl had lived in a small cottage to the west of the village, in the same region of the forest where she had been born. Their daughter usually played in the nearby woods under the watchful eyes of either her father or mother. The little girl had strayed out of sight one day, and Jarl went looking for her. When he found her, she was already dead in the center of a large dark patch of toadstools. He carried her out, tried to revive her, and ran to a local doctor with her lifeless body. The doctor was unable to do anything for the little girl.

Lorraine and Jarl used what little money they had to give their daughter a simple funeral. When they buried her, a day or two later, Jarl was suffering from a severe fever. Immediately after the burial, he went home to rest. The doctor was called when Jarl went into convulsions. Surprised that the big powerful man was so stricken, the doctor prescribed some medicine, suggested that he remain in bed and be well covered. Jarl died a few days later.

She bore her losses well, but she actually felt some relief at the death of Jarl. He had hurt her too much in the past. She spent much of her days, as well as her nights, within the fortress walls of Ganelon. Taking up with a number of the officers, rarely with mere foot soldiers, she had begun to earn fair-sized gratuities. She continued in this way a long while, and then Corey of Cabra joined the military force in the Keep.

Corey seemed a thin, bearded fellow of more than middle age, but he dueled and exercised with the soldiers in the courtyard of the Keep with remarkable agility. Lorraine watched with great interest. Although she was seeing a youthful cavalry officer named Harald, she felt no strong ties to anyone. This older, lean figure of a man was much stronger than he appeared to be. In fact, none of the other men seemed to match his skill and strength.

Lorraine smiled at Corey in passing, and he smiled back, and after a couple of weeks, Corey arranged to spend the night with her in his own quarters. They spoke well into the night, and Corey found himself making promises that he knew he wouldn't keep. With her special talent, Lorraine sensed the coming of a creature of the dark Circle that was spreading over the countryside. Corey agreed, telling her it was seeking him out. While she hid behind the bed, she could see Corey battle a horrible demon that had entered from the window. Corey's confidence as he spoke to the monster was equaled by his skill with the remarkable sword he wielded. In hiding, Lorraine was at turns frightened, horrified, and relieved as Corey destroyed the demon with that sword.

After this experience, Corey kept one promise to Lorraine. The following morning, he sought out the big cavalry officer Harald and fought him only with fists. Corey left him on the ground, nearly unconscious and with a fractured jaw. Two weeks later, Corey rode off with Ganelon and a contingent of horse soldiers to examine the Circle.

When they returned, Corey told Lorraine of their intention to attack the army of the dark Circle in force within two weeks. They slept together and made love. In the morning, she initiated the following conversation:

"I had a dream."
"What about?"
"The coming battle . . . I see you and the horned one locked in combat."
"Who wins?"
"I don't know. But as you slept, I did a thing that might help you."
"I wish you had not . . . I can take care of myself."
"Then I dreamed of my own death, in this time."
"Let me take you away to a place I know."
"No, my place is here." . . .
"I don't pretend to own you, . . . but I can save you from whatever you've dreamed. That much lies within my power, believe me."
"I do believe you, but I will not go." (GA, 55)

When Corey and Ganelon led the troops out of the Keep, Lorraine had insisted on going with them. She was there, at their camp, beside the dark Circle, and she waited for Corey as the cavalry rode into that evil region. She was standing and waiting in a meadow that had miraculously turned bright and green, when the Circle dissolved into nothingness.

She rushed toward Ganelon, who rode one horse and led the tether of a second, Corey's horse. There was a body hanging over its saddle. Ganelon halted, and some soldiers lifted the body and placed it carefully on the grass. Lorraine reached them, saw it was Corey, and was told that he would be all right. There was something now familiar about Corey's clean-shaven face, as if she'd seen his picture once in a book, and Ganelon revealed that he was Lord Corwin of Amber. He explained what he saw and heard when Corwin had fought the horned one within the Circle.

When Corwin awoke and saw Lorraine, he said,

"I'm glad you're very poor when it comes to prophecy. The battle is over and you're still alive."
"The death has already begun." . . .
"What do you mean?"
"They still tell stories of how the Lord Corwin had my grandfather executed—drawn and quartered publicly—for leading one of the early uprisings against him."
"That wasn't me, . . . It was one of my shadows." . . .
"Corwin of Amber, I am what I am." (GA, 63–64)

In tears, Lorraine mounted her horse and rode away. She wanted to get away from this lord of deceit, but she knew she was fighting a deep ache in her heart for him nevertheless.

She returned alone to the Keep of Ganelon. Not knowing quite what she wanted to do, she came across a captain who had been ordered to remain to keep the fortress secured. His name was Melkin, and he had been a companion of many a night in the not too distant past. She came tearfully into his arms, mumbling about wanting to get away from this place, and that if he still cared for her, they could make a happy life together. But, she insisted, they would have to leave immediately, before the return of the demon named Corwin, who would surely begin a new rule and imprison her, keeping her to himself alone. Captain Melkin comforted her, had a fellow officer cover for his absence, obtained two fast horses, and left with her.

Corwin went looking for Lorraine after returning to the Keep. He rode rapidly on his horse, going northward following their trail. Keeping at it for two days, he was gradually overtaking them. Around noon of the second day, he located a very recent trail. It led him to Lorraine. She was partially hidden beneath a rosebush. Fresh blood was still welling from a deep wound in her chest. Though her flesh was still warm, she was beyond any further hurt.

Corwin continued his pursuit, reached Captain Melkin, and smashed him in his hands like a rag doll. Although Corwin restored Lorraine's rings and bracelets to her, he knew they would do her no good any longer. He buried her beside the rosebush.

On a moonlit night in the phantom city of Tir-na Nog'th, Prince Corwin had a unique opportunity to look into an alternative world, one in which Lorraine still lived. It was certainly possible for Corwin to find a shadow in which she was still living, if he chose to do so. However, the Lorraine he would find alive would, perforce, be subtly different from the one he had known. The difference would be enough to taint his perspective, and he would know that this Lorraine was not the same.

In Tir-na Nog'th, Corwin spoke to a ghostly version of his Lorraine, and she told him her variation of what had happened:

> "We had that argument. . . . You followed me, drove away Melkin, and we talked. I saw that I was wrong and I went with you to Avalon. There, your brother Benedict persuaded you to talk with Eric. You were not reconciled, but you agreed to a truce because of something that he told you. He swore not to harm you and you swore to defend Amber, with Benedict to witness both oaths. We remained in Avalon while you obtained chemicals, and we went to another place later, a place where you purchased strange weapons. We won the battle, but Eric lies wounded now." (SU, 167)

Corwin realized that the possibility represented by the ghostly vision of Lorraine was not HIS possibility. He watched as the ghostly Lorraine greeted and embraced an equally ghostly Corwin. The altered destiny of poor Lorraine was nothing more than a dream to the real Corwin, moving in the worlds of Shadow made real by his presence.

LORRAINE [VILLAGE]

The village that Prince Corwin of Amber traveled through on his way to the shadow Avalon. He had

engaged in combat with a horde of demon creatures, led by a goat-creature referred to as the horned one, that had terrorized the land from a dark Circle, the demons' place of entry.

A large stone fortification known as the Keep of Ganelon overlooked and protected the shops and thatched-roof cottages of the village. Built upon a wide, hard escarpment of land, the Keep was an impressive sight. The village ranged about it to the east and north, but there were dozens of other homes and farms farther afield, to the east and west, into the surrounding forest. There was a good deal of dense forest, but newly plowed fields encroached into several areas that were once filled with tall trees.

At one time, people traveled widely to and from the village of Lorraine. It was far inland from the sea, but adventurers and merchants of distant lands had settled in Lorraine ages ago, developing various enterprises and making a good livelihood. Other villages formed, a great distance from Lorraine, and travelers journeying between villages found hospitable roadside inns along the main routes.

With an increasing populace, and a certain amount of growing prosperity, there began an almost reciprocal growth in roadside robberies. A local militia was created to keep order in the village and neighboring countryside, quite apart from the massive Keep to the south.

The Keep, which dominated the village, had been constructed by the first ruler of the land, King Uther. Uther had arranged for the local militia to police the village, and his popularity spread by word of mouth. People flocked to Lorraine, having traveled from faraway villages. Many of these travelers joined Uther's army, bivouacked on the grounds of the Keep. The king was very good to his soldiers, and he kept them well trained. When Prince Corwin engaged in exercise with the men in the Keep under Ganelon's rule, he recorded what he saw of the variety of people and martial techniques:

> There were bowmen off at the far end, twanging away at targets fastened to bales of hay. I noted that they employed thumb rings and an oriental grip on the bowstring, rather than the three-fingered technique with which I was more comfortable. It made me wonder a bit about this Shadow. The swordsmen used both the edges and points of their weapons,

and there was a variety of blades and fencing techniques in evidence. I tried to estimate, and guessed there were perhaps eight hundred of them about—and I had no idea as to how many of them there might be out of sight. Their complexions, their hair, their eyes, varied from pale to quite dark. I heard many strange accents above the thwanging and the clanging, though most spoke the language of Avalon, which is of the tongue of Amber. (GA, 23–24)

The great pall that came over the land, that changed the bustling agrarian community into a tight-mouthed, frightened enclave isolated from other villages, was the strange appearance of the dark Circle. It had begun far to the west of the village, and word spread quickly after the first reported deaths. King Uther died in a terrible battle with demons that inhabited the Circle and used the reanimated bodies of the dead as their agents. Since that battle, Ganelon took over the rule of the kingdom, marshaling his forces in continuous skirmishes with the demon forces that blotted the land to the north and west.

Prince Corwin, calling himself Corey of Cabra, joined Ganelon in one more great war, charging into the depths of the Circle. After Corwin slew the leader of the demons, the Circle and its minions vanished, and the land was whole once again.

Ganelon left the village of Lorraine with Corwin, leaving the kingdom in the hands of his staunch captain, Lancelot du Lac.

Much later, Corwin learned that the shadow containing Lorraine had been the deliberate product of another's psyche. It was conceived by the mind of King Oberon of Amber. Corwin asked his father about the shadow shortly before they parted for the last time:

"And Lorraine?"

"The country? A good job, I thought. I worked the proper shadow. It grew in strength by my very presence, as any will if one of us stays around for long—as with you in Avalon, and later that other place. And I saw that I had a long while there by exercising my will upon its time-stream."

"I did not know that could be done."

"You grow in strength slowly, beginning with your initiation into the Pattern. There are many things you have yet to learn. Yes, I strengthened Lorraine, and made it especially vulnerable to the growing force of the black road. I saw that it would lie in your path, no matter where you went. After your escape, all roads led to Lorraine."

"Why?"

"It was a trap I had set for you, and maybe a test. I wanted to be with you when you met the forces of Chaos. I also wanted to travel with you for a time." (CC, 27)

And yet, of course, the village of Lorraine still exists in that shadow, as real and living as any shadow one inhabits. If one were to visit Lorraine now, one might still find Lancelot residing there.

MAGICAL SPELLS

These refer to the manifestations and/or the processes invoked by beings initiated in the Magic Arts. We usually think of supernormal beings as having the ability to wield magical spells; adepts such as sorcerers, demons, ephemeral entities, and magical beings, like the unicorn. The spells that are produced are often directed at an individual or object, causing a distinct alteration that appears to be beyond natural principles. Usually, a spell directed at another individual is offensive, while one directed at oneself or, perhaps, an object, would be defensive.

The keystone or foundation of the magical abilities of those of royal blood in Amber is the Pattern. In the Courts of Chaos, the foundation of those nobles skilled in the Arts is the Logrus. However, we have discovered that there are other sources generating enormous power that an astute disciple of the Arts can harness. Merlin had described a number of such sources: the Black Stone Fount at the Keep of the Four Worlds, the Way of the Broken Pattern, the blue stones of the blue crystal cave, the rings called spikards that draw energy from multifarious shadows, and the Land Between Shadows, also known as the Undershadow.

Those who become initiates of the Logrus, according to Merlin's journals, usually carry some ordinary object with them. This object becomes transformed in the initiation, enhanced to act as a supernatural aide for the initiate. Merlin had obtained his protective entity Frakir in this way. His stepbrother Mandor utilized dark-colored metal balls as a means of working his influence over people and the environment. Those who become initiates of the Pattern are able to use a number of devices that are composed of some aspect of the Pattern. The Trumps, for instance, contain elements of the Pattern. Corwin's sword Grayswandir, Brand's blade Werewindle, and Merlin's construct Ghostwheel all bear elements of the Pattern. The Jewel of Judgment, of course, is the artifact that had originally inscribed the Pattern of Amber. It is of a higher order than the Pattern. When an initiate becomes attuned to the Jewel, he increases his potential tremendously. An attuned initiate's control of meteorological conditions is only the most superficial invocation one is able to perform.

Among the children of Oberon, Brand, Fiona, and Bleys had the most interest in delving into the Art and experimenting with their powers over the stuff of Shadow. Brand had the additional benefit of undergoing the ritual bathing at the Black Fount of the Keep of the Four Worlds, attaining near-invincibility as well as instantaneous transport through Shadow. Bleys was extraordinarily capable of playing with shadows, based on his initiation of the Pattern only. He created the shadow of unstable formations in which he and Fiona imprisoned Brand. Fiona had learned how to shift people and objects from one position to another, and maintain control over their movements, as she did with Brand at Patternfall. Neither Bleys nor Fiona had been attuned to the Jewel of Judgment.

Corwin had been able to call forth incantations that affected others, understanding some of the principles involved but not having a deep mastery of the processes. He influenced the anatomy of the demon Strygalldwir with the force of a simple statement in Thari. When Eric had Corwin blinded, Corwin uttered a curse vehemently, a curse which he believed caused the twisted, sinister atmosphere of the Valley in Garnath and helped let into Amber horrible beasts from other shadows. In his Chronicles, Corwin indicated that "the curse of a prince of Amber, pronounced in a fullness of fury, is always potent." (NP, 147) Years after the fact, the Lady Dara confirmed this: "No, it helped—in a metaphysical way—making it easier to extend the Black Road to Amber." (PC, 115)

Merlin considered himself a professional in matters concerning wizardry. It was the reason why, he believed, Queen Vialle had summoned him instead of any of the other members of the Family when Dalt and his mercenaries marched on Amber (SC, 134). His talents were based on his Logrus initiation mainly, though he was also versed in the Pattern and, later, the independent energies of a spikard. He was able to call up an image of the Logrus in heightening his perceptions and extending his physical control over objects and people. But, aside from that uncanny harnessing of power, he had vast arcane knowledge in arranging spells.

In his journals, Merlin described the process he used to prepare a spell to evict a body-possessing entity:

> I lined up the spoken signatures and edited them into a spell. Suhuy would probably have gotten it down even shorter, but there is a point of diminishing returns on these things, and I had mine figured to where it should work if my main guesses were correct. So I collated it and assembled it. It was fairly long—too long to rattle off in its entirety if I were in the hurry I probably would be. Studying it, I saw that three linchpins would probable hold it, though four would be better.
>
> I summoned the Logrus and extended my tongue into its moving pattern. Then I spoke the spell, slowly and clearly, leaving out the four key words I had chosen to omit. The woods grew absolutely still about me as the words rang out. The spell hung before me like a crippled butterfly of sound and color, trapped within the synesthetic web of my personal vision of the Logrus, to come again when I summoned it, to be released when I uttered the four omitted words.
>
> I banished the vision and let my tongue relax. (BA, 153)

In the actual performance of his spell, Merlin's reflexes automatically work in concert with his uttering the key words. His gesture is a integral part of the working of the incantation.

As a professional adept, Merlin had this advice for anyone working in the Art: "A good sorcerer should have one attack, one defense, and one escape spell hanging around at all times.'' (BA, 158) However, he also admitted that he was somewhat lazy about maintaining that kind of preparation. When he joined with Jasra and Mandor to go after Mask and Jurt at the Keep of the Four Worlds, Merlin depended upon a finite number of spells he had set up from his Logrus base. These invocations were virtually all offensive in nature; spells with names like the Falling Wall, Icy Path, and Fantasia-for-Six-Acetylene-Torches. For defense, Merlin simply dodged or used the side of the Black Stone Fountain as a shield. At one point, Mask produced a spell which struck Merlin: ''Mask hit me with a Klaxon spell which temporarily deafened me while bursting blood vessels in my nose.'' (SC, 215)

The conjurations which may be more appealing than offensive and defensive spells are those which have a measure of wish fulfillment. Merlin's Invisibility spell was quite useful to him in sneaking past guards in the Keep of the Four Worlds, but as he told Flora, it was not an easy spell to learn. For an individual of a devious bent, a spell of Invisibility would seem a clever way to win friends and influence people, as long as its potency does not wear off in midstream. Merlin mentioned another quaint, minor spell that would seem to be useful for similar purposes: ''Then I brushed off my deep purple jacket, the one on which I'd once laid a spell to make the wearer seem a little more charming, witty, and trustworthy than is actually the case.'' (SC, 116) That might be just the sort of enchantment one needs when setting out on a social engagement.

While the source or foundation of magical incantations derives mainly from either the Pattern or Logrus, in the journals of Merlin we have glimpsed that ordinary people on shadow Earth, for instance, have acquired the ability to work the shadows. Often, people who have a deep interest in studying mystical systems also have an aptitude for them. This isn't always true, of course, but often the talent is already within an individual who is prepared to pursue the necessary steps. In the case of Rick Kinsky, for instance, he lacked the needed spark that would allow him to make the leap into invoking psychic energies, even though his interest was keen. On the other hand, Victor Melman and Julia Barnes had natural talent, and when shown the way, they both were able to tap into resources not readily available to ordinary people.

In Julia Barnes, to pursue one example, we see an ordinary young woman who had a latent talent that she hadn't been aware of. She was given an enlightenment when Merlin took her on an inexplicable journey through Shadow. Not only was her interest in the mystical aroused, but also her latent ability was awakened. She had made the crossover, recognizing that the unknowable was possible. This was the first step in her growing awareness of powers beyond the norm. An individual must accept this knowledge to reach beyond a single shadow world, relying on innate psychic qualities that, through training, permit the kind of interplay with Shadow that invokes magic. Indeed, while Julia was seeking studies in mystical systems, she actually performed a magical feat for Merlin:

> An over-friendly Irish setter approached us about then. She placed her hand on its head and said, ''Sit!'' and it did. It became still as a statue at her side, and remained when we left later. For all I know, there's a dog skeleton still crouched there, near the cart return area, like a piece of modern sculpture. (BA, 103)

The example of Julia Barnes offers any of us the hope to control the phenomenal forces formed by the workings of Shadow. Knowledge of multishadows, in itself, might raise one above others going through their everyday lives expecting nothing of a spectacular nature. Bill Roth, the middle-aged attorney from shadow Earth who settled in the true city, has a higher understanding of the nature of Shadows than those he knew back in that shadow. Mr. Roth has no inclinations in the direction of performing wizardry, but his knowledge of the infinitude of shadows and their workings places him in a position above the ordinary human being of Earth.

Some who read this work may aspire to the knowledge and practice of occult systems referred to here. As a means of beginning the process, seek for the cosmic principles within yourself. The ability to manipulate the stuff of Shadow may develop of its own accord.

MANDOR

Son of Gramble, Lord Sawall, and Gride. Sometime in his young manhood, his mother died. Lord

Sawall subsequently married Dara, who already had a son, Merlin. Although Lord Sawall had two other sons with Dara, Mandor felt closest to Merlin. Since they were centuries apart in age, Mandor often took the role of advisor to his stepbrother.

While Mandor often maintained a benign posture with Merlin, it was later shown that he had engaged in covert activities and underhanded political machinations in the Courts of Chaos. After the death of King Swayvill, Merlin discovered that his older brother was behind several political deaths in his attempt to place the House of Sawall in a favorable position in the royal succession.

From our vantage point in Amber, it is not known what role Mandor may have had in the Patternfall War, although he was certainly of an age to participate actively. However, the journals of Merlin that have been published indicate something of his activities around that period. Prior to Patternfall, Mandor countenanced a duel between Merlin and his hot-headed youngest half brother, Jurt. He helped officiate as they pretended to a sporting duel with trisliver and trisp, riding the air currents above the great Abyss. Even after realizing that Jurt meant to kill, Mandor was a study in forbearance. Only when a bloodletting outcome was reached did he and Despil intervene. Quietly attentive, Mandor watched as Despil took the wounded Jurt away. At Merlin's request, he joined him on a visit to see Suhuy, Master of the Logrus. It was apparent that in his maturity Mandor had learned patience and tolerance for his younger siblings.

After Patternfall, Mandor, like many others in the Courts, took up the worship of a member of the Royal Family in Amber. Mandor had constructed a chapel to the Princess Fiona and invited friends to light candles to her. For a time, he was fixated upon the study and contemplation of Fiona of Amber. When the edict from the king proscribing such practices came, Mandor declared that he had destroyed his shrine. It may be that he had simply relocated the chapel to a hidden Way. Interestingly, Mandor did later meet his patron, and they spent some little time together.

Mandor became involved in the problems of his stepbrother, and, perhaps, became interested in his welfare, when Merlin contacted him by Trump after leaving his friend Luke in an Alice in Wonderland bar. The Trump that Merlin used showed Mandor in this way:

. . . blue eyes and the young, hard, slightly sharp features beneath a mass of pure white hair. He was dressed all in black, save for a bit of white collar and sleeve showing beneath the glossy tight-fitting jacket. He held three dark steel balls in his gloved hand. (SC, 28–29)

When Merlin reached him, Mandor was relaxing with a book, seated on a balcony at Mandorways. He was quite willing to put down his book, join Merlin, and listen to his adventures.

After a satisfying exchange of information, enhanced by a meal that Mandor enjoyed putting together by magical means, Merlin was reached by Trump by his aunt, Fiona. It marked the first time Mandor met his worshiped patron.

Fiona told them of her concern of increasing Shadow-storms and other phenomena, which she attributed to the new Pattern created by Corwin. She showed them a tornado that was gradually devastating a shadow that she had been observing. Using his skills, Mandor was able to prove that the occurrence had nothing to do with Corwin's Pattern, but was developed by some intelligence on the Chaos side of things. However, Fiona was persistent enough in her concerns that Mandor chose to join her in investigating other strange phenomena and seeking some connection with an imbalance caused by the new Pattern.

Somewhat later, Merlin received Trump contact from Fiona and Mandor. Mandor said that their investigation into shadow disturbances had been interesting but inconclusive. Fiona added that they had come across Merlin's special data-processing construct, Ghostwheel. She warned Merlin that Ghostwheel was potentially dangerous and should not be trusted. During Fiona's conversation, Mandor stood by silently. Apparently, he was reserving judgment about Ghostwheel, and instead, assessing Merlin's reactions to Fiona's warnings.

Merlin's journals later record that Mandor and Fiona had gathered sufficient observed data to make a preliminary report to Suhuy in the Courts of Chaos. Their findings had confirmed that the Pattern created by Corwin was causing some kind of upset. Based on their findings, Suhuy traveled in Shadow to verify matters for himself. He returned to the Courts, convinced that Mandor and Fiona were correct. He had undisclosed evidence that there was an imbalance between the two poles of existence, and the new Pattern was a key factor in that problem.

Merlin required his older stepbrother in Amber once again on an urgent matter. When Mandor trumped in, he met a possessing demon inhabiting the body of an attractive young lady. Using the dark metal balls that he always carried with him, Mandor kept her imprisoned while he spoke with Merlin. Mandor recognized the entity as a being known in the Courts as a ty'iga. With his unique powers, Mandor questioned the ty'iga. Although it told them that it was there to protect Merlin, it was patently unable to reveal who had sent it while Merlin remained in the room. Only after Merlin had left did the entity inform Mandor of the name of the person who had sent it.

On further occasions when Mandor lent support to Merlin, he continued to keep himself in reserve, never revealing more of his powers than was necessary. This was the case when he joined Merlin and Jasra in storming the Keep of the Four Worlds. While Jasra and Merlin took on the sorcerer known as Mask, Mandor refrained from exerting the forces he held. Although Mandor had told Merlin that he would kill Jurt, who had become Mask's ally, he said to Jurt when they confronted one another, "I am here to preserve your life, if at all possible." (SC, 212) Jurt and Mask escaped the assault, but Mandor brought the Black Fount within the Keep into ruin using his metal balls.

Much later, when Merlin once more called his brother back to Amber, he was soon met by another catastrophe. The Powers of the Pattern and the Logrus came together in a terrifying explosion that wrecked portions of the Royal Palace. Mandor was slightly injured, but he endured his pain to help those around him. He used his magical balls to levitate himself and an injured woman to the apartments of King Random. The king's wife, Vialle, ministered to the unconscious lady. As some rather interesting participants entered and left, Mandor stood by passively. No doubt he learned a great deal about matters in the true city as he quietly waited his turn to be nursed.

Those of us who have little firsthand knowledge of the Courts of Chaos, know of the politics there only through rare sources, such as Merlin's journals. Apparently, Mandor indicated some of his true nature to Merlin only when he was fully in his element, as he was in the Courts.

With hindsight, it is clear that Mandor had been scheming for a measure of control in the Courts long before the death of King Swayvill. Also, in hindsight, it would seem that Merlin figured in his plans soon after Mandor became enmeshed in the petty conflicts of his sibling. For example, Mandor used his knowledge of the arcane spikards that were known by the lords of the Courts to place Merlin under his control while he was in Amber. This occurred at the time that Merlin brought Jasra out of her immobile state. Merlin allowed his older brother the freedom to walk about the palace for a brief time. He even referred to Mandor as "a lord of deception," (SC, 198) when Mandor made himself invisible. It is likely that Mandor used those few minutes of undetected liberty to plant the ring of Swayvill in Brand's bedchamber. If that was indeed the case, then Mandor was deliberately plotting to ensnare Merlin as a pawn in his larger scheme with remarkable foresight into possible eventualities.

While in the Courts, Merlin decided that Mandor was involved in a conspiracy to place the House of Sawall as the prime candidate for the royal succession. Mandor had been present during the sudden deaths of the two last rivals to the throne. Merlin overheard a discussion between Mandor and the high priest of the Serpent, acting as temporary head of the Courts, that sounded, if subtly, to be conspiratorial in nature. In fact, when Merlin had a conversation with his mother, they both intimated that Mandor was responsible for the deaths of candidates to the succession (PC, 111).

In spite of all his machinations, Mandor preferred not to be recognized as the head of state. Merlin understood this quite well when he spoke of the politics of his House with his friend Luke:

"By rights, Mandor should be first in line of succession from our House. He'd removed himself from the line years ago, though."
"Why?"
"I believe he claimed he was unfit to rule."
"No offense, Merle. But he seems like the only one of you who *is* fit for the job."
"Oh, without a doubt ... Most of the Houses have someone like him, though. There's usually a nominal head and a de facto one, someone for show and someone for scheming. Mandor likes the climate behind the scenes." (PC, 183)

In a sorcerous confrontation with Merlin, even with Dara as an ally, Mandor found himself defeated. By the conclusion of their battle, the Power of the Logrus was at a stalemate against Merlin and his construct, Ghostwheel, as well. When the Logrus Sign acceded to Merlin's wishes to have the throne without anyone else's manipulations, Mandor accepted the circumstances. Graciously, he took his leave of Merlin, offering, to the last, to help him with advice should he need it.

It is almost a certainty that Mandor continues to be a frequent visitor to the royal residence, offering suggestions to the new ruler, and making his mark, subtly, behind the scenes.

MANTICORA

A creature with the face of a man, body of a lion, and wings of an eagle. Measuring twelve feet in length, it has such ferocity that many believe it lacks human intelligence despite its human-seeming face. Corwin encountered a manticora on two occasions, once when he was leading an expedition against Eric in Amber, and a second time when he met Julian and his patrol chasing one in the Forest of Arden.

The manticora prefers to inhabit immense forests in tropical regions, where unwary prey is plentiful. While its face resembles a man's, its gaping mouth is filled with three rows of deadly, razor-sharp teeth. It fears no animal that wanders into the forest. While it enjoys consuming large animals, it seems to take special satisfaction in stalking humans. Once it has pinned its prey beneath its massive paws, it uses its terrifyingly effective teeth to crunch up its victim entirely. Skull, bones, clothing, and even such items as gourds carried by women when going for water, all vanish down the manticora's voracious gullet.

Although the manticora is not indigenous to Amber, Corwin reported having seen one at a distance in the isles far to the south. That was quite a while before he encountered any in Amber proper.

It was during Corwin's second expedition against his brother Eric that he was confronted by these vicious beasts. Accompanied by Ganelon and an army of men out of shadow Ri'ik bearing rifles that fired in Amber, Corwin watched as a manticora lay dying of a rifle shot on a rocky ridge. His men informed him that the beast had torn one of their number, a man named Rall, apart (GA, 22). Later, as they approached Mt. Kolvir, they were attacked by a flock of manticoras. The beasts did much damage. They slaughtered seven of the men from Ri'ik, seriously injured numerous others, and caused many others to flee. However, Corwin and his men shot down sixteen of the manticoras. Corwin was somewhat hurt in the attack. They stopped to rest and minister to each other before continuing on their way.

Initially, Corwin thought that Eric had summoned the manticoras out of some distant shadow to harass them. But when Corwin reached Kolvir and saw the Valley of Garnath, he realized that the manticoras and other creatures had a different source. They were invading Amber from the black road. Corwin saw Eric and his soldiers battling the varied creatures all about Kolvir. With the advantage of his firepower, Corwin entered the battle and supported Eric's forces. That turned the tide of the skirmish on Kolvir.

In Corwin's second encounter with a manticora, he was riding on horseback through Arden, ready to begin a hellride to shadow Earth. As he rode, he heard the horn of Julian. Fearing that he was the object of a hunt, Corwin attempted to outride Julian's patrol. Shortly, Corwin learned that he was not the target of the hunt. Behind him, and perhaps in pursuit of him, was a manticora. Remembering the former encounter, Corwin reflected:

> There was no reason to believe all of them had been accounted for, save that none had been reported since that time and no evidence of their continued existence in the vicinity of Amber had come to light. Apparently, this one had wandered down into Arden and been living in the forest since that time. (HO, 117)

Corwin watched as Julian's hellhounds reached the lone manticora and began attacking it. The beast used its scorpion-like tail both to sting and strike fatal blows against several of the dogs. Still, the dogs were wearing it down. It seemed likely that the fierce dogs would bring down the manticora. However, Julian reached them and called off his dogs. The manticora, badly hurt, charged at Julian.

Julian lunged with a long lance, piercing the creature through the chest. Seeing Corwin, Julian pulled out the lance from the dying body and thrust it into the ground. He smiled in triumph.

Fortunately, to the present time, that hunt seems to have produced the last manticora within Amber's preserve.

MARTIN

Son of Random and Morganthe, born in the undersea city of Rebma. He grew up never having met his father nor knowing his mother, who killed herself soon after his birth. He lived with his mother's mother, Queen Moire, until he was old enough to walk the Pattern there. Able to travel the shadows, he learned more of his heritage from his uncle Benedict before going off on his own. He had a disastrous encounter with Brand, which made him all the more wary of those who reside in Amber. In his travels, he met Dara, who took care of him for a time, confiding in him about plans to destroy Amber. Even when he became reconciled with his father, he continued to travel frequently to a variety of shadows, searching, in a sense, for his identity.

When Random was a wild, undisciplined young man, he had gone to Rebma under a pretense of friendship. He succeeded in seducing Morganthe, young daughter of the queen. Corwin's Chronicles describe the following exchange, when Random had been coerced into returning to Moire's realm:

> "Surely you recall," she [Moire] said, "that one time Prince Random came into my realm as a friend, and did thereafter depart in haste with my daughter Morganthe."
>
> [Deirdre said] "I have heard this said, Lady Moire, but I am not aware of the truth or the baseness of the tale."
>
> "It is true," said Moire, "and a month thereafter was she returned to me. Her suicide came some months after the birth of her son Martin. What have you to say to that, Prince Random?"
>
> "Nothing," said Random.
>
> "When Martin came of age," said Moire, "because he was of the blood of Amber, he

determined to walk the Pattern. He is the only of my people to have succeeded. Thereafter, he walked in Shadow and I have not seen him since. What have you to say to that, Lord Random?"
>
> "Nothing," Random replied. (NP, 81–82)

The blind noblewoman who was married to Random at that time, Vialle, later spoke to Corwin about Martin: "You see, I knew Martin in Rebma, when he was but a small boy. I was there while he was growing up. I liked him then. Even if he were not Random's son he would still be dear to me." (HO, 53)

When he was still young and living in Rebma, Martin was visited by Benedict. After becoming initiated in the Pattern, Martin chose to see his uncle Benedict, who was residing in shadow Avalon at that time. Benedict explained some of Martin's reasons for coming to him upon gaining his ability to walk in shadows:

> "He had to go somewhere, you know . . . He was sick of his position in Rebma, ambivalent toward Amber, young, free, and just come into his power through the Pattern. He wanted to get away, see new things, travel in Shadow—as we all did. I had taken him to Avalon once when he was a small boy, to let him walk on dry land of a summer, to teach him to ride a horse, to have him see a crop harvested. When he was suddenly in a position to go anywhere he would in an instant, his choices were still restricted to the few places of which he had knowledge. True, he might have dreamed up a place in that instant and gone there—creating it, as it were. But he was also aware that he still had many things to learn, to ensure his safety in Shadow. So he elected to come to me, to ask me to teach him. And I did. He spent the better part of a year at my place. I taught him to fight, taught him of the ways of the Trumps and of Shadow, instructed him in those things an Amberite must know if he is to survive. . . .
>
> ". . . Once he had obtained some confidence in his abilities, he wanted to exercise them. In the course of instructing him, I had taken him on journeys in Shadow myself, had introduced him to people of my acquaintance at various

places. But there came a time when he wanted to make his own way. One day then, he bade me good-by and fared forth. . . .

". . . He returned periodically, staying with me for a time, to tell me of his adventures, his discoveries. It was always clear that it was just a visit. After a time, he would get restless and depart again." (HO, 37–38)

During the time that Martin was traveling in Shadow, Brand began to show an interest in him. Random recalled a time, long ago, when Brand queried him about Martin. Although Brand indicated that he had never met the youth, he asked Random a number of questions about him, actually taking quite a long time for someone who professed no special interest in him. Llewella, who had preferred living in Rebma to residing in Amber, spoke further of Brand's interest in Martin:

"It was in the interim, and it may have no bearing," she went on. "It is just something that struck me as peculiar. Brand came to Rebma long ago—"

"How long ago?" I [Corwin] asked.

She furrowed her brow.

"Fifty, sixty, seventy years . . . I am not certain. . . .

"Whatever the date," she said, "he came and visited me. Stayed for several weeks." She glanced at Random then. "He was asking about Martin."

Random narrowed his eyes and cocked his head.

"Did he say why?" he asked her.

"Not exactly," she said. "He implied that he had met Martin somewhere in his travels, and he gave the impression that he would like to get in touch with him again. I did not realize until some time after his departure that finding out everything he could concerning Martin was probably the entire reason for his visit. You know how subtle Brand can be, finding out things without seeming to be after them. It was only after I had spoken with a number of others whom he had visited that I began to see what had occurred." (SU, 99–100)

When Corwin met Martin for the first time, the young man filled in the blank spaces of what hap-

pened at the time that Brand finally caught up with him:

"I was camped on a little hillside, just resting from a long ride and taking my lunch, on my way to visit my friends the Tecys. Brand contacted me then. I had reached Benedict with his Trump, when he was teaching me how to use them, and other times when I had traveled. He had even transported me through occasionally, so I knew what it felt like, knew what it was all about. This felt the same way, and for a moment I thought that somehow it was Benedict calling me. But no. It was Brand—I recognized him from his picture in the deck. He was standing in the midst of what seemed to be the Pattern. I was curious. I did not know how he had reached me. So far as I knew, there was no Trump for me. He talked for a minute—I forget what he said—and when everything was firm and clear, he—he stabbed me. I pushed him and pulled away then. He held the contact somehow. It was hard for me to break it—and when I did, he tried to reach me again. But I was able to block him. Benedict had taught me that. He tried again, several times, but I kept blocking. Finally, he stopped. I was near to the Tecys. I managed to get onto my horse and make it to their place. I thought I was going to die, because I had never been hurt that badly before. But after a time, I began to recover. Then I grew afraid once again, afraid that Brand would find me and finish what he had begun. . . .

". . . I left the Tecys before I was completely recovered and rode off to lose myself in Shadow." (HO, 163–64)

In his discussion, Martin told Corwin of his finding a black road that seemed to wind its way through all the shadows he traveled. Riding hard to trace it, he became weak and feverish, suffering from his not fully healed injury. As he rested, only half-conscious, a young woman came to him and took care of him. She said her name was Dara. She said she was descended from Benedict, that she was also related to the lords in the Courts of Chaos, and that the Courts were intent upon destroying Amber. She had been very curious to learn more about Benedict, and Martin told her of the many good things

Benedict had done for him. Martin had a sense that his talk of Benedict may have swayed Dara to have sympathies for Amber. Dara remained with him for a week, until he had fully recovered, and then she departed without bidding him farewell.

Martin's father first became concerned about his son when he, Corwin, and Ganelon discovered the primal Pattern. Random had realized that his son's blood had been shed to cause the blot on the Pattern when he saw the pierced Trump of Martin that Ganelon had retrieved. The picture resembled him enough that Random recognized his own son.

After returning to Amber, Random asked Benedict to take him to the shadow where the Tecys resided. He wanted to find Martin and reconcile with him. Benedict agreed, and they left at once. Their journey took them well into Shadow. They reached a place called Heerat, and learned that Martin had been there but had traveled on. Random continued the search, but Benedict was anxious to return to Amber to find out more about Dara. They parted company at Heerat.

Random finally overtook his son, met him, and sought an end to their estrangement. Happy to be thus reunited, Martin gladly returned to Amber with his father. Random contacted Corwin and arranged to meet with him at the site of Corwin's cenotaph to introduce him to Martin. Still unnerved by Brand's attack, Martin had been leery about meeting all of his relatives at one time in Amber proper. Martin told much of his background to Corwin at that time.

Soon afterward, while Martin had been familiarizing himself with his new environs, Dara contacted him by Trump. He brought her to the Royal Palace, then he brought Benedict to them to meet Dara. A strange tableau was reenacted in the throne room then, one that Corwin recognized as a replay of something he took part in in Tir-na Nog'th. It caused the loss of Benedict's mechanical arm, which Corwin had brought back from the ghost city, and it permitted Random and Corwin to question Dara about the plans of the Chaos lords.

Dara told her side of the conspiracy between Brand and the leaders of the insurrection at the Courts of Chaos. Her contact with Martin had dissuaded her from pursuing the ends that the Chaos lords had been seeking. Dara showed evidence that she was currently working with King Oberon, and

the king confirmed this. She credited Martin as a key factor in altering her alliance.

It is unclear what part Martin took in the Patternfall War that followed this juncture. Perhaps he had remained in Amber along with Gérard during the great cataclysm. Once Random was installed as king of Amber, Martin, of course spent much time in residence in the Royal Palace. He needed to become reacquainted with his stepmother, Vialle, as much as with his father.

Martin had been in Amber when Merlin had abruptly returned from shadow Earth, bringing Bill Roth with him. Of course, he had an interest in affairs that touched upon Amber, and he cared very much about those things which affected his father. He was no doubt privy to much of the information that Random received, and Random would confide in his son about things that bothered him. Thus, Martin would have known about the murder of Caine and the attempted murder of Bleys in different shadows. He was at dinner with his father, Merlin, Bill Roth, Julian, Gérard, Fiona, and Flora the evening that Merlin and Mr. Roth had arrived. After dinner, he had joined his father and Merlin as they tested the ammunition that Merlin had brought with him from shadow Earth. He joined in firing a rifle, an exhilarating experience. While Merlin went over recent events in his life on shadow Earth, he noted about Martin: "He had spent the past few years off in a more pastoral setting, I learned. I got the impression that he was more fond of the countryside than of cities." (TD, 122)

However, Merlin's impression of Martin was not quite accurate. Although Martin was happy to have found a home and family in Amber, he was still restless. He was, it would seem, seeking to find himself, and he wouldn't be content until he tried a wide variety of lifestyles in shadows far afield. Sometime later, Merlin had run into Martin in the palace, and he almost hadn't recognized him. He was dressed "in black leathers and various pieces of rusty and shiny chain. . . . His hair was of an orange Mohawk cut and there were several silver rings in his left ear near what looked like an electrical outlet of some sort." (SC, 99) Martin told him that he had spent well over a year in another time stream in a noisy city of a distant shadow with variant forms of high-tech music. He discovered that he enjoyed the noise and crowds and music of large urban areas.

Nevertheless, Martin remained intimate with those in Amber. He attended official diplomatic functions, and he enjoyed playing a musical set with his father every so often. He attended the funeral for Caine, which had been momentarily disrupted by an intruder tossing a bomb. He had seen Merlin trumping into the main hall of the palace carrying the frozen form of Jasra, and he was nearby when Merlin was taken away by means of a giant Trump. He attended the banquet that Vialle presided over for members of the Begman Embassy, and heard later of the confrontation of military troops in Arden, when Dalt and his forces faced the armies of Julian and Benedict. And, of course, he was with his father, enjoying a musical set in the library, at the time when the Signs of the Logrus and the Pattern had their violent confrontation.

Oddly, Martin hadn't involved himself directly in the more critical aspects of these affairs. In spite of his love for his father and stepmother, and his obvious concern for Amber, something in his personality kept him aloof, a need to distance himself from those events in his past that had hurt him, emotionally as well as physically.

MARTINEZ, DAN

A well-dressed businessman in Santa Fe, New Mexico. He approached Merlin of the Courts of Chaos in a bar in the Santa Fe Hilton, asking about Merlin's friend, Luke Raynard. He appeared again, later the same night, firing a pistol at Luke and Merlin.

While Merlin had been waiting in the Hilton bar for his friend to shower and change clothes, Martinez came up to his table. In his journals, Merlin described him as

> a short, thin man of Spanish appearance, his hair and mustache flecked with gray. He was sufficiently well dressed and groomed to seem a local business type. I noted a chipped front tooth when he smiled so briefly—just a twitch—as to indicate nervousness. (TD, 64)

Their conversation before Luke's joining Merlin in the bar marks the only actual acquaintance we have with Dan Martinez. Aside from that fact, however, his questions and seeming knowledge of things beyond the earthbound are rather interesting. Following is a transcript of their discussion:

MARTINEZ: My name's Dan Martinez. Could I sit down a minute?

MERLIN: What's this about? If you're selling something, I'm not interested. I'm waiting for somebody and—

MARTINEZ: No, nothing like that. I know you're waiting for someone—a Mr. Lucas Raynard. It involves him, actually.

MERLIN: Okay. Sit down and ask your question.

MARTINEZ: I overheard you talking in the lobby, and I got the impression you knew him fairly well. Would you mind telling me for about how long you've known him?

MERLIN: If that's all you want to know, for about eight years. We went to college together, and we worked for the same company for several years after that.

MARTINEZ: Grand Design, the San Francisco computer firm. Didn't know him before college, huh?

MERLIN: It seems you already know quite a bit. What do you want, anyway? Are you some kind of cop?

MARTINEZ: No, nothing like that. I assure you I'm not trying to get your friend into trouble. I am simply trying to save myself some. Let me just ask you—

MERLIN: No more freebies. I don't care to talk to strangers about my friends without some pretty good reasons.

MARTINEZ: I'm not being underhanded, when I know you'll tell him about it. In fact, I want you to. He knows me. I want him to know I'm asking around about him, okay? It'll actually be to his benefit. Hell, I'm even asking a friend, aren't I? Someone who might be willing to lie to help him out. And I just need a couple simple facts—

MERLIN: And I just need one simple reason: why do you want this information?

MARTINEZ: Okay. He offered me—tentatively, mind you—a very interesting investment opportunity. It would involve a large sum of money. There is an element of risk, as in most ventures involving new companies in a highly competitive area, but the possible returns do make it tempting.

MERLIN: And you want to know whether he's honest.

MARTINEZ: I don't really care whether he's honest. My only concern is whether he can deliver a product with no strings on it.

MERLIN: Ah. I'm slow today. Sorry. Of course this deal involves computers.

MARTINEZ: Of course.

MERLIN: You want to know whether his present employer can nail him if he goes into business out here with whatever he's bringing with him.

MARTINEZ: In a word, yes.

MERLIN: I give up. It would take a better man than me to answer that. Intellectual properties represent a tricky area of law. I don't know what he's selling and I don't know where it comes from— he gets around a lot. But even if I did know, I have no idea what your legal position would be.

MARTINEZ: I didn't expect anything beyond that.

MERLIN: So you've sent your message.

MARTINEZ [rising]: Oh, just one thing more.

MERLIN: Yes?

MARTINEZ: Did he ever mention places called Amber or the Courts of Chaos?

MERLIN: No, I never heard him refer to them. Why do you ask?

MARTINEZ: It's not important. Thank you, Mr. Corey. *Nus a dhabzhun dhuilsha.* (TD, 64–66)

Before Merlin could question Martinez further, the businessman had rushed off and disappeared into the crowd. It seemed that Martinez wasn't what he seemed to be, since his last words had been spoken in Thari.

Later, when Luke was taking Merlin for a drive around the outskirts of Santa Fe, Merlin mentioned Dan Martinez. Luke claimed he had no idea who Martinez was, nor had he spoken with anyone about a business deal involving computers. Nevertheless, it was an odd coincidence that Luke had asked Merlin about combining their talents to incorporate and market a project involving a unique computer that Luke believed his friend to be working on.

While they stood talking off the shoulder of a cliffside road, someone began firing gunshots at

them. Merlin dodged and hit the ground, but Luke took out a pistol and returned fire. Luke's shots found their target. As they reached the body, Merlin noted a bluish mist rising from the mouth of the dead man. He identified the dead man as Martinez.

Although Luke said he didn't know the man, he forced Merlin to take his car and leave. Merlin did so, but returned on foot to find his friend and Martinez's body gone. On a later occasion, Luke admitted that he had taken the body with him to avoid leaving any evidence of the incident.

The mystery of Dan Martinez was resolved sometime later in Merlin's journals. During the time that Merlin had encountered him, the Santa Fe resident had been possessed by an entity that was attempting to protect Merlin from perceived dangers. This entity had been loath to harm either Luke or Merlin, so it deliberately missed striking Luke with its gunshots. It had acted as it did because it believed Merlin to be in deadly peril from Luke, but its actions resulted in the death of the host body.

The entity's involvement, using the guise of Dan Martinez, was indeed most unfortunate for the ordinary businessman. While it may have been convenient for the entity to take on the role of a local businessman in order to approach and follow Merlin, there had not been anything to connect the real Martinez to the activities of Luke or Merlin.

This may have been a case of an innocent being made an unaware dupe in the name of causes beyond any human ability at intervention.

MASK

An unknown wizard who had wrested control of the Keep of the Four Worlds from Jasra of Kashfa.

Merlin first encountered Mask as a projection after discovering a mystical route from the apartment of his deceased girlfriend, Julia Barnes, to the mountain range overlooking the Keep. Besides being a formidable structure against military siege, the Keep of the Four Worlds contained a power source that would make an initiate invincible.

After learning some of the history of the Keep from a hermit in the mountains, Merlin examined the surrounding landscape. When he moved a boundary marker from the ground in an ice region, there was an earth tremor and the projection appeared before him.

> "The head was cowled; the mask was full and
> cobalt bright and strongly reminiscent of the
> sort worn by goalies in ice hockey; there were
> two vertical breathing slits from which pale
> smoke emerged . . . lower series of random
> punctures was designed to give the impression
> of a sardonically lopsided mouth. A distorted
> sound of laughter came down to me from it."
> (BA, 54)

Mask threatened Merlin's destruction. Before Mask could act on his threat, Merlin used his Logrus powers to send an electrical charge through the projection to the actual person behind it. Mask screamed, and Merlin took the opportunity to contact King Random of Amber by Trump. Although he escaped Mask's clutches, Merlin was followed through his Trump leap by a force that dropped flowers on him as he reached Random.

The flowers were a motif that Mask became associated with in his encounters with Merlin. But they also showed that Merlin had met this presence previously. When Merlin had joined his aunt Flora in San Francisco on shadow Earth, he had received a strange communication, like a Trump contact. A telepathic voice promised they would meet again, but it simply wanted to observe Merlin on this occasion. Merlin used his Logrus skills to pull a small, hard substance from the body of the unknown presence. When Merlin pulled away, Flora's apartment was showered with a multitude of flowers. Merlin found in his hands a small blue button, with a stone similar to a kind he had seen elsewhere.

Merlin engaged in a sorcerous duel with Mask after using the Pattern in Amber to bring him inside the Keep of the Four Worlds. He had come to a huge chamber that had as its centerpiece a large, Black Stone Fountain. At one corner of the chamber were two statues, one of Sharu Garrul, former ruler of the Keep, and one of Jasra. It was Merlin's intention to carry the frozen Jasra back to Amber with him. As Merlin reached the frozen figures, the Black Fountain came to life, and Mask stood on a landing above him. They exchanged magical spells against each other. Merlin paused long enough to question the sorcerer, and Mask responded:

> "What do you want, anyway?" . . .
> "Your blood, your soul, your mind and
> your body."
> "What about my stamp collection? . . . Do I
> get to keep the First Day Covers?"
> "What do you want with that one, funny
> man? . . . She is the most worthless property
> in this place."
> "Then why should you object to my taking
> her off your hands?"
> "You collect stamps. I collect presumptuous
> sorcerers. She's mine, and you're next." . . .
> "What have you got against your brothers
> and sisters in the Art? . . .
> "By what name shall I call you?"
> "Mask!" . . . —Not very original, I thought.
> I'd half expected a John D. MacDonald appellation—Nightmare Mauve or Cobalt Casque,
> perhaps. (BA, 206–7)

Before exiting by Trump to the main hall of the palace of Amber, Merlin used a spell to drop a pile of flowers on Mask. Before Mask could shake off the flowers, Merlin dumped a load of manure on him, then completed his passage through the Trump.

On a later occasion, Merlin allied himself with Jasra, after he had revived her to mobility, and his stepbrother Mandor, in another attack upon the Keep. They were concerned that Merlin's other brother on the Chaos side, Jurt, would attain the power of the Black Fount. Mandor, Jasra, and Merlin joined forces to prevent that from occurring.

In the chamber of the fountain, Merlin was faced with handling Mask while Jasra and Mandor dealt with Jurt. During their separate battles of mystical forces, Mask brought Sharu Garrul to mobility, and Jasra was forced to pit her energies against him.

Fighting in close quarters with Mask, Merlin pulled a dagger from under his cloak as Mask attempted to slay him with a fiery sword.

> And so, turning, I struck with my own more
> mundane dagger of steel, driving its full length
> up into Mask's left kidney.
> There followed a scream as the sorcerer stiffened and slumped beside me. (SC, 216)

Jurt interceded against Merlin at that moment, then rescued Mask, carrying him away from the Keep. But, in the couple of seconds that Mask lay helpless beside him, Merlin had seen the identity of Mask. He recognized Mask to be a former friend from shadow Earth. Merlin didn't have an opportunity to speak to Mask again directly until much later, under quite different circumstances.

Once Jasra had subdued Sharu Garrul and taken command of the Keep once again, she discussed her connection to Mask with Merlin and Mandor. Seeking vengeance against Merlin for his father's role in the slaying of Brand of Amber, Jasra trained an occultist named Victor Melman. Jasra intended to teach Melman the Art so that he would act as the instrument of Merlin's death on shadow Earth. However, Jasra observed that a close friend of Merlin's had a more personal stake in causing Merlin harm. Their friendship had ended abruptly after a serious argument. This former friend had shown an interest in the occult, so Jasra acted to have the friend meet Melman. The friend showed genuine talent and proved to be a better adept than Melman. When she deemed the friend ready, Jasra took him through the initiation of the Way of the Broken Pattern. What Jasra had not anticipated was that the friend would use the powers gained to double-cross Jasra. The friend used the special locating powers of two blue crystal stones to trace his way back to the Keep of the Four Worlds. He hid his appearance behind the goalie mask and learned further of the energies of the Keep. He surprised Jasra upon her return and turned her into a frozen statue. When Merlin showed up at the Keep, Mask turned his attention to him, partly out of hatred and partly to prove to Merlin that he was equal to him in power. Although Jasra didn't know how Mask formed an alliance with Jurt, both Mandor and Jasra concurred that a significant reason for Mask's doing so was Jurt's physical resemblance to Merlin. Despite Mask's actions against Merlin, he seemed to have retained strong feelings of friendship for him.

When Merlin returned to the Courts of Chaos for the funeral of the late king, he encountered Jurt again. Jurt prevailed upon him to end their enmity, and they spoke briefly of Mask. Jurt informed Merlin that Mask was staying in the House of Sawall with him and was recovering from the wound. At a later time, Merlin encountered Mask himself in the House of Sawall. Merlin initiated a reconciliation:

> "I owe you several apologies . . . I'm ready to make them."

> "I'd heard you were back. I heard you were to be king."
>
> "Funny, I heard that, too."
>
> "Then it would be unpatriotic of me to stay mad, wouldn't it?"
>
> "I never meant to hurt you . . . Physically, or any other way." . . .
>
> "Jurt says you're friends now."
>
> "I guess we sort of are." . . .
>
> "If we got back together again, . . . he'd probably try to kill you again."
>
> "I know. This time the consequences could really be cataclysmic, too."
>
> "Where are you going right now?"
>
> "I'm on an errand, and it's going to take me several hours."
>
> "Why don't you stop by when you're finished? We've got a lot to talk about. I'm staying in a place called the Wisteria Room for now. Know where that is?"
>
> "Yes . . . This is crazy."
>
> "See you later?"
>
> "Maybe." (PC, 228–29)

This brief meeting may indeed have been the beginning of a new alliance between the one who called himself Mask and the new king of the Courts of Chaos.

MAZE OF ART

A large gallery of fascinating artifacts found in the House of Sawall. Its numerous hallways and artistic creations, such as tapestries and draperies, conceal hidden Ways that lead to other shadows. Since young Merlin grew up in the Courts, he often wandered through his stepfather's Maze of Art. Shortly before accepting the kingship in the Courts, Merlin had discovered a secret Way that helped him to find his father, Corwin of Amber.

Merlin recorded his thoughts about his early wanderings in that place:

> I recalled the many times I had been lost in that maze as a child. The House of Sawall had been a serious collector of art for ages, and the collection was so vast that there were several

ways into which one was cast within the maze itself, leading one through tunnels, a huge spiral, and what seemed an old train station before being shunted back to miss the next turn. I had been lost in it for days on one occasion, and was finally found crying before an assemblage of blue shoes nailed to a board ... There were ... strikingly lovely pieces mixed in, such as the huge vase that looked as if it had been carved from a single fire opal, and a set of odd enameled tablets from a distant shadow whose meaning and function no one in the family could be found to recall. (PC, 96)

As Merlin had explained, people visited the Maze of Art, not only from the Courts, but from nearby shadows as well. Lord Sawall had the gallery lovingly stitched together by Shadowmasters in his younger days, before he took ill. One of Sawall's crowning achievements was the sculpture garden.

The floor was uneven—concave, convex, stepped, ridged—with concavity being the dominant curve. It was difficult to guess at its dimensions, for it seemed of different size and contour depending upon where one stood. Gramble, Lord Sawall, had caused it to be constructed without any plane surfaces—and I believe the job involved some unique shadow-mastery. (PC, 120)

In another part of the gallery, Merlin was shown a Way that had been constructed much more recently. His old friend of the Courts, Glait, showed Merlin the Way. Glait led him to a hall of trees made of many metals. They climbed the trunk of the tallest tree, and Merlin was able to push through a Way. It led to a hidden chapel dedicated to Corwin. According to Glait, who had observed its construction, the Shadowmaster was murdered after completing the task. Within that chapel was the means of locating Merlin's missing father.

The Maze of Art remains one of those lovely enigmas that those who visit from the near shadows often attempt to unravel by the most casual of investigations. Its intricacy defies fathoming, however, and, for most, it will always contain those diverse qualities of beauty and intrigue.

MELKIN

Officer assigned to the Keep of Ganelon and one of several former lovers of Lorraine of the village of Lorraine.

After the great battle of the dark Circle, Lorraine returned to Ganelon's Keep with confused feelings of anger, hatred, and longing for Corey of Cabra. She had just learned that he was really Corwin, the Demon Lord, who had long ago executed her grandfather. When she reached the Keep, Lorraine turned to Melkin for comfort.

Melkin was more mercenary than commissioned officer, so he felt little compunction about deserting his duties. Filled with loathing, and perhaps some fear, Lorraine insisted that Melkin take her away. She hoped to start a new life in another village, and if Melkin truly loved her, he would gladly help her. It was likely that he intended to return to the Keep without the girl and in timely fashion, so that he would not be missed by his superiors.

Melkin obtained two fresh horses from the stables, and he and Lorraine headed north with dispatch. By the end of the first day's ride, Lorraine sensed that they were being followed and said so. The officer feared it also, and encouraged them to move more quickly. They rode until it was too dark to continue and made camp well off the pathway they had been traveling. Melkin kept vigil most of the night.

Corwin reached them on the afternoon of the second day:

When I found her, I leaped down from my mount and ran to where she lay, beneath a wild rosebush without flowers, the thorns of which had scratched her cheek and shoulder. Dead, she had not been so for long, for the blood was still damp upon her breast where the blade had entered, and her flesh yet warm.

There were no rocks with which to build her a cairn, so I cut away the sod with Grayswandir and laid her there to rest. He had removed her bracelets, her rings, and her jeweled combs, which had held all she possessed of fortune. . . .

I rode on, and it was not long before I overtook him, riding as though he were pursued by the Devil, which he was. I spoke not a word when I unhorsed him, nor afterward, and I did not use my blade, though he drew his own. I hurled his broken body into a high oak tree, and when I looked back it was dark with birds. (GA, 67)

When Corwin, Lord of Amber, returned to the Keep of Ganelon alone, none of the military officers questioned what had happened to Captain Melkin. Gossip spread among the common soldiers, but the matter was probably settled only upon the discovery of Melkin's body at some later time.

The incident occasioned a bit of philosophy on Corwin's part about his role in things.

A prince of Amber is part and party to all the rottenness that is in the world. . . . In the mirrors of the many judgments, my hands are the color of blood. I am a part of the evil . . . which exists to oppose other evils. I destroy Melkins when I find them, and on that Great Day when the world is completely cleansed of evil, then I, too, will go down into darkness. (GA, 67–68)

MELMAN, VICTOR

Artist and occultist who underwent training from a high master of the Arts. Melman was obsessed with obtaining power, and he fought a sorcerous duel with Merlin of the Courts of Chaos in an attempt to gain that power.

Merlin first learned of Victor Melman from Rick Kinsky, a young man who was dating Merlin's former girlfriend. Kinsky gave this background information about Melman:

"Strange man . . . I—I've heard it said—by a number of people, some of them fairly reliable—that he really has something going for him, that he has a hold on a piece of something, that he's known a kind of enlightenment, has been initiated, has a sort of power and is sometimes a great teacher. But he's got these ego problems, too, that seem to go along with that sort of thing. And there's a touch of the seamy side there. I've even heard it said that that's not his real name, that he's got a record,

and there's more of Manson to him than Magus. . . . He's nominally a painter—actually a pretty good one. His stuff does sell." (TD, 21–22)

It was because of Melman's talent as a painter that he came under the tutelage of a master of the occult. Merlin's friend Lucas Raynard was an artist interested in improving his own work. Living in San Francisco, Raynard had seen some of Melman's paintings. They were quite accomplished, and Raynard decided to look up the artist. When they got together, they showed each other their work. Melman was impressed and suggested giving Raynard lessons that would enhance his skills. Raynard agreed.

Melman may have been more interested in Raynard's money, as he had divined Luke was wealthy, than in improving his techniques. However, he thought there was something special about Luke Raynard beyond his artistry alone. He began talking of developing personal power through the occult. Believing himself to have psychic gifts already, Melman offered to share his understandings with Luke. These talks probably turned Luke off, for soon thereafter, he stopped taking lessons from Melman.

However, Raynard talked to his mother, Jasra of Kashfa, about his experience with Victor Melman. Jasra conceived of a plan to use Victor Melman as a means of placing Merlin in a vulnerable position. Although she shared her plan with her son, she handled most of Melman's training after their initial overtures. Luke, and then Jasra, visited Melman in a cloaked outfit, hiding their features and disguising their voices. At first, Luke undertook this task, but soon Jasra continued these visits on her own.

In her guise, Jasra spoke to Melman of Merlin, referring to him as a creature out of Chaos and Hell. She persuaded Melman that if he learned his lessons well, he would be given all the power that Merlin of Chaos possessed. Melman was to play a role in capturing Merlin and then aid the Master in sacrificing him, after which Merlin's supernatural powers would be transferred to him.

Knowing that Melman leaned toward cabalistic tendencies, Jasra encouraged her son to do a large painting of the Cabalistic Tree of Life, which Luke, in disguise, then presented to Melman. Luke, as the Master, showed Melman how to put his concentration into each of the sephiroth in turn. Melman found himself existing in the worlds depicted within each one. He found he could transport himself to any of them at will, controlling the environment, making objects appear and disappear. It gave him power.

Having observed the breakup of Merlin with Julia Barnes, Jasra decided to exert her influence over her. Secretly, Jasra affected Julia's search for occult knowledge, leading her to meet Victor Melman. Jasra had told Melman of Julia, wanting him to speed the girl into the ways of power. On a much later occasion, when Jasra had formed an alliance with Merlin, she explained her earlier intent:

> "I saw that I would have to get her together with Victor, to have him train her, to teach her a few simple effects, to capitalize on her unhappiness at your parting, to turn it into a full-blown hatred so intense that she would be willing to cut your throat when the time came for the sacrifice." (KS, 25)

However, Melman was too presumptuous. When Merlin came by his studio asking questions about Julia, Melman decided to take action. He spoke cryptically to Merlin, insisting that he look at a painting that he had covered. Melman revealed the Tree of Life painting. Using his powers, Melman brought himself and Merlin into one of the sephira and attempted to perform the sacrifice himself. He simply hadn't expected Merlin's power to be more potent than his own.

Merlin took control. He brought both of them to a tiny, shriveling island on the verge of Chaos. In terror, Melman called to a Master who would not come. Under Merlin's questioning, Melman told him about his Master, about his being set up to mentor Julia, and about the promise of power with Merlin's death.

Seeing a chance to succeed in killing Merlin, Melman attacked him with a black dagger. Merlin found a way to put him off-balance, lift him, and toss him away from him. Too late, Merlin realized he had tossed Melman too far. With a curse, Melman was flung into the reaches of oblivion.

MENILLAN, KING OF KASHFA

Monarch of the shadow kingdom of Kashfa in a long-ago time.

Kashfa was continually at war with its neighbor shadows, Begma in particular. King Menillan had ruled for many years and grown old and fat on the heavy taxation of his subjects and the tribute of conquered realms. Complacently living off his gathered wealth, he even made some conciliatory gestures toward Begma before illness overtook him.

The aging king became enamored of a young foreign woman from an unspecified land. Her name was Jasra. When she received old Menillan's attentions, numerous rumors about her origins abounded. Some said she had been brought into Kashfa in a slave caravan; some that she was a witch or sorceress; some that she was a prostitute of highborn blood; others that she had served in a Royal House in the Courts of Chaos. Virtually everyone agreed that she had old Menillan wrapped about her little finger.

She lived in the king's household and was his constant companion. Shortly thereafter, Menillan became ill. His physician suspected food poisoning, but he could detect none as he pursued a careful analysis of foods passed to the king. Some members of Menillan's court had later informed courtiers from Amber that the physician, a friend to the king, had appeared to have dropped out of sight.

Jasra was by the dying king's bedside constantly. Although servants were in attendance, none had heard any pronouncements from their liege about the status of his consort. As King Menillan remained adamantly silent about her, Jasra paved her own way by other means.

Menillan died quietly in his sleep. A maid found him in the morning and gave the alarm. His personal servants were in tears throughout the funeral services.

Using the term "Royal Consort" as her personal banner, Jasra announced to Kashfa's peoples that she had been made successor and queen of the realm. She had the support of the royal army to back up her claim.

Soon after Menillan's death, Queen Jasra engaged in diplomatic negotiations with Begma, arranging policies of which the former king would, in all likelihood, not have approved.

MERLIN

Son of Prince Corwin of Amber and Lady Dara of the Courts of Chaos. As a member of the Royal

Family in Amber, he had been vested with the titles of duke of the Western Marches and earl of Kolvir, granted to him by his uncle, King Random. While these titles place Merlin in the Royal Line, he is not a candidate for the succession in any direct way. On the other hand, he had been a member of one of the Royal Houses in the Courts of Chaos: the House of Sawall. In that position, he was in line to the Royal Throne of the Courts.

In his journals, Merlin set down the account of his travels, beginning with his life in San Francisco on the same shadow Earth where his father dwelled for centuries. He recounts brief instances of his earlier life in the Courts of Chaos throughout the journals, but he expounded upon the situation in that place more thoroughly in his most recent tellings, seasoning the story with larger glimpses of his past there.

For a detailed history of Merlin's life, as far as we have comprehended it, one may look at the scope of his account as it relates to the multifarious places he visited. Our discovery of the events in Merlin's life is related to shadows, some of which he had longed to visit as a youth: Earth, Kashfa, the primal Pattern, the Keep of the Four Worlds, the crystal cave, Corwin's Pattern, the Courts, and, of course, Amber and its environs. If we were to devise a model of Merlin's life, as a means of clearly envisioning the account he has put in writing, we might think of it as a circle in which the circumference is composed of many colorations. Imagine a long strip of the circumference as containing a grayish black color representing the Courts of Chaos. This would likely be the lengthiest portion of the circumference. A bright green might represent Amber, spread out in varying lengths throughout the circle, some longer than others. Blue could be the color for shadow Earth, concentrated mainly in one long section, but also dappled in other areas. White and black zebra stripes splattered in several disparate areas represent the Keep of the Four Worlds. Kashfa shines in strident purple here and there. The Pattern of Corwin's design is silvered with a unique sheen. The Alice in Wonderland bar is shown in a splash of pink and bright yellow. The many worlds that color the circle enable us to define the composite that Merlin makes of himself in his journals. His adventures, and his responses to perils and pleasures, seem less chaotic and enigmatic if we use this model as a reference point.

Set out at any point and one will be able to make one's way to the Courts of Chaos, the beginning and the terminus of Merlin's history. Merlin wrote his accounts from a point near the end of his stay on shadow Earth, so that the distance along the circumference to the Courts would not be so great. It would be proper, for this record, to commence with Merlin's youth in the Courts, doing so by relying upon Merlin's own journals, since few of us in Amber have seen that unique realm.

Merlin's birth was the result of trickery and deliberate scheming, though it is difficult to determine the root of such a plan. The late King Oberon had admitted that he murdered innocent people in order to join Corwin with Dara. Dara claimed to have rescued the late king of Amber from his Chaos captors and subsequently worked with him to arrange her tryst with Oberon's son. Much later, Dara admitted to Merlin that the plan had a deeper layer than that: "The Logrus assured me that such a child would be uniquely qualified to reign here [in the Courts of Chaos]." (PC, 112) Merlin has confirmed that the Logrus, like the Pattern of Amber, is a sentient being, thus adding strength to the idea that Dara had plotted Merlin's birth with its aid.

The Courts of Chaos, colored in sinister shades of gray and black: Merlin spent his boyhood and adolescence there. It has been described as a non-Euclidean realm, where a downward movement past a solid-looking floor leads one upward through a cylindrical tunnel. Disorienting to any who dwell in the true city. For Merlin, it was home. It was familiar ground. He trusted that world and the people who cared for him.

Although the journals give no explanation of who raised Merlin in Dara's absence, it seems probable that his uncle Suhuy had guardianship of the child for a large part of the time. Merlin has indicated that he enjoyed a happy childhood, consorting with strange entities without inhibition. Of his boyhood, Merlin wrote: "I always seemed to have more fun playing with demons than with my mother's relatives by blood or marriage. I even based my main Chaos form upon one of their kind." (PC, 7) In a childhood that must have seemed long and pleasant to Merlin, his playmates were mostly nonhuman. Gryll was a demon servant of Suhuy's who taught him the Bonedance Game, reanimating the skeletal remains of the dead. Glait was a female Chaosite snake that loved to listen to Merlin's tales. Merlin would often hunt for mice with Glait, who wrapped herself in his clothing. Kergma was a game-loving entity and a shapeshifter. Merlin had no idea what its true form was, but it has been described as nearly being a mathematical abstraction. These were the friends of his early boyhood.

Though often left to himself in adolescence, Merlin found companionship with at least two females in and around the Courts. One was Gilva of the House of Hendrake. Little more is known about their relationship except that they had been acquainted in the Courts. The other was a young girl of a shadow near to the Courts: Rhanda. In childlike innocence, they played together in a cemetery in Shadow, beneath a fairy circle surrounding a tree. One day, Rhanda stopped coming. Years later, Merlin discovered that her parents had halted her from continuing their play, warning her away from him because he was a demon.

Merlin's mother had married Gramble, Lord Sawall and, although he was a much older man, she bore him two sons, Despil and Jurt. Lord Sawall had been married before and had a son named Mandor. Because Merlin was not fully a Chaosite by birth, his siblings kept him at a certain distance. Mandor was the friendliest, though he may have been somewhat condescending in his treatment of Merlin. Despil seemed to be sympathetic, but he closed out any chance of friendship by siding with his full brother Jurt in any conflicts between Jurt and Merlin. As for his youngest sibling, Merlin has expressed the relationship this way: "Jurt had hated me from sometime before he had learned to walk, for reasons entirely his own. While I did not hate Jurt, liking him was totally beyond my ability." (BA, 83)

Sawall, the old Rim Duke, had been ailing a long time. He remained in seclusion for much of Merlin's cognizant life. While the Lady Dara spent much time in the Courts during Merlin's late adolescence, Merlin's upbringing was mainly in the hands of Suhuy, Master of the Logrus. Suhuy is an ancient relative on Sawalls' side of the family. He is so many generations removed from any of Merlin's other living relatives in the Courts that it is convenient for Merlin to refer to him simply as "uncle."

Merlin knew of his father, of course, through Suhuy and others. In his youth, he rode with one of his few friends, a young Chaosite named Kwan, along a filmy outside the Courts. They were in training, riding routine patrol, when they noted an anomaly in the mountains. Kwan was the more experienced and rode his mount faster. Merlin reached the mountains after seeing his friend slain by a tall warrior from another place. He would have fired an arrow from his crossbow as soon as he reached the man, but he looked into the man's face and relented. The sword he wielded was like no other, and Merlin thought he recognized it from Suhuy's descriptions. He asked the man if the sword was called Grayswandir. The stranger's answer confirmed for Merlin that this was his father. He let him depart unharmed.

While he was not a party to the conspiracy arranged between some of the Chaos lords under King Swayvill and Prince Brand of Amber, Merlin was kept informed of events by Suhuy and his stepbrother Mandor. For a time, Merlin was kept under protective custody by emissaries of the aged king, restricted to the House of Sawall but prevented from visiting his stepfather's Maze of Art. He was told that he was born to rule from the Amber side of things. In brief, furtive moments, Dara came to him, telling him of the shadowlands, of Amber, and the prince named Corwin.

Merlin knew the war was imminent, and when it came the household was in sudden flurry. Security relaxed, Merlin found he was left to himself as members of the House rushed hither and yon. Flames in the distant horizon denoted a battle begun.

It is not known how Merlin arrived at the field of battle nor how he made introduction to Fiona of Amber as the fighting subsided. Nevertheless, Fiona took Merlin to see his father, resting on the near hills. They spoke together for long hours, and Corwin told of his convoluted history. Sometime afterward, Merlin committed his father's story to writing. Meeting his father in that way, and watching as the unicorn appointed Random king of Amber, affected Merlin deeply enough to accept Amber as a second homeland. He had been taught to view Amber as the enemy, but that now was changed irrevocably.

The last time Merlin saw his father, Corwin was going to the royal residence of Thelbane. Corwin's brothers Random and Benedict were already there, negotiating the peace treaty with King Swayvill. Not permitted to engage in these activities, Merlin went his own ways.

Early in his education, Merlin learned shapeshifting, so that changing his form became second nature to him. Suhuy taught him of the Logrus, explained the method by which he could be initiated when the time was right. Merlin found himself adept in artistic pursuits, and Suhuy promised to teach him the art of drawing Trumps when he was ready. Since meeting his father at the Patternfall battle, he was eager to walk in Shadow. He continued to press Suhuy to allow him to try the Logrus.

Jurt challenged Merlin to a sporting duel with trisp and trisliver, and he accepted with honorable intentions. Both Mandor and Despil joined them above the Abyss, gliding upon floating stones they guided with shapeshifted feet. When Jurt took the duel to greater extremes than Merlin intended, and was hurt through his own arrogance, Merlin determined to see Suhuy. He hoped to persuade the Logrus Master to allow him to see the Logrus. He wanted to try it, soon.

Sometime after this, Suhuy deemed Merlin almost ready to try the Logrus. The skeletons of the dead who tried it and failed are strewn about the cavern, hidden by Ways within Ways. The Logrus in the cavern has never been seen by any living outsiders, but it has been described as being utterly different from the Pattern of Amber. According to Merlin's accounts, it is a three-dimensional geometrical form, much larger than is at first apparent. Trying the Logrus is less a walk and more a climb through rising hollow boles and sharply descending wells of great vastnesses. One must make choices between ways within the Logrus, for the easier way might lead one to death. Merlin recorded his trial through the Logrus, the physical effort rivaling the effort of will necessary to choose the proper entryway, even as fatigue weakens leg and arm muscles. Even though he made it through, the Master of the Logrus called him a fool, for Merlin tried the Logrus on his own.

Suhuy may have covered up some hidden pride for the youth, but he expressed annoyance that he went to try the Logrus without him. Merlin may have been ready, but Suhuy hadn't been quite certain. It seemed foolish to the Logrus Master that his young disciple hadn't brought a worthy weapon or amulet, for the Logrus would have enchanted anything carried into it by the initiate. Merlin has not explained why he chose a cord of rope to take into that trial, but he seems not to have regretted the choice.

Having mastered the Logrus, Merlin intended to travel the shadows, and he wanted to see the land that his father had called home.

Amber, livid green on the spectrum of our circle: Merlin visited there often once he learned to walk the Shadows. He met his relatives firsthand, walked the streets of the city, and enjoyed the courtesies of its people. At first, his visits were few and far between, for he felt awkward being among former enemies, and he would then return to House of Sawall. However, King Random's conviviality, and the attentions of his aunt Fiona, brought Merlin back for longer stretches of time. He came to think of Amber as a home in spirit, a restful spot to come to for recreation. He enjoyed losing himself in numerous sporting activities, dallying with a young girl or two in town. He found Random's looseness and sense of playfulness a welcome respite from the restrictive urging of order and duty practiced by Suhuy, who frequently reminded him of his responsibility to the High Art.

During this time in his life, Merlin often returned to the Courts after visiting in Amber. It is likely he stopped at other shadows as well, eager to experience the wonders of shadow-walking.

Sometime after he initiated plans to live on shadow Earth for a time, he went through a number of unusual events in a somewhat indeterminate succession. The events may have been further apart than Merlin had recalled in his journals.

One was an invitation from his brother Jurt to hunt zhind in the Black Zone. Merlin believed that Jurt wanted to reconcile their differences before Merlin's departure for shadow Earth. As they rested from their tracking of zhind, Jurt asked about the power of the Logrus and what it felt like to travel in Shadow. After they continued the hunt, Merlin's enchanted piece of rope, named Frakir, gave Merlin warning. Merlin survived a murder attempt by his brother, but in the subsequent fight, Jurt lost an eye. The incident gave Merlin further incentive to hasten his departure from the Courts.

One morning, while Merlin was preparing applications for the college he had planned to attend on shadow Earth, Suhuy visited him in his quarters. Taking Merlin through Shadow, Suhuy showed him a barren, rocky land devoid of all life. There Suhuy illustrated the final lesson of Merlin's power. Merlin used his Logrus sight to join Suhuy as the aged

sorcerer called forth the great destructive force of
Chaos. Suhuy taught him how to direct the power,
to learn how to control the ultimate annihilation that
can come from Chaos itself.

In their conversation about the power of the Logrus, Suhuy questioned whether one may hold the
power of the Pattern while also containing the Logrus. Suhuy's doubts were settled subsequently,
when Merlin contacted him by Trump from within
the palace of Amber. Merlin was visiting his Amber
relatives again, before taking up residence on
shadow Earth, in a place called San Francisco. Merlin gives the following account:

> "Random, Fiona, and Gérard had taken me
> down to show me the Pattern. I got in touch
> with Suhuy then and gave him a look at it. He
> said that they seemed antithetical, and that I
> would either be destroyed by the attempt or the
> Pattern would drive the image of the Logrus
> from me ... But Fiona said that the Pattern
> should be able to encompass anything, even the
> Logrus, and from what she understood of the
> Logrus it should be able to work its way
> around anything, even the Pattern. So they left
> it up to me, and I knew that I had to walk it.
> So I did. I made it, and I still bear the Logrus
> as well as the Pattern. Suhuy acknowledged
> that Fi had been right, and he speculated that
> it had to do with my mixed parentage."
> (TD, 87–88)

Another important incident of this period occurred shortly after Merlin began college at Berkeley. During spring break, he returned to Amber.
When Fiona could get him alone, she requested he
accompany her to a distant place. She took him to
a fogbound valley with a great tree looming above
the mist. He didn't know the place, but Fiona prod-
ded him to recall the description given him by his
father of this special realm. It was where Corwin
had drawn a Pattern of his own, leading to a new,
unexplored universe. Fiona wanted him to walk his
father's Pattern, explaining that neither she nor
Bleys was permitted to step upon it, and King Random had demurred from making an attempt. Although Fiona insisted that this new Pattern needed
to be explored because it represented a danger to
the equilibrium of the worlds, Merlin was doubtful
that there was any imminent danger. Because his

break from school was nearly over, Merlin pretended that the Pattern prevented him from walking
it. Fiona remained concerned about Corwin's Pattern, but Merlin allowed its existence to take a lower
priority as he returned to the business of college life.

Earth. A shadow of the real. Yet the people there
are so egocentric that they believe themselves superior to any other form of life. How very like those
of Amber, and yet how self-deceived they are. They
believe that knowledge can be contained in a book
and, therefore, is all there is to knowledge. They're
so very confident, so very knowing, but knowing is
not knowledge, and knowledge is unrestricted and
cannot be contained between covers.

Perhaps, though, this knowingness of people of
shadow Earth is what charms so many Amberites.
It may have been the reason for so many of us
wishing to attend their universities. Pretense can be
charming. Particularly a pretense toward knowledge.
Merlin went there to learn at their universities, but
he was also attracted by the desire to learn from the
people there, just as his father had done before him.

Berkeley University in California seemed the
place to be, even though Merlin missed the era of
student protests. The dynamism and enthusiasm
were still there, as young men and women pretended
to be cerebral and scholarly while barely covering
their sexual excitement for one another. Merlin
sought a liberal education indeed.

A tall, red-haired young man named Lucas Raynard attended many of the same freshman classes
that Merlin did. They fenced together in Fencing
Club, and Merlin attempted to speak to him there.
Luke Raynard spoke tersely, eyeing him with suspicion. In spite of this, Merlin admired his skill,
strength, and intelligence. He kept a watchful eye
on Raynard, but he maintained a certain distance.
This is how he explained his relationship with
Raynard:

> "We barely talked to each other. I thought he
> was an arrogant bastard who felt he was ten
> times better than anybody he'd ever met. I
> didn't like him, and he didn't like me much
> either. . . .
> ". . . We got to know each other by trying
> to show each other up. If I'd do something
> kind of—outstanding—he'd try to top it. And
> vice versa. We got so we'd go out for the same

sport, try to date the same girls, try to beat each other's grades. . . .

"Somewhere along the line I guess we started to respect each other. When we both made the Olympic finals something broke. We started slapping each other on the back and laughing, and we went out and had dinner and sat up all night talking and he said he didn't give a shit about the Olympics and I said I didn't either. He said he'd just wanted to show me he was a better man and now he didn't care anymore. He'd decided we were both good enough, and he'd just as soon let the matter stand at that. I felt exactly the same way and told him so. That was when we got to be friends." (TD, 85)

Since that time, Merlin hasn't questioned the close friendship he formed with Luke Raynard. They both excelled in track and field events, and Merlin attributed Luke's superior stamina to athletic conditioning and practice. Although they shared an interest in paintings, attending galleries and museums together, he knew remarkably little about Luke's background. Merlin accepted his friendship without stipulation, remaining naively unsuspicious of Luke, even when a series of dread accidents began occurring shortly after they met.

Every year on the same date, April 30, near-fatal accidents placed Merlin on his guard. The first two incidents seemed like mere happenstance, but the third year's occurrence was apparently a deliberate attempt at murder. He waited resignedly for each year's incident, and in warding off disaster, Merlin decided that there were other agents who were protecting him from death. These yearly attacks continued to plague him for eight years, the last occurring just as he planned to leave shadow Earth. Shortly after this last attempt on his life, he gradually learned who was behind them and reached a resolution with the agent involved.

In those eight years on shadow Earth, Merlin completed his course of study at the university and began working for a computer firm called Grand Design in San Francisco. Luke Raynard was also employed by the company.

Early in their college days, however, both Luke and Merlin became involved with girls; Luke with Gail Lampron, and Merlin with Julia Barnes. They made an intellectual foursome, based on Merlin's account of a weekend venture they had. Luke and Merlin spent part of a Saturday together, then met with Julia and Gail. They ate dinner at the marina where Merlin kept his sailboat, *The Starburst*. While their conversation was rather philosophical, a contention about the various shadings of duty, morality, and power, their perspectives seemed to be coming from entirely different directions. Merlin remained largely in the background, as Luke argued for a definition of personal morality that implied an origin in another world. Gail appeared defensive, supporting a need for maintaining communal values and a sense of duty to society. Julia preferred a sticking to an individual morality that was separate from society, so that one would be free to seek power. These disparate perspectives hint at secret truths about Luke, Gail, and Julia. Luke was related to Merlin on the Amber side; Julia discovered herself to be a talented adept in the Arts; and Gail was a unique entity from the Chaos side of things. Morality, duty, and power were very important facets to the lives they led and were to lead.

Merlin had first met Julia in a Computer Science course at Berkeley. They met casually after class, but soon started seeing each other frequently. When they felt comfortable with each other, they occasionally double-dated with Luke and Gail. They saw a lot of each other alone, too.

At the end of a particularly bright and pleasant day, Julia and Merlin went to a deserted beach. Then, Merlin led her on a walk, a rather special one. He took her through Shadow, and they viewed impossible landscapes in fantastic lands. The next morning when they awoke on the beach, Julia remembered, and she knew that the visions he showed her were not a dream. Some time later, after much thought, she questioned him about that night. She had investigated, found that none of the landscapes she had been shown that night could have existed. In spite of his refusal to explain, she persisted in demanding an explanation.

"You have some power that you will not share."

"Call it that, then."

"I would do whatever you say, promise whatever you want promised."

"There is a reason, Julia." . . .

"And you won't even share that. . . .

"It must be a lonely world you inhabit, magician, if even those who love you are barred from it.'' . . .

''I didn't say that.''

''You didn't have to. It is your silence that tells me. If you know the road to Hell too, why not head that way? Good-bye!'' (BA, 57–58)

A few nights after their breakup, Merlin met Julia in a supermarket parking lot. She was calm, speaking about having studied a number of surprising things. As they talked, she petted an Irish setter that had come over. Before they parted, she had said to the dog: ''Sit!'' Merlin felt vaguely surprised, especially in retrospect, at the way the dog seemed to remain immobile. Although Merlin didn't see her again, he learned that she was dating another young man by the name of Rick Kinsky.

When Merlin completed his course of study at Berkeley, he was hired as a computer programmer at Grand Design in San Francisco. Soon afterward, he discovered that Lucas Raynard had begun working there as a sales representative. With his aptitude for computers, Merlin mapped out a scheme to develop a new form of computer. Over a matter of years, he put together a remarkable device that was composed partly of elements of the Pattern of Amber. Dubbing the device Ghostwheel, he placed it in a unique environment, where no one could access it but himself. After working on it for four years, he felt that Ghostwheel was ready to perform its primary function. Merlin quit Grand Design and packed his belongings with the intention of leaving California for good.

For a long time, Merlin had wondered over the whereabouts of his father, Prince Corwin of Amber. He had been back to the true city several times during breaks from college classes, and later, on vacations from his job. Gathering up bits of gossip about his father, Merlin could find nothing substantial about what happened to Corwin since the time he entered the Courts of Chaos. No one had been able to reach him by Trump either. Wonder turned to concern, and Merlin created his Ghostwheel project as a means of seeking out Corwin in Shadow, wherever he was.

He waited until April 30, after having completed Ghostwheel, intending to resolve the business of the yearly murder attempts before departing the West Coast. Bothered as he had been by the annual attacks on his life, he expected that they would end

with his departure, even if he couldn't trace the perpetrator. Up to that point in time, there was nothing otherworldly about them.

On this eighth year, however, elements beyond the mundane took effect.

After receiving a message from Julia Barnes, Merlin went to her apartment. She was dead; her face and arm torn apart. The attacker was still in the room with her.

The huge doglike beast that waited and pounced on Merlin was not native to shadow Earth. After killing it, Merlin discovered several Trumps very much like those used by Amberites. Examining the Trumps closely, he found himself viewing a distant shadow of a much faster time stream. The discovery showed him that agents other than those of the ordinary variety were at work here. Saddened by Julia's death, and feeling a new urgency about solving a mystery with possible origins in the true city, Merlin engaged in an odyssey. It had its beginnings on mundane Earth, but the mysteries within mysteries carried him to multishadows along our symbolic sphere.

Merlin's journals, published in numbers of shadows, including the North American Continent of shadow Earth, give explicit details of Merlin's odyssey. Rather than review those details here, it would be more appropriate to present an overview, one that emphasizes his movements from shadow to shadow as Merlin completes the circuit of the representational wheel posited earlier. For Merlin's father, Prince Corwin, all roads led to Amber. Interestingly, by following this circuitous route on a rounded model, all ways lead back to the Courts of Chaos. For Merlin, this is certainly the case.

1. **Shadow Earth.** San Francisco; Merlin meets Victor Melman, then Jasra, and finds himself on a side trip to a shadow where a sphinx awaits travelers. In Santa Fe, New Mexico, while seeking Luke, Merlin encounters Dan Martinez. Visiting Bill Roth in upstate New York, he meets with George Hansen. Hansen's strangeness is the catalyst for Merlin's sudden decision to introduce Roth to the land of Amber.

2. **Amber.** While Bill Roth takes the royal tour, King Random acquaints Merlin with the facts of assassination and near-assassination against the Royal Family.

3. **Shadow Earth.** Upstate New York; Merlin enjoys a pleasant dalliance with Meg Devlin. Afterward, he suspects she was the agent who contacted him for a meeting.

4. **Amber.** At the funeral for Prince Caine, there is an attempt at assassination thwarted. After telling Random of the Ghostwheel Project, Merlin is ordered to shut it down. Merlin departs for the unique environment in which he had placed his project.

5. **The Shadows.** Between Amber and a unique hydrogen-helium Lake: Luke rescues Merlin from the destructive tendencies of Ghostwheel. However, Ghostwheel unleashes a Shadow-storm that tosses them helplessly through Shadow, until Merlin drifts into unconsciousness.

6. **Blue Crystal Cave.** Luke entraps Merlin within the sealed environment where magical inducements will not work. Before doing so, Luke admits his culpability in the April 30 attacks and explains the reason behind them. Much later, Merlin finds escape through the clumsy interjection of two minor henchmen working for Jasra.

7. **Shadow Earth.** San Francisco; Flora aids Merlin as he returns to Julia's apartment. They discover a magical entranceway hidden there.

8. **Enchanted Pathway and Keep of the Four Worlds.** Merlin discovers the pathway from Julia's apartment leads to the Keep, a center for powerful forces. Along the way, he encounters Scrof, Dave the hermit, and a unique projection dubbed Mask. Merlin uses a Trump of Random to find his way out of Mask's grasp.

9. **Amber.** After a pleasant repast at Bloody Bill's in the city, Merlin is attacked by four robbers. He is helped by Vinta Bayle, girl-friend of the late Prince Caine, and he joins her on a brief sailing trip to Arbor House, her father's country estate. While there, Merlin reconciles with his contrite pet project Ghostwheel, and comes to realize that Vinta Bayle is a body-possessing entity who has intervened in his life previously. Receiving a Trump contact from an injured Luke, Merlin brings him to Arbor House. They make a side trip back to the Blue Crystal Cave so that Luke can recover more quickly than elsewhere. After returning to Arbor House, Merlin finds that Vinta has no memory of having been possessed nor of what transpired during that time. Traveling back to the true city on horseback, he encounters a shapeshifting wolf that has access to a Trump Gate for escape. In the city, he runs into Bill Roth, then goes on to Corwin's sarcophagus on Mt. Kolvir to hide one of the potent stones from the crystal cave. Back in the Royal Palace, he walks the Pattern.

10. **Keep of the Four Worlds.** Using his memory of the room in which he had seen Dalt, Merlin teleports to the Keep. Finding his way to a large chamber containing a black fountain, he locates the immobile figures of Jasra and Sharu Garrul. Mask confronts and attacks Merlin with various incantations, but Merlin prevails. He grabs up the form of Jasra and Trumps back to the palace of Amber.

11. **Amber.** After catching up on some much-needed sleep, Merlin encounters a large-sized Trump of himself, with Luke's voice emanating from it. Luke reaches out for Merlin, and Merlin grabs his arm intending to bring him to Amber. Instead, Luke pulls Merlin through the giant Trump to his location.

12. **Lewis Carroll Bar.** Merlin finds himself suffering from symptoms of an hallucinogenic stupor that Luke is in. Having been dosed with LSD, Luke has entrapped himself in a strange bar with creatures out of *Alice in Wonderland*. Reality of a kind impinges when a Jabberwock and a Fire Angel from the region of Chaos pursue them down a tunnel. As they fall, Merlin summons vitamins and other stimulants from Shadow in order to revive Luke. Once they have landed and Merlin dispenses with the pursuing creatures, he returns with Luke to the Wonderland bar. Merlin leaves him there while he walks out into a fog. He walks on until the fog clears and he can shift through the shadows.

13. **Bridge Spanning two Floating Mountains.** Merlin stops here to contact his step-brother Mandor by Trump. Bringing Mandor to him, Merlin summarizes recent events, seeking advice from his brother. After an exchange of information, Merlin receives a Trump contact from his aunt Fiona, calling from a faraway shadow. She speaks of a problem that needs Merlin's attention, and brings both of them to her location.

14. **Shadow of Rock and Green Sky.** Fiona shows Mandor and Merlin a strange tornado growing in a nearby valley. She claims a connection between disturbances called Shadow-storms and the mysterious new Pattern created by Corwin. Merlin minimizes the threat, and he is supported by Mandor. Merlin leaves Fiona and Mandor, who intend to work together on further investigations of the agent behind the disturbances. Merlin shifts through Shadow, then halts to concentrate on his Trump of the main hall of the palace in Amber.

15. **Amber.** After a rest, Merlin brings the frozen figure of Jasra to his room and explores the spell upon it. Afterward, he becomes caught up in a political situation involving the shadow realms of Begma and Kashfa. He plays politics at a dinner party with Queen Vialle and the Begman prime minister, Orkuz, and his daughters, Coral and Nayda. After dinner, Merlin escorts Coral on a tour of the town and the sea caves, where they encounter his half brother Jurt. Showing Coral the Pattern deep within the bowels of the Royal Palace, Merlin is surprised when Coral survives a walk on it. Coral disappears after allowing the Pattern itself to transport her. In the palace, Merlin hears from Fiona and Mandor, and from Ghostwheel, both sides warning caution against the other. Preparing for a second formal dinner with members of the Begman Embassy, Merlin meets Bill Roth again. They learn of possible trouble of a military kind from Benedict just before joining the dinner guests. In private, Merlin learns from Queen Vialle that Dalt and an army of mercenaries have arrived at the Forest of Arden. Dalt demands the cus-

tody of Luke, and Merlin brings his friend in by Trump to arrange a meeting between them. The arrangement is for a personal hand-to-hand combat between Dalt and Luke. At the conclusion of the fight, Luke is beaten, and Dalt takes his men in retreat with the unconscious Luke. Later, Merlin meets with Nayda, shows her the unmoving form of Jasra, and Nayda admits that she is the body-possessing entity that he had encountered previously. Merlin makes contact with Mandor, who comes through to Merlin's room. Mandor places Nayda under a quieting spell, and Merlin proceeds to revive Jasra. Conferring with Mandor and Jasra, Merlin gets them to agree to an assault on Mask at the Keep of the Four Worlds. Using Ghostwheel's abilities for their transport, the three of them are teleported to the mountains overlooking the Keep.

16. **Keep of the Four Worlds.** Reaching the Black Fountain, Merlin, Jasra, and Mandor engage in sorcerous battle with Mask, Sharu Garrul, and Jurt. Just before Jurt and Mask flee from the crumbling edifice, Merlin discovers the identity of Mask. Jasra takes control over the Keep once again, enslaving Sharu as guardian of the Fount. Enjoying a leisurely meal prepared by Mandor, the three of them discuss several matters. Jasra recounts her connection with Julia, Merlin's former girlfriend, and how she attained her arcane skills. Jasra and Mandor agree to help Merlin locate Coral, the Begman prime minister's missing daughter, by means of her Trump. They manage to see her by Trump, but in doing so, have alerted the power that holds her captive. The unknown power rushes to their location, and Ghostwheel intervenes to send Merlin and the others to different shadows.

17. **Cave of a Distant Shadow.** Ghostwheel transports Merlin to this distant but undisclosed realm for his own protection. Merlin is confronted by images of Dworkin, Oberon, and Corwin. The Corwin-image knocks Merlin unconscious.

18. **Land Between Shadows [Undershadow].** Merlin awakens in a realm of negative im-

ages; what should be dark in color is white and what should be light-colored is black. Attempting to leave, Merlin summons the Logrus. He blacks out again in an explosion. Becoming conscious again, he discovers that the Logrus summoning enhanced Frakir, his strangling cord. Frakir can communicate with Merlin telepathically, and it has an increased understanding of what is going on around them. With Frakir's guidance, Merlin learns that the powers of the Pattern and the Logrus are at war with each other. The Undershadow is a region between the Shadows that neither power can reach directly, but both can send artificial constructs of people who had been imprinted on them. These constructs, either Pattern-ghosts or Logrus-ghosts, act as agents for their respective Powers, programmed to do their Powers' bidding. Merlin meets a number of these ghost-images, realizing himself to be a pawn in the game between the Logrus and the Pattern. When he meets a Logrus-ghost of Jurt, they join forces, and they are led to a Broken Pattern that holds Coral trapped in its center. In their rescue of Coral, the ghost-Jurt dies in an encounter with a threatening ghost-Merlin. Once Merlin performs an oddly exhibitionist ritual with a semiconscious Coral, the Broken Pattern, now made whole, sends them to Amber.

19. **Amber.** Finding that they have been transported to the Pattern in the Royal Palace, Merlin has it send Coral and himself to his quarters. There, Merlin communicates with Ghostwheel, who informs Merlin that it had been the Pattern that held Coral captive and had sought for him at the Keep of the Four Worlds. Merlin discovers the aged Dworkin seeking him out. Dworkin suggests that Merlin should protect himself from the destructive power of the Pattern by attuning himself to the Jewel of Judgment. Merlin agrees to do so.

20. **Blue Crystal Cave.** Merlin voluntarily goes there to rest, undisturbed by any magics. Once rested, he attunes himself to the Jewel of Judgment. He then has Ghostwheel return him to his quarters in Amber.

21. **Amber.** As Merlin walks by the library in the palace, he observes Random and Martin sharing a moment together at musical play. Merlin leaves Grayswandir in his father's room, then makes Trump contact with Luke. After listening to Luke's sketchy explanations about Dalt's actions, Merlin discovers Coral tampering with the spell on Nayda in his room. He brings Mandor to his room and finds that Nayda is able to move about. She grabs the Jewel of Judgment that he has in his possession and runs out of the room. Merlin gives chase and learns from her that his mother Dara had placed a *geas,* that is, an involuntary compulsion, on the possessing entity to protect him in his travels. In the hallway, they confront a huge representation of the Logrus. A second image, an immense unicorn, appears, representing the Pattern. Both Powers demand the Jewel of Judgment, and Ghostwheel intervenes to prevent them from obtaining it. When Ghostwheel disappears with the Nayda/entity and the Jewel, the two Powers come together, causing a minor cataclysm. Dworkin brings Merlin to his den, saving him from the general destruction. They return to a partially ruined palace, where Queen Vialle treats Mandor's broken arm and Dworkin tends to a badly injured Coral. In private, Random gives Merlin new information he just received about matters in Kashfa. Luke Raynard had just taken over the kingdom in Kashfa. Random suggests that Merlin attend the coronation there as a private citizen. Before preparing to leave for Kashfa, Merlin goes through the Hall of Mirrors, bringing him a brief adventure with the women in his life. The adventure seems real enough when he is returned to the palace bleeding from several cuts. He enters Brand's room, finds a sword and a potent magical ring. Because Frakir fights to remove the ring from his finger, Merlin ties Frakir around a bedpost in his uncle's room. Merlin chooses to use the ring to teleport himself to the capital city of Kashfa.

22. **Jidrash, Capital of Kashfa.** Outside the palace, Merlin contacts Luke by Trump.

They meet together in the First Unicornian Church. Merlin offers Luke Brand's sword, and Luke recognizes it, calling it Werewindle. Jurt appears in the church, fights with Merlin, obtains Werewindle, and disappears. In the church, Merlin discovers that Coral is there, that Dworkin had implanted the Jewel of Judgment into her eye socket, and that she and Luke are betrothed. He remains for their coronation, and he spends most of a night with Coral. She explains that their marriage had been arranged when she and Luke were children, as a means of sealing a bond between Kashfa and Begma. Early in the morning, while Coral still sleeps, a demon arrives in their bedchamber, summoning Merlin. It is an old friend, Gryll, a servant of his uncle Suhuy. Merlin is being called back to the Courts of Chaos, upon the death of old King Swayvill. Climbing onto Gryll, Merlin is carried back through Shadow, along a thin Black Thread, to the Courts.

23. **Ways of Suhuy in the Courts of Chaos.** Suhuy greets Merlin warmly and speaks briefly of the political situation there. Mandor arrives to greet him, followed by Merlin's mother, Dara. They speak of the succession to the throne of the Courts, and Merlin asks his mother about the protective entity, known as a ty'iga. When he is alone, Merlin meets briefly with Ghostwheel. Merlin's artificial construct wants to learn more about the Logrus, and Merlin points the way for Ghostwheel to find it. Merlin then makes a tentative Trump contact with his father, trapped in some dark place. He asks Suhuy to tell him what he knows of Corwin's activities the last time Corwin had been to the Courts.

24. **Mandorways.** Merlin meets with Mandor for breakfast. Mandor fills him in on matters of the succession, and that Merlin might indeed be the next king of the Courts. Mandor mentions that Jurt has also returned to the Courts to attend the late king's funeral. Not making any commitment about accepting the crown, Merlin takes his leave of Mandor.

25. **Underground Mausoleum Near the Courts.** In a reflective mood, Merlin walks to a childhood play area he frequented as a boy. He recalls a young girl named Rhanda with whom he played there. He discovers a note left by her long ago, which explains the reasons why she stopped meeting with him. While in the mausoleum, a Pattern-ghost of Luke greets Merlin. Luke tells something of Jasra's origins in the Courts, and Merlin uses his own blood to sustain the Pattern-ghost Luke. Together, they encounter a Logrus-ghost Borel, bent on ending the Pattern-ghost Luke's life. A special Pattern-ghost of Corwin intercedes, and Merlin, Luke, and Corwin flee. Six unknown figures pursue them as the Pattern-ghost Corwin follows the essence of a Pattern force into Shadow.

26. **Pattern-like Tunnel.** The ghost-Corwin leads them into an image of the Pattern that becomes a kind of tunnel. The power of the Logrus, however, attempts to break up the tunnel as the three run through it. The tunnel is rent apart, and the three begin drifting.

27. **Shadow of Fog.** Drifting in fog, they spot a definite shape a distance away. Merlin uses his ring to levitate the three of them toward the shape. They find that it is an objectified version of a painting that Merlin is fond of—a red '57 Chevy. They climb into the automobile, and Merlin finds he is able to drive it. They move along until the fog lifts somewhat and they seem to be driving on a surface. They seem to drive along ground familiar to Merlin, and he recognizes a large tree next to a gleaming area of ground.

28. **Corwin's Pattern.** The ghost-Corwin confirms that they have arrived at the new Pattern created by Merlin's father. Because the ghost-Corwin is the only image that this particular Pattern can create, it has maintained the ghost-Corwin for a very long period. It was this ghost-Corwin that Merlin had encountered previously. Communicating with his Pattern, the ghost-Corwin is able to suggest their next course of action. All three of them are to walk the Pattern. They reach the center, and Luke, protected by the Pattern, is willing to share the duty of guarding it. He teleports out to stand by the '57 Chevy, then gets in to sit in the passenger seat for

the duration. Merlin has the Pattern send him as close to the Courts of Chaos as it is willing to go.

29. **Fire Gate.** Corwin's Pattern delivers Merlin to a high promontory of white stone next to a black sea. Merlin recognizes the place as a way station named Fire Gate, not too far from the Courts. He walks the shadows from there.

30. **Ways of Sawall.** Finding himself early for his lunch date with Dara, Merlin decides to explore the Maze of Art, a huge area within House Sawall that includes Shadowmastered Ways as part of its artwork. He meets another old friend of his boyhood, a snakelike creature named Glait. Glait shows him a hidden chapel in a secret Way that is dedicated to Corwin. Most telling about the chapel is that the actual sword Grayswandir lay before the altar. Afterward, Merlin joins his mother in the main hall, and they talk as they eat. Dara wants to see Merlin on the throne in the Courts. As they talk, the sign of the Logrus appears before them, having chased Ghostwheel across the nearby ocean in their direction. Merlin protects his construct, refusing to give him up. Dara speaks of more important plans to the Logrus, and the power acquiesces. It leaves them. Merlin turns the conversation to his father, and Dara becomes increasingly annoyed at his questions. When he accuses her of imprisoning Corwin, she haughtily rises and disappears in a fiery flame. Merlin shows Ghostwheel the Maze of Art, and the artificial construct goes off to explore it. Still in the Maze of Art, Merlin encounters Jurt, who claims he wants a truce so they could talk. Jurt has been in close contact with Dara and learned that the Logrus chooses Merlin to serve on the throne. That fact, and his own introspection about his motives, has caused Jurt to decide to end his conflict with Merlin for the throne. They decide to join forces to prevent Dara from exerting control over Merlin's reign, which includes a plot to kidnap Coral to be Merlin's queen. Jurt uses his Trump-like abilities to transfer them to his quarters, where they change to prepare for Swayvill's funeral.

After dressing, Jurt brings them to the plaza, where the funeral procession will cross.

31. **Plaza at the End of the World.** Upon arriving, Merlin and Jurt greet acquaintances who have gathered for the procession. Mandor contacts Merlin by Trump and asks both of them to join him.

32. **Main Hall of Thelbane.** After Mandor brings Jurt and Merlin to him, he has them join the procession, which will cross the plaza from Thelbane, the royal residence. Using his spikard, the magical ring he found in Brand's room, Merlin transforms two men in front of them to appear as them. Then Jurt uses his abilities to teleport Merlin and himself away.

33. **Jidrash, in Kashfa.** In a series of "Trump Jumps," Jurt takes them back to the capital city in Kashfa. They discover that Coral is already missing, and they contact Luke. When Merlin brings Luke to him, Luke tells of Coral's kidnapping. Merlin uses the spikard to take Luke, Jurt, and himself away from Kashfa.

34. **Corwin's Pattern.** Merlin introduces the real Luke to the ghost-Luke guarding the Pattern. Since the ghost-Luke is unable to leave his duties to join them, Merlin leaves the two Lukes there, while he and Jurt initiate their series of jumps back to the Courts.

35. **Ways of Sawall and Thelbane.** Jurt and Merlin change clothes and their forms in Jurt's quarters. Jurt returns them to Thelbane, which is deserted. There is a crowd in the Plaza, however, gathered in confusion. Merlin has Jurt take them to the outer edge of the crowd.

36. **Plaza at the End of the World.** The casket of the deceased king is carefully guarded, as a mob gathers around the two men resembling Merlin and Jurt. Merlin takes away his spell upon them and returns Jurt and himself to their proper appearance. Mandor believes some unknown person has done the deed to create confusion. Calling Merlin over, Mandor informs him that Tmer, another successor to the throne, has just been stabbed to death during the procession. Mandor sug-

gests that Merlin leave, to return to the Cathedral of the Serpent later, under greater security. Merlin rejoins Jurt in the crowd, and Jurt returns them to his quarters.

37. **Ways of Sawall.** As Merlin and Jurt change again, they discuss the succession and the danger posed by the Logrus if Merlin chooses not to follow the Power's dictates. Merlin uses the spikard to take them to the new Pattern.

38. **Corwin's Pattern.** The two Lukes greet Merlin and Jurt. The ghost-Luke has been able to communicate with the Pattern, and the Pattern has given permission for him to join the others once the ghost-Corwin returns. Jurt offers to remain on guard while the others search for the kidnapped girl Coral. The ghost-Luke communicates with the Pattern about it, and the Pattern agrees. After showing Jurt where to obtain food and water, the ghost-Luke joins the real Luke and Merlin. Using the spikard, Merlin brings them to Kashfa.

39. **Jidrash in Kashfa.** Before returning to the palace, Luke shows them where the Black Trail had been, a telltale sign of the route the kidnappers of Coral had taken. Unable to locate the trail, Luke asks Merlin to take them to his apartments in the palace. To avoid confusion, Luke asks Merlin to change the ghost-Luke's appearance. Merlin transforms him to resemble Oberon of Amber. They make their way to another room, where they meet Nayda. Merlin returns the ghost-Luke to his normal appearance. They plan to have the ghost-Luke remain in Kashfa as its king, while the real Luke, with Nayda, begins searching for Coral. Merlin chooses this time to return to the Courts, asking Luke to contact him as they close in on the kidnappers.

40. **Ways of Sawall.** Returning alone to Jurt's quarters, Merlin senses the presence of a Way. He finds it deep inside Jurt's armoire, enters, and discovers a chapel dedicated to Brand. Brand's sword, Werewindle, is on the altar. Returning to Jurt's room, Merlin changes, pondering the origin of the spikard

on his finger. He has the spikard bring him outside the great Cathedral at the farthest edge of the Plaza.

41. **Cathedral of the Serpent at the outer edge of the Plaza at the End of the World.** Sitting in the rear of the Temple, Merlin observes the formalities of the funeral service. Bances of Amblerash, High Priest of the Serpent, reads from the Book of the Serpent Hung upon the Tree of Matter. He, with Mandor, Dara, and Lord Tubble, the only other remaining successor to the throne, lifts the casket bearing Swayvill. The candlelight is purposely dimmed as they carry the casket to the very Rim of Chaos. As the last candle is snuffed, there is a shuffling and a cry. When the Cathedral is illumined again, everyone can see that the casket and Lord Tubble are gone. Before feeling the need to leave, Merlin speaks to an old friend, Gilva of the House of Hendrake. With her permission, Merlin brings Gilva and himself to a chamber of metal trees, a sculpture garden, in Lord Sawall's Maze of Art.

42. **Ways of Sawall.** Merlin shows Gilva the hidden Way and the secret chapel dedicated to his father. She explains how cults grew in which citizens of the Courts created personal chapels in worship of the royal members of Amber. Old King Swayvill had banned the chapels because they conflicted with the worship of the Serpent, the principal religion of the Courts. Secret chapels then became all the more prevalent as acts of rebellion in response to the ban. According to Gilva, even Mandor has a personal chapel, one dedicated to Princess Fiona. Merlin's snakelike friend, Glait, enters the hidden Way to inform him that Dara is coming through the Maze of Art in their direction. Merlin uses his spikard to lead them through a Way to a wooded area. From there, Merlin sends Gilva back to the Cathedral of the Serpent. Then, Merlin and Glait return to the sculpture garden of the Maze of Art. He summons fresh clothing and weapons from Shadow, preparing to return to Kashfa. Before departing, he contacts Luke by Trump. Luke is traveling in Shadow with Nayda, who is

able to track the black path. Luke brings Merlin through.

43. **Shadows some distance from the direction of Kashfa.** As Merlin joins them, he finds that Dalt is with Luke and Nayda. Merlin summons a horse he names Tiger, and he rides with the others as they pick up their pace. They continue on the Black Trail as it widens. Nayda, using unique senses, is able to tell that Coral and her captors have settled in in a tall gray tower. As they ride, Merlin fills Luke in about his position in the line of succession in the Courts. Luke comes around to discussing the spikard on Merlin's finger. Merlin allows him to examine it, and Luke recognizes the potent spells upon it. Nayda is able to tell them that there are six kidnappers with Coral in the tower. They are defending against a small party of attackers. When they reach the gray tower, they see that Pattern-ghost relatives of Merlin are attacking Logrus-ghosts protecting the tower. Merlin uses an invisibility spell to rescue Coral while the Logrus- and Pattern-ghosts fight each other. Although Merlin escapes the Logrus-ghosts, he has to face battle with the Pattern-ghosts. Dalt joins him in the fight. After Merlin banishes the Pattern-ghosts with his spikard, the Sign of the Pattern comes before them. Merlin challenges the right of the Pattern to use Coral as a game piece in its conflict with the Logrus. He decides to test the effect of opening all the channels of the spikard against the Pattern. He is rushed into unconsciousness along with the others.

44. **Primal Pattern.** Merlin awakens to find that the Pattern Sign has brought him and his companions to this place. The Sign intends to keep all of them imprisoned at the primal Pattern so that it can regain a greater measure of power than that of the Logrus. Merlin takes control of the situation by cutting his hand with a dagger and sitting poised over the Pattern. The Sign tries to reason with him, pointing out that the Logrus also wants Coral and will attempt anything to get her. She and Merlin would be safer at the primal Pattern than under the Power of the Logrus. The Pattern promises them a Golden Age if they side with it. Merlin continues to demand unconditional freedom, and the Sign acquiesces. In order to hold the Sign to its word, Luke cuts his own hand, holding it over the Pattern as Merlin is doing. Taking one of the Trumps of Doom from Merlin, Luke holds it as his personal means of escape while the Sign sends the others to a place of their desire. Merlin has the Sign send them to Kashfa.

45. **Jidrash in Kashfa.** Merlin intends to leave Nayda and Dalt here while he and Coral Trump to a safe place. Both Dalt and Nayda refuse to be left behind. Merlin maintains a contact with Luke, still holding the Sign at bay at the primal Pattern. When Luke's Trump goes black, Merlin takes himself and his companions far away from Kashfa.

46. **Corwin's Pattern.** As soon as Merlin reaches the place of his father's Pattern, he stretches on the grass and goes to sleep, leaving Nayda, Coral, and Dalt with Jurt to discuss recent events. He dreams of the Hall of Mirrors, and familiar faces speak to him from various mirrors. One image is Delwin, who reveals some information about the spikard. An image of Bleys in another mirror elaborates further, speaking of nine spikards. He awakens to earth tremors, and the ghost-Corwin is standing over him. The ghost-Corwin tells him that the Logrus has caused the tremors, trying to destroy the Pattern. Merlin uses his spikard to halt the process deep underground. Realizing where his imprisoned father must be, he tells the others that he and the ghost-Corwin are returning to the Courts of Chaos to rescue him. After saying his farewells to Coral, Nayda, Jurt, and Dalt, he opens a doorway into Shadow for himself and the ghost-Corwin.

47. **Ways of Sawall.** Merlin and the ghost-Corwin step into the Sculpture Garden in the Maze of Art. Merlin overhears Mandor and Bances of Amblerash talking as they pass by, seeming to be combined in a conspiracy of some sort. When Merlin finds a second spikard in his pocket, the ghost-Corwin remarks about it, seeming to know something

of the origin of the spikards. When they reach the area of the chamber where the hidden Way should be located, Merlin discovers that the sculpture had been changed. Using the spikard, Merlin levitates the ghost-Corwin and himself into the Way. They locate a second hidden Way in the floor design of the Abyss of Chaos. They use it to find the real Corwin. After releasing him from a darkened room, the ghost-Corwin takes his place, suitably transformed to resemble the disheveled figure of the real Corwin. Merlin levitates the real Corwin and himself out of the chapel, then, still levitated, brings them quickly to Jurt's quarters. While Corwin rests, Merlin goes to bring back food for his father. He runs into his old girlfriend, Julia, who has forgiven Merlin for past actions. She asks him to come by when his problems are resolved.

48. **Rim of the Abyss.** Merlin comes to this place for solitude, the chance to consider his options, and to examine the two spikards in his possession. The ring planted by Mandor in Brand's room has a spell commanding the wearer to follow Mandor's orders. Merlin ponders his need to work out his personal problems so that his home would be secure here as well as in Amber.

49. **Ways of Sawall.** In the Maze of Art, Merlin calls for Ghostwheel. He uses both the Trump he had drawn of his construct and the energies of the spikard to make contact. Ghostwheel returns contact to say he is trapped in a spinning force caused by an entity named Kergma, a being that Merlin is familiar with. Merlin helps Ghostwheel, bringing him through the Trump. Merlin asks his construct to hide on his wrist, requesting that Ghostwheel be prepared to support him in a showdown with Mandor and Dara. Mandor arrives in response to the energies he had felt emanating from the spikard. Speaking with Mandor about accepting the throne, Merlin uses the spikard to hold Mandor. Then, creating a Trump in the air of his mother, Merlin summons her. Merlin holds his stepbrother and mother in their human forms as he questions them

about the control they had intended to exert upon him as king. Arguing, Mandor initiates a spell against Merlin. Dara uses her powers against Merlin also, and they fight a sorcerous duel. His spikard allows Merlin greater resources than either Dara or Mandor, and he is able to defeat them. As Merlin begins a spell that would place them in his control, Dara calls forth the Sign of the Logrus. The Sign would have acted against Merlin, but Ghostwheel uses mirror images of itself, from a shattered exhibit, to abate the Sign's energies against it. Seeing that it faces a stalemate, the Sign orders Dara to permit Merlin's reign without restriction. After they depart, Merlin obtains suitable apparel for his father. He brings the clothes back to Jurt's rooms, where he tells his story to Corwin.

50. **Patternfall Battlefield.** Merlin shows his father some of the Ways of the Courts, finally bringing him to the now-healed site where the greatest battle between Amber and the Courts had been fought. Corwin and Merlin agree to work from the two poles of existence to maintain the peace and seek a balance between the controlling forces. Merlin sends his father back to Amber.

Because Merlin hadn't been back to Amber during these later events, we of the true city must depend on his published journals to appraise the man he has become. Based on his writings, the wheel of many colors seems to hold. Merlin may still step forth from the Courts of Chaos and traverse the shadows depicted on our representational sphere, skipping some altogether, staying longer in one shadow, thus lengthening the color spectrum at that point. His actions have become the guide for transforming the hypothetical turning of this sphere.

In a retrospective viewing of Merlin's life, his movements from place to place appear to have been made with striding self-confidence. Even at the end, facing Mandor and Dara in a final showdown, he acted with utter assurance. Yet his questions of their intentions for him, and his need to try to dissuade them from manipulating him, illustrate an ingenuousness on his part. Those seem to be twin characteristics of this young mage: a naïveté in understanding the

TABLE OF PLACES DESCRIBED IN MERLIN'S JOURNALS
AND CORRESPONDING PAGE NUMBERS
FROM PUBLISHED AVON BOOKS PAPERBACKS IN ENGLISH ON SHADOW EARTH

The following listing corresponds to the summation of places and events described in the entry for MERLIN:

Place	Published Work/ Page Number	Place	Published Work/ Page Number
1. Shadow Earth	TD/ 10–110	23. Ways of Suhuy	PC/ 13–55
2. Amber	TD/ 111–24	24. Mandorways	PC/ 55–71
3. Shadow Earth	TD/ 124–34	25. Underground Mausoleum	PC/ 71–81
4. Amber	TD/ 135–52	26. Pattern-like Tunnel	PC/ 82
5. Shadows Between Amber and Hydrogen-Helium Lake	TD/ 153–77	27. Shadow of Fog	PC/ 82–86
		28. Corwin's Pattern	PC/ 86–94
		29. Fire Gate	PC/ 94
6. Blue Crystal Cave	TD/ 178–83; BA/ 7–15	30. Ways of Sawall	PC/ 96–132
		31. Plaza at End of World	PC/ 132
7. Shadow Earth	BA/ 16–34	32. Main Hall of Thelbane	PC/ 132–37
8. Pathway and Keep of the Four Worlds	BA/ 35–55	33. Jidrash in Kashfa	PC/ 137–43
9. Amber	BA/ 58–197	34. Corwin's Pattern	PC/ 143–44
10. Keep of Four Worlds	BA/ 197–208	35. Ways of Sawall/Thelbane	PC/ 145
11. Amber	BA/ 208–15	36. Plaza at End of World	PC/ 145–46
12. Lewis Carroll Bar	BA/ 215; SC/ 1–26	37. Ways of Sawall	PC/ 147–49
		38. Corwin's Pattern	PC/ 149–52
13. Bridge spanning Floating Mountains	SC/ 27–36	39. Jidrash in Kashfa	PC/ 152–54
14. Shadow of Rock and Green Sky	SC/ 36–48	40. Ways of Sawall	PC/ 154–58
		41. Cathedral of the Serpent	PC/ 158–61
15. Amber	SC/ 48–203	42. Ways of Sawall	PC/ 162–71
16. Keep of Four Worlds	SC/ 203–17; KS/ 9–51	43. Shadows, from Kashfa	PC/ 170–96
		44. Primal Pattern	PC/ 196–205
17. Cave of Distant Shadow	KS/ 52–63	45. Jidrash in Kashfa	PC/ 205
18. Land Between Shadows	KS/ 64–164	46. Corwin's Pattern	PC/ 206–17
19. Amber	KS/ 165–72	47. Ways of Sawall	PC/ 218–29
20. Blue Crystal Cave	KS/ 173–79	48. Rim of Abyss	PC /229–30
21. Amber	KS/ 179–238	49. Ways of Sawall	PC/ 230–40
22. Jidrash in Kashfa	KS/ 239–51; PC/ 1–7	50. Patternfall Battlefield	PC/ 240

relationships of beings, and a high confidence in the actions he takes. These traits should serve him well in his new position. He learns from others around him, accepting easily the knowledge others pass to him, but he will not be readily influenced by that knowledge to act against others.

His work is surely not over, and if change does come to the poles of existence, it will have to pass with his acknowledged regard.

METAL BALLS, MANDOR'S

Dark metallic spheres that Mandor, oldest stepbrother of Merlin, had carried with him when he first walked the Logrus in the Courts of Chaos. They are used to gain control over another being and influence him or her in certain ways. They have other unique capabilities, as well. The metal balls have become so closely associated with Mandor that his Trump, held by Merlin, shows him with three of them in his gloved hand. (SC, 29)

We have a clear example of the usefulness of these dark metal balls in the journals written by Merlin. After Merlin discovered that Nayda, older daughter of the Begman prime minister, was a possessing entity, he surreptitiously contacted Mandor by Trump. When Merlin brought Mandor through to his room in Amber, Mandor used the balls immediately to incapacitate the entity. Mandor sent a metal ball to circle the air around Nayda so that she would be unable to move but could still answer questions put to her. The encirclement appeared to involve some pain, or, at least, physical distress, because the entity moaned, fell to her knees, and dribbled spittle from her mouth uncontrollably. While in that position, the entity told Mandor what kind of being it was.

At Merlin's request, Mandor allowed the entity a measure of relief, letting the metal sphere drop to the floor and circle her at ground level. Mandor ordered the entity to sit in a chair, and the sphere followed and continued to circle her and the chair as she moved.

Mandor spoke to Merlin about the control he had over her:

"It cannot vacate that body . . . unless I release it. And I can cause it any amount of torment within my sphere of power. I can get you your answers now. Tell me what the questions are."

"Can she hear us right now?"

"Yes, but it cannot speak unless I permit it."

"Well, there's no point to causing unnecessary pain. The threat itself may be sufficient. I want to know why she's been following me about." (SC, 180)

Although they put this question to her more than once, she either refused or was unable to explain her purposes. Mandor propelled a second ball to hover in front of her face, saying, "Let the doors of pain be opened." (SC, 181)

The ball began circling her head, and she cried out in pain. Unable to watch her suffering, Merlin asked his brother to halt the process. At Merlin's request, Mandor allowed Nayda to speak freely, and she asked for a towel to wipe her face. Mandor stopped Merlin from passing the towel to her, explaining that he shouldn't reach within the circling balls. Mandor tossed the towel to Nayda.

Even under Mandor's threat of killing the entity with his balls, it or she indicated it was under a compulsion that prevented its telling its purpose before Merlin. However, Nayda came up with the solution of confiding in Mandor privately, and he agreed. Afterward, Mandor told Merlin that it was best that he not learn of the entity's purposes. When Mandor and Merlin had finished with her, Mandor placed Nayda in a deep sleep and put her on Merlin's bed in a second room.

Somewhat later, Merlin surprised Coral, Nayda's younger sister, when she was examining her sleeping sister. Coral had removed a metal ball, which she said had been in Nayda's hand, resting across her chest. The removal of the ball permitted the entity to speak, although she seemed unable to move and her eyes remained closed. After Mandor returned and noted that Merlin had the Jewel of Judgment, Nayda sat up and called out.

Nayda was able to stand and move freely. Mandor called out, "Who's been tampering with my spell?" (KS, 193) Merlin opened his hand containing the metal ball that Coral had removed. It flew directly to its master.

Nayda suddenly rushed toward Merlin, grabbed the Jewel of Judgment, and ran out of the rooms into the corridor. Mandor sent his balls after her, and Merlin's artificial construct, Ghostwheel, also gave chase.

In the face of an immense representation of the Logrus, Mandor's balls acted to halt the entity, now carrying the Jewel of Judgment. In spite of the potency of the metal balls, Ghostwheel was able to nullify their hold on the entity by slipping into a tighter circle around her. The three metal balls dropped to the floor and rolled ineffectually away, while Ghostwheel took control and gave protection to the entity.

After a confrontation between the Powers that destroyed part of Castle Amber, Mandor recalled his balls. He used them to levitate himself and the injured Coral to King Random's quarters.

At the Keep of the Four Worlds, Mandor made use of the metal balls in various ways. They can grow in size and smash through walls, so that a mage could use them as a means of escape from confinement. In order to allay the fiery destruction of the Keep, Mandor tossed a ball toward the burning structure. It bounced, grew, made a tremendous noise at each bounce, and rumbled through the Keep. The fires abated, dampened by the rolling ball. When the huge ball had quieted the flames, it returned to its normal size and bounced back to Mandor's hand.

This is the extent of our understanding of Mandor's balls. In spite of our limited knowledge, it is clear that they represent Mandor's personal method of magical performance, and they continue to serve him well.

MINOBEE, DUCHESS BELISSA

Head of the House of Hendrake in the Courts of Chaos. The husband of Duchess Belissa, Duke Larsus, was killed at the Patternfall War at the hands of Prince Julian.

The duchess, like most of the men and women of the Ways of Hendrake, was inured to the fortunes of war. In fact, Belissa Minobee was as redoubtable and sanguine as her husband had been in all things military. She took pride in her martial prowess and her warrior integrity. Thus, she held no grudge against those who had been the adversaries of the

Courts, but were now allies. This was a beneficial attribute, since she also lost her eldest son, Lord Borel, Master of Arms of Hendrake, in the same war.

Duchess Belissa countenanced the forming of a chapel dedicated to Prince Benedict of Amber by members of the House of Hendrake. Benedict had been the acknowledged commander of Amber's forces at the Patternfall battle, and it may be that the late duke had had some admiration for the Amberite leader before that engagement. Of course, the duchess has expressed admiration for the military skills exhibited by Benedict at the great battle. It is even conceivable that she has made a study of all of Benedict's campaigns.

Besides the late Borel, Duchess Belissa had given birth to two other sons who reside in House Hendrake. She also has a stepson and stepdaughter who were her husband's children from a previous marriage. The House is quite large, consisting of many cousins, aunts, and uncles. They are such a large and close-knit House that, in a sense, the duchess's influence in the Courts is bolstered by that. Belissa even counts the House's lineage to Amber as being significant: Benedict had brought forth heirs in House Hendrake through his link to Lintra, great-grandmother of Dara. Since Dara of the House of Sawall is associated with Hendrake on her maternal side, and Merlin is the son of Corwin of Amber, Hendrake's sphere of influence is even stronger.

While Belissa Minobee has not expressed an interest in succeeding to the Crown in the Courts, certain quarters acknowledge the right of the House of Hendrake to rule after the House of Sawall has relinquished its power. However, the duchess remains discreetly aloof to such future possibilities.

MOIRE

Queen of the undersea city of Rebma, the mirror image of Amber. She permitted Corwin to walk the Pattern there when he had lost his memory. Moire had punished Random at that time for having taken her daughter from Rebma and then abandoning her. His punishment was to remain in Rebma for one year after being wed to a blind noblewoman of the realm. For a time, when Eric was ruling in the true city, there were rumors that Moire was to become

Eric's consort. This was never realized, and Moire has rarely left her kingdom under the sea.

A strikingly beautiful woman, Moire was best described by Corwin, who was suffering from amnesia and thus was seeing her with fresh eyes when brought to Rebma.

> "A woman sat upon the throne in the glassite room I almost recalled, and her hair was green, though streaked with silver, and her eyes were round as moons of jade and her brows rose like the wings of olive gulls. Her mouth was small, her chin was small; her cheeks were high and wide and rounded. A circlet of white gold crossed her brow and there was a crystal necklace about her neck. At its tip there flashed a sapphire between her sweet bare breasts, whose nipples were also a pale green. She wore scaled trunks of blue and a silver belt, and she held a scepter of pink coral in her right hand and had a ring upon every finger, and each ring had a stone of a different blue within it."
> (NP, 79–80)

While Corwin described Moire's voice as a "lisping, soft, flowing thing," (NP, 80) she spoke severely to them. Her reproof that the three of them were "outcasts of Amber" (NP, 80) hints that she may have known a good deal of the political maneuverings evolving in the true city at that time.

Deirdre pleaded their case, and the Queen of Rebma was attentive when she learned that Eric of Amber would be adversely affected by what they intended. In Rebma, as Moire stated, the usurping ruler of Amber was hated almost as much as Random was. As Deirdre explained about Corwin's loss of memory, Moire became sympathetic. She was willing to allow Corwin to walk the Pattern in Rebma to restore his memory.

As for Random, she was quite stern and uncompromising about his fate. In brief, she recounted the story of Random's seduction of her daughter Morganthe. Random came as a friend and charmed her daughter to go with him to visit other shadows. She had returned alone to Rebma, pregnant with Random's child. After the birth of their son, Morganthe had killed herself. Queen Moire had seen to the raising of her grandson, Martin. Of all the citizens of the undersea city, Martin was the only one who successfully walked the Pattern there. With his new-

found power, Martin had bidden farewell to Moire and the only home he had known and went off to travel in Shadow.

Moire's pronouncement to Random, standing before her, was unyielding: "Therefore, I will punish thee . . . You shall marry the woman of my choice and remain with her in my realm for a year's time, or you will forfeit your life." (NP, 82)

She was gentler and kinder in her dealings with Corwin. When she visited Corwin in his bedchamber, Moire spoke of the music of the legendary Corwin. Although she told him that she couldn't imagine a prince of Amber feeling love, she recognized that ability in Corwin. If it came to supporting a successor to the throne of the true city, she would willingly throw her support to him. Before Moire showed Corwin, Deirdre, and Random the way to the Pattern, she had shared intimacies with Corwin in his room.

We have no record of Moire's responses to the further endangerment of Corwin, nor of Random's actions, during Eric's rule in Amber. She may have remained aloof and silent when Random walked Rebma's Pattern with a crossbow, determined to end Eric's reign. Perhaps Moire quietly observed the change in him while he lived with her blind kin, the Lady Vialle. It's even possible that she approved of Random's attempt to assassinate Eric, particularly when Vialle encouraged the act. All of this, however, is uncertain.

She has remained close with Llewella, sister of Corwin, who was born in Rebma, and with Vialle, who became queen of Amber. They frequently visited Moire, and she welcomed them enthusiastically. In spite of her desire for isolation from the political climate of the true city, she continued to feel concern for the fortunes of Corwin. She was eager to hear what Vialle and Llewella could tell of the shadows and King Random's problems. However one views Moire's coldness toward Amber and the other shadows, she has always been loyal and caring toward Llewella and Vialle. Their concerns about the realms above the sea would surely be reflected in Moire's heart.

MOONRIDERS OF GHENESH

A barbaric people who had attempted an invasion of Amber long ago and were repelled by the combined armies under the leadership of King Oberon and his son Benedict.

They were called "Moonriders" because many of them were seen riding large spherical beasts that flew the skies during their attack. Those who fought and died in Amber were all male, so it has been surmised that their females were subservient and remained in their homeland, tending to household chores and caring for children. While the males had distinctly individual features, in the main they were short by Amberite standards, quite broad with as much fat as muscle on their frames, and were covered with short but thickly matted hair. Their noses were thick and blunt, and their eyes were far apart, with large black pupils.

All that we know about the Moonriders out of Ghenesh comes to us secondhand from reports written after the fact and from soldiers who had been told about the battle by older soldiers who, in turn, had heard about it from aged veterans of the campaign.

In order to accomplish the defeat of the Moonriders, Benedict had traveled to Ghenesh to learn what he could. When he returned, he informed his men about just those things they needed to know to plan their strategy. Apparently, the Moonriders were the most savage of several tribal clans that settled in various regions of Ghenesh. The other tribes were just as primitive, but those in contact with the Moonriders had developed a servile posture in order to prevent wholesale slaughter at the hands of the Moonriders. They had an uneasy peace with that savage clan because the Moonriders preferred to live off the labor of others instead of systematically gathering foodstuffs and other necessities for themselves. Thus, the neighboring clans were coerced into offering tribute periodically, avoiding any further contact than was needed.

Early in their prehistory, the Moonriders had evolved a symbiosis with numerous kinds of wildlife that foraged in and around the vast forests. This symbiosis enabled them to become dominant over the other clansmen, which led to the arrangement of plunder and tribute that was their way of life. One of the more vicious animal-symbiots in their employ was the bulbous, flight-bound creature from which the name "Moonrider" was derived. This beast has a brain that is not quite half the size of a scavenging vulture, with instincts that are similar. Unlike the vulture, however, it will strike at a living

prey, tearing the flesh with pincerlike mandibles at its "head." It has no other friend except the savage males of this single clan on their entire world. Nothing has ever been learned about this beast's method of propulsion and flight, but its appearance suggests locomotion on the order of balloons releasing air.

In Benedict's discreet observation of the Moonriders in their native habitat, he had found himself hard-pressed to keep hidden from the tribesmen and women. They had an uncanny knack of discerning an alien presence. When he recounted this to his officers, Benedict suggested that this unique sense may have been the way they had followed a route into Amber, for the Amberites had recently concluded certain transactions with a shadow congruent to Ghenesh.

Although it is difficult to determine why the Moonriders mounted an organized attack on Amber, it was probably akin to their instinctual need to plunder once they had discovered the affluence of other peoples. It may have been that small scouting parties had slipped into Amber before the large invasion force, and they had reported back to their fellow tribesmen of the wonders they had seen.

Once the main force of the Moonriders had entered Amber, their activities made their presence known rapidly to the Amberites, and soon afterward King Oberon prepared for war against them. While the Moonriders were versed in the use of crossbow, swords, and knives, they were ingenuous enough to believe that their numbers and sheer brutality were sufficient to conquering any enemy defenses. They remained oblivious to any surveillance and intelligence-gathering about themselves by agents of the enemy until they were trapped in a narrow pass above the Forest of Arden. Only a few men made an escape from death, never to return.

MORGANTHE

Daughter of Moire, Queen of Rebma, the city under the sea.

She was a delicate young girl when Random visited Rebma that first time. His easy manner and quick-witted charm engaged her completely. Initially, Morganthe's mother, Queen Moire, was also taken in by the young prince. This was soon changed, though.

One morning, Morganthe was not in her room. The young prince, who was also staying in the undersea palace, was not to be found. When the queen inquired, a very nervous servant informed her that Morganthe and Random had been seen leaving together through the golden gates of the city. A guard had just left his post and informed the first palace official he had seen, the servant who nervously told Moire.

A month later, a servant in Random's employ in Amber returned a sobbing Morganthe to her city. They placed her in the company of Rebma's guard with no explanation and departed again. Little was known of what happened thereafter until Queen Moire herself told the account to Corwin, Random, and Deirdre on their visit to Rebma. Moire had said,

> "Her suicide came some months after the birth of her son Martin. . . .
>
> "When Martin came of age. . . . because he was of the blood of Amber, he determined to walk the Pattern. He is the only of my people to have succeeded. Thereafter, he walked in Shadow and I have not seen him since." (NP, 82)

Shame was no doubt a powerful motivation for the young woman's decision to take her life. Considering the reconciliation and close bond that grew between Random and Martin, more is the pity.

MORGENSTERN

The mighty horse that was created by Julian of Amber. Larger than any ordinary horse, Morgenstern was a fearful sight chasing down any prey, Julian mounted lightly on his back. Julian had usually kept watch in the Forest of Arden for intruders during the reigns of Oberon, Eric, and Corwin. When not pursuing an invader to the realm, Julian rode Morgenstern on many a hunting expedition. The tables in the Royal Palace frequently were laid out with fresh meats from these hunts.

In his Chronicles, Corwin gave this description of the great beast: "Morgenstern was six hands higher than any other horse I'd ever seen, and his eyes were the dead color of a Weimaraner dog's and his coat was all gray and his hooves looked like polished steel." (NP, 57) On one occasion, Corwin found himself chased down by Julian on Morgenstern. This was when Corwin was driving a Mercedes-Benz with Random, finding their way through Shadow to Amber. Morgenstern raced along like a steam locomotive bearing down on them. At one point, he leapt over their Mercedes, forcing Corwin to swerve in order to avoid a collision.

Julian had trained Morgenstern quite deliberately to hate his brother Corwin. Dressing a captive in some of Corwin's old clothes, Julian had the man come at Morgenstern with a whip and a short pike. Morgenstern maimed the man, who subsequently died of his wounds, but the beast continued to despise the scent. Sometime afterward, when Corwin had joined Julian on a hunt, the great horse attempted to run Corwin down, very nearly trampling him to death.

Like so many enigmas in the true city, Morgenstern's origins are shrouded in speculation and rumor. Corwin searched his fragmented memory, at a time when he suffered from amnesia, to recall that Julian had created Morgenstern "out of Shadows, fusing into the beast the strength and speed of a hurricane and a pile driver." (NP, 56) While this is poetic, it doesn't explain anything of the manner in which Julian obtained his creation. Several members of Julian's patrol have put forward a variety of beliefs on the subject. Consequently, a scholar residing in Amber had published a letter presenting some of these beliefs. A portion of this document follows:

> "Julian's steed Morgenstern has been said to be a demon he had defeated and forced to take on the form of a horse and to serve him; while the late Prince Caine had once remarked to Vinta Bayle that Morgenstern had been the mount of a Valkyrie Julian had loved and lost in the destroyed Gotterdammerung shadow. . . . In general, the latter story is deemed to have more to it than the former, considering its source." (LETTER, ROGER ZELAZNY, 27 JUNE 1988)

Whatever the truth may be of Morgenstern's origins, he has proven himself to be loyal to no other master but Julian.

MURN

A small dairy village in the northern provinces of Amber.

Merlin, son of Corwin, had come across a stone marker at a crossroads, bearing the sign showing the distance to Murn, when he was near Baylesport. He had been horseback riding with Vinta Bayle, not far from her home, Arbor House.

Murn is one of many such farming communities in the north. The villagers subsist on crops they grow, and they trade much of their produce for other goods in neighboring townships. In order to keep up with a profit market, the farmers of Murn specialize in raising cows and goats for milk and milk products. Supply led to demand, and the village thrived and grew. Most of the large farm owners developed large tracts of grazing land for their animals, maintaining crops on the remainder of their land.

The fertility of the northlands provide for great opportunities for hardworking citizens. Not a few farmworkers earned enough to purchase their own land. The entrepreneur has been known to cultivate some unique product from his crops, and has progressed sufficiently to become a gentleman farmer.

Most of the milk and milk products of Amber come from Murn.

NAYDA

Older daughter of Prime Minister Orkuz of Begma. From the time she was old enough to do so, Nayda acted as her father's secretary, handling much of the documentation of his political affairs.

While no one in the Royal Palace remembers meeting Nayda on any former visits to the true city, she had some brief conversations with servants and courtiers when she accompanied her father on his last official visit. However, it has since come to light that a possessing entity had inhabited Nayda's body on that visit, so that any impressions given to those in the Royal Court were false.

On the occasion of Orkuz's state visit, Merlin recorded his first impressions of Nayda:

"Nayda's was a more pleasingly sculpted version of his [Orkuz's] face, and though she showed the same tendency toward corpulence, it was held firmly in check at an attractive level of roundedness. Also, she smiled a lot and she had pretty teeth." (SC, 56)

Merlin indicated that she had very dark hair and a full-length red-and-yellow gown that allowed her shoulders to go bare. Because she was possessed of a demon-entity at that time, she queried Merlin about his enemies and the dangers in which he had recently been involved. The entity was there to protect Merlin from harm, and, obviously, this possessed Nayda simply echoed those concerns.

Nevertheless, the entity that has been described in Merlin's journals is known to make use of its host's knowledge for its own ends. Therefore, given our understanding of Begman politics, it appears likely that the real Nayda was privy to files, kept in her home shadow, on various members of the Royal Family. Nayda spoke of having studied such files:

"I read through your [Merlin's] file several times. It's kind of fascinating." . . .

"It's no secret that we keep files on people we're likely to encounter in our line of work. There's a file on everyone in the House of Amber, of course, even those who don't have much to do with diplomacy. . . .

"Your early days are glossed over, of course, and your recent troubles are very confusing. . . .

". . . If your problems have ramifications that may involve Begma, we have an interest in them. . . .

"We have very good intelligence sources. Small kingdoms often do. . . .

". . . I was trying to discover whether I might be able to offer you assistance." (SC, 110-11)

At dinner in the Royal Palace, the possessed Nayda asked Merlin about the whereabouts of her sister Coral. Of course, the entity was concerned about any peril that would involve Merlin. Coral's disappearance while having been seen accompanied by the young lord would be worrisome to the possessing creature within Nayda. During the state banquet, the possessing entity continued to press Merlin for information. She indicated that she could help in eliminating persons that Merlin felt endangered him. There may have been something in that comment that implied the particular methods that might conceivably be used in Begma, and to which the true Nayda would have been privy. On the other hand, the creature may have been referring to its own unique powers. The possessed Nayda was, after all, maintaining a clandestine exchange with Merlin, wary of eavesdroppers from among the others in the Begman party.

While Merlin was conversing with Nayda on several occasions in the Royal Palace, he wondered at her relationship with her sister Coral. She seemed not to care about any immediate danger that Coral was in after Merlin explained the manner of her disappearance. Nayda seemed equally unconcerned when he told her that Coral's actual father appeared to be the late King Oberon.

Much later, while revealing the truth to Coral about Nayda, Merlin learned about the sisters' relationship:

> "Your sister was very ill awhile back, wasn't she?"
>
> "Yes," she [Coral] replied.
>
> "She was near death. At that time her body was possessed by a *ty'iga* spirit—a kind of demon—as Nayda no longer had any use for it."
>
> "What do you mean by that?"
>
> "I understand that she actually died."
>
> Coral stared into my eyes. She didn't find whatever she sought, and she took a drink instead.
>
> "I'd known something was wrong," she said. "She hasn't really been herself since the illness."
>
> "She became nasty? Sneaky?"
>
> "No, a lot nicer. Nayda was always a bitch."
>
> "You didn't get along?"
>
> "Not till recently." (KS, 165–66)

Although it is virtually impossible to separate the entity's interest in Merlin from any romantic interests that Nayda may have had in him, Merlin recorded a poignant statement that she made. One may view this confession as having some remnant of truth, if one accepts the possibility that the creature was drawing upon Nayda's true background:

> "Your file . . . It was . . . fascinating reading it. You're one of the few people here close to my own age, and you've led such an interesting life. You can't imagine how dull most of the things I have to read are—agricultural reports, trade figures, appropriations studies. I have no social life whatsoever. I am always on call. Every party I attend is really a state function in one form or another. I read your file over and over and I wondered about you. I . . . I have something of a crush on you. I know it sounds silly, but it's true. When I saw some of the recent reports and realized that you might be in great danger, I decided I would help you if I could. I have access to all sorts of state secrets. One of them would provide me with the means of helping you. Using it would benefit you without damaging Begma, but it would be disloyal of me to discuss it further. I've always wanted to meet you, and I was very jealous of my sister when you took her out today." (SC, 131)

The death of the actual Nayda is certainly a tragedy for the Begman prime minister and his family. It is an odd circumstance, if Orkuz will ever be made aware of it, in which his older daughter no longer remains alive; yet a magical being in her form and voice remains active and aware. None in Amber at this time knows whether or not the prime minister has been told. It is a very delicate matter, and it would probably be best if Orkuz remembers his daughter as she was in earlier days.

NEVER WED A HENDRAKE LASS

One of several songs well-known in the Courts of Chaos. This particular song refers to the House of Hendrake. It appears to be an ode to the military spirit of both men and women in that House.

Our knowledge of the music of the Courts is quite limited. In recent years, however, Merlin had brought some of their musical compositions to the Royal Palace in Amber. King Random, on occasion, had expressed an interest in hearing melodies of that distant realm.

NEVER WED A HENDRAKE LASS

Tread light o'er when 'y go to the bat-tle field.

Hen-drake folk when they go, die be-side their wo-men.

On the field Hen-drake men fight be-side their wo-men.

War like form in the clash, Hen-drake wo men

in their ar-mor de fend. Oh, brave las-ses to the

end, brave-ly fight-ing to the end. Dough-ty souls to the

last. No, ne-ver do 'y wed a Hen-drake lass.

© 1995   Alice Christy

Counter to what the title of this song suggests, its lyrics are not cautionary in nature. A pleasantly rhythmic tune, its lyrics describe the women of the House of Hendrake as sharing the pride of battle with their men. No special privilege is given to, nor is any accepted by, the females when they join in a military engagement. They bear the hardships and burdens of war as well as any man.

The caution of the title is not directed to a nobleman of the Courts who wishes to take marriage vows with a woman of Hendrake. Rather, it is a warning to any warrior on the battlefield not to take too lightly the prowess and rigor of a female adversary of the House of Hendrake.

OBERON

Royal liege of Amber for millennia. Much of the conflict in the true city in his latter days was caused by discord among the legitimate heirs to his throne. These troubles were accelerated by the machinations of lords of the Courts of Chaos who intended to destroy Amber and rule over the remaining Shadows. Oberon was able to free himself from captors in a shadow near the Courts, and he traveled with his son Corwin for a time in a shapeshifted form. After regaining the Jewel of Judgment, King Oberon revealed himself to his children. Asserting martial law, he orchestrated the Patternfall battle, then attempted to repair the damaged primal Pattern in order to restore Order. Although the Amberites won the battle at Patternfall, and the king succeeded in clearing the Pattern, Oberon died in the process.

Much of King Oberon's early days have been made so much a part of an arcane, mystical past that it is virtually impossible to separate historical fact from bygone lore. In an historian's eyes, the belief that Oberon was born of Dworkin and the unicorn would be seen as dubious at best. Some scholars maintain that the unicorn has shapeshifting abilities and was therefore able to bear Dworkin's child while in the form of a lovely young maiden. Those who scoff at this notion speculate that the unicorn may have led a young lady to Dworkin, but otherwise the patron beast of Amber had nothing to do with the birth of Oberon.

When he was quite young, Oberon took over the governing of Amber from Dworkin, who never was too interested in administering to a whole society of people. He willingly let young Oberon handle the details of government. Aside from formalizing many of the legal and commercial affairs that continue to be followed to this day, Oberon often visited other shadows. His dalliance with women in the shadows was, quite literally, legion. He also spent a long enough term in shadows of a given time period, usually involved in some military campaign of conquest, that shadow vesions of himself influenced whole nations and affected their history. Thus, he, or a shadow of himself, had become Gilgamesh of Uruk, Alexander of Macedon, Henry of Navarre, and any number of others on more than one shadow Earth.

Even among his own children Oberon was an enigma. Corwin thought of him with a sense of ambivalence, as indicated in his Chronicles:

"I do not really know what Dad was. He never encouraged intimacy, though he was not an unkind father. Whenever he took note of us, he was quite lavish with gifts and diversions. But

he left our upbringing to various members of his court. He tolerated us, I feel, as occasionally inevitable consequences of passion. Actually, I am quite surprised that the family is not much larger. The thirteen of us, plus two brothers and a sister I knew who were now dead, represent close to fifteen hundred years of parental production. There had been a few others also, of whom I had heard, long before us, who had not survived. Not a tremendous batting average for so lusty a liege, but then none of us had proved excessively fertile either. As soon as we were able to fend for ourselves and walk in Shadow, Dad had encouraged us to do so, find places where we would be happy and settle there. This was my connection with the Avalon which is no more. So far as I knew, Dad's own origins were known only to himself. I had never encountered anyone whose memory stretched back to a time when there had been no Oberon. Strange? Not to know where one's own father comes from, when one has had centuries in which to exercise one's curiosity? Yes. But he was secretive, powerful, shrewd—traits we all possess to some degree. He wanted us well situated and satisfied, I feel—but never so endowed as to present a threat to his own reign. There was in him, I guessed, an element of uneasiness, a not unjustifiable sense of caution with respect to our learning too much concerning himself and times long gone by. I do not believe that he had ever truly envisioned a time when he would not rule in Amber. He occasionally spoke, jokingly or grumblingly, of abdication. But I always felt this to be a calculated thing, to see what responses it would provoke. He must have realized the state of affairs his passing would produce, but refused to believe that the situation would ever occur.''
(GA, 92–93)

Although Oberon was not intentionally cruel to the women with whom he engaged in sexual liaisons, he was, for the most part, uncaring. In some cases, he acted out of a willful urge for sexual gratification without concern for the consequences, as when he raped Deela the Desacratrix while she was his prisoner. He may never have realized that Dalt, who attempted an invasion of Amber, was his son. His ignoble treatment of a few of his wives has

been documented, showing something of a raffish nature. There were such instances as his controversial marriage to Harla, when his wife Rilga had grown old and was coerced into leaving the true city for a country retreat. Before that, Oberon ended his marriage to Cymnea, as if it had never occurred, and married Faiella, creating much distress among the children of those unions. A vague rumor of an indiscretion in the shadow called Begma was recently proved true. The younger daughter of Prime Minister Orkuz and his wife Kinta was able to walk the Pattern in Amber, offering proof to local gossip that her biological father was King Oberon. As a Pattern-ghost version of Oberon told Merlin, he had sired forty-seven illegitimate children in his travels to various shadows. (KS, 57) Those are the ones he knew of.

While Oberon had quite different interests from Dworkin, he nevertheless learned much from his father about the arcane Arts. Even later in life, he showed his grown children that he retained fantastic powers that were beyond their own considerable talents. He seemed to have as much knowledge as Dworkin about the potentials of the Jewel of Judgment. Besides having shapeshifting ability, Oberon was able to work the shadows even upon Mt. Kolvir; he influenced the actions of others as much through personal appeal as through some incomprehensible foreknowledge of events; and, he illustrated his physical prowess by subduing Gérard, the most physically indomitable of his sons, in a fistfight that no other person could have won.

In spite of the vastness of his knowledge and strengths, and also, in spite of his seeming lack of concern for his wives and their issue, Oberon showed his frustration and worry over an errant son: Corwin. Late in his life, Oberon told Corwin that he had settled upon him as his successor. This awakening feeling for Corwin may have been felt initially at the time of Corwin's disappearance centuries ago. Corwin had gone hunting with Eric shortly after they had had a heated argument. Eric returned alone, claiming that Corwin had decided to go wandering in Shadow for a substantial length of time. Long after the fact, Brand explained to Corwin what had happened as Corwin's absence grew overlong:

"Dad suspected Eric of having slain you. But there was no evidence. We worked on this feeling, though—a word here and there, every now and then. Years passed, with you unreachable by any means, and it seemed more and more likely that you were indeed dead. Dad looked upon Eric with growing disfavor. Then, one night, pursuant to a discussion I had begun on a totally neutral matter—most of us present at the table—he said that no fratricide would ever take the throne, and he was looking at Eric as he said it. You know how his eyes could get. Eric grew bright as a sunset and could not swallow for a long while. But then Dad took things much further than any of us had anticipated or desired. In fairness to you [Corwin], I do not know whether he spoke solely to vent his feelings, or whether he actually meant what he said. But he told us that he had more than half decided upon you as his successor, so that he took whatever misadventure had befallen you quite personally. He would not have spoken of it, but that he was convinced as to your passing." (SU, 153)

Troubled as he was by the unresolved disappearance of Corwin, Oberon was also concerned with the erratic activities of Dworkin. During his reign, Oberon had had to get his father out of one difficulty or another, sometimes having to mediate with officials in another shadow to accomplish Dworkin's release into his custody. Dworkin began spending much time in the unique region of the primal Pattern. Oberon wondered about his preoccupation, went there, and had a long conversation with him. Becoming increasingly uncomfortable with Dworkin's fixation on the original Pattern, and his philosophical talk of his mind affecting the Pattern in the same way the Pattern affects his mind, Oberon asked him directly why he was so obsessed with the place. Dworkin later told Corwin: "I told him I'd thought of a way to destroy Amber. I described it to him, and he locked me in." (NP, 162) Actually, Oberon wanted to keep Dworkin secured for his own safety, and he had arranged quarters deep within a cave of the mountainside near the original Pattern. He provided his father with all the comforts he could desire, and he visited him often.

A new set of problems began to emerge, quite literally into Amber. Strange creatures seemed to be slipping into the true city from other shadows, and Oberon, as well as the rest of the Family, found the occurrences worrisome. Flora had talked about the situation to Corwin:

"We have always been alert for peculiar things slipping through. Well, for several years prior to your recovery, more such things than usual seemed to be showing up in the vicinity of Amber. Dangerous things, almost invariably. Many were recognizable creatures from nearby realms. After a time, though, things kept coming in from farther and farther afield. Eventually, some which were totally unknown made it through. No reason could be found for this sudden transportation of menaces, although we sought fairly far for disturbances which might be driving them this way." (SU, 104)

In Oberon's search for the cause of these "monster migrations," (SU, 104) he may have gone to examine the primal Pattern, or else Dworkin may have summoned him. At that point, Oberon would likely have discovered the blot on the Pattern and recognized that as the primary cause for the disturbances. With Dworkin talking of having to destroy the Pattern by his walking it and killing himself, Oberon arranged a guard for the primal Pattern. It is not known how Oberon summoned Wixer, the purple griffin, or if he created the beast from Shadow, but he assigned Wixer to watch the Pattern and prevent Dworkin from setting forth upon it.

Brand admitted to Corwin that he had planned to get Oberon out of Amber with the help of the lords of the Courts of Chaos. It is likely that Fiona also assisted in this part of his plan. The method used to draw the king away has always been unclear. More than one factor may have been involved in assuring Oberon's departure, particularly in leading him in the proper direction. Dara spoke of what may have been the strategy:

"I only know that Brand effected his presence in a shadow far enough from Amber that he could be taken there. I believe it involved a fake quest for a nonexistent magical tool which might heal the Pattern. He realizes now that only the Jewel can do it." (CC, 19)

Since Oberon left abruptly, without leaving orders, those of the Family not involved in the plot were extremely doubtful. Benedict told Corwin that the king had simply vanished from his quarters one morning, his bed still made. (GA, 86) Julian spoke to Random about their father's disappearance, saying that Eric had been acting on his behalf, but they were operating without any real authority. (SU, 34) Since they had been trying to raise Oberon on his Trump for many months without success, they believed him dead. Gérard remembered seeing his father in the library of the palace on the night before he disappeared. He recalled that Oberon was wearing the Jewel of Judgment, but Gérard later saw it in Eric's possession. (SU, 106) These various perspectives made Oberon's departure appear suspiciously forced and part of some insidious intrigue.

When Corwin joined Bleys in Avernus, he tried to reach his absent father by Trump. He was surprised to have made contact, and he recounted their brief exchange in his Chronicles:

"Father?" . . .

"Yes . . ." Very faint and distant, as though through a seashell, immersed in its monotone humming.

"Where are you? What has happened?"

"I . . ." Long pause.

"Yes? This is Corwin, your son. What came to pass in Amber, that you are gone?"

"My time," he said, sounding even further away.

"Do you mean that you abdicated? None of my brothers has given me the tale, and I do not trust them sufficiently to ask them. I only know that the throne seems open to all grabbers. Eric now holds the city and Julian guards the Forest of Arden. Caine and Gérard maintain the seas. Bleys would oppose all and I am allied with him. What are your wishes in this matter?"

"You are the only one—who—has asked," he gasped. "Yes . . ."

" 'Yes' what?"

"Yes, oppose—them. . . ."

"What of you? How can I help you?"

"I am—beyond help. Take the throne. . . ."

"I? Or Bleys and I?"

"You!" he said.

"Yes?"

"You have my blessing. . . . Take the throne—and be quick—about it!"

"Why, Father?"

"I lack the breath—Take it!" (NP, 110)

Thus, Corwin learned that his father was still alive. When he saw Benedict in Avalon, Benedict said that he had received some tentative contact from Oberon also. They were both at a loss, however, as to how to help him.

In some undisclosed manner, Oberon was able to escape from the shadow where he was kept prisoner. He may have been preparing some form of deception, using abilities of which the leaders of the Courts of Chaos were unaware. Oberon was also assisted by Dara, after she had met Random's son Martin and decided to shift allegiance. Dara may have known his secret location and managed to reach him without interference. Once they joined together, Oberon was able to flee. It was then that he chose an unusual course of action.

Using his ability to change his form, Oberon altered his appearance to become an old foe of Corwin's: Ganelon. It may be difficult for us to comprehend the processes he undertook, or even to be sure how he might have begun. Apparently, he learned of Corwin's predicament in the dungeons of Amber, perhaps from Dworkin. Prior to the Patternfall battle, he spoke to Corwin about the shadow that Corwin had traveled to after escaping from Amber:

"The country [of Lorraine]? A good job, I thought. I worked the proper shadow. It grew in strength by my very presence, as any will if one of us stays around for long—as with you in Avalon, and later that other place. And I saw that I had a long while there by exercising my will upon its timestream." (CC, 27)

As Ganelon, Oberon was able to travel with Corwin, guiding him to discover certain truths, and assisting him in facing obstacles that needed to be overcome before the final stages of the Patternfall War could be put into motion. Along the way, Ganelon made sure that Corwin returned from Tir-na Nog'th with a tool that Benedict would later be able to use to wrest the Jewel of Judgment from Brand. He saw to it that Corwin and Random would locate the primal Pattern and realize what had been done there to create the problems facing Amber. And he arranged for Corwin to meet Dara, and engage in a union that led to the birth of Merlin, an heir to the realms of the Courts of Chaos and Amber.

By pretending to be Ganelon, Oberon was able

to actualize events that otherwise would have been left to mere chance. A grander scheme would be accomplished as a result of each of the little incidents that Oberon had directed in his role as Ganelon. However, his guise had a secondary benefit, one that touched Corwin on a personal level. Corwin spoke of this to the now-revealed Oberon:

> "For a time we rode as comrades . . . Damned if I did not come to like you then. I never had before, you know. Never had guts enough to say that before either, but you know it is true. I like to think that that is how things could have been, if we had not been what we are to each other." (CC, 24)

Deliberate plans were set into motion even before Oberon revealed his true self. While he was still disguised, he received a Trump contact from Bleys. Reverting to his true form, Oberon discussed some of his plans with Bleys. The plans he carried forward with Bleys meant his creating a special shadow in a location that would not be swept up by the Storm of Chaos. Only he and Bleys would have access to that shadow.

He met with Dworkin and with Dara, then assigned Dara to present his orders to those of his children he had not already spoken to personally. When Corwin made Trump contact, then came to Oberon at the primal Pattern, Oberon wasn't entirely prepared for what his son attempted. Corwin grabbed the Jewel of Judgment and ran for the Pattern, intending to repair the blotted area himself. Both Oberon and Dworkin exerted their psychic powers to prevent Corwin from accomplishing this. Still, Oberon was gratified by his son's gesture. He gave Corwin orders to await him in a private place, and Corwin told him he would be at his cenotaph.

Before going to meet Corwin, Oberon prepared a special projected image of himself with a message, fixed to take effect automatically within a specific time frame outside the Courts of Chaos. Then he went to Kolvir to meet with his son. Using Corwin's blood, Oberon created a small red bird that would know Corwin and be able to find him in any shadow to which he traveled. Oberon wanted Corwin to hell-ride through Shadow in order to create an appropriate distance. Corwin would need that distance to keep ahead of the destructive Death Storm that would inevitably come. The red bird would convey the Jewel of Judgment to Corwin, wherever he was, when Oberon had finished with it. That arranged, Oberon returned to the primal Pattern.

Dworkin may or may not have been a witness to Oberon's walking the primal Pattern with the Jewel of Judgment. Although we know that Oberon succeeded in repairing the Pattern, we cannot be sure that place remained standing while the Death Storm arose and swept over the shadows. In the projected message that Oberon had prepared, which appeared in the sky above the battlefield, Oberon's voice announced:

> "I send you this message . . . before undertaking the repair of the Pattern. By the time you receive it, I will already have succeeded or failed. It will precede the Wave of Chaos which must accompany my endeavor. I have reason to believe the effort will prove fatal to me." (CC, 113)

Soon after, when the funeral procession passed along the black road toward the Citadel of the Courts, it was confirmed that King Oberon's life had ended. Corwin recorded:

> Then, as my eyes drifted back along those lines, another shape emerged from the glistening curtain. It was a cart draped all in black and drawn by a team of black horses. At each corner rose a staff which glowed with blue fire, and atop it rested what could only be a casket, draped with our Unicorn flag. The driver was a hunchback clad in purple and orange garments, and I knew even at that distance that it was Dworkin. (CC, 121–22)

With due reverence, the body of Oberon was returned to the realm that gave us all birth.

At the far end of the Main Concourse in the true city, a statue of King Oberon was erected, its eyes gazing regally over the people he governed for so long.

OLD JOHN

Veteran soldier and emissary to the late King Oberon and King Random of Amber.

In younger days, Old John (simply John then) had been a very close friend to the youthful Oberon. Oberon often took him on his travels through Shadow. They fought together in many battles, and it is believed that John commanded one of the regiments that helped Benedict rout the Moonriders of Ghenesh. After Oberon ruled Amber for quite some time, Old John remained one of his few confidants. Often the king would send Old John on clandestine missions in other shadows, usually to gather information for use in some future military campaign. Old John proved his efficiency many times over.

During the reigns of King Eric and Lord Corwin, Old John remained in the background. He preferred to keep silent counsel and be wary of the shift of the political wind. Although there is no clear record of it, it is believed that he served in Benedict's troops during the Patternfall battle. With the matters of Oberon's death and Random's new kingship settled, Old John made it a point to let King Random know that he was giving his total allegiance to him. Random appreciated this, knowing of his long friendship with Oberon. After taking up his duties as king, Random included Old John on diplomatic missions with him.

Old John was most instrumental in expediting matters during the time of shadow Kashfa's political unrest. Given political immunity, he was able to take action that would not, under ordinary circumstances, be officially sanctioned. Such was the case in his "unofficial" activities in Kashfa while in the king's employ, for which he was fully protected although no attachment was made to any party's jurisdiction.

King Random had taken Old John into his confidence about his wishes concerning Kashfa at that time. Basically, the king wanted Old John to find some information that would be useful in preventing the former queen of Kashfa, Jasra, and her son, from regaining the throne. Old John had to surreptitiously ask around in Kashfa's capital city about influential people who might have governmental connections. On his agenda, also, was to seek some detail that would act as a linchpin for Amber's becoming the benefactor of Kashfa. Understanding the task in hand, Old John traveled to Kashfa and quietly plied his way through its thoroughfares.

When he returned to Amber, Old John brought some worthwhile news with him. He informed the king of the situation concerning Eregnor. Random had heard of it before, through his experience with the shadow kingdom Begma. Both Begma and Kashfa claimed the piece of land known as Eregnor, and they had gone to war over it for several centuries. Just at that time, however, the present ruler of Kashfa, General Jaston, was negotiating with Begma over Eregnor. Jaston was willing to give it up for the payment of old war debts. From Old John's sources, it appeared that these negotiations were widely unpopular among the upper classes of Kashfa.

By Old John's estimation, Kashfa was on the verge of civil war. Such an event would make for a perfect climate for the return of Queen Jasra, who would unite the people by eschewing these dealings with Begma. Random wanted to avoid this at all costs. He asked Old John for recommendations. The emissary presented a list of nobles who had some association with the government over the years. He recommended that Random support one of the men that he had marked and find a way to depose General Jaston.

Old John had another piece of news, incidental in nature. Dalt the mercenary, son of the late Deela, who often harassed Begma, was still around causing trouble. In addition, it was rumored that he was a son of King Oberon from the days when Deela had been captured and imprisoned in Amber.

The king thanked Old John, praising his efforts, and dismissed him. Old John promptly headed for town, eager to take in some ale and a good meal.

It was on this occasion that Merlin, son of Corwin, encountered the emissary at Bloody Bill's, in the Harbor District. Old John was already there, enjoying his dinner, when Merlin entered and took a nearby table. Old John was maintaining the custom of keeping his sword half out of his scabbard beside him, noticed that the young man was not aware of the custom, and also saw two unsavory-looking sailors eyeing them.

Not turning to look at the young man, Old John quietly spoke to him: "Free advice. I think those two guys at the bar noticed you're not wearing a blade, and they've marked you for trouble."

"Thanks." (BA, 65)

Old John did not show any of his fascination in his expression as he watched the young man cause a long sword, scabbard, and belt to appear from nowhere.

Old John said:

"Neat trick, that ... I don't suppose it's an easy one to learn."

"Nope."

"It figures. Most good things aren't, or everybody'd do 'em. They may still go after you, though, seeing as you're alone. Depends on how much they drink and how reckless they get. You worried?"

"Nope."

"Didn't think so. But they'll hit someone tonight." (BA, 66)

As it happens, the sailors followed Old John out of the restaurant. The veteran of Amber's wars dispatched them outside, and the fact that one of the would-be thieves made it back to Bloody Bill's before he died spoke more of the man's stamina than any mistake on Old John's part.

When Random called Old John to his quarters, he had a new set of orders for him. Old John was to accompany Random, Benedict, and a small diplomatic party (which included bodyguards from Amber's Royal Guard) to Kashfa. In making clear Old John's part in the business, the king explained that he was throwing his support to one of the nobles on the emissary's list, Arkans, duke of Shadburne. Cautioning care and subtlety, Random explained that Old John was to await his signal and then precipitate an accident that would remove Jaston from the throne.

With his usual quiet mien, Old John joined the small expedition. In Kashfa, he showed no expression and spoke to no one while Jaston hosted a state dinner for the Amberites. Old John pretended to drink heartily from his goblet of wine, but actually it was left untouched.

At the end of the meal, Old John seemed to dally, standing off in a corner, as people rose and departed the hall. He watched and waited, while Random and Benedict continued sitting and talking to Jaston. He saw Random begin to yawn, observed as the general reciprocated. Smiling, Jaston rose, bade them goodnight, and left the room. Old John noted when Random gave him a slight nod. Quietly, he left the hall.

People heard a brief scream and a heavy impact shortly thereafter. Palace servants were first to find the body of their king below a winding staircase.

On orders, Old John returned to Amber with Benedict and his contingency force. He continues to serve King Random in the true city, living a life of solitude and stealth.

ORKUZ, DOMINÉO

Prime minister of Begma, recipient of the silver Gedering Award for International Relations from the Royal Diplomatic Society of Begma.

Prior to King Random's interest in forming a treaty with the country of Kashfa, Amber's policies had been quite acceptable to the nation of Begma and its prime minister. Orkuz became directly involved in applying an influence in Amber when Random acted to form peaceful relations with the newly proclaimed monarch of Kashfa. Concern over the effects of a treaty with Kashfa brought Prime Minister Orkuz and his party to the Royal Palace in Amber unexpectedly earlier than had been arranged officially. Although little is known on record of the prime minister's motives for arriving unannounced at the Royal Palace, and at a time when King Random was known to be in Kashfa, certain rumors have been acknowledged as strong possibilities. In fact, it is uncertain whether Orkuz had been attempting to embarrass the absent sovereign by inducing some scandal during his stay in the palace, or if he simply hoped to present a strong enough protest against a treaty with Kashfa that King Random would be willing to rescind any agreement already made with Kashfa.

The following background information on Prime Minister Orkuz comes from official files to which the Begman government allows access by members of the Royal Court of Amber and their designates:

Dominéo Orkuz inherited his position as prime minister from his father, Frekalin Orkuz, who had inherited it in turn from his father, Podrely Orkuz. Although part of the public record, the history of Dominéo Orkuz's great-grandfather is never spoken of, and it remains surreptitiously hidden on a separate, yellowed document kept in the back of the official file. It was the great-grandfather, Roddrin Orkuz, who had been the impetus for turning the family toward public office. When Roddrin Orkuz died, he had been a judge advocate, scholar of international law, and a highly respected ambassador.

However, he had begun life as an orphan and ward of the state. As a boy, he was troublesome, ran away from the state institution where he lived, and took to begging and stealing. Some undetermined factor changed him when he reached adolescence, and he spent much of his time reading books of law in the libraries in and around Begma. He had a great affinity for legal studies, and this led to his being apprenticed to a minor government official who practiced international law. Although Roddrin Orkuz held many menial jobs in his young adulthood, including those of hired farmhand and gravedigger, he also pursued a career in various law offices, mainly in a clerical position. His brilliant mind and pleasant appearance eventually led to his applying for a battery of exams in international law, which he passed splendidly. From that point on, his career moved from one success to another. The family name was not merely a respected one, but during his lifetime, it became synonymous with public service and diplomacy. His son carried on the family legacy, and his son after him, but each of them endeavored to conceal in some dark recess of time the mean beginnings of the great Roddrin Orkuz. His great-grandson, Dominéo, often felt the insecurity of that open secret, and feared that some action of his might betray that impoverished, menial background. Thus, snobbery and haughtiness had become a characteristic part of him. He would never allow any tincture of crudeness to show through his icy exterior.

Dominéo Orkuz married late in life to a young woman named Kinta Boecton, fifteen years his junior. He was delighted when their union brought them a daughter, Nayda, although he soon after became fully immersed in the politics of the state and had little time for his family. With the birth of his second daughter, Coral, several years later, Orkuz showed a fondness for her that was, nevertheless, somewhat distant. In truth, he seemed quite surprised at this second birth, but he treated both daughters with equal detachment.

Absorbed as he was with important matters of state, Orkuz built his personal success on the development of a vast file of governmental personnel, in Begma and environs, but also in Amber. Acknowledgment of the true city, after all, invites comparison; and, by comparison, Begma is a small kingdom. Orkuz knew that the Begman military capability could in no way compare to Amber's might.

As a small kingdom, and one with old ties to Amber in trading agreements, maintaining intelligence was more than a prime factor in diplomatic relations, it was a practical necessity. Thus, Orkuz worked hard to maintain and update his files, and his influence grew in accordance with the growth of classified data on personnel in Begma, Kashfa, Deiga, several other nations of the Golden Circle, and, of course, Amber.

Although Prime Minister Orkuz has been known to be quite charming in public, he is known as a solemn individual whom it would be better not to cross. Not very tall and tending to be stocky, Orkuz seldom smiled. His frown, actually, masked much inner turmoil in recent times, caused by both personal and political troubles.

Troubles with the nearby country of Kashfa have been long-standing. In the past, Begma and Kashfa had times of peace, and harmonious trade agreements had been reached. But there were frequent occasions of hostility between the two neighbors. Their rivalry, in part, was due to Begma's long association with Amber as an ancient member of the Golden Circle. Kashfa enjoyed no such arrangement, and this was a primary cause of dissension between them. Political intrigues, spying, and covert activities have become part of the fabric of relations between Begma and Kashfa. At times, some secret maneuver has turned into a public skirmish and led, in turn, to a bloody war. The smoothing-over process between these times of bloodshed has become less frequent during the course of Orkuz's tenure.

While Begma has jealously guarded its status in the Golden Circle for centuries, the Begmans' concern over the problem of Eregnor has lasted nearly as long. During Orkuz's term of office, Eregnor has also been a sore point in any argument with the Kashfans. Most recently, when King Random of Amber intervened to form an alliance with Kashfa, the situation with Eregnor and Kashfa's joining the Golden Circle have been worrisome dilemmas fixed prominently in the prime minister's mind.

These several troubles aside, other areas in Begma have added frown lines to Orkuz's grim face. The comparatively recent phenomenon of Begman women taking a great interest in political affairs may be traced back to the time of the Days of Darkness, when Amber was at war with the army of the Courts of Chaos. Shadow worlds, like Begma, that were close enough to Amber to be aware of this cataclysmic upset, wished to exert an influence over affairs touching upon Amber to a greater extent than ever before. All the citizenry in Begma felt the need to have their voices heard in any future confluence of interests between Amber and Begma. One significant result of this general sentiment was an influx of women into the political sphere. Since Orkuz is a confirmed member of the old school, he had initially found this state of affairs, with women holding positions of power in the government, abhorrent. In later years, he has allowed his attitude to soften, so that he merely finds the situation distasteful. He has had little choice, when the Begman ambassador to Amber, and her assistant, are both females, and the president of his advisory council, Edena Cortz, who reports directly to the Begman king, is also a female. In the face of all this, Orkuz keeps his distress hidden, while dealing with the feminine gender in his government as little as possible.

Almost in self-defense, Orkuz insisted on engaging his daughters in affairs of state at a young age. He proved a lenient mentor, allowing his daughters to choose their separate interests of their own accord, as long as such interests also served the state. His older daughter, Nayda, proved very adept in handling documentation; researching and filing the minutiae of appropriations, agricultural reports, and trade figures. On the other hand, his younger daughter, Coral, thirsted for activity, exploration, and physical challenge. Orkuz encouraged this "tomboy" quality in Coral, and supported her in her training in armed and unarmed combat.

While Orkuz does not seem the fatherly type, he has taken pleasure in the way his daughters have grown into roles befitting the children of a statesman. When Nayda became deathly ill a short time before Orkuz's planned visit to Amber, the prime minister was dreadfully worried. While his wife Kinta remained in Nayda's room almost constantly, Orkuz paced his own room restlessly, unable to sleep, and frequently looked in on his daughter. His eyes reflected his worry and sleeplessness as he prepared for his state visit to Amber. It was with great relief that he greeted the news of Nayda's rallying. His pleasure was apparent when Nayda insisted on accompanying him on his trip in her official capacity as secretary. When Coral also requested to join them, eager to visit the true city, Orkuz was more than willing to take her. This sudden good fortune

in his household changed him enormously: rather than dreading a distasteful but necessary journey to assert their rights of state, he felt nearly magnanimous in deciding to make friendly gestures to the royal household, knowing that Random would be absent. He decided to agree with an old proverb that, translated to English, would be closest in meaning to: "You can catch more flies with honey than with vinegar."

No doubt all these troubles: family, domestic, and political, weighed heavily on Orkuz's mind as he greeted Queen Vialle and the members of the court on his visit to Amber. As soon as diplomatically feasible, he spoke to the queen about "recent distressing news concerning Kashfa," (SC, 57) and tried to further smooth the way by proposing a toast "to the ancient alliance between Amber and Begma." While clearly expressing his concern about the proposed alliance between Kashfa and Amber openly, he was attempting to address the problem with restraint and good grace. He was frankly charmed by Queen Vialle and found himself entranced by the remarkable stories of Bill Roth who described, in detail, life in the shadow called Earth.

Astute in understanding human nature, Prime Minister Orkuz hoped that the presence of his two daughters would help open the means for resolving the Kashfa problem. In the back of his mind was the possibility that Coral and Nayda would fix their eye on the younger members of the court in order to uncover data that would be useful in negotiation. At the same time, he hoped to learn enough about Amber's stance from those most likely to know the maneuverings of Amber's politics. By making his visit without prior warning, he hoped to encounter some ingenuousness on the part of the queen. However, he found her rather intractable. He had more luck learning about military tactics from Gérard and several minor legal problems with which Mr. Roth had been involved.

The success of Orkuz's visit has not been fully assayed, but he has seemed satisfied that his course of action has been correct, and he would like to continue a fact-finding tour of the true city as a means of protecting the Begmans further in Amber's future plans.

OSRIC AND FINNDO

The two eldest sons acknowledged as being the late King Oberon's issue. They died in a long-ago war against Shadow-beings that attacked Amber's borders on flying wyvern.

Of those still living in Amber today, only Lord Benedict and the demented wizard Dworkin remember the brothers Osric and Finndo. For his own reasons, Benedict refuses to shed any light on the history of his two older brothers.

These few bare facts remain in official records kept by anonymous scribes writing several centuries after the deaths of Finndo and Osric:

"Finndo is firstborn to Cymnea of Karm and Oberon of Amber. Osric is name of second son, born————years later.... Osric and Finndo continue to live within the palace and retain rights as princes of the realm, although their mother is banished.... Lady Gea, sister of Cymnea, is forced to take her own life by her uncle, King Lasli of Karm. Prince Osric proclaims vendetta; kills Lasli's two sons and a loyal councillor before he is taken prisoner. Oberon claims right of judgment; finds Osric innocent of wrongdoing under ancient custom allowing rights of personal combat in such matters.... Oberon orders his two oldest sons to the Northern front during fiercest of the battles with the Spotted Men of Gahmery.... Osric and Finndo are buried with full honors on the Northern Plain."

Long ages ago, Dworkin told numerous stories in court of people and events of the early days in Amber. Several of these included tales of young Oberon, of his lustiness with women, and the consequences thereof. Often these tales were bawdy and riotous, but sometimes Dworkin spoke with such seriousness that one might take an odd story or two for fact. Since it is believed that Dworkin's mind was addled even that long ago, it is nearly impossible to determine the truth of any of the sorcerer's accounts.

Here, distilled from stories told over a great span of time, is Dworkin's history of Osric and Finndo:

"There were other sons born to Oberon before Finndo. At least three others. I don't remember their names. They all died young—accidents or disease. I remember there was one daughter. Delicate little creature. She died in a boating accident when she was a mere child.

"From what these courtiers and scribes say today, you would think that Finndo and Osric were twins. They were born nearly ten years apart, did you know that? They were as far apart as they could possibly be in the way they acted, their feelings about things. Finndo was older; not wiser, but more stable, willing to accept things as they were. Osric was the hothead, always arguing with his father, his brother, others in the court. He was a royal troublemaker, no doubt about that.

"Little Benedict was a mere toddler when Oberon first began sneaking off into Shadow and returned with that little black-haired vixen Faiella. Hot-tempered Osric argued fiercely with the king, while his older brother stood glaring, holding his mother closely to give her comfort. Quite a tableau, that. The truth was, Cymnea was terrified of Oberon by that time. Kings lopping off the heads of their wives for the sake of convenience was in fashion just then. Finndo was trying to allay her fears. He was convinced this was a mere flirtation on his father's part. He tried to persuade his younger brother not to take any drastic action. It was through Finndo's intercession that Osric had not acted at once against their father. Only infrequent shouting matches marred the tense silences between father and sons.

"During the time that Benedict grew to adolescence, Oberon spent more time away, and when he was back, he was in his chambers dallying with the same dark-haired girl. Cymnea had since taken up quarters in another wing of the palace.

"As infrequently as Oberon appeared in court at this time, young Finndo tried to be politic. He probed his father about his intentions with this young lady, but the king's explanations were not forthcoming.

"With all the best intentions, Finndo went seeking the young lady. I know, for I was a fly on the wall of Faiella's chamber when Finndo came knocking. Faiella was quite some lady, I can tell you, for she had that poor boy seduced and lying in bed with her when Oberon walked in. The king raged at them with such a furor that they both gathered up their clothes and ran out of the chamber and down the corridor in separate directions.

"Later, of course, Faiella calmed the king, placing the blame firmly on Finndo's momentary passion. Oberon believed her every word. He agreed to do nothing to harm his errant son, but Oberon never forgot.

"That delightful young vixen worked her charms on Oberon, smoothing over his sometime outbursts about finding her sleeping with his son. Faiella used his jealousy to her advantage; she urged him to consider ending his marriage with Cymnea and marrying her. The king had been reluctant to formally file for divorce from Cymnea because of old trade relations he had with her uncle, King Lasli of Karm.

"Faiella decided on a drastic strategy to remove such cautious considerations from Oberon's mind: she became pregnant.

"Eric's birth was the impetus for Oberon's calling for a unique contingency meeting of his cabinet. Besides legal advisors and royal councillors, Oberon requested the attendance of the foremost religious officials of the Way of the Unicorn. The session continued for days behind closed doors, and Osric, Finndo, and their mother waited with irritated impatience, having heard the gossip about the meeting's purpose.

"When the cabinet had ended the session, no word was spoken of any decision. Not until a fortnight later, when public proclamation was posted, did Cymnea and her sons learn of the judgment.

" 'According to Royal Charter,' the proclamation read, 'and in accordance with the laws set down by the sacred Way of the Unicorn; when a queen has brought grievous displeasure on the person of the king, her husband, her life is forfeit. Inasmuch as the king does not wish to visit too harsh a judgment on his wife, the queen, he may declare the marriage nullified *ab initio,* to the extent that the state declares that no such marriage has ever taken place. In necessity thereof, the queen must absent herself forever from the court and from the farthest precincts of the royal state of Amber. Decision effective immediately; any disobedience of these terms means immediate forfeiture of life

of the aforementioned person heretofore referred to as "queen." End of proclamation.'

"The next day, the royal nuptials were announced. Oberon and Faiella were married six days later.

"Osric would have murdered Oberon immediately after seeing the proclamation were it not that his older brother informed him of their mother's disappearance. She had taken what she could carry and fled. No one knew where she had gone. She had vanished completely. Osric and Finndo searched for her in all the shadows in which she was known to have occupied herself. Their search was as thorough as anyone's could have been. They returned to Amber distraught and exhausted, to learn that the royal wedding had taken place in their absence.

"When the king's messenger and an escort of six royal guards found the two brothers and led them to the King, Finndo and Osric presumed they were about to be executed. They entered the king's presence resigned to their fate. Instead, they were greeted with exuberant cordiality. Oberon had wisely given them an audience without the presence of the new queen, but with all the other members of the court in attendance. Smiling widely, Oberon assured the brothers that they were welcome guests and were invited to remain in the Royal Palace for as long as they wished. No mention was made of their mother nor of the status of their inheritance to the throne. Oberon continued to wear a smile as he summarily dismissed them with a gesture. Osric and Finndo were escorted back to their chambers by the guard.

"While these matters stood in an arena of tension and uncertainty, several other events were occurring at about the same time. Fierce half-men/half-leopard creatures had found an entrance from their shadow, Gahmery, into Amber. They massacred a couple of villages in the north before they were discovered by the vigiles of Amber. The Spotted Men of Gahmery were vicious fighters who used crossbows and rode on the backs of wyvern in their attacks on the villagers. Oberon had to mobilize much of his military might to fight the Spotted Men. The wars against Gahmery forced Oberon to concentrate all his efforts on the northern plains. For a long while in the early stages of the warfare, Oberon quartered himself with his men on the field of battle. The fighting was so heated and terrible, though, that after several months Oberon's generals insisted that he return to the safety of the Royal Palace. Oberon reluctantly agreed.

"During the period of this attack from Shadow, problems had erupted in the near shadow of Karm. Although the details are unclear, apparently the niece of King Lasli of Karm, a young girl named Gea, had disgraced herself. Whatever had happened, Lasli had been angered and intended to mete out stringent punishment. In order to avoid facing his punishment, the Lady Gea drank poison and died. It happened that Lady Gea was the sister of Cymnea, mother of Osric and Finndo. This time, Osric did not wait to be appeased by his brother and went off seeking blood. In the palace of Karm, the guards made note of Osric racing toward the king's throne room, but, as he was a frequent visitor known to them, they did not halt his progress. When he reached the throne room, Osric demanded to see King Lasli. Councillor Gorbae of Fienwuhl, Lasli's closest advisor and friend, did not give Osric a satisfactory answer, and Osric killed him. It happened that this was a festival day in Karm, and most of the court, including the king, was in the town square, so that the palace was nearly deserted. Osric went storming through the palace rooms, his fury increasing as he found no one else upon whom to vent his anger.

"It is said that King Lasli's young sons were at play in rooms adjacent to the king's, and they had been left unattended by the Court matron for a few minutes. When they heard Osric's noisy approach, they hid. Incensed as he was, Osric didn't bother to check who he murdered as he thrust his sword into each small boy in hiding. He stormed away, not knowing he murdered the two young princes of Karm.

"Before Osric had left the palace, the matron gave loud alarm, and the guards seized the visitor, who was striding through the halls in such fury.

"King Lasli, in his grief and anger, made brief work of a compulsory trial, and Osric was prepared for execution. Only when Oberon himself, under royal guard, marched to the palace of Karm, was Lasli reluctantly willing to give up his charge.

"No one knows what was said between Oberon and Osric when they were alone in the palace of Amber upon their return, but Oberon convened a hearing with members of the court attending shortly thereafter. After several hours of testimony by various witnesses, Oberon dismissed the case. He cited the Code Duello, which allowed for vendetta between parties when a legitimate grievance had been proven. Such was the situation between Osric and the House of Karm. The decision was addended to the Royal Charter, and the case formed a precedent still referred to today.

"Did I tell you of Lady Cymnea? I think not. She was found, you see. By Oberon. Or perhaps she was never really gone. I never knew all the facts. I can tell you, however, that King Oberon summoned Finndo by secret messenger to his chambers. Oberon acted deliberately cryptic as he swore Finndo to absolute confidence. He led the young man through dark passages, down a circuitous route to the dungeons below. There, in a small filthy cell, was Finndo's mother, in chains and unconscious. Finndo cried out and Cymnea stirred but was too weak to respond.

"Oberon's proposal was simple and straightforward. Oberon would free Cymnea, have her secretly escorted to Karm where she could live out a comfortable life, on condition that Finndo volunteer to join the front lines on the Northern Plain against the Spotted Men. Finndo quietly accepted.

"When these things came to pass, Osric was greatly surprised to find his mother alive and well and on her way to Karm, and his older brother missing. His hatred of Oberon had been quelled, you see, after his acquittal. Naturally, he had hoped for an opportunity to avenge his mother's disgrace, but his need for vengeance had been blunted by the vague possibility that he might find himself in favor again in the Royal Court.

"Uncertain as to why Oberon would order his older brother to a terrible and bloody war, Osric found himself unable to address the king about the matter. When attempting to see Oberon in his rooms, he was told that Oberon had gone to some distant shadow. No, they couldn't say where. Osric was kept entirely in the dark.

"He couldn't find anyone willing to carry a message to his mother in Karm, and he could not travel there himself in safety. His only alternative, an alternative that was probably left open intentionally by the king, was to seek his brother on the northern plains.

"No actual witnesses can be found to tell what happened when Osric reached the battlefield. Too much was going on for anyone to take particular note, you see. One wounded sergeant who was sent back to Amber proper reported a man fitting Osric's description asking about his brother. That was all.

"Only after the attackers from Gahmery were killed to the last man, were accounts made of the dead. The military corps that was gathering the bodies made the claim that Finndo's body was found just six feet away from his brother's. When informed of the recovery of his sons' bodies, Oberon sent a brief message that they were to be given full military honors by the army. And then they were to be buried at the site of battle. This was done; stone markers with the royal banner of Amber over them, remain there to this day.

"From then until the day of his death, Oberon never spoke the names of Finndo and Osric."

PATTERN OF AMBER, THE

The great design of Order, which resides in a large chamber far below the Royal Palace in Amber. Those of the blood of Oberon walked this Pattern ages ago to become Pattern-initiates, able to walk in Shadow and draw from its supernal forces to summon up inner reserves. Those in Amber have always known about the reflected forms of the Pattern that lay in Rebma and Tir-na Nog'th, holding the same potentialities as the one in Amber. Somewhat later, it was discovered that there is an underlying reality to Amber, and that reality is where the primal Pattern is located. That original design had

been devised by Dworkin in bare rock under an open sky. Aside from these forms of the Pattern, there are shadows near to Amber which contain imperfect designs upon congruent sites of the original. These representations have been called Broken Patterns, and there is danger in trying to walk them and hold the image of such a design, even for a talented adept.

The Grand Pattern in Amber can only be reached from inside the Royal Palace. One must take a major corridor toward the rear of the palace to the marble dining hall. Walking through the dining area to the rear, one will find a dark narrow corridor where a guard is posted. The guard would readily permit any member of the Royal Family to enter beyond that point, but he would log one's entry, to be reported to the captain of the guards. There is a door and a platform before the stairs. At that passage, one can usually find a lantern to take along. From there, one must descend a long, winding stair deep into the recesses of Mt. Kolvir in almost-complete darkness. Lanterns are set along the walls at intervals of forty feet. At the bottom of the stairs is a guard station, consisting of a table, a bench, some racks, and a number of footlockers. The cells of the dungeons are to the left of this area. One would head to the right to locate a large, dark tunnel. Using a lantern, one could make out the gray stone of the cave walls, and would have to watch carefully the progress of side passages as one continues. At the seventh side passage, one need go only a short distance to reach the heavy, metal-bound door. A large key hangs from a steel hook in the wall to the right. After unlocking the door, one must push very hard with all one's strength. It opens inward, into the chamber. As one steps inside, the heavy door slowly closes.

The Pattern has a bluish glow on the black, shimmering floor. It takes up nearly all of the chamber, 150 yards long and a hundred yards in diameter. One's first impression is that it resembles an intricate maze of the kind one draws upon with a pencil on paper. There are numerous curves and some straight lines one can see clearly. A person could feel the potent forces welling from the design. One of the Blood Royal would begin the Pattern walk at the far corner of the room from the doorway.

One needs to be composed when one comes to the decision to step upon that gleaming design embedded in the polished black floor. The initiation is

quite difficult, no matter how many times one engages in it. Against those areas of great resistance
on the Pattern, one must continue to breathe normally and keep moving at a steady pace. Electrical
sparks and accompanying shocks might be dis-
tracting, at times rising all about one, but these
should be ignored. Memories will begin to flow
through one's mind, and one should accept these,
but continue the walk. Stopping on the Pattern
would be disastrous.

If one wished to have a set of directions for walking the Pattern, from the far corner to its center,
those directions might be given in the following
way:

1. Place one's left foot upon the single line that
begins the Pattern at the corner. One will
feel the energy surging immediately, apparent in the sparks given off.

2. Take a second step, and the crackling of
electrical energy continues. At the third step,
one begins to feel the pressure of resistance.

3. Move along a line that curves abruptly back
upon itself. Resistance will increase.

4. Proceed into the First Veil, taking ten steady
paces against heightened resistance. One
must apply a continuous forward pressure
against it to keep moving.

5. Making it through the First Veil is an
achievement. When past it, the pressure is
eased for a while. One will find a flood of
memories filling one's thoughts.

6. Follow a long curve, then a sharp switch-
back. Take two steps, a turn, three more
steps, and the pressures increase again.
Sparks of energy rise to the level of one's
knees. One is well into the Pattern at this
point, and it is difficult to see out at the rest
of the chamber.

7. One reaches a straight line which is the beginning of the Second Veil. As the electrical
energies rise to one's waist, the resistance
becomes terrible.

8. Take three sharp turns. One's effort will be
taxed to the limit as one presses through
these turns.

9. As one steps into a curve, the resistance will

gradually lessen. One has prevailed over the
Second Veil.

10. Proceed for ten paces, going through a swirling filigree of fire.

11. Emerging from this filigree, one commences
the Grand Curve. The sparks continue to
crackle about one's waist, and one feels hot
and cold in turns.

12. Advance into three more curves, a straight
line, a series of sharp arcs. At this point, one
has power over shadows.

13. Step into ten dizzying turns, a short arc, a
straight line, and one is before the Final
Veil.

14. Take ten paces through the Final Veil, needing enormous effort against awful pressure.
The electrical energies rise to one's shoulders, then to one's eyes.

15. Leaving the Final Veil, there is a short arc,
then three steps more, and one must struggle
against heavy resistance, after which, one
has reached the center of the Pattern.

Having completed the circuit, standing in the center of the Pattern, one is changed. The Pattern leaves
its mark upon one. The process that occurs is like
being torn apart and then reassembled into a purer
form. As a result, a person can travel the shadows,
or imagine any shadow of one's desire and transport
there at will. One's endurance and physical stamina
are greatly enhanced, so that one appears to remain
youthful for a much longer time and have greater
strength than an ordinary human.

Once a person reaches the Pattern's center, one
must teleport away. One may transport anywhere
within the palace, or Amber, or any shadow of one's
dreams. That is part of the gain one has achieved
by the initiation. This means that one has power
over Shadow, and over the beings that inhabit it. A
curse would have actual effect, even upon Amber
itself to some extent.

With training, one can summon up the Sign of
the Pattern in the preparation of magical incantations, which may be used defensively or offensively
against adversaries. Other powers seem to vary from
person to person, perhaps determined as much by
genetic predisposition as by the variety of skills that
one may choose to develop. For instance, there is

a high variance in individual initiates' abilities to regenerate parts of their own bodies, although the capacity to do this seems present in all the members of the Royal Family.

Some of the potentialities of initiation in the Pattern were not readily apparent to many of the children of Oberon, but they have since learned that they are empowered to perform them. A Pattern-initiate can learn to draw Trumps of his own style that he may use to transport himself instantly to another location. These Trumps are also routinely used for communication. One may also focus one's energies to alter one's own form. This skill depends a great deal on practice as well as concentration, and one must spend time in a shapeshifted form to learn to facilitate the altered sensory apparatus at one's disposal.

It is imperative for those who read this to understand that not everyone has the qualifications to walk the Pattern. A person not descended from Dworkin, or from the royalty in the Courts of Chaos, will be instantly destroyed upon setting foot on the Pattern in Amber. If those of the Royal Family seem superior to the rest of us, it is because, in truth, they are. The Pattern gives them that superiority, by virtue of their capability to change shadows and remake them in their own image.

PATTERNFALL WAR

The conflict between the lords of the Courts of Chaos and the Royal Family in Amber which culminated in an armed battle on a plain outside of the Courts. The existence of all of the shadows, as well as the true city, was at stake in the mounting incursion. Beginning as a collusion between the Chaos lords and members of the Family in Amber, the actual battle was a military tactic used to draw attention away from the repair of the primal Pattern by King Oberon.

For a long time, Prince Corwin believed that the curse he had spoken against the usurper Eric and Amber was the cause of the dark changes in the realm. He blamed his curse for the sinister appearance of the Valley of Garnath and for the terrible beasts that began to invade Amber from other shadows. When he discovered the smeared stain of blood on the primal Pattern, Corwin began to realize that other forces were at work as well. He learned that the blotted stain had opened a way, along a black road, for the minions of the Courts to pass into the true city. That stain was formed from the stabbing of Random's son Martin. The perpetrator, the conspirator who cooperated with the Chaos lords, was Brand.

Originally, Brand had been part of a triad in Amber, formed of Brand, Bleys, and Fiona, that had contacted the Courts in order to seek support in claiming the rule of Amber. Fiona and Bleys soon severed their interest in such an alliance, believing that Brand and those of the Courts were seeking something quite beyond their original intentions. Dara, who had been a vital part of the conspiracy, clarified the way that the Chaos lords saw the situation:

"Brand was given what he wanted, ... but he was not trusted. It was feared that once he possessed the power to shape the world as he would, he would not stop with ruling over a revised Amber. He would attempt to extend his dominion over Chaos as well. A weakened Amber was what was desired, so that Chaos would be stronger than it now is—the striking of a new balance, giving to us more of the shadowlands that lie between our realms. It was realized long ago that the two kingdoms can never be merged, or one destroyed, without also disrupting all the processes that lie in flux between us. Total stasis or complete chaos would be the result. Yet, though it was seen what Brand had in mind, our leaders came to terms with him. It was the best opportunity to present itself in ages. It had to be seized. It was felt that Brand could be dealt with, and finally replaced, when the time came....

"... I began to feel that the changes I had been told would be for the better would not simply result in a revision of Amber more along the lines of my elders' liking. They would, instead, turn Amber into a mere extension of the Courts, most of the shadows would boil away to join with Chaos. Amber would become an island. Some of my seniors who still smart at Dworkin's having created Amber in the first place are really seeking a return to the days before this happened. Total Chaos, from which all things arose. I see the present condition as superior and I wish to preserve it.'' (CC, 17–18)

Dara's change of heart toward Amber occurred after meeting Random's son, Martin, and King Oberon. Oberon had been led away to a distant shadow on a pretext arranged by Brand's cabal. There, Oberon was supposed to be kept confined while the Chaos lords enabled Brand to take control of Amber. Dara spoke of her contact with the late king:

"I met him during his—difficulties—some time back ... In fact, you might say that I helped to deliver him from them. This was after I had met Martin, and I was inclined to be more sympathetic toward Amber. But then, your father is also a charming and persuasive man. I decided that I could not simply stand by and see him remain prisoner to my kin."
(CC, 18–19)

Once freed, Oberon was able to maintain a measure of control over events on the Amber side of things that led to the great battle.

Traveling incognito, Oberon was with Corwin, observing his actions and those of his other children in and around the true city. Oberon arranged for the love affair between Dara and Corwin, which produced an offspring who could succeed Corwin to the throne. Through some means beyond mere providence, Oberon had seen to it that Corwin and Random discovered the blotted stain on the primal Pattern, and that Benedict received the odd, mechanical arm from Tir-na Nog'th. That strange arm provided the means by which Oberon regained the Jewel of Judgment. Only through the use of his mechanical arm was Benedict able to obtain the Jewel in a deadly confrontation with Brand.

When the Jewel of Judgment was again in his possession, King Oberon made himself known to his Family in Amber. Maintaining his secrecy, he continued clandestine plans already put into motion while telling Corwin and the others a bare minimum. He told Benedict to ready his troops in the mountains of the Courts of Chaos to prepare "a peremptory strike" (CC, 9). Similarly, Julian was to prepare to take his men through Shadow to the Courts. Random was assigned to join Julian in

Arden and depart with him. Through Dara, Oberon gave these orders to Gérard: "You are to remain here, Gérard, and see to the safety of Amber herself." (CC, 30) Oberon had also met secretly with Bleys, who everyone thought had died in a fall from Mt. Kolvir. The king had been supplying Bleys with men and provisions in a shadow of his own creation, coordinating Bleys's movements with the plans for Benedict's attack in the Courts.

Standing by at the primal Pattern, Fiona reported to Corwin what she had learned of Oberon's intentions there:

"I think Dad is going to try to repair the Pattern. He has the Jewel with him, and I overheard some of the things he said to Dworkin. If he makes the attempt, they will be aware of it in the Courts of Chaos the moment that he begins. They will try to stop him. He would want to strike first to keep them occupied."
(CC, 21–22)

Meeting with Corwin, Oberon prepared for a conveyance that would bring the Jewel of Judgment to Corwin once Oberon had completed his task at the primal Pattern. Corwin's orders were to hellride across Shadow to the Courts, bringing the Jewel with him in that roundabout way as a means of protecting it. Before initiating the process of repairing the Pattern, Oberon set into operation the presentation of his final words to all his kin at the Patternfall battle in the event he did not survive.

Corwin had hellrode ahead of the storm of Chaos, which was sweeping across the shadows behind him, ending their existence. Oberon's plan to have Corwin convey the Jewel of Judgment to the Courts was ruined by Brand. However, after snatching the Jewel away from an exhausted Corwin, Brand transported to the battle with it, thus fulfilling the king's goals, if inadvertently.

Reaching the mountains above the battlefield, Corwin had an excellent view of the fighting, which was already in progress. Here, therefore, is his perspective on the progress of that engagement:

I stood upon a hilltop beside a plain, a cold wind whipping my cloak about me. The sky was that crazy, turning, stippled thing I remembered from last time—half-black, half-psychedelic rainbows. There were unpleasant fumes in the air. The black road was off to the right now, crossing that plain and passing beyond it over the abyss toward that nighted citadel, firefly gleams flickering about it. Gauzy bridges drifted in the air, extending from far in that darkness, and strange forms traveled upon them as well as upon the black road. Below me on the field was what seemed to be the main concentration of troops. (CC, 102)

I saw Deirdre in black armor, swinging an ax; Llewella and Flora were among the archers, Fiona was nowhere in sight. Gérard was not there either. Then I saw Random on horseback, swinging a heavy blade, leading an assault toward the enemy's high ground. Near him was a knight clad in green whom I did not recognize. The man swung a mace with deadly efficiency. He wore a bow upon his back, and he'd a quiver of gleaming arrows at his hip. . . .
. . . They [the beast-men of the Courts] advanced, sweeping down the slope, reinforcing their lines, pushing our troops back, driving ahead. And more were arriving from beyond the dark abyss. Our own troops began a reasonably orderly retreat. The enemy pressed harder, and when things seemed about ready to be turned into a rout an order must have been given.
I heard the sound of Julian's horn, and shortly thereafter I saw him astride Morgenstern leading the men of Arden onto the field. This balanced the opposing forces almost exactly and the noise level rose and rose while the sky turned above us.
I watched the conflict for perhaps a quarter of an hour, as our own forces slowly withdrew across the field. Then I saw a one-armed figure on a fiery striped horse suddenly appear atop a distant hill. He bore a raised blade in his hand and he was faced away from me, toward the west. He stood unmoving for several long moments. Then he lowered the blade.
I heard trumpets in the west, and at first I saw nothing. Then a line of cavalry came into view. I started. For a moment, I thought Brand was there. Then I realized it was Bleys leading his troops to strike at the enemy's exposed flank.
And suddenly, our troops in the field were no longer retreating. They were holding their line. Then, they were pressing forward.

Bleys and his riders came on, and I realized that Benedict had the day again. The enemy was about to be ground to pieces. (CC, 105–7)

That stage in the battle, with the surprise onslaught of Bleys's cavalry out of Shadow, was the turning point. Benedict, Bleys, and Julian continued to lead the combined troops and prevailed over the Chaos forces.

Besides Corwin, several other members of the Royal Family detected the presence of Brand, wielding the Jewel of Judgment, in the heights near the Abyss. While Amber's armies overran the battlefield, Random, Deirdre, Fiona, and a number of others converged upon those heights. The problem of Brand came to a head when he managed to hold Deirdre hostage against any attack from his kin.

With Brand facing off against Random and the others in a stalemate, a huge projection of Oberon's face appeared above that great teeming plain. Fighting men on the field halted their skirmishes as the voice of Amber's king spoke. It addressed his children in the main. It began by explaining that he had prepared this message prior to walking the Pattern. Although he expected the arrival of the storm of Chaos, he expected that Corwin would use the Jewel to repel its ultimate destruction. Cryptically, Oberon's voice indicated that the choice of the succession in Amber would be left "on the horn of the Unicorn." (CC, 113) When the speech ended, and the form dissipated, Brand did not relent. He laughed at his siblings, uninterested in helping to rid the Death Storm that was rapidly approaching. In a surprising way, Brand was dispensed with, but it resulted in the loss of Deirdre's life and the Jewel of Judgment. The knight in green fired two silver-tipped arrows into Brand, and Brand died, falling into the Abyss, taking Deirdre and the Jewel with him.

Without the Jewel of Judgment to turn back the Death Storm, Amber's victory over the armies of the Courts seemed pointless. Resting amid the other members of the Family, Corwin observed the remainder of the battle on the plain:

The fighting appeared to be over except for a few isolated pockets of resistance by the enemy, and these were rapidly being enveloped, their combatants slain or captured, everyone moving in this direction, withdrawing before the advancing wave which had reached the far end of the field. Soon our height would be crowded with all the survivors from both sides. I looked behind us. No new forces were approaching from the dark citadel. Could we retreat to that place when the wave finally reached us here? Then what? The abyss seemed the ultimate answer. (CC, 116)

Corwin was filled with despair and fatigue as incidents unfolded before him on the heights. The knight in green, who had slain Brand, revealed himself to be Caine. He had used a shadow of himself to pretend his own death, so that he could observe his kin in secret. Then, Corwin and the others saw the long funeral procession of beings from the shadows, slowly marching along the black road toward the citadel. The aged Dworkin drove the funeral carriage that bore the coffin of Oberon. Shortly after the last of the procession entered the dark structure, a remarkable thing occurred.

The lovely white unicorn of Amber climbed out of the Abyss. Approaching the small group standing near that edge of the worlds, the unicorn could be seen wearing the Jewel around its neck. The beautiful creature came gingerly toward the Family, then knelt before Random, its horn nearly touching him. Random removed the Jewel from the unicorn, and then the creature galloped down the slope of the hill, disappearing. The members of the Family who stood beside him offered Random their allegiance.

Corwin helped Random become attuned to the Jewel, and then Random put all his efforts into turning back that storm. He succeeded, and the Trumps became active once more. Random was able to contact Gérard in Amber. Thus, the shadows stood once again.

The Concord between Amber and the Courts of Chaos was drawn up. King Swayvill and his councillors had met with King Random, with Benedict sitting in as counsel to the king. After careful review, the Concord was agreed to, and both parties signed. To this day, neither side has acted to breach the faith given with that signing.

PATTERN-GHOSTS

Artificial constructs of living beings created by the Pattern in order to do its will. Essentially,

Pattern-ghosts are agents of the Pattern used to interact with other humans directly when the Pattern has difficulty in doing so.

In his journals, Merlin described his first encounters with Pattern-ghosts as he traversed the unusual realm later referred to as the Undershadow. He had recently discovered that the Pattern was a sentient entity, and it was seeking his help. Since the Power known as the Pattern could not reach Merlin in the Undershadow, it employed the Pattern-ghosts to persuade Merlin to join it and make it stronger.

A Pattern-ghost of Corwin's dead sister Deirdre explained to Merlin what a Pattern-ghost was:

> "An artifact created by the Pattern. It [the Pattern] records everyone who walks it. It can call us back whenever it wants, as we were at one of the times we walked it. It can use us as it would, send us where it will with a task laid upon us—a *geas*, if you like. Destroy us, and it can create us over again." (KS, 108)

Merlin's unique entity Frakir noted that the Pattern-ghosts of Oberon and Dworkin that they had witnessed

> were pulsing energy fields within geometrical constructs . . . [and] the swirls—the geometrical constructs on which the figures were based—they reproduced sections of the Pattern at Amber. . . . Both figures were three-dimensional twistings of Pattern segments. (KS, 85)

Although the existence of a Pattern-ghost appears to be of short duration, its life can be extended, perhaps indefinitely. Merlin was able to maintain a Pattern-ghost version of his friend Luke Raynard by giving him his own blood to drink. The blood of one of royalty from Amber sustains a Pattern-ghost's existence, but only if drunk in sufficient quantities and within a limited time. The Pattern-ghost Deirdre took some of Merlin's blood, but it was not sufficient and she evaporated in smoke.

In Merlin's case, his veins also contain the blood of a Chaosite. If the fiery blood of a Chaosite touches a Pattern-ghost, he becomes a vortex of flame and enters oblivion. This was true for a Pattern-ghost version of Brand, who made the mistake of requesting blood in a place where it was volatile.

TABLE OF PATTERN-GHOSTS AS THEY APPEAR
IN DOCUMENTED CITATIONS
FROM THE JOURNALS OF MERLIN OF AMBER
AND THE COURTS OF CHAOS

Pattern-Ghost	Mission	Action Taken	Citation
Dworkin	Bring Merlin within the power of the Pattern	Reaching through Merlin's wards, begins to melt. Disappears when Merlin uses Logrus.	KS 55–56
Oberon	Set up Merlin as champion in conflict against Logrus	Merlin sends Logrus against it, causing explosion that ends its existence	KS 57–59
Corwin (A)	Bring Merlin beyond reach of both Pattern and Logrus	Using sword to break wards, duels with Merlin and knocks him out with sword's pommel	KS 61–63
Deirdre (A)	Make Merlin aware of his ability to intervene in scenes; Merlin discovers he can speak aloud	Negative image of Brand sacrifices her on bare slab and she screams while red blood ebbs from wound	KS 92–93
Brand	Obtain some of Merlin's blood to become more permanent; inform Merlin of the nature of Pattern-ghosts	After discussing Luke/Rinaldo, Merlin cuts wrist to give him blood, but Chaosite blood spreads fire that consumes him, turning him into a vortex that disappears	KS 96–102
Deirdre (B)	Inform Merlin of nature of Pattern-ghosts; direct him to right path of crossroads	After realizing Merlin is not Pattern-ghost, she takes some of his blood, but it is insufficient to maintain her. She disappears in a vortex.	KS 106–109
Caine (A)	Kill Logrus-ghost Jurt, who accompanies Merlin	Confirming Jurt's identity, he tosses a dagger at him. Merlin simultaneously throws a Chaos knife at Caine. He erupts into pieces which blow apart.	KS 117–118
Benedict (A)	Protect Merlin from Logrus-ghost Borel and allow him time to complete mission	Seeing that Merlin wears Jewel of Judgment, he duels with Logrus-ghost Borel to keep him occupied while Merlin and Jurt continue their mission	KS 141–142
Luke (A)	Warn Merlin away from Courts of Chaos. (Personal curiosity causes him to procrastinate on this mission.)	Joins Merlin in underground mausoleum, allies himself with Merlin and Pattern-ghost Corwin against Logrus-ghosts, accepts the task of guarding Corwin's Pattern after walking it with ghost-Corwin and Merlin	PC 72–95

Pattern-Ghost	Mission	Action Taken	Citation
Corwin (A)	Join Merlin and protect Pattern-ghost Luke from Logrus-ghost Borel; lead them to Corwin's Pattern	Knocks down Borel and flees with Merlin and Luke. After reaching new Pattern, admits to having been previous incarnations of Corwin seen by Merlin. Leads Merlin and Luke on walk of Pattern. Talks about Dara, then sets up Luke at '57 Chevy before going off.	PC 81–95
Luke (A)	Meet the real Luke Raynard and seek to aid him	After finding out about recent events from real Luke, agrees to take Luke's place in Kashfa after Pattern accepts Jurt as guardian	PC 143–44; 149–54
Benedict (B), Eric, Caine (B), and Gérard	Retrieve Coral from agents of Logrus at gray tower, to return her to Sign of Pattern	Gérard fights Logrus-ghost Chinaway and defeats him; others fight remaining Logrus-ghosts and defeat them with Merlin's help; Eric fights Dalt for Coral; Pattern-ghosts vanish when Sign of Pattern appears	PC 187–90; 192–94
Corwin (A)	Warn of Logrus intrusion via earth tremors under Corwin's Pattern; join Merlin to rescue real Corwin	Wakes Merlin to stop tremors from destroying Corwin's Pattern; goes with Merlin to Courts of Chaos; takes real Corwin's place when Merlin frees him	PC 212–26

It may be that the creation of ghosts taxes the Pattern. That is one reason why Pattern-ghosts, under normal circumstances, last only briefly. When Merlin used his special talents against four Pattern-ghosts, the Sign of the Pattern seemed coerced into making them vanish in order to make an appearance itself.

Interestingly, some of these ghosts appear to be strongly independent, while others are fully controlled and directed by the Pattern. While a ghost of Caine came into existence solely to kill the Logrus-ghost of Jurt, the Pattern-ghost of Luke was confused and uncertain of its origins, knowing only that it had a message to deliver to Merlin. This ghost-Luke avoided giving its message, hoping to maintain its existence by procrastinating the mission it was on. When Merlin gave it a sufficient quantity of blood, the ghost-Luke gained a full measure of autonomy from the Pattern. Its existence continued long after its mission was accomplished.

Currently, the absolute monarch of the shadow Kashfa may be a Pattern-ghost. Thus, one might say, a Pattern-ghost has an independent life after all.

PATTERN-LOGRUS CONFLICT

The ancient conflict between the unicorn of Order and the Serpent of Chaos. It had been considered that the shadows and their people were an afterthought, providing agents that could be manipulated to act out the continuing conflict. Because of recent disturbances in the balance between the two Powers, the hostilities have become much more agressive in the involvement of human agents. Merlin had become a focus for both Powers because he bears both the Pattern and the Logrus within him.

Dworkin certainly had an intimate understanding of the ages-long clash between the Powers, and he appears to be still around, having recently advised Merlin on the matter. In some mysterious way, Dworkin had consorted with the unicorn, giving birth to his son Oberon. Of course, Dworkin had created the primal Pattern with the help of the unicorn, which formed Amber and all of the shadows. He knew the true nature of the Jewel of Judgment, which was needed to formulate the Pattern.

In his journals, Merlin wrote of the unheard-of confrontation between the Signs of the Logrus and the Pattern within the Royal Palace in Amber. The Powers spoke, venting their wrath with accusations as to who caused the imbalance between them:

"Return the Eye of Chaos," it [the Sign of the Logrus] said. "The Unicorn took it from the Serpent when they fought, in the beginning. It was stolen. Return it. Return it."

The blue face I had seen above the Pattern did not materialize, but the voice I'd heard at that time responded, "It was paid for with blood and pain. Title passed."

"The Jewel of Judgment and the Eye of Chaos or Eye of the Serpent are different names for the same stone?" I said.

"Yes," Dworkin replied.

"What happens if the Serpent gets its eye back?" I inquired.

"The universe will probably come to an end." . . .

"The balance was tipped against me by recent actions of this turncoat," the Logrus replied—a burst of fire occurring above my [Merlin's] head, presumably to demonstrate the identity of the turncoat in question. . . .

"Just a minute!" I cried. "I wasn't given much choice in the matter!"

"But there was a choice," wailed the Logrus, "and you made it."

"Indeed, he did," responded the Pattern. "But it served only to redress the balance you'd tipped in your own favor."

"Redress? You overcompensated! Now it's tipped in your favor! Besides, it was accidentally tipped my way, by the traitor's father." Another fireball followed, and I warded again. "It was not my doing."

"You probably inspired it." (KS, 197–99)

Dworkin tried to give Merlin a broader perspective on their argument than might have been readily comprehensible:

"The biggest bar to understanding is the interpretation they put on each other's doings. That, and the fact that everything can always be pushed another step backward—such as the break in the Pattern having strengthened the

Logrus and the possibility that the Logrus actively influenced Brand into doing it. But then the Logrus might claim this was in retaliation for the Day of the Broken Branches several centuries ago. . . .

". . . It wasn't all that important a matter, except to them. What I'm saying is that to argue as they do is to head into an infinite regression—back to first causes, which are always untrustworthy." (KS, 200)

Although Dworkin may know a great deal about the earliest hostilities between the Serpent and the unicorn, and he may have imparted that knowledge to his son, the late King Oberon, we of Amber have not been privy to such arcane information. For our purposes, which is to clarify the current state of affairs in all the shadows between the two poles of existence, we need only refer to the documents set down by Corwin and Merlin.

Thus, a cause of these disturbances reverberating throughout Shadow may be traced to Brand's shedding of an Amberite's blood on the primal Pattern. This seems to be a reasonable point of origin for the problems experienced in our age. That stain of blood on the Pattern affected the originator of that design, Dworkin, and it permitted foul monsters to roam freely through the shadows into Amber.

At the time when that blotted area of the primal Pattern was cleared away, Corwin designed a new Pattern. Corwin's Pattern became a third Power that began to take part in the conflict. Fiona had brought the potential danger of the new Pattern to Merlin's attention. She feared that it was affecting the "fabric of Shadow," (BA, 162) and that Shadow-storms were one symptom of the disturbances it was generating. Fiona joined Merlin's stepbrother Mandor to investigate phenomena that might have been caused by Corwin's Pattern. They determined that the third Power had become a significant factor, and they reported their findings to Suhuy, Master of the Logrus. Suhuy came to the same conclusion after independent research. There was indeed a definite imbalance of forces affecting Shadow. All the shadows complained of disasters, both natural and societal in nature.

Merlin first discovered that the Pattern in Amber was a sentient being when he brought Coral of Begma to view it. When Coral survived her initiation into the Pattern, she chose to allow the Pattern itself to send her someplace. After she disappeared, Merlin addressed himself to the Pattern directly, and the Pattern responded. Aside from this revelation on Merlin's part, Coral became an important "pawn" in the maneuvering of the Pattern and the Logrus.

Using a Trump he had drawn of Coral, Merlin enlisted the aid of Mandor and Jasra to concentrate on reaching the girl. They managed a clear but brief connection, and the Pattern became aware of their combined effort. The Pattern, having deliberately kept Coral imprisoned, sought for Merlin. Through the intervention, first, of Ghostwheel, and second, an agent of the third Power, Merlin was isolated from the reach of both the Pattern and the Logrus in a realm called the Undershadow. In spite of the two Powers' inability to make direct contact with Merlin, they expended what energies they could to try to influence him to select one Power above the other. Ultimately, the Pattern succeeded. Leading Merlin to a chamber where a Broken Pattern resided, the Pattern had positioned Coral, unconscious, in its center. It became Merlin's task to make the Broken Pattern whole by walking it in order to reach the girl. When he did so, Merlin found himself and Coral back in the Royal Palace in Amber. By Merlin's action, the Sign of the Pattern was able to absorb the newly repaired Broken Pattern, and the shadow in which it was placed, within itself. Thus, the Power of the Pattern had a much greater advantage over the Power of the Logrus.

When he had been in the Undershadow, Merlin had been coerced to hold a vigil in a chapel carved into a negatively brightened mountainside. While in the chapel, the imposing forms of the unicorn and the Serpent entered. They communicated with Merlin through his special entity Frakir. In his journal, Merlin noted that the Serpent of Chaos had only one eye. (KS, 80)

The attempt of the Sign of the Logrus to regain the Eye of the Serpent in the Royal Palace of Amber, within the domain of the Pattern Sign, was certainly a desperate move. The explosion that destroyed sections of the Royal Palace caused harmful consequences, but it also provided the aged Dworkin with a unique opportunity. Dworkin was able to act to prevent the Logrus from tilting the balance of Powers back to its own side. Coral had been seriously hurt in the cataclysmic explosion. Performing a surgical operation on the girl, Dworkin hid his procedures from the others. Once he had completed the operation, he removed himself and the girl from the scene. Merlin learned that Dworkin had placed the Jewel of Judgment, or the Eye of Chaos, in Coral's eye socket.

Using human-formed constructs, the Pattern and the Logrus focused their attention on Coral. Logrus-ghosts kidnapped Coral, who had become queen of Kashfa. Because she bore the Eye of the Serpent, the Logrus intended to make her queen in his domain. After Merlin was able to rescue her, and with the help of several others, he brought her to the new Pattern, where she could be protected from both the Logrus and the Pattern. At one point, the Logrus attempted to undermine Corwin's Pattern by sending its forces to rend the ground beneath the new Power. Fortunately, Merlin halted its progress and put up blockages under the ground to prevent the Logrus's incursion from that direction again.

Merlin had faced both Powers individually. Rather than responding fearfully to either Power, Merlin stood up to them, speaking forthrightly of what he hoped to gain in the outcome. He understood the need to resolve the conflict between the Logrus and the Pattern in order to end the turbulence that was spread throughout the shadows. Finding that his mother Dara was on intimate terms with the Sign of the Logrus, Merlin confidently dealt with it, going so far as to make the following assurance:

> The Sign slid past her [Dara], a tiny sun turning itself into a succession of ideograms.
> "Merlin, you will take the throne and serve me when the time comes?"
> "I will do what is necessary to redress the balance of power," I replied.
> "That is not what I asked! Will you take the throne under the terms I set?"
> "If that is what is needed to set things right," I answered.
> "This pleases me," it said. (PC, 114)

In Merlin's last confrontation with the Logrus, when he held Mandor and Dara in abeyance, his artificial construct Ghostwheel supported his position. The Power acceded to Merlin, permitting him to rule in the Courts of Chaos without its influence, or the influence of Dara or Mandor. As the Sign of the Logrus expressed to Dara: "You must honor Merlin's wishes. If his reign be a foolish thing, he will destroy himself by his own actions. If it be prudent, you will have gained what you sought without interference.'' (PC, 239)

Merlin had been placed in the best possible position, at the far pole of existence, for initiating the smoothing=over process. Working in concert with King Random and others of integrity at our pole, Merlin is empowered to ameliorate the disruptions to the shadows between, at least in terms of people and societies. Perhaps the enmity of the two Powers could be affected inversely, that is, through the spread of harmony from the shadows outward, to the poles.

PHYSICAL REGENERATION

The ability to regrow living tissue that has been diseased, severed, or otherwise atrophied into disuse. This regeneration occurs with a greater propensity among those of the Blood Royal of Amber than among other human beings.

Prince Corwin of Amber had been deliberately blinded by his brother Eric during the succession wars. Eric's guards had used white-hot irons, which touched Corwin's eyeballs. Nevertheless, after a number of years, Corwin regained his sight, and his vision gradually returned to normal a short time after.

Corwin's Chronicles recount his delighted realization that sight was returning after three years in the dungeons of Amber:

I'd discovered a tiny patch of brightness, off somewhere to my right. [Do you know what that meant to me?] Well, let's take it like this: I had awakened in a hospital bed and learned that I had recovered all too soon. Dig?

I heal faster than others who have been broken. All the lords and ladies of Amber have something of this capacity.

I'd lived through the Plague, I'd lived through the march on Moscow. . . .

I regenerate faster and better than anybody I've ever known.

Napoleon had once made a remark about it. So had General MacArthur.

With nerve tissue it takes me a bit longer, that's all. . . .

I had grown new eyes, my fingers told me. It had taken me over three years, but I had done it. It was the million-in-one thing I spoke of earlier, the thing which even Eric could not properly assess, because of the variances of powers among the individual members of the family. I had beaten him to this extent: I had learned that I could grow new eyeballs. I had always known that I could regenerate nerve tissues, given sufficient time. I had been left paraplegic from a spine injury received during the Franco-Prussian wars. After two years, it had gone away. (NP, 157–58)

Much later, Corwin learned more of the reasons for Eric having decided to put out his eyes rather than kill him. He learned this from the sibling who suggested blinding Corwin: Julian. As Julian explained:

''Eric . . . figured that your eyesight might eventually be restored—knowing the way we regenerate—given time. It was a very delicate situation. If Dad [Oberon] were to return, Eric could step down and justify all of his actions to anyone's satisfaction—except for killing you. . . .

''. . . Blinded, however, there was no need to slay you and you were of no use for anything else they [the opposing cabal] might have in mind. It saved you by taking you out of the picture for a time, and it saved us from a more egregious act which might one day be held against us.'' (HO, 122)

Conversing with his brother Benedict, who had recently lost an arm, in the shadow Avalon, Corwin spoke of the likelihood that his brother would regain his limb.

Benedict asked:

''And how long did the regeneration take?''

''It was close to four years before I could see again, and my vision is just getting back to normal now. So—about five years altogether, I would say.''

''Good . . . You give me some small hope.

Others of us have lost portions of their anatomy and experienced regeneration also, of course, but I never lost anything significant—until now."

"Oh yes . . . It is a most impressive record. I reviewed it regularly for years. A collection of bits and pieces, many of them forgotten I daresay, but by the principals and myself: fingertips, toes, ear lobes. I would say that there is hope for your arm. Not for a long while, of course." (GA, 91)

It should be understood that this regenerative power holds true for beings of noble blood in the Courts of Chaos also. Merlin, son of Corwin, has reported as much in his written accounts. His brother Jurt, born of Dara and Lord Sawall, had severed most of his left ear in a duel with Merlin, and later, lost his right eye in a second attempt to kill Merlin while they were hunting in the Black Zone. The oldest son of Lord Sawall, Mandor, reported the progress of Jurt's regeneration: "Oh, he's grown about half the ear back. It's pretty ragged and ugly-looking. Generally, his hair covers it. The eyeball is regenerated, but he can't see out of it yet. He usually wears a patch." (SC, 34) When Merlin confronted Jurt inside the First Unicornian Church in Kashfa, Jurt seemed to have a fully grown eye, his ear was covered and hidden by his longish hair, and a finger he had lost subsequently had partially regenerated.

This power of regeneration is apparently related to the long-lived quality of those who rule over Shadow and can move from one shadow to another. More than a simple, commonplace accident is needed to destroy a person who can control the lives of lesser beings.

PIT OF CHAOS

The vast emptiness that marks the ultimate terminus of the universe at the Courts of Chaos. It has also been referred to as the Rim and the Abyss.

When Corwin first looked upon the Abyss in the Courts of Chaos, he felt the fearfulness of the prospect, as shown in his description in the Chronicles:

I looked down upon what at first seemed a valley filled with countless explosions of color; but when the advancing darkness faced this display away the stars danced and burned within its depths as well as above, giving then the impression of a bottomless chasm. It was as if I stood at the end of the world, the end of the universe, the end of everything. (HO, 79)

At the farther reaches of the chasm, Corwin was able to see a dark structure on top of a black mountain jutting up from its greater blackness. Later, he saw gauzy strips floating outward from that region, and men riding demonlike horses upon those floating strips.

When Corwin again saw the Abyss, it was during the Patternfall battle, in which the forces of Amber were led by his brother Benedict against the armies of the Courts. Incongruously, the black road, which stretched through all the shadows to the foot of Mt. Kolvir, hung above the black Pit, crossing over and into that dark dominion. To Corwin and his siblings, the Abyss seemed a terrible and awesome place, a complete anathema to any known reality.

The majesty and inscrutability of the Pit of Chaos appeared entirely beyond human ken when Brand and Deirdre were lost to its depths. The Jewel of Judgment, which fell with them, had been apparently lost to the Amberites forever. Thus, it was all the more astounding for Corwin and the others to witness the great unicorn climbing out of the chasm, bearing the Jewel about her neck.

Corwin expressed his personal impression of the Rim as a great unfathomable precipice. It was unknowable, illimitable, and absolutely nihilistic. It was inviolable by the presence of man.

Not so in the journals of Merlin, son of Corwin. The Rim was sanctified, a place to worship and bid farewell to the deceased when they depart the Courts of Chaos. The Cathedral of the Serpent, at the farthest point of the Plaza at the End of the World, rests at the very Rim. As a culmination of the funeral service, the casket bearing the deceased is slid along a track through an opening that sends it to the depths. It is a solemn ceremony, but one which all who reside in the Courts accept with a measure of hope and pride.

In some areas of the Abyss the wind currents are so great that youthful residents have sport above it. As a young man, Merlin engaged in a sporting duel with his half brother Jurt. They rode upon stones using shapeshifted feet, fencing with trisliver and trisp. Heedless of the immense void beneath them, they fought. When the sport turned to something more dangerous, Merlin's stepbrother, Mandor, and his half brother Despil, intervened. Although Jurt had been hurt, he was in no peril of dropping into the chasm. With his feet clinging tightly to the small stone he rode, he drifted briefly until Despil reached him, and then he guided Jurt to an edge of the Rim. Such play among the air currents over portions of the Pit has always occurred among the daring and the youthful.

The Pit offers employment to those of an icono-clastic nature. Unconcerned with the sacredness of the Abyss, and venturesome enough to traverse it as if in mundane occupation, the Pit-divers of the realm plumb its depths continuously. Sometimes these Pit-divers are hired by others to seek artifacts for study or ferret out trophies for a collector. More often, though, the diver has a mercenary spirit and will hunt up objects to be sold to any who see value in them through private commercial means.

In his journals, Merlin makes mention of knowing a Pit-diver: "... [I] located a small dagger I had brought with me from Chaos—a gift from the Pit-diver Borquist, whom I'd once fixed up with an introduction that led to a patronage. He was a middling-good poet." (BA, 190) More recently, when the conflict between the Logrus and the Pat-tern had reached a boiling point, Merlin visited an area of the Abyss where Pit-divers often plummet into its depths. Merlin recorded: "The Pit-divers ... had suspended operations for the first time in a gen-eration. When I questioned them they told me of dangerous activities in the depths—whirlwinds, wings of fire, blasts of new-minted matter." (PC, 229) Apparently, the disharmony between the op-posing Powers was reflected even in the great void, which we, hithertofore, believed to be nothingness.

The Pit-divers, the sport of his youth, the famil-iarity with all of the region that included the great Pit, this was part of the homeland that Merlin knew and loved. After learning of the disruptions of the Pit from the mouths of the divers, Merlin decided that he would act to bring peace to this pole of his existence.

PLAZA AT THE END OF THE WORLD

The wide courtyard that stretched between the royal residence of Thelbane and the Cathedral of the Serpent in the Courts of Chaos. The funeral procession for the late King Swayvill had proceeded along the Plaza from Thelbane.

When Merlin, son of Corwin, had been called back to the Courts to attend the funeral of the late king, an incident occurred in the Plaza. As a mem-ber of one of the Houses in the Royal Succession, Merlin participated in the procession of people fol-lowing the casket along a route across the Plaza to the Cathedral which faced the great Rim of Chaos. Merlin used a spell to absent himself and his brother Jurt while two other members of the procession were transformed to resemble them. Merlin's ruse would not have been discovered, except for the sud-den attack of an assassin on a member of another House in their absence. When Merlin and Jurt re-turned to the Plaza, they found the members of the procession stopped about a quarter of the way from Thelbane. Swayvill's casket rested on the ground of the Plaza, the dead body of Tmer of the House of Jesby lying several feet away. Mandor, Merlin's stepbrother, explained his view of the incident:

"Someone gave two of the security guards your [Merlin's] appearance and Jurt's. This was obviously intended to create confusion when the assassin struck. They rushed forward insisting they were guards. Obviously, they weren't. Clever—especially with you and Jurt on their black watch list." (PC, 146)

Mandor ordered that Merlin and Jurt, as well as another candidate for the succession, leave immedi-ately for security reasons. Once the candidates were safely away, the procession continued along the Plaza.

The incident remained mysteriously unexplained, but Merlin felt uncomfortable about it. He saw to it that the two guards taken into custody were exon-erated, since they were innocent of any knowledge of Tmer's murder.

Before transporting away from the Plaza, Merlin gave a brief greeting to a young woman he had been acquainted with in his youth, Gilva of the House of

Hendrake. He made tentative plans to speak with her at a later time.

The assassin was not uncovered, and it may be that it was the daring act of a member of an important House in the succession whom no one would have suspected. From other reports about the political conflicts in the Courts, the Plaza at the End of the World was likely to have been the scene of other acts of subterfuge and fatal ends in the past, and the custom may certainly continue in the future.

PRIMAL PATTERN

The true Pattern that had been designed by Dworkin. With its completion, Order, and the universe as we know it, had been formed. The unicorn helped point the way for Corwin, Random, and Ganelon when they first discovered the primal Pattern. Brand had begun walking it in order to become attuned to the Jewel of Judgment, but he was prevented from completing the circuit by Corwin. The Sign of the Pattern had brought Merlin and his companions there, intent on keeping them there to protect them from the Sign of the Logrus.

The primal Pattern resides upon a barren rock's surface in a location that is congruent to the site of Amber's Pattern, deep within Mt. Kolvir. The Chronicles written by Corwin describe what he saw when he and Random and Ganelon approached the true Pattern on horseback:

> The sky was a deeper blue than that of Amber, and there were no clouds in it. That sea was a matching blue, unspecked by sail or island. I saw no birds, and I heard no sounds other than our own. An enormous silence lay upon this place, this day. In the bowl of my suddenly clear vision, the Pattern at last achieved its disposition upon the surface below. I thought at first that it was inscribed in the rock, but as we drew nearer I saw that it was contained within it—gold-pink swirls, like veining in an exotic marble, natural-seeming despite the obvious purpose to the design.... We regarded it in silence for a long while. A dark, rough-edged smudge had obliterated an area of the section immediately beneath us, running from its outer rim to the center. (SU, 191)

This Pattern, Corwin, Random, and Ganelon realized, was the actual beginning of all things. Amber was merely the first, if special, shadow of the shadows that were cast by this design. The smudged area, they soon learned, was the blood of an Amberite. That blotted area was the primal cause of the black road that was allowing passage for strange creatures to travel the shadows into Amber.

Since some enemy of Amber had caused the blotted stain, a special guard was set to prevent others from acting similarly. A purple-colored griffin was guardian of the primal Pattern. It was leashed with a long chain to a cave in the nearby rock wall. Although it was friendly toward those of Royal Blood, it began shrieking and set about in nervous movements when Random allowed a drop of his blood to fall upon the design.

In a chamber connected to the cave tunnel where the griffin dwelled, the aged wizard Dworkin resided in a den containing numbers of ancient books. It was Dworkin's belief that King Oberon had placed the griffin there to prevent him from trying to clear the blotted stain from the Pattern, fearing for the old wizard's life. Dworkin had befriended the griffin, dubbing it Wixer, and so had more freedom of movement than Oberon had actually intended.

When Brand sought to attune himself to the Jewel of Judgment, he tried to do so by walking the primal Pattern. Corwin was aware that Brand was seeking the power to re-form a new Amber, and so he had warned the other members of the Family to guard the Pattern in Amber and in Rebma. Corwin arrived at the primal Pattern with Fiona on horseback. They found Wixer slain, its head cut off. Brand was already well into the Pattern, gaining strength in his attunement. The only way Corwin could reach him to prevent him from completing the attunement was to walk the Pattern himself. He began the travail.

Corwin found that he could pass along the stained area by using the point of his sword Grayswandir. This cleared a tracery that Corwin was able to follow. Finally, after much effort, Corwin was near enough to Brand to attack him with his sword. They dueled, while still maintaining their respective positions on the Pattern. Unable to best Brand in those circumstances, Corwin drew on the power of the

Jewel of Judgment in Brand's possession. He was able to create a tornado-like funnel from the sky that closed upon Brand. Before it could reach Brand, however, he stepped into the blotted area, and he seemed to shrink. He was gone before the funnel reached him. Corwin could do nothing more, other than complete the circuit himself. He had some slight satisfaction, at least, in preventing his outlaw brother from becoming entirely attuned to the Jewel.

When King Oberon revealed to his kin that he was alive and well, he had come to the decision to repair the blotted area of the primal Pattern himself. Corwin and Benedict had succeeded in regaining the Jewel of Judgment. It was the key factor that Oberon required to clear the way on the true design. Although he had told his son Corwin that in repairing the Pattern he would likely die, he had prevented Corwin from trying to do it in his place. Instead, Oberon arranged for Benedict to mount a battle at the Courts of Chaos. This would distract the lords of the Courts, while the king took the initial steps to clear away the blot. After sending Corwin on a hellride from Amber toward the battlefield at the Courts, Oberon commenced.

At first, it was unclear whether or not Oberon had succeeded. As planned, a red bird carried the Jewel from Oberon to Corwin. However, a terrible storm of Chaos was sweeping over all the shadows, obliterating them. That storm was an inevitable part of the process that would have occurred even if the primal Pattern still stood. Later, after the new king of Amber dispelled the Death Storm, it was found that the true Pattern survived, clean once again.

Much later, when the conflict between the Pattern and the Logrus had escalated, the Sign of the Pattern brought Merlin and several others to the primal Pattern. With Merlin were Luke Raynard, Dalt, Coral, who wore the Jewel of Judgment in her eye socket, and a body-possessing demon in the body of Nayda. The Sign of the Pattern addressed Nayda: "No, I will not harm [you or] your companions. But I must detain Coral and Merlin here as power counters, and the rest of you for political reasons, until this dispute with my adversary is settled." (PC, 198)

Merlin used the primal Pattern to arrange a standoff. He cut his hand with a dagger and held it, cupped, over the design, knowing full well what would happen if his blood spilled on it. Merlin proceeded to negotiate with the Sign of the Pattern for their freedom.

Unable to persuade Merlin that it could protect him and Coral from harm if they remained at the primal Pattern, the Sign acquiesced. Luke suspected, though, that the Sign would not permit all of them their freedom once the Pattern was out of danger. So, Luke cut his own hand and took Merlin's place upon the primal Pattern. In this way, the Sign was coerced to send the others wherever they wished. Luke would remain to see that it kept its word. This was done, although it became unclear how successful Luke was in eluding the Sign of the Pattern after his comrades were safely away.

It is said that the primal Pattern remains clear and safe, in spite of rumors to the contrary. It is securely ensconced at that pole of the universe, though the shadows may continue to go through tumultuous times.

PRIVATE CHAPELS IN THE COURTS OF CHAOS

A significant cult that grew out of political unrest in the Courts of Chaos after the defeat of the Chaosites at the Patternfall battle.

In the accounts of Merlin, citizen of both the Courts of Chaos and Amber, he tells of first learning about these private chapels that are dedicated to members of the Royal Family in Amber. His Chaosite stepbrother Mandor described one he had seen:

> "I recall a social visit to the Ways of Hendrake one time, . . . when I wandered into a small, chapellike room. In a niche in one wall there hung a portrait of General Benedict, in full battle regalia. There was an altarlike shelf below it bearing several weapons, and upon which a number of candles were burning. Your mother's [Dara's] picture was there, too." (PC, 66)

Merlin had seen two such chapels himself, both hidden in secret Ways where they could not be easily discovered. One of these was a chapel dedicated to Merlin's father, Corwin. It was hidden in a Way in the ceiling of an exhibit called the Sculpture Garden in the House of Sawall. A friend of Merlin's had observed the construction of the Way. The

Shadowmaster who devised it was slain afterward. A second chapel that Merlin found was in the room of his brother Jurt in House Sawall. The Way had been sloppily constructed, deep within Jurt's armoire. His chapel worshiped Brand of Amber.

By speaking in confidence with an old friend from the Courts, Merlin learned how the private chapels evolved and the significance of worshiping the Royals of Amber. Herein is Merlin's record of his friend's explanation:

"Nobody thought we would actually lose that war, though it had long been argued that Amber would be a formidable adversary. Afterward, there was considerable unrest over the policies that had led to it and the treaty that followed it. No single house or grouping could hope for a deposition against the royal coalition, though. You know the conservatism of the Rim Lords. It would take much, much more to unite a majority against the Crown. Instead, their discontent took another form. There grew up a brisk trade in Amber memorabilia from the war. People became fascinated by our conquerors. Biographical studies of Amber's royal family sold very well. Something like a cult began to take shape. Private chapels such as this began to appear, dedicated to a particular Amberite whose virtues appealed to someone.

"It smacked too much of a religion, . . . and for time out of mind the Way of the Serpent had been the only significant religion in the Courts. So Swayvill outlawed the Amber cult as heretical, for obvious political reasons. That proved a mistake. Had he done nothing it might have passed quickly. I don't really know, of course. But outlawing it drove it underground, made people take it more seriously as a rebellious thing. I've no idea how many cult chapels there are among the Houses, but that's obviously what this is." (PC, 165)

Interestingly, Merlin's friend indicated that his brother Mandor was not as innocent of knowledge about the cult as he seemed when he described the chapel dedicated to Benedict. Before the prohibition, Mandor had been a known cultist. He maintained a hidden chapel worshiping Princess Fiona.

Before the ban, it was a common practice to invite friends over to a private chapel and perform a service. If this was done at all after the ban, it was done with a very select group of friends. When they can be had, personal possessions belonging to the patron are kept in the chapel. The patron's spirit is venerated, but the patron need not be living. In fact, Merlin discovered that, in one special case, the individual worshiped in a secret chapel in House Sawall was actually a prisoner of the devotee.

When Merlin realized that his father was alive but was being held prisoner, he was able to use his knowledge of the private chapels to pinpoint Corwin's location:

"I figured out something I think my mother really meant when she told me, 'Seek him in the Pit,' . . . The floor of the chapel [dedicated to Corwin] bears stylized representations of the Courts and of Amber worked out in tiles. At the extreme of the Courts' end is a representation of the Pit. I never set foot in that area when I visited the chapel. I'm willing to bet there's a way located there, and at the other end is the place of his imprisonment." (PC, 222–23)

As far as is known, the practice of maintaining secret chapels continues in the Courts. Perhaps more recent events have demystified the objects of veneration to some extent, however.

QUIST, FERLA

Ambassador of Begma assigned to the true city.

A rather tall, imposing woman approaching middle age, Ferla Quist had spent a number of years residing in the Begman Embassy, located on the Main Concourse in Amber. It had been some months since she had visited her homeland when the Begman prime minister, Orkuz, made his unexpected visit to the Royal Palace.

Having received reports from Begma concerning clandestine negotiations that King Random had initiated with the shadow kingdom of Kashfa, Quist had submitted messages of protest with Queen Vialle. These messages were received and responded to graciously, with no substantial comment on policies. It was promised that the ambassador would be notified immediately upon the return of the king from a "state visit," and that she would then be able to address her concerns to him directly.

It was reported that Ferla Quist viewed Prime Minister Orkuz's sudden visit to the palace with consternation. The Begman Embassy had not been informed of his appearance before the queen, and the ambassador moved to remedy the situation as soon as she received word. She sent a hasty message to Queen Vialle, apologizing for any possible unseemly show made by the prime minister. She indicated that Orkuz had acted on his own and without notifying the embassy. She ended with a request to correct any former misunderstandings with the arrival of an official embassy delegation. Quist was ready to depart for the palace even before receiving Queen Vialle's response.

Attending the formal dinner party prepared for her and her official entourage, Ferla Quist was the very epitome of grace and diplomacy in the presence of her hosts. However, a couple of servants in the palace reported that, in her private quarters, she had spoken harshly with Prime Minister Orkuz about his haste. She had softened her reprimand, though, when he spoke of his concern for the whereabouts of his younger daughter Coral.

Haughty by nature, Quist prefers to speak with a softness that reflects quiet authority. Few would care to raise her ire with an ill-conceived opinion, nevertheless.

RANDOM

King of shadow Amber as determined by the choice of the unicorn.

Although Random was not directly heir to the throne, the late King Oberon indicated to his sons that the choice of his successor would be accomplished in a unique way.

The youngest surviving son of King Oberon, he was often the butt of jokes played by his male siblings. His mother had been a woman of shadow Earth, where Oberon often traveled. Her name was Paulette, and she had been characterized as being nervous and high-strung. After Random was born, it is believed Paulette gave birth to a daughter, Mirelle, who died shortly thereafter. Random was not old enough to have been able to remember his mother, for she committed suicide while he was quite young.

Among all the sons of Oberon, Random had undoubtedly changed the most with the years. Irresponsible and reckless as a youth, he grew into a caring, almost-sentimental man in maturity. Many factors were involved: the love of his blind wife Vialle; the rediscovery of his illegitimate son Martin; his part in the Patternfall battle; and the burden of kingship thrust upon him from a strange and heretofore unknown quarter. Writing with the objectivity that comes from a difference in generations and time, Merlin, son of Corwin, said this of the Royal Liege:

> "I understood that he had once been pretty wild and footloose and nasty, that he hadn't really wanted the job of ruling this archetypal world. But parenthood, marriage, and the Unicorn's choice seemed to have laid a lot on him—deepening his character, I suppose, at the price of a lot of the fun things in his life."
> (KS, 184)

At a time closer to the youthful Random, his brother Corwin referred to him as "a homicidal little fink," (NP, 55) and characterized Random in this way:

> I knew that on the one hand he was nobody's fool; he was resourceful, shrewd, strangely sentimental over the damnedest things; and on the other hand, his word wasn't worth the spit behind it, and he'd probably sell my corpse to the medical school of his choice if he could get much for it. (NP, 33)

Later, in a more conciliatory tone, Corwin described him in this manner: "Younger, smaller ... he might have had it a bit rougher than the rest of us ... Nothing quite as useless as another prince when there is already a crowd of them about." (HO, 51)

Testimony given by Random's sister Flora showed that he was not likable in his younger days for other reasons:

> "It is too late to start pretending I like him ... I just don't like the people he associates with—

assorted criminals, jazz musicians. . . . I had to show him family courtesy when he was visiting my shadow, but he put a big strain on my nerves, bringing those people around at all hours—jam sessions, poker parties. The place usually reeked for weeks afterward and I was always glad to see him go." (SU, 61–62)

In his Chronicles, Corwin recalled a harsh practical joke he and his brother Bleys played on Random. The three of them sailed to a tiny island in the south, and the two older youths stranded the boy Random there. It was days before Gérard rescued him when he learned of it. During Corwin's recollection, he found out from Random's wife that Random had placed a spike in Corwin's boot in retaliation. Still, Corwin also thought back over fond memories of their adolescence, even to the point of feeling, mistakenly, that they shared the same parents.

It is likely that Random was quite young when Dworkin directed him through his walk of the Pattern in Amber. Nevertheless, it was probably at a later time than Corwin and the others. Random recalled that moment of his past:

"You never forget the day you come of age and walk the Pattern . . . I remember it as though it were last year. When I had succeeded—all flushed with excitement, with glory—Dworkin presented me with my first set of Trumps and instructed me in their use. I distinctly recall asking him whether they worked everywhere. And I remember his answer: 'No,' he said. 'But they should serve in any place you will ever be.' He never much liked me, you know." (SU, 185)

Gambling and music have certainly been a part of Amber and its environs, but young Random was more likely to have picked up those interests in his travels in lands of shadow. Just as for his older siblings, Random obtained a liberal education by attending to other realms. His interests grew with those experiences.

In a pleasant interlude overheard by Merlin, King Random played a musical set on drums while his son joined him on a saxophone. Random was showing Martin a trick he learned long ago: rapidly changing five drumsticks in quick succession as he beat the drums. Random explained:

"Learned it from Freddie Moore, in the thirties, either at the Victoria or the Village Vanguard, when he was with Art Hodes and Max Kaminsky. I forget which place. It goes back to vaudeville, when they didn't have any mikes and the lighting was bad. Had to do show-off things like that, or dress funny, he told me, to keep the audience paying attention." (KS, 181–82)

Once he was initiated in the Pattern, Random spent more time walking the shadows than he did in Amber. However, he was also known for a brief sojourn he took in the undersea city named Rebma. It had been an infamous dalliance that has been spread through gossip in the realm even to this day. Young Random had visited the queen of Rebma, Moire. He paid ardent interest to her daughter Morganthe, and persuaded her to elope with him, promising her any number of shadow worlds in which to live. Ignominiously, Random had her returned with a lowly servant he employed. This was a mere month after their "elopement," in Amber-time. Morganthe learned shortly thereafter that she was pregnant. Several months after the birth of a son, whom she named Martin, Morganthe committed suicide. Except, perhaps, with his wife Vialle, Random has always remained silent about this early disgrace.

He described his discovery of the shadow named Texorami as being more than mere accident. In his own words:

I was here in Amber some years ago. Not doing much of anything. Just visiting and being a nuisance. Dad was still around, and when I noticed that he was getting into one of his grumpy moods, I decided it was time to take a walk. A long one. I had often noticed that his fondness for me tended to increase as an inverse function of my proximity. . . . I had decided to go looking for an assemblage of all my simple pleasures in one small nook of Shadow.

It was a long ride . . . and it was pretty far from Amber, as such things go. This time, I was not looking for a place where I would be especially important. That can get either boring or difficult fairly quickly, depending on how responsible you want to be. I wanted to be an irresponsible nonentity and just enjoy myself. (SU, 15)

It was an untamed town. Although Texorami was a port city, full of exotic merchants and wide-ranging sailors, it had all the ingredients of a village in a wilderness frontier, barely on the edge of civilization. Fistfights and duels with swords were as much a part of its charm as the willing women and accessible gambling. Random even took to a sport that the powerful winds in the city allowed: sky surfing on sailplanes.

Random recounted how a game of poker with a small group of ill-reputed acquaintances in Texorami brought him back into the Family's problems. One of the cards in his hand, the Jack of Diamonds, began communicating to Random, as from a great distance. He discovered it was his brother Brand, who had been missing for some time. Random's remembrance of subsequent events have been placed in the public record, through Corwin's Chronicles, so they do not bear repeating here. However, in brief, the Chronicles describe Random's futile attempt to rescue his brother, who was trapped in a tower within a strange shadow of immense floating boulders and guarded by a huge, transparent serpent. Escaping from Brand's guards, Random found that the partial men-beings of that shadow were capable of tracking him through every shadow to which he shifted.

During his flight, Random received Trump contact from another brother, Julian. Through him, Random learned that their father had been missing for more than a year. Julian informed him that Eric intended to be crowned king of Amber in the near future. His intention in communicating this to Random was to find out where he stood on Eric's taking over the throne. Julian seemed satisfied with Random's response: "I have always been able to detect the quarter of the wind. I do not sail against it." (SU, 36)

After this Trump contact, Random discovered that the half-men were again in pursuit. In his attempt to rid himself of his pursuers, Random shifted to shadow Earth. From the West Coast of the North American Continent, he made a telephone call to the only relative he knew resided in that shadow who might be willing to give him sanctuary: his

sister Flora. That was when he discovered that Corwin was still alive, apparently under Flora's protection also.

When he reached New York State, Random made it to Flora's home in Westchester, but the shadow men remained close behind. With Corwin, Flora, and her guard dogs, they faced the shadow men's attack and were victorious.

At that point, Random became allied to Corwin, though he was somewhat suspicious of his older brother. He hadn't suspected that Corwin was suffering from amnesia, but he was concerned that the half-men of that strange shadow keeping Brand prisoner were Corwin's. He wanted to remain on Corwin's good side because he believed Corwin intended to use such creatures as an invasion force against Eric. And Random wanted to be on the winning side. That was why Random willingly led Corwin on an automobile excursion through shadowlands, in the direction of Amber. He mistook Corwin's sly comments as the craftiness of ulterior motivations, and not what they really were: the false bravado of someone who had no idea what was going on.

Nearing the realm of Amber through shadows of the Forest of Arden, Random and Corwin came across Julian. Corwin managed to capture Julian so that he could question him on conditions in the true city. After releasing Julian, Corwin and Random eluded patrols as they reached Amber. They rescued their sister Deirdre from four of Eric's men and learned more about Eric's status from her.

While they rested, Corwin made a startling confession. Initially, Random thought he was about to turn against them and was ready to kill Corwin with his sword. He was completely taken by surprise, then, when Corwin announced he had no idea who any of them were, who he was himself, nor what Amber was all about.

With what must have seemed remarkable courage to Deirdre, Random told them they would head for the sea in order to take Corwin to Rebma. Rather than retreat through Shadow, Random was willing to take some chances to see Corwin on the throne. When Deirdre cautioned that the citizens of Rebma would likely have Random cut up into pieces to be fed to the fish, he told her that he didn't intend to travel all the way, but that she would have to take Corwin into the undersea city.

That option became less tenable for Random

when one of Julian's patrols caught the three of them along the beach. The horsemen gave chase as Random, Corwin, and Deirdre ran into the sea. They fought off the horsemen even as they traveled down the undersea stair known as Faiella-bionin. There was no other route for Random to take but to enter the city of Rebma with Deirdre and Corwin.

Although Queen Moire was quite civil with the three members of the true city, she coldly presented punishment for Random's misdeed of years earlier. She proclaimed that he was to marry a woman of her choosing and remain in Rebma for a duration of one year. Random calmly accepted this judgment.

At the same time, Moire was kindly disposed toward Corwin and Deirdre. She willingly permitted Corwin to walk the Pattern there so he would regain his memory. He did so, as Deirdre, Random, and Moire watched. On the way down to where the Pattern resided, Corwin spoke briefly with Random. He asked Random to do his time there and he could look forward to a regency in Amber if Corwin won the throne. At that point, Corwin told Random the name of his bride, and that she was blind. Random agreed to accept his situation gracefully. Then Corwin walked the Pattern, completed the circuit, and disappeared, leaving Deirdre and Random behind in the reflected city in the sea.

Random remained in Rebma, but he kept abreast of events in Amber. He had occasion to speak to Corwin again about such matters when Corwin contacted him by Trump. At the time, Corwin was traveling on a warship, heading a fleet organized by their brother Bleys on its way to invade Amber. Random initiated the discussion as soon as he knew who it was who contacted him:

"Turn back . . .

". . . According to Llewella, Eric can cream you now. She says wait a while, till he relaxes, and hit him then—like a year from now, maybe." . . .

"Sorry . . . Can't. Too many losses involved in getting us this far. It's a now-or-never situation. . . . Why, though?" . . .

"Mainly because I just learned he can control the weather around here." . . .

"We'll still have to chance it." . . .

"Don't say I didn't tell you."

"He definitely knows we're coming?"

"What do you think? Is he a cretin?"

"No."

"Then he knows. If I could guess it in Rebma, then he knows in Amber—and I *did* guess, from a wavering of Shadow."

"Unfortunately, . . . I have some misgivings about this expedition, but it's Bleys' show."

"You cop out and let him get axed."

"Sorry, but I can't take the chance. He might win. I'm bringing in the fleet."

"You've spoken with Caine, with Gérard?"

"Yes."

"Then you must think you have a chance upon the waters. But listen, Eric has figured a way to control the Jewel of Judgment, I gather, from court gossip about its double. He *can* use it to control the weather here. That's definite. God knows what else he might be able to do with it."

"Pity . . . We'll have to suffer it. Can't let a few storms demoralize us."

"Corwin, I'll confess. I spoke with Eric himself three days ago."

"Why?"

"He asked me. I spoke with him out of boredom. He went into great detail concerning his defenses."

"That's because he learned from Julian that we came in together. He's sure it'll get back to me."

"Probably . . . But that doesn't change what he said."

"No." . . .

"Then let Bleys fight his own war . . . You can hit Eric later."

"He's about to be crowned in Amber."

"I know, I know. It's as easy to attack a king, though, as a prince, isn't it? What difference does it make what he calls himself at the time, so long as you take him? It'll still be Eric."

"True . . . but I've committed myself."

"Then uncommit yourself." . . .

" 'Fraid I can't do that."

"Then you're crazy, Charlie."

"Probably."

"Well, good luck, anyhow."

"Thanks."

"See you around." (NP, 116–17)

It is part of the public record that Corwin lost his bid against Eric. Rebma, as well as most of the shadows congruent to Amber, watched the coronation, and Random and his wife Vialle witnessed Eric's pronouncement that the captured Corwin was to be blinded and thrown into a dungeon.

A little over three months after Corwin was blinded and imprisoned, Random used the Pattern in Rebma to appear within Castle Amber. He hadn't come empty-handed. He sought out Eric with a crossbow and shafts. Before being taken by the royal guards, Random had fired a shaft into Eric, wounding him. Under other circumstances, Eric would have had Random summarily executed. However, Queen Moire of Rebma interceded. Because Eric hoped to curry favor with the queen, he chose to be merciful. Random was tossed into a dungeon not far from Corwin's. A week after Random's capture, the queen contacted Eric again. This time, she wished Eric to hear the plea of Vialle, wife of Random. Vialle requested that she be allowed to join her husband in prison. Eric seemed somewhat moved, but he told her he needed time to consider her appeal. Some months later, Eric arranged for slightly larger quarters in the dungeon area, and Vialle joined Random there.

While Eric became more and more occupied with strange invading creatures out of Shadow, he became more lax in his wardenship over Random and Vialle. Since Corwin had mysteriously escaped, the invasion of horrible beasts had become quite frequent. Citizens dared not leave their homes at night for fear of attack. Violence and murder were occurring so often that even local police mobilization was insufficient to the task. Although guards were placed on Random and Vialle, they soon were enabled to roam freely within the confines of the palace.

When haphazard invasions turned into all-out war, Random was told very little about specific incidents. If he saw Eric or his other siblings in the palace, they were so busy making preparations that he was made to feel he was in the way. Instead of making direct inquiries, Random and one or two faithful servants kept an ear at the ready for any overheard conversations among the guards and the sons of Oberon. In this way, listening as Julian spoke with Gérard by Trump in a hallway, or as a guard spoke with another at the armory, Random learned of the most recent skirmishes. He heard also that it was believed Corwin was leading a fresh army through Shadow.

Therefore, it was not extraordinarily surprising to Random when he received a Trump contact from Corwin. Only the circumstances were surprising. Random knew that the heart of the battle with the Shadow invaders was going on. Nearly every able-bodied man was outside fighting. A bare skeleton crew of armed guards remained about the palace, and only a handful of these were assigned to watch Random.

Corwin demanded to be brought inside the palace. He was not surrounded by Eric's soldiers; he was not battling beasts nor men; he was not under any special duress. He stood alone and seemingly unharmed. This was surprising.

In his Trump message, Corwin told Random that Eric was dead and he was in charge. Random reached forward and brought Corwin to him.

Corwin moved Random quickly, saying there was a danger and they had to get to the Pattern. On the way, Random spoke of his love for Vialle:

> "She really cares for me . . . Like nobody else ever has before."
> "I'm glad for you." . . .
> "I'm not . . . I didn't want to fall in love. Not then. We've been prisoners the whole time, you know. How can she be proud of that?"
> "That is over now . . . You became a prisoner because you followed me and tried to kill Eric, didn't you?"
> "Yes. Then she joined me here."
> "I will not forget." (GA, 220)

Then Corwin told Random of the girl named Dara. She claimed to be the great-granddaughter of Benedict, but Benedict knew nothing about her. Corwin was worried that she would attempt to walk the Pattern in Amber. On the way down the long winding stairs, they found a dead guard. When they reached the room containing the Pattern, they saw a being that was not quite human nearing its center. The being spoke to Corwin. Before disappearing, it said, "Amber will be destroyed." (GA, 223)

Random remained loyal to Corwin during his very troubled rule. The mystery of Dara was just one small aspect of the whole. There was also the matter of the black road, which had reached the foot of Mt. Kolvir and stretched into Shadow. Corwin had amassed an enormous army of strange shadow beings, and they brought with them a cache of rifles that would fire in Amber. What was to be done with these strange new soldiers? And, early on in his rule, Corwin brought home another mystery to show to Random.

Corwin deliberately involved Random in this last mystery because Random had some familiarity with features of it. Carrying something into the palace with some haste, Corwin asked Random to join him. Alone in a small sitting room, Corwin revealed to Random the body of a dead man. Asking Random to examine the body, Corwin pointed out that this man had many of the same peculiarities as the shadow men they had fought at Flora's home on shadow Earth.

Corwin's account about his coming across this being involved the murder of their brother Caine. Someone was trying to frame Corwin for Caine's death, having set up messages to both parties to meet in secret at the Grove of the Unicorn. The creature of Shadow had apparently cut Caine's throat and was hiding when Corwin arrived. The creature fought with Corwin, and Corwin was unable to subdue him with anything less than breaking his neck. Then, Corwin decided to cover up Caine's body in the dirt and return to the palace with the corpse of the shadow creature.

At this point, Random filled him in on his attempt to rescue Brand, which had been the first time he had encountered this particular breed of Shadow-being.

At the conclusion of Random's tale, Corwin sent him on a brief mission. He asked Random to go into town to get Flora, and bring her back to Corwin's quarters so that he could question her. Then they parted.

Although Corwin had found a new confidant in the man named Ganelon, he grew to rely a great deal on Random during this time. Their common hardship in opposition to the late King Eric gave them a close bond. Also, Random's marriage to Vialle gave his personality a stability and confidence that he had been lacking prior to this time. Now, Corwin could look to him as a man trustworthy and loyal.

When Corwin met with Random and Flora a little later, Random noted that he wore the Jewel of Judgment. Random left Flora alone with Corwin to deal with as he wished. He returned to his own rooms.

Random, along with his other siblings, was listening and watching through their Trumps of Gérard

the following day. Early that morning, Gérard had come to Random, asking that he maintain a contact with him by Trump as he joined Corwin. They were riding to the Grove of the Unicorn to fetch the dead body of Caine.

Random, with the others, watched as Gérard and Corwin fought. He saw Gérard hold Corwin upside down at the brink of Kolvir. He heard as Gérard expressed his suspicions that Corwin was behind the shadow invasions; that Corwin was behind the creation of the black road; and that Corwin had engineered the absences of Oberon and Brand, and the deaths of Caine and Benedict's servants in Avalon. Gérard made a solemn promise that if Corwin were guilty, he would kill him. He told Corwin, then, of the insurance he had drawn to protect himself: that their siblings were watching these actions via the Trumps.

Certainly, Random never revealed to anyone publicly what his feelings were when Gérard placed Corwin in such dire circumstances. It is possible that Gérard had earlier made assurances that he wouldn't cause any harm to befall Corwin. After all, Gérard was a stalwart, blunt fellow who wanted to get at the truth. He wasn't out to murder his brothers, even if there were others who would resort to such devious methods.

Events seemed to move quickly after this. They can almost be told in a blur, with each succeeding incident eclipsing the last. The sighting of the unicorn by Gérard and Corwin, of such immense significance, went nearly forgotten when Corwin gathered up his brothers and sisters in the library of the Royal Palace. Random's taking center stage to tell what he knew of recent occurrences was set aside with the rescue and near-assassination of Brand, their long-lost brother. Even though Random showed courage in helping Gérard battle Brand's jailors and return him to Amber, Gérard refused to put his trust in Random or any of his siblings. The question of Random's son Martin came up again, in regard to Brand. Random was very concerned as he questioned his sister Llewella about a long-ago visit by Brand to Rebma, and Brand's interest in Martin. This became highly important to Random, who recalled that Brand had also questioned him about Martin. Knowing more about Martin, and of any connection with Brand, grew into an obsessive need for Random.

The only hint that Random had that something

was wrong with Corwin was Corwin's movements as they left the library. On the stairs, Corwin moved with greater than ordinary speed, so that Random had difficulty keeping up. Nevertheless, Random hadn't thought much about the incident at the time. They parted on the stair when they reached the floor of Corwin's quarters. Random continued up the stairs to his rooms.

Only when Random was knocking continuously on the door to Corwin's quarters the next day did he suspect something was wrong. When there was no response from Corwin's rooms, he decided to use Corwin's Trump. He reached Corwin, who told him he was in another shadow. Random returned to his own rooms to receive him. When Corwin appeared, he was unsteady. He told Random he had been knifed in his room just after they had parted.

Random had news for Corwin. A servant had come to Random saying that Brand was conscious and wanted to speak to Corwin. The same servant mentioned that Julian was nowhere to be found.

As Random helped lead the weakened Corwin to Brand's rooms, they spoke of possible culprits. Corwin asked Random not to reveal his injury to anyone. Corwin intended to cover up his weakness from his other siblings. Perhaps an inadvertent remark from some quarter would answer Corwin's apparently normal appearance.

Gérard met them at the door to the library. Brand wanted to see Corwin alone, so Random left him there, returning to his own quarters. It's likely that Random told Vialle about these incidents. Vialle certainly would have an interest in finding out more about Random's son, since she knew him as a boy in Rebma.

Later in the day, Random received Trump contact from Corwin. Corwin asked him to join him in his quarters. Random complied, and they were soon joined by Ganelon. Corwin informed them of his conversation with Brand. Brand had been part of a secret cabal working against Eric. Brand's cabal had made allies of the lords at the Courts of Chaos and was responsible for the opening of the black road.

Before dusk began to gather on Mt. Kolvir, Corwin, Random, and Ganelon rode on horseback to the uppermost point of the mountain. It was Corwin's intention to walk the stair that appears only in moonlight into the sometime city of the sky, Tir-na Nog'th. Images appear in that mystical reflection of Amber that may or may not be true. What Corwin

hoped to achieve was some insight into the way of things in the true city. At worst, it would be an illusion, a distortion of facts as he would know them. At best, it would bring him revelation. And a direction to take in future occurrences.

As Corwin walked into that city of mists, Random maintained contact through his Trump, while he and Ganelon remained at the high point of Kolvir. Unable to see or hear what Corwin could in that place, Random waited patiently, keeping his brother informed of the progress of the night.

With the growing of dawn, Random became more and more concerned about Corwin. He sensed some violence in the ghost city, and he began to call more frantically to Corwin as the sun tipped its face in the horizon. He tried to reach Corwin through the Trump. He saw his image. It needed Corwin's grasp to bring him back from the city that began to evaporate. Corwin's image became clearer, an alien object clutching his shoulder. Corwin reached. His feet went out from under him and he began a sudden drop. Random grabbed and pulled toward himself. Tir-na Nog'th was no more. But Corwin had fallen beside Random on the ledge. Something else was with him too.

Random was more concerned about Corwin's well-being than the unique mechanical arm he had brought back. He may have been listening, however, while Ganelon asked Corwin about it. Random was nearby, preparing breakfast for them. While they ate, the three of them discussed the struggle for power among the members of their Family. Their ponderings about who would do what to gain the throne left open more questions than were answered.

On the way down the mountain, headed toward the Royal Palace, the way, somehow, became confused. Familiar demarcations were not where they were supposed to be. Nothing was where it should be. They were lost. Random tried his Trumps, but was unable to reach anybody. The Trumps themselves seemed inactive.

Ready to allow any powers at work to lead them where they wished, they began to dismount. Random was first to see it. Not very distant stood the unicorn. It moved away, but Corwin, Random, and Ganelon knew it was meant to be followed. The unicorn remained in sight, but always partially obscured as it led them. It led them to a low shelf in the mountain. Then the unicorn disappeared in a blaze of light. The three men found themselves at the primal Pattern, the true etching in rock that created the universe, Amber included.

There was much significance in what Corwin, Random, and Ganelon found at the primal Pattern. For instance, they were able to determine that a darkened area they saw on this Pattern corresponded to the black road that ran through all the shadows to Amber. They discovered a purple-winged griffin at the end of a leash guarding the Pattern. It both amazed and amused them that the creature was friendly toward them. In helpless fascination they watched the destructive force of the Pattern. Frightened by the griffin, Random's horse Iago had retreated onto the edge of the Pattern. The Pattern began its eerie workings, and the horse gradually dissolved into nothing.

What took greater precedence at this crossing for Random, however, was the Trump with a dagger through it. Ganelon had retrieved it from the Pattern. Then Ganelon showed Random how a drop of his blood had a "blotting" effect on the Pattern, similar to the much larger blot near its center. Examining the face of the young man on the Trump more closely, Random came to an alarming revelation. He shared it with Corwin and Ganelon. He pointed out the resemblance of the picture to himself. The Trump was that of Martin, Random's son.

After Corwin told Random that there had been a connection between Benedict and Martin, Random chose to try Benedict's Trump. He found it active once more, and Benedict brought them to his location. Once they had joined Benedict on another part of the mountain, Random told of their adventure since leaving Tir-na Nog'th.

In his turn, Benedict explained how Martin had come to him in Avalon, and how he had taken the boy under his wing. Benedict had introduced Martin to the Tecys in a special shadow, and Martin spent much time there. Although Martin decided to travel in Shadow, he often sent messages to Benedict. Some years ago, Martin had returned to the Tecys injured with a serious sword wound. He had recovered and left again, leaving word for Benedict not to worry.

That was the extent of Benedict's knowledge of Martin's whereabouts. Random decided that he wanted to seek out his son. He asked Benedict to take him to the Tecys, and he asked Corwin if he could use his horse Star for the Shadow ride. Before departing with Benedict, Random requested that Corwin inform Vialle of these latest events. Then Random and Benedict began their journey through Shadow.

On their Shadow ride, Random spoke much, and Benedict was impressed by the changes he saw in him. When Random described what he had seen at the Pattern in Amber on the day Eric had died, and what he had learned of Dara from Corwin, Benedict was inclined to believe him. In fact, Benedict's interest was piqued to the extent that he intended to seek Dara out, just as Random was seeking Martin.

Random had done another small favor for Benedict. Using whatever technical knowledge he had gained in Shadow, Random attached the arm that Corwin brought back from Tir-na Nog'th to Benedict's stump. It fit as naturally as if it belonged there. Although Random hadn't thought of it at the time, it was a special providence that brought Benedict and that arm together. After their last breakfast on that lost trail of Kolvir, Random had no room in his own saddlebags for the mechanical arm. So, instead of stowing it with his horse, Iago, Random had placed it with Star, Corwin's horse. Then he forgot all about it, even when Iago died in the Pattern and he borrowed Star to make this trip. Providence was at work.

When Benedict returned from the hellride alone, he told Corwin that he had traveled with Random as far as a city named Heerat. Benedict had been anxious to return to Amber, largely in order to learn more about Dara from Corwin. Meanwhile, Random continued on his own, following a lead he had picked up in Heerat.

Once Random found his son in a distant shadow, Martin agreed to return to Amber with him. At Martin's request, they met with Corwin at the cenotaph erected for Corwin long ago.

In brief, Corwin explained that their brother Brand was presently intent on destroying the universe. With this in mind, Brand had sought the Jewel of Judgment. Brand wanted to attune to the Jewel so that he could inscribe a new Pattern with himself as leader. Martin confirmed that it was Brand who tried to kill him, leaving his blood on the Primal Pattern.

Young Martin then told his past history. He described how Brand had managed to trick him, got him close enough through a Trump contact to stab him. After Martin had escaped, he went to the Tecys, recovered somewhat, and went off into

Shadow again. He didn't want to contact Benedict because he didn't want to do anything to tip Brand off that he was still alive. In his discourse, Martin told of his meeting the girl Dara, who cared for him for a time. She had confirmed that she was descended from Benedict, but also had her lineage with the Courts of Chaos.

As their conversation concluded, Random told Corwin he intended to bring Martin to meet Vialle, and then, gradually, the others in the Family. Corwin asked Martin pointedly if he had seen Dara since, and Martin quickly responded that he had only been with her that one time. It seemed to Corwin to be too rapid a denial. Corwin had hoped to put Random on his guard concerning this newfound relative, but it is uncertain if Random recognized Corwin's intent.

They were interrupted by Trump contact from Ganelon, and Corwin stepped aside to receive his message. Neither Random nor Martin could hear what transpired. When Corwin ended his contact, he hurriedly asked Random for his mount Star. He hadn't the time to explain and rode off, leaving Random and Martin on their own to reach the Royal Palace.

It was only a short interim during which Random reintroduced Martin to his wife. There was not much time for Martin to meet many of the others. A surprising turn of events had happened: Oberon had returned.

The king didn't give any explanation as to where he had been, and Random was as perplexed as anyone about Oberon's sudden reappearance. He had given individual orders to his children, making it clear that they would launch an attack against the Courts of Chaos in three days' time.

Random discussed Oberon's return, and the impending war, with a disgruntled Corwin over lunch. Random's discussion of Oberon's actions turned to personal matters:

"The part that bothers me . . . After Dad had mounted and waved a good-bye, he looked back at me and said, 'And keep an eye on Martin.' "

"That is all?"

"That is all. But he was laughing as he said it."

"Just natural suspicion at a newcomer, I guess."

"Then why the laugh?"

"I give up. . . .

"Might not be a bad idea, though. It might not be suspicion. Maybe he feels Martin needs to be protected from something. Or both. Or neither. You know how he sometimes is." . . .

"I had not thought through to the alternative. Come with me now, huh? . . . You have been up here all morning."

"All right. . . . Where is Martin, anyway?"

"I left him down on the first floor. He was talking with Gérard."

"He is in good hands, then. Is Gérard going to be staying here, or will he be returning to the fleet?"

"I do not know. He would not discuss his orders." (CC, 9–10)

As Random and Corwin walked down the stairs, they heard some noise below. Rushing down, they reached Gérard outside the throne room. He pointed out an inexplicable situation. An invisible barrier prevented anyone's entry into the throne room. Inside, sealed off from them, were Martin, Benedict, and Dara. They were speaking but could not be heard.

When a sword suspended in air appeared before Dara, Random was completely mystified. He thought he recognized it as Grayswandir and asked Corwin about it. Corwin spoke as if he knew what would happen. He told Random and Gérard that they would not be permitted to enter until two objects disappeared from the throne room.

Benedict lost his mechanical arm to the suspended duplicate of Grayswandir. Those two objects sank into the floor and disappeared. Suddenly, the way was clear for Random, Corwin, and Gérard to enter the room.

Dara was caring for Benedict when they reached them. Random questioned his son. Martin explained that he had communicated with Dara by Trump. She asked to see Amber, and he brought her there. Then Random contacted Benedict and brought him to meet Dara. Martin didn't go into the mystery of the sealed room, if he knew it, because Random and Corwin were more interested in the Trumps he carried. They were drawn in a different style than was known to them: cards of Martin, Dara, and an unknown youth. Martin said it was this young man who had drawn the Trumps. Dara told them that the image was that of her son by Corwin, Merlin.

Benedict urged that they move to a room down the hall where the Family could talk more privately. They did, and Dara explained the situation. In spite of past alliances, she claimed she was cooperating with King Oberon in preparing for war against the Courts of Chaos. Her feelings had been changed through her association with Martin and Oberon. She showed them Oberon's signet ring, saying she was presently acting under his orders. She told them that Oberon wanted Benedict to mount his attack of the Courts of Chaos immediately.

Benedict made it clear that he would not take such an action without confirmation from the king. Random asked if their sister Fiona was still at the primal Pattern, where Corwin had said she had been. Since Oberon was there with Dworkin, as Dara had said, Random suggested they reach him through their sister. Random, Corwin, Benedict, and Gérard concentrated on a Trump of Fiona. With their combined efforts, they reached her at the primal Pattern.

Fiona was near the primal Pattern while Oberon and Dworkin were inside the cave. She told Corwin she would go to Oberon to get confirmation and then contact him again. She ended their contact, and they remained waiting for her return message. A while later, Fiona contacted Corwin. She was with Dworkin and Oberon in Dworkin's sitting room. Corwin asked to be brought through. As Fiona obliged, Random called out, asking what was going on. Before fading, Corwin said that he would be back to tell them shortly.

When Corwin returned it was through some special power of Oberon's, sending him through Shadow back to the room where the others waited. Corwin confirmed that Dara was working with their father. Dara gave Benedict some final orders, and then Benedict trumped out to join his men stationed at the Courts of Chaos.

Dara transmitted orders to Random as well: He was to join Julian and his troops at the Forest of Arden, which led to the ways of Shadow. Gérard was to remain in Amber as its custodian. They parted, initiating the business at hand.

Of course, Amber and all the shadows up to the Courts were not aware of the Patternfall battle until after it ended. However, all accounts of it show that Random's life was forever changed during its course.

With Julian and his forces, Random had ridden into the battle. He had chosen a heavy sword in his fight against these lords of darkness. In the major part of the battle, Random led troops on horseback near the high ground of the enemy camp. A knight dressed in green was in his company.

Early in the fighting, it seemed that the troops of Amber were falling back. This was overturned when Benedict signaled with his sword off to the west. Seemingly out of nowhere, Bleys led troops in a flanking maneuver that took the enemy by surprise.

The fighting continued in earnest even while Random and others saw Brand using the Jewel of Judgment against them from a mountain cliff. Random, Deirdre, Fiona, and several other horsemen rode through the enemy lines to reach Brand. As they approached, Brand discharged a bolt of lightning that unhorsed their group, tossing them to the ground.

Using her special powers, Fiona held Brand against the edge of the Abyss, while Random attempted to reason with him. Brand held Deirdre captive in his grasp.

Random reached an impasse with Brand, neither one willing to give in to the other. Their negotiations were halted when the recorded face of Oberon appeared in the sky and spoke to them. Among the things that image had spoken was the prophecy that came to mean so much in regard to Random: "With my passing, . . . the problem of the succession will be upon you. I had wishes in this regard, but I see now that these were futile. Therefore, I have no choice but to leave this on the horn of the Unicorn." (CC, 113)

When the image of their father was gone, Fiona and Random tried to persuade Brand to join them in ending the Death Storm that was destroying the universe. Brand would have none of it. Not forgiveness nor praise from his siblings. Before he could act to carry out his threat to kill Deirdre, however, Brand's expression changed to one of fear. He seemed to be literally burning from within. Random may have surmised the cause, but Brand began calling out to Corwin to stop his spell. Brand carved his knife edge along Deirdre's face. Deirdre bit his arm, pushed him, and pulled away. An arrow appeared, protruding from Brand's throat. Brand dropped the knife. A second arrow pierced his chest. Tipping toward the very edge, Brand reached forward, grabbed Deirdre, and before anyone could move, he took her over the cliff edge with him.

Corwin had started running up the ledge toward where Brand and Deirdre had been. He easily would have gone over the ledge after them. Random jumped to intervene and struck Corwin in the jaw.

When Corwin regained consciousness, lying on his back farther back from the edge of the Abyss, Random was caring for him. At that point, the knight in green who slew Brand with silver-tipped arrows revealed himself. It was Caine, alive and well. Caine explained that he used a shadow of himself to fake his death, then listened to the Trumps of his siblings while in hiding. He hadn't been sure whom to trust and used this method to try to learn some of the secret dealings going on. Caine admitted to Random that he had been the one who stabbed Corwin in his room.

All proceedings halted a second time when the funeral procession for Oberon crossed along the black road to the Citadel of the Courts of Chaos. They could see that the driver of the horse-drawn carriage containing Oberon's coffin was Dworkin.

As the procession passed, Fiona asked if Order had been reestablished on the other side of the storm. Corwin revealed to them that even if the late king hadn't succeeded in repairing the Pattern, he had created a new Pattern himself. Although Random remained silent on the matter, he listened as the others pondered the possibilities of two Patterns coexisting. No definite conclusions were drawn.

Random, with the others, quietly observed the visits of Dara and the young man named Merlin to the resting Corwin. Like the others, Random very likely occupied himself in some small way concerning the final "cleaning up" of the battle.

As Merlin spoke quietly with Corwin some distance away, several nobles and members of the Family, grouped together, pointed toward the Abyss. A dust cloud had risen, and there was the soft sound of horse's hooves against stone. Random and the others watched as their patron creature climbed over the edge and stood before them: the unicorn.

The unicorn took a step forward and turned to look toward Corwin and Merlin. It stared calmly at them. Then it turned and took some further steps toward Random and the small group he was with. It moved closer, and Random could see that it wore the Jewel of Judgment around its neck.

Cautiously, the unicorn stepped toward the small crowd. Grtradually, it came close enough to be touched. It knelt, its forelegs bending, its head lowering. The Jewel had slid to the base of its single horn, and that horn was barely touching the person before whom it knelt. Random reached for the Jewel, removed it, and said, "Thank you."

Julian was first to place his sword at Random's feet to show his allegiance. He was followed by Bleys, Benedict, Caine, Fiona, Llewella, Corwin, and Merlin. Random accepted their expression of loyalty. Suddenly, the unicorn rose and ran down the slope of the mountain. Minutes later, it was out of sight.

As his first official statement as liege of Amber, Random initially addressed all of his followers, but then quickly addressed himself to Corwin:

"I had never expected anything like this to happen . . . Corwin, can you take this thing and stop that storm?"

"It is yours now, . . . and I do not know how extensive the disturbance is. It occurs to me that in my present condition I might not be able to hold up long enough to keep us all safe. I think it is going to have to be your first regal act."

"Then you are going to have to show me how to work it. I thought we needed a Pattern to perform the attunement."

"I think not. Brand indicated that a person who was already attuned could attune another. I have given it some thought since then, and I believe I know how to go about it. Let's get off to one side somewhere."

"Okay. Come on."

[Random led the way farther down the slope where someone had kept a cooking fire going. Corwin sat with Random as the new king began again:]

"About this king business; . . . What am I going to do, Corwin? It caught me totally unprepared."

"Do? Probably a very good job." . . .

"Do you think there were many hard feelings?"

"If there were, they did not show . . . You were a good choice, Random. So much has happened recently . . . Dad sheltered us actually, maybe more than was good for us. The throne is obviously no plum. You have a lot of hard work ahead of you. I think the others have come to realize this.''

"And yourself?''

''I wanted it only because Eric did. I did not realize it at the time, but it is true. . . . But after his death, I kept finding reasons for not taking the throne. Finally, it dawned on me that it was not really what I wanted. No. You are welcome to it. Rule well, brother. I am sure that you will.'' (CC, 132–33)

Remembering the limits of their time because of the approaching storm, Random asked Corwin to begin his attunement to the Jewel of Judgment. They leaned close over the Jewel and Corwin guided him. It was like traveling along a three-dimensional version of the Pattern. The effort was as great as any actual traversing of Amber's Pattern, and both Random and Corwin were strained to their limits.

Random became attuned, but his brother collapsed with the effort. He carried the unconscious Corwin back to the others. Benedict and the others listened with new respect as Random discussed matters with them. The Amberites had won, and many of the Chaos soldiers were in custody. Random ordered Benedict to lead all the troops to the dark Citadel. If Random failed to turn back the storm, those remaining on this field of battle at least would be saved within the Courts. When Corwin regained consciousness, he saw that Random had set to work turning back the annihilating storm. He stood on a shelf of rock several meters closer to the storm, where he remained in sight.

Deep in concentration, Random may not have paid attention to Corwin, Fiona, and Merlin, who had remained behind with him. The storm required all his attention, and he used every measure of his will to move it, his back to his remaining kin.

In his Chronicles, Corwin recounted the aftermath of Random's efforts:

The sky turned, and turned again as I spoke. Standing against the storm, Random prevailed. It broke before us, parting as if cloven by a giant's axblade. It rolled back at either hand, finally sweeping off to the north and south, fading, diminishing, gone. The landscape it had masked endured, and with it went the black road. Merlin tells me that this is no problem, though, for he will summon a strand of gossamer when the time comes for us to cross over.

Random is gone now. The strain upon him was immense. In repose, he no longer looked as once he did—the brash younger brother we delighted in tormenting—for there were lines upon his face which I had never noticed before, signs of some depth to which I had paid no heed. Perhaps my vision has been colored by recent events, but he seemed somehow nobler and stronger. Does a new role work some alchemy? Appointed by the Unicorn, anointed by the storm, it seems that he had indeed assumed a kingly mien, even in slumber. (CC, 139)

Once Random was revived, he and Corwin attempted to reach Gérard by Trump back in Amber. Gérard responded, and this in itself told them that Amber and the shadows were again in existence. They learned from Gérard that years had passed in Amber during their absence.

Random joined Benedict in the Courts. They met with the king there and began the long process of drafting the Concord between Amber and Chaos. After the initial discussions, allowing for certain concessions and compromises on both sides, the scribes of both realms were left to their tasks. Random, Benedict, and the others returned to Amber. It was Random's understanding that Corwin wished to remain to visit the land of his son.

Random took up his duties in a cleaner, fresher Amber. The black road was gone. His siblings appeared willingly consolidated under his rule. At least, no hard feelings were shown. Benedict remained by his side to make sure things ran smoothly, and for a long while, they seemed to.

Merlin, Corwin's son, came to visit numerous times, and Random and Vialle made him feel welcome. Random grew used to the affairs of state, but he often found himself so busy with them that he gratefully allowed others to look after his nephew.

There were many happy times for Random, even though he was immersed in work. He enjoyed a pleasant family life with Vialle and Martin. Together, they made official visits to various shadow kingdoms, where Random hoped to bring closer ties. His keen interest in forming stronger bonds with other realms led to his being given a semiofficial nickname for the history books: The Great Conciliator.

After Random read Merlin's account of his father's adventures, he thought of making contact with Corwin's old friend on shadow Earth, Bill Roth. The arbitration for a Concord with King Swayvill had been going well, but Random felt the need of a legal advisor to go through the immense volume of verbiage manufactured by Swayvill's scribes. Asking his sister Fiona to meet with him, Random gathered up these papers into a kind of satchel. Since Fiona had met with Bill Roth once before, Random thought it would be politic, if not polite, to have her be the bearer of the draft. Fiona agreed, and suggested that King Swayvil accompany her on her visit to shadow Earth. Random saw no reason to disallow that.

In fact, the matter of the Concord was handled so well by Mr. Roth, that Random didn't mind his dealing with other legal matters from time to time, even though he himself had not met the man.

Early in his reign, Random arranged for the establishment of embassies from a number of shadow kingdoms. Most of them were located along and around the Main Concourse in town. In short order, the people of Amber accepted the members of these embassies and their families, particularly since they contributed so well to the local economy.

Many consider Random's establishment of foreign embassies on Amber's soil a shrewd move. King Oberon had made it a practice not to interfere in regional disputes between shadows. Even those realms with secured Golden Circle status had to plead their case for support—military or otherwise—and win approval of a royal committee, before the late king would provide manpower or provisions. This kind of caution was necessary, and King Random felt that too radical a change in protocol would be met with popular protest. However, a slower form of change, a policy of openness, for example, would help to avert any gross disapproval of future policies. Hence, setting up embassies.

This also allowed the king an access to information about current affairs in other realms that he would not otherwise have.

Diplomatic missions to other shadows became part of the norm. When the king himself couldn't take the time to travel, he sent one or more of his siblings to handle mundane matters, or sent one of them as a specialist in a certain area of commerce. Caine or Gérard, for example, to handle details of shipping, or Julian when an operation involved horse trading.

Random's reign had been going so well that he became particularly worried when two similar incidents occurred at roughly the same time in two different places. Caine and Gérard had been in the distant port of shadow Deiga, and Bleys was in another shadow kingdom. All had been involved in simple diplomatic missions. However, in the same day, Bleys was shot and wounded, and Caine was killed. The assassin had fired from a rifle. Random wasn't certain that ordinary gunpowder would work in Deiga, raising the suspicion that the killer knew of Corwin's special gunpowder. In addition, the fact that the killer attacked in two different shadows showed that he was a Shadow traveler; therefore, he may have been an initiate of the Pattern. The problem, thus compounded, left Random with much to worry about.

Knowing that Merlin still resided on shadow Earth, Random decided to contact him. The possibility that Corwin's gunpowder had something to do with these incidents urged Random to bring them to Merlin's attention. It seemed possible that Merlin might know something more.

Using Merlin's Trump, Random made contact while sitting in the Royal Library. Merlin came into view. He was outdoors with a slightly older man. Merlin responded to Random's calling his name, and the image became clearer. Random said, "I want you back in Amber right away. . . . Come on through." (TD, 110) Through the contact, Random could hear the sudden splashing of water just out of his range of vision. Merlin was momentarily distracted, but he reached forward to meet Random's grasp. Oddly, Merlin had his hand on the older man's shoulder, so that, inevitably, he also would be drawn through with Merlin.

Random was quite surprised to find the older man appearing with Merlin in the library of the Royal Palace. Merlin introduced the man as Bill Roth. It pleased Random finally to meet him, although he hadn't expected the odd formality that Roth presented. Roth fell to one knee, bowing his head low, and murmured, "Your Majesty." Random realized it was merely the unnecessary modesty that ordinary citizens attempt to profess before royalty. It was certainly unnecessary to act so in Random's presence.

Merlin explained the need to bring Mr. Roth to Amber at that moment. He was being pursued by someone he felt was dangerous to himself and Roth.

He also told Random, without having time to elaborate, that someone had been trying to kill him. This deeply disturbed Random, but he wanted Merlin to wait for a bit more privacy before sharing his account. Fortunately, Random's sister Flora entered the library, greeting the newcomers warmly. Flora had taken some of her legal business to Mr. Roth on shadow Earth, and so already knew him. Random permitted her to take Roth on a tour of Amber so that he could speak to Merlin alone.

Describing the murder of Caine and the attempted murder of Bleys, Random told Merlin that he had two great fears. One was that his siblings would take action on their own, possibly against each other, and against Random as well, for no greater reason than suspicion. The second was the rumor, being quickly spread in Amber, that Corwin was behind it. While Random refused to believe it, others suspected that Corwin had gone mad and was now taking vengeance on those siblings he perceived as having acted against him in the past.

Although Merlin was annoyed at hearing this rumor, Random placated him, explaining that his brothers and sisters were all on edge because of Caine's murder and Bleys's wounding. Then Random asked to hear Merlin's story.

Merlin recounted the near-misses on his life, perpetrated by some unknown assailant every April 30. He described the people he had become acquainted with while living in San Francisco on shadow Earth, including Julia Barnes and Lucas Raynard. He talked of Julia's horrible death, and the possibility of its having an otherworldly cause. He told of his subsequent encounter with Victor Melman, an artist and occultist, which had led to Melman's death under unusual circumstances. He went into the story of finding the building in which Melmen lived burned down and discovering bullets with pink powder in them. He concluded with the final remarks of his friend Luke Raynard, when they had been driving in Santa Fe, New Mexico. Luke had said that it was Victor Melman who told him of Amber, but Luke himself called Merlin "son of Corwin."

Merlin showed the bullets he carried in his pockets to Random. Although they took the time to enjoy a pleasant dinner with family, Random wanted to test the bullets as soon as possible. Using one of the rifles that Corwin had long ago brought into Amber, Random, Martin, and Merlin tried the bullets. First Random fired at an empty suit of armor and was surprised, though hardly delighted, that it worked. Martin tried a second round, which also fired. A third bullet was fired by Random, confirming the fact that they all contained the special gunpowder discovered by Corwin.

Merlin explained that the third bullet came from his friend Luke's pants pocket, something he discovered in Luke's hotel room in Santa Fe. With the connection made between Luke Raynard, the special bullets, and the warehouse where Victor Melman lived, Random needed to research the company on shadow Earth that manufactured the bullets. He chose to assign Flora to the job and left Merlin with his son while he went to find her.

The following morning was the funeral for Caine. Since he had been a son of the sea, Caine had expressed a wish to be buried near it. Hence, his coffin was to be placed in one of the sea caves that faced the vast watery expanse at the bottom of Mt. Kolvir.

The ceremony began at a chapel dedicated to the unicorn at the southern foot of Mt. Kolvir. As high priest of the realm of Amber, Random read passages from the Passing of Princes in The Book of the Unicorn. After completing those parts, he turned the rest of the service over to Gérard, who had been closest to Caine. Besides the Family, there were about fifty people in attendance. Nobles and merchants of Amber were there, as well as representatives from other shadows.

Four members of Caine's crew from his flagship lifted up his coffin. Slowly, they left the chapel and carried the coffin toward the sea caves. Random led the procession behind them. Julian, on horseback, led his mounted troops alongside the procession.

Random started slightly when Merlin put his hand on his shoulder. Merlin pointed upward toward a cliff face, and Random followed the line of his arm. A figure wearing a black cloak stood just a little ahead and above them, seemingly waiting for them to pass below him. Immediately, Random halted the procession and raised one hand to the Jewel of Judgment around his neck. He held the Jewel and concentrated his will. The dark figure began to move just as an ominous cloud formed above. The figure tossed a small black object at the procession. Gérard shouted for everyone to get down. Random remained standing, working his mental powers against the object flying through the air toward them. Lightning thrust out from the cloud, directed toward that object. It exploded, high enough and distant enough so that no one on the ground was harmed. The dark figure was gone though.

The funeral ceremony was duly concluded, and all the guests returned to the Royal Palace. A reception was given in the dining hall, which was noisy with conversation. Random caught Merlin long enough to say that he wanted to continue their earlier discussion in private after the meal. He told Merlin he would send for him later.

That night, Random used his Trump of Merlin to contact him. He felt the jarring pain of loud animal howls and saw immense doglike beasts as he reached Merlin's mind. It had been a dream, and Merlin was just waking from it. Recovering, Random asked Merlin to join him in a sitting room to the south of the main hall.

Over cups of coffee, Random asked Merlin to tell him about his project on shadow Earth, Ghostwheel. Merlin explained that Ghostwheel was a special kind of computer. He had incorporated elements of the Pattern into it, so that it had the same properties that the Trumps have. He constructed it in a unique, virtually unreachable environment so that no one else could access it. The purpose of Ghostwheel was to riffle through Shadow, so that it could find any specific shadow one might be looking for, and then it could set up a surveillance of that shadow. In his explanation, Merlin stopped short of telling Random that he had intended it for one very specific purpose: to seek out his father, Corwin.

At Random's request, Merlin summoned a remote terminal of Ghostwheel through its Trump. Although Merlin remained unconcerned, Random saw immediately the potential for danger in it. As Merlin explained, Ghostwheel could draw upon the energy of an entire planet as part of its function, and then discharge that energy. This was not its purpose, as Merlin explained, just the necessary power to enable it to shift through Shadow. Random couldn't believe Merlin's naïveté.

Random ordered Merlin to shut down Ghostwheel. His fears seemed verified when the remote terminal responded to Random, saying it had done nothing to offend him. It seemed as if the computer had a mind of its own. Random insisted, and Merlin told him he would make contact when it was shut down. Then he bade Random good-night and departed.

When Flora reported her findings about Brutus Storage Company to Random from San Francisco,

it began a chain of revealing facts. She told him that Brutus Storage was owned by J.B. Rand, Incorporated. She checked the office of J.B. Rand in Sausalito and found that it had been vacated two months earlier. Talking to the owners of the building which had housed J.B. Rand led Flora to an empty post office box. Payment for the box had been discontinued, the key returned, and it was not in use by another renter at that time.

Random remembered where he had seen a name very similar to J.B. Rand before. In the days when Corwin was suffering from amnesia on shadow Earth, their wayward brother Brand had posed as a psychiatrist named Hillary B. Rand. Under that guise, Brand had committed Corwin to Porter Sanitarium.

Whoever was behind the warehousing of special ammunition that could only be fired in Amber and environs knew of Brand's former impersonation.

At that point, Random began sending emissaries to several shadows that enjoyed Golden Circle status. He hoped to discover anything about living relatives of Brand's that Amber was not aware of. He was still waiting for news when he received contact from Flora again.

Her news was quite disturbing. According to Merlin, Lucas Raynard was actually Rinaldo, son of Brand. He had killed Caine and shot Bleys out of revenge for his father's death. Rinaldo had imprisoned Merlin in a cave of blue crystal before he could reach his Ghostwheel. When Merlin had contacted Flora by Trump, she had glimpsed both Rinaldo and a woman she recognized. She told Random that the woman was Jasra of Kashfa. She jogged Random's memory about the kingdom of Kashfa and how Jasra had become its queen. Although Random didn't know what connection Rinaldo had with Jasra, he decided that it would be worth investigating the political situation in Kashfa.

A servant led Old John to Random's quarters. Old John was a war-scarred veteran of many a campaign. Often, in the days when Oberon ruled, he had been sent on hazardous missions of a secret nature. Although Old John had been loyal to the Crown, he maintained a low profile during the reigns of Eric and Corwin. He did not care to serve a liege whose authority was in doubt. Random, of course, knew of him, and Old John saw fit to make his services available to the one chosen by the unicorn.

The king explained his need to Old John. An important part of his task was to examine possible alternate candidates for the rulership of that shadow. Random also needed to know what political factors were at stake that might be used to bring about a closer bond with Kashfa. The king had every confidence that Old John would fulfill his mission expeditiously. With dispatch, the emissary left on his information-gathering visit.

Random was enjoying an all too brief sojourn in the music room when he received contact from Merlin. As soon as he saw Merlin's image, he put down the drumsticks in his hands, stood, and said, "It's about time." He reached as Merlin reached for him, and, as Merlin stepped through, a tremendous cascade of flowers fell upon them. Looking at Merlin half-seriously, he said, "I'd rather you said it with words." (BA, 55)

Merlin spent hours telling Random what he had learned. Jasra had met and married Brand in a secret ceremony. Jasra had given birth to Rinaldo, known to Merlin as Luke Raynard. Luke had a close friend named Dalt, a mercenary with whom he campaigned on occasion. Luke and Dalt had been involved in a campaign to assault and take over a fortress called the Keep of the Four Worlds.

In light of Merlin's story, Random seemed less concerned about Ghostwheel and more concerned about the sudden appearance of a mercenary named Dalt. If he was the same man, Random had seen Benedict run him through with his sword in battle. Although the Amberites hadn't recovered the body, Random had thought that Dalt was permanently out of the picture. Random knew Dalt's history and told it to Merlin. His mother was Deela the Desacratrix, who had made attacks on the shadow Begma. The late King Oberon had led an army against her, defeating and capturing her. Deela escaped, and she returned several years later to pillage Begma. This time, Oberon sent Bleys to lead an army against her. Deela died in battle against Bleys and his men. Years later, Dalt began making attacks against Amber out of revenge. Dalt took his fight right up to the foot of Mt. Kolvir, but Benedict personally finished Dalt, and his mercenary soldiers were routed by the combined armies of the realm.

Random was quite worried. Dalt and Jasra and Rinaldo made for a dangerous combination. It didn't matter, as Merlin had indicated, that Jasra did not like Dalt. The association, in itself, was dangerous

enough. It seemed apparent to Random that Jasra and Rinaldo would continue to act against Amber out of revenge for Brand's death. And Dalt, of course, had his own ax to grind.

One fact was clear: Random had to do whatever was necessary to keep Jasra away from the throne of Kashfa. Just about that time, Old John returned and reported to Random. Old John told him of the Eregnor situation. It was a piece of land between Kashfa and Begma that both realms had been fighting over for centuries. Random had heard about it before, through his contacts with Begma. However, Random didn't know that the current ruler of Kashfa, a general named Jaston, was willing to give up Eregnor for payment of ancient war damage claims and a peace agreement with Begma. Old John explained that many of the Kashfan nobles were against Jaston's conciliatory policy. If Jaston continued in this way, someone among the nobles might lead a revolt, and the result could enable Jasra to regain power. No one enjoys a civil war, and a strong leader with a rightful claim, like Jasra, would be welcome if her presence ended the strife.

So Random saw clearly the path he would have to take. To prevent Jasra from returning to power, he would have to stop Jaston.

Old John also had an interesting piece of news to share with Random. It seemed to be fairly common knowledge in Kashfa, but not often spoken aloud, that Dalt the mercenary was an illegitimate son of Oberon of Amber. The lusty old liege had his way with Deela the Desacratrix while she was his prisoner. She gave birth to Dalt in Kashfa after she escaped.

After Old John departed, Random used his Trump of Merlin to try to reach him. He had heard that he was in Amber, and he felt it urgent to tell him what he learned of Dalt. Through the Trump, Random was nearly certain that he sensed Merlin's presence, but no connection was made, and the sensation faded.

A delegation from Kashfa wished to see King Random. Random told his servant to have the delegation meet him in the throne room. When he entered the room, the men of Kashfa were already seated. He was introduced to Arkans, the duke of Shadburne.

Arkans was an elder statesman, well-spoken and reasonable. He said he hoped that the citizens of Amber would be willing to put aside any old antagonisms they had with Kashfa. He hoped they could reach a reconciliation, and, if King Random saw fit, perhaps they could reach an agreement that would allow Golden Circle status. He then spoke of their current leader Jaston. The nobles, represented by this delegation, were concerned that Jaston's concessions to the people of Begma would make Kashfa weak. Arkans and the other representatives with him explained that divisive factions were growing. They were worried that the political situation would lead to civil war.

Having heard most of this before through Old John, Random expressed sympathy for their position. He was grateful, he told them, that they had come to see him about their problem. Random said he wanted to look further into the matter, that he wanted to consult his own advisors. Before departing, he made it clear that he would contact Arkans again. In fact, he would only help them if the duke of Shadburne was the principal spokesperson for Kashfa. The delegation agreed, and Random left the room.

Shortly after this, Martin came looking for his father. When he found Random, he told him that Merlin had returned to the palace, bringing an interesting artifact with him. Martin led Random to the main hall. Near the doorway was the lifelike statue of a woman, a cloak thrown over her left shoulder. Random had not actually seen her, but the face matched the description he had heard of Jasra.

The court jester found Random and Martin in the main hall and told them that Merlin was in a small room to the right. Random would have gone there directly, but the jester told him that Merlin was asleep. Random posted the court jester in the room with Merlin with orders to get him when Merlin awoke.

Random was talking to Benedict about recent events when the court jester's screams, growing louder as he approached, were heard. The jester nearly collided with them as he ran. Random quieted him, and the jester rapidly told a fantastic yarn about the wall of a room melting, just after Merlin woke up. Random, Benedict, and the jester rushed back to the room. It was empty. Suddenly, the floor shook as if from an earthquake. Noises seemed to emanate from the main hall. They rushed there to find Merlin talking to a disembodied voice. After a moment, Random recognized the voice as Rinaldo's.

Merlin's journals record this interchange:

"Merle!" Random called to me. "What's going on?"

I shook my head. "Don't know," I said.

"Sure, I'll buy you a drink," Luke's voice came very faintly.

A fiery blizzard swept through the center of the hall. It lasted only a moment, and then a large rectangle appeared in its place.

"You're the sorcerer," Random said. "Do something!"

"I don't know what the hell it is," I replied. "I've never seen anything like it. It's like magic gone wild." (BA, 213)

From where he stood, Random could see the large rectangle turn into a giant Trump of Merlin. The huge card rotated on an axis, and Random could see strange images in its face. As a human hand reached out from the face of the Trump, Benedict began to move, his sword in hand. Random stopped him, and they continued to watch.

Merlin asked Rinaldo about a secret he knew vital to the safety of Amber. Rinaldo told them what Random already knew about Dalt the mercenary. Although Random knew that Dalt was a son of Oberon, he didn't know that Dalt had proved it to Rinaldo by walking the Pattern in Tir-na Nog'th. Rinaldo added that Dalt had stolen the weapons and ammunition from Brutus Storage in San Francisco, then burned down the warehouse. When Rinaldo told them that Dalt would probably be heading for Amber, Random said wryly, "Another relative coming to visit . . . Why couldn't I have been an only child?" (BA, 214)

Rinaldo asked Merlin to give him a hand. Merlin reached for the disembodied hand coming out of the giant Trump. Instead of retrieving Rinaldo, Merlin found himself irresistibly drawn in. As he disappeared into the suspended Trump, Random shouted for his guards. However, there was little anyone could do. After Merlin disappeared, the giant Trump vanished as well.

With Merlin's disappearance, Random had three major concerns. The first had to do with whatever devious plans Rinaldo had for Merlin. The second had to do with the necessity of dealing with Dalt. The third involved finding a way to prevent Rinaldo from rescuing his frozen mother in Amber's custody and block their return to power in Kashfa. It was absolutely necessary for Random to take positive action.

He sent an emissary to Kashfa to ask Duke Arkans to meet with him in Amber. Arkans returned with the emissary and met privately with the king. After many hours, Random and Arkans had drawn up a treaty agreement that gave Kashfa Golden Circle Status in exchange for certain entitlements for Amber. Random had Bill Roth, his legal advisor, look over the draft. Mr. Roth told Merlin what he learned through his examination:

> "In the papers I got from Random, Amber specifically recognizes Kashfa as including the area of Eregnor. Arkans had insisted that go into the treaty. Usually—from everything I've been able to find in the archives—Amber avoids getting involved in touchy situations like this between allies. Oberon seldom went looking for trouble. But Random seems to be in a hurry, and he let this guy drive a hard bargain." (SC, 133)

Shortly thereafter, Random left for Kashfa with a small contingency force, headed by Benedict. Old John was a member of this party. The ruler of Kashfa, General Jaston, was pleased by Random's formal visit. It was rumored that the king of Amber planned to discuss the possibility of giving Kashfa Golden Circle status. Random and his party met with Jaston in conference. Although Random and Benedict spoke long and avidly about their desire for closer bonds with Kashfa and the need to smooth over the many problems that Kashfa faced in its history, neither spoke specifically about forming a treaty of commerce. King Random suggested they adjourn for the day and continue discussions on the morrow. Jaston maintained an amiable front, but it is likely that he was somewhat perplexed.

That evening, Jaston served up a state dinner for the Amberites. It was a pleasant social occasion, and the general enjoyed himself immensely. That night, as he was retiring, he had an unfortunate fall from a balcony. He never recovered.

As word spread of the general's death, Random met with Arkans. Even as a hasty state funeral was arranged, the palace guards were announcing their allegiance to Arkans, duke of Shadburne. Certain other nobles in the city proclaimed their support of Arkans. Eventually, word returned to the palace that many of the citizens supported the advancement of Duke Arkans.

Random remained in Kashfa an extra two days in order to iron out plans with Arkans. As the second day wore on, Random gave Benedict his orders to return with the rest of the party to Amber. One member of the party stayed behind to report to Random as needed. The king intended to return to Amber later in the evening. Meeting with Arkans again, Random enjoyed a long discussion with him over supper. He returned to Amber quite late, and Vialle was already asleep. He joined her without waking her.

He was up before his wife awoke, dressed, and went to the kitchens for some breakfast. When he finished, he thought he'd relax in the library, where he had placed some musical instruments, and he met Martin along the way. They talked quite a bit in the library while Random did some tricks on the drums. Martin joined in, playing a saxophone.

The eruption that occurred threw Random off his seat and left him scrambling on the floor. The entire palace seemed to have been rent as if it were being ripped apart by a giant hand. The door to the library and, in fact, the entire wall were gone, fallen into rubble somewhere below. Edging forward, Random looked over the empty space where the wall had been. He stared amazed into open-walled rooms across a wide abyss.

He cursed loudly at the lord of Chaos (Merlin, perhaps?), but was distracted by the voice and appearance of a handsome man holding an unconscious girl in a room across from the library. The stranger said, "The lady is injured, Your Highness." (KS, 202) Random directed him to his quarters, where Vialle would be able to help. He was much too worn to be amazed as the stranger and the unconscious girl levitated through the air to his quarters. Turning to Martin, Random saw that he was unhurt. He told his son that he had to take care of some matters in his quarters and departed, making his way as best he could.

Reaching his quarters, Random saw that Vialle was already tending to the girl. His wife told him she was Coral, the younger daughter of the Begman prime minister. The stranger sat in a chair by the foot of the bed on which Coral lay. He introduced himself as Merlin's stepbrother Mandor. As Vialle worked, she spoke to Random briefly about the early visit of the Begman delegation. He listened carefully, letting Vialle tell her story in her own way as she cared for Coral.

Out of the corner of his eye, Random saw Merlin talking to Mandor. He turned to confront Merlin about this sudden disaster to the palace, but he stopped when he saw, standing beside Merlin, the old mage Dworkin.

After greeting Random, Dworkin asked to examine the unconscious girl. While Dworkin joined his wife by the bed, Random received a Trump sending and moved away from the others to make contact. Vialle joined him as they received information from the remaining emissary in Kashfa. When he finished with the Trump, he spoke with Vialle a moment, then called to Merlin. Wanting to speak to Merlin privately, Random asked Vialle if they could confer in her studio.

Alone with his nephew, Random restated some of the facts that Merlin already knew about the Kashfa situation. He had planned to return to Kashfa that day to attend the coronation of Duke Arkans. Unfortunately, according to his messenger, something had happened to change all his plans. There had been a military coup. Rinaldo and Dalt had led a mercenary force that overtook the palace of Kashfa. Arkans was in custody, and Rinaldo would soon become the new king.

Merlin related some of the events that happened while Random had been in Kashfa. He explained that Vialle had placed Rinaldo under royal protection during the time he confronted Dalt and his mercenaries in the Forest of Arden. Together, Random and Merlin pondered how cleverly Rinaldo had fooled Merlin and Vialle into thinking he hadn't been in control of the situation. Rinaldo intentionally lost his fight with Dalt so they could go off together and plan their coup. In the meantime, it would appear that Rinaldo was temporarily out of the picture, seemingly unable to affect Random's political maneuver.

Although Random made it clear that he would not deal with Rinaldo for any trade agreements, he asked Merlin to attend his coronation unofficially. Merlin agreed.

In a strange interval, Random saw Merlin disappear down a hall that vanished. Half a minute later, Merlin reappeared below him. In talking to Merlin, Random revealed that he had been briefed about the cause of the explosion that destroyed parts of the palace. He had been told about the confrontation of the Sign of the Pattern and the Sign of the Logrus near Merlin's quarters. At that point, no doubt, Random had a glimmer of the greater problem facing the realm. Soon, the matter of Rinaldo's taking the kingship of Kashfa would be supplanted by the power struggle between the Logrus and the Pattern. And what was King Random supposed to do about that?

More strange events seemed to come to Random that were beyond his control. While Random was still in Vialle's studio, Dworkin took Coral away to some undisclosed place. Mandor had seen it, and told Random that Dworkin had deliberately vanished. There had been no coercion by the Powers. Dworkin had left behind the chain and setting of the Jewel of Judgment. The Jewel itself was gone.

When Merlin returned, Random asked him to use his talents to see where Dworkin had taken Coral. They learned that Coral had been taken to Kashfa. Since Merlin was ready to leave for Rinaldo's coronation, Random asked him to find out the status of Coral and Rinaldo and report back. Using a Trump, Merlin departed from them. Sometime later, when Vialle and Random were alone, she told him that mystical forces other than Trumps had been at work while Merlin conjured.

If Random depended solely on Merlin for the latest news from Kashfa, he would be frustrated indeed. Through his faithful emissary in Kashfa, Random learned of the nuptials of King Rinaldo and Coral. Long ago, when Kashfa and Begma were on relatively peaceful terms, Jasra had prearranged this marriage with Prime Minister Orkuz of Begma. The completion of that early agreement took the matter of Eregnor, once again, out of Random's hands.

Through the same source, Random discovered that Coral wore the Jewel of Judgment as an eye. Dworkin's mysterious operation in Random's quarters had been to replace her damaged eye with the Jewel. It is likely that Random became quite worried when he later learned that Coral had been kidnapped. From what he heard, it would appear that Coral, bearing the Jewel, was a playing piece in the struggle between the two Powers.

It was quite wondrous to Random, naturally, when Corwin made his return to Amber. Over a meal, Corwin told Random of being trapped in the Courts of Chaos for all these years. The Pattern that he had created had initiated the creation of a Pattern-ghost of himself, and the ghost-Corwin had been helping Merlin. He had been rescued by Merlin and the ghost-Corwin, who took his place in his black prison. After a long talk with his father at the old battlefield of the Patternfall battle, Merlin sent Corwin through Shadow back to Amber.

The news of current status at the Courts which Corwin brought back probably struck King Random as remarkable and surprising. His nephew, Corwin's son, had become King Merlin of the Courts of Chaos.

With Corwin joining Random at one pole as advisor, and Merlin ruling at the other pole, it seemed possible that the Powers would be in balance once again. Because he had a relative at the other side of things, Random hoped that he wouldn't have to work so hard at political maneuvering at this juncture in order to form an alliance between Amber and the Courts.

REBMA

The city under the sea that is a reflection of Amber.

Sometimes referred to as the Ghost City, Rebma is one of two realms that bears a replica of the Pattern. The other is the city in the sky, Tir-na Nog'th. Rebma is a mirror image of Amber, so that its architecture, landscape, and the Pattern itself, are the reverse of their counterparts in Amber.

It is located in the great sea, on the eastern shore of Amber. The only way for a traveler to reach it safely is by walking down to the bottom of the sea on Faiella-bionin, the stairway to Rebma. By keeping to the stairway, one may breathe freely and maintain normal body pressure in spite of the watery depths surrounding the traveler. Although gravity along Faiella-bionin is also maintained at Amber-normal, if one should jump or fall away from it, he would be instantly crushed by the pressure, even before drowning could occur.

Upon reaching the bottom of the staircase, one must walk a direct route toward elegantly carved arches, approximately two hundred feet farther. One must continue walking the ocean floor for a brief span of time until one reaches the golden gates of the city. Because of its watery environment, everything in Rebma is covered with a green haze. Tall,

fragile buildings form its skyline, and the palace lies in the center of the city. The palace duplicates the original, but differs from it in that mirrors are set in its walls, both inside and out.

Corwin's sister Llewella makes her home there. The leader of the city is the Lady Moire. Lord Corwin had occasion to visit there at the suggestion of his brother Random. At that time, while Eric ruled in the true city, Corwin was suffering from amnesia, and Random suggested that he walk the Pattern as a means of regaining his memory. Since the Pattern in Amber was out of reach of them, Random and Deirdre accompanied Corwin to the Ghost City under the sea.

Although Queen Moire gave them a cool reception upon their arrival, she felt an attraction for Corwin, whom she had not met previously. However, Random had come at his own risk, and Moire placed him under arrest. Years before, Random had lived in Rebma. He had run away with Moire's young daughter, Morganthe, without promising her the permanent bond of marriage. Morganthe returned to her homeland alone, and it was there that she gave birth to a son, who was given the name Martin. Months after Martin's birth, his distraught mother took her own life. When Martin grew to young manhood, he walked the Pattern of Rebma, which gave him as great a power as the Pattern in Amber would have. Having gained the talents of a prince of the true city, Martin left Rebma to walk in Shadow. His whereabouts were unknown to Queen Moire.

With Random's return to her city, Moire tempered her desire for vengeance with the calming effect of the distance of years. His punishment was to marry a blind girl, Vialle, and remain in Rebma for a year's time.

Moire led Corwin to the Pattern, which was in a corresponding place to the one in the deep recesses of the dungeons of Amber. Descending a spiral staircase that entered the black depths below the sea bottom, she took Corwin, Deirdre, and Random to an immense room bearing the black, shining image of the Pattern on its floor. Corwin was able to walk the Pattern, finding resistance in its electrical charges and invisible force fields. As a true prince of Amber, however, Corwin surmounted the difficulties of the walk and recovered both his memory and his powers. He used the forces of the Pattern to transport him to the true Pattern in Amber, where he intended to face his evil brother Eric.

RED BIRD

The large-crested bird created by King Oberon from the blood of his son Corwin. Its purpose was to convey the Jewel of Judgment to Corwin after Oberon used the Jewel in an attempt to repair the primal Pattern.

In his Chronicles, Corwin recorded the occasion of the red bird's birth:

> I watched as he cut my arm, then resheathed his blade. The blood came forth, and he cupped his left hand and caught it. He released my arm, covered his left hand with his right and drew away from me. Raising his hands to his face, he blew his breath into them and drew them quickly apart.
>
> A crested red bird the size of a raven, its feathers all the color of my blood, stood on his hand, moved to his wrist, looked at me. Even its eyes were red, and there was a look of familiarity as it cocked its head and regarded me.
>
> "He is Corwin, the one you must follow," he told the bird. "Remember him." (CC, 32)

The red bird accompanied Oberon while Corwin began a hellride south through Shadow, making his way to the Courts of Chaos. Corwin had stopped to rest in a desolate rocky region under a sky of green. It was a shadow of great distance from Amber, farther than he had needed to go before. But he knew he was well on the way to the Courts.

As Corwin rested and stretched, he heard a shriek from above. The red bird circled closer, then landed on his arm. Looking at its red-in-red eyes, Corwin sensed that the bird had a "peculiar intelligence." It allowed Corwin to reach over and take the Jewel of Judgment that it carried. When he mounted his horse to continue his hellride, the bird called out again and flew into the sky.

Sometime later, Corwin was riding through a narrow pass between high mountains beneath a black-and-red-streaked sky. He was suddenly assailed by someone firing a crossbow. He discovered that the attacker was his brother Brand. Brand slew Corwin's horse and was continuing to send bolts at Corwin. Although Corwin tried to ward him off with stones, Brand was able to pin him down and readied a death strike. Corwin was using the power of the Jewel to create storm clouds, and he stalled his brother's last firing of his crossbow. After replying with scorn, Brand aimed his crossbow.

The red bird gave a shriek and flew at Brand. Its suddenness caused Brand to drop the crossbow. As Brand fended off the bird, Corwin strode toward him, pulling out his sword from its scabbard. The bird flew off, circled, and dived again. Although Brand raised his arms to cover his face, the bird managed to tear out his left eye. Using special abilities he had acquired, Brand began to fade from sight. The bird continued to strike at his head with its talons, and both bird and man disappeared before Corwin could reach them.

Corwin never saw the bird of his blood again. It is unlikely that it could have survived whatever vengeance Brand meted out to it once he had control of the situation again.

RED '57 CHEVY

Originally an oil painting by Polly Jackson, an artist living in Santa Fe, New Mexico, on shadow Earth. It took on real proportions for Merlin of the Courts of Chaos, however, becoming the means of transportation to his father's Pattern.

Merlin had purchased the painting during a showing of Jackson's work at the Santa Fe East Gallery when he and Lucas Raynard were passing through on a cross-country trip. Both admired the work greatly, and it apparently left a strong impression on Merlin. Before leaving shadow Earth, Merlin placed the painting in storage in San Francisco, where he had lived for a number of years.

The red '57 Chevy became a physical object when Merlin found himself in a strange universe of negative images, later referred to as the Undershadow. The automobile, with snow partially covering it, was off to the side of a dark ribbon of road that Merlin was walking. It had been one of several areas of light that revealed images not completely formed. The Chevy was among the first images to take on a clarity and color. He reached toward it with his hand, touched the car, and brought back a handful of snow into the Undershadow. It was real, and some unknown power had objectified it out of Merlin's recent thoughts of the Jackson painting.

Sometime later, the '57 Chevy appeared again as a real vehicle. Merlin had encountered constructs of the Pattern, or Pattern-ghosts, of both his friend Luke and his father Corwin. They were chased by unknown assailants in a realm very near to the Courts of Chaos, but the Pattern-ghost Corwin seemed to know where he was going as he led Merlin and the ghost-Luke. From a realm of fog in which the three floated, Merlin saw a shapeless form in the distance. Using his unique powers, Merlin carried them toward it. It took form as the red Chevy. They climbed in, and Merlin discovered he was able to turn on the ignition and drive it. The car radio worked, and they listened to music that had appeal for Merlin. They seemed to be driving on an actual surface, and the all-encompassing fog lifted a bit, allowing them to see trees and landscape. The ghost-Corwin appeared confident in trusting the Chevy to take them to a definite place, and this was confirmed when Merlin recognized a large tree beside a shining patch of land. The automobile had conveyed them to Corwin's Pattern, the new Pattern that he created out of his own psyche. The ghost-Corwin had Merlin park the car in a relatively flat area beside the tree.

Corwin's Pattern had acted on its own to create the ghost-Corwin, maintaining him to give him lasting endurance. It had also reached Merlin when he was being sought by both Powers, projecting the ghost-Corwin to him at an appropriate time. This special Pattern had also read Merlin's thoughts, creating the red Chevy and projecting it to Merlin's location as an aid in bringing him to the Pattern.

The red '57 Chevy became a way station, associated intimately with Corwin's Pattern, in which the ghost-Luke could stay to help act as guardian for the Pattern. The ghost-Luke willingly accepted this role, so that the Pattern would continue to sustain him. The ghost-Corwin explained that it was necessary to guard the place because the Powers would likely make an attempt to disrupt it and destroy this Pattern. After walking the Pattern with Merlin and the ghost-Corwin, the ghost-Luke transported to the car, got into the passenger side, turned on the radio,

and began his guardianship. The ghost-Corwin joined him just long enough to show him where food caches were placed. They shook hands, and the ghost-Corwin walked off into the fog.

When Merlin returned, he brought with him his brother Jurt and the real Luke Raynard. The ghost-Luke was listening to Renbourn's "Nine Maidens" on the car radio when they appeared. Unwilling to leave his duties beside the Pattern without the ghost-Corwin's knowledge, the ghost-Luke remained with his alter ego to compare notes, while Merlin and Jurt returned to the Courts of Chaos for a time. After a while, Merlin returned with his brother Jurt, who volunteered to take over as guardian of the Pattern. The others went off, with the Pattern in agreement, leaving Jurt at the Chevy. When, again, Merlin arrived, he brought with him Coral, Nayda, and Dalt. At this point, Merlin was exhausted, made the introductions, and went to sleep on the grass beneath the tree.

He was aroused by earth tremors, noticed a newly formed crack in the ground near him, and saw the ghost-Luke, Dalt, Coral, and Nayda attempting a picnic on a blanket, being disrupted. The ghost-Corwin had returned and bent to talk to Merlin about this new problem. Standing, alert and aware, Merlin used a magical ring he wore to battle the Logrus, which had caused the earthquake in its attempt to destroy Corwin's Pattern. Merlin's magical abilities were equal to the Logrus forces, and he stopped the quake.

Merlin told the ghost-Corwin and the others of his plan to free the real Corwin in the Courts of Chaos, with the ghost-Corwin's help. The ghost-Luke, Jurt, Dalt, Nayda, and Coral remained behind, by the '57 Chevy, while the ghost-Corwin left with Merlin for the Courts.

The painting by Polly Jackson should still be in storage in San Francisco on shadow Earth. However, it has been claimed that the painting hangs in the home of a well-known writer living in Santa Fe. It is also believed that the artist painted only one such automobile, as part of a series of car paintings that had been on exhibit.

Mrs. Jackson, strictly a studio painter, had used a photograph of an actual '57 Chevy she had taken beside an adobe house in Santa Fe. She created the artwork in her studio using the photograph.

Since the red Chevy has now become an integral part of Corwin's Pattern, perhaps there are many such vehicles on many shadow Earths, and these inspired numerous Polly Jacksons to paint numerous red Chevys from a variety of angles and in a variety of styles.

REIN, LORD

Minstrel to the Royal Court of Amber, knighted on the battlefield at Jones Falls by Lord Corwin. The composer of numerous ballads, he is working on a long epic entitled "The Siege of Amber."

Lord Rein had befriended young Prince Corwin when he was just a child and Corwin was fully grown. As a child, Lord Rein had been a candidate for court jester. Others in the Royal Court played practical jokes on him, making him the butt of their humor. He took them in stride however, presenting to the world a thoughtful, almost solomn demeanor, with an extremely thin frame that complemented the intellectual yearnings of his spirit. Corwin accepted the boy as a companion out of a sense of guilt for being one of those who made Rein the butt of his jokes.

Rein followed Corwin about, particularly enchanted by the youthful prince's musical compositions. Having been given a lute by one of his teachers, Rein learned to play it fairly quickly. Shortly thereafter, Rein began to accompany Corwin's singing with his instrument.

In the passing years, their friendship grew, and the music and voices of the two were frequently heard in the halls and gardens of the Royal Palace. Since music was only one small part of Corwin's interests, he attempted to teach his companion some of his other avocations. Rein valiantly played in matches of wrestling and boxing, but his tiny, thin physique made for no contest against the strength of his elder friend. But Rein continued to pursue the rigorous training that Corwin enjoyed, if only to please his friend of long standing. Eventually, Corwin showed him what he learned of the martial arts from his time spent on the Shadow Earth. Although Rein was rather bad at the practice, he worked hard to develop some style. Seeing the need for learning some kind of self-defense, Rein allowed Corwin to coax him into practicing the procedures of these exotic arts until he knew them well and

could, at least, appear graceful in their performance. Rein also learned to use the saber, an exercise that he much preferred since it depended more on agility and skill than physical strength. Sword in hand, he was able to offer a passing challenge to Corwin, who otherwise could defeat him in any other form of combat.

During this time, Rein's position in court was as page to Prince Corwin, and he graduated to court minstrel as young manhood came upon him. When dark things out of a shadow called Weirmonken invaded the outer regions of Amber, Corwin made Rein his squire and they went off to war. Following Corwin and a company of men into a large, hidden encampment of the shadow beings of Weirmonken, Rein proved himself an able soldier. Corwin called the charge, and the battle was a long and bloody one. Corwin's men were outnumbered four-to-one, but they were better trained in tactics and dicipline. The shadow beings depended on brute strength and superior numbers, but this was their downfall. Late in the battle, when it looked like the creatures of Weirmonken would defeat the soldiers of Amber, Corwin had been cornered by a dozen of them. By dint of fearful blows, the shadow beings had separated Corwin from the others, forcing him back to the roaring falls, where he would be trapped. At the very edge of the roiling waters, Corwin was bleeding from several nasty gashes, and one particularly large and hefty being had come close to decapitating him. Corwin was ready to jump the falls and take his chances there when three or four creatures cried out and fell dead from some turbulence behind. Corwin saw the bloodstained face of young Rein, slashing out with his saber, a terrible grimace on his face. Rein's sudden assault brought a momentary confusion upon the creatures who surrounded Corwin, and Corwin took the advantage. The prince's first maneuver was to behead the huge shadow being who would have done the same to him. After that, fighting inward from both ends of the remaining group, Corwin and Rein slaughtered the others. As they met in the middle, when the last enemy had fallen, Rein and Corwin embraced and laughed loudly. When they returned to the main part of the battlefield, they found the creatures of Weirmonken in defeat: those that remained alive were held captive, including two or three high officers.

While his men acted as witnesses, Corwin gave Rein the title of "Lord," dubbing him with his sword Grayswandir, for his actions in saving his life. The onlookers, save for the captives, applauded and shouted their approbations to the young new lord.

After the Battle of Jones Falls, they returned to enjoy a victory celebration in the Royal Palace. Lord Rein was looked upon with new regard, and although he acted as the king's official minstrel, he proved himself a fine spokesman as well. He became a trusted advisor to the court and was often assigned to diplomatic tasks of welcoming guests upon arrival to the palace.

Taking pleasure in his duties, Lord Rein remained impeccably loyal to King Oberon. Dressed in crimson, he would often soothe the troubled mind of the king with his gentle, lilting ballads. He lost touch with his friend Corwin, who spent centuries away on the shadow Earth. Rein chose to remain close to the throne of Amber, working quietly and unobtrusively. In his solemn, unpretentious manner, he maintained a semblance of normality in the Royal Court during the time when Oberon had mysteriously wandered off. His efforts at statesmanship were so unobtrusive that he was able to remain a close observer of the court even when the succession to the throne was in question.

When Oberon's son, Eric, forcibly took the crown of kingship in his father's absence, Rein was not even thought of as a figure to be feared in the court. Eric and his loyal constituents accepted Rein as a trusty member of the nobility, ignoring his former friendship with Corwin. For his part, Rein accepted the prevelent conditions of the court, but was biding his time, hoping for the safe return of Oberon.

With Corwin's capture and imprisonment, Rein felt terrible anguish. The usurpation of the throne by Eric and the blinding of Corwin were unforeseen by Lord Rein. When these events occurred, Rein was unable to act to prevent them. However, staunchly true to his friend of long standing, he brought the blinded Corwin food, clothes, wine, cigarettes, and matches. For anyone else, such actions, if detected, would have led to arrest and execution, but for Lord Rein such considerations seemed incomprehensible. His dedication to the kingdom was beyond reproach, and even Eric himself would have sought some other solution if confronted with Rein's acts other than invoking the death sentence. As it happened, Lord Rein needed only to elicit a promise of silence from the guard on duty to obtain safe passage for himself and his smuggled bounty.

Of course, Lord Rein offered Corwin much more than food, clothing, and physical ease: He gave his old friend solace in having at least one loyal friend in Amber. Lord Corwin eagerly listened as Rein told him the latest news of Amber, which included tidbits of gossip along with details of important matters of state. Hearing that genial voice of long ago did much to boost Corwin's spirits. It may be said that the Lord Rein rescued Lord Corwin from near-certain death a second time.

Lore Rein continues to reside in his quarters within the Royal Palace. He serves as court minstrel and advisor to King Random, endeavoring inconspicuously in much the same capacity as he had under King Oberon. Never having married, he remains loyal to his single love: the kingdom of the true city.

REVERSE OF SHADOW WALK

The capability of a being of Chaos to reach into Shadow to obtain some material object and bring it back with him to his precise locality.

In order to manipulate Shadow in this way, one must walk the Logrus in the Courts of Chaos. Although the Logrus is the counterpart of the Pattern in Amber, and therefore imprints upon those who walk it similar abilities, this particular skill is in varience to those powers given to an initiate of the Pattern.

Merlin, son of Corwin of Amber and Dara of the Courts of Chaos, clearly documents, in subjective terms, the sensations involved in calling forth this ability:

> I closed my eyes and visualized an image of the Logrus—shifting, ever shifting. I framed my desire and two of the swimming lines within the eidolon increased in brightness and thickness. I moved my arms slowly, imitating their undulations, their jerkings. Finally, the lines and my arms seemed to be one, and I opened my hands and extended the lines outward, outward through Shadow.... The lines would keep extending through an infinitude of

Shadow till they encountered the objects of my desire—or until I ran out of patience or concentration. Finally, I felt the jerks, like bites on a pair of fishing lines. (TD, 89-90)

As an initiate of both the Logrus and the Pattern, Merlin is particularly adept at this skill. In spite of the seeming effort with which he descibes the use of the "reverse Shadow walk" above, he is usually quite successful, and he accomplishes it with greater ease than it takes to describe the process.

RHANDA

A young girl from the shadows close to the Courts of Chaos with whom Merlin played when he was a boy. He had taught her the Bonedance Game in an underground mausoleum, where they had met almost every day for dozens of cycles, as time was measured in the Courts.

In his journals, Merlin expressed a nostalgic fondness for that early period in his life, before shadow walking and relatives from the Amber side of things complicated his life. He returned to the underground play area of his youth when he visited the Courts after the death of King Swayvill. He reflected upon the sudden loss of his friendship with Rhanda there:

One day Rhanda had simply stopped coming, and after a time I had, too. I'd often wondered what sort of woman she had become. I'd left her a note in our hiding place, beneath a loose floor stone, I recalled. I wondered whether she'd ever found it.

I raised the stone. My filthy envelope still lay there, unsealed. I took it out, shook it off, slid out my folded sheet.

I unfolded it, read my faded childish scrawl: *What happened Rhanda? I waited and you didn't come.* Beneath it, in a far neater hand, was written: *I can't come anymore because my folks say you are a demon or a vampire. I'm sorry because you are the nicest demon or vampire I know.* (PC, 71-72)

A while later, Merlin had a dream that included Rhanda. Since the dream was influenced by the magic of his uncle Suhuy, it is likely that there were elements of fact integrated with the fancy.

He saw her as a grown woman, looking back at him from a mirror, with "long, coal-black hair and eyes so dark I could not tell where the pupils left off and the irises began. Her complexion was very pale, emphasized perhaps by her pink eye shadow and lip coloring." (PC, 210) When she explained about her parents' attitude toward him, she said, "They would rather I cultivated the acquaintance of the sons and daughters of men and women, than of our own kind." (PC, 210)

She revealed then that she had the long, extended fangs of a vampire herself. Before she departed the realm of Merlin's dream, she invited him to visit her in her shadow, named Wildwood.

RI'IK

A shadow that is a great distance from Amber but somewhat closer to the shadow Avernus, where Corwin conspired with Bleys against Eric. Corwin had reached Ri'ik in order to raise an army to dethrone Eric the Usurper.

Ri'ik is a cold shadow with short, hairy humans who subsist as hunter-gatherers. Only the hardiest of crops grow in the frost-covered soil, so most of the menfolk hunt small predators while the women farm the land and gather the rough-skinned fruit of the small, gnarled trees.

When Corwin first entered one of their camps, tall and lean and hairless, dressed in remarkably soft woven garments, the people of Ri'ik thought him a god. They spoke a harsh, guttural form of Thari, and Corwin was able to make himself understood by their leaders. In rather callous terms, Corwin had described this first encounter:

"I walked among Shadows, and found a race of furry creatures, dark and clawed and fanged, reasonably manlike, and about as intelligent as a freshman in the high school of your choice—sorry, kids, but what I mean is they were loyal, devoted, honest, and too easily screwed by bastards like me and my brother. I felt like the dee-jay of your choice.

Around a hundred thousand worshiped us to the extent of taking up arms.'' (NP, 106)

The short, hairy men of Ri'ik were comfortable working side by side with the tall, red-skinned natives of Avernus as Bleys and Corwin trained them. When the training was complete, Corwin took most of the men of Ri'ik on board the warships Bleys had constructed. Bleys marched overland with the remainder of the beings from Ri'ik, relying more heavily on his already-disciplined infantry of Avernus.

Corwin's vessels were ultimately defeated by Amber's fleet under Caine's command. Before abandoning his crew, Corwin promised them that Caine would spare their lives. Only nine men of Avernus and three of Ri'ik remained on Corwin's flagship. Corwin joined Bleys and his army traveling by land. All but Corwin had been slaughtered on the climb up Kolvir. Bleys's fate had been uncertain.

Corwin sought the people of Ri'ik a second time, accompanied by Ganelon of Lorraine. This time, they drove two trucks loaded with rifles and specially made ammunition from shadow Earth. These folk of Ri'ik were enthusiastic at the sight of Corwin, seeming to forget the loss of their hundred thousand good men years earlier. In fact, they were disappointed that Corwin wanted to recruit only a few hundred men.

Most of this second army survived the second assault. Believing they were embattled in a holy war in heaven, they took orders easily as Corwin and Ganelon commanded they fire their strange weapons at hideous flying creatures and beings that burst into flames upon impact. When that great battle was over, those of Ri'ik were unsure as to who the enemy had been. It seemed to them that human soldiers remained alive and unharmed when they were supposed to be part of the enemy camp.

Most of the soldiers of Ri'ik remained in Amber, under the direction of Ganelon, while preparations were under way for an even greater war. However, they were kept separate from the regular army of Amber, whose members were growing resentful of the presence of the creatures of Ri'ik.

Corwin moved the men of Ri'ik to the Forest of Arden, to be kept in training by Ganelon and away from the main portion of the population of Amber. When the Patternfall War took place, it is certain that many of these beings joined forces with the troops under Julian. As a result of their courage in that final conflict between the poles of existence, those of Ri'ik gained acceptance by the Amberites. Afterward, a large proportion of the survivors returned to their homeland. Still, on occasion, one will come across a farmer or tradesman on the outskirts of Amber who had been a citizen of Ri'ik.

RILGA

Wife of King Oberon of Amber and mother of Julian and Gérard.

As a young woman, Rilga was brought back to Amber from a distant shadow by Oberon. They were wed in the Royal Palace and spent a number of happy years together. Within a short time, she gave birth to her two sons, who were fairly close in age, Julian being the older. During this time, Oberon remained in Amber close to his family.

The metabolism of most people from Rilga's homeland is much more rapid than that of those from Amber. This biological factor caused Rilga to age at a much greater rate than those who had spent their lives in the true city. Unfortunately, this affected the relationship she had with her husband. Oberon moved to separate quarters and made frequent excuses to avoid being with her. She suffered greatly from his lost affection, but she bore her sorrow well. Rather than remain in the palace under such conditions, she notified her husband by court messenger that she intended to leave the city to live at a shrine dedicated to the unicorn in the countryside.

Seizing the opportunity, Oberon gave way to his wanderlust and, offering up as a rationale the necessity of handling some diplomatic matters in a shadow with Golden Circle status, went away for a while. He returned with a new bride that he had married in the shadow he visited. This caused a great deal of controversy with his council and the noble classes, and nearly erupted into a scandal of bigamy. Oberon and his new wife, a lovely woman named Harla, claimed that they had been married for many years in the shadow of her birth. Since Oberon never offered any documents, and Rilga was living at a distant shrine, growing quite old and senile, the scandal died down.

Rilga received her children only once or twice in her remaining life. She died a lonely old recluse in a small thatched cottage beside the unicorn shrine. The priests who acted as caretakers of the shrine had her buried in a small cemetery on a hilltop overlooking her home.

RINALDO [A.K.A. LUCAS RAYNARD]

Son of Queen Jasra of Kashfa and Brand of Amber. Born within recognized marital and religious proprieties, Rinaldo had a clear claim to the kingship of Kashfa.

Rinaldo lived in San Francisco on shadow Earth for eight years, befriending Merlin, son of Corwin of Amber. While there, he used the name Lucas (Luke) Raynard, hiding his parentage from Merlin. Although he came to enjoy his sojourn on shadow Earth, his main purpose for residing there was to avenge the ignoble death of his father on the son of an Amberite. A secondary purpose was to use a wilderness area of the American Southwest to train mercenaries for military assaults in other shadows.

Merlin's journals piece together some of the early history of Rinaldo, deferring to various sources of information. For instance: It was a hermit named Dave outside of the Keep of the Four Worlds who told him of the secret wedding ceremony of Brand and Jasra, and of Luke's upbringing and his friendship with the mercenary named Dalt. Much later, Merlin learned from a Pattern-ghost version of Luke that Jasra had been the maidservant of Merlin's mother in the House of Helgram in the Courts of Chaos. According to the ghost-Luke, Brand had met Jasra there when he was plotting against Amber. From his Aunt Flora, Merlin discovered the manner in which Jasra had become queen of shadow Kashfa. Tracing these several factors would support both Rinaldo's right to personal vendetta and his claim to Kashfa's throne.

When Rinaldo was a boy, he lived in and around Kashfa, but he also spent time with Jasra in a stronghold, the Keep of the Four Worlds, that she

and Brand had wrested from another wizard. Rinaldo recalled carving his initials in the leg of the former owner, Sharu Garrul, whom his parents had placed in a frozen state. Brand was away much of the time, and Jasra taught him her Arts. On those rare occasions when his father was around, he taught Rinaldo how to draw Trumps of the kind used by the Amberites. When Brand deemed his son old enough, he took him to the ghost city in the sky above Amber, Tir-na Nog'th. Without anyone in Amber learning of it, Brand guided his son in walking the Pattern there. Rinaldo has not indicated where he asked the Pattern to send him once he was initiated. Afterward, he was able to draw Trumps on his own with great proficiency.

The younger daughter of the prime minister of the shadow Begma, Coral, knew Rinaldo quite well. She described what the young prince was like to Merlin:

> "Rinny? Sure I know him. He didn't like us to call him Rinny, though. . . ."
>
> "You really *do* know him? Personally, I mean?"
>
> "Yes, . . . though it's been a long time. Kashfa's pretty close to Begma. Sometimes we were on good terms, sometimes not so good. You know how it is. Politics. When I was little there were long spells when we were pretty friendly. There were lots of state visits, both ways. We kids would often get dumped together."
>
> "What was he like in those days?"
>
> "Oh, a big, gawky, red-haired boy. Liked to show off a lot—how strong he was, how fast he was. I remember how mad he got at me once because I beat him in a footrace."
>
> "You beat Luke in a race?"
>
> "Yes. I'm a very good runner."
>
> "You must be." (SC, 64–65)

Much later, Merlin learned that the relationship between Rinaldo and Coral had been closely bound to the politics of Kashfa and Begma. When the two kingdoms had been undergoing a period of peace, Jasra had made an arrangement with Coral's father, who was an ambassador at the time, to cement their alliance. A marriage decree had been drawn up, and young Rinaldo and Coral were married by proxy. However, diplomatic relations between the two shadows fell apart again, and the liaison was all but forgotten. Coral and Rinaldo did not see each other again for many years.

The friendship between Dalt and Rinaldo probably began when they were very young, especially since they both came from the same area. Dalt had lived in a region between the two shadows named Eregnor, and he also spent time in Begma. According to Dave the hermit, Rinaldo had been a wild youth who frequently ran away from his mother in Kashfa to join with Dalt's band of mercenaries. He had ridden with them, even though Jasra had put bounties on the heads of Dalt and his men. As Dave explained: "I think she didn't like it that he'd run to them and they'd take him in whenever he had a falling out with her." (BA, 50)

Aside from growing up in and around Kashfa, and spending a little time residing in the Keep of the Four Worlds as a boy, Rinaldo also was shown the Cave of Blue Crystal by his mother. Jasra had taught him its usefulness as a sanctuary against magical intrusion. Its crystalline walls prevent the passage of anything of a psychical nature, making it impregnable to sorcerous attack. Rinaldo also learned of the linking quality of stones from the crystal cave. Any stones kept in proximity for a length of time would maintain a connection, so that an individual holding one stone could trace his way to another stone, even through Shadow. Rinaldo remembered these lessons and made use of them later.

After becoming an initiate of the Pattern, Rinaldo took to drawing Trumps of useful places and people. He may have begun under the guidance of his father, but he was extremely skillful, and Brand was around less often after their walk in Tir-na Nog'th. When Merlin found Luke's personal Trumps, done in his own hand, he saw Trumps of the crystal cave, Luke's apartment in San Francisco on shadow Earth, a former apartment of Merlin's, an unfamiliar palace, Dalt, Jasra, Merlin, Victor Melman, Julia Barnes, a partly finished one of Bleys, three uncompleted sketches of Ghostwheel, and several duplicated editions of cards left at Julia's apartment, dubbed Trumps of Doom by Merlin. Among these Trumps were two drawn by Brand. They bore the likenesses of two distant relations on the Amber side: Delwin and his sister Sand. (BA, 111–12)

It is not known exactly how Rinaldo was told of his father's death. Nor is it known where Rinaldo and Jasra were during the Patternfall battle and

thereafter, when the news probably reached them. If they were not within the Courts of Chaos, then they were swept into nonexistence for a time along with all the other shadows that were touched by the all-consuming Death Storm.

It is clear, however, that Rinaldo learned of Brand's death on an April 30, Earth-time. That date was significant because Rinaldo and Jasra chose to make attempts on Merlin's life on that date every year for the eight years that Merlin resided on shadow Earth. Again, it is unclear why they decided to take revenge on Merlin, son of Corwin, before trying to assassinate the other members of Amber's Royal Family. Perhaps it was because Prince Corwin was hailed as a hero of the battle, and his son seemed vulnerable outside the protective reach of Amber. Rinaldo said that his mother had him make the deadly attempts on Merlin as practice before striking directly at Oberon's children.

While there were political problems facing Jasra and Rinaldo in Kashfa, Rinaldo had also arranged to attend Berkeley University on shadow Earth, initiating his plans to meet Merlin as a fellow student. If we believe all that Dave the hermit told Merlin at the Keep of the Four Worlds, then there is some confusion about the order of events. According to Dave, Jasra had gone to the Keep, leaving Prince Rinaldo in charge of Kashfa, while she charmed Sharu Garrul. Jasra was gone a long time, and Rinaldo became concerned. He raised an army of Kashfans to march on the Keep, but he wasn't satisfied with the numbers. He contacted Dalt, had Dalt and his mercenaries join his regular army, and promised to pay them with treasure from the Keep. Dave had been a foot soldier in this campaign. Rinaldo led the way through Shadow to the Keep. When they attacked, the Kashfans and mercenaries had heavy losses. That was when Dave deserted, hiding in the nearby mountains. From his mountain sanctuary, Dave observed the turn of events: the Kashfans were winning over the Keep's army. He learned more about the changes at the Keep from other deserters. According to Dave:

"I got the impression that the attack forced Jasra's hand. She'd apparently been planning to do away with Sharu Garrul all along and take over the place herself. I think she'd been setting him up, gaining his confidence before she struck. I believe she was a little afraid of the old man. But when her army appeared on the doorstep she had to move, even though she wasn't ready. She took him on in a sorcerous duel while her guard held his men at bay. She won, though I gather she was somewhat injured. Mad as hell, too, at her son—for bringing in an army without her ordering it. Anyway, her guard opened the gates to them, and she took over the Keep. That's what I meant about no army taking the place. That one was an inside job.'' (BA, 47)

Rinaldo paid Dalt and his men as he had promised, against Jasra's wishes.

"Big argument at the time, too, [Dave had told Merlin] between Rinaldo and his mom, over just that point. And she finally gave in. That's the way I heard it from a couple of guys who were there. One of the few times the boy actually stood up to her and won, they say. In fact, that's why the guys deserted. She ordered all witnesses to their argument executed, they told me. They were the only ones managed to get away.'' (BA, 50)

After Jasra established herself at the Keep, Rinaldo went off. It's likely he returned to San Francisco on shadow Earth, where he had begun his college studies and spotted Merlin. Since both he and Jasra also began their conspiracy against Merlin, they may or may not have known about continuing attacks against the Keep of the Four Worlds, assaults made by a usurper to the throne in Kashfa.

In his freshmen year at Berkeley, Rinaldo, calling himself Luke Raynard, took many of the same classes that Merlin took. While Luke decided he would seek to excel in his classes, he determinedly showed his dislike for Merlin. Luke felt a genuine hatred for the family that was responsible for his father's death, possibly fueled by the influence of Jasra as well. Although Jasra acted as advisor, Luke himself planned and executed the first murder attempt on Merlin. It involved placing a spell on an ordinary truck driver. Luke put him in a trance with the posthypnotic suggestions that directed the driver to Merlin. Luke fully intended to kill Merlin, but, unfortunately, Merlin saw the truck driver bearing down on him in time to leap away. The driver died in the hospital, never regaining consciousness.

Sometime after this, Luke gradually felt a growing respect for Merlin. Going for the same sporting events, competing against each other for the highest grades in their courses, and even dating some of the same college girls, Luke's interest in the young man, so much like himself, continued to grow. In his journals, Merlin traced the sealing of their friendship to the time they both succeeded at the Olympic finals. Just as Merlin remained silent about his past, Luke told Merlin very little about his family background. He said only that he had come from the Midwest, never even pinpointing where.

Luke met Gail Lampron at college in some unspecified way. They became close shortly thereafter. Since Luke and Merlin became friends, it soon was common for them to double-date: Luke with Gail, and Merlin with another student named Julia Barnes. Both Gail and Julia were attractive, but neither was the cheerleader type. They were engaging young ladies who spoke their minds on a wide variety of subjects. Merlin recorded a discussion they had together at dinner. The four of them had spent the day sailing on Merlin's sailboat, and that evening they ate at the marina. In their talk, Luke was making the point that morality is guided by one's personal need to act out of duty to something that one honors. Society does not dictate morality, in his mind, so much as one's duty to a cause dictates morality. That was Luke's argument, and with our perspective on his true background, it is understandable why he would feel that way.

From the information that Jasra gave Merlin, Luke first met the artist Victor Melman while still in college. Herein is Jasra's account:

"He [Rinaldo] took a few lessons from the man. He'd liked some of his paintings and looked him up. Perhaps he bought something of his, too. I don't know. But at some point he mentioned his own work and Victor asked to see it. He told Rinaldo he liked it and said he thought he could teach him a few things that might be of help. . . .

"After a time he [Melman] began speaking of the development of personal power, using all those circumlocutions the half-enlightened love to play with. He wanted Rinaldo to know he was an occultist with something pretty strong going for him. Then he began to hint that he might be willing to pass it along to the right person. . . .

"It was because he realized Rinaldo was rich, of course . . . Victor was, as usual, broke himself at the time. Rinaldo showed no interest, though, and simply stopped taking painting lessons from him shortly after that—as he felt he'd learned all he could from him. When he told me about it later, however, I realized that the man could be made into a perfect cat's-paw. I was certain such a person would do anything for a taste of real power. . . .

". . . I handled most of his training. Rinaldo was usually too busy studying for exams. His point average was generally a little higher than yours, wasn't it?" (KS, 23–24)

In spite of the fact that Jasra was disparaging about her son's talent in painting, she urged him to create a unique work to give to Melman. Disguised by a hood and trench coat, Luke presented Melman with a large painting of the Cabalistic Tree of Life, an artistic achievement containing the same potency as the Trumps. On other occasions, Jasra disguised herself in the same way when she visited the artist, fooling him into believing he was dealing with a single "master." Jasra and Luke were grooming Melman to be a part of a deadly game of sorcery meant to lead to Merlin's death. The conspiracy was extended beyond Merlin's college years.

When Luke and Merlin graduated from Berkeley, they were such promising candidates in the computer field that they were hired by the same company, Grand Design. Merlin rose rather quickly in their ranks as a computer programmer, and Luke earned their esteem as an enterprising salesman and marketing analyst. Luke and Merlin remained good friends in spite of the fact that Luke traveled out of town often, bringing in new prospects and expanding his sales territory greatly.

Keeping in touch with both Jasra and Dalt, Luke was mindful of the politics back in Kashfa and at the Keep. He used his travel opportunities to stake out an isolated region in New Mexico for paramilitary training, bringing in mercenaries, with Dalt's help, from other shadows.

Whenever Luke was back in San Francisco, he and Merle would frequent art galleries and museums. They shared an interest in art, and Luke kept up with his own painting. Somewhere along the

way, although it is uncertain when, Luke broke up with Gail.

Luke and Jasra had purchased a warehouse on the east end of San Francisco, under the name of J.B. Rand. They used the warehouse to store the same kind of specialized ammunition and weapons that Corwin of Amber had once used. Maintaining that cache was one more reason for Luke to hold on to his connections in that city.

It is likely that Luke was responsible for the second April 30 attack on Merlin, but that his mother continued them thereafter. Luke may even have acted on at least one occasion to prevent an assassination attempt against his friend. Apparently, other agents also aided Merlin on subsequent April 30 attempts.

Luke may have begun having doubts about killing Merlin because they had become friends. His reconsideration may also have been part of a natural rebelliousness he felt for all demands his mother made upon him. Then again, he may have formed some more deliberate course of action that precluded Merlin's death. He had seen drafts of Merle's plans for Ghostwheel at Grand Design. Knowing Merle's true background, Luke was intrigued with the potential of the device. He broached the subject with Merle while he drove Merle in his station wagon around Santa Fe, New Mexico:

"What is Ghostwheel?" . . .

"What?"

"Top secret, hush-hush, Merle Corey project. Ghostwheel. . . . Computer design incorporating shit nobody's ever seen before. Liquid semiconductors, cryogenic tanks, plasma—" . . .

"My God! . . . It's a joke, that's what it is. Just a crazy hobby thing. It was a design game—a machine that could never be built on Earth. Well, maybe most of it could. But it wouldn't function. It's like an Escher drawing—looks great on paper, but it can't be done in real life. . . . How is it you even know about it? I've never mentioned it to anyone." . . .

"Well, you weren't all that secret about it . . . There were designs and graphs and notes all over your work table and drawing board any number of times I was at your place. I could hardly help but notice. Most of them were even labeled 'Ghostwheel.' And nothing anything like it ever showed up at Grand D, so I simply assumed it was your pet project and your ticket to security. You never impressed me as the impractical dreamer type. Are you sure you're giving this to me straight?''

''If we were to sit down and build as much as could be constructed of that thing right here, it would just sit there and look weird and wouldn't do a damned thing.'' (TD, 72-73)

Since Merlin didn't know Luke's real identity at the time, Luke simply played the game. He acted mystified about Merle's creating an ''impossible'' project and tried to draw him out further. Merlin didn't offer any additional information, and their conversation turned to other matters. However, Luke was convinced that Ghostwheel was real and complete. He needed to learn more about it, and so it was necessary that Merle not come to harm until he did.

On the morning before Merlin intended to leave San Francisco and travel cross-country, Luke found him in a diner he used to frequent. Luke told him he had returned to San Francisco from a successful business trip two days earlier. He had been to Julia's apartment the night before for a visit, and she had given him a note for Merlin. Julia's note made it seem important that Merle see her before he left.

During their breakfast, Luke tried to ascertain why Merlin had decided to quit his job and leave town so suddenly. He was persistent in trying to find out what kind of work Merle had finished and where he intended to go. Since Merle was staying one more day, Luke offered to treat him to dinner and gave him a matchbook for the address of the motel in which he was staying. At the diner, Merle happened to notice Luke playing with his key ring. Besides the keys, it contained a pendant with a blue crystalline stone.

It's possible that Jasra was speaking to Luke by telephone from Victor Melman's apartment when she had Merlin incapacitated. When Merlin managed to disappear by Trump, the act may have set both Jasra and Luke into motion. On Luke's part, he may have considered that Merle would return to Amber and report back about his knowledge of Luke. Someone in Amber might have known about Brand and Jasra, about Dalt, and about Luke himself. That person could then help Merle put things together, uncovering Luke's actual identity and deciphering his intentions to murder the members of

the Royal Family. Luke's subsequent steps may have been intended to prepare a military force to march against Amber. Still, he seemed to move with a measure of caution.

Before leaving his motel in San Francisco, Luke left two items with the desk clerk to give to Merle Corey. One was a gold ring with a blue crystal stone. The other was a brief note. It read:

> Merle,
> Too bad about dinner. I did wait around. Hope everything's okay. I'm leaving in the morning for Albuquerque. I'll be there three days. Then up to Santa Fe for three more. Staying at the Hilton in both towns. I did have some more things I wanted to talk about. Please get in touch.
>
> Luke (TD, 59–60)

Merle caught up with Luke in the hotel lobby in Santa Fe. Luke was dressed in fatigues and boots, covered with dirt. He explained that he had been hiking in the Pecos, needed a few minutes to shower and change, and would meet Merle in the hotel bar.

Refreshed, Luke caught Merle just as he seemed to be running off. Merle returned to the table he was saving and Luke joined him. Noting that Merle was wearing the ring he had left in San Francisco, Luke didn't appear very surprised when Merle couldn't easily pull it off his finger. He offered to sell Merle the ring. Merle excused himself and headed for the bathroom. Again, supposition might claim that the blue crystal ring had its mate on Luke's key ring. He might have been able to track Merle's progress, and know something of his whereabouts, through the unique affinity of the blue stones.

When Merle returned, he had gotten the ring off, and he handed it to Luke. Instead of wearing it, Luke wrapped it in a handkerchief and put it in his pocket, saying it was a gift for someone.

They went to dinner at a local restaurant. Merle commented on the way several people greeted Luke. He was clearly well-known. Luke told him it was because he did a great deal of business in Santa Fe. It was conceivable that those who stopped to talk to Luke were less business people and more recruited personnel involved in tactical maneuvers.

After dinner, Luke proposed their taking a ride,

during which time he asked Merle about the Ghostwheel Project. Merle told Luke about being approached by a well-dressed businessman named Dan Martinez just before Luke arrived at the bar. Luke had no idea who Martinez was, but their discussion of Martinez's knowledge of Amber led Luke into revealing that he had known the artist Victor Melman, who, Luke said, also spoke of the land of Amber.

Merle told him that Melman and Julia Barnes were both dead. Luke appeared to be genuinely surprised. When Merle showed Luke the Trumps he had found in Julia's apartment, Luke admitted that he had delivered them to her, but that they were given to him by Melman. Luke may not have expected that Merlin would have ended up with the Trumps, for he made a peculiar request:

"First, give me those cards."
"Why?"
"I'm going to tear them into confetti."
"The hell you are. Why?"
"They're dangerous."
"I already know that. I'll hang onto them."
"You don't understand."
"So explain."
"It's not that easy. I have to decide what to tell you and what not to." (TD, 77)

Before Luke could go any further, someone began shooting at them. Luke had a gun and shot back, hitting the assailant. They discovered it was Dan Martinez. Luke ordered Merlin to leave immediately, taking the car back to the hotel. Threatening him with his gun, Luke said, "Merlin, son of Corwin, . . . if you don't start running right now you're a dead man!" (TD, 78) Merlin quickly drove away. Silently, he walked back after pulling the car off the road. Neither Luke nor the body of Martinez was to be found.

Although Merle didn't see Luke again for quite a while, he was able to trace Luke's activities in retrospect after Luke made several significant admissions. Apparently, Luke decided to take direct action against the Amberites, possibly because Merle was temporarily out of reach and he realized that Merle would soon be joining them.

When Merle returned to Amber with his friend Bill Roth, King Random informed him of the assassination of Caine and the attempted murder of Bleys. Caine had been with Gérard in shadow Deiga negotiating a new treaty. He was killed by a rifleman on a roof. Although Random couldn't be certain, the shot fired may have contained the same special gunpowder that Corwin had discovered for use in Amber and its environs. Someone with that special means would have been behind Caine's death. Bleys had also been shot by a gunman in another shadow, but Bleys was not badly injured.

During the funeral for Caine, a cloaked figure on a hilltop tossed an explosive at the procession. Bill Roth had spotted the suspicious individual in time, and Random used the power of the Jewel of Judgment to cause the bomb to detonate before it reached them. The mysterious form on the hill disappeared.

On Random's orders, Merle traveled through Shadow to approach his Ghostwheel Project in order to shut it down. As he traveled closer to the realm of his construct, he found that Luke was following him. Luke joined him, rescuing him from the hazardous warnings of Ghostwheel to keep away. They traveled on together. Luke explained very little of his actions on the night he had hidden the body of Dan Martinez and run away. Only after Merle used a Trump to escape a Shadow-storm caused by Ghostwheel, and subsequently fell under Luke's power, did Luke reveal the truth about himself.

"I am your cousin Rinaldo . . . I killed Caine, and I came close with Bleys. I missed with the bomb at the funeral, though. Someone spotted me. I will destroy the House of Amber with or without your Ghostwheel—but it would make things a lot easier if I had that kind of power. . . .
"I went after Caine first . . . because he's the one who actually killed my father." (TD, 182–83)

Using a large boulder to block the sole entrance, Luke trapped Merle in the blue crystal cave.

While it cannot be verified, Luke was likely in contact with both Jasra and Dalt, becoming updated on political matters in Kashfa. Since Jasra had maintained her rule in the Keep of the Four Worlds, she had lost in popular influence in Kashfa. A series of military leaders had retained the kingship there, and the people had grown accustomed to such authority. Generals of armies who become kings run things in an orderly way. If they seem somewhat tyrannical at times, at least they tend to deal with transgressors directly and with a minimum of intrigue.

At this point, Jasra must have urged her son to make certain arrangements with Dalt to assure Luke's gaining kingship of his home shadow. Luke would then have conferred with Dalt, and Dalt would have agreed to set in motion specific contingencies for the future. None of them knew just how long their tactics would be delayed, but a paramilitary staff would certainly be put in readiness.

Either Luke had his mother under surveillance, or else he happened to contact her by Trump just at a moment when she was in danger. Merlin had hold of her in some way near the crystal cave. Luke reached for his mother through the Trump connection, not fully formed yet. Jasra seemed to be struggling for air, although the reason may not have been readily apparent to Luke. He may not have seen the woman in a bedroom of another shadow, rising upward and punching Jasra full in the face. Merlin released his hold on Jasra, and she fell backward to Luke's location. No doubt, Jasra was able to fill Luke in on Merle's escape from the blue crystal cave.

Merlin was in Baron Bayle's home in the northern wine country of Amber when he received a Trump contact from Luke. He was hurt and needed sanctuary quickly, so Merle brought him through. Luke had a serious chest wound, and Merle learned that Dalt had caused it while they were in battle at the Keep. After Merle cared for him, and he was somewhat recovered, Luke explained some of his activities:

"Well, I'd been having trouble with Ghostwheel. I thought I almost had him talked into coming over to our side, but she [Jasra] probably thought I wasn't making progress fast enough and apparently decided to try binding him with a massive spell after—"

"Wait a minute. You were talking to Ghost? How did you get in touch? Those Trumps you drew are no good."

"I know. I went in."

"How'd you manage it?"

"In scuba gear. I wore a wet suit and oxygen tanks."

"Son of a gun. That's an interesting approach."

"I wasn't Grand D's top salesman for noth-

ing. I almost had him convinced, too. But she'd learned where I'd stashed you, and she decided to try expediting matters by putting you under control, then using you to clinch the deal—as if you'd come over to our side. Anyhow, when that plan fell through and I had to go and get her away from you, we split up again. I thought she was headed for Kashfa, but she went to the Keep instead. Like I said, I think it was to try a massive working against Ghostwheel. I believe something that she did there inadvertently freed Sharu, and he took the place over again and captured her. Anyhow, I got this frantic sending from her." (BA, 125)

Their conversation was interrupted for a time. Later, Luke told Merle about contacting Dalt and traveling to the Keep of the Four Worlds to rescue Jasra. Luke mentioned that Merlin had probably observed their attack on the Keep at the time that Merle encountered Dave the hermit. As for Dalt's wounding Luke, this is the way Luke described it:

"We were doing all right. Their defense was crumbling and we were pushing right along, when suddenly Dalt turned on me. We'd been separated for a time; then he appeared again and attacked me. At first I thought he'd made a mistake—we were all grimy and bloody—and I shouted to him that it was me. But he just kept coming. That's how he was able to do a job like this on me. For a while I didn't want to strike back because I thought it was a misunderstanding and he'd realize his mistake in a few seconds." (BA, 136)

While under Merle's ministrations, Luke met the possessing entity that had once been Gail Lampron on shadow Earth. It was presently inhabiting the body of Vinta Bayle. Vinta exhibited a knowledge of Luke during his years on shadow Earth that confirmed her being there. Luke took an opportunity to hold and kiss her for a moment, for old times' sake.

Luke offered a deal to Merle. He would reveal something vital to Amber's security if Merle would help rescue his mother from the Keep. Merle told him he would have to consider it, but he was willing to take Luke to a place where he would heal quickly in a different time stream. He took Luke to the Cave of Blue Crystal, left him with sufficient supplies, and allowed him the added courtesy of not imprisoning him.

After Luke had recovered sufficiently from his wounds, he gathered up his mercenaries, probably from New Mexico on shadow Earth, and went ahead with an assault on the Keep. Deciding on a surprise attack, they had come into the fortress on hang gliders. The attack was a disaster. The army of the Keep was bolstered by someone with sorcerous powers, and they easily defeated Luke's paramilitary force. Luke was captured and imprisoned. It may have been that the sorcerer of the Keep deliberately sought him out during the early stages of the mercenary campaign, avoiding doing injury to Luke.

Merle rediscovered Luke when Luke made Trump contact with him in the palace of Amber. Luke was rambling, talking as a disembodied voice, but he was able to see Merle in the palace. Merle showed him the frozen figure of Jasra, explaining that he had gone inside the Keep and stolen her from the sorcerer named Mask. In a disjointed way, Luke told of his defeat at the Keep.

Since King Random was in the room with Merle, Luke disclosed the information he had withheld about something vital to Amber. Dalt was an Amberite who had walked the Pattern in Tir-na Nog'th. Dalt had been to shadow Earth, stolen the rifles and ammunition from Brutus Storage, and burned down the building. Luke had found out about it afterward from witnesses to the fire.

Through a giant Trump of Merlin, Luke pulled Merle through to his location: an Alice in Wonderland bar, where their problems didn't seem so immediate.

If Luke remembered the incident of the Fire Angel and Bandersnatch chasing Merle and himself down a tunnel in freefall, it was probably a very blurred memory. Fortunately, Merle thought of the possibility that Luke had been drugged. He reached through Shadow for appropriate medicines to bring Luke out of his euphoric state. Merle then returned him to the Lewis Carroll bar, where Luke could remain in relative safety until his mind cleared and he could travel the shadows again.

In his journals, Merlin analyzed Luke's situation, as he saw it:

"Luke had told me that his attempted invasion of the Keep of the Four Worlds, by means of a glider-borne commando team, had been smashed. Since I had seen the broken gliders at various points within the walls during my own visit to that place, it was logical to assume that Luke had been captured. Therefore, it seemed a fairly strong assumption that the sorcerer Mask had done whatever had been done to him to bring him to this state. It would seem that this simply involved introducing a dose of a hallucinogen to his prison fare and turning him loose to wander and look at the pretty lights. Fortunately, unlike myself, his mental travelings had involved nothing more threatening than the brighter aspects of Lewis Carroll." (SC, 19–20)

The next time Merlin heard from Luke, Luke was relaxing beside a swimming pool and a bikini-clad girl. He had contacted Merle by Trump from a shadow in which the time streams were much faster than at the Lewis Carroll bar, so that he had recovered his mental awareness and made physical adjustment more rapidly after coming out of his drugged state. Although Luke had interrupted another Trump contact that Merle had been engaged in, Merle and he had a long conversation, exchanging some important facts.

Luke made clear his decision to call off his vendetta against the House of Amber. With Caine's death, honor was satisfied. However, he wasn't eager to turn himself over to King Random at this juncture. He asked about his mother, and Merle was unwilling to release her, both from the spell she was under and from his custody in Amber. When Merle explained that Mask could not be the wizard Sharu Garrul, Luke suggested that Jasra might prove a needed ally, since she knew the Keep, and the magical processes of bathing in the Black Fount, so well. Merle wondered about what he could offer her to secure her alliance. Luke said she would be willing to settle for permanent management of the Keep. Merle was doubtful, but he said he would think over the proposal.

In their talk, Merle inadvertently let slip the fact that Random was in Kashfa, on a mission related to the sudden death of Kashfa's ruler, General Jaston. Luke said, "I can see what's going on. I've got to admit Random's got style. Listen, when you find out who he puts on the throne let me know, will you? I like to keep abreast of doings in the old hometown." (SC, 103) Based on our knowledge of subsequent events, we can see that Luke's interest was more than academic.

When Merle told Luke of his added problem of Jurt, his half brother bent on killing him, Luke discussed the nature of the power of the Black Fount at the Keep. During his explanation, Luke let slip the fact that when he and his mercenaries attacked the Keep on gliders, they had used Corwin's special ammunition and rifles. The weapons were ineffectual there. Nevertheless, Merle should have picked up on the clue: If, as Luke had said earlier, Dalt had stolen the rifles and ammo before destroying Brutus Storage on shadow Earth, then Luke could not have had access to them if Dalt and Luke were enemies. Thus, Luke and Dalt must have reestablished their alliance when their mercenary force had gone against Mask and Luke was captured. This would explain Dalt's appearance at the Forest of Arden shortly after the conversation between Merle and Luke by Trump.

While Merle was entertaining a delegation from Begma with Queen Vialle, and in Random's absence, the queen was called away. A few minutes later, she sent for Merle. She informed him that Dalt and his mercenaries were camped near Arden, and Dalt was demanding that the Amberites turn over Rinaldo and Jasra.

At Vialle's request, Merle used a Trump to contact Luke. Luke was outdoors, by a campfire, dressed in green, and ready to join Merle in a fresh assault on the Keep of the Four Worlds.

Merle explained the situation and brought Luke to him to meet Vialle. After briefly talking to Luke, Vialle chose to place him under Amber's protection by giving him her ring. Luke received the queen's permission to join Julian at Arden, where Amber's troops were at a standoff with Dalt's men.

Merle took Luke aside, on the pretense of getting warmer clothes from his quarters, so that they could converse privately. Luke seemed too ready to say that he knew nothing of Dalt's march on Amber. After seeing the frozen Jasra in Merle's room, Luke renewed his efforts in trying to convince Merle to free his mother.

When they returned to Queen Vialle, she opened contact with Julian and allowed for Luke's passage. As Luke entered the Trump transfer, Merle joined him, so that both appeared at Julian's camp.

After Julian apprised them of negotiations and current status, Luke asked that he meet with Dalt immediately, even though it was after dark. The meeting was set up, Julian and Merlin acting as Luke's retainers, carrying torches to light the area, while two men with torches accompanied Dalt to the meeting place. Luke and Dalt spoke alone, out of Merle's earshot, then Luke returned. It seemed a small matter at the time, but before the meeting Merle had told Luke that Random had arranged for the crowning of a new king in Kashfa: Arkans, duke of Shadburne.

Luke told Julian and Merle that he had found a way to avoid a war between the two sides. He and Dalt would fight in hand-to-hand combat, without weapons. If Dalt were to win, Luke was to accompany him as his prisoner as they withdrew. If Luke should win, Dalt would allow himself to become Luke's prisoner while his officers led the mercenaries away. Although Merlin was against the deal, Julian found it quite reasonable.

The combat proceeded. As Merle began to cheer Luke on, the troops on both sides took up cheering, as if it were a sporting competition. Dalt defeated Luke, knocking him into unconsciousness. Both sides honored their agreement, and Dalt had Luke carried away as his men began their retreat. Afterward, when Merle returned to Queen Vialle, she said that she believed Luke had planned on making his challenge of personal combat from the start.

Sometime afterward, Merle had brought Nayda, older daughter of Prime Minister Orkuz of Begma, to his quarters. After he showed her the frozen form of Jasra, Merle attempted to contact Luke by Trump. Nayda seemed to have some secret knowledge that Luke would deliberately block Merle's sending. She was right.

Merlin tried Luke's Trump again at a time when he had attuned himself to the Jewel of Judgment as an added measure of protection. This is Merlin's account of that brief contact:

> I felt Luke's awareness, though no vision of his circumstances reached me.
> "Luke, you hear me?" I inquired.
> "Yep," he answered. "You okay, Merle?"
> "I'm all right," I said. "How about yourself? That was quite a fight you—"
> "I'm fine."
> "I hear your voice, but I can't see a thing."
> "Got a blackout on the Trumps. You don't know how to do that?"

"Never looked into the matter. Have to get you to teach me sometime. Uh, why are they blacked out anyway?"

"Somebody might get in touch and figure what I'm up to."

"If you're about to lead a commando raid on Amber, I'm going to be highly pissed."

"Come on! You know I swore off! This is something entirely different."

"Thought you were a prisoner of Dalt's."

"My status is unchanged."

"Well, he damn near killed you once and he just beat the shit out of you the other day."

"The first time he'd stumbled into an old berserker spell Sharu'd left behind for a trap; the second time was business. I'll be okay. But right now everything I'm up to is hush-hush, and I've got to run. G'bye."

Gone Luke, the presence. (KS, 187–188)

Shortly after the palace of Amber was partly destroyed by terrible forces, King Random received a Trump message concerning Luke's activities. Although a couple of residents were being given medical treatment for injuries suffered in the major upheaval, Random took Merlin into a more private room. He revealed certain of his political plans to Merlin, plans that a military coup at the royal palace in Kashfa had altered completely. Luke Raynard, working with Dalt and his mercenary band, had taken command of the little kingdom. Random's emissary in Jidrash, the capital of Kashfa, had told him by Trump that Luke would be crowned King Rinaldo I.

Random was unwilling to take a military force into Kashfa to uproot Luke, particularly since he had learned that Queen Vialle had given him her protection. After Merlin gave the king further details of the events that occurred when Dalt and his men had marched on Amber, they mulled over the unfolding situation that ultimately worked to Luke's benefit. Random began by saying:

"It was pretty smoothly done ... Dalt must have been operating under old orders. Not being certain how to collect Luke or locate Jasra for fresh instructions, he took a chance with that feint on Amber. Benedict might have spitted him again, with equal skill and greater effect."

"True. I guess you have to give the devil his due when it comes to guts. It also means that Luke must have done a lot of fast plotting and laid that fixed fight out during their brief conference in Arden. So he was really in control there, and he conned us into thinking he was a prisoner, which precluded his being the threat to Kashfa that he really was." (KS, 212–213)

In spite of King Random's very natural urge to put up a brick wall against Kashfa in terms of any treaty negotiations, Merlin convinced him that Luke would try to be conciliatory. The life of Duke Arkans, after all, did hang in the balance, and Random felt he owed Arkans that consideration. Random suggested that Merlin attend Luke's coronation in Kashfa as a private individual, bearing no powers to act on Amber's behalf. Merlin agreed.

When Merlin contacted Luke by Trump, Luke appeared pleased to hear from him. Luke said he needed his friend's advice, and he was pleasantly surprised to learn that Merle was in Kashfa, just outside the royal palace. They met privately in the First Unicornian Church.

As a gift, Merlin handed Luke the sword of Brand, Werewindle, which Merlin had recently discovered. In the church, the two old friends had a long discussion about the political situation, initiated by Luke:

"I've been had ... That woman has done it again, and I am peeved to the extreme. I don't know how to handle this."

"What? What are you talking about?"

"My mother ... She's done it again. Just when I thought I'd taken the reins and was riding my own course, she's come along and messed up my life."

"How'd she do that?"

"She hired Dalt and his boys to take over here."

"Yeah, we sort of figured that out. By the way, what happened to Arkans?"

"Oh, he's okay. I've got him under arrest, of course. But he's in good quarters and he can have anything he wants. I wouldn't hurt him. I always kind of liked the guy."

"So what's the problem? You win. You've got your own kingdom now."

"Hell, . . . I think I was conned, but I'm not exactly sure. See, I never wanted this job. Dalt told me we were taking over for Mom. I was coming in with him to establish order, claim the place for the family again, then welcome her back with a lot of pomp and crap. I figured once she had her throne back, she'd be off my case for good. I'd hit it out of here for more congenial turf, and she'd have a whole kingdom to occupy her attention. Nothing was said about me getting stuck with this lousy job." . . .

"I don't understand at all. You got it for her. Why not just turn it over to her and do as you planned?" . . .

"Arkans they liked . . . Me they like. Mom they're not so fond of. Nobody seems that enthusiastic about having her back. In fact, there were strong indications that if she tried it, there would indeed be a coup-coup."

"I suppose you could still step aside and give it to Arkans." . . .

"I don't know whether she'd be madder at me or at herself for having paid Dalt as much as she did to throw Arkans out. But she'd tell me it's my duty to do it, and I don't know— maybe it is." (KS, 242-44)

Luke continued to speculate about possible consequences if he refused the coronation. It may have been posturing on his part, but Luke claimed that he would rather act as Kashfa's representative in other shadows, taking on the role of a salesman of sorts, a role he knew best. After presenting himself as a reluctant liege, Luke asked about the possibility of continuing negotiations with Amber for Golden Circle status and for Kashfa's annexing the shadow realm of Eregnor. Merle related Random's stance: no deal.

As they came to the end of their discussion, Merle's half brother Jurt appeared out of nowhere to threaten Merle. To Luke, Jurt probably seemed manic and disturbed. Jurt was initially interested in pursuing Merle to the death, but he became entranced by the sword Werewindle as soon as he saw it in Luke's possession.

Merlin fought with Jurt, but Jurt managed to hold a hooded woman in the church captive, while he demanded the sword. The hooded woman was revealed to be Coral of Begma. When Jurt escaped with Werewindle, he left Coral unharmed. Luke introduced Coral anew to Merlin as his bride.

As an unofficial representative of Amber, Merlin took part in the coronation ceremony of Rinaldo and Coral. Later that night, Merle learned from Coral about her marriage by proxy to Luke when they were very young. Beyond the formality of sealing relations between Kashfa and Begma, Coral and Luke had no strong romantic inclinations toward one another. Coral proved this by spending the night with Merle, and Luke never raised any objections, nor even an acknowledgment, assuming he knew of it at all.

Luke took on the routine duties of a monarch in Kashfa.

Before running into Luke again, Merle heard from a different source that his mother, Dara of the House of Hendrake, intended to have Coral kidnapped. Dara planned to hold Coral because she possessed the Jewel of Judgment, known in the Courts as the Eye of the Serpent. This made Coral extremely valuable. Dara was intent on making her Merlin's queen in the Courts in spite of the fact that she was Luke's bride.

When Merle contacted Luke by Trump once more, it was to surprise him that he was inside the palace in Kashfa. Merle surprised him further by saying he had his half brother Jurt with him. Before Luke joined them in the chamber Merle had occupied with Coral, Merle noted that someone had been in the bed behind Luke.

Luke was happy to see Merle, and their conversation yielded some useful facts:

"Where've you been, anyway?" he asked.
"The Courts of Chaos," I replied. "I was summoned from here at the death of Swayvill. The funeral's in progress right now. We sneaked away when I learned that Coral was in danger."
"I know that—now," Luke said. "She's gone. Kidnapped, I think."
"When did it happen?"
"Night before last, I'd judge. What do you know of it?"
I glanced at Jurt. "Time differential," he said.
"She represented a chance to pick up a few points," I explained, "in the ongoing game between the Pattern and the Logrus. So agents of

Chaos were sent for her. They wanted her intact, though. She should be okay.''

"What do they want her for?"

"Seems they feel she's specially suited to
be queen in Thelbane, what with the Jewel of
Judgment as a piece of her anatomy and all.''

"Who's going to be the new king?''

My face felt warm of a sudden.

"Well, the people who came for her had me
in mind for the job,'' I replied.

"Hey, congratulations!'' he said. "Now I
don't have to be the only one having all this
fun.''

"What do you mean?''

.''This king business ain't worth shit, man. I
wish I'd never gotten sucked into the deal in
the first place. Everybody's got a piece of your
time, and when they don't someone still has to
know where you are.''

"Hell, you were just crowned. Give it a
chance to shake down.''

" 'Just'? It's been over a month!''

"Time differential," Jurt repeated.

"Come on. I'll buy you a cup of coffee,''
Luke said.

"You've got coffee here?''

"I require it, man. This way." (PC, 140–41)

Reverting to a typical "salesman pitch," Luke
suggested that he have his own marriage to Coral
annulled so that Merlin would be free to take her
as his queen. Luke was willing, he said, if it would
mean that Kashfa could enter the Golden Circle,
enjoying commerce with Amber.

Merlin explained that he wasn't in control of the
situation; that Coral and he were pawns in a power
play between the Logrus and the Pattern. Coral
would be in great danger if she came under the
power of the Courts at this time. Jurt had joined
Merle in this venture because he, too, was afraid of
the powers at work in the Courts.

After hearing Merle's explanation, Luke asked
him to try to contact Coral by Trump. No answer.
Luke told them that the trail of the kidnappers was
not yet entirely cold. The fading image of a black
pathway going off into Shadow remained in the city.
They could use it to track Coral and her captors.

Merlin asked Luke to take a walk with Jurt and
himself. He said he wanted Luke to meet someone.
When they reached an obscured portion of the castle, Merle used his powers to transport them
elsewhere.

They appeared near the Pattern created by Merlin's father. A Pattern-ghost version of Luke was
sitting in a red Chevy. Luke stared a moment at his
double. Merlin greeted the Pattern-ghost: "Hi . . .
Meet each other. You hardly need an introduction,
though. You have so much in common." (PC, 143)

It was Merle's intention that the ghost-Luke take
Luke's place as ruler of Kashfa. That way, Luke
wouldn't be missed as he went off in search of
Coral. There was a slight obstacle, however, in that
the ghost-Luke was unwilling to vacate his guardianship of the Pattern, leaving it open to challenge
by the other Great Powers. Merlin decided to return
with Jurt to the Courts of Chaos for a time, allowing
the two Lukes to become better acquainted.

About six hours later, Pattern-time, Merlin and
Jurt returned to Corwin's Pattern. The ghost-Luke
had communicated with the Pattern, and it indicated
its willingness to release him from his duty, once a
suitable replacement turned up. At that, Jurt offered
himself as temporary guardian of the Pattern. The
ghost-Luke obtained the Pattern's permission,
showed Jurt where provisions were kept, and joined
Merle and Luke on the journey to Kashfa.

Before returning to the palace, Luke pointed the
way to the place where he had seen the black pathway. It was no longer noticeable. Merle transported
them back to the palace, where Luke led them to
the room occupied by Nayda, the older sister of
Coral, although that was not quite so, anymore.
Nayda had been possessed by a ty'iga, one who had
been with Luke and Merle on shadow Earth. When
she was freed of any compulsions upon her, Nayda
had been brought to the blue crystal cave by
Ghostwheel. She had the ability to travel through
Shadow. It seems likely that she chose to seek out
Luke. The tracking abilities of the crystal stones
may even have been utilized to bring her to Luke.

From Nayda, they learned that two days had
elapsed in Kashfa while Luke had been at Corwin's
Pattern. That accounted for the disappearance of the
black pathway. Luke asked her if her psychic powers could be used in tracking Coral, and she said
they could. In fact, she sensed that Coral was not
in any immediate danger. While Luke intended to
brief his Pattern-ghost double on matters touching
Kashfa, Merle decided to return to the Courts. Luke
said he would probably start his search for Coral in

the morning, with or without Merlin. If Merle didn't return by then, Luke would try to call him by Trump.

When Merlin made Trump contact with Luke again, Luke had been following the black path for days. He brought Merle through to his location. With Luke, traveling on horses, were Nayda and Dalt. Nayda greeted Merle warmly, and Dalt made a terse remark that may have been meant as a friendly rejoinder to an earlier, passing comment of Merle's.

Nayda had been able to tell them that demonformed warriors from the Courts of Chaos had been Coral's kidnappers. Since Nayda was actually a demon herself, her presence assured a certain amount of protection as they traveled the black path.

Merlin sent a summons through Shadow. He went off the trail and entered the woods. He returned with a colorfully striped horse that he named Tiger. When he rejoined the party and mounted, they rode hurriedly to make up some time.

As they rode, Merle and Luke talked of a number of things: the spikard on Merle's finger, Merle's father, the royal succession in the Courts, and some of the political maneuvering there.

They reached a tower where the kidnappers had placed Coral. Nayda was able to determine that six demon lords held her. They had been pursued by Pattern-ghosts, who were mounting an attack at the tower. Nayda didn't want Luke to find out just then that she had been Gail Lampron, and was actually a possessing demon, so she let Merlin take credit for the knowledge she gave him. From his horse, Merle turned around and called to Luke:

"Luke! . . . I just probed ahead, learned the attackers are Pattern ghosts!"

"You don't say? . . . Think we should be taking their side? It's probably better for the Pattern to take her back than for the Courts to get her, wouldn't you think?"

"She shouldn't be used that way . . . Let's take her away from both of them."

"I agree with your feelings . . . But what if we succeed? I don't really care to be struck by a meteor or transported to the bottom of the nearest ocean."

"As near as I can tell, the spikard doesn't draw its power from the Pattern or the Logrus. Its sources are scattered through Shadow."

"So? I'm sure it's not a match for either one, let alone both."

"No, but I can use it to start an evasion course. They'll be getting in each other's way if they decide to pursue us."

"But eventually they'd find us, wouldn't they?"

"Maybe, maybe not . . . I have some ideas, but we're running out of time."

"Dalt, did you hear all that?" . . .

"I did." . . .

"If you want out, now's your chance."

"And miss an opportunity to twist the Unicorn's tail? . . . Keep riding!" (PC, 186–87)

They made their way through some trees on foot to an area overlooking the tower. They saw demon guards at the tower's entrance and, in the clearing before the structure, the Pattern-ghosts of Benedict, Eric, and Caine. In the center of the clearing stood a Pattern-ghost of Gérard and a Chaos lord named Chinaway. These two figures were preparing for unarmed combat.

Luke and the others stood by while Merlin used a spell to become invisible. While the fight proceeded, Merlin made his way unseen to the tower. From his vantage point, Luke could see the bundled form of Coral seemingly floating out the tower door.

When the demon captors burst into flames, Merlin became visible again. He was faced with the four Pattern-ghosts, who halted all motion to ask who he was. As the Pattern-ghosts came toward him to claim the girl, Luke, Dalt, and Nayda joined Merlin, armed and ready. Dalt and Eric engaged in a duel as the others watched. When Eric wounded Dalt, and appeared to be besting him, Merlin used his spikard to discharge them. At first, the Pattern-ghosts seemed unaffected. They began to fade to nothingness, however, when the Sign of the Pattern took form.

Luke let Merle do all the talking, since he wasn't well acquainted with the living embodiment of the Pattern. Merle stated his case well. Luke may have noted that Merle was attempting something, but thought ended with a shuddering explosion and blackness.

When he recovered, Luke, like the others, realized that the Pattern Sign had moved them. Nayda stood before the prone form of Merlin, protecting him from the Sign. The Sign told Nayda that it was at the other end of the universe from where such demons as she originated. They were at the primal Pattern.

The Sign revealed that it intended to keep them confined at the primal Pattern, but none of them would be harmed. Luke checked on Coral, finding her awake and alert.

As the Sign indicated the caves nearby, where they could be quartered, Merle moved toward the great design of the Pattern, and cut his hand with a dagger. He stood with his cupped hand over the Pattern, ready to spill some of his blood if the Sign made any threatening movement.

Supplied with a glass of iced tea and a cushion, Merlin settled in, holding his hand over the Pattern. Merle told the Sign that to resolve their impasse, it would have to allow all of them to depart. During negotiations, the Pattern kept referring to Nayda as a demon lady. Luke asked Nayda about it, and she indicated that she would tell him the story at a later time.

The Sign attempted to persuade Merlin and the others to join with it; humor it for the moment and be rewarded with a Golden Age. Luke called it what it apparently was: a good sales pitch.

To assure that the Sign would allow all the others safe passage, Luke slashed his hand and took a position before the Pattern. Luke told Merlin to have a Trump of him ready so that they could communicate when they'd trumped away. He asked Merle to lay out the several cards he had in his possession known as the Trumps of Doom. Luke took one of these at random, not revealing what the card depicted. That way, the Sign would not know where he transported to when his turn came. He also asked the Pattern for a glass of iced tea, as well.

When Merle asked to be sent to Jidrash in Kashfa, the Pattern complied. Luke was left alone at the primal Pattern, but he maintained his link with Merle and the others. He heard Merle telling the others that he wanted to put Coral in a place of safety, but that Dalt and Nayda need not leave Kashfa. Both Nayda and Dalt objected, saying they wanted to remain together with Coral and Merlin.

Through the Trump contact, Merle said, "Hey, Luke! You hear all that?"

Luke answered, "Yeah . . . Better be about your business then. Shit! I spilled it—" (PC, 205)

Contact with Luke was severed.

Whatever happened at the primal Pattern, Luke

no doubt made use of the Trump he himself had drawn, the unknown card in his possession. As on previous occasions, he very likely had figured all the angles, and any risk he was taking was presumably a carefully calculated one.

RODERICK

Physician in attendance at the Keep of Ganelon in the village of Lorraine.

When Corey of Cabra brought Lancelot du Lac to the Keep, Roderick was with his master, Lord Ganelon, in his room. Although Corey was uncertain of Roderick's medical competence, he relinquished the badly wounded Lancelot into his care. Ganelon, on the other hand, appeared quite confident in his physician, telling him in an offhanded manner: "Roderick, tend to him." (GA, 21)

While the Chronicles of Prince Corwin describe Roderick as an old man, little is known of his background. Given the nature of his situation, serving a lord under feudal conditions, he was likely a man not academically trained in any formal way. More likely, his training was of a practical type, treating battle wounds and the common ailments affecting families living in less sanitary conditions than other communities that did not live under continuous siege.

He may have had a multigenerational family, being a man of advanced years, or he may have been an old bachelor. It doesn't matter. Roderick lived a long, full life. His entire existence, from birth to some final end, occurred during the briefest part of another's millennia-long range of activity. It may be said Roderick lived to fulfill his purpose to suit another man's whims. He was there, he was called, he did his duty, and he left. On occasion, such a life is all there need be.

ROGER

Guard of the royal dungeons in the palace of Amber. His last name is known, but is of foreign origin, difficult to pronounce, and nearly impossible to spell.

Although Roger could have risen to captain of the guards, owing to his kinship with Lord Corwin, he chose to accept a lesser position as chief guard of the dungeons of Kolvir. Being of a contemplative air, he is less interested in the excitement and intrigue of guardship in the palace proper, which would have been an important part of his role as captain. He prefers to spend his spare time writing fictional works of horror and melodramatic romances, partly for personal pleasure and partly for publication in his shadow of origin, where he is known as an adventurer and explorer.

The shadow of his birth is an adjacent shadow Earth, where Lord Corwin spent so much of his time. Roger's shadow was named Ikseth, which may have been a slight distortion of "Earth." On one of Oberon's many travels through Shadow as a young man, he came across Ikseth and came to know Roger's parents. Even as a small boy, Roger resembled Oberon's son Corwin: He had a long, angular head, wide, intelligent eyes, narrow lips that easily turned to a self-deprecating grin, and a longish nose. He was also lean of body and tall for his age. Thinking that he might be an excellent playmate for his son, Oberon struck a deal with Roger's parents, who were flattered that the king of Amber wished to bring their son to the true city. Oberon had also crossed their palms generously.

In many forms of play, Roger was equal to the young prince, but, being a human of ordinary strength, he was at a disadvantage. Sometimes Corwin would forget his great strength, and this once caused Roger a dislocated shoulder. Although they remained on friendly terms, Roger remained cautiously distant from his boyhood friend for many years.

On occasion, Roger would return to Ikseth to visit his parents, and, once or twice, Corwin accompanied him. Through Corwin, Roger learned some of the distinctions between his world and the shadow Earth that the young prince was familiar with. Although Ikseth was a world composed of a similar water-to-land proportion, its outer atmosphere had a weaker ozone layer and a lesser atmospheric pressure. This caused a greater imbalance in meteorological conditions, so that storms of various kinds were frequent. The seasons were similar to those on the shadow Earth, but the summers were generally hotter and more humid, while the winters were harsher, bitterly cold, and subject to icy hail storms. The lighter atmospheric pressure allowed for an occasional pelting of meteor rocks, and every so often, a village or town was destroyed by a meteor shower. Much rarer, but still a possibility, was the flattening of an entire city by an oversize meteor, or even a series of such meteors, that would effectively wipe out the culture of centuries.

Roger was a son of Ikseth, and as such he was of hardy stock. That shadow breeds men and women who could not settle down to fixed homes and professions that were totally deskbound and dependent on a physical niche in society. Rather, the realm encouraged risk-taking and the seeking of adventure. The people of Ikseth were natural doers, adaptable to abrupt changes in their lives. This endeared them to Oberon, and he maintained friendly relations with them for generations. He frequently invited members of Ikseth society to join his military, often allowing whole families to live in the countryside of Amber.

Roger continues to write novels and philosophical tracts for publication in his home world, while loyally serving as chief guard in the royal dungeons of Amber.

ROTH, BILL [WILLIAM]

A citizen of shadow Earth who became a close friend of Corwin, prince of Amber, during his stay in upstate New York. Eventually, Bill Roth became counsel to the Court of Amber, and took up residence in the true city.

Merlin, son of Corwin, described him as "a short, heavy-set man with a somewhat florid complexion, his dark hair streaked with white and perhaps a bit thin on top." (TD, 82) He had been a member of a country club that Corwin, as Carl Corey, also attended on occasion. Initially, Roth and Carl Corey were only passing acquaintances. They happened to be standing at the bar of the country club one night when Roth, talking to another friend, launched into a heated discussion on a point about the Napoleonic Wars. This piqued Corey's interest, and Corey responded knowledgeably to one of Roth's contentions. Friends they had in common drifted to and from the bar as Corey and Roth continued their exchange. They took a table and talked through the night, fairly oblivious to people around them. Of all the people that Corey became acquainted with in that shadow, he felt he could put his trust in Bill Roth more than any other individual.

Bill Roth had always lived in the same undisclosed area of New York State, somewhere between Albany and Westchester. He had been away when he studied law in Buffalo, but he returned to marry his childhood sweetheart, a girl named Alice, and entered the family law practice. He was a successful attorney who enjoyed small-town life. However, he was very curious about the somewhat mysterious Carl Corey, and balanced his curiosity with professional restraint.

Roth's curiosity led him to investigate Carl Corey's disappearance after he had been hospitalized following an automobile accident. Roth hadn't known about Corey's accident and hospital stay until after the fact. It was a matter of Roth's concern over Corey's prolonged absence from the country club, leading him to investigate Corey's financial affairs while caring for his home. When he learned of Corey's hospitalization, he investigated further. Although he didn't allow his imagination to go wild, Roth was able to see that unknown agents were at work to do harm to his friend. He had learned that Corey had been committed to Porter Sanitarium in Albany by someone assuming the role of a psychiatrist. Roth acted to have a falsified court order declaring Corey's insanity vacated, even though Corey was nowhere to be found. Roth kept his records of the investigation for years, wondering if the unknown agent or agents ever caught up with the mysterious Mr. Corey.

When Corey appeared one night on the snowy road beside his home, Roth was driving by. He was amazed at rediscovering his old friend, and greatly worried over his condition. Corey was bleeding profusely from a knife wound. Roth drove him to a nearby hospital and stayed the night. When Corey recovered, Roth had a frank talk with him. He discussed the contents of his investigative notes with Corey in his hospital room. Expressing the hope that Corey would one day explain the details surrounding those past events, Roth told him he was satisfied to have helped his friend. They arranged for the sale of Corey's house, but more significantly, Roth had the opportunity to examine the unique tarots that were among Corey's personal effects. They, and the mystery of Corey's strange appearances and disappearances, prompted Roth to say: "It is as if I were one of those minor characters in a melodrama who gets shuffled offstage without ever learning how things turn out." (SU, 139)

When one day Corey showed up at his doorstep with a horse, dressed in his Amber clothes and bearing a sword, Roth discovered that he was somewhat more than a minor character in a melodrama. Corey was there on an urgent mission, in search of a valuable jewel that had been hidden in a compost heap. Only Roth could help him locate it. Quite a melodrama!

The adventure started rather mundanely, with Corey riding horseback while Roth drove to the contractor's farm where the compost heap had ended up. Roth was intrigued, however, by discussion of the red-bearded figure who had appeared twice. Corey explained that this person had been the pretended psychiatrist years before and was his brother Brand. Carrying tools and an electric lantern, Roth accompanied Corey to the field at Ed Wellen's farm to locate the compost. Finding it, they saw that it had been gone through, but they searched anyway. Then things became really strange . . .

Corey began talking to someone, seeming to speak and respond as if talking on some invisible telephone. Then he seemed to be talking to a different person, making slightly different responses. Roth would have doubted Corey's sanity if the weirdness of the situation hadn't been followed by a phenomenon that was certainly otherworldly. Corey raised his right arm to eye level, seemed to reach out and pull slowly back. A hand, an arm, held in Corey's, appeared out of nothingness. A lovely young lady followed. She appeared fully before them, moving, turning, offering a smile to Roth. He recognized her as being on one of Corey's unusual tarots. Corey introduced her as his sister, Fiona. While Corey went to get his horse, Roth spent a few brief minutes speaking to Fiona. She spoke of a place called Amber; that their brother Brand was endangering the entire realm; and that only Corwin was in a position to prevent that danger. With Corey's return, Roth bade them farewell, saying he wanted the whole story someday. He watched as Fiona and Corey rode together on the horse named Drum. He continued to watch as they began to grow smaller with distance, crossing the farmland. They disappeared before reaching the horizon.

Roth might well have gone back to a placid, complex but ordinary way of life if sometime later he hadn't had a couple of unusual visitors to his home. Alice answered the door one evening on a young woman and an elderly man wearing oddly medieval clothing. They said they had urgent business with Mr. Roth. When Roth met them in his study, he was pleased that the young lady was Fiona. She introduced the older man as His Royal Highness, Swayvil, king of the Courts of Chaos. Speechless for a moment, Roth took a step back, then bowed on one knee, lowering his head. The monarch spoke in an unfamiliar tongue, and Fiona explained that His Highness had bidden him to rise. Formalities aside, Fiona presented a lengthy document that she translated for Roth, and the three of them settled at a large desk to work.

The document, as became readily apparent to Roth, was a declaration of peace and consent for mutual obligations between the realms of Amber and the Courts of Chaos. Fiona used the term Concord in referring to it. Roth went through the conditions set up by both parties, and with Fiona's translations, he specified certain additions that made clearer terms to which King Swayvil agreed. After several hours of reading and revising, His Majesty stood and took his leave of Mr. Roth. Fiona thanked him, saying that she hoped their relationship might continue in kind. She took his hand warmly and left a gold ingot in it. The next day, Roth had it appraised. It was valued at five thousand dollars.

This was the first of several occasions when Mr. Roth performed services for the royal citizens of Amber. Fiona returned several more times to review several terms and phrases of the Concord, and Roth began a study of the language Thari. At one point, Fiona introduced her sister Flora to him, who offered a retainer to have him handle some of her personal affairs—matters that had been unresolved during her stay on shadow Earth.

When Fiona introduced Roth to Merlin, the son of his friend, he was delighted. He was somewhat disturbed that no one had heard from Corwin since the signing of the Concord, and he expressed his concern to Merlin. Merlin said that he intended to learn of his father's whereabouts, but he felt certain his father was well. It was simply part of his father's

habits to wander widely in Shadow. Roth, remembering the Carl Corey he knew, had to concur.

Merlin visited with Roth a few times over a period of eight years. Attending Berkeley University in California, Merlin would usually drop by during summer vacation, when he felt he could leave his studies for a while. On one occasion, unhappily, Merlin had been notified by telephone of the death of Alice Roth. He flew in for the funeral, met Bill Roth, Jr., and his family, who had flown in from the Midwest, and spent a couple of days reminiscing with Roth over absent friends.

Before his planned departure from shadow Earth, Merlin came to visit Roth in New York again. Merlin discussed his recent troubles in San Francisco, and Roth astutely questioned him about his relationship with Lucas Raynard. By this time, Merlin invested great trust in Roth, speaking openly of the arcane workings of the Pattern and the Logrus. Roth listened critically, asking questions and offering suggestions as they pondered the mystery of murder attempts on Merlin's life.

They hadn't arrived at anything conclusive, but a couple of troubling matters occurred during Merlin's stay. One of them, the odd behavior of a young neighbor, resulted in an unforeseen contingency. Roth and Merlin were walking outdoors, when Merlin received an urgent Trump contact from King Random in Amber. Because this singular neighbor seemed about to assault them, Merlin brought Bill Roth with him as he trumped into the library of the Royal Palace. Random was as surprised as Roth when they confronted each other:

> "Merlin, who's this?" . . .
> "Your attorney, Bill Roth . . . You've always dealt with him through agents in the past. I thought you might like to—"
> Bill began dropping to one knee. "Your Majesty . . ."
> "Cut the crap . . . We're not in Court . . . Call me Random. I've always intended to thank you personally for the work you did on that treaty. Never got around to it, though. Good to meet you." (TD, 111)

Roth stood quietly by as Random told Merlin about the murder of Caine in a distant shadow. Before he could offer any help, Roth was greeted by Flora, who had rushed into the room. With Random's permission, Flora was allowed to lead Roth on a tour of Amber. Roth accepted the experience with delight. He later joined Random, Merlin, and several of the others for a banquet. He remarked about the comic routines of the court jester, Droppa MaPantz. Merlin confirmed that Roth had probably heard the jokes before from some shadow Earth comedian—Droppa had visited the place to obtain fresh jokes on occasion.

At Caine's funeral, Roth pointed out to Merlin a lone stranger on a near ledge of Mt. Kolvir. When Merlin told Random, the king halted the procession. Using the Jewel of Judgment, Random was able to cause a tossed bomb to explode before it reached them. The stranger on the ledge escaped, however.

No longer having any close ties to anyone in New York, and relishing a new kind of life in Amber, Roth decided to remain. Random was magnanimous in accepting Roth as counsel to the Court, and assigned him quarters in the palace. Partly because Roth was a very recent and, therefore, rare visitor from shadow Earth, he found the other members of the Court to be eager to show him around. Gérard brought him to his prized ship, taking him out to sea a few times. Once, Roth traveled with him to the shadow called Deiga. One of the other sisters of his friend Corwin, Llewella, took him to Rebma. Initially, he was extremely disoriented in traveling to the undersea city, but he grew to love its uniqueness.

Gradually, Roth became proficient with foils, learned Thari fluently, and changed his wardrobe completely. Keenly observant of customs and manners, he let his whiskers go, grew a mustache, and dressed in boots, cloak, and sheathed sword.

Although he enjoyed the company of Flora, he felt she was slightly too overbearing at times. Besides, she left on a mission to shadow Earth. He began spending time with Droppa, who proved to be an interesting and enterprising individual. The next time he happened to see Merlin, Roth was enjoying a lunch at a café that Droppa co-owned, a place in town called the Pit.

Merlin told him of his latest adventures; most particularly about his changing relationship with Luke Raynard. Roth's interest was piqued when Merlin suggested he represent Luke if he were to be granted a formal hearing with Random under House Law. While Merlin made it clear that such an event was highly tentative, Roth was intrigued

enough to study the matter in the library of the Royal Palace.

While Roth began occupying himself with the study of House Law in the palace library, he was also given employment by Random on other matters. The king chose to take Roth into his confidence about some of the political maneuvering he was involved in. Since Queen Jasra was no longer ruling in the shadow called Kashfa, Random believed it was advantageous to gain a measure of control in that realm. Because of longtime ties to a neighboring shadow, Begma, with which Kashfa was in conflict, Amber had not considered Kashfa for membership in the Golden Circle. However, Kashfa had much potential for trade, and Random hoped to prevent the possibility of Jasra's regaining power, so that he opened up talks with the present king of Kashfa.

Random gave Bill Roth access to documents concerning the histories of Kashfa and Begma, as well as several historical texts kept in the Royal Library. Leaving him to his research, the king suggested that Roth study the details of the Eregnor situation and the background of Kashfa's current ruler, General Jaston. Roth agreed, beginning a long sojourn of poring over texts and documents.

Although Roth spent many long hours, sometimes well into the night, at his research, he still occasionally joined Droppa on little jaunts into town. He was preparing to go with Droppa to the Pit when a messenger came to his quarters. The king wished to see him. When Roth arrived in the throne room, Random motioned for him, handing over several handwritten documents. The ink seemed fresh.

Random told him he would be away for a time, visiting shadow Kashfa. In the meantime, the king requested that Roth go over the papers. They were drafts of a tentative trade agreement, granting Kashfa entrance into the Golden Circle. When Random dismissed him, Roth canceled his appointment with Droppa and headed for his own quarters. Referring to numerous legal texts he now kept there, Roth went through the various points of the treaty. It was curious to him that on a couple of the later drafts, a new name was appended to the party conjoined with the authority of Kashfa. Roth went back to the historical texts in Thari to learn what he could of the man known as Duke Arkans.

An invitation for an official state dinner was delivered to Roth. The messenger waited while he signed a brief note to Queen Vialle, indicating that he would be delighted to attend. Later that day, Roth spoke with Hendon, the head steward for the Court, and learned that the banquet was for the prime minister of Begma and his party. Hendon mentioned that Merlin was also part of the official reception. Before parting, Hendon carelessly spoke of the sudden death of Jaston of Kashfa. Roth asked further of this, and the news served to confirm some of his own suspicions, based on certain delineations stated in the drafts of the papers he had been reading.

On his way toward the wing of the palace housing the royal quarters, Roth heard much movement and clanging metal, as if weapons were being gathered. He backtracked and turned a corner to look down a long corridor from which the activity seemed to be coming. Several guards were rushing about. Roth, out of curiosity, might have questioned one of them, but he froze at the sight of one man. He hadn't actually been introduced to the tall, impressive-looking man dressed in rustic colors. But he knew him by reputation and by Trump. His lacking one arm, while still appearing quite formidable, made identification unmistakable. Roth turned and rushed away.

Slightly unnerved, but beginning to calm down, Roth made his way to a familiar part of the castle. He found Merlin's room and knocked. He was glad when Merlin came to the door and greeted him warmly. As they started out together, Roth led Merlin to the area where all the activity had been going on, in order to get Merlin's opinion. Merlin told him of the latest news about Luke Raynard: that his personal vendetta against Amber was at an end.

When they reached the armory, Merlin tried to question his uncle Benedict about any possible military escalation. Laconic as ever, Benedict simply said they were not to worry. Merlin had to let it go at that. Privately, Merlin told Roth that he suspected that Dalt the mercenary might be in the realm, and that was the reason for the activity they had seen. It was troubling to them because Roth and Merlin both knew that Benedict had accompanied King Random to Kashfa, and Random had not yet returned.

At the formal dinner, seating had to be arranged, so the guests were milling around, socializing. Roth went with Merlin to the bar, and Merlin pointed out the Begman officials to him. Hendon announced the seating arrangements, and everyone went to the table. Roth was seated between Merlin and Dretha

Gannell, assistant to the Begman ambassador. Roth found himself vying for Merlin's attention with one of the daughters of the prime minister of Begma. Concerned that Merlin might inadvertently say something compromising to current political affairs, Roth wanted to fill him in as quickly as possible. Seeing that the other guests were occupied in their own conversations, Roth leaned over and spoke to Merlin about the situation, as he had been studying it. He told Merlin of the drafts of a new trade agreement to be signed between Amber and Kashfa, the positioning of a new, Amber-backed ruler there, and the conceding of Eregnor to the Kashfans. Roth had noted with some relief that Merlin had given a noncommittal response when asked by another member of the Begman delegation about his views of the Eregnor situation. Even when Queen Vialle was called away, followed by Merlin's being notified by a servant that the queen wished to see him, Bill Roth felt reasonably assured that he had helped keep the lid on an international incident.

After dinner, Roth took a stroll with Gérard and the Begman prime minister, a short, dour man named Orkuz. Roth found he could be quite entertaining simply by recounting some of the mundane events that are common to shadow Earth.

He completed his corrections and drew up a final draft of the treaty with Kashfa, having it delivered to the king and queen by messenger. This same messenger, a servant who had been assigned to him, informed Roth about the armed mercenary troop that had faced Julian's soldiers at the Forest of Arden. Roth regretted not being there, especially when he heard of the bare-handed combat between Dalt and Luke Raynard. Since he had learned of this after the fact, Roth saw little use in seeking out further information about the aftermath of Random's political dealings. He certainly didn't want to run into Prime Minister Orkuz again, who seemed increasingly suspicious of secret meetings, such as had occurred at the banquet between Vialle and Merlin.

Roth decided it would be best to take a little vacation from House politics. He didn't want to be in the way, and he felt it was time that he seek a measure of independence from his royal hosts. It is believed that Roth went into town with Droppa and took up residence in a small manor house to the west of the town. He maintained a watchful but remote eye on proceedings in the Royal Palace through the connections of his servant, who came to like Roth, and Droppa. He knew that Random was back, and Merlin was about, at the time when he was awakened by a sudden explosion from the direction of the palace. The townspeople felt the tremors, and Roth was reminded of an earthquake he once experienced. However, his servant assured him that no one in the palace had been badly injured. Keeping apprised of the situation, Roth remained in town. If he were needed by the king, his servant made a promise to notify him immediately.

His servant mentioned in passing that Roth had wondered aloud at one juncture about his son's reaction if he should suggest inviting Bill, Jr., and his family to relocate in Amber.

RUSHING FORCE, THE

One of the Supreme Powers that sought out Merlin of Amber and the Courts of Chaos. It wanted to coerce Merlin into joining its side against the other Power.

This Rushing Force was initiated when Merlin attempted to reach a young woman named Coral by Trump. Coral had fallen under the spell of this Power when she foolhardily permitted it to send her wherever it wished. The Power chose to entrap her and prevent contact by others by placing her in utter darkness.

Merlin combined his effort to reach Coral with the skills of his stepbrother Mandor and Jasra of Kashfa. Concentrating on a Trump of Coral, the three of them brought forth a transitory image of the girl. Merlin's powerful construct Ghostwheel was with them, informing them of what was happening:

"The force that holds her has become aware of your interest and even now is reaching toward you. Is there some way you can turn off that Trump?"

I passed my hand across its face, which is usually sufficient. Nothing happened. The cold breeze even seemed to increase in intensity. I repeated the gesture along with a mental order. I began to feel whatever it was, focusing upon me.

Then the Sign of the Logrus fell upon the Trump, and the card was torn from my hand

as I was cast backward, striking my shoulder against the edge of the door. Mandor lurched to his right as this occurred, catching hold of the table to steady himself. In my Logrus vision I had seen wild lines of light flash outward from the card before it fell away.

"Did that do the trick?" I called out.

"It broke the connection," Ghost replied.

"Thanks, Mandor," I said.

"But the power that was reaching for you through the Trump knows where you are now," Ghost said.

"What makes you privy to its awareness?" I inquired.

"It is a surmise, based upon the fact that it's still reaching for you. It is coming the long way round—across space—though. It could take as long as a quarter of a minute before it reaches you."

"Your use of the pronoun is a little indefinite," Jasra said. "Is it just Merlin that it wants? Or is it coming for all of us?"

"Uncertain. Merlin is the focus. I've no idea what it will do to you." (KS, 50–51)

Ghostwheel was able to protect Merlin, Jasra, and Mandor by sending them separately to distant shadows.

Although Merlin was secured in a cave of a distant shadow and had put up warding spells, agents of the Power did reach him. These agents attempted to talk him into joining them, and Merlin had no idea what would have happened if he consented. His wards and the Sign of the Logrus dispensed with two of these agents. A third agent, claiming to need Merlin's help, got the better of Merlin, knocking him into unconsciousness.

However, instead of finding himself trapped under the influence of the unknown Rushing Force, Merlin awoke in a strange, remote realm different from any other he had experienced. Nevertheless, it was a place that offered him a measure of protection against the Rushing Force that had tried to reach him and place him under its power.

S

The nomenclature assigned by Merlin Corey to an unknown assailant who deliberately pursued him with the intent of causing him bodily harm every year on a specific date.

Merlin recorded the problem of S in this way:

> Someone enjoyed trying to kill me once a year, it was as simple as that. The effort failing, there would be another year's pause before an attempt was made again. It seemed almost a game.

> But this year I wanted to play, too. My main concern was that he, she, or it seemed never to be present when the event occurred, favoring stealth and gimmicks or agents. I will refer to this person as S (which sometimes stands for "sneak" and sometimes for "shithead" in my private cosmology), because X has been overworked and because I do not like to screw around with pronouns with disputable antecedents. (TD, 3)

The attempts on Merlin's life began shortly after he had come to San Francisco, taking up college studies at Berkeley. For seven years, always on April 30, accidents occurred that were too coincidental and mysterious not to have been caused by a specific agent. Since the assaults began soon after he arrived on the shadow Earth, Merlin suspected that S was someone he had gotten to know while living in San Francisco.

It wasn't until the third year of the presumed "accidents" that Merlin came to the conclusion that they were deliberate acts against him by an unknown agent. The first year's occurrence was an out-of-control truck that nearly crushed him against a wall. The second year involved an attack by would-be muggers. Both incidents had the markings of being only slightly out of the ordinary: The truck driver who nearly ran him down seemed to have been in a trance; and a shadowy figure appeared out of the darkness, watching Merlin, after he had disposed of the muggers.

On the third occasion, however, there was little room for doubt. A package received in the first class mail exploded in Merlin's apartment. Only the ringing of the telephone in another room saved him from being splattered about his apartment.

Most troubling to Merlin was the reason for the attempts on his life, occurring, as they did, with such odd regularity. What was the significance of the date April 30?

When Merlin discovered the dead body of his former girlfriend, Julia, and a doglike beast that was distinctly alien to the shadow Earth on the most recent April 30, he suspected the agent had reasons having roots in Merlin's former life. A deadly conflict with an occultist named Victor Melman confirmed that the agent dubbed S was from some other shadow.

Although Merlin speculated on possible candidates from his past who might be behind the attacks, he seemed naive in not recognizing the obvious. Bill Roth, a New York attorney who had befriended Merlin's father, guided him to realize how little he knew about his best friend on the shadow Earth, Luke Raynard. While Merlin knew nothing of Luke's family, nor the exact location of his hometown, and readily accepted the fact that Luke could run as fast as an Amberite, he never questioned the coincidence that they had known each other for the same length of time as the murder attempts.

Merlin remained mystified about S's identity until he fell under his power, and then S willingly acknowledged his actions. The murder attempts had been planned by Jasra, former queen of the shadow Kashfa. She involved her son in the initial attempts as a means of seeking revenge against Corwin, Merlin's father, because of his complicity in the death of Brand. Jasra had been married to Brand in a private ceremony in Kashfa. Although her son shared her desire for vengeance against those of Amber, he recanted after becoming friendly with Merlin. Jasra continued the planned assaults on her own, but some of the later ones may actually have been deflected by the intervention of her son.

For a time, Merlin became the prisoner of S and his mother, trapped by S in a cave of blue crystal. Ironically, his escape was effected by the interference of Jasra, who sought Merlin out, sending two incompetent henchmen to do her bidding.

SAND

Daughter in a so-called bigamous marriage between Oberon, king of Amber, and a woman of a distant shadow, Harla. After the death of her mother, Sand and her brother Delwin were subtly coerced into leaving Amber. They returned to Harla's homeland, refusing to have anything to do with the Royal Family of the true city.

Sand was very close to her brother, often taking his lead, as if they were of one mind. When discovering Trumps drawn of Delwin and Sand, Merlin noted that the "one of a woman resembled this man [Delwin] so closely it would seem they must be related." (BA, 111) Like her brother, Sand was slender, with russet-colored hair and green eyes. Like him, she often dressed in browns and blacks.

Merlin had learned of Sand, Delwin, and the questionable marriage of their mother to King Oberon from his aunt, Flora. In Amber-time, or so it had been explained, Oberon had been married to Rilga, mother of Gérard and Julian. Then Oberon married Harla in her shadow, a place where the time streams flowed much faster. In his journals, Merlin recorded:

> Interesting arguments both for and against the bigamous nature of his marriage to Harla may be made. I'm in no position to judge. I had the story from Flora years ago, and in that she'd never gotten along too well with Delwin and Sand, the offspring of that union, she was inclined to the pro-bigamy interpretation. I'd never seen pictures of Delwin or Sand until now. There weren't any hanging around the palace, and they were seldom mentioned. But they had lived in Amber for the relatively short time Harla was queen there. Following her death, they grew unhappy with Oberon's policies toward her homeland—which they visited often—and after a time they departed, vowing not to have anything to do with Amber again. At least that's the way I'd heard it. There could easily have been all sorts of sibling politicking involved, too. (BA, 115)

In fact, we have no other documentation concerning Oberon's marriage to Harla nor the disposition of her children. Thus, Merlin's account is enlightening in expressing a hint of the difficulties under which Sand and her brother felt burdened while residing in Amber.

Although Sand and her brother left Amber, never to return, they took with them some of the arcane secrets of the realm. As a young attractive woman, Sand found ways to learn secrets that were not readily available to Delwin. Through her sources within the Royal Palace during her stay there, she uncovered the account of nine very special rings, called spikards, that drew upon vast powers. She confided her knowledge to Delwin. Having no intention of dealing with Amber or its minions ever again, she and her brother chose not to divulge any of the useful bits of knowledge they were taking with them when they left the true realm. Sand's feeling was that it was better to keep such knowledge in reserve, even if no opportunity to utilize it ever presented itself.

While Sand was generally known to accede to Delwin's wishes in most things, it seems possible that she influenced him to help Bleys of Amber in his time of need. Such intercession, however, was a rare exception.

SAWALL

Nominal head of the Ways of Sawall in the Courts of Chaos. His extreme old age and physical impairments have caused him to remain reclusive for several years. He has virtually given the power of authority over the House of Sawall to his eldest son, Mandor.

When he was a young nobleman, given the title of Rim Duke, Gramble, Lord Sawall, married Gride, who gave birth to Mandor. They had a good life together, and Lord Sawall showed his interest in sculpture and unique artistic devices early on. Using Shadowmasters, he planned a special wing to the House which he called the Maze of Art. After seeing it executed, Lord Sawall invited people from all over the Courts and the near shadows to wander its many Ways. One area in particular, according to Merlin's journals, was of special delight to Sawall: the Sculpture Garden. Some of its mysteriousness has been expressed by Merlin:

> "The floor was uneven—concave, convex, stepped, ridged—with concavity being the dominant curve. It was difficult to guess at its dimensions, for it seemed of different size and contour depending upon where one stood. Gramble, Lord Sawall, had caused it to be constructed without any plane surfaces—and I

believe the job involved some unique shadowmastery....

...As I strolled, what had seemed walls became floor to me. The pieces that had seemed floored now jutted or depended. The room changed shape as I went, and a breeze blew through it, causing sighs, hums, buzzes, chimes. Gramble, my stepfather, had taken a certain delight in this hall, whereas for me it had long represented an exercise in intrepidity to venture beyond its threshold." (PC, 120–21)

It was many years later, after enjoying a full life with her husband and son, that Gride died. Perhaps, the ailments that harrassed Lord Sawall and drove him into isolation had begun with the grief he suffered at her death.

Sometime afterward, Lord Sawall met Dara of the Houses of Hendrake and Helgram. Although he knew some of her history—that she had given birth to an illegitimate son through one of the princes of Amber—he was quite taken with her. Soon they were married. The Lady Dara gave him two more sons, Despil and Jurt.

Already too old to be much of a father to his sons, Sawall gave Jurt and Despil into their mother's care almost exclusively. In spite of his infrequent appearance with family members, Sawall apparently had some influence over his sons. Merlin recorded that Jurt, at least, had felt Sawall's influence: "I could remember how much the old man's approval had meant to him [Jurt]." (PC, 124) At another time, Merlin learned from his stepbrother Mandor about some surprising actions taken by the "old Rim Duke":

"You are not aware that Sawall adopted you, formally, after your departure [from the Courts to shadow Earth]?"

"What?"

"Yes. I was never certain as to his exact motives. But you are a legitimate heir. You follow me but take precedence over Jurt and Despil." (SC, 33)

Thus, we see that old Sawall had an interest in Merlin, as well as his other sons. It is uncertain, but perhaps the Rim Lord developed a fondness for Dara's son while he grew up in the Courts.

As to how ill Lord Sawall is, very little is known.

Mandor gave the merest hint of old Sawall's condition when he spoke to Merlin about seeking out their mad brother Jurt with the intent of killing him: "I'm afraid that the news of his [Jurt's] death could push our father over the edge." (SC, 194)

While little more is known about Sawall's condition, it is likely he still resides somewhere within the House of Sawall. It may well be that he is often visited by the Lady Dara. Since his second son, Despil, is rumored to be traveling in Shadow, it is conceivable that he pays frequent visits to his father in secret.

SCROF

A magical being created out of the primal Chaos. Its main function was to prevent the passage of any living being, with the exception of other magical beings, through the tunnel between the shadow Earth and the Keep of the Four Worlds.

Also known as the Dweller on the Threshold, Scrof took great joy in its work, eating sorcerers and their magic, while adhering to a set of rules that it made plain to intruders before they transgressed the Threshold.

Scrof's nature and origins are open to speculation, since there is only one report of its existence: the journals kept by Merlin, son of Prince Corwin of Amber. The fact that Merlin's journal is the only record of Scrof's existence leads to two diverse theories. One theory is that whoever ruled at the Keep of the Four Worlds during this period of time found it convenient to have a ready passage to the shadow Earth, and therefore created Scrof to guard that passage from any intrusion and, very likely, from any living creature seeking escape from the Keep by that egress. The second theory, first put forth by Merlin in retrospect, was that the tunnel and its guardian were deliberately placed there with the intention of luring Merlin to the Keep in the hope of making him a captive.

An important factor that troubled Merlin was what possible connection there might be between the Keep and the apartment of his girlfriend Julia on shadow Earth.

Whoever was responsible for the creation of the mystical tunnel placed Scrof there in anticipation of one or more specific people coming across its Threshold. It is likely that the sorcerer named Mask, if he indeed was the tunnel's creator, anticipated its discovery by Jasra, Victor Melman, or Merlin. Therefore, Scrof's appearance may have been deliberately planned to be both formidable and offensive. By giving Scrof the ability to make caustic gibes and witty rebuffs, its master may have intended to express a sense of humor. The Dweller was huge, well-rounded, with purple skin, fangs, and claws. While menacing in its immensity, it had an aura of potential vulnerability: it was naked, seemingly immobile, as its protruding belly rested upon its knees, and its putrid odor was noticeably malodorous.

Scrof had only come into existence recently. Its recognition of the sphinx and its riddle may hint at a connection between the individual who created the tunnel and the one who designed the magical cards that Merlin had named "Trumps of Doom." More likely, however, was that Scrof's range of experience included knowledge of other magical beings.

In a small way, Scrof offered an interesting diversion for Merlin, one in which he was able to utilize his remarkable, preternatural muscles. Unwilling to let the Dweller deter him from passing through, Merlin revealed his mystical entity Frakir, preparing for a fight. His journals describe what followed:

> Scrof smiled. "I not only eat sorcerers, I eat their magic, too. Only a being torn from the primal Chaos can make that claim. So come ahead, if you think you can face that."
>
> "Chaos, eh? Torn from the primal Chaos?"
>
> "Yep. There's not much can stand against it."
>
> "Except maybe a Lord of Chaos," I replied, as I shifted my awareness to various points within my body. Rough work. The faster you do it the more painful it is. . . .
>
> "You know what the odds are against a Chaos Lord coming this far to go two out of three with a Dweller?" Scrof said.
>
> My arms began to lengthen and I felt my shirt tear across my back as I leaned forward. The bones in my face shifted about and my chest expanded and expanded. . . .
>
> "One out of one should be enough," I replied, when the transformation was complete.

> "Shit," Scrof said as I crossed the line. (BA, 38)

While Scrof's fate was uncertain, it seems likely that the transformed Merlin would have left it defeated but alive. Ultimately, it would seem, Scrof's existence was dependent on the continuance of the tunnel's duration. Once that mystic avenue faded into nothingness, Scrof, too, would be gone.

SECTIONS OF AMBER'S PALACE DESTROYED

In the awesome confrontation between the Signs of the Pattern and Logrus within the Royal Palace of Amber, rooms, corridors, and supporting archways were ripped apart. The destruction was so great that the reconstruction went on for quite some time afterward. It was fortunate that the foundation itself was not weakened, so that the rebuilding could go on in an orderly fashion without the necessity of evacuating residents from the structure entirely for the duration.

The explosion initiated by the meeting of Powers took place near one of the central staircases close to one of the rooms of Bleys's quarters. Merlin gave a reasonably accurate inventory of the destruction and the affected areas in his journals:

> That long section of hallway where the encounter had occurred had been destroyed, along with the stairs, Benedict's apartment, and possibly Gérard's as well. Also, Bleys's rooms, portions of my own, the sitting room I had been occupying but a short time before, and the northeast corner of the library were missing, as were the floor and ceiling. Below, I could see that sections of the kitchen and armory had been hit, and possibly more across the way. Looking upward . . . I could see sky, which meant that the blast had gone through the third and fourth floors, possibly damaging the royal suite along with the upper stairways and maybe the laboratory. (KS, 201)

In the quarters of King Random, part of one wall was missing in the bedroom, but an inner room, containing Queen Vialle's art studio, seemed intact but for a hole in one wall. There was no easy access from the royal quarters to Merlin's rooms, for instance, but a standing beam was solid enough to permit Merlin to slide down and reach a hallway between an inner and outer door of his quarters. However, the outer door was gone, as was the outer wall of that entrance.

Merlin found that the far wall of his apartment was also damaged, and he could see into the adjacent room, which was Brand's quarters. Merlin tried fitting a piece of stone he had recovered from a strange dream into the partially destroyed archway to Brand's room. In examining the damaged archway, Merlin detected some kind of healing process occurring in the stones of the arch. He could tell that there were numerous magical enchantments in and around Brand's rooms. After several minutes, more of the wall was repaired, as if by invisible workmen.

Nearly all of the major chambers have been rebuilt, as well as new stairways constructed where huge gaps had been. This reconstruction necessitated the movement of certain rooms, expanding some and diminishing others. Nevertheless, its occupants have become quite used to the changes, and are even somewhat inured to the possibility of future alterations that may be incorporated.

SENTIENT TREE AT DIVISION OF CHAOS AND ORDER/ OLD YGG

The aged tree that addressed Corwin on his way to the Courts of Chaos at the time of the Patternfall War. Corwin broke off one of its limbs to use as a staff, and later planted it in the ground to mark the beginning of the new Pattern he created.

The speaking bird Hugi referred to the tree as old Ygg. In many shadows, the Yggdrasil has come to refer to the great Tree of the World, whose branches encompass the universe. It is a great ash tree whose roots extend into three distinct realms: Asgard; the land of the Frost Giants; and the Kingdom of the Dead. Legend in a number of shadows purports that the Yggdrasil will remain after humankind destroys

itself in dreadful wars. After the great cataclysm, the gods Lif and Lifdrasir, hiding in Yggdrasil's branches, will emerge and create a new world.

Trees that possess the power of speech seem to have been documented in a number of shadows. Some who claim to have spoken to these sentient trees describe the responding voice as the sound of a combination of sighs, murmurs, and groans. Large trees have thick, deep voices, whereas smaller, slimmer trees whisper so quietly as to be almost inaudible.

In his Chronicles, Corwin recounted his talk with old Ygg:

> I spotted an ancient tree and cut myself a staff. The tree seemed to shriek as I severed its limb.
>
> "Damn you!" came something like a voice from within it.
>
> "You're sentient? . . . I'm sorry . . ."
>
> "I spent a long time growing that branch. I suppose you are going to burn it now?"
>
> "No," I said. "I needed a staff. I've a long walk before me."
>
> "Through this valley?"
>
> "That's right."
>
> "Come closer, that I may better sense your presence. There is something about you that glows."
>
> I took a step forward.
>
> "Oberon!" it said. "I know thy Jewel."
>
> "Not Oberon," I said. "I am his son. I wear it on his mission, though."
>
> "Then take my limb, and have my blessing with it. I've sheltered your father on many a strange day. He planted me, you see."
>
> "Really? Planting a tree is one of the few things I never saw Dad do."
>
> "I am no ordinary tree. He placed me here to mark a boundary."
>
> "Of what sort?"
>
> "I am the end of Chaos and of Order, depending upon how you view me. I mark a division. Beyond me other rules apply."
>
> "What rules?"
>
> "Who can say? Not I. I am only a growing tower of sentient lumber. My staff may comfort you, however. Planted, it may blossom in strange climes. Then again, it may not. Who can say? Bear it with you, however, son of Oberon, into the place where you journey now.

I feel a storm approaching. Good-bye.'' (CC, 75–76)

Of course, no one of Amber has ever seen old Ygg again, and it falls to us to wonder if, like the Yggdrasill of legend, it survived the absolute destruction of that storm.

Then again, the limb of that aged tree that Corwin carried with him took root beside his Pattern. The tree grew tall and leafy, alive, acting, for a time, as a lone guardian beside Corwin's Pattern. Fiona had found the spot, and she had shown it to Random and Bleys and Corwin's son, Merlin. Much later, a special image of Corwin led Merlin and others to that remarkable place. The tree continues to give shelter to the companions of Merlin.

This new tree stands as a mute legacy to its sentient forebear. It remains there, to be seen by those who know the way.

SHADOW EARTH

A shadow that exists quite far from Amber, in a direction that removes it from realms of magic. Corwin spent centuries residing there after his brother Eric placed him there in an unconscious state. While on shadow Earth, Corwin joined a number of military campaigns. His son, Merlin, chose to live there also. Merlin attended Berkeley University in California, then worked for a computer firm for several years. Bill Roth, a fairly new resident of Amber, was originally from New York on shadow Earth.

Actually, that shadow became a favorite place for several of the Royal Family: Flora enjoyed living in France during its eighteenth century and returned in recent times to San Francisco to take up residence for a while; Random visited Flora in France in his younger days; Brand spent time in New York while working his intrigues against Corwin; and Droppa MaPantz, the court jester, returns there every so often, especially to Las Vegas, Nevada, in order to pick up fresh comedy routines.

The major question, of course, is why do the royal members of Amber, and others besides, find shadow Earth so fascinating? So much of that shadow's culture have been introduced in Amber, after all. Books, art, music, military tactics. One of the

reasons for there not being institutions of higher learning in Amber is because those with connections to the Royal Court are able to send their sons and daughters to universities on shadow Earth. Most agree that the place offers a richness, a diversity of knowledge, that cannot be easily found in other shadows.

When Corwin spoke of his life in that shadow, he expressed some of the variety of activities he engaged in: ''It occurs to me that I was a professional soldier, madam. I fought for whoever would pay me. Also, I composed the words and music to many popular songs.'' (NP, 83) One can speculate that those who visited Earth were more greatly influenced by their surroundings than ever they could influence that land and its people.

Lacking in the arcane Art, those of shadow Earth show remarkable creative talents using mere rational, physical means. In counterpoint to the natural beauty of mountains and trees and rivers and sky, the people of Earth construct immense objects of man-made beauty and function. There is magic in an enormously complex bridge of steel and wire crossing a river and gargantuan buildings of glass and metal piercing a blue sky. Much of that realm is a unique paradoxical mix of artificial construction set against natural elegance. These objects of creativity are all the more remarkable because of the capacity of many of its people for violence and destruction. Sometimes, it seems, both tendencies go hand in hand, the tendency to create and the tendency to destroy. It is easier for people to tear down what others create than to create something special with their own hands. Thus, it would appear, those of shadow Earth have a keen propensity for war. Wars between people may simply be a reflection of the war within oneself, the war between destructive urges and the need to create.

This is not to say that shadow Earth is atypical, or that its people are quite unlike those of the true city. Quite the contrary. In matters of conflict and warfare, Earth is a clear reflection of Amber. As Corwin has said: ''The same conflicts exist everywhere, in various forms. They are all about you, always, for all places take their form from Amber.'' (GA, 150) In his younger days, it has been said, Oberon traveled upon the Earth in the infancy of its history. If it is so, no doubt he sought conquests that led nations to battle one another in those early times. His eldest surviving son, Benedict, experienced warfare on shadow Earth and its shadows in order to observe the tactics of a Caesar. No, shadow Earth is not alone in evolving new methods for making war and engaging in mutual destruction.

A quality that Amberites have found endearing about those of shadow Earth is their cynicism about the rationally inexplicable. They are so steeped in their worldly smugness that, more often than not, they utterly refuse to accept supernatural explanations for bizarre events. No matter that they have found no rational explanation for some strange occurrence, they are firm in their faith that the solution is rooted in science. There was a certain nurse, for instance, working in a city hospital in upstate New York. She claimed she saw a patient, Carl Corey, vanish from his room, within a sudden, rainbowlike glow. Doubting her own vision, she had her eyes checked for glaucoma. Her eyes were perfectly normal. (SU, 145; HO, 135) Still, from the account of Bill Roth, the nurse stopped speaking of the incident within a short time. No one believed what she described, except for Bill Roth. Soon, the nurse herself doubted that it ever really happened.

For those of us who reside in Amber, there is a fascination in the apparent substitution of technology on shadow Earth for the mystical effects of our realm. Earth has electricity; we have pet dragons. Earth possesses vehicles that run by means of combustion engines; we have commerce with other shadows. Yet, for all their ingenuous pragmatism, some people of shadow Earth acknowledge the possibility that there are forces of magical enchantment. Many spend a large part of their lives seeking to set in motion such forces themselves. Merlin, son of Corwin, met one of these people. He was a young man who believed fervently in supernatural influences, but he failed in finding the truth for himself. Completely disheartened, the young man told Merlin:

> "Sometimes I felt that I was close, that there was some power, some vision that I could almost touch or see. Almost. Then it was gone. It's all a lot of crap. You just delude yourself. . . .
>
> "You know, it's really sad . . .
>
> "That there's no magic, that there never was, there probably never will be." (TD, 22–23)

Corwin had been literally tossed into the shadow of Earth. It had not been his choice. Without mem-

ory, he simply managed a full, rich life without benefit of knowing his heritage. On the other hand, Flora deliberately selected Earth as a respite from the intrigues of Amber. Flora explained to Corwin: "I had been wandering, looking for something novel, something that suited my fancy. . . .

". . . It was, if you like, my Avalon, my Amber surrogate, my home away from home." (SU, 58–59) The period during which Flora and Corwin lived on shadow Earth was a wonderfully dynamic time. Unaccountably living an incredibly long time compared to his acquaintances, Corwin met a remarkably diverse number of renowned people. He knew Vincent van Gogh, Bertolt Brecht, and Sigmund Freud. He served in military campaigns under Napoleon Bonaparte, Robert E. Lee, and Douglas MacArthur. He lived through the black plague of London, the French Revolution, the two world wars, and, when he moved to the United States, the Kennedy years. In spite of his memory loss of his past in Amber, Corwin enriched his life immeasurably in the world of shadow Earth. As Bill Roth has said, "He was never just plain Carl Corey. He had a few centuries' worth of Earth memory when I knew him. That makes for a character too complex to be easily predictable." (SC, 120)

As a consequence of having visited Earth, Corwin, his son Merlin, and Random, among others, have assimilated numerous American phrases into their own speech. Whether they express these idioms in Thari or in English, they often slip out with amusing effect. Julian was slightly perplexed when Corwin maintained his secrecy by uttering in Thari: "Does Macy's tell Gimbel's?" (HO, 123) Random spoke bemusedly to Merlin when his nephew arrived in Amber by a Trump connection amid a shower of flowers: "I'd rather you said it with words." (BA, 55) Merlin's wit may have been inadvertent when he called after a fleeing entity in a human form: "Hold that ty'iga!" (KS, 194) But he was speaking more deliberately, hoping to halt an enemy in puzzlement, when he called out on separate occasions: "Your shoelace is untied," (SC, 208) and "Banzai!" (BA, 176)

Books and music and art have all found a place in the hearts of Amberites who know something of shadow Earth. When an angry Alice in a mock courtroom called out, "Who cares for you. You're nothing but a pack of cards!" in *Alice's Adventures in Wonderland,* it was remarkably representative of

the way members of Amber's Royal Family sometimes perceive themselves. Aside from the obvious
associations to be made with the Trumps that the
Family uses, Corwin may have been considering Alice's comment as he reflected on his siblings in his
Chronicles: "I deal you out like a hand of cards,
my brothers and sisters." (CC, 140) Merlin's friend
Luke Raynard was influenced enough by the creatures imagined by that author that he created a
shadow filled with them out of a drugged, subconscious mind. One way or another, the world of
Lewis Carroll even touched the Courts of Chaos. In
Lord Sawall's Maze of Art was a room "which
contained the skeleton of a Jabberwock painted in
orange, blue, and yellow, Early Psychedelic."
(PC, 219)

Certainly, Shakespeare excited much interest in
Amber, and some who are familiar with his words
have quoted or paraphrased them to their own purpose. When Brand was about to kill a transfixed
Benedict, he sneered, "Good night, sweet Prince."
(HO, 183) Deciding to join in the battle of Eric's
army against creatures from the black road, Corwin
paraphrased the Bard in thinking: "I could not hate
thee, Eric, so much, loved I not Amber more."
(GA, 210)

Since Merlin had been a student in a prestigious
college on shadow Earth, it is reasonable to assume
that he had read widely, and he included some references to his readings in his journals. He shows passing knowledge of Thomas of Erceldoune, or
Thomas the Rhymer, (TD, 88) James Joyce's *Ulys-
ses,* (TD, 135) Jamaica Kincaid, (SC, 12) and John
D. MacDonald. (BA, 206–7) He had given a copy
of the book *Praise* by Robert Hass (perhaps a Thari
edition) to his stepbrother Mandor. (PC, 56) His
college classmate, Luke Raynard, was reading a
copy of B.H. Liddell Hart's *Strategy* (TD, 80) while
training mercenary troops in the New Mexican
wilderness.

Music of that shadow has been very important to
members of the Family. King Random, having been
a musician himself, brought back the music of
"Greensleeves" from shadow Earth, which was
performed during the banquet in honor of the delegation from Begma. (SC, 128) Droppa MaPantz fled
the scene of the two Powers confronting each other
in the Royal Palace, singing the lyrics of "Rock of
Ages." (KS, 197) In a drugged stupor, Luke Raynard echoed the sentiments of the title song from
Cabaret while toasting Merlin in the Wonderland
bar. (BA, 215)

In a concrete argument of whether art imitates
life, or life imitates art, Merlin saw a favorite painting actualized and made utilitarian. Merlin bought
a painting done by a New Mexican artist named
Polly Jackson. It was a rendition of a red '57 Chevy.
Because the painting was on his mind, Merlin discovered that a third Power took it from his thoughts
and created its form in reality. The red '57 Chevy
became a useful conveyance and was incorporated
into a way station for Merlin and his friends.

Those who are able to visit the shadows from
Amber apparently have a great appreciation of what
they have learned on shadow Earth. It is likely an
important reason why King Random has agreed to
have this compendium published in English on the
North American Continent of that world. Repaying
a long-felt debt, we carry the hope that more people
of that land of skeptics will come to believe in
Shadow.

SHADOWMASTERS

Citizens of the Courts of Chaos who have a special aptitude in maneuvering Shadow stress points
in order to create a passage into the shadows.

As Merlin of the Courts and Amber has written
in his journal: "The stuff of Shadow is so docile at
this end of reality [at the Courts of Chaos] that it
can be easily manipulated by a Shadowmaster—who
can stitch together their fabrics to create a way."
(PC, 15–16) Anyone who succeeds in walking the
Logrus automatically becomes a member of the
Shadowmaster Guild. However, one does not have
to be an initiate of the Logrus to become a Shadowmaster. Although a Shadowmaster's skill derives
from the Logrus, his individual talents and understanding of the weaving of these stress points, or
ways, makes him an effective technician.

Our understanding of the process of constructing
a Way is lacking, but Merlin has offered some striking perspectives of movement through Ways in his
journals. In his ancestral home in the Courts, Merlin
found a hidden Way in the armoire of his brother
Jurt's room:

"I pushed garments aside, making a way clear to the back of the thing. I could feel it strongly. A final shove at the garments, a quick shuffle to the rear, and I was at the focus. I let it take me away.

Once there was a forward yielding, the pressure of the garments at my back gave me a small push. That, plus the fact that someone (Jurt, himself?) had done a sloppy shadowmastering job resulting in mismatched floor levels, sent me sprawling as I achieved destination." (PC, 155)

Here, thus, we have an inkling of the greater or lesser qualities of shadowmastering, and what errors a poor job may bring.

As shown through the journals of Merlin, there is danger in being a Shadowmaster. The danger comes from a specific instance, one not at all related with the manipulating of Ways. A snakelike creature named Glait, a childhood friend of Merlin's, told of watching a Shadowmaster open a Way high in a chamber of Sawall's Maze of Art. Those who had hired the Shadowmaster killed him after he had done his work, maintaining the secret of a hidden Way at the cost of a life. This deed may remind one of the lot of slaves of ancient Egypt on shadow Earth. It was customary for house servants who supervised the construction of burial tombs for their royal masters to slay the enslaved workers in order to keep the exact location of the tomb secret.

The work of Shadowmasters is so common in the Courts, where Ways are frequently the only means of entry or exit in most enclosures, that they are no more revered than electricians or plumbers on shadow Earth.

SHADOWS

In the most general sense, shadows are the innumerable worlds that are reflections of the true city, Amber. The shadows were formed at the moment that Dworkin Barimen drew the Pattern on a bare rock, creating Amber, Order, the universes as we understand them. In a more philosophical, or perhaps, psychological, sense, there is Shadow. That is, the form that can be actualized by an initiate of

the Pattern into a real world of his or her imagining. Any kind of place that a Pattern-initiate can think of will then become real, and that person can go to it.

Corwin, a Pattern-initiate, had long contemplated the nature of Shadow and the shadows, expressing his thoughts of them in his Chronicles:

"I can find, somewhere, off in Shadow, anything I can visualize. Any of us [the Royal Family in Amber] can.... It may be argued, and in fact has, by most of us, that we create the shadows we visit out of the stuff of our own psyches, that we alone truly exist, that the shadows we traverse are but projections of our own desires.... it does go far toward explaining much of the family's attitude toward people, places, and things outside of Amber. Namely, we are toymakers and they, our playthings." (SU, 164–65)

Someone like Corwin, who can move through Shadow, has the ability to lead ordinary people, the "playthings" of shadow worlds, into various shadows as well. Corwin's Chronicles state:

"Now, it is written that only a prince of Amber may walk among Shadows, though of course he may lead or direct as many as he chooses along such courses. We led our troops and saw them die, but of Shadow I have this to say: there is Shadow and there is Substance, and this is the root of all things. Of Substance, there is only Amber, the real city, upon the real Earth, which contains everything. Of Shadow, there is an infinitude of things. Every possibility exists somewhere as a Shadow of the real. Amber, by its very existence, has cast such in all directions. And what may one say of it beyond? Shadow extends from Amber to Chaos, and all things are possible within it." (NP, 113–14)

The Chronicles explain the means that a prince or princess of Amber has to traverse Shadow. One may move on foot or on horseback and exert one's mental focus to change aspects of the scenery. This is commonly referred to as a hellride. One may use the Trumps to reach another initiate of the Pattern, having that person bring one to his location. And, one may walk the Pattern again, and use its energies directly to send one to any shadow of one's desire.

Many of the early problems faced by Corwin developed because of a power struggle between himself and several of his siblings. They had sought to rule in Amber at a time when King Oberon was seriously considering abdicating his throne. At one point, Vialle, the blind wife of Random, questioned Corwin about the nature of Shadow and the Royal Family's lust for power:

> "Lord Corwin, my knowledge of the philosophical bases of these things is limited, but it is my understanding that you are able to find anything you wish within Shadow. This has troubled me for a long while, and I never fully understood Random's explanations. If you wished, could not each of you walk in Shadow and find yourself another Amber—like this one in all respects, save that you ruled there or enjoyed whatever other status you might desire?"
>
> "Yes, we can locate such places," I said.
>
> "Then why is this not done, to have an end of strife?"
>
> "It is because a place could be found which *seemed* to be the same—but that would be all. We are a part of this Amber as surely as it is a part of us. Any shadow of Amber would have to be populated with shadows of ourselves to seem worthwhile. We could even except the shadow of our own person should we choose to move into a ready realm. However, the shadow folk would not be exactly like the other people here. A shadow is never precisely like that which casts it. These little differences add up. They are actually worse than major ones. It would amount to entering a nation of strangers. . . . Personality is the one thing we cannot control in our manipulations of Shadow. In fact, it is the means by which we can tell one another from shadows of ourselves. This is why Flora could not decide about me for so long, back on the shadow Earth: my new personality was sufficiently different."
>
> "I begin to understand," she said. "It is not just Amber for you. It is the place plus everything else."
>
> "The place plus everything else . . . *That* is Amber," I agreed. (HO, 55–56)

In his youth, Corwin had ruled in a place called Avalon. He has said that the Avalon he knew was destroyed, but he believed that he resided there long enough that shadows of himself also existed, ruling in shadows of that Avalon. In his travels, Corwin reached a land where the people remembered a Corwin that was not him:

> "They still tell stories of how the Lord Corwin had my grandfather executed—drawn and quartered publicly—for leading one of the early uprisings against him."
>
> "That wasn't me," I said. "It was one of my shadows." (GA, 63)

An individual adept at moving through Shadow can seem to be making no effort whatsoever. He or she need not be traveling very fast in order to make a hellride, nor be conveyed by any vehicle; walking will suffice. At a time when Corwin was suffering from amnesia, and thus everything that was occurring was fresh to him, he was led on a hellride by his brother Random. Corwin was driving a Mercedes from shadow Earth while Random was influencing the shadows around them:

> "Turn right at the crossroads," he decided.
>
> What was happening? I knew he was in some way responsible for the exotic changes going on about us, but I couldn't determine how he was doing it. . . . He seemed to do nothing but smoke and stare, but coming up out of a dip in the road we entered a blue desert and the sun was now pink above our heads within the shimmering sky. . . .
>
> The steering wheel changed shape beneath my hands.
>
> It became a crescent; and the seat seemed further back, the car seemed closer to the road, and the windshield had more of a slant to it. . . .
>
> . . . Something told me that whatever Shadows were, we moved among them even now. How? It was something Random was doing, and since he seemed at rest physically, his hands in plain sight, I decided it was something he did with his mind. . . .
>
> . . . I'd heard him speak of "adding" and "subtracting," as though the universe in which he moved were a big equation. (NP, 47–48)

Naturally, those who are able to play with Shadow find it pleasurable. The ability reinforces one's sense of superiority. An initiate may even find some distinct advantages in using the "playthings" of other shadows. For instance, Caine pretended his own murder by substituting a shadow of himself as the "victim." In that way, he was able to observe the actions of his siblings without arousing their suspicions.

Frequently, members of the Royal Family have revealed the secrets of traveling through shadows to others who were uninitiated. Benedict trained young Martin in the ways of Shadow when the youth came to him for advice. Corwin showed a seemingly ingenuous Dara what it was like to walk the shadows. And Merlin, feeling, perhaps, the need to show off, took his girlfriend Julia to strange realms from shadow Earth.

Late one evening while Merlin and Julia were lying on a beach in San Francisco, he decided to take her on a trip she would remember all her life. Without explaining, Merlin took her by the hand and led her from the beach, through a cave, and . . .

> . . . through a canyon of colored rocks and grasses, beside a stream that flowed into a river. . . .
>
> . . . to a precipice from whence it plunged a mighty distance, casting rainbows and fogs. Standing there, staring out across the great valley that lay below, we beheld a city of spires and cupolas, gilt and crystal, through morning and mist.
>
> "Where—are we?" she asked.
>
> "Just around the corner," I [Merlin] said. "Come." . . .
>
> . . . It was an enormous prospect, blazing with new constellations, their light sufficient to cast our shadows onto the wall behind us. She leaned over the low parapet, her skin some rare polished marble, and she looked downward.
>
> "They're down there, too," she said. "And to both sides! There is nothing below but more stars." (TD, 25)

Sometime later, when Julia had time to consider what Merlin had shown her, she reacted quite differently than he expected. She questioned him about it angrily:

> "What kind of an idiot do you take me for? That walk we took isn't on the maps. Nobody around here's ever heard of anything like those places. It was geographically impossible. The times of day and the seasons kept shifting. The only explanation is supernatural or paranormal." (BA, 57)

Unfortunately, despite Merlin's reluctance to discuss it, Julia would not let it rest. In consequence, their relationship ended. Of course, something more resulted from that hellride Merlin led Julia on. It had, indeed, influenced her entire life.

We have learned, of course, since those earlier days before the Patternfall War, that the Amber we are familiar with is not the true "casting off" point of Shadow. A deeper layer of reality, wherein resides the primal Pattern, the one drawn by Dworkin, is the actual point of departure for all Shadow. Our Amber is, essentially, the first shadow, a very special one. That is the reason why it is so difficult for a Pattern-initiate to shift through Shadow in Amber: It is so close to the true state of Order. However, Oberon was able to lead Corwin and Random into Shadow on Mt. Kolvir. Though difficult, it is not impossible to hellride from our Amber. In fact, Corwin attempted to alter Shadow while still on Kolvir:

> While Dad [Oberon] was able to play with the stuff of Shadow atop Kolvir, I had never been able to. I required a greater distance from Amber in order to work the shifts.
>
> Still, knowing that it could be done, I felt that I ought to try. So, working my way southward across bare stone and down rocky passes where the wind howled, I sought to warp the fabric or being about me as I headed toward the trail that led to Garnath.
>
> . . . A small clump of blue flowers as I rounded a stony shoulder.
>
> I grew excited at this, for they were a modest part of my working. I continued to lay my will upon the world to come beyond each twisting of my way. . . .
>
> Some of the smaller ones were indeed working. . . . An ancient bird's nest, high on a rocky shelf . . . More of the blue flowers . . .
>
> Why not? A tree . . . Another . . .
>
> I felt the power moving within me. I worked more changes. (CC, 33–34)

The nature of Shadow will remain one of the great mysteries of our universe. We of Amber have learned a great deal about it; many have traveled to other shadows on board ships led by Gérard, for example. For us, the shadow worlds are an accepted part of reality. Nevertheless, the fact that there are endless possibilities out there—unimagined perils and unknown denizens vastly different from any seen by the well traveled among us—that is a fact that is difficult to grasp. Those with an adventurous spirit continue to explore those limitless possibilities, following, quite literally, in the footsteps of those of Royal blood.

The larger concerns of Place (or, rather, Other Places) still seem an abstraction to many of us. Until and unless the workings of the Powers cause some alteration in shadows, we simply cannot be apprehensive about those things over which we have no control. Shadows, after all, do not touch the ordinary individual on a daily basis. Only when the shadows impinge upon us on a personal level need we consider them as a real and intrusive concern.

SHADOW-STORMS

A natural phenomenon involving wavelike motions that flow outward from both Amber and the Courts of Chaos. The waves of such a storm usually move through Shadow and can cause great damage in some shadows along the way, although other shadows might suffer little or no damage. Quite often, any number of things can be transported from one shadow to another by a Shadow-storm, and these may include a displacement of people.

Merlin explained the nature of Shadow-storms to his father's friend, Bill Roth, in this way:

> "It's a natural but not too well-understood phenomenon. The best comparison I can think of is a tropical storm. One theory as to their origin has to do with the beat frequencies of waves that pulse outward from Amber and from the Courts, shaping the nature of shadows. Whatever, when such a storm rises it can flow through a large number of shadows before it plays itself out." (TD, 88–89)

While Shadow-storms were known to those in the Courts and in Amber for a long time, Princess Fiona of Amber looked upon their increased incidence as a danger to both poles of reality. In fact, the nature of these Shadow-storms as a significant threat was a point of contention between Fiona and her nephew Merlin. Fiona felt the conviction that Prince Corwin's new Pattern had set up an imbalance between the poles, and the Shadow-storms were a manifestation of that possibly disastrous imbalance. Merlin sought elsewhere for a simpler, less dramatic explanation of the increased phenomena. In Merlin's accounts, he expressed quite well the opposing positions that he and Fiona had taken:

Fiona told Merlin:

> "Amber and Chaos are the two poles of existence, as we understand it, . . . housing as they do the Pattern and the Logrus. For ages there has been something of an equilibrium between them. Now, I believe, this bastard Pattern of your father's is undermining their balance."
>
> "In what fashion?"
>
> "There have always been wavelike exchanges between Amber and Chaos. This seems to be setting up some interference."
>
> "It sounds more like tossing an extra ice cube into a drink . . . It should settle down after a while." . . .
>
> "Things are not settling. There have been far more shadow-storms since this thing was created. They rend the fabric of Shadow. They affect the nature of reality itself."
>
> "No good. . . . Another event a lot more important along these lines occurred at the same time. The original Pattern in Amber was damaged and Oberon repaired it. The wave of Chaos which came out of that swept through all of Shadow. Everything was affected. But the Pattern held and things settled again. I'd be more inclined to think of all those extra shadow storms as being in the nature of aftershocks." (BA, 162)

On a later occasion, Fiona pursued her belief in the danger of the Shadow-storms by making Trump contact with Merlin from a distant shadow. Merlin introduced Fiona to his stepbrother Mandor, and both of them joined her in a shadow of green skies and craggy mountains. There, she presented a finding that she believed justified her fears. She pointed out a huge black tornado on a distant plain below them. Her argument revolved around the fact that this particular Shadow-storm was unwavering and unmoving. It was not manifesting itself in its usual manner, which was to move in waves through Shadow. Its stationary field indicated that this Shadow-storm had undergone a fundamental change in nature. Behind Fiona's conjecture was the implication that some force or agent was harnessing the power of Shadow-storms for some unknown purpose. If such were the case, the result could become as catastrophic as the Death Storm that erased Amber and all the shadows during the Patternfall.

Fiona proposed that Merlin walk Corwin's Pattern, allow Fiona to trump to him in its center, and together transport to its primal Pattern. In that way, they could fathom its magical source and correct the growing imbalance of the realities known to them. If the black tornado was manifested by the third Pattern, Fiona and Merlin could learn to control its destructive power.

Taking matters into his own hands, Mandor conducted an experiment with the Shadow-storm/tornado. Using his Logrus powers, he threw the all-consuming annihilating force of Chaos at the tornado. The manifested storm grew immensely for several moments, then tossed aside the accumulated mass to return to the same size and shape it had been before. Based on their observations, this is the conclusion reached by Mandor:

> "It is a Chaos phenomenon . . . You could see that in the way it drew upon Chaos when I provided the means. But that pushed it past some limit, and there was a correction. Someone is playing with the primal forces themselves out there. Who or what or why, I cannot say. But I think it's strong testimony that the Pattern isn't involved. Not with Chaos games. So Merlin is probably correct. I think that this business has its origin elsewhere." (SC, 44)

Shortly thereafter, the tornado disappeared entirely.

A significant factor that Merlin chose not to reveal was that he had actually experienced a Shadow-storm himself, and it had been caused by a construct other than Corwin's Pattern. Merlin's unique computer Ghostwheel had once called up such a storm to prevent him from shutting it down. Hurtling directionless through the air, Merlin noted the strange confluence of matter around him:

> "In the distance, I seemed to see a tiny steam locomotive negotiating a mountainside at an impossible angle, then an upside-down waterfall, a skyline beneath green waters. A park bench passed us quickly, a blue-skinned woman seated upon it, clutching at it, a horrified expression on her face. . . .
>
> A batlike creature was blown into my face, was gone an instant later, leaving a wet slash upon my right cheek. . . .
>
> An inverted mountain range flowed past us, buckling and rippling." (TD, 176–77)

From Merlin's description, it seems only a being of supernatural abilities could survive the experience intact.

We can think of Shadow-storms as being the natural outcome of the sometimes delicate tension between the poles of the Courts and Amber. Their increased frequency and altering character, however, may be attributable to principles or intelligences not readily understood by us.

SHAPESHIFTING

The ability to alter one's appearance at will. Those who are initiates of the Logrus apparently have this ability, but it seems likely that those who walk the Pattern may also be able to change their shape. Because Dworkin was affected by the blot on the Pattern, he shapeshifted involuntarily when undergoing great emotional stress.

Prior to Patternfall, Dara spoke to several members of the Royal Family in Amber about this talent:

> "All whose origins involve Chaos are shapeshifters," she replied.
>
> I [Corwin] thought of Dworkin's performance the night he had impersonated me.
>
> Benedict nodded.
>
> "Dad fooled us with his Ganelon disguise."
>
> "Oberon is a son of Chaos," Dara said, "a rebel son of a rebel father. But the power is still there."

"Then why is it we cannot do it?" Random asked.

She shrugged.

"Have you ever tried? Perhaps you can. On the other hand, it may have died out with your generation. I do not know. As to myself, however, I have certain favored shapes to which I revert in times of stress. I grew up where this was the rule, where the other shape was actually sometimes dominant. It is still a reflex with me." (CC, 16)

Corwin and his siblings had a very limited experience with shapeshifting. Even if they had the power to do so, they did not practice it with any acuity, and certainly not when there was somebody to record the event. The children of Oberon are apparently content to maintain their usual semblance.

Merlin, son of Corwin, unlike his father, had a wide experience with the phenomenon. Because he was brought up in the Courts of Chaos and had walked the Logrus, he was entirely used to the concept of transforming himself at will. He documented his shapeshifting abilities on several occasions in his published journals. When he needed to get past Scrof, the Dweller on the Threshold between shadow Earth and the Keep of the Four Worlds, he transformed into one of his Chaosian demonforms. As a youth, he had altered the shape of his feet so that they would cling effortlessly to a boulder soaring above the Pit of Chaos in a sporting duel with his brother Jurt.

When Merlin fought an enemy who had shapeshifted into a wolf, he described his understanding of such workings:

Most people who daydream of transforming themselves into some vicious beast and going about tearing people's throats out, dismembering them, disfiguring them and perhaps devouring them tend mainly to dwell upon how much fun it would be and generally neglect the practicalities of the situation. When you find yourself a quadruped, with a completely different center of gravity and a novel array of sensory input, it is not all that easy to get around for a time with any measure of grace. One is generally far more vulnerable than one's appearance would lead others to believe. And certainly one is nowhere near as lethal and

efficient as the real thing with a lifetime of practice behind it. (BA, 180–81)

Indeed, Merlin has shown himself to be quite knowledgeable about how best to utilize the talent. When he and Jurt were faced with crossing a large field of ice, he made a prudent suggestion:

"Looks slippery," Jurt said. "I'm going to shapeshift my feet, make them broader."

"It'll destroy your boots and leave you with cold feet," I [Merlin] said. "Why not just shift some of your weight downward, lower your center of gravity?" (KS, 123)

Clearly, a shapeshifter need not alter his entire physical appearance to obtain a desired effect. When Merlin chased after the shapeshifted wolf, he was barefooted. Having no time for anything else, Merlin simply hardened the soles of his feet as he ran through the forest.

As Merlin has commented in his journals, one who often transforms his physical appearance usually does so to cause an emotional reaction, such as fear. The effect is frequently temporary and somewhat illusory. A shapeshifter really needs to know what he or she is doing, if that person wants to create a longer-lasting impression of competence.

SIEGE OF AMBER, THE (BY LORD REIN)

A martial ballad composed by Lord Rein while Corwin was languishing in a dungeon of the Royal Palace. The ballad recounted the assault that Corwin and Bleys made against the armies of Eric the Usurper, especially their valiant climb up the steps of Mt. Kolvir.

The balladeer hadn't completed the lyric, and he decided against publishing the composition. While Eric was alive, it certainly wouldn't have been popular in the Royal Court. The song cast Bleys and Corwin as "enemies of the Crown," but it also glorified their efforts in fighting their way up Kolvir against overwhelming forces.

Its melody quite strident, "The Siege of Amber" seemed strangely out of place during the time that

THE SIEGE OF AMBER

by
Lord Rein

© 1995   Alice Christy

Eric ruled, since he had wide popular support. It is interesting to us now for its marking of an historical event that was, in some ways, ignominious, and was ultimately futile. Bleys was leading an army of men from distant shadows against the army of Amber. Although Amber's soldiers were fighting in defense of a prince who has been considered a usurper in retrospect, they were still the same soldiers that Bleys and Corwin had known in the days of King Oberon. Thus, Lord Rein was never able to foresee a time when the ballad would be appropriate for a public audience.

SPHINX

A blue-colored creature on a rocky ledge that confronted Merlin with its riddle. As in days long ago, the sphinx intended to consume the young man if he was unable to answer its riddle correctly. The sphinx had been depicted on a card that was one of several that came into Merlin's possession. Merlin had named the cards Trumps of Doom. Apparently, the sphinx represented a booby trap meant to ensnare those attempting to use the Trump without understanding the peril involved.

The Sphinx crouched on top of a blue-gray wall in a rocky region under a lemon yellow sky. It was located in a desertlike area of variously colored rocks and short, spiked bushes. The creature resembled the horrid sphinx of ancient Thebes in legends of several shadow worlds, but this one appeared to be genderless. It had a lion's body, huge eagle wings, and long, sharp teeth.

Although the sphinx was hungry, it permitted Merlin to recover fully from an artificially induced narcosis. It even allowed the young man freedom of movement while they spoke.

Although it seems possible that Merlin could have defeated the sphinx if the creature chose to attack the young man, Merlin decided to use wit and logic against the creature. Their conversation, therefore, makes for some intriguing banter, as well as helping to define the sphinx's personality and purpose:

"You seem to lack something of the proper spirit . . . But here it is: I rise in flame from the earth. The wind assails me and waters lash me. Soon I will oversee all things. . . .

"Well?"

"Well what?"

"Have you the answer?"

"To what?"

"The riddle, of course!"

"I was waiting. There was no question, only a series of statements. I can't answer a question if I don't know what it is."

"It's a time-honored format. The interrogative is implied by the context. Obviously, the question is, 'What am I?' "

"It could just as easily be, 'Who is buried in Grant's tomb?' But okay. What is it? The phoenix, of course—nested upon the earth, rising in flames above it, passing through the air, the clouds, to a great height—"

"Wrong." . . .

"Hold on . . . It is not wrong. It fits. It may

not be the answer you want, but it is an answer that meets the requirements.'' . . .

''I am the final authority on these answers. I do the defining.''

''Then you cheat.''

''I do not!''

''I drink off half the contents of a flask. Does that make it half full or half empty?''

''Either. Both.''

''Exactly. Same thing. If more than one answer fits, you have to buy them all. It's like waves and particles.''

''I don't like that approach . . . It would open all sorts of doors to ambiguity. It could spoil the riddling business.''

''Not my fault.'' (TD, 47–48)

The sphinx's code of ethics caused it to reach a compromise. It permitted Merlin to ask it a riddle of his own. After spending an entire night puzzling over Merlin's riddle, the sphinx admitted defeat. However, the sphinx felt it was deceived when it heard Merlin's solution and made to attack him. Using the special entity that he carried, Merlin revealed some of his true power to the sphinx. At that point, the sphinx allowed his departure.

A significant outcome of this encounter was that Merlin learned of a traveler passing the sphinx who knew of the Keep of the Four Worlds. The traveler had also gone on his way, unmolested. It seemed likely that the unknown traveler had an intimate knowledge of the special Trump for the sphinx and knew his way around the danger it represented.

SPIKARDS

There are nine such spikards known to exist. Each is a ring with tremendous power that extends into Shadow, independent of both the Pattern and the Logrus. One of these spikards was worn by King Swayvill of the Courts of Chaos. Another member of the Courts meant this ring for Merlin and hid it to be found in the quarters of Brand of Amber. Merlin used a spikard in numerous ways as an alternative to the two Powers during their most recent conflict.

Merlin of Amber and the Courts of Chaos was

meant to find one of the spikards. It had been planted in the palace of Amber by Merlin's stepbrother, Mandor. Merlin described his first impressions of the ring in his journals:

The band was wide, possibly of platinum. It bore a wheellike device of some reddish metal, with countless tiny spokes, many of them hairfine. And each of these spokes extended a line of power leading off somewhere, quite possibly into Shadow, where some power cache or spell source lay. . . . When I slipped it on, it seemed to extend roots to the very center of my body. I could feel my way back along them to the ring and then out along those connections. I was impressed by the variety of energies it reached and controlled—from simple chthonic forces to sophisticated constructs of High Magic, from elementals to things that seemed like lobotomized gods. . . . The ring was a beautiful alternative to Pattern Power or Logrus Power, hooked in as it was with so many sources. (KS, 232–33)

Intriguingly, Merlin felt compelled to stop his mystical entity, Frakir, from removing the ring from his finger. Suddenly quite annoyed with her, Merlin tied Frakir around the bedpost in Brand's room and left her there.

Beginning to rely on the spikard's powers to move him by levitation or direct transport from place to place, Merlin's change was detectable. Vialle, the blind wife of King Random of Amber, immediately sensed a difference in Merlin after he found the spikard. She made note of it, but Mandor intervened, attributing any change to Merlin's having gone through several traumatic experiences.

Through a dream of enlightenment that was placed on him, Merlin learned more of the spikards. The ring hidden in Brand's bedpost had been worn by the late king of the Courts of Chaos. Spells had been placed on it to compel the wearer to obey two members of the Courts: Mandor and Dara, Merlin's mother. However, the spikard meant to enslave Merlin had been switched. His uncle, Bleys of Amber, had access to a second spikard, and he placed that one in the bedpost. In the dream, Bleys handed him the ring that Mandor had planted. Bleys told him never to wear it, but to keep it with him. From Bleys, Merlin learned there were nine spikards in all. When Merlin awoke, he had the second spikard in his pocket.

The spikards were ancient artifacts that other members of the Royal Family in Amber were cognizant of. Merlin found out the background of the spikards from someone very close to him:

> "They were said to be very early power objects, from the days when the universe was still a murky place and the Shadow realms less clearly defined. When the time came, their wielders slept or dissolved or whatever such figures do, and the spikards were withdrawn or stashed or transformed, or whatever becomes of such things when the story's over. There are many versions, of course." (PC, 220)

Whatever the deeper secrets of the spikards may be, Merlin quickly grew accustomed to using the spikard exchanged by Bleys. Indeed, there was some magical enchantment that bound Merlin to the ring, but it apparently gave him confidence in its use. He used it variously to scrutinize other magical objects; to carry himself and others great distances through Shadow; to arrange directional guidance for his Ghostwheel to find the Logrus; to change the flow of his own blood from fire to liquid; to create illumination in a darkened area; to change the physical appearance of others; to call forth objects, animate as well as inanimate, from distant shadows; and to hold and transform Dara and Mandor against their wills. Still, his spikard had limitations. Opening all its channels against the Sign of the Pattern, Merlin was knocked into unconsciousness in an explosion of forces. The Pattern was then in control of him.

In a large way, Merlin was able to balance the influence of both the Pattern and the Logrus over him through his use of the spikard. Other allies, of course, enabled Merlin to keep the Powers at bay, but the spikard in hand was just the accommodation he needed to attain his autonomy from them.

STORM OF CHAOS

Variously called "Wave of Chaos," "devil-storm," and "Death Storm."

The storm was caused by King Oberon's attempt to repair the primal Pattern. Whether he cleared the blot upon it or not, the Wave of Chaos gradually spread from that source of order, enveloping all the shadows between Amber and the Courts of Chaos. Before undertaking the task, the late king told Corwin that "the entire fabric of existence will be undergoing an alteration." (CC, 33) Insisting that their father had died in the attempt, Brand explained the coming of the Death Storm to his brother:

> "Things fall apart . . . Even now, Chaos wells up to fill the vacuum back at Amber. A great vortex has come into being, and it grows. It spreads ever outward, destroying the shadow worlds, and it will not stop until it meets with the Courts of Chaos, bringing all of creation full circle, with Chaos once more to reign over all." (CC, 45)

To Corwin, it seemed that Brand was lying about Oberon's death and the coming destruction of the Wave of Chaos in order to obtain the Jewel of Judgment in Corwin's possession. He learned of the actuality of the eerie storm approaching from a stranger in a cave, where they both had sought shelter. The stranger described it in this way:

> "This is no natural storm . . .
> "For one thing, it is coming out of the north. They never come out of the north, here, this time of year. . . .
> "For another, I have never seen a storm behave this way. I have been watching it advance all day—just a steady line, moving slowly, front like a sheet of glass. So much lightning, it looks like a monstrous insect with hundreds of shiny legs. Most unnatural. And behind it, things have grown very distorted. . . .
> ". . . Everything seems to be changing its shape. Flowing. As if it is melting the world—or stamping away its forms." (CC, 51–52)

Before Corwin departed, the stranger spoke of an Archangel Corwin mentioned in the "Holy Book." The passage foretold Corwin's coming and that "this is the way that the world ends—beginning with a strange storm from out of the north." (CC, 52–53)

At that time, Corwin used the Jewel of Judgment to consciously push away the storm. He found that he had succeeded in maintaining an area of ground, a valley, that was untouched by the storm. If anything could repel that destroying wave, it was the power of the Jewel around Corwin's neck.

As he continued his hellride ahead of the oncoming storm, Corwin met a lady dressed in white. He realized she was deliberately keeping him from continuing his journey as she fed him, but he "kept an eye on the progress of that inexorable-seeming stormfront." (CC, 68) He was almost persuaded by Lady to remain with her. When Lady believed it too late for Corwin to effectuate any remedy, she told him:

> "There is no need to delay you now. I see by this that the Courts have won. There is nothing anyone can do to halt the advance of the Chaos. . . .
> "But I would rather you did not leave me at this time . . . It will reach us here in a matter of hours. What better way to spend this final time than in one another's company?" (CC, 68)

Nevertheless, Corwin traveled on. Looking back at the storm as he moved ahead, he watched it pass the spot where he dallied with Lady. He recounted: "I halted to look back, and perhaps a third of the valley now lay behind the shimmering screen of that advancing stormthing. I wondered about Lady and her lake, her pavilion. I shook my head and continued." (CC, 70)

In the face of the approaching storm and at the verge of a vast wasteland, Corwin decided that he must design a new Pattern in the event that the original no longer existed. He did so, creating a Pattern out of his own psyche on a bare, fogbound plateau. The new Pattern held, and the destroying storm was not part of the prospect. The Death Storm could not touch this place. Yet, it still threatened the Amber he knew, and all the shadows between Amber and the Courts. Corwin used the power of his Pattern to send him to Patternfall.

On a hilltop in the Courts, Corwin was able to see the army of Amber battling the Chaos soldiers on a plain below him. He also found the storm, still approaching:

> "Turning toward what must have been north by a succession of previous reckonings regarding its course, I beheld the advance of that

devil-storm through distant mountains, flashing and growling, coming on like a sky-high glacier.
> So I had not stopped it with the creation of a new Pattern. It seemed that it had simply passed by my protected area and would continue until it got to wherever it was going." (CC, 102–3)

For a brief time, the Jewel of Judgment was lost to Corwin and the other Amberites. It looked as if the storm would bring oblivion to everyone and everything that remained outside of the Courts of Chaos. Corwin's Chronicle records:

> The sky had rotated completely and the darkness was now above us, the colors passing over the Courts. The steady advance of the flashing stormfront was emphasized by this. I leaned forward and reached for my boots, began pulling them on. Soon it would be time to begin our retreat. (CC, 129)

When the Jewel was recovered, it was again possible to turn back the Wave of Chaos, end its existence, and gradually re-form Amber and its shadows. However, Corwin was completely exhausted, unable to gather the strength to repel the storm. He found it necessary to attune his brother Random to the Jewel, so that Random could use its power to turn the storm away. The two of them moved away from the others to begin the attunement. Afterward, Corwin collapsed.

When he regained consciousness, Corwin saw Random standing before the onslaught of the wave, working with the Jewel. The Chronicles describe it thusly:

> Standing against the storm, Random prevailed. It broke before us, parting as if cloven by a giant's axblade. It rolled back at either hand, finally sweeping off to the north and south, fading, diminishing, gone. The landscape it had masked endured. (CC, 139)

That was how the Storm of Chaos wiped all the shadows out of existence, even yours, though you did not know it. The shadow worlds were purged and then re-formed. They continue to endure, even though new struggles threaten them. Still, it is believed, they will thrive.

STRYGALLDWIR

One of the high servants of the demon known as the horned one from the dark Circle outside of the village of Lorraine. It was sent by the horned one to learn more of the stranger who came to Lorraine. This stranger had accomplished the killing of two beasts from the dark Circle and had carried a man several leagues to the Keep of Ganelon. If he was a new ally to Ganelon, the demon of the Circle needed to know. Strygalldwir was his ablest servant.

The description of Strygalldwir comes to us through the record of Corwin of Amber, later transcribed by his son:

> It was well over six feet in height, with great branches of antlers growing out of its forehead. Nude, its flesh was a uniform ash-gray in color. It appeared to be sexless, and it had gray, leathery wings extending far out behind it and joining with the night. It held a short, heavy sword of dark metal in its right hand, and there were runes carved all along the blade. (GA, 48)

It hovered outside the window of the stranger's bedroom, trying to determine if the human could conceivably be the mage who had opened up the way from the dominion of the Courts of Chaos to the shadow of Lorraine. Strygalldwir was disappointed. The man looked too frail and old to be the opener of the way. Still, the human blandished a sword that resembled the great blade Grayswandir. As required, Strygalldwir asked four times, "Who are you?" to which it needed a response from the one within before it could enter the chamber.

While the human in the bedchamber did not seem formidable, he knew the words to a spell in Thari that affected the demon. In fact, the human appeared to be quite presumptuous and fearless. Upon breaking through the latticework of the window, Strygalldwir engaged in battle with the aged human with the unique sword.

Bewildered, Strygalldwir found the stranger an able opponent. He caused a couple of deep gashes to well out in flame from the demon's body as they fought. The human impaled it on his blade, but Strygalldwir became more enraged. It lunged at the human, seeking to crush flesh and bone beneath its immensely powerful hands. Remarkably, the human was equal to the attack. The seemingly old man quickly got the advantage of the demon. He grasped the demon's throat in a death grip. It was the demon's first opportunity to really look into the human's eyes. Before death enveloped it, Strygalldwir knew that the man was indeed the Opener. It died not knowing why the Opener had joined the camp of the enemy.

SUHUY

Master of the Logrus in the Courts of Chaos. He is related to Merlin through Lord Sawall's side of the family, but he is so extremely old that no one knows how many "greats" to put before "uncle." He has excluded himself from the matter of the succession in the Courts, pleading that his age and infirmity prevent him. It has been documented that Suhuy oversaw the training of Merlin and Jurt in the initiation of the Logrus, and it is likely that he did the same for Mandor and Despil, as well. While Suhuy does not take an active part in the politics of the Courts, he continues to show great interest in recent events in the royal succession, and, perhaps, hopes to be of some influence in the final outcome.

Although Merlin underwent training with Suhuy in the initiation of the Logrus since early youth, Suhuy was somewhat displeased when he walked the Logrus on his own. Somehow sensing the energies of the Logrus being used, deep within a cavern in the Ways of Suhuy, Suhuy rushed to the site. Merlin had just completed the wild, labyrinthine circuit of the Logrus and had collapsed onto the rock floor. Suhuy stood before him and said:

> "You are a fool. A lucky fool. I had not judged you ready to essay the Logrus for a long while yet. . . . And a fool not to have borne a blade and so enchanted it—or a mirror, a chalice or a wand to brace your magic. No, all I see is a piece of rope. You should have waited, for

more instruction, for greater strength.'' (TD,
UNDERWOOD-MILLER, x–xi)

While he was a stern taskmaster, Suhuy cared
very much for his young nephew of mixed parentage. In his journals, Merlin recalled the day of Suhuy's last lesson in the power of the Logrus, shortly
before Merlin went off to shadow Earth:

I remembered Uncle Suhuy's final lesson. He
had spent some time following my completion
of the Logrus in teaching me things I could not
have learned before then. There came a time
when I thought I was finished. I had been confirmed in the Art and dismissed. It seemed I
had covered all the basics and anything more
would be mere elaboration. I began making
preparations for my journey to the shadow
Earth. Then one morning Suhuy sent for me. I
assumed that he just wanted to say good-bye
and give me a few friendly words of advice.
His hair is white, he is somewhat stooped
and there are days when he carries a staff. This
was one of them. He had on his yellow caftan,
which I had always thought of as a working
garment rather than a social one.
"Are you ready for a short trip?'' he
asked me.
"Actually, it's going to be a long one,'' I
said. "But I'm almost ready.''
"No,'' he said. "That was not the journey
I meant.''
"Oh. You mean you want to go somewhere
right now?''
"Come,'' he said. (BA, 171)

Suhuy brought him through Shadow to a remote
rocky place devoid of life. After talking briefly of
what he had taught Merlin, he showed him something that could be drawn from the Sign of Chaos
that is beyond the powers of Pattern-initiates. Suhuy
summoned Logrus extensions, then ordered Merlin
to use his own, passively, to observe and then take
over when he was called to do so. Out of the image
of the Logrus, Suhuy formed an inky blackness of
seething turbulence, directed at a large boulder.
Merlin's journal indicates:

"The boulder became one with the turmoil,
joined it and was gone. There was no explo-

sion, no implosion, only the sensation of great
cold winds and cacophonous sounds. Then my
uncle moved his hands slowly apart, and the
lines of seething blackness followed them,
flowing out in both directions from that area of
chaos which had been the boulder, producing a
long dark trench wherein I beheld the paradox
of both nothingness and activity.'' (BA, 173)

Suhuy relinquished the power of Chaos to Merlin.
In his hands, the Chaos went wild, consuming the
entire region around them in an ever-approaching
blackness. After retreating to another shadow,
Suhuy allowed Merlin to work the Chaos alone, and
Merlin learned to control it. That was the lesson
Suhuy felt it necessary to teach him before Merlin's
departure from the Courts.

Rarely visiting other shadows, Suhuy is rather reclusive. However, he did come to Amber on one
occasion, at Merlin's invitation. Merlin contacted
Suhuy by Trump while he was with King Random,
Fiona, and Gérard in the chamber of the Pattern in
the Royal Palace. Since Merlin already bore the Logrus within him, they were concerned about the effect of his walking the Pattern, thus becoming a
Pattern-initiate as well. After coming to the chamber
of the Pattern, Suhuy examined it, then concluded
that the Logrus and the Pattern were antithetical. If
Merlin walked the Pattern, it would either kill him
or purge him of the image of the Logrus. Fiona, on
the other hand, held a completely different belief.
She felt that both the Pattern and the Logrus should
be capable of withstanding each other, that one
could encompass the other without any harmful effects. (TD, 87) All parties left the decision to try
the Pattern up to Merlin. He decided to walk it, and
his attempt was successful. Since that time, contrary
to Suhuy's educated assumption, Merlin has held
the images of both Powers within him.

Shortly before the death of King Swayvill of the
Courts of Chaos, Suhuy gave an audience to
Mandor and Fiona. They presented evidence of phenomena in various shadows that appeared to trace
their causes to the Pattern created by Corwin. "He
made several journeys into Shadow and became persuaded that this is the case. He was preparing his
findings for presentation to the king when Swayvill
suffered his final illness.'' (PC, 10) At that time,
Suhuy sent his demonic servant Gryll to locate Merlin and bring him to his Ways.

When Merlin arrived, Suhuy greeted him in his natural form: "A large, stooped, gray and red demonic form, horned and half-scaled, regarded me with elliptically pupiled yellow eyes. Its fangs were bared in a smile." (PC, 14) We must assume that when Suhuy appeared earlier in more human proportions, he was merely practicing the height of politeness. No doubt, he was more comfortable in his Chaosian Demonform.

Clearly, Suhuy enjoyed having his nephew as his guest, and he played the role of host to the fullest. He led Merlin through Shadow stress points within his Ways to feed him and give him drink. Merlin was given a pleasant room in a high tower in which to sleep.

Whether or not Suhuy was privy to some of the nastier political maneuverings occurring during Swayvill's recent illness and after his death, he didn't say. But he did inform Merlin that he was under black watch during his stay in the Courts. Rather than explain anything further in a direct manner, Suhuy relied on two spells he passed to Merlin: the images in reflections of a dark green pool beneath a rock ledge; and the familiar people who spoke to him from the Corridor of Mirrors in a dream of enlightenment. Suhuy claimed that the pronouncements made in that dream were as real as they could be, a rather cryptic remark. Nevertheless, later on, Merlin obtained some tangible proof from a recurrence of Suhuy's dream-spell that revealed that there was a definite reality to it.

In hosting Merlin, he had also invited Mandor and Dara to his Ways to welcome him. As Mandor begged forgiveness to depart, the following interesting exchange occurred:

> "You've barely arrived," Suhuy said, "and you've taken no refreshment. You make me a poor host."
>
> "Rest assured, old friend, there is none could perform such a transformation," he [Mandor] stated. He looked at me as he backed toward the opening way. "Till later," he said, and I [Merlin] nodded.
>
> He passed into the way, and the rock solidified with his vanishment.
>
> "One wonders at his deliveries," my mother said, "without apparent rehearsal."
>
> "Grace," Suhuy commented. "He was born with an abundance."

> "I wonder who will die today?" she said.
>
> "I am not certain the implication is warranted," Suhuy replied. (PC, 29–30)

Suhuy may have simply been continuing in his role as the good host, avoiding any offensive conversation. However, he may also have been sincerely defending Mandor as someone he liked and had sympathies for.

From all that Merlin has indicated in his journals, Suhuy was not one to practice mendacity. He relied on his uncle to give him honest estimations of people and events, and thus, we also must feel Suhuy's word is reliable. For instance, Merlin asked him about his father Corwin. Suhuy answered that he had never met Corwin, but that he had heard that Corwin had attended a conference with Swayvill after the Patternfall War. He had been there with King Random as they began talks leading to the drafting of the Concord. When Random returned to Amber, Corwin had gone his own ways, and Suhuy didn't know where they might have led him.

Merlin did not make any note in his journals to indicate that Suhuy was in the funeral procession for Swayvill, nor that he was in attendance in the solemn ceremony in the Cathedral of the Serpent. Presumably, Suhuy chose to maintain his solitude, seeking quiet contemplation.

SWAYVILL

King of the Courts of Chaos for many more generations than Oberon's kingship in Amber. Considered the late King Oberon's nemesis, Swayvill never reconciled with Amber's liege. Swayvill later came to terms with King Random after the Patternfall War, signing a peace agreement that came to be called the Concord.

He was quite old at the time of the Patternfall. Although he was still active, it's likely that most of his administrative duties had been allocated to his ministers. While he no doubt gave his consent to the leaders of the Patternfall attempt, he was probably influenced by those who were entrusted with affairs of state in the Courts.

The old king would rarely shapeshift from his demonform into a human form; it would be unnec-

essary for one of his age who remained within the
Courts. However, he did agree to appear in human
form when he accompanied Princess Fiona to
shadow Earth to work out the details of the Concord. According to Fiona, the old king of Chaos
was enthusiastic about making the journey, although
his concern for the provisions of the treaty may
have been at the heart of the matter. In Fiona's
company, old Swayvill seemed eager to meet a
human of that shadow and visit that place for the
brief time he did. He appeared quite amused at the
solemn courtesy offered him by the attorney Bill
Roth.

After finalizing the Concord, Swayvill suffered
the first of a new series of bouts with illness that
left him bedridden. Several trusted ministers took
on more of his authority, although he continued as
supreme monarch. Mandor of the House of Sawall
may have been assigned certain areas of jurisdiction
within the Courts at this time. It is possible that
Mandor used his position to affect the infirm monarch by casting a spell upon the ancient spikard
he wore.

King Swayvill suffered for many years, and there
were several periods when his illness became highly
critical. At one point, Mandor spoke to his stepbrother Merlin about it: "He's gotten much worse.
Some think it has to do with the death curse of Eric
of Amber. Whatever, I really believe he hasn't much
longer." (SC, 32)

Numerous Houses in the Courts boasted descendants related in one way or another to Swayvill.
Perhaps under the influence of advisors who saw
their own advancement given a boost if no direct
heir were named, the king never indicated a successor. Duels and suicides and sudden accidents grew
beyond mere coincidence while Swayvill languished
on his deathbed. Those closest to him waited patiently for the final end. While the old king drifted
in and out of consciousness, the spikard he wore on
his finger inconspicuously disappeared.

Upon the death of Swayvill, Suhuy of House of
Sawall sent a messenger to Merlin, to inform him
of the king's passing. This messenger, Gryll, a loyal
servant and an old friend, found Merlin in shadow
Kashfa. Returning with Merlin, Gryll spoke of the
significance of Swayvill's death:

"It is as major an upheaval as the death of
Oberon," Gryll volunteered. "Its effects are
rippling across Shadow."

"But Oberon's death coincided with the recreation of the Pattern," I [Merlin] said.
"There was more to it than the death of a monarch of one of the extremes."

"True," Gryll replied, "but now is a time
of imbalance among the forces. This adds to
it. It will be even more severe." (PC, 9)

In retrospect, it seems clear that Gryll's estimation of the general state of affairs was correct. The
opposing Powers of the Pattern and the Logrus had
manifested themselves more openly after King
Swayvill's death. The imbalance between the poles
that had been increasing over the years had widened
enormously with his death, and the two Powers felt
the need to interract more overtly with the inferior
beings of the worlds to resolve that imbalance.

Merlin attended the funeral service for the late
king and reported his observations in his journals.
He described the shrunken, demonic body of Swayvill lying in state. The deceased was dressed in
robes of yellow and black, "resplendently garbed,
serpent of red-gold laid upon his breast, there in the
flame-formed coffin." (PC, 136)

Attending the solemn ceremony inside the Cathedral of the Serpent, situated at the very edge of the
world, Merlin watched as Lord Bances, High Priest
of the Serpent and old friend of Swayvill, pronounced the final Consignment of the body in its
casket. With the aid of Mandor, Dara, and Lord
Tubble of Chanicut, Bances slid the casket along a
grooved track toward the Rim at the end of everything. The illumination of candlelight was gradually
being dimmed by servants, and as the last candle
was snuffed out, there was the sudden sound of
shuffling. The casket had struck hard upon the
flooring, but it continued to fall toward oblivion.
Several of the spectators provided their own lights,
and it was seen that the coffin had completed its
journey, but one of the four participants had also
fallen beyond all hope of recovery.

While this incident was sacrilegious, most of
those in attendance maintained that the solemnity
and sanctity of the occasion were not diminished.
King Swayvill went peacefully to his final rest, joining his old enemy, King Oberon, and was sleeping
"with the ancestors of darkness." (PC, 6)

TECYS, THE [FAMILY NAME]

A middle-aged couple who live in an unnamed shadow, they are loyal friends of Benedict of Amber.

To the Tecys and the other several people who make up the village, Benedict is their god. It is entirely possible—and very likely—that Lord Benedict created the shadow in which the Tecys live full-blown out of his imagination. Although he spent much time there, he allowed the village and its people to continue without having any urge to learn more about Amber and other shadows. The sparse population remained an incurious people and fully accepted the god Benedict and any of the people he brought to the shadow from the holy realms of Amber and Avalon.

Inasmuch as Lord Benedict viewed the shadow of the Tecys as a place safe from all intrusion, one that was secret even from the near-paradise he had formed in shadow Avalon, we may refer to the Tecys' shadow as Sanctuary. The village functioned very much as a personal sanctuary for Benedict, who felt confident in bringing any relative or friend to either recuperate from the ills of the worlds, or have a perfectly safe haven. In creating the shadow Sanctuary, Benedict imbued the sky and land with certain innate properties that would be nearly impossible for any other practitioner of Shadow to duplicate. This amounted to a personal signature existing on a molecular level, so that Benedict would be the only individual able to locate Sanctuary.

Benedict has been so secretive about the Tecys that he has refused even to indicate what their first names are. Other sources, such as King Random and his son, Prince Martin, are more forthcoming in giving details about the Tecys. They appear to be a husband and wife in their mid to late fifties. Instead of being an elderly couple, they are rather youthful and vigorous. Like most of the people in Sanctuary, they are hardworking people who live off the land. The Tecys live on a farm that is about five miles from the village, which is a small town containing about half a dozen little shops run by people of the same peasant stock as the Tecys. These townsfolk are given to exchanging local gossip about goings-on in the area and work at their jobs from dawn to dusk. The little leisure they have they spend either talking to friends and neighbors at the local pub or with their families.

Anyone brought by Benedict to the Tecys has been struck by their open friendliness. They never put questions to anyone who stays under their roof and are perfectly content to follow whatever instructions Benedict gives them. While Random has said that he is certain the Tecys are husband and wife, Prince Martin has stated that they seem more like brother and sister to him. Both are short, though Mr. Tecy is about three inches taller than Mrs. (Miss?) Tecy. Mr. Tecy has thinning black hair and Mrs. Tecy is prematurely gray-haired. Both have rounded faces that are unlined and easily given to smiling.

On one of his frequent visits to Sanctuary long ago, Benedict had brought Martin when he was little more than a boy. Martin spent much time with the Tecys while his uncle taught him about Shadow and the uses of the Trumps. Mr. Tecy taught Martin love of the land and the self-worth engendered by using one's hands to accomplish tasks. They always were delighted when Martin returned for a visit, and their love for him was obvious. In a sense, they had adopted him, and he is forever grateful.

Of course, when Martin came to the Tecys with a serious injury, they were terribly upset and gave him all the medical attention at their disposal. This was just after Martin had been summoned by Trump by his uncle Brand, who then attacked him. As Benedict has recorded Martin's situation at the time:

> "He did show up injured at a friend's place— off in Shadow—some years ago. It was a body wound, caused by the thrust of a blade. They said he came to them in very bad shape and did not go into details as to what had occurred. He remained for a few days—until he was able to get around again—and departed before he was really fully recovered. That was the last they heard of him. . . .
> "... He did leave a message for me with the Tecys, saying that when I learned of what had happened I was not to worry, that he knew what he was about." (HO, 39–40)

In attempting to reconcile the story told to Corwin by Dara of Chaos with Benedict's account, it remains unclear just what role the Tecys played. When Benedict checked with his friends in Sanctuary, they admitted caring for a wandering young girl named Dara who didn't seem to know where she was. This young girl claimed to be related to Benedict but was vague about her connection. She wandered off as mysteriously as she had come. Benedict and Random came to the conclusion that Dara was spying on Benedict and his activities for some time after she learned how she was related to him. As part of her long-term surveillance, she discovered the shadow Sanctuary. She spent some days with the Tecys so that she could include them more easily in her account to Corwin at their first meeting. Nevertheless, the facts she gave Corwin about her attempts to learn more about Sanctuary have been verified through Benedict, who questioned the Tecys on this point. As a matter of general interest, this is Dara's account as recorded in Corwin's Chronicles:

"I spent the next day trying to get more information out of the Tecys and the other people in the village. But it was like a bad dream. Either they were stupid or they were purposely trying to confuse me. Not only was there no way to get from here [the shadow Avalon] to there, they had no idea where 'here' was and were none too certain about 'there.' " (GA, 113)

Benedict has no intention of ever revealing the whereabouts of his shadow Sanctuary, and the Tecys remain safe and innocent of the ways of Shadow.

TEXORAMI

A port city far from Amber in Shadow. It catered to sailors and travelers mainly, though it wasn't notable for tourism. Those who resided there full-time were merchants, artists, musicians, prostitutes, and a number who lived in hovels and lived by their wits.

Among the shop owners was a small syndicate of entrepreneurs that developed several gambling casinos along the main thoroughfares of the town. These establishments accounted for a bustling trade, maintaining a healthy commerce for the townspeople generally. Seamen on furlough often stopped by in Texorami between assignments, and most of Amber's seafaring vessels included it on their tour

of duty. The chandlers kept well supplied in shipboard necessities, and general stores were able to be resupplied in coffee, spices, and other foodstuffs that ships exported. Pubs and saloons kept sailors supplied with alcoholic beverages while gaining a high revenue for services rendered.

Some of the more artistic types of Texorami had initiated the sport of sky surfing, making use of the phenomenal air currents that swept the skies just above most buildings. Younger sailors who tried the sport brought word of it to acquaintances in other shadows. This resulted in a new trade as young travelers ventured in to ride the currents on homemade sailplanes. A couple of artists got together, constructed their own sailplanes, and began selling them on the open market. Most of the youthful travelers who came for the sky surfing returned yearly, but there was a great turnover of this population.

The town would have been an ideal coastal resort except for the roughness of its indigenous population. Although Texorami was by no means a lawless hamlet, there were deeply ingrained moral codes that were understood rather than stated. These codes depended upon the frontier spirit of its people, and matters of honor were usually settled with a pistol or a sword. Things were resolved in simple, straightforward ways, and fistfights often broke out in the small pubs or on the streets. Those who survived the revelry apologized to shop owners and paid the bills. The local undertaker was kept occupied, and new residents joined the cemetery on the western hillside almost every day.

As a young man, King Random of Amber spent a few years in Texorami. His natural wildness and love of gambling made it a perfect refuge for him. He partook of the favorite sporting activity of the youths of the city, and he enjoyed sky surfing also. Lucky at cards, he spent whole nights at a favorite table in one of the large casinos. Other times, he entertained himself and others by playing the drums in a smoke-filled nightspot overlooking the river.

Random had rented a small room in a rooming house near the docks. He became known as a very good gambler and a fair musician, but few people inquired further, and he didn't give out additional information. He liked the place for its incuriosity and enjoyed remaining an ordinary traveler staying to see the sights for a while. After two years of the carefree life, however, he received an urgent call from a sibling that took him away from the pleasures of the city for quite a long time.

THARI

The language universally spoken in Amber. Thari is spoken by all the peoples in shadows who have commerce with Amber, but of course, some may have formed variations of dialect which would be strange to our ears. It is generally believed that the spoken Thari of today has been virtually unchanged since the time that Dworkin created Order. As a member of the Courts of Chaos, Dworkin spoke the same language as the other nobles of that realm; however, it seems likely that other forms of Thari, or perhaps even languages quite different from it, were spoken by the numerous other folk and entities that reside in that distant pole of existence.

Because the Royal Family is quite lenient about the migration of people to and from Amber, most of the documentation for such comings and goings falls on local magistrates and those serving in their offices. Thus, many Amberites have traveled with reasonable freedom to other shadows, and a percentage of these remain in other realms for the rest of their lives. Shadow Earth, for one, has been the beneficiary of a large number of such visitations all through its history.

A young man of Amber by the name of Kuno left the true city and settled in an island realm on shadow Earth known as Britain. According to some of Kuno's early records that were sent back to Amber, that nation was widely uncultivated and under threat of invasion by seagoing invaders of many countries. It has since been understood that Kuno taught the rudiments of Thari to a number of the bards among the ancient tribe called the Picts. While those people readily accepted the new tongue, they transposed many of the common phrasings, altered pronunciation somewhat, and recast much of the grammatical formations to conform better to more familiar languages. Thari never really spread among the peoples of that island nation very widely. It did, however, come into minimal usage as a coded form of speech used by the tinker caste of Ireland.

Naturally, the work before you has been studiously translated into English from the original Thari set down by Gaem dau'Basvl, the Royal Scribe. In spite of that, a couple of statements in Thari were kept intact because their effective meaning would have been lost if translated. One statement is found in the Chronicles of Lord Corwin. In its original context, it is an incantation that has a physical effect upon the person or subject to whom it is directed. In that instance, Corwin was focusing its influence upon a demon out of Chaos (GA, 49). The second statement was spoken by a demonic entity possessing a human body, addressed to Merlin, son of Corwin (TD, 66). Since the incident took place on shadow Earth, the utterance in Thari of a sudden was meant to have a disorienting effect on Merlin, as it momentarily did.

The following are the two statements in Thari, the first from Corwin's Chronicles, the second from the journals of Merlin. Following each is a literal translation in English, followed by an idiomatic translation:

1. Misli, gammi gra'dil
   Go, bad luck you (to)
   Be off, and bad luck to you
2. Nus a dhabshun dhuilsha
   Blessing of God you (on)
   The blessing of God on you

From these two brief samples, one may deduce certain constructions and the beginnings of a vocabulary, at least on an elementary level. The words "dhuisha" and "dil" are clearly related. Actually, "dil" is a shortened form of "dhi-il," and this makes the connection clearer. The "dhi" root refers to the second person pronoun "you." The two variant endings, "sha" and "il," are prepositions attached as suffixes to the pronoun.

From these two statements, we arrive at the following Thari words and their meanings:

misli = to go
gami = bad
gra = luck
nus = blessing
dhabzhun = God

In order to see some word and structural relationships better, let us examine the following statements with their idiomatic English translations:

1. Stimera dhi-ilsha, stimera aga dhi-ilsha
   If you're a piper, have your own pipe
2. Nap gredhurn churi nijesh muni
   A white-faced horse is never any good
3. Mislo granhes thaber
   The traveler knows the road
4. Thari shirth gather od kam
   A speech, come down from father to son

From these statements, we are able to compile the following additional words and definitions:

stimera = a piper; pipe
muni = good
mislo = traveler
thari = speech; language
granhes; grani = know
churi = horse
nap = white
gredhurn = face
gather = father
kam = son
shirth = down; downward

From these statements, we can recognize how the words of the first two statements relate to those in the second group. Thari, of course, is the word for language. It also is used to mean "speech" and "talk." The words "misli" and "mislo" are clearly related; again, the suffix effects a change in usage. "Gami" and "muni" are antonyms. The word "dhi-ilsha," repeated twice in the same statement, is apparently used to mean both "your" and the contraction "you're."

If one intends to practice speaking Thari, it is necessary then to discuss the pronunciation of its vowels and consonants, and proceed from there. The following are the phonetic symbols used to pronounce the vowel sounds in Thari:

a	Short a, as in "pan"
ā	Long a, as in "father"
å	A more closed long a, as in "awe"
e	Short e, as in "pen"
ē	Long e, as in "pain"
i	Short i, as in "pin"
ī	Long i, as in "machine"
o	Short o, as in "pod"
ō	Long o, as in "mode"

u	Short u, as in "pun"
ū	Long u, as in "moon"
ə	The neutral vowel-sound

The diphthongs are:

ai; ei	i, as in "pine"
oi	oy, as in "boy"
au	ow, as in "cow"

The consonants are pronounced in the following ways:

b, p, k	same as in English
g	always hard g
d, t	pressing the tip of the tongue against the teeth, forming a sound similar to: dh, th [The ordinary English d and t do not exist in Thari].

All consonants have a second set of palatalized sounds. Essentially, they consist of a slightly extended sound: "cyow" for "cow," and "cyard" for "card." These palatalized consonants are indicated by an accent mark: c´ow; c´ard.

The liquid consonants of l, n, r, when following a long vowel, become vocalic; that is, an added syllable is formed. For instance, "aeroplane" would be pronounced "eī-ō-plā-n," and the phrase "It's going to rain" becomes pronounced "əts gōn to rē-n." This extended syllabication is indicated with an apostrophe, as in "di'l."

Assuming that this little primer in Thari phonetics has been helpful in the practice of spoken Thari, we should turn our attention to sentence structure. It is common for an adjective to follow the noun it describes in Thari, but there is no definite rule involved, so that adjectives, just as often, precede the noun. While the syntax of a sentence appears to be very close to English as written on shadow Earth, there are some marked differences.

There is no definite or indefinite article in Thari. It is simply assumed, so that a sentence may be constructed thusly: " 'Tell me price,' said woman." On occasion, the Thari word "in" is placed to form a definite article where the need arises. An example would be the phrase: "tripus in gloch," meaning "fight the man," where the article is needed for clarification of purpose. The Thari word "a" is used in the genitive case, that is, when needed to express possession. We see this in the phrase: "b'or a k'ena," which means "(the) woman of the house."

In noun forms, a suffix usually indicates a change in number; that is, whether a noun is singular or plural. The Thari "gloch," meaning "a man," becomes "glochi" for "men." "Gloch" is placed before a second noun to denote occupations or specific kinds of men:

gloch gut = policeman   gloch tom = rich man
gloch srugad = doctor   gloch rilu = madman

As stated before, adjectives are often positioned after the nouns they specify, as in "k'en toms," meaning "house of great [folks]," and "k'en ned'as" for "a lodging house." However, they just as frequently precede the noun they modify: "tom gured" for "big money," and "tom g'uk" for "big man."

The personal pronouns are combined with the word "d'il," meaning "self." First, second, and third person singular and plural possessive forms are "mo," "do," and "a" respectively. These correspond to "I, we," "you," and "he, she, they." Because "mo" and "do" produce a blend with the consonant "d" that is too awkward, the "d" is changed to a "y." Thus, we have "mo d'ill" becoming "mo yil," and "do d'ill" becoming "do yil." These forms, in turn, have been combined, generating the forms "mwil" and "dil" (with an unpalatalized d). Sometimes, a suffix is added to give emphasis to the pronoun, the suffix "sa." This would change the first and second person forms to "mwilsa" and "dilsa."

The tenses of verbs are formed by specific suffixes added to the verb. Present tense uses the suffix "-s," as in "taris b'or," meaning "says (the) woman." Past tense uses "-d," as in "mwilsa sunid," meaning "I saw." Present participle uses "-in," as in "misli-in," meaning "going." Future tense uses "-a," as in "grucha se," meaning "he will shoot."

The formation of a verbal noun makes use of the suffix "-al," so that the Thari for "seeing or sight" becomes "sunal," and for "speech," it becomes "taral." The participle form "-in" is also used to form verbal nouns, as in "tari-in a midril," which means "talking of the devil; blasphemy."

There are verbal stems that are identical to substantive forms to which they are related. Examples

of this are the Thari verb "laburt," which means "to swear," but which is also used to mean "an oath; a curse," and the Thari "gruber," meaning both "to work" and "a job."

The simplicity of the language of Thari may be a significant reason why it is so widely used in Amber and the shadows most congruent to it. However, this same simplicity can lead to confusion for an individual just learning the language. In some cases, a sentence may read like a string of roots without connecting articles. We see this in a sentence like, "Dilsa tari g'ami laburt," which, translated literally would be, "Thou. Speak. Bad. Swear." However, in context, and with proper inflection, it is asking, "Did you say a bad curse?" In the Thari sentence string, there is nothing to indicate whether the speaker is asking a question, making a statement, or issuing a command. In such an instance, the spoken tone becomes absolutely essential.

Nus a Dhalzhun, misli.

THELBANE

Residence of His Royal Majesty, king of the Courts of Chaos. It is a tall, narrow structure ending in a long spire. Thelbane stands at one end of the great Plaza at the End of the World, while at the other end lies the Cathedral of the Serpent, open directly to the Abyss of Chaos.

The exterior of Thelbane resembled a long black needle piercing the sky. Merlin's journal describes the inside of its first level this way:

> ... the slick and gleaming interior of Thelbane's main hall at ground level, a study in black, gray, mossy green, deep red, chandeliers like stalactites, fire sculptures about the walls, scaly hides hung behind them, drifting globes of water in the middle air, creatures swimming within them. The place was filled with nobles, relatives, courtiers, stirring like a field of flame about the catafalque at the hall's center. (PC, 133–34)

The catafalque contained the body of the late King Swayvill, lying in state.

It can be inferred, from Merlin's record of his ancestral homeland, that Thelbane is more than a mere residence. It represents the seat of royal authority for all of the Courts. Merlin spoke to his friend Luke Raynard concerning the kidnapping of Luke's bride. He explained that a faction in the Courts wanted Coral to occupy the throne in the Courts beside their king. In Merlin's words: ''Seems they feel she's specially suited to be queen in Thelbane.'' (PC, 140) In that context, Thelbane is used symbolically to delineate the heart of the Courts of Chaos.

TIME STREAMS [TIME FLOWS]

The time differential that one notices when traveling from one shadow to another.

The phenomenon is not observable within a single shadow, so it can only be examined by one capable of shifting through shadows. For those who are not aware that other shadows exist, the concept of time flows may be thought of as nothing more than an abstract theory of physics with no basis in fact. However, those of the shadows can recognize analogous situations within the limits of their worlds.

Take for example, the life cycle of an insect. The smaller varieties may have a fragile life cycle in which they are born, develop into adulthood, and die, all within the course of several weeks (in terms of shadow Earth). If an individual had the ability to transmute himself into a kind of insectlike being and live in the insect world for a time, then revert to his normal state, and then return again to that insect state later that same day, he would discover that his insect friends had grown much older than he had been on his first trip. From the viewpoint of his insect friends, he may have been gone for years, when, to him, only several hours have passed. That, essentially, is the nature of time streams.

Tha variations in time flows in different shadows cannot be accurately measured. If one thinks of time in the present, that is, time passing this very moment, as the NOW, then one would discover that the NOW is different in different shadows, even if the time is clocked instantaneously. This has been attempted by two experimenters during the reign of Oberon—Baphon and Feyhlir. Keeping in contact by means of Trumps, Feyhlir traveled to a shadow with a much more rapid time stream than Amber. While maintaining constant contact, the experimenter in shadow set a kind of stopwatch while simultaneously counting off one-second beats. The one in Amber, Baphon, counted off one-second beats in time to the other experimenter. At the same time, Feyhlir set up an audio recorder to record the counted beats in both places. The experiment continued to fall awry, because Baphon found that before reaching the count of thirty, his verbal beat had fallen behind the count of the experimenter in shadow. The audio recorder bore this up. No matter how often they repeated the experiment, their verbal count would not remain synchronized. Of course, they attempted to use a stopwatch in Amber, but no timepiece, regardless of how simple a mechanism, would function within the realm of the true city.

In addition to this empirical inability to measure the variation of time flows, the idea of NOW itself comes under question. It is part of the nature of Amber's casting of shadows that there is an infinity of possible shadows cast. Therefore, the NOW of a particular shadow cannot be gauged in comparison with other shadows, nor with Amber itself. There are any number of Earths, for instance, that are contiguous to the shadow Earth upon which resides the twentieth century North American Continent. On one such shadow, the Native American roams freely over the whole wilderness that would be that same continent, knowing nothing about a race of ''Europeans.'' Although this is their NOW, it need not resemble twentieth century America as you know it, nor need there be any means of comparing their time scheme to yours. A shadow that is somewhat farther distant would contain a European continent in which the Roman Empire holds sway over the known world. The emperor Caesar would be totally incapable of understanding that there is another Earth that includes a technology that has harnessed nuclear energy to derive a weapon of such catastrophic potential as to be able to wipe out his entire empire in a single moment. His NOW would be measured in quite different terms than ours, and there would be no way to induce any Roman citizen that his NOW is another Earth's THEN. What's more, it wouldn't be strictly true. Events unfolding on the Earth of the Roman Empire would follow its own pattern. Although history may repeat itself for the first time there, it also may not. Then again, any number of possibilities exist on shadows of the Roman Empire contiguous with that one. And they all might have wide variations in the flow of time. It can be quite complicated.

Early in his wanderings through shadow, Oberon accidentally uncovered another aspect of the time streams that had been heretofore unexplored. By visiting Shadows that exist under a much more rapid time flow, he discovered upon his return to Amber that a much smaller amount of time had passed than the amount of time that he lived through in his subjective NOW. The margin of actual time passing in Amber decreased proportionately as he traveled further into shadows of varying rapid time flows. This resulted in a blurring of the chronological passage of time. In other words, the true chronology of an action taking place across shadows of widely different time flows cannot be accurately determined.

Oberon later used this knowledge to compound the confusion about the rightful heir to the throne of Amber. His propensity for frequent shadow-walking, combined with a natural lustiness, created some interesting legal twists involving marriages to women of other Shadows. Merlin, grandson of Oberon, recorded his own ponderings about the effect of time streams on the legal questions of Oberon's intimate liaisons:

> When Oberon's wife Rilga had shown less hardiness than many by aging rapidly and retiring to a reclusive life at a country shrine, he had gone off and remarried, somewhat to the chagrin of their children—Caine, Julian, and Gérard. But to confuse genealogists and sticklers for family legality, he had done it in a place where time flowed more rapidly than in Amber. Interesting arguments both for and against the bigamous nature of his marriage to Harla may be made. (BA, 114–15)

Although one may argue that the actions of Oberon can be measured by their chronological order, the legality of birthright must take into account the legitimacy of the marriages from the wife's perspective as well. Here, the lines are no longer clearly drawn. Thus, the dual question of legitimacy

and birthright as a matter of law cannot be easily determined.

TIR-NA NOG'TH

The ghost city in the sky above Amber. It only appears on moonlit nights. Corwin brought back a mechanical arm from Tir-na Nog'th, which was worn by his brother Benedict for a time.

In his Chronicles, Corwin described a strange visit he made to Tir-na Nog'th at the time when Brand was rescued from captivity and subsequently stabbed. Corwin sought enlightenment from the city in the sky after learning from the injured Brand about the two cabals within the Family seeking to take the throne of Amber. Although Corwin claimed that he didn't expect a revelation in the ghost city, as other Amberites did, certain visions proved later to be valid.

One reached Tir-na Nog'th by foot, climbing to the topmost peak of Kolvir. Three rough steps of flattened stone jut slightly upward from the cliff face. Corwin described how the stone steps meet the city of illusion in nighttime:

> "When the moonlight touched them, the outline of the entire stairway began to take shape, spanning the great gulf to that point above the sea the vision city held. When the moonlight fell full upon it, the stair had taken as much of substance as it would ever possess, and I set my foot on the stone. . . . If I looked too hard at any portion of the stair, it lost its shimmering opacity and I saw the ocean far below as through a translucent lens. . . . I lost track of time, though it seems it's never long, afterward . . .
> "At the head of the stair, I entered, coming into the ghost city as one would enter Amber after mounting the great forestair up Kolvir's seaward face." (SU, 163–64)

Corwin continued to describe his trek through that landscape, watching the minions of the ghost city moving about, but unseen himself. He walked through parks and gardens, passed small homes with terraces. Those he passed remained unseeing, for he was of another world. Only his sword Grayswandir, created long before by the Phantom Smith of Tir-na Nog'th, could allow him communication with those around him.

As he approached a figure on a stone bench, Corwin recognized a girl named Lorraine, whom he had loved. She had died though, in another shadow. But in this strange land of new probabilities, of opportunities lost and possibilities recaptured, Lorraine was alive and waiting for him. Our Corwin was able to speak to her by placing Grayswandir on the ground between them, nearly touching the image of Lorraine. There, in that ghost realm, alternate events had come to pass. A ghostly version of Corwin had brought a living Lorraine back with him to this version of Amber. The state of Amber, as Corwin knew it, was changed. However, this was a transitory vision, and he soon moved on.

Reaching the image of the Royal Palace, and then inside, Corwin found a Benedict wielding a unique arm of metal talking to Dara in the throne room. With the use of his sword, Corwin spoke to Dara. Benedict intervened, and Corwin was forced to duel with the image of his brother. Benedict grasped Corwin upon the shoulder with his strange new arm. Just before the ghost city faded with the dawn, Corwin used his sword to remove that mechanical arm. It came with him as Random, atop Kolvir, pulled him to safety.

The mechanical arm that Corwin brought back from Tir-na Nog'th continued to exist in the light of day in the true city. Upon the smooth-surfaced palm of that strange hand was a bit of a scribbled design, permanently engraved within it. It was a portion of the Pattern, and this gave that metal arm its permanence.

Corwin became involved in that mystical realm again, but in a more peripheral way. He stood waiting at the three steps atop Kolvir, while his brother Benedict engaged in a deadly duel within the newly formed sky city. Acting as guide and watchdog, Corwin held Benedict's Trump. At the moment when the stair of Tir-na Nog'th solidified, he informed Benedict, who transported himself from the center of Amber's Pattern to its counterpart in the sky. There, Benedict confronted their renegade brother Brand, who had intended to walk the Pattern there. Brand fought his brother beside the Pattern with sorcery, and it seemed Benedict was helpless. However, his mechanical arm, the same that Corwin

had brought back from that place, had a motive force that could not be held captive by Brand. With it, Benedict was able to defeat him. Corwin brought Benedict back to Kolvir's peak just as the ghost city faded to nothingness.

As is true for many things in Amber, Tir-na Nog'th has been made the stuff of legend in numerous shadows. Often, the stories are distorted versions of the truth. In some shadows, a realm named Tir-Na N-Og is the favorite habitation of fairies. In several others, it is a land of living beings under the sea, perhaps a misconstruction of Rebma.

On shadow Earth, for instance, people speak of a mythical Country of the Young, where the inhabitants never age nor die. According to one tale, a poet by the name of Oisin wandered there on a white horse and remained in Tir-na-n-Og for three hundred years. When he finally returned to his homeland, he withered with extreme old age. Before dying, he imparted his knowledge of the Country of the Young to the young great-grandson of a former comrade.

People from other shadows, visiting Amber, have claimed to have seen a wondrous floating island in the sky in their own homelands. The appearance of the island is often accompanied by the soft chime of distant bells.

For those of royal blood who wish to walk the Pattern surreptitiously, Tir-na Nog'th has proven an accessible alternative. Unlike the Patterns in Amber and Rebma, which are locked and under guard, the Pattern in the sky cannot be protected from trespass. Its residents cannot see or interact with the sons and daughters of Oberon. Thus, it was a convenient place for both Rinaldo, Brand's son, and Dalt the mercenary to reach undetected. Rinaldo and Dalt each succeeded in walking the Pattern there, enabling them to walk freely in Shadow of their own volition, and proving their royal parentage.

TMER

Lord of the House of Jesby in the Courts of Chaos. Although he was near the end of a long line of possible successors to King Swayvill of the Courts, he came very close to the throne before his life ended suddenly.

The eldest son of the late Prince Rolovians, Tmer continued his father's heritage of bravery mixed with sensitivity. He sported a closely trimmed beard, thick brows, was of a stout build, and considered by some to be quite handsome.

Lord Tmer was placed under black watch by Lord Bances of Amblerash after the death of King Swayvill. He was one of three men placed in black watch as a means of protecting him. At the time of Swayvill's death, Tmer was second in line to be crowned the new king.

While there had been deaths among the successors to the throne for some time, a small number had been assassinated around the time of the old king's death. According to Mandor of the House of Sawall, the more recent assassins either escaped or were killed, leaving no trail as to who might be behind the murders. The prime suspect, therefore, was the nobleman who was next in line: Tubble of Chanicut. Tmer of Jesby, though, was also considered a possible suspect. However, Mandor discounted him by describing Tmer in this way:

> "He's a very private man. But he was never associated with such extremes [such as resorting to assassination] in the past. I do not know him all that well, but he has always struck me as a simpler, more direct person than Tubble. He seems the sort who'd simply attempt a coup if he wanted the throne badly enough, rather than spend a lot of time intriguing." (PC, 25)

Tmer's end came tragically. He was part of the funeral procession for the late king as it moved along the Plaza at the End of the World. The guards of his black watch were on either side of him. An unknown assailant seemed to get pass Merlin and Jurt of House Sawall, murdered Tmer with one swift stroke of a dagger, and disappeared within the procession. Because Jurt and Merlin were so close to the fallen Tmer, they were held by members of the crowd. Remarkably, these two changed form, becoming guards meant to protect Tmer. Mandor explained the situation to the real Merlin: "Someone gave two of the security guards your appearance and Jurt's. This was obviously intended to create confusion when the assassin struck. They rushed forward insisting they were guards." (PC, 146) This confusion also permitted the murderer to escape.

Tmer's death brought the Crown a step closer to those who would take any ruthless action to see their man have it.

TRISLIVER

An energy-emitting short weapon used mainly in challenges between opponents in a duel in the Courts of Chaos.

A trisliver is used in similar fashion to a knife or dagger. It is a squat, handheld device with a trigger-like lever on one side, usually held inward and pressed with the thumb in a slight movement. A tubular nozzle allows for a thin beam of energy to radiate a short distance and only at three-second intervals, necessary for the recharging of its energy-accumulation source pack. It is used most effectively in making feints, rather than in direct assaults.

"The *trisliver* only cuts to a depth of about three quarters of an inch through flesh, which is why the throat, eyes, temples, inner wrists, and femoral arteries are particularly favored targets." (BA, 83) By feinting at any of these vital areas, a duelist can anticipate his opponent's involuntarily protecting himself with his fandon. Such a reflex action would allow the duelist to thrust at an undefended area with his primary assault weapon, the trisp.

The trisliver is rarely, if ever, used under conditions other than as a secondary dueling weapon, as described above.

TRISP

A weapon used in dueling in and around the Courts of Chaos.

Its description and use are known to us mainly through the accounts of Merlin, son of Prince Corwin, who was raised in the ways of Chaos. In describing its function as a dueling weapon, Merlin indicated that it is not meant to be used in a duel to the death. The survivor of such a duel would be considered an outcast and banished from the realm.

The trisp is a kind of laser weapon with a short range. It is held like a rifle rather than a sword, with the haft secured to the right hand by three flexible finger loops. Remarkably lightweight, the narrow, balanced haft of the trisp leads to three curved projections through which the energy thrust is generated. The triggering mechanism is in the haft and is squeezed like a rifle trigger, firing pulsed beams of light from three hair-fine blades.

While the trisp resembles a rifle, it is used like a foil, the triple laser beams cutting with their terminating points of light. Easy mobility is the key in dueling with this weapon, since the combatants usually engage each other while floating upon air currents above the Abyss of Chaos, clinging to small stones with their feet. In this manner, one's entire body rotates and maneuvers in 360-degree pivots in relation to one's opponent, taking offensive and defensive positions all the while. One engages an opponent in middle attack position, but feints, parries, and ripostes may occur from upper, lower, extreme right, or extreme left thrusts. The slight curvature of the projections allows a cut either high or low, for instance, above or below an opponent's guard, with a slight rotation of wrist and elbow.

If a beam were focused on a specific region of an opponent unimpeded for longer than five seconds, it would be capable of causing death by piercing a vital organ. This would only be possible if an opponent is entirely unprotected and immobile, and the pulse beam of the attacker's weapon is deliberately adjusted to a continued high-intensity thrust. Normally, a touch would burn an opponent's skin, causing pain but little other damage beyond some scarring. Each combatant has effective means of warding off this danger with the use of a shielding device called a fandon.

When not in use, the three-pronged head of the trisp is turned counterclockwise forty-five degrees to be placed into a safety-lock position.

TRUMP GATE

A doorway to another place that had been opened through the use of a Trump of the kind used by those of royal blood in Amber. Rather than an initiate holding contact with the person or place on the Trump by direct visual concentration, an adept must expend considerable psychic energy to maintain a Trump Gate under its own volition for a period of time.

In his journals, Merlin recorded an instance of a mysterious shapeshifting mage using a Trump Gate as a quick means of escape. He recognized its manifestation as he chased the shapeshifted form of a lop-eared wolf. The Trump Gate appeared as a square of pale light from a distance, but as Merlin came closer, he was able to judge its dimensions more accurately. It was a large rectangular form about nine feet in height and five feet wide. Within its brightness, Merlin was able to see a low stone building on a hillside, with stone steps and a walkway. This picture-framed image was in marked contrast to the surroundings of forest, bushes, and a dirt clearing around it. The Trump that generated the Gate was on the ground at the threshold of the bright rectangle. When the shapeshifter reached the threshold, it picked up the Trump from the ground in its teeth and plunged into the image. The retrieval of the Trump, and its removal to the imaged place, caused the Trump Gate to implode silently, sending shock waves that felt like earth tremors in the immediate vicinity. There was no trace of the gateway remaining.

Afterward, Merlin pondered over the shapeshifter's use of such a means of escape:

> It had employed a Trump Gate, which is not a thing one does lightly—or at all, for that matter, if it can be avoided. It is a flashy and spectacular thing to make Trump contact with some distant place and then pour tons of power into the objectification of such a gateway as a form possessed for a time of an independent existence. It is exceedingly profligate of energy and effort—even a hellrun is much easier—to create one which will stand for even fifteen minutes. It can drain most of your resources for a long while. Yet this was what had occurred. The reason behind it did not trouble me, as much as the fact that it had happened at all. For the only people capable of the feat were genuine initiates of the Trumps. It couldn't be done by someone who just happened to come into possession of a card. (BA, 181)

The creation of a Trump Gate is such an exhaustive drain on an adept's personal resources that one is forced to take a period of rest, both physically and mentally, during which time all magical defenses are down, leaving one vulnerable to adversarial breach. This makes the use of such a gateway very unprofitable, and thus, it is rarely used except in the most extreme of circumstances.

TRUMPS

The special cards on the order of the Major Arcana of the Tarot, originally drawn by Dworkin Barimen. They were designed as a means of communication and teleportation among King Oberon and his sons and daughters, no matter the distance from one place to another. As had been discovered by Oberon's offspring, the Trumps could be used in other ways as well.

The packs that were drawn and arranged by Dworkin contained cards emulating the configuration of the Minor Arcana, with the special cards only thinly disguised as the usual Greater Trumps, so that the uninitiated would not realize their significance. In his Chronicles, Corwin explained:

> They were on the order of Tarots, with their wands, pentacles, cups, and swords, but the Greater Trumps were quite different. . . .
> They were almost lifelike in appearance, the Greater Trumps ready to step right out through those glistening surfaces. The cards seemed quite cold to my touch, and it gave me a distinct pleasure to handle them. (NP, 27)

In order to work his strange power, Dworkin had hand-drawn them, making numerous sets. There is some confusion about the number he originally prepared, and, of course, several packs have been lost. When Corwin sought a replacement pack in the Royal Library of Amber's palace, he indicated that there were four decks in the crystal case where they were kept. (NP, 93) Much later, Corwin contradicted this when he spoke of the Trumps to his companion Ganelon:

> "Well, everyone in the family has a pack or two and there were a dozen or so spares in the

library. I don't really know whether there are any others. . . .
> "... Dad's deck, Brand's, my original pack, the one Random lost—Hell! There are quite a number unaccounted for these days." (SU, 68–69)

The circumstances of the creation of the Trumps have been lost in the remoteness of time. Some say that Oberon commanded that Dworkin design them, knowing the special powers the old man possessed. It is more likely that Dworkin and Oberon conferred, coming to an agreement to form the Trumps, initially as a means of communication. Oberon would certainly have deemed such a thing necessary once his children walked the Pattern and were able to travel to any shadow of their desire.

Then: At what point would Dworkin, of necessity, have sketched the sons and daughters of Oberon? Using speculation as much as informed sources, it would seem that the original Trumps were drawn just prior to their coming of age and being deemed ready to walk the Pattern. In fact, King Oberon's Trump was probably drawn first, just before Dworkin went about sketching his other subjects. Since Dworkin intended to draw all of the required Trumps by hand, he was likely to have begun by sketching each of his subjects rather quickly over a short period of time. He would then, with greater care, transmute them (so to speak) onto the cards that would become the finished product. The drawings are done in fine lines, with uniform shadings showing barely perceptible lines. The coloring of the clothing was purposely selected by each subject and became emblematic in identifying each of the princes and princesses. While each knew he or she was being sketched, Dworkin apparently asked them to pose in certain specified ways. Much speculation has been passed down through the generations concerning which of the original tarots of the Major Arcana Dworkin had in mind as he posed each of them. Some of these will be speculated upon (again) below.

Corwin was quite thorough in describing the appearance of the princes and princesses on the cards when he narrated his Chronicles. Instead of being redundant here, it would be more fruitful to consider the setting, as well as the manner, in which each subject was drawn.

Benedict, the oldest at the time the Trumps were begun, was caught outdoors with one of his favorite horses beside him. Having a restless spirit, he was probably leading his horse from the stables when Dworkin stopped him to pose for the sketch. Thus, the dour look, though, in truth, he seldom smiled. With the rustic colors Benedict wore, and the long staff he leaned upon, his Trump reminds one of the Knight or Page of Wands from the Minor Arcana. Of course, this correspondence may not have been deliberate on Dworkin's part.

Eric was accoutered for dueling and gaming. Wearing a leather jacket, cloak, and high black boots, he was likely headed outdoors, perhaps into town to join some friends. Although the bit of wall behind his heroic pose is not easily identifiable, it may be a portion of the main hall. It would seem he was posing just before leaving through the main doorway.

Corwin had been outdoors on some unrecognizable part of Kolvir. It is not at all certain where he was going or what he was doing, but he, too, like Benedict, had a restless spirit. At times, Corwin would often walk about the varied range of Kolvir. While some scholars have compared Corwin to the Fool of the Tarot, it seems unlikely that this was the way Dworkin saw him. Corwin was not nearly foolish enough to stand so unheedingly near a precipice.

Caine had been dressed for dinner, ready to dine out with one of several young ladies from town. He was standing in, or perhaps just outside of, his quarters in the palace. Bemused by Dworkin's insistence of a sketch, he chose to stand in profile and tilted his feathered cap at an angle.

Deirdre was seated beside a bureau, evidently in her bedchamber. Her black hair hung long, as if she had just brushed it. While her eyes of deep blue held a frankness about them, they also seemed quite knowing. It is unclear if it was late evening and she was preparing to retire, or early morning and she had just risen. Some have compared her image to that of the quietly contemplative high priestess.

Leaning with seeming reluctance against a dark wall of her quarters was Fiona. Her green eyes and slightly puckered lips shone with an attitude of disdain. The bright russet, unkempt hair hanging carelessly somehow gave her an ennobled appearance. Though her posture was quite different, the quality of her supreme confidence reminds one of the Trump for Strength.

Full-bearded Bleys, with a gleam in his blue eyes and the beginnings of a leer on his lips, was seated on a mahogany chair in the dining hall. Turned slightly askew in the chair, with his knees apart and his ankles crossed, Bleys held a cup of wine up in his left hand. In his right, he clenched the hilt of a sword, holding the blade upright and angled away from him. There were elements of carelessness and caution in this posture, of craftiness and suspicion. Perhaps his posture, deliberate or not, was inspired by a crossing of the King of Swords and the King of Cups.

In a room of a greenish tinge that seemed unlike any of the quarters in Amber sat Llewella. She stared wistfully at the artist, almost expectantly, from a small, cushioned sofa. There was a tension there, or perhaps merely a slight discomfort. It seems that Llewella rarely poses for any portraiture, and this was one of those rare occasions.

Brand had been riding, his face agleam with perspiration and exultation. Sitting on his white horse, he was simply resting from his exertions while allowing Dworkin to draw him. His eyes looked past the artist, to something beyond and to the right. Although scribes have thought of his Trump as representing the Devil, it is more likely that his positioning was more symbolic of Death. After all, the Tarot does not depict Death as an absolute ending of life; it symbolizes renewal and change. In a large sense, Brand had come to represent those things himself.

Flora stood, looking upward from a room lit by candles. She seemed to be looking at the sky through a window behind the artist. Her wide blue eyes were a brilliant contrast to her shimmering crimson bangs and shoulder-length red hair. Her gaze and posture made her seem both vulnerable and as wise as the ages. In her features were perceptiveness, ingenuousness, and a sense of awe of the worlds.

Julian stood at the ready, near attention, a group of trees and a tethered horse behind him. His blue eyes revealed no emotion, signaled no comment of the moment. Dressed entirely in a white, enamel-like armor, he was obviously a man one did not easily halt in order to be sketched. He acted out of duty, and he stood transfixed, as a true soldier, giving the impression that he would not be moved unless it was his will.

The jutting, rough edge of a dock, with the sea behind it, was immediately behind Gérard. He stood leaning against a wooden post, an aged bronze goblet of wine, perhaps just gotten from a nearby café, in his right hand. He was dressed casually, probably overseeing the ships in a less toilsome capacity than was the usual. The silver hunting horn around his neck was, in all likelihood, being used to call to his friends rather than to laborers on board any of the ships.

Random sat lightly on a high wooden bench. He appeared to be in one of the tower rooms, probably gaming with the guards. As was often true of him, he was dressed to attract the young ladies about the court, and it was indeed possible that he was caught between these two pastimes when Dworkin requested his modeling for a Trump.

Since Dworkin drew his son just prior to the sketchings of Oberon's children, the Oberon he delineated was in his youthful middle age. Unlike the manner of the Trump of the Emperor (or, in fact, any of the Kings of the Minor Arcana), Oberon had insisted that Dworkin draw him standing. His thick beard was still black, tinged with gray. The golden sword in his right hand was held blade downward, touching the ground. He was standing outdoors, in the gardens, so that the green of his robes and the large gems in his rings combined with the varicolored greens and yellows of the flowers about him. His long black, gray-tinged hair seemed to ripple as in a slight breeze. He wore no crown upon his head.

Though Dworkin himself would certainly see an association between himself and the Tarot card of The Hermit, it would have been difficult for him to design it that way, since his Trump was a self-portrait. In a room with a shelf of books behind him, Dworkin stared directly ahead, as if looking carefully into a mirror. He stood pensively, tensing against the slope of his back in order to get the features done with clarity. Deep gray eyes stared out of a hooded and cloaked form, his white beard and mustache masking much of his sharp facial structure. Thus, he was dressed as The Hermit, but in full form rather than profile, his hands hanging at his sides so as not to be distinguished. It was, indeed, the face and form of the aged artist, but done in such simplicity of style that the same hand could readily duplicate the image on numerous cards without the need of a mirror.

In his den deep within the cave beside the primal Pattern, Dworkin kept other Trumps he had designed. Corwin had discovered them when he visited Dworkin in that place. It was a moment when haste was needed, and Corwin could not examine them carefully. He used one to transport him elsewhere, and he was able to retain that card. Corwin described what he found in this way:

> To the desk. I tore open the drawer and snatched at some Trumps which lay scattered within it. . . . I raised the cards before me and regarded the one on top. It was an unfamiliar scene, but I opened my mind immediately and reached for it. A mountain crag, something indistinct beyond it, a strangely stippled sky, a scattering of stars to the left . . . The card was alternately hot and cold to my touch, and a heavy wind seemed to come blowing through it as I stared, somehow rearranging the prospect. . . .
> . . . The vision seemed ready, and I rushed forward into it. Then I halted and stood stock-still, to let my senses adjust to the new locale.
> I knew. From snatches of legend, bits of family gossip, and from a general feeling which came over me, I knew the place to which I had come. It was with full certainty that I raised my eyes to look upon the Courts of Chaos. (HO, 76–77)

Corwin kept this card and later lent it to Benedict so that he could use it to transport troops to that place.

Only a person who has succeeded in walking the Pattern could then be enabled to draw Trumps with their special potency. For a millennium or more Dworkin was the only artist in Amber with that skill. However, other Pattern-initiates were able to acquire the knowledge, and even pass that talent on to their offspring.

In the instance of the Trump of Martin, Corwin first discovered that others could design a potent card. He, Random, and Ganelon had found the card on the primal Pattern, near the point where the dark blot had originated. While Random was able to determine that the image on it was of his son Martin, Corwin realized that the style of the drawing was quite different from Dworkin's. And yet, it seemed familiar to him (HO, 21). Later, Corwin showed the card to Dworkin:

"It is not your work, is it?"

"Of course not. I have never set eyes on the boy." . . .

"If you did not prepare that Trump, who did?" . . .

"My best pupil. . . . Brand. That is his style. See what they do as soon as they gain a little power?" (HO, 72–73)

Another artist was found who learned his art from a separate source. Martin had used a Trump to bring Dara to the Royal Palace, and he was questioned closely by Random and Corwin. Martin was carrying a distinctly different trio of cards from any that Corwin had seen previously. One was of Dara, one of Martin, and one of Corwin's son Merlin. Corwin was informed that the cards were drawn by Merlin. He had learned his artistry in the Courts of Chaos, where he had grown up. (CC, 14) Merlin's ability, however, came from walking the Logrus, the counterpart of the Pattern. In the Courts, it was the Master of the Logrus, Suhuy, who taught Merlin how to draw Tarot-like cards that consisted of the same potency as Dworkin's.

The cards of Martin, as drawn by Brand and by Merlin, were quite different in style from one another. Brand had designed his without having met his subject. He had deftly pieced together the memories of other people whom he questioned in order to develop a composite image. In his Chronicles, Corwin noted this fact:

Where had I seen that deliberate line before, less spontaneous than the master's, as though every movement had been totally intellectualized before the pen touched the paper? And there was something else wrong with it—a quality of idealization of a different order from that of our own Trumps, almost as if the artist had been working with old memories, glimpses, or descriptions rather than a living subject. (HO, 20)

Thus, Brand's depiction of Martin shows a wan face, dull eyes staring ahead, dressed in dark clothes covering an undefined form, with a simple background of dark shading hinting at drapery.

The Trump of Martin drawn by Merlin was quite different. Dara had brought Martin to meet Corwin's son without explaining their relationship. Perhaps it was at Dara's request that Merlin drew the Trumps of each of them, sketching his own portrait last. While Merlin didn't know Martin at that point, his drawing was of a livelier sort than Brand's. He drew Martin standing on a rock-strewn cliff, one foot raised upon a stone and his arms leaning on the bent knee. A slight grin appeared at the corners of Martin's face as he looked frankly at the artist. His hair was a light reddish color similar to Random's, but he wore clothes of a somber brown and red combination.

Wearing a longish dress of green and blue, Dara held an air of authority as much as casualness. The background was clearly the same rocky promontory as shown in the card for Martin. Her brown hair was nearly shoulder-length, and despite the youthful presence of freckles on her nose and cheeks, Dara's eyes had a hardness that bespoke the accumulation of years of wisdom. She stood with one hand at the hilt of her sword in its scabbard at her waist, her legs slightly apart. Looking at a point just behind the artist, she appeared relaxed in her pose, and supremely confident.

In his self-portrait, Merlin sat astride a boulder, his legs wide apart, his arms slightly bent inward, and the hands apparently holding a small card and writing utensil below the range of the drawing. He was looking intently at something just in front of him; in all likelihood, a small mirror held by Dara. He wore a riding suit of gray and black, with an oddly long tunic with a high collar of a silvery sheen.

All three Trumps were done in long, sweeping lines; informal yet competent. One had the impression that the artist understood each stroke, knew every line and curve, even before he touched any of the cards.

Merlin had come across another artist of the special Trumps, as he recounted in his published journals. This was Rinaldo, the son of Brand. Initially, Merlin knew him as Lucas Raynard. Rinaldo had been taught to draw Trumps by his father, and he was tutored in the Pattern walk by Brand as well, who saw him through the Pattern in Tir-na Nog'th.

Since neither Merlin nor Rinaldo has shown these new Trumps to anyone in Amber, we have only Merlin's description of them. His journals describe the cards Rinaldo carried in this way:

I turned up a set of Trumps in a side pocket [of Luke's clothing], along with several blank cards and a pencil—and yes, they seemed to be rendered in the same style as the ones I had come to call the Trumps of Doom. I added to the packet the one depicting myself, which Luke had been holding in his hand when he had trumped in.

His were a fascinating lot. There was one of Jasra, and one of Victor Melman. There was also one of Julia, and a partly completed one of Bleys. There was one for the crystal cave, another for Luke's old apartment. There were several duplicated from the Trumps of Doom themselves, one for a palace I did not recognize, one for one of my old pads, one for a rugged-looking blond guy in green and black, another of a slim, russet-haired man in brown and black, and one of a woman who resembled this man so closely it would seem they must be related. These last two, strangely, were done in a different style; even by a different hand, I'd say. The only unknown one I felt relatively certain about was the blond fellow, who, from his colors, I would assume to be Luke's old friend Dalt, the mercenary. There were also three separate attempts at something resembling Ghostwheel—none of them, I would guess, completely successful. (BA, 110–11)

From Luke, Merlin learned that Brand had drawn Trumps of two previously unmentioned relatives: Sand and Delwin, daughter and son of Oberon and Harla. Brand had sketched them in the hope of using them as allies against the Amberites before the Patternfall battle. They had declined, indicating they wanted nothing to do with Amber whatsoever.

Of course, through Merlin, we have learned that similar sets of Trumps had been designed in the Courts of Chaos. Such special cards with like potencies probably existed for as long as Amber itself existed. Perhaps even longer. In the journals, Merlin explained that he knew that Bleys and Fiona were expert at drawing Trumps. They were even teaching King Random by that point in time. Aside from several Logrus-initiates in the Courts with that skill, there were talented mages in adjacent shadows capable of preparing Trumps. Merlin has recorded:

"It is my understanding that you have to be an initiate of either the Pattern or the Logrus to do them properly. Some of them could do a sort of half-assed set, though, one you'd be taking your chances on using—maybe winding up dead or in some limbo, sometimes getting where you were headed." (TD, 89)

As has been indicated earlier, a depiction on a card need not involve a portrait of a person. Trumps have been designed bearing a scene, as the aforementioned card of the Courts of Chaos. One need only concentrate on the image to bring it into vividness, and then step forward into the scene. Dworkin had been the author of a Trump of the main hall in the Royal Palace, used when a practitioner wished to return to Amber without contacting a member of the Royal Family directly. Old Dworkin was able to sketch a scene on any medium with any utensil, obtaining the same power as on the Trumps. He did this when Corwin had been imprisoned by Eric. Although faded, Dworkin's scratches of the Lighthouse at Cabra and his own den on the walls of a dungeon cell retain their potential.

There are all manner of ways to make use of the Trumps. It is certain, in fact, that not all of the possibilities have yet been utilized. When Corwin allied himself with Bleys, he had a literal battle of wills with Eric through the Trumps. Pain on a psychic level could be thrust at one person by another who focused on that person's image. If the victim also has a strong will, as Eric had, the psychic duel could be carried on both ways. Such a contest could be broken off by a simple movement of a hand over the face of the card. Usually, both parties feel drained by the effort of wills.

The late Prince Caine had discovered another use for the cards. Intriguingly, Oberon had suspected the specific use that Caine was attempting and tried to warn Corwin about it while in disguise. Pretending to be dead, Caine had listened in on the Trumps, maintaining his own remoteness, hoping to discover ulterior motives and secret yearnings of his brothers and sisters. Revealing his plan at the Courts of Chaos at the conclusion of the great battle, Caine described the technique:

"I had learned to be completely passive about it. I had taught myself to deal them all out and touch all of them lightly at the same time, waiting for a stirring. When it came, I would shift my attention to the speakers. Taking you one at a time, I even found I could sometimes get

into your minds when you were not using the Trumps yourselves—if you were sufficiently distracted and I allowed myself no reaction.''
(CC, 117–18)

Luke Raynard had found a way to create a blackout on his own Trump, so that he could make contact with someone else without being seen himself. On the other hand, Corwin urged his brothers and sisters to combine their psychic strength to make contact with their imprisoned brother Brand, who was beyond anyone's individual reach. This proved successful: a link was established, and they were able to reach Brand's location and rescue him from his captors.

Speaking to Bill Roth of shadow Earth, Merlin stated that anyone could operate a Trump merely by concentrating on the depicted image. Someone finding a card in a shadow, even one lacking the potential for magic, could conceivably make contact with the image on it. Such a person might be drawn into a place in a far-distant shadow by such a simple method as stepping forward into the growing three-dimensionality of such a scene. For this reason, as speculative as it may be, it seems odd that the widely ranging offspring of Oberon should be so casual about the maintenance of the Trumps.

As more Pattern- and Logrus-initiates become skillful in designing Trumps, it certainly seems necessary to promote greater awareness of the potentials involved—both for beneficent and for malevolent outcomes. Those who read this work in the shadows: Be wary of that oddly cold, pleasantly real–appearing Tarot card. Do not stare too long.

TRUMPS OF DOOM

A small, incomplete set of Tarot-like cards that Merlin, son of Corwin, found in the apartment of his former girlfriend, Julia Barnes, in San Francisco on shadow Earth. Like the Trumps of Amber, these cards permit an initiate of the Pattern to teleport to the places depicted on them. Merlin had used one of them as a means of escaping a deadly encounter. It led him into further peril, but the danger was less immediate, and Merlin was able to extricate himself from the situation. As Bill Roth, a friend of both

Corwin and Merlin on shadow Earth, had said about the strange Trumps: "I'll bet they're all that way—traps of some kind." (TD, 95) Hence, Merlin dubbed the handful of cards "Trumps of Doom."

In his published accounts, Merlin described only a couple of these unusual Trumps. They were drawn in a style he didn't recognize, but he referred to some of them as seeming half-familiar. One of them he described as

"depicting a small grassy point jutting out into a quiet lake, a sliver of something bright, glistening, unidentifiable, off to the right. I exhaled heavily upon it, fogging it for an instant, and struck it with my fingernail. It rang like a glass bell and flickered to life. Shadows swam and pulsed as the scene inched into evening. I passed my hand over it and it grew still once again—back to lake, grasses, daytime.

Very distant. Time's stream flowed faster there in relationship to my present situation.''
(TD, 16)

He used this particular Trump later to break out of a Shadow-storm in which he was caught.

Merlin used a second Trump under unusual duress. He was becoming paralyzed by a poisonous bite. His only easy means of escape was to pull out one of the Trumps in his possession, focus on it, and be transported before the agent could finish the job. Reaching through the Trump, Merlin lay on a blue ledge beside a large, crouching sphinx with the body of a lion, a human face, and an eagle's wings. Relatively safe from further attack by the agent who bit him, Merlin slept off his paralysis. Once recovered, however, he was coerced into resolving the sphinx's riddle, or else become its next meal. Using guile, logic, and a bit of humor, he was able to thwart the sphinx and make his way out of that shadow. In any event, he seemed confident that he could handle the awesome ferocity of the sphinx merely because he was a lord of Chaos.

As Merlin learned, the Trumps were drawn by his friend Luke Raynard, who had secretly been indoctrinated with the Pattern when his father, Brand, took him to Tir-na Nog'th. Luke found them useful for his own purposes, for Merlin had discovered duplicates of the Trumps of Doom on Luke while he came under Merlin's care. On a later occasion, Luke made use of one of them at random, without having much concern about which one he selected. When they were involuntarily transported to the primal Pattern, he had asked Merlin to take out the few cards he had with him. Luke asked his friend to shuffle the cards and hold them facedown for him to choose from. When he did, he felt confident that he had his own private means of escape, while allowing Merlin and their friends to depart from the grasp of a sentient power. This use of the "Trumps of Doom" may have been Luke's true purpose in drawing them. They permitted him safe passage, as long as he knew the key element for averting danger to himself. Anyone following him through the Trump, though, would face serious difficulties without necessarily having the means to avoid them. The "Doom" aspect was really a safety feature that Luke had set in place.

These special Trumps had been planted in Julia Barnes's apartment under unusual circumstances. Merlin had found them on the mantelpiece in her living room, between a clock and a stack of books on the occult. As soon as Merlin handled them, he felt the familiar coldness that signaled their unique properties. There was something more to it also. That morning, Luke Raynard had given him a note from Julia. In part, it read: "I have something you will need." (TD, 6) It seemed obvious to him that Julia had been referring to the Trumps. She had wanted him to have them.

Questions remain about Julia's reasons for wanting Merlin to have these somewhat hazardous cards and about how they came into her possession. Luke gave Merlin an answer to the latter. He said: "I knew Julia was seeing Melman, okay? I went to see her the night after I'd seen him, okay? I even delivered a small parcel he'd asked me to take her, okay?" (TD, 76–77) He confirmed that the parcel contained the special Trumps.

Earlier, however, Merlin had questioned Victor Melman. Melman claimed that he had never seen any such Trumps, and he had no need to lie about them since he admitted to other matters. Since Luke had been the artist who drew the Trumps in the first place, it is more logical that he had given Julia the Trumps on his own. Based on what we know of Julia's subsequent actions, she seems to have devised a complicated plot to place Merlin in danger. The Trumps of Doom were a small part of that plot. Since she apparently had to work within a tight time frame, she may have manipulated Luke in some way

to visit her, turn over the Trumps to her, and accept a brief message to give to Merlin, a message designed to draw Merlin to the cards and also into a deadly series of events. She had to act quickly because Merlin was planning to leave San Francisco when Luke came to him with her message.

Although it may appear that Luke was a party to Julia's plan to put the Trumps in Merlin's hands, the later account of Luke's mother indicates that that wasn't the case. When Jasra and Merlin had become allies, she admitted wanting to use Julia as an agent to murder him. Merlin asked if Luke had been a part of the conspiracy between Julia and Jasra. Jasra replied: "No, you two had grown too chummy by then. I was afraid he'd warn you." (KS, 26)

It appears, then, that the Trumps of Doom placed in Merlin's possession was entirely Julia's idea. Although they are far from harmless, in the hands of a skillful adept they could be the source of "a merry chase." Possibly, Julia saw them as a means of giving Merlin an additional puzzle to solve, designed to throw him off track in deducing that she was behind further schemes involving him.

TUBBLE

Prince of the House of Chanicut in the Courts of Chaos. He was well down in the line of succession to the throne of the Courts until shortly after the death of King Swayvill. A number of assassinations at that time brought Tubble into the number one spot to succeed Swayvill.

Tubble was an extremely clever and devious man who had lived for centuries. Known for his wiliness, he had the mild appearance of one who was innocent and peaceful. He was heavily built and wore a fringe beard.

As next in line, he was placed under black watch by the high priest Lord Bances. This placed him under protection against assassination, as were the second and third men in line of succession, Tmer of Jesby and Merlin of Sawall.

There had been no clue as to who was behind the recent assassinations of candidates to the throne, but this only meant that Tubble was under suspicion. In discussing the current situation with Merlin, his older stepbrother Mandor told him:

> "Tubble himself is of course suspect, though it is not a good idea to say it aloud. He stood to benefit the most, and now he's in a position to do so. Also, there is much in his career of political connivance, double-dealing, assassination. But that was long ago. Everyone has a few skeletons in the cellar. He has been a quiet and conservative man for many years." (PC, 25)

During the funeral procession for the late king along the Plaza at the End of the World, an assassin murdered Tmer of House Jesby. For his own welfare, Tubble was spirited away under heavy guard.

However, Prince Tubble felt obligated to take part in the ceremony in the Cathedral of the Serpent. He sat with Dara and Mandor of the House of Sawall at the front of the chapel. Lord Bances intoned the Consignment of the dead. On signal, Mandor, Dara, and Tubble stood and joined Bances at the casket containing King Swayvill. Tubble stood opposite Bances at the front sides of the casket as the four slid it into a groove on the floor, ready to slide it to the edge of the Abyss of Chaos. The many candles in the Cathedral were slowly put out by assistants of the service. As the last candle was put out, the four slid the casket out and over the Abyss. In the darkness, someone stumbled, the casket fell to the floor heavily, and a cry was heard. The cry continued, growing distant, fading into silence. When the lighting was restored, it could be seen that both the casket and Prince Tubble were gone. They had fallen into the Abyss.

As a result of Prince Tubble's ignominious death, the House of Sawall came into control of the rights of succession.

TY'IGA

A race of demons that exists in bodiless forms in the blackness beyond the great Abyss of the Courts of Chaos. One of these demons was placed under a compulsion to protect the son of Dara while he attended college on shadow Earth. The ty'iga remained near Dara's son by occupying the corporeal

forms of various humans while he traveled in Shadow.

In its several human forms, and when it manipulated to get close to the son of Dara, the ty'iga questioned the human's parentage. It was able to detect an initiate of the Pattern in Amber, but it had no way to differentiate which male initiate was related to Dara. When the ty'iga took possession of the body of a human female attending Berkeley University on shadow Earth, it could not determine which of two young male initiates it was required to protect.

Dara of the Courts of Chaos had used some potent means to bind the ty'iga so that it was compelled to obey her will. There is no way we can know how this was done, for Merlin's journals indicate that these demons "were very powerful and very difficult to control." (SC, 179) While the ty'iga had not had dealings with humans before, nor with other kinds of demons for that matter, this particular demon adjusted to living corporeally on shadow Earth after inhabiting the body of Gail Lampron. Once possessing a human form, it also retained the knowledge of the person as well. As Gail, the ty'iga became acquainted with Lucas Raynard, one of the two Pattern-initiates it had sensed in that place.

The ty'iga had a very difficult time trying to determine which of the two Pattern-initiates she was supposed to protect, Luke or Merlin Corey. She spent years watching both, and she was placed in distress numerous times as a result. Much later, when it was trapped in the body of a human female who had died just before its possession, the ty'iga told Merlin of that early time on shadow Earth:

> "Those were the happiest days in my life, with you and Luke, back in school. For years I tried to learn your mothers' names so I'd know who I was supposed to be protecting. You were both so cagey, though. . . .
>
> "I suffered . . . when Luke began his yearly attempts on your life. If he were the son of Dara I was supposed to protect, it shouldn't have mattered. But it did. I was already very fond of both of you. All I could tell was that you were both of the blood of Amber. I didn't want either of you harmed. The hardest thing was when you went away, and I was sure Luke had lured you into the mountains of New Mexico to kill you. By then, I suspected very

strongly that you were the one, but I was not certain. I was in love with Luke, I had taken over the body of Dan Martinez, and I was carrying a pistol. I followed you everywhere I could, knowing that if he tried to harm you the *geas* I was under would force me to shoot the man I loved.'' (PC, 176–77)

When the ty'iga had been in possession of Gail's body, she rescued Merlin from Luke's April 30 attacks on at least two occasions. Rather than reveal herself, she had used the telephone to reach Merlin, bringing him out of the path of danger. Even after Luke decided to discontinue their relationship, the ty'iga remained in Gail's body to watch over both of them.

Following Merlin to New Mexico, it took possession of the body of an ordinary businessman, Dan Martinez, probably because Martinez carried a pistol. It is unclear what had happened to Gail Lampron at that time. It seems likely that the ty'iga vacated her body and tracked Merlin in a formless state. As Martinez, the entity decided to approach Merlin to attempt to learn if it was meant to protect Merlin or Luke. Not having resolved the question, the ty'iga observed both of them in Santa Fe. For the first time, Merlin had a glance at the entity in its natural form. Martinez had shot at Luke, but Luke fired back and fatally shot him. Merlin described what he saw: ''I reached him just as he [Luke] was turning the body over, in time to see what seemed a faint cloud of blue or gray mist emerge from the man's mouth past his chipped tooth and drift away.'' (TD, 78)

The entity approached Merlin again in New York, while Merlin was visiting his father's friend, Bill Roth. It appeared as a neighbor named George Hansen and a lovely young woman named Meg Devlin. In both guises, the ty'iga asked directly who Merlin's mother was. Alone with Meg Devlin in her bedroom, Merlin admitted that his mother was Dara. Finally, the entity knew who it was supposed to protect from harm.

Picking up Merlin's trail as he hellrode through Shadow, the ty'iga entered the form of a dark-haired woman on horseback. It had sensed that Merlin was engaged in a perilous journey, and it probably recognized that Luke was following also. As the woman on horseback, the ty'iga sped to help Merlin when it sensed that some remarkable energy source

had set fire to Merlin's surroundings. Unable to control the horse when it reached the area, the ty'iga was thrown. The woman's back was broken in the fall, and she died in Merlin's arms. He detected the ty'iga exiting the body only as a slight billowing cloud. The smoke of the fire around them obscured anything else.

Vinta Bayle was merely a convenient vessel for the ty'iga to enter because she was in the city of Amber when Merlin walked to Death Alley. Speculation would suggest that the entity located Merlin in the city, sensed the fact that others had been tracking him as he entered Bloody Bill's, and took possession of Vinta's body. It was simply coincidence that it chose Vinta, who had been Caine's mistress and had met Merlin at the Royal Palace briefly.

Having Vinta's knowledge of her country home, it was able to persuade Merlin to travel there with her. As Vinta, the ty'iga found it extraordinarily opportune to exchange information with Merlin, thus learning more precisely the nature of the dangers facing him. Finding itself in sudden proximity to Luke as well was an added bonus. For a brief while, it was quite enjoyable for the entity to reminisce and share pleasantries with both acquaintances at one time.

Perhaps the ty'iga did some investigating in other shadows after vacating Vinta Bayle's body. It may have learned something from Merlin, or have been tracing the movements of blue crystal stones. Whatever the reason, the formless demon traveled to Begma. Since it apparently spent time observing the family of the Begman prime minister, it may have found out that the minister was planning an official visit to Amber. Prime Minister Orkuz's plans seemed in jeopardy when his older daughter, Nayda, became extremely ill. Again, supposition hints that the ty'iga sensed Nayda's closeness to death and decided to use her body for a dual purpose. It entered Nayda, but, although it could heal her body, it was too late to save her life. Still, as Nayda, it could accompany Orkuz to Amber and become reacquainted with Merlin in this new form.

As Nayda, visiting in Amber, the entity attempted to urge Merlin to speak of his current situation, particularly those matters that were most troubling to him. It pretended that Nayda was informed of Merlin's activities through a file to which she had access in Begma. She also asked about her sister Coral, who had earlier gone off with Merlin, but seemed to have disappeared.

After a while, Merlin came to realize that Nayda wasn't what she seemed. In his quarters in the Royal Palace, he used a Trump to summon his stepbrother Mandor. As soon as Mandor stepped into the room, Merlin had him place the entity under an enchantment. Mandor recognized immediately that it was a ty'iga in a human body.

Even under hard questioning, the ty'iga was unable to name the person who had sent it to protect Merlin. Mandor learned the truth only after Merlin left the room and the ty'iga spoke to him alone. Much later, Nayda was brought out of the spell that Mandor had placed upon her through the intervention of Coral. Able to move about once again, Nayda saw that Merlin had the Jewel of Judgment in his possession. Recognizing the Jewel as the Eye of the Serpent, as it was referred to in the Courts of Chaos, the entity seized it and raced out of Merlin's quarters. Merlin went after her, and Nayda explained:

> "This takes precedence . . . over your mother's binding. . . .
>
>   "She placed me under a *geas* to take care of you when you went off to school. . . . This breaks it! Free at last!" (KS, 195)

Perhaps because of the movement and use of the Jewel of Judgment, the Powers of the Pattern and the Logrus came together in the Royal Palace. Both Powers demanded the Jewel in Nayda's possession. She was protected by Merlin's artificial construct, Ghostwheel, however, who removed her from the scene during the explosive confluence of the two Powers.

When Merlin rejoined Ghostwheel later, his construct told him that he had left Nayda near the blue crystal cave, and she had wandered off into Shadow. Because the real Nayda was dead, the ty'iga was trapped within her body, but she/it still retained its powers. Thus, although in human form, she had become "something of a magical being," (KS, 206) unique to our knowledge.

The ty'iga, as Nayda, appeared to Merlin in an enchanted dream, speaking to him in the Corridor of Mirrors. She claimed to be real even though she had come to him while he dreamed. Professing her love for Luke, the entity asked where it could locate him. Merlin told it that Luke had been crowned king of Kashfa. The ty'iga thanked Merlin and then continued its journey.

The ty'iga found its way to Kashfa and became reacquainted with Luke in her new form. Luke didn't seem to realize that Nayda was the entity that had possessed the bodies of Gail Lampron and Vinta Bayle. The entity explained to Merlin that it didn't want Luke to know who it had been previously. Although it was no longer under any compulsion, it was still in love with Luke. As Nayda, it could continue to be with him, perhaps giving him the opportunity to fall in love with it anew.

Merlin joined the entity/Nayda as it traveled with Luke, seeking to rescue Coral from agents of the Logrus. Luke had reason to become suspicious of Nayda's true nature when the Sign of the Pattern addressed her as "Creature of the Pit." (PC, 198) Luke indicated that he cared for Nayda, even if she was a "demon lady," but circumstances separated them for a time. While Luke maintained a standoff with the Sign of the Pattern, Nayda was placed under the protection of Corwin's Pattern, along with Coral, Dalt, and Jurt. Until the conflict between the Pattern and the Logrus could be resolved, the ty'iga would probably remain with her companions at Corwin's Pattern, protecting them as much as being protected in turn by that greater force.

UNDERSHADOW/LAND BETWEEN SHADOWS

A place with a landscape that was like a photographic negative. Objects that normally were light in color were black; objects that were normally dark were white. There was no color whatsoever in this Land Between Shadows, only white, black, and gray. Under these specific conditions, no sounds could be heard either.

No magical influences could operate in this negative realm. Although the Supreme Powers of the Pattern and the Logrus had found a way to penetrate the Undershadow, they were extremely limited in the effect they could have. In fact, the place prevents activity from the Powers, unless certain conditions exist.

An odd set of circumstances made Merlin of Amber and the Courts of Chaos aware of the Undershadow. In fact, several factors were at play in moving Merlin, interfering, as it were, with different potencies. To clarify: Merlin, his stepbrother Mandor, and Jasra, former queen of Kashfa, attempted to reach a Begman girl named Coral through their combined efforts. Their attempt released some unknown Power that had been confining her. This Power sought out Merlin and was approaching his location. As a means of protecting Merlin and his comrades, the artificial construct named Ghostwheel sent them separately to distant shadows. Merlin found himself in a cave where he was visited by images of Amber relatives. The last of these, in the form of his father, Corwin, seemed more substantial than the other images. This Corwin proved himself to be fairly substantial by knocking out Merlin. After Merlin regained consciousness, he found himself in the Undershadow.

It appeared that the image of Corwin, later referred to as a Pattern-ghost, had deliberately sent Merlin to this negative land. Merlin tried to use the magical means at his disposal in order to leave the remote, disorienting place. His Trumps, both for Amber and Chaos relatives, were inoperable. His attempt to take a Shadow walk, influencing the landscape as he walked, was met with a throbbing headache. His search through his pockets for a grain of the magical blue crystal stones turned up nothing. His final attempt to leave, by summoning the Sign of the Logrus, caused a startling change. He was still trapped in the negative realm, but factors had been altered that would bring him a degree closer to finding a way out.

While Merlin's calling the Logrus to the Undershadow created an enormous explosion, it allowed the Logrus to leave one slight influence behind. It enhanced the talents of Merlin's Logrus protector, the piece of rope called Frakir. She (Frakir was a feminine entity) received a greater intelligence than previously, and she was able to communicate telepathically with Merlin.

Through Frakir, Merlin learned more about the Undershadow and his purpose there. In this place, according to Frakir, Merlin was on a quest. There would be stations in the Undershadow where Merlin would have to choose between the two Powers. Communicating telepathically, Merlin asked his enhanced cord:

Any idea what we're actually doing?
One of those damned quest-things, I think.
Vision? Or practical?
It was my understanding that they all partake of both, though I feel this one is heavily weighted toward the latter. On the other wrist, anything you encounter between shadows is likely to partake of the allegorical, the emblematic—all that crap people bury in the nonconscious parts of their beings. (KS, 74)

Aside from the choices Merlin was given, he met other conditions which widened his limitations within this realm. Merlin had been walking a bland path when he saw a stone altar to one side. He watched as a half-black, half-white man raised a long dagger above a bound woman:

My Concerto for Cuisinart and Microwave spell would have minced him and parboiled him in an instant, but it was useless to me when I could not speak the guide words.

. . . And then the knife hand descended and the blade entered her breast beneath the sternum with an arcing movement. At that instant she screamed, and the blood spurted and it was red against all those blacks and whites, and I realized as it covered the man's hand that had I tried, I might have uttered my spell and saved her. (KS, 93)

From this point on, with the appearance of real color and the actual sound of a human scream, other shadows were able to impinge upon the Undershadow. Merlin was able to speak aloud to his magical cord, and he was able to interact with beings and locales that appeared from the periphery of the path he walked.

Although we know of the Undershadow only through Merlin's journals, it may not be too presumptuous to make some reasonable statements about its origin. For instance, it would be reasonable to assume that this Land Between Shadows had not existed until recently. We may further assume that it only came into existence after the creation of the new Pattern designed by Corwin of Amber. This seems likely because it was the Pattern-ghost Corwin of this new Pattern that sent Merlin there. Apparently, the Pattern-ghost Corwin was trying to protect Merlin from the two Powers just as Merlin's Ghostwheel had done.

Of course, these speculations are contrary to the suppositions made by Frakir under her enhancement. But even Merlin came up with an explanation for Frakir's way of thinking. Frakir, still communicating telepathically, expressed her ideas thusly:

> But I've been thinking, now I know how to do it, and this place gets more and more fascinating. This whole business of Pattern-ghosts, for instance. If the Pattern can't penetrate here directly, it can at least employ agents. Wouldn't you think the Logrus might have some way of doing the same?
>
> "I suppose it's possible."
>
> I get the impression there's some sort of duel going on between them here, on the underside of reality, between shadows. What if this place came first? Before Shadow, even? What if they've been fighting here since the very beginning, in some strange metaphysical way?
>
> "What if they have?"
>
> That could almost make Shadow an afterthought, a by-product of the tension between the poles.
>
> "I'm afraid you've lost me, Frakir."
>
> What if Amber and the Courts of Chaos were created only to provide agents for this conflict?
>
> "And what if this idea were placed within you by the Logrus during your recent enhancement?"
>
> Why?
>
> "Another way to make me think that the conflict is more important than the people. Another pressure to make me choose a side."
>
> (KS, 110–11)

We know so little about this phenomenon that either possibility is open for further speculation. Perhaps it is simply harder for the ordinary citizen of Amber to accept the notion that we are mere playthings of all-powerful deities.

The unchanging Land Between Shadows must still be there, part of the problem of having two Designs of Order. For the ordinary mortal wandering into that place, with no method of contacting either the Pattern or the Logrus, that strange world of negative images would be of terrifying permanency.

UNICORN OF AMBER, THE

A magical creature that rarely allows itself to be seen by human eyes. In Amber, it holds a special place. Legend tells us that ages ago, before there was Time or Order, Dworkin first encountered the unicorn. Their relationship was inexplicable, but it is conceivable that the creature could change its form. She (the unicorn being feminine in gender) obtained the Jewel of Judgment, enabling Dworkin to create the Pattern in bare rock on an island floating in the void of Chaos. This act established Order, and Amber, and all the shadows between Order and Chaos. Before wandering off to gambol in the Shadows, the unicorn bore a son of Dworkin's, thus beginning the Royal Line in Amber.

There are no recorded facts to dispute the legend. We must accept the tale as a matter of faith. Those who have actually sighted the unicorn have no uncertainty about this acceptance.

Dworkin's son, Oberon, may have had doubts himself about the remarkable union. He seldom spoke of it, and with the passing of millennia, even Oberon's children consigned the story to that impersonal region we call myth.

In his Chronicles, Corwin mentions Oberon's naming of the Grove of the Unicorn and a sighting he had made long ago:

> The Grove of the Unicorn lies in Arden to the southwest of Kolvir, near to that jutting place where the land begins its final descent into the valley called Garnath. While Garnath had been cursed, burned, invaded, and fought through in recent years, the adjacent highlands stood unmolested. The grove where Dad [Oberon] claimed to have seen the unicorn ages before and to have experienced the peculiar events which led to his adopting the beast as the patron of Amber and placing it on his coat of arms, was, as near as we could tell, a spot now but slightly screened from the long view across Garnath to the sea—twenty or thirty paces in from the upper edge of things: an asymmetrical glade where a small spring trickled from a mass of rock, formed a clear pool, brimmed into a tiny creek, made its way off toward Garnath and on down. (SU, 73)

Wherever the unicorn has been sighted, the scene is nearly always pastoral and pleasing. The effect on those who have seen her appears to be one of calming; the easing of woes, the soothing of discontent, the healing of pain.

Corwin's reference to "peculiar events" may allude to one of several unverified stories about early encounters with the magical beast. It seems possible that Corwin's allusion was to the time when Oberon, as a young man, was terribly maimed by a dire wolf. He was near death, alone in the woods. Some bards wrote, many years after the fact, that the unicorn found him lying upon a smooth rock by some trees. She touched him with her horn, and he was revived from a state of near-death. His wounds closed up, and, still very weak, he was able to crawl away until he reached a more inhabited area. After his recovery, Oberon returned to the wood, recognizing the bloodied place where he had been attacked. A small stream of clear water flowed between the rocks, the very same place where he had lain dying.

Corwin recorded seeing the unicorn himself, and others were with him to verify it. In Corwin's experience, the sightings were at crucial times, when the Family was undergoing a crisis, and, in the aftermath of the unicorn's appearance, those who saw her felt a serenity beyond measure.

Gérard and Corwin had gone to the Grove of the Unicorn to retrieve the murdered body of Caine that Corwin had found there. Gérard was extremely suspicious of Corwin, believing that he had been the murderer. While other members of the Family watched by Trump, Gérard put Corwin in a precarious situation, explaining that the others were observing. It was Gérard's belief that Corwin would not be able to act against him without arousing the suspicions of the others.

Following those tense moments, while they covered Caine's body in a sheet, Gérard drew Corwin's attention to a remarkable vision:

> Neither of us moved as we regarded the apparition: a soft, shimmering white encompassed it, as if it were covered with down rather than fur and maning; its tiny, cloven hooves were golden, as was the delicate, whorled horn that rose from its narrow head. It stood atop one of the lesser rocks, nibbling at the lichen that grew there. Its eyes, when it raised them and

looked in our direction, were a bright, emerald green. It joined us in immobility for a pair of instants. Then it made a quick, nervous gesture with its front feet, pawing the air and striking the stone, three times. And then it blurred and vanished like a snowflake, silently, perhaps in the woods to our right. (SU, 79)

As Corwin chronicled them, there were two other significant occasions when the unicorn appeared. With each appearance, the creature affected them deeply, but this was much more than in a personal, emotional way. Each time, the unicorn brought with her a revelation, one that influenced the Family's conception of the world.

She appeared before Corwin next as he, Random, and Ganelon were riding down Mt. Kolvir from the mountain's highest point, where three stones touch the ghostly stair of Tir-na Nog'th in the moonlight. She appeared and led them along a strangely changed Kolvir to the place where they discovered, for the first time, the primal Pattern. (SU, 187–92) They were able to share the knowledge with the others of the Family that they had seen the true, underlying level of reality, and they could see the cause of all Amber's troubles exposed upon that original design.

The last occasion upon which Corwin saw the unicorn was at the conclusion of the Patternfall battle. At a time when Amber and the shadows seemed lost to the surviving members of the Family, she came before them. The all-consuming storm was about to wipe out the final vestiges of existence but for the Courts of Chaos. Corwin and the others waited upon the heights before the Abyss, with no hope of restoring Order. Suddenly, unbelievably, the unicorn climbed out of the Abyss, bearing the Jewel of Judgment around her neck.

She approached Corwin and the others on the heights gingerly. Without showing fear, she came directly to one of the members of the Family and knelt before him, so that her horn nearly touched him. It was Random who stood before the unicorn. He reached out and carefully removed the Jewel from around the creature's neck. After Random placed the Jewel around his own neck, the unicorn stepped away, then galloped down the slope and vanished.

The unicorn had shown all the other members of the Royal Family who was to be the successor to the late King Oberon, and she also provided the means for eradicating the Death Storm. The occasion had been humbling, but it also was cause for exaltation and reflection.

The tradition of the unicorn as a supernatural being to be worshiped continues to this day in Amber and a number of shadows. In Jidrash, capital city of Kashfa, the First Unicornian Church holds services that reflect the Kashfans' belief that the unicorn plays a part in every aspect of their lives.

In Amber, chapels dedicated to the unicorn are placed in sites where she has been spotted, sightings confirmed by several witnesses. The funeral services for Caine took place at one of these chapels, along the southern foot of Mt. Kolvir. King Random read a passage from The Book of the Unicorn as part of the service. As Merlin had written in his journals: "It was said that Dworkin himself had penned the Book in his saner days, and that long passages had come direct from the unicorn." (TD, 136) Sometime later, when Merlin sailed along the coast with Vinta Bayle, he thought he saw the unicorn momentarily, near the sea cave where Caine's body had been interred. (BA, 80)

The many tales of unicorns that are retold in the shadows speak of the creature's beauty, gentleness, purity, and ability to heal with its wondrous horn. There is scant mention of a unicorn's fierceness and aggressiveness. The creature is known, in some stories, to protect its territory with such terrible fury that even elephants would flee in terror. Interestingly, lions have been said to live in the same territory harmoniously with unicorns. Lions and unicorns, it seems, do not threaten each other's food supplies. This is of particular interest, since Dalt the mercenary, who often conducted raids in and around shadow Begma and hated the Amberites, designed his martial banner to show a lion rending a unicorn.

In more recent times, of course, we have learned through Merlin's journals that there is much more to the legends of the unicorn than was previously understood. This new information lends credence to the perception of the unicorn of Amber as a creature to be feared by ordinary people. Merlin reported seeing an immense image of the unicorn in several rather dire circumstances. Those who resided in the Royal Palace at the time of the great meeting of the Powers of the unicorn and the Logrus, have spoken with absolute certitude of the awesomeness of that unworldly presence.

UTHER

King of the shadow named Lorraine. Late in his rule, he fought strange forces that emerged from an expanding dark Circle. In a great battle, in which he was supported by Ganelon and his men, King Uther was struck down. He died from his wounds.

Although little is known about Uther in this shadow, other shadows carried stories of a King Uther protecting his realm from evil invaders. On shadow Earth, for instance, a King Uther Pendragon of Britain is said to have battled an alliance of kings from the northern reaches that was continually harassing the land. At the Battle of St. Albans, the aged Uther defeated the northern kings. However, his age and infirmities caught up with him. The old king was carried off the battlefield and tended, but it was already too late. Legend has it that before Uther died, the mage Merlin appeared before him. The wizard asked him to declare his estranged son Arthur the successor to the throne. Before dying, King Uther responded, "I give him God's blessing and my own, and bid him pray for my soul, and . . . claim the crown."

We know of King Uther of Lorraine through the story that Ganelon told Corwin, when Corwin visited that shadow under the name Corey of Cabra. The following is what Ganelon related about the late king of Lorraine:

"But now all manner of raiders emerged from it [the dark Circle]—some even faring forth during the day—laying waste to the countryside about its borders. When they had devastated the land about its entire circumference, the Circle moved to encompass those areas also. And so its growth began again, in this fashion. The old king, Uther, who had long hunted me forgot all about me and set his forces to patrolling that damned Circle. . . . There were cats such as you slew, and snakes and hopping things, and God knows what all else. As we neared the edge of the Circle [from within], one of King Uther's patrols saw us and came to our aid. . . . When they saw who I was, they hustled me off to court. Here. This used to be Uther's palace. Told him what I had done, what I had seen and heard. . . . He offered full pardon to me and to my men if we would join with him against the Wardens of the Circle. Having gone through what I had gone through, I realized that the thing had to be stopped. So I agreed. . . . We fought many skirmishes. I was promoted until I stood at Uther's right hand, as once I had at Corwin's. Then the skirmishes became more than skirmishes. Larger and larger parties emerged from that hellhole. We lost a few battles. They took some of our outposts. Then one night an army emerged, an army—a horde—of both men and the other things that dwelled there. That night we met the largest force we had ever engaged. King Uther himself rode to battle, against my advice—for he was advanced in years—and he fell that night and the land was without a ruler.'' (GA, 33–35)

King Uther had died in that confrontation more than three years before the arrival of Corey of Cabra. And Ganelon had been carrying on the fight all that time. As Ganelon recounted, they had won the battle the night Uther had fallen, and Ganelon believed the enemy was a little afraid as a consequence.

Further warfare proved inconclusive, but Ganelon attributed his dedication to defeating the minions of the Circle, in part, to the legacy of King Uther.

VIALLE

Wife of Random and reigning queen of Amber.
Vialle was born blind in the undersea city of Rebma. Her background did not come to the fore until her liaison with Random, but it is known that she was of noble birth. Queen Moire of Rebma felt high esteem for Vialle, and it was likely this esteem, rather than a spitefulness on Moire's part against Random, motivated her to force his marriage to Vialle. Although we have no records for verification, it is possible that Vialle is related to Moire of Rebma. At the time, it might have been hoped that their marriage would produce offspring who would succeed in walking Rebma's Pattern and expand its citizens' understanding of the shadows.

Even before she came to know Random, Vialle knew his son. She had informed Corwin of Amber:

"I knew Martin in Rebma, when he was but a small boy. I was there while he was growing up. I liked him then. Even if he were not Random's son he would still be dear to me.'' (HO, 53)

Because of her blindness, Vialle compensated by a greater acuity of her other senses. She was extremely talented in creating sculpture of people by the use of touch alone. People have marveled at how closely her sculpted busts resembled those whom she portrayed. Corwin noted this when he visited her in the Royal Palace and saw a bust of Random (HO, 49). Early in her life, she seemed gifted in the healing arts. Since her parents were affluent in Rebma, they engaged the best available tutors to educate Vialle. She received medical training through the services of one of these tutors. Her natural skills enabled her to ease the suffering of numbers of citizens in Rebma. She was relied upon almost as frequently as any surgeon of the realm, and she was often asked into consultation with other medical experts.

Virtually nothing is known of how Queen Moire broached the subject of marriage to Vialle, nor of the year that Random and Vialle spent together in that undersea realm when Random was coerced to marry and live there. Corwin and Random had a brief conversation about that early period of time, however.

Corwin had asked,

"I thought you were going to get the year over with and be done with it.''
"So did I . . . But I fell in love with her. I really did. . . .
"She really cares for me . . . like nobody else ever has before.'' (GA, 220)

In Vialle, Random found a stalwart confidante. As she had revealed to Corwin: "He [Random] tells me most things. I know your story and most of the others'. He keeps me aware of events, suspicions, conjectures.'' (HO, 52) On the occasion when Corwin spoke at some length with Vialle in her husband's absence, Corwin discovered her to be an intelligent, knowledgeable person. She asked him of Shadow and the possibility of finding another Amber elsewhere. It was obvious that she understood the philosophical basis, and that she had considered deeply the subject of moving through worlds of Shadow. She had learned a great deal from Random, but she kept her own counsel as well.

We do not know what counsel Vialle gave Random in Rebma when he determined to walk the Pattern, go to Amber Castle, and attempt to assassinate his brother Eric, who ruled there. As public as Random and Vialle have since become, both of them maintain a privacy in matters of family. However, it was quite risky of Random to decide to assassinate Eric after Eric had crowned himself. The denizens of Rebma had been spectators to the ceremony of Eric's coronation, as were numerous shadows that were contiguous with Amber. Random, Vialle, and the others of Rebma also witnessed Eric's public pronouncement that the captured Corwin have his eyes put out, and that he was to languish in darkness in a dungeon. If we can presume anything about the private affairs of Vialle and Random at this point in time, it can be asserted that Random saw a good reason in Corwin's predicament to take the action he did. While Vialle might have argued against her husband's taking such a risk, she would certainly have felt empathy for Corwin. Whatever speculations may be raised, Random, armed with a crossbow and shafts, used Rebma's Pattern to seek out and kill Eric in Amber. He succeeded in wounding Eric, but was himself captured and thrown in a dungeon not far from Corwin's.

Queen Moire interceded on Vialle's behalf, speaking to Eric by Trump. For his part, Eric imagined he had gained a possible romantic interest from the queen of the undersea city, so he was inclined to listen. When the blind girl addressed the self-proclaimed ruler of Amber by Trump, one might believe he felt some sympathy for her. Nevertheless, he refused to grant Vialle's request immediately. It was something he wished to consider. Vialle's request was to be allowed to join her husband in Amber's dungeons. Eric's assertion that he needed to ponder her request may, indeed, have been a sign of sympathy on his part.

While Corwin was still a prisoner, probably sometime during his first two years of blindness, Eric allowed Vialle to join Random. They were moved to a larger cell, and gradually were given some of the basic amenities. Little else has been recorded of their days of imprisonment.

As the frequency of strange and terrible creatures from Shadow increased, Random and Vialle were gradually given greater freedom to move within the Royal Palace. Guards were assigned to them at all times, but, as Eric became increasingly involved in warfare with the gathering denizens of other shadows, he maintained less vigilance over his brother and sister-in-law. In light of the perils to be faced by these intruders, conflicts among the Family became inconsequential.

Remaining in the background and without influence, Vialle was likely to have absorbed all that her husband had to say about events during the Shadow Wars, Eric's death, and Corwin's subsequent rule. No doubt Random told her of his sighting of Dara in Amber's Pattern, when he stood beside the victorious Corwin; about the dead half-man and Caine's death, planned in such a way as to implicate Corwin; about the rescue of Brand from a distant shadow, and the cabals Brand had described to Corwin after reviving; and about the conjectures and suspicions his siblings expressed in the Royal Library that had put everybody on his guard.

For her part, Vialle probably talked of Rebma, and of Random's son Martin. Certainly, Random would have been curious about his son and would ask further of him, knowing, as he would, that Vialle had known Martin.

Therefore, it was not too surprising for her to receive Corwin calmly, when he came to tell her of her husband's journey to seek his son. Healer that she is, she expressed more of an interest in Corwin than in the errant wanderings of Random and Benedict through lands of Shadow. It was a mark of her trust and confidence in her husband that she merely listened to Corwin's explanations without questioning Random's impulsiveness in departing. Instead, she asked Corwin about Amber and about his relationship to it. She spoke with a mixture of humility and assurance that is a recognizable part of her character. While she and Corwin sat together in her apartment, she had told him:

> "I want to understand you . . . Ever since I first heard of you back in Rebma, even before Random told me stories, I wondered what it was that drove you. Now I've the opportunity—no right, of course, just the opportunity—I felt it worth speaking out of turn and order beyond my station simply to ask you."
> (HO, 54)

This wonderful combination of disarming honesty and tactful curiosity has served her in good stead in more recent times, as well.

When Random found his son, they returned to Amber. They met with Corwin on Mt. Kolvir by Corwin's cenotaph, and Martin told Corwin of his story since leaving Rebma. Along the path he took, Martin encountered Benedict, Brand, and Dara, all important shapers of his life. While Corwin went off to join Benedict in attempting to trap Brand, Random took his son to Vialle. It is unfortunate that no one has recorded that meeting between stepson and stepmother, she, who had been a friend of his youth.

One cannot help but feel that Random was echoing Vialle's advice when he spoke to Corwin about their father's sudden return to the throne. King Oberon had revealed himself as having played Corwin's friend Ganelon, and Corwin took this new matter badly. He locked himself in the library of the Royal Palace, but allowed entry to his brother Random. Random's calm and rational demeanor bespoke a maturity that hadn't appeared before. His experiences, of course, would explain this new maturity. But it is suspected that Vialle's great inner calm and her supportive nature had an enormous influence on him, even in that earlier time.

Again, we do not know of Vialle's opinion of the strange vision of Benedict's duel with an invisible sword wielder in the throne room, nor of Martin's part in it. It is likely, however, that she had been supportive of King Oberon's plans and activities, even to the extent of trusting Dara. Mere speculation, certainly. Still, Random's role in the shaping of Amber may have depended, in some small measure, on the perceptions of several forces concerning Vialle's influence.

When the Death Storm swept away all the shadows, Amber was eradicated as well. Random fought with his brothers and sisters outside the Courts of Chaos at the Patternfall battle, but Vialle remained in Amber. For an empty, immeasurable period, life did not exist beyond the Courts of Chaos. By Corwin's account, years had run their course in the indefinable interim back in the true city.

The Chronicles of Corwin tell us something of the return to normalcy:

> "Random's last act after defeating the storm was to join with me, drawing power from the Jewel [of Judgment], to reach Gérard through his Trump. They are cold once more, the cards, and the shadows are themselves again. Amber stands. Years have passed since we departed it, and more may elapse before I return. The others may already have Trumped home, as Random has done, to take up his duties.'' (CC, 141–42)

With kingship, and the routine of diplomacy, domesticity returned for Random and Vialle. Although Random may have felt an uncertainty about his rule during that early time, the comfort and support of his wife may well have given him balance and confidence.

Vialle had never been one to overnurture and smother others with love. She wished to maintain her own independence, and she accepted that same independence in others. Thus, her relationship with her stepson, Martin, seemed not to rise above friendship and genuine caring. She recognized his need to search for himself in shadows. Some say she even encouraged him to seek his own truth in those other realms. Still, she kept such matters private, and it is not for us to say what occurred behind closed doors.

Those infrequent times when young Merlin, son of Corwin, visited Amber, Vialle welcomed him, made him feel comfortable, and allowed him to choose his own recreation. She never seemed bothered if he chose to spend time with his aunts or uncles rather than with her. Her own interests in sculpture and music occupied much of her time.

Naturally, Vialle remained Random's closest confidante. She often acted as hostess at diplomatic gatherings in the Royal Palace. Usually, she saw to the innumerable arrangements of state dinners and residential accommodations when ambassadorial contingents visited Amber. She charmed such visitors and provided informed conversation that enhanced the guests' good opinion of the royal couple.

However, she also missed her homeland of Rebma, and the king willingly gave her leave to visit Queen Moire and her many friends who resided in the undersea city. She had long known Llewella, sister of Random, who also divided her time between Rebma and the true city. They were welcome traveling companions for each other over the years. Quite often, if Vialle were absent from official affairs of state, it was because she was visiting in Rebma.

She was away when her husband received word of the death of Caine and the wounding of Bleys in separate incidents in different shadows. Random informed her by Trump of the situation, and the disturbing news that someone had also been trying to murder Merlin on shadow Earth. When she suggested that she return, Random indicated that he preferred she remain in Rebma. He was concerned for her safety, of course, but her being away also gave him one less thing to worry about. Vialle realized all this and consented to remain in the reflected city.

When Random became aware of certain political facts, he did request that Vialle return to Amber as soon as possible. After learning from Merlin that Luke Raynard was actually Prince Rinaldo of Kashfa, Random set certain contingencies in motion. These involved a bit of devious intrigue concerning the shadow Kashfa. When Vialle returned, Random informed her of the current, very tentative, status of Kashfa and the political connections to Rinaldo and his mother, Queen Jasra. To take control of Kashfa out of Jasra's hands, Random needed to embark for that shadow with Benedict and a small force. He needed Vialle in Amber in order to fend off any queries concerning his whereabouts. Random also mentioned the sudden death of Kashfa's current ruler, and Vialle was able to infer that her husband had been involved covertly in this new death.

Vialle was sharing some of her personal concerns about her husband's absence with Llewella over a small meal in a drawing room of the palace when Merlin entered. Vialle allowed Merlin to tell of his own recent adventures while she listened quietly.

When Merlin asked about the other family members, Vialle told him of their fortifying for a possible siege and Random's trip in her singular, quiet manner. She was taken by surprise, though, when the courtier Randel announced the arrival of the Begman prime minister and his party. While she was surprised at the timing, she did know something of their reasons for coming. She explained to Merlin:

"They've never been friendly with Kashfa, but I'm not sure now whether they're here to protest Kashfa's possible admission to the Golden Circle or whether they're upset about our interfering in Kashfa's domestic affairs. It could be they're afraid they'll lose business with such a close neighbor suddenly enjoying the same preferred trade status they have. Or it may be they had different plans for Kashfa's throne and we just foreclosed them. Maybe both." (SC, 55–56)

Her expressing these several possibilities reveal that she has an astute political mind. She told Llewella and Merlin not to volunteer any information when meeting with the Begman party, but to accept any forthcoming information they may have about the Kashfan situation.

Upon greeting Prime Minister Orkuz in the Yellow Room, Vialle was met with comments about distressing news involving Kashfa. Llewella and Merlin offered their presence for support, but Vialle calmly handled Orkuz's concerns, saying that these matters would have to wait for the return of King Random. Vialle and Llewella engaged Orkuz and his staff in conversation of lesser import, and Merlin became involved with the younger of Orkuz's two daughters, Coral.

Vialle arranged for a state dinner for the guests and the ambassador of Begma attached to Amber, allowing Henden, the head steward, to handle most of the details. In the dining hall prior to dinner, Vialle kept Prime Minister Orkuz occupied, while keeping the Begman ambassador, a tall woman named Ferla Quist, from making vehement protests to the prime minister about his tactless avoidance of official protocol. He hadn't informed the embassy of his arrival, and the ambassador had been furious. Vialle acted to maintain the decorum of these two officials, while also handling the ordinary duties of hosting the contingent of people.

She may have been slightly disturbed that the prime minister's younger daughter was not in attendance, but she didn't indicate it. She helped Henden rearrange the seating at the dinner table, and her new arrangements were inconspicuously diplomatic. She was seated at the head and Merlin faced her from the other end. On her left was Orkuz, and on her right, Llewella. Ferla Quist was placed next to Orkuz, then Martin, Cade, the ambassador's secretary, and Orkuz's older daughter Nayda. Beside Llewella were Gérard, Dretha Gannell, assistant to Ambassador Quist, and Bill Roth. All in all, a reasonable seating plan, considering the possibilities and checks for intrigues between interested parties.

Avoiding them entirely was, most assuredly, out of the question.

During dinner, three musicians played from a corner of the room, limiting the chances for an exchange of anything more indiscreet than a bit of gossip.

Vialle was pleased to have Bill Roth present. Not only was he an interesting conversationalist, coming as he did from that favorite shadow of the Amberites, Earth, but he was also naturally amusing. He kept relations with Nayda, and later, with Orkuz, on a lighthearted and good-natured level. As an attorney, he also had good sense, and he knew when to be discreet.

The only incident of note, from Vialle's standpoint, was Cade's mention to Merlin about the Eregnor situation. Talking around the table stopped momentarily, and the secretary seemed slightly shaken. Fortunately, Merlin saved the moment by responding that there were things to be said for both sides of most matters. (SC, 127) This was noncommittal enough, but with the ring of condescending understanding, that the statement smoothed an awkward silence.

Well into the meal, Vialle sensed a subtle vibration with variant tonal qualities. She recognized the sensation as a Trump sending and excused herself. Llewella started to get up with her, but Vialle bent to whisper something that kept Llewella there. She left for a small sitting room, where she would be undisturbed. She permitted the sender to reach for her and complete his contact.

Julian reached her from Arden, bringing news of a sudden crisis. After conversing with him for several minutes, Vialle asked him to maintain his position in the field, and she would contact him again shortly. She called for one of the servants and asked her to bring Merlin to the sitting room. Once Merlin arrived, Vialle apprised him of the situation:

"Dalt's men are dug in near the western edge of Arden ... Julian's are strung out facing them. Benedict has taken Julian additional men and weapons. He says he can execute a flanking movement that will take Dalt's line apart. But I told him not to."

"I don't understand. Why not?"

"Men will die." ...

"That's the way it is in war. Sometimes you have no choice."

"But we do have a choice, of sorts ... one that I don't understand. And I do want to understand it before I give an order that will result in numerous deaths."

"What is the choice?" ...

"I came here to respond to a Trump message from Julian ... He had just spoken with Dalt under a flag of truce. Dalt told him that his objective was not, at this time, the destruction of Amber. He pointed out that he could conduct an expensive attack, though, in terms of our manpower and equipment. He said he'd rather save himself and us the expense, however. What he really wants is for us to turn two prisoners over to him—Rinaldo and Jasra."

"Huh? ... Even if we wanted to, we can't give him Luke. He's not here."

"That is what Julian told him. He seemed very surprised. For some reason, he believed we had Rinaldo in custody."

"Well, we're not obliged to provide the man with an education. I gather he's been something of a pain for years. I think Benedict has the right answer for him."

"I did not call you in for advice." ...

"Sorry ... It's just that I don't like seeing someone trying to pull a stunt like this and actually believing he has a chance of success."

"He has no chance of success ... But if we kill him now, we learn nothing. I would like to find out what is behind this."

"Have Benedict bring him in. I have spells that will open him up." ...

"Too risky ... Once bullets start flying, there's the chance one might find him. Then we lose even though we win."

"I don't understand what it is that you want of me."

"He asked Julian to get in touch with us and relay his demand. He's promised to hold the truce until we give him some sort of official answer. Julian says he has the impression that Dalt would settle for either one of them."

"I don't want to give him Jasra either."

"Neither do I. What I do want very badly is to know what is going on. There would be small point in releasing Jasra and asking her, since this is a recent development. I want to know whether you have means of getting in touch with Rinaldo. I want to talk to him.''

"Well, uh . . . yes . . . I have a Trump for him.''

"Use it.'' (SC 136–38)

When Merlin contacted Luke Raynard/Rinaldo and brought him to Amber, Vialle touched his face as he knelt before her. She told him she sensed both strength and sorrow in his face. Luke told her that his vendetta against Amber was ended, largely because of his friendship with Merlin. She responded: "You must trust him [Merlin], to come here. I respect that . . . Take this,'' (SC 139) and gave him her ring. This act offered Rinaldo the queen's protection, so that no liegeman of Amber would cause him harm. Then she explained the situation concerning Dalt to him.

Luke made the suggestion that he go to the Forest of Arden to speak to Dalt. Both Merlin and Vialle were concerned that Luke's presence might escalate the conflict, but Luke assured them that he would simply parley, avoiding any chance of battle between their armies. Although the queen was not certain of the terminology, Merlin explained that Luke was the best salesman in the southwest, and was capable of achieving anything he wanted though palaver.

Vialle agreed to permit Luke to trump to Arden and meet with Dalt. Before she made contact with Julian, however, Merlin suggested he take Luke to his quarters to find a warm cloak to wear in the wintry night. All concerned were aware that it was a subtle pretext for Merlin and Luke to speak privately, but the queen allowed it.

Upon their return, Vialle asked Luke to join her, placing his hand on her shoulder. She held a Trump of Julian, and, sightless, she used it to call up the contact. It is unclear exactly what she must do to make a Trump contact, but it is likely that a strong mental image is sufficient to the task. In his journal, Merlin pondered the question of what Vialle sensed when one of the Family attempted Trump contact with her:

I found myself wondering, not for the first time, just what it was that Vialle sensed when it came to a Trump contact. I always see the other person myself, and all of the others say that they do, too. But Vialle, as I understood

it, had been blind from birth. I've always felt it would be impolite to ask her, and for that matter it's occurred to me that her answer probably wouldn't make much sense to a sighted person. (SC 165–66)

Together, Vialle and Luke spoke to Julian, explaining Luke's plan. At the conclusion of their talk, Luke used the contact to reach toward Julian, who, in turn, reached for the young man. Before Vialle could prevent it, Merlin joined Luke, and they disappeared together to Julian's position in Arden. Vialle remained behind in the sitting room.

There is no official record of Vialle's activities during this interval. It is likely, though, that she saw to her guests, or at least inquired after them, before returning to the sitting room to await further contact.

When Julian made Trump contact, she accepted the sensation calmly. She listened intently to his report, making very few comments. Julian described the meeting between Rinaldo and Dalt, and their one-on-one fight, and its outcome. He mentioned Merlin's exhibiting his arcane knowledge in scooping out a grave in the earth before the enemy. Vialle may have even agreed with Julian that it was a foolish move on Merlin's part, making the enemy aware of his powers.

Upon Merlin's return to the sitting room, he spoke with Vialle about Rinaldo. Vialle told him she believed Rinaldo had planned the challenge against Dalt all along. As soon as he heard from his friend again, Vialle wanted Merlin to inform her immediately.

Then, Merlin brought up other matters:

"It concerns Coral's not being present at dinner this evening.''

"Go on.'' . . .

"You are aware that we took a long walk about town today?'

"I am.'' . . .

"We wound up below . . . in the chamber of the Pattern. She'd expressed a desire to see it.''

"Many visitors do. It is pretty much a matter of judgment whether to take them. Often they lose interest, though, when they learn about the stairway.''

"I did tell her about it . . . but it didn't discourage her. When she got there, she set foot upon the Pattern—''

"No! ... You should have watched her more closely! All that other trouble with Begma ... and now this! Where is her body?"

"Good question ... I don't know. But she was alive the last time I saw her. You see, she claimed Oberon was her father, and then she proceeded to walk the Pattern. When she'd finished, she had it transport her somewhere. Now, her sister—who is aware that we went off together—is concerned. She was pestering me through dinner as to where Coral might be."

"What did you tell her?"

"I told her that I'd left her sister enjoying some of the beauties of the palace and that she might be a bit late to dinner. As things wore on, though, she seemed to grow more concerned and made me promise to search for her tonight if she didn't turn up. I didn't want to talk about what really happened because I didn't want to go into the business of Coral's parentage."

"Understandable ... Oh, my....

... "I was not aware of our late king's affair in Begma ... So it is difficult to assess the impact of this revelation. Did Coral give you any indication as to how long she intended to stay away? And for that matter, did you provide her with any means of return?"

"I gave her my Trump ... but she hasn't been in touch. I got the impression she didn't intend to be away for too long, though."

"This could be serious ... for reasons other than the obvious. How does Nayda strike you?"

"She seemed quite sensible ... Also, I believe she rather likes me." ...

"If word of this gets to Orkuz, he could well get the impression that we are holding her hostage against his proper performance in any negotiations which might arise out of the situation in Kashfa."

"You're right. I hadn't thought of that."

"He will. People tend to think of such matters when dealing with us. So what we need to do is buy some time and try to turn her up before this begins looking suspicious."

"I understand." ...

"Most likely, he will send to her quarters soon—if he hasn't already done so—to dis-cover why she was not present at dinner. If he can be satisfied now, you will have the entire night in which to try to locate her."

"How?"

"You're the magician. You figure it out. In the meantime, you say that Nayda is sympathetic?"

"Very much so."

"Good. It seems to me that the best course of action then would be to attempt to enlist her aid. I trust you to be tactful and do this in the least distressing manner possible, of course—"

"Naturally—" ...

"—because of her recent illness ... All we need to do now is give the second daughter a heart attack."

"Illness? ... She hadn't mentioned anything about that."

"I'd imagine the memory is still distressing. She was apparently quite close to death until very recently, then rallied suddenly and insisted on accompanying her father on this mission. He's the one who told me about it."

"She seemed fine at dinner." ...

"Well, try to keep her that way. I want you to go to her immediately, tell her what happened as diplomatically as possible, and try to get her to cover for her sister while you search for her. There is, of course, the risk that she will not believe you and that she will go directly to Orkuz. Perhaps you might employ a spell to prevent this. But we have no other choice that I can see. Tell me whether I'm wrong."

"You're not wrong." ...

"Then I suggest you be about it ... and report back to me immediately if there are any problems, or any progress, no matter what the hour."

"I'm on my way." (SC, 167–69)

After leaving Vialle, Merlin made arrangements with Orkuz's older daughter, Nayda, allaying the prime minister's concerns for his younger daughter. Matters between Orkuz and the Royal Family were further smoothed over when Coral turned up sometime later, explaining that she had been wandering in a strange area within the palace called the Corridor of Mirrors. Vialle learned of these developments through Prime Minister Orkuz, and she shared his relief.

In the interim, King Random returned from his mission, and Vialle told him of the events that occurred in his absence. The king had been informed of the incident between Dalt and Rinaldo by Benedict as soon as he had trumped back. Random had been more concerned about Rinaldo's activities than about Orkuz and his errant daughter. Still, the king visited the prime minister's quarters, attempting to alleviate his fears by being quite conciliatory.

Queen Vialle was pleased to be able to take a step back from her major role as political arbiter, allowing her husband to handle these primary matters of state once again.

At a time before Coral had reappeared at her father's door, Vialle had an eerie encounter. She was in the sitting room outside the bedchamber of the royal quarters, preparing to retire, when she heard a shout from within. It had sounded like: "Come out fighting!"

As she approached the door to her bedchamber, she heard a second voice. It seemed quite familiar. She paused and listened. After a moment, she continued to the door and opened it. There was the slight grating noise of some fixture being moved, and then a movement of feet, the rustle of garments. Someone was in the room she knew. Not completely certain, she believed there were two people. She sensed that one was pushing another toward the far wall. She heard a soft explosion of air, as if one of these were about to say something. She called out, "Who's there?"

There was a sharp concussion, as if someone tripped another. Another explosion of sudden breath expelled, the vibration of a body falling toward the floor, then, strangely, not hitting. With that one strange motion of bodily movement, followed by the lack of any follow-through, the presence, or presences, were gone. She had reached toward the movement, calling out again, "Who's there?" but she knew it was to no avail.

Carefully checking the room, Vialle discovered that a brick had been removed from a low section of wall just to the right of the fireplace. She replaced the brick. She did not confide in anyone about the incident, even after the publication of Merlin's journal. It remains unclear whether or not she recognized the familiar presence as Merlin, or if she knew that the Jewel of Judgment had been taken.

When the forces of the Logrus and the Pattern collided in the corridor near Merlin's quarters, the explosion that followed tore through the wall containing the outer door to the royal chambers (KS, 201). Vialle had been safe in the bedchamber. She communicated with her husband by Trump, finding him and Martin unhurt one floor below.

Vialle received Mandor, Merlin's stepbrother from the Courts, and Coral, who was unconscious. Although Vialle could tell that Mandor was injured by the way he moved, she turned her attention to the prime minister's daughter. Random joined them as Mandor placed Coral on the bed. Gently touching the girl, Vialle could tell that she suffered a head injury, and there was some superficial facial damage. It seemed as if Coral had lost her right eye. She realized the damage was more extensive than her healing powers alone could handle.

Vialle was aware that Merlin had entered, and she recognized the name when her husband called out "Dworkin," but she was preoccupied with Coral's injuries. Vialle recognized that it was Dworkin who joined her at Coral's bedside even though they had not met before. She sensed enormous power in him as he began to minister to the girl.

As Dworkin worked, using some object of power that Merlin had given him, Vialle joined her husband. She listened when Random received a Trump contact. A courier in Kashfa had made the contact. Vialle understood quite well the implications when Random learned that the Kashfan palace had been taken over by a mercenary force led by Dalt and Rinaldo. She also heard that Duke Arkans had been taken into custody and was being held within the palace.

Vialle nodded slightly to Random as he looked toward Merlin. The king halted the young man, then asked Vialle for the use of her art studio to speak privately with Merlin. She assented, and remained close by the bed where Dworkin worked on Coral. Nearly forgotten, Mandor spoke to the queen, and she noticed again that he was injured. Checking him lightly, she realized he had a simple fracture of his right arm. She tended to it while Dworkin remained occupied.

Before Random returned from the studio, Dworkin gently lifted Coral by the hand, while Mandor watched and Vialle sensed the event. Dworkin held the girl by the hand as they stood a moment beside the bed. Dworkin smiled slightly at Mandor, then he vanished with the girl. Random joined Mandor and his wife, wonderingly, and Mandor informed him of the disappearance (KS, 235).

Upon Merlin's return before departing for Kashfa, Vialle felt a strong sensation of magical impulses surrounding him, chiefly about his head. She remarked that she wasn't certain it was him when he stepped past her. His use of some newer enchantments may have puzzled Vialle all the more since she had not sensed them in Merlin before. He used one of these to show Random where Dworkin had taken the girl. As Random commented, they had gone to Kashfa.

Readying to leave for Kashfa also, Merlin was mildly surprised when Vialle came over and pointedly took his hand.

"Gloves," she commented.

"Trying to look a little formal," I explained.

"There is something in Kashfa that Coral seems to fear," she whispered. "She muttered about it in her sleep."

"Thanks," I said. "I'm ready for anything now."

"You may say that for confidence," she said, "but never believe it." (KS, 237–38)

One can't help feeling, with the advantage of hindsight, that Vialle sensed that Merlin was using powers other than those given by the Pattern and the Logrus. And if one were to credit her that far, it could also be that somewhere in her being she had an inkling that greater forces were at play than those governing the petty political maneuvering of her husband and men like Prime Minister Orkuz. Perhaps Queen Vialle had some prescience of things to come, if only to confirm what Merlin later recounted in his journals.

WARDENS OF THE CIRCLE

Humans of the countryside outside of the village of Lorraine who had come under the influence of the dark Circle. They were once ordinary people, but they became possessed by the demon creatures that ruled the Circle in that shadow. These Wardens became the agents of the other creatures that dwelled within the Circle.

Ganelon of Lorraine described what he knew of the Wardens:

"The Circle continued to grow, and those who lived near it fled—mostly. A few remained. It was said that those who remained had struck some bargain with the dark things.... More and more people remained, living, within it. I have spoken with these people, fought with them, slain them. It is as if there is something dead inside them all. Their voices lack the thrust and dip of men chewing over their words and tasting them. They seldom do much with their faces, but wear them like death masks. They began to leave the Circle in bands, marauding. They slew wantonly. They committed many atrocities and defiled places of worship. They put things to the torch when they left them. They never stole objects of silver." (GA, 33)

Ganelon told Corwin of his encounter with a group of Wardens within the Circle who were sacrificing a goat on a stone altar. With more than fifty of his men, Ganelon fought and killed all but one of them. The remaining Warden was questioned, then one of Ganelon's men killed him on the altar.

"He really died, for I know a dead man when I see one.... But as his blood fell upon the stone, his mouth opened and out came the loudest laugh I ever heard in my life. It was like thunder all about us. Then he sat up, unbreathing, and began to burn. As he burned, his form changed, until it was like that of the burning goat—only larger—there upon the altar. Then a voice came from the thing. It said, 'Flee, mortal man! But you shall never leave this Circle!' And believe me, we fled!" (GA, 34)

When Corwin of Amber first came upon the land of Lorraine, he met a seriously wounded captain of Ganelon's army, Lancelot du Lac. This loyal officer had been attacked by six Wardens of the Circle as he was returning to the Keep of Ganelon. Lancelot killed the six possessed men, but he sustained a wound that would have caused him to bleed to death if Corwin hadn't come along. Later, Ganelon had explained that Lancelot had been on his mission, and the leader of the dark Circle was cognizant of Ganelon's activities. Ganelon told Corwin,

> "If I were to leave this land, another such army—one that is readying even now—would come forth. That thing would somehow know of my departure—just as it knew that Lance was bringing me another report on the disposition of troops within the Circle, sending those Wardens to destroy him as he returned. It knows of you [Corwin] by now, and surely it must wonder over this development. It must wonder who you are, for all your strength."
> (GA, 36–37)

After Corwin slew the goat-creature that Ganelon had seen, the Wardens of the Circle collapsed into lifeless corpses. The hold of the Circle and its denizens was gone.

WAY OF THE BROKEN PATTERN

The means to an initiation into the magical arts that draws upon the power of imperfect shadow Patterns.

The shadows closest to Amber contain imitations of the Pattern of Amber, deeply embedded within Mt. Kolvir. These imitations are not true reflections, and therefore are different from the counterparts of the Pattern found in Rebma and Tir-na Nog'th. Instead, the imitations have marked defects that leave the Patterns incomplete. The first three shadows that are most congruent to Amber contain imperfect Patterns that appear to be very similar to Amber's except for sudden breaks or spaces in the design. As one moves farther away from Amber, these artificial Patterns have more pronounced breaks in the lines that an initiate would normally walk to gain power. In theory, one can gain power from the first nine of these Broken Patterns, but beyond that, the distortions are so great that one could not survive an attempt to traverse them.

Jasra of Kashfa had discovered the method and usefulness of the Way of the Broken Pattern. Since she originally came from the Courts of Chaos, she knew something of arcane arts and was able to travel the shadows. She had used her knowledge of the Broken Patterns to initiate two humans from the shadow Earth in their Way: Victor Melman and Julia Barnes.

Instead of stepping upon the lines of the complex design, an initiate of the Broken Pattern must walk in the interstices between half-formed lines. One first steps onto the Broken Pattern at the closest break in the lines, then proceeds along the spaces until reaching the center. When one has succeeded in completing the circuit, one has the ability to conjure through the imperfection, having the image of the Broken Pattern within one's psyche. When an initiate summons the image, "it is like a dark well from which you draw power." (KS, 32) Such a person could travel Shadow in much the same way as an initiate of Amber's Pattern, but the defect of the Pattern is always a part of any magical working, including shadow-walking. This defect takes on a physical reality in every shadow one visits, and it is present in every spell one casts. It may appear as a tiny crack running through ground, horizon, and sky beside the initiate, or it may be a huge chasm in the fabric of the world, off to one side. The danger is in its coming too close; the initiate's fall into the imperfection is the final death.

Jasra had spoken to Merlin, son of Corwin of Amber, about the probabilities of an ordinary mortal becoming initiated in the Way of the Broken Pattern:

> "Only a few of them . . . [can traverse a broken image of the Pattern and live]. The others step on a line or die mysteriously in the broken area. Ten percent make it, maybe. That isn't bad. Keeps it somewhat exclusive. Of them, only a few can learn the proper mantic skills to amount to anything as an adept." (KS, 34)

She claimed that Merlin's former girlfriend on shadow Earth, Julia, was her best pupil, having a knack for learning the magics involved. Julia was able to draw raw power from the Broken Pattern. She used its image for magical sight and preparing incantations. Her skills made her quite adept at finding her way through Shadow also, while remaining wary of the physical manifestation of the imperfection.

Merlin had seen the Broken Pattern in a shadow that was nearest to Amber. In order to rescue Coral, one of the daughters of Ambassador Orkuz of Begma, Merlin was coerced into traversing the Broken Pattern. He wore the Jewel of Judgment, and it instructed Merlin to walk along the lines just as one would in walking its counterpart. Merlin described the sensations that occurred as he walked the lines of the Broken Pattern:

> The black line did not have the same feeling to it as the blazing ones back under Amber. My feet came down as if on dead ground, though there was a tug and a crackle when I raised them. . . .
>
> . . . There came small crackling sounds whenever I raised my feet now. . . .
>
> I came to the first break in the Pattern. A quick consultation of the Jewel showed me where the line should lie. With some trepidation I took my first step beyond the visible marking. Then another. And another. . . . I saw then that the entire line I had walked thus far had begun to glow, just like the real thing. The spilled luminescence seemed to have been absorbed within it, darkening the interstitial ground area. . . .
>
> . . . I came to another break in the Pattern and felt it knit as I crossed it. A barely audible music seemed to occur as I did so. The tempo of the flux within the lighted area seemed to increase also, as it flowed into the lines, etching a sharp, bright trail behind me. (KS, 153–56)

In walking the lines of the Broken Pattern, guided by the Jewel of Judgment, Merlin repaired the imperfections, making this imitative Pattern whole. It is believed that, in so doing, he tilted the balance of the poles of Order and Chaos away from the Courts of Chaos and in favor of Amber and the Pattern. This alteration was likely to add to the rift between the Powers of the Pattern and the Logrus, a rift that would be felt in all the shadows between.

WAYS OF CHAOS, THE

In and around the realm known as the Courts of Chaos, Shadow stress points, or "Ways," permit transport from one region to another. The nature of the Courts makes doors and vehicles for transportation superfluous. Instead, movement through stress points can bring one thousands of miles away from the entry point, or to some other shadow, or simply to the next room, depending upon how the way has been manipulated.

Merlin, of the House of Sawall in the Courts, offers this description of the nature of ways and their proper manipulation:

> While it's awfully hard to pass through Shadow in Amber, the shadows are like frayed curtains in the Courts—often, you can look right through into another reality without even trying. And, sometimes, something in the other reality may be looking at you. Care must be taken, too, not to step through into a place where you will find yourself in the middle of the air, underwater, or in the path of a raging beast. The Courts were never big on tourism.
>
> Fortunately, the stuff of Shadow is so docile at this end of reality that it can be easily manipulated by a shadowmaster—who can stitch together their fabrics to create a way. Shadowmasters are technicians of locally potent skill, whose ability derives from the Logrus, though they need not be initiates. Very few are, although all initiates are automatically members of the Shadowmaster Guild. They're like plumbers or electricians about the Courts, and their skills vary as much as their counterparts on the Shadow Earth—a combination of aptitude and experience. (PC, 15–16)

While visiting the Courts to attend the funeral of the late King Swayvill, Merlin described the castle of his uncle Suhuy as containing "places from all over Chaos and Shadow, stitched together into a crazy-quilt pattern of ways within ways." (PC, 17) In passing through a way, Merlin has indicated that a solid-seeming surface often masks a stress point. One may pass through by reaching into the surface, and as one's hands pass into it, one feels a kind of pressure or tugging sensation. One may resist this tugging until one steadies one's legs and feet, so as not to fall upon gaining entry. When one relaxes within the focal point, the pressure and the forward momentum pass one through to the other end of the Way.

Ways can be constructed within ceilings, floors, even cabinets, as shown by the reports of Merlin. For one of ordinary orientation, traveling through Ways can be confusing, since they often distort one's perception of space. As an illustration of this distortion of ordinary perception, Merlin gives this description of his visit to Suhuy's palace:

> We adjourned to the kitchen for further sustenance, then took another way to a floating balcony above a lime-colored ocean breaking upon pink rocks and beaches under a twilit or otherwise indigo sky without stars. . . .
> He extended a hand and I took hold of it. Together, we sank through the floor. (PC, 34–35)

On another occasion, Merlin describes walking through an intricate variety of Ways as he went from Suhuy's Ways to the home of his older stepbrother in Mandorways. He had to remember the proper paths, and they included crossing a glade, walking a mountain trail, passing a blue beach and lava field, and moving along the Rim before reaching the receiving area of Mandorways.

Ways are sometimes celebrated and appreciated in combination with forms of art, as in the Ways of Sawall, which contains an area called the Maze of Art. The Maze consists of numbers of ways within it, included with the works of art, so that one visits other worlds as one wends his way through the exhibition.

Merlin also discovered that there are secret Ways, created to serve a hidden purpose. In at least one case, he learned that a Shadowmaster had been killed after engineering a hidden Way so that its location would remain secret. The use of such Ways had become a part of the politics of the Courts that eventually involved Merlin on a personal, as well as a political, level.

WEREWINDLE

The Daysword, brother to the Nightblade, Grayswandir. Apparently, it once belonged to the late Prince Brand of Amber, although he did not exhibit it prominently during his lifetime. Merlin, son of Corwin, discovered it in Brand's room at the time of the terrible confrontation between the Pattern Sign and the Logrus Sign in the Royal Palace.

Finding the sword in his uncle's armoire in his bedchamber, Merlin gave this description:

> It was a long and lovely gold-chased sheath of dark green, and the hilt of the blade which protruded from it appeared to be goldplated, with an enormous emerald set in its pommel. I took hold of it and drew it partway, half expecting it to wail like a demon on whom one has dropped a balloon filled with holy water. Instead, it merely hissed and smoked a little. And there was a bright design worked into the metal of its blade—almost recognizable. Yes, a section of the Pattern. Only this excerpting was from the Pattern's end, whereas Grayswandir's was from a point near the beginning. (KS, 231)

While vague and inconclusive, most versions of the story of Werewindle's origins connect it with the creation of Grayswandir, the sword of Corwin of Amber. Nevertheless, the existence of the Daysword was withheld from the Amberites quite deliberately. Those with associations with the Courts of Chaos became cognizant of the sword Werewindle at a much earlier time.

If we synthesize the variant forms of the tale about its beginnings, a good story teller might tell the following around a campfire, late at night:

> A lovely young maiden named Ewaedan enchanted a Chaos lord named Duke Namo. Ewaedan seemed to come out of nowhere, and soon after returned to the same. In the interim, however, she held the attention of the adoring Namo.
> One evening, she came to him, her eyes agleam with tears, and her face filled with desperation. She told her lover of her two brothers, princes in a distant shadow engaged in war with a ruthless king of a neighboring shadow. This king had recently slain their father, who ruled in their kingdom. The weapon used by the wicked tyrant was a fire-filled globe that seemed to fly of its own volition and sent out a devastating bolt of lightning, seemingly at the will of the evil king.
> Ewaedan's brothers had consulted a wizard of their land named Owain. This wizard proph-

esied that the globe of the evil one would be destroyed by twin blades, one of the sun and the other of the moon. These twin swords could only be fashioned by a lord of the Courts, one with intimate knowledge of the great Serpent.

Now, it was known by all that Duke Namo was a favored initiate of the Logrus. Often, he had conferred with the Serpent. That was why Ewaedan came to him at that time, to plead for him to have the twin swords prepared for her brothers.

As enamored of Ewaedan as he was, Duke Namo agreed. He sought out a blacksmith in a shadow near the Courts who had been known to be a maker of remarkable artifacts. Never having dealt with the blacksmith himself, the duke was wary. When the blacksmith produced a set of beautifully crafted rings, and demonstrated a number of their potent capabilities, Namo made his compact.

The compact included Namo's swearing an oath to supply the blacksmith with whatever raw materials were needed to forge the two blades. Now, according to some versions, the blacksmith was Ewaedan transformed; in others, he was the wizard Owain; in still others, it was the unicorn in another guise, having been a secret force directing Namo's movements.

Whatever version one finds acceptable, the situation was that Namo bound himself by word and deed to a compact planned by the Sign of the Pattern. Corwin of Amber had already set in motion, unwittingly, his part in the forging of the twin swords in Tir-na Nog'th. Duke Namo's actions completed the cycle.

It is believed that the duke stood by, watching the blacksmith heating the metals Namo had brought. In the brightness of the sunlight, the smith went to work. He bent the slowly hardening alloy to his will as Namo observed.

When the gleaming sword began to cool, the smith carefully lifted it by its hilt, and gestured for Namo to follow him inside. They stood together by a lathe, where the smith honed the edge of the blade. Its metal leavenings fell into a large clay receptacle, as long in diameter as a man's length, on the floor beside the lathe.

In a moment, the smith pushed Namo down onto the clay receptacle. Before the duke could resist, the smith had pierced his heart with the newly made sword. The duke had fulfilled the compact by giving his life.

As conjectured by many a storyteller, the unicorn directed the smith to melt the blade once more. Using the blood of Duke Namo, and some object taken from the cavern of the Logrus that Namo had supplied before his death, the Daysword was forged. Afterward, the Nightblade was created, using those things which Prince Corwin had supplied in Tir-na Nog'th. Thus, the Daysword and the Nightblade are inextricably conjoined.

And so, Corwin was given Grayswandir, and Brand received Werewindle. Separated, the twin swords traveled different paths to fulfill separate destinies.

Stories do abound, and they do not always agree. Nevertheless, most concur that Werewindle and Grayswandir are brother swords, bound together in some way.

While Merlin, who discovered Werewindle in Brand's bedchamber in Amber, had not known of the sword before, both Rinaldo and Jurt had. Rinaldo, as Brand's son, would likely heve been cognizant of the weapon. He named it for Merlin, connecting it to Corwin's blade (KS, 242). Soon after, Merlin's half brother Jurt recognized the sheathed sword in Rinaldo's possession. After a bold fight against Rinaldo and Merlin, Jurt escaped with Werewindle.

. Much later, Merlin reconciled with his errant brother Jurt. However, the sword of Brand was not in Jurt's possession. Looking through the garments of Jurt's armoire within the House of Sawall in the Courts, Merlin located a secret way. It was a sloppily constructed one, perhaps devised by Jurt himself. Pushing through the way, Merlin found himself in a chapel dedicated to the late Prince Brand. At the altar, half-drawn from its scabbard, was Werewindle. As he held it in his hands once more, Merlin thought: "It contained a similar feeling of power to that which Grayswandir bore, only somehow brighter, less tragedy-touched and brooding. Ironic. It seemed an ideal blade for a hero." (PC, 156)

By all accounts, Duke Namo had been a great hero in the Courts of Chaos. A sometime-told tale even has Namo live on to a ripe old age, having enjoyed the long companionship of his beloved Ewaedan. A similar story explains that the duke had also walked the primal Pattern in young adulthood, perhaps making him the first to bear the Signs of the Logrus and the Pattern in harmony.

Werewindle, like its brother sword, has more of its destiny yet to satisfy.

WIXER

A domesticated griffin set by the late King Oberon near the primal Pattern. Its apparent purpose was to protect the Pattern from intrusion after one of royal blood bled on it, causing a disturbance of primal forces in the universe. The late king may also have placed Wixer there to prevent the ancient mage Dworkin from reaching the Pattern in an attempt to repair it.

It was Random of Amber who identified Wixer as a griffin, although the creature was not precisely formed like the traditional beast of lore. Nevertheless, Prince Corwin, author of the published Chronicles, accepted Random's identification. In his Chronicles, Corwin described Wixer in detail:

My first impression of the beast was that it was snakelike, both from its movements and because of the fact that its long thick tail seemed more a continuation of its long thin body than a mere appendage. It moved on four double-jointed legs, however, large-footed and wickedly clawed. Its narrow head was beaked, and it swung from side to side as it advanced, showing us one pale blue eye and then the other. Large wings were folded against its sides, purple and leathery. It possessed neither hair nor feathers, though there were scaled areas across its breast, shoulders, back, and along the length of its tail. From beak-bayonet to twisting tail-tip it seemed a little over three meters. There was a small tinkling sound as it moved, and I caught a flash of something bright at its throat. (HO, 13)

In spite of all the wondrous creatures to be found in Amber, the sight of this particular one was unique. Random's words upon seeing it express the rarity of the vision: "Closest thing I know . . . is a heraldic beast—the griffin. Only this one is bald

and purple.'' (HO, 13) Random, Corwin, and his companion Ganelon found that Wixer, as it was later named, had been deliberately placed there as a protector of the Amberites. It had been chained to the cave near the primal Pattern, and was able to reach a distance of only thirty meters.

When Wixer first appeared, striding ominously out of its cave, it was a terrifying sight. It threatened the horses, not paying attention to the three men initially. As the horses rushed away, Wixer took notice of the men, but its attitude was not hostile. It seemed to examine Corwin, Random, and Ganelon curiously. It made a soft cawing sound, lowered its head, tapped the ground lightly with its beak, and swung its tail rapidly from side to side. Before Corwin and the others could make much of its behavior, the horse upon which Random was riding cried out in terror. In its fear, the horse accidentally stepped onto the primal Pattern. Unable to prevent it, Corwin and the others watched helplessly as the horse was consumed.

With his hand on his sword hilt, Corwin stepped cautiously closer to Wixer. Corwin found the beast willing to be touched about the head. Like an oversize but friendly dog, the beast moved its head with pleasure as Corwin stroked its neck. Random was able to do the same. Ganelon declined, however, speculating that it would be tame only with those of royal blood.

Based on the beast's behavior and the proximity of the primal Pattern, Corwin suggested to Random and Ganelon that it had been purposely placed there to prevent anyone from tampering a second time with the Pattern. When Random let a small drop of his blood fall upon an edge of the Pattern, Wixer shrieked and had to be calmed. Further speculation and examination led them to conclude that Wixer had been placed there sometime AFTER the large blot had formed on the Pattern.

In his Chronicles, Corwin referred to a strong, unpleasant odor that he attached to the beast. That odor served him a second time, when Dworkin led Corwin from his den to the interior of a cave. Corwin recognized the smell before actually seeing the beast, and it helped orient him as to his location. Dworkin's den was in the deeper recesses of the cave adjacent to the primal Pattern.

Dworkin called the griffin Wixer, and offered it something to eat out of his hand. Believing that

Corwin was really Oberon in disguise, Dworkin told him:

> "Surprised? . . .
> "You thought I was afraid of him. You thought I would never make friends with him. You set him out here to keep me in there—away from the Pattern." (HO, 70)

Although Dworkin managed to win the beast over, it kept a wary eye on Corwin and Dworkin as they walked to the Pattern. As they stood near an edge of the Pattern, Corwin realized that Wixer was behind them. Dworkin turned to him and said, "He knows . . . He can sense it when I begin to change. He will not let me near the Pattern then. . . . Good Wixer. We are returning now. It is all right." (HO, 74)

Good beast that it was, Wixer died in service to the Royal Family. With ruthless disregard, Brand, late brother of Corwin, hacked off Wixer's head while seeking to walk the primal Pattern.

WONDERLAND BAR

Variously called Alice in Wonderland bar and Lewis Carroll bar. Merlin was brought into the strangely effervescent bar by his friend Luke Raynard. Merlin had been immediately affected by the euphoria of the place. The place was peopled by characters out of Lewis Carroll's works and from nursery rhymes. While there, a Fire Angel from the Courts of Chaos located Merlin and pursued him with deadly intent.

Merlin was resting in Amber after a successful venture at the Keep of the Four Worlds, when Luke began making contact with him. The contact was strange from the beginning, because a witness informed Merlin that he had begun to fade out, then reappear, as he slept. Luke's voice came from a giant Trump card with Merlin's image on its face. Merlin reached for Luke's extended hand from the card to bring him to the Royal Palace. Instead, Merlin found himself drawn into Luke's location. He felt released from all troubles as he observed his surroundings:

> I put my own foot up on the rail as the Hatter poured me a drink and topped off Luke's. Luke gestured to his left and the March Hare got a refill too. Humpty was fine, balanced there near the end of things. Tweedledum, Tweedledee, the Dodo and the Frog Footman kept the music moving. And the Caterpillar just kept puffing away. (BA, 215)

Merlin was caught up in a "contagious trap," (SC, 4) as the Cheshire Cat told him before fading away. Unable to clear his mind, Merlin simply took in the odd sights for a time, drinking tankards of beer with Luke. Most interesting to him was a wall-sized mural that extended into an actual landscape. The artist John Tenniel stood there with his palette and a paintbrush, adding to the mural. As Merlin watched, a frightening creature slowly stepped out of the painting, taking form as it did so. It was a Bandersnatch. "A frumious Bandersnatch," (SC, 6) as Humpty Dumpty pointed out. Because the creature seemed real enough to do harm, Merlin shrugged off his lethargy and called up the image of the Logrus. Using a cardiac arrest spell that he had prepared at an earlier time, he did in the beast. Disposing of the Bandersnatch in that way served to clear Merlin's mind.

> The image of the Logrus which had appeared to me during the spell's operation had also served the purpose of switching on a small light in the musty attic of my mind. . . .
> . . . the Cat, who seemed somewhat sophisticated in these matters, could well have been correct in assessing our situation as the interior of a spell. Such a location is one of the few environments where my sensitivity and training would do little to inform me as to the nature of my predicament. This, because my faculties would also be caught up in the manifestation and subject to its forces, if the thing were at all self-consistent. It struck me as something similar to color blindness. I could think of no way of telling for certain what was going on, without outside help. (SC, 6–7)

The bar, of course, was a shadow out of Lewis Carroll's writings. It was created by Luke Raynard, who was not fully in control of events in that place. Luke's mind was the key, and Merlin soon became aware that Luke was devising some of the danger as well:

> Luke strolled up, smiling.
> "So that was a Bandersnatch," he observed. "I'd always wondered what they were like. Now, if we could just get a Jabberwock to stop by—"
> "Sh!" cautioned the Cat. "It must be off in the mural somewhere, and likely it's been listening. Don't stir it up! It may come whiffling through the tulgey wood after your ass." (SC, 7)

The Jabberwock began to move through the wall painting as they were speaking. Somehow, Luke's mind had called it into their reality. Merlin decided on drastic action. Calling Luke over to move closer to him, Merlin threw his fist into his jaw with all the force he could muster. Luke crumpled into unconsciousness.

As Merlin lifted Luke's body over his shoulder, Mr. Tenniel pointed out the arrival of a new creature that caused the Jabberwock to retreat. Merlin recognized the creature as something that decidedly was not a figment of the imagination of Charles Dodgson. It was a Fire Angel, a powerful predator found only in uninhabited regions of the Courts of Chaos. Its only purpose, apparently, was to hunt down and kill Merlin. Carrying Luke, Merlin rushed to the rabbit hole in the rear of the bar and began to descend.

The rabbit hole began as a slight decline, but it became ever steeper. Merlin could hear the sounds of the Fire Angel in pursuit. Suddenly, Merlin lost his footing, and he and Luke were in freefall down a long, well-lighted tunnel. Passing through a lighted area, Merlin was able to see the Fire Angel above him, and just above that creature was the Jabberwock.

Only later, when the Fire Angel had disposed of the Wonderland beast, and Merlin, in turn, had dispatched the Fire Angel, did Merlin have the opportunity to consider what had happened. For a brief time, Luke had been held captive by Mask at the Keep of the Four Worlds. Before releasing Luke to wander about on his own, Mask had secretly given him some form of hallucinogen in his food. In a euphoric, drugged state, Luke's imagination could have considered any nightmarish realm and made it into a real place. An initiate of the Pattern could bring any shadow he thought of into actuality. As Merlin had recorded: "Fortunately . . . his mental travelings had involved nothing more threatening than the brighter aspects of Lewis Carroll." (SC, 19–20)

Merlin returned Luke to the Wonderland bar to recover, after having given him some medicine that would gradually bring him back to a normal mental state.

Interesting, that a couple of storybooks for children, written by a Victorian on shadow Earth with dubious fascinations for children, should have such an immense readership. Nevertheless, Merlin's father Corwin had read Lewis Carroll's works, and the library of the Royal Palace boasts several editions of *Alice's Adventures in Wonderland,* written in Thari.

WYVERN

Also, wivern. A fabulous beast out of the mythology of many shadows. Often, the image of a wyvern is used on an heraldic charge placed on the shield of a nobleman. It is a terrifying creature resembling a two-legged dragon with wings and a barbed tail.

The minions of the Courts of Chaos used wyverns in their attack on Mt. Kolvir when Eric ruled in Amber. Coming from the black road, numbers of beast-men rode on the backs of these flying dragons. Eric had soldiers stationed along the cliff face to repel the wyvern and their riders, while Benedict led the cavalry against other invaders in the valley. Eric was using the Jewel of Judgment to send out bolts of lightning against the wyvern, while his archers along the cliff slew many of the beasts and their riders. Corwin reached the site of battle from the western mountains. He described what he observed of the fighting on the mountainside:

> I saw the leader of the nearest party of defenders behead a landing wyvern with a single sword stroke. With his left hand, he seized the harness of its rider and hurled him over thirty feet, out beyond the lip-like brink of the place. As he turned then to shout an order, I saw that it was Gérard. (GA, 208)

Corwin's expedition carried rifles with ammunition that would fire in Amber. He brought his men close to the battle on Kolvir, and they fired upon both the beast-men and the wyvern. As the wyvern fell from the skies, they began to burn. Their volatile blood indicated that their native habitat was very close to the Courts of Chaos. In a few minutes' time, the wyvern and their riders began to flee under the barrage from Corwin's rifles. Most of the fleeing attackers were slaughtered, falling and burning on the rocks below.

If any of the wyvern survived, it is likely they returned from whence they came. None has been found in Amber since that time.

ZHIND

Horned, carnivorous beasts indigenous to the region of Chaos known as the Black Zone. The name zhind is both singular and plural. Since zhind commonly travel in drifts of six or more, they are usually spoken of in the plural.

Belonging to the order of carnivora, zhind have long snouts, retractable claws, and a thick, pointed horn above the nostrils. Though the size of a wild boar, they resemble the rhinoceros of shadow Earth. Their skin has a toughness and texture similar to the skin of an elephant. They are hairless, and have a pigmentation that colors their flesh in shades from a dark brown to a buffed black. While they eat the flesh of other animals, they subsist largely on insects, rodents, and vegetation. When frightened, they can attain a speed of thirty miles per hour on an open plain.

On one occasion, young Merlin, son of Prince Corwin of Amber and Dara of the House of Helgram, was hunting zhind with bow and arrow with his brother Jurt. Although it may be considered dangerous and foolhardy to hunt zhind armed only with bow and arrow, because of the toughness of the animal's skin, it is more likely that zhind will flee from attack. Only when greatly angered, as when one of their young is threatened or harmed, would zhind prove ferocious and attack in deadly earnest. Even an injured beast would tend to skulk away quickly under cover, hide, and lick its wounds.

When Jurt and Merlin hunted zhind, they didn't really have much hope of making a kill. Zhind are simply too fast to become easy prey to bipedal hunters, and their meat is too leathery and salty to make for an easily digestible meal. The two young hunters tracked some zhind through a heavy thicket for some time. They located a lone beast and followed its trail. Reaching a point where they couldn't tell the direction it had taken, Merlin and Jurt stood still to listen. Several yards ahead, they heard the thrashing of thick branches flung aside, and Merlin moved cautiously ahead to determine its course. It was then that Merlin nearly became a victim himself, when an arrow fired from behind narrowly missed him.

Merlin never successfully killed any zhind.

APPENDIX A
SHADOW WORLDS

Shadow	*Description*	*Documented Record*
Amber	A special shadow cast by the primal Pattern on an oval shelf beneath/above a strange sky-sea	*The Hand of Oberon*, 9
Avalon	A shadow of silver and shade and cool waters, where the green of day was always the green of spring; Corwin had long ago been ruler of that place; Benedict acted as Protector of a slightly different shadow of it	*The Guns of Avalon*, 27, 31, 71–151
Avernus	The shadow where Bleys gathered an army of seven-foot-tall beings to attack Eric in Amber; it is a land of smoking craters, dark sand, icy nights and hot days	*Nine Princes in Amber*, 104–112
Begma	A long-standing member of the Golden Circle; it is the nearest point on the Circle to Kashfa; Orkuz, the prime minister, and his two daughters, paid a surprise visit to Amber while King Random was absent	*Blood of Amber*, 52; *Sign of Chaos*, 54–57, 67–68, 121–129
Brand's Prison Shadow	A stark land with shifting colors, having no sun in the sky although there is daylight; while rocks glide across the land like sailboats, the tower in which Brand was imprisoned was the only point of stability	*Sign of the Unicorn*, 18, 21–26
Deiga	A distant port with which Amber had commerce; Caine and Gérard had gone there to renegotiate an old trade agreement when Caine was assassinated by a rifleman	*Trumps of Doom*, 112
Earth	The shadow where Corwin had dwelled for centuries with amnesia; Flora found him accidentally in Paris, France during the eighteenth century; Merlin also lived there while attending college and beginning a mundane career in San Francisco, California	*Nine Princes in Amber*, 5–44, 87–89; *The Guns of Avalon*, 85, 194–201; *Sign of the Unicorn*, 38–39, 58–59, 121–144; *Trumps of Doom*, 1–45, 56–110, 124–134; *Blood of Amber*, 14–28

Shadow	_Description_	_Documented Record_
Eregnor	A large, rich area between Kashfa and Begma, described as being their Alsace-Lorraine; both shadows had tried to claim it as their own and it had long been an area of contention and a cause for open warfare between Begma and Kashfa	_Sign of Chaos,_ 133–134
Ghenesh	A shadow from which beings known as "Moonriders" had once attacked Amber during the reign of King Oberon	_Nine Princes in Amber,_ 138 _The Guns of Avalon,_ 85
Heerat	A commercial center at the junction of several trade routes; a block city of adobe and stone	_The Hand of Oberon,_ 101
Karm	The shadow from which Cymnea, mother of Benedict, Osric, and Finndo, came; Osric had been taken into custody for killing three members of the House of Karm ages ago, but he was acquitted by King Oberon	_Sign of Chaos,_ 117
Kashfa	A shadow kingdom that had been conducting negotiations to enter the Golden Circle during the reign of King Random; for a time, Jasra ruled there as its queen	_Blood of Amber,_ 16–17, 40–42; _Sign of Chaos,_ 52–54, 64, 123–124, 132–133; _Knight of Shadows,_ 209–215, 239–251
Keep of the Four Worlds	Four worlds come together at this point, so that one moves into a different shadow from it, depending on the direction one takes; the energy released there manifests itself within a Black Fountain, and it is a source of tremendous power; Sharu Garrul once ruled there, and the place had been under siege various times by Queen Jasra of Kashfa, her son, Prince Rinaldo/ Lucas Raynard, and Dalt, son of Deela the Desacratrix	_Blood of Amber,_ 33–46, 105, 114–118; _Sign of Chaos,_ 105, 145, 203–217; _Knight of Shadows,_ 10–19
Land Between Shadows	A place that lies between shadows and consists of negative space—that is, light and dark are reversed; also, sound cannot be heard there; it is a place that is inaccessible to the Pattern and to the Logrus in a direct manner	_Knight of Shadows,_ 71–74
Lewis Carroll Bar	In a drugged state, Rinaldo/Lucas Raynard created a place fashioned out of Alice in Wonderland images; in this place, a Fire Angel from the realm of Chaos found and attacked Merlin	_Sign of Chaos,_ 1–10
Lorraine	The land to which Corwin of Avalon had exiled Ganelon; the place near which the dark Circle manifested itself; Corwin helped his former general to rid the land of the half-beast/half-men of the Circle; Corwin fell in love with a girl of the same name	_The Guns of Avalon,_ 20–68; _The Courts of Chaos,_ 27–28
Martin's Shadow	A high-tech, urban shadow that Martin, son of Random, traveled to; time ran very quickly there, and Martin experimented with a number of fashion changes	_Sign of Chaos,_ 99, 122

Shadow	*Description*	*Documented Record*
Rebma	The reflection of Amber within the sea; everything in Amber is duplicated like a mirror; Corwin was brought there by Random and Deirdre so that he could walk the Pattern there and regain his memory	*Nine Princes in Amber,* 71–92
Ri'ik	The shadow where Corwin recruited short, hairy men, as loyal and gullible as high school freshmen, to join with Bleys's army in the assault against Eric	*Nine Princes in Amber,* 106, 108
Shadows of the Broken Pattern	There are shadow worlds that contain imperfect versions of the Pattern; one may be initiated with some little hazard by the first nine shadows that contain such a Pattern, but the first three shadows afford the least danger; Jasra initiated Julia Barnes in one of these shadows	*Knight of Shadows,* 31–34, 148–154
Texorami	A port city of warm days and long nights, music, gambling, duels in the morning, fabulous air currents for sky surfing in sailplanes, palm trees and the mixed smells of coffee, spices, and salt; peopled by merchants, sailors, and assorted travelers; once it had been a place where Random felt perfectly at home	*Sign of the Unicorn,* 15–17
Tir-na Nog'th	A special sphere of Shadow in the real world, swayed by the promptings of the id—a full-sized projective test in the sky; only a person of the Blood Royal of Amber can walk its ghostly avenues in the sky above Kolvir; Corwin was able to obtain a mechanical arm there that replaced Benedict's lost arm for a time	*Sign of the Unicorn,* 161–173; *The Hand of Oberon,* 142, 168–182
The Village [*see* TECYS]	The place in the mountains where Benedict's friends, the Tecys, reside; Dara claimed to have spent time there; Martin was cared for by the Tecys when he was badly wounded	*The Guns of Avalon,* 112; *The Hand of Oberon,* 40

NOTE: Pagination for the above documented records come from Avon Books editions on the North American continent known as the United States on the shadow Earth and are available in English.

TABLE OF CORRESPONDENCE
BETWEEN AMBER-TIME AND TIME ON THE SHADOW EARTH

Shadow Earth	*Amber*
4000 B.C: The first cities were developed by human beings.	1 d'L: Dworkin Barimen drew the Pattern on bare rock on an island floating in Chaos
330 B.C: Alexander of Macedon ruled over the known world.	1468 d'L ogan >//: Oberon, son of Dworkin, was made king of Amber in a formal coronation
A.D. 1664: The plague in London was rampant; thousands of people died and their bodies were burned to prevent the spread of infection	2265.5 d'L maga ~////: While Oberon talked openly about retiring from the throne, Eric and Corwin argued over the succession. They contrived to go hunting together in the Forest of Arden. They fought, and Eric was able to knock Corwin unconscious. Searching through Shadow carrying Corwin's body, Eric found the London of the shadow Earth. Eric left the unconscious Corwin there, expecting that the plague would kill him.
A.D. 1761: The Star of Bethlehem Hospital in London was an established asylum for the insane, more widely known as Bedlam	2304 d'L djaya /<: Brand fled from the surveillance of Julian, Eric, and Caine in the Royal Palace. He traveled to London, located Corwin, and had him committed to Bedlam.
A.D. 1787–1799: The French Revolution. The storming of the French prison, the Bastille (July 14, 1789) allowed the commoners the beginning of control over the government. The Reign of Terror began in June, 1793, and reached its conclusion in July, 1794.	2314 d'L kanam ~/ to 2316 d'L dewa ~///: Flora had traveled widely in Shadow to find a special place of her own and settled upon Paris, France, on the shadow Earth. She arrived in A.D. 1785 Earth-time. In October, 1790, at a party given by Monsieur Focault, she saw Corwin arrive with a redheaded French girl named Jacqueline. Corwin introduced himself as Cordell Fenneval. When Flora reported this to Eric in Amber, Eric arranged for her to continue a surveillance of Corwin on the shadow Earth.
June, 1791: The French king, Louis XVI, fled from France with the royal family. His carriage was stopped in Varennes, near the German border, and they were escorted back to Paris under armed guard.	2316.2 d'L asada >//: Having a unique insight of events taking place in France, Corwin as Cordell Fenneval, stole a horse and raced toward the German border. French soldiers were in pursuit, and he downed three of them with his sabre as they closed upon him. The rest of the men seemed intent in pursuing a distant carriage and veered away from the trail Corwin had taken in his escape.
A.D. 1812–1813: Napoleon Bonaparte led his army into Russia. When his exhausted troops reached the city of Moscow, they found it deserted. Demoralized, Napoleon and his men faced a terrible march through Russia's frozen wasteland during its winter. In October of 1813, the armies of Austria, Prussia, and Russia defeated Napoleon's army at the Battle of Leipzig.	2324.2 d'L wadra ~// to 2324.4 d'L djaya /<: Corwin became a commissioned officer in Napoleon's army. He was with Napoleon when they made the long march on Russia. The next year, Corwin was seriously wounded in the Battle of Leipzig. Although Corwin had a bad chest wound, Napoleon was surprised to find Corwin up and about and nearly healed within a matter of weeks.

Shadow Earth

A.D. 1800–1850: The beginnings of the Industrial Revolution in Europe and America; invention of photography and the steam locomotive; wars of revolution in Europe and the Near East; growth of Romanticism in art, music, and literature; British poet William Wordsworth died in 1850

July, 1870–May 1871: The Franco-German War, also known as the Franco-Prussian War. France stood alone in its conflict against the European nations of Germany, Russia, Prussia, and Great Britain. A leading figure in the provisional French government, Leon Gambetta, escaped in a hot-air balloon when Paris was surrounded by the German army. In the countryside outside of Paris, Gambetta organized a new army and engaged the German forces in Paris. Gambetta's men were unable to defeat the Germans. Marshal Bazaine of the French field army capitulated at Metz on October 27, 1870, and Paris surrendered on January 28, 1871.

A.D. 1897–1904: Sigmund Freud began to set down his principles of psychoanalysis in 1897. In 1902, he was appointed professor of neuropathology at the University of Vienna, a post he held until 1938.

A.D. 1905: While France enjoyed the Entente Cordiale with Great Britain, it also suffered a conflict with Germany over Morocco. In the beginning of the following year, the Moroccan crisis was resolved at an international meeting in Algeciras, at which French rights were recognized.

A.D. 1918: Young Douglas MacArthur was given command of the Rainbow Division's 84th Infantry Brigade. During the first World War, he led offensives in St. Mihiel, Meuse-Argonne, and Sedan.

Amber

2320 d'L to 2340 d'L: Llewella has reported that Brand visited Rebma during this time. Brand showed much interest in learning about Random's son, Martin.

2348 d'L posya >/ to 2348.2 d'L asada ˜///: Corwin joined the provisional troops of Leon Gambetta. While engaging the Germans in battle outside of Paris, Corwin received a spinal injury that left him a paraplegic. Although provincial doctors said he would never walk again, Corwin recovered completely after two years, in 1872, Earth-time.

2360 d'L posya >// to 2361.5 d'L kanam /<: Corwin followed with interest the career of Freud with the hope that the doctor could help him regain his memory. In the years 1903 and 1904, Earth-time, Corwin, using the name of Carl Corey, consulted with Freud in Vienna a number of times.

2362 d'L desta ˜///: Corwin recalls the pleasant interlude he had in the spring of 1905, Earth-time, in Paris. During that year, he was a regular patron of the Café de la Regence, where he played chess games with actors from the Comédie Française that drew crowds. He recalls a fight he had in the bar under the Olympia Music Hall, and a kind French girl who bandaged his bloodied hand, then led him to her apartments. He enjoyed the company of many French girls, and he thought fondly of the music of gypsy travelers and cocktails at Louis' Cafe.

2367.1 d'L dewa >/: Carl Corey was an American soldier serving in World War I. While providing covering fire for his platoon in the Argonne, Corey was shot in the legs, abdomen, and chest. Despite tremendous loss of blood, he survived his wounds and was taken to an army field hospital. His recovery was so rapid that he was brought to the attention of MacArthur, who personally awarded him the Medal of Honor. Captain Carl Corey was one of 123 soldiers in World War I to be so decorated.

Shadow Earth	Amber
November, 1945–October, 1946: The Nuremberg War Crimes Trials. In the town of Nuremberg, West Germany, twenty-four leading Nazis were tried as war criminals for acts of atrocity against humanity.	2378 d'L maga ˜// to 2378.4 djaya >///: Carl Corey served during World War II in France with the Resistance for two years prior to the invasion of Normandy. Taking on an assignment as a war correspondent at the end of the war, Corey recorded the trials at Nuremberg.
January, 1949: While living in Berlin, Bertolt Brecht staged his play *Mother Courage*. This led to the formation of his own acting company, the Berliner Ensemble, for which he directed twelve of his own plays.	2379.5 d'L wadra ˜////: Corwin had become friends with playwright Brecht. He sat in the audience and watched Brecht's wife, Helene Weigel, play the title role in *Mother Courage*.
Circa 1960: John F. Kennedy became the thirty-fifth president of the United States; the first atomic-powered aircraft carrier, the *US Enterprise,* is launched; in Africa, numerous countries changed their names as they gained their independence; the USSR shot down a US aircraft over the Barents Sea, stepping up political tensions between the two countries	2384 d'L: Carl Corey bought a large six-room house on a hilltop in upstate New York. He lived there alone, spending much of his time in his workshop and den. Although he kept to himself, he met and became friends with Bill Roth, an attorney, whom he met at the local country club. Corey intrduced himself as a retired Army officer who must frequently travel abroad on business.
A.D. 1968: President Lyndon B. Johnson ordered a total halt to US bombing of North Vietnam; the American intelligence ship *Pueblo,* with eighty-two crew members, was seized by North Korean forces. In December, the *Pueblo* crew members were released and returned to the US. In April, Martin Luther King, Jr. was assassinated, and in June Robert F. Kennedy was also assassinated.	2387.4 d'L raksasa >/: Brand became suspicious of Eric's continued communication with Flora on the shadow Earth. Investigating, Brand discovered Corwin alive in New York State. Posing as Dr. Hillary B. Rand, psychiatrist, Brand drugged Corwin and had him committed to Porter Sanitarium in Albany, New York. As Dr. Rand, Brand subjected Corwin to electric shock therapy, intending to destroy his memory permanently. After two days, Corwin escaped from Porter. He was tracked by Brand, who caused Corwin's automobile accident. Corwin was taken to a local hospital, treated, and released into the custody of Flora, masquerading as Evelyn Flaumel. Flora committed Corwin to Greenwood Private Hospital, where he remained for two weeks, until he recovered sufficiently from his injuries to escape.

Alternate 1870s South Africa: Corwin traveled through Shadow from the shadow Avalon to an alternate shadow Earth. In Earth-time, diamonds were discovered at Kimberley, South Africa, in 1869, and gold was discovered on the Witwatersrand in 1886. The British government took control of mining operations, and the conflicts that ensued between British outsiders and colonists led to the Anglo-Boer War. Corwin found an alternate shadow of the African desert, four hundred miles northwest of Cape Town, untouched by human habitation. Diamonds were strewn across the sand, and Corwin was able to take advantage of this unmined wealth to make an exchange for weapons to use against Eric in Amber.

Shadow Earth

Autumn 1972: The XXth Olympic Games were held in Munich, West Germany. In September, at the Olympic Village, Arab terrorists killed two members of the Olympic team and held nine others hostage. In a fight with the German police, all nine hostages were killed, and also a German policeman and five of the eight terrorists.

In a referendum, Norway voted against joining the Common Market, while Denmark voted in favor of joining.

April 1977: Severe storms caused flooding along the entire eastern coast of the United States, from New England to Florida; tornadoes destroyed thousands of homes from Western Pennsylvania to Kansas; flash fires raged through the Western states and Mexico; earthquakes wiped out whole villages in eastern Europe, including the USSR, India, Iran, Iraq, and much of Asia; tidal waves swept over many island nations, including Japan, Cuba, the Phillipines, the Jamaican isles, and the Hawaiian Islands; hundreds of acres of tropical rain forests in South America were destroyed by fire

April 1984: Newspaper article: Louise Maria Cruz, twenty-five, a nurse at Good Samaritan Hospital in San Jose, California, disappeared after leaving the hospital building at the end of her shift on the morning of April 29.

Miss Cruz, a naturalized citizen originally from Mexico, lived alone in an apartment on Alameda Street. She left Mexico two years ago, at age twenty-three, when her parents were killed in an automobile accident.

She had been scheduled to assist in surgery the following day. When she didn't show up for work, inquiries were made, and the police were called in after repeated attempts to reach her at her apartment were fruitless. Her whereabouts remain a mystery.

May, 1984: The San Francisco police department described the fire that destroyed the building which was the address of the Brutus Storage Company, owned by J.B. Rand, Inc., of Sausalito, as arson. The warehouse stood at Powell and Clay Streets, near Chinatown. An artist by the name of Victor Melman lived in the two upper floors of the building. His body was never recovered from the debris.

Witnesses claimed to have seen a big man with blond hair leaving the building shortly before the fire began. These eyewitnesses would not have noticed the man except for his hard-to-place uniform and that he carried a large case with ease.

Amber

2388.8 d'L ogan //<: Corwin and Ganelon traveled to Antwerp, Belgium to exchange the diamonds in their possession for almost seven hundred thousand dollars. Then they went to Brussels to order a shipment of rifles from an ex-RAF officer named Arthur. After closing the deal, Corwin and Ganelon spent three weeks in Switzerland working with a Swiss arms outfit in preparing the special ammunition.

2390.5 d'L desta ~//: In an attempt to repair the primal Pattern, Oberon died. Outside of the Courts of Chaos, Benedict directed the army of Amber against the forces of Chaos in the Patternfall battle. Brand was killed, and Deirdre inadvertently with him, when Caine fired an arrow that pierced his throat and a second that struck him in the heart. Random was made king of Amber.

2393.5 d'L desta >//: Merlin, son of Corwin, discovered the dead body of his girlfriend Julia in her apartment in San Francisco. She had apparently been killed by a doglike creature he found and killed in Julia's apartment. Her death occurred on the day that Merlin anticipated an attempt on his life, April 30, Earth-time.

2393.5 d'L desta /<: Dalt, son of Deela and Oberon, broke into the warehouse that housed Brutus Storage in San Francisco. Helped by two or three others, Dalt emptied the warehouse of an unknown quantity of rifles and ammunition. He started the fire to cover up any evidence of what had been taken. The apartment and studio of Victor Melman were on the upper two floors of the same building and were also destroyed.

APPENDIX B
EXPLANATION OF AMBER'S SYSTEM
OF CHRONOLOGICAL DATING

Early in King Oberon's rule, a committee of ecclesiastical officials and scribes systematized the chronology still used today. It should be understood, however, that in most cases, when arranging appointments with other shadows, the calendar of the shadow is used as a reference that those in Amber educate themselves to follow.

The period in which order was established is called the Era of the Pattern; in Thari, dlennic Lefing. For the sake of convenience, the first dlennic Lefing (d'L) had been set at 4000 B.C. Earth-time, reflecting the direct connection between Dworkin's act and the growth of intelligent human activity in all shadows. (For further information, see the entry on AMBER, sub-heading HISTORY AND MYTH)

In devising a correspondence between historical dates on shadow Earth and the dlennic Lefig of Amber, the rule of thumb has been that one day in Amber is equal to two and a half days in Earth-time. This is an approximation; however, the correspondence proceeds from this to the equation that for every one thousand years that passes on shadow Earth, only four hundred years have passed in Amber.

There are ten ngans that make up the Cycle of the Unicorn. A ngan is the Thari word that expresses a set period of time, somewhat like a week or a month on shadow Earth. In truth, a ngan is neither a week nor a month, but it possesses attributes of both. Anywhere from six Amber days up to forty-two Amber days, in multiples of six, could make up a ngan. This period of days depends primarily on three factors: 1) religious observance and holidays (such as the celebration of a sighting of the unicorn); 2) agricultural concerns (planting and harvesting of crops); and 3) mercantile requirements (periods of greatest congruence between Amber and certain shadows that allow for easy access trade routes). The period of days that make up a given ngan varies greatly, so that a ngan of twenty-four days' duration can be followed by a ngan of six days, followed by a ngan of eighteen days.

The ten ngans that make up the Cycle of the Unicorn, and their accompanying seasonal occurrences, follow:

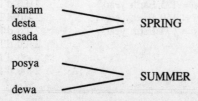

kanam
desta   SPRING
asada

posya
           SUMMER
dewa

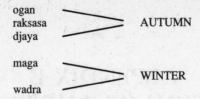

```
ogan
raksasa   >———   AUTUMN
djaya

maga      ———
          >———   WINTER
wadra     ———
```

A final element that affects the codifying of a chronology in Amber relates to the stresses felt in the "tuggings" of Shadow on Amber. Just as tides of an ocean can affect the shape of a shoreline, so the tuggings of Shadow can alter, imperceptibly perhaps, the edges of Amber. Each day in Amber has a unique signature that cannot be duplicated because of the variance of these distortions. The date 2391 d'L desta is NOT the first anniversary of the date 2390 d'L desta, even if the ngan cycle were exactly the same, because the spatial-temporal distortion, or "tugging," is completely different.

The following is a representative breakdown of this spatio-temporal distortion. These configurations are commonly used for the sake of convenience, but they are not complete. To reflect a true representation of each factor, a string of sixty-plus characters would be needed.

SPATIAL-TEMPORAL DISTORTION FACTORS {REPRESENTATIONAL}

~/	>/	/<
~//	>//	//<
~///	>///	///<
~////	>////	////<

We may be able to devise a correspondence between the day of the Patternfall battle and the calendar date in Earth-time as April, 1977. However, the Amber date 2390.5 d'L desta ~// can never be more than a written approximation of the actual event. Even the date 2391.5 d'L desta ~// would not be anywhere near in time to the anniversary of the Patternfall because of the variations in the entire string not shown in the symbolic configuration ~//.

BRIEF TABLE OF EQUIVALENTS

1.5 Amber years = 4 shadow Earth years	1 d'L = 4000 B.C.
4 Amber years = 10 Earth years	1600 d'L = A.D. 1
12 Amber years = 30 Earth years	2000 d'L = A.D. 1000
30 Amber years = 75 Earth years	2120 d'L = A.D. 1300
50 Amber years = 125 Earth years	2180 d'L = A.D. 1450
60 Amber years = 150 Earth years	2240 d'L = A.D. 1600
70 Amber years = 175 Earth years	2300 d'L = A.D. 1750
	2320 d'L = A.D. 1800
	2360 d'L = A.D. 1900
	2400 d'L = A.D. 2000

WORKS CONSULTED

In order to make the detailed notes and records of Gaem dau'Basvl comprehensible to readers of shadow Earth, I have made use of a number of reference sources. These sources not only enhanced my efforts, but also enabled me to draw comparisons for a rational-minded, technologically oriented populace. The following bibliographic listing excludes the published documents of Corwin and Merlin, so often referred to in this compilation, and known collectively on shadow Earth as The Chronicles of Amber and The New Amber Series.

Bulfinch, Thomas. *The Age of Chivalry and Legends of Charlemagne*. New York: New American Library, 1962.

Carroll, Lewis. *Alice in Wonderland*. New York: Clarkson N. Potter, Inc., 1973.

Davis, William Stearns. *A Day in Old Rome*. Boston, Mass: Allyn and Bacon, Inc., 1966.

Gray, Eden. *Mastering the Tarot*. New York: New American Library, 1971.

Griffith, Samuel B., trans. *Sun Tzu: The Art of War*. London, Oxford, New York: Oxford University Press, 1971.

Hamilton, Edith. *Mythology*. New York: New American Library, 1969.

Hobson, Burton. *Coin Collecting as a Hobby*. New York: Sterling Publishing, 1980.

Hopfe, Lewis M. *Religions of the World,* Third Edition. New York: Macmillian Publishing Company, 1983.

Lacy, Norris J., ed. *The Arthurian Encyclopedia*. New York & London: Garland Publishing, 1986.

Lewis, John. *The Religions of the World Made Simple,* Revised Edition. New York: Doubleday & Company, 1968.

Macalister, R.A. *The Secret Languages of Ireland*. New York: AMS Press, 1937.

Muller, Robert A., and Theodore M. Oberlander. *Physical Geography Today: A Portrait of a Planet,* Third Edition. New York: Random House, 1984.

Page, Michael, and Robert Ingpen. *Encyclopedia of Things That Never Were.* New York: Viking Penguin Inc., 1987.

Sandars, N.K., trans. *The Epic of Gilgamesh.* New York: Viking Penguin Inc., 1985.

Yeats, W.B., ed. *Fairy and Folk Tales of Ireland.* New York: Macmillan Company, 1973.

Zacour, Norman. *An Introduction to Medieval Institutions,* Second Edition. New York: St. Martin's Press, 1976.